Discover Lakota Native Americans in History

Big Picture and Key Facts

Written by Elke Sündermann

D1496458

1

A Little Bit about the Book

This book was written to give basic information to young readers about Lakota Native Americans in U.S. history, aligned with current education standards.

As a teacher, I am on a mission to make teaching reading and social studies go hand-in-hand, while laying a solid foundation of the understanding of history and our place in it.

I welcome any feedback, or addition and revision ideas, as all of my books are a work in progress! Please contact me at elke@anyone-can-learn.com with a subject line of **help revise books,** and let me know which book you are giving feedback for.

Thank you!

- Elke Sündermann

Table of Contents

Native Americans in U.S. History................4

Plains – Lakota...............................12

Day Trips....................................22

Glossary.....................................23

References...................................25

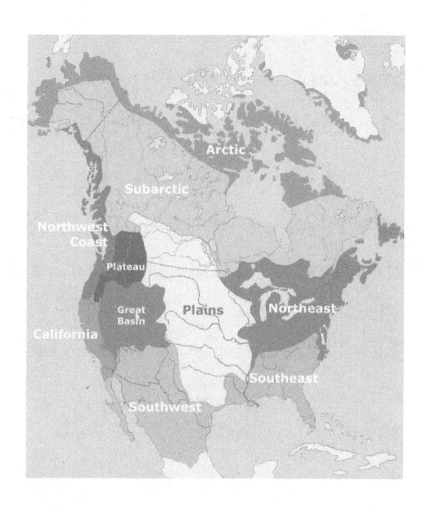

Regions of U.S. Native Americans

Native Americans in U.S. History

Have you ever wondered what the U.S. was like long ago? Native Americans were the first people to live on this land, hundreds of years before anyone else discovered it.

There are still many Native American tribes, and they are not all alike. Depending on where they live, many things are different for each tribe: food, shelter, clothing, and language.

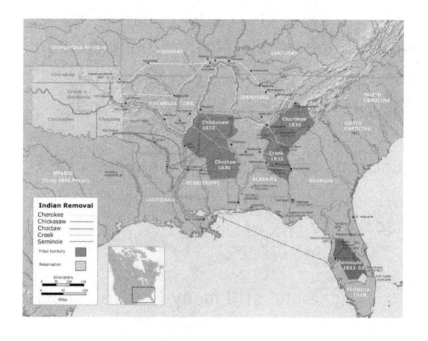

Cherokee Trail of Tears

Things changed a lot when the settlers came to start their own government. When they met natives, some greetings were peaceful, and some weren't. Many natives died in battles, or from diseases. Many were forced to move from their homes, like the Cherokee on the Trail of Tears. Those that survived learned how to live off the new land. Many of these tribes still live in these areas, called "reservations."

Honey bee carrying pollen

The settlers learned many things from Native Americans. They learned how to grow plants for food, like corn, squash, beans, and peanuts. They also learned how to raise turkeys and honeybees for food, and how to use cotton from plants. Even the government we have in the U.S. today is very much like the one the Iroquois tribes used long ago. Some Native Americans today continue to live much like they did hundreds of years ago.

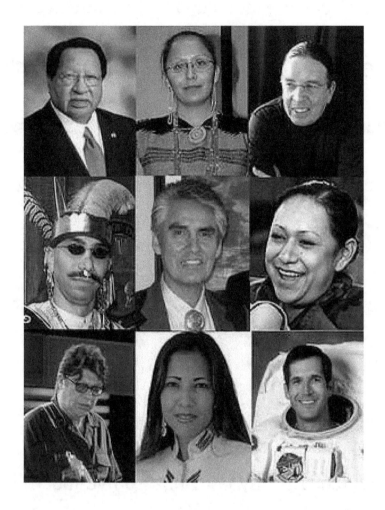

Modern Native Americans Today

Others live in communities and live more modern lives. Their **cultures** are very strong, adding **diversity** in the world today.

The information in this book is organized by **region**, or area, that the tribes lived in. We'll focus on Lakota Native Americans, and at the end of the book is a chart to help review.

Region	Tribe	Food	Shelter	Clothing	Other facts

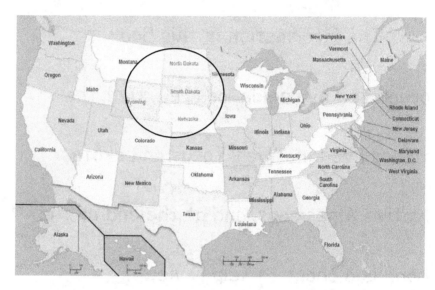

Location of Lakota highlighted

Plains Native Americans - Lakota

One of the many Plains tribes was the Lakota, ("**Allies**") who were part of a group of seven Sioux (soo) tribes. They lived in North Central U.S, in mostly the Dakota area. It is believed the Lakota may have come from the Ohio Valley and could be part of the ancient mound-building tribes.

Some Lakota war chiefs and medicine men were Crazy Horse, Sitting Bull, and Black Elk, who helped protect the land.

Buffalo (bison) hunt

During the 1800s, the Lakota and Cheyenne agreed to let travelers through on the Oregon Trail. Until then, they had battled those who tried. The Lakota were **nomads**, following the buffalo. They hunted buffalo for food, shelter, and warmth. They used every part of the **bison:** clothes, bags, blankets, moccasins, and tipi covers from hide, rope from the hair, glue from the hooves, cups and toys from horns, and they ate the meat! Then, there were over 50 million bison. Now there are hardly any.

Lakota used par fleche saddlebags (in the picture) made of buffalo skin, to carry medicine and dry food on their long travels. The hide was so strong it could be used as a shield to arrows! Many times the drawings on them were maps of the area!

Their homes were seasonal: tipis with buffalo hides and a center pole of wood in the summer, so they could move them easily. In the winter, they made shelters out of mud to keep them warmer.

Lakota men and boys playing lacrosse

Lakota children played all of the usual games other children did at the time. One game that the men and older boys played was lacrosse. This was played with a stick that had a net tied to the end of it, a ball, and a goal. Lacrosse is a popular sport in the world, even today! Competitive sports were even used to settle arguments! What a great idea!

Lakota portraits

Today, many Lakota live in Denver and other towns. Those that live on the reservations are mostly in South Dakota. There are about 70,000 Lakota now, and over 20,000 speak the Lakota language!

What do you know?

List 5 things Lakota made from buffalo. Cite the evidence.

Lakota Snapshot					
Region	Tribe name	Food	Shelter	Clothing	Other facts
Plains	Lakota	Buffalo, fruit, veg	Buffalo tipis	Buffalo	Lacrosse, parfleche

Lakota Day Trips!

If you live near any of the towns below, you are close enough for a day's drive to Lakota land:

- Bismarck, ND
- Williston, ND
- Casper, WY
- Sheridan, WY
- Rapid City, SD
- Pierre, SD
- Billings, MT
- Glasgow, MT
- Pretty much all of Nebraska!

Glossary

Allies – joined in a close relationship; friends

Bison – another word for buffalo

Culture – group with similar beliefs and behaviors

Diversity – variety and differences objects

Govern – to control or rule a place or people and their behaviors

Nomads – people who have no permanent home, who move from place to place for food, water, and land

Region – a large area of land

Reservation – a piece of land set apart by the government for the use of Native Americans

References

All information in this book comes from

Wikipedia, Facts for Kids, Yahoo Kids

Dictionary Search websites, and from

several years of teaching this unit of

learning with miscellaneous materials and

sources. Photos credited to Wikimedia

Commons.

CPSIA information can be obtained
at www.ICGtesting.com
Printed in the USA
LVHW082150130321
681492LV00032B/878

HOBBES

Unhuman

I
Inspector Hobbes and the Blood

II
Inspector Hobbes and the Curse

III
Inspector Hobbes and the Gold Diggers

IV
Inspector Hobbes and the Bones

Poetry

Relative Disasters

HOBBES

Unhuman Collection – Books I—IV

Wilkie Martin

The Witcherley Book Company
United Kingdom

Published in United Kingdom
by The Witcherley Book Company

Hobbes
Published by The Witcherley Book Company in 2017
Copyright © 2017 The Witcherley Book Company.

Inspector Hobbes and the Blood
First published in paperback and ebook (Kindle)
by The Witcherley Book Company in 2013
Copyright © 2013 The Witcherley Book Company.

Inspector Hobbes and the Curse
First published in paperback and ebook (Kindle)
by The Witcherley Book Company in 2013
Copyright 2013 The Witcherley Book Company.

Inspector Hobbes and the Gold Diggers
First published in paperback and ebook (Kindle, ePub)
by The Witcherley Book Company in 2014
Copyright 2014 The Witcherley Book Company.

Inspector Hobbes and the Bones
First published in paperback and ebook (Kindle, ePub)
by The Witcherley Book Company in 2016
Copyright 2016 The Witcherley Book Company.

The right of Martin J Wilkinson (Wilkie Martin) to be
identified as the author of this work has been asserted by him in
accordance with the Copyright, Designs and Patents Act 1988.

British Library Cataloguing in Publication Data.
A catalogue record for this book is available from the British Library.

ISBN 9781912348084 (paperback)
ISBN 9781912348107 (hardback)
ISBN 9781912348114 / 9781912348121 (ebook)
ISBN 9781912348169 / 9781912348176 (audio)

Contents

Inspector Hobbes and the Blood   1

     Unhuman I

Inspector Hobbes and the Curse   195

     Unhuman II

Inspector Hobbes and the Gold Diggers   411

     Unhuman III

Inspector Hobbes and the Bones   611

     Unhuman IV

Inspector Hobbes

and the Blood

Unhuman I

1

As I paused beneath the sodium glare of a streetlight to pull a crumpled Post-it note from my jeans, for the fifth time in as many minutes I read the fateful words I'd jotted down earlier: *Meet Inspector Hobbes. 5.30 at 13 Blackdog Street.*

The ranks of smart Cotswold stone shops flanking the broad avenue known as The Shambles were funnelling wind down my neck, and rain, or maybe sleet, was spotting my sweatshirt. I shivered, wishing I'd stayed in the office long enough to pick up my cagoule, but, having missed deadline with my piece on the senior citizens' whist drive, the Editorsaurus was on the rampage and a discreet, rapid withdrawal had been the sensible option.

The church clock striking the quarter hour, I took a deep breath, and resumed my walk, knowing I couldn't afford another screw-up. With fifteen minutes to spare, though, I would at least be early, which would be no bad thing. Still, I wished I was heading almost anywhere else.

Turning right past the church tower, I entered Pound Street, where an arthritic yew tree had survived the centuries and paving slabs. A set of traffic lights shone red to dam the flow of early evening traffic, so, taking my chance, I crossed into Blackdog Street.

A shambling old man in a shabby raincoat, clutching a paper carrier bag to his chest, hobbled to the front door of a tall, drab building, struggling with his keys. Walking past, I hesitated, before turning back, smiling, helpful.

'Excuse me,' I said. 'You … umm … look like you could do with a hand.'

He glared over his shoulder. 'Are you trying to be funny?'

'No,' I said, taken aback. 'I just thought you might need a hand.'

He turned to face me, the bag slipping to the pavement with an ominous shattering of glass. Where his left forearm should have been was a hook.

'Ah … umm …' My cheeks were heating up, reddening.

'Get lost!'

'Sorry … I hadn't noticed.' I'd embarrassed myself again, and it didn't get any easier with practice. 'I just thought you might need some help with the door.'

'You're the one who needs help, mate.'

As he raised his hook and shook it, I, cowed beneath a storm of imaginative and anatomical abuse, left at an undignified pace. When certain he wasn't in pursuit, I slowed down, catching my breath, resolving, not for the first time, to get fit, to spend less time in pubs.

I ran my fingers through my damp hair in an effort to make it presentable and found myself outside a terrace of old stone houses, almost threatening, like cliffs looming over the narrow street. I counted down to number 13. Three steps led towards a black door with a brass knocker, glinting beneath the white streetlights of this ancient part of town.

I still had plenty of time, or so I reckoned, being without a watch. Mine had blown up in the microwave, slipping off when I was bunging in a frozen curry on return from the pub. The acrid, black, plasticky smoke had completely spoiled my supper, not to mention killing my microwave. A month later, I was still living off sandwiches and takeaways.

A sharp gust spattered stinging raindrops into my face, goose pimples crawled across my skin and, since it seemed foolish to hang around outside, I made a firm decision to ring the doorbell. But, striding up the steps, raising my ringing finger, I found I couldn't go through with it. Standing outside Inspector Hobbes's door was as close to him as I wanted to get.

I was scared of him, or, rather, of his reputation, yet the Editorsaurus had decreed we should meet. This, he'd stated, was neither a punishment, nor that my name had sprung to mind as a competent and reliable reporter. It was because no one else was available. Such remarks, typical of the man, made me question why I worked for him. I wouldn't have, had I believed anyone else would employ me, and had I dared hand in my notice, for the Editorsaurus was a big, scary man, yet neither as big or scary as Hobbes, if rumours were to be believed … and I believed them.

The rain was beginning to penetrate my sweatshirt so, with a shudder and a muttered prayer to whatever gods might protect local newspaper reporters, I leaned forward and jabbed at the bell.

Before I made contact, the door swung open. Recoiling, I stumbled back down the steps as a diminutive figure smiled at me, her face, a toothless network of fine wrinkles and deep ravines, was framed by a green headscarf. Wiping her hands on a pink pinafore, patterned with red flowers, she stared at me, a pair of twinkling blue eyes behind thick spectacles.

'Hello, dear,' she said, her voice high and quavery. 'You must be Mr Donahue. Please, come in.'

'Umm … I'm not Mr Donahue, actually … he couldn't make it. I'm … umm … Andy from the *Sorenchester and District Bugle*.' Fumbling for my card, I realised I'd left it in my cagoule. She didn't seem to mind.

'In that case, come in, Andy.' She gestured me inside. 'Get a move on, I've got a stew on the hob. I wouldn't want it to spoil.'

'Oh … right … the hob … which reminds me, is Inspector Hobbes in?'

As I entered, she closed the door with a crash.

'Not yet, dear but he'll be back shortly. Please take a seat.'

Sitting down on a worn, if surprisingly comfortable, red-velour sofa as the strange old woman left via a door in the corner, I surveyed my surroundings. I was in a small, plain, yet neat, sitting room, containing a pair of old oak chairs and a coffee table with a copy of *Sorenchester Life* magazine on top. An incongruous widescreen television stood in one corner and an old-fashioned standard lamp in another. The walls were papered in a faded yellow pattern, depicting various exotic plants. I experienced an odd twinge of disappointment: from the rumours, I'd expected something out of the Addams Family. Still, beneath the sweet scent of lavender and wax polish, the room held a faint, feral taint, reminiscent of the wildlife park, and which topped up my nervousness.

Allowing myself to relax into the softness, I sighed, for it had already been a difficult day. The Editorsaurus had made some caustic, not to say brutal, remarks on realising my article wasn't finished and his language had deteriorated further when I'd confessed to having not actually started it. He hadn't been impressed by my argument that no one really wanted to read about whist drives.

At least Ingrid had been a comfort, and a vision of her lovely face beneath its thicket of blondish hair proved life at the *Bugle* wasn't all bad. She had a bright, sympathetic smile, was neat and efficient, smelled of soap, and would often make time for a chat. After the Editorsaurus had, temporarily I feared, exhausted his ranting, she'd made me a mug of coffee, sharing her packet of Bourbon Creams. I never felt guilty about taking her biscuits, feeling, in fact, that I was doing her a favour: losing a little weight would not hurt her.

Picking up *Sorenchester Life*, I flicked through its heavy, glossy pages until reaching a section devoted to Colonel Squire's latest charity ball at the Manor. My suspicion that it might merely have been an excuse for a bunch of rich blokes and their toffee-nosed wives to flaunt their wealth and feel good about themselves was confirmed by the magazine's failure to mention the charity the extravaganza had supposedly been aiding. In the midst of sneering at the hypocrisy, my attention was caught by a familiar figure. Before me, in full colour, magnificent in a crisp dinner jacket, stood Editorsaurus Rex, barrel gut precariously restrained by a crimson cummerbund, an expensive-looking blonde woman leaning on the arm not occupied by holding a drink. 'Mr Rex Witcherley and wife, Narcisa, enjoy a joke', claimed the caption. I wondered whether wife, Narcisa, would be entirely happy with the photograph, which showed her baring her teeth like a wolf.

A high, quavering voice rang in my ear. 'I've got all my own teeth, you know.'

I couldn't have leaped up any faster had I sat on a pin. As I landed and turned around, the magazine fluttering to the carpet like a dying pigeon, the blood pounding through my skull, my shin bruised from a sharp encounter with the table, the old lady, standing by the sofa, gave me a gummy smile. Though I could have sworn she did not have a single tooth left in her head, I thought a positive response was appropriate.

'What?' I said. 'All your own teeth? How wonderful.'

'Isn't it?' Reaching into the pocket of her pinafore, she pulled out a jar, rattling it.

I took a step back as the horror hit. It was full of teeth. Lots of teeth. Hundreds of human teeth.

The gummy grin broadened. 'I collect them. Aren't they beautiful?'

Nodding queasily, humouring the crazy woman, I looked around for an exit.

'Of course,' she said, 'they do take such a lot of polishing but they're worth it.'

'That's excellent,' I said, with what I hoped would develop into a reassuring, calming smile. 'Everybody should have a hobby.'

She stepped towards me. 'Do you keep teeth, dear?'

'Only the ones in my mouth.' My smile grew more alarmed.

She peered up. 'Ooh yes! Aren't they beautiful? I can see you've really looked after them.'

'Umm … yes, my father's a dentist,' I said, attempting to put the coffee table between us. 'He's always been a great believer in looking after one's teeth.'

'Can I have 'em?' Her bright little eyes widening, she took another step towards me. 'When you've finished with them, of course.' She laughed.

I did too, for panic was not far off. 'Why, certainly, you can have them all, when I've done with them. Please, help yourself.'

'Ooh, you're a lovely young man. I got these beauties the other night.' Upending the jar, she poured a pile of discoloured teeth into her hand. 'Mr Binks at the pub lets me have the ones that come out on his premises. He's a very nice man. Do you know him?'

'Featherlight Binks? At the Feathers on Mosse Lane?'

'That's the one, dear. I often get teeth from the Feathers.'

I nodded, knowing the place rather too well. It was a disreputable dive full of seedy low-lifes, while Featherlight, its landlord, not at all a nice man in my opinion, was a surly brute who never showed reluctance when it came to fisticuffs. I could guess to whose head those teeth had belonged. A customer, not a regular who would have known better, had complained about the head on his beer. When Featherlight, purple-faced and twitching, had asked what was wrong with having a head on beer, the customer had retorted, not unreasonably, that everything was wrong when the head had once belonged to a mouse. I'd slipped away on hearing him demand a fresh pint in a clean glass. Featherlight doesn't like that sort of thing and the heaviness of his brow and the stormy tinge of his skin had led me to forecast imminent violence.

Cackling, the crazy woman held out the teeth, some still showing traces of blood, for inspection. I swallowed the hot taste of vomit and, on the verge of flight, glanced towards the front door.

It swung open.

A vast figure in well-polished black boots, baggy brown trousers and a flapping gabardine raincoat, stood framed in the doorway. As he pulled the door behind him, his blood-red eyes scrutinised me from beneath a tangle of dark, bristly eyebrows. 'I'm Inspector Hobbes. You must be Mr Caplet?'

His voice rumbled through my chest, as if a heavy lorry was passing. I nodded and he stepped towards me, holding out his hand, which I shook with trepidation, mine feeling tiny, soft and feeble, like a baby's, compared to his, as hard and as hairy as a coconut.

'Pleased to meet you, Inspector.'

'Likewise. How is Mr Donahue?'

'Mr Donahue? Oh … Duncan? He's fine.'

Hobbes, frowning, released my hand. 'Fine? I heard he's got two broken legs?'

'Ah … umm … yes.' The question had thrown me for a second, in a similar way that someone had thrown Duncan, the *Bugle's* crime reporter, from a speeding car, which was just my luck, for otherwise it would have been his responsibility to cover Hobbes. 'I mean apart from that, he's OK. Oh … and he broke his jaw, too, so that's all wired up.'

Hobbes raised his eyebrows, the eyeballs beneath exceedingly red. Reaching into his pocket, he pulled out a bottle of Optrex. 'Well, I hope the poor man gets better soon. It was a nasty incident but, at least, I was able to make a quick arrest since the perpetrator is an old acquaintance of mine, one Gordon Bennet, a ne'er-do-well who decided to try his hand at carjacking. The last time I had occasion to arrest him was for persistent indecent exposure. He claimed he'd considered giving up but wanted to stick it out for a little longer. I dissuaded him. Now, if you'll excuse me, I'd better go and bathe my eyes.'

'Oh, right … too many late nights?'

He grinned. 'No, too many camels. I have an allergy.' He turned to the old girl. 'Could I trouble you to make a pot of tea? I'm parched and I'm sure Mr Caplet would like a drink too.'

'Of course,' she said.

They both departed, leaving me to my thoughts. Though I had a feeling getting on his wrong side would be a foolish idea, it seemed he might not be as bad as I'd heard. Yet, on reflection, I wasn't quite sure if I'd heard much at all; I'd just seen the expressions on the faces of those who'd met him professionally. The old lady, on the other hand, scared the wits out of me.

I tried to calm down by concentrating on *Sorenchester Life*, its glossy pages, filled with nothing of consequence, having a restful effect, so I was well relaxed by the time Hobbes strolled back into the room.

'Well, Mr Caplet,' he said, 'Superintendent Cooper informs me that, due to Mr Donahue's accident, you will be my shadow for the next week.'

I nodded. 'That's right. Ed … umm … Mr Witcherley … told me to report on local policing from your perspective. He wants really in-depth stuff to enlighten and enthral our readers.'

I tried to speak with a confidence I didn't feel, yet, only that morning, I'd been complaining to Ingrid about never getting important assignments. Certainly, I'd made the odd cock-up in the past, but I felt I'd learned enough in eight years as a cub reporter to be entrusted with something meaty, though I hadn't envisaged anything quite as meaty as Hobbes.

'Enthral, eh?' he said. 'I'll see what I can do. However, you never know what will turn up and, though much of our work is routine, I ought to warn you it can occasionally be dangerous or shocking, even in such a quiet little town as this.'

I nodded, making a show of nonchalance, though his words chilled me even more than had the November air. I was not good with danger.

He sat beside me and continued. 'What's more, we don't work office hours.'

'Nor do reporters,' I said, which was true, for Phil Waring, the Editorsaurus's blue-eyed boy, was working round the clock on a story that kept him away from the office, sometimes for days at a time. More importantly, so far as I was concerned, it kept the git away from Ingrid.

'Good.' He smiled, giving me a closer view than I wanted of great, yellow fangs.

I wondered how my father would react if faced with such a mouth, and felt my left hand creeping up to protect my throat. Hobbes, not appearing to notice, sitting back with a huge sigh, closing his eyes, rested his feet on the coffee table. He'd changed his heavy boots for a huge pair of slippers: they were pale-blue with a dinky little kitten pattern. I stared, shocked.

He stretched, yawning. 'Caplet is quite an unusual name. French?'

'It was originally but, please, just call me Andy.'

'Very well, Andy. I expect you'll want to hear about what I'm working on at the moment?'

'Yes, please … umm … the Editorsaur … Mr Witcherley said you were investigating the Violin Case.'

'Correct,' said Hobbes, 'according to the *Bugle's* headline yesterday.'

'Oh, yes. Body Found in Violin Case – most amusing.' I laughed. 'It was like you'd really found a body in a violin case.'

He gave me a funny look. 'We did. Didn't you read the article?'

'No, I was too busy,' I said truthfully, for Rex had assigned me to sorting out the stationery cupboard. 'I mean it sounded like someone's body had been found in a violin case. You know, where you'd normally find a violin?'

He frowned. 'It was precisely where we did find the body.'

'Oh, I'm sorry.' I grinned, still not grasping the point. 'It must have been a very small body, or an outsize case. You're sure it wasn't a double bass case?'

'It,' said Hobbes, scowling, 'was a very small body.'

Shock hit me like a slap round the ears. A sick feeling welled up from my stomach. 'Not a child?'

He shook his head.

'Whose body?'

'That,' he said, 'is what we need to establish.'

'But if it wasn't a child … how could an adult fit into a violin case? And was it a man or a woman?'

He pulled his feet off the table, a strange, knowing expression, half a smile, appearing on his face. I gulped, my flippant mood shattered.

'It's not easy to fit even a child's body into a violin case, at least without boning it first. In fact, this body had been mutilated but there was enough left to prove it was neither a man, nor a woman.'

I shook my head in confusion. What he was saying made no sense and his casual reference to boning a child had unsettled me. 'I don't get it,' I said.

'I'm not surprised. I don't think I do. Would you like to see it?'

'The body?'

As he nodded, I flinched as if he'd threatened to nut me, an icy tingle chilling my spine. I took a deep breath to steady myself. I'd never set eyes on a real corpse, though, of course, I'd seen plenty in films and on the news when they'd never seemed real. They'd always felt too far away, always somebody else's problem, even when the stories had struck me as especially sad or horrific.

Yet, I was there to show interest. 'Yes, I'd love to see it,' I said.

Hobbes's frown made me wonder if perhaps I'd sounded over-enthusiastic.

I bit my lip. 'I mean, I'd be delighted, no … glad … happy … damn it!' I was babbling, intimidated by the frown that appeared to be deepening. 'Look, I don't actually *want* to see the body but if it might help me to understand the case, I think, perhaps, I should. Where is it?'

At that moment, the clink of crockery announced that the old woman was at my side. Though the suddenness of her arrival made me gasp, I calmed down on realising she was carrying a metal tray with a vast brown teapot and essentials, including a plain, giant mug, a normal-sized mug, decorated with a picture of a cat, a silver bowl of sugar lumps and a milk jug in the shape of a cow. In addition, my greedy gaze locked onto a white plate, layered with what must have been an entire packet of Hobnobs – chocolate ones, I noticed with some approval and more drool. Their scent made me realise just how long it had been since I'd scoffed my lunchtime sandwiches.

'Thank you.' Hobbes beamed, with no trace of anger on his face.

Still, it was not a pleasant face and I doubted whether even his mother would have considered him good looking, assuming he actually had a mother. I supposed he must have, or have had. How old was he? I couldn't have said, for though his face might have been described as craggy, or possibly leathery, I couldn't detect any grey in the black bristle of his hair. The dark stubble on his chin, protruding like spines on a cactus, made me pity any poor razor having to cope with it.

'Did you two have time to introduce yourselves?' he asked, as the old woman poured the tea.

'Umm … no … not properly.'

'Right then. Andy Caplet, this is Mrs Goodfellow, my housekeeper. Mrs Goodfellow, this is Mr Caplet, whom we will call Andy. He'll be working with me for a few days.'

'Delighted,' said Mrs Goodfellow.

'So am I,' said I, keeping a wary eye on her.

Her work done, she drifted away. Hobbes leaning forward, heaping a pyramid of sugar cubes in his great paw, tipping them into the big mug, stirred the scalding liquid with his finger.

'Help yourself,' he said, helping himself to a Hobnob and sliding back into the sofa.

Without the covering of mugs, the tray revealed its decoration, a chipped portrait of Queen Victoria. Still, there's no accounting for taste and, despite everything, Mrs Goodfellow made a brilliant cup of tea. Taking a sip from the cat mug, I crammed a biscuit into my mouth. Hobbes was still nibbling his as I took another, trying to fill a chasm within and, for a few minutes, we sat without talking, just slurping and munching and I could almost have forgotten the body.

Then, thumping his mug back onto Queen Victoria's lumpy face, Hobbes arose. 'Come on, Andy. Let's take a look at it. And quickly.'

Putting my empty mug down, grabbing another biscuit, though only a couple remained, I realised I'd guzzled nearly the entire packet. Hobbes, I think, had taken only one.

'Right then,' I said, lifted by the sugar steaming through my veins. 'Where is it?'

'This way, I'll show you.'

His slippered feet scuffing the carpet, he led me through a door, down a short corridor and into the kitchen. My initial impression was of a cheerful, old-fashioned sort of room, mellowed red bricks echoing beneath my feet, the gas cooker looking like a museum piece, a deep, white enamelled sink standing beneath the window, the shelf of which supported a miniature, yet prolific, jungle of pot plants. There was no sign of Mrs Goodfellow. The odd, feral smell I'd noticed earlier seemed stronger, despite a mouth-watering savour bubbling from a stew pot on the hob.

I'd assumed the body would be kept in the morgue or a forensic laboratory or something, so it would not be a lie to say I was surprised, if not alarmed, when he opened the fridge door and reached inside. I couldn't see over his shoulder but when he turned he was carrying a metal dish covered in Clingfilm, misted by condensation. As he clunked it onto the scrubbed wooden table in the centre of the room, I leaned forward for a better look.

He peeled back the film. I gasped, horrified, for a body, naked, hairless, not even two-foot long, filled the dish. It still had four limbs, though the hands and feet had been hacked off, as had the head; I had no doubt it wasn't human. When Hobbes turned it onto its back, there was a long gash down the front where someone had eviscerated it. I turned away, both hands covering my mouth.

'Oh, my God!' I forced myself to look again. 'What is it?'

Hobbes shook his head, a strange expression in his eyes, which were no longer red. 'It looks like a gnome.'

'A gnome? That's ridiculous. There's no such thing. Is there?'

He shrugged.

The horror was growing inside. 'I don't get it. Why would anyone want to kill a gnome?'

'For illegally fishing in a garden pond? And, if you don't believe it's a gnome, what else do you think it might be?' He waved his thick, hairy finger at the abomination.

I shrugged, trembling, feeling as if I might be sick, or faint, or both, yet I couldn't help thinking what a fantastic story this would make, one that would even impress E. Rex. It could be my ticket to fame and fortune. I could become known as the reporter who uncovered the gnome.

'The trouble is,' said Hobbes, rubbing his chin thoughtfully, 'that I can't afford to spend any time investigating. After all, has a crime actually been committed? There's no law against killing gnomes. Indeed the law does not officially recognise them.'

'There must be something you can do. Have you any idea who could have done such a terrible thing?'

'Well,' he said, slowly, eyes wide, 'I suspect it might have been the Butcher of Barnley. Last time I saw anything like this, he was the culprit for sure, though he was never charged.'

'The Butcher of Barnley?' I shuddered, horrid thoughts fluttering into my mind like bats into an attic, images of blood and guts and death flapping behind my eyes. 'And you said last time – do you mean this sort of thing has happened before?'

He nodded.

'What happened?'

'Money changed hands and the Butcher of Barnley was free to go about his bloody business.'

'And what did you do with the body? Poor little thing.'

'I did the only thing I could.' He grunted. 'What anyone would have done in the circumstances. I ate it.'

'What?'

'Stewed in cider with onions and carrots. Very tasty. Very tender. Mrs Goodfellow had some too, though only the juice. She can't chew you know.' He licked his lips.

I stared at him, disgusted, scared by the sly, crazy look in his eyes, feeling totally lost for words. I mean, what can you say to someone who has just admitted to eating stewed gnome? I became aware my mouth had fallen open.

'What's that doing out?' Mrs Goodfellow had materialised behind us. 'It's for your supper tomorrow.' She glared at Hobbes with an expression of half-amused exasperation, like a mother gives to a naughty child. 'I thought I'd stew it in cider again. I remember how much you enjoyed it last time.'

I stared at the old woman and then at Hobbes. I'd fallen among despicable people and didn't like it. I now understood why everyone spoke of him in hushed tones. I'd known he had a reputation, everyone knew it, but I'd never guessed he'd be the sort to devour a gnome. Three minutes earlier, I hadn't even realised the poor little creatures existed, except in fairy tales and suburban rockeries, yet these horrible people relished them stewed. I wanted to leave and began to feel vulnerable. Why, I wondered, had he let me eat so many of the biscuits? For what was he saving his appetite?

'The butcher said he'd send his bill next week, if it's convenient,' said Mrs Goodfellow.

'Yes, of course.' Hobbes glanced at me.

'He says he'll let me know next time he gets any in, because he knows how much you like a bit of rabbit.'

'Rabbit?' I said.

He shook silently, an expression of manic glee on his face, an explosive guffaw bursting forth, followed by a long, rumbling laugh.

'Sorry Andy,' he said after a while and started again. 'Your face, you should have seen your face! Gotcha.'

He'd gotcha'd me alright. I'm no cook, so how could I have guessed what it was? But a gnome? Feeling an utter fool, I tried to laugh it off. 'Yeah, you really had me going. I don't know what I was thinking. It's obviously a rabbit.'

'Yes,' he agreed, 'gnomes are much squatter and,' he paused, smacking his lips, 'they're not such good eating: a little on the stringy side.'

I forced a laugh through clamped teeth.

'Right,' he said, 'I'll just put it back and then I'll really tell you about the case.'

Returning to the sitting room, I slumped back with a sigh and a touch of indigestion. A few seconds later Hobbes came in, grinning as if he'd done something clever, sitting next to me with a slow laugh, patting me gently on the shoulder. It felt like it would leave a fine bruise.

'The Violin Case, as your paper calls it, has led to the apparent suicide of Mr Roman, a gentleman who lived in Fenderton. It's all quite tragic. Someone broke into his house, causing some damage. However, according to Mr Roman, the only thing stolen was his violin.'

'Was it a Stradivarius or something?'

'So far as we know, it was just an ordinary modern instrument, not a cheap one, in fact rather a good one and more than acceptable for playing in amateur orchestras. However, it was nothing out of the ordinary. Mr Roman played in the Fenderton Ensemble and normally played well, according to the other musicians, though he'd not been up to his usual standard in the day's rehearsals.'

'But surely he could buy another? Why kill himself?'

'That's what I want to know. Unfortunately, he wasn't very helpful when I spoke to him. He seemed overly distressed, even though he was insured. Anyway, a couple of days after the burglary he disappeared and a woman walking her dog found him hanging from a tree in Ride Park.'

Though sorry for Mr Roman and the dog walker, I felt it was going too far to kill oneself over a lost violin. I said as much.

Hobbes agreed. 'I suspect there was something else. Maybe he'd had something stolen he shouldn't have had in the first place: something illegal or embarrassing perhaps? Or, possibly, someone was after him.'

'An assassin? Surely not.'

He shrugged. 'Just speculation, and, though we don't get many assassins around these parts, a copper's got to keep an open mind. Anyway, the burglary was the real crime and that's what the lads are investigating. It looks fairly straightforward. Someone waited till Mr Roman drove out to rehearsal one evening, climbed over the back gate and snagged his trousers on a splinter. Forensics has a few fibres to keep 'em happy. It looked to me like our culprit wore old blue jeans, so I'm not expecting they'll learn much. Once he was in the back garden, the burglar chucked an ornamental birdbath through the window to get in.'

'Did no one hear it being smashed, or see anything?'

'No. The house is set back from the road and his neighbours are on holiday. I found quite a pile of cigarette butts and chocolate wrappers under a bush in the front, so it looks like the perpetrator watched and waited for Mr Roman to go out. He must have realised there was no one in next door and yet didn't break in there.'

'So, Mr Roman was targeted.'

'Very good, Andy.' He grinned. 'That is what I suspect, though most of the lads reckon the burglar was disturbed and ran off. They may be right but parts of the house were well-ransacked so he must have been inside for some time. Oddly, some unusual jewellery had been tipped out on the bed and left behind.'

'Unusual?'

'Yes, big and heavy. Middle-European and rather old I'd guess. Probably rather valuable, too.'

'So, he left valuable jewellery and stole an ordinary violin. It's crazy.'

'I agree. That's if he did take the violin, because, how could he have done, if Mr Roman was playing it at rehearsal?'

I raised my eyebrows in what I hoped looked like a perceptive manner.

Hobbes continued. 'I reckon the burglar found something he wanted more, something he was searching for, perhaps. Oddly, Mr Roman wouldn't say anything and I got the impression he wouldn't even have called us if he'd had his way.'

All the tea I'd drunk began to make its presence known. 'May I use your bathroom?' I asked.

He looked surprised. 'If you want. There's plenty of hot water.'

He may have been joking, I didn't think so. 'What I mean is that … umm … I need to use your … umm … toilet.'

'Well, you might have said. Upstairs and first on the left. It's in the bathroom.'

I walked up the gloomy staircase. There were four doors at the top, all closed. I entered the first, a small room containing a gleaming white bath, a large hand basin and a toilet with an overhead cistern and chain, a sort I hadn't seen since I was a boy. As I stood over it, I noticed a chipped mug with a single toothbrush, a burst tube of toothpaste, two towels with portraits of cats, soap and some rose-scented talc. Some of the stuff belonged to Mrs Goodfellow, I supposed. There was nothing unusual, except for the electric sander on the lino beneath the basin. I speculated that Hobbes used it instead of a razor. I finished, flushing the toilet, which thundered like Niagara Falls, walked out and started down the stairs.

'You forgot to wash your hands, dear.'

I spun on the spot, maintaining my balance with difficulty. Mrs Goodfellow stood on the landing, looking me right in the eye, her expression stern.

'What?'

'You didn't wash your hands.' She tapped her foot impatiently. For some reason she was wearing wellingtons. She gestured towards the bathroom and frowned.

Meek and embarrassed, I turned around, washing my hands and drying them. She'd vanished by the time I headed back down.

I got back to business. 'Who was with Mr Roman when he discovered the break-in?'

'Some of the Fenderton Ensemble: its fiddle section to be precise. They'd insisted on going back with him to practice a piece he'd had trouble with. When they got inside it was obvious a burglary had taken place and one of them called us. Mr Roman was in a terrible state, shaking and nearly hysterical when uniform got there. He was worse when I turned up. Those are the bare bones of it, except his car hasn't been found yet.'

'It's very puzzling.'

Hobbes grinned. 'Aye, lad, isn't it just? Isn't it great?'

I nodded. I wasn't sure I agreed, even though I'd just experienced a frisson of excitement, as if I was getting into some real journalism. The last 'big' reporting job Rex had assigned to me was the Moorend Pet Show. Hamsters, not the fluffy balls of fun they appear, have teeth like needles, as I'd discovered when playfully pulling the winner of the rodents' section from his cage to conduct a mock interview. The kids had loved it when I asked the beast how it felt to be a champion, holding it up to my ear as if awaiting a reply. They'd loved it even more when its jaws clamped onto my earlobe, like a bulldog onto a bull, before seizing my finger which was trying to prise it off. The *Bugle* had never even printed my article, preferring the photograph of me, cowering in a corner, the blood-slathered brute bearing down on me. Readers had apparently found it highly amusing, yet all I remembered was the pain and the humiliation. For days afterwards laughing people would point at me in the street.

'Anyway, Andy,' said Hobbes, 'that's what we'll be working on tomorrow. Now, I've my supper to eat and then I've got to see a dog about a man. I'll see you at the station, tomorrow morning at eight.'

He rose like a wardrobe and the interview, if that's what it was, terminated. I had intended to ask some penetrating questions but they would have to wait. He showed me to the door and I stepped into the street, silvery light reflecting from the damp surfaces as I walked away. All in all, the day had not gone so badly, even though I'd been shouted at, been made a fool of and had been alarmed, horrified and disgusted. Hobbes had not been as bad as I'd feared. Nonetheless, I did not fancy meeting him again next morning and, hoping it might help me sleep, decided to dose myself with a few strong drinks. Not at the Feathers, though, for Mrs Goodfellow's teeth haunted me.

I paid a visit to the Bellman's on The Shambles, a pub with little to recommend it other than being located just down the road from the *Bugle's* offices and supplying food of a sort. Despite the biscuits, I felt the urge for a slap-up meal and, popping a couple of Rennies from my pocket to ease the indigestion, I scurried out of the rain.

The tough, tasteless chop, the cold, limp, over-boiled vegetables and the lumpy mashed potato from a packet failed to meet expectations, though I had expected little. I still ate it all, because I'd paid for it, and even told the fat, gravy-stained barman it was 'very nice'.

However, the drink was good and, having knocked back several bottles of strong lager, I made my way home to Spire Street, number 2, flat 2 and passed out on the sofa, where I was afflicted by nightmares in which Mrs Goodfellow and my father argued about the most excruciating method for extracting my teeth.

2

The sofa was vibrating, a noise like thunder pounded through my head and I didn't know what the hell was happening. Only one thing was clear; I stank of stale pub. It felt like the whole world was shaking and the only explanation making any sense was that I was in the middle of an earthquake. Panic dragged me to the front door, unlocked it and wrenched it open. I ran.

After half a step, something as solid as a wall bounced me back inside.

Hobbes, standing in the doorway, his great, hairy fist raised for knocking, a scowl the size of a continent corrugating his brow, greeted me. 'Good morning, Andy. You're late.'

Swallowing a scream, I slumped back onto the sofa, my entire body shaking, struggling for breath as his laughter rumbled through me.

'Did I alarm you? I did knock.'

I kept my mouth firmly clamped, certain I would scream if I didn't, not convinced I'd be able to stop once I'd started. My head ached.

'At least you're dressed,' he observed, 'but you'd better move yourself, and quickly; villains don't catch themselves.'

Nodding, I took a deep breath, trying to calm down, waiting until I'd regained the power of speech.

'Umm … what time is it?' I asked.

'Eight-thirty. You were supposed to be at the police station by eight.'

I stood up. 'Sorry. I need the bathroom.'

I fled for sanctuary, last night's lager throbbing in my skull, bladder close to overflowing, guts ready to burst. For some time, sitting on the toilet, I held my head, biding my time, trying to round up my stampeded wits. Occasionally, I heard Hobbes snort like an impatient bull.

Finished at last, I washed my hands, splashed cold water into my eyes, brushed my teeth and gazed into the mirror. My face was pastry-white beneath ragged stubble, my eyeballs, glistening like pink mushrooms, stared back. I groaned, finding it difficult to believe I could feel even rougher than I looked. On bending to drink from the tap, my brains felt like they would explode and I had to swallow hard so as not to throw up. The water was cool and, gulping it down, I berated myself, hating that I'd drunk so much again. Only then did I remember that I should have drafted and delivered a succinct account of my meeting with Hobbes to the *Bugle*. Cringing at what the Editorsaurus would say, I hoped to redeem myself with something brilliant later.

'Hurry up.' Hobbes's voice reverberated through my soul.

Opening the bathroom door, I stepped out, attempting to smile through the nausea, intending to explain that I needed a long, hot shower and a long, slow breakfast but, before I could start, he seized my shoulder, hauling me from the flat, down the stairs and into the street. The morning sun, reflecting off the damp pavement, left me blinking and rubbing my eyes, nearly blind and helpless. As my vision adjusted, I noticed he was dragging me towards a battered, rusty Ford Fiesta by the kerb. Opening the passenger door, he pushed me into it.

'Make yourself comfy and don't forget your seatbelt,' he said, getting in the other side, grinning, his mouth a mass of yellow fangs.

Fighting the impulse to protect my throat, I nodded, trying to project an image of polite alertness and interest. The belt clicked around my belly and he started the engine with a roar. Why he roared, I'll never know and I came within a whisker of wetting myself. I felt how I imagined I'd feel if someone locked me in a cage with a tiger, except tigers are beautiful. The car screeched away and, before I could plead for release, we were speeding to work.

He was really speeding, not simply exceeding the speed limit. Gripping my seat, wrestling with the urge to bail out, I hoped that, with luck, I might end up in hospital with nice nurses to look after me and no Hobbes to worry about. Yet, as I stared at the road flying past, I knew I couldn't do it; even if I survived the leap and the inevitable splat, I'd have trouble explaining my actions. After all, he'd never done anything to threaten me and flinging oneself from a moving vehicle because of a vague feeling of horror is a sure way into the nuthouse. Instead, I shut my eyes, letting my crazy thoughts divert me from his driving and, eventually, when it looked as if I might survive, it occurred to me I had no idea where we were heading.

Opening my eyes, peering around, I saw we were out of town, passing between avenues of tall, bleak trees, somewhere, I guessed, on the Stillingham Road. 'Umm … where are we going?'

Hobbes turned to face me, the car swooping back and forth across the road like a drunken swallow, causing a van coming the other way to flash its lights. 'To where Mr Roman's body was found. It's not far. Hang on and relax.'

He chuckled and, briefly, the idea of leaping from the car regained its appeal as it crossed my mind that Duncan's so-called 'accident' might have been a cunning ploy to get out of this assignment. Making an attempt at a smile, sitting back, I closed my eyes and thought of Ingrid, who sometimes spoke to me. I couldn't understand what she saw in that smarmy Phil.

Our brakes screeched, jerking me from my reverie. We swerved, accompanied by the long braying of the horn from a big, shiny, black car, and both vehicles, pulling into a lay-by, stopped.

A furious, red-faced, young man stepped out. He looked like trouble. So did the other three, their appearances perfectly matching my definition of 'yobs', especially the one twiddling a baseball bat. As they approached, Hobbes was fiddling with a map, while I cringed into my seat, aiming for invisibility. The red-faced one rapped on the door with heavy brass rings.

Hobbes wound down the window. 'Can I help you, sir?'

'What the hell d'you think you're playing at, arsehole? You forced us off the bloody road. You need a lesson.'

'Mind your language, please, sir,' Hobbes's voice rumbled. 'I wasn't playing. It appeared to me that you weren't paying due attention to the road conditions. In fact I considered you were driving to the imperilment of the public and so I forced you here so I could tell you to drive more responsibly.'

'No one tells me nothing.' The man cracked his knuckles.

'We'll see,' said Hobbes, unbuckling his seat belt, opening the door.

I slid further down, a cold, sick feeling entering my belly.

Taking a step back, beckoning with both hands, the red-faced man laughed. 'C'mon then, granddad, if you think you're hard enough.'

Hobbes, squeezing from the car, straightened up. He was a bulky bloke, I knew, yet it was surprising how big he'd become, though it was still four against one, and one of the four was armed. Swallowing as Hobbes advanced, the red-faced man took another step backwards, looking to his mates, who showed little inclination to be heroes, except for the one with the baseball bat, who, lunging forward, yelling fiercely, took a great swing at Hobbes's head. I turned my face away, hearing a cry of pain; when I looked back, Hobbes was on his knees, the gang standing around him. Fearing it wouldn't be long before they started on me, I made up my mind to leg it. After all, what point would there be in me getting beaten up, too?

Leaping from the car, glancing over my shoulder, I stopped, for, although Hobbes was kneeling, his legs were straddling the man who'd swung the bat and who now appeared to be unconscious. He was gently slapping the man's cheek. At least, I supposed it was meant to be gently.

'Wakey, wakey,' he said.

The man groaned, and came to, the splintered stump of his baseball bat beside him.

'I'm sorry,' said Hobbes, 'I broke your stick.'

Standing up, he lifted the groggy man to his feet, holding him by the scruff of the neck, and addressed the yobs. 'Your mate needs a bit of a lie down. Now, you will all be certain to drive sensibly in future won't you?'

The man with the red face had changed, his expression of fury replaced by one of bewilderment, his complexion turned white, with a hint of muddy-green, reminiscent of some toothpaste I'd once bought in a hippy shop. He nodded.

'Promise?' said Hobbes.

'I promise.'

'Okey-dokey.' Hobbes smiling, swung the patient into the back of the big, black car. 'You may go now.'

Meekly, the men got in and drove away.

'That was fun,' said Hobbes, 'but I should get to work. Come along.'

Where we'd parked, the road cut through an expanse of desolate, grey, woodland. Hobbes, sniffing the air, strode into it with me on his tail. The season's fallen leaves were mouldering in deep drifts around our ankles, the closeness of the trees making everything gloomy and oppressive, an odour of damp decay filling my nostrils.

While he moved swiftly, quiet as a wood mouse, I stumbled over roots, banging my head on low branches. I was gasping for breath by the time the woods opened out into a clearing, in which stood a single oak tree, encircled by police tape.

Hobbes stepped over it. 'Stay where you are. This is where the body was found, hanged by the neck until dead.'

Although sweat was already trickling down my back, I shivered, as he squatted on all fours like a monstrous toad, appearing to sniff the grass. After a few seconds, he ducked back under the tape, loping into the woods, his knuckles brushing the ground. I toiled after him as well as I could, for he was following an erratic course at a deceptive pace, though, as far as I could tell, we were always heading away from the hanging tree. I blundered along behind, sweating, cursing, struggling to keep him in sight, already uncertain of finding my way back to the clearing, never mind to the car, and fearing I'd be in real trouble if I lost him. My rising fears kept me lumbering forward while too many lagers, takeaways and days sat on my backside slowed me down. I puffed and gasped, the blood throbbing in my aching head.

After stumbling over a crumbling, mossy log, I leaned against a green-streaked tree trunk, catching my breath, and, by the time I was able to stand upright again, he'd gone. He'd abandoned me in the woods, in the wild, where anything might happen. My legs giving way, I knelt in the sodden leaf mould, feeling the damp and cold spreading through my jeans, longing for the familiarity of town, particularly that bit where my bed offered warmth and security. I didn't even know why we'd been running. I'd just been following because I couldn't help myself.

'Come on, Andy, keep up, lad.' He was standing over me, not even breathing heavily.

Shocked beyond speaking, filled with an adrenalin rush, I sprang back to my feet. Nodding, he set off again in the same hunched run, if just a little slower and, somehow, I did keep up for what I guessed was about twenty minutes. When he stopped and straightened up, I ran into him.

Without appearing to notice, he stepped away. Bending forward, resting my hands on my knees, dripping with sweat, throwing up water, I gulped down air, waiting for my pulse rate to drop to something feasible, and realising I wasn't as fit as I'd thought, though I'd thought I was pretty unfit.

'Found it,' said Hobbes.

Raising my head, I let my gaze follow his pointing finger towards a silver Audi, parked down a rutted track through the trees.

'That's Mr Roman's car.' He shambled towards it, rubbing his huge, hairy hands together in triumph. 'He must have parked here and wandered through the woods before hanging himself. There are no signs anyone was with him, so the suicide theory looks solid.'

He'd impressed me. I'd seen no trace of any trail.

'Right, I'll take a look.' He turned to me, efficient and commanding. 'You stay where you are, and don't touch anything.'

'OK.' Despite the nausea and headache, I was excited, seeing some real police work. Reaching into my jeans pocket for my notebook, I remembered it was still in my cagoule, still in the *Bugle's* office.

Hobbes, taking a large, red handkerchief, or possibly a small, red tea towel, from his coat, used it to open the car's door. Scanning the interior, he bent forward, and the boot opened with a click. There lay a violin case. Opening it, Hobbes revealed a violin.

'Interesting,' he said. 'Someone broke into his house, ransacked it and he claimed the only thing stolen was his violin, which was really in the boot of his car. Mr Roman was fibbing.'

'But why?' My teeth had started chattering as the heat of my exertions dissipated and cold air penetrated my clammy sweatshirt.

He shrugged. 'Who knows? Possibly he really did have something to hide.'

'It must have been something serious if it made him kill himself.'

Hobbes frowned. 'That seems likely. Maybe the burglar discovered a secret and tried to blackmail him, or perhaps the burglar took something so important he couldn't live without it.'

Pulling a mobile phone from his bulging coat pocket, he pressed a few buttons using the sharp, yellow nail on his little finger. I hadn't really noticed his fingernails before, which puzzled me, as they seemed to protrude like claws but, when he put the phone to his hairy ear, they appeared normal, if thick, horny and yellow is normal.

Having issued orders to someone, he thrust the phone back into his pocket. 'A couple of the lads will be here soon,' he said. 'Stay put while I have a poke around.'

Getting down on hands and knees, he crawled, sniffing and touching. Although fascinated, I couldn't settle, for throwing up had made me feel better, despite the chill, and my stomach, now empty, was demanding a fill.

The lads, actually a gangly constable and a fierce-looking young woman, drove down the track towards us about twenty minutes later. After briefing them, leaving them in charge, taking a glance at the sky and a sniff of the air, Hobbes led me straight back through the woods to the car.

As he squeezed inside and let me in, my stomach rumbling, I realised just how sharp hunger pangs could be, though I was glad the excitement and exertion had overwhelmed my hangover. My head felt clear, my brain ticked over sweetly: all the fresh air and exercise must have done me a deal of good. All the same, I would have preferred a couple of aspirins, several mugs of strong coffee and a relaxing morning in bed. I risked a question.

'Is there any chance of getting a bit of breakfast? I'm starving and a cup of coffee would be nice, too.'

He looked astonished. 'Have you not had breakfast? I thought you must have done, with those grease stains down your front.' He paused. 'I'll tell you what, we're heading back to the station and the canteen hasn't killed anyone recently. They'll do you some grub. I wouldn't touch the coffee but there's a kettle and stuff in my office.'

He started the engine and we sped back to Sorenchester, stopping with a squeal of brakes. Opening my eyes, I got out, wrinkling my nose on account of the stench of burned rubber, noticing the bumper touching the police station wall. He led me through a side-entrance straight to his office.

It was not the first time I'd been in a police station. I'd once become involved in an unfortunate incident at the Wildlife Park, although I have always maintained my innocence; my arrival and the hippopotamus's disappearance being entirely coincidental, but that's another story, one entirely different to what the *Bugle* published, without my contribution. Yet, Hobbes's office looked unlike anything I'd seen before, except, perhaps, when I'd watched reruns of *Dixon of Dock Green*. The furniture, not that there was much, would have been at home in a junk shop: a battered and dented mahogany desk with brass fittings, two substantial oak chairs, looking as though they might once have been upholstered, a rusting filing cabinet, with a black, Bakelite telephone on top. Cardboard boxes had been stacked in one corner and a hat stand, constructed from lustrous dark wood with bullhorns for hooks, lurked behind the door. A vast aspidistra on the window ledge, gave the room a gloomy, greenish tinge like being in the jungle. A small table with a gas ring stood in the corner opposite the entrance, supporting a dented copper kettle, a stained white teapot, a few tins and two chipped mugs. The room smelt of dust, old books and, of course, the feral scent of Hobbes. Mounds of papers littered the desk, along with a solitary picture frame. I glanced at it, expecting a photograph of … actually, I'm not sure what I'd expected: maybe his family, assuming he had one. I wouldn't have bet on a sepia photograph of Queen Victoria.

'I see you're admiring my picture of the queer old dean.' The room shook as he laughed. 'Right, d'you fancy a cup of tea?'

'Yes, please,' I said.

'Good. Make me one as well, would you?' A banana-sized finger pointed to the kettle.

'Oh, right. Of course. Umm … do you take milk or sugar?'

'Two lumps of each, please. When you're done, I'll show you to the canteen.'

The kettle, being already full, and discovering a box of matches on top of one of the tins, I lit the gas and rummaged for tea bags. There weren't any, just loose leaves in a tin caddy, for which my training as tea-boy at the *Bugle* had not prepared me. Still, I had learned of the possibility of making tea without bags; Phil had been telling Ingrid how tea tasted 'so much nicer if made properly', while I'd listened sarcastically, never thinking I might one day be grateful. When the kettle boiled, I poured a little into the pot, swirling it round to warm it and then, since there wasn't a sink, opened the window, flinging out the contents. A roar of anger followed, prompting me to slam it shut and duck out of sight. Hobbes, sitting behind his desk, writing on a form, merely snorted. I tipped three spoons of tea into the pot, inundating it with boiling water and picked up the chipped mugs.

'Careful with those,' said Hobbes, 'they're Chippendale.'

'Oh right, of course.'

I held them with exaggerated care. They showed images of Chip and Dale, the cartoon chipmunks. I grimaced, putting them down, Hobbes grinning as he returned to his paperwork. Sprawling in the spare chair, I waited while the tea mashed.

His fountain pen looked the size of a matchstick in his great paw, and he wrote slowly, his brow furrowed, the pink tip of his tongue between his lips, looking like a monstrous schoolboy, lost in a world of his own. Occasionally, he would hum a few bars of a tune I thought I nearly recognised. For those few quiet minutes he looked at peace with the world and himself and had a strange air of vulnerability. I almost felt friendly towards him.

The tea smelt fantastic as I poured it out and placed the Chip mug on the desk beside him. He was dreamily stirring it with a finger as I sat back down, taking a sip from the Dale mug, the fragrance steaming away any last vestiges of hangover. I relaxed, closing my eyes, leaning back in my chair. The office was warm, the distant hum of the world seemed far away and I felt strangely happy until, upending my mug, I got a mouthful of tealeaves. Spluttering, I spat the dregs back.

'Manners, Andy,' said Hobbes, shooting me a disapproving look, putting down his pen, picking up his mug and standing up. 'Right, give me a top-up and have one yourself if you like and I'll take you to the canteen.'

Having drained the teapot into our mugs, I followed him through the dark panelled doorway into a large, airy and untidy room where half a dozen officers and civilians were hard at work. Some looked up from their computer screens as we passed, seeming surprised to see me, one or two nodding as Hobbes acknowledged them with a gesture like a benediction. Turning into a corridor, he pushed open a double door and the rich warm scent of fried bacon overwhelmed me. I'd quite obviously not really been hungry earlier. What I'd experienced then had been a passing peckishness, but this was the real thing. Ordering an all-day breakfast, though lunchtime approached, I proceeded to stuff my face, while Hobbes sat quietly, as if in deep thought. When I'd eaten enough to allow some of my attention to wander from the plate, I noticed, with suppressed amusement, that his little finger, on raising his mug, was crooked like that of an old lady at a vicarage tea party. He left the canteen as I polished the plate clean, returning as I finished off the last slice of toast and marmalade.

'Right, Andy, I want to take a proper look at Roman's house. Let's see what we can find.' He hustled me from the canteen to the car.

Feeling fully awake and fit by then, I was really able to appreciate the journey, which only went to show the advantage of having felt like death earlier. Hobbes, I decided, knew only one way to drive: with the accelerator pressed flat against the mat. For him, speed limits were restrictions applying, and only applying, to other road users. It was the same with one-way signs and he regarded red lights as optional. As we hurtled past the speed camera on Fenderton Road, he waved his warrant card in the instant it flashed. Gripping my seat, wide-eyed, speechless, I sat, anticipating a violent end at any second. As we passed the cemetery, I tried to take my mind off the fear by imagining which plot I'd fill, assuming they didn't cremate me. Would, in fact, enough of me survive the inevitable smash to make a funeral worthwhile? My strategy was not working so well as I'd hoped and, once again, I was considering flinging myself into the road when Hobbes, with a crazed chuckle, spun the wheel to the right.

'This is it,' I said to myself, shutting my eyes as we turned in front of a council lorry, 'I'm going to die.'

I didn't and, when I looked again we'd made it into Alexander Court, a quiet side road lined with tall trees, behind which stood a scattering of large, old houses. Hobbes braked as we approached the end of the road, gravel crunched, and he skidded to a halt on the drive of a house, impressive, even by comparison to the others.

He smiled as we got out. 'Roman's empire. Nice isn't it?'

'Not bad,' I said.

From its high gables, its banks of chimneys, rising like towers, its neat rows of glittering, leaded windows, looking out over formal gardens, seemingly large enough to form a small farm, I guessed it dated from Victorian times.

'He was well off, then?'

'Rolling in it,' said Hobbes. 'At least by normal standards. He admitted, if that's the right word, that he was a wealthy man, though I gather times had been harder in the recent past. He wasn't forthcoming on the source of his wealth, though I suspect his parents left him plenty. They certainly bought this place just after the last war and he inherited it. Mr Roman lived quietly and rather well and, for the most part, without the necessity of having to work for a living. He enjoyed foreign holidays, good restaurants, Saville Row suits and those sorts of things and, until fairly recently, kept a cook, a maid and a gardener. It seems he spent his time playing the fiddle and painting.'

21

'A gentleman of leisure? Lucky bastard.' I grinned. 'I've always wanted to be like that.'

'May I remind you the lucky bastard hanged himself?' Hobbes's stare nearly knocked me backwards.

'Sorry,' I mumbled, 'was he … umm … a good painter?'

He shrugged. 'From what I've seen, he was a decent draughtsman with a real eye for colour, though with something of a magpie style. One work would be reminiscent of Cézanne, the next Rousseau or maybe Matisse. He even appears to have gone through a Daliesque phase. In my estimation, his paintings look good but reveal little of the artist, except to suggest he was intimately acquainted with the works of the masters. His work is more pastiche than original, if you follow me.'

Though my knowledge of art is poor, in truth almost non-existent, I nodded as Hobbes stood before me, his voice soft, his demeanour thoughtful. It was hard to believe he was the same man who'd just threatened my life with his lunatic driving.

'Come on,' he said, approaching the front door. 'Let's take a look inside. Stay behind me and don't touch anything. Right?'

I stood back, expecting him to have a key. Instead, he thumped the door once with both fists and, as it swung open with a tortured creak, I followed him inside.

Mr Roman obviously hadn't tidied up after the burglary. The finely patterned carpet, though well worn, was deep and soft, sprinkled with shards of broken china. Hobbes strode into what he called the drawing room, where the French window had been boarded up and slivers of glass glittered on the floor. Dropping to his hands and knees, he crawled about, apparently oblivious to the risk of cuts. He searched thoroughly, occasionally grunting, once or twice sounding as if he was sniffing, while picking up a number of wedge-shaped slivers of dried mud from the carpet, which, he remarked, came from the soles of a well-worn pair of boots.

I soon grew bored watching his broad backside and studied the room, which, though a mess, was a rich mess. However, something about the old ornaments and furniture, something to do with their colours and chunkiness, suggested they weren't British. Engaging my brain for a moment, I remembered Hobbes talking about the foreign-looking jewellery left behind in the burglary and Roman's parents having bought the house just after the war. Perhaps, I thought, they had been foreigners who'd arrived in Britain at the time and, perhaps, they'd done something bad, or had acquired something they shouldn't have, when Europe was in turmoil. And what if someone had tracked the hiding place down after all these years? I tried my theory out on Hobbes, who sniffed and stuck his head under a sideboard.

Crawling backwards, he squatted on his haunches, staring up at the panelled wall and down at the turquoise patterned carpet, scratching his chin with a sound like someone sawing wood. At first, I couldn't see what had interested him. Then I became aware of faint scuffs on the carpet, suggesting the sideboard had been pulled away from the wall on one side and then pushed back. As I turned my head, the light striking the wall revealed a thin vertical crack along one side of the panelling. My heart lurched with excitement.

Hobbes stood up, hauling the sideboard out the way, poking the panelling with his thumbnail until a section swung back with a ping, revealing a wall safe. It wasn't locked but it was empty. He glanced at me over his shoulder, raising his shaggy eyebrows.

Leaning forward, he sniffed and poked the combination lock with the tip of a fingernail. 'There's no sign of forced entry but the burglar's been in here alright. Hallo, what's this?'

There was a scrap of screwed up paper in an ashtray. He picked it up, spreading it out, revealing a page from a small, cheap, wired jotting pad, much like journalists used at the *Bugle*, just like I should have had with me. Someone with large, sprawling, handwriting had scrawled five numbers on it in black biro. Hobbes, after studying them for a second or two, twiddled the combination dial, using the tips of his horny nails, smiling when the lock clicked.

'What does it mean?' I asked.

'It means the burglar knew the combination to the safe, which suggests an inside job – except it wasn't, unless Mr Roman burgled his own house. Besides, whoever did it didn't have a door key.' He nodded at the boarded-up French window.

'What about the servants?'

'He'd got rid of 'em about a year ago during a temporary financial problem. Still, it might be worth having a word with them at some point. Well, well, well, there's something else here.'

Taking the paper, he turned it over, holding it up to the light, laying it down on the sideboard, pulling a pencil from his coat pocket. As he delicately rubbed the lead over the page, faint, white indentations began to stand out, slowly turning themselves into letters. Even I could tell the small, neat, carefully formed capitals were in a different hand to the one that had jotted down the numbers.

'What does it say?' I said, struggling to look over Hobbes's bulging shoulder.

He stood aside, frowning, puzzled. 'See for yourself.'

I could make out, quite clearly, that the letters formed the words, though oddly spaced, *EX WITCH IS A JOY OK.*

'What on earth does that mean?'

He shrugged. 'No idea, but it might all become clear, eventually. Then again, it mightn't. What is most interesting is that I'm certain this bit of paper wasn't here on my last visit. Anyway, I'm done in this room and at least I now know someone, other than Mr Roman, knew how to open the safe and they've been back, assuming it was the same person.'

'So will it help you solve the case?'

'It may provide a lead. Possibly more than one. I'm going to take a look in his files.'

Folding the paper carefully, shoving it into his pocket, he led me to a small study, a smart, cosy, little retreat with a green leather chair on casters behind a leather-topped desk, with a laptop computer and a modern telephone. Rows of books lined the walls, obscuring polished oak panelling. A fax-machine rested on a small table in a corner by the desk, beside a brim-full shredder; a filing cabinet locked by a steel bar occupied another corner. The carpets, as rich and luxurious as in the rest of the house, gave the impression of comfortable, modern wealth. There was no sign of the burglary.

Hobbes, muttering about not having the key, wrenched the locking bar from the filing cabinet, propping it against the wall, rummaging through the folders inside.

Taking a seat, I stared out into the back gardens, imagining them in the springtime, an explosion of colour and life, wondering what fate held for them. Few houses possessed such a space and I suspected it might all be sold off for development, which I thought a shame. Hobbes, switching on the laptop, began tapping at the keys.

'Well, well,' he said after a few minutes.

'What have you found?'

'Nothing of interest, which may be significant.'

I shrugged. Finding nothing didn't sound very significant to me. It more or less summed up my journalistic career. The *Bugle* had only ever printed my stuff when desperate for fillers, or one time, after the office party, when everyone was a little drunk, and my article sneaked in. At least my piece on the history of smoking had prompted more letters to the editor than he'd ever received before. I blamed bloody Phil, who, swaying under the influence of several crème de menthes, had told me tobacco came from potatoes and was introduced into the country by Mr Chips, who'd also invented the Raleigh bicycle. I should never have trusted the git, even though he claimed he'd been joking.

'By the way,' said Hobbes, 'when you were staring out the window, did you notice how soggy the patch of lawn by the French doors looked?'

I shook my head. 'Is that significant?'

'Probably not. Right, let's get out of here.'

We got out. The last thing he did was to pull the front door back into place, wedging it shut with a piece of wood he broke from a small occasional table.

'Fake Chippendale,' he grinned. 'It's worthless. Especially now.'

As we got back into the car and he started the engine, the butterflies in my stomach began fluttering. The feeling was getting too familiar.

'Where to?' I asked, expecting to be heading back into town, probably to the police station.

'To the cinema in Pigton.' He glanced at his watch. 'We'll be just in time for the late afternoon show.'

'Are you off duty?' I asked, hacked off that, if so, he was taking my presence for granted – not that I had anything planned.

'I'm never really off duty, but I find films relax the mind and allow me to think. By the way, I'm on the graveyard shift later and you're welcome to come along. I've had a tip off and it might be fun.'

The journey to Pigton proceeded without incident until, as we were hurtling down the dual carriageway, a white Mercedes van had the temerity to pass us.

'Did you see that clown speeding?' asked Hobbes, crushing the poor accelerator under his foot.

'No.' I stared ahead, helpless.

Despite the engine squealing like a soul in torment, we would never have caught up had there not been a steady line of lorries in the inside lane and had not a yellow Citroen in the outside slowed down, signalling to turn right, blocking the van's progress.

Hobbes shook his head. 'Now what's he doing?'

The van driver made an attempt to squeeze into an inadequate gap in the inside lane, 'undertaking' the Citroen. He failed and red brake lights stabbed through the gloom.

Hobbes chuckled. 'Now I've got him.'

I didn't mean to, but I whimpered as he squeezed us between two lorries, filling a gap barely big enough for a skateboard. The driver behind hooted and I turned to see him gesticulating and swearing. Hobbes acknowledged him with a cheery wave and waited his chance, managing to sneak in front of the van as it tried to accelerate, controlling its speed and position until, as soon as the inside lane was clear, he forced it to stop on the verge.

'Right,' he said, 'let's see what this clown's problem is.'

Once the immediate prospect of death had receded, I was horrified to hear him speak so disrespectfully about a member of the public, and might have said something, had he not already burst from the car and been marching towards the van. Scrambling after him, I was glad, at least, that the wrath of Hobbes would be directed at someone else. Despite the glare of the red dipping sun on the windscreen, the van driver's face was pale and I wondered how I'd look after being stopped in such a manner.

Hobbes rapped on the window, which hummed open, and leant into the van. What he said next took me completely by surprise.

'Who d'you think you are? Stirling Moss?'

A soft Irish voice replied, 'No, Inspector, it's Pete Moss – as you well know.'

'You're a clown.'

I winced.

'I am that.'

The man was wearing full clown make-up and regalia, except for the big boots, which were lying along the passenger seat, on top of a huge suitcase.

'Why are you in such a hurry?' asked Hobbes. 'Don't you know speed kills?'

I nodded vigorous agreement.

'Actually, Inspector, it's usually the abrupt cessation of speed that kills, but I take your point. I'm rushing because I'm booked to entertain some sick children at Pigton Hospital and I'm running late. I got delayed by … business and I'm not sure quite where I'm going. I'd hate to disappoint those poor kids.'

Hobbes, smiling, nodded. 'Alright, Pete. Follow me. Move yourself, Andy – and quickly.'

He hustled me back to the car and I threw myself into the passenger seat, just in time. From somewhere, he whipped out a blue-flashing light, sticking it on the roof, and speeding off, Pete Moss's van close behind. He turned on a siren and we hurtled towards the big town, ignoring traffic lights and give-way signs, forcing other vehicles out of our way. A sign flashed by saying 'Pigton 10', yet I could have sworn that within five minutes we were screeching into the hospital car park.

Hobbes opened the window, pointing to a low, modern building as the clown got out. 'The children's ward's over there. Mind how you go in future.'

'I will that,' said Pete, running towards the hospital, struggling with his case, a giant boot wedged beneath each arm.

'Nice chap,' said Hobbes, accelerating away, cutting through the traffic like a scimitar through tissue paper. 'I barely recognised him under all the makeup. I knew him when he was a lad, you know.'

'Shouldn't you turn the siren off?' I asked, embarrassed, as well as scared.

'All in good time. We've got a film to catch.'

He turned it off as we reached the cinema car park. I barely had time to get out before he'd locked up and was marching towards the foyer, pulling out his wallet and removing some cash. The wallet was small and hairy and strangely disturbing. I wished I hadn't seen it.

'Two for screen one, please, miss.' He slapped his money down in front of the cashier.

Her hands shook as she handed him the tickets.

'Let's go.'

I followed because I'd had no time to consider my options. I didn't even know what was showing. When we took our seats in the gloom, the auditorium was half-empty, which was fortunate as he overspilled his seat and I had to make myself comfortable in the next but one. Though the film was already in progress, he shuffled out for a quiet word with the projectionist and very soon it restarted. I don't remember its name: it was a Western and not the sort of thing I'd normally go for, though it passed the time enjoyably enough. Hobbes barely moved during the next hour and a half and once or twice I glanced at him as he watched the screen through narrowed eyes, apparently entranced.

He emerged from his trance only once, when a spiky-haired, baggy-shirted youth in the seat in front opened a bumper-sized packet of crisps. From deep inside Hobbes's chest emerged a rumble of disapproval. The youth, ignoring it, munching his crisps, kept scrunching the bag, until, after a few seconds, Hobbes leaned forward and tapped him a crushing blow on the shoulder.

'I am a police officer,' he whispered, his voice as soft as a hurricane, 'and I must warn you, that unless you desist from making that noise, and quickly, I will arrest you.'

The youth had guts. He rubbed his shoulder, looking back over it, barely flinching. 'On what charge?'

'Rustling,' Hobbes drawled. 'See there?' He pointed to the screen, where the broken body of Luke Kinkade dangled from the gallows. 'Some places you can still be hung for rustling and don't you forget it, boy.'

The youth had the good sense to turn away and keep quiet. Hobbes settled back with a contented sigh, watching in rapt silence until a shootout signalled the end. As we got up to leave, the youth turned, as if planning to say something. Hobbes put his head to one side, sticking out his tongue, twisting his mouth horribly, making a hanged man gesture, until the youth fled. I felt rather sorry for him but Hobbes was smiling like a cheerful wolf.

There was something of a nip in the air as we left the cinema under a sky seemingly weighed down with cloud.

'I enjoyed that,' said Hobbes, walking to the car. 'Now it's time to go home for supper. A nice dish of gnome, I expect.' He grinned evilly. 'Hop in and I'll drop you off at your flat or anywhere else you like. I expect you'll be hungry again by now.'

I nodded, the hot scent of charred steak from some nearby eatery moistening my mouth. Swallowing, I got into the car, as if hypnotised. 'Can you drop me at the Greasy Pole?'

Hobbes was easing the car through the car park as he waited his opportunity to flatten the accelerator pedal. 'The Greasy Pole! By heck, Andy, you do like flirting with danger. Have you heard what Eric does with his—? No, that's unfair, it was never proven, although you won't ever find one of our lads in there, except when we have to escort the rat catchers.'

'I ate a burger and chips there a couple of days ago,' I said.

'And you're still with us?' There was a hint of admiration in his voice. 'Isn't nature wonderful?'

As we reached the main road, the car leaped forward, weaving through the traffic like a skier down the slalom.

Clutching the seat until we were back on the dual carriageway and there seemed less immediate chance of being smashed into eternal darkness, I had a few minutes for reflection. 'Actually, could you drop me at the Cheery Chippy? I'm not sure I fancy the Greasy Pole tonight.'

When at last we stopped, I opened my eyes to find we were outside the Cheery Chippy. Something seemed odd, disorienting, until I realised he'd gone the wrong way down a one way street. I didn't know why I was surprised.

'D'you know this is a one way street?' I asked.

'Of course. I was only going one way.'

'But don't the arrows mean anything to you?'

'Arrows usually mean an attack by them pesky redskins. There ain't too many redskins in Sorenchester.'

I nodded, knowing I was wasting my time.

'Right, Andy, off you go and get your chips. I'll pick you up at your place at ten.' He drove off up the road, forcing two cars and a bus onto the pavement, and turned out of sight. I heard a screech of brakes as I stepped into the warm, greasy interior.

Carrying my haddock and chips home, I turned on the television, eating, relaxing in the pool of normality. On finishing my meal, I took a leisurely shower, changed my clothes and watched more telly, luxuriating in my vegetative state, relieved to forget all about Hobbes for a few minutes. Of course, that careless thought took me straight back to thinking about him. There was something about him I didn't understand at all, something that made me want to run and hide. In his company I felt like a nervous climber must feel on a snowfield, where any false move or noise might set off the avalanche. I'd been terrified half the day, yet I'd come to no actual harm, though I feared for the state of my nervous system. I guessed that with luck, in time, assuming I survived, I would get used to him. Oh God! I hoped I wouldn't have time to get used to him. I raised my hands. They appeared steady and for a moment I felt good about my nerves of steel, until I realised my whole body was trembling in time.

Finding my way to the bedroom, lying on the bed, burying my face in the pillow, I let loose the fear that had been growing throughout the day. It emerged as a long, long, long scream, from the soul, from the guts and most of all from the lungs. I counted myself fortunate I'd had the foresight to muffle it, just in case anyone heard and called the police, for Hobbes might have been sent round to investigate and might have been angry I'd disturbed his supper. He might … in fact, what might he do? In truth, and in his own way, he'd looked after me. He was an enigma. He was a monster. He was a policeman. He was someone I ought to be writing about.

A sharp crackle of rain on the window and the wind humming and whistling drove me to snuggle under the duvet. It sounded as if we were in for a fine storm and my tatty little flat had never felt so cosy or so safe.

Not meaning to fall asleep, I awoke to the storm rattling the windows and beating against my front door. As consciousness slowly returned I wondered how that could be, for my flat was upstairs and down a corridor. Raising my head, I glanced at the alarm clock, which showed *2200*, ten o'clock, triggering an alarm in my brain that resulted in an attempt at a vertical take-off. I'd been lying on one arm, which felt all big and clumsy and useless, as far as I could feel it at all. It tingled back to life as I ran, jerking open the front door. Hobbes was standing there, his fist again raised for knocking and, though I'd been expecting him, I gasped and cringed.

'Evening,' he said. 'Good chips?'

'Oh … umm … yes. Very good.'

'Excellent.' He smiled. 'D'you fancy the graveyard shift?'

Not really, I thought, the rain pounding down with renewed vigour. Nevertheless, I nodded, for the evening might lead to a fantastic article, assuming I ever got down to writing anything.

'Great, get your things and we'll be off.'

Grabbing a thick jumper, the front curry-stained, stinking a bit of sweat under the arms, yet the warmest top I'd got, and pulling it on, I looked around for my cagoule, before remembering it was still in the office. I disinterred a dusty old anorak from under the bed and, before I'd really woken up, found myself back in the car, hurtling through the darkness. After a short while we turned onto the Fenderton Road.

'Are we going to Mr Roman's house again?'

'No,' said Hobbes, sounding puzzled, 'we're on the graveyard shift.'

'Yeah, so you said, but where are we going?'

He gave me a glance and replied slowly, as if to a simpleton, 'To the graveyard.'

'Umm … the cemetery?'

The night was very dark and very stormy.

'Precisely. We're going to be doing some surveillance.'

'In the cemetery? Why?'

'I have received information that a person, or persons well-known, might attempt a little grave robbing. We're going to watch and ensure no harm is done.'

I wished I were back in my flat.

'It might be a long night,' he said, turning onto a side road with a squeal of tyres.

After a short distance, he stopped on the kerb in a spot offering a panoramic view of the cemetery, if it hadn't been so dark, and, reaching into the back, pulled out a paper bag. 'Have a doughnut. Mrs Goodfellow made them.'

I took one, though I wasn't hungry. It was rather good and cheered me up a little. Then we sat and stared into the darkness, the windows steaming up, time crawling into the bleak, small hours. When I couldn't take any more, I flopped into the back, huddling beneath a musty old tartan blanket and dozing.

The car was buffeted by the pounding fist of a wind, howling in rage that anything dared stand in its way. Hobbes flicked on the windscreen wipers, combatting a fresh spattering of rain, sitting up abruptly as distant white headlights pierced the sodden darkness, illuminating the grinning grey headstones. When the lights turned away down Tompot Lane, he sighed, slouching back into his seat.

'It's on nights like this,' he remarked, 'that I wish I was tucked up in bed with the wife.'

'Really? I didn't think you were married?'

'I'm not but I can wish, can't I? Any doughnuts left?'

'No, sorry.' I emerged from the comforting warmth of the blanket, shivering. 'What time is it?'

'Nearly two. Looks like they're not coming. Hold on … what's this?'

He leaned forward, peering in the mirror, and I turned to see the vague shape of a car rolling down the hill towards us, lights off, vanishing now and again in the shadows. Hobbes sank down his seat, presumably in an effort to remain inconspicuous and, despite my fatigue and the cold, I chuckled. There could never be the remotest chance of him hiding in such a small car; it would be like trying to conceal a warthog in a wheelbarrow. Yet, I had little time for amusement with the other car approaching slowly, silently, as the hairs on my scalp stiffened. I couldn't see the driver and had a sudden horror that it was a ghost car. Although I'd heard whispers of strangeness happening in the vicinity of Hobbes, I'd never expected anything like this. When it drew alongside, I nearly wet myself. It was a hearse.

My mouth, opening and shutting involuntarily, only a feeble, stuttering whimper escaping, I stared wide-eyed over the edge of the window as the driver's door opened. The shriek that had been growing inside burst from dry lips and I fell back quivering.

'Oh, do be quiet, Andy,' Hobbes growled. 'This is supposed to be covert surveillance.'

I'd read books in which a character supposedly growls but, before meeting Hobbes, I'd just taken it as a literary affectation. Dogs and lions might growl but people didn't, except for him; he could growl fiercer than any of them.

Still, it had its effect and shut me up. I'd discovered one of the advantages of working with him that I failed to appreciate for some time: no matter how scary things got, he could always be scarier.

I heard a click, the front passenger door opened, clean night air blowing away the greasy doughnut fug and the faint animal odour.

'Evening,' said Hobbes.

He'd spoken to no one. At least, to no one I could see.

'Wotcha,' said a high-pitched voice.

'What's the word on the street?'

I struggled up, staring through the open door into the black night. The driver wasn't, in fact, invisible, he was just short: very short. I'd seen him in town, now and again, mostly at the Feathers, where, bizarrely, he seemed to get on well with Featherlight, often working behind the bar.

'I can't stop, guv, but I thought you might be interested in some news. You scratch my back, y'know? Cos I'm a bit short this month.'

'Cheers, Billy,' said Hobbes, handing him a twenty pound note.

Billy grinning, screwed it up, thrusting it into his trouser pocket. 'Ta, guv. Right, the guys are gonna do it tonight, like I told you, but they're gonna do it in St Stephen's down Moorend. The rain's made it too wet to dig here and there's better drainage at St Stephens. Plus, their bike broke and it ain't so far for 'em to walk.'

'Great work.'

The dwarf nodded, returned to his hearse and drove away. It seemed to dissolve into the night.

'Good man, that,' said Hobbes. 'He keeps his ear close to the ground.'

I nearly remarked that he kept all of himself pretty close to the ground, but something in Hobbes's expression suggested it might not go down too well. Instead, I asked a question. 'Why did he come here in a hearse?'

'Because it was too far to walk.' His reply had an unanswerable logic.

The engine bursting into life, the acceleration flinging me back into my seat, we roared through the rain to St Stephens, a Victorian churchyard on the Moorend edge of town.

'It's a thirty,' I squeaked, as Hobbes's buttress foot squashed the accelerator.

He flashed his yellow teeth in what I supposed was a grin. 'What's a thirty?'

'The speed limit.'

'Well, I never.'

'And wouldn't headlights be useful?' I asked, rechecking my seatbelt, clinging to the passenger seat in front.

'If we weren't on covert surveillance.' He was grinning like a maniac.

I groaned, shutting my eyes, holding on, cursing myself for accepting the assignment. If I'd just resigned on the spot, I'd be safe and warm back home in bed.

The car, stopping abruptly, I opened my eyes, blinked and tried again. It was just as dark as when they'd been shut.

'Where are we?' I whispered.

'Just outside St Stephens in a derelict garage. No one comes here but derelicts. You may find the aroma is rather … pungent. Now, let's move, we're supposed to be on watch. Be quiet and follow me. And quickly.'

We left the car and, he was right, it didn't half pong. Holding my breath, I followed the sound of his footsteps until we were in the open air, where a glimmer revealed the silhouette of a kneeling angel, marking the edge of the churchyard. I could just about pick out Hobbes's hunched form.

I wiped rain from my eyes. 'Shouldn't we have back-up?'

'I don't normally require it. Anyway, I have you.' I caught a vague glint of teeth.

'Mightn't it be dangerous?'

'Let's hope so.'

As he slouched forward, a huge, creeping gargoyle, I shuffled after him. I didn't want to be with him, yet daren't lose him.

Lights flashed from behind a huddle of overgrown gravestones. I froze, heart pounding, as the rumble of chanting male voices reached me, making the hairs on my neck quiver, starting a dull ache in my stomach. Hobbes had melted into the blackness. I blundered forward, close to panic, needing the reassurance of his hulking presence and, unfortunately, he wasn't present. He'd left me, lost and alone, in a churchyard at night and my head was filled with chanting that chilled even more than the icy stab of the rain.

'Turn the bleeding music off, you daft berk,' said a rough voice, like someone was gargling with hot gravel. With a click, the chanting ceased and, at the same instant, a light shone in my face.

Dazzled and disoriented, I turned to run, my heart racing like a dog's at the vets. My feet missing the ground, I dropped through blackness until something hard transformed my gasp of terror into a groan of pain, leaving me to endure a few seconds of stunned confusion.

My groping hands touched wet, muddy walls. A sharp, earthy odour filled my nostrils. I'd tumbled into an open grave. The next horror was discovering I had an audience. As the grave filled with light, voices coming from above, I rolled onto my back, blinking, temporarily blinded. After a few moments, I began to make out two faces that, if I hadn't spent the past day with Inspector Hobbes, would surely have given me an immediate cardiac arrest.

'Blimey, this one's still moving. What we gonna do with it?' The gravel voice I'd heard earlier sounded hesitant.

Another voice, softer, yet creepy, replied. 'Dunno. Maybe if we fill it in again, it won't be next time. Nuffing like this ever 'appened to me before. They've always been still … and packed inside the box.'

'Good evening,' I said, putting my hope in politeness and affability. At least I had the satisfaction of making them jump.

'Wah!' said Gravel Voice. 'It talks.'

'Certainly, I talk. Look, I appear to have stumbled into this hole and I wonder if you could see your way to giving me a hand out?'

'Give you a 'andout?' said Creepy Voice. 'Do I look like I'm a charity? What are you? A bleeding scrounger?'

'No, sir, I mean, could you help me to get out?'

''elp you to get out?' Creepy Voice sounded shocked. 'I'm not sure that's allowed. What are you in for anyway?'

'It was an accident. I slipped and fell. I shouldn't really be here.'

'That's what they all say,' said Gravel Voice, knowingly.

'Oh,' I said as I pushed myself onto my knees, 'it's most remiss of me. You must think I'm terribly rude. I haven't introduced myself. I'm Andrew Caplet, Andy. And you are?'

'I am not,' said Creepy Voice, 'you're wrong there, mate. I'm not Andrew Caplet Andy.'

'No.' I forced a smile, struggling to my feet, for the muddy coffin top was as slippery as an ice rink. 'I meant, who are you?'

'Ghouls,' said Gravel Voice.

I held up a hand. 'Nice to meet you. Umm … I'd appreciate a bit of help, it's getting very wet down here.'

The two faces looked at me, then at each other. They whispered a few words.

Creepy Voice nodded and spoke. 'Er, look, mate, we'd like to 'elp but we're worried that if we was to let you out, then all of them would want out and then what would we 'ave to eat?'

'Yes,' said Gravel Voice. 'And we 'ave our reputations to fink of. We wouldn't want anyone to fink we're just a couple of ghouls who can't say no.'

'So, we're gonna 'ave to bury you again,' said Creepy Voice. 'It's for the best. I'm sure you'll understand. No 'ard feelings, eh?'

'You can't bury me again. I haven't been buried at all.'

'Then what are you doing in a grave?' Gravel Voice was mocking. 'Now, enough of your nonsense. Lie down and get buried before this 'ole fills up with water and we 'ave to bury you at sea.'

Mud began to thud around me as the ghouls set to work with shovels. No matter that I screamed for help and sobbed for mercy, they shook their heads and carried on. Black despair and terror took me, madness seemed my only escape, and I was considering taking that dark path when I heard two metallic clangs, two grunts, two soggy thuds. A massive hand engulfed mine and before I knew what had happened, I was dangling over the open grave while Hobbes inspected me for damage. He set me down on solid ground, the two ghouls stretched out at his feet.

'Thank you.' My voice quavered. 'That was horrible.'

'Was it?' He shrugged. 'Well, it's all over now, so you can help me tidy up.'

He set to work, filling in the grave, stamping down the black, oozing mud, refitting the toppled headstone. I helped as much as my trembling body would allow. One of the ghouls groaned.

'What are they?' I asked at last.

'Just a couple of local ghouls. They eat old skeletons and they're quite harmless really, providing a valuable service to the community. Otherwise, we'd be knee-deep in bones and no one would like that, except for dogs. Still, I like to make sure these lads tidy up afterwards. If they don't, folk get upset and I won't stand for bad feelings between them and the ghoul community. Not on my patch.'

'Old bones? Aren't they rather hard?'

'They grind 'em up and make a sort of ghoul hash.'

I nodded. 'Do you know their names?' I reached for my non-existent notebook, believing I'd got a major scoop on only the second night of my assignment. With luck, it would make Editorsaurus Rex forgive me.

'They don't have names like you and I, though you could call them Doug and Phil.'

'Why?'

'Well that one,' he said, pointing at Creepy Voice with an inappropriate snigger, 'dug the grave and this one,' he poked Gravel Voice with his boot, 'was going to fill it.'

I sighed. 'What are we going to do now?'

'Take them home.' Bending, he hoisted both of them over one shoulder and straightened up. 'Then I'll make my report and we can call it a night. By the way, tonight's little escapade will not be appearing in the *Bugle*. As far as that's concerned, we had a quiet night, apart from having to take a couple of drunks home. Understand?'

'But …'

'Understand?' Hobbes repeated, standing a little closer than was necessary.

'I understand.' Self-preservation had asserted itself. I wanted to ask questions, wanted to know so many things, yet I was afraid, as if I'd fallen into a nightmare. My perception of Sorenchester as a nice, cosy, little town had been blown to pieces, I'd seen things I shouldn't have, and had a terrible sickly feeling my life had changed forever.

My old anorak proving no match for the storm, icy water trickled down my back, making me shudder. Though the rain was as heavy as a tropical downpour, the cold and a wind, too powerful to even consider going around me, blew that idea away.

Hobbes loped to the edge of the churchyard, the limp ghouls bouncing on his shoulder. 'Follow me. We'll take care of these two and then we're done and can head back to the station.'

As I jogged after him, a worrying habit I had no intention of forming, the effort started giving me just a little wonderful warmth. Still, my feet skidded and squelched inside my shoes, while my trousers, clammy and stiff, flapped whenever they took a break from clinging to and squeezing my poor legs. I wasn't used to the kind of activity to which I'd been subjected in the last few hours and every muscle was aching. I muttered to myself about what I'd do to Editorsaurus Rex should I ever chance upon him in a darkened churchyard – not that I could imagine him ever allowing himself to fall into such an awkward or uncomfortable situation, never mind into an open grave. Besides, I wouldn't really have done anything: I wasn't like that at all, and not merely because he was bigger than me.

We passed through a covered gateway into a deserted street, where sad cars dripped into oily puddles, glinting under orange streetlights. A shredded plastic carrier bag, pale and ghostly, flapped into my face. Flinching, I beat it off, watching it skid along the gutter, twirling in eddies, vanishing as it rose over the rooftops. Crossing the street, we plunged down an alley that funnelled the wind into such a full-frontal gale I found it a struggle to get through. Hobbes, oblivious, turned left along a pot-holed back lane, ducking beneath a broken fence into the overgrown backyard of a decayed terraced house. He proceeded without problem. I, however, in following, snagged my trousers, my anorak and my skin on the sickle thorns of the brambles that infested the yard. I sucked a scratch on the back of my hand, while he opened the rotting door, lugging the two ghouls into the darkness within. A gut-turning stench billowed out and only Hobbes's urging made me enter.

'Come in,' he said, 'and mind how you come down the steps. You'd better turn on the light. You'll find the switch by your hand ... left a bit ... a bigger bit ... and down.'

I groped and turned it on. The narrow room didn't exactly flood with light, because the grime-encrusted, bare bulb dangling above us failed to match up to the task. Nonetheless, it dribbled out sufficient illumination to show a bleak, damp cellar, the crude painting of a funeral on the far wall doing nothing to improve it. Hobbes deposited the ghouls onto two filthy beds, tucked into a corner, where they lay messily, matching everything else down there. Their's was a cheerless, comfortless home, black with mould, a sticky nastiness coating the bare brick floor. All it contained was a pair of plain stools, a grubby, slimy-looking table, apparently constructed from coffin lids, some gruesome pans and bowls, a sink I doubted had ever been washed and, bizarrely, a stuffed crocodile.

While Hobbes rinsed out a pan and filled it with water, I took a proper look at the ghouls: thin, insipid creatures, dressed in filthy overalls and muddy boots, from which fetid white toes peeped. One was bald, while the other sported a greasy comb-over plastered across his translucent scalp. Yet, it was their faces that stuck in my memory and, although I'd formed an impression when I'd been in the grave, I wasn't prepared for their full awfulness. They looked like what would happen if some ham-fisted incompetent, having carved a pair of pumpkin lanterns, had left them outside for a week or two to moulder and fall in on themselves. The only parts that appeared substantial and healthy were their small, sharp, white teeth, set in jaws a bulldog might have been proud of. Yet, no dog had ever been cursed with breath like these two.

The one with the comb-over groaned as Hobbes splashed water in its face. Eyes, as cold and dark as those of a shark, opened and it sat up, rubbing its head with its claws. Looking up at Hobbes, it laughed, its mouth open, causing me to turn my head away as the charnel stench wreaked havoc on my stomach. Tottering upstairs into the garden, I threw up and leaned against the wall. Strange noises rose from the cellar as if two people were burping while a cat and a dog fought to the death. I stayed in the clean air, glad now of the cleansing rain and wind, until Hobbes emerged, pulling the door behind him, his brow corrugated in deep thought.

'What was that horrible noise?' I asked as he led the way back.

'I expect you mean my conversation with the ghoul. I don't get a chance to practise my Ghoulish very often and I think my accent amused him. However, the young fellow did tell me something interesting. Let's get out of this storm and I'll tell you. Hurry up.'

We jogged back through the rain, Hobbes silent until we were back in the car and on the move.

'The young ghoul,' he said, 'denies opening the grave you were mucking around in.'

'They must have. Who else would have done it?'

'Ghouls may have their faults but they don't lie. I don't think they understand the concept. No, as far as I could gather, the grave you were in was one they'd emptied years ago after the bones had matured; they prefer them dry.'

I winced. 'They're horrible.'

'They're not so bad, really. Live and let live. They only eat a few old bones their owners are done with and, mostly, they tidy up afterwards. Tonight, though, they were delayed because someone else was digging in their pantry.'

'Another ghoul?' I yawned, longing to be warm and dry and asleep.

'No, not a ghoul, a man. They watched him digging, apparently rather amateurishly and the interesting thing is that he removed something from the grave before running off without bothering to refill it.'

'Well, the last part's true. I really thought I was going to die down there.'

'These things happen.' He swerved and stopped the car. 'This sort of thing shouldn't, though.'

He got out, dragged an enormous branch from the road, and slid back in. 'Someone should have been taking care of that. It was rotten and could have caused an accident to the public.'

'Yeah ... but any idea who was robbing the grave?'

The car shot forward.

He shrugged. 'I don't know. Ghouls aren't good at describing humans. He was wearing a black balaclava, though.'

'Well, that narrows it down.' My heavy irony went unremarked, so I continued. 'And what did he take?'

'Something small and shiny and, since it didn't look edible, the ghouls weren't interested. They lurked in the shadows until he'd gone before starting on the grave they wanted. Unfortunately, you blundered in and ruined their plans. They'll go hungry tonight, poor things.'

'Poor things? They're disgusting. They shouldn't be allowed amongst ordinary, decent people. Aren't there laws against grave robbing?'

'You get used to them and there are many humans who aren't pleasant: humans such as the grave robber tonight. I hope we catch him.'

'But you took the ghouls home. You didn't even arrest them.'

He laughed. 'As you should know by now, most laws in this country are specific to humans. They simply don't apply to ghouls. The law doesn't recognise them.'

'Like it doesn't recognise gnomes?'

'You're catching on.'

I nodded. Since I'd met him, reality and dreams, or nightmares, had become intertwined. 'Umm …' I said, 'do you know whose grave it was? Might that be important?'

'Good lad.' He nodded, slapping me on the back as he swung the car round a bend. 'It belongs to a chap called Lucian Mondragon who, according to the gravestone, departed this life on the thirty-first of October 1905. I don't believe I ever met him.'

'1905? Why would anyone dig up such an old grave?'

'I wish I knew,' he said. 'Oddly, the ghouls said they smelled fresh meat. And, come to think of it, whatever you were jumping about on was still solid. What's more, it didn't sound like wood did it?'

'I don't know. Are you getting at something?'

'I suspect there's more in that grave than mud, more than there ought to be.' He pondered. 'I think I'd better take another look.'

'No, please.' I heard the panic rising in my voice. 'I'm cold, wet and tired. I can't do anymore tonight. I really can't.'

Hobbes nodded. 'I understand. Tell you what, I'll drop you back at your place. You take it easy and have a lie-in and I'll pick you up at … let's say ten tomorrow. OK?'

'Thank you.' I nearly wept. Fatigue was overwhelming me and I hadn't expected kindness.

Hobbes chuckled. 'Hang on.'

I'd barely noticed that, up to then, he'd been driving relatively slowly, almost with due care and attention, but he made up for it and I could hardly express my relief when he stopped and I was still alive. As I got out, he accelerated away between the lines of parked cars before I could even say goodnight. Trudging upstairs to my flat, switching on the electric fire, I stripped, washed off the worst of the mud, and collapsed into bed. It had been a horrible night.

A crash burst into my dreams and I awoke with blurred mind and senses, squinting at the alarm clock; it was just gone four. Why was there an orange light glowing under the bedroom door, and why could I smell smoke?

'Fire!' I screeched, leaping up, lurching towards the bedroom door, grabbing the handle and letting go with a yelp of pain. The handle was red hot and I was in deep trouble. Up till then, I'd been acting on instinct but cold terror was growing inside, weighing down my legs and stomach. Choking fumes tormented my throat and I began to cough uncontrollably. I pulled myself to the window, struggling to open it. Everything began to happen too fast. My head was spinning and I knew I was going to die. It was ironic, I thought, falling to my knees, that I'd only just returned from the grave. The window burst inwards as I slumped onto my face to sleep.

On opening my eyes again, I appeared to be outside, in mid-air, looking onto the patio beneath my window. It got closer, yet slowly. I was dropping gently, like a leaf.

I awoke in a bed. I knew it wasn't mine because of the clean, white sheets, though I was certain I'd crawled under my own duvet, with the familiar pong of stale curry and socks. A screen surrounded me and a table stood by my bedside. I groaned and a face appeared, a young woman's face, and I remembered being too tired to put on pyjamas. As I pulled the sheets around my chin, I found I was dressed in a sort of dress.

'Good afternoon, Mr Caplet.' The face spoke, its smile pushing through the screen.

A woman's body, dressed in nurse's uniform, followed the smile. It was all very puzzling. I was, it appeared, in hospital, but how? A memory surfaced, an idea of flinging myself from a speeding car to get away from Hobbes. Yes, Hobbes! Sitting upright abruptly, I groaned.

'How are you feeling?'

'Ohhhh!'

'Are you alright?'

'Ohhhh.'

'I'll get the doctor.' The nurse hurried away as I struggled to pull my wits within touching distance.

Coughing up something disgusting and acrid, brought back a hazy memory of fire. A quick check indicated that all of me was still present, though I'd acquired a white dressing on my right hand.

A boy in a white coat approached. 'Hello, Mr Caplet, I'm Dr Finlay. No jokes please. How are you this afternoon?'

My voice came out as a croak. 'OK, but my throat and chest are sore. So's my hand.'

'A bit of smoke inhalation and a minor burn. You were lucky the policeman was passing and got you out before there was any lasting harm.'

'Policeman?'

'Yes, apparently he was going off duty when, noticing the smoke, he broke in and got you out, before alerting the other residents and calling the Fire Brigade.'

'What policeman?' I had to ask, though I was sure I already knew.

'An officer named Hobbes brought you in. You're lucky to be alive but you'll be alright. We'll keep you in for observation overnight, though I doubt there'll be any problems. You'll probably cough a bit and you might feel a bit confused during the next few hours.'

'I've been feeling a bit confused ever since I met Hobbes.'

'You know him then?' Doctor Finlay's voice registered surprise. 'He's obviously a great bloke.'

'Obviously. What about my flat?'

'I'm afraid you don't have one anymore.'

'What happened?'

'It caught fire. You must know better than I how it might have started.'

Maybe the doc was right but I didn't wish to think about it. Not then.

I spent the rest of the day in hospital. Most of the time I was sleeping or drinking pints of water to wash the smoke taint from my tubes. The rest of the time seemed to involve me tottering round, looking for the bathroom. In my more lucid moments I wondered where I might stay when it was time to leave.

In the early evening I had a visitor. It was Ingrid. She was looking very pretty and worried and joy erupted at the sight of her. She sat beside me, asked how I felt, patting my hand, making sympathetic noises, finally crushing me by saying she couldn't stay long, as Phil was taking her to the opera. What a git he was.

I barely had a chance to say anything before she rose to leave. Then, as she turned, she hesitated and handed me a carrier bag. 'Mr Witcherley asked me to give you this.'

Inside were my cagoule, and a brown envelope.

'Rex? I didn't think he'd remember me. That's nice of him.'

She smiled. 'See you.'

'Goodbye, Ingrid. Thanks for coming.' I deflated as soon as she was out of sight.

A couple of minutes later, I tore open the envelope with a warm feeling of gratitude. Perhaps Rex wasn't as bad as I'd thought.

Dear Mr Capstan.

It got up my nose that he'd got my name wrong, and not for the first time.

The Sorenchester and District Bugle has been undertaking a review. As a result of this, and because of your continued failure to produce requested articles on time, I regret to inform you that your services are no longer required. Please find enclosed a cheque for one month's salary in lieu of notice. Many thanks for your contribution and get well soon.

Yours,

Rex Witcherley.

I'd never exactly been a high-flyer, yet the thud of my ego hitting rock bottom left me stunned. I had no job, no home, no girlfriend and, I realised, no clothes, apart from a short cagoule. At least things couldn't get any worse.

Rock bottom split apart and plunged me into Hell.

'Evening, Andy. How are you?' asked Hobbes cheerfully, approaching.

'Not bad,' I said. 'More like bloody awful.'

'I'm sorry to hear that. Dr Finlay informed me you were on the mend.'

I was ashamed. After all, Hobbes had saved my life, such as it was. Still, I couldn't help but feel he was partly to blame for my misfortunes and that, if I'd died, things might have been better. No matter how hard I tried to look on the bright side, I couldn't see round the dark side. 'I'm sorry,' I said, 'but the last couple of days have been a bit traumatic. I didn't have much and now I've got nothing. I've got nowhere to live, Ingrid's going to the opera with Phil and I've just been sacked.'

Hobbes shrugged. 'Don't despair,' he said. 'Adversity often brings out the best in people. You'll be alright, your friends will help out.'

That didn't improve my state of mind, merely bringing home the fact that I had no friends, not real ones, anyway. Apart from Ingrid and some blokes I sometimes talked to in the pub, there was no one to turn to.

'Anyway,' he continued, 'you'll be out of here in the morning and you'll have to stay with someone until you can sort out another place.'

I tried to think. There were my parents of course. They would take me in. She'd be delighted to have me to mother again. She meant well but it had been such a struggle to escape her stifling affections the last time my life had gone belly up. As for him? He'd love letting me know just how useless I was, pointing out every mistake I'd ever made from childhood onwards. I couldn't do it to myself; there had to be another option.

'If you're really stuck,' said Hobbes, 'I've got a spare room.'

I listened, considering the proposal, highlighting just how low I'd sunk. Those were my choices: Hobbes or my parents.

'Thank you,' I said at last. 'I am really stuck and your spare room seems my best option.' God help me, I thought.

'Great.' He grinned. 'I'll let Mrs Goodfellow know, so she can make up a bed.'

'Oh good,' I said. Incredible though it might seem, I'd forgotten her. Maybe it was self-defence, for there are only so many horrors a mind can hold. 'I've got no clothes, or money, apart from this cheque.' I read it. It was for five hundred pounds and made out to Andrew Capstan. The Editorsaurus had got my first name right.

'I'll get Mrs Goodfellow to sort you out some clothes and pick you up tomorrow.'

'Thank you.' Despite everything, I really meant it.

Then I slept.

Shortly after breakfast, a cheerful Dr Finlay told me I was fit to go, though he advised taking it easy and keeping the dressing on my hand for a day or two. I sat up in bed, wishing I didn't have to leave. It had been pleasant to lie between clean sheets and have nurses caring for me.

'Hello, dear.' Mrs Goodfellow was standing by my bed, her eyes bright as a cat's in the morning sun. My body jolted with the shock and my heart thumped like a drum roll. Somehow, I found myself standing on the floor with the bed between us.

'Did I shock you?' she beamed. 'That's a nice frock you're wearing. I didn't know you liked women's clothing or I'd have brought you some.'

'I don't normally wear this sort of stuff,' I explained. 'This is just a gown they put on me because I lost all my clothes, man clothes, in the fire.'

'Have it your own way, dear. I don't mind. The old fellow says we have to live and let live and I reckon he's right. I hope these suit you.'

Hauling a battered leather case onto the bed, she opened it, pulling out a carefully folded tweed suit in rusty-herringbone, a gleaming white shirt, a silk tie with a subtle flower pattern that matched the suit exactly, a pair of thick black socks, white cotton underwear, a pair of glossy brown brogues and a white linen handkerchief. Everything looked old-fashioned and I was more a jeans and sweater person, yet they were all I'd got and, until I could get Rex to change the name on the cheque, all I seemed likely to get. It struck me I really was penniless and destitute and reliant on Hobbes's charity.

'They look OK, thanks,' I said. 'Umm … would you mind turning your back while I put them on?'

'Bashful are you, dear?' she twinkled but turned around and sat on the bed.

I dressed, surprised how everything fitted perfectly, though it felt stiff and heavy compared to my usual garb. I noticed the faint odours of cigar smoke and lavender and wished I could see myself.

'Very smart, dear, now, come along and I'll take you home.'

'Thank you.'

She led the way from the hospital at a surprising pace, down the hill, past the supermarket, up Goat Street, along Rampart Street, Golden Gate Lane and finally to Blackdog Street. Though, she'd swapped her wellingtons for a pair of trainers, the rest of her, apart from the absence of a pinafore, was as I remembered: a green headscarf that didn't quite match her woolly, yellow cardigan and a voluminous, brown and cream checked skirt. The sun shone on my arrival at Hobbes's.

'Here we are.' Unlocking the door to number 13, she stepped inside.

Taking a deep breath, I followed as she led me upstairs, opening the door into the end room. I was pleasantly surprised, if puzzled. It was a good size, with bare white walls, low black beams, a polished wood floor, a dressing table with a stool and a small wardrobe. What it lacked, was a bed.

'The old fellow,' she said, 'asked me to make up a bed for you. I haven't had time yet, but all the bits are in the attic.'

I offered to go up and fetch them down but she said some of the planking was rather ropey and might be dangerous.

'I'll do it, dear, and it won't take five minutes.'

She was right. It took the best part of an hour because, having hauled herself up the foldaway ladder into the attic, she discovered an extended family of mice had taken up residence, and took up the pursuit with gusto and a wooden tennis racquet. I could hear her feet thumping above, interspersed with occasional thwacks as she found a target. At any minute, I expected to see her plunge through the ceiling. Eventually, everything went quiet: too quiet. I waited a couple of minutes.

'Umm … Mrs Goodfellow? Are you alright?' Not a sound.

Hesitating for a few more seconds, I started up the ladder. The faint light in the attic was squeezing through the bars of a tiny window, dust dancing in its beam, and I glimpsed wonderful things in the instant my head poked through the hatch. Hearing a thwack and a mad cackle, I lost my grip, stretching my length on the landing rug.

A wizened face poked through the hatch upside down. 'Got the little devil! Are you alright, dear?'

I nodded, standing up, feeling a little groggy.

'Can you catch with that bandage on?'

'Umm … yes well, probably.'

'Good,' she said, 'catch these.'

She patted a small brown object with her racquet. It twisted through the air and, despite fumbling, I grabbed it before it hit the floor. It was a limp mouse.

'Next one.' She patted another.

In the end, I had eight little bodies in my hands. I stared at them, aghast, not knowing what to do as she slid down the ladder.

'Better hurry,' she said. 'Let's get 'em to the park before they wake up.'

They were already stirring when we got there, one taking a speculative nibble at my finger. I released them and they disappeared into a hedge and began a frantic rustling. I sucked away a bead of blood as Mrs Goodfellow took my arm.

'Come along, dear. It's time I had you in bed.'

A smart, young woman, wheeling a child in a pushchair, gave me a most peculiar look. Though I tried a tentative smile, she turned away as Mrs Goodfellow propelled me back to Blackdog Street.

Once we were inside, I watched amazed as she disappeared into the attic and emerged with bits of iron, slats of wood and a mattress, building the bed in five minutes, making it up with sheets, blankets and an eiderdown. It all looked antique, yet was clean and smelled of fresh lavender.

'There you are, dear,' she said. 'I hope you'll be comfortable. You'll find more clothes in the wardrobe. Help yourself.'

'Thank you. Umm … whose are they?' I knew they weren't Hobbes's; I doubted whether he'd even be able to pull the trousers over his arms.

'Yours, if you want 'em.' She grinned her toothless grin. 'They belonged to my husband but he doesn't need 'em anymore.'

'You're very kind.' I assumed Mr Goodfellow had passed away.

'Kind? Not really. It's more of an advanced payment for when you let me have your teeth.'

As I smiled, I noticed the gleam in her eyes, examining my mouth like a connoisseur. I snapped the display shut.

'I can't wait to get my hands on that lot,' she said as she left the room.

I sat on the bed and tried to get my thoughts in order.

'Liver? What about liver?'

I flinched and leaped to my feet as she leaned towards me. 'You can't have my liver!'

She laughed. 'I don't want your liver, I was asking if you like to eat liver, because not everyone does, you know. I'm planning a liver and bacon casserole for supper and was wondering if you like good, old-fashioned food.'

'Oh,' I said, ashamed, 'it sounds lovely. Are you sure Hobbes … are you sure Inspector Hobbes won't mind?'

'Mind? Of course he won't. He'll be glad of the company. He doesn't get too many visitors, more's the pity.'

'Well,' I said, because I had not yet given food a thought, 'in that case, I would be delighted.' I made an attempt at a smile.

'Ooh,' she said peering up at me, 'you do have a really lovely smile. I can hardly wait.'

I forced a laugh, which sounded rather hysterical. 'Well, let's hope it won't be for many years.'

She cackled and patted my arm. 'Lovely smile, lovely smile.' She walked away. 'Likes liver, too. Lovely boy, lovely smile.'

I sat on the bed, trembling. In happier times I would sometimes sit and think. On this occasion I just sat and stared at the wall, my mind cowering in a dark corner of my skull, refusing to come out.

I must have been there for a couple of hours when I heard the tortured whine of a car's engine, followed by the sound of brakes, and I knew Hobbes had returned. Gulping, taking a deep breath, I went downstairs.

'Good afternoon,' Hobbes boomed. 'Has Mrs Goodfellow made you comfortable?'

'Yes,' I said, 'very comfortable, thank you.' Truthfully, she made me feel exceedingly uncomfortable, but it would have been churlish to say so.

'Good.' He rubbed his hands together, making a sound like someone vigorously wiping their feet on a coconut doormat. 'What are you going to do with yourself for the rest of the day?'

He had me there. What was I going to do? Obviously, I needed the Editorsaurus to amend the cheque, yet I didn't feel up to confronting him just then, if ever. I supposed I ought to sign on as unemployed, except I guessed that, being a Saturday, the job centre would be shut, and, besides, I hadn't the foggiest where it was or what to do. I wondered about taking myself round town to see if there were any vacancy ads in shop windows, though I wasn't sure anyone did that sort of thing anymore.

'I don't know,' I admitted.

'In which case, how about coming with me, if you're still interested in police work now you're not working for the *Bugle*?'

I pondered for a moment. I had more than a few misgivings, but then I realised he'd shown me things that had rocked my perception of the world and, deep within, a seed of curiosity had sprouted. I was astonished to discover how much I wanted it to grow, for it might change my life, which, just then, felt like a great idea.

'I'd like that,' I said and, though a sensible part of me was screaming no, my new spirit of curiosity, proving more powerful, stifled it. 'And, if the *Bugle* doesn't want me, maybe I can go freelance.'

Hobbes, nodding approvingly, patted me on the back, knocking me to the floor, and helped me back to my feet. 'Take a seat. I've got a few things to tell you.' He indicated the sofa.

We sat side by side and he turned to me with a grin that might have revived my sensible part, had the scent of baking bread, wafting in from the kitchen, not soothed my nerves.

'I took another look into the grave the other night,' he said, 'and the box you'd been jumping around on was, in fact, a plastic wheelie bin, resting on the remains of the original coffin, which the ghouls had evidently broken into decades ago. However, the wheelie bin contained a fresh body. Well, fairly fresh.'

'Murder, then?' The thought of how close I'd been to a corpse, not to mention how close I'd been to becoming one, made me feel sick. Fighting back the feeling, I forced myself to concentrate.

'Almost certainly, though let's not be too hasty.'

'It could hardly have been suicide.'

'No, I think we can rule out suicide.' He looked thoughtful. 'That's unless he was very inventive. It seems to me that, if someone wants to hide a body, where better than in a grave? It's the last place anyone would look for one and, if it hadn't been for us keeping an eye on those ghouls, someone would probably have got away with it. It still begs the question of why anyone would dig it up again.'

'Umm … whose body was it? You say it was a he?'

'He was an adult male and, apart from that, it's hard to tell. There was no ID or anything and his face was bashed in, so I've got our forensic lads checking dental records, DNA, prints and so on. The corpse's clothes were muddy, yet the mud wasn't the same as that in the graveyard. Plus, he was wearing wellington boots with worn soles.'

'Cheese and pickle?' said Mrs Goodfellow's shrill voice from behind.

Gasping, shocked by the suddenness of her voice and how silently she'd got there, I stared at her over my shoulder. Her head was tilted to one side, her eyes glittering like a sparrow's.

'Would you boys like a cheese and pickle sandwich? Or are you going out for your dinner?'

'A sandwich would be lovely,' said Hobbes.

'It would be very nice,' I said, voice quavering to match hers.

'I'll do it right away. I expect you'll be hungry.'

She was correct. Hospital breakfasts are inadequate, at least for me. I turned back to Hobbes, expecting her to leave.

'Tea? Or coffee?' Her voice rang in my ear.

My heart jumped and I clutched my chest, which must have looked somewhat theatrical, yet was genuine. I had a sudden panic that my much-abused ticker was going to burst from my rib cage. Unexpected noises had always alarmed me and I seemed to be getting worse at dealing with them.

'Tea, please,' said Hobbes.

'Hahaha,' said I, nodding my head, 'and the same for me.'

She smiled and I watched her walk towards the kitchen, making sure she left the sitting room. Her startling appearances were doing me no good at all.

'With all the excitement recently,' said Hobbes, 'I haven't had time to interview Mr Roman's staff, so I thought we might do that this afternoon. Unfortunately, Superintendent Cooper has suggested I should concentrate on the grave case and let sleeping Mr Roman's lie. She believes it was just a minor burglary case, that I've already proved no one else was involved in Roman's death, and that there are more important cases to attend to.' He paused, looking thoughtful. 'The trouble is, I'm intrigued, because, though it may only have been a break-in, it led to suicide; I want to know why.'

'So, what are you going to do?'

'Interview Roman's staff, as I said.'

'Won't the superintendent be angry?'

'Not if I don't tell her.' He grinned. 'And I'm not really supposed to have you working with me now you've got the push from the *Bugle*. I'm not planning on telling her about that either.'

'Will there be any danger?'

'If we're lucky.'

Nodding, I wondered again why I'd agreed to go with him. Perhaps, I was crazy. More likely, I just wasn't good at saying no.

'Tell me,' I asked, as a thought occurred, 'what, exactly, is your job?'

He looked at me, obviously puzzled. 'I'm a police officer, a detective inspector to be precise.'

'I know that but, what I mean is, don't you get assigned to things like the flying squad, or traffic, or fraud, or something? That is to say, don't you have a speciality?'

Hobbes displayed his happy wolf grin. 'You sound just like my old Super. He would demand that I stuck to his orders, even when I pointed out that policing was policing and that I would always do whatever it took. He kept insisting that I was wilfully disobeying his orders, even when I pointed out how foolish they were.'

'Did he get mad?'

'Yes,' said Hobbes, 'he got quite mad in the end, poor chap. Still it was only when he took to throwing pointy cabbages at passers-by from the station roof that they had to take him away – not that they were much danger to anyone, because he'd over-boiled them.'

'You mean he literally went mad?' The news shocked and scared me. If Hobbes had been responsible for driving a police superintendent mad, what chance did I have of keeping my sanity? Of course, I'd already agreed to stay in his house and to continue working with him when I didn't need to, so already I wasn't acting entirely rationally. Thinking about it, I had, in the last few hours, been nearly buried alive by ghouls, burned in my own bedroom, and caught handfuls of live mice patted to me by an old lady in an attic. Perhaps there was no reason to fear going mad, maybe I had already tipped over the edge. I chuckled as Hobbes continued.

'Went mad? I don't know if he actually went mad, because the lads reckoned he must already have been mad to try and tell me what to do in the first place.'

'What about your new superintendent?'

'Superintendent Cooper is a very sensible woman and only makes suggestions and I can't wilfully disobey a suggestion. Besides, I think she's mostly happy to let me police in my own way.'

'Sensible indeed.' I knew I wouldn't care, or dare, to reprimand him.

'Your dinners are on the table,' Mrs Goodfellow piped up by my right ear.

'Aghh!' Springing lightly across the room, catching my foot on the coffee table, I stumbled against the standard lamp.

Hobbes caught the lamp before it fell and guffawed, shaking his head. 'By heck, Andy,' he said, wiping his eyes, 'your comic tumbling turn ought to be shown on the telly. Funniest thing I've seen since they took the old superintendent away.'

Mrs Goodfellow beaming, nudging me in the ribs, whispered, 'I'm glad to see you getting on so well with the old fellow. I haven't heard him laugh so much for months.'

After rubbing my bruised shin, I followed the laughter into the kitchen, Mrs Goodfellow reaching up and patting my back.

Still, there were compensations to staying at Hobbes's, as I discovered on the kitchen table. The old woman had prepared a huge plateful of sandwiches and, sitting down, I grabbed one from the top, took a bite and savoured the wonderful carnival of textures and flavours filling my mouth. Now, cheese and pickle sandwiches were not something I'd normally rave about, but, the crusty bread still being warm and fragrant from the oven, the primrose-yellow butter dripping through like honey, the cheese tasting tangy and sweet, and all cut to a satisfying thickness, then it was a meal fit for a king.

Mrs Goodfellow clicked her tongue and Hobbes frowned, gesturing for me to stand. He lowered his head. 'For what we are about to receive, may the Good Lord make us truly thankful. Amen.'

'Amen,' said Mrs Goodfellow.

I felt the blood rushing to my face.

'Don't worry,' said Hobbes, sitting and helping himself to a sandwich, 'you weren't to know our customs, but you will next time. Now, tuck in.'

I tucked in. The steaming mug of tea Mrs Goodfellow poured for me was excellent, too. Hobbes was well looked after and, evidently, so would I be during my stay. I quite forgot my embarrassment and my problems at that scrubbed table. Perhaps madness had something going for it.

Eventually Hobbes finished and pushed his chair back. 'Thank you,' he told his housekeeper, 'that was most excellent.'

'Yes, indeed,' I enthused, 'it was really good.'

She grinned gummily and blushed like a schoolgirl.

'Right, then,' said Hobbes, 'to business.'

'To business!' I raised my mug in a facetious toast.

A baffled frown wrinkled his forehead.

As he got up from the table and left the house, I followed, meek as a lamb, though the butterflies were, once again, taking wing in my stomach at the prospect of more of his driving. I was, however, spared, at least temporarily, for he led me down The Shambles in a brisk five-minute walk. Despite the pale sun shining in a watery sky, a fierce north-easterly wind obliterated any warmth and I was glad of my tweed suit, which, in addition to its insulating properties, must, I felt, be giving me a most distinguished air. When a couple of women chatting outside the church smiled as we walked by, my back straightened and my chin lifted, until self-doubt launched a counter attack: they'd probably smiled because I looked so ridiculous and old-fashioned. Yet there was no time to brood for Hobbes, shoulders hunched, shambling but surprisingly fast, was getting ahead of me. I took great, long, strides to keep up, stumbling on a cracked paving stone.

A portly youth smirked. 'Enjoy your trip?'

Ignoring him, I hurried after Hobbes, who having turned onto Up Way, entered the Bear with a Sore Head. It was great to slam the door in the face of the biting wind and appreciate the log fire glowing from the far side, casting shadows against the low-beamed ceiling. Customers lounged in pairs or small groups around brass-rimmed tables, a shaven-headed barman in a gaudy silk waistcoat pulled a pint of cider for a red-faced, giggling girl, and a plump, pretty woman, probably in her late-forties, in a white apron, chatted to a tall, slim man in a smart, grey suit, who was leaning against the bar. He turned as we approached and stepped towards me, hand outstretched. It was bloody Phil.

Grinning, he shook my hand, squeezing my fingers, maintaining his grip for slightly longer than felt comfortable.

'Hiya, Andy. I hardly recognised you. Nice clothes.'

'Hello,' I said.

'I was very sorry to hear about your flat.' He smirked. 'It must have been a real bummer, and then losing your job! Rex might have been a bit kinder.'

'Thanks,' I said, hating his smug concern.

'Still, you're looking good and that suit really is something else, very much the country gent.'

I snarled internally. 'Did you enjoy the opera?' I asked, with a friendly smile.

'Not much. The tenor tended to sing flat and it turns out that poor Ingrid is allergic to lobster. We had to leave before the interval and she threw up all over me.'

'Poor girl,' I sympathised, concealing my delight.

Hobbes beckoned.

'I'm sorry,' I said. 'I've got to go. See you.'

I stepped round Phil to where Hobbes was introducing himself to the lady in the white apron.

He smiled as I approached. 'A friend of yours?' He nodded towards Phil, who was just leaving the pub.

'No,' I said, 'that was Phil. He's a git.'

The lady frowned. 'He seemed a very pleasant young man to me. He's a reporter but very polite and well-spoken, unlike that one at the pet show. My sister said she'd never heard such language, and in front of the kiddies, too, and all because a hamster nipped him.'

'Mrs Tomkins,' said Hobbes, 'may I introduce Andy Caplet, who's assisting me on this case? Andy, this is Mrs Tomkins, who used to be Mr Roman's cook. She has graciously agreed to talk to me for a few minutes. Would anyone like a drink?'

'A coffee please,' she said.

'A pint of lager.' I reckoned I could do with a drink.

'And I'll have a quart of bitter. No, better make it a lashing of ginger beer, I'll be driving soon.' Hobbes nodded at the barman and placed his order.

'How much?' he asked when the drinks were poured.

The barman shook his head. 'On the house, Inspector.'

I smiled at Mrs Tomkins who did not reciprocate; evidently she had not yet forgiven me for my remark about Phil. Hobbes, escorting her to a round table, pulling out a chair for her, sat down opposite.

After a few pleasantries, he got down to business.

'How long did you cook for Mr Roman?'

'Twelve years. It was part-time; I didn't live in like in the old days. None of us did.'

'And why did you leave?'

'Because we were no longer required. That was almost a year ago now, I suppose.'

Hobbes nodded. 'So I'd heard. Do you know why?'

'No.' She shook her head. 'At least, not for certain. I believe he might have had some money troubles. He had to sell a painting, but not one he'd done, one of the good, old ones he was fond of, one his parents had brought from wherever they came from. Did you know they weren't British? To be honest, I was glad it had gone: it gave me the creeps. It was a nasty, evil-looking king holding a dagger. I suppose it must have been worth a bob or two.'

'Though,' said Hobbes, 'not enough to enable him to keep his staff on.'

'Apparently not,' said Mrs Tomkins.

He continued. 'What did you feel about Mr Roman when he sacked you?'

Her face flushed. 'I was pretty angry. We all were, especially Jimmy, the gardener. It was all so sudden. One day we had jobs, next day he called us in and gave us our marching orders and a cheque for a month's pay. Two thousand quid doesn't go far and I had a lad at college to support. Still, it all worked out pretty well in the end. I got a job here. It's close enough to walk to and the pay's better. So's the company.'

I'd been listening, nodding and sipping lager quite happily, until she mentioned her pay. Two thousand pounds a month? For a cook? For a part-time cook! I'd been getting a quarter of that at the *Bugle*. It wasn't fair. I muttered under my breath, railing against Editorsaurus Rex and his antediluvian pay scales, until Hobbes growled at me to shut up.

He turned back to Mrs Tomkins. She'd not much liked Mr Roman, who'd been brusque, though not actually rude, to her and to the other staff. She believed Anna Nicholls, the maid, and Jimmy Pinker, the gardener, had also disliked him. She had, however, loved the house and mentioned how conscientious Anna had been with her dusting and vacuuming, moving the furniture nearly every day, despite its bulk. Hobbes listened intently, occasionally scratching with a pencil in a small leather-bound notebook he'd taken from his coat pocket. She could cast no light on why Mr Roman had been burgled, or why he might have committed suicide. Neither Anna nor Jimmy had kept in touch, though she'd heard they shared a flat in Pigton. Eventually, Hobbes thanking her, drained his ginger beer, rose from the chair and led me out.

Still fuming about my wretched cheque, I came close to marching into the *Bugle's* offices to confront the Editorsaurus, but Hobbes was restless, itching to interview Anna Nicholls and Jimmy Pinker. My resolve proved as firm as wet tissue paper and I found myself walking beside him to his car.

I cursed my weakness as we set off to Pigton. Very quickly though, I was cursing his driving. What on Earth was wrong with me? I didn't need to be with him, I could have been cadging a lager off someone, somewhere with a fire and a jukebox, somewhere where I was not in constant fear.

I gritted my teeth, clinging to the seat as we hurtled into Pigton, stopping outside a damp-stained, concrete block of flats. Getting out, I followed him up the steps to the door, which, though it had once been an electronic security door, was hanging open from one twisted hinge, a stench of smoke and stale urine emerging from inside. We entered, heading towards a concrete staircase, where three boys, about fourteen years old, slouched on the tiled floor below, smoking and giggling. Hobbes approached them.

'Hullo, hullo, hullo,' he said, and I swear that's what he said, 'what's going on here then?'

One of the boys spoke from deep within a grey hood. 'We're just chilling, so don't go giving us no hassle, man.' His two companions giggled again and I caught a whiff of their smoke. It wasn't tobacco.

'It doesn't surprise me you're chilly,' said Hobbes. 'It is draughty out here and a seat on cold tiles could give you piles. Why don't you go to a nice warm café?'

'Ain't got no money, 'ave we?' The biggest of the lads, sporting a stud through his lip, his face erupting with pimples and pale whiskers, sneered.

'Tell you what,' said Hobbes, squatting down to their level, 'I'll trade you.'

His right hand flashed forward, ripping the spliffs from their mouths. He stubbed them out on the palm of his left hand, the three lads staring open-mouthed and wide eyed, and reached into his coat pocket for his horrid, hairy, little wallet, removing a ten-pound note, handing it to the smallest youth. 'There you go, boys. Remember, smoking can damage your health. And now you can have a nice warm drink in the café. Can't you?'

There was a moment's silence and all three stood up, obediently, looking completely bemused, being quite polite. The one in the hood even said, 'Thanks,' as they walked away.

'Just chilling.' Hobbes snorted and chuckled. 'Where do they pick up these expressions? In Pigton of all places?' Scrunching up the remains of the cigarettes, he took them outside and let them blow away on the wind. When he returned to the lobby, he bounded up the stairs onto the second floor. I puffed after him.

He knocked on a door. After a short pause it opened a little, restrained by a chain. A scared young woman, with short dark hair and huge blue eyes, tear-stained behind heavy glasses, peered through. On seeing Hobbes, she gasped, recoiling, trying to slam the door. He used his fingers to keep it open.

'Sorry to bother you, Miss Nichols.' He showed her his ID with his free hand. 'I'm Detective Inspector Hobbes from Sorenchester. I was wondering if I might have a word with you?'

'Oh, you're the police.' She smiled. 'Please come in.'

Unchaining the door, she let us in. She was small, dark and neat, dressed in old jeans and a faded T-shirt, her smile transforming her into something of beauty. 'I'm ever so sorry about your fingers,' she said, 'but we've had some trouble with burglars in the flats, I thought you might be them.'

'Fingers?' Hobbes looked intrigued. 'What's wrong with my fingers?'

'I trapped them in the door.'

'Think no more of it. By the way, the young fellow lurking behind me is Andy, who's assisting with my enquiries into a burglary at Mr Roman's house.'

'Mr Roman's been burgled? How dreadful. How's he taking it? Please take a seat.'

Indicating a saggy, threadbare old sofa, she seated herself in a corduroy beanbag. Everything was clean and orderly, the scent of Flash and polish trying hard to mask the stink of boiled cabbage from the tight, ugly kitchenette, yet it was a poky little flat, with threadbare carpets, mouldy walls and sparse furniture. Piled in the far corner, still in their boxes, were iPods, laptops, a plasma television and various other items I couldn't make out.

'I'm afraid to say,' said Hobbes, 'that Mr Roman took it rather badly and committed suicide.'

'How awful.' She wiped away tears. 'Poor man.'

'Hadn't you seen anything about it in the news?' I asked.

'No, I've been busy. I clean at the hospital and I'm doing all the overtime I can get. Money's been so tight since we lost our jobs at Mr Roman's.'

She noticed Hobbes's glance at the boxes.

'Jimmy picked those up. He said he'd had a bit of luck on the horses.' She turned her face away, wiping her eyes.

'Where is Jimmy?' Hobbes's voice was gentle.

'I don't know.' Her tears began to flow. 'He's gone. We'd argued about money and things and he stormed out saying someone in Sorenchester owed him and it was time he paid up. He never came back.'

'When was that?'

'Last week.' She sniffed. 'On Thursday. I don't know what to do.'

'Do you have a photo I could take?' Hobbes looked troubled.

Nodding, she pulled one from her handbag.

He studied it and grimaced. 'Thank you. I'll look into it. In the meantime, do you know any reason why Mr Roman might have been burgled or killed himself?'

'No.' She shook her head. 'He wasn't the sort who'd make enemies, though I don't think he had many friends either. Some of his stuff must have been worth a bit, but I don't believe he had much spare money.'

'Were you upset when you lost your job with him?'

She nodded.

'And Jimmy?'

She closed her eyes a moment and spoke in a quiet, controlled voice. 'Jimmy was furious and said some wild things, but he wouldn't do anything like burglary … I don't think so … would he?' She hesitated and even I could see the appeal for reassurance in her eyes. She must have had suspicions.

Hobbes shrugged. 'People sometimes do desperate or silly things when they need money badly.'

'You think Jimmy did it?' Her face was a mask of misery.

'I don't know,' said Hobbes. 'However, he seems to have gone missing the day Roman's place was burgled. It may just be coincidence.'

He asked me to give her some privacy, so I stood outside, while he spoke softly to her. I couldn't hear very much, yet her tears had stopped by the time he left and she gave him a grateful smile. It struck me as peculiar how she'd responded to him. Though her first reaction had been terror, as soon as he'd shown his ID it was as if all she could see was the reassuring bulk of a policeman.

It was starting to get dark when we left the flats, and the pavements were awash with people, many spilling over into the road. Most, those wearing dark blue, looked morose, but small groups sporting red and white favours were smiling and making all the noise.

Hobbes sighed. 'The football's finished already. I'd hoped to get away before the crowds. Oh, well, it can't be helped. Looks like Pigton lost again and to Hedbury Rovers, too.'

To my astonishment, he eased the car through the crowds with care and consideration. I pointed this out.

'There are far too many uncertainties to proceed any faster with safety,' he said, 'there's too much I can't predict and too many variables to consider. A member of the public might step into the road or stumble or get pushed and the public is astonishingly prone to damage if hit by a car, even a small one such as this.'

I would have liked to question him more about his philosophy on driving, because, it seemed to me that he was normally close to the edge of disaster and, in my opinion, the public, specifically myself, was astonishingly prone to damage if smashed into a tree or a wall or an oncoming vehicle at the speeds he went.

I was trying to phrase a question in such a way as not to offend him when the trouble started.

A bottle flew from the mass of Pigton supporters, glancing off the shoulder of one of the red and white Hedbury fans, shattering the plate-glass window of a shop, Sharif Electrical Supplies. The fan turned with an expression of anger and pain, hesitated, shook his head and continued walking, rubbing his shoulder. Someone in the crowd, leaning through the shattered window, grabbed a watch. Someone went for an iPod and within a few seconds it had become a free-for-all. People seized radios, food mixers, steam irons, anything. The shopkeeper, a plump, bearded guy in a white robe, ran out, waving his arms, shouting, trying to save his goods.

A fist struck the side of his head. I felt a sick sensation of utter helplessness, chilling like ice in my stomach as the shopkeeper fell, a pack forming around him. When one beer-bellied, tattooed lout raised his booted foot to deliver a kick, I couldn't watch and turned away. Though most of the onlookers looked as horrified as I was, no one was going to the poor man's aid.

'Can't you do anything?' I asked, but the car had already stopped, the door was open and Hobbes was gone. It all went quiet.

Three men were lying motionless on the pavement as he helped the shopkeeper to his feet. A phalanx of about a dozen shaven-headed thugs, muscling through the crowd, charged as Hobbes pushed the shopkeeper behind him. I'm not quite sure what happened next, since those in the rear of the charge blocked my view. There was a loud crack, as if heads had knocked together, and then most of those who'd been following were sprawling over those who'd been in front. Hobbes was standing exactly where he had been, his great teeth glinting red in a shaft of light from the setting sun that had just peeped below the evening clouds.

By the time two police vans arrived, uniformed officers bursting from them, looking mean, the trouble had ceased. All was weirdly quiet, except for the moaning of the debris piled at Hobbes's feet. The police looked at the shop front, then at the groaning heap, and then at Hobbes. I sensed indecision. They must have suspected him of being responsible, yet no one appeared willing to accost him. Their relief was evident when he flashed his ID.

'These men attacked the shop,' he said. 'It was a set-up, using the cover of the football crowds. Fortunately, I happened to be passing and prevented the situation getting too ugly, though Mr Sharif was assaulted by this gentleman.' He poked a groaning man near the bottom of the heap with his boot. 'This man broke the window.' He pointed at a body near the top. 'This one,' he hauled one from the middle, collapsing the pile into individual moaning invalids, 'tried to put the boot in.'

'These good people,' said Hobbes, pointing at a group, shamefacedly holding electrical goods, 'witnessed the attack. Didn't you, lads?'

They stared, dumbfounded and, one by one, nodded.

'I see they've picked up a few items for safekeeping with the intent of returning them to Mr Sharif. If they put them back immediately, we will say no more about it. Right?'

They returned the goods.

'Great.' Hobbes turned his bulk towards the police officers. 'I'll leave it in your hands.'

Smiling, he strode back to the car, got in and began threading it through the crowd. People, talking in small groups, pointing at us, raised their thumbs or nodded as we passed. I acknowledged their gestures, feeling the warm glow of satisfaction and reflected heroism.

All too soon, the crowds thinning and Hobbes's foot growing heavier, we were hurtling back down the dual carriageway towards Sorenchester. He was humming sonorously over the engine. It was a tune I thought I ought to recognise and I tried to decipher it, since it took my mind off the speed, though, whenever I was getting close, the car would swerve or brake and my thought process would tumble like a pile of child's bricks. I never did get it.

6

We'd parked outside the police station and were heading for the entrance when it occurred to me to ask to see what Jimmy looked like. Hobbes, stopping, fished in his coat pocket, pulling out the photograph and holding it under a light. Jimmy, more than a little pie-eyed to judge by his expression and the number of empty glasses heaped around him, was smiling. I'd guess he was about thirty, small, with dark, slicked-back hair, an undergrowth of stubble sprouting from chin and cheeks. He was in a black shirt and jacket and, since the flash had turned his eyes red and his skin deathly pale, looked extraordinarily sinister.

'I wouldn't want to meet him on a dark night,' I said, sniggering, unthinking.

'I suspect you already have,' said Hobbes.

Realisation hit me like a punch to the stomach. 'It was Jimmy in the bin?'

He nodded. 'I fear so, though I won't know for certain until the forensic lads report. Of course, his face had been bashed in, but the bits left looked like bits on the photograph, though not necessarily in the same place.'

'Poor Anna,' I said, feeling sorry for the little woman. 'Who could have done it?'

He shrugged. 'I don't know yet, but I agree, Miss Nicholls will be distraught. Still, in my opinion, she could do far better than Jimmy Pinker.'

'Umm … d'you think Jimmy is connected with the burglary?'

'I'll be surprised if there isn't a connection, but shouldn't we go to my office? Or do you prefer standing out here?'

The wind, whistling around my ears, left them feeling as though they'd been boxed. I shivered. 'Let's go in. I'm getting cold.'

'Not as cold as Jimmy.' Putting the photograph back in his pocket, he turned towards his office, sniffing the air. 'I wouldn't be at all surprised if there was a frost tonight.'

All I could smell was car fumes, burnt rubber and, blown in from afar, a subtle hint of chips. I followed him inside, making tea, while he, slouching at his desk, wrote laboriously on a sheet of paper. I supposed it was a report, although I wasn't sure he actually reported to anyone.

It gave me time to sit and think about the case. If Jimmy had been the burglar, then who'd killed him? Perhaps, whoever it was had wanted to get their hands on his swag, if he'd actually stolen anything that was. But why? And who had buried the body? And why in that particular grave? What really puzzled me was why whoever had done it had then returned and dug it up again. The whole affair was grotesque, yet it felt right that Hobbes was investigating. I just wondered what my role was.

Though no answers came, more questions did. Was the body, in fact, that of the burglar and, if so, had Mr Roman been responsible? It might explain why Hobbes had found him so distracted, why he'd made up such a bizarre story and killed himself. Still,

I found it incredible that a respectable man would murder and dispose of the body in such a crazy manner. Why would he? And, of course, it couldn't possibly have been Roman who'd dug it up again, because he was dead by then. So, perhaps Roman hadn't killed Jimmy at all and we were looking for someone else. I concluded that I didn't know what the hell was going on and that merely thinking about it would give me a headache.

Hobbes, still engrossed in his paperwork, I placed a mug of tea beside him, looking around for distraction. There was a pile of books on the rug by my chair and, sitting back down, I selected a leather-bound, musty volume from the top of the pile and flicked through. It was filled with pages of old-fashioned handwriting, a mess of loops and blots and the occasional smudge, and appeared to be a record of old Sorenchester crimes. Heinous offences they'd been too, judging by the first item to catch my attention, one about a certain Thomas 'Porky' Parker who'd been arrested on suspicion of pig stealing. Though the pig had never been recovered, a substantial quantity of sausage had been returned to its rightful owner. I chuckled, looking at the following page, where Mistress Katherine Boot, having been discovered intoxicated in the parish church, tried to put the blame on her next door neighbour, Gramma Black, claiming she'd cursed her.

As I bent to replace the book, a scrap of yellowed paper, a cutting from the *Bugle*, fluttered to the floor. Picking it up, I noticed it was from August 1912 and about an aerobatic display in the church grounds. Though marvelling at the blurry photograph of the aeroplane, a flimsy structure of wood, canvas and wire, with an astonishing curved propeller, it was the women's enormous hats and the men's vast whiskers that struck me as most remarkable.

Or so I thought, until, when about to return the cutting, I noticed the police constable holding back the crowd. The unfortunate fellow was almost a dead ringer for Hobbes, though not quite so bulky, and with his face partly concealed behind a dark, drooping moustache. Finishing my tea, I speculated whether he might have been an ancestor. Hobbes laid down his pen and sat back.

'Was your grandfather a policeman as well?' I asked.

He looked up with a small frown. 'As well as what?'

I held out the cutting. 'This policeman looks a bit like you and I was just wondering if he was a relation?'

'No.' He pushed aside his papers and leaned back in his chair with a strange grin. 'He's no relation. I never knew my grandparents, or my parents for that matter; I was adopted.'

'I'm sorry.'

'Don't be. My adoptive parents were kind and looked after me as if I was really their own. They forced me onto the straight and narrow and held me there long enough that I wanted to stay. They were good people and it's a shame there aren't a few more like Uncle Jack and Auntie Elsie.'

'I sometimes wish I'd been adopted,' I said. '"They fuck you up, your mum and dad," to quote Jim Betjeman … or was it L S Eliot?'

'Larkin, I think you'll find.' He shook his head, sighing. 'It's always easy to blame others, particularly parents, for one's own shortcomings. I have observed that bringing up a child is never easy and that the majority of parents and adoptive parents do their

54

best, most of the time. People just find it difficult to take responsibility for themselves and their own mistakes.'

'Do you ever make mistakes?' I was astonished to hear him speak in such a way.

'Of course, though not so many as I used to. For instance, in my younger days I would sometimes miss mealtimes when on a case. I don't do that anymore, unless it's an emergency, which is why we are leaving now.'

'Are we leaving?'

He was on his feet, nodding. 'Put the cutting away, it's time to go home. Mrs Goodfellow will have our suppers ready.'

I did as instructed, happy at the prospect of being fed, for I'd had a growing feeling of hunger, and followed him into the night air. A few shreds of cloud, clinging to the face of the half-moon, were torn away as I looked up, and were lost in the darkness. Despite the town's brightness, stars glittered in the open sky and I blessed the thick tweed suit, shrugging into it as the rising wind chucked leaves and grit into my face.

I expected we'd drive but Hobbes wanted, he said, 'a brisk walk to blow away the cobwebs and stir the juices before supper'. Turning up my collar, taking an almost wistful glance at the car and its promise of shelter, I followed down an alley into The Shambles, where a handful of Saturday night revellers were braving the chill in their search for fun and alcohol. Pub windows glowed with welcome. Passing whiffs of cooking piqued the appetite.

'Are you originally from Sorenchester?' I asked, struggling to keep up.

'No. We had to move around a lot when I was young. They were troubled times. I first remember living near the Blacker Mountains on the Welsh borders. Afterwards we lived near Hedbury in a cottage in the woods until there was some trouble and we had to move to London, where Auntie Elsie worked in a hat shop and Uncle Jack became a docker. I went to school there until there was some trouble and we left for Wales. I used to love the mountains and the green valleys and the singing. After the trouble in Tenby, we lived in a caravan, touring round the shows and carnivals. Later, Uncle Jack worked at a factory in Pigton, where we lived until there was some trouble, and moved here when I was eleven. There was never much trouble here, so we stayed.'

'Trouble seemed to follow you around.'

He chuckled. 'So they told me. I regret being the cause of much of it, in the days when I was young and wild.'

We crossed The Shambles opposite the church, from where we could hear a choir practising. Hobbes, dawdling outside the great studded doors, closed his eyes, evidently enjoying the sound. Being no fan of choirs, preferring a good stonking beat in my music and lots of volume, I was glad when the song ended and we could get on. I shivered, hoping there might be an overcoat hanging in the wardrobe.

'I know you were adopted,' I said, as we turned up Pound Street past the old yew tree, 'but did you ever try to trace your real parents?'

Hobbes shook his head. 'Uncle Jack said they were killed.'

'An accident?'

'No.'

'What? D'you mean someone killed them?'

'That's enough. They died. Uncle Jack and Aunt Elsie looked after me.'

'But—'

'Enough.' He scowled and I shut up.

Though curious to know more about him, and pleasantly surprised at his brief openness, I knew he'd closed up again, and feared my probing had touched a sore spot. I consoled myself that there would be plenty of time for further investigations for, though my remark about going freelance had been no more than bravado, the thought had been growing. I really could write something about Hobbes, something to amaze the people in Sorenchester and, maybe, those as far away as Pigton, or even further, would find him fascinating. I could make a name for myself with a racy article in the national press. Or why not a series of articles? Or a book? Hobbes could be my ticket to fame and fortune. I'd have a flat in London, probably a penthouse, a mansion in the country, a villa in Spain and there'd be girls and parties and designer suits. Editorsaurus Rex would grovel to get my reports and he'd be sorry he sacked me. Plus, I'd be able to sneer at my father's pathetic little dental practice from a safe distance. I felt I was scaling new heights.

Arrival at 13 Blackdog Street brought me down to earth. My penthouse and all the rest were way over the horizon. For now, I'd have to make do with Hobbes's spare room, Mrs Goodfellow, suppers in the kitchen and Mr Goodfellow's old suits. I hoped it would be worth it.

The door opening, an enticing savoury aroma welcomed us and my mouth was awash by the time Hobbes shut the door on the cruel night. As we took our places at the kitchen table, I restrained myself until he'd said grace and then got stuck into the casserole, as if I hadn't eaten all day. Mrs Goodfellow, opening a bottle of red wine, left us to it. When I'd slowed down a little, had enjoyed a sip of the smooth, fruity wine and the kitchen's warmth had soaked into my core, my optimism began to rise, for Hobbes wasn't so bad when you got to know him and Mrs Goodfellow was just a harmless old biddy who fed me and brought me drinks.

So, she wanted my teeth? Well, she could want. I intended hanging on to them as long as I could. I was attached to them and they were deeply attached to me, apart from one in front that was a little wobbly since I'd fallen down the cellar at the Feathers. Featherlight Binks, who'd been changing a barrel, had broken my fall. A moment later he'd broken my lip and loosened the tooth with an uppercut. I always knew where I stood with Featherlight, or on this occasion, where I lay. He had a regrettable tendency to lash out without thinking. He did most things without thinking.

'Excuse me,' I said, on finishing eating, 'what do you make of Featherlight Binks at the Feathers?'

'He is a thoughtless, charmless, soap-less, hopeless lout, who runs a squalid drinking hole and can't even keep his beer well. He should not be allowed to meet the public and has been arrested more than anyone else in town.'

'Ah,' I said, 'though I've heard he has a bad side, too.'

'That is his bad side.' Hobbes frowned. He must have noticed my grin because he nodded. 'I see, that was a joke. In fact, he's not all bad: he just reacts like an animal. To give him his due, he doesn't have an ounce of real malice in his entire corpulent frame. Yet, he can be dangerous, especially when he's full of drink, which is most of the time.'

He pondered a moment. 'There is some good in him. In a way, he's like a child and genuinely dislikes hurting people, though he doesn't often remember until after he's clobbered them. A couple of years ago he was the one who told me Billy Shawcroft had gone missing.'

'The dwarf in the hearse?' The memory of the silent, sinister shape rolling towards us was imprinted on my mind.

Hobbes nodded. 'Once again, Featherlight had been brought into the station for assaulting a customer. This one had complained about his jacket potato having skin on it.'

'Jacket potatoes should have skin on them. Isn't that the point?'

'But not cat skin. The customer put two and two together and made certain allegations about the spicy meat stew that Featherlight took rather badly, being proud of having once served as an Army cook. To cut a long story short, he rammed the customer's head into the stew pot.'

'Was he hurt?'

'The customer? No, not much. It wasn't very hot, though the pot became well and truly stuck and he had to go to hospital to have it removed. When they got it off, they found a little collar and bell at the bottom.'

'No!' I said, horrified. 'I once had his spicy meat stew.'

'The worst part,' Hobbes continued, 'was that the customer worked for the Food Standards Agency and happened to be a keen supporter of the RSPCA and Featherlight ended up in court again. However, he was only prosecuted for serving unfit food, as there'd been no animal cruelty. A dustbin lorry had run over the cat and Featherlight was just being thrifty. He claimed he'd eaten far worse in the Army and didn't see what all the fuss was about.'

I grimaced, wishing I'd had the sense to keep away. 'But what had happened to Billy?'

'I was coming to that,' said Hobbes. 'Billy's a regular at the Feathers, often helping out behind the bar, but hadn't been seen for a couple of days. Featherlight grew concerned. At his trial, he claimed to have been too distracted by worry to buy meat and had been forced to use the cat. The point is, he informed me about Billy's disappearance and, thanks to his information, I was able to trace the poor little chap. He'd been kidnapped and was being held in a cage. I got him out and closed the case.'

'Who kidnapped him?' I didn't remember hearing anything about it.

'A kidnapper, who would have become a murderer had I not got there when I did. If it hadn't been for Featherlight, I doubt there'd have been a happy ending.'

'So, umm … who kidnapped him? And why?'

'That's all I'm prepared to say. Ask Billy if you want more of the story. It was a good thing for me that I rescued him because he's since proved a most valuable ally. When you're in a tight spot, Billy's the sort of man you want with you, because there's so little of him. Mind you, he can put away a surprising amount of beer, which reminds me, if you fancy a drink later tonight, I haven't looked in on Featherlight for a while.'

'Sounds good to me.'

'In the meantime, let's go through to the sitting room. The lass will bring us tea and she says she's got me a bone to pick.' As he drained his glass, a drop of blood-red wine ran down his chin.

I took my place on the sofa, wondering why sheets of newspaper had been spread in the corner of the normally immaculate room.

I glanced at Hobbes, who, all of a sudden, seemed twitchy and tense.

Mrs Goodfellow came in, carrying a huge bone in both hands. Raising it above her head, she tossed it towards the newspapers.

Hobbes growled like a dog. The sofa jolted backwards.

I jerked my head to see what he was up to. He was a blur on the edge of vision. My eyes focussed just in time to see him roll with the bone into the corner. He'd caught it in mid-air. In his jaws.

Slavering, he crouched over the bone on all fours and the crunching began. His teeth, tearing off great lumps of bloody, raw meat, he swallowed without chewing. The feral smell grew stronger, wilder and more predatory. His eyes flashed red and his upper lip pulled up in a snarl, like a hyena's. I couldn't stop myself from hugging my knees. A strange whimpering filled the room, as if a frightened animal had come in, and it was a few seconds before I realised I was responsible. Though within a minute or two he'd stripped the bone of meat, he continued gnawing until he'd cracked it open and could slurp the oozing marrow.

'Cup of tea, dear?' She was back.

My normal, civilised inhibitions taking fright, I cried out in horror. What had I let myself in for? Why had I ever considered that staying in this madhouse would be a doddle? I must have been mad. What the Hell was happening?

Mrs Goodfellow, placing a steaming mug at my side, glanced at me, then at Hobbes, and shrugged. 'Don't you go letting the old fellow worry you. It's just his way. He'll not hurt you … probably.' She patted my shoulder.

I nodded feebly, understanding how a lamb must feel inside the lion's den. Yet lambs don't drink tea. That's what an Englishman does in a crisis. Reaching out with unsteady hands, picking up the mug, I took a sip and turned to thank her but she'd already gone. The tea was hot and sweet, ideal for cases of shock. The old girl knew what she was doing. I tried and failed to ignore the crunching and sucking from the corner. I drank and concentrated on not spilling any, though my whole body was quivering. In times of stress, say the experts, our physiology prepares us for fight or flight. Mine didn't. I couldn't force any bits to move at all. I couldn't even look away. It made no sense whatsoever.

Aeons passed. At some point Mrs Goodfellow materialised and refilled my mug. I didn't jump and hardly even noticed, though conditioned reflexes kept me sipping. By then, my vision was narrowing and I felt as if I was cowering, trembling and sweating, in a long, narrow tunnel, with Hobbes at its mouth, shattering raw, white bone with his teeth. From behind, unseen demons urged me to retreat into the blackness and hide forever. Then, I could no longer see him and the dread grew that he was creeping up, preparing to spring. My breathing grew rapid and shallow and the blood pounded in my head like tom-toms. Darkness folded around and embraced me.

'Are you alright, Andy?'

I recognised the rumbling voice.

'Wake up.'

I opened my eyes to see Hobbes frowning down at me, his eyes dark, his teeth concealed behind bulldog lips. I gasped and flinched and found I was still on the sofa. My mug was empty.

'Are you alright?' he repeated.

I decided his frown was one of concern and nodded, while striving to rediscover my power of speech. The room was bright and warm. There were no tunnels or demons, just a heap of torn and scrunched newspaper in the corner. Something small, warm and soft patted the back of my hand and Mrs Goodfellow gave me a gummy smile.

'Good lad,' she said. 'All this excitement's been too much for you. You just sit a while and you'll feel better.'

'Thank you.' I shut my eyes. The animal odour faded.

I did begin to feel better. I don't know how long it took, yet when I opened my eyes again the newspapers had been removed and Hobbes was sitting beside me, engrossed in *The Times*.

'What happened?' I asked.

'You had a turn. Don't you remember?'

'Yes, of course. What I mean is, what happened to you? I mean the bone and … and everything?'

He shrugged. 'I just enjoy a bit of a chew sometimes. It's good for the teeth and exercise for the jaws. It stops me getting a double chin.' He peered at my face and grinned. 'Maybe you should give it a try.'

'But, you went strange.'

'Sorry. There's a lot of stress in police work and we all have our little methods for coping with it. It's best to let loose the beast within on a bone rather than on a member of the public.'

'That's true,' I said, imagining horrible things.

He smiled. 'You've had a tricky few days too, and dealt with it by having a funny turn. Each to his own. By heck, though, you had me worried when your eyes turned in on themselves.'

'I had you worried? Good.' I tried to appear nonchalant, though I was still trembling. In all honesty, I'd never been so terrified in my life for, though the ghouls had been horrible, they'd been strangers and I'd thought I was getting to know Hobbes.

He smiled, putting down his paper. 'These crosswords are getting too easy. I remember when one might take me as much as fifteen minutes. Now, how about that drink?'

I don't remember much about walking to the Feathers, except feeling cold and detached. Hobbes talked about aubergines, and I think I nodded a few times. Now and again I wanted to cry. It was a relief when he opened the door and ushered me into the warm, smelly fug. Featherlight lounged behind the bar, flouting the law by smoking a stinking pipe, while taking great swigs from a pewter tankard and snubbing any customers demanding drinks. Nonetheless, pints of beer kept appearing on the counter and cash disappeared behind it, though no one appeared to be serving. Featherlight, ignoring me, glowered at Hobbes.

'What are you here for? I've done nothing.'

'Nothing?' said Hobbes. 'I'm not sure about that. Didn't you knock out a customer's teeth on Wednesday?'

Featherlight scowled. 'That's a lie. I did no such thing – it was on Tuesday and it wasn't all of them. I didn't hear the customer complain.'

'He was unconscious.'

'He was out of order, whinging about a dead mouse in his beer when it was only a bit of one.'

Hobbes raised his eyebrows. 'Well, fair enough, but this is just a social visit.'

Featherlight, grunting, concentrated on his beer, several of his bellies resting on the counter. At least he'd changed his vest since the last time I'd been in, though it didn't smell as if he'd washed it and a dark patch down the front looked rather like blood.

'What are you gawping at?' he glared. 'D'you fancy a knuckle sandwich?'

'We've already eaten, thank you,' said Hobbes, 'but a couple of beers would go down well. We'll have two pints of this.' He tapped a handle.

'No, I'd rather have a lager.'

'… and a pint of lager for Andy.'

'Coming right up, Mr Hobbes,' said a piping voice with no body.

I leaned over the bar to find Billy Shawcroft grinning up at me. 'Hello, ice cream man.' He turned on the lager tap and simultaneously pulled Hobbes's pints.

'I'm not an ice cream man,' I said, puzzled. 'I'm a journalist … or was.'

Billy chuckled. 'No, I mean 'I scream, man'. You were screaming your head off in Mr Hobbes's car the other night.'

'Oh!' I blushed. 'I suppose I might have cried out when I saw you roll up and couldn't see anyone driving. I was tired and it was a dark and stormy night and it just got to me. It was nothing.'

'Well, you gave me a laugh anyway.' Smiling, he pushed a glass of lager towards me. 'There you go.' Turning away, he topped off Hobbes's glasses and lifted them onto the counter.

'Cheers Billy.' Hobbes handed over some cash.

'Very kind of you, Mr Hobbes,' said Billy, putting a little of it into the till and the rest, including at least one twenty pound note, into his pocket.

Sitting down at a greasy table by the bar, Hobbes drained one of his glasses in a single slow movement. Joining him, I was about to make a comment when he raised his hand to shut me up. He appeared to be listening, though I could hear nothing other than the usual bar noises. Looking around the shabby pub, filled with its usual mix of lowlifes, students and weirdoes, I doubted that Featherlight had ever decorated the place, apart from periodically replacing the dartboard in the corner. The pub was impregnated with decades of smoke, spilt beer, sweat and Featherlight's cooking, the furniture was chipped, dented and stained, the floor covered in a grey-brown growth that might once have been carpet. It was a gruesome place with a foul-tempered landlord, yet retaining a loyal clientele. I wondered whether they went there through choice, or bravado, or simply because nowhere else would have them.

Hobbes, still listening, I spotted a knothole in the side of the bar near to his ear and surmised Billy was on the other side. Hobbes's gaze flicked round the room before settling on one of the group playing darts, a medium-sized man in his mid-thirties with short hair, long sideburns and tinted spectacles. Despite the cold outside, he was wearing a flowery blue Hawaiian shirt, showing off a chunky gold chain around his neck and the matching Rolex on his wrist. I'd seen him around town, I was nearly certain, but couldn't quite remember when.

As Hobbes stood up and ambled towards him, the man's eyes widened, he turned and ran. Although, he was at least six strides nearer to the door than Hobbes and wearing expensive-looking trainers, Hobbes came within a shoelace of grabbing him. The man slammed the door behind him.

'I only wanted to play darts with him,' said Hobbes.

Featherlight scowled. 'Don't you go scaring away my customers.'

'I'll see if he wants to come back.' Hobbes opened the door, stepping into the night. Throwing back the dregs of my lager, I followed.

He was thundering up Vermin Street, hot in pursuit of the man in the shirt. I jogged after them, the lager sloshing uncomfortably round in my stomach, noticing that, despite the man's head start, Hobbes was gaining on him fast. I puffed along as well as I could but there was no way I could keep up. I'm sure I'd have fallen behind at the best of times and, with the earlier horror, a full meal and the lager, not to mention my heavy tweed suit, I had no chance at all. Turning sharp left into Rampart Street, the fugitive barged through a group of young ladies waiting at the Pelican crossing, knocking two to the ground. Hobbes stopped to help them, letting me catch up.

'Are you alright?' he asked.

'Just out of breath,' I gasped, leaning against a shop's wall.

'I wasn't talking to you.' He stepped into the road, halting the traffic to allow one of the girls to retrieve the scattered contents of her handbag.

A car driver, held up for a few seconds, honked his horn repeatedly, leaning out the window, shouting abuse. Hobbes waited, smiling, as the girl picked up her belongings. Then, having escorted her back to the pavement, he sauntered towards Mr Impatience, drawing himself up to his full height. The man cringed, his face turning as pale as the moon as Hobbes bent and looked in at his window. I couldn't make out what he said. I did, however, hear the driver yelp, 'Have mercy.'

Hobbes nodded and let him drive off. 'A little courtesy goes a long way,' he remarked and, having assured himself of the girls' well-being, saluted and loped off along Rampart Street. The fugitive was long out of sight. I offered a sickly smile to the ladies, who seemed more stunned by Hobbes's intervention than by the collision, and toiled behind him as he sped up Hedbury Road. It wasn't long before I gave up; all the exercise was killing me and I had to rest, bending forward with my hands on my knees, gasping, contemplating the cracks in the pavement and wondering whether I should throw up. By the time I felt better, Hobbes had vanished. Though I began walking towards where I'd last seen him, it wasn't long before I realised it was pointless. I rested on the wall by the Records Office.

Then I spotted the guy we'd been chasing. He'd doubled back and was sneaking into the town centre. He crossed the road and into the Records Office car park, ignoring me completely.

A wild thought entered my head; I could arrest him. I'd heard of a citizen's arrest, though I wasn't really sure what one was. Nor had I any clue why we'd been pursuing him, yet Hobbes was a policeman and, therefore, must have had a reason, probably a good one. The man's shirt was drenched with sweat despite the first crystalline hints of frost and he looked exhausted. I stepped towards him at the same moment he glanced over his shoulder. His eyes bulging behind his tinted lenses, he gasped and ran before I could lay hands on him. Hobbes was still on his trail. I started after the man as he fled downhill through the car park, by the side of the wall, and out the far gate. Hobbes passed me, his stride long and loping and, despite his heavy boots, almost silent. He didn't appear to be breathing hard, though his coat flapped around him like an enormous bat's wings. As he disappeared through the gate, I realised they were getting away from me again and reckoned I might save a few seconds by going straight over the wall. Taking a running jump, I scrambled up and over.

'Look before you leap' is a wise maxim, though I doubt whoever coined the phrase knew anything of supermarket trolleys. I didn't hit the ground running as I'd expected, I hit a supermarket trolley, sprawling. The lazy individual who'd abandoned it there instead of returning it to the trolley park probably never thought of the danger, that someone might drop into it, that the impetus of that someone's landing would set the trolley rolling downhill. Despite frantic struggles, I was stuck on my back in the wire shell, legs in the air, helpless as an overturned tortoise as the speed inexorably picked up. Typically, I'd fallen into that rare breed of supermarket trolley that runs freely, and my teeth rattled with every crack in the pavement. There was an instant when I experienced the sensation of flying, followed by a bone-jarring smack as the trolley left the kerb and landed in the road. Raising my head, peering between my knees, I could see the cars hurtling along Beechcroft Road directly ahead. I gulped and my struggles grew frantic though no more productive. I shouted for help.

It was no use. The front wheels hitting a pothole, the trolley tipped over, flinging me in front of a speeding van. Too dazed to move, all I could do was close my eyes and prepare to be smashed into oblivion. I heard the screeching of brakes before something seized my legs.

I found myself flat on my back on the pavement, winded and shocked, smelling hot metal and burnt rubber.

Hobbes squatting next to me, grinned. 'By heck, Andy, you do lead an exciting life. Are you alright?'

I nodded as well as I could and sat up, rubbing bruises and grazes. The van driver and crowd of concerned onlookers began dispersing when they saw I was still alive.

'Did you catch him?'

'No,' said Hobbes. 'I thought I'd be able to talk to him any time, whereas I only had one opportunity to save you.'

'Thanks.' I really was grateful because, for the third time in as many days, I'd been sure I was going to die. 'And … umm … sorry about the one that got away.'

'Don't mention it.'

The pavement was seeping coldness into my bones and I was glad when Hobbes helped me to my feet, though I needed his support for a while. As I was counting my injuries, bloody Phil drove past in a new blue Audi and stared. What a day I was having! Still, enough was enough. 'I want to go home now.' My words came out perilously close to being a sob.

'OK,' said Hobbes. 'I'll come back with you.'

Strangely, I was pleased, although only an hour or two earlier he'd been crunching bone like a wild animal. I was happy I was going to sleep under his roof and that Mrs Goodfellow would be after my teeth. He led me back, humming to himself.

'What's the tune?'

'Ribena Wild.'

'I don't think I know it.'

'You must do,' he said. 'It was playing on Pete Moss's car stereo. You know, Ribena wild rover for many a year?'

I grimaced and was relieved to get back to 13 Blackdog Street. I went straight to my room, dressing in thick, stripy pyjamas and, despite the horrors of the day and the not-so-distant thump of music, quickly fell into a deep sleep.

Coming awake to the faint tang of smoke triggered a memory of fear. I jerked upright with a racing heart, yet there was no fire, just a lingering hint of cigars, noticeable over the scent of lavender. Though my eyes were open, I could see nothing apart from a feeble glimmer of street lighting through heavy curtains. The lack of curry and sock pong made me realise I was not in my own room, or even in my own flat. The time, I guessed, was somewhere in the aptly-named wee hours, and I desperately needed to relieve myself, but, apart from the fact of being in a bed, I had no point of reference. It took a couple of minutes of disorientation to work out I was in Hobbes's spare bedroom, and that my room had burned, along with my socks.

My drowsy brain failing to remember where the door was, I was forced to fumble and grope around the walls until locating it allowed me to lurch towards the bathroom, getting there in the nick of time. Afterwards, I washed my hands, in case Mrs Goodfellow was lurking, although the faint, ladylike snores from her room were reassuring. On the way back, and considerably more at ease, I noticed Hobbes's door was open. Greatly daring, I peeped inside. The curtains had not been drawn and light from Blackdog Street showed he wasn't there. I was blurry with fatigue, a biting draught from his open window making me shiver, so I groped my way back to bed, instantly dropping back into sleep. At some point, I was vaguely aware of a clunk, as if a window was closing, and it was light when I woke again.

Yawning and stretching was good, despite a superficial tenderness from a hundred bruises and scrapes. My burned hand didn't feel too bad beneath its dressing, just a little stiff and tight. I hadn't slept so well for ages and was able to take pleasure in the ache of muscles, muscles that had barely been active during most of the previous decade. My stomach being empty, I lay a while, relishing the anticipation of what Mrs Goodfellow would prepare for breakfast. There was sufficient light for me to notice that yesterday's underwear and shirt, carelessly tossed into the corner, had vanished and miraculously been replaced with clean, pressed garments, lying neatly folded on the dressing table, alongside a fluffy white towel. I got up and went to the bathroom.

Both Hobbes's and Mrs Goodfellow's doors were shut and the house had an odd stillness, suggesting I was alone. After washing, returning to my room and dressing, I went downstairs, to find that the kitchen, apart from a mouth-watering aroma of roasting beef, was empty. A note lay in the middle of the table. It had been written on pink paper with a fountain pen and the writing was infested with loops and the occasional blot.

Dear Andy,

I trust you slept well. The lass and I have gone to the Remembrance service and didn't want to disturb you. We will be back around noon. Please help yourself to breakfast – there's bacon and eggs in the pantry and a loaf in the bread bin. I recommend the marmalade. The lass makes it herself out of oranges.

Hobbes.

PS. There was a break-in at the museum last night.

I shrugged away a sense of disappointment. There was nothing for it but to look after myself. I've never been a dab hand at cooking and reckoned marmalade sandwiches would do me well enough. A pat of primrose-yellow butter lay in a white china dish on the table, alongside a pot with a hand-written label declaring its contents as marmalade. Filling the kettle, setting it on the hob and lighting the gas, I located the bread in a cream-coloured, enamel bread bin with a wooden lid. On opening it, I hit a snag: the bread was all in one lump — and I'd usually known it to come in slices. A childhood memory surfaced from when I was staying at Granny Caplet's while mother was in hospital having my baby sister, who died. Granny was using a big, shiny knife with a serrated edge to cut a Hovis loaf. A similar knife lay on a gleaming, wooden breadboard next to the marmalade.

Sawing energetically produced two slices or, more accurately, wedges of the fragrant, crusty, brown bread, which I buttered and marmaladed while waiting for the kettle to boil. As soon as it did, I made tea, taking the loose leaves in my stride. Then, satisfied with my achievements, sitting down at the table, I tucked in. Hobbes had been right to claim the marmalade was excellent. It held just a hint of whisky smokiness, lending a satisfying warmth and depth to the citrus tang and sweetness.

I drank a mug of tea, cut another hunk of bread and remembered the last breakfast in my flat: left-over chop suey, still in its foil box. Washing down the congealed mess with the warm, flat, dregs of a can of Special Brew, I was blissfully unaware of the cigarette butt until it caught in my throat. As smoking is a vice I've never indulged in, and I was pretty sure I'd been alone when I got home from Aye Ching's takeaway, it was a mystery. I never did get to the bottom of it, unlike the bottom of the can. At least, I couldn't imagine anything quite so horrible happening in Mrs Goodfellow's kitchen.

Smoke seemed to be on my mind a lot and it was almost as if I could smell it again. Actually, I could. The kettle was glowing red, its wooden handle carbonising. I'd forgotten to turn off the gas, though in my defence, I was more used to electric kettles. Jumping up, I grabbed the smoking handle, releasing it with a yelp, lucky my hand was still partially protected by its dressing. A souvenir of Margate tea towel was hanging on a rail by the sink and, grabbing it, wrapping it around the handle, I hurled the incandescent kettle into the sink and turned on the tap.

My cheerful waking mood dissipated, unlike the cloud of steam that arose around me with a hiss. I flapped the tea towel to clear the air, bewildered why it was making things worse, nearly setting the curtains alight before realising it was on fire. It, too, ended up in the sink. I opened the back door and, when the smoke and steam finally cleared, grew even more miserable on seeing the red, plastic washing-up bowl with a perfectly circular hole right through it. I spent the next half-hour with the bread knife, cursing and muttering as I chipped and peeled congealed lumps of red plastic from the sink and from the bottom of the kettle.

I could just imagine Phil's smug grin should he ever find out about my misfortunes, which reminded me of seeing him in his new car the previous evening. He hadn't been alone: someone had been in the passenger seat, someone with a ratty face and tinted glasses. It had been the man we were chasing and I felt guilty about not mentioning it to Hobbes, though I had been a little distracted at the time.

'I said get yourself some breakfast, not set fire to the kitchen.' Hobbes was standing framed in the kitchen doorway. He was wearing a smart, if old-fashioned, suit with a dark-blue pinstripe and a poppy in the buttonhole, his cheeks were shaved smooth and his hair was plastered flat.

I gasped and the knife clattered into the sink. 'I'm sorry,' I said, 'I … umm … had an accident.'

'Just the one?' He looked around, frowning. 'Tell me.'

As I did, he roared with laughter. I had to repeat my tale of woe for Mrs Goodfellow. Doubling the audience doubled the mirth.

Hobbes wiped his eyes, shaking his head. 'By heck, Andy, if laughter's the best medicine, you should be available on prescription. Aye well, there's no real harm done. I'd better go and change into my work things.' He went up to his room.

Mrs Goodfellow winked as she headed towards the stove, pulling on her pinafore. 'Well done, dear, you've snapped the old fellow out of it. He usually becomes quite morose on Remembrance Sunday.'

'Oh,' I said. 'Is that today? I … umm … used to keep an old poppy in my flat, one I'd found. It saved me having to buy new ones.'

Mrs Goodfellow was bending down to open the oven with her back to me and I still felt the reflected force of her frown.

'I was joking,' I said, though I had actually neglected to buy one. 'Why does it make him morose?'

'It brings back memories.' She basted the joint, poking it with a fork. 'He remembers too many faces from the past. Old comrades, old enemies, old times.'

'Was he in the forces?'

Shutting the oven, she straightened up and faced me. 'He was a soldier, a decorated war hero, though he doesn't talk about it much. Now, I've got the vegetables and Yorkshire puds to see to.'

Hobbes a war hero? There was more to him than I'd supposed. His heavy footsteps clumped down the stairs and he reappeared in everyday apparel before I could ask any more.

'Let's leave the lass to get on with dinner,' he said, 'and I'll tell you what's happened at the museum.'

'Oh, yes. The break-in.' Following him through to the sitting room, I made myself comfortable on the sofa.

Hobbes rested his boots on the coffee table. 'Since it's just round the corner, I took a quick look while you were still snoring. It's rather a peculiar case. Someone dug a hole through the wall to get in.'

'It sounds like hard work. Why not just break a window or force a door?'

'The windows and doors have alarms fitted. Whoever got in must have known – though any visitor might have noticed.'

'Do you know who did it? Surely they've got CCTV?'

'They do, but only on what are regarded as valuable exhibits. None of them was taken, so nothing was recorded.'

'It sounds like something was taken.'

'Correct,' said Hobbes. 'The only item that appears to be missing is a bronze bracelet from the store, an interesting piece, according to Mr Biggs, the curator, though of no great value, worth a few hundred pounds at most.'

'Someone put in a lot of effort to steal a piece of no great worth. Why?'

He shrugged. 'I don't know yet. Mr Biggs says the bracelet is probably fifteenth century and of central European origin. The museum only received it a few weeks ago and he hadn't got round to classifying it. It's in the shape of a sleeping dragon, with its tail coiled around its neck. Unusual.'

'Whoever went to so much bother to nick it must be a nutter,' I said, scratching my head. 'One thing, though – wouldn't he have made a lot of noise digging through a wall? Did no one hear anything?'

Hobbes shook his head. 'Not so far as we know. There was a private party at the Black Dog Café last night and they were playing loud music.'

'Yeah,' I said, 'I heard. It had stopped when I went to the bathroom.'

'When was that?'

'I don't know. The middle of the night? It was dark and you weren't in your room.'

'I was out looking for the gentleman in the flowery shirt.'

'Did you find him?'

'Not yet.'

'Why were you after him?'

Hobbes grinned. 'I'd received information that he'd suddenly come into money and wanted to ask him about it.'

'Did Billy tell you? Is that why you paid him?'

Hobbes nodded. 'Billy is a valuable ally in the fight against crime, and the man we were after, he's called Tony Derrick, has never done an honest day's work in his life, yet has suddenly acquired a wallet full of cash.'

'Tony Derrick, eh? It sounds like you know him.'

'Yes, he's lived around here for most of his life and was involved in Billy's kidnapping, which is why Billy has issues with him, and why Tony wasn't pleased to see me again.'

I was indignant. 'You said the kidnapping nearly became a murder. If the bastard tried to kill Billy, how come he's not in prison?'

'Tony wasn't going to kill him. He might be a loathsome, sneaking rotter, but he's not a killer, just an opportunist. If he sees a chance, he'll steal. Billy was blind drunk and Tony robbed him. That would normally have been as far as it went had someone not made it clear that she was willing to pay good money for someone like Billy.'

'He sold him? That's outrageous, yet who would want to buy him? And why?'

'Dinner's ready.' Mrs Goodfellow was just behind my right ear.

I leaped up, twisting in mid-air, landing and facing her, wishing she'd stop doing it.

'You're keen, dear, I can see you're hungry.' She turned to Hobbes. 'Did you see how fast the young fellow was?'

Hobbes chuckled as he stood up. 'He's fast enough on his feet where vittles are concerned, yet maybe not so nippy when chasing villains, eh, Andy?'

I made a weak attempt at a laugh while he told her about my misadventure with the supermarket trolley. Her reedy cackle joined his deep guffaws. Entering the kitchen, I was feeling more than usually ridiculous. But no one would laugh when my book came out. I would edit out the unflattering parts, make myself the hero. I would be cool, debonair, successful and people would respect me.

Still, I forgave their laughter when Mrs Goodfellow served lunch, a sirloin of beef, cooked to a succulent, tender perfection, fiery horse-radish to die for (or of, perhaps, if you were reckless with your helpings), crispy roast-potatoes and parsnips, and the most gorgeous, lightest, tastiest Yorkshire puddings in the whole world. Her gravy was the most delicious ever made, without even a hint of Bisto, and even the cabbage tasted special. She was an expert and I'd never before been presented with such a meal. For afters, she served the best rice pudding in the universe, one for which you would not blame little green men from Mars for invading merely in order to sample a spoonful. Nothing was quirky or exotic, everything was just superb and my palate, more used to dodgy pub grub and takeaways, went into overload. I couldn't talk, even if I'd wanted to, while the meal lasted, lost in my own little ecstasy. Only when I'd finished did I realise she was no longer with us, and that I'd never yet seen her eat anything. I sat back in my chair with a feeling of enormous well-being.

'Coffee?' She'd done it again.

'Yes, please,' said Hobbes. 'Thank you for dinner, lass.'

I nodded, too shocked to speak. She smiled, bustling around, as Hobbes took me back to the sitting room and resumed talking, as if there'd been no interruption.

'Strange individuals find their way to Sorenchester,' he said.

I looked at him and agreed.

'And strange events happen. Billy was caught up in one with a very weird individual until I put a stop to it. A clue pointed to Tony's involvement and, after I'd nabbed him, he made some amends by providing vital information. After I'd persuaded him, of course. I can be very persuasive.'

'Umm … why didn't he go to prison? And who was the weird individual? And—'

'One at a time, Andy,' said Hobbes with a smile. 'Firstly, Tony did not go to prison because he was never charged. Any evidence was burned in the rescue. However, shortly after our little chat, Tony enrolled in a monastery. I hoped he'd go straight but it was a forlorn hope; Tony will always be what he is. It's not all his fault, he had a difficult childhood, but he's always been one to make the worst of things. At least in the monastery he was delivered from temptation for a short time. I didn't know he'd come back, though Billy says he reappeared about a month ago. He was broke then.'

'Tony broke, you could say,' I smirked.

Hobbes nodded. 'Yet, in the last few days, he's been flashing handfuls of cash around and I don't believe he's got himself a proper job.'

'I'm sure I've seen him around town before,' I said slowly. 'I thought so in the pub and I'm surer now. What's more I think I saw him again last night.'

Hobbes shrugged. 'Of course you did. We were chasing him.'

'Yeah, I know. It was when I was lying on the pavement.' I paused. I'd be dropping Phil in it, right up to his silk-collared neck. Could I do such a thing to a former colleague? Of course I could. 'One of the cars that went by,' I said, 'belonged to Phil from the *Bugle* and I'm pretty certain Tony was in the passenger seat.'

'Really?' Hobbes raised his eyebrows. 'Then I'd better have a word with this Phil some time. Do you know his surname and where he lives?'

He nearly had me there. I'd grown so accustomed to thinking of him as 'Bloody Phil' or 'Phil the Git' that it took me a few moments to remember. 'It's Waring. I don't know his address, though they'll have it at the *Bugle*.'

'Thanks. Your information might prove useful.'

Gotcha you smug git! I thought. Maybe Ingrid would now see him for what he was. I just hoped I'd be there when Hobbes had his word with him. It might be entertaining.

'Here are your coffees,' said Mrs Goodfellow in my ear. She placed the tray on the table before us.

Hobbes laughed and took a great slurp from his mug. I poured a drop of milk into mine, took a sip and gasped.

He poured himself a second mug from the huge cafetiere. 'Mind, it's hot.'

It certainly was; the tip of my tongue was par-boiled and tender and it was a few minutes before I risked another sip, by which time he was well down his third mug. When mine was cool enough to enjoy without agony, he was becoming twitchy and tense. Though I had a few moments of horror in case he was going to do the bone thing again, all he wanted was to get out and take another look at the museum. Having nothing better to do, I drained my mug and went with him.

The biting wind of the previous day had lost its teeth and grown gentle under a pale sun. It only took us five minutes to walk down Blackdog Street, turn right up Ride Street, past the Black Dog Café, and reach the museum, which was just opening its iron gates for the afternoon. A small group of visitors started moving inside and we joined them, passing beneath a genuine Roman arch into the foyer. I expected Hobbes to push past the tourists, yet he seemed content to wait his turn. When he showed his ID, the woman behind the desk nodded and waved him through with a smile. All she could see was the reassuring presence of a policeman. And me. All I warranted was a suspicious glance.

'It's alright,' Hobbes explained. 'He's with me.'

She smiled at him and let me in. I admit to feeling disgruntled. Surely, in my tweed suit and tie, I looked most respectable? More respectable than he did in his flappy old gabardine coat.

'C'mon Andy,' he beckoned. 'This way.'

We walked through a hall filled with Roman antiquities and, though I'm not much of a history student, I wished I could have stayed for a proper look. For some reason, I'd never visited before, which, seeing all the wonderful things on display, struck me as foolish. A bit of history would undoubtedly have been healthier than spending so long in pubs, especially in the Feathers. The thought of the cat in the stew pot turned my stomach. What had ever possessed me to eat there? I knew what Featherlight was like.

Hobbes, pushing open a door marked 'private', loped down a short corridor into a storeroom, filled from floor to ceiling with loaded shelves and boxes, apart from the space by the window, where a worried little man sat at a desk, leafing through papers.

He looked up, forcing a smile. 'Good afternoon, Inspector. Any developments?'

'Not yet, sir.'

Hobbes introduced me to the curator, Mr Biggs. An ironic name I thought, shaking his podgy hand, for Mr Biggs was small. Everything about him was small, except for spectacles that made his pale blue eyes goggle like a goldfish's. He must have been getting on for two feet taller than Billy Shawcroft, yet Billy was larger than life and seemed to occupy more than his own small volume. The curator, by contrast, looked like he'd collapsed into himself and his thin, white hair was dishevelled.

'A terrible thing, Inspector,' he said. 'No one's ever broken into my museum before. Dreadful times we live in.'

'Indeed, sir.' Hobbes nodded. 'However, don't despair. We may be able to trace the thief and recover the item.'

Mr Biggs snorted, shaking his head.

'Now,' said Hobbes, 'I need to look into the hole.'

He walked along an aisle, lined on both sides with plain cardboard boxes that, no doubt, concealed a host of wonders. A cold draught blew around my ankles, a mess of rubble littered the beige carpet. There was, as he'd said, a hole in the wall.

'Stand back and don't touch anything,' he commanded.

I nodded, already used to the routine. Squatting on his haunches, he began moving slowly and deliberately forward over the rubble towards the wall, shifting his feet so as to leave no marks. On reaching the wall, he crouched and poked his head into the hole. He began humming his 'Ribena Wild' song again.

'I went to an ale house I used to frequent,' he murmured, reaching out for something. When he straightened up he held a sticky-looking, grey-brown tuft of fibre between his nails. He sniffed it, his nose wrinkling.

'What is it?'

'Fluff from a carpet, a pub carpet and I'd stake my reputation it's from the Feathers.'

'Do you think Featherlight robbed the place?'

'I doubt it,' said Hobbes, pointing at the hole, 'and there's no chance he could squeeze through that.'

'Billy could.'

He shook his head. 'Billy has his faults but he's one hundred per cent honest, except, possibly, when he plays cards. Not that I've ever caught him out.' He paused, 'No, I suspect someone else who's been at the Feathers.'

'Tony Derrick then?'

He shrugged. 'Could be. He's skinny enough to squeeze through. Unfortunately, uniform tramped around in here before I got a proper look. Those lads have big feet, though they do their best.' He stopped and thought for a moment. 'The only thing is, it doesn't feel right. Tony's a nasty little sneak thief, an opportunist, and this took time, planning and knowledge. I can't see him doing this. Unless …'

'Unless what?'

'Unless, he's working for someone again.' His forehead furrowed in thought and he muttered something under his breath. I didn't catch it all and had to try filling in the gaps. I think he said, though I couldn't swear to it, 'You'd have thought he'd have had enough after the old witch.'

'Excuse me?'

'Just thinking out loud,' said Hobbes. 'No, I'm sure, if Tony Derrick was involved, he didn't plan it. Someone else did.'

A happy thought came into my mind. 'Phil?'

'Possibly.' He grinned. 'Unfortunately, apart from being in a car with Tony, there's no evidence against him. I will talk to him, though he's not high on my suspect list. Just because you don't like him, Andy, it doesn't mean he's a criminal.'

'Oh,' I said, surprised by his perspicacity, 'I suppose that might be true. He is a git, though!'

'Mrs Tomkins didn't think so and Ingrid likes him.'

I glowered. 'Only because he's a smooth-talking, flash git.'

'And you're jealous?' He raised his eyebrows.

'Of course not.' Though part of me I tried to ignore agreed Hobbes had a point, I wouldn't admit it. 'There's nothing to be jealous of.'

His eyebrows twitched, making me think of a pair of bristly caterpillars wrestling. 'So you don't mind him going out with Ingrid?'

'No. Well, yes, I do. Umm … it's up to her.'

He walked back to the desk. 'From where was the bracelet taken, sir?'

'I'll show you.' Mr Biggs stood up. With his fluffy white hair, it was like watching a tuft of thistledown wafting in a breeze. He was obviously still in some distress and drifted up and down the aisle until he found the right box. He tapped it with a brittle finger. 'From here, Inspector.'

Hobbes leaned forward, sniffing the outside of the box, a box identical to the hundreds of others in the storeroom.

'Were any of the others touched?' he asked.

Mr Biggs shook his head. 'No. At least, it doesn't appear so.'

'So, what drew your attention to this one?'

Mr Biggs looked puzzled. 'What do you mean? The bracelet was missing that's all.'

Hobbes, frowning, glanced along the rows of boxes. 'How did you know something was taken from this particular one? Did you check all of them?'

It sounded like a good point to me.

Mr Biggs's face, which had been as pale and lumpy as uncooked pastry, reddened. 'What are you trying to say? Are you accusing me of something?'

'No,' said Hobbes mildly. 'Is there something I should be accusing you of? I was merely trying to establish a fact. How did you know something had been taken from this particular box?'

'This is outrageous.' Mr Biggs was getting himself into a strop. His little feet stamping on the ground, he puffed out his chest like a robin. 'I shall have a strong word with your superiors, Inspector. I don't expect to be treated like a criminal in my own museum. Now get out!'

Hobbes scowled, leaning ever so slightly towards him, looming like an elephant's foot over an anthill. 'I am investigating a crime. Please answer my questions, sir.'

Mr Biggs's bluster collapsed. 'Don't hurt me!'

'I never intend to hurt anyone.' Hobbes's smile held all the friendliness of a hyena.

Though he hadn't done or said anything threatening, I felt the intimidation like an approaching storm at sea. Mr Biggs's eyes goggled behind his spectacles, his jaw moved up and down wordlessly and he staggered as if he'd been punched.

Hobbes helped him to his chair. 'Now, sir,' he asked, his voice gentle, 'how did you know something had been taken from this box?'

'I didn't know.' Biggs's voice grew shrill. 'I just suspected something when I saw the hole.' His breathing had become heavy and runnels of sweat streaked his face.

'What did you suspect?'

'That the bracelet had gone. It's an unusual piece. I don't mean the workmanship or the materials. They are not exceptional. It's the design.'

'Go on,' said Hobbes.

'The … er … Order of St George used the symbol of a dragon with the tail coiled round its neck in the fifteenth century. It is rare to come across them nowadays: unique, I believe, in Sorenchester. Though they have little intrinsic value, they are worth a great deal to collectors interested in the Order.'

'What is the Order of St George?' I asked, too intrigued to keep shtum.

'All in good time, Andy,' said Hobbes, raising his hand. He turned to Mr Biggs, 'How did you know it had gone missing, sir?'

'I saw the hole and guessed it had been stolen.'

Hobbes persisted. 'Why?'

'I don't know. It was a guess.'

Hobbes stared at Biggs who squirmed and twisted like a worm caught in the midday sun. 'What made you think the thief would bypass all the other boxes and go straight for this one?'

It was obvious even to me that Biggs was hiding something, yet the man looked so deflated and shrivelled I couldn't help feeling sorry for him. He was gulping like a fish, his face pale again, with an unhealthy sheen like on a lump of putty and the thought occurred that he was going to pass out, just as he passed out. His eyes rolling, his mouth dropping open, he clattered from his chair with all the elegance of a sack of potatoes.

'Oops,' said Hobbes. 'I didn't think I was pressing him too hard.' He knelt, loosening the man's collar, checking his pulse. 'Still alive at any rate, though I'd better phone for an ambulance.'

He did so and prowled round the storeroom for a few minutes until the paramedics turned up. They bustled in, performing some quick tests on the patient, and wheeled him away. They obviously knew Hobbes of old and gave no indication of surprise to see him beside an unconscious witness.

Hobbes grinned. 'Well, that's mucked things up. Still, it wasn't my fault. I suppose he just fainted. It's a shame, because he knows a lot more than he wants to tell.'

I nodded, shaken by the little man's collapse. I'd never seen anyone go down in such a way before, yet Hobbes was right, he hadn't touched or threatened him. Not exactly.

'Have you ever heard of the Order of St George?' I asked, since it meant nothing to me.

'No more than Biggs told us.' He shrugged. 'Still, it might be worth finding out whether anyone does collect that sort of stuff around here. I rather formed the opinion that someone does.'

I agreed. 'It was as if he expected someone to steal it.'

'Right, and yet he didn't try to stop it, though I think he was upset it had gone.'

'He looked frightened to me,' I said, 'even before you interrogated him.'

'It was hardly an interrogation, but it's an interesting observation. Frightened, you think? I wonder why? Anyway, we'd better go.'

We left the storeroom, passing some of the museum staff who'd gathered to watch their curator being removed. Some angry comments were directed at Hobbes but I don't think he heard them. It was a relief to get outside into the fresh, cool air. Still, the day was proving more exciting than the previous Sunday afternoon, when I'd had my lunch in the Bellman's, drunk too much, returned to my flat and fallen asleep on the carpet in front of my telly. My ex-telly, I reminded myself, on my ex-carpet in my ex-flat.

Hobbes, staring at the railings around the museum, began crawling slowly along the pavement. I watched, fascinated, once again reminded of an enormous bloated toad, though toads don't sniff.

'Aha.' He stopped, squatting before a section of railings.

'What is it?'

He pointed. 'Look, the paint's chipped near the base and there's no sign of rust, so it must be recent – and look up there. Can you see the smudges? That must be where the thief climbed over to get access to the wall. Hallo, hallo, hallo, what have we here then?' Reaching round the back of the railings, he held up a pair of latex gloves between dagger-like fingernails. 'He was careful not to leave any prints anyway. Still, though this isn't a busy road at night, there would have been a risk of being seen, unless there was a lookout.' He sniffed at the gloves and wrinkled his nose. 'Too much powder in these.'

'Phil and Tony Derrick?' I said, more as an accusation than a suggestion.

'Perhaps,' he said, 'but don't jump the gun. It may not have anything to do with either of them. Coincidences can happen.'

'Now what?' I asked. 'Do we go and find Phil?'

'Later. First, I'd rather have another chat with Mr Biggs, when he's in a more cooperative frame of mind.'

'You mean a conscious one?'

He grinned. 'That would, of course, be an advantage. Until then, there's one or two things I must do back home and I ought to go and make some notes back at the station. What do you want to do?'

'Actually, I think I might go and have a look at my flat. What's left of it.'

'Fine,' said Hobbes. 'I'll see you at suppertime. At six o'clock.'

We parted and I walked through town to the remains of my former home. From a distance – and from the right angle – the block looked the same as always. Then the outside of my flat came into view, the walls stained with great, heavy swathes of smoke, as if some careless painter had used a huge, broad brush to streak black paint. Every window was shattered and the roof had partly collapsed. The whole block had been boarded up and tape was stretched across the front door, warning that the structure was unstable. I realised I had not been the only victim: all the other flats had been evacuated, too. I had a sickening suspicion that I'd started it, certain I'd left the electric fire on when I'd crashed out, remembering being careless when discarding my clothes. As I gazed up at the ruined first floor window, I realised just how lucky I'd been that Hobbes was passing, because I doubted anyone else could have done what he'd done. In fact, if he hadn't actually done it, I wouldn't have believed anyone, least of all a big bloke like him, could have scaled the wall and carried me down. There really was something strange about him.

During the following hour or so I mooched about, staring at the block, kicking up leaves in the overgrown communal garden, thinking about Hobbes, while trying to remain inconspicuous in case any of my fellow former residents showed up. Though I didn't know any of them, except to nod to on the steps, I had a feeling they might not be happy to see me.

8

Dusk descended, dragging the temperature down with it, making my breath steam and curl. I shivered, thrusting my hands into my pockets, trying to turn my mind to Ingrid, as my feet turned homewards. Home? I was already thinking of Hobbes's place as home. I put it down to shock.

Ingrid was the only thing I missed from the office, apart from the pay, which reminded me of the urgent need to see Editorsaurus Rex and force him to change my cheque. Then I could give him a piece of my mind, if I dared, though it would have to be a small piece: the way things had been going I couldn't afford to lose much more.

I was fond of Ingrid's soft brown eyes and friendly smile. I liked to think of her hair as blonde, though I suspected an impartial observer might callously describe it as mousy. Again, some might have considered her a little short for symmetry; I suspected my impartial observer might even consider her dumpy, the boorish lout. 'You, sir, are no gentleman,' I would tell the swine before thrashing him within an inch of his life. My problem was that, since I no longer worked for the *Bugle*, I wouldn't be able to impress her with my ardour and prove I was 'arder than Phil. I was worried he'd be able to have his wicked way without me to protect her.

I wondered about her motives for going out with him. Sure, my impartial observer might consider him good-looking – and he did keep himself fit and dressed well and had nice manners and a smart new car – but the impartial observer was a fool, as he'd shown with his views on Ingrid. He didn't recognise Phil was a git. He was always smiling, feigning friendliness, ready to help anyone. He'd be the first to dig his wallet from his trendy trouser pocket and buy a round at the Bellman's, or to contribute to a birthday present, or to make a donation to charity. I despised him and every little thing he did to show-off to Ingrid.

And now he'd started taking her to the opera. Well, at least she'd had enough taste to throw up on him, if not enough to avoid lobster. That, at least, gave me a reason to cheer up.

A treacherous part of my mind interrupted the mental rant with a suggestion that, maybe, she would have gone out with me had I ever taken the trouble to ask her and that, maybe, I should have bought her a birthday present, or, at least, a card. I laughed it out of sight. Why should I have to act flash like Phil? I reckoned she only liked him because he was nice to her and bought her presents and took her to the opera. I was who I was and she ought to appreciate it. The treacherous part rallied and whispered that I'd never even hinted that I liked her, and asked why she should have gone out with me if I'd never asked her. I squashed the notions with ease; we were living in the twenty-first century and a woman could ask a bloke out perfectly easily. No, though she might be gorgeous, in her dumpy, mousy way, the girl had no taste in men and I sometimes wondered if she was right for me.

It came as something of a surprise to find my feet had carried me into Blackdog Street, for I'd hardly been aware of walking with all the turmoil in my mind. It was satisfying to know that Hobbes planned having a word with Phil and that, with luck, I'd be present to see him squirm. With more luck, he'd collapse like old Biggs or, even better, Hobbes might tear out his throat. I chuckled, wondering whether I might be able to give a little shove, something to ensure Phil dropped right in the shit. Then I'd have a free run at Ingrid, because there was no way a girl as pure and intelligent as her would associate with a criminal. My treacherous part made a final effort. What made me think she was pure? A bastard like Phil would, surely, have got into her pants at the first opportunity and, therefore, deserved everything he'd got coming.

Reaching number 13, I raised my fist to knock.

'Hello, dear,' said Mrs Goodfellow's voice.

My stomach contracting, I spun around, unable to see her anywhere, yet sure I'd heard her. I couldn't have imagined it.

'You'll be wanting to come in I expect.'

She couldn't have become invisible. I looked behind me, along the street and even up the side of the house, as if she might be hanging there like a monkey.

'Down here, dear.'

A wizened face, pale in the streetlights, winked up at me from behind the bars covering the cellar.

She grinned. 'Just seeing to the mushrooms. I'll be up in a minute.'

'Oh, good,' I gasped. 'Mushrooms. Very nice. I'm sorry, I didn't see you there.'

She chuckled. 'I expect you thought I was invisible, or hanging around like a monkey?'

'No, of course not,' I lied, laughing, but she'd gone. I stared into the black hole by my feet.

'Come in, dear.'

I hadn't heard her approaching the front door and my jump wouldn't have disgraced the Olympics. I forced a smile, stepping into the warmth.

She pushed the door to. 'The old fellow's not home yet, but he's normally back in time for his supper. By the way, dear, he asked me to give you this.'

Reaching into the pocket of her pinafore, pulling out a key, she handed it to me. 'He said it was best if you had your own, so you aren't locked out if no one's home. He said to treat the house like your own.'

'Thanks,' I said, touched that he trusted me.

'Mind you, he also said how you wasn't to go burning the house down, like your last place.' She chuckled.

I grimaced.

'Would you like a cup of tea, while you're waiting?'

'No thanks. I didn't know you'd got a cellar.'

'Oh yes. All the houses down the street had cellars, though most have been turned into basements or filled in. The old fellow sometimes likes the peace of being underground and it's where he keeps his wines and where I grow my mushrooms and force my rhubarb.'

I wondered what on earth she was forcing it to do. There had been, I remembered, a frisson when venturing into Granny Caplet's cellar, all dark and mysterious, when I was very small. 'Can I see the cellar?'

'Of course, dear.' Taking me into the kitchen, she opened what I'd assumed was a cupboard door. 'Down there. Will you be wanting the light on? The old fellow fitted an electric one.'

'Oh no,' I said, intending humorous sarcasm, 'I'd much rather flounder around in the dark.'

'Suit yourself,' she said. 'Just beware the pit of doom. They do say it's bottomless.'

'What?'

'Oh sorry, dear. Did I say the pit of doom? I meant to say mind your head. The ceiling's a little low in parts.'

Smiling, she flicked a light switch and let me descend the creaky, narrow, wooden staircase. It was cool down there, yet dryer than I'd expected, with a pleasant, earthy odour and just a hint of damp, coming from trays of compost in a corner, some covered in mushrooms as big as cauliflowers. Beneath the grille, next to where I'd seen Mrs Goodfellow, was a pile of coal and against the near wall stood a great rack loaded with bottles. Unable to see any rhubarb, I guessed the old girl must have forced it into hiding. I'd been down there some minutes before it struck me just how cavernous it was. It appeared far wider than the house.

I was considering returning upstairs when I noticed what appeared to be another door, partially concealed by coal. It puzzled me because, if it actually was a door, then it led in the direction of the road.

Hobbes's voice rumbled from above. 'Who's that down there?'

'It's me, Andy.' I peered up through the grille at his face, cratered like the moon.

'Oh dear,' he sighed. 'I thought the lass had given up on locking men in the cellar. She hasn't done it for ages. I'll come and let you out.'

'It's alright. I asked to come down.'

'Really?' His face ascended as he straightened up. I heard the front door open and shut and his heavy footfall as I headed back to the stairs. She had locked me in.

He released me, rolling his eyes skywards. 'Sorry. She's got a thing about locking men in the cellar. I wouldn't worry about it though. I'm sure she means well.'

'But why?'

'I think it's because her father went away when she was a little girl and she reasoned that if he'd been locked in the cellar he wouldn't have been able to go. She only does it to men she likes. It's a compliment really.'

'Not the sort of compliment I like,' I said, though in all honesty it was about the only one I'd ever received from a woman, except from mother. 'Is she safe?'

'Oh, I shouldn't think so.' He grinned. 'She's only human after all. Are they ever safe?'

I shrugged. 'Dunno. Has she ever locked you in?'

'Oh yes,' he said airily, 'she used to do it all the time but I kept escaping and, since I always came back, I think she decided I was here to stay.'

'Well, it is your house.'

'True,' said Hobbes, 'and it's her home. Yours, too, as long as you want it.'

Again, I was touched. 'Thank you,' I said, though I still planned to write the book and was glad of any scraps of information about him and his crazed household. 'Umm ... I noticed a door in the cellar.'

'Well of course you did.' He frowned. 'Which is how you were able to enter and exit.'

'No. Another door.'

'Are you sure?' Without apparently doing anything, he seemed suddenly threatening.

'Yes,' I said, though his reply and manner had confused me and made me unsure. 'I've just seen it.'

'I don't think you should have just seen it.' He leaned towards me a fraction, the animal scent strengthening. 'It would be far better if you hadn't just seen it. If I were you, I'd forget about it. That door is not for you. Not yet. Maybe never.'

He patted me on the shoulder. It felt like being cudgelled.

'Now, come along, Andy.' He spoke slowly and emphatically. 'There is no other door in the cellar and you didn't see one because there was nothing to see. Do you understand?'

I knew how Biggs had felt. I was trembling all over, my knees knocking together, yet I managed to nod.

He smiled. 'Good man.'

The animal odour dissipating, my knees settled back into their accustomed supporting roles.

'Supper'll be ready soon. In the meantime, why not take a seat and take the weight off your mind.' Propelling me into the sitting room, he sat me on the sofa.

'Thank you,' I said, as he left and bounded upstairs. Though I tried to stop thinking about the door, I couldn't understand why he'd reacted in such a way. A horrible thought made me clutch at the lapel of my tweed jacket. What had happened to its original owner, Mr Goodfellow? Was he locked behind the door, walled up, never to escape? Or maybe his mortal remains were hidden there … or was there something worse? I sat in an ecstasy of doubt and fear until supper was ready when Hobbes reappeared, guided me into the kitchen and said grace.

I wouldn't have said I was hungry until I saw what lay on the table. It was what is sometimes referred to as a spread. There was a plate of sandwiches, generously cut from Mrs Goodfellow's still-warm crusty bread and packed with ham and mustard or cheese and pickle. Then there was egg and cress, cucumber and salmon, paté, cheeses, cold tongue and homemade pickles. To follow, she produced a cream trifle, drowning in sherry, a coffee cake smelling as fragrant as if the coffee had been freshly ground and was as light as air, a luscious dark fruit cake and a bowl of tinned pears. The latter surprised me, yet turned out to be Hobbes's favourite. I made myself at home. So what if I spent half my time in a state of fear and horror? I could at least eat well. And, by golly, I did eat well.

Afterwards, I sat back in my chair, hands folded across a distended stomach and belched happily.

'Manners, Andy. Manners.' Hobbes wagged a finger at me. He looked almost friendly, yet a glint in his eyes reminded me of Granny's cat. That evil orange beast used to slink towards me, exuding bonhomie, purring, begging to be stroked. As soon as I touched him, he'd roll onto his back in ecstasy, dig his claws into my hand and bite my thumb. He'd got me every time, and I was determined to stay on my guard with Hobbes. Though I'd once overheard a drunk in the Feathers state that Hobbes's bark was worse than his bite, I'd bet Hobbes had never bitten him, and my fear of being bitten was not the least of my worries about him. Even so, I was managing to live in his house, was fit and well, and gathering material for a book that could be the making of me, though a doubt had begun to take root; would anyone believe it?

I'd fully expected Hobbes to want to talk about the break-in after tea but, to my surprise, Mrs Goodfellow, bringing out a Scrabble board, invited me to join them in a game. I agreed. I was, after all, a journalist, one who'd increased his word power with *Reader's Digest* often enough. Though my confidence was high, humiliation was on its way as they thrashed me using words I'd never heard. Early on I challenged Hobbes over 'quitch', which he claimed was a type of grass, giving him a triple word score, and demanded a dictionary. He proved to be correct and, furthermore had just ruined my next move; all I could do was add an 's' to the word 'rat'. 'Rats.' At least it summed up my feelings. When Mrs Goodfellow followed my brilliant addition of 'san' to a 'g' to get 'sang' by expanding it to 'sanguineous' I knew I was in trouble. We played four games over the evening, Hobbes and Mrs Goodfellow winning two each, while I came a poor third every time. And that was to flatter myself, for in the final game, my total score was less than either of them achieved in a single move and, even worse, I was convinced they were trying to let me do well, giving me plenty of opportunities that I didn't, or couldn't, take.

'Bad luck, Andy.' Hobbes sounded sympathetic. 'Sometimes the letters run against you. Anyway, we're older than you and have had longer to pick up vocabulary.'

I nodded. 'Well done both of you.' At least I could play at being a good loser. I went up to bed shortly afterwards with a mug of cocoa.

'Make sure you clean your teeth when you've finished.' Mrs Goodfellow looked stern. 'We wouldn't want them rotting away would we?'

'No, we wouldn't.' I made a special trip to the bathroom just to make sure she didn't have an excuse for leaping out on me. Then I slept until late on Monday morning.

Once again, fresh clothes had been left on the dressing table. I supposed I ought to thank the old girl for that and for the meals, and for making my bed, too. When I was enjoying a leisurely bath, I noticed the sander still tucked under the sink and I wondered what Hobbes used it for. I wondered what was behind the door in the cellar. I wondered what was up in the loft. I wondered if I'd been born under a wondering star.

Though I'd only glimpsed inside the loft, I'd had an eyeful of colours and pictures. There was much to look into in this house, yet, now he'd entrusted me with a key, I had access all the time.

So did Mrs Goodfellow. The bathroom door swung open. 'No need to get up, dear.' She beamed her toothless smile, flicking a duster around.

I dropped back into the water, covering myself with my hands, squirming. 'Do you mind?'

'Of course not, dear.' She fixed her bright little eyes on me and chuckled. 'And don't mind me either. I'll only be a few minutes.'

'Couldn't you dust later? It's rather embarrassing.'

She tittered. 'From what I've seen, there's no reason for you to be embarrassed, dear. Now, Mr Goodfellow, he might have been embarrassed.'

'Mrs Goodfellow, please!'

'Oh alright, dear. Don't get into a state. I'll go and dust the old fellow's room. He's out already, you know.' She sat on the corner of the bath. 'Do you know, someone broke into the church last night? He's gone to investigate and he's upset. He doesn't like crimes on his patch and there have been a few recently. Now, the other year, there was a spate of car break-ins and—'

'Mrs Goodfellow,' I squeaked, 'please!'

'Oh, sorry, dear, I'm going.' She left me, closing the door behind her; her grin was the last thing to vanish, like she was a toothless, wrinkled, Cheshire cat.

Washing in haste, getting out the bath, I dried myself and scurried to my room where I tried to dress while leaning against the door. I could hear her flapping round in the bathroom as I went downstairs. At least I thought I'd heard her, for when I walked into the kitchen, she was stirring a copper pot.

'All dressed and safe from prying eyes, eh?'

I nodded, forcing a laugh to show how nonchalant I felt.

'Lovely teeth,' she cackled. 'Now would you like to get them stuck into something?'

'Like what?' I asked, nervously.

'Like bacon and eggs with mushrooms. It's what the old fellow had.'

'Mmm, it sounds lovely,' I said. I was wrong. It was better than that; it was divine. The scent of the frying mushrooms started me drooling and, when the bacon and eggs had been added, I feared my mouth would spill over. It tasted even better than it smelled and then I stuffed myself with toast and her superb marmalade, all washed down with fresh orange juice and as much tea as I could fit in. A little embarrassment seemed a small payment for such a breakfast.

'The old fellow asked what you were going to do today,' said Mrs Goodfellow when, having finished eating, my mouth became available for talking. 'He says he'll be down the church for a while if you want to meet him there. Mind you, he said it a while back when you were sleeping like a puppy. Then he said he'd have to go to Pigton, so, if he wasn't at the church, he'd be somewhere else and you were to do what you wanted to do. He reckoned you had to go to the *Bugle* sometime to get a name changed on a cheque, so he wouldn't be worried if you didn't show up. And he asked, if you were in the *Bugle's* office, if you'd find out where someone called Philip Waring lives. And—'

'Say no more,' I said, desperately trying to hold back the torrent of words. 'I'd better go.'

Standing up, I nodded and walked away, stepping out into the street, shutting the front door behind me, jumping down the steps. A flurry of sleet spattered the icy pavement at my feet and the cold wind had returned. Despite shivering, I was too proud to go back and pick up the old overcoat I'd found in the wardrobe. Since I had to pass the church on the way to the *Bugle*, it struck me as a good idea to look in. Hobbes might still be there and, even if he'd already gone, someone should be able to tell me what had happened. And if no one could then, maybe, I'd pick up sufficient divine inspiration to deal with Editorsaurus Rex. I'd bet bloody Phil, the editor's blue-eyed boy, never had problems like mine. Bastards the both of them. Still, I might be able to find Phil's address and then I'd do my best to ensure he had a really hard time at Hobbes's hands and, with luck, at his feet too.

Cold thoughts almost took my mind off the cold wind and, besides, it was only a short walk to the church. I was still glad to rush inside, pushing through a party of tourists, grateful for shelter. I can't claim I knew the church all that well, as I'd only been in once before, during a sudden downpour when returning from the pub. The dark, sombre atmosphere combined with the massive, mediaeval architecture and ancient treasures had impressed me then and still did.

A guy in a dog collar minced by. 'Excuse me, Vicar,' I said, 'has Inspector Hobbes left already?'

'Indeed he has,' he replied in a voice often described as fruity.

'Oh well. I'd hoped to catch him. I hear there was a break-in last night?'

'I'm afraid so.'

'Was anything taken, Vicar?'

He nodded.

'What?'

'Who wants to know?'

'I do. My name's Andy Caplet and I've been helping the Inspector for the last few days.'

'You don't look like a policeman and, I'm not the vicar, by the way, I'm the curate. The name's Kevin Godley; just call me Kev.'

I shook the hand he held out. It was cold, limp and flabby like a dead man's and gripped for rather longer than I liked. I jerked my arm away.

'I'm not a policeman. I'm just hanging out with Hobbes.'

'Oh, I see. A camp follower.'

I wasn't too chuffed with the stress he put on the word 'camp'.

I asked again. 'Can you tell me what was taken?'

'I can. Some lost sheep has swiped our Roman cup.'

'A Roman cup? Was it valuable?'

He nodded. 'I should think so. It was made of gold.'

'Wasn't it protected?'

'Yes, of course. It was displayed in a safe built into the wall, with a bullet-proof glass front until someone got it out last night.'

'How?'

He shrugged. 'They ignored the glass and cut through the mortar. Your Inspector mentioned an angle grinder but I don't really know what that is.'

'I think it's a tool.' I scratched my head. 'What's this cup look like anyway?'

Kev nodded towards a desk by the main door, where there were piles of books and pamphlets for sale. 'There's a photo in one of those pamphlets. Now, if you'll excuse me, I really must go, I've got a service to arrange.'

'It's OK,' I said. 'For Vespers?' I felt rather proud at my display of ecclesiastical knowledge.

'No.' Kev grinned. 'I meant a service for my motorbike and it's a Honda, not a Vespa. I can't abide those scooters with their piddly little motors. No, give me seven-fifty CCs throbbing between my thighs and I'm a happy curate. See you, Andy.' He patted my shoulder and walked away.

He disappeared behind a screen and I turned towards the desk, flicking through a pamphlet until coming across a photograph of the Roman cup, a large, heavy-looking goblet, plain, apart from a few foreign words in the form of a cross on the base. The pamphlet cost 50p and I was, literally, penniless but, as the severe, blue-rinsed woman in charge was occupied with a visitor, I folded the pamphlet, slipping it surreptitiously into my trouser pocket.

'That's fifty pee, sir.' The severe woman glared at me, her angry eyes glittering through horn-rimmed glasses.

'What is?' It was a feeble bluff but I'd never stolen anything before and I could feel the adrenalin coursing through my veins.

'The pamphlet in your pocket. Please pay for it or put it back. If not, I'll call the police.'

Panicking, I ran for it and, once I'd started, I couldn't stop. It was a stupid thing to do and I wouldn't dream of doing anything like it again and I would have paid if I could have and, anyway, the pamphlet was overpriced. In truth, I had no excuse – and I didn't even manage to keep it. It must have fallen from my pocket when, barging through a group of pensioners by the front door, I stumbled up the steps, before fleeing down The Shambles, weaving through the hordes of shoppers. Then, stunned by my own folly, heart pounding, I ducked down an alley, scrambling over a tall wooden fence, cowering in the backyard of a house. Out of sight, I got my breath back and listened for any sign of pursuit. I was just beginning to believe I'd got away with it when someone let the dog out.

It was a big animal, with rough, black hair and gleaming white fangs, and a deep prejudice against trespassers in tweed and I amazed myself at how fast I could move with a beast with the bulk and temperament of an angry bear snapping at my vitals. I jumped up, straddling the top of the fence, pulling up my leg before the brute could take a chunk out of it. The creature howled its disappointment and I thought I was safe. However, the fence was obviously in league with him. With a crack and a lurch, it buckled and collapsed beneath me. For a moment dog and I stared at each other. Then it gave a deep, resounding woof and I took to my heels with a yelp of terror.

I put it down to the beneficial effects of all my recent exercise that I made it from the alley before he caught me and brought me down at the feet of the gangly policeman. The severe woman was with him.

She pointed at me. 'That's him, officer, he's the one. Arrest him.'

The policeman, grabbing the dog's collar, pulled him off, handing him to his owner who had just emerged from the house, his fat red face quivering with rage.

'That's him.' He pointed at me. 'Arrest him for breaking my fence and cruelty to animals.'

'But …' I said. It was too late.

My hands were suddenly and surprisingly restrained by handcuffs and I was being led through the streets by the policeman, escorted by an angry woman, a furious man and a frustrated dog. People enjoy a good spectacle and I soon became the centre of a crowd, as wild and inaccurate rumours flew around. My sole consolation was that the excited dog, deprived of my blood, turned on his master, sinking his teeth into a fatted calf. The fat man, bleeding, roared and smacked the dog round its ears, while the woman denounced me as Sorenchester's answer to the Antichrist.

'What *have* you been doing, Andy?' asked a soft, familiar voice.

I turned and smiled weakly. 'Oh hi, Ingrid.' I made an attempt at nonchalance. 'It's just a misunderstanding. I'm sure it'll be sorted out soon.'

'He robbed the church!' the severe woman shouted.

'He smashed my fence down and he's been tormenting my dog. Aghh!' The angry man grew angrier as the dog nipped his other calf. 'Get off you brute.' He aimed a kick, losing the crowd's sympathy.

The woman was screaming, 'Search his pockets! Search his pockets!' at the policeman, who looked stunned by the whole procedure.

'All in good time, madam,' he said. 'At the station.'

'Don't you "madam" me. If you won't search him, I will.'

She pounced on me, and the dog, recognising a fresh target, pounced on her, growling like an over-revved scooter.

The crowd was taking sides. A spotty youth cheered on the dog and the angry man floored him with a punch. The youth's friend knocked the angry man onto his back and then it was mayhem. Quite a few joined in and even the dog had his day, snarling and snapping at random. Ingrid was swept away in a torrent of retreating townsfolk. The policeman gasped, 'Christ!' as the angry man, having staggered back to his feet, was hurled through the plate glass window of a dress shop. Fists and feet flew and a thrown bottle knocked the policeman cold. By then I was in a state of pure terror, my heart pounding, my mouth dry, doing whatever I could to protect myself, which was not easy in handcuffs. I don't know what came over me but, noticing the policeman was in real danger of being trampled, I somehow hoisted his limp body over my shoulder and staggered through the affray, taking several hits as I did so.

A voice boomed, echoing off the buildings as if a cannon had been fired. 'Stop this at once.'

The crowd went quiet. The dog fled. I looked up with my left eye, the right one, having taken a punch, had closed as tight as a clam. It was Hobbes, standing before us, hands thrust in the pockets of his coat, a scowl sculpting his face into that of a gargoyle.

'This is the police. I order you to disperse immediately or there will be trouble.'

'There's only one of him. Get him!' A big man in a red sweater incited the mob from the back. At least, he started at the back but the general retreat was so fast, he quickly found himself alone at the front.

He stared at Hobbes, quivering. He looked at the crowd.

'You were saying?' said Hobbes, conversationally.

The idiot was brave, I'll give him that. Brave, if not bright. Screaming incomprehensibly, putting his head down, he charged. Hobbes stood, watching. What happened next was a surprise. I expected Hobbes to hit him, yet all he did was shift his weight and pivot like a bullfighter as the idiot hurtled past, head-butting a lamppost, flopping back into his arms.

'This young fellow's going to have a headache,' said Hobbes, examining a gaping, oozing wound on the man's forehead and lying him down on the kerb. He gave a wolfish grin. 'Still, I doubt he had much brain to damage. Are you alright, Andy?'

I nodded and sank to the pavement with the policeman still over my shoulder, groaning as I helped him down.

'It was brave, rescuing Constable Poll like that,' said Hobbes. 'He might have been badly hurt if you hadn't. How are you doing, Bean?'

PC Poll's eyes opened. 'Could be better, sir.'

By then more police officers were appearing and the crowd had dispersed, except for a few onlookers gawping from a distance. Several dismembered bodies lay scattered in the road. I gasped; I hadn't realised things had got so bad. Hobbes picked up one, twisting its head round. 'Gottla geer,' he said like a bad ventriloquist, 'gottla geer.'

I stared, horrified. It took several long dark moments before I worked out that the bodies were mannequins from the dress shop. When the relief hit me, I must have fainted.

9

The world looked strange. My knees were pressed into my armpits, my knuckles scraped against a tatty rug and a great weight was forcing my head down. I could see my feet and the bottom drawer of a rusty filing cabinet upside down between the legs of a chair. As I groaned, the weight lifted, a hairy hand took me by the shoulder, easing me upright and, though I'd seen some strange things when waking, Hobbes's leathery face peering into mine was the most unnerving. Yet, I was sitting in his office, the handcuffs were off, and he was looking at me with an expression wavering between concern and amusement.

'How are you feeling?' he asked.

'Not too bad. What happened?' I was determined to act cool, despite not understanding what I was doing there.

'You fainted. Now put this on your eye and cover it up. It looks like a baboon's backside.'

He handed me an ice pack and I applied it with another groan.

'That's some shiner you've got.' He grinned. 'We had a doc take a look at it and it's only bruised. By heck though, you do have an eye for trouble.'

'It wasn't my fault.'

'No. Not entirely. I had the story from young Poll before they carted him off to the hospital. He's got a touch of concussion and it might have been a lot worse if you hadn't got him out when you did. Mind you,' he said and chuckled, 'it might have been a lot better if you hadn't got him into it in the first place.'

'I didn't mean to. I didn't want to be arrested. Will I be charged?'

'Of course not. I can't have it said that I harbour criminals under my own roof. I gave the gentleman twenty pounds towards fixing his fence and we agreed he won't be taking the matter any further. In addition, your pockets being empty, there was no evidence of theft and, besides, the lady is currently undergoing treatment for shock and dog bites and is unwilling to talk.'

'What about the dog?'

'I had a word with the man about his dog, just before the ambulance came for the worst casualties.' Hobbes's grin grew broader. 'We agreed he should never have been keeping a dog that is so evidently a danger to himself and the public.'

'What's going to happen to it? It's mad and vicious and should be put down.'

'So the man said,' said Hobbes, 'but I pleaded for a reprieve.'

'What? Why? It's dangerous.'

'Probably, which is why I'm going to look after him. His name's Dregs, according to his former master.'

I groaned, not being keen on dogs since one ate my football when I was six. I've always blamed it for my failure to shine as a sportsman. At least, I've blamed it when not blaming my father. 'Where is he now?' I looked suspiciously round the office.

'They patched him up, though he wasn't much hurt and he's taking Mrs Goodfellow to the shops. They're going to pick up some dog biscuits. He says he's a bit fussy and won't touch the cheapuns, so they're off to the posh shop.'

'He told you that did he?'

'Yes.'

'So you've talked to him?' Now, it seemed Hobbes was speaking with animals. I wasn't as surprised as I would have been when I'd first met him.

'He says I'm welcome to take his basket and any leftover food and reckons his wife will be glad to see the back of him.'

'His wife? He can't have a wife. It's impossible.'

'I admit it's unlikely,' said Hobbes, 'though I understand the dog was what made him so angry, and the fact that his wife hated it didn't help his temper.'

'Oh. I understand now. I thought you'd been talking to the …' I let the sentence fade away as the colour rose to my cheeks.

He laughed. 'Maybe that knock on your head is more serious than it seems.'

'Sorry. I got a bit confused.'

'As if I'd have a conversation with the dog.' He chuckled. 'I wouldn't do such a thing – not till we've been properly introduced.'

He guffawed and I responded with a feeble twitch of the lips.

'Anyway,' he said, changing the subject, 'did you get the editor to rewrite your cheque, or were you too busy fomenting civil unrest?'

'No, not yet.' I felt a sinking sensation in the stomach. I didn't fancy confronting Editorsaurus Rex just then, with an ice pack pressed to my throbbing eye, with torn knees on my trousers and blood splashed over my shirt – at least it wasn't mine.

'Right then,' said Hobbes. 'If you're feeling better, there's no time like the present. Come on.'

I followed him of course. By then I didn't even think about it, though I'd have much preferred to curl up quietly somewhere in the dark. I struggled to keep up, while attempting a cool and heroic demeanour for the shoppers. He burst through the doors of the *Bugle* building, bounding upstairs to the main office.

'Can I help you?' asked a male voice on my ice-packed side.

'I doubt it,' said Hobbes, marching straight towards Rex's door.

'You can't go in. He's busy,' said the voice. I didn't recognise it. Rex hadn't wasted any time in replacing me.

Hobbes opened the door and walked in, with me bobbing in after him, shrugging apologetically. Rex rose from behind his desk as if someone had cut loose a hot-air balloon.

'What do you mean by this interruption?' His stare fixed on me. 'It's Capstan, isn't it? Didn't I sack you? What are you doing here?'

'Sit,' said Hobbes. 'We'll not take long. I am Inspector Hobbes, of the Sorenchester Police.'

Rex, deflating, slumped into his chair. A skinny woman sitting opposite him turned to stare at us and I recognised her from *Sorenchester Life*: she was Mrs Witcherley. Her face, beneath a trowel-full of makeup, looked young and soft, her blonde hair shone with youthful lustre, yet her neck, though concealed under strings of lustrous pearls, suggested she was approaching sixty. She sat, legs crossed, cigarette in hand, pungent fumes coiling from between her glossy red lips. Apart from the smoker's pout, she showed no expression.

'Firstly,' Hobbes continued, 'Mr Caplet requires you to amend a cheque. Andy?' His hand propelled me towards the desk.

'Sorry to disturb you, sir.' I felt very much the humble supplicant. 'Umm … you appear to have written the wrong name on my severance cheque.'

'So what do you expect me to do about it?'

'Umm … change it, please.'

'You're damn lucky I gave you a cheque at all.' Rex scowled. 'You misled me about your interests and abilities, you consistently failed to file reports on time, if at all, and you were a constant drain on the resources of this newspaper. Now, run along.'

Hobbes leaned over the desk. 'It would be advisable to pay him, sir.' Without apparently doing anything, he reeked of menace.

Rex, jerking back into his chair as if he'd been punched, nodded. 'Only joking, Capstan. I will, of course, write you another immediately. What name should I put on it?'

'Andrew Caplet,' said Hobbes. 'And, if I were you, I would amend the figure, too, just in case anyone happened to let slip what a deplorable and possibly illegal wage you've been paying him.'

Rex, nodding again, pulled a chequebook from his desk, popping the top off his fountain pen, writing on a cheque, blotting it carefully, tearing it off and handing it to me.

'Thank you, sir,' I said as I glanced at it. It was for two thousand pounds. 'Thank you very much.' Folding it, I put it in my inside pocket.

'Good,' said Hobbes. 'Now I'd like to have a word about a member of your staff.'

'Oh yes?' said Rex. 'By the way, may I introduce Mrs Witcherley, my wife.' He gestured towards the woman who, nodding, exhaled an acrid cloud.

'Delighted to meet you, Mrs Witcherley,' said Hobbes, taking her hand, raising it to his lips. For a moment I thought he was going to bite her and, from the way her eyes widened, I suspected the same thought had crossed her mind, yet her lips unpuckered into a smile.

'Delighted, Inspector,' she murmured.

'Mrs Witcherley and I have no secrets,' Rex said. 'Please feel free to ask anything.'

'Andy, you'd better step outside.' Hobbes strode across the carpet and opened Rex's door. 'I'll see you at home for lunch.'

Raising a hand in an ignored gesture of farewell, I cringed back into the main office. All eyes were looking at me, except for Basil Dean's strange one that always did its own thing.

Ingrid bustled towards me. 'Hi, Andy. What's happened to Phil?'

'Eh?' I asked, coherently, taken aback.

'Phil. What's happened to him?'

'Something's happened to him?'

'What?'

'I … umm … don't know.'

Oh,' she said, 'I thought you'd come here because of him.'

I was confused. 'Has something happened to Phil?'

'We don't know, which is why I'm asking you. I assumed the Inspector had come to investigate.'

'Investigate what?' I was enormously miffed to find her concerned about Phil when I was so obviously battered and bruised and she'd last seen me handcuffed in the middle of a riot.

There were tears in her eyes. 'He hasn't turned up for work today, and he's not at home.'

'Bloody Phil,' I muttered.

She stared at me as if I'd just booted a puppy.

'I meant, bloody hell, Phil's missing.' I said, trying to inject the authentic note of concern for the git.

She was crying, looking worried. 'No one knows what's happened to him. I went round to his house when he didn't ring in. His milk's still outside, he didn't respond when I knocked and he's not answering his mobile.'

'Oh,' I said, 'I wouldn't worry. He's probably working on a story and if he is missing, Hobbes'll find him, or someone will – like with the body last week.'

She didn't appear to find my words very comforting. 'You think he might be dead?' She sobbed, her pudgy little hands covering her mouth. 'Poor Phil.'

'Oh no,' I said, attempting reassurance, 'I'm sure he's not dead. Not yet. Well, probably not anyway. Look, I'm sure there's a perfectly reasonable explanation. He'll turn up, just you wait and see.'

He probably would turn up, I thought, though I wished he wouldn't. Yet, I smiled, Hobbes would still want a word with him when he reappeared.

'I suppose you're right.' She sniffed and moved slightly closer.

I raised my arm on impulse, with the idea of wrapping it around her shoulders, to comfort her, yet I couldn't see past her swollen red eyes and the little bead of mucus glistening at the corner of her nose. I recoiled, my arm dropping to my side.

'Sorry,' I said, 'but I've got to go.' It occurred to me that this was a good time to start undermining Phil. 'I'm sure Hobbes will find him. He probably guessed Hobbes wants to see him, to grill him about a serious crime, and has done a runner.'

'Is he in trouble?' asked Ingrid. 'I don't believe it.'

'You'd better believe it,' I said, raising my voice so everyone could hear. 'I'm afraid Phil is wanted for questioning about some pretty heavy stuff and could go down for a long time. He's been linked to some despicable characters involved in theft and kidnapping and now he's disappeared. Well, it doesn't prove anything, but it makes you think.'

On that climactic note I left, well satisfied with the shocked look on Ingrid's face and the interest I'd stirred up in the others. Phil would have a job explaining his way out of it. I gloated as I strolled along The Shambles back to Blackdog Street. I heard footsteps running as I reached the church.

The dog brushed past me, with Mrs Goodfellow clinging to his lead like a water-skier behind a speedboat, except water-skiers aren't known to carry big red shopping bags.

'Alright, dear? What have you been doing to yourself?'

'I, umm …' I said, and she was gone.

I heard a cry of 'Whoa!' as they flashed past the front door, heading down Ride Street in the direction of the park, making me wonder what I would do for lunch.

I needn't have worried. They'd reappeared by the time I got home, the dog trotting obediently to heel, tail wagging, tongue lolling, the epitome of friendliness. They pushed by when I opened the door. As I followed them into the kitchen, she put down a bowl of water, which he lapped up noisily, before sprawling under the table.

Mrs Goodfellow attended to lunch, which had been slowly cooking in the oven and filling the house with enticing smells. It was just a cottage pie, though not like the soggy, tasteless travesties in the Bellman's. This was a pie of delights, as I discovered on Hobbes's return. As usual, we ate in silence, which felt right, because Mrs Goodfellow's meals were deserving of reverence. Still, it bothered me that she never took food with us.

Hobbes and I finished, sitting back with a pair of contented sighs, rising from the table, taking our positions in the sitting room as normal, except that Dregs padded in after us, sitting with his head on Hobbes's knees and his big, heavy, hairy backside crushing my left foot. When Hobbes rested his hand on the dog's head it was barely noticeable among the mass of wiry hairs. Though I tried shuffling my foot, the blasted mutt seemed to like it and began wriggling in ecstasy, contriving to pin both my feet down, as well as wedging my knees against the sofa.

Mrs Goodfellow cackled as she carried in the tea tray. For probably the first time since I'd been there, I didn't jump; I couldn't.

'He seems to like you, dear.'

Hobbes smiled. 'I'm glad you two are getting on so well, Andy.'

I grimaced, which was all I could do by then as the bloody thing had managed to wriggle up my legs and was lying across me. The more I tried, the less I could move and soon, the brute's weight, being concentrated on my chest, it became increasingly difficult to breathe. In fact, I saw clearly that I was going to expire beneath him and couldn't even find enough breath to complain. What a way to go, I would have laughed if I could. The colours in the room were fading to a dull grey and I was looking at the world through a rapidly narrowing tunnel. I could see brightness at the end and seemed to be rushing towards it. My consciousness flew up, fluttering round the light shade like a large moth and I watched with moth's eyes and purely academic interest as Hobbes pushed the dog from my body. It did look battered, with the huge bruise around its right eye already showing more shades of colour than a sunset. Battered and blue. I remembered a lecture on first aid. Blue indicated cyanosis, which is what happens to a body when it's been deprived of oxygen for too long. I wondered why Hobbes was lifting me in such a way.

I came to, dangling upside down, my ankles squeezed in his left hand, my buttocks stinging, squirming, squawking like a chicken when I saw his right hand lifted to deliver another blow. I cried like a baby when it landed.

'Told you it'd work,' said Mrs Goodfellow. 'It always got 'em breathing when I was a midwife. You can put him down now. He's alright. His face is going red.'

I found myself swinging like a pendulum, the arcs growing wider until I was fully upright when he released his grip. I experienced a brief moment of weightlessness, as if becoming a moth again, before, catching my shoulders, he dropped me onto the sofa. Then the blasted dog leaped up, licking my face, making me wish I couldn't breathe again. It came as a great relief when Mrs Goodfellow dragged him off and led him to the kitchen.

'Sorry about that,' said Hobbes. 'I thought you were playing until you turned blue. It was quite unusual; your lips matched your eyes. You don't see that every day.'

I shook my head and groaned.

'Glad you're better. You should be more careful, though. Dogs can be dangerous. Right then, I was going to tell you about the theft from the church. The first one that is, not the one by the despicable pamphlet pilferer.'

I laughed bitterly. I was not having a good day. The church clock struck two – two o'clock in the afternoon and I'd already been pursued by a dog, handcuffed by a policeman, reviled by a mob, been in a riot and been unconscious twice.

'Someone, as you know, broke into the wall safe and pinched the Roman cup. As far as I can make out, the person, or persons, did not break into the church, so, unless they had a key, which is unlikely, it's probable they attended the service on Sunday evening and hid until everything was quiet. Then they must have broken into the safe and slipped out when the warden opened the doors this morning.'

'Aha! That bloody Phil's gone missing. He must have done it.'

'I think we do need to find him,' said Hobbes, 'because he may know something of significance. It's probably more than coincidence that he went missing right after the robbery.'

'Let's hunt him down like the dog he is.' I felt the thrill of the chase rising within.

'Calm down, Andy, I didn't say he did it. There are some interesting aspects to this theft. Firstly, look at these.' Delving into his jacket pocket, he pulled out a sealed plastic bag, containing cigarette butts and chocolate wrappers.

'Interesting? Why?'

'I found them in a pew.'

'Well? So what? Doesn't it just mean someone's been smoking and eating in church?'

'It does, yet the pews are always swept after the service. Therefore, someone must have left them there after the sweeping and the church was closed to the public immediately afterwards.'

'Then,' I said, 'the burglar left them there. All it means is that he smokes and eats chocolate.' I realised Phil didn't smoke. 'Phil eats chocolate.'

'So do I,' said Hobbes, 'and I'm not going to arrest every chocolate-eating smoker in Sorenchester and district. There's another interesting little fact. D'you remember the break in at Mr Roman's house?'

'Of course.'

'Well, don't you remember what I found under the tree to suggest the burglar had been watching the house?'

I thought a moment, creasing my forehead in concentration. 'Yeah. I remember: cigarette butts and chocolate wrappers.'

'Correct, and they were the same brand of cigarettes and the same wrappers as in the church. What's more, the cigarette butts are from a brand I'm not familiar with. They've mostly been smoked well down but there's a bit of writing on one of them. See here? It says "pati".'

'So it's likely the same person did both crimes.'

'So I suspect. I wonder why they wanted the Roman cup, though? What's so special about it? There are plenty of other, much more valuable, treasures in there that weren't stolen, just like at the museum. In both cases someone knew just what they were looking for and where to find it and everything else was apparently untouched.'

I nodded. 'So you think the same burglar has done Mr Roman's house, the museum and the church? All within a week. That's three crimes linked.'

'Four,' said Hobbes. 'The death of Jimmy the gardener is another obvious link, though I don't yet know why. If only Roman had told us what really happened.'

'And Phil has done a runner.' I thought I should remind him.

'He's certainly gone missing, which brings me to another coincidence. Mr Biggs from the museum discharged himself from the hospital last evening, against medical advice, and he, too, has vanished. I visited his flat this morning. He'd taken clothes as well as his passport.'

'He must have been in league with Phil.'

'Now, now, Andy.' Hobbes frowned. 'Still, I ought to have a look at Mr Waring's house and see if I can discover a reason for his disappearance. I'd be glad of your company if you want to come.'

'I'd love to.' I was convinced, or nearly convinced, that Phil had done it and dearly wanted to be there when justice caught up with him. With any luck, he was the one who'd killed Jimmy; a conviction for murder would keep him away from Ingrid for life. Even so, deep down, a persistent suspicion lurked that maybe I was only trying to convince Hobbes of Phil's guilt, because, if he believed it, then I, too, could legitimately believe it. A nasty, nagging question popped up from the uncharted depths of my mind and wouldn't go away; was I, in some way, jealous of Phil with his looks and charm and talent and easy, courteous way with women? I had to keep reminding myself that he was a smarmy git who deserved everything coming to him and that I deserved so much more, which Hobbes would help me to achieve.

'C'mon, Andy. There's no time for daydreaming, there are crimes to be solved. Mr Witcherley gave me Mr Waring's address. It's number two, Aristotle Drive.'

'Where's that?'

'Part of the new estate on the edge of town, out Sorington way.'

I nodded. 'Oh yeah, I know. They're rather smart.' Typical, I thought that Phil would live there. I remembered my late-lamented, grotty, little flat. Life wasn't fair but I wasn't jealous: I just don't like flash gits.

'We'd better take the car,' said Hobbes.

'Oh, great,' I muttered, my stomach churning, my pulse starting to race in emulation of his driving.

'You'd better change your suit first.' He glanced at my knees. 'You're a mess.'

Going up to my room, opening the wardrobe, I picked one of the half dozen suits hanging there at random. It was dark grey, fitting like it was bespoke. It gave me the shivers that someone else's clothes could be such an amazing fit. I'd always worn off-the-peg stuff and it had never been entirely satisfactory. 'It fits where it touches,' as Granny Caplet used to remark.

When I went down, Hobbes was standing by the door, the car keys dangling from his monstrous hand like an earring on a wild boar. 'Hurry up. I haven't got all day.'

I scurried to the car after him and climbed in. 'It's a one-way street,' I moaned as we set off.

Hobbes turned, grinning. 'And?'

I shut my eyes. 'I know, I know. You're only going one way.'

He laughed like a maniac.

'And the speed limit's thirty miles per hour.' I had to say it, though I recognised the futility.

'Don't worry,' he said over the screech of tyres and the blaring of a horn, 'we won't be driving anywhere near thirty miles in the next hour, so there's no chance of exceeding the speed limit.'

'Oh, that's alright, then,' I said, my sarcasm unremarked and wasted. I wondered if he really believed what he'd said.

When I opened my eyes, we were hurtling towards a crossroads – and we were on the minor road. Whimpering, I tried to close my eyes again, finding all my muscles had taken fright and refused to comply. As we crossed the dotted line, a blue car sped towards us from one direction, a white van approaching from the other. Though I don't know how, we avoided them both by the thickness of a layer of paint, zipping up the road ahead, leaping the traffic-calming bumps with the exuberance of a spring lamb and landing with a sickening thud. I know it was sickening because it made me sick. I only just managed to wind down the window in time. Mrs Goodfellow's cottage pie decorated the side of the car like lumpy go-faster stripes.

'Are you alright?' Hobbes asked.

'Never felt better in my entire life,' I said, my groan becoming a retch, ending as a hysterical laugh. I flopped back in the seat. He was staring at me, with a puzzled expression.

'Everything's just wonderful,' I giggled. 'Live fast. Die young. Leave a beautiful corpse. Or one smashed into a million bloody quivering fragments. Oh, yes, everything in the garden's roses.'

Hobbes was still frowning as we took the next speed bump. I guessed we were doing seventy. We'd have been faster if the wheels had stayed in contact with the road for longer.

'Yeehah!' I screamed.

Without looking away from me, Hobbes spun the wheel, skidded into Cranberry Lane and braked rapidly and smoothly. Only my seat belt prevented a close encounter of the painful kind with the windscreen. I stopped my crazed giggling, watching a small, dishevelled, black cat flee across the road in front of us, pursued by a fat ginger tom. At least we hadn't killed them and the thought calmed me until his foot stamped on the accelerator and the car leaped forward. Just to think, a couple of days earlier I'd believed I'd been getting used to his driving. No way. It's just that nerves can only take so much before exhaustion leads to acquiescence.

'I can go faster if you like.' At least he was looking the way we were going.

'No. Please.' I gulped. 'How did you do that?'

'Do what?'

'Stop before those cats ran out! You weren't even looking, for God's sake.'

'Language, Andy. I stopped the usual way, by pressing on the brake pedal and I don't need to look to find it, it's always in the same place.'

'Umm … why did you stop?'

'Because I didn't want to run over the animals.' He looked puzzled.

'What I mean is, how did you know they were there?'

'Oh, I see. Well, you learn to anticipate such things when you've been driving as long as I have.'

I thought, just for a moment, before he turned away, I could detect a hint of embarrassment in his expression. As he tugged the wheel, the car danced into Aristotle Drive. Phil's driveway was the first on the right, which meant we had to cross the road. Hobbes could have waited until the post-office van had passed but, no, he turned in front of it, the brakes screeching as we came to a standstill.

'Here we are,' he said. 'Not too bad a journey, eh?'

My head shook. I wasn't disagreeing, it was just that every part of me was shaking. Taking several long, deep breaths to calm myself, I staggered from the car, making sure not to look at my mess down the side, still queasy.

Phil's house looked as smart as all the others along the road. There was a small garden in the front and the brown, brittle leaves of the neatly trimmed beech hedge rattled in the breeze. The grass had grown long and straggly. Phil was evidently not a conscientious gardener, at least not in November. Two milk bottles stood, pale and neglected, by the doorstep.

'How do we get in? Have you got a key? Or one of those big metal rams they use on the telly?'

'Usually,' said Hobbes, 'I ring the doorbell first.'

He raised his hand, his fingernail appearing to slide forward like the point on a biro, and pressed the button. The bell rang somewhere inside. We waited in silence.

'Then, I usually knock.'

He raised his hand again, forming a mighty fist and knocked. The door shuddered, flying open, revealing a hall painted in magnolia, carpeted in beige, with a wooden door on the left side, a glass door leading into the kitchen at the far end and a staircase on the right. As we stepped inside, it was quiet: as quiet as the grave and nearly as cold. Everything was very neat and clean, smelling of bleach and detergent, without even a hint of socks. Hobbes opened the door on the left and I glanced into the lounge, disgusted by the enormous television, the hi-fi, the black leather suite and the deep, cream carpet.

'Stay there.' He prowled through the lounge, disappearing through an archway at the far end, reappearing a few moments later through the kitchen door.

'No one in there,' he said, 'though there's a defrosted single-portion lasagne on top of the oven. Let's take a look upstairs.'

He led the way. A fish tank stood on a windowsill halfway up and its inhabitants danced and fluttered as we approached.

'They're hungry.' He sprinkled the water with flakes from a tub by the side. As the fish gorged amid an ecstasy of splashing and popping, he nodded, carrying on to the landing.

Five closed doors stood before us. Opening them one by one, he revealed first a bathroom and then four other rooms, one, stinking of cologne, with an en-suite bathroom, obviously Phil's bedroom. I sniffed in disapproval. The double bed with its black satin sheets had not been made and raised the question of why he needed a double bed. If he'd laid a finger on Ingrid … never mind his finger, if he'd laid anything on her, there was going to be trouble. Hobbes moved on, barely glancing into the sparsely furnished spare room and a box-room filled with sports gear and heavily loaded bookcases.

He headed straight into the last room, done out as an office, starting the computer in the corner, leafing through a diary while it warmed up, or whatever computers do. I'd never quite come to terms with them. I wasn't technophobic or anything, but machines just hated me. One computer had lost an article I'd struggled with for over two hours. I still maintain it wasn't my fault, it was just that the can of lager had got all shaken up as I ran from the Old Folks' Origami Extravaganza to file my report before deadline and it could have happened to anyone. Rex didn't see it like that, of course. After a long and vicious rant he'd assigned Phil to be my mentor. I couldn't believe it, for I'd been working for the *Bugle* far longer than he, and the worst part was when the bastard agreed. Rex loved Phil, just because he got reports in the paper every day. Luck always seemed to be on his side.

While Hobbes was hunched over the computer, jabbing away at the keys, I stood looking out the window, watching the expectant birds hopping around on the empty bird table in the back garden. A fluffy grey cat, springing from a shrub, completely missed them all as they scattered into the bushes.

Phil's business cards were stacked on the windowsill. Typical, I thought, for him to have business cards. For what reason? He didn't need that sort of thing to prove what a pretentious bastard he was. As I sneered, a thought occurred. They might have a use, one he would never have thought of. Hobbes, appearing engrossed by something on the screen, I slipped a few into my pocket.

'That's interesting,' said Hobbes.

I started guiltily but he was still looking at the screen.

'It appears Mr Waring was researching an article on Mr Roman's death and had linked it to the body in the graveyard, too.'

'Oh?' I said. 'He was probably trying to give himself an alibi.'

'Enough, Andy,' Hobbes growled.

I flinched.

'There's no evidence that Philip Waring has committed any crime and it appears more likely he has been a victim of one. Investigative journalism can be dangerous, you know.'

Of course I knew. I had, after all, been mauled by a hamster in the course of my work. Besides, I was working with Hobbes. How much more dangerous could it get?

He looked at the diary again. 'Last night he was going to meet someone called "T".'

'"T" for Tony?'

'Possibly,' he mused. 'However, there may be other possibilities. Mr Waring obviously expected to return, otherwise he wouldn't have defrosted the lasagne. There's no evidence of a struggle or of anyone else being here in the last few days, so he left of his own accord. I think we ought to catch up with Tony Derrick and see if he is the contact.'

'So how are we going to find him?'

'With patience and skill,' he grinned. 'I called in on Billy earlier. Tony wasn't in last night and no one had heard from him. Mind you, Tony's not the sort to have friends and most of his acquaintances are not the sort to talk.'

'He was in Phil's car on Saturday night and Phil is always pretending to be friendly.'

'Pretending?' He grimaced. 'Everyone else I've spoken to remarked on his friendliness.'

'That's cos he's a phoney.'

'Well, someone is,' said Hobbes with a scowl. 'It hardly matters anyway. He's a member of the public and I suspect he's in trouble. Therefore, it's my job to get him out of trouble.'

Affronted by Hobbes's implication that I might be the phoney, I made up my mind to show him evidence proving how much of a git Phil was, even if I had to make it myself. All of a sudden in a sulky mood, I followed him around the house, barely noticing what he was up to, silently sneering at Phil's taste in everything, especially his cabinet filled with sporting trophies. The guy was unbelievable, even owning Wagner CDs and no one has that sort of crap, except to impress the feeble minded. Well, it didn't work on me. And then there was his book collection. Why have all those volumes on Roman Sorenchester? As for his spice rack and everything else in the sodding house, I found it all too much.

I was happy to leave. The whole house reeked of his achievements. I wasn't jealous; I was just glad he was out of the picture.

Still in a deep sulk when we got back into the car, not inclined to pay attention to anything, I was barely aware of Hobbes's mobile chirruping and him answering.

Turning towards me, putting the phone back in his pocket, sticking the key in the ignition, he said, 'There's been a robbery with violence.'

'Oh.'

'I don't like such crimes on my patch. They make me angry and that is a bad thing … for someone.'

'Oh.'

'Don't you want to hear about it?' He sounded puzzled. 'I thought you'd be interested.'

With a huge effort, I forced myself to be fair. 'Sorry,' I said, 'I'm just upset about Phil.' I was being truthful, in a way.

'I understand,' he said. 'It's a bad feeling when a comrade goes missing, though, for some reason, I'd formed an opinion that you didn't like him. I believe everyone deals with bad news in their own way.'

I nodded. Again, I felt I might not be entirely in the right. Ignoring the feeling, I asked about the robbery.

'I'll tell you on the way over.' He started the car's engine with a throbbing series of revs and in moments we were hurtling along the road. I didn't know where, because with Hobbes behind the wheel, ignorance was, if not blissful, less terrifying.

'It happened this morning,' he said, 'just out of town on the Green Way.'

'The Green Way? Isn't that an old Roman road?'

'So it's said. Why?'

'Oh, I don't know. It's just with the Roman Cup going missing and the bracelet – wasn't that something to do with the Order of St George? – and wasn't St George a Roman?'

'I am aware,' said Hobbes, 'that St George is venerated by Eastern European churches, who believe he was a tribune in the Roman army. If I remember rightly, the despotic Emperor Diocletian had him beheaded.'

'So he was a Roman.' I enjoyed the brief elation of triumph.

'If the old tales are true.' He shrugged. 'What are you getting at?'

'Well, everything seems to have a Roman connection: Roman cups, Roman saints, Roman roads.'

'Not to forget the unfortunate Mr Roman,' said Hobbes with a grin.

'Yes, well. Though it does make you think, doesn't it?'

'It does. And I expect you're going to tell me all about Mr Waring's collection of books on Roman Sorenchester.'

'Does he have one?' I asked, innocently. 'Well, how strange, he never told me he was interested in antiquities. I wonder where he got them from.'

'He is a Friend of Sorenchester Museum and many of the books are on loan from there.'

'Then he'd have known all about the museum and he'd be likely to know what was in the store.'

'Quite possibly and I'm sure it will be extremely useful to have a word with him. However, it's really not difficult to make all sorts of dubious Roman connections round here. After all, they founded the town. And there are three hundred and twenty-seven Friends of the Museum. I checked because, you're absolutely right, the burglars knew exactly what they were looking for and where to find it.'

'OK,' I said, 'I was only saying. It just hit me, that's all. Now, what happened this morning?'

The car's engine roared. Now and again car horns blared, sometimes coinciding with wild and erratic movements. I, however, saw no evil, though it is amazingly difficult to keep your eyes closed when peril is all around.

'What I know,' said Hobbes, 'is that a robbery occurred at a house used by a Mr Arthur Barrington-Oddy – and I have no evidence to suggest he's a Roman. Apparently, when Mr Barrington-Oddy opened his front door to answer the doorbell, two masked men were standing there …'

'Two men? How very interesting.'

'…and, before he had a chance to defend himself, they overpowered him, rendering him unconscious by means of a noxious substance that caused minor burns to the skin around his mouth and nose.'

'What would do that?'

'Chloroform sounds most plausible at this stage. Mr Barrington-Oddy woke some time later feeling giddy and ill but managed to reach a telephone and call for help. He is now recuperating in hospital.'

'So, what was stolen?'

'He doesn't know, because he's only renting the house. However, he could tell a display cabinet had been broken into.'

'So, whose house is it?'

He laughed. 'Give us a break, Andy, I was only on the phone a minute, not long enough to ascertain all the facts. Anyway, if detecting was that easy then anyone could do it.'

'Even me, you mean?'

'Well perhaps not everyone. Now, hold tight!'

The car, lurching and banking, gravel scrunching, we stopped with a skid and I opened my eyes. We'd stopped within an inch of a police car, from which a pale-faced, grey-haired constable was emerging.

'Here we are.' Stopping the engine, Hobbes opened the door.

Undoing my seat belt with shaky hands, I got out onto a gravelled drive. A turreted old house stood in front of us, lurking in the shadows of a large, tree-infested garden that I suspected would look right impressive in the summer, though it was desolate in grey November. A gleaming plaque on the studded door, above a polished brass knocker in the shape of a bear's head, indicated the house was called Brancastle.

The constable saluted. 'Good afternoon, sir.'

'Afternoon, George,' Hobbes nodded. 'What's going on here then?'

'A forced entry, sir, and a robbery. Mr Barrington-Oddy has already been released from hospital and is returning by taxi. He may be able to answer some of your questions.'

'Good,' said Hobbes. 'In the meantime, I'd better take a look around. Andy, would you stay here with PC Wilkes?'

'Yeah, OK.'

Hobbes squatted down, crawling over the gravel towards the front door, PC Wilkes and I, standing by the police car, watching until he disappeared inside the house.

'Weird,' said Wilkes. 'Was he sniffing then?'

'Umm … it sounded like it.'

'I don't know what it is but something about him gives me the creeps.'

'I know what you mean,' I said.

'Yeah.' Wilkes grimaced. 'I know he's a copper, and a good one, and there's less crime on his patch than most others and a better clean up rate, but there's something unnatural about him. No … not unnatural; if anything he's too natural. Unhuman, is that the right word?'

'Inhuman?' I suggested.

Wilkes pondered. 'Maybe not – inhuman sounds like he's cruel or something and he isn't. Well, not really.'

I agreed. 'I see what you're getting at.' I thought for a moment about all his oddities. 'Unhuman sums him up rather well.'

'Still,' said Wilkes, 'he's a feature of Sorenchester Police. All the regional coppers know him by reputation at least. I guess he must be about due for retirement. Mind you, that's what I thought when I transferred here, nearly twenty years ago. What's your connection with him?'

'I'm staying with him temporarily, because my flat burned down last week. By the way, my name's Andy. Andy Caplet.'

'George Wilkes.' He nodded, his broad, slow face brightening with a smile of recognition. 'You're the journalist aren't you? The bloke from the *Bugle*? I've heard about you. What on earth did you do to get saddled with the Inspector?'

'I don't know.' I frowned. 'I've left the *Bugle* now. I'm freelance.'

'Yeah, I heard you'd got the boot. And aren't you the guy that got his ear chomped at the pet show?'

I acknowledged the fact.

He laughed. 'I can still remember your photo in the paper: what an expression! Yeah, that's it, you're doing it again.' He continued to laugh, leaning against the police car, until a taxi turned into the drive, scattering gravel. Then wiping his eyes, grinning, he stood upright, patted me on the back and stepped towards the taxi.

Rage and fury built within me and, though I wanted to say something fine and biting, a retort to cut him down to size, I couldn't think of anything. 'Hah!' I said, frustrated, turning away, wishing I had something to kick. Anything.

Then I had a brilliant idea. Walking towards the door of the house, my hand casually thrust into my jacket pocket, climbing up the steps, I peeked into the entrance hall, seeing no sign of Hobbes. Casually, removing my hand from the pocket, letting one of Phil's cards flutter to the dark, parquet floor, I used my foot to push it partly under the rug.

It was a lovely rug with a startling pattern of flowers, trees and birds woven amid brilliant colours and I guessed it was very old. My parents' friends, the Moffatts, used to have one a bit like it, which they'd picked up in Turkey, having beaten a desperate peasant down to a ludicrously low price. I'd heard them boast about it many times, yet this was far finer than theirs.

I heard a clatter from within. 'Mr Barrington-Oddy's returned,' I shouted.

'Thanks.' Hobbes's voice replied from behind a tall, dark dresser, glittering with expensive looking knick-knacks. 'I'll just be a minute.'

I went back down the steps, strolling towards the cars, my heart thumping, knowing I'd dropped Phil right in it, convinced Hobbes would now see him for what he was. Yet, I already felt guilty, and might have turned back and retrieved the card had Hobbes not appeared in the doorway, flattening my good intentions under his heavy boots. I'd really done it, for good or ill; I half hoped he wouldn't notice it.

Wilkes was assisting Mr Barrington-Oddy from the taxi as Hobbes came alongside and introduced himself. Barrington-Oddy shook his hand without even flinching, obviously a man with great stiffness in his upper lip. He was very tall, very thin and very grey, wore a heavy, dark suit with a waistcoat and regimental tie and I wasn't at all surprised to learn he was a retired barrister, though barristers are rarely portrayed with angry-looking blisters around their mouths and noses.

When Hobbes introduced me, I didn't warrant a handshake, just a curt nod.

Barrington-Oddy, possessing a clipped, posh voice, the sort rarely heard except in parody, addressed Hobbes. 'I trust you will brook no delay in apprehending the miscreants. In the meantime, shall we go inside? I find the clammy chill this time of year to be exceedingly bad for my constitution.'

Hobbes and I followed him inside, Wilkes taking up his position by the car. He grinned sarcastically, while I smirked, glad he was being left outside in the cold. As Hobbes shut the front door behind us, I was astonished how gloomy it became.

'Take a seat,' said Barrington-Oddy, entering a room, turning on the lights.

It was, I guessed, a drawing room, impressive in an oppressive way. Everything looked heavy and fussy. Dark panelling lined the walls, on which hung dark portraits of stern, humourless individuals in rich, dark clothing. An old black clock, intricately carved with grotesque demon shapes ticked on the mantelpiece, looking both fascinating and repulsive. The only thing in the room I could admire without condition was the carpet, similar to the rug in the entrance hall, though even richer and heavier. A sad fire glowed in the grate and I was grateful when Barrington-Oddy stirred it with a poker and placed a couple of chunky logs on top; the place certainly needed some heat. Shivering, I almost envied Wilkes who was, no doubt, lounging comfortably in his police car. I sat next to Hobbes on a solid, leather-backed chair in front of a solid, leather-covered table. Nothing in the room looked even vaguely Roman, with the exception of Barrington-Oddy's nose.

'I apologise. My man, Errol, would normally have attended to the fire but he's been called away on urgent family business.' Barrington-Oddy, straightening up, shut the drawing room door and relaxed into a deep, dark armchair.

I wished I'd positioned myself a little closer to the heat as I had to keep clamping my jaws together to stop my teeth rattling. Hobbes never appeared to notice the cold.

'Right, Inspector,' Barrington-Oddy began, his tone suggesting he was in charge, 'I suppose I ought to inform you of what happened. I might as well, as I'm sure I've already told most of your colleagues.'

'If you would be so good, sir,' said Hobbes.

'Let me begin. I intend residing in Sorenchester until the New Year while researching a book concerning the influence of Roman law on aspects of modern English jurisprudence.'

Jumping at the mention of Roman law, I glanced significantly at Hobbes, who ignored me.

'I chose this place,' Barrington-Oddy continued, 'because the local museum has a number of fascinating artefacts and documents that are proving exceedingly valuable.'

The museum connection had reappeared and I wasted another significant glance on Hobbes. Somehow, I felt as if I was trying to build a jigsaw puzzle from a handful of pieces and no idea of the overall picture. Yet, everything had to fit together.

'I was transcribing some notes I'd made last week and was indexing the details when the doorbell rang,' said Barrington-Oddy. 'I waited, expecting Errol to answer and when it rang again I recalled he was absent. I was somewhat annoyed as I dislike being interrupted when at work, yet I thought I ought to go. I rather wish I hadn't.'

'I'm not surprised, sir,' Hobbes said, 'you've had a most unpleasant experience.'

'Most unpleasant indeed. When I opened the door, two masked figures were standing there and before I could react they sprang on me. A pad impregnated, so I am informed, with chloroform was clamped over my face, the world began spinning and that is all I can remember until I awoke in the entrance hall. As soon as I felt able, I contacted the police and made a quick surveillance of the house. I am not aware of anything being taken. However, that cabinet,' he pointed towards a mahogany and glass monstrosity in the corner, 'has been broken into. As far as I can tell, nothing else was touched. The two men had gone.'

'Thank you, sir,' Hobbes said gravely. 'A most succinct account. Now, sir, could you describe your attackers?'

'Well,' said Barrington-Oddy with a frown, 'I didn't have long enough to form anything other than the slightest impression of them. As I said, they wore masks, or rather, one wore something like a balaclava with eyeholes and the other had a brown scarf around his face and a trilby hat pulled down low. I can't recall anything further.'

'Any idea of their sizes or ages?' Hobbes asked.

'Sorry, not much. Though I believe neither was as tall as I, the taller of the two, the one wearing the scarf, appeared somewhat skinny. That's really your lot, except, yes, there was a faint smell like flowers before they got the pad over my nose. They took me entirely by surprise, I regret to say.'

'Any idea how long you were unconscious, sir?'

'No, though it can't have been long because I'd just prepared a pot of coffee and it was still warm when I came back in here. I took a sip because of an unpleasant taste in my mouth, which felt as dry as water biscuits.'

'Do you have any idea what was taken, sir?'

'Not really. There are a number of antiques in the cabinet but I'm not so familiar with them that I can identify what has been removed, though there may be a space where there wasn't one before. Errol could probably tell you, because he dusted in here.

Unfortunately he's in Jamaica.'

'What about the house's owner?'

'She would probably know,' said Barrington-Oddy. 'Unfortunately, she's in Switzerland, I believe.'

'That is unfortunate,' said Hobbes. 'Do you happen to know how I can contact her? And what her name might be?'

'It's Mrs Jane Ilionescu. I don't know the woman – I'm renting through an agent. The number's on this.' Mr Barrington-Oddy reached into a drawer and handed a card to Hobbes.

All through the interview I'd kept quiet but I ventured a question. 'Is the owner a foreigner then? I mean with a surname like that?'

'I believe she is English,' said Barrington-Oddy. 'She married a foreign gentleman, now unfortunately deceased. If you require any further information, I would advise contacting the agent.'

'Thank you, sir.' Hobbes nodded, rising to his feet. 'Now, would you mind if I take a closer look at the cabinet?'

'Please do,' said Barrington-Oddy. 'My daily routine has been entirely disrupted already. If you have any questions, please feel free to ask. I doubt, though, that I will be of much help. I am not, I regret, an observant man. I focus only on what is important to my work.'

'Very good, sir,' Hobbes said, approaching the display cabinet as if stalking a deer. He squatted onto his haunches, creeping forward, examining the carpet, sniffing the air and apparently listening.

I sat still, glad the fire had begun to compete with the damp chill. Brancastle was a grand old house in its way, yet I hated it and couldn't blame Mrs Whatsaname for going away. Mr Barrington-Oddy, lighting a pipe, sank back into his armchair, eyes closed, hands folded over his stomach, almost as if he'd fallen asleep. A heavy cloud billowed about him, curling tendrils reaching out into the room.

Hobbes, unfolding into his usual hunched stance as he reached the cabinet, opened its door, peering at the damaged lock. 'This was forced using a knife with a broad blade. I can't see any sign of fingerprints. Your man Errol obviously dusts well and the burglars wore gloves, which isn't surprising, as it's winter. Hallo, hallo, hallo. What's this?'

Frowning with concentration, leaning forward, he plucked at the cabinet, close to where the knife had been forced in. I was astonished how delicate and precise he could be, although, when he raised his fingers to the light, I could see nothing.

'What is it?'

'Some fibres were caught where the wood's splintered. I'll bet they came off a glove. A black one: woollen.' Dropping them into a polythene bag, he sniffed. 'Hmm. There's a faint hint of flowers.'

I couldn't smell anything other than Barrington-Oddy's suffocating pipe smoke that, having formed a dense layer at head height, was stinging my eyes and making my nose run.

'Two people,' said Hobbes, staring at the carpet, 'one tall, wearing shoes with a smooth sole and a bit of a heel. He was light of build, soft treading, and wore black woollen gloves smelling of flowers, a scarf and a trilby. The other one was of medium build, wearing new trainers and a balaclava with eyeholes. Well, if I see anyone fitting those descriptions, I'll be sure to arrest them.'

The doorbell rang. Barrington-Oddy's eyes opened, holding a momentary look of concern, unsurprising in the circumstances. 'I wonder who it could be.'

'Could you get it, Andy?' asked Hobbes.

PC Wilkes stood at the door. 'Sir!' he called across the hall. 'I've been ordered back to the station and thought I'd better tell you. Hallo.' He glanced down by his feet. 'What's this?' Stooping, he picked up Phil's card.

I'd nearly forgotten about it. A sudden cold feeling gripped my stomach and again, for a moment, I wished I hadn't done it.

'What is it, George?' Hobbes walked towards us.

'A business card, sir. The name on it is Philip Waring of the *Sorenchester and District Bugle*. Isn't he the journalist who's gone missing? I wonder what he was doing here.'

'I've never heard of the chap,' said Barrington-Oddy, from the drawing room.

Hobbes took the card with a glance that made my stomach leap in terror. Had my little ploy backfired?

'Perhaps,' said PC Wilkes, 'it was dropped during the struggle with Mr Barrington-Oddy. Perhaps this Waring was one of the men who did it.'

'Precisely what I was thinking, constable,' said Barrington-Oddy, approaching, looking at the card in Hobbes's hand. 'It's screwed up and grubby: hardly what a chap would leave if he desired an appointment.'

Saying nothing, my pulse racing, my breath coming in rapid gasps, I turned away so it wouldn't be obvious, trying to feel triumphant that my scheme was working. I'd dropped Phil right into the shit and Ingrid would be mine. Yet, somehow, I felt no pleasure. Now I'd really got him, confusion overwhelmed me and, though part of me was cheering, another part cowered in fear of discovery. I made a decision to dispose of his other cards as soon as possible.

In addition, my conscience was insisting that I stop right there, confessing my little ruse before any harm came of it. Yet, if I did, I'd be a laughing stock to the police, Hobbes would be furious and I wondered whether I might even have committed a crime. Besides, I daren't let Barrington-Oddy know; there'd always been something about a barrister's eyes that gave me the creeps.

'Very interesting,' said Hobbes. 'Well spotted, Wilkes. Now you'd better be getting back to the station.' He turned towards Barrington-Oddy. 'We'll be on the lookout for Philip Waring. There is a good chance he can help us with this investigation. And I'll be in contact with the house agent to find out what's been taken. Good afternoon, sir.'

He shook Mr Barrington-Oddy's hand and we left him framed in the doorway of a house that might have featured in a gothic horror film. I was glad to be out of it, glad to leave his fierce barrister's eyes behind. Wilkes, saluting, slipped into his car and headed back to Sorenchester. I expected we'd follow him back to the station. Instead, on leaving the gardens, we turned left.

'Where are we going?'

'To have a word with the next door neighbour. The evidence suddenly seems to be pointing at Philip Waring, doesn't it?'

'Apparently,' I said, 'though I don't think we should jump to conclusions.'

'Oh,' said Hobbes quietly, 'I never do that. However, I thought you'd be overjoyed your suspicions appear to be well-founded.'

I nodded, feeling sick – and not from his driving. We'd only gone a couple of hundred yards when he turned left down a narrow, rutted lane, pulling up next to an angular stone building a few bumpy moments later.

'This,' he said, 'is the Olde Toll House. Of course, it was never really a tollhouse. It's a deliberate misspelling, because people were alarmed by its original name.'

'Why? What's was it called before?'

'The Olde Troll House. We're going to have a quick word with the Olde Troll himself. His name's Leroy but he likes to be called Rocky.'

'We're going to see a troll?'

'Not just any old troll.' He grinned. 'Rocky is a friend of mine, so be careful what you say; he's a little sensitive about his appearance.'

I didn't know what to think. Life had not prepared me for meeting trolls. Still, come to think of it, life hadn't prepared me for meeting ghouls either and I'd got away with it: just about, anyway.

'This way.' Hobbes, springing from the car, beckoned me through the deepening gloom. I followed, my breath curling like dragon smoke in the clammy air as he headed towards an open porch, where a king-sized pair of green wellingtons stood beside a heavy walking stick. Though the bright red door was closed, someone had pinned a note to it, saying, 'I'm in.' A great chain hung from the ceiling. Hobbes pulled it and a low chime I could feel through my feet bonged through the structure. There were a few seconds of vibration and then silence. The door opened.

'It's a bit late for trick or treating,' said a guttural voice. A face, pale and round as the full moon before age had cratered its surface appeared, smiling, from the blackness within. ''ello, 'obbes. 'ow the devil are you old boy?'

'Pretty well, Rocky.' Hobbes shook his hand. 'This is Andy who's helping me with some cases.'

'Delighted to meet you, laddie,' Rocky beamed. 'Now come on into the parlour. I've just made a pot of tea.'

We followed him into a small room, where a cheerful fire made the shadows dance. It felt so much cosier than Barrington-Oddy's dank study.

'Please make yourselves comfortable,' said Rocky, 'and I'll get some light.' Poking a taper into the fire, he lit an oil lamp, placing it on a low sideboard.

Only then did I get a proper sight of him and gasped, because he looked so normal. That is, he would have passed for a rather chubby, human male, six foot tall, broad, bald, clean shaven, wearing well-worn khaki corduroy trousers, a checked shirt and a blue cardigan with a hole in the left elbow. I guessed he was in his mid-sixties.

'I'll fetch the tea,' he said, leaving the parlour through a door opposite to where we'd entered.

'He doesn't look like a troll,' I whispered.

'Shhh,' said Hobbes. 'As I said, he's sensitive about his appearance. Please don't bring it up again.'

I shut up, wondering whether Hobbes was having another joke at my expense, like with the so-called gnome, yet, when Rocky returned with the tea tray, there was something odd about him, though it was difficult to say quite what. His movements weren't right, his arms and legs not bending quite as they should have, while his shovel hands were huge, even bigger than Hobbes's great paws, though hairless and pale. When he handed me a mug of tea I discovered they were as smooth as marble. And, despite the roaring fire in the grate, as cold as marble, too.

'There are biscuits if you want some. I've got a tin of them 'obnobs, or there's crumpets for toasting, if you'd prefer.'

'Just a cup of tea,' said Hobbes. 'Oh, go on then, let's have a crumpet.'

Rocky returned to the kitchen, coming back carrying another tray with a full butter-dish, a smoke-blackened toasting fork and a plate of crumpets. A delicious, warm aroma filled the little room as he toasted them at the fire, while Hobbes informed him about the recent crimes, culminating in the attack on Barrington-Oddy.

'D'you know Mr Barrington-Oddy?' Hobbes asked.

Rocky shook his head. 'I've seen 'im out in 'is car once or twice but 'aven't spoken to 'im. 'e keeps 'is self to 'is self.'

'What about the owner?'

Rocky buttered a crumpet, passing it to me on a plate before answering. 'I don't know the missus too well. She's much younger than 'e was and I reckon she only married the old boy for 'is money. Mind you, 'e 'ad a lot and no one to share it with. I know 'e thought 'e'd made a good bargain and, to be fair, she stuck to it and made 'is last years 'appy ones. I knew the old man well enough. 'e came 'ere after the last war, did old Nenea. Poor as a church mouse 'e was then, though 'e 'ad a way with business and was pretty well set up in the end. 'e never married 'till 'is declining years.'

'D'you know where he came from?' Hobbes asked.

'Nenea? Yes of course. Now where was it? 'e used to call it the old country. It was where Dracula came from, though 'e said 'e wasn't from that part. Romania, that's it.'

'Interesting,' said Hobbes. 'Now, have you seen any suspicious strangers around these parts in the last day or two?'

Rocky handed him a crumpet.

I'd already sunk my teeth into mine. It was warm, the butter dripping from it like honey from a honeycomb. Hobbes took a bite. 'Excellent,' he pronounced.

'Strangers?' Rocky scratched his head with a sound like two pebbles rubbing together. 'Well, there was a car as went speeding off down the lane this morning. Blue it was. One of them German ones. An Audi. Old Fred in the village, 'is son used to 'ave one like it. Nice car. It 'ad two folks in it and they was goin' real fast so as I couldn't recognise 'em and I 'adn't seen the car round 'ere before.'

My mouth dropped open. Phil's car was a blue Audi. Maybe the seed of guilt that had sprouted in my conscience would shrivel and die. Maybe, I'd been right all along and my prejudice against him didn't necessarily mean he wasn't a genuine villain. It was only then that I finally acknowledged to myself that I had been prejudiced. It was because he was slim, because he was better educated, better spoken and, I winced, a better journalist than I would ever be. It was no wonder Ingrid preferred him. I began to wallow in self-pity.

Hobbes, having finished his crumpet, was talking. 'That's most helpful. You see an individual I wish to interview owns a blue Audi. I don't suppose you were able to get its number?'

'Sorry, old boy, it was all covered in muck: too thick to see through. Fancy another crumpet?'

'Though it's tempting, we'd better not.' Hobbes smiled. 'I've got to think of my figure and Mrs Goodfellow doesn't like it if I ruin my appetite by eating between meals.'

''ow is the young lass?' asked Rocky. ''as she got over losing that daft 'usband of 'ers?'

'She's doing well,' Hobbes said, 'and rather enjoying having a young man around the house. Mind, she's only locked him in the cellar the once. So far.'

I smiled, stupidly pleased to be described as a young man. No one had called me that for a decade. I confess a little anxiety was there, too. How many more times was I likely to be locked down there?

'Still,' Hobbes continued, 'she hasn't actually got over losing Mr Goodfellow; she can't because she hasn't really lost him. She knows exactly where he is and can't be bothered to fetch him back. She reckons he's happy where he is and she's happy he's not getting under her feet.'

'Glad to 'ear it.' Rocky laughed, reminiscently. 'I remember the first time you brought 'er round 'ere. A skinny little lass, cooing over 'er rag dolly. We 'ad crumpets then an' all. They grow up so fast.'

'Indeed they do.' Hobbes chuckled. 'You must come round to supper sometime. I'm sure she'd be delighted.'

Rocky smiled. 'That'd be nice, old boy. I 'aven't been gettin' around so much recently, cos me old joints are turning to chalk but I'd like to see the lass again.'

I gawped in astonishment and confusion. Not for the first time since I'd met Hobbes, I didn't get it. I mean, how old was this Rocky? And why did both he and Hobbes refer to Mrs Goodfellow as 'the lass'? And as for Mr Goodfellow, what on God's good earth had happened to him? I'd assumed he was dead and had accepted his old suits without too much thought, except for a vague feeling of spookiness.

It struck me how peculiar it was to feel so comfortable, so at home, in Rocky's parlour. He was a bloody troll, for Christ's sake and trolls, at least in all the stories I could remember, were bad things, savage, wild creatures who killed people and threatened to gobble up Billy Goatgruff, or whatever his name was. Yet, this one was giving me tea and crumpets in a cosy parlour while chatting with an old friend. It was all far too difficult to comprehend. Still, it says something about the change in me that, despite appearances, I had no doubt Rocky wasn't human and, what's more, was sanguine about it. What a difference a few days with Hobbes had made to my life! There was so much more going on than I'd ever imagined. Mind you, I never entirely discounted the likelihood that I'd gone quietly insane. And, if I had, so what? Things were still looking up.

Hobbes and Rocky plunged into a deep conversation about the old days and though I started to listen, the warmth and the crumpets conspired to make me drowsy. I remained vaguely aware of the trickle of melted butter down my chin and the rise and fall of their talk. I think they were discussing a mutual friend, who'd gone down with the Titanic and turned up in Bournemouth but it's possible I was dreaming.

I awoke to total confusion and the chimes of Big Ben, apparently coming from the clock on the mantelpiece.

'Six o'clock already,' said Hobbes. 'Time we were getting back for our suppers. Time for Andy to wake up.'

Hobbes got to his feet, shaking Rocky's hand. I followed his lead. It was like shaking hands with a statue, except there was flexibility and a pulse, and I was grateful for his gentleness, my bandaged hand still being a little sore.

'Thank you for your hospitality,' Hobbes said and I nodded my agreement. Stepping outside, we made our farewells, got into the car and sped home.

'A nice man … umm … chap, Rocky,' I said, as we narrowly avoided a wall.

'Indeed. He's the white sheep of his family; some of the others aren't quite so civilised but the Olde Troll's always been a good friend.'

Hobbes swerved to avoid a tractor and began humming 'Dooby Dun' under his breath. Though I thought I almost recognised the tune, I couldn't quite get it.

'What's the song?'

'Dooby Dun,' he replied, 'by Gill Butt and Sully Van.'

'Strange. I thought I knew it. How's it go?'

'When constabulary duties dooby dun, dooby dun,' he sang in a surprisingly mellow, if noisy, baritone.

I joined in. 'A policeman's lot is not an happy one.'

'All wrong of course,' he said. 'It's fun being a policeman.'

Looking at his manic grin as he hurtled past the red light at the end of the Green Way, I could believe it.

We made a brief stop at the police station and, since he said he'd only be a short while, I decided to wait in the car. After a couple of minutes, PC Wilkes walked past, grinning and waving, while I pretended to be engrossed in a map book.

A few moments later, Hobbes returned. 'We might as well leave the car here. There's plenty of time for a brisk walk home before supper and I haven't had my exercise today. Come along, and quickly.'

Understanding how a fat, lazy cat must feel when plucked from its cosy doze by the fire and turfed out into the night, I got out with as much enthusiasm as I could muster, which wasn't much, although the relief of not having to endure his driving again was some comfort.

'PC Poll's much better,' said Hobbes as we set off for Blackdog Street. 'He suffered a very minor concussion and is resting at home now.'

Though I'm sure he wasn't trying, his stride was just long enough to compel me to scurry in an undignified fashion to keep up. 'Good,' I said, two steps behind.

'Actually, they're all out of hospital and there's a nice little article about the riot in the *Bugle* – George Wilkes showed me – and there's a fine photograph of you. Here, take a look.' Rummaging in his coat pocket, pulling out the evening paper, he handed it to me.

A fine photograph? I could see why Wilkes had grinned. Cringing, open-mouthed, handcuffed, gormless, I dominated the front page, Constable Poll's long arm feeling my collar, an angry woman waving a bony finger under my nose. My expression was similar to the one I'd displayed when the bloodthirsty hamster had savaged my ear. I gritted my teeth, thinking what a proud man my father would be if he ever saw it. Still, I didn't look as agonised as Dregs' former master, who was brandishing a bit of fence while the dog ripped his trouser leg.

A teenaged-boy, all zits, lank hair and dandruff, glanced at me in passing. He nudged his mate and his mate nudged another mate who was holding the *Bugle*. They all sniggered.

'There's still no sign of Mr Waring, or of Mr Biggs from the museum,' said Hobbes, seemingly oblivious to my embarrassment.

'Oh, isn't there?' Trying to play it cool, I caught my foot on a cracked paving slab and stumbled. As the sniggers ripened into jeers and laughter, I was glad I was making someone happy. Actually, I wasn't. I'd have much preferred to make them very miserable with my boot. However, I kept running after Hobbes, trying to pretend I never noticed lower forms of life. 'Dignity is the ticket to success,' my father used to say, though I never believed there was much dignity poking around in people's mouths.

'The forensic lads got back about the body,' Hobbes continued, 'and made a positive DNA match with Jimmy Pinker, so there's no doubt he was the victim. He'd been killed by a single thrust of an extremely sharp blade into his heart. There's no sign of the weapon yet. What's more, whoever messed up his face did it with a shovel after he was dead.

'They also tested the mud on his wellingtons; it was probably from Mr Roman's garden, and the dried stuff I found in the house fits the tread, plus there were fibres from the carpet, proving Jimmy was at Mr Roman's shortly before he was killed, so it is likely he was the one that broke in. However, as he wasn't a smoker, the cigarette butts in the bush suggest an accomplice, unless by coincidence another individual hid there at roughly the same time.'

'Oh, right.' I tried to throw my mind back to the body in the grave case. All the break-ins and the attack on Mr Barrington-Oddy had almost driven it from my mind and I was surprised Hobbes was still interested. 'Poor Anna,' I said, remembering her big eyes and smile.

Hobbes nodded. 'I'd already warned her to expect the worst. She took it as badly as you might expect. She's a soft-hearted young lady and I've arranged for a friend to stay with her; she'll need one. If there's one thing I don't like about policing, it's telling bad news to people. Still, she deserves much better than poor Jimmy and maybe she'll be luckier next time around.'

I was touched by his thoughtfulness; sometimes he appeared almost human. With that, a thought, germinating in a dark corner of my brain, sprouted making me gasp and my head spin as I struggled to comprehend what it meant. PC Wilkes had suggested Hobbes was unhuman. Hell's Bells! Though, almost from the start I'd realised he was different, it had never crossed my mind that he might really not be a human being. After all, being human was the least anyone might expect from a policeman.

I doubt the possibility would ever have crossed my mind had I not already met the ghouls and Rocky, the Olde Troll, who looked like a man. Shaking my head, I tried to dismiss the idea, yet, in a crazy way, it made sense. It was more than possible Hobbes wasn't human. Yet, if not, what was he? And how would I be able to find out? Suddenly, I was trembling: not with fear but with a strange excitement.

Hobbes's great hand patted me gently on the shoulder and I stumbled. 'Chin up, Andy. It's difficult being around murder cases when you're not used to them – it's bad enough when you are used to them. I'm sure Anna will come through this ordeal and we will catch the culprit.'

I nodded, my thought processes temporarily scrambled. 'Good,' I said, flattered by the 'we', until I realised he meant 'we, the police'.

'Evening all,' said a slurred voice from ankle level.

Billy Shawcroft sprawled on his back in the doorway of the teashop, a blissful smile splitting his face.

'Hello, Billy. Are you drunk?' asked Hobbes.

'Yes,' said Billy, 'and in the morning I shall be hung-over. Featherlight's got some cheap new beer called "Draclea's Bite". It's strong shtuff, though it tashtes of oven cleaner and nobody will buy it. He shays I can 'ave it.' He shivered.

'Very good.' Hobbes, bending, lifted Billy to his feet. 'Now, mind how you go and be careful where you go to sleep. It's cold at night.'

'Tha's alright.' Billy smiled. 'I'm gonna work now. It's warm enough in the

Feathersh.' A frown congealed his face. 'I got shomething to tell you.' There was a pause and an hiccup. 'Tony Derrick was in town today. Thish afternoon. He was driving a big blue car along The Shambles. I thought I should tell you.'

'What sort of car?' asked Hobbes.

'I told you, a big blue one. I dunno the make. Bye Bye.'

He began his journey to the Feathers, taking the long route, via both sides of the road, once colliding with a lamppost, and apologising profusely for his 'clumsinesh.'

'He likes a drink rather too much,' said Hobbes, unnecessarily. 'Still, he's a good man. We now have further evidence of Tony Derrick's involvement in the attack on Mr Barrington-Oddy. Now hurry up, or we'll be late and I'm getting hungry.'

As he increased the length of his stride, I alternated between a jog and a scurry to keep up. We passed the front of the church where Kev, leather clad and helmeted was revving up an enormous motorbike. With a cheery thumbs up, he roared off down the road.

Hobbes chuckled. 'There goes our curate. He used to be known as Kev the rev in the old days, when he was in a biker gang and a bit of a bad lad. It was just foolish pranks for the most part and nothing malicious, though I had to have a stern word with him in the end. Shortly afterwards, he found religion and now he's Kev the reverend. He still likes his bike though.'

I was panting by then. 'I met him this morning. He's the one who pointed me to the pamphlets about the Roman Cup.'

Hobbes turned to nod. 'Yes, he'd need to. He's only been back in town a few weeks and is still learning. If you really want to learn about the church's history you should have a word with Augustus Godley, his great grandfather. He was church warden for many years and what he doesn't know about the old place isn't worth knowing.'

We turned into Blackdog Street as the rain, which had been threatening violence for hours, began its attack. Apart from a glance at the frowning sky, Hobbes didn't appear concerned but I scuttled for the front door of number 13, the key already in my hand. Heavy drops were already spattering the pavement as, opening the door, I dived for cover. There was a deep, booming woof, as if from an aggressive tuba, a pair of big black paws thudded into my chest, knocking me back through the door, down the steps, onto the pavement at Hobbes's feet.

He laughed. 'Beware of the dog! He's a bundle of fun isn't he?'

Pinned to the ground, on my back like a defeated wrestler, stunned and winded, I tried to work out if Hobbes's last remark had been directed at me or the dog, who had begun worrying my tie, though the tie wasn't half as worried as I was, even though he didn't hurt me.

'Drop him,' said Hobbes, 'and get inside out the rain.'

Dregs, tail wagging like he'd just done something clever, bounded up the steps with Hobbes, leaving me to stare into the night sky, rain water pooling in my eye sockets.

A middle-aged couple passed by on the other side, tutting in disapproval. The woman had a penetrating whisper. 'That one's started early. Disgusting! Someone really ought to do something about people like him.'

'I haven't been drinking. I've been steamrollered by a huge, hairy, horrible animal. I need help.' That's what I wanted to say but the only sound I could force out was a piteous little whine.

'Are you going to lie out there all night?' asked Hobbes, looking down from the doorway. 'You'll get wet and miss your supper.'

Struggling to my feet, I stumbled up the steps, the bloody dog cocking an evil eye at me as I entered the sitting room. Hobbes patted its head and it followed him into the kitchen, while I dripped upstairs to change my wet clothes, to wash away the street. In my bedroom, I unwrapped the soiled bandage from my hand, pleased the skin beneath was pink and shiny and, though it felt stiff, it appeared to be healing well. I removed my jacket, all grimy and soggy, stinking of wet sheep and, more worryingly, urine, and dropped my trousers. They were round my ankles, I was bending to remove them, when the door opened, striking me firmly on the backside.

Mrs Goodfellow entered with the trousers I'd ruined in the morning hanging from her skinny arm. 'They're all cleaned and repaired. Have you lost something?'

'Only my dignity, though there wasn't much to worry about.' I tried to cover myself and look cool. It wasn't easy.

She smiled, not at all embarrassed. 'You'd better give me those dirty trousers, dear.' Folding the clean ones, placing them neatly on the dressing table, she picked up my muddied jacket. 'Cor, you are a mucky lad. It's a good job the old fellow knows a good tailor and dry-cleaner.'

Resistance was obviously useless, so, giving up, I handed over my trousers.

'Ooh, you've got legs like pipe cleaners, dear. They're all thin and white and fluffy.'

I said nothing; nothing in life had prepared me for a comment like that. However, my legs blushed. I'd never suspected they were so bashful.

'They've gone all pink like Dregs's tongue.' She laughed. 'Now, get dressed, there's chicken curry for supper.'

All the meals she'd made so far had scaled previously unimaginable heights of excellence, yet, as a long-time addict, I needed the occasional curry fix and it might have become a serious matter of concern if she hadn't cooked one just in time. I could have kissed her had my legs not objected, refusing to take a step until she'd left the room. Then, dressing quickly, I bounded downstairs, only just avoiding Dregs who'd fallen asleep halfway.

The curry, after the inevitable delay for grace, was a truly sensational meld of mysterious spices, flavours and piquancy that nearly made me cry in ecstasy. I like to think she'd surpassed herself, though I thought the same at every meal. Hobbes, too, seemed in dreamy mood as, finishing his last chapatti, he sat back with a sigh. Someday, I thought, I would have to leave, find a place of my own, eat normally. The thought was hard to bear and I felt tears starting in my eyes.

Hobbes grinned. 'Curry too hot?'

'No,' I defended it, 'it's wonderful but I fear it's too good for this world.'

'If you like this, then you should try her vindaloo. That'll bring more than a tear to your eyes.'

I expected we'd adjourn to the sitting room as usual. Instead, Hobbes, picking up the dishes, carried them to the sink.

'The lass has her Kung Fu class on Monday nights,' he said, 'so I do a bit of washing up.'

'She does Kung Fu?' My voice soared incredulously. 'I'm surprised they let anyone her age learn a martial art. Isn't it dangerous?'

'You don't understand,' said Hobbes, 'she's the teacher and an honorary Master of the Secret Arts. She combines her class with sex education as a sort of spin-off. It was all the printer's fault; he made a mistake and some folk turned up hoping to learn the marital arts. She didn't like to disappoint them.'

I was so flabbergasted I volunteered to do the washing up myself and Hobbes, to his credit, did not stand in my way, taking himself and Dregs off for a walk. The bowl I'd melted had been replaced and I washed the dishes with a virtuous feeling. Afterwards, I dried and put everything away methodically, some of it, I flattered myself, in the right place.

Hobbes had not returned when I'd finished and I guessed Mrs Goodfellow would be busy for some time. Finding myself at a loose end, alone in the kitchen, my mind kept returning to the cellar below, the darkness beckoning me to adventure, to discover what might be hidden behind the nearly secret door below. Yet, I couldn't do it. When it came to the crunch, I was too chicken to venture down there, especially at night. I tried to convince myself I was worried that the light would shine through the grille, revealing my actions to Hobbes when he returned. In reality, I was just scared.

A happier idea struck: I'd glimpsed intriguing things in the attic, which wasn't nearly so scary. Besides, apart from Mrs Goodfellow's warning about the planks, there seemed to be no reason why I shouldn't go up there. Tearing myself away from the cellar door, I climbed upstairs.

As I pulled a cord, the ladder slid down towards me, clicking into place. I started up the rungs, breathing hard, as if doing something wrong, though no one had told me not to. When my head and shoulders poked through into the blackness, air, as cold as if blown from mountain peaks, cascading down, made me shiver. I groped for the switch, the light clicked on and I was staring into the gaping maw of a huge bear.

'Jesus Christ!' I gasped and damn near fell down the ladder. The bear was stuffed of course, its moth-eaten carcass lashed to a timber frame. Trying to control my rushing heart, I climbed up and examined a tarnished disc on its cracked, leather collar. 'Cuddles', it read and, on the reverse, 'Please return to Hobbes, 13 Blackdog Street'. Nerves made me giggle like a schoolgirl.

The place was infested with junk. I could see neatly stacked brass bedsteads, what appeared to be a penny-farthing that had come off second best in a brawl with a steamroller, boxes, crates and racks of canvasses. A threadbare cloak lay across a stack of old records and I wrapped it around myself to keep out the chill, before sitting down on an old trunk, wondering whether any other bits of elephant were concealed up there.

I eased one of the canvasses from its rack. It was a painting of a hilly landscape with an old man repairing a dry stone wall, a small town nestling in the background. Though I'm not an art buff, I found the colours, the contrasts, the vibrancy of the scene quite disturbing. It was almost photographic in its detail but there was more; the scene appeared real, yet more vivid than life and, gazing into the picture, I had an impression almost of flying above the landscape, like a kestrel, soaring and hovering on a whim, while my eyes picked out the tiniest details. The church tower seemed familiar and I realised the town was Sorenchester, though not as I knew it, as it had once been. I fancied I could make out Blackdog Street and even the number 13 on the door, such was the artist's skill. Wondering who'd painted it and why it had been confined to the attic, I looked for a signature.

In the bottom right-hand corner, a mess of loops and blots, it said W.M. Hobbes. I whistled, trying to make myself believe it had been painted by one of Hobbes's relations. I might have succeeded had he not told me he'd been adopted. Still in denial, I reasoned that he'd probably purchased the painting because of the coincidence of names and, yet, something about it made me suspect he was the artist. I realised then that I didn't actually know his first name – I assumed he had one – or his second name, assuming W.M. Hobbes really was him. To me, he was just Hobbes, or possibly Inspector Hobbes, or even, if Mrs G was correct, the old fellow. There was, to use Wilkes's word again, something unhuman about the painting, something suggestive of wildness, as if the artist related more to the natural world than to the world of the town, or even to the man working on the wall. Though they were there, and skilfully depicted, the grass, the trees, the sky and even the rocks felt more important.

Putting it back, I selected another. Again it was by W.M. Hobbes, this one showing a moonlit night in town. The details were every bit as vivid as the first, though the colours were muted and, again, it was disturbing, for there was too much in the picture, almost as if the artist had been using a night-vision scope. I shivered as my glance strayed to the shadows, for there was a suggestion of danger, of unseen beings lurking, waiting for the moon to be shrouded by the threatening clouds. It was eerie and yet compelling, exciting even.

I couldn't tell how old the paintings were, though they gave an impression of antiquity, which made me curious about Hobbes's age. I'd have guessed he was in his mid-fifties, yet Wilkes had mentioned how he'd looked about ready for retirement twenty years earlier. Recalling the newspaper cutting in Hobbes's office, I realised, assuming the policeman in the picture wasn't his ancestor, or an unfortunate look-alike, but Hobbes himself, that it would make him well over a hundred years old. I tried reasoning, to convince myself it was impossible, that his weirdness was messing up my head, and that there was no way he could be so ancient and still working. Surely, I thought, the police had to retire at a certain age, and definitely before they were one hundred. I decided he couldn't really be unhuman: it would be too stupid. I just wished I believed it.

The next painting was of Rocky wearing a military uniform, looking as if he was off to fight the Great War. Impossible, I told myself. Stop imagining things, he's not a troll, he's just a man in fancy dress.

It was then I heard an altercation in the street outside, the sound filtered into the attic. A man shouted, 'Get your dog off my bloody leg!'

Hobbes's voice came next. 'Your leg's not bloody yet. However, it might be if you don't pick it up.'

'You can't make me.'

'Can't I? My dog doesn't like litter louts, so pick up that cigarette packet or you'll discover there can be painful side effects to smoking.'

I heard a cry but that was all because, for some reason, I felt uncomfortable at the thought of Hobbes knowing I'd been in the attic. Sliding the portrait back into the rack, squeezing past the junk, I slid down the ladder and shut the hatch. As casually as could be, I strolled downstairs and towards the sitting room. All had gone quiet in the street and a key turned in the lock. The front door opened, there was an enormous woof and, as the bloody dog leaped at me, I sidestepped, dodging behind the table. The next few seconds featured a chase round and around the sofa to the accompaniment of a wailing moan, sounding as if it might be coming out of my mouth. I was vaguely aware of words in it. 'Get off! Get off! Get off! Get off!' In addition, there was, I regret, a selection of choicest swear words to fill any gaps.

'Get down,' said Hobbes.

I dropped to all fours. The dog came down on me, wagging his tail as if we'd been enjoying a great game.

Hobbes looked thoughtful. 'He does seem to like you. However, you shouldn't encourage him. Now leave him alone.'

I thought he was talking to me first and the dog second but I may have been wrong. Dregs and I parted with a relieved snivel from me and a sad whine from him. I stood up.

'Go to the kitchen,' said Hobbes.

I turned towards the door.

'Not you, Andy. Yes you, Dregs. Sit down. Not you, Dregs. Yes you, Andy.'

I sat as the dog left the sitting room with a mournful tail.

Hobbes subsided onto the sofa beside me. 'Were you looking for something?'

'When?' I replied, puzzled.

'Two minutes ago, when you were in the attic.'

'I wasn't in the attic,' I began, until I caught the look in his eye. 'Oh, you mean just then? No, I wasn't looking for anything as such. I just wondered what was up there. I hope you don't mind?'

'Oh no, not at all. Only I'm replacing some of the flooring up there. It's why I've got the sander in the bathroom, for when I have the time.'

I felt ashamed I'd suspected him of using it for shaving, though I still couldn't believe any normal razor could cope with bristles as thick as cactus spines. 'Umm … how did you know I'd been up there?'

He grinned. 'I'm a detective. Your skin is paler than normal, suggesting you've been somewhere cold, there's a speck of sawdust on your right shoe, hinting that you've been where someone has been woodworking and, what clinches it for me, you are wearing an old cloak from the attic.'

I slapped my forehead. I'd forgotten all about it. Taking it off, I draped it over the coffee table.

'Besides, I saw the light shining from the attic window.'

He'd got me bang to rights, whatever that meant and I thought I'd better explain. 'I was curious what was up there and I … umm … put the cloak on because of the cold.'

He nodded.

'There were some paintings, next to the bear,' I said. 'They were rather good. Did you do them?'

I was astonished to see his face turn pink. Surely he wasn't embarrassed? Not Hobbes, the man with the thickest skin in Sorenchester?

He avoided my stare. 'I dabble. It's merely a foolish hobby. By the way, did you like my bear? His name's Cuddles.'

'He frightened the life out of me, when I turned the light on and all I could see was his whopping great mouth.'

Hobbes chuckled. 'Cuddles was a fine bear; he used to have your room once, many years ago, after he'd retired from the circus.'

'A bear?' I gasped. 'Living here? What about the neighbours?'

'Oh,' he said, with a reminiscent smile, 'they weren't happy. They objected most strongly, so I told them he was my pal and that he was staying. They came to accept him in time.'

'But what about the smell?'

He shrugged. 'Cuddles got used to it. They're tolerant creatures, bears and well-behaved, except where salmon are concerned. He did invade the fishmongers once or twice, though I always paid for what he ate and, in time, he became quite friendly with the fishmonger, even having his photograph used in the advertisement, "He can't bear to miss his weekly fish, can you?"'

I laughed. Not that I really believed him.

'He left his mark on Sorenchester,' he said. 'You know the Bear with a Sore Head pub?'

'Yeah, of course.'

'Well, in the old days it was called the Ram but they renamed it in his honour. He often used to drink there.'

'The bear used to drink there?' I was fascinated.

'I'm afraid so. Alcohol was his weakness. I mean, many of us enjoy a beer or two but Cuddles couldn't hold his drink, which was something to do with having claws and no opposable thumbs. He had to sup from a bucket with a tap on it and they used to hang it by the dartboard, just above the number eight. He'd swig it all down, getting very drunk: hence the expression "to drink one over the eight". Incidentally, it was also the origin of pail ale. In the end, though, the drink caused his downfall.'

'Why, what happened?' I sat as still as a child who has been entranced by a fabulous tale.

Hobbes, shaking his head, sighed. 'It was very sad. One evening he fancied a drink and went down to the Ram, as it was then, and ordered a beer.'

'How?' I asked. 'Could he talk?'

'Don't be silly, he was a bear and bears can't talk, so he used sign language.'

'Ah,' I said, 'that explains it.' Actually, it didn't, though I failed to spot the flaw until afterwards.

'It,' he continued, 'was tragic. The Ram having quite run out of best bitter, they had to serve him a bucketful of worst bitter and Cuddles wasn't happy.'

'I bet he wasn't. There's nothing worse than bad beer.'

'Precisely,' said Hobbes, 'it was appalling.'

'The beer?'

'Yes. Well, to continue, though the story's harrowing, they hung his bucket up.'

'Over the eight?'

'Over the eight. By chance, there was a big grudge darts match underway. Poor Cuddles supped his beer, which was so horrific that he turned away in disgust. Unfortunately, he turned towards the dartboard and a dart aimed at the bull's-eye struck his nose.'

'Oh no.'

'Oh yes.' He nodded. 'It was awful. He staggered away, roaring in pain, and collapsed in the skittle alley, where a speeding ball struck him on the head. Hence, the pub was renamed the "Bear with a Sore Head".'

'What happened to him?' I asked, agog.

'He died,' said Hobbes, sorrowfully, 'three years later. A salmon stuck in his throat and he choked.'

'He choked to death?'

'No, it was worse than that. You see, when the fishmonger began hitting him on the back, trying to remove the blockage, poor Cuddles thought he was being assaulted and ran straight out in the road, where he was struck by a bus.'

'Oh no,' I said. 'How awful.'

'I told you so.' Hobbes's eyes filled with tears.

'And that's what killed him?'

'Not exactly. Yet, we are approaching the really dreadful bit. The bus knocked him into a music shop, where his muzzle became entangled in an antique stringed instrument that suffocated him. And so my sad tale ends, with a bear-faced lyre.'

'Wow,' I said. 'Who'd have thought it?'

'There you go. I told you it was tragic.' He sniffed back tears that, if I hadn't seen the sorrow in his face, I might have thought sounded like a snigger.

In my defence, having pondered the story for a while, I became less than convinced of its veracity. Later, I asked Mrs Goodfellow, who said the old fellow had found the bear in a skip and brought it home – but she wouldn't have it in the sitting room because its stuffing was coming out.

The rest of the evening passed quietly. Hobbes turned on the television and watched a documentary about 'The Secret Life of Aubergines', which he appeared to find gripping. Not many people know the aubergine is related to Deadly Nightshade and is not technically a vegetable but a fruit. Spread the word.

Mrs Goodfellow returned from her class and, after setting my heart pounding with her abrupt appearance, soothed it with a large mug of cocoa. Afterwards, I brushed my teeth and went to bed and, though it was barely ten o'clock, I dropped asleep in seconds. I had survived a very full day.

Something, either a sound or a feeling, woke me. I lay, listening to the silence, trying to get back to sleep. Unfortunately, my bladder had reached the awkward stage and I dithered, unsure whether to get up and empty it or to try ignoring it until daylight. When the church clock bonged only twice, morning seemed uncomfortably distant, so I got up, groping my way to the bathroom. On the way back, still drowsy, barely aware of anything, cold air blew across my bare feet.

Hobbes's door was open and in the faint light from the street, I could make out the curtains flapping. A dark figure, cloaked like Dracula, lurked in the corner by the wardrobe.

'Who's there?' The words trembled from my shivering jaw and received no reply. I tried again. 'What are you doing here?' This time, though my voice sounded firmer, more manly even, there was still no response, apart from a swaying of the cloak. Nor was there any sound from Hobbes.

A sudden horror struck that the shadowy figure might be an assassin. Fear kicked in for Hobbes, as well as for myself, yet there was also an overwhelming anger. With a yell, I dived headlong at the intruder. There was a stunning crash and pain and fairy lights danced behind my eyes before everything went black and I was struggling against an overwhelming, smothering force. Something sharp jabbing my neck, I gasped in pain and horror. Had that been the vampire's bite? Would my existence continue as some sort of half-life, one of the undead? The fight left me, my body going limp. So, to my confusion, did my assailant's.

Standing up, holding my neck, there was just enough light to see that I'd attacked the cloak I'd taken from the attic and which Hobbes must have hung on a sharp wire coat hanger from his wardrobe door. It was no wonder my head hurt and I didn't half feel a twerp, but at least I hadn't disturbed Hobbes; he wasn't in.

I walked towards the window, taking deep breaths of the clean, night air, shivering, picking up the cloak, wrapping it around me and peering out over the street. The rain had passed and everything was grey and damp. The half-moon, partly hidden by wisps of dark cloud, lit up a shadowy figure clambering up the roof on the house opposite. The way the thing moved reminded me of an orang-utan, except its hairy back was black.

Despite the cloak, I felt goose pimples erupting as the creature moved from the shadow of the chimney onto the ridge. The shock was palpable when I saw it was wearing stripy pyjama bottoms. It stood, raising its head, apparently looking for something, or sniffing, and crept along the ridge. It turned towards me and for an instant I could see its face. It was Hobbes.

The bedroom lights coming on, I spun around with a gasp as a foot hurtled towards my head. The lights went out.

My eyes felt as if they'd been gummed shut, while my waking mind echoed with confusion and fear. The side of my face was sore and my brain sort of connected the fact with a hazy recollection of a bad dream that made no sense. Getting out of bed, I prised open my eyelids, peering at the mirror, shocked to discover I'd become the proud owner of another black eye, a close match for the first one.

I had a vague image of a foot powering towards my head and my mind was awash with even vaguer fragments of images.

I was trying to rearrange them into coherent pictures when the bedroom door opened and Mrs Goodfellow peeped in.

'Did you sleep well, dear?'

'I'm not sure,' I said. 'I got up in the night and things went a bit strange.'

'I expect they did,' she said, 'though I'm sorry I kicked you. I heard a noise and saw a figure dressed in a black cloak and I thought to myself, there's one of them ninjas, and I reckoned I'd see if they was as good as in the movies. I was a little disappointed; you didn't put up much of a fight, dear.'

'I ... umm ... sorry.' So, it had been her foot. I hung my battered head. What else could I do when I'd been beaten up by a skinny old woman?

'Never mind,' she said. 'Though, why were you lurking in the old fellow's room dressed in a cloak?'

I told her the truth because I couldn't think of a more plausible explanation.

She laughed. Then she laughed a whole lot more. 'So, you nutted the wardrobe, thinking it was Count Dracula? You are a one, dear.' She grinned all the time she wasn't laughing and I attempted to show that I, too, was amused. Becoming suddenly serious, she said, 'It was a brave thing to do, if you really thought the old fellow was in trouble. It's not everyone who'd put themselves on the line for him.'

The vision of Hobbes crawling on the rooftops exploded into my brain, taking my breath away. I had to sit down on the bed, never again doubting that he wasn't human, except when doubting my own sanity.

'I saw him out on the roof over there. He was wearing stripy pyjama bottoms.'

'Of course, he'd hardly go out in his bare skin would he? There are laws against that sort of thing. Anyway, it's time for breakfast; he's having a bit of a lie-in. He usually does after a night on the tiles.'

'What was he doing out there?'

'How should I know? He's still asleep.'

'Does he go out on the tiles often?'

'Only when he wants to, or has to. Now get dressed. I'll make you a nice breakfast and then I'll see if I can find something to put on your eyes.'

'A bit of raw steak?'

'I was thinking more of bacon and eggs,' she said. 'I don't think we've got any steak, though the old fellow likes one for his breakfast, sometimes. Mind you, sometimes he prefers Sugar Puffs. I could nip into the butcher's? I was going out later, anyway.'

'Stop,' I said, 'I don't want raw steak for breakfast. I was asking if you were going to put it on my eyes.'

'I could if you really wanted, though it wouldn't do you much good. It might amuse Dregs, though. No, dear, I was thinking of my special tincture that I prepare from herbs and stuff: it's very good. Now, hurry up.' She turned and left the room.

I scratched my head, still the stranger in this bizarre world. Nevertheless, breakfast was breakfast, so having a wash, getting dressed, I went downstairs. Despite the ache of my swollen face, the fry-up was just what I needed, leaving me deeply indebted to the pig who'd laid down his life so I could enjoy the best bacon ever. I hoped he'd thought it was worth the sacrifice. I knew I did.

I finished off with toast and marmalade and, while I was wolfing down the last fragments, Mrs Goodfellow rummaged in a drawer. Pulling out a small, glass bottle and uncorking it, she shook a couple of drops of pungent, green sludge onto a wad of cotton wool and handed it to me.

'Go to the sitting room, dear, and press this gently against your eyes and they'll soon be as right as reindeer. You'd best keep the bottle; you're a little accident prone.'

Dregs was occupying the sofa and, when I tried to persuade him to move over, he went limp and immovable, growling, baring his teeth, something he'd never have dared had Hobbes or the old girl been there. I gave up, sitting down on one of the hard oak chairs, holding the pad against my face. Hell, it stung! I gasped and nearly threw it down in disgust yet, as I persevered, it began to soothe and relax the skin. It was good stuff, if a little on the stinky side of ripe, and I never did discover what she put in it. All she'd say was that it was based on a recipe her Kung Fu master had taught her and that she could tell me the ingredients but then she'd have to kill me. I didn't press.

For an hour or more I sat still, the pad to my face, peeping out just once to see Mrs Goodfellow climbing upstairs with an armful of neatly pressed sheets. Shortly afterwards, hearing Hobbes's roar, I gathered he didn't appreciate his bedding being changed when still in occupancy. For some reason, Dregs held me responsible for the altercation. He emitted a deep woof and an angry growl and I uncovered my eyes to see the horrible creature leaping from the sofa, approaching, bristling and stiff-legged. His teeth looked awfully big, his snarl reminiscent of Hobbes, who sounded as if he was coming off second best in the struggle for mastery of the bed. Dregs looked ready to spring and, in desperation, I thrust the pad towards his nose. Taking one sniff, he sneezed and fled, yelping, tail squeezed between his legs as a thump from above, suggested a heavy body had rolled out of bed.

A few moments later, Hobbes slouched downstairs in his stripy pyjamas and slippers and, nodding to acknowledge me, disappeared into the kitchen. By then I reckoned I'd had enough of the stinking tincture. Standing up, walking to the stairs, intending to dispose of the cotton wool and to wash my face, I glanced into the kitchen where Hobbes, frowning and growling, his face dark and bristly, was hunched at the table over an enormous bowl of Sugar Puffs. Dregs, slumped in the corner, whimpered when he saw me. I climbed the stairs with some satisfaction.

Heading to the bathroom, I examined my face in the mirror, amazed at what a remarkable a job the gunge had done, delighted the soreness and swelling had all but vanished. What remained was a slight, barely noticeable, greenish discoloration beneath my eyes and I wasn't sure if it was a residual effect of the tincture or the remains of bruises. If the old girl had ever marketed the stuff, she'd have made a fortune.

Sometime later, when the Sugar Puffs and several mugs of tea had raised his spirits and he was washed and dressed, Hobbes called me down to the sitting room. Dregs was there too, but maintained a respectful distance from me, which felt like a victory.

A strange light was glinting in Hobbes's eyes. 'Would you like to see an arrest?'

'I'd love to,' I said, 'unless it's me getting arrested.'

He smiled. 'No, you're safe enough for now. I'm going to nab Tony Derrick.'

'Good,' I said. 'Umm ... where is he?'

'He's squatting in a house over on the Elms Estate.'

The clock on the mantelpiece showed ten-thirty. 'Don't you normally make dawn raids?' I asked.

'As far as a sluggard like Tony Derrick is concerned, any time before lunchtime is as good as dawn.'

'Great. When are we off?'

'Now,' said Hobbes, 'so get your jacket on.'

'Right ... umm ... how did you find him?'

He shrugged, 'I did a bit of overtime last night and picked up his trail near the Feathers. I found this in the alley.' He reached into his pocket and pulled out a crumpled cigarette packet. 'What d'you make of it?'

'It's an old cigarette packet,' I said, puzzled as to why he'd been collecting junk. 'Is that all?'

The way he was looking suggested I should be seeing much more.

'Well, yes.'

'What about the label? Doesn't it suggest anything to you?'

It read 'Carpati', with some foreign words underneath 'They're foreign cigarettes?' I said.

'Very true, but is that all?' He raised incredulous eyebrows.

'Yes.'

'Alright.' He shook his head. 'Now look again.' He held the packet with his thumb over the first three letters.

'Aha,' I said, as the penny dropped. 'Pati – the same as on the cigarette butt you picked up at the museum.'

'Correct.' He grinned.

'So the burglar smokes foreign cigarettes?'

'Carpati cigarettes from Romania to be precise. Now shift yourself – we've got to walk to the station for the car.'

I was soon in the street, jogging at Hobbes's side, not really understanding what was going on, except with an idea that, as Mr Barrington-Oddy's house had been filled with Romanian stuff, then, perhaps, my Roman connection should have been a Romanian one. There was, though, something more important.

'Do you think Phil might be with Tony Derrick?' I asked, panting.

'Not as far as I could tell,' said Hobbes. 'Let's see.'

He strode ahead, not talking again until we were in the car, speeding towards Tony Derrick's squat. With my eyes firmly closed, I tried to distract myself by fretting about what would happen if Phil was there.

'Right,' said Hobbes, after a few minutes. 'Here we are.'

The car jerking to a standstill, I opened my eyes. We were parked outside a small house on an estate, one that appeared to have been built in the 1960s and neglected ever since. Though a few cars rusted on nearby drives or by the kerb, no people were about. A cat, curled up on an old mattress in the cracked concrete and weed garden, opened suspicious eyes, fleeing when Hobbes emerged. As I got out, my foot scrunching on a litter of old lager cans in the gutter, noticing a lack of police vehicles, I felt suddenly vulnerable.

'Umm … don't you have any back-up?'

He grinned horribly. 'Of course I do, I've got you. What more could I possibly want?'

'Me? What can I do?'

'You can watch.'

'Mightn't it be dangerous?'

Hobbes clapped his hands together like an excited child. 'For somebody. Stay behind me and let's nab him.'

As he strode towards the front door, I expected he'd knock it open like at Phil's but, instead, after standing quietly for a moment, as if listening, he raised a cudgel fist and knocked hard, though not so hard as to damage anything.

'Open up, it's the police!' he bellowed, turning round, loping past me in his usual hunched fashion.

For a moment I thought he was playing the old kids' trick of ringing the bell and running away. Instead, he ran towards the back of the house down a scruffy alley. I trotted after him, scrambling past the battered sofa partly blocking the way, hearing a door open at the back and the sound of running feet. It wasn't Hobbes's, because he was nearly silent, despite his great, heavy boots. As I reached the end of the alley, a gate in a rotting fence flew open and Tony Derrick, vivid in a pink Hawaiian shirt, rushed out. He turned towards me, pausing, a smile creeping over his face as he removed his glasses and tucked them into his shirt pocket. Lowering his head, he charged.

At least that's what he'd planned, because he'd failed to spot what had come to a halt on the other side of the gate. He only managed two steps before Hobbes landed on him. The impact was not like being hit by a ton of bricks, for Hobbes was more solid than that; it must have been more like being flattened by a paving slab and, although he was undoubtedly a nasty, sneaky, horrible villain with a bad taste in shirts, Tony had my sympathy.

Hobbes stood up, holding him by the collar as if he were a bundle of rags. 'Were you planning on going somewhere?'

Tony groaned.

'Anthony Stephen Derrick,' said Hobbes, 'consider that you have just had your collar felt. You've been nabbed in other words. You are currently incapable of saying anything, though, when you are able to speak again, you may come to harm if you do not mention, when questioned, something which I later find to be of relevance. Anything you do say may be given in evidence. Anything you do say that subsequently proves incorrect may result in … unpleasantness.'

He lifted Tony a little higher so he could look into his face. 'D'you understand?' Still keeping a firm grip on him, he used a massive finger to make the lolling head nod. 'Good.'

Though I was certain he hadn't used the correct form of words for cautioning a suspect under arrest, Tony didn't complain.

'Now let's take a look inside your house,' said Hobbes, heaving him across his shoulder and letting him dangle.

Tony looked as if he was still wondering what had hit him as I followed them through the concrete backyard, a mess of sickly grass with stinking rubbish, spewing from tattered black bin bags. The house was hardly any better, though the stench of rot was partially concealed under cigarette smoke and stale beer. Cans and bottles littered the floor, along with takeaway cartons and pizza boxes. I'd had my eyes tight shut on the way to this hovel – I felt justified in calling it that, because it was far worse than my flat had ever been – and now I wished I could close my nostrils. I did what I could by pinching them and breathing through my mouth.

Hobbes was wearing Tony round his neck like a loud scarf – loud in both appearance and moaning, since he'd come to and was demanding to be put down.

'Language, Tony, please,' said Hobbes after one exceptionally foul-mouthed outburst.

We conducted a short tour of the downstairs with Tony yelling and cursing and occasionally wriggling, until, banging his head on a doorframe, he hung limp again.

'Oops,' said Hobbes, carrying him upstairs.

It wasn't quite so disgusting up there, if you could ignore the bathroom, which I couldn't and, though I'd never been the world's tidiest or most hygienic man, it sickened me that anyone would choose to live in such squalor. There were three bedrooms, two of them empty apart from beer cans, the third containing a mattress, a stained sleeping bag, a lop-sided pile of dog-eared porn mags and screwed up tissues scattered over the bare boards.

'Well, there's no sign of Mr Waring,' said Hobbes, bounding downstairs, three at a time, Tony bouncing on his shoulders, 'and there's nothing to make me believe he's ever been here. Now, let's see what this rogue has in his pockets.'

Turning Tony upside down, holding his ankles, he bounced him gently on a manky rug, bits and pieces dropping like apples in a storm. There wasn't much, a few coins, his glasses, a penknife, a fat nylon wallet, some keys, a lighter, a very upsetting handkerchief and a half-empty packet of cigarettes. Hobbes grunted, tossing Tony onto a burst beanbag, and picking through the spoils. The cigarette packet said Carpati, two of the keys were obviously for the front and back doors, another appeared to be for a heavy padlock and the final one, attached to a plastic key fob was a car key. The wallet when he opened it made me gasp as if entering Ali Baba's cave; it was stuffed with bank notes.

'That must be a thousand pounds!' I said, hoping it was finder's keepers and that I'd be in for a cut.

'More than that,' said Hobbes, flicking a callused thumb over the top, 'I'd say about four thousand, three hundred and fifteen pounds.' Tony wasn't doing so badly.

Looking through the rest of the wallet, he found nothing except for a plastic card, which he held out between his fingernails, letting me see. 'Hallo, hallo, hallo,' he said, 'what d'you make of this?'

'Umm … it's a credit card,' I said. 'Oh, I see! It's Phil's. I knew he was involved, I just knew it.' A surge of relief rushing though me washed away some of the guilt about the dropped business card, for this, surely, was genuine evidence that Phil was connected to the thefts. My suspicions, based only on prejudice and dislike, appeared to have been vindicated.

'However, I don't think he was involved, at least, not in the way you mean,' said Hobbes. 'I can't see him having business with a wretch like Tony, apart from as a source of information for a story. In my experience, people don't normally give their credit cards away: someone usually takes them, by fraud or force.' He dropped the wallet into a polythene bag, which disappeared into his pocket.

Tony groaned.

'He's coming round,' I said. 'Shouldn't you cuff him?'

'No, that would be police brutality, something that is frowned on these days, although, when I joined the force, the odd cuff round the ear was permitted, if not encouraged. I never favoured it myself but some of the lads used to like it.'

'No, I didn't mean that. What I meant was, shouldn't you handcuff him so he can't get away?'

'Oh, I see. No, I don't like to do that. It's undignified and I mostly find suspects are willing to come quietly.'

Another groan emerged.

'You'll come quietly, won't you, Tony?'

Raising his head, staring at Hobbes through bleary, blue eyes, he nodded, saying, 'Yeah, I suppose I will. I don't have much choice, do I?'

'Of course you do,' said Hobbes with a smile. 'You have many choices. You could come quietly, in which case it's traditional for you to say, "it's a fair cop, Guv'nor". Or you could fight and scream, which is resisting arrest, in which case I am required to restrain you, with the minimum of force necessary. Or you could try to run away and then I'm obliged to pursue you, stop you and restrain you, with the minimum of force. The end result is much the same.'

'I'll come quietly … it's a fair cop, Guv'nor.'

He didn't appear to be very happy, yet I think he made the right choice.

'Good lad,' said Hobbes, his face a mass of happy teeth. 'Now would you like to answer a few questions here? Or would you rather answer them in the nice, comfortable police station? You see? More choices.'

Tony frowned in dazed confusion. 'Uh, the station.'

'The station what?'

'The station, please?' Tony's lip curled into what was probably meant as an ingratiating smile.

'That's better,' said Hobbes cheerfully, 'good manners don't hurt do they? Oh, and before we go, do you happen to know the whereabouts of Mr Philip Waring?

Tony shook his head. 'I ain't seen the git since Saturday.'

I warmed to him, snivelling, dirty thief though he was, for he'd at least got Phil pegged right. Still, I did experience another twinge of guilt and regret.

'Let's be having you, then.'

Hobbes, pulling Tony upright, took us outside, leading him, meek as a beaten puppy, from the house, locking the back door behind us. I was expecting Hobbes to head back to the car but he went the other way, along a cracked, concrete path to a square surrounded by garages. After scanning the flaking, wooden doors, he settled on one and strode towards it, pulling the padlock key from his pocket, opening the door with a flourish like a stage magician, revealing Phil's Audi, encrusted with mud, squeezed into the garage, as tight as a piston in a cylinder.

'We'll take this,' said Hobbes. 'It's evidence. Besides, it's much bigger than mine and we'll all be more comfortable.'

'You can't take it, it's mine,' Tony whined.

'I can if I want to.' Hobbes smiled. 'Besides, I'm not convinced it's yours at all. Doesn't it belong to Mr Waring?'

'He gave it to me.'

Hobbes raised an eyebrow. 'Did he really? Like he gave you his credit card? He's a very generous man, this Mr Waring. He must be a great friend of yours.'

'Yes.'

'And yet you still called him a git?' Hobbes shook his head. 'You know something my lad? You don't deserve such a friend. Now stand back and I'll drive it out ... a little further back would be better.'

Somehow, flattening his bulk against the garage wall, he squeezed into the car. A few seconds and a puff of grey smoke later, the Audi lurched forth, like a greyhound from the trap, and came to a halt. Hobbes, getting out, examined it, while Tony slouched beside me, looking as if someone had just made off with his wallet. I wondered how often it had been the other way round.

I suffered a moment of heart-stopping horror when Hobbes, opening the boot, tugged aside a frayed green tarpaulin. I don't know why, but I half expected to see Phil's bloated corpse beneath; it was only a collection of power tools. Without being aware, I'd been holding my breath, which escaped in one long, relieved stream. There wasn't much else in the car besides an empty Carpati cigarette packet and a fragment of a chocolate wrapper under the passenger seat. Phil liked things neat.

'All aboard,' said Hobbes. 'Next stop's the cop shop.'

As I got in the front seat, Tony shuffled into the back, like a condemned man.

'Seat belt, Tony,' said Hobbes. 'I wouldn't want any harm to come to you.'

The car sprang forward again and, as I closed my eyes, I heard a whimper as if from a scared baby. Tony would have to come to terms with Hobbes's driving in his own way. The ride seeming smoother than normal, I considered opening my eyes until Hobbes spoke.

'One hundred and forty. That's quite fast, eh, Tony?'

He did not reply.

Not surprisingly, we made the five miles back to the police station in three minutes, which I supposed meant we'd slowed down at times. The car pulled up abruptly and with barely a screech.

'The brakes aren't bad either,' said Hobbes, as I opened my eyes.

He had to lift the pale-faced, trembling Tony from the back seat and carry him into the police station. On reaching the interview room, he plopped him onto a chair with a soft thud, watching as he slithered to the floor like a sack-full of quivering jelly. My legs, though shaking, still held me up and I looked down on the sad mess with a heady feeling of superiority.

'It's a bit nippy in here,' I shivered.

'Would you like a cup of tea?' asked Hobbes.

'I'd love one,' I said.

'Great,' he smiled. 'So would I and you'd better make one for our guest as well. He looks like he could do with one. Make it a sweet one; he's looking somewhat stressed.'

Having descended from superior being to tea-boy in less than fifteen seconds, I muttered under my breath as I headed for Hobbes's office to perform my menial task, though I perked up on realising I'd been presented with an opportunity. While the kettle got hot, I rummaged through some of his things, although I felt guilty, almost as if I was committing burglary. At first, I didn't find a great deal of interest, since nearly everything was locked away, apart from the piles of old reports and other such stuff on the floor. Yet, taking another look at the newspaper cutting, I was staggered how much the moustached, uniformed policeman looked like a younger version of Hobbes.

Then, not expecting much, I tugged at the drawer in his desk, a spine-tingling thrill of naughtiness running through me as it opened. I found more or less what I expected in a desk drawer: a variety of junk, some stationery, pencil stubs, a chipped twelve-inch wooden ruler and a battered tobacco tin. However, the contents of the tin were interesting. On top lay a handful of bent, flattened and distorted bits of metal, looking very much like damaged bullets. Underneath, was a faded, purple ribbon attached to a dull, black cross, bearing the legend 'For Valour', beneath images of a crown and a lion. It took a few moments for the meaning to sink in: it was a Victoria Cross, Britain's highest military decoration. Stunned, I remembered Mrs Goodfellow telling me that he'd been decorated, and I didn't feel the need to turn it over to know whose name was engraved on the back.

Yet, I was puzzled why he kept such a glorious award in a tin at the back of a drawer filled with rubbish. If I'd ever won something like that, if I'd ever won anything at all, I'd have it displayed where it might impress people. My father proudly showed off his dental certificates, yet I'd never even passed my cycling proficiency test.

At least, I didn't think so, because when the badges were handed out I was in hospital with a broken collarbone and cracked pelvis after having failed to notice the road works in time, crashing through a wooden barrier and plummeting down a hole. Though it had hurt like hell, I didn't cry when they pulled me out, or laid me in the ambulance, or during treatment. It wasn't until I lay in the hospital bed, plastered and helpless, that the tears overwhelmed me. My parents had been visiting and I'd wet the bed, because I didn't know how to get to the toilet and couldn't speak over mother's crying and father's sarcasm.

Footsteps approaching, I crammed everything back, scuttling towards the kettle, which had started to boil. I was pouring it out when Hobbes entered, giving me a quizzical look.

'Alright, Andy?'

'Umm … yeah. Why d'you ask?'

'Because you're pouring boiling water into the tea caddy. Never mind, I expect a good strong cup of tea will do us all a power of good.'

'Oh, bugger, I'm sorry!'

I poured the run off into the teapot, trying to retrieve the situation while he rummaged behind the filing cabinet, pulling out a side-handled baton.

'I always enjoy using this,' he said, whacking it into the palm of his left hand.

'You can't,' I cried, appalled. Although I didn't think much of Tony Derrick, I was damn sure Hobbes shouldn't use a baton on him.

'Why not? It does the job and it's quicker than getting someone in.'

'No, it's wrong.'

'Of course it isn't. And even if it was, who's to know?'

'I'd know,' I said. 'I really don't think you should do it.'

'OK,' he shrugged. 'You can do it.'

'Me?'

'Why not?' He grinned. 'It makes a smashing noise, you'll enjoy it.'

'No.' He was going to overstep the mark and my hands trembled because I was going to stop him. 'I absolutely refuse to do anything of the sort.' My sentiments were strong, though my voice was a squeak.

'Well, in that case, shut up and let me get on with it. Just bring the tea in, if you can salvage any, and I'll get to work.'

Managing to squeeze something vaguely tea-like from the brown sludge I'd created, I filled three mugs and carried them through, unsure what else to do.

Hobbes held the door of the interview room to let me in. I put the tray close to Tony, who sat slouched at the desk and, who, to judge by his grimace, was not impressed by my efforts. His eyes widened when Hobbes stepped inside, twiddling the baton between his fingers as though it weighed no more than a chopstick.

'Right, this won't take long,' said Hobbes, eyeing the baton, swinging it round in a circle above Tony's head. 'These things are ever so good. We got 'em for testing but weren't allowed to keep 'em, apart from this one that accidently fell behind my cabinet. Right, a couple of good, sharp whacks should get things going. It usually does.'

I felt a numbing chill along my spine. Though it was cold in there, I don't think that was the reason. Tony shivered, looking like he was going to cry and I gulped, stepping towards him, certain that any protection I might offer would be about as much use as a soggy cardboard shield against a battle-axe, yet determined to do something.

The baton, whooshing through the air, rapped hard against the radiator. Tony, jumping from his seat, slumped to the floor with a low groan, nearly matching the gurgles of the heating pipes.

'What's up with him?' asked Hobbes, looking surprised. 'He was the one moaning about the chill in here. A good whack usually shifts the air-lock in these old pipes.'

I sagged back into a chair, shaking my head. It would have been far too difficult to explain. At least, I think it would have been. I wondered how Hobbes managed to live among ordinary people, although no one else appeared to doubt his humanity. Even PC Wilkes, who had sussed his 'unhumanity', hadn't taken the next step to enlightenment. I pondered the question of whether Hobbes knew the truth about himself. He'd told me he'd been adopted; if he'd been raised as a human, perhaps he regarded himself as one of us.

'Daydreaming again, Andy?' He ran his hand along the radiator. 'Ah, good, can you feel the heat, Tony?' He turned, lifting the whining figure back into his seat.

I emerged from my deep thoughts with a jerk.

'I've done nothing,' Tony shouted. 'I want a lawyer and I want to make a phone call.'

'And I want a decent cup of tea,' said Hobbes. 'Sadly, we can't always get what we want. So shut up, have a drink and then we'll enjoy a pleasant chat. Won't we?'

'I've done nothing.'

Hobbes, sitting across the desk from him, took a sip of tea and grimaced, his eyes widening. Standing up, clutching his throat, he dropped to the ground and lay still.

'You've done him in,' Tony jumped up, pointing a shaking finger at me. 'You've poisoned him.' He flung away his mug, slopping tea across the floor.

I sat as if I'd been nailed to the chair, unable to speak, unable to do anything other than stare at the inert body, sprawled like a clubbed elephant seal. What had I done? I knew I wasn't much cop at making tea, yet …

Hobbes sat up with an evil grin. 'Andy, I've had better bilge water than this. It's worse than the stuff from the canteen, which is saying a lot.'

'I thought you were dead.' A muscle in my cheek twitched.

'No thanks to your tea that I'm not. I'll get George Wilkes to make some; he's not bad.' Rising with a smirk, he called for Wilkes. Tony was shaking like he'd just emerged from an icy pond and had forgotten his towel.

Hobbes sat down and smiled at him. 'It's time we had a good chat.'

'Right then,' said Hobbes, sitting back in the chair, clasping his great hands behind his head. 'Let's treat this as a friendly little chat between old friends who happened to bump into each other.' Frowning at the quivering wretch, he leaned across the table. 'I take it, that you have no objection to a chat between old friends.'

Tony shook his head, a portrait of misery.

Hobbes grinned. 'Good. Are you sitting comfortably? Then I'll begin. What have you been doing with yourself since the little misunderstanding over Billy Shawcroft? I heard you'd gone into a monastery.'

Tony nodded. 'I did, only I didn't stay long. I couldn't be doing with all the praying and getting up early, though I kinda liked wearing those robe thingies.'

'Cassocks?' I suggested.

'No, it's true.' He gave me an angry glare. 'But the thing is, I thought a monastery'd be more fun. I'd heard they, like, brewed beer and stuff but my lot didn't. They dug gardens and kept bees and went to church, every day – several sodding times! We didn't even get Sundays off. I mean to say, it's a bit bloody over the top, isn't it?'

Hobbes nodded, rocking back in his chair, which, teetering on two legs, emitted alarming creaks.

'They wouldn't even let me eat chocolate, so after about six weeks, I gave them the shove.'

'That's funny,' said Hobbes, 'I was informed that they asked you to leave following some inappropriate remarks to a nun.'

Tony flinched. 'That's not true. Well, it is sort of true, though it wasn't my fault, was it? I thought nuns would be a bit like the girls in "Naughty Naturist Nuns". Have you seen it?'

Hobbes shook his head.

'Ah, you should,' said Tony and sighed. 'Bloody good it is. But they're nothing like that. All I did was tell one of them about it and, next thing I knew, the chief monk was calling me in for a bollocking. Afterwards, we agreed I wasn't quite ready for monastic life. Do you know, monks aren't supposed to think carnal thoughts? Not even about nuns. So I left.'

'Incredible,' said Hobbes. 'Do go on.'

'Then I did some stuff. This and that, you know. I worked as a barman, worked in a shop and worked my way back here.'

'And who are you working for now?' asked Hobbes, as PC Wilkes entered, bearing three steaming mugs of tea.

He placed them on the table, departing with a grin, which I ignored.

'No one,' said Tony. His hand shook as he reached for a mug and spilt a few drops. Taking a sip, he pulled a face and put the mug down.

'And yet you had thousands of pounds in your wallet,' Hobbes pointed out, 'how come?'

Tony took another slurp of tea. 'I've got generous friends.'

'Like Philip Waring?'

'Yeah, he's a good mate. Very generous.'

'How long have you known him?'

'Years and years.'

Hobbes, taking a gulp from his mug, turning towards me, grimaced. 'Nearly as bad as yours,' he said, turning back towards Tony, with what I guess he believed was a friendly smile. 'Years and years? Really? I find that an intriguing remark. You know, of course, that Mr Waring only came to live in Sorenchester a year ago? But I suppose you must have met him somewhere else?'

'Uh, yeah.' Tony nodded, slouching. 'That's right.'

'Where did you meet him?'

'It was so long ago, I can't quite remember.'

'Try.'

I had an inkling Tony wasn't being completely honest.

'Uh … I'm thinking.'

His eyes widened as Hobbes stared at him with a deepening frown that threatened to rival the Grand Canyon.

'Do go on.' Hobbes growled softly, like a lion on the hunt. 'Where did you first meet your most generous friend, Mr Waring? I'd love to know.'

'Uh … Blackpool.' Tony was no longer slouching but leaning back as far as he could.

'Blackpool?' Hobbes sounded almost amused, though his brows were still furrowed.

'Yeah.' Tony clutched at straws. 'Blackpool. I was working on the … uh … donkeys and we got chatting and he invited me for a beer. Yeah, that's how it was.'

'What did you chat about?'

'Uh … this and that.' He nodded, as if reassuring himself of the facts. 'Deckchairs … candyfloss … seaweed. Those sorts of things I expect.'

Hobbes snorted. 'Of course, that makes it all clear. Just one thing, when, exactly, was this?'

'Uh … twenty years ago.' Tony, scratching his head theatrically, screwed up his weasely face. 'More or less.'

'So you really have known him a long time,' said Hobbes. 'He must have been really generous taking you for a beer, so soon after meeting you. It sounds like you two hit it off. Good for you.' He paused, looking thoughtful. 'Though, I suppose you actually bought the beers?'

Tony looked confused. 'Why me? He was flush. As I remember, he'd just had a win on the geegees and insisted on getting the beers in.'

'A win on the geegees? How amazing,' said Hobbes. 'What a lucky lad – winning on the geegees and then meeting you. Incredible, some might say, as he must have been about ten years old at the time. I know modern kids grow up fast but it's not really likely is it?'

'I don't know. Maybe I got my sums wrong.'

'By a decade?' Hobbes raised his eyebrows. 'D'you know what I think?'

'No.'

'I think, you're not telling me the truth.' His eyebrows puckered into a savage scowl. 'I would advise you to be honest. You know I like honest people.'

He sprang with such predatory intent that it made me gasp. Tony, jerking backwards, would have fallen had Hobbes not grabbed his shirtfront. The frightened man clutched at Hobbes's hand as he was dragged upright, dangling, his trainers barely scuffing the lino, his watery eyes bulging like a rabbit's with myxomatosis as Hobbes, grinning, pulled him closer, his teeth looking as sharp as steak knives. Tony whimpered, hanging limp like a rag doll.

'You nearly hurt yourself,' said Hobbes. 'It's lucky I caught you. I knew a fellow once who broke his spine falling off a chair and never walked again. Still, such is life. Accidents can happen at any time. Now, are you ready to tell me the truth about Philip Waring?'

Hobbes, setting Tony's feet back onto the floor, held him up by the head. Though the room had begun to warm up, I shivered again, because of a horrible vision of the ratty skull, cracking like a new-laid egg, spilling its contents over the floor. I could only imagine what was passing through Tony's mind – and hope it wasn't Hobbes's fingers.

'Alright,' Tony squeaked as if the words were being squeezed from him. 'I'll tell you what I can.'

Hobbes shoved him back into the chair. There were dents in his forehead, the size and colour of plums.

'That's better,' said Hobbes, quietly resuming his seat, pulling a tattered notebook and a pencil stub from his pocket. 'Now, when did you really meet him?'

Tony swallowed. 'Uh … about two weeks ago.'

'Go on,' said Hobbes.

'It was like this. I was back in town and had got myself the squat but I was broke and on the lookout for some fast cash. Anyway, I'd got just enough for a pint in the Feathers, so I was supping it, keeping my ears open, thinking what to do, when this posh ponce walks in, taking off his jacket, hanging it over a stool and ordering a single malt.'

A slight smirk flickered across Tony's face. 'Featherlight slipped him a malt vinegar and it didn't half make his eyes water. Anyway, when he was spluttering, I sort of noticed his wallet was still on the bar. Taking my chance, I grabbed it and ran. I thought I'd got away but he collared me in the car park.'

Tony took a sip from his mug. Hobbes sat quietly, occasionally scratching in his notebook. I relaxed and the room grew warm and stuffy.

Tony continued. 'I reckoned I was in for it, cos he was a fit bugger. He'd either give me a bloody good shoeing or turn me over to you bastards, or both. He didn't, though. He took his wallet back, said he was a reporter and offered me twenty quid for my story, cos he was writing a piece about crime in the town. Well, I was hardly going to turn down twenty quid, was I?'

'I noticed,' said Hobbes, 'that you said he *was* a fit bugger. Why?'

'Well he was a fit bugger.' Tony looked puzzled for a moment. A look of shock erupted across his pasty face. 'Hey! I don't like what you're getting at. I've done nothing to him. I'm not a killer. You know I'm not.'

Hobbes snarled. 'I don't know any such thing. Billy would have been dead if I hadn't turned up in time – and it was you who'd put him in harm's way.'

'I never knew what she was up to. I swear I didn't – and I did help you find him, which was why you let me off. All I knew was that the old witch was willing to pay good money for him, cos he's so bloody small. She said a kid would've been better, though she didn't want no kids, cos of all the fuss when one goes missing.'

'You didn't care what was going to happen to him,' said Hobbes. 'You sold him and forgot about him.'

'I never hurt him.'

'Did you hurt Philip Waring?' He leaned towards Tony like a tiger preparing to pounce on a tethered lamb.

'No, not me.' Tony's face was as white as a sheep.

'So who did?' asked Hobbes quietly, sitting back.

'No one.' Tony looked more disconcerted by Hobbes's sudden quietness than by his aggression.

'So,' said Hobbes and smiled, though his unblinking gaze was merciless, 'where is he?'

'Don't ask me.'

'I am asking you. Where is he? What's happened to him?'

'I don't know. Honest.' Tony's face had taken on a greenish hue and he looked as if he might be sick.

I wouldn't have blamed him; I was shaking and sweating, even though it wasn't me on the heavy, knobbly end of Hobbes's cudgel stare.

'You can do better than that.' Hobbes was as unblinking as a cobra.

'I can't.' Tony shook his head as if he hoped his neck would break. 'She told me …' His eyes were wild and scared. 'I can't say.'

'Tell me who *she* is? Does *she* know where Mr Waring is?'

The room became very quiet. I was holding my breath and you might have heard the proverbial pin drop if it hadn't been for the slither of Tony falling from his chair and the dull, soggy thump as his body hit the floor. He lay still.

'He's scared of someone,' said Hobbes.

I nodded. He wasn't the only one.

Hobbes stood up, poking the inert body once or twice without response, waving a sharp-nailed finger close to Tony's throat. 'His heart's beating and he's still breathing. He's just fainted I expect. Such a pity. I was enjoying our little chat.'

'Who do you think he could mean by *she*?' I asked.

He paused thoughtfully. 'I don't know. Last time there was a *she* in his life, apart from those unfortunate nuns, it was the wicked old witch who wanted Billy's blood. We believe she died in the inferno when I was getting Billy out, although there was no trace of her afterwards.'

'What did she want his blood for?' I asked, appalled.

'We never found out for sure, though Billy reckoned he'd heard her muttering about a blood-bath.'

'A blood-bath?'

Hobbes nodded. 'She had some crazy notion it would make her young again. I've never heard of it working, though, and it's more orthodox to use a child's blood. I'm pretty certain it wouldn't have worked using dwarf blood.'

My mind struggled to compute the data. 'When you said "the wicked old witch", I thought you just meant a nasty woman. Are you telling me she was a real witch?'

'No, I'm not telling you. I've already told you.'

'So, let's get this straight. There are witches in Sorenchester?'

'Not anymore,' he said, 'unless she resurrected herself.'

'This is too much. Witches aren't real … are they?'

'Oh, they're real enough, they are just rare – they should be treated as an endangered species, the genuine wicked ones that is, not the harmless ladies and gentlemen who enjoy prancing around in their birthday suits; there's a few of them still around and you should see Hedbury Common at mid-summer. It's an eye opener and no mistake.'

I shook my head, struggling to make sense of the world. It was no use.

Hobbes stood with one foot on Tony's chest, like a big-game hunter with a trophy. 'I can't believe,' he said, 'that the old witch is behind this. I know we found no trace of her body, but the fire was intense. Foolishly, she'd built her house from gingerbread. It defies all logic and it's incredibly inflammable when mixed with brandy. It's a wonder she obtained planning permission.'

I thought I detected a twinkle in his eye. Perhaps he was winding me up, or perhaps not. I was becoming more and more inclined to believe the previously unbelievable. Maybe I was gullible, yet I had seen and heard things I would have considered incredible before meeting him. I realised, of course, that he made jokes at my expense but I think, in part, he was using them to prepare me for the weirdness of the world he inhabited. There were strange parallel lives being lived all around us, if only we knew where and how to look. Yet, humans have proved themselves adept at ignoring whatever does not fit with their simplistic views of the way things ought to be. Or rather, humans have proved *ourselves* adept at ignoring whatever does not fit with *our* simplistic views. Hobbes was getting to me; I hoped unhumanity wasn't catching.

'Right,' said Hobbes. 'I suppose, we'd better drop Tony off in a cell until he feels better.' Slinging the limp body over his shoulder, turning towards the door, he strolled to the cells.

The desk sergeant glanced up as we approached. 'Morning, sir. Another one fainted? Drop him in number two and I'll keep an eye on him.'

'Thanks, Bert,' said Hobbes. 'Right, Andy, since we won't get any more out of him for a while, I propose having a word with Augustus Godley.'

'Who's Augustus Godley?' My mind was blank.

'Do keep up. He's the old churchwarden. He lives only a couple of minutes away.'

'Oh, yes, I remember. The one who knows everything about the church. Umm … will he know anything about Phil?'

Hobbes shrugged. 'I doubt it. However, he does make a really good cup of tea and he's generous with the biscuits. Now walk this way.' He turned towards the door.

If I'd tried to walk that way I'd have done myself a mischief, so I contented myself with my usual scurry, interspersed with bursts of jogging. Leaving the station, turning through an alley into the bottom of Vermin Street, we crossed into Moorend Road, where a row of impossibly cute alms-houses stood. Hobbes held open the gate, ushering me onto the garden path of the first house. Four steps took us to the diminutive stone porch, blotched and camouflaged with decades of lichen and moss.

Hobbes rang the bell and we waited. And waited. He rang again.

'There's no one in,' I said after about a minute.

'He's coming. Just be patient.'

He was right. A few seconds later I could hear a shuffling sound and the door creaked open.

'Hello?' A face, crinkled as a pickled chestnut and a similar colour, surrounded by a fuzz of white whiskers and eyebrows, poked out. 'Hello?' he said again, peering at us through alert blue eyes. 'Why, it's PC Hobbes.' He grinned, revealing a mouth as free of teeth as his skin was free of smoothness. Every line on his face was wrinkled, every fold was furrowed. 'I should say Inspector Hobbes. Come in, my dear fellow, and bring the boy with you.'

I glanced over my shoulder before realising he meant me. Hobbes introduced us and I trundled after them down a gloomy stone-paved corridor that was even gloomier when I'd pulled the door behind us. Though the house smelled musty and dusty, Augustus was smartly dressed in a black suit, as if he was off to a funeral. After a minute or two, and all of ten steps, he led us into a small room in which a coal fire glowed like a small volcano. A blue budgie in a cage by the window greeted us with a chirrup as the old man waved us towards a couple of faded velvet armchairs.

'I was just going to make a cup of tea,' said Augustus. 'Would you care to join me?

'Yes please,' said Hobbes, while I nodded hopefully.

As the old man shuffled off to the kitchen, I wondered how long he'd take, realising how parched I'd become. I'd hardly drunk anything at the station; my concoction had been too disgusting and I'd been too enthralled and terrified by Hobbes's friendly little chat to take more than a sip of PC Wilkes's version.

In the meantime, I relaxed, enjoying the fire and glancing round the little room. It held three armchairs, a battered old dining table with matching chairs and a small bureau covered in loose papers. To the right of the fireplace, a bookcase sagged beneath yellowing old books that I suspected were the source of the mustiness. On a shelf to the left stood a small television set that looked prehistoric and which was so encrusted in dust I doubted it would show a picture should it ever be turned on. Further to the left, a window looked out over a tiny lawn, glowing green as northern seas in the sun, which was just peeking out from beneath blanket cloud. There was a clattering from the kitchen, followed by the cheery whistle of a boiling kettle and the budgie's impression of it.

'Should I go and help?' I asked Hobbes, who was sitting with eyes closed, and breathing as deeply as if he'd fallen sleep.

'Eh? What? Oh no. He likes to look after himself. He'll be alright. You'll have to be patient. He doesn't need any help, providing he's allowed to go at his own pace.'

'He looks as old as Methuselah,' I whispered.

'He's not even close. He won't be a hundred until next August.'

'Have you known him long?'

'Since boyhood.'

The kitchen door opening, Augustus shuffled in, shaking a tray piled with tea things, plates and a heap of biscuits. When I made a move to offer assistance, Hobbes raised a finger and an eyebrow and I sat back, twitching and fretting, desperate to hurry him up. Still, it was worth the wait for the tea tasted nearly as delicious and fragrant as

Mrs Goodfellow's and there were heaps of biscuits to dunk and suck.

The old man, sat next to Hobbes, and they chatted briefly about the weather and aubergines. Then he fixed Hobbes with a steady gaze. 'Now,' he said, 'you always come here for a reason. What do you want to know?'

'Could you tell us about the Roman Cup at the church?'

Augustus frowned. 'The Roman Cup? Ah yes, I remember, I hear it has been stolen. Such a pity. It was a fine bit of work.'

'Do you know anything about it?' Hobbes took a sip of tea.

'Not much, I'm afraid,' said Augustus, stroking his whiskers between thumb and forefinger of his knobbly hand. 'It is, of course, not a Roman relic.'

Hobbes glanced at me.

'It's only been in the church for a few years. It was a gift in, let me think, 1953, I believe.'

'A gift to the church?' Hobbes raised his eyebrows.

'Yes, yes. It was the year the young queen got crowned. That's why I got that.' He pointed a bulbous finger at the television. 'There hasn't been much worth watching since. Now then, if I remember right, and I usually do, the cup was given by a young couple. Foreigners they were, but very pleasant and most respectable. They wanted to make a gesture of thanks to the good folk of Sorenchester who'd looked after them when they first arrived here. Just after the war, it would have been.'

Hobbes took out his notebook. 'Would you remember the name of the couple?'

'Of course I would. I may be old but I'm not yet in my dotage, I'll have you know.'

'Sorry. What was their name?'

Augustus chuckled. 'Do you really mean to say you don't know? I thought you were trying to trick me and you call yourself a detective? Dear oh dear. Mr and Mrs Roman donated it, so we called it the "Roman Cup". I'd have thought that might have been a clue.'

'It might have been,' said Hobbes, looking comically crestfallen, 'if we'd known it wasn't a cup made by the Romans.'

'Well, you know now,' said Augustus laughing into his tea. 'Just wait till I tell the boys about this.'

'Do you know where the Romans came from? The couple I mean not the empire builders,' asked Hobbes, not appearing at all put out by his mistake.

'They were from Romania.'

I gasped. 'Romania.'

'The boy can speak then?' Augustus smiled. 'Yes, they were Romanians, on the run first from the Nazis and then from the Communists. I used to see them at the church for many years. They had a young lad, too. I wonder what happened to them?'

'They've all passed away,' said Hobbes.

'I'm not surprised,' said Augustus, nodding. 'Some reckoned it was a communion chalice that had once belonged to a king and there was some doubt as to whether the Romans really owned it, yet, since no one else claimed it and they weren't trying to profit from it, the church accepted it in the spirit in which it was offered. It became quite an attraction, you know. However, I'm afraid that is really as much as I know about the cup, except that they'd brought it with them and it was very old.'

'Well thank you,' said Hobbes. 'That was most illuminating.'

'Would you like more tea?'

'No, thank you, I'm afraid there's important work to be done and we'd better be going.'

'So soon?' asked Augustus. 'Ah well, I was only going to ask how your painting was getting on. Do you still do it?'

To my surprise, Hobbes blushed. 'No, well, not often anyway.'

'A pity. You were showing promise. Still, maybe you can take it up again when you retire.'

'Maybe. We really must go.'

We said our goodbyes and left.

'What the hell's going on?' I asked as we stepped into Moorend Road.

'I don't know yet, though I've got a hunch it's something rather unusual. I was slow not picking up the link between Mr Roman and the cup but I still can't work out what it means. With luck we'll get more information from Tony. He's hard work, though. It's just a good job he's such a bad liar. A little more pressure might squeeze something useful from him.'

'So, what about Phil?' We crossed back into Vermin Street towards the shops and the police station.

Hobbes was walking at my pace, hunched up as though under a heavy load. I had never seen him look so worried before. 'Mr Waring?' he said, 'I'm beginning to fear the worst.'

'Do you think he's dead then?' An icy coldness seemed to have invaded my blood.

'I said, I feared the worst. You've seen enough to know death is not the worst that can happen.'

My blood would have run cold if it hadn't already been frozen. I was frightened for Phil, thoroughly ashamed of my silly, spiteful trick, wishing I could have taken the card back. If I'd had the courage, I would have told Hobbes.

A woman's voice called, 'Andy! Mr Hobbes!'

Ingrid had just stepped out of Boots. She wore a long, dark coat and a beige woolly hat that emphasised her pallor. She looked tired.

'Hello,' I said, trying to sound cheerful.

Hobbes stopped, saluting as she approached. 'Good day, Miss Jones.'

'Have you discovered anything about Phil?' she asked. 'I'm dreadfully worried.'

'We've found his car,' said Hobbes, 'and the person who took it will be answering a few questions shortly. I'm afraid I have no other news, although there is some evidence to link Mr Waring to a serious criminal offence yesterday.'

'Phil?' Frowning, she shook her head. 'There's no way he'd be involved in crime. He's not the sort. Maybe he was on a story?'

Hobbes nodded. 'That is likely, though we found an item of his at the crime scene.'

'I don't believe it.'

'I'm not sure I do either, miss. I smell a rat!'

A woman screamed; another joined her. Hobbes was right, a rat the size of a terrier was sauntering down the middle of the road, as if it owned the county. Certainly, no one seemed willing to block its path or to offer any sort of challenge.

Not until there was an explosive woof and a flurry of head shaking that ended with Dregs strolling towards us, tail wagging ecstatically, rat dangling limply. I don't know how he'd got out but he was evidently trying to ingratiate himself now I had the power of Mrs Goodfellow's tincture, and dropped the corpse onto my foot.

Hobbes chuckled. 'Sorry, Miss, I'd better be getting back to the station and look after the dog. He shouldn't be out on his own. Clear it up, Andy.' He pointed to the rat, turning away, continuing with his hunched walk. Dregs, to my relief, followed him.

I was left with Ingrid and a dead rat. Somehow, she never saw me at my best. I shrugged, smiling, trying to make light of the situation. 'I seem to have got ratted. I'd better get rid of it.' Fortunately, the large bin standing down the alley next to Boots looked suitable for a last resting-place. Bending, shuddering, I picked the rat up by the tip of its tail, praying it was really dead. I'd had enough pain from a hamster a tenth its size to feel completely at ease, though Dregs had broken its neck for sure. I held it at arm's length with an attempt at nonchalance.

'You horrible man,' said a woman, driving her words home with solid whacks from her rolled umbrella, 'murdering God's creatures without a second thought.'

I turned towards her.

It was the blue-rinsed woman from the church. 'You again,' she said, 'I might have known.'

With solid blows raining down on my head and shoulders, I raised my arm to protect myself. The rat's tail slipping through my fingers, it flew through the air, striking the woman full in the face. Screaming, she backed off. People had stopped in the street to watch the fun, yet now, somehow, their amusement evaporating, they saw me as the aggressor. Fingers pointed, hard words were flung as, forgetting Ingrid, I fled.

Cries of 'police', 'stop that man', 'knock him down', and 'three for a pound', pursued me as I plunged into the alley. I'd only gone a couple of steps before I was in an arm-lock, my face pressed against the wall. The mossy brickwork was damp against my cheek, while its odour, a medley of stale urine, vomit and chips, made me feel ill.

'Well done, constable,' said a pompous male voice. 'I witnessed the incident. He assaulted the lady with a dead rat. She was forced to beat him off with her umbrella.'

'No,' said a shrill female voice, 'I saw it all. He was torturing a poor dumb animal and, when the lady tried to stop him, he threw it in her face.'

'That's not what happened at all,' said Ingrid. 'A dog killed the rat and Andy was trying to dispose of the body when the woman attacked him, without provocation. He was only trying to protect himself.'

I nodded. Good old Ingrid, she'd get me out of the mess.

'Be quiet.' The police officer bellowed. It was Wilkes. It had to be Wilkes.

The crowd around the alley's entrance shut up.

Wilkes, turning me round to face him, winked and murmured, 'Nice to see you again. What is it with you and rodents?' He glanced at the crowd, raising his voice. 'There's nothing to see here. If anyone has anything to say, follow me to the station and say it.'

Placing a heavy hand on my shoulder, he frogmarched me to the station, only a couple of minutes away. I only managed one glance back as he thrust me through the station doorway, relieved that only Ingrid had followed. I hoped it was a sign that I was starting to make progress with her, though my thoughts were mostly concentrated on what Wilkes would do. I needn't have worried. Releasing me, he smiled and patted my back as we moved inside.

'Sorry about that, mate. I saw it all, so don't worry. The show of authority was to appease the mob – it usually works better than reasoning. Now, mind how you go.' He stepped back into the street.

I smiled at Ingrid, embarrassed as usual. 'I'm glad that's over.'

She seemed genuinely concerned. 'Are you alright? It was lucky the policeman saw what happened.'

'I'm fine and George Wilkes,' I said, nonchalantly, 'is a good man.' Maybe, I thought, he wasn't so bad.

Ingrid smiled. 'Great ... but I was going to ask you to let me know when you find anything out about Phil.'

Though I heard what she said, a thought gripped me. Perhaps Wilkes had only laughed at me when we first met because I was so funny. For the first time, I managed to see the hamster incident from another's viewpoint, seeing that it had been amusing, or would have been if it had happened to someone else. And the riot I'd accidentally sparked, maybe that had a funny side, too. Recalling the pained expression on my face in the newspaper, a snigger sneaked out and then laughter engulfed me.

Ingrid's pretty face contorted in outrage and, for some stupid reason, that boosted the hilarity. Leaning on the counter, I tried to stop myself collapsing into a giggling heap. I was a joke and life was a joke and she couldn't see it.

'What's wrong with you?' Her voice veered towards fury. 'How can you laugh when poor Phil's in trouble? It's not funny. You disgust me. At least the Inspector's taking it seriously and he doesn't even know him. Goodbye!'

Opening the door, she stamped away, leaving me helpless, half-blind with tears, struggling for breath, with no chance of explaining myself. Then, at last, a wave of despair broke over me, submerging the hysterics. If I'd been alone, I might have cried. The sergeant sat watching, as if he saw the same sort of thing every day.

I pulled myself upright, taking a deep breath, smoothing my emotions into a superficial calm. Remorse about Phil's card was gnawing at my conscience and it was getting harder to keep it caged at the back of my mind.

'Are you alright now, sir?' asked the desk sergeant, 'because the Inspector would like a word with you. He'll be in his office.'

'I'm OK,' I said.

Trying to stroll casually through the police station, I stubbed my foot on the carpet and stumbled. Ignoring the smirks, I carried on until, reaching Hobbes's door, I jerked it open before stepping briskly inside. At least, I envisaged it that way. In reality the door opened inwards and I nearly tore my shoulder from its socket as my head banged against wood. Hearing a snigger, embarrassment heated my face.

'Come in,' said Hobbes.

He looked up from behind his desk, a sheet of paper in his hand. 'Oh, it's you. There was no need to knock.' He peered at me. 'Are you feeling alright? Your face is extraordinarily red.'

'I'm fine. It's just a little warm in here.'

A smile flickered. 'Sit,' he said. 'I've just received this.' He waved the paper at me. 'The house agent faxed the inventory through for Brancastle.'

I made myself comfortable. 'Oh yes? What was stolen then?'

'It's long and detailed though, so far as I can tell, only one item is missing.'

'That's what old Barrington-Oddy thought.'

Hobbes nodded. 'Apparently he is more observant than he claims. It looks like the only thing stolen was a ring.'

'A ring? Is that all? There were all sorts of valuable things in the house.'

'Indeed,' he said. 'It is suggestive.'

'So, what's so special about a ring?' I attempted humour. 'Is it a ring of power, forged by the evil Lord Sauron to control mortal men, doomed to die?'

He looked puzzled. 'No. At least I don't think so. Why do you mention Sauron?'

'Sorry. He's just a character in a film about rings.'

'I know. You need to learn to separate fact from fiction, or you'll go the same way as PC Norman, who used to work with me until he started insisting he was communicating with goblins. It was ridiculous yet, as he was still capable of doing his job reasonably well, I kept him on until the day the goblins told him to take his clothes off and direct the traffic onto the golf course.'

'What happened to him?'

Hobbes sighed. 'We found him standing stark naked in the middle of the ring road, waving his truncheon and screaming, "No man is an island." When I asked, "What about the Isle of Man?" he went to pieces and we had to scoop him up and take him away for his own safety. The superintendent put the whole incident down to a PC gone mad.'

'What,' I asked, 'has that to do with the ring?'

'About as much as your remark about Lord Sauron. Now listen, Rocky was correct to say a Romanian gentleman owned the house and, according to the inventory, the missing ring is Romanian, too. It is very old, made of gold and in the form of a dragon with ruby eyes.'

'A dragon? Like the bracelet? So, it's something to do with the Order of St George?'

'It sounds plausible. I'll get one of the lads to call the agent to see if there's any more information.'

'I bet it is,' I said. 'I bet this case is all to do with Romania and the Order of St George.'

Hobbes shrugged. 'We'll see. We have Mr Roman's suicide following the break-in at his house. Jimmy, the gardener, the probable culprit, was stabbed to death, buried and dug up so something could be removed from his grave. Afterwards came the break-in at the museum to steal a bracelet. Then the Roman cup was taken and now this ring has been stolen.'

Seeing that he was thinking aloud, I kept quiet.

He scratched his ear. 'What puzzles me is how Mr Waring fits into all this and where he's got to. The discarded cigarette butts suggest Tony Derrick was involved with, at least, the break-ins at Mr Roman's, the church and at the museum. Plus, he knows Mr Waring, whose business card was discovered at Brancastle.'

I nodded, shifting uncomfortably. In my heart, I'd already accepted that Phil wasn't a criminal, that I'd just resented him because he was the better man and, though deep down I still held a grudge, my malice didn't go so far as to wish him real harm. I hoped he was still alive. 'D'you really think Phil's involved?'

Hobbes's expression was thoughtful. 'Let's just say there are no indications that he is, except for circumstantial evidence. There is, of course, the business card that would seem to place him at one of the incidents.' He paused, staring hard at me. 'I can't work that one out.'

This was it. I gulped. 'I think I can.'

'Go on, then.' Leaning forward, he rested his head on one hairy paw.

I couldn't look him in the eye and, my lungs seemingly too tight to breathe, it was an age before I forced a faint voice. 'It's … umm … my fault.'

'Yours, Andy? I am surprised.'

'Yes. Oh God, I don't know how to say this.'

'Take your time.'

'OK. I'd better just spit it out. It's no use putting it off any longer. It's my fault.'

'So you said.'

I thought I could detect the beginnings of a growl.

'Oh God.' I stared at my hands. They were shaking and fluttering in time with the butterflies in my stomach.

'OK. I'd better just get it off my chest. It's my fault.'

'I'm sure it is,' said Hobbes and I was sure the growl was present.

'I … umm … really don't know how to say this.'

'I know I said take your time but I didn't mean take all day. Out with it. And quickly.'

'Right … umm … you know Phil's business card? The one Wilkes found under the mat?'

'Yes.'

'Right. OK. Oh God. Umm … well, it was like this. I put it there.'

'You, Andy? Why?'

What else could I do except tell the truth?

'Because I … umm … because I was jealous, I suppose. Phil is everything I'm not. He's like what I want to be, yet I can't be like him and, because I can't, I came to detest him, to hate his success, to hate that people liked him. And then there was Ingrid.'

'Do go on,' said Hobbes, and I felt sure I detected rising anger in his voice.

Still unable to look at him, I took another deep, gulping breath. 'When we were round at Phil's place and you were looking at his computer, I picked up a couple of his cards. The thing is, I'd kind of convinced myself he was a villain and thought that if I put his card at the scene then you'd see him in the same light. I'm sorry.'

'Sorry?' roared Hobbes, his voice rumbling like a volcano, 'I should think you are sorry. It was a despicable act.'

Flinching, nodding agreement, I lifted my head, still unable to raise my eyes above his chest, bracing myself for when he blew his top. 'I really am sorry. I was sorry from the moment Wilkes found it and I keep wishing I hadn't done it. If there's anything I can do to help make amends?'

And then he exploded.

I cringed, sweating, caught between running for my life and curling up and taking his wrath. Yet, when I finally dared to look up, he was laughing. Tears poured down the furrows in his face as he rocked back and forth in his chair.

'By heck, Andy!' He guffawed. 'Promise me you'll never be a criminal. You'd make things far too easy for us. We do like some sort of challenge, you know?'

'Umm … I don't understand.'

He wiped his eyes. 'Did you honestly believe I'd fallen for your silly trick? I am a detective you know. I should feel insulted; I might have been if you weren't so funny.'

Stunned, shocked, confused, humiliated, relieved and indignant in quick succession, I finally settled on being relieved, with a seasoning of confusion. It seemed he did not intend tearing me limb from limb. 'But how?'

'How? Well, firstly, I observed you removing the cards from the box.'

I didn't see how he could have done, unless he'd got eyes in the back of his head, which he hadn't. I didn't think so, anyway.

'Secondly, the card was not under the mat when I entered Brancastle and only appeared after you came looking for me. Thirdly, Mrs Goodfellow found several other cards in your jacket pocket when she took it away for cleaning. Fourthly, you had not exactly hidden your feelings towards Mr Waring and, fifthly, I've heard you muttering under your breath more than once that you wished you'd never hidden "the bloody card." Excuse my language.'

'So you knew it was me all the time? Why didn't you say anything?'

'Because it amused me and gave you the chance to make good.' He chuckled. 'The lass and I had a talk about it and decided you weren't a bad lad really. Still, I'm glad you've owned up at last. She'll be pleased when I tell her.'

'Not as pleased as I am,' I said, dizzy with relief. 'It's been horrible, especially when Phil went missing. It's true I wanted him out the way, though not like this, and, anyway, I don't think Ingrid likes me very much.'

'That's a shame. However, you can't make people like you,' he said, 'and sometimes the more you try the less they do. It's the way things are. You have to be yourself and be hopeful.'

I nodded, looking into his corrugated mess of a face, wondering how it felt to be Hobbes, feeling an overwhelming sense of loneliness. Who, I thought, could befriend him? I supposed Mrs Goodfellow, the olde troll, Augustus and maybe Billy Shawcroft might, but they were all outsiders and oddities. Everyone else just seemed to regard him either with respect as a copper who got the job done, or as a figure of fear. Surfing a wave of sympathy and well-being, I reminded myself that, in his own grotesque way, he'd shown me nothing but kindness, except for when he'd shown me terror and horror. Still, with the chains of my guilt released, the world felt a lighter, more hopeful place.

'I still don't really understand what's going on,' I said.

'D'you mean with life, the universe and everything? Or with these crimes?'

'The crimes.'

'So you understand life, the universe and everything?' He grinned. 'You're a genius on the quiet then?'

'No, I didn't mean that. I mean I'm often confused and I'm specifically confused about all these robberies. As far as I can see, there's some Romanian thing connecting them all, yet it doesn't explain why anyone would want the things they took.'

'You're right,' he said. 'I have a bad feeling, though. I fear trouble is afoot and I'm rarely wrong. Anyway, first things first; I ought to see how Tony's getting on and have another word with him.'

We headed for cell number 2. When the sergeant opened it, there was a woof and a black, hairy creature bounded out, bouncing around us.

'I put Dregs with him so he wouldn't feel lonely,' said Hobbes.

I was shocked. 'Couldn't he have hurt him?'

'Most unlikely. He's a big dog and can look after himself.'

'I meant the other way round.'

'I never thought of that,' he said, chewing his lip, peering into the cell and patting the dog's head. 'However, Tony appears to be in one piece.'

He stepped into the cell. 'How are you feeling? A little better? Good. It's not pleasant to faint. So I've been told.'

Tony was sitting on the bench, his back against the wall, his knees drawn up to his chest. When Dregs squeezed past me and bounded in, he squealed, 'Keep it away.'

Hobbes grabbed Dregs's collar. 'Sit,' he said.

The dog sat, wagging his tail, staring at Tony who cringed further up the wall.

'Now then, Tony, are you ready to continue our friendly little chat? Or would you like a bit of dinner? I am obliged to warn you that the stew from our canteen might be construed as cruel and unusual punishment, yet some of the lads seem to thrive on it. At least, they go back for more.'

'I am hungry,' said Tony, adding pathetically, 'I never had no breakfast.'

'No problem,' said Hobbes. 'I'll ask the sergeant to arrange something. We'll continue our talk later, eh? It's a shame I'm not going to let you out because my housekeeper's made chicken soup for lunch. At least I think so, because I heard her plucking the chicken this morning. Would you like Dregs to stay with you? No? Suit yourself. He probably should go home anyway.'

Hobbes turned away, Dregs walking to heel like the hero of an obedience school, as the sergeant locked the door.

'See he gets some grub,' said Hobbes and turned to me. 'We'll leave him to stew and get our dinners.'

The thin November sun radiated genuine warmth, though a chill wind dominated the shadows as we proceeded along The Shambles towards the church, the clock striking one as we waited to cross the road into Blackdog Street. I was far away, thinking of chicken soup, when a woman in a black Volvo drove past, her dull eyes staring at me from a dead head. I shivered, yet, it must have been some sort of illusion, for the driver turned her head and drove away.

'Did you see that?' I asked, as the traffic lights changed and allowed us to cross.

'What?'

'I don't really know.'

'Then, nor do I,' said Hobbes with a frown.

I shrugged, yet something still troubled me, as if she ought to have been familiar.

Lunch was nearly ready when we got in. Hobbes messed about in the back garden with Dregs, while I flopped down on the sofa, flicking through *Sorenchester Life*, stopping when I reached the photo of Editorsaurus Rex. 'Mr Rex Witcherley and wife, Narcisa, enjoy a joke,' I read and slapped the open magazine down on the table, afraid I'd been the joke. Everyone else apparently found me a source of amusement, yet, I had to admit, in my heart of hearts, that I doubted Rex would ever have given me so much thought. I'd just been an employee, a useless oaf he'd finally got rid of. Perhaps I was laughable as a journalist, a complete fool. Still, at least now I'd confessed my appalling trick, I could be an honest fool and, maybe, I could even help to put things right.

I tried to think deeply about the cases and see what I could make of them. The only connection seemed to be something to do with Romania – and Phil didn't fit, unless he was Romanian and I had no reason to suspect so.

'It's on the table!' A shrill voice rang in my ear.

I gasped, collapsing into the sofa. I had not yet developed immunity to Mrs Goodfellow's sudden appearances.

'Thank you,' I said, rising on shaking legs, sure that one day I'd suffer heart failure. At least, it would stop people laughing at me.

As I joined Hobbes in the kitchen, it occurred to me that, if I expired, I wouldn't be able to enjoy Mrs Goodfellow's cooking any more. Her chicken soup was to die for, or, more rationally, a great reason to live. As usual, she disappeared when we were eating. Unusually, I could hear her rummaging round in the cellar.

'She's searching for her roots,' said Hobbes, dunking a chunk of crusty bread into his soup and slurping with massive enjoyment.

I nodded, trying to make sense of his enigmatic statement, speculating whether it might have something to do with whatever lay behind the mysterious door. However, when she emerged after a few minutes with a basket of turnips and parsnips, I understood. Yet, the door still irked me. What did it conceal and would I ever get the chance to find out? Should I even try when it might be dangerous? Whatever the answers, there were other more important puzzles to solve first, not to mention concentrating on maximising my enjoyment of the soup.

We'd finished and were sitting on the sofa drinking tea, when a yawn erupted from deep within. A disturbed night, an exciting morning and a belly tight with chicken soup combined to induce an overwhelming fatigue and that first yawn was like the pattering of small pebbles that presage a landslide. Within moments I was engulfed and yawning uncontrollably.

'Ooh.' Mrs Goodfellow's voice seemed to reach me from a distance. 'Hasn't he got lovely teeth? And so many of 'em.'

I made a feeble attempt to clamp my mouth shut and vaguely noticed Hobbes carrying me upstairs over his shoulder. That was all until I woke up, the gloom and stillness suggesting dusk. I lay in bed in my pyjamas with no memory of changing; I'd bet Mrs Goodfellow had looked after me.

I shrugged; she'd seen more of me than any woman since I was eight. Still half asleep, I winced as an old memory forced itself to the forefront of my thoughts. Though Father didn't believe in wasting good money on holidays, the doctor had insisted that Mother needed a break, because of what had happened to my sister. So, Mother, Father and I went to Tenby. We were sitting on the beach in late September and I decided I wanted a swim, though the sea was foaming as a teasing wind goaded it to a fury. While changing, goose pimples modestly concealed behind the soft folds of a towel, having just reached the awkward point, having stepped out of my pants, I was bending to pick up my new, stripy swimming trunks when a vindictive gust tore along the beach, whipping up the sand into a stinging cloud. Turning my face away, seeing my trunks taxiing for take-off, I tried to pin them down with my foot, but only stepped on the edge of the towel, tugging it from my hand. My despairing lunge for the trunks failing, they accelerated, skimming the sand and flying. A moment later, my towel, too, took flight like a fluffy seagull, its edge slapping my cheek in farewell. I stood, exposed and humiliated, convinced the eyes of the entire world were pointed at me. All my clothes were blowing away as well.

'Don't just stand there, boy,' said Father, 'go and fetch them.'

Though I tried to argue, he wouldn't listen. He sent me running along the beach, trying to retrieve my clothes, my towel and my dignity, while the bullying wind kept tossing everything just out of my reach and the tourists pointed and laughed. It had been so long ago and yet it still made me cringe.

Still, it was all in the past, irrelevant to my current life and, cramming the thoughts back into a dark recess, I indulged my body with a long stretch. Clean sheets were still a novelty and the faint fragrance of lavender was relaxing. I thought I should get up. I'd obviously missed the afternoon and wondered what we might be getting for supper.

Apart from a faint murmur of traffic rising from the street outside, the house lay in silence. Barefoot, I padded across to the window, poking my head between the curtains, looking out on the twilit town where the streetlights had just flickered into life, a handful of huddled people hurrying beneath their glow. A glimmer off the window of a parked car suggested there might already be a hint of frost. A movement from the roof opposite made me jump and my thoughts flew towards Hobbes, though it was only a ragged flock of starlings practising touch and go before roosting.

Somehow, Hobbes had tracked down Tony Derrick; somehow his bizarre crawling around on rooftops had contributed. I supposed he might have spotted Tony during his nocturnal excursion and followed him, or possibly he'd picked up his scent – I could hardly fail to have noticed that he appeared to use his nose rather like a dog – and, perhaps, an unhuman possessed other senses, ones I couldn't even imagine. Yet I knew speculation would not get me anywhere.

I guessed he'd been interviewing Tony Derrick as I slept, which was good, for the atmosphere in the interview room had grown too heavy for comfort. It was also a disappointment, since I'd have liked to see how he prised further information from the human rat. I hoped he'd found Phil, alive and well, even if it meant I'd lose any chance of hitting it off with Ingrid. Sighing, I drew the curtains and dressed, not bothering to turn on the light. Muzzy-headed and heavy after my nap, I thought a cup of tea might perk me up. There were no lights on and no sound of movement as I picked my way downstairs, though something delicious was cooking in the kitchen.

I put the kettle on, trying to avoid looking at the cellar door, for one day, I feared curiosity would drive me down there. A click suggested the front door had opened, the kitchen door, pushed to, flew open and I was engulfed in dog. Though Dregs had apparently decided I was one of the pack, a friend, and showed delight at seeing me, his enthusiasm seemed almost as bad as his earlier aggression. He was exuding tail-wagging bonhomie and an overpowering doggy odour as he alternately thrust his head into my groin or leaped at my face to favour me with a good licking. Behind the disgust, I almost felt pleased.

'Get down, you daft brute,' I said, patting his head, making an effort to keep it where it could do least harm.

'Hello, dear.' Mrs Goodfellow materialised at my side.

As I flinched, the dog took the opportunity for one last lick.

She smiled. 'Did you sleep well? You've got to be careful not to overdo things. There's not many can keep up with the old fellow.'

'Yes, I think I needed it. Now I need a cup of tea.'

'I'll make it,' she said. 'I don't want you setting fire to anything.'

Afterwards, filled with tea, I felt better until she sidled up.

'Would you give me a hand, dear?'

'No.' I recoiled. 'You've got enough. You can have my teeth when I've finished with them but not my hands.'

She hooted with laughter, her gummy mouth beaming hilarity. 'No, dear. Could you give me a hand to wash Dregs? He stinks and I don't want a dirty dog in my nice, clean house.'

'Oh. I see what you mean … umm … do you think it's wise? He's a big dog.'

'That's why I need help. I'll hold him down and you can wash him. I've got some special dog shampoo.'

I didn't really have a choice. 'OK.'

'Right, let's get him up to the bathroom. I'll carry him and you can open the doors. Alright?'

Dregs was sniffing the flip-top bin in the corner when she bent and took him by surprise. He yelped and kicked as her scrawny arms seized him, sweeping him off his feet. Big, frightened eyes looked to me for sympathy, as I led the way upstairs.

I shrugged. 'Sorry mate, but she's right, you do stink.'

Part of me thought I ought to be carrying him, yet the old girl was already jogging upstairs as fast as I could go. At the top, I flung open the bathroom door and, as I shut it behind us, the prisoner, recognising his cruel fate, howled.

After I'd filled the bath with lukewarm water, Mrs Goodfellow dunked him like a biscuit, amid a frenzy of splashing and kicking until the futility of resistance struck him, making him stand stock still, a picture of abject misery. Lathering his rough coat with dog shampoo, I rubbed it in. Now and again, his memory failing, he restarted the struggle, yet he stood no chance and, in a strange way, it made me feel better that I'd been knocked out by her; I, too, had stood no chance.

Eventually, as she lifted the defeated creature from the water, I helped towel him down. When freed from her iron grip, he still retained sufficient sogginess to drench us as he shook his coat, shedding all gloom and resentment in that glorious act of sweet revenge, scampering round the bathroom, rubbing himself on every surface, playful as a puppy, until Mrs Goodfellow, opening the door, released him into the community. He threw himself downstairs while we did our best to dry ourselves and clean up.

'The old fellow will be back for his supper soon,' she said, scrubbing away a muddy patch.

'Good,' I said, 'what is it?'

She smiled. 'I like to see a young man with a healthy appetite. It's steak and kidney pudding, one of his favourites. I hope you like it?'

'I don't know. I've had steak and kidney pie and that was alright.'

'The old fellow likes the pudding best – it was his first decent meal after getting out of hospital in the war.'

'Was he wounded?'

'He was shot as full of holes as a colander.'

'Where was he shot?'

'In the Arras area. They thought he'd die until one of his mates patched him up and held him together.'

I was shocked, finding it difficult to imagine him ever being hurt, for he exuded such an air of invulnerability that it didn't seem right that he could bleed like anyone else. Yet, I'd recognised the sensitivity in his paintings and seen occasional compassion in his actions. Perhaps, he wasn't so very different.

Arras? I groped in the haze of memory; surely it had been a battle in the First World War? Hobbes was amazing.

'I'm glad he pulled through,' I said.

Mrs Goodfellow beamed. 'So am I dear, otherwise neither of us would be here.'

I couldn't disagree. He'd saved my skin three times already. 'Has he ever rescued you?' I asked.

She nodded, giving the bath a final wipe and standing up. 'It was during the Blitz. Our house got bombed and my family was killed. All I remember is a horrible noise and the ceiling falling down. I was buried and it felt like I lay in the dark forever. Then everything lifted and the big policeman was kind. That was the old fellow.'

It was another shock, for, although I'd worked out that Hobbes was ridiculously old, I'd assumed she was as well, because she looked ancient. The idea of her being so much younger flabbergasted me.

'I'm sorry about your family,' I said, 'but he's good at saving people isn't he?

'Yes, and it didn't stop there, because he looked after me right up to my marriage.'

I would have liked to ask her about that, specifically what had happened to Mr Goodfellow and why I'd acquired his clothes but the chimes of the church clock, striking six, put an end to our chat.

'I'd better get back down to the kitchen. I don't like to keep him waiting.'

He didn't turn up. About quarter to seven, she fed me, saying it was a pity to let good food spoil when I was so obviously starving yet, despite the steak and kidney pudding tasting truly, fantastically delicious, I didn't really enjoy it, because she never went away and kept looking at the clock and checking the oven.

He still hadn't appeared by the time I'd finished.

'I hope he's alright,' she said. 'He's not normally late for his supper and if he is, he lets me know.'

'I expect he's just busy and has lost track of time. He'll be back soon, I'm sure.'

He wasn't. She tried his mobile without reply. I phoned the station, learning that he hadn't been seen since mid-afternoon when he'd released Tony Derrick. By half-past eight, Mrs Goodfellow looked frantic. Dregs, on the other hand, had fallen asleep in a corner and snored, as if his inner pig was trying to emerge.

At last I made a decision. The snoring had started to bug me and I couldn't stand any more of Mrs Goodfellow sitting down, standing up, looking at the clock and going to peer out the front door. Her nervousness was infectious. 'I'll go and see if he left a note at the station, and I might have a word with Billy Shawcroft. Hobbes says he knows what's going down.'

Mrs Goodfellow looked grateful and I felt relieved to be out of the house, though I was glad of the long overcoat I'd found. Turning up the collar, an icy wind slapping my ears, I wished I had a hat. Actually, Mrs Goodfellow had dug out a rather fine trilby, which I'd been too embarrassed to wear in public, even if I'd thought it made me look rather cool when posing before the mirror. Returning briefly, jamming the hat onto my head, thrusting my hands into my pockets, I strode towards the police station, my breath curling like smoke. Catching a glimpse of myself in a shop window, I thought I looked a bit like Sam Spade or some other hero of film noir. Even though I laughed at myself, some of the image and attitude stuck.

Though the streets were quiet, I couldn't ignore an impression that dark things lurked in the shadows. It was fanciful, maybe, but I was beginning to see Sorenchester differently, to see the world differently. There were more things in heaven and earth than I'd dreamt of before Hobbes. I hoped he was alright.

A verbal altercation was taking place by the desk when I reached the police station. Though keeping my distance, I gathered it had kicked off after a van was pulled over for speeding. The cops, looking in the back, finding it loaded with suspected contraband, had arrested the driver, who was insisting loudly and coherently that it wasn't contraband at all but props for his clown act. The Irish accent being familiar, I swiftly recognised it as belonging to Pete Moss.

No one having eyes for me, I slipped past.

The rest of the station was deserted, the big office standing in darkness. Without an audience, I opened Hobbes's door with no problem and turned on the light. His room appeared the same as always and I began to suspect I was on a fool's errand. Still, I decided, I might as well have a bit of a nose around, though I felt reluctant to rummage too deeply, in case he returned. A mess of papers littered the desktop and I was about to push them aside when I noticed the doodle. Actually, it was far better than a mere doodle, more like a portrait in ink, unmistakably the face of Narcisa Witcherley, which puzzled me. Why her? I wondered. It occurred to me, thinking back to his rather gallant manner on meeting her in Rex's office, that he might have the hots for her, for she did possess a certain feminine charm, though she'd not impressed me, being too stretched, too plastered with make-up, and being a smoker of unusually noxious cigarettes. There was another sketch of her with Tony Derrick of all people, and I wished I had Hobbes's ability for, although the portraits were accurate, Tony's held a hint of weasel, while Narcisa's suggested arrogance and coldness.

Yet it made no sense to have wasted his time drawing when he was working on a case. Maybe, he'd done it subconsciously, as I'm prone to do, though my doodles look like doodles.

I uncovered another sketch showing two men standing together, one wearing a long coat, a trilby hat pulled low and a scarf wrapped around his face, the other sporting a short jacket and a balaclava to conceal the bits of his face not obscured by sunglasses. The significance was clear; they were the villains who'd attacked Mr Barrington-Oddy.

On pushing the drawings aside, I noticed the fax from the house agent, confirming the ring was fifteenth-century Romanian, yet disputing that it had anything to do with the Order of St George. It was, in fact, a relic of a different order, the Order of the Dragon and, according to the agent, a rare and valuable object. However, Mrs Iliescu, loathing it and needing the money, had offered it for sale. The fax incorporated a copy of her advert, including historical details about Sigismund, the Holy Roman Emperor establishing the Order of the Dragon in 1408 and having the dragon ring fashioned for one of his vassals, a chap with the unfortunate name of Vlad, in about AD 1430. I felt a wavelet of satisfaction that I hadn't been entirely wrong about the Roman connection after all.

Skipping the baffling details about the Troy weight in gold and the quality of the rubies, I found a photograph of the ring, an exquisite object, shaped like a winged dragon, its tail coiled around its neck, resembling the bracelet. Despite the fax being rather blurred, I could understand Mrs Iliescu's point of view, because there was something loathsome about it, despite the quality of the craftsmanship. Yet, she obviously had great faith in its value, for its price was fifty thousand pounds – a hell of a lot of money for such a small item.

I speculated that the bracelet, though only of bronze, might be worth a similar amount to, say, a collector. Few have such money available and anyone really desiring it, my putative collector for instance, might resort to stealing as the better option. I was impressed by my insight: I was starting to think like a detective. Hobbes was starting to rub off on me.

Yet all my brilliant reasoning had got me no closer to finding him. Deciding I might as well head to the Feathers and ask Billy, I was on the point of leaving when I noticed a copy of *Sorenchester Life* beside the desk, open on the picture of Editorsaurus Rex and wife. Bafflingly, Hobbes had underlined some of the letters in the caption, presumably, I thought, subconsciously, for they made no sense to me.

Still, it refuelled my speculation that he'd developed some sort of crush on Narcisa and led to a sort of reluctant curiosity about the sort of sex life he enjoyed, if he enjoyed one at all. Maybe, if there were any females of his kind he could, though I felt almost certain any human female would be repulsed by his looks, if not by his Hobbesishness. Not that I was in any position for smugness, since my last hint of an amorous encounter had been when Dregs had become affectionate. I left the police station deep in thought.

It was a quiet night at the Feathers. That is, no one was actually fighting. Featherlight Binks was in an unusually convivial mood, acknowledging my arrival with a grunt that I took as a welcome. On reaching the bar, Billy Shawcroft approached, his pale face evidence of yesterday's drinking binge.

'Evening,' I said. 'Can I have a nice pint of lager?'

'Of course you can, mate,' said Billy and, under his breath, 'though it's not so nice in this dump.'

'Thanks,' I said. 'Did you enjoy your free beer last night?'

He shuddered. 'Enjoy is not the word. I must have been mad. That Romanian stuff's corrosive.'

'Romanian?' Everything was Romanian.

'Yes, Romanian,' Billy whispered, one eye watching Binks, pouring my pint. '"Dracula's Bite" they call it and, though it's got a nice label, it's bloody awful and I've still got a man-sized hangover. If you think I look bad, you should see it from my side.'

Smiling, speculating about whether a dwarf-sized hangover should be a hangunder, I reached into my pocket, completely forgetting I was broke. Embarrassed, I admitted my predicament, 'Umm … I'm really sorry but I'm right out of cash.'

'Forget it. It's on me,' said Billy. 'I'm glad to do a favour for a friend of Hobbes. I'm indebted to the old devil.'

'Thanks, you're very kind.'

'You might not think so after you've tasted it.' He frowned. 'I feel like death.'

'I'm sorry to hear it, but you'll live.'

He groaned. 'Will I? Please say I won't. It's bloody well-named that Dracula's Bite; it makes you feel undead and you just long for a stake and I don't mean the sort you have with chips.'

'Why did Featherlight buy such bad beer?'

'It was cheap. Some Irish guy turns up from time to time selling dodgy cigarettes and last time he'd got some crates of beer. The boss bought 'em, thinking he was being shrewd but the stuff's terrible, even by our standards.'

'Would that be Pete Moss?' I asked, leaning on the bar so I could hear Billy more easily.

'Yeah, that's him. The boss is gonna punch his lights out next time he turns up, which is why he's so cheerful tonight.'

'He might have a bit of a wait,' I said. 'Pete was at the police station. He's been nicked for smuggling.'

'Lucky bastard,' said Billy, grinning. Then, clutching his head, he moaned. 'Oh God, I shouldn't move my face in the state I'm in.'

'You'll be OK,' I reassured him and took a slurp of lager, which wiped the smile off my face. Standing upright, I peeled my sleeves off the bar. 'By the way, have you seen anything of Hobbes today?'

'No. Why?'

'Well,' I said, 'he didn't turn up for his supper and didn't phone to say he'd be late. His housekeeper says it's not normal and she's worried.'

'He can look after himself. He'll turn up.'

'You're probably right. Except … umm … he was last seen with Tony Derrick.'

Billy, grimacing, held his head again. 'Well in that case, I hope Hobbes gives the bastard a right good walloping. Tell you what, I'll keep my eyes open and my ear to the ground and let you know if anything turns up, OK?'

He turned to serve an impatient customer.

I finished my drink, apart from the mysterious selection of brown lumps at the bottom. 'Goodnight,' I said, walking towards the door.

Featherlight responded by merrily chucking a soggy rag at me. When I saw what came out as it splattered against the wall, I was mightily relieved he'd missed. Slithering down the wall like a giant slug, it flopped onto a chair, just as the bloke Billy had served sat on it. I closed the door behind me, stepping into the frosty street, as a bellow of rage rang out and Featherlight answered with a roar. Normal service had resumed and I wondered whether Mrs Goodfellow would shortly be adding to her collection.

As I hurried away, the lager sloshing in my stomach, my foot struck an empty bottle on the kerb, which, rolling into the gutter, shattered. Stopping to kick the broken glass down a nearby drain where it wouldn't be of danger, I noticed the label.

'Dracula's Bite Romanian Export Beer', it said in blood-red gothic letters. Stepping into the road, I picked it up, examining it beneath a streetlight. Billy had been right to claim the label, showing a white-walled, red-turreted castle on a hill surrounded by trees, was picturesque. 'Castle Bran, legendary Carpathian home of Count Dracula', I read. I don't mind admitting it worried me. What worried me more was the roar of the swerving motorbike.

As I flung myself back onto the pavement, the bike screeched to a stop. A menacing, helmeted figure in black leathers stepped off, coming towards me, removing his heavy gauntlets. I thought I was in for it.

'It's Andy isn't it? Are you alright?' asked the figure, removing his helmet, revealing himself as Kev the Rev.

'Oh,' I said, relieved, 'umm … yes I'm alright. I'm sorry if I got in your way.'

'You didn't really. I was just passing and, seeing you looked kind of lost, I thought I'd better stop and see if I could help.'

'It's good of you.'

'Well I am a reverend, I'm meant to be good, though it's not always easy. Anyway, to coin a phrase, why the long face?'

'It's not me, I'm alright. I'm worried about Inspector Hobbes.'

'I'm not surprised,' said Kev, 'he's a very worrying bloke. What's he done to you?'

'Nothing.'

'Nothing yet you mean. I remember him putting the fear of God into me when I started getting into trouble, which is why I ended up doing what I do.'

I understood what he meant. Hobbes had the power to terrify with a glance, a word or an action, though it was not only Mrs Goodfellow who was worried about him. I had to admit it; so was I.

'No, he's gone missing and I'm looking for him.'

'Fuckrying out loud. How can he go missing? He's about as inconspicuous as a tiara on a turtle. Have you asked anyone?'

'Yeah, he was last seen leaving the station with a guy called Tony Derrick who's a right little weasel.'

'Now, now,' said Kev, 'we are all God's children. Mind you, I know what you mean. I've known Tony since I was a boy and he really is a nasty little shit. They say he had it tough; his mum left when he was a nipper and his dad was a violent alcoholic swine, but, may God forgive me, every time I meet him, I struggle against an urge to throttle the bugger. Tell you what, though, if you like, I know where he's been living, I'll give you a lift there, and you can ask him. I've got a spare lid in the box.'

'Thank you,' I said.

'You can hold onto me if you like.'

A couple of minutes later I was sitting on the back of his bike, my trilby replaced by a smelly helmet, thinking that Hobbes's driving hadn't been so bad after all. It wasn't that Kev did anything unusual for a motorcyclist, it was just that I'd never been on a bike before and was wishing I'd never been on one at all. Clinging to the back stanchion, refusing to put my arms around Kev, I hoped I'd live long enough to die of the frostbite I was convinced was eating my extremities. Yet, in a few minutes, we were safely outside Tony's.

The street was still deserted except for the cat on the mattress and there was no sign of anyone being home. Getting off the bike, approaching the front door, I knocked. Total silence. Total darkness. I returned to Kev.

'No luck?'

I shook my head. 'Umm … you don't happen to know anything about Romania, do you?'

He frowned. 'That's an odd question. Why do you want to know?'

I didn't tell him everything, though I did mention that Hobbes had been, or, I

149

hoped, still was, working on a case involving Romania. And I did tell him about Dracula's Bite beer and Pete Moss.

'I know Pete,' said Kev, 'he's a rogue, though one with a good heart.'

'He was arrested tonight,' I said, 'for smuggling.'

'It's not the first time.' Kev's breath curled in the breeze and his mouth curled into a smile. 'He once had the brilliant notion of smuggling fake Viagra into the country. He stuffed the pills into condoms and swallowed them. The trouble was, one burst and, well, he rather stood out when he tried to get through Customs. He was so obviously a hardened criminal.'

'Leave it out. I'm not in the mood.'

'Which is precisely what his girlfriend told him when he got home.'

'Shut up.'

'Sorry,' Kev shrugged, 'I was only trying to cheer you up. Tell you what, I'll give you a lift home. I wouldn't worry about Hobbes, he can handle himself, which is, incidentally, what Pete had to do. Sorry. No, I bet he's back home right now. Jump on.'

Dropping me outside the front door of Blackdog Street, he drove away with a cheery wave. I went inside, to be greeted by Dregs as a long-lost friend. A glance at Mrs Goodfellow's face sufficed to tell me Hobbes hadn't returned. Sitting together on the sofa, we talked occasionally, flicking between television channels, starting at every sound from outside. Despite my afternoon nap, I was still whacked and went up to bed before midnight. She said she'd wait up a little longer.

As I lay in bed, dozing, I couldn't stop myself listening for the front door opening. Sleep kept its distance, my mind ticking over, trying to make sense of everything and I was still awake when the church clock struck one and the old girl came upstairs. I awoke with daylight filtering into the room through inadequately closed curtains. Swirling inside my head were dream images as substantial as mist and, like early morning mist, they soon evaporated, leaving only a residue of unease.

The clock said it was nine-thirty. I got up, opening the curtains, sitting back on the bed, yawning and stretching. Hearing movement from Hobbes's room, I leaped back to my feet, with a punch of the air and a suppressed cheer. It would have been far too embarrassing to let him know I'd been worried, so I pulled myself together and strolled out, as if on my way to the bathroom, intending to look in and say Good Morning, before finding out where he'd been and what he'd been doing.

His door, standing ajar, I poked my head inside. Hobbes wasn't there but Dregs was, walking round and round, sniffing and whimpering like a lost puppy. He was delighted to see me and even more delighted to smell me. Secretly gratified, I tried to push the beast down and keep his cold nose from my groin. I succeeded, though his long wet tongue curled across my face in a sneak attack.

'Get down,' I said and he sat, looking up as if expecting me to do something. I wasn't used to dogs and my first experiences with him had been unpleasant, yet, now I felt safe, there was something reassuring about his presence. 'So Hobbes isn't back?'

Dregs's ears perked up and he began sniffing round the room again.

'He must be somewhere,' I said. 'A bloke like him can't just vanish.' The dog tilted his head to one side as I explained. 'He's too big to hide, though I still don't know how to find him.'

Dregs wagged his tail, sniffing the carpet and giving me an idea. Dogs, I knew, could follow trails, so maybe Dregs could find Hobbes. But first I needed breakfast.

When washed and dressed I went downstairs. Mrs Goodfellow being out, I was forced to make my own tea and toast, managing the feat without any involuntary arson, eating and drinking in silence, vaguely aware of Dregs padding about above. My mind was apparently in neutral, yet something must have been going on behind the scenes because, to my surprise, I experienced a moment of inspiration. It felt almost as if someone had flicked a switch in my brain, turning on a floodlight, letting me realise what a spluttering, smoky, little candle normally illuminated my thoughts. Hurrying to the sitting room, I searched for *Sorenchester Life*, needing to see the photo of the Editorsaurus and wife. The magazine had gone; Mrs Goodfellow must have thrown it away.

A minute or two later, and to my surprise, I was running down Blackdog Street heading for the police station, barely noticing the icy air whipping my face, the slippery pavements still white with frost and the grey, frigid sky. I was gasping and sweaty when I arrived but I'd run all the way and felt mightily impressed with myself.

'Has Hobbes been in?'

The desk sergeant shook his head. 'Not yet. Can I help you, sir?'

'No, not really. I need something from his office.'

'Sorry, sir, I can't allow you in, if you're not with the Inspector. I'm afraid it's no entry.'

'It's important.' I raised my voice. 'Very important.'

'Sorry, sir, and I'd be obliged if you'd stop shouting and go about your business.'

'But it is my business! He's gone missing and there's something in his office I think might be a clue.'

'The Inspector can look after himself. He probably has good reasons for being absent and if he really has gone missing then it's police business.'

Though I argued, the sergeant was immovable. 'It's only a magazine I want.' When I tried to push past, he moved surprisingly quickly, holding me in an arm lock.

'Please leave, sir,' he said, still polite, though the pressure on my arm hinted it could become extremely painful.

Leaving, muttering furiously, yet afraid of getting myself banged up in a cell, I stamped up and down outside, fuming and fretting, unsure what to do next. Someone walked out and stood in my way.

A soft Irish accent addressed me. 'Are you alright, there?'

I stopped and Pete Moss, clown, entertainer and smuggler grinned at me.

'Yes,' I said. 'Or rather, no… umm … maybe.'

'It's best to cover all your options,' said Pete with a nod. 'Don't I know you? Yeah, weren't you with Hobbes the other day? You're not a copper, right?'

'That's right. I'm Andy.'

Reaching for my hand, shaking it, he said, 'Hobbes is a decent fellow, for a copper. He's pretty straight, even if he always makes me feel like a naughty schoolboy before the headmaster, though I've never seen a headmaster as ugly as he is. Jaysus! He gave me a turn the night I was discovered at the theatre.'

'Were you auditioning?'

'Not exactly. He discovered me backstage when I was … acquiring some bits for my act. I thought I was for the high jump and ran for it, fancying myself as an athlete in those days. Once, I even entered the London marathon.'

I was impressed. 'How did you do?'

'I walked it.'

'You won?'

He laughed. 'No. I really did walk most of it.'

'Is that a joke?'

'Actually, no.' He shrugged. 'I did try, only I hadn't run in my shoes enough and got blisters, hence, my abysmal performance. Even so, I was well fit when Hobbes came after me and, seeing the size of him, I reckoned I'd get away easily but – Jaysus! – he's bloody fast, like an avalanche.'

'What happened?' I was fascinated despite the urgency and the frost nipping my ears.

'He collared me pretty damn quick and I thought he'd run me in but he didn't. He made me put all the stuff back, gave me a good talking to and then, I don't know why, he took me shopping and paid for the stuff I needed from his own wallet.'

'Amazing,' I said because there were no words to do justice to my thoughts.

'I reckoned I was for it again when he pulled me over the other week,' said Pete, 'yet he got me to the gig on time. Sadly, I reckon I'm really in trouble after this latest incident. They caught me red-handed with contraband cigarettes and bloody awful beer.'

'Carpati cigarettes and Dracula's Bite beer?'

He nodded. 'Correct. The fags aren't so bad if you like that sort of thing but the beer is …' He tailed off. 'Well, let's just say it's not Guinness.'

'So I've heard, from someone who got drunk on it.'

He looked shocked. 'Someone got drunk on it? Jaysus! Is he alright? He must be made of sterner stuff than me. I can only manage to force down a few sips, to impress customers with its hoppy, fruity characteristics.'

'Billy said it tasted of oven cleaner.'

'He's the little fellow at the Feathers?'

I nodded.

Pete shrugged. 'I've heard tell he'll drink anything. I wouldn't put it past him to have tried oven cleaner.' He grimaced. 'How is Hobbes?'

'He's gone missing. I'm worried.'

'Don't be, he can look after himself if anyone can.'

I shook my head and told of my concerns. I probably said more than I should have, though I had the feeling I could trust Pete.

His blue eyes looked grave. 'I wish I could help but I've got to make a few arrangements before my case comes up. Look, I don't know if it's of any use, I've only sold a few of those Carpati cigarettes round here recently. Most were to Featherlight or to a lady who was arranging a party. She was a skinny old biddy. I can't remember her name, though she drives a black Volvo. I only met her because she was with a ratty-looking fellow I'd bumped into at the Feathers. He told her my fags were OK and she bought a load of boxes. It was a nice profit and all tax-free, so I wasn't going to complain.'

Pete, I decided, though a nice enough guy for a criminal, didn't half go on when I wanted to hurry. Besides, I was getting cold. 'Sorry,' I said, 'I've got to go. Thanks for your information.' I didn't think it would be much use.

I hurried to a newsagent on the lower part of The Shambles, spending a frustrating ten minutes looking through the magazine racks for *Sorenchester Life*.

The girl manicuring her nails behind the till acknowledged my existence when I'd got to the muttering stage. 'Can I help you?'

'I'm looking for *Sorenchester Life*.'

'Is there life in Sorenchester?' She smirked.

'I mean the magazine *Sorenchester Life*.' I almost growled. Hobbes was definitely catching.

'You're standing right in front of it. On the third shelf.'

I'd been looking straight at it, only not at the issue I wanted. 'I was looking for last month's. Have you got it?'

'We did have. Last month.'

'Do you know where I could get it?'

'Haven't a clue.'

'Thanks, you've been a great help.'

I stomped out the shop as the girl went back to her nails. For want of anything better to do, feeling helpless, I started walking back towards Blackdog Street, looking around, hoping to spot Hobbes. I was out of luck. However, I did spot a plaque for a dental surgery and, on impulse, stepped inside. The waiting room was nearly full. Although it smelled of fear and sounded of drills, I ignored everything, except for the table upon which teetered a tower of dog-eared magazines. I found the right issue of *Sorenchester Life* near the top, flicking through until I came to the picture of the Editorsaurus and Narcisa.

As I stared at the caption, *Mr Rex Witcherley and wife, Narcisa, enjoy a joke,* I tried to remember which letters Hobbes had underlined, with an idea that something was starting to make sense at last. I thought back to Hobbes highlighting the faint impressions on the scrap of paper he'd found at Mr Roman's, the few letters standing out forming the enigmatic message, *EX WITCH IS A JOY OK* and read the caption again to make sure. *Mr Rex Witcherley and wife, Narcisa, enjoy a joke.*

An ashen-faced man spoke to the pretty young receptionist. 'I've got to make an appointment for root canal surgery.'

'Brilliant! That's fantastic!' I cried.

Shocked faces stared at me.

'Sorry.' Replacing the magazine, I hurried away, glad to escape; dentists reminded me of my father and made me edgy. Nonetheless, I was almost dancing on reaching the street, where a few dusty snowflakes were swirling. I had solved a clue and the fact that Hobbes had done it first hardly detracted from the satisfaction.

I could have cheered until I realised I still didn't understand anything. All I knew was that someone had written out the caption from the magazine, leaving an impression on the paper, which had then been used for writing down the combination of Mr Roman's safe. So what?

My sense of satisfaction having died by the time I reached the church, I sneaked inside, hoping for divine inspiration. I really wanted to be up and searching for Hobbes but I'd got nothing to go on except for the one clue, assuming it was a clue, and my hare-brained notion of Dregs as a tracker-dog.

The blue-haired lady at the book counter was belittling a confused Japanese couple, and didn't notice me creep into a pew where I sat, head bowed. Somehow, it felt even colder in the church than outside and I wished I'd taken the time to put on my overcoat.

All I had to work on was my clue and Hobbes's sudden obsession with Narcisa. It was time for deep thinking. So, someone had written the caption on the note pad and someone with different handwriting had scrawled the combination for the safe on the sheet below. But why would anyone copy such a caption? It wasn't interesting, just a few bland words in a dull magazine. I couldn't imagine anyone doing it.

Then it struck me and it was obvious. The reporter who'd covered the ball would have made notes, as most reporters didn't forget their notebooks, and I remembered thinking at the time that the paper had been torn from a small, cheap, wired jotting pad, much like we used at the *Bugle*.

Feeling like a bloodhound finally picking up the trail, I understood why they bayed, and might have yelled in triumph had I not been in church. Clenching my fists and shaking them at the ceiling was as far as I let myself go. I was convinced a reporter had jotted down the caption in the notebook and that whoever had written the combination to Mr Roman's safe on the following leaf had access to the notebook. Therefore, it was probable the reporter had been involved with the break-in at Mr Roman's!

A mischievous part of my brain reminded me that Phil was a reporter. However, I knew his writing and was pretty sure he was in the clear. Therefore, I needed to discover who had actually written the article. I ground my teeth because I hadn't thought to look before.

I'd have to return to the dentist's. 'Damn.' My mutter came out louder than anticipated.

'I'll trouble you to watch your language in the House of the Lord, young man.'

Glancing up to apologise, I met the glare of the blue-haired woman.

'You,' she said with a look of contempt, 'I might have known. I'm going to call the police.'

'Oh no you're not,' I said, suppressing my instinct to flee, standing up, looking her right in the eye, 'I'm leaving now on important police business. Do not interfere.' It must have been the way I said it, for she was speechless as I strode from the church.

Heading back to the dentist's, I picked up *Sorenchester Life*.

'Are you here for an appointment?' asked the receptionist.

'No, I've come for this.' I said, holding up the magazine. 'I need to borrow it. I'll bring it back.'

Hurrying into the street before she could protest, I turned to the article, which was only accredited to NW. Looking in the index, I discovered that Witcherley Publications, Editor R. Witcherley, Contributing Editor N. Witcherley, owned the magazine and, since none of the other contributors had the initials NW, concluded that Narcisa was the author. I couldn't help noticing the names of other *Bugle* journalists, including Phil Waring and even Ingrid on the list of writers. I'd never realised there was a connection between the *Bugle* and *Sorenchester Life*, much less been invited to write for it, and resentment began to bubble until I forced myself to simmer down and consider.

'OK,' I said, thinking out loud, 'she wrote it and then what? Did she give the notebook to someone else?'

'I'm sorry, I don't know,' said a little old guy in a flat cap and muffler, scuttling away, as if I was the loony that sits next to you on the bus.

A bizarre thought sprouted. Perhaps Editorsaurus Rex was behind the crimes. He would certainly have access to Narcisa's notebook and could easily have hired someone to carry out the dirty deeds. It was possible, of course, that Narcisa was, herself, the master criminal, though I didn't think she looked the type. Still, I could think of no sensible reasons why either of them would have done it. Why would they need to steal? I knew they were wealthy enough to own a holiday home abroad.

I decided to approach the Editorsaurus. My next stop would be the *Bugle's* offices.

16

I'd always suffered with butterflies in my stomach when entering Editorsaurus Rex's presence. On the whole, this had been because I was trying to work out what I'd done wrong. This time, I was pretty much going to accuse him or his wife of stealing, or worse, and it felt like I'd got a flock of vultures flapping around inside. Nevertheless, despite a brief, panicky dither on the stairs, I was determined to give it my best shot.

Taking a deep breath, I strode into the main office, looking like I meant business. Ingrid turned away as I headed for Rex's den, which hurt more than my fist when I thumped on his door in the style of Hobbes. There was no reply. I hesitated, caught between knocking again and barging straight in.

'He's not in.'

Though she was still talking to me, there was no smile, just polite indifference.

'Rex is away. Duncan's in charge.'

I grimaced. So, Duncan was back already; he had stitched me up with Hobbes.

'But I need to talk to Rex … umm … or Mrs Witcherley,' I said. 'It's important.'

'Then you're out of luck. They're away together.'

My plan had fallen at the first hurdle. 'I don't suppose you know where?'

She shrugged. 'Romania, I suppose.'

'Romania? Why Romania?' It seemed I couldn't get away from the place.

'It's where she comes from, or at least, her family did. They've got a holiday home in the mountains out there. Now, excuse me, I've work to do.' Spinning back to her computer, she stabbed at the keys.

I slouched away, no longer the hound hot on the trail, more like a whipped puppy. Leaving the building, I stopped, uncertain what to do, the fires of enthusiasm having been all but extinguished, shivering as the wind flung hard, stinging nodules of snow into my face. For want of a better idea, I headed back to Blackdog Street where, with luck I'd hear some good news and, if not, at least I'd get a cup of tea.

I opened the door of number 13, bracing myself when I saw Dregs lying there, watching and waiting, but he greeted me with a single wag of his tail, a mournful look in his eyes, almost as if it was bath time again. Mrs Goodfellow was stirring a pot on the stove when I entered the kitchen and, whatever it was smelt delicious, though I was never destined to taste it. She'd been shopping and piles of groceries were heaped on nearly every surface.

'Any news?' I asked, though her expression had already told me.

She shook her head. 'I'm cooking his favourites for when he comes back. What about you, dear? Have you found out anything?' Her voice shook, as if she'd been crying, though there were no tears.

'Not much.' I sat at the table in front of a huge, bloody leg of lamb in a dish. 'I think my editor and his wife might know something, only they've gone to Romania.'

She sighed. 'Have they, dear? Well, I expect you'd like a cup of tea and a bit of dinner?'

Glancing at the clock, I nodded. It was nearly one.

Though the cup of tea was up to standard, the bread in the cheese and pickle sandwiches was, perhaps, a little dry. This wasn't a complaint, merely an indication of her state of mind. I covered up my disappointment, eating to fill the emptiness.

I was still at the table, comfortably full and warm, when, my brain, unfreezing, started working. If Hobbes had been onto something, perhaps that had led to his disappearance. Perhaps he, too, had uncovered the link between Romania and the Witcherleys, who, of course, employed Phil, who had some connection to Tony Derrick. It struck me then that Hobbes's sketches might have been more than idle doodles. The fact of his having drawn Tony and Narcisa together, and then sketching Barrington-Oddy's attackers, sparked a possibility. I'd just assumed both assailants were men, but could one have been a woman? The taller, skinny one, whose face had been hidden by a scarf and a hat might have been. Another idea nudged into my head: Hobbes had discovered fibres with the faint scent of flowers. Could that have been Narcisa's perfume?

Then, of course, Pete Moss had sold some of his foul Carpati cigarettes to a woman who was organising a party, and had mentioned that she'd been with a ratty bloke. It had to be Narcisa and Tony. Probably, anyway. I'd even heard her party at the Black Dog Café and was willing to bet all the thumping music was to cover the break-in at the museum. By then, I'd nearly convinced myself the Witcherleys were up to their necks in crime, with Tony as their accomplice. A deluge of congratulation and excitement bursting over me, left me gasping with self-admiration, thinking I was really getting the hang of the detective game.

Unfortunately, I couldn't see how my brilliance would help, especially now the Witcherleys were in Romania and Phil and Hobbes were still missing. I discounted the idea that Hobbes had gone after them – he wouldn't without telling Mrs Goodfellow. It was then I realised his car had vanished as well. We'd left it outside Tony's squalid squat and it hadn't been there when I'd gone back with Kev. Nor had it been at the police station. Had he retrieved it and then gone missing? Or had Tony stolen it? Or was there another explanation? Detecting wasn't so easy after all.

Dregs padded in, sitting gloomily on my foot, sighing, and I wondered whether my initial idea had merit.

I jumped up. 'Where's his lead? I'm going to see if he can find Hobbes.'

'Are you, dear?' The old girl was attacking a vegetable with a cleaver. 'It's on the hook by the back door. I hope you find him, because he'll be hungry and I ought to tell you, dear, he can get rather wild when he's hungry. You'd best take the leg of lamb. I'll wrap it for you.'

'But it's not cook—' I began. 'Oh, yeah. Right.'

Wrapping the bloody leg in a tea towel, she dropped it into a carrier bag. Though Dregs watched, he'd been fed and was far too interested in the prospect of a walk to spare a thought for raw meat. Besides, he preferred his meals nicely cooked. Mindful of the cold, I donned my overcoat and trilby, and clipped him to the chunky length of chain and led him out.

'Take care, dear,' she said as I shut the door, 'and good luck.'

'Right then, Dregs,' I said. 'Find Hobbes. Got it? Find Hobbes.'

He looked at me and then bounded down the road with a woof. I struggled to hold him back, pleased how well my experiment was working, until he came to an abrupt halt by the nearest lamppost and gave vent to pent-up emotions, letting off steam in the cold air. I'd not taken into account that he'd been inside all morning. At last he finished and, after a rapturous bout of sniffing, set off with an excited woof.

Though I'd got him on a short chain and was hauling back with all my strength, I struggled to keep up, my strides growing longer and longer, sure that, sooner or later, I'd crash to the pavement, yet, amazingly, keeping going. My hat blew off as we turned into Pound Street; I never saw it again. On reaching the main Fenderton Road, Dregs had enough sense to keep away from the traffic because, so far as I could see, the only way I could even slow him was by flinging myself to the ground and acting as an anchor.

The overcoat had been a mistake, for sweat was already trickling down my chest, sticking the shirt to my back. I glimpsed my reflection in a car's tinted window; my face was puffed out, as red as a robin's chest, my hair was sticking up in damp clumps. When I managed to unbutton the coat, it flapped like heavy wings. I wasn't used to such exercise, and the cheese sandwiches were making sure I couldn't forget them.

I kept going, though my head, in contrast to my leaden body, felt light and I wondered when my lungs would give up the struggle. It was, surely, a race between them and my heart as to which exploded first. I think the speed camera on the outskirts of Fenderton flashed as we went by, although it might just have been the lights in my head. My tongue lolled like the dog's, though he was in his element, running with boundless enjoyment, apparently oblivious to the dying man he was dragging behind.

When he made a sharp turn to the right, darting across the road, I didn't. Inertia, plus both feet happening to be off the ground, meant I carried straight on until the chain, jerking in my hand as it twisted round a pole, snapped tight. The next thing I remember, I was sprawling on my side on the pavement, gasping for breath like a landed fish, panicking that my lungs had collapsed under the impact. Cars and lorries thundered past. No one stopped to help.

Though I guess I was just winded, it was ages before I could breathe normally, sit up and audit my other injuries. My wrist was raw and tender where the lead had chafed, my shoulder felt as if it had been wrenched from its socket, the side of my face was bruised and bleeding, my hip was throbbing and sore, blood was pounding through my head, and I hoped the stickiness inside my clothes was only sweat. Nothing seemed too serious but the experience gave me an insight into how Tony must have felt when Hobbes tackled him. Using the pole as support, I climbed back to my feet. A sign on top thanked me for driving safely.

I brushed myself down as well as I could, while my pulse and breathing dropped to sustainable levels. The clip on the chain had snapped off and there was no sign of Dregs, which was good, because I'd half-expected to see him flattened in the middle of the busy road. I was furious, coming close to abandoning him, going home, licking my wounds. Yet, worst luck, I recognised my responsibility for the daft brute. Groaning and swearing, picking up the bag of lamb from the gutter, I hobbled across the road into a quiet, tree-lined cul-de-sac that looked familiar. It was Alexander Court, where

Mr Roman had lived.

'Dregs!' I yelled and no dog appeared. 'Where are you?'

The net curtains of number 2 opened and a tubby grey-haired woman stared out. I could feel her suspicion burning into me.

'Here boy!' I held up the lead, making a pantomime of searching before turning towards her with a smile and a shrug. Though the curtains closed, I could feel eyes watching as I walked away.

I'd been impressed by Roman's house, yet it was rather small compared to one or two of the others. Most were set well back from the road as if they had something to hide and I caught myself staring at one that lurked behind a high yew hedge. With its Cotswold stone walls and chimneys like turrets, it might have passed as a small castle. Its front lawn, as smooth and neat as a bowling green, was edged with exotic shrubs and naked flowerbeds. A brushed gravel drive led towards a double garage, outside of which stood a Volvo, as glossy and black as a raven.

Carrying on up the road, I called again for the dog, as memory dropped a reminder into my consciousness; a black Volvo – I couldn't help thinking it ought to ring a bell.

Bong! Pete Moss had said the thin woman who'd bought his cigarettes drove a black Volvo. Coincidence? Maybe.

Bong! A second bell rang. A black Volvo had passed us yesterday, a thin woman with eyes like death staring out at me. An image formed in my mind, slowly twisting into shape. It could easily have been Narcisa, camouflaged by lack of makeup. I was almost sure.

Which meant she hadn't been in Romania then and, perhaps, still wasn't. To my surprise, I had a hunch. Perhaps, I'd just seen the same car and therefore, perhaps, it was parked on the Witcherleys' drive.

Needing to know, I turned back. A quick ring on the doorbell would show whether my guess was correct and, if not, which seemed more likely, I could use my lost dog as an excuse for disturbing the occupants. Scrunching though the deep gravel, I reached the polished oak and gleaming brass front door. Behind it was a porch roughly the same size as the lounge in my poor old flat. I caught a faint tang of metal polish as I reached out to press the glinting doorbell.

I waited. And waited, wondering if it had worked. Pressing again, I was on the point of giving up when Editorsaurus Rex appeared, dressed in jeans and a faded red sweatshirt. I'd never seen him casual before and the sight made me even more nervous than usual. A faint frown crossed his jowly face as, shuffling across the porch, he opened the front door. He was wearing fluffy white socks and sported a lurid mark on his neck, like a love-bite. I gulped, astonished my guesswork had paid off.

'Capstan?' his voice boomed. 'What the devil do you want? Have you been fighting? You're not getting your job back if that's what you think.'

It didn't seem worthwhile correcting him. 'Good Afternoon,' I said. 'I was … umm … wondering if you'd seen Inspector Hobbes today?'

Rex shook his head. 'Hobbes? I haven't seen him since you brought him along to my office. Damn it, Capstan, you should have learned to fight your own battles at your age. How old are you? Twenty-nine? Thirty?'

'Thirty-seven.'

He shook his head again. 'Is that it, then? And, please tell me, why you've got a dog chain in your hand?'

'I've lost a dog.'

'As well as Hobbes? It smacks of gross carelessness. Well, I'm sure when you find Hobbes he'll find your dog for you. Good Afternoon.' He closed the door in my face.

My mouth opened and closed, my hands fluttering stupidly. There'd been so much I'd wanted to ask, yet, as usual, he'd steamrollered me. Frustrated and angry, I started back down the drive, pausing by the garage, its doors gleaming with brass fittings set in varnished, panelled wood, below a row of glinting windows. Curiosity prompted a peek inside. To the left was a large silver car, a Daimler I think. Far more interesting to me was Hobbes's small car on the right.

I tried the garage doors. They were locked. I dithered, trying to think. Rex, it seemed, had lied and, unless he'd stolen the car, Hobbes must have been there, and, perhaps, still was. Maybe I'd been correct to think Rex was up to no good. My best course of action, I came to the conclusion, was to call the police and get professional help.

Jogging back along the drive, heading down the road to number 2, I presumed, in the circumstances, she'd allow me to use her phone. The net curtains moved as I trotted down the garden path by the side of a lawn, heavily decorated with gnomes. Though I rang the bell and waited, the door didn't open. Stepping back, I unleashed my most ingratiating smile on the window. The net curtains twitched again.

'Good afternoon. I wonder if I might … umm … use your phone? It's a sort of an emergency.'

Nothing happened. I rang the bell again and waited. A car, speeding up the road, stopped. A door slammed.

'Please can I come in? It's rather import … oof!'

A heavy hand, seizing my shoulder, turned me round. It belonged to a large, hard-faced, young policeman, though not one I recognised. For no reason, I felt guilty.

'Now, what d'you think you're up to, sir?' he said, politely enough but without removing his hand.

'I wanted to use the telephone.'

'There's a public call box opposite the village shop. Why don't you use that?'

'Because it's an emergency and I haven't got any money.'

'So you thought you'd get some here, did you?'

I was confident I could explain myself. 'No, I just wanted to use the phone. You see …'

The front door opening, the fat woman stood before me, red-faced, quivering with rage. 'Well done, officer,' she said. 'I've been watching him. He's been up and down the road, casing the joints. I'll bet he was the one who broke into poor Mr Roman's.'

'Look …'

'You can tell at a glance he's up to no good. What a scruffy, dirty, ugly, little man! He's obviously had a go at someone and been given a taste of his own medicine. What a brute! It wouldn't surprise me to learn he's a murderer, too. It's a good job I spotted him in time.'

'But …'

'And he's armed, just look at that vicious chain.'

'It's for …'

'Thank you, Madam.' The policeman, raising his hand to dam the torrent, looked me straight in the eye and smiled. 'Now, what have you got to say for yourself, sir?'

'I'm not a burglar. The chain's for my dog.'

'Oh really?' he said. 'I see no dog. Would you mind if I take a look in your bag, sir?'

I'd almost forgotten about it. 'It's not important,' I said.

'I'll be the judge of that, sir.' Taking it from me, he tipped it out.

A bundle wrapped in a blood-stained tea towel rolled down the path.

'Murder!' screamed the fat woman.

The policeman stepped back, a look of shock on his face. He poked the bundle with his foot and the meat jutted out.

'What is that?'

'It's a leg of lamb.'

'Why?'

'To feed a police inspector,' I said. I might have phrased it better.

'What?'

'It's for Inspector Hobbes, I'm looking for him.'

'Hobbes? Are you sure he's not looking for you, sir? In connection with the break-in down the road on the afternoon of the second of this month?'

'No, he's disappeared and I'm trying to find him.'

'I've heard no reports of the Inspector disappearing. He's not the sort.'

'This blackguard has probably murdered him,' said the woman, 'so he can escape justice. I bet he's the one who burgled Mr Roman's.'

'Have you been in Mr Roman's house, sir?'

'No, well … umm … yes. I was with Hobbes at the time. It was after the break-in; it was part of his investigation.'

'I was there when the Inspector investigated and don't recall seeing you. You admit you were inside?' The policeman's expression turned as hard as his grip on my shoulder. 'I think, perhaps, you'd better come along to the station and answer a few questions.'

'No, I was there when he went back for another look. I need to find him, he may be in trouble.'

'I know Inspector Hobbes. He can look after himself, if anyone can. I'm afraid you're the one in trouble.' The policeman reached for his handcuffs.

In fact, the young policeman was the one in trouble, for at that moment the cavalry arrived. Or rather, Dregs did. Loping down the garden path with a deep woof, obviously believing I was in danger, he launched himself like a hairy black missile. The policeman, turning too late, Dregs thumped into his midriff with the pace and power of a punch. The poor man, doubling up, grunted, falling backwards into the house, banging his head on an occasional table as he rolled inside. The table collapsed under the impact and became a pile of occasional firewood. The woman screamed again – she was having a most exhilarating afternoon – and slammed the door.

Dregs bounced round me, butting and licking, as if he'd done something clever. I calculated that, though he had stopped me being arrested, he'd probably not improved my situation and I wasn't sure I'd now be able to convince the police to help me. In fact, the way things were going, I felt it more likely they'd arrest me for assaulting a policeman with an offensive weapon, namely a large, hairy dog and, if they banged me up in the cells, I'd have no chance of helping Hobbes. It appeared I was on my own, apart from Dregs, which was a dubious advantage.

I was about to flee the scene, when I remembered the leg of lamb. As I bent to pick it up, Dregs sniffed it and kicked soil over it in apparent disdain. Maybe he thought it would smell better after being buried for a few days. Still, he let me bag it and I scarpered, while he sat down, staring at the door, with his head on one side as if listening. I left him to it. He'd be able to find me if he wanted and I'd be better off without him.

I had to find out what was happening, though I had little idea how to go about it. Reason suggested that, if I sneaked into the Witcherleys' garden and kept out of sight, I'd at least have time to think. I darted up the road, taking some comfort no one else was about, concealing myself between the hedge and a bush. I seemed to be putting myself into, at best, an embarrassing situation and the pressure of thinking I ought to do something was crushing. My face grew hot and my stomach quivered at the thought of what would happen if I'd misread the situation. Yet, the longer I dithered the more I'd get the wind up. I had to be positive.

All the running and stress had left my mouth as dry as chalk, yet slaking my thirst was not my priority. Firstly, I had to relieve my bladder, a regular consequence of meeting Rex. Taking a quiet leak in the hedge, I began operations, deciding, as a start, to scout the garden, to get the lie of the land. Basing my movements on what I'd seen Red Indians do in old westerns, though I doubted they'd ever made so much noise, I stumbled, pushed and crawled through the undergrowth. In such situations, buckskins have distinct advantages over long overcoats. I kept kneeling on its edge or snagging it on branches and thorns, dampness spreading from the tweed knees of my trousers. When a trunk of a huge evergreen tree concealed me, I stood up, wiping the cobwebs from my face, a putrid stench making me retch. My hands were plastered in slimy, disgusting, sticky, brown gloop. I'd got it all over me, the pigeons flapping overhead suggesting the source. I wiped my hands down my trousers, which were already beyond hope, trying not to throw up. There was a downside to being a detective, yet I was not deterred.

I began my reconnaissance with a closer look at the house. The lowering sun, glinting off an array of windows on a single-storey modern extension, connecting the old part of the house to the garage, meant I was too dazzled to see much and my teeth chattered as, scurrying across the lawn, I pressed myself against the wall. Gulping like a goldfish, I peeped into the extension. It was the kitchen, though it looked more like a glossy advert, with lustrous blacks contrasting with creamy whites and the glitter of stainless steel. Although it looked impressive, almost like a work of art, I'd have taken Hobbes's homely kitchen any day, especially with Mrs Goodfellow's cooking.

My anger flared. How dare Rex pay me such a meagre wage when he could afford all this? The kitchen alone must have cost many times my annual salary and then they'd got the house and the cars and the holiday home and everything. It wasn't fair. Yet it was nothing compared to my rage at Rex's lie. How dare he lie to me? How dare he put me through all the crawling round in pigeon shit? How dare he put Mrs Goodfellow through all the worry? And how dare he do anything to Hobbes?

I stopped myself. He obviously dared a lot but what might he have done to Hobbes? How, in fact, could he have done anything? Even though the Editorsaurus was a big bloke, even heavier than Hobbes I guessed, he was fat and lumbering, whereas Hobbes was …Hobbes.

The door, leading into the kitchen, swinging open, I dropped to my knees in the rich loam of a border, flattening myself against the wall, praying nobody decided to venture out.

A whiny voice spoke. 'Shouldn't I at least give him a drink?' It was Tony Derrick.

'He's been in there for ages and …' he paused and muttered. 'OK. Keep your hair on. I was only asking.'

I could hear him moving about, splashing water, opening and shutting doors.

'Where d'you keep your coffee? Thanks … sugar? Milk? OK … cream it is then. Uh, which one's the fridge? I got it … single or double? Chocolate biscuits? Right … can I have one? I'm starving.'

The stream of questions continued for a minute or two and then there was silence. After a while, risking poking my head up, I satisfied myself the kitchen was empty again. Tony had spilt coffee by the sink and a couple of broken biscuits were valiantly attempting to soak up a dribble of cream splashed on the floor beneath the stainless steel door of what I took to be the fridge.

It meant there were at least two people inside, Editorsaurus Rex and Tony and, since Narcisa's car was parked outside, it was likely she was home, too. In which case, who was the 'he' Tony had mentioned? Hobbes? Or Phil?

A timid part of my brain suggested I was jumping to all the wrong conclusions. I tried to ignore it, because part of me was convinced Hobbes was inside and, since he'd been looking for Phil, he might also be there.

Keeping my head below the windows, I crept along the side of the wall like a commando, except commandos usually carry weapons they're trained to use and are not dressed in soggy tweed that's growing ever soggier. The shadows were lengthening and I guessed it had gone four o'clock. Though the huge, red sun was blinding, it wouldn't be long before it no longer peeped over the hedge.

On reaching the spot where the kitchen-extension met the old part of the house, I stood up straight, stretching cramped muscles, noticing a small, dilapidated shed in the far corner of the back lawn, somewhere I thought would make a brilliant hiding place. Scurrying behind it, I looked back, shocked to realise I'd been in full view of the upper windows of the house, but it seemed I'd got away with it. I resolved to be more vigilant, for a momentary carelessness might waste all my efforts and would lead, at best, to intense embarrassment.

Two fears were competing: first, if Hobbes and Phil were being held captive, I, too, soon might be; second, if, by chance or stupidity, I'd got everything wrong, Rex might simply spot me trespassing, call the police and I'd be a laughing stock again. My timid side just wouldn't shut up, urging me to run before I got into something I couldn't get out of. I forced myself to ignore what seemed only common sense, feeling I owed Hobbes something. Yet for a while, all I could do was lurk behind the shed, where the shadows concealed me.

Buttoning my coat, pulling up the collar, thrusting my hands into the pockets, I looked around in the half-light. To one side was a steaming compost heap, to the other, a heavy lawn roller, smothered under a blanket of enormous spiders' webs. Imagining the enormous spiders that had created it, I couldn't stop shuddering, so I forced myself to concentrate on my mission. I peeked round the side of the shed, observing the garden, bright and ruddy in the glow of the setting sun, encircled by a hedge, dotted here and there with tall trees. There was an ornamental pond, a covered swimming pool and a tennis court. A strange vision of Rex floundering about in white shorts, or diving into the water made me snigger, despite, or because of, my nerves. My imagination failed to conjure up an image of Narcisa doing anything similar.

A light coming on in one of house's upper windows, I jerked back behind the shed, very cautiously risking another look, hoping the dusk would conceal me. Narcisa, clad in a glossy blue gown, sat down in front of a dressing table by the window, dabbing something behind her ears, turning as if to speak to someone. Another figure moved into view and, though I could only see his back, his green Hawaiian shirt screamed it was Tony Derrick. He leaned on the window ledge, seemingly entirely at home in her bedroom. When she finished speaking he, nodded, kissing her on the lips and left.

I couldn't take that sort of thing standing up and had to sit on the roller, despite the spiders. Surely, Narcisa and Tony weren't lovers? What could she see in the weasely, whiney, grubby lowlife? If it came to that, what could he see in her? To be fair, she'd looked OK, elegant even, in the *Sorenchester Life* photo, if only because of the crust of makeup. Yet, perhaps neither was fussy. I couldn't understand how Rex fitted in and why he didn't just throw Tony out. I shook my head, glad I didn't live that way.

When I looked again, she'd removed her robe and was wearing only a flimsy, shimmering slip, held up by coat hanger shoulders. Her neck was scrawny, as if it had been stretched, and encircled by a triple string of pearls. As she ran a bony hand through her hair, I turned away, feeling like a peeping Tom. Yet, I had to take another look and this time, to my horror, she was quite bald, apart from a few fluffy, brittle tufts reminiscent of a lawn in a drought. Her sleek blonde hair was nowhere to be seen as she touched up her makeup. Then she stood, disappearing from view for a minute or so, returning in a loose, purple robe with a heavy gold chain around her neck. Bending, picking up her wig, she sat at the table to fit it, the sleeves of her robe slipping down revealing a bracelet. Even from such a distance I was sure it was the one stolen from the museum.

She walked away and the light went out.

As the last lingering tentacles of sunlight slithered below the hedge, I berated myself for failing to make real progress. I was convinced Narcisa had the dragon bracelet and reckoned it was a safe bet she'd stolen the other articles as well. So what? I didn't know why she'd taken them, or why Phil and Hobbes had vanished, or even if there was a genuine connection between the events. Of course, her ancestry might explain her interest in Romanian artefacts but why those particular ones? Surely, there were millions of old Romanian bits and pieces in the world? There had, in fact, been a fair number in Mr Barrington-Oddy's cabinet, yet only one had been taken. It dawned on me that asking unanswerable questions and beating myself up wasn't helping. I was prevaricating, yet I couldn't really blame myself, since I'd never done anything so frightening before. My nervous terrors were not at all alleviated by being alone in the dark.

A childhood memory returned, of an old book of fairy stories at Granny Caplet's, its grotesque illustrations scaring me silly. In particular, the skinny old witch in *Hansel and Gretel* had such a look of cruel wickedness she had haunted my dreams for months. I began to understand my unease, for the shed bore an uncomfortable resemblance to her tumbledown cottage, or it did in my imagination. I tried to laugh it off, for I was starting to believe Hobbes's tall tales. Even so, I couldn't stop myself patting the rotting wood, as if to reassure myself it was not built of gingerbread. He'd really had me going about that, and, despite everything, I smiled, coming to a decision.

'Right then, Andy,' I addressed myself, 'let's get out of here. It won't get any easier.' Forcing my mouth into a determined, devil-may care grin, I stood up, just as something rushed towards me, something too black to be mere shadow. I gasped as it sprang, knocking me onto my back.

It could have been worse, I thought, as Dregs's long, stinky tongue snaked over my face.

'Bloody dog,' I muttered, patting his hairy head.

I was all over dog drool and he was all over exuberance.

The back door of the house opened and Tony Derrick spoke. 'No, I'm not getting twitchy. I really heard something. I'm gonna take a look.'

A torch beam flashed across the lawn. Dregs, releasing me, loped towards it with a woof. Diving back behind the shed, I lay still, trembling.

Dregs growled the way he did when he wanted to play.

Tony screamed. 'Get it off!'

'Shut up,' said Narcisa, 'or the neighbours will be round complaining.'

A bright light flooding the garden, my hidey-hole was no longer dark.

'Get it off me!' Tony sounded as if he was going to cry.

'It's only a dog.'

'Get the bastard off!'

'Shut up, he's not hurting you.'

Something hissed and Dregs yelped.

'That's got rid of him,' said Narcisa.

'About bloody time. What is that stuff?'

'Pepper spray. It's not nice but he'll get over it, poor mutt.'

'Poor mutt?' Tony spluttered. 'It was Hobbes's bloody dog, you know? And Hobbes won't be too far away. You'd better hide the spray.'

She laughed. 'You're right, he isn't far away but, don't worry, he'll be no trouble.'

'What d'you mean?'

'You'll see,' she said. 'Now come along. There's still plenty to do.'

Their footsteps receded and a moment later the light went out. Dregs had come to my rescue again and I just hoped he wasn't going to suffer too much for it. Standing up, I brushed myself down. Narcisa's assertion that Hobbes wasn't far away gave me reason to believe I was doing the right thing, yet her confidence that he'd be no trouble had me worried, even more worried than the prospect of running into her pepper spray.

Drawing a deep breath, I tiptoed across the darkened lawn, creeping around the outside of the house, peeping into every room. The furniture and carpets looked expensive and comfortable and nothing seemed out of place, except that I couldn't see anyone. As the upstairs lights were off, it was a puzzle, because, so far as I could tell, no one had left the house. I was baffled, though I was sure of one thing – I didn't want to be standing outside for too long. A brutal gust caught me in the back of the neck and goose pimples erupted over my skin.

'C'mon, you idiot,' I muttered, my breath steaming, 'you've got to do something.'

I stole round to the back door, which was locked. The kitchen behind it lay in darkness, though a small ventilation window above my head was open. Pulling myself up by the frame, kneeling on the narrow sill, I squeezed my head and shoulders through the window, standing up, carefully, wriggling and squirming. I'd got so far through that I was starting to worry about what I was going to land on, when something snagged. I couldn't slither forwards or push myself back and, losing my footing, ended up balanced on my ribs, a hard, pointy knob sticking into my solar plexus, despite the layers of clothes. An involuntary groan, partly pain, mostly despair, squeezed out and a new proverb came to mind: 'Don't try to squeeze through inadequate gaps in inappropriate clothing.' It wasn't snappy, yet I wished I'd thought of it beforehand. I writhed and wriggled and it made no difference.

Soft, heavy footsteps approached and there was nothing I could do except cringe and wait for whatever happened next.

'What's going on in here?' asked Editorsaurus Rex.

At such times it's impossible to be nonchalant, though I did my best, smiling, keeping my chin up, as the kitchen light flickered on. I'd been discovered in a most embarrassing position. Slumping, dangling, I awaited my doom. A pair of fluffy white socks sailed into view across a sea of glossy black and white tiles and a soft, moist hand lifted my head.

'Capstan, what the Devil are you doing?' The Editorsaurus's voice sounded strange and there was curiosity instead of the fury I'd anticipated. My head dropped.

'Just hanging about,' I said, attempting an ingratiating grin.

'Oh, that's all right then. So long as you're not burgling.'

'Oh no, sir. I'd never do such a thing.'

'I'm very glad to hear it. Now, are you going to stay there all day, or are you coming in for a drinkie?'

I realised why he sounded so odd – he was dead drunk, though his speech was controlled and precise rather than slurred.

'I'd love a drink, sir, only I appear to be stuck.'

'I'm not surprised, it's far too small for you.' His voice grew angry. 'Not too small for Narcisa's rat-boy, though. Oh no, he squeezed himself in all right. Nasty, dirty, little sneak. Are you sure you're not burgling?'

'No, sir, I'm here for a drink. If you wouldn't mind giving me a hand?'

'Sorry Capstan. Of course, you are. It's very good of you to visit me on my birthday and I see you've brought a present. Thank you.' He took the plastic bag from me. It had been dangling from my arm for so long it was almost part of me.

The next few moments were painful and undignified. He lifted and shoved me, the window frame creaking, as if on the point of collapse. There was a tearing sound, a handful of buttons clattered across the tiles and I slithered backwards, feet scrabbling, landing heavily on my back in the garden. By the time I'd recovered my breath and got to my feet, Rex was lumbering away, swaying like an elephant, my bag twisting in his hand. I banged on the door but he was oblivious.

My skin, apart from the odd, additional scrape, had survived intact, yet most of the buttons from my coat, jacket and shirt were gone and my clothes were flapping in the breeze. After a few moments to recover, I had what I considered a great idea. Stripping my top half down to my vest, I made another attempt on the window. Though it was still a squeeze, after grunting and groaning and sweating like a wrestler, I began to slide through.

Then I stopped. The knob thing had snagged me again and my entire weight was suspended on my trouser waistband. I writhed and wriggled until, with a long, slow, zip-rending rip, I slid forwards, shedding my trousers as a snake sheds its skin. Gently, sedately even, I slithered onto the kitchen floor, looking back to where the tattered remnants of a once fine piece of tailoring fluttered in the breeze.

At such times it's important to count your blessings. I could count one: my underwear had survived. Apart from that, my situation was desperate. I glanced down at my muddy shoes, tartan socks and the long white underpants and realised I could count two blessings: they were clean on that morning. Still, if anyone caught me, how could I explain skulking in my ex-boss's house in my underwear? Besides, I still had to get home somehow. My face glowed as I imagined the photos in the *Bugle* and the sarcastic comments PC Wilkes would throw at me in the cell. Why did these things keep happening to me? All I'd ever wanted was a quiet life and I didn't deserve this. At least, though, I was in a place where I could wash my filthy hands and have a glass of water, both of which I did.

Then, with a lump of fear in my stomach and a cringe in my walk, I began to prowl through the house.

I found Rex in the next room, lying flat on his back on the deep, soft cream carpet, an empty gin bottle clutched to his heart, looking as peaceful as a sleeping baby, though no infant could fill the room with the noises he was producing. He snored, gurgling and farting like a flatulent hippopotamus and I doubted he'd regain consciousness for many hours. Retrieving my carrier bag, I left him to sleep it off, though, before going, I made free with his drinks cabinet. Opening a bottle of whisky, pouring a considerable measure into a crystal tumbler, I gulped it down. The liquid fire, searing its way towards my stomach, felt good.

I carried out a rapid search downstairs, where everything, apart from Rex, was quiet. Then, finding myself in the hall at the bottom of the stairs, I began to climb into the darkness, my footsteps muffled by the deep pale-yellow carpet, an admirable aid to sneaking, or so I thought until, reaching a landing where the stairs turned at a right angle, I glanced back. I'd left a muddy trail and there was nothing I could do about it, so wiping my feet, I carried on to the first floor, where a brass candelabra with three flickering candles rested on a small wooden table, providing the only illumination. I picked it up, surprised by its weight, and took it with me, since I feared turning on a light would draw attention to me. Candlelit exploration of an old unfamiliar house where I had no right to be was not a soothing occupation, every movement of the flickering shadows, every creak of a floorboard, making my heart race.

I looked into three empty bedrooms before finding the one in which I'd seen Narcisa and Tony. A flowery scent, overly sweet and cloying, seemed strongest by a small bottle on the dressing table. When I removed the stopper, I sneezed. It was a powerful scent, yet familiar. Averting my eyes from the crumpled white sheets on the four-poster bed, I noticed an ancient leather-bound book on a small table at its side. Putting down the candelabra, I opened it, a sheet of paper fluttering to the carpet.

It was a letter, written on Sorenchester Museum paper. Picking it up, I read:

Dear Mrs Witcherley,

I have acquired this volume, which I believe to be the one detailing the ritual in which you expressed an interest. My asking price for this exceedingly fine and rare copy is £10,000 in cash. In addition, I have knowledge of a fine bracelet with an established provenance to the Order of the Dragon. I am confident I can put it your way, for the right price. I must once again emphasise the importance of treating any such transactions in strict confidence.

Yours sincerely,

Ray Biggs, Curator.

Hobbes's suspicion about Mr Biggs appeared to have been justified. Replacing the letter, I examined the book. It was made of parchment or something, with heavy, black gothic printing and a smell of dust and age. On the first page was a woodcut of a castle, familiar to me from the label on the Romanian beer bottle and, a couple of pages further on, I came across an illustration of a dragon with its tail in its mouth. The text was incomprehensible, in a foreign language, yet, on seeing the word 'Dracul' several times, the hairs on the back of my neck rose and stiffened.

My worry and fear levels rising to critical, the animal part of my brain tried to convince me that Narcisa was a vampire and that I should run away. Though a more rational part tried to point out that vampires were fictional, I couldn't stop myself wondering if I'd ever seen her in full daylight. My teeth were chattering, my mouth was as dry as chalk and I was trembling all over. In fairness, I was in a weird Romanian woman's bedroom, lit only by flickering candlelight and I'd just discovered a book, apparently about vampires. Furthermore, convinced she was a thief, I hoped that was the worst of it, though I had a terrible fear she'd done something dreadful to Hobbes. Finally, I was dressed only in my underwear, which always puts one at a disadvantage.

In the circumstances, I think my nerves were entirely justified. Sitting down on the chair by the dressing table, I glanced in the mirror, shocked by how scared I looked, unable to suppress a paralysing horror that something was creeping up behind, yet, when I forced myself to turn and face it, there was nothing.

I heard a click and a stair creaked. Someone was coming. Or was it something? Wanting to scream and run, I made do with diving under the bed and cowering like a coward.

'Where did you say you put it?' shouted Tony.

'On the table on the landing,' Narcisa replied from downstairs, 'and bring the book too – it's in the bedroom.'

'The candelabra's not here. Anyway, haven't we got enough already?'

'Don't be stupid. Just fetch it.'

'I'm not being stupid.' Cursing softly, he entered the bedroom and shouted, 'it was in your room all the time.'

His footsteps drawing close, I held my breath. When they moved away, the candlelight faded, leaving me in utter darkness and confusion. Tony had come from downstairs and Narcisa was downstairs, though I was certain only Rex had been down there. Where had they been hiding?

'There's mud on the stairs,' said Tony. 'Someone's in the house.'

My whole body going into an ecstasy of terror, I thought I was going to be sick. I wanted a wee; I wanted a crucifix; I wanted garlic; I wanted Buffy the Vampire slayer; most of all, I wanted to be out of there.

'It'll just be Fatso staggering around drunk,' said Narcisa. 'Now, hurry up. It's nearly time.'

I lay still until I regained control of my limbs. What was it nearly time for?

I crawled out, creeping towards the staircase, my legs wobbling as I stood up and tiptoed downstairs, which was now in darkness, apart from the glimmer of a distant street lamp lighting up the porch and hall. The mystery of Narcisa and Tony's whereabouts held no interest for me just then. I wanted out. Slipping into the porch, fumbling with the latch, almost sobbing with relief, I opened the front door, shivering as my body was exposed to the night air. I was about to run when, hearing muffled sounds from below, I realised they were coming from the cellars. I could have kicked myself; of course a house of this age would have cellars. I just hadn't seen the door.

The revelation didn't stop me fleeing. What did stop me was the chanting of deep male voices from below ground, making my legs all wobbly again. How many people were down there? Had I stumbled into some sort of Satanic Mass? Then, to my surprise, I chuckled, recognising the chanting as the same recording I'd heard the ghouls playing. Somehow, I found it soothing, because the ghouls, though terrifying, had as Hobbes pointed out, not been so bad. Not really. In fact, other than trying to bury me alive, they'd been pretty harmless. With any luck vampires, or Satanists, were similar.

Forcing myself back inside, fortifying my courage with another raid on the whisky bottle, I searched for the cellar door, finding it under the stairs, in plain view, if only I'd been looking.

As I put my ear against it to listen, it clicked open and I stumbled through onto a creaky wooden staircase, cool, damp air and an earthy odour surrounding me. There was light down there, candlelight, to judge from the flickering. I swallowed, tiptoeing down, as the chanting grew louder. A familiar scent struck me, the same cloying, flowery scent as in Narcisa's room, though heavier, if it were possible.

On reaching the bottom, I saw I'd entered a vaulted cellar, similar to, though even larger than Hobbes's. To start with, I was amazed at the quantity of wine down there. Hundreds, possibly thousands, of bottles were laid to rest in racks on the smooth limestone floor.

The light emanated from an archway at the far end. Creeping towards it, my footsteps echoing treacherously, I hoped the chanting would drown them out.

Flattening myself against the wall by the arch, taking a vast breath, I poked my head round the corner, jerking back, dazzled and shaking, as if I'd gone down with malaria. On the other side was a cavernous chamber packed with burning candles, where a forest of sturdy limestone buttresses supported a low ceiling. In the middle, in a space like a clearing, stood a stone altar. Next to it, on a wooden table, the Roman cup reflected red in the candlelight. What had scared me most, though, was the long, naked, glinting dagger, lying with its point to the cup. Though I'd not seen or heard Narcisa or Tony down there, in my imagination they were lurking in every shadow, waiting to do me harm. An incongruous thought occurred: I'd always enjoyed watching this sort of thing in films and on telly. It wasn't the same in real life.

Curiosity, wrestling with cowardice, got it, rather to my astonishment, in an arm-lock, yet without quite gaining total submission. The chanting rang even louder, muffling my clumsy footsteps, which was good, reducing my chances of hearing movement, which wasn't. As I slipped into the chamber and cringed behind the nearest pillar, I heard a cry of despair from a man, though not from Hobbes. It turned into a scream, taking all my strength, even as it blew the fog of trivia from my mind.

The cry echoed above the chanting. 'Water! Please! Oh Christ, it burns.'

Though pain and fear had distorted it, I knew the voice and any remaining animosity washed away in a flood of sympathy. It was Phil Waring and he was in big trouble. Fighting an impulse to rush blindly to the rescue, I told myself that getting both of us into a mess would not help. Despite my innate cowardice suggesting immediate flight, I steadied myself, acknowledging the importance of finding out precisely what I was up against, and where he was, since his cries, echoing round the smooth curved walls, confused my senses. As I became aware of other voices, quieter and indistinct, I wished I had Hobbes with me.

I sneaked a glance round the pillar, seeing no one, although a dark painting of a mediaeval king, hanging in an alcove behind the altar, made me start. Recalling Mrs Tomkins, the cook, telling Hobbes that Mr Roman had sold a creepy painting, I could easily believe it was this one, for there was nothing but malice in the King's eyes, nothing but threat in the way he held the long, naked, glinting dagger over a golden chalice. Dagger and chalice looked identical to the ones on the altar.

I shuddered as the chanting faded away. In the ensuing stillness, footsteps approached.

'Move!' yelled Tony.

My heart leapt and, for a moment, I thought I'd been discovered but he was shouting at Phil, whom he was goading into a stumbling walk with a spiked pole. His strange gait seemed to be more because he couldn't see than because of the chains weighing down his wrists and ankles. It was almost as strange to see him unshaven, tieless and dirty, with sweat stains around his armpits, as to see him in a dungeon. He flinched as the chanting started again.

I shivered, wishing I'd been more careful with my clothes, that I'd had the sense to bring the whisky bottle, something far more useful than the leg of lamb I was still carting around like an idiot.

Tony, enveloped in a long, heavy, grey robe, with a deep hood, and only his beaky nose jutting out, reminded me of a vulture. Narcisa was close behind, wrapped in the deep folds of the purple gown I'd seen earlier, walking slowly, majestically, with bowed head, her arms folded across her chest, holding the book I'd seen in the bedroom.

Tony forced Phil to lie on the altar. Staying in the shadows, sneaking a little closer, praying they wouldn't see me, I slipped behind another pillar. When I risked a look, Phil was stretched on his back as Tony secured his chains. Narcisa stood over him, facing me. I jerked back, amazed she hadn't noticed me. Taking a moment for a better look around the chamber, I noted the small barred cell at the far end, presumably where they'd been holding Phil, but saw no sign of Hobbes. I couldn't grasp why they'd made Phil a prisoner, though it was not difficult to surmise that whatever they were planning would not be to his benefit. Only one person could put a stop to whatever was going to happen. Me.

I risked another glance. Narcisa was in the same position, Tony at her side. A few candles flickered close to where Phil was writhing uselessly against his chains yet, otherwise, the air was still. Narcisa raised her skinny arms, the heavy ring on her finger and the dragon bracelet on her wrist glinted; the chanting stopped.

She spoke into the sudden silence, reading from the book, her voice tremulous at first, as if she, too, was nervous. I couldn't understand the foreign words.

'What are you going to do?' Phil's voice cracked into a squeak.

She ignored him. Tony sniggered, glanced at her and went quiet.

'You can't do this.' Anger and fear competed in Phil's voice.

'Shut it,' said Tony.

Narcisa's incantation grew more confident, powerful, drowning out Phil's protestations, as I cursed myself, wishing I'd thought to pick up some sort of weapon in my search round the house. I didn't like the look of things one little bit, and the glittering dagger was never far from my mind. There was something in the way it sliced the light to suggest its blade was razor sharp: not something you'd choose for cleaning your nails but ideal for a human sacrifice.

'Hand me the sanguinary chalice,' said Narcisa.

'The what?' asked Tony from the darkness of his hood.

'The sanguinary chalice.'

'Uh … you mean this old cup thing?'

'Just give me the bloody cup.'

'OK, keep your hair on.' He handed it to her.

'What do you mean by that?' Her voice was sharp.

'Nothing, just be cool. Can I open a bottle of plonk now?'

'If you must.' Narcisa, raising the cup in both hands, continued speaking in the strange, droning language. I saw she was wearing the gleaming dragon ring on her middle finger.

Holding my breath, I squeezed deeper into the shadows, as Tony walked past towards the wine cellar, returning with a bottle, opening it with the corkscrew on his penknife. She lowered the cup, placing it on the altar by Phil's head.

'Hand me the Dagger of Tepes,' she said.

'Uh … the big knife?' asked Tony.

'Of course.'

Picking it up by the blade, presenting the hilt to her, he yelped as she grasped it.

'Ow! You nearly had my bloody finger off. You'd better be careful or you might really hurt someone.' He groped inside his robe and wrapped a handkerchief round his hand. The grubby cloth darkened.

'What are you doing?' Phil blinked at the dagger through red-rimmed eyes.

My eyes watered in sympathy.

'Shut up!' shouted Tony.

'It's all right,' said Narcisa. 'There's no reason why he shouldn't know. Not now. Mr Waring, I must apologise for detaining you like this, but you did poke your nose into my affairs at an awkward time. Yet, in its way, your arrival has proved most opportune. The ritual demands blood and your sacrifice will give me new life, so I must thank you.'

'Mrs Witcherley, what are you talking about?'

'Simply, you will die for me. Greater love has no man than to lay down his life.'

'You're going to murder me?' Unsurprisingly, Phil sounded terrified.

'No, not murder, sacrifice. Don't worry, the blade is razor sharp, as Igor has discovered to his cost. You'll not feel much and the expenditure of your blood will not be in vain. Think of it as an honour.'

Phil said nothing, shaking even more than I was.

'What d'you mean, calling me Igor?' asked Tony, whining. 'That's an insult that is. It's adding insult to injury. My finger's bloody sore.'

'Just a joke,' she said.

'But you're not really going to kill him are you? You're just going to frighten him? Make sure he shuts up?'

'Oh, wake up, you idiot. Do you really imagine I'd go to these lengths to frighten a journalist? If I'd only wanted to shut him up, I'd have got Rex to have a word with him. My husband is a fat old goat but he has his uses.'

'You told me no one was going to get hurt. You said red wine would do as well as blood.'

'You heard what you wanted to hear. Now, be quiet, I need to concentrate.' She resumed her chanting.

'No.' Tony faced up to her, pointing his finger. 'You called me an idiot and that's not nice. I thought we had something together, you and me.'

'Think what you want and be quiet.'

'I won't. You lied to me.'

'You were useful. That's enough.'

'You used me.'

'If I did, you had your fun and were handsomely paid. Rex's bank account is another of his good features.'

I wish I could claim I was planning a brave and intelligent intervention but, the truth is, I was cowering in the darkness, too terrified to move, yet holding a faint hope that Tony would somehow prevail.

'It's not right,' he whined. 'You said you loved me and that we were made for each other. It's why I helped you steal everything. It wasn't the money.'

Unable to believe his claim, to my horror, I snorted with disdain.

'What was that? I heard someone. Honest.'

'It doesn't matter,' said Narcisa. 'Just shut up and let me get on.'

'But someone's in here.'

I retreated deeper into the shadows, awaiting discovery and whatever came of it.

'It'll just be Hobbes,' she laughed.

'Hobbes? What d'you mean Hobbes?' Tony, pulling his hood back, stared around wildly.

'Mr Waring wasn't the only one snooping into my business. Hobbes turned up too, shortly after he'd let you go.'

'Where is he?'

'That's not your concern, he'll not interfere. Now shut up.'

So, Hobbes was down there and I couldn't guess what she might have done to him to be so confident. I stole towards the very back of the chamber, where there were no candles and the gloom became blackness. The heavy, almost narcotic, scent of flowers faded and I became aware, ever so faintly at first, of the feral odour I associated with Hobbes.

As Narcisa resumed her chanting, the strange words echoing hypnotically round the chamber, I hesitated, torn between trying to find Hobbes and trying to rescue Phil. The latter was in imminent peril, assuming Narcisa meant what she said, and I had no doubt she intended to kill, yet Hobbes would be able to stop her far better than I could. In all honesty, I'm not a fighter; I doubted I could overcome Tony and, as for Narcisa, something about her made me suspect she knew how to hurt a man. Besides, she'd got the pepper spray and the dagger. Again, I dithered, though I was starting to think that, if I couldn't find Hobbes very soon, I would have to do something.

Do or die – it wasn't a happy prospect.

'You're going too far,' yelled Tony, sounding angry and scared. 'Stop it now, or I'll stop you myself.'

Narcisa laughed. 'You're too late.'

Clasping the dagger with both hands, she raised it above her head. Phil screamed.

Tony, as fast as a weasel, caught her wrist, forcing her backwards. The hood of her gown fell back and for a moment her blonde wig clung to the top of her skull before sliding to the floor. Tony grunted, maintaining his grip, making her cry out, making her drop the dagger, barely managing to twist his foot out of the way as it stuck in the floor. His movement allowed her to break free, to pull something from her gown. Her back being towards me, I guessed she'd gone for her pepper spray.

Tony, his eyes bulging with fear, spun round and bolted. Narcisa turning after him, was not holding the spray but a small revolver. There were two explosions, shocking and painful in the confined space, sparks sprayed from the wall above Tony's head as he scurried through the arch, fleeing like a hunted rat. If she intended hitting him, and I'm sure she did, she was a rotten shot. I dropped to the floor like a pile of dirty washing.

It took a few moments to work out why I'd got a dead leg, and why a hole had appeared at the top of my left thigh, oozing blood and burning. A ricochet must have hit me, though it must have been nearly spent, because I could touch the bullet's distorted shape, slightly proud of my skin. It still felt red-hot. Licking my fingers, as you do when snuffing a candle, I tugged at it, almost fainting as it popped out with a sucking sound. Unable to suppress a groan, I lay, panting as the agony slowly subsided.

'Well, well,' said Narcisa looking down on me, her gun pointing at my face, 'fancy meeting you here, Mr Caplet. And dressed so formally, too.'

'The name's Capstan,' I said. 'I mean, no it isn't. It is Caplet.'

As she smiled, I stared at her teeth, trying to see if they were suspiciously sharp.

'Make up your mind. Rex said you were a ditherer. He still gave you many chances, the soft fool. I see you've been injured – a couple of inches over and you'd be a gelding. Well, never mind. Stand up.'

My wound throbbing, blood trickling down my leg, I pulled myself upright, leaning against a pillar for support. 'What are you going to do? Are you going to call the police?'

She laughed. 'Your reputation for stupidity doesn't do you justice. I'm going to have to shoot you. You've seen far too much.'

I rested my forehead on the pillar, its rough, cool solidity somehow soothing, though my heart was thumping, as if I'd run a marathon with Dregs. My breathing was fast and shallow and not enough and I could see Narcisa, as if at the end of a tunnel, raising her revolver, taking a step closer, taking aim. I thought she must really be a rotten shot to do that. But it put her within range. Swinging my arm, I watched the carrier bag, as if in slow motion, straining under the weight of the leg of lamb, describing a perfect arc straight into the side of her head. The revolver, flying from her hand, clattered on the stone floor as she went down like the great white hope.

A strange mix of elation and horror combined with sharp pain as I swayed over Narcisa.

'Who's stupid now?' I asked, silently thanking Mrs Goodfellow for my unlikely weapon.

Phil's voice brought me back to myself. 'What's happening? Andy, is it you? What are you doing here?'

Before I could respond, my leg buckling, I stumbled backwards into heavy, musty cloth, like a curtain, grabbing at it for balance. As it ripped away, I plunged into emptiness.

I dropped a long way before hitting something hard, if not as hard as I feared, and came to rest on a cold stone floor, lying flat on my back, stunned and winded. As breathing returned, I sucked in lungfuls of cool, fetid air, sitting up, still clutching a fragment of cloth, wondering what had happened, while my eyes adjusted to the faint light filtering in from somewhere above. I'd fallen into a pit, four or five metres deep at a guess, and, maybe three metres across. A pile of leaves in the corner had saved me from harm.

The leaves moved and an animal odour filled my nostrils. Something snarled and I leaped to my feet, despite the agony shooting through my leg, as an unkempt, ugly head emerged.

'Hobbes!' I gasped. 'Are you alright?'

Growling, he stood up, sniffing the air like a dog, staring without apparent recognition. It worried me. Even worse, he was looking at me the way a starving man looks at a steak dinner. Flattening myself against the wall, I edged away.

'It's me,' I said, 'you know ... Andy.'

He was following my every movement, tense like a predator, licking his lips and swallowing.

'What's wrong? I'm sorry I fell on you ... stay back!'

Blood, trickling into my sock, it felt as if I'd stepped into a warm, sticky puddle as I began to panic, fearing what the scent of blood might do to him. Then some words I'd heard a few hours earlier, when the world had been a friendlier place, came into my head, 'He'll be hungry and I ought to tell you, dear, he can get rather wild when he's hungry. You'd best take the leg of lamb.'

As I upended the bag, Hobbes pounced. I screamed as, with one hand, he tossed me over my shoulder into the leaves. Snarling, he turned his back on me, like a lion shielding a carcass from a jackal. Covering my ears to drown out the growls, the slurping, the tearing of flesh, the crunching of bone, I prayed the lamb wouldn't just be the appetiser. Nightmare minutes passed as the slobbering and cracking continued.

I had to get out of the pit or die, yet the walls were smooth and sheer, unclimbable except, maybe, to a gecko. I contemplated yelling for help, yet Phil was chained up, Tony had run away and Rex, even if my voice could reach him, was dead drunk. Accepting my fate with all the dignity I could muster, I began to cry like a snotty little kid. It wasn't fair after all I'd done.

That thought snapped me out of it. All my imagined brilliance in finding Hobbes and Phil, in knocking out Narcisa, came to nothing now I was stuck in that dismal hole. I hadn't actually rescued anyone, but at least I'd tried, which was no comfort whatsoever.

Hobbes stood up, loping towards me, still carrying a hefty chunk of bone. I shrank back.

'Thanks for that,' he said, 'I was rather peckish.'

'Hobbes?' I stared into his face. Bristles sprouted from his chin and flecks of raw meat were stuck to his lips and between his teeth as he smiled. By God, I had never been so pleased to see a smile in all my life!

'Yes. Sorry if I alarmed you.'

Getting to my feet, I damn near hugged the bastard. 'You scared the life out of me,' I said, damn near to kicking the bastard.

'Oops,' he said. 'We'd better get out of here, and quickly. Your leg needs treatment and Mrs Witcherley is waking up.'

'How can you possibly know that?'

'Trust me.'

'Umm … we can't get out of here.'

'We can try.'

'Haven't you tried already? You must've been down here for ages?'

He nodded. 'I did have a go, of course, but the rock's too hard and brittle.' He showed me his hands, his nails all torn and bloody. 'However, you may have provided a solution.'

Taking the bone, which he'd gnawed into a crude pick, he attacked the wall.

Stone chips flying in all directions, I hung back out of harm's way, sticking a finger into the hole in my leg to slow the oozing, though the sensation made my head float. I had to close my eyes until the nausea and faintness abated, yet it wasn't long before I could pay attention. He was not, as I'd supposed, making a mad assault on the wall. He was excavating ledges to serve as toe and finger holds.

'She's got Phil chained to an altar,' I said. 'She was going to kill us so I knocked her out.'

Hobbes, grunting, pulled himself up, wedging his feet into a small hole at waist-height. Bits of stone fell at my feet. 'I know,' he said. 'He's very frightened and she's regaining consciousness. I must work harder.'

I didn't bother asking how he knew. He was speeding up, despite having to hold on with one hand, the sinews on the back of his neck bulging with the effort. He still had a long way to go. Above us, Narcisa groaned and muttered.

Two thirds of the way up, he paused, gnawing at the bone's edge, sharpening it I guessed. As he examined it, he slipped, falling at my feet. Though he leaped back up in an instant, I'd seen the sweat streaming down his face and neck and heard how hard and fast he was breathing.

A light shone into the pit.

'Stop right there,' said Narcisa, standing above us, the revolver in one hand, a candelabra in the other.

Without thinking, I began hurling debris and, though I don't think I actually hit her, she obviously hadn't expected resistance and ducked back. Her head appeared twice more and volleys of rocks kept her at bay. Hobbes, ignoring her, was making astonishing progress. She didn't return again but once more, from a distance, I heard her intoning the strange words of her ritual.

'Hurry! She's going to kill him.' I nearly wept.

Stone chips flew as the incantation continued. I couldn't stop myself hopping in a frenzy of agonised helplessness, wishing I had some inkling what she was on about, wishing I could do something.

At last, Hobbes, stretching out a long arm, grabbed the edge of the pit, hanging for a moment by his fingertips. With a grunt, he swung up and onto the floor.

He beckoned. 'C'mon, Andy, and quickly.' Then he was gone.

My leg throbbed and spasmed as I began to climb, yet the holds were so far apart and so narrow, I only managed a couple before falling. Though pain made me cry out, I had another go and was balanced on a narrow ledge, stretching for a handhold when a shot rang out. The shock making me lose my grip, I slid down the wall, skinning my elbows and jarring my leg. I barely noticed the pain, as another shot echoed around, followed by a succession of shots.

'Hobbes!' I yelled and, forgetting impossibility, launched myself up the wall and over the edge. Narcisa screamed as I got to my feet. Hobbes had his back to me and he'd got her by the throat. She kicked and howled as he jerked her above his head, as if he meant to dash her brains out against the wall.

'No,' I said. 'Don't!'

He turned, staring at me for a long moment, as if puzzled, blood soaking his shirt front, dripping onto the stone floor. 'You're right,' he said. 'I should never hurt a lady. Thank you.'

He fell onto his face. She skidded across the floor like a stone, bouncing over a frozen pond until she came to rest against the altar and lay still. As still as Hobbes.

'Andy!' Phil cried, sounding desperate, 'get these bloody chains off me. Please.'

'Hold on,' I shouted, hurrying towards Hobbes. 'Are you alright?'

He wasn't. Kneeling, sweating with the strain, I rolled him onto his back. He didn't even twitch. Four neat round holes pierced his front and my hands were red and sticky with hot blood.

Putting my face in my hands, I groaned, knowing I'd failed. Yet Phil was sobbing and begging for release and, after what he'd been through, I couldn't blame him. My leg throbbed like a voodoo drum as, pulling myself together, I stumbled towards him. Hobbes, after all, had come here to rescue him, so it was the least I could do and the least seemed to be the most I would achieve.

Phil gasped as I reached him. 'Your face! What's wrong with your face?'

'There's nothing wrong with it,' I said, infuriated. I was trying to save his life and all he could do was insult me.

'It's covered in blood. Have you been shot?'

'Yes, in the leg.'

'But your face?'

'Oh … umm … it's Hobbes's mostly. He's hurt.'

Although I couldn't find the keys to the padlocks securing Phil's chains, I managed to unbolt the shackles that anchored them. He sat up, clanking and groaning like Marley's ghost, staring at me, looking puzzled.

'Andy,' he asked. 'Where are your trousers?'

'In the kitchen window.'

He nodded. 'Great. How did you get here? I thought I was going to die. It's been awful.'

As he sobbed, I wrapped an awkward arm around his shoulders, despite his stink.

'There, there,' I said, feeling useless and embarrassed, 'but I've got to help Hobbes now. She shot him.'

'Why? And why did she want to kill me? And why here? Like this? What's going on?'

Unable to give a satisfactory reply, I shrugged, hobbling back towards Hobbes, kneeling beside him, wishing I could remember what to do. The thing was, Rex, insisting that everyone working for the *Bugle* should know at least basic first aid, had made everyone take a course. Ingrid had been on mine, and having been far too interested in her short skirt to pay attention to anything else, the ABC of resuscitation was all that came to mind, the instructor having banged on about it for long enough. Unfortunately, unable to remember why, I could have kicked myself as the blood spread and steamed.

Phil knew what to do, of course. Clanking his chains, kneeling opposite me, pulling Hobbes's head back, he peered into his mouth. 'His airway's clear,' he said, 'and he's breathing, though not very well. I'll check his circulation.' He poked around Hobbes's neck. 'I can't find a pulse.'

My leg kept erupting into spasms of hurt and my body shook with cold and shock. The stink of hot, fresh blood and its tacky feel as it dried on my hands was getting to me, so, feeling my head floating, I closed my eyes and, had Phil not grunted unexpectedly, might have fainted. On opening my eyes, I found he'd beaten me to it, slumping across Hobbes like a wet blanket. I shook him. 'Wake up.' There was no response, except that he slipped to the floor, leaving it all up to me. I gritted my teeth.

At least I now knew the ABC stood for Airways, Breathing and Circulation and, though I couldn't find a pulse either, the blood still pumping from the holes suggested he was still alive and that I should plug the leaks. Without bandages or dressings, I had to improvise. Picking up the dagger, cutting strips from Phil's nice silk shirt, I removed my vest and, folding it into a pad, used the strips to bind it over Hobbes's wounds.

'Right,' I said out loud, though I doubted he could hear, 'that should staunch the bleeding while I go and phone for an ambulance. Don't worry.'

Pushing myself up, I staggered towards the arch, convinced Hobbes was a goner.

'Stop right there,' said Narcisa.

Her makeup had run, she had a lump the size of a duck egg on her forehead, a purple bruise on the cheek where I'd hit her, and she'd put her wig on askew. Though she looked grotesque and battered, she was holding the revolver in a steady hand. I had a vision of myself standing before her, facing death, bloodied and shocked and surprisingly heroic. Strangely, I felt little fear.

'You couldn't hit a barn door at this distance.'

'You could be right,' she said grinning and her teeth looked uncannily white in the candlelight, 'so, you'd better come closer.'

'I'm not that stupid.'

She laughed and sneered, 'Oh, but you are. If you don't, I'll shoot him.' She pointed the gun at Phil's head.

Even she couldn't possibly miss at that range, so forced to comply, I limped towards her as slowly as possible, hoping for the best.

'Good boy,' she said. 'Now, if you don't mind, or, let's face it, even if you do, I want you to lift Mr Waring back onto the altar.'

'No,' I said.

'No is not the answer I expect when I've got a gun in my hand. Do you imagine you're being heroic? You ought to take a look in the mirror sometime. You're a mess. Now, move him before I get angry.'

'No.'

'There's no chivalry in young men these days. Are you sure you mean no?'

'No. I mean, yes, I'm sure I mean no.'

'Oh, well,' she said and raised the gun. 'Parting is such sweet sorrow.'

'And parkin is such sweet cake.' I couldn't help thinking that my attempt at a James Bond-style witty riposte hadn't quite reached the standard. They were hardly famous last words and I grimaced, though I didn't anticipate them being either famous or last.

She squeezed the trigger.

Nothing happened. She squeezed it again and again.

My mind was clear and any fear was minimal. I'd counted how many shots she'd fired. 'You're out of ammo,' I said.

Screaming, she hurled the revolver at me but it was a real girlie throw, one even I might have bettered. It clattered to the floor behind.

'Missed!' I glanced over my shoulder to see where it had landed and, in case she'd got more bullets, picked it up, finding it heavier than I'd imagined. Realising she was too dangerous to leave on her own, I knew she'd have to come with me while I phoned for help. I congratulated myself on forgetting nothing.

Except for one thing: the dagger. Terror chewed my guts, yet it was still lying beside Hobbes, out of her view. Unfortunately, it was not the only thing I'd forgotten.

She stuck the can of pepper spray in my face, squeezing the release, and it would have done for me, had the liquid burst out in a powerful jet instead of dribbling and dripping harmlessly to the ground.

'It's all gone,' I said, laughing, which was a mistake.

She leaped on me like an infuriated cat and, though I did my best against the clawing, spitting and biting, she'd taken me by surprise. A well-manicured talon, slashing at my eyes, I covered up as well as I could, feeling her sharp, varnished nails tearing my face. Squealing like a stuck pig, I shoved her down. She sprang back, this time more like an enraged leopard and, my injured leg failing, I fell. She was all over me in an instant, hissing, screeching, gouging, biting. Her sharp teeth piercing my neck, I screamed, pushing and kicking her off, struggling to my feet, clutching the wound, sick and scared within. She'd bitten me and, as the realisation hit home, horror overwhelmed me. I feared I was doomed to become like her, one of the undead, her slave forever. I may not have been entirely rational.

'Help!' I cried.

Though she was sprawling on the ground at Hobbes's side, her teeth were still locked in my neck and, as I clawed at them, they dropped, clacking on the stone floor. I might have laughed if not for the pain and fear. False ones! Yet even as the relief hit me, she sprang up, wielding the dagger. Jumping backwards to avoid a slash, twisting to one side as she stabbed at me, I ducked and squirmed, fending her off with the brass candelabra. Too heavy and clumsy to be an effective weapon, it treacherously shed its load across the floor and, as I parried a lunge at my face, I stepped on a candle, skidding into a pillar. The candelabra clattered to the floor and, like a striking cobra, the dagger stabbed towards my throat. I took what I expected to be my last breath.

Fortunately, some things move even faster than cobras. The dagger, ceasing its attempt to skewer my larynx, flew upwards like a rocket, twisting through the air, sticking in the ceiling. A moment later, Narcisa, following a similar, if lower, trajectory, landed on her back in the middle of the altar, groaning. Her eyes opened with a look of puzzlement as if she was wondering how she'd got there and the Dagger of Tepes, falling loose in a shower of stone fragments, dropped towards her head. She screamed and was quiet.

'Hello, dear,' said Mrs Goodfellow.

'You?' I replied as intelligently as I could in the circumstances. 'How? You?'

'Well spotted, dear, it is me. Has she hurt you?'

'Yes, but Hobbes needs help.' I lurched towards him. 'She shot him.'

'Then I wish I'd hit her harder. Who's the attractive young man in the chains?'

'It's Phil – he was missing. We need to get Hobbes to hospital.'

'No.' I felt a faint rumble as if a heavy vehicle had passed on the edge of hearing. It came from Hobbes. 'No hospital.' The words emerged slowly. 'Fetch Rocky.'

'You have to go to hospital.'

'No. Rocky.'

'But …' I began.

Mrs Goodfellow shushed me. 'He's right, dear, we need Rocky.'

'But …'

'The old fellow knows what he's saying. Hospitals can't help. He's different to you and me.'

I sort of understood what she meant and one look at her persuaded me there was no room for argument. 'What can Rocky do?'

'Same as last time. Patch him up and fix him.'

'He's not a doctor, he's a troll. And how do we get to him? Is he on the phone?'

'No. Can you drive, dear?'

'Umm … no … not really. I had a couple of lessons once. How about you?'

'I don't know, I've never tried.' She nibbled her lip, looking worried.

'Phil could drive when he comes round … or there's the Editorsaurus.'

'Who, dear?'

'Upstairs. Her husband.'

'The fat, snoring one?'

'Yes.'

She shook her head. 'He's out for the count.'

'A taxi then?' I said.

'No, taxi drivers are reluctant to carry trolls, even civilised ones like Rocky and we need to hurry. You'll have to drive.'

'I can't … I won't. It's out of the question.'

She gave me the look and knelt by Hobbes. Hobbling upstairs, finding the keys to the Volvo on a small table, I set off on my mission of mercy, no less scared than I'd been all evening.

To my amazement, the car started first time, though when I tried to turn on the lights, the windscreen wipers started instead. After a lot of stirring, I found a gear, stalling three times before getting going. My progress was reminiscent of a drunken kangaroo; I bounced, lurched and skidded down the drive. When I reached the end, I turned into Alexander Court, having first turned into the gatepost. The car rumbled and grumbled into the night and I allowed it to coast down the slope towards Fenderton Road until I had to brake.

Though I had to brake, I couldn't since my foot, hitting the accelerator instead, refused point blank to try another pedal. My hands locked onto the steering wheel and I wailed like a frightened baby as Fenderton Road came towards me at a surprising pace.

Headlights flashed as in desperation I turned the wheel, making the tyres squeal in agony. I thought the car was going to roll as it swung into the main road, just missing a van and a big green car, though not the tree.

There was a horrible crunch and the airbag pinned me to my seat, leaving me winded and shocked, yet unhurt, except for all the hurts I'd already got. My leg throbbed and oozed and the bite in my neck was stinging as if a giant wasp had scored a hit. I was light-headed, though glad to be alive, if only temporarily, for who knew whether false teeth could transmit the curse of vampirism?

The door of the Volvo opened with a crunch.

'Were you trying to kill yourself? Or are you just a bloody idiot?' A high-pitched voice berated me, though I couldn't see anyone.

I groaned, wondering if the first stage in being undead was not being able to see the living. Unbuckling my seat belt, I rolled out onto wet grass, icy cold on my exposed skin, making me leap up with a yell.

'Well you're alive and, bloody hell, you are bloody.'

I looked down into a small, worried face.

'Billy, thank God.'

'Are you alright? Did you find Hobbes?'

'He's been shot and I'm going for help, only I can't drive.'

He glanced at the wreck of the Volvo, his expression saying it all.

'I need to fetch a troll called Rocky who can save him, and you'll have to get me there before I change into a vampire, because I think I've been bitten by one. Don't look at me like that, it's true.'

'You'd better hop into the hearse,' said Billy with a look suggesting he might be humouring me. Nevertheless, I noticed him finger the small silver cross round his neck. A minute later we were hurtling towards Sorenchester.

'Where am I going?' he asked.

'Left at the traffic lights and you'd better be quick. Hobbes is in a bad way.'

'OK then,' said Billy, calmly as if this sort of thing often happened on his nights out. 'Just one thing, though. Why are you running round in your underpants?'

'Because my trousers came off in the kitchen window, and would you mind turning the heating up? It's freezing.'

'Fair enough. Could happen I suppose.' Though he sounded sceptical, he did turn the heating up, as well as offering me a rug from the back.

We turned onto Green Way, flying past a long row of houses into the darkness of the countryside. He kept his foot down until we passed Brancastle, which lay in utter blackness apart from a lamp on the porch.

'Next turn on the left,' I said.

We swung onto the track towards the Olde Troll House.

I leaped from the car before it had even stopped, landing on my bad leg with a howling jolt, hobbling towards the front door, pounding on it like a Japanese drummer, ringing the doorbell frantically and then spotting the note pinned to the frame. It was too dark to read, so, tearing it down, I took it back to the hearse, which Billy had already swung round for the return journey.

'He's not answering,' I said, thrusting the note into Billy's hands. 'What's it say?'

Turning on the light, he screwed up his face. 'It says he's outstanding in his field.'

'Well I'm glad he's so modest,' I roared, 'but where is he?'

'Out in his field,' Billy replied, as if talking to an imbecile. 'He's standing in it. Actually, he might not be. Some big fellow's coming this way ... doesn't look much like a troll to me.'

Rocky came striding towards us.

''Oo's tryin' to knock my front door down?' he asked in his guttural voice.

'It's me, Andy, I came here with Hobbes a couple of days ago.'

'Andy? 'ow the Devil are you?' A huge smile spread like a ravine across his face.

'I'm fine,' I lied, unable to spare any time for explanations of my state.

'You don't look fine, and I take it this is not a formal visit? You'll catch your death if you go running round dressed like that at this time of year. You'd best come in and bring your little friend. I'll put the kettle on.'

'Sorry, there's no time. It's Hobbes.'

''ow is the old boy?'

'He's been shot.'

'What? Again?' Rocky's smile snapped shut.

'Yes, he asked for you and he's in a bad way. Hurry ... please!'

'Righto, lad. I'll get my things.' Running inside, he returned two interminable minutes later carrying a selection of small leather bags.

The hearse suited Rocky and appeared to amuse him. He lay down in the back. 'Most comfortable,' he said. 'Now, tell me what's 'appened.'

I told him as we sped back towards town. Billy nodded significantly when I mentioned Tony Derrick's involvement. Rocky was silent. The traffic lights onto Fenderton Road turning against us, we had to stop while a bulging, crop-headed youth in low-slung jeans swaggered unsteadily across in front of us just as the lights changed back to green.

'Shift your fat arse!' I yelled, furious at any delay.

Billy pumped the horn and the youth, turning, lurched towards us with an expression hinting at imminent drunken violence. It took him a couple of seconds to notice he was approaching a hearse. He hesitated, his glare fixed on Billy, propped up on a pile of cushions in the driving seat. His expression turned to puzzlement as he looked at me, covered in blood and half-naked. When Rocky sat up he fled. Billy flattened the accelerator.

'Fast as you can,' I said, 'and take a right into Alexander Court, just after the "Thank You for Driving Safely" sign.'

'Righto, Chief,' said Billy. 'Just past the broken Volvo, eh?'

I doubted I'd been away more than twenty minutes, yet I'd begrudged every second and, though Billy was by no means slow, I longed for the sort of speed Hobbes could squeeze from a vehicle. At last we turned into Alexander Court and into the Witcherleys' drive.

I leaped from the car, urging Rocky to move before Billy even had time to tug on the parking brake. 'C'mon,' I said over my shoulder, 'this way.'

Running into the house, I had to go back for the olde troll who was still sliding out, as slow as a slug. Despite my sore leg, I caught myself in a little jig of despair and frustration.

'Calm down, Laddie. I'm moving as fast as I can but there've been too many years and there's too much chalk in my joints.'

When, eventually, I reached Hobbes, his breathing was slow and ragged with bright blood bubbling round his mouth. Mrs Goodfellow had applied a new and improved dressing, discarding my blood soaked vest in a corner, placing a pillow behind his head, covering him in blankets. Narcisa was still sprawled on the altar where the Dagger of Tepes had ended her part in the story. I barely spared her a glance.

'How is he?' I asked.

'Not so good. So you found Rocky?'

''e did.' The olde troll creaked as, kneeling beside us with a cracking of knees like a ragged volley of shots, he began examining him.

It was too much for me, so I hobbled towards Phil, who, sitting against a pillar, his head in his hands, was groaning, his face as white as a vampire's, his eyes strawberry red, though I didn't think he'd been bitten. I wondered how long it would take me to turn evil.

'Someone had better fetch a stake,' I said, 'I'm going to need one soon.'

'Don't mention food,' said Phil. 'I'll be sick again.'

Billy joined us. 'Old Hobbesie doesn't look too good.' He wrinkled his nose. 'And someone doesn't smell too good.' He looked at Phil. 'I know you – you're the newspaper bloke who was hanging round with Tony Derrick. I told you he was a wrong 'un, didn't I?'

Phil nodded.

Billy returned to his hearse, coming back with a hacksaw that made short work of Phil's chains. Then he went upstairs, bringing us glasses of water, for which I was truly grateful, while Rocky set to work on Hobbes, the gleam of polished blades turning my stomach.

'What's been going on here?' asked Billy. 'This place is weird.'

'I don't really know,' said Phil, 'except Mrs Witcherley was trying to kill me, to use me as a sacrifice. She sounded insane. I'd been investigating her, not realising Tony was her stooge. I think he slipped something into my drink and next thing I knew I was stuck in the horrible cage. They got the Inspector too. He fell through the ceiling and I thought he must be dead. I don't know how long I was down here but she was just about to murder me when he reappeared like a demon from the black pit … and then Andy turned up.'

Though I wanted to play up my heroic part in the rescue, an urgent call made me jump to my feet.

'Come on, boys,' said Mrs Goodfellow, 'Rocky says the old fellow's got to be moved.'

Under Rocky's command, Billy unscrewed the cellar door, we loaded Hobbes onto it and carried him carefully upstairs. He was muscle-achingly heavy even for four of us – there were only four, because Billy couldn't reach. Lying Hobbes gently in the back of the hearse, his breathing sounding better, though his face was as pale as the moon, we piled into the front, a tight squeeze.

As we left I'd seen Rex, still snoring peacefully and felt strangely sorry for him: he'd have one hell of a headache in the morning.

We drove back to Blackdog Street at a funeral pace to avoid jarring Hobbes, who was limp when we carried him inside, placing him on the kitchen table like a huge turkey. Rocky, grim-faced and intense, assisted by Mrs Goodfellow, performed a variety of gruesome operations. I went to check on Phil, who having long since fled the gory scene, was slumped in the corner of the sitting room with Dregs, both looking mournful and blinking, presumably due to the effects of the pepper spray, but they appeared to be weeping. I returned to the kitchen where Billy busied himself with tidying up my bloody leg and applying stinging antiseptic to all my bumps and grazes. It was over an hour before Rocky finished, stitching Hobbes up with what appeared to be leather shoelaces, straightening up with a percussive rattle and, I hoped, a hint of a smile.

'Is he alright?'

The olde troll nodded.

'I reckon 'e should be just fine,' said Rocky, with a sudden grin that lent his time-smoothed face the illusion of softness, 'yet it was a close thing. You did well to get to me so quick, cos 'e wouldn't 'ave lasted much longer. And 'e was lucky she was a bad shot and ran out of ammo.'

'Wouldn't it have been better to get him to hospital?' asked Billy

'Not at all, young man,' said Rocky. 'They really wouldn't know 'ow to deal with 'is ... Well, let's just say, 'obbes would be beyond their experience.'

'Umm ... how did you know what to do?' I asked.

Under the table stood a bucket brimming with blood-sodden rags. Not so many days ago, it would have made me sick.

'Aye, well, I 'ad to patch 'im up last time 'e got a belly full o' lead – at Arras it was. The sawbones reckoned 'e was already a goner, cos 'e was so full of 'oles but 'e was one o' my lads, so I did what I could to 'elp and saw 'e wasn't like the rest of 'em. 'e pulled through then and 'e'll pull through now.'

A weight lifted from my soul and, though his big hand was covered in gore, I shook it.

'I'm only glad I could 'elp. 'e's a goodun. Now, I'll wash myself and we'll take 'im upstairs to bed. Then I must get back to my field, if your little friend wouldn't mind giving me a lift?'

Billy nodded.

'Thank you, young man. I'll stop round tomorrow and make sure all's well but 'obbes is as tough as old boots. 'e'll get better, though it'll take a few days.'

We carried Hobbes to his bed and Mrs Goodfellow tucked him in. Though he lay as still as a corpse, his face greenish, his soft, regular breathing was reassuring.

Rocky and Billy left together and Phil took himself straight to the police station to inform them he was no longer missing and explain why they should pay an immediate visit to the Witcherleys, leaving me alone with Hobbes and Mrs Goodfellow.

'Why does Rocky stand out in his field?' I asked, as she smoothed the sheets.

'It's just that his sort ...'

'Trolls?'

She shrugged, stroking Hobbes's brow. 'His sort enjoys communion with the earth. They say they like to stand and think, though mostly I reckon they just like to stand. They're good at it. Still, Rocky has a talent for patching up wounds and the old fellow reckons he was a damn fine sergeant in his day – excuse my language. Now, you'd best have a wash and get some sleep. You've had a rough day, too. I'll sit with him.'

'Thanks,' I said, for the church clock was striking two and I'd been stifling yawns for over an hour. As I started towards the bathroom, a thought stopped me in the doorway. 'D'you know, you're the only one who didn't ask why I wasn't wearing my trousers.'

'I expect you had your reasons. Now, hurry up, have a wash and turn in.' She smiled.

I followed her advice and very soon, and just in time, pulled myself into bed. Billy had been lavish with his first aid, covering me in a patchwork of plasters, bandages and antiseptic cream. Everywhere was sore and the bite in my neck throbbed even more than the wound in my leg. Despite this, I fell asleep in no time.

Something was tapping at my window. Getting up, drawing back the curtains, seeing Narcisa floating out there, her purple robe flapping like wings in the spangled sky, I shuddered and was trying to shut out the sight when her dead eyes met mine. She smiled, two rows of sharp wolf's teeth glinting in the starlight, pointing a blood red fingernail at the window. My neck burning, pleading with her to leave me in peace, I shook my head, yet had no power to resist as it opened. She glided in on a chilling breeze, clutching my hand, her grip so cold it burned, her glazed eyes staring into mine. I was paralysed as her thin lips, scarlet in a ghastly, white face, opened to speak and I knew, when they did, I would become like her. I heard words as if from a great distance …

'Wakey, wakey, dear. It's nearly eleven o'clock.'

I jerked into consciousness, my heart thumping. I was in bed.

'You were having a bad dream. Never mind, it's a fine bright day and your breakfast will be ready in ten minutes. Look sharp. I've laid out clean clothes for you.'

Narcisa wasn't there, just Mrs Goodfellow and Dregs, who'd been licking my hand. At least, I assumed it had been the dog. The curtains being drawn back, winter sunlight drenched me and I did not crumble into dust. My stomach grumbled to confirm I wasn't undead and, in the rush of relief, I whooped like an idiot before remembering Hobbes.

'How is he?'

'Not so bad now.'

She smiled and there was something strange, yet oddly familiar, about her. She had teeth in her mouth: the same ones I'd had stuck in my neck. I tried to ignore my horror.

'He had four mugs of tea,' she continued, 'and Sugar Puffs for his breakfast and now he's sleeping like a kitten. He said you saved him from the beast.'

'The beast? Narcisa?'

'I think he meant you saved him from himself. Now come on.' She left, taking the dog, now, to my delight, fully recovered.

After washing and dressing, I limped down to the kitchen for a cooked breakfast as delicious and necessary as a breakfast could be. Finishing, I brushed the crumbs from my front as Mrs Goodfellow started on the dishes.

'I was really glad to see you last night,' I said. 'How did you find us?'

'Well, dear,' she said, picking up my plate, 'when you weren't back for your supper, I thought I'd better find you, so I called the station, who said someone answering to your description had run amuck in Fenderton with a dangerous dog, and I was just getting ready to leave when poor Dregs came home in a terrible state. I had to clean him up first. What happened?'

'Mrs Witcherley pepper sprayed him, which probably saved me, because she'd run out when it was my turn.'

Mrs Goodfellow nodded, tight-lipped, scrubbing the frying pan furiously. 'That new curate gave me a ride on his motorbike. He's got nice teeth – nearly as nice as yours, dear. He dropped me off in Fenderton and I was wondering what to do next when a ratty little fellow ran from the big house, screaming like his pants were on fire. I reckoned the old fellow sometimes has that effect on folk, so I took a look inside. The fat man was snoring his head off and I searched all through the house without finding anyone sensible. Someone had muddied up the stair carpet and I was looking at it when I heard noises from the cellar and went downstairs.'

'You got there just in time. The dagger was far too close.' I took a deep breath. 'I'll dry. Where's the tea towel?'

'Thank you, dear. There are clean ones in the drawer.'

Choosing one with a nice view of the Blacker Mountains, I began wiping a mug. 'Who'd have thought Narcisa would be killed by her own dagger?'

'She wasn't killed, dear.'

'But it stuck in her head, didn't it?' I hung the mug on the mug tree, where, clinking tunefully against another, it knocked off its handle. I pushed the evidence behind the packet of Sugar Puffs.

'No, only her ear. It pinned her to the table thing. She started moaning, trying to pull it out when you were away, so I had to give her a little tap to quiet her down. She's in hospital now, under police guard, more's the pity. After what she did to my boys, I'd like to have words with her.'

'She bit my neck and I was scared I'd become a vampire like her.' In fact, I was still nervous in case the change had merely been delayed.

Mrs Goodfellow, spitting out Narcisa's teeth into her hand, held them up to the light. 'With these? No, dear, she's no vampire. The real ones don't go in for all the Gothic nonsense, they don't need daggers or rituals and they always have lovely, gleaming, pearly whites. They shed the old worn out ones and new ones pop up, a bit like with sharks. I've got some in a jar – I'll show you later if you like.'

'Thanks.' I smiled, drying the last plate and stacking it on the dresser. 'Umm ... is Sorenchester normal? I mean to say, is it worse than other places, you know, with all these ghouls and trolls and vampires and things?'

'I don't know quite what you mean. They're just folk, same as you and me, though a bit different, like the old fellow and Rocky. Most of 'em are no worse than anyone else and some are better. However, you're correct in thinking there are more round these parts than most places. That's because of the old fellow. He polices them fairly and they know there'll be no trouble unless they break the rules and, just as important, they know just what'll happen if they step too far out of line. He might appear soft-hearted to you, dear, but he can be quite strict when he has to be.'

'Thank you for helping with the dishes. Now, I've got to take the dog for his walk and then I'd better get down to the shops.' She smiled. 'I'm right out of garlic.'

Life went on and I never developed a taste for blood.

Hobbes was very quiet and weak on the first day of his recovery, sleeping most of the time, waking to drink lashings of tea or Mrs Goodfellow's ginger beer. By the second day he was a little more alert, though his voice had diminished to a soft grumble I had to strain to hear. Not that he spoke much, relying on nods or shakes of his head to respond to questions. Now and again, furious growls, as if someone had kicked a wasps' nest, would explode from his room when Mrs Goodfellow gave him a bed-bath or fussed too much. I looked in from time to time, though it was clear he was only tolerating me. I think he was embarrassed at being seen in such a frail state.

Over the next few days, Mrs Goodfellow surpassed herself in preparing feasts fit for a king, though I can't imagine how she got her hands on swan and sturgeon. To start with, Hobbes ate comparatively little, so Dregs and I were well-stuffed with leftovers. Now and again, always after dark, Rocky turned up to check on progress, to eat crumpets and to express quiet pleasure at his patient's rate of recovery. His visits ceased after the fifth evening.

As my injuries healed, Dregs and I enjoyed long walks in Ride Park. One day, cashing in Rex's cheque, I paid off my debts. What little was left over, I offered to Mrs Goodfellow for my keep but she refused to take it. As a gesture of thanks, I tried to fix the loose floorboards in the loft and don't think I did too much damage.

One morning, from Tahiti, came a postcard, reeking of cigar smoke. I read it, though it wasn't for me.

Dearest Wife,

It's been nearly ten years since I went away to find myself. I now find myself in Tahiti where I have founded a naturist colony. So far I'm the only one. One day I hope you'll join me.

Your loving husband,

Robin.

The mystery of why he no longer required clothes was solved, though why they were such a good fit was still baffling. When I handed the card to the old girl she read it, chuckling.

'He's quite mad, you know? Still, I think he's happy.' She stuck it into a scrapbook with many others.

Hobbes began to sit up in bed with the aid of pillows, even getting up for short periods, though he was shaky and soon became grumpy. Still it was clear he was recovering at an astonishing speed – but, then, he was Hobbes.

On occasion, he received visitors. Though there weren't many, he seemed to appreciate them, especially a plump old guy called Sid who wore a black cape and had the whitest teeth I'd ever seen. Like Rocky, he only turned up at night. Superintendent Cooper paid a visit one afternoon. I'd expected someone fierce, whereas she was plump and motherly; she stayed with him for over an hour and he was thoughtful when she left.

One morning Phil came round, and it came as a jaw-dropping surprise when he introduced a tanned and fit-looking young man, who'd just returned from Hollywood, as Tom, his boyfriend, a nice enough chap – not my sort of course. I was happy for

188

them. Admittedly, this was partly because it seemed to have removed one major barrier to Ingrid, or so I thought until Phil handed me an envelope. My delusion lasted until, opening it, I found an invitation to her wedding.

Phil, guessing the reason for my sudden dejection, pointed out that Ingrid had been engaged for a year and that I'd attended her engagement party. I could vaguely remember an evening at the Bear with a Sore Head when I hadn't had to pay for my lager, when some affable Scottish guy had been hanging around Ingrid, buying drinks for everybody. I'd not paid him much attention, being focussed, so far as I could focus, on preventing Phil getting too close. I could have wept, yet couldn't help feeling she'd found a far better man than me and, though I wished them both well, it felt like I'd been punched in the gut – except the ache lasted far longer.

Hobbes didn't speak about what had happened until, a day of winter sunshine cheering him up, he got out of bed, dressed in a shapeless brown dressing gown and strolled with me around the back garden. After a few minutes he sat on a bench, which was cunningly situated where it would capture any warmth from the pale sun. I sat beside him as he breathed deeply for a few moments.

'Well,' he said at last, 'I expect you'd like to know what happened?'

'I would. The suspense has been killing me.'

He chuckled, deep and soft as distant thunder. 'I'll start from when I got back to the station. I had a short, if informative, chat with Tony before releasing him. I couldn't detain him any longer. After all, he had come in voluntarily.'

I said nothing.

A faint grin twitched on his lips. 'At the time, I entertained suspicions that Rex Witcherley had used the noisy party to cover the museum break-in and it hadn't occurred to me that Mrs Witcherley might be the villain. She seemed such a nice lady, though I'm no expert. I was planning to get my car and go straight round to see Mr Witcherley when I had a thought. Do you remember the scent of flowers on the glove fibres?'

I nodded.

'I knew I'd smelt it somewhere before and, finally, it came to me. It had been in Mr Witcherley's office and it was her perfume, only the cigarette smoke had masked it. I made sketches of Tony and Mrs Witcherley together and fell to speculating whether one of Mr Barrington-Oddy's assailants might have been a woman. His description of the taller one, vague though it was, fitted Mrs Witcherley and the other assailant could easily have been Tony.'

'Who you'd just released.'

He shrugged. 'I thought he might lead me to Mr Waring.'

'You were going to see Rex. How could he lead you if you weren't following him?'

He tapped the side of his nose. 'Tony's trail's is not difficult to pick up when you know where he started and I did go round to the Witcherley's eventually. Their house is smart, isn't it?'

I nodded. 'Too smart.'

'Mrs Witcherley came to the door and must have known why I was there, because she confused me by bursting into tears, confessing and begging for forgiveness. She said her husband had made her do it and offered to take me to see Mr Waring. Something about a woman in tears makes me soft-hearted, and it seems to have made me soft-headed as well. I believed her. She asked me to follow her to the garage, where she would show me something. She did.'

'What?'

'That I was a fool to trust her. Telling me to stand aside, she unlocked the garage doors and next thing I knew she'd squirted pepper spray into my face. I took a step back and I guess she must have opened a trap-door because I dropped through into the pit.'

'Why would she have a pit?'

'It was an ice store. There used to be a millpond in Lower Fenderton, down by the river, from where they'd cut ice blocks in winter, storing them underground to keep things cool before we had fridges. She must have adapted it. I don't know why, though I'm certain it wasn't done for my benefit. Anyway, it was a long drop and, though some old leaves broke my fall, it knocked me out, I think.'

'Phil said you'd dropped in.'

'Yes, and I felt he was there, though he wasn't making much sense. They'd doped him and, when he came to and complained, she sprayed him.'

I grimaced in sympathy.

Hobbes continued. 'Being stuck in the pit with no way out, unable to get a signal on my mobile, all I could do was wait and see what she had in store for me. At least it gave me time to listen, to think and to piece together the story. It was clear she was the villain and Mr Witcherley was not involved at all. I grew hungry, thirsty, furious and desperate until you dropped in with the leg of lamb, which was most welcome. How did you get there?'

I related my own sorry exploits and, despite skipping the most embarrassing bits, still felt like a bumbling incompetent. He didn't see it that way.

'You did well,' he said.

Though I don't know if he meant it, it cheered me up.

'You know,' I said, 'I really thought you were going to attack me when I fell in.'

'Well,' he said, 'I didn't.'

Something in his eyes stopped any further questioning along that line.

'Thank you,' I said. 'So, what was Narcisa trying to achieve?'

'Ah, now that is interesting. You know her family comes from Romania? Well, she seems to have got it into her head that she was descended from Vlad Tepes …'

'It was his dagger?'

'Possibly. It certainly looks like the one in his portrait. You saw it?'

I nodded.

'Vlad's father, being a member of the Order of the Dragon, Vlad was known as Dracula, which translates as "son of the dragon".'

'What's that got to do with Narcisa?'

'I'm afraid Mrs Witcherley, driven mad by increasing signs of her own mortality, became convinced a blood ritual would help her regain her youth.'

'Why Phil's blood?'

'His investigations were becoming a danger to her and his blood was as good as anyone's.'

'Tony thought they were only going to frighten him,' I said, 'and tried to stop her.'

Hobbes nodded. 'I'm not surprised. Though he is nasty, vindictive and greedy, he's not a killer.

'From what I heard, Mrs Witcherley had an old book detailing a blood-ritual, which seems to have put the idea into her head and began collecting specific artefacts that were, on the face of it, connected with Vlad Tepes. They were certainly Romanian and date from roughly the right period and, although it's anyone's guess how authentic they are, they undeniably match items shown in the portrait, which Mr Roman had sold her. I believe he elevated the value of his dagger by modifying the painting – he was good at copying and pastiche.'

'I saw the book,' I said. 'Biggs from the museum sold it to her and offered her the bracelet.'

'So the superintendent informed me,' said Hobbes. 'Mr Biggs and Mr Roman were in cahoots but failed to realise how dangerous she was. Anyway, as you know, Mrs Witcherley eventually got her hands on the Roman Cup, the ring and the bracelet. She picked up the altar at a church jumble, though it wasn't for sale.'

'What about Jimmy? Who killed him? And buried him? And then dug him up?' I shook my head, still baffled.

'I never believed Mr Roman's account of the break-in,' said Hobbes, 'and we proved he'd lied when we found the violin in his car boot. As I see it, Mr Roman refused to listen to Jimmy when he demanded money and threatened to call the police. Jimmy left in a fury, ending up getting drunk at the Feathers, where he had the misfortune to fall in with Tony, who'd been working for Mrs Witcherley since she caught him breaking into their house.

'Jimmy made some wild threats about what he'd like to do with Mr Roman's dagger, though I doubt he meant them, and let slip that he knew the combination to Mr Roman's safe. Tony told Mrs Witcherley, who was desperate to get hold of the dagger and promised Jimmy money to steal it, which must have sounded like the answer to his problems. For her, it was considerably cheaper than paying what Mr Roman was demanding. Sadly, he caught Jimmy in the act and there was a struggle. I suspect the fatal injury occurred on the lawn outside the French windows. Do you remember I draw your attention to that soggy patch?'

'Yes,' I nodded. 'Oh, I get it! It was soggy because Roman had swilled all the blood away.'

'I fear so, and I believe he did it immediately after killing Jimmy.'

'With the Dagger of Tepes?'

'Indeed.' Hobbes looked grave. 'Poor, silly Jimmy.'

'And poor Anna.' I still felt sorry for the sweet-faced little woman.

A thin film of cloud dimming the sun, I shivered. A murder story is no longer a mere shock-horror entertainment when you know someone involved in it.

Hobbes sighed. 'Mr Roman, panicking, buried the body in the grave, which I suspect he'd previously used as a hiding place for smuggled antiques. He was not as respectable as he made out.'

'But why that particular grave?'

'Simply, it was hidden from the road, yet Mondragon is a Romanian name and there may have been a deeper reason. The secret probably died with Mr Roman. Tony, who had been keeping an eye on things, witnessed the killing and the disposal of the body and tried to blackmail him into handing over the dagger.'

'Which was still in Jimmy's back.'

'Right.' Hobbes nodded. 'Tony didn't know that at first. He had, however made a note of the safe's combination and broke in himself when Mr Roman refused to hand it over.'

'Ah,' I said, 'so, there were two break-ins and Tony was the one who left the piece of paper behind. It was clever to spot the clue on the back.'

'Thank you.' He looked pleased. 'Carelessness has always been Tony's downfall. Anyway, Mr Roman must have felt the pressure building, what with the killing and the blackmail and a second break-in. It was the final straw when the violin section came to his house and called the police.

'It was obvious where the dagger was hidden, so Tony dug it up – on the very night we happened to be in the same graveyard.'

'That was a lucky break,' I said.

'Lucky?' He winked and his smile broadened. 'Yes, it could have been luck.'

The cloud passing, a haze of gnats took the opportunity to dance in the sun's spotlight and, for some obscure doggy reason, Dregs began digging a patch of garden, a cone of mud balanced on his nose. Mrs Goodfellow called us for lunch and, since she regarded Hobbes as an invalid, fed us the world's tastiest, creamiest, chicken soup. Speaking was out of the question, for it demanded total dedication. Dregs was far too muddy to be allowed inside and his dismal howls were the only sounds, apart from those of eating. He howled even more when Mrs Goodfellow pounced, hauling him upstairs for a bath. By then, he'd learned the futility of trying to escape.

On ending our meal, we adjourned to the sofa, where Hobbes continued his summing up.

'We come now,' he said, 'to the museum break-in.'

'It still seems ludicrous,' I said, 'to go to all that trouble for one bracelet.'

'But not to Mrs Witcherley who had lost all sense of proportion. In fact, it was only after learning about the Order of the Dragon that I began to get an inkling of what was really going on and felt old Romanian superstitions might be at the bottom of it.'

'Why did Biggs tell us the bracelet was from the Order of St George? Didn't he know?'

'Of course he knew. He was trying to mislead me. He'd learned of Mrs Witcherley's obsession from Mr Roman, acquired the bracelet with museum funds and was attempting to sell it to her. He was too greedy, so she stole it, which explains why he knew only one particular article out of all the thousands in the boxes had been stolen. Knowing he'd lose his position and reputation if the truth came out, he tried to throw me off the scent.'

'Where is he now?'

'Lying low and hoping everything will blow over. He'll have some awkward questions to answer when he returns.'

Mrs Goodfellow brought us tea. Hobbes's injuries had scared her and she was still subdued, which, at least, meant she didn't keep materialising by my ear with a shrill, 'Hello, dear.' I was grateful.

Hobbes, thanking her, took a huge swig and sighed. 'The lass makes superb tea. I really missed it when I was down the hole.'

I nodded and took a sip. 'What about the Roman cup?'

'That puzzled me,' he said, 'until Augustus explained its origins. I came across an old tale about Vlad Tepes ordering a gold cup to be left next to a fountain in his kingdom. Anyone was free to use it, but anyone foolish enough to steal it would be impaled, which must have been an excellent deterrent. In addition, there were rumours that Vlad drank the blood of his enemies to keep young. The cup vanished after his death and Mrs Witcherley got it into her head that the Roman cup and Vlad's cup were one and the same. I wouldn't be at all surprised if Mr Roman had led her to the conclusion.

'Next came the attack on Mr Barrington-Oddy and the theft of the dragon ring, which was when I began to pick up the chain that led, link by link, to Mrs Witcherley.'

'And Phil?'

'Well, Andy,' he said with a ferocious frown, 'if you hadn't been stealing his business cards to further your nefarious schemes, you might have seen his note on the computer, suggesting he was investigating Mrs Witcherley.'

I hung my head. 'I'm really sorry.'

Laughing, he patted me on the back. I could tell he was still weak because I stayed on the sofa. 'Only joking. No harm came of it and you learned something about yourself. No one's perfect, we're all a mess of contradictions and impulses and yet we can train ourselves to rise above them. At least, for most of the time.

'Mr Waring, who was trying to work out precisely what Mrs Witcherley was up to, unfortunately, trusted Tony, who was apparently a valuable source of information, for the right price. Tony played along, taking his money, remaining loyal to Mrs Witcherley. He doped Mr Waring, and the rest you know.'

I nodded. 'Tony claimed he wasn't doing it for the money and thought she loved him. I think he changed his mind when she started shooting.'

Hobbes chuckled. 'Well, perhaps he does have a better side. Let's hope he chooses his next lady more wisely.'

'Where is he now?'

'Gone,' said Hobbes. 'The superintendent said he'd packed his bags and fled. He'll be back. He always comes back.'

'What'll happen to Narcisa? Will she go to prison?'

He shrugged. 'Maybe, though she'll have good lawyers and the most likely verdict is "not guilty by reason of insanity", or whatever they say these days. That's assuming she's in a fit condition to stand trial.'

'There's one other thing,' I said. 'Would the blood ritual have actually achieved anything?'

'Yes, it would have killed Mr Waring.'

'No, what I mean is, if she had drunk his blood would it have given her youth back?'

'I doubt it. Leastways, I've never known that sort of thing to work. Drinking a goblet of warm blood is enough to make most people sick, which is why they normally swap it for red wine, though Ribena will do at a pinch.'

'Oh. Umm … there's one more other thing.'

'Make it the last then,' he said, 'I'm going for a lie-down.'

'OK. What was she going to do with you?'

'I don't know.' He yawned. 'Happily, thanks to you, I never found out.'

'It was nothing,' I said. 'And I'd have been killed if it hadn't have been for Mrs

Goodfellow. She deserves the credit.'

He stood up. 'What you did was a great deal more than nothing. The lass did well, but Philip Waring and I would have been dead without you. I told him what you'd done.'

He turned away, walking slowly upstairs, leaving me in silence, partly basking in the praise, partly embarrassed, finding it hard to cope with praise after a lifetime of criticism. I was overwhelmed by a strange emotion that felt like happiness and lasted far longer than on the previous occasion.

Next morning when I went down, Hobbes was dressed in his work clothes, as if nothing had happened. Mrs Goodfellow, materialising under my ear with a joyful, 'Good morning, dear,' cackled at my jump.

I enjoyed breakfast, though not as much as Hobbes, who wolfed down three full plates of bacon and eggs and several mugs of scalding tea. Afterwards, I walked with him into town and, though icy rain was blowing into my face, I was smiling, feeling like a hero.

We stopped off at the *Bugle*, where I congratulated Ingrid. She smiled, blushing, and it hurt, though I was, genuinely, happy for her and only a little jealous of the lucky Scottish guy. She told us Rex wasn't in because he was looking after Narcisa, who'd had a breakdown. Phil caught my eye and grinned. I grinned back, happy to see him alive and well, wondering what I'd ever had against him.

As we were leaving, Ingrid stopped me. 'Andy,' she said, 'I'm sorry I got so upset with you the last time. Phil told me that you helped rescue him and Mr Hobbes. Thank you.' She kissed me on the cheek.

I walked away in a daze. I wished her well, I really did, yet there was an aching emptiness inside where something was missing. For the first time I could see her for what she was: small, dumpy and worth a million times more than my idealised portrait.

'Never mind,' said Hobbes as we stepped out into the street, ''tis better to have loved and lost than to have been shot by a crazy woman.'

Though I smiled, my mind turned back to dark places. 'Umm … there's a question I must ask. It's really been bugging me.'

'Fire away.'

'Could you tell me what's behind the door in the cellar?'

'Of course I could.'

We walked in silence for a few moments.

'Umm … will you tell me?'

'I will … probably.'

In the distance, somebody shouted and glass shattered.

'When?'

'At the appropriate time. However, right now there's constabulary duty to be done.' As he loped away, he was grinning.

Inspector Hobbes

and the Curse

Unhuman II

When I drew Hobbes's attention to the unpleasant, if somewhat underwhelming, article on the front page of the *Sorenchester and District Bugle*, neither of us could have foreseen the deadly and bizarre events it heralded. The next few weeks were to prove among the most painful, frightening and horrific of my life, taking me to dark places I would have given almost anything to have avoided.

I was, at the time, having to live at Hobbes's, sleeping in his spare room, jobless, broke and pretty low. Mrs Goodfellow, his housekeeper, had left us to fend for ourselves while she attended a dental conference in Norwich: she wasn't actually a dentist, merely obsessed by teeth, having amassed a collection of several thousand. To start with, things had been fine, for she'd prepared meals to heat up, but we'd devoured the last one the previous night and I'd volunteered as stand-in cook, having made a passing study of the old girl's culinary technique during the months I'd been staying there. Admittedly, my experience had been mostly confined to hanging around, getting in her way and eating whatever she prepared, yet I'd been quietly confident I'd absorbed enough and could cope so it had seemed only fair that I, as a non-paying guest, should help out. Hobbes, to his credit, had let me get on with it, on a trial basis. Breakfast had been a doddle, there being little I could do wrong with Sugar Puffs and marmalade on toast; my first big test was lunch.

Since we'd been surprised by a burst of intense summer, I had opted, as a first attempt, for simplicity. I threw together a salad and cold meats, using up a few leftovers and adding some green stuff from the garden. Unfortunately, it hadn't looked sufficient for me, never mind for Hobbes's vast appetite, and so I'd decided to make a nice gazpacho, using a recipe I'd spotted in *Sorenchester Life*. This, I thought, combined with our remaining bread, would fill the void.

Taking advantage of the fine weather, I served the meal beneath the fractured shade of the knobbly, old apple tree in the middle of the luxuriant, flower-scented back garden. After Hobbes, according to his custom, had said grace, his voice competing against the buzzing of countless bees, I handed him the salad, which was, in my opinion, not bad. Certainly, he ate his without fuss, seeming not to mind the big green caterpillar on the lettuce, and he even complimented me on its freshness. He did, however, point out that the potatoes in a potato salad are better when cooked.

Then, proudly, I ladled out the gazpacho, its blood-red hue and tingling aroma of herbs and spice a promise of excellence, yet, from my first spoonful, it was obvious something had gone terribly wrong, resulting in a weirdly unpleasant meaty flavour that, combined with a nasty grittiness, caught the throat and turned the stomach. Hobbes only got as far as sniffing his before, aiming a puzzled frown in my direction, he headed towards the kitchen.

Sitting on the garden bench, watching the ants avoiding a spot of soup I'd spilled, I tried to figure out where I'd gone wrong, following a recipe the magazine claimed to be foolproof. So far as I could remember, I'd followed the instructions precisely, using only fresh vegetables, and, being short of tomatoes, a big squirt of tomato purée. Although my soup had come out considerably redder than the photograph, I'd put it down to the printers saving on red ink.

When Hobbes returned, carrying an immense slab of cheese and pickle sandwich, he tossed the tomato purée tube in front of me with an amused snort, except it wasn't tomato purée at all but the dog's meat-flavoured toothpaste. Hobbes, grinning at my shudder of revulsion, my look of despair, took a big bite from his sandwich and sat chewing.

On finishing, he suggested it would be better if we ate out, or bought in takeaways until the old girl got home. I didn't argue, merely taking myself to the kitchen to make a pot of tea, a task at which I'd become reasonably adept.

I'd just picked up the *Sorenchester and District Bugle* when Hobbes, sauntering in from the garden, helped himself to a steaming mugful of tea from the pot I'd made. Chucking in a handful of sugar, he stirred it with his great, hairy forefinger, relaxed into the battered, old chair next to mine, stretched out his thick legs, took a quick slurp, and placed his mug on the kitchen table.

'Let's hope,' he said, grimacing, 'that the lass returns before you finish both of us off.'

I shrugged, trying not to feel more inadequate than usual, for I was really doing my best in the absence of Mrs Goodfellow and, pointing at the front page, changed the subject. 'Umm … According to this, there was blood everywhere.'

'Whose blood?'

'The sheep's I suppose. What d'you reckon did it?'

Frowning, he scratched the side of his bull neck. 'The very beginning is a very good place to start. About what are you talking?'

'This.' I pushed the paper towards him.

Taking it, he scanned the article, his bristling eyebrows plunging into a scowl. 'You want *me* to tell *you* what killed it, even though you've got all the information I have?'

I nodded. 'Well, you are a detective.'

He smiled. 'Alright, I'll do what I can, though there's precious little to go on. First point: yesterday morning, a farmer found a dead sheep in a field just off the main road to Pigton. Second point: its throat had been torn out. Third point: it had been partially eaten. Those are the facts; the rest is filler.'

It was, I thought, a good summary, though the reporter had managed to inflate the story to cover half the front page, while hinting at dark mysteries. Still, 'Sheep Killed' was not among the snappiest headlines Rex Witcherley, the editor, or Editorsaurus as I called him, had come up with and the blurry photograph of a sheep in a field, entitled 'A Sheep in a Field' that occupied most of the rest of the page, was not the most creative idea he'd had. To be fair to the Editorsaurus, it wasn't always easy to find hot news in a small Cotswold town like Sorenchester. Furthermore, he'd been going through a tough time since his wife got herself locked up in a secure unit for attempting to murder Hobbes, me and others the previous November, and wasn't yet back on form.

Hobbes, taking another swig from his mug, continued. 'I suspect a dog might be to blame, possibly a stray, because when pet dogs run wild they are less likely to eat what they kill. Anyway, there's nothing I can do about it, unless there are further incidents.'

Dregs, Hobbes's delinquent dog, padded in through the open back door, his long pink tongue snaking out to lick a blood-red globule dripping from his shaggy black muzzle. He slumped onto the cool red-brick floor with a sigh, wagging his tail as if he'd just done something clever.

'Look!' I cried, my finger trembling as I pointed, 'It was him, but he's always well fed.'

Hobbes's laugh rumbled round the kitchen. 'You'd be hard pressed to make the charge stick, since he was with me at the station at the alleged time of the incident. Furthermore, if you observe more closely, you'll notice that it's not blood but your … interesting tomato soup round his chops. You shouldn't jump to wild conclusions.'

I flinched and said nothing, wallowing in a familiar sense of failure. It was worse that, this time, I had really tried.

At length, draining his mug, he got to his feet. 'I'd better be off,' he said, 'Superintendent Cooper asked me to have a word with Skeleton Bob Nibblet. Do you fancy a trip out?'

'Umm … Yeah. Why not? What's he been up to this time?'

'Same as usual – poaching.'

'Well,' I said, 'you can't blame him; he looks like he needs the meat.'

Bob's hollow eyes, sparse frame and skull-like head were familiar to *Bugle* readers, his frequent appearances before the magistrate providing the crime desk with a constant trickle of small news. His offences, always petty, usually detected early in their inception, meant he would never be regarded as a criminal genius, yet he had a reputation as an excellent poacher and, according to pub rumours, supplied many respectable people with illicit game.

Hobbes led Dregs and me from number 13 Blackdog Street towards his rusting blue Ford Fiesta. As we got in, I wondered why I was always relegated to the cramped back seat whenever the dog travelled with us. In a way I was glad of this inferior position, for Hobbes's maniacal driving, showing no signs of abating, meant I enjoyed a slight sense of security when cowering in the rear, reasoning that the chances of him reversing into a tree at breakneck speed were considerably less than those of smacking into one at full speed ahead. Dregs, on the other hand, showed every confidence in Hobbes's abilities and, to give him his due, the facts backed up his nonchalance, for no one I'd asked could recall Hobbes ever being involved in a road accident. Apparently, the time to worry was when he went off road; more than one vehicle had allegedly disintegrated about him while he was hot on some miscreant's trail.

The engine growled into life. Dregs growled back in challenge, barking madly until we yelled at him to shut up. The ritual complete, we hurtled along Blackdog Street, screeched round the corner, flew along Pound Street and Spittoon Way, ignored the red traffic light onto the main road and sped in the general direction of Pigton.

Despite the open windows directing a hurricane of miscellaneous insects into my face, sweat was soon trickling down inside my loose white shirt and pooling around the belt of my khaki chinos, which, like all my clothes, had once belonged to Mrs Goodfellow's husband, last heard of attempting to set up a naturist colony on Tahiti. Dregs's long tongue was lolling like a pink snake as he stuck his black head out the window, enjoying the jet stream. Hobbes, though apparently unaffected, still wearing his usual heavy, bristly tweed jacket and baggy flannels, making me sweat even more whenever I glanced at him, had, as a concession to the heatwave, ventured out without his battered gabardine mac.

At least with him driving, it only took a few desperate minutes before we were turning off the main road into a tree-shadowed lane. After a couple of hundred yards and a sharp turn, we bounced onto a track, stopping in a fog of dust. Back home on the kitchen wall, Mrs Goodfellow had put up a calendar showing glossy images of romantic cottages, all black and white walls, thatched roofs and roses round their doors, but Bob's cottage would never have got anywhere near the long list, though, what it lacked in roses it more than made up for in brambles. It was, in fact, a crumbling, red-brick hovel amidst a small yard overflowing with rusting bits of car, and mysterious remnants of machines that might once have had an agricultural purpose. In the corner, a rotting shed slouched against a crumbling brick wall and next to it stood a cage, shiny and clean and looking well out of place.

As we got out the car, Skeleton Bob, filthy string vest drooping from bony shoulders, was perched on an upturned beer keg in the porch. A faint, musky odour tainted the breeze.

Hobbes nodded. 'Good afternoon, Bob.'

Bob grunted.

'Who is it?' asked a woman's breathless voice from inside.

'It looks like the circus has come to see us,' said Bob grinning, displaying a spectacular set of discoloured and broken teeth. 'Leastways, we've got the strongman, the lion and the clown.'

A spherical, red-faced woman immersed in a billowing purple tent rolled from the cottage, coming to rest beside Bob, her hands on where her hips might have been.

'Good afternoon, Mrs Nibblet,' said Hobbes, touching his forehead.

'Oh, it's you. What's he done this time?'

'I've done nothing,' said Bob.

She frowned. 'You can shut up!'

Bob shrugged.

'It's been brought to my attention that someone's been poaching in these parts,' said Hobbes, shambling towards the Nibblets.

Mrs Nibblet sniffed. 'Oh, is that all? Can't a poor man take the odd rabbit to feed his starving family?'

'If,' said Hobbes, 'only the odd rabbit had been taken, I very much doubt I'd be here. Unfortunately, there's been a sudden and dramatic reduction in the pheasant population. Colonel Squire has been objecting. In fact, he's been objecting very loudly to Superintendent Cooper, demanding action. He says there's a lot of money in pheasants.'

'In which case,' said Bob, 'the odd one or two going missing won't hurt him.'

'Keep quiet, you,' said Mrs Nibblet, glaring at her husband, turning back towards Hobbes. 'Look, Bob only takes the odd bird or two that he comes across. Loads more get killed on the roads.'

'However many he takes, poaching is still against the law. Yet, in this case, Mrs Nibblet, dozens of young birds have vanished without trace, while a similar number have been found without heads. Do you know anything about it?'

Bob and wife spoke together, 'Dozens?'

'Yes, dozens.'

Bob shook his skull head. 'Honestly, Mr Hobbes, it's got nothing to do with me.'

Hobbes frowned. 'Fair enough, but perhaps you know something about it?'

Bob glanced at his wife as if seeking permission.

'We know nothing,' she said before he could open his mouth.

'Nothing,' said Bob after a moment's hesitation.

Dregs yelped and I turned in time to see him leap away from the cage, blood oozing from the black tip of his nose and dripping onto the grass.

'You ought to keep that dog away from my ferrets, or he'll get hurt,' said Bob, shuffling off his beer keg, approaching Dregs.

'Careful,' I warned, 'he's fierce.'

Bob ignored me, taking Dregs's head in his hands and examining the injury. 'That's no more than a love-bite,' he said, reaching into the pocket of his threadbare jeans, pulling out a battered tobacco tin and handing it to me. 'Open it, please.'

I screwed off the lid. The waxy brown goo inside stank of garlic and stuff. I wrinkled my nose. 'What's in this muck?'

'Garlic and stuff, but it's not muck.' Scooping up a globule with a bony, nicotine-stained finger, he massaged it into the wound.

To my astonishment, Dregs, after a faint whimper, allowed the indignity. I knew I'd never let the gunk get any closer to my nose than arm's length.

'Won't he just lick it off?'

'Would you lick it off?' asked Bob, his grin exuding his habitual good nature.

'Thank you,' said Hobbes. 'He'll not do that again. I doubt he's ever seen a ferret before.'

Dregs's tail thumped a staccato beat as Bob stroked him; I wondered how he would have reacted six months ago when Hobbes had first brought him home, a savage, vicious, malevolent creature. It had only been a few days after I'd moved in and, without exaggerating, I'd been in fear for my health and safety, if not for my life. In fairness, Dregs had only nearly killed me twice and neither time had it been on purpose. Since then we'd become friends.

'We'd better be on our way,' said Hobbes. 'Sorry to disturb you, Mrs Nibblet.' Again he touched his forehead in an old-fashioned salute.

She nodded, waddling back into the cottage as Hobbes turned, strolling towards his car, gripping Bob's arm. Dregs and I walked beside them.

'Right, then, Bob,' said Hobbes, 'you want to tell me something.'

'Do I?' asked Bob, biting his lip, looking shifty, which was normal for him.

'You do. I saw the look you gave Mrs Nibblet.'

'I try not to look at her.'

'You can tell me in confidence,' said Hobbes. He chuckled, his arm encircling Bob's skinny shoulders, like a python round a fawn.

Bob squeaked and found himself in agreement. 'OK, OK, I'll tell you ... just give me a moment to catch my breath.'

Hobbes releasing him, Bob talked. 'Look, don't think I'm going funny or nothing and I don't really know if it's important or not, but I did see something the other night … something strange.'

'Go on,' said Hobbes, slowing to snail-pace.

'I was out for a quiet walk in the woods a couple of nights ago.'

Hobbes raised his eyebrows.

'And you'll never guess what I saw.'

'What?' I asked.

'A big cat.'

'A big cat?'

'Yes, a big cat.'

'How big?'

'Andy, shut up a minute,' said Hobbes. 'How big was it?'

'Much bigger than this dog of yours but it was black like him.' Bob glanced around as if hidden ears might be listening. 'I reckon it was one of them panthers.'

'So,' said Hobbes as he reached his car, 'you reckon a big cat's been taking the pheasants?'

Bob nodded and then shook his head. 'Yes … no … er … could be.'

'Go on,' said Hobbes.

'Look,' Bob whispered, 'I didn't see it do anything; it was just slinking through Loop Woods, that's all. It might just be a coincidence.' He stopped and frowned. 'You don't believe me do you?'

Hobbes looked thoughtful. 'Let's say I don't not believe you. Thank you for your help and if you see anything else you know where to get hold of me. By the way, I'd lay off the night-time excursions on Colonel Squire's land for the time being if I were you. I'd hate to hear you'd been eaten by a stray cat. Goodbye.'

With a nod, he squeezed into the driver's seat and, as soon as Dregs and I had taken our places, started the engine, waving as we lurched and bumped back down the track. Bob was standing still, rubbing his shoulders, wearing an anxious frown on his bony face.

'What d'you make of that?' I asked.

'I don't know yet,' said Hobbes. 'There have been plenty of reports of mysterious big cats over the years, so it's not out of the question, but Bob's never been the most reliable of witnesses.'

'I reckon he was just trying to cover his tracks,' I said. 'It's hardly likely that a big cat would eat loads of pheasants.'

'It depends on how hungry it was and, if we allow the possibility that one big cat's on the loose, there's a chance there may be others. And don't forget that dead sheep; that could conceivably have been the work of a big cat.'

'It's a bit far-fetched. Surely, you don't believe him?'

'As I said, I don't not believe him. In fact, it wouldn't be the first time there've been big cats on the loose around here.'

'Really?' I said. 'I don't remember.'

'It was a few years ago, just after I'd been made up to sergeant, and it all happened up by the Elms estate, which in those days was a quiet, pretty place with lots of beautiful elms and very few houses. It was, by all accounts, a lovely spring day and no one could have anticipated the terrible events. Do you want to hear it?'

'Yes.'

'I wasn't there, being on holiday in Rhyll at the time, and only heard the story when I got back. Apparently a small travelling circus had come to town, featuring among the usual acts, a pair of lions in the charge of Claude the lion-tamer.' He paused, frowning. 'Actually, that might not have been his name, but he was definitely clawed, and had to be taken to hospital with multiple lacerations, leaving the other circus folk to look after his animals. They didn't do a very good job.'

The car bumped along the track, stopping at the end of the lane, the bleating of nearby sheep drifting in through the window.

'Go on,' I urged, meaning to continue his story, not to pull out in front of the lorry that was powering towards us. Brakes shrieked, the engine roared and somehow we were still alive.

He continued. 'They forgot to feed them for a few days and, when they remembered, both lions lay limp in their cage, as if dead. A juggler and a clown went in to check – the clown had nicked himself shaving and was bleeding. Anyway, to cut a long story short, the lions weren't dead; they'd merely been sleeping and woke to find two men in their cage and the door wide open.'

'Gosh,' I said. 'That must have been scary, especially for the bleeding clown.'

'Language, Andy. As it happens, the lions, ignoring the clown, went straight for the juggler, who was in front of the door, and knocked him to the ground. Yet, the lure of freedom proved stronger than hunger and they fled without harming him. The circus folk contacted the police, who organised a big search but found no sign of the beasts.

'They turned up on Sunday morning. Back then there was a pleasant little church on the estate and a service was in progress when the lions walked in. The story goes that the vicar looked up to see them bounding towards him down the aisle. "Oh Lord," he prayed in his terror, "turn these ravenous beasts into Christians."'

'What happened?' I asked, agog.

'Well,' said Hobbes, 'on hearing his words, the lions stopped, bowing their heads before the altar. The vicar rejoiced, certain a miracle had been granted to him, until he heard what they were saying.'

'The lions could speak? What did they say?'

'For what we are about to receive …'

I laughed. 'No! I don't believe you.'

Hobbes chuckled. 'Oh well, you're learning. Actually, most of the story is true, just not that last bit. In reality, old General Squire, Colonel Squire's grandfather, shot them both in the apse. A pity as they weren't doing any harm.'

'What next?' I asked.

'I think we should pay a visit to the Wildlife Park and have a quiet word.'

'You do think there's a big cat on the loose.'

'I would merely like to eliminate the possibility from my enquiries.'

The road to the Wildlife Park, being quiet, presented Hobbes with an opportunity for some brutal accelerator crushing. I clung to my seat, sweating, wishing I could be as cool as Dregs whose head was stuck out the window, ears flapping like bats in a hurricane. Now and again, Hobbes insisted on looking over his shoulder to talk to me, allowing the car to swoop wildly across the road, taking the shortest route. Responding only encouraged him; keeping quiet only made him turn to check nothing was wrong.

Fortunately for my well-being, the ten-mile journey could only have lasted five minutes, since the more I got used to his driving, the more frightening it became. Turning into the Wildlife Park, we slowed down, having, as always, made it without harm to ourselves or others. A small herd of antelope stared at us, acting skittishly as if we might be predators. To the left, half a dozen two-humped camels lounged in the shade of a mighty tree, watching the world with total disdain.

'I'd best keep well away from that lot,' said Hobbes, a look of concern on his face.

'Why? They're not dangerous are they?'

'Not as such, but unfortunately I have an allergy to camels; at least they're not dromedaries, because they can make me really bad.'

'Well, at least you're not allergic to something common, like dogs or cats. You can't run into camels very often.'

'You'd be surprised.'

The car park was guarded by a broad, red-faced man in a narrow, green booth. Standing up, he emerged, ticket machine swinging from his bulging neck.

'Be careful,' I said, 'he's going to charge.'

Hobbes, stopping the car, smiling, held out his ID. 'I'd like a word with the manager.'

'Very good, sir. Try the main office in the big house, but dogs aren't allowed.' He pointed to a large sign confirming his statement.

'It's alright,' said Hobbes, 'he's with me.'

'But …'

'He's with me,' said Hobbes, his tone leaving no room for argument.

'Fine. In that case, you'd better leave your car by the coaches,' said the poor man pointing vaguely behind him, mopping his forehead with a red handkerchief, 'because the parking by the house is rather limited at the moment. We're expecting delivery of a kangaroo.'

Hobbes thanked him and parked and we piled out of the oven. I felt as limp as a month-old lettuce and even Dregs was drooping.

'You two look like you could do with a drink,' said Hobbes, parting the flock of excited school children loitering in front of the kiosk, deciding which sweets would rot their teeth best. He returned with a large lemonade for me and an ice cream carton filled with water for the dog. Dregs lapped it up, splashing almost as much as he drank.

'We'd best find the manager,' Hobbes said when I'd drained my paper cup and Dregs had licked the carton dry. 'Come on. And quickly.'

We headed towards the house, an impressive, turreted, stone edifice with fine mullioned windows and ivy draped around the porch, where a sign directed us inside to the main office. Going inside was almost like stepping into a cave, the coolness coming as a blessed relief, the shade delightful. The problem was my eyes, taking a few moments to recover from the glare, failed to spot the sign advising visitors to mind the step.

I didn't mind it. Stumbling down, struggling to regain my balance, I might have succeeded had it not been for the rug slipping beneath my feet. My legs began a desperate race, trying to keep up as my upper body lurched headfirst towards a door that was, fortunately, ajar. Bursting through, sprawling full length, skidding across the marble floor on my belly, I came to rest a few centimetres from a pair of elegant ladies' shoes. On pushing myself to my knees, I couldn't fail to notice the equally elegant pair of legs, clad in sheer black nylon. An intoxicating, powerful perfume filled the air.

I'd never had much luck when meeting attractive women, somehow never appearing at my best, as if cursed to be a buffoon, a klutz. Yet, as I looked up, the smile on her face suggested amused sympathy, rather than the horrified contempt I'd expected.

'Are you alright?' she asked, her voice soft and gentle with rather a posh accent, suiting her look of quiet sophistication. She wore a black skirt and a pale-green silk blouse, which clung around her. My eyes, briefly meeting hers, stared at the carpet, yet I retained an image of full red lips, sleek, dark hair surrounding a face suggestive of Mediterranean ancestry, eyes flashing green like northern seas in the sunlight, beneath fine quizzical eyebrows, and …

'Andy?' Hobbes arrived in a more conventional manner, his voice bursting into my reverie like a hippo into a paddling pool. 'Are you hurt?'

'Umm … er …'

'Do you think we should call an ambulance?' asked the woman, sounding concerned. 'He might have hit his head.'

A great muscular paw dragged me to my feet. An electric fan whirred, blowing cool air into my back.

'He probably should get his head examined,' said Hobbes, 'but I don't think he's hurt himself.' He sniffed, rubbing his nose.

'I'm alright,' I said. 'I … umm … fell.'

When the woman smiled at me, my knees came close to giving way.

Another woman spoke. 'Can I help you?'

An older woman, flecks of grey in her short, gingery hair, wearing round, red-rimmed spectacles, sat behind a desk. I had found the main office.

'Forgive me,' said Hobbes in his official voice, showing his ID, 'I'm Inspector Hobbes and this young oaf,' he patted my back, 'is Andy.' He sneezed. 'Excuse me.'

I flinched, but not from the suddenness of the sneeze. Being labelled an oaf in front of such a beautiful woman was not good for the ego, especially when the accolade was well deserved. Yet, she smiled again before turning to the other woman.

'Thanks, Ellen,' she said. 'I can see you'll be busy with these two gentlemen so I'll come back later.' She walked away, with an elegant swing of the hips.

'Good afternoon, Inspector,' said the older woman, rising from her chair, 'I'm Ellen Bloom, Mr Catt's secretary. How can I help you?'

She smiled at him; I still wondered how he managed to conceal his otherness behind his policeman's façade.

'It's merely a routine enquiry. I wondered whether you might have lost any big cats recently?'

'I wouldn't have thought so. We are not in the habit of losing animals, especially big ones.'

'No, I thought not,' said Hobbes, nodding. 'However, I needed to check. I wonder if I might have a word with your boss?'

'Mr Catt is not in his office. I'll find him.' Sitting back in her chair, picking up a walkie-talkie, she pressed a button and spoke. 'Mr Catt? It's Ellen.'

The walkie-talkie crackled and buzzed in response but Mrs Bloom seemed to understand it.

'I have an Inspector Hobbes here, who wants to talk about big cats … OK, I'll tell him … goodbye.' She released the button, looking up at Hobbes. 'Mr Catt is in the reptile house attending to the crocodiles. Go out the front door, turn left and left again. You can't miss it.'

'Thank you,' said Hobbes as we left.

'Wasn't she gorgeous?' I murmured.

'Mrs Bloom?'

'No, the other lady. I wonder what she's called?'

He grinned. 'It's like that is it? And there was I thinking you'd thrown yourself at her feet by accident.'

'I did … D'you think I made a fool of myself?'

'No,' he said with a chuckle, 'almost certainly not.' Pulling a handkerchief from his pocket, he blew his nose like a foghorn. 'I think the rug you slid on must be made of camel hair. It's good to get some fresh air.'

I nodded, unable to take my mind from the woman, who, though she must have seen me as a clumsy oaf, had smiled at me. It had been a smile of sympathy but it had shown off her perfect white teeth, lovely lips, the way her eyes crinkled at the corners …

'Where's Dregs got to?' asked Hobbes, looking around.

He'd definitely been with us when we'd entered the house but I couldn't recall seeing him since. There was no sign of him.

'We'd better find him,' said Hobbes, 'and quickly. Otherwise he'll end up in the lion's den – or worse.'

He loped away in a crouch, his hairy hands nearly brushing the dusty concrete and, though he looked awkward, I had to jog to keep up. At least I could keep up for a short while. When I'd first met him, I wouldn't have stood a chance, but Mrs Goodfellow's good food, combined with running after him and Dregs, had lifted me to a level of fitness that was still a novelty. Nevertheless, I was puffing and sweating like a Turkish wrestler when we found the dog, cowering under the car, trembling, showing the whites of his eyes, licking his lips. He seemed pleased that we were there and crawled out, whining like a frightened puppy. I'd never seen him like it before and it came as a shock, for I wouldn't have believed anything could scare him.

'What's up with him?' I asked, stroking his hairy head.

'I don't know but something's obviously given him a fright.'

'Perhaps it's the scent of all the animals round here?'

'I doubt it. He normally likes that sort of thing.'

'I suppose so. Perhaps my fall upset him?' Even I was sceptical about this theory for, judging by past experience, Dregs regarded any trip or pratfall with great, tail-wagging amusement.

'Who knows, but whatever was up with him, he's better now.'

It was true, for Dregs's whiplash tail was working overtime and he was now bouncing around us as if nothing had happened.

Hobbes shrugged. 'Oh well, let's find Mr Catt.'

As we headed towards a long, low-slung building, my stomach started turning somersaults because I'd always had a thing about reptiles, and particularly snakes, even the little ones. I had a moment of hope on spotting a sign saying the reptile house was temporarily closed to the public, but it didn't deter Hobbes or Dregs who plunged inside, while I dithered, scared to enter, yet unwilling to miss out on whatever transpired. At length, screwing up my courage, I ran after them. It was bad, as bad as I'd feared. There was a boa constrictor slithering in my direction in the first tank and a pair of anacondas, sleeping but sinister in the second. Then came smaller tanks, writhing with all sorts of venomous serpents but the worst was a massive reticulated python, its belly swollen to the size and shape of a small pig. I shivered, avoiding eye contact, trying to hurry past, while Hobbes peered at it, obviously fascinated, and Dregs bounced, barking in excitement.

'This fellow's enjoyed a good lunch and no mistake,' said Hobbes, 'and it's obviously not the snakes that frightened Dregs.'

'C'mon,' I urged, 'let's find Mr Catt.'

'There's no hurry,' said Hobbes, putting his great, hairy paw up to the glass and waving. 'Hello, Mr Python, curling round a tree.'

The snake, responding, slithered towards us, making me feel sick and wobbly, scarcely able to breathe, as its unblinking gaze locked onto me, following my every movement. Though my rational mind knew it was safely behind the thick glass, I couldn't help myself wondering what would happen if the glass broke, or if some careless keeper had left the door open.

'Can we go now?' I asked, backing away.

'I think she's got a crush on you,' said Hobbes with an evil grin.

Turning, I fled towards a walled pen at the rear, where a pair of crocodiles lurked. Hobbes followed, chuckling.

The larger of the crocodiles raised his head as we drew close. 'Ah,' it said, 'you must be Inspector Hobbes. I'll be with you in a moment.'

I was so startled that, forgetting my panic, I stood still as a statue, gaping like an idiot, until a chubby, little man, red-faced, dressed in a dishevelled safari suit, stood up abruptly from behind the wall, seized the smaller croc by the tail and plunged a syringe into it. The beast thrashed and snapped but the man had moved on.

Sauntering away, he climbed back over the wall, dropping the syringe into a yellow plastic box. 'A jab well done,' he said, rubbing his hands together, chuckling at his own joke. 'I'm Francis Catt, the director. How may I help you?'

'I'm sorry to disturb you, sir,' said Hobbes, 'but have you lost any cats?'

'Felines, nothing more than felines,' Mr Catt sang in a wavering tenor and grinned. 'No, we haven't lost any. Have you found some?'

'Possibly,' said Hobbes, 'according to Mr Nibblet.'

'Would that be "Skeleton" Bob Nibblet?'

'Yes,' said Hobbes. 'I take it that you know him?'

'Oh yes. He's turned up here several times recently, fretting that we'd lost a black panther. We haven't of course. The only thing we've ever lost is a grass snake.'

I couldn't stop myself from looking around, preparing to run. Grass snakes, I knew, were mostly harmless, but they were still snakes.

'Do you think,' asked Hobbes, 'that he was making it up?'

Mr Catt thought for a moment. 'I wouldn't go so far as to say that but he always seems to run across big cats on Friday nights and Ellen – you've met my secretary? – she lives not far from him and says he's usually rolling drunk on Friday evenings.'

'I see,' said Hobbes.

Mr Catt continued. 'I'm not saying he's lying deliberately but I wouldn't rely on him. He's not so bright at the best of times and with a skinful of beer, well, I think it's likely that he's just seen a normal black moggy and blown it up out of all proportion.'

'That would seem likely,' said Hobbes, nodding. 'Still, while we're here, would you mind if we take a look at your big cats. What have you got?'

Mr Catt, escorting us from the reptile house, took us along a dusty path, past groups of happy visitors, heading for the cats. 'We've got lions,' he said. 'Tony, the lonesome tiger, and a pair of leopards – you might find them interesting. Zoologically speaking they are synonymous with panthers, the so-called black panthers, merely being melanistic variants. We have a couple of fine specimens but they're safe in their pen. Anyway, even if they did escape, they wouldn't get far; leopards are always spotted.' He sniggered like a schoolboy. 'By the way, did you know lions are so called because they're always lion around?'

'Huh!' I said and, to distract him, pointed towards a pen where some white birds with long beaks were standing round a pond. 'Are those storks?'

'No, they're Egrets. Egrets, I've had a few, but then again too few to mention.'

I sighed. We were passing the rhino enclosure when Hobbes stopped walking. I continued, chatting to Mr Catt.

'What's a melanistic variant?' I asked, more as an attempt to halt his little 'jokes' than because of a thirst for knowledge.

'It's merely an animal that possesses an increased amount of black, or dark, pigmentation. Interestingly enough it can occur in many felines and, it's not generally known but …'

'How dangerous are rhinoceroses?' asked Hobbes, frowning.

Mr Catt looked puzzled. 'The rhinos? They're not really dangerous at all, so long as they're confined to their enclosure and we're safely out here. Why do you ask?'

'I wondered if that little girl was safe,' said Hobbes.

'What? Oh hell!' Mr Catt groaned.

The child was running through the enclosure, presumably having squeezed under the wire and clambered across a ditch. She was heading for her sunhat which must have blown off. One of the rhinos raised its head, staring, ears twitching, ambling towards her. The other, looking up, trotted after it.

'If something startles them, they might charge,' said Mr Catt, his ruddy complexion having turned the same greenish colour as the dried mud caked on the rhino's backside.

'Then I'd better get her out,' said Hobbes, 'because she's public and it's my job to protect her.'

'No!' said Mr Catt, his voice almost a shriek, 'you might alarm them and …'

But Hobbes, vaulting the high steel gate into the enclosure, was already speeding towards the girl. Then a tall, thin woman, unmistakeably a schoolteacher, even at a distance, noticing her charge, called out a sharp command. The child, running towards the wall, was pulled to safety and given a stern rebuke. Mr Catt and I had barely moved, understanding how it felt to be rooted to the spot.

Hobbes, slowing to a jog as he saw the girl was safe, bent to pick up her hat.

Both rhinos charged.

Mr Catt and I yelled in unison. 'Look out!'

Though the rhinos' massive feet were kicking up dust and turf as they pounded the dry pasture into a thundering rhythm, like a troupe of Japanese drummers, Hobbes didn't appear to have noticed. Cold horror clutched my insides, for surely not even he could withstand a direct hit from a pair of three-ton rhinos. The first one lowered its horn and I shuddered, imagining the scene when I told Mrs Goodfellow of his untimely and messy end.

Then, straightening up, brushing the dust from the hat, he sprang into a twisting somersault, carrying him straight over the first rhino. Landing with a gymnast's poise in time to meet the second one, he vaulted it, as if playing leapfrog, his teeth glittering in a grin of pure exhilaration. Before the bewildered creatures had skidded to a halt, he'd hauled himself from the enclosure and was handing the hat back to the little girl, touching his forehead in salute as she and her friends goggled, open-mouthed. The rhinos, seeing no sign of their target, obviously assuming they'd pulped him into oblivion, swaggered back across their field. If they'd exchanged high fives, I wouldn't have been surprised. Actually, I would have been, but, there was no denying, they were exuding an air of smug achievement.

The grin was still on Hobbes's face when he rejoined us. 'You can have a lot of fun with rhinos,' he said, 'but we're here for a look at your leopards.'

'Oh, yes, alright,' said Mr Catt, rubbing his sleeve over his face. 'That was a remarkable thing you just did.'

'Not really. The child needs her hat on such a hot day. Anyone would have done the same.'

'Of course they would,' I said, nodding my agreement.

Hobbes chuckled, patting me on the back. I picked myself up, brushing down my trousers, following as he propelled a shaking Mr Catt towards the leopard enclosure. Dregs, who'd been investigating a lamppost, appeared not to have noticed anything out of the ordinary.

'You should have seen that,' I told him. 'Who'd have thought a big bastard like him could do a backward somersault in mid-air? From a standing start, too!'

Dregs wagged his tail to indicate he'd have thought it.

Mr Catt was in lecture mode as we caught up. 'Of course,' he said, 'leopards are by far the most adaptable of the big cats, being equally at home in forests, savannahs, semi-deserts and mountains. If any big cat could survive in this country I feel it would have to be a leopard, but I'm sure they'd leave signs. I can't believe they'd go undetected for long.'

Hobbes nodded. 'I agree. Most of England is too crowded to shelter large wild beasts. It's a shame there's no room for animals these days.'

'Well,' said Mr Catt, 'I, for one, am pleased. No one would pay to come here if they could see the exhibits roaming outside for free. Anyway, it'd be dangerous. Our male leopard weighs as much as the average man and can easily overpower prey much larger than himself. He could kill or seriously injure someone.'

'There is that to consider,' said Hobbes thoughtfully, as if the idea hadn't occurred to him. 'Human beings are annoyingly fragile and it's a good job they've got good brains.' He glanced at me. 'Most of them, anyway.'

Mr Catt smiled at my affronted expression but I was playing along with Hobbes's joke. I assumed he'd been joking.

'Our leopards,' Mr Catt continued, 'are particularly fine specimens and we're hoping they'll breed soon. The female has already had a couple of litters at her previous zoo but, for some reason, our male doesn't seem capable of making her pregnant, appearing to prefer cheetahs.' He sniggered. 'We think he might be trying to pull a fast one. Anyway, we've got the vet coming here next week. We're hoping he might be able to do something to get her in cub.'

'Will she let him?' I asked, smirking.

Mr Catt rolled his eyes. 'Don't be silly,' he said, as if talking to an imbecile. 'The vet's going to check if there are any physiological or nutritional reasons for their failure to copulate.'

'I was joking. But ... where are your leopards?'

The pen appeared empty apart from trees and stumps, a variety of wooden platforms at different levels and tufts of tawny and grey fur, blowing in the breeze.

'Eh?' said Mr Catt with a look of wide-eyed panic.

'Up there,' said Hobbes, pointing to the topmost platform where two pairs of furry ears twitched in the shade. 'They're having a lie down.'

'Of course,' said Mr Catt, regaining his composure, 'they spend about twenty hours a day sleeping and lounging and prefer to do it at height. Unfortunately, it's not so good for the visitors but the animals' welfare must come first.'

'Of course it must,' said Hobbes.

The walkie-talkie crackled and Ellen's distorted voice informed Mr Catt that the kangaroo had arrived.

'I'd better go and see to it,' said Mr Catt. 'Bruce, our marsupial keeper, is laid up in a coma after Rufus the red kangaroo jumped on him during his first day with us.'

'How did that happen?' I asked.

'It's actually a very sad tale. Rufus, who was our alpha-male, was an orphan who'd been hand-reared at Walkabout Zoo where he was born. It turned out that Bruce had started his career at Walkabout, one of his first jobs being to hand-rear young Rufus.

Apparently, he used to wear a sort of apron with a pouch for Rufus to jump into. When he started work here, he didn't recognise Rufus but Rufus recognised him and tried to leap into the bag of food Bruce was carrying. Being hit full on by two hundred pounds of solid kangaroo is not good for a man.'

'I understand why Bruce isn't here,' I said, 'but why do you need another kangaroo?'

'Because, before uncovering the full story, assuming Rufus had just gone berserk, we thought it best to shoot him. Ellen ordered a sane one on eBay.'

'That's really sad,' I said. 'Poor Rufus.'

'True, but every cloud has a silver lining. The leopards did rather well out of it.' He pointed towards the clumps of fur.

'Well, thank you for your time,' said Hobbes. 'It has been most instructive. Do you mind if we look around on our own?'

'Be my guests.' Mr Catt bustled away.

We strolled round the park for an hour or so, Hobbes studying each animal with keen interest, now and again licking his lips and swallowing, as if hungry. Dregs slouched alongside with an expression of acute boredom that only lifted when he saw the tortoises; they caused great and noisy excitement. He obviously held the opinion that rocks should stay put and should not sprout legs and lumber around. Hobbes had to grab him by the scruff of the neck and drag him away. Otherwise, I think he'd be there still. Other than that, we came across nothing of great interest, though Hobbes appeared to be deep in thought about something. I contented myself with walking at his side, occasionally kicking stones for Dregs to chase.

A barbed-wire fence eventually indicated the limits of public access. I noticed one or two matted tufts of brown fur snagged on the barbs, as a pair of Bactrian camels, appearing from the shade under an oak tree, began pulling at a bale of hay.

'I'd be a bit careful if I were you,' I said. 'That could be camel hair.'

My warning came too late. Hobbes had already plucked a tuft from the wire and sniffed it. He looked up. 'I wish I hadn't just done that.' He reached for his handkerchief.

He sneezed so violently that Dregs fled a hundred yards up the path, loping back towards us suspiciously, growling. Hobbes sneezed again. And again. He blew his nose, which, I swear, though prominent enough at the best of times, was growing and ripening.

'I've got some stuff that helps in the car,' he said, snuffling. 'I'd better get back there … and quickly.'

By the time we reached the car park his eyes had swollen shut as if he'd come off worse in a punch-up and his nose shone like a baboon's bottom. I had to guide him as he groped for the car.

Reaching into his pocket, he handed me the keys. 'Look in the boot. There should be a black bag. I'd be obliged if you'd open it for me.'

I did as he asked. The bag contained a bottle of Optrex, half a dozen handkerchiefs and an assortment of glass vials filled with a coloured liquid.

'Could I have one of the green ones, please? And a fresh handkerchief. This one's ripped.'

Ripped wasn't really the word: it had been blown to shreds. I handed the things to him. Between explosions, he bit the top off the vial, tilting back his head, gulping down the contents. Then he sneezed again. Then he howled like a wolf. Then he collapsed like a factory chimney that had been dynamited.

Though Hobbes came down with a thud, a desperate dive saved me from being completely crushed. Even so, I ended up flat on my front, my legs trapped beneath him. As I pushed myself up on my elbows, Dregs ran up, nosing me, wagging his tail, as if it was all a jolly game.

'What do I do now?' I asked.

He made a strange snicker that I interpreted as, 'You're the human. You do something.'

'A great help you are.'

Neither education nor experience had prepared me for how to act when my legs were pinned beneath a hefty, unconscious police inspector. Groaning, wriggling and straining proved to be of no avail; I might just as well have tried to break free from the stocks. Yet, most of all, I was worried about Hobbes. Unable to tell how sick he was, though able to feel the rise and fall of his chest, I felt utterly helpless, not to mention ridiculous. Dregs, thumping his tail on the ground, eager for further entertainment, sat by us, expectantly. I had a great idea.

'Go and fetch help,' I said in my most commanding voice.

He listened, his head on one side, his tail beating faster and then, to my amazement, ran off, as if on a mission. 'Good dog!' I cried, impressed.

Sadly, he had not turned into a latter-day Lassie and, returning, he dropped one of the chewed rubber balls he kept in the car in front of me, bullying me until I threw it. As soon as I did, he bounded after it with a joyous bark.

Fearing rescue would not come until I gave up on dignity, I decided to call for help, though the car park was deserted.

'Excuse me, anybody,' I cried, at a polite volume. 'I could do with a little help here.' Since there was no response, I concluded a more effective option might be to scream with all the force of my lungs. For me, to think was to act and so, throwing back my head, opening my mouth, I sucked down air in preparation for a titanic bellow. As I did, Dregs, scampering back, dropped the ball. My mouth wasn't big enough to take it in, at least not in one bite, but it stuck between my upper and lower teeth, gagging me. Spluttering, I spat it out, wiping my mouth in a frantic bid to remove any dangles of dog drool, as a low, rumbling groan emerged from Hobbes.

'Are you alright?' I asked, continuing to wipe away with the backs of my hands, while Dregs, barking excitedly, stared at the ball, waiting.

'Ugh,' said Hobbes, pushing himself into a kneeling position.

Pulling my legs to safety, I rubbed the life back into them.

'Are you alright?' I repeated.

He turned towards me, his face pale, skin glistening like moist putty, eyes damp and red, though, at least, his nose had shrunk to its normal dimensions. He nodded and we helped each other up. Then he leant against the car, every breath bubbling and popping, as if he were sucking through a part-flooded snorkel.

'Optrex!'

I handed him the bottle. His hands shook and he must have spilled half of it as he filled the bath to rinse his eyes.

'That's better.' He sighed.

Maybe he really did feel better, but he still looked as if someone had scooped out his eyeballs and filled the sockets with overripe strawberries. It was a most striking effect, causing my own eyes to water in sympathy and a small group of respectable elderly visitors strolling by to gasp and hurry away.

'Andy,' said Hobbes in a loud, nasal voice, 'a word of advice. It's never a good idea to let the dog drop his balls into your mouth; you don't know where they've been.'

The blood boiling in my cheeks, all I could do was nod and grin inanely.

The pensioners departed even more rapidly, muttering, shaking their heads.

'I'd like to go home now,' said Hobbes, 'but I can't drive like this. I wonder if Billy's free?'

Billy Shawcroft was a binge-drinking dwarf, who, for reasons I'd never fathomed, drove a reconditioned hearse and claimed Hobbes had once saved him from the clutches of a witch. Whether or not his grasp of reality could be trusted, he seemed to like Hobbes, often providing valuable information and other help. There was no point in asking me to drive; the last time I'd tried I'd demolished a Volvo while creating the 'Leaning Tree of Fenderton', as the *Bugle* dubbed it. Not that it leaned anymore; last January, having decided enough was enough during a storm, it had lain down across the main Fenderton Road, holding up the rush-hour traffic for several hours while the chainsaws reduced it to bite-sized chunks. Hobbes had since offered me driving lessons, but I'd declined. It seemed wisest.

Pulling his mobile phone from his pocket, he handed it to me. 'See if he can pick us up. His number's in the menu under "D".'

'OK. "D" for dwarf.'

'No, "D" for driver,' said Hobbes and attempted a smile. 'You're under "D" too.'

'Eh?'

'No, not "A"; "D" for don't let him drive.' His attempted chuckle turned into a soggy cough. Those pensioners didn't know how lucky they were to be out of earshot.

As I phoned Billy, who was available, didn't sound as if he'd been drinking and reckoned he'd be with us in about half an hour, Hobbes slumped in the shade of a tree, groaning that he wished to be left alone.

As we waited, I chucked the ball round the field, keeping Dregs entertained, mostly thinking about the wonderful woman, kicking myself for not asking her name, though my father would, no doubt, have pointed out that she was way out of my league. I had to admit he might have been correct, but I could dream and hope, which are two things I was rather good at. After all, there was no accounting for taste and, one never knew, she might have fallen under a curse, compelling her to fancy an out-of-work, crap journalist. I might have been just her type. These things can happen … really. In fact, at the very same moment, she might have been feeling similar regret at not having asked for my name and telephone number. My hand feeling the smoothness of my chin, I was grateful for Hobbes's Christmas gift of an electric razor, something I used nearly every day. I wished I'd managed to buy him a little more than a bumper bag of walnuts, which had been all I could afford. Still, he'd appeared rather pleased and had eaten them all, though I would have preferred it if he'd removed the shells first.

The image of the woman's loveliness, having burned into my brain, I knew I'd never forget her face, her eyes, her hair, her figure, her clothes, her everything. She'd smiled at me and moved with such grace, her voice as warm and soft as a kitten's purr, and I realised with stomach-churning certainty I'd never see her again, unless, of course, I could persuade Ellen Bloom to give me her name and number, an act of bravery that would risk embarrassing myself further. Remembering the old saying that faint heart never won fair lady, time and again, in between throwing the ball for Dregs, I tried to revive my fainting heart and had probably nearly succeeded when Billy's hearse showed up.

He waved, sitting atop the pile of cushions he needed to see over the steering wheel, operating the pedals by means of long wooden extensions. It must have been illegal but no police officer had ever brought him to book, which I suspected was something to do with Hobbes's influence. Even so, Billy was an excellent and careful driver, who retained enough sense never to try when he was on a bender. On those occasions, he might sometimes be seen flailing down The Shambles on a pair of roller blades that scared him silly when sober. I had long suspected that at least part of the reason for his headaches after a night on the booze was because he'd fallen over so often, but at least he didn't have far to fall.

He chugged towards us, stopped and jumped out. Dregs bounded up to him, an old friend, greeting him exuberantly, jumping into the front seat, chewing his ball.

'Hiya,' said Billy, in his high-pitched, piping voice. 'How ya doing? You don't look so good.'

'Thanks,' said Hobbes with a grimace.

'Have you been messing with camels again?'

Hobbes nodded.

'I've told you before they're no good for you,' said Billy, with a stern frown.

'I made a mistake.'

'You're telling me? Oh well, I'd best get you home. You'll have to pick up your car tomorrow.'

Billy helped Hobbes stand, trying to support him as he struggled to the hearse, the pair making an entirely ludicrous tableau. I helped get Hobbes into the back, where he lay flat, groaning, and joined Dregs and Billy in the front, there being plenty of room for three to sit abreast. Following a brief scuffle, I had to take the middle seat, so Dregs could stick his head out. An elderly gentleman raised his sunhat respectfully as we pulled away at a speed in keeping with the vehicle's original use.

'Has he taken one of the green bottles?' asked Billy.

'Yes,' I said. 'What on earth is in that stuff?'

'Mysterious herbs from the East, so I was told. Mrs Goodfellow makes it and it's powerful stuff, though the side effects can be alarming.'

'I've seen them,' I said, nodding.

'Did he howl?'

'Yes. It didn't half give me a turn.'

'Not as much as it gave me,' said Hobbes and coughed horribly.

'At least he's compost mental again,' said Billy.

'That's compos mentis,' said Hobbes.

'Which proves my point.' Billy chuckled.

Hobbes didn't speak for the rest of the journey, except for a snuffly complaint about a headache. I wondered about the green stuff he'd taken, alarmed that its side effects were presumably better than not drinking it. On reaching Blackdog Street, he rolled from the hearse with a brief word of thanks and went straight upstairs to bed. I checked on him from time to time but he was fast asleep, still bubbling like a cauldron on the boil.

I was, therefore, by default, back in charge of catering and, despite the lure of the pubs, I decided it wouldn't be fair to desert Hobbes. Besides, I had no money. Dregs's dinner was not a problem; opening a tin of dog food, I spooned it into his bowl and watched him wolf it down in half a dozen noisy bites, before taking himself upstairs to lie at Hobbes's door. Next came the important thing: my supper. A rummage through Mrs Goodfellow's cupboards revealed surprising quantities of tins, mostly ancient ones. I was amazed she kept so many for I'd hardly ever known her use one – except for tins of pears, which Hobbes liked with his Sunday tea. None of them appealed.

Then I had a brainwave. A jacket potato with cheese would taste great and be highly nutritious. Selecting a brick-sized spud from Mrs Goodfellow's store, scrubbing it clean, I sliced it down the middle. Next, taking a nice chunk of the wonderful, crumbly Sorenchester cheese from the pantry, grating it with a potato peeler, I heaped a generous amount onto the potato halves and shoved them under the grill. After lighting it, reckoning they'd take about half an hour to cook, I sauntered into the sitting room and turned on the telly. As I sat down, the regional news came on, making no mention of dead sheep or big cats.

However, one item caught my attention, a report on the First Annual Great Sorenchester Music Festival. I watched with increasing interest, despite the inane and annoying presence of Jeremy, a reporter who clearly imagined himself the epitome of cool. He might have been twenty or more years earlier, though I doubted it and his three-minute slot showed him to be a patronising, smug, ignorant twit. He interviewed the festival's organisers, a pair of local farmers, clearly not gentleman farmers but genuine, horny-handed sons of the soil, though I couldn't imagine how they'd managed to get so encrusted in mud when it hadn't rained for weeks.

Why the report piqued my interest so much mystified me for, although I had attended the occasional music gig over the years, I'd not really enjoyed them and the last time I'd gone out to see a band had been quite painful when a careless, or vindictive, person had dropped a full drink from the balcony and, though I'd been fortunate a safety-conscious management had replaced glasses with plastics, it had left a deep impression on the bridge of my nose and a bloody mess down my shirt.

The acrid stink of smoke in my nose, my eyes were already running with tears as I leapt up, running to the kitchen, where heavy, yellowish, greasy smoke was billowing from the grill. I was coughing like a sixty-a-day man, my potato and cheese belching fumes like a pair of miniature volcanoes, erupting into orange flame as I tugged the pan from under the heat. I tipped the whole lot into the sink, spinning the taps to full throttle, watching as, with a sad hiss, the fires dying, the potato halves collapsed in on themselves, leaving a blackened, soggy mess. Throwing open the back door and window, I flapped a tea towel to disperse the smog, dreading what Hobbes would say when he woke up, for it wasn't the first time I'd nearly set fire to his kitchen and, since the reason I was staying there was because I'd accidentally burned my old flat down, I feared he might regard me as a liability.

Though I was fortunate there were two closed doors between him and the kitchen, I was sure he'd notice the smell, unless I cleaned up as well as possible. Finding a bucket and cleaning stuff, I scrubbed every surface I could reach until I was dripping with sweat, and then spritzed air freshener all around; it turned out to be fly spray but it did mask the pong quite effectively.

Afterwards, my culinary confidence dented beyond repair, I resorted to cold baked beans à la tin, eating in the garden, resolving to pay much more attention next time Mrs G was cooking. Then, before turning in, and much to Dregs's disgust, I splashed bleach around, hoping the pungent fumes would mask any underlying odours and that Hobbes would think I'd merely decided to clean up.

As I lay in bed that night, thinking of the music festival, I hoped I'd find a way to get there, despite what had happened at the last one I'd sort of been to as a schoolboy. It had started when my mate Baz, spotting a poster for a free festival, grew really excited at the bands listed and, though they'd meant little to me, I'd allowed myself to be dragged along in the slipstream of his enthusiasm. I'd agreed to go with him, providing I could get father's permission, something I'd thought unlikely with the festival taking place during term time, albeit over a weekend. To my surprise, he'd said yes.

Just after tea on the Friday evening, Baz's mum had given us a lift to the farm hosting the event, dropping us off with our rucksacks and a tent we'd borrowed from Baz's sister. We'd been surprised – and not a little proud – to be the first arrivals. Tramping across a squelchy field that had quite obviously been home for many cows, we found what we considered a suitable spot and set to pitching the tent. The sky was already darkening when we started the argument about which one of us should have brought a torch and, by the time we'd called a truce, we could really have done with one, if only to read the instructions. Instead, opening the tent bag, tipping everything out, we used the grope, stumble and curse method, taking an hour at least to contrive something tent-like.

Then, while I held it together, Baz, picking up the rubber mallet, attempted to knock in the pegs. Taking a massive overhead swing, he struck the first peg a mighty blow, bending it in half, as the mallet, rebounding, gave him a fat lip. Our strained friendship could have done without my heartless laughter. Still, in the end, we succeeded in pegging it down. We then spent another half-hour discussing whether we needed the flysheet; Baz, insisting that we wouldn't since it was too cold for flies, won the argument on the grounds that it was his sister's tent. We were well past the tetchy stage when, at last, we chucked our gear inside and set out for a recce.

Still no one else had arrived and we slipped and squelched through mud that would have been ideal for a First World War movie, searching with increasing desperation by the flickering light of a match for a signpost, or anything to direct us to the facilities. I'd begun to get a very bad feeling by the time we were forced to pee in a hedge.

The downpour started as we groped our way back to the tent, where we discovered what a flysheet was for, how badly we'd put up the tent and how thin were our sleeping bags. That night had been the longest, the most uncomfortable and the most miserable of my life, up to that point.

Having finally got to sleep in the dawn's grey light, we were woken by a grinning farmhand who, roaring up in a tractor, told us, through tears of laughter, that we were a month too early. By the time Baz and I managed to get a lift home, a tedious process in the days before mobile phones, we were no longer on speaking terms.

I sighed. I've never been very good at keeping friends, or making them for that matter. In fact, by then, my best friend was either Hobbes, or Dregs, something I didn't like to dwell on. Nevertheless, hope was prevailing over experience and, having recently seen a film clip on telly about Woodstock, the idea of sitting in a sunny field with a few beers amidst friendly, peace-loving fans appealed and, maybe, my lovely woman would turn up.

Waking next morning, after a sweaty night of broken sleep and hot dreams, I washed, dressed and strolled down to the kitchen. Hobbes was already up. His eyes had lost their strawberry look, though they still retained a delicate pink tinge. He was growling to himself, eating Sugar Puffs straight from a large bowl with 'DOG' written on the side. Sometimes I wondered how much of his weird stuff was done for effect.

'Morning,' he said, still snuffling.

I felt some guilt at my relief when he didn't mention the stink of smoke or fly spray or bleach. 'Good morning,' I said. 'Did you sleep well?'

'Yes, thank you and thanks for helping out yesterday. I really should take more care with camels.'

'You should.' I nodded. 'Umm ... what was in the vial? It seemed to have a terrible effect.'

'Mysterious herbs from the East: Norfolk, I think. The lass makes it, and it does me a power of good, though it tastes vile.'

'It didn't appear to do much good.'

'You haven't seen what I'm like without it. You should see what happens to my ...' He paused.

'To your what?'

'You're sure you want to know?'

'Yes ... umm ... probably.'

He shook his head. 'I think it best that you don't.'

After breakfast, he led Dregs and me to the car. I'd climbed into the back and put on my seat belt before it struck me that it shouldn't have been there.

'How did this get back?' I asked

'I expect the car fairy brought it,' he said, with a strange grin.

I think he was joking but I wasn't entirely sure. One day, I probably would meet a car fairy and many things would become clear. The thought had occurred more than once that I was stuck in a dream, for there was no way someone like Hobbes could exist and, yet, there he sat, as solid as a pile of bricks.

We left town, heading roughly in the direction of Skeleton Bob's place, but Hobbes said he was planning to ask around some of the farms and cottages in that area and see if they'd noticed anything out of the ordinary.

'Are you still worried about the panther?' I asked.

'I'm not worried. I want to know if there is any truth in Bob's story – and I still need to find out what happened to those missing pheasants.'

The odd thing was that, though he was driving, I could talk with him, look about and enjoy the ride since he was driving safely, within the speed limit, keeping an eye on the road. In a way, I almost found it more disconcerting than his usual maniac style.

We stopped at several farms and homes in the area; no one claimed to have seen any big cats or, indeed, anything unusual at all, most regarding the suggestion with amused scepticism. I, for one, didn't feel in the least surprised.

Then, a couple of miles beyond Bob's place, we visited a small farm bordering the woods where he'd claimed his sighting. It was Loop's Farm, according to a blue enamelled sign by the entrance. Rattling over a cattle grid, we bumped along a dusty drive towards the lichen-encrusted walls of an old stone farmhouse, where two men were leaning against a gate into a field, dotted with Sorenchester Old Spot pigs. We pulled up next to them.

The younger man nodded. 'G'day.' A length of orange twine substituted for a belt round his mud-spattered moleskin trousers, his bare chest was nearly as hairy as Hobbes's and he was wearing a tatty, broad-brimmed straw hat.

'Good day,' said Hobbes as he got out.

The older man smiled. He was dressed like the first one, except for a red-checked shirt with the sleeves rolled up. He gave the impression of being even muddier, as if he'd been rolling in muck with the pigs. 'What can we do you for?' he asked.

Hobbes was introducing himself as I slithered from the car. Dregs, who had fallen asleep with his bottom half on the front passenger seat, his top half in the footwell, awoke with a resounding woof and bounded into the yard, upending me as he sprang towards the farmers. I sprawled in the dust, fearing he was going to attack, but his tail span like a propeller as he danced around them, as if meeting old friends.

'Nice doggie,' said the older man, patting him. He held out a big, grey-haired hand towards Hobbes. 'Bernie Bullimore and this is my son-in-law, Les – Les Bashem. Now, how can we help you?'

Hobbes shook hands. 'I have a few routine questions.' He hauled me to my feet. 'There have been reports of pheasant poaching in these parts and I wondered if you'd had any problems?'

'No, not really,' said Les, 'but, then, we're not a shooting estate and there's not much for 'em to take. Bob Nibblet takes the odd rabbit now and again but we don't object to that.'

'Does he have permission to be on your land?'

'Not as such but we know he does it and he knows we know and we know he knows we know, if you know what I mean. It's an informal arrangement. Old Skelly Bob don't do much harm.'

Hobbes nodded and I brushed the dust and dung from my trousers. Dregs was rolling on his back at Les's feet, like an excited puppy.

'Funny you should mention Mr Nibblet,' said Hobbes, 'because he reported seeing what might have been a big cat in Loop Woods. I don't suppose you've seen anything out of the ordinary?'

'No,' said Bernie, shaking his head so emphatically that his hat spun away like a Frisbee. I thought he glanced at his son-in-law.

'Mind you,' said Les, 'we was wondering what'd killed that sheep, 'cos we ain't seen no stray dogs around here, not this year anyhow. And it was found on Henry Bishop's land and that's right close to Loop Woods. Of course, Henry's not the sort to let dogs get at his beasts. He's always ready with his shotgun – a bit too ready if you ask me.'

'That's right.' Bernie nodded. 'He damn near blew my head off once, when I was picking nuts in the woods by his hedge.'

'Why?' asked Hobbes.

'Because I like nuts.'

Hobbes chuckled. 'No, why did he shoot at you?'

'He said he mistook me for a stray dog.'

'But dogs don't pick nuts.'

'That's what I told him.'

'How did he respond?'

'He said, "Get off my land" and popped in another couple of shells. Of course, I wasn't actually on his land, but Henry's not one to let facts get in the way of a good catchphrase. He enjoys having something to moan about.'

Hobbes looked stern. 'Did you report the incident to the police?'

'No. The way I saw it, there was no harm done, but I make sure the kids keep well away from him.'

'That's right,' said Les. 'The nippers can go where they like on the farm, except near that old bugger's place. It's best for everyone. He's not the easiest of neighbours.' He grinned. 'Mind you, he might say the same about us when we hold our festival.'

Only then did the recognition circuits in my brain connect. 'I know you!' I said, 'I saw you talking to that twerp on the telly last night before I set f …' I glanced at Hobbes. 'That is … umm … before I … umm… set the table for my tea.'

Bernie took a bow. 'That's right. Me and Les are celebrities now. You can have our autographs for a fiver.'

I smiled. 'I'll remember that when I've got one. I would like to see the festival though. Unfortunately, I'm skint.'

'Quiet, Andy,' said Hobbes. 'We're here on police business, if you remember?'

'Sorry.' I shut up.

The festival's appeal was growing, though money would be a problem. Since losing my job at the *Bugle*, I'd been unemployed, except for a disastrous two weeks as stand-in waiter at the Black Dog Café. They gave me a uniform but the trousers, being very much on the tight side, I'd had to wear them with caution and much stomach sucking. Though the memory was as painful as the trouser squeeze, by the end of the second week, I'd believed I was getting the hang of things. Then, one busy lunchtime, came a moment of explosive release, a feeling of freedom, which lasted until a lady started making a fuss about flies in her soup. Since the teeth of my zip were grinning up from her bowl and my predicament was obvious, there'd been no point in denying ownership. I hadn't regarded it as my fault but the manager, taking a different view, had sent me on my way.

I could perhaps have got another job since then, but Hobbes seemed to need my help and, despite everything, I enjoyed being out with him and Dregs. It was far more exciting than working as a not-very-good journalist or as a waiter and, thanks entirely to Hobbes's and Mrs Goodfellow's generosity, I lived better and healthier than ever before. I just wished I had some money.

Hobbes and the farmers were now discussing the forthcoming event. 'So,' he said, 'it's all happening over the last weekend in July? What's your security like?'

'It should be fine,' said Bernie. 'It's not as if we're trying to compete with Glastonbury or anything, we're just getting in a bunch of local acts and the Kung Fu club are willing to act as stewards. We were willing to pay normal rates but the lady I spoke to didn't want paying, so long as we allowed her to keep any teeth she found.'

Hobbes nodded with a grin that almost made him look human. 'Ah, yes,' he said. 'I think I know the lady.'

Of course he knew her. Mrs Goodfellow, besides looking after us and collecting teeth, taught Kung Fu and gave instruction (as a result of a printing error) in the marital arts.

'It sounds like you've got it sorted,' said Hobbes, 'but I think it would be a good idea for me to be here, in an unofficial capacity. It's not the big cat that worries me so much as Henry Bishop's short temper and shotgun.'

Bernie smiled. 'I really don't think it's necessary but we'd be happy to have you here.'

'I'll want Andy and the dog with me, if that's alright,' said Hobbes.

'Fine by us, Inspector,' Les said. 'He's a fine dog.'

'We'll bring a tent,' said Hobbes, 'mingle with the crowd and I'll keep myself inconspicuous.'

I suppressed a grin. Hobbes in a crowd was about as inconspicuous as a gorilla in the ballet. Still, he had solved my problem of how to get in, though he was not a regular fairy godmother.

'That's sorted then,' he said, rubbing his hands together. 'Will I know anyone taking part?'

'We're expecting No One You Ever Heard Of,' said Les.

'Excellent. I read about the jig they did at the Feathers.'

'The *gig* they did,' I corrected. He knew of course; it was all an act, almost certainly. And it had, reportedly, been some gig: never before in Sorenchester had a band generated so much raw emotion, never before had so many instruments been smashed in such a short time. The band really should have asked 'Featherlight' Binks, the landlord, before starting to play. If they had, he wouldn't have said no; he'd have said a whole lot more, though the meaning would have been much the same, but asking would have saved a great deal of suffering. Featherlight had only got away with it because the magistrates refused to believe the band's injuries had been caused in a brawl and assumed they must all have been in a car crash or two. Presumably, since the band had been booked, they'd been discharged from hospital.

Les continued. 'There's gonna be all sorts of bands and singers for every taste. So far we've booked Tiny Tim Jones, Mad Donna, the Delius Myth, Lou Pole and the Lawyers and Stink – you might remember him – he used to be in the police.'

Hobbes nodded. 'Yes, I know him. He wasn't, in fact, a police officer. He worked in the canteen for a while, but never quite mastered basic hygiene.'

'There are more bands and singers that haven't yet confirmed and we're also going to have fire-eaters and jugglers and magicians and lots of things.'

'I can see you've got it all running smoothly,' said Hobbes, touching his forehead in salute. 'Well, you must be busy so we'll leave you to get on with it. If you do see any big cats, you know where to find me. Goodbye.' He turned away. 'C'mon you two.'

Dregs was reluctant to leave but I managed to coax him into the car with half a biscuit I found in the glove compartment. As we pulled away, I looked back. Les and Bernie had returned to business. Leaning on gates must have been a vital part of farming.

Our next stop was at Henry Bishop's overgrown smallholding, outside the house, a house that looked as if it was still in the process of falling on hard times. So did Henry Bishop who burst from his tumbledown barn, an open shotgun over the crook of his arm, his unshaven face as red and as dirty as the handkerchief round his short, thick neck. His nose might have been mistaken for a giant blackberry.

Dregs, I noticed, was staying close to Hobbes. I couldn't blame him. I was keeping pretty close myself.

'Get off my land!' Henry shouted. 'I'll have the law on you!'

'I am the law, sir,' said Hobbes with what passed for a pleasant smile as he showed his ID. 'I'd just like to ask you a couple of questions. I take it that you are Mr Henry Bishop?'

Henry glowered. 'That I am. Now, get on with it. I haven't got all day.'

'Firstly, do you have a valid certificate for that shotgun?'

'What? Of course I do.'

'May I see it, sir?'

'I'm not sure where it is. Somewhere inside, I expect. It may take some time.'

'We're not in a hurry,' said Hobbes, his smile broadening. 'I can help you find it.'

Henry scratched his bald head, frowning in thought for a moment. 'I'll get it myself,' he said, spitting, slouching away, and closing the front door behind him.

'I don't think he's pleased to see us,' Hobbes remarked as we waited in the shade of a worm-eaten, old apple tree.

Henry's furious shouting penetrated the door, though I couldn't make out any words. He reappeared, thrusting a plastic wallet into Hobbes's great paw.

Hobbes, opening it, nodded. 'Thank you, sir. That appears to be all in order, except for the date. This expired two years ago. You shouldn't try to amend it with a biro, it doesn't work.'

'Well, I forgot,' said Henry, spitting again. 'It happens. I'll renew it tomorrow. I never use it anyway.'

'Very good, sir,' said Hobbes, 'but I'd better take the shotgun for the time being. I'm sure you don't mind and it will stop you from inadvertently breaking the law any further.'

'Very well.' He handed it to Hobbes.

'And I'd better take the others.'

'What others?'

'The ones in your cabinet. I really ought to check that, too. Do you mind if I take a look inside?'

'Yes,' growled Henry, his ruddy complexion darkening like an impending storm, 'I bloody well do mind.'

'I'm sorry to hear that, sir,' said Hobbes, shrugging, pushing open the front door, stepping into the house.

With another spit and a curse, Henry followed.

Dregs and I looked at each other, agreeing to keep out. Henry Bishop was a nasty piece of work and both of us were happy to keep our acquaintance with him to the minimum. Mopping the sweat from my forehead with a handkerchief, I lounged against the tree, contemplating lunchtime, thinking of the pleasant little pubs that weren't far away, hoping Hobbes would decide to stop at one or other, relishing the prospect of a nice, cold lager and a bite to eat.

The sudden commotion inside the house made Dregs bark and retreat and made me quake. The front door jerked open. Henry ran through with a terrified howl. He hadn't gone more than a couple of steps when Hobbes burst out, catching him within a couple of loping strides, seizing his collar and swinging him off his feet. Henry's legs kept moving, his eyes bulging like a rabbit's, as Hobbes twisted him round and dropped him. He fell to his knees but Hobbes lifted him by the lapels on his jacket, shaking him like a duster.

'I'm not going to do anything to you now,' said Hobbes, speaking slowly and at terrifying volume, his face showing a rage I'd never seen before, 'but if it comes to my attention that you ever do anything like that again, I will dismember you. Is that clear?'

The front of Henry's trousers darkened and he moaned as a wet patch spread down his leg. I felt some sympathy for him, no matter what he'd done, because Hobbes was at his terrifying best and, even as an innocent bystander, the collateral fear almost overwhelmed me, making my legs shake. God alone knew what Henry was feeling.

'Is that clear, sir?'

A squeak emerged from Henry's bloodless lips. His flour-white face looked as if he'd suffered an extreme vampire attack. 'Yes. Yes. It's clear. I won't do it again, I swear I won't.'

Hobbes, increasing the ferocity of his glare to force twelve, released the hapless man, who, dropping to the ground, lay in a quivering foetal position, sucking his thumb like a baby.

'You'd better not sir, because I mean what I say.'

I, for one, didn't doubt it. Hobbes, turning his back on the human detritus, returned to the house, remaining inside for a few minutes. I could hear his voice rising and falling gently. He reappeared, carrying three shotguns.

'If you obtain a valid certificate and behave yourself,' he said, looking down, 'I may let you have them back. Right, my next question is, have you seen any big cats around here?'

Henry, still lying in the dirt, shook his head and whimpered.

'Thank you, sir,' said Hobbes, walking back to the car, dropping the guns into the boot. As Dregs and I crept in, he started the engine and moved off. Looking back, I glimpsed a woman at the upstairs window. She was pale, thin and grey-haired, her most outstanding feature being the grotesque swelling of her right eye. Understanding, I shared Hobbes's anger. We drove away in silence, broken only by the sound of Dregs licking himself.

Despite the angry feelings, I was extremely pleased when Hobbes pulled up outside

The Crown at Dumpster. He ushered us into the cool gloom of the bar where horse brasses gleamed and the smell of cooking made my mouth water. 'A double lashing of ginger beer for me, a pint of mild in a bowl for the dog and a pint of lager in a glass for the lad.'

The rosy-cheeked barmaid poured out our drinks.

'And I'll order three steak and kidney pies with all the trimmings and one for the dog too. Do you want anything, Andy?'

I sipped my lager. 'I'll have the same.'

'Same as me or same as Dregs?'

'Same as Dregs.'

He smiled. 'That'll be five steak and kidney pies then please, miss.'

4

Both outside and in, The Crown gave the impression of unchanging permanence. Hobbes and I took opposite seats on a pair of creaking, old settles in the corner, while Dregs stood on the timeworn flagstones, lapping at his bowl of mild. Though Hobbes smiled, commenting on the horse brasses around the bar, the bunches of hops hanging from the beams, there was something tense in his hunched posture as if he was not quite at ease. That, combined with his strange feral odour, always there, but seeming suddenly stronger, made me nervous and I was relieved that, when the barmaid served our meals, he thanked her with his normal gentle, old-fashioned courtesy. For the next few minutes as he shovelled down his three substantial, steaming pies, I ate mine with quiet appreciation. Though it wasn't up to Mrs G's standards, it was good – and hunger adds relish to any meal. Dregs, wolfing down his lunch and licking his bowl dry, took himself out through the open front door. A few moments later, there was a furious, imaginative and prolonged outbreak of swearing from some man in the garden.

Hobbes, a semi-circle of empty plates in front of him, ignored the commotion, mopping up any remaining gravy with his fingers and sucking them clean. He drained his glass in one long, slow movement, putting it down carefully on a beermat. The rank, feral taint in the air grew stronger.

'That sort of thing makes me angry,' he said, his voice rumbling. 'In fact, it makes me very angry.' He thumped the table and a plate, bouncing off it, hitting the stone floor, exploded into jagged splinters. He grimaced, glancing apologetically at the barmaid. 'Sorry, miss, it was an accident. I'll pay for it.'

She stared at him, as if at a diabolical manifestation.

'What does?' I asked, in case it was something I'd done, fearing he was going to blow his top because I'd nearly set fire to his kitchen again, coming over all sweaty and breathless. It brought back a memory of how I'd felt as a ten-year old when I'd been summoned to the headmaster's office to explain why I'd broken the windows in the gym. Although, I'd had absolutely nothing to do with it, someone had reported seeing me in the vicinity and, despite all my denials, I was forced to take the blame, all my pocket money for the next few months going to pay for the repairs. It still rankled.

'Bullying,' said Hobbes.

I was able to breathe again. I'd never done anything like that. 'Do you mean what Henry Bishop did?'

'I do. He hit Mrs Bishop in the face just because she had to stop and think where he might have put the key to the gun cabinet. It was such a casual thing, even with me standing there, and her eye was already bruised. If he's like that when the police are with him, what's he like when they're on their own?'

'Worse?'

'Damn right!'

He'd never before sworn in my presence and, though it was mild by most standards, the shock hit so hard I struggled to breathe, having to force myself to speak.

'You won't really dismember him if he hits her again, though?'

'Won't I?' His scowl was as deep as the ocean.

'You scared him pretty well. He'll behave himself, won't he?'

'Oh yes, he will for a while, a few days, maybe for a week or two, but bullies like him don't change. Still, having their arms and legs torn off usually slows them down.'

His laugh was deep, long and wicked. The barmaid, dropping a tray of glasses, scurried, wide-eyed towards the kitchen; a man walking in, an empty glass in his hand, turned, heading straight back out.

'Right,' said Hobbes, his hands twitching and clutching, as if they were already squeezing Henry's throat, 'I think a visit to the butcher's is in order. And quickly.'

I nodded. 'Are you alright to drive?'

'Never better.'

Indeed, having stopped snuffling, his eyes, no longer retaining the pink tinge, having instead turned a furious, burning red, he appeared fully recovered from his allergic attack. Despite being reasonably confident that he wouldn't harm me, I felt like a kid in the tiger's den. Standing up, dropping a handful of money onto the bar, he dragged me from the settle, to which I'd become quite attached, and dumped me in the back of the car. Dregs jumped into the front, his panting almost as loud as the engine.

I closed my eyes, clinging to the seat as we accelerated away from the pub onto the road, realising just how wrong I'd been to suggest his careful driving of the morning might have been more alarming than his usual style. I knew we were going fast, overtaking in places where no one in their right mind should overtake but, when the car seemed to jump, landing heavily, my head banged the ceiling and my eyes opened involuntarily, I saw he was taking a short cut through what I guessed was Barnley Copse. Trees and shrubs whizzed past only millimetres away, as we plunged into hollows, leaped over mounds, swerved past fallen logs. But we didn't hit anything, not even Bob Nibblet, who was staring open-mouthed, a sack over his shoulder, as we skirted the hulk of a vast, rotting trunk.

After a few minutes, a stomach-churning bounce and the wail of car horns, we left the bumps and ruts behind, meaning my teeth were only chattering with terror. When he stamped on the brake, stopping the car, I cannoned into the seat in front, sprawling back, stunned, into the footwell, wishing I'd got round to doing up my seat belt. As Hobbes got out, slamming the door behind him, Dregs stuck his head between the seats to snicker at my predicament. By the time I'd extricated myself and had struggled back into a sitting position, Hobbes was striding back, a bulky parcel wrapped in white paper and string balanced on his shoulder. Slinging it down beside me, he started the engine, and the nightmare journey continued. Fortunately, it didn't take long to get home and as I clambered from the car I reflected, not without a degree of horror, that I did regard 13 Blackdog Street as home.

Hobbes was already bounding up the steps to the door, the parcel tucked under his arm, Dregs very attentive at his heels. At the top, he turned, tossing me the car keys. I caught them – on the bridge of my nose, which didn't half smart. After wiping away the tears, I retrieved the keys from the gutter, locked the car and prepared myself for the sitting room. I knew what was happening and intended keeping out of the way.

As I entered, Hobbes having already spread newspapers in the corner of the sitting room, lobbed his parcel onto the paper, springing after it, like a lion onto a wildebeest. The bag disintegrated, spilling a dozen or so cow tails, as, shutting the front door behind me, edging past, I fled towards the kitchen, cringing at the sound of his great jaws crunching hide and bone. Dregs prowled round the edge of the paper like a jackal hoping for scraps. When he'd first joined us, he'd refused raw meat in favour of gourmet meals, but acquaintance with Hobbes had broadened his horizons.

Hobbes's face was already slathered with blood and hide and bits of bone, the hairy end of a cow's tail protruding from his mouth, as I made it to sanctuary. I shut myself in the kitchen until it was all over. Though I'd seen him the same way several times and no longer experienced the same paralysis of horror as on the first occasion, I did my best to keep out of his way whenever he was enjoying one of his 'little turns', as Mrs Goodfellow described them. She reckoned it was just his way of ridding himself of built-up anger and frustration and it seemed to work, for he was always most affable after a good session of bone crunching. Frankly, the whole procedure turned my stomach and I couldn't rid myself of the fear that, one day, having run out of bones, he'd start on me.

I shuddered, turning my attention to tea: hot, sweet tea being unbeatable in times of stress. Sitting down at the table, clutching my mug, I pondered where Hobbes put it all, for he'd polished off three large steak and kidney pies and within half an hour he was stuffing his face with cow tails. Yet he wasn't fat, though there was a hell of a lot of him. I put it down to his unhuman metabolism.

He was still a mystery. I'd only known him a few days when I came to the unlikely, if undeniable, conclusion that he wasn't actually human, yet I'd never quite worked out what he might be. Sometimes, on waking in the night from disturbed dreams, I'd felt close to a great revelation but it always slipped away before I could grasp it. One thing was certain, I'd never met anyone like him, even in Sorenchester, a town with more than its fair share of individuals who were different, though none of them seemed different in the same way that Hobbes was different. During my time with him I'd nearly been buried alive by ghouls, had tea and crumpets with a troll and been told about a witch, but what other types of being might be lurking on the edge of perception, I couldn't guess. Sometimes I feared the vague, hazy images that haunted my nightmares might not be far from the truth.

I'd just finished my second mug of tea when I heard Hobbes's footsteps walking upstairs and, a couple of minutes later, the new shower starting. He was very proud of the shower, having installed it himself, like most of the plumbing in the house. Never before had I seen anyone crimp copper pipes with his fingers, but it appeared to work, for nothing dripped. Having only used the shower once, coming within an inch of drowning as alternate blasts of icy and boiling water flattened me, I now stuck to the bath, in a manner of speaking. Though he would roar as the hot and cold torrents found their mark, he always emerged from the bathroom with a happy grin.

It wasn't long before he strolled into the kitchen, clean and glowing, dressed for work, as if nothing unusual had happened. 'I ought to go into the station for a couple of hours,' he said, helping himself to tea, 'I have some paperwork to catch up with, worse luck. Do you want to come?'

I shook my head.

'OK – I'll get a takeaway on the way back. What d'you fancy?'

'Fish and chips, probably.' After the cow tails, I didn't fancy burgers.

'Right. Oh, would you mind clearing up?' Pointing to the sitting room, he quaffed his tea. 'Cheerio.'

He strode away, Dregs walking obediently to heel, behaving well as he always behaved for Hobbes and Mrs Goodfellow, while doing what he liked with me. Not that I really minded, for we were on friendly terms, quite accustomed to each other's roles, and I'd come to enjoy taking him for walks, his zest for living being infectious. Walking with him in the park or out in the countryside offered a rare kind of freedom, allowing me time to think and reflect on life, though, for the most part, my brain ticked over in pleasant idleness. Apart from that, his exuberant behaviour meant other dog walkers, even women, sometimes talked to me. It was as if I'd joined a club, with the advantage of not having to pay for the privilege.

Taking a bin liner from a cupboard, I went to clean up the sitting room, which didn't look too bad, considering; apart from the torn and bloodied newspapers and the occasional cow hair, little evidence remained of what had gone on in there. As I stuffed the papers into the bag I shuddered, with a sudden fear that Henry Bishop could go the way of the cow tails, should he dare to transgress Hobbes's law again. I don't know what put that in my mind, for Hobbes had not, to my knowledge, killed anyone, apart from those in the First World War, who didn't really count.

Yet, there'd been this guy called Arthur Crud, who, a few months ago, having got off a rape charge on a technicality and having celebrated his lucky acquittal with a few beers in the Feathers, had never made it back home. My suspicions had been raised earlier that same evening when Hobbes had phoned to tell Mrs Goodfellow he wouldn't be home for supper. As the only other time I'd know him miss his evening meal was when he'd been trapped in a hole, I'd wondered what was up. Since then, no one had found any sign of Arthur, though I doubted anyone had bothered looking and, though I supposed he might have just left town or been abducted by aliens, I couldn't quite rid myself of the absurd notion that Hobbes had, not to put too fine a point on it, eaten him.

After tidying up and disposing of the bag, I switched on the telly, sprawling on the sofa, relaxing. Nothing grabbed me, so I watched some awful chat show until my head drooped. I must have fallen asleep, for I dreamt of bone-crunching, hairy terrors creeping up on me, while I groped with increasing urgency for the fly spray that would defeat them. Finally, my fingers chancing upon the can, I jerked up with a roar of defiance and, still half asleep, rolled off the sofa.

Hearing a slight movement, I looked up, straight into a jawful of huge brown teeth, only a few inches from my face. I gasped, recoiling, trying to squirt the fly spray, finding it wasn't fly spray at all but the telly's remote control. The jaw pulled back; it was attached to a skull, appearing to float in mid-air.

'Hello, dear,' said Mrs Goodfellow, 'did I wake you?' Her smiling, wrinkled face came into focus next to the monstrosity. 'Look what those nice dentists let me have.'

Holding the skull aloft like it was the World Cup, she leaned over me, exuding the peculiar, sweet scent of dental surgery, a smell I hated, for not only did it unlock memories of pain but it reminded me of my father's surgery, a place I'd spent many a miserable day while he tried to interest me in his profession.

'Hello,' I said, climbing back onto the sofa, fighting to control my breathing and racing heart. 'You're back early. I thought you were finishing tomorrow?'

'Yes, dear, that was the plan but the hall was overrun with flies, so we called it a day.'

'Flies?'

'Yes, dear, there were horrible, buzzing bluebottles everywhere.'

'Umm … Where'd they come from?' I asked, awake but still confused.

'From the air conditioning. There was a dead cat in it.'

'Oh, well. It's good to have you back.' I meant it, for apart from her unnerving habit of appearing from nowhere, scaring the shivers out of me, she treated me with enormous toleration and kindness and cooked like a goddess.

'Thank you, dear.'

'That's a very fine skull,' I said, trying not to make it too obvious that I was humouring her. 'Whose is it?'

'It's mine.'

'But … umm … where did you get it from?'

'The dentists said I could have it. They were using it in a seminar to demonstrate the effects of a rare dental condition. Just look at these.' She pointed to the malformed canines. 'Don't they look like Dregs's?'

'Yes, very nice,' I said, 'but didn't they want to keep it?'

'No. Just after I told them my opinion, the chairman asked if someone would have the goodness to get rid of the old relic. So, I did.'

'I see.' I smiled.

'Where's the old fellow?' She polished the dome of the skull with a delicate, lacy handkerchief.

'At the station, doing some paperwork. He's just eaten a bag of cow tails.'

'I expect he needed them. Shall I make you a nice cup of tea?'

'No thanks. I'm going out for a walk. Umm … By the way, he said he'd bring fish and chips back tonight, so there's no need to cook.' I spoke with some regret, for fish and chips, though delicious in their way, just didn't compare to a Mrs Goodfellow special, or even to a Mrs Goodfellow ordinary, if such a thing existed.

I needed to get out; the skull had unsettled me. Something didn't look right about it; it wasn't just the horrible, discoloured canines, though they were bad enough, but the shape was all wrong. It looked nearly human, in some way reminding me of Hobbes and yet it was almost completely unlike him. I wondered if it might have belonged to another 'unhuman' being, though, I guessed it was more likely to have come from an unfortunate human with a nasty dental condition.

Leaving the house, I walked towards the centre of Sorenchester, trying not to think about the skull, happy for it to remain a mystery, insoluble and forgotten, except by Mrs G and possibly the dentists. One more mystery wouldn't make much difference to me.

The sun was dazzling as I left the shade of Blackdog Street for the broad stretch of road known as The Shambles, where it occurred to me that I had no idea why it was called The Shambles; there was nothing shambolic about the neat rows of Cotswold-stone shops or the hulking tower of the parish church. Turning down Vermin Street, I headed for the bookshop, hoping to find a local history book – not that I could buy it, of course, but a little browsing wouldn't hurt.

Going into the smart, modern, airy interior, it only took a couple of minutes to find *A Concise History of Sorenchester* by local historian, Spiridion Konstantinopoulos. According to this, Shambles was an ancient term for the meat market or slaughterhouse which had occupied an area in the centre of town until the early nineteenth century. I nodded, appreciating Spiridion's scholarship, flicking through a few more pages until chancing on a selection of black and white photos. In one, dated 1902, I spotted Hobbes, lurking behind a luxuriant moustache. He was in uniform, standing as stiff as a fence post, his hand resting on the shoulder of a wide-eyed, grubby-faced schoolboy in a too-small blazer and a too-big cap. In the background, a building, the 'derelict Firkin public house,' said the caption, lay in ruins. The boy, Frederick Godley, had been playing inside when it had started to collapse and only the timely arrival of Constable Hobbes had saved him from being crushed.

'Do you intend to buy that book?' asked a severe man, in a rainbow bow tie and a brown woollen cardigan.

'Umm … no. I was just browsing.'

'Well, this is a bookshop, not a public library. Either buy it or get out.'

'I'm sorry. I was only looking.'

Grabbing the book, he thrust it back onto the shelf. The cover, catching against another book, creased.

'Vandal!' cried the man, pulling the book back out, shaking it in front of me, its cover flapping like a broken wing. 'Look at the damage you've caused. You'll have to pay for it.'

'But …'

'It'll cost you fourteen pounds and ninety-five pence.'

'But I didn't do it and, anyway … umm … I haven't any money.'

The small group of bibliophiles who had gathered to watch the fun stared at me with deep loathing.

'I didn't do anything,' I insisted.

'Just look at it,' cried the man, holding up the book like exhibit A.

There was a collective intake of breath and much shaking of heads among the jury.

'It wasn't my fault.'

'I'm going to call the police.'

The man's hand gripped my shoulder and the jury murmured with intent. As far as they were concerned, I'd been caught red-handed, though I could feel my face was even redder. The injustice was horrible.

I evaluated my options: I could run for it, though a couple of blokes in the crowd looked big and fit, like rugby players, I could feign a sudden, severe illness, or I could await my fate with equanimity and contempt for the mob. In the end, I dithered and gibbered, letting myself get hauled towards a side office.

A deep, authoritative voice rang out from the back of the crowd. 'Release that man at once.'

'I will do no such thing,' said the man in the brown cardigan.

'You are laying yourself open to a charge of assault and false imprisonment if you choose to continue this ridiculous charade.'

Twisting free, I turned to face the voice.

'He damaged this book and refuses to pay for it,' said the man in the cardigan.

'No, he didn't. I chanced to see what really happened,' said a tall man, with sleek, dark hair and striking, green eyes, parting the mob. 'You took the book from this unfortunate man's hand and damaged it yourself before putting the blame on him.'

I nodded. The man in the cardigan, his face as red as I imagined mine was, backed away. 'That's a lie. He did it.'

'No doubt you have security tapes,' said the tall man. 'Can we perhaps examine them and see who's telling the truth?'

'Oh. Well, perhaps I was mistaken. Perhaps it would be best to say no more about it then,' said the man in the cardigan, retreating behind his counter, breathing hard, his face now white.

The crowd dispersed, disappointed.

'Thank you,' I said to my rescuer.

'Don't mention it,' he replied, turning away, walking towards the exit.

Although I knew with absolute certainty I'd never seen him before, for some reason he seemed extraordinarily familiar. I watched him leave the shop, impressed by his easy walk, the cut of his black suit, how he looked so cool despite the heat and, most of all, by his confident manner. I envied his elegance, something to which I could never aspire, for even if the cream of Savile Row tailors had poured their expertise into a suit for me, I'd still have looked like a sack of potatoes with a belt round the middle. Then, since the man in the cardigan was giving me the evil eye again, I walked out before he could rally and launch a fresh, unprovoked attack.

My feet, with little input from my brain, carried me to the recreation ground just off Moorend Road, where, sitting on a bench in the shade of a conker tree, I watched two guys knocking a ball around on the tennis court. I paid them little attention, since my mind was circling in a galaxy far, far away, trying to work out why my benefactor in the shop had seemed familiar. I returned to earth with a bang as a tennis ball struck me on the nose, exactly where the car keys had hit earlier. Putting my hands to my face, I felt no surprise at the smear of blood as I pulled them away.

A harsh voice bellowed from the tennis court. 'Oi, Caplet, you dozy git! Wake up and chuck the ball back.'

There was no hint of apology and though my eyes watered so I could only see blurs, I knew it was Len 'Featherlight' Binks, the gross landlord of the Feathers public house. I would never have suspected him capable of playing tennis, or of engaging in any physical exertion, other than raising a glass or brawling with his customers; Mrs Goodfellow had picked much of her tooth collection from the floor of his establishment. Pulling a handkerchief from my pocket, I clamped it to my nose.

'Come on Caplet, shift your lazy arse.'

My vision clearing, I found the sight of Featherlight in pink, flowery shorts almost as disconcerting as the blood pumping from my nose. I picked up the ball, throwing it back, staring in horror. His shorts, obviously designed for a person of considerably inferior girth, had perhaps fitted him a quarter of a century ago, when such garments had briefly and inexplicably achieved fashionable status. In addition, he was wearing a pair of mildewed plimsolls and his habitual stained vest, through which gingery chest hairs protruded. His opponent, by comparison, was a young, athletic man, clad in the sort of gleaming whites that detergent manufacturers often promise but rarely deliver.

If ever there was a mismatch, this was it. Featherlight, his belly swinging low, twirling a warped wooden racket between sausage fingers, was puffing and wheezing, looking done in even before they'd completed the knock up. At last they started. He served, tossing the ball high into the air, raising his racket, swinging like a professional, giving his opponent no chance; the match was over before the ball even hit the ground. He'd won by a knockout. Raising his massive, mottled arms to the sky in triumph, picking up the ball, he lumbered to the other end of the court to retrieve his racket. It was lying beside his fallen opponent. Squatting, he removed a ten pound note from the man's top pocket, grunted and strode away, without looking back.

As I hurried to the victim to see if I could be of assistance, he sat up, spitting blood and groaning. We made a fine pair.

'Umm … Are you alright?' I asked.

'Do I look alright?'

'Sorry.'

He held out his hand and I shook it.

'Actually,' he said, 'I was hoping for a hand up.'

I helped him to his feet. 'Why were you playing Featherlight?'

'For a bet.'

'You should never bet against him,' I said. 'You can't win. One way or another, even if he loses, he comes out on top. I once got lucky and beat him at darts and won a fiver. When he actually paid up, I felt pretty pleased but, when I was taking my darts from the board, he threw one of his, and pinned my hand to it. Then he charged me ten pounds for cleaning off the blood.'

The man snorted and packed his kit away into a smart leather bag bearing a crown symbol and a King Enterprises logo. 'Binks might have won the bet but he won't win in the end. Mr King wants to take over his pub and Mr King always gets his way.' With a curt nod, he walked away, holding a tissue to his mouth.

He left me with a puzzle. Why would anyone wish to buy the Feathers? It had a reputation as far and away the nastiest, most dangerous pub in Sorenchester, though it retained a loyal clientele. In addition, Featherlight, to the despair of the council, had become a sort of unofficial tourist attraction, with people visiting the Feathers because they couldn't believe the rumours. Few left disappointed, for Featherlight really was the vilest slob of a landlord you could hope never to meet. He kept his beer badly, refused to serve wine or soft drinks and his spirits were 'interesting', and I knew of one customer who, having asked for a glass of his best malt, had been given malt vinegar. The fun really began if anyone complained; few dared and fewer dared a second time. The really intrepid even ate there. No one had died yet.

By then my nose had stopped bleeding, so I decided to head home and clean up. Though the sun had dipped well into the west, the afternoon's heat continued to build. If I'd had any lager money I would have visited the Feathers to find out about the take-over. However, I was broke and it wasn't wise to ask for credit. There was a hand-written sign over the bar with the legend, 'If you ask for credit, you'll get a punch in the mouth'. It wasn't a joke.

When I got home, it seemed very still, so I assumed Mrs Goodfellow had gone out and that Hobbes and Dregs weren't back. I went upstairs, washed my face, came back down and poured myself a glass of Mrs G's ginger beer, which she made in the cellar but stored in the fridge. I made a point of avoiding the cellar, because the old girl had a tendency to lock me in. According to Hobbes, this was a result of a childhood trauma and I wasn't to take it seriously. It was, he claimed, just a sign of affection but it didn't stop him moaning whenever she did it to him. Besides, there was another reason for avoiding the cellar: it contained a hidden door that Hobbes had warned me against opening. He gave good warnings and my stomach still quaked when I remembered it. I reasoned that, if I kept away, I wouldn't be tempted to explore, but sometimes, waking at night, I lay and wondered about its secrets.

The ginger beer, tingling on my tongue, cooled my throat. Emptying the glass, I refilled it and sat at the kitchen table with the *Sorenchester and District Bugle*, amazed to see the image of the man who'd helped me in the bookshop smiling from the front page. It was millionaire Felix King, head of King Enterprises, who, according to the report, was looking to develop properties in the area. He had already acquired the old cinema, intending to demolish it to make way for luxury flats and claimed the scheme would provide plenty of jobs for locals and that no one would miss the cinema since everyone preferred to watch DVDs at home. In truth, the article interested me less than Felix King himself. He was a remarkably good-looking man in his late thirties, I guessed, impeccably dressed, slim and masterful. I stared at his picture, perplexed. Something about his face was definitely familiar but what was it? Resting my chin on my hand, I dug through layers of memory.

'Did you have a nice walk, dear?'

An involuntary leg spasm launching me upwards, my knees struck the bottom of the kitchen table, knocking it at least six inches into the air before coming down hard, as if retaliating. Missing my chair on re-entry, I sprawled on the red-brick floor, gasping like a fish. Ginger beer dripped onto my stomach.

'Did I surprise you, dear?'

I nodded, puzzled, unable to see her.

'Sorry.'

I sat up. 'Where are you? I thought you'd gone out.'

'No, dear, I've been cleaning the tin cupboard.'

Smiling happily, she was kneeling on the shelf, half-hidden behind the cupboard door, a bucket and a sponge in front of her.

'From inside? Why?'

'Why not? Would you clean a room from outside?'

It was true but, then, I probably wouldn't clean a room at all, if I could help it.

'It's the best way to reach into those awkward little corners. And someone had messed up all the tins.'

I climbed to my feet.

'Anyway, dear, I'd best get the kettle on. The old fellow will be home soon.'

Clearing up my spillage, I helped her set the table. When, at half-past six precisely, Hobbes returned, bearing fish and chips, Dregs insisted on a five-minute dance of tail-wagging welcome for Mrs G, while Hobbes engulfed her in an enormous bear hug that had me worried. She emerged red-faced and beaming a vast toothless smile.

As always, when eating at home, Hobbes said grace. Then we could tuck in – and about time too – my walk and the shock having left me ravenous. The fish was fragrant and flaky, the chips crisp and hot and liberally vinegared. It was nowhere near as good as what Mrs G would have produced, but still pretty good.

Afterwards, Hobbes picked up the newspaper. 'This chap on the front,' he remarked, 'must be related to the lass who took your fancy at the Wildlife Park. They've got the same eyes. I'd guess they're brother and sister.'

He was right.

Mrs Goodfellow gave me a gummy twinkle. 'You've found yourself a lady-friend then? It's about time, too.'

I shook my head. 'No, I'm afraid not. She's lovely.' I could feel a blush coming on. 'But if that really is her brother and she's a millionaire too, she's never going to be interested in someone like me.'

Leaving the kitchen, I sat and moped in front of the telly.

The evening, bringing in heavy cloud, wind and rain, conspired with my feelings of hopeless inadequacy, to push me into a dark, moody place where I spent the next two days. The fact that the woman's brother was super-rich had, I knew, only reduced my chances of getting to know her from next to none to none, but it had slashed through a slim thread of hope, a thread I'd been holding onto. I brooded on my life, raking up embers of failure and misery from the ashes of cold despair, wondering how much I could blame the misfortune of my birth date for my situation. Why, I thought, had I, a man seemingly incapable of being punctual for anything, allowed myself to be born precisely on time? If I'd only held on for a few more hours, I wouldn't have been an April fool, wouldn't have been such an object of derision to my schoolmates.

That April I'd celebrated, if that was the word, my thirty-eighth birthday. By that age, a man should have achieved something: a decent job, a home, a wife, perhaps a family, whereas all I had I owed to Hobbes. Despite my enormous gratitude for his kindness, I was scared resentment might erupt from the seething magma chamber of my past failures and make me say something I shouldn't. I kept to my room, only emerging for meals, toilet breaks and long, damp walks in long, damp grass with Dregs.

On the third day, the wet weather having apparently doused the nefarious schemes of local villains, Hobbes joined us as we headed to Ride Park. When I let Dregs run free, he set off like a guided weapon, targeting a small white cat, rubbing its whiskers against a holly bush, apparently daydreaming until, spotting the incoming dog just in time, it leapt into a tree. Dregs's momentum carried him, scrabbling madly, well above head height, until gravity, realising what was up, pulled him down. The cat mewed from the topmost branches.

'I suppose,' said Hobbes, looking up, 'that I should rescue it.'

He jumped, grasping a branch, pulling himself into the tree, swinging from arm to arm like a great ape, disappearing among the greenery. I did what I could to calm Dregs who, thinking we'd started a wonderful game, was making bounding attempts to join him. From above, came rustling and the occasional creak and, now and again, Hobbes's grinning face emerging from the foliage.

'Here, kitty, kitty,' he called in a voice that would surely have driven even a fierce creature further into the canopy. There was a pause. 'Aha!' he said, as something cracked. 'Oops.'

A drum-roll of thuds and crashes coincided with a shower of leaves, twigs and drops of water. Then came Hobbes.

'Oof!' He chuckled as he lay on his back in the grass, the cat clamped in one hand, a broken branch in the other. Tossing the branch aside, he sprang to his feet. 'Make sure you've got hold of Dregs,' he said, 'and I'll let kitty go.'

'Umm,' I said, grabbing Dregs's collar, 'wouldn't it be better if …'

Too late. Putting the struggling cat back onto the ground, he released it. It hissed, bolting straight back up as Hobbes, brushing moss from behind his ear, laughed. 'Kitty appears to like it up there.'

'Are you alright?' I asked, shaken. 'I suppose you must know how to fall?'

'I'm fine and any fool knows how to fall; the trick is in knowing how to land. It's not the first time I've fallen from a tree.' He glanced upwards. 'In fact, I fancy it's not the first time I've fallen from this one – and I dare say it won't be the last.' He coughed and spat into a patch of nettles. 'It clears the tubes out most wonderfully. You should try it, but start with a small tree, because you need to build up your resistance and make sure there's a nice, thick layer of leaf mould in the landing area.'

I nodded, taking a decision to ignore his advice. 'Are you going to get the cat down again?'

'No, she can look after herself.'

'Then why fetch it down in the first place?'

'I needed the exercise.'

The shock of his plunge did, at least, jolt me from my brooding, and, though I still felt the ache of thwarted desire, I continued living. Unfortunately, this meant I had no excuse for getting out of St. Stephen's Church Fete when Hobbes asked me, saying he'd be showing off his King-Size Scarlets. These he declared were a sort of delphinium and nothing to snigger about. As I couldn't tell the difference between lavenders and lupins, I had no reason to doubt it and, assuming they were the ones he'd been growing for the last few months, they were eye-catching plants, their vivid scarlet spikes standing up to my shoulders and adding ranks of regimented colour to the exuberant scruffiness of the back garden.

Waking early on Saturday morning, I drew back the curtains and was greeted by sunlight glinting off the damp street and the roofs opposite and, despite my impending fete, I was filled with an unexpected sense of well-being. My feelings had been very different the previous year, when, as a very badly paid reporter, I'd attended the fete, which alongside pet shows and beetle drives had been my speciality, since Editorsaurus Rex had rarely trusted me with real news. I remembered arriving and shaking hands with the new vicar of St. Stephen's, before a downpour of biblical proportions forced us into the refreshment tent.

When, somehow, I made it back to the office, my recollection of the event was hazy, possibly on account of the farmhouse cider stall I'd discovered, I had nothing to report and Editorsaurus Rex was on the rampage. However, always resourceful in a crisis, and working on the theory that all church fetes were basically the same, I wrote a few inconsequential words about rain and then cut and pasted an article my colleague, Phil, had written the previous year. If I'd read it first, I might have remembered that not all fetes were the same, for that particular one had been remarkable for the untimely and, indeed, unlikely, death of the old vicar who, having just awarded first prize in the flower show, had been struck down by a bolt from the blue. Though some had considered it a sign of the wrath of God, it turned out to have been debris from an ex-Soviet satellite. Obviously, this meant my subterfuge didn't pass unnoticed and I had to endure a most unpleasant and prolonged showdown with the Editorsaurus. Still, the event summed up my life at the time: a succession of lousy assignments, failures, drunkenness and apoplectic editors.

Such problems hadn't afflicted me since the fiasco of my last mission, which had been to report on Hobbes. Since then, life wasn't bad at all, though it might have been better, and very soon did get better, the scent of frying bacon greeting my nostrils as I hurried downstairs.

After breakfast, I helped Hobbes as he worked in the greenhouse, a structure he'd thrown together from odds and ends picked out of skips, but it wasn't long before he suggested that I might try getting under someone else's feet for a change. So, grabbing myself a glass of ginger beer, I sat on a bench, enjoying the sun, watching his pest control procedure. Refusing to use chemicals, he examined each plant from leaf to stem, removing any aphids and harmful bugs by hand, his patience amazing me. Still, it looked like he would produce a bumper crop of aubergines.

When satisfied, he left the aubergines and felled a small forest of King-Size Scarlets, sticking them into a black plastic bin, filled with water. Then, after a mug of tea, he prized me from my seat, ready to go to the fete. Grasping the bin to his chest, he set off for St. Stephen's. Mrs Goodfellow held the back door for him, while I rushed to open the front door. Though I doubted I'd be able to move such a weight, never mind carry it, I could still barely keep up with him as he marched through the centre of town, down Vermin Street, weaving through the Saturday shoppers, as if he wasn't carrying a flower shop. Sweat dripped off me but he looked just as cool as ever in his tweed jacket.

Although the sun was high and hot as we reached St. Stephen's, I couldn't suppress a shiver, for the last time I'd been there, on a dark and stormy night, a pair of ghouls had tried to bury me alive, until Hobbes intervened, dissuading them with a spade. Taking a deep breath, I followed him into the marquee, where the noise and migrations of herds of roaming exhibitors drove the horrifying memory back to its dark recess. He found a space, marked W.M. Hobbes, and set about arranging his blooms while I, finding I was superfluous, wandered off to take a look around. Apart from the bustle in the marquee, loads of other people were setting up all sorts of stalls, including one where customers could bowl for a pig. What the lucky winner would do with a pig, I hadn't a clue.

I moved on, fascinated by a small brown wigwam staggering from place to place until it found a spot to settle near the front gates. A woman, magnificent in purple and lace, emerging like a butterfly from a chrysalis, erected a cardboard sign that read, 'Madame Eccles, palms read, fortunes told, medium.' She looked more like a large, or even an extra-large to me. I looked like a customer to her.

'Can I read your palm, love? Or would you prefer to talk to loved ones who have passed over? Cross my palm with silver – or paper money would be better – and all proceeds to charity.'

'I'm sorry … I'm … umm … skint.'

'Never mind, love. Step inside and I'll give you one for free.'

It was an offer I couldn't refuse.

I followed her inside. In actual fact, since she occupied most of the interior, I perched on a three-legged stool in the entrance as she, forcing her ample backside into a fold-up chair that groaned most piteously, drew a small crystal ball from deep within her robes and placed it on her lap.

'Palm reading? Divination? Or would you prefer an encounter with the spirit world?'

'Palm reading.' I said; it sounded safest. I held out my hand.

'Oh no,' she said, shaking her head, 'that's not right.'

'What's the matter?' I asked, feeling a lurch of fear, though I knew it was all bunkum.

'Wrong hand, love.'

I gave her the other one.

'Let's see. Aha! That's interesting … But that's not so good. Do you know, I've never seen such a varied fate line.'

'What's going to happen to me?'

'You will live an unusual life. I see fear and laughter, delight and horror. Love may be on the horizon but, beware, something wicked this way comes.'

Though I normally had no truck with this kind of nonsense, a sudden cold sensation up my spine made me shudder. The feeling persisting, I looked behind me. It was Dregs, his nose stuck where my shirt had rucked up, looking sheepish, as well he should have been, for Mrs Goodfellow had harnessed him to a small cart loaded with bottles of ginger beer. She'd brushed his wiry black coat till it shone and, as a final indignity, had garlanded him with ribbons. He looked at me with mournful eyes and, though I sympathised, I couldn't help; he was in the clutches of a far greater power. I was glad the old girl was there though, because she was helping out with the refreshments and I hoped I might be in for a few freebies.

'Hello, dear,' said Mrs Goodfellow, as I jumped up, tucking my shirt back in. 'Has he been pestering you, Edna?'

'Not in the least,' said Madame Eccles. 'He's a very interesting young man and is going to lead an eventful life.'

Dregs sighed as I made my excuses and left them talking.

I looked in on Hobbes who'd completed his arrangement. It was breath-taking for, as well as his King-Size Scarlets, he'd worked in daisies, producing a flower sculpture of a sheep with its throat torn out. There was blood everywhere. 'That's amazing,' I said.

'Thanks.' He blushed.

Although he had a superb eye for detail and his great paws could work with amazing delicacy, he seemed to think that art wasn't quite manly. I wished I had a fraction of his skill, even though his creations gave me the creeps.

'Let's get some grub,' he said, before I could embarrass him any further. 'The fete opens at two, so we've got about an hour. We could try the Cat and the Fiddle. I haven't dropped in for ages and I hear they've got a decent menu.'

'Great,' I said, already feeling hunger pangs.

We left the marquee but never made it to the Cat and the Fiddle. 'Just-call-me-Dave', the vicar, approached. He was a pale and nervous man at the best of times and I could tell that times were not the best.

His voice trembled. 'Excuse me, Inspector, I wonder if I might call on your expertise?'

'Of course, vicar. What's the matter?'

'It was like this … A group of young men bumped into me in town. They apologised and I didn't think anything of it, but I'm afraid my wallet and car keys have gone. The worst thing is that I'd picked up a load of cream cakes for the cake stand and now they're locked in the boot of my car. The cream will go off in this heat and they'll all be spoiled.' He wrung his hands. 'Can you help me?'

'Of course,' said Hobbes. 'That's my job.'

'Unfortunately, my car's parked in town.'

'That's not a problem,' said Hobbes. 'I'll give you a hand. C'mon, vicar. And quickly.'

As he turned to go, he paused. 'Sorry, Andy,' he said, 'the pub's off.' Reaching into his pocket for the small, hairy and deeply disturbing pouch that served him as a wallet, he removed a twenty-pound note, thrust it into my hand and loped away with Just-call-me-Dave.

It was a heady feeling to once more have money in my pocket. I headed for the Cat and Fiddle, intending to spend it wisely on food and a pint, or possibly two, of lager. However, I hadn't gone far, the pub still out of sight, when my nostrils detected the scent of frying onions. It was like a Siren song, luring me down an alley towards the lurking burger van, a greasy little man with a stained white coat and discoloured grin watching me approach.

'What can I do for you, squire?' He stirred the onions.

The sizzling overcame any remaining resistance. 'I'll have a jumbo hotdog,' I said, 'with mustard and loads of onions.'

'Good choice, squire. That'll be three-fifty.'

Handing over the money, I gloated as I received my change, sixteen pounds and fifty pence, money to spend on refreshments. I'd noticed a keg and several crates being loaded into the beer tent and could believe it wasn't going to be a fete worse than death after all.

Carrying my hotdog back, I sat on a low wall overlooking the road in the shade outside the church. Saliva flooded my mouth as I inhaled the aroma. However, on taking a bite, the bun, aided by a sausage with the texture of cotton wool, sucked up moisture, leaving my mouth as dry as blotting paper. It became a struggle to force the stuff down my reluctant throat and I had to spit out a couple of mouthfuls of gristle. Still, the hotdog served two purposes: it filled me up pretty well and made me appreciate Mrs G's cooking even more. I'd just finished and was beginning to wish I hadn't started, when a skinny young man in shorts, t-shirt and trainers shot past, breathing hard, going like a whippet down the road. Shamed by his commitment to fitness, I wondered how he motivated himself.

A moment later, Hobbes loped into view, a couple of hundred yards behind, catching up, despite having a cursing youth tucked under each arm. They didn't look like they were enjoying themselves.

'A couple of bad lads,' said Hobbes with a grin as he passed.

I stepped down, running after him to see what was happening, until the hotdog made its presence known. I slowed to a jog and then to a brisk walk. I wasn't following to offer my assistance – he only had three to deal with – but to see how the hunt ended. I was far too slow. Within a couple of minutes, I met him coming back, lecturing his prisoners, who were walking in front, hanging their heads like naughty three-year olds. One of them appeared to be crying.

'I'm just taking these boys to apologise to the vicar,' said Hobbes. 'They picked his pockets and were trying to steal his car. They might have got away with it if the vicar had remembered to fill up with petrol. They didn't get very far.'

I followed them back as far as the church wall where, indigestion claiming me, I sat back down, stomach churning, watching them out of sight. A few minutes later, Just-call-me-Dave reappeared, driving his little red car at a sedate pace, as fast as the sweating lads could push it. Hobbes ambled behind, offering encouragement and good advice.

'Right, boys,' he said as the vicar parked by the kerb, 'I hope you've learned a good lesson today. Crime does not pay, especially when I'm around. However, it's far too nice a day to go inside and mess with paperwork, so I'm going to let you go away and reflect on what you've done. If you behave yourselves, there'll be no need for me to pay any unexpected visits, which, I ought to point out, you wouldn't enjoy at all. Now, give the vicar a hand with his cakes. Then run along, and mind how you go.'

After profuse apologies and some serious grovelling, they hurried away.

The church clock striking two, the vicar opened proceedings with a speech that must have been a contender for the most boring ever, still rambling on twenty minutes later, by which time almost everyone had left him to it. The stalls began to get busy and, by three o'clock, the fete was swinging as well as any fete swings.

A pushy old man in a striped, multi-coloured waistcoat and a straw hat persuaded me, against all reason, to bowl for the pig; my attempt was humiliating, painful and best forgotten. Afterwards, I headed to the refreshments tent, still suffering from the hotdog, needing a drink to take away a lingering taste. Mrs Goodfellow's ginger beer stall, conducting a brisk trade, I bypassed it, since I could enjoy it for free back home, and went to the bar for a lager. They only had the bottled kind, and since the bottles were small and expensive, and the day was hot and humid, I changed my mind, heading for a table where a red-faced, tubby woman was selling Brain-Damage Farmhouse Cider, kept under restraint inside a large plastic tub. Ordering a pint, I was delighted to find it considerably cheaper than the lager, with a fruity, rich, refreshing, innocuous taste. I had another and a third, by when the world was taking on a golden haze of well-being. I began to enjoy the fete, exuding a sort of paternal benevolence, a smile for everyone.

A young lady walked up to me, carrying a tray loaded with ginger beers. Her friendly smile was, I thought, a good sign, even if she failed to live up to the woman at the Wildlife Park's standard, being a little plump and disfigured by tattoos. However, I wasn't fussy: I couldn't afford to be.

'Hello,' I said, trying my best to look interesting.

'Oh, hello,' she said. 'Would you mind moving aside? You're in my way.'

'Oh ... umm ... yes, of course.'

As I stepped back, a man yelped and swore.

'Sorry,' I said, moving my foot.

The cider chose that moment to show off its strength. Co-ordination failing, I stumbled into the young lady, knocking the tray from her hands.

'Sorry.'

As I squatted to pick it up, I found my legs wouldn't work properly. Rocking backwards, slightly overcompensating, I lurched forward. Next thing I knew, I was lying across the young lady, who was face down in a sticky puddle of ginger beer.

'I really must apologise,' is what I wanted to say, but it came out slurred and incomprehensible. Anything I attempted seemed to require considerable concentration. I pushed myself upright, vaguely aware of my hands pressing on something soft.

'Take your filthy hands off my arse,' she said.

Her words were a little crude for a lady, but making allowances for the circumstances, I did as she asked, as hands grabbed my shoulders, pulling me up. Considering it a diabolical liberty, I wriggled free and, slumping forward, found I was lying across the young woman again, who made such unpleasant remarks I could no longer think of her as a lady. Somebody shoved me and I rolled off her onto my back. A big hand grabbed my shirtfront, jerking me to my feet, so I was looking into the face of a burly man, his head shaved as smooth as a hard-boiled egg.

'I'd be obliged if you'd leave my wife alone,' he said.

'Don't you tell me what to do.' I wagged my finger in his face.

'Look mate, I can see you've had too much to drink, so I'm not going to make a fuss. Just leave her alone, walk away and try to sober up.'

He had a dotted line tattooed round his neck above the words, 'cut here'. It struck me as rather amusing and I giggled.

His frown deepened. 'D'you think I'm being funny?'

It deepened even more when my wagging finger found its own way up his nostril.

'Right, that's it.' He raised his fist, 'love' tattooed across the knuckles.

The realisation that I was in for a pasting almost sobered me up. I squealed like a snared rabbit, cringing, anticipating pain as the fist drew back. The punch never came. Hobbes was holding it in his own great hand.

'Calm down, sir,' he said with a shake of his head, 'there's no need for violence. We're all friends here. Andy, get your finger out. And quickly.'

'Sorry.' Freeing it, I wiped it down my trousers.

'Now,' said Hobbes, 'what's going on here then?'

The woman got to her feet. 'He knocked me over, spilt our drinks and pinned me to the ground.'

'Is that true, Andy?'

'No. Well … umm … yes. It's sort of true but it was all an accident. I stepped back to get out of her way like this …'

A man yelped and swore.

'Sorry.' The cider still had me in its grasp. Stepping off his foot, I stumbled, the edge of a table coming up at me.

I came to, lying on my side on a hard bench somewhere cool and gloomy, my head throbbing, women's voices echoing as I tried to sit up. It appeared I was inside the church. I shook my head to clear the fuzziness, a bad mistake, only amplifying the pain, slumping back as waves of nausea overwhelmed me.

'How are you?' a woman asked.

'I'm going to be sick.' Sitting up abruptly, I threw up.

Someone thoughtful had placed a bucket next to the bench. I missed, distributing my hotdog and cider over the stone floor, splashing a pair of elegant ladies' shoes.

'I'm sorry,' I said, encoring with another deluge. Closing my eyes, I held my head in both hands, hoping the pain would subside. Someone had tied a rag round my forehead. It felt sticky.

'The ambulance will be here in a minute. How are you feeling?' asked Mrs Goodfellow.

'Awful,' I groaned.

'I'm not surprised. I'll go and find a mop and something to wipe your shoes.'

'What's wrong with my shoes?'

'Nothing, dear, I was talking to this young lady.'

I was intrigued, though everything seemed to be very distant and getting further away. 'Umm … good. Who's the ambulance for?'

'For you,' said a woman with a soft, comforting purr that made me think of rich velvet.

'For me?' It sounded unlikely. All I needed was a rest and maybe a new brain.

'Yes. You banged your head.'

She sounded like the beautiful lady at the Wildlife Park. I risked opening my eyes. It was her. Again, I retched, the hot, sharp taste of vomit stinging my throat. 'I'm so sorry.'

'Mind yourself, dear,' said Mrs Goodfellow, clattering a metal bucket, wielding a dreadlocked mop. I lay back, groaning, as she swilled away my mess. What would the beautiful lady think of me now? It had been bad enough throwing myself at her feet but throwing up on her feet was such a horrible thing to do. I wondered if I was cursed. I always messed up with women.

The church doors opened and a man and woman dressed in green entered. The light hurt my eyes and blurred my vision.

'Hello, sir' said the green man. 'What's your name?'

'It's …' I said, 'it's on the tip of my tongue.'

'How are you feeling?'

'I have a headache but I think someone's had an accident.'

'How many fingers am I holding up?'

'Yes. Why not?'

'I think we'd better get him to casualty,' said the green woman.

I wondered about whom she was talking. 'Has there been an accident?'

'Yes,' said the green man, untying the rag round my head. It came away red.

'Someone's cut themselves,' I said. 'You'd better make sure they're OK.'

My recollection after that is fragmentary. They wheeled me to an ambulance and a pigeon flew overhead, while a man with a bald head said 'sorry.' I couldn't imagine why. When they loaded me into the back, the beautiful lady looked in, looking worried. It felt good until Mrs Goodfellow's voice impinged.

'I wouldn't worry about him too much, he's got a good, thick skull. Do you think they'll give him a brain scan? I wonder if they'll find anything?'

'Poor man,' said the lady.

The doors closed.

The rocking motion would have put me to sleep had the green man, who seemed to think he was in an ambulance, not insisted on talking to me. When, at last, everything went still, the door opened and they wheeled me into an echoing building with a white ceiling. Now and then something bumped and pain jolted through my head, making it spin, yet, on another level, everything seemed a long way away, as if I were drifting like a balloon. A Casualty sign hanging from shiny chains above my head, it dawned on me that there'd been an accident and, since my head was hurting, I wondered whether I might have been involved.

A thin lad in a white coat, a stethoscope dangling around his neck, appeared above me. 'Hello,' he said. 'Don't I know you?'

He was familiar, though last time I'd seen him he'd been less blurry and there'd been only one of him. My head throbbed, throwing up a memory. 'You're Dr Finlay and you've heard all the jokes.'

'That's correct and you're Mr Andrew Caplet. I remember meeting you after the fire. Nice to see you again. Now, I want you to lie still while I take a look at you. A nasty bang on the head, wasn't it? I'm sure you'll soon be on the mend.'

Flashing a torch into my eyes, he asked loads of questions. I answered those I could but he seemed to think I should know something about a fete, when all I wanted to talk about was a beautiful woman. Apparently, I spent the afternoon and evening under observation, though I slept through most of it when my headache allowed, for they wouldn't let me take anything for the pain. I was told I also underwent a CT scan and that I cheered when Dr Finlay said it showed absolutely nothing wrong with my brain that a couple of days of rest and quiet wouldn't cure. I asked him to let Mrs Goodfellow know.

Next morning, still delicate, though feeling much better, I lay in a white bed behind curtains, a pretty nurse with a sympathetic smile and a scent of soap, checking up on me from time to time. At some point, with a clattering and a nauseating smell of burned grease, my breakfast, charred bacon and leathery eggs, with bread that had been toasted just enough to dry out, without browning, arrived. I made an attempt at it but didn't much fancy staying for lunch. However, Dr Finlay, looking in, allayed my worries.

'Good morning,' he said. 'How are you today?'

'Not too bad, apart from a sore head and feeling a bit confused.'

'That's perfectly normal after a minor head injury, though I expect it feels like a major injury from your side. Tilt your head, please ... good. You have a magnificent goose egg on your forehead, or it would be magnificent if we hadn't put a couple of stitches in – they'll drop out in a few days.'

Nodding, I yawned. I couldn't remember being stitched, which was good because

I'd always feared needles. The lump, beneath a sticking plaster, was very tender.

'You'll probably notice that you tire easily in the next week or so. Listen to your body and take plenty of rest. How's your vision?'

'It's … umm … fine now. It was all fuzzy yesterday, I think. Like my memory.'

'Excellent. And your speech patterns are normal. You were perseverating yesterday.'

The blood rose to my cheeks. 'Oh God, I wasn't, was I? I'm ever so sorry, I didn't know what I was doing … Umm … What was I doing?'

'Perseverating – you had a tendency to repeat yourself – a classic symptom of a concussion.'

'Oh, is that all?'

'Yes. Well, Mr Caplet, in my opinion you'll be fit enough to go home in a couple of hours. Will there be anyone to look after you?'

I nodded, cheered by the prospect of getting home for Sunday lunch, wondering what the old girl was cooking, hoping there'd be plenty for me.

'Excellent. Remember, plenty of rest and quiet and don't go back to work for at least five days.'

I smiled, approving Dr Finlay's instructions, the sort I could agree to follow without hesitation or guilt. His bleeper sounding, he left me to doze.

Just after twelve o'clock, Hobbes stomped into the ward, his head appearing round the curtain. 'The hospital called to say you can come home. How are you?'

'Much better, but the doctor says I need rest and quiet.' I was hoping to influence his driving.

I needn't have worried. On leaving the hospital, I found he hadn't come in the car, instead bringing Dregs and the little cart, to which he'd fitted a three-legged stool from the kitchen. Dregs, taking it all in his stride as I sat down, set off, trotting by Hobbes's side. At first, I squirmed with embarrassment, though few people were out and about in town, but after a while, to my amazement, I began to enjoy the ride, feeling safe and comfortable, if eccentric. The town glistened with the sprinklings of an overnight downpour, the streets steaming under the sun's power.

'It's a fine cart,' I said.

Hobbes agreed. 'It is. If you'd hung around a little longer yesterday, you'd have seen him giving rides round the fete in it. The children loved him and he raised more money than any other attraction, though the lass might have matched him if she hadn't run out of ginger beer.'

'She makes good stuff,' I said. 'I wish I'd stuck to it. That cider was lethal.'

Hobbes chuckled. 'It nearly was, wasn't it? They're talking about renaming it "Dozy Headbanger" in your memory.'

I grimaced. 'How did you get on in the flower show? Did you win?'

He shook his head. 'I'm afraid not, though they awarded me a certificate for the most original use of delphiniums, which was nice of them.'

'Shame. Umm … by the way, have there been any more big cat sightings?'

'Not as such, but a bird watcher reported a large paw-print in Loop Woods. I took Dregs up to have a look this morning but, unfortunately, some lads had been motor biking and everything was churned up. There were no signs of cats and the whole place stank of two-stroke.'

'If there really was a big cat on the loose, would they get someone to shoot it?'

'Not if I had my way,' said Hobbes.

'What would you do?'

'Catch it.'

'How?'

'With stealth, cunning and a big sack.'

'Then what?'

'Find it somewhere to live where it can't be hurt by anyone and where it can't hurt the public.'

His answer came as some relief, for I'd got it into my head that, if he found one, and caught it, he'd bring it home. Having a panther in the house would not be good for my state of mind, especially when I needed to rest.

All went well until, reaching Blackdog Street, Hobbes, pulling the keys from his pocket, strode up the steps to the front door. Dregs, forgetting what he was doing, bounded after him. The cart's wheels bounced and skipped and, though I grasped the stool with desperate hands, I tipped out backwards with a yelp, bracing myself for a heavy fall. I never hit the floor. Hobbes, diving full length down the steps, caught me.

'Sorry,' he said, standing up, setting me down. 'That wasn't much of a start to your course of peace and rest. Are you alright?'

'I'm alright, but what about you?'

The knees of his baggy, old trousers were torn and his elbows, poking through the sleeves of his tweed jacket, were dripping blood.

'I'm fine,' he said. 'The odd scrape won't do me any harm. Mind you, I'll need to get these clothes fixed.'

Springing back up the steps, he opened the door and let us in. A delicious scent of roasting meat welcomed us.

'It's good to be home,' I said, with some difficulty for my mouth was flooding.

'Good,' said Hobbes, 'and now you need to take yourself up to bed.'

'But I'm alright … and hungry.'

'Doctor's orders. Up you go. And quickly.'

Arguing with Hobbes never worked, so I went up to my room, undressed, climbed into bed and hoped the old girl wouldn't forget me. The next thing I knew, I'd woken up. From the light outside, the emptiness of my stomach, I guessed it was late afternoon. As I stretched and sat up, still a little weak, I became aware of soft breathing. A little man was sitting cross-legged on a stool in the window, sewing. He had a big head and a long, thin nose, supporting a pair of half-moon glasses. Looking up, he grinned and nodded.

'Good afternoon,' he said, the guttural tone of his voice suggesting he was foreign. 'I am not, I hope, disturbing you?'

'No.'

'That is good.'

As he returned to his sewing, I closed my eyes, convinced I was dreaming, but when I looked again he was still there.

'Who are you?'

'I am the tailor, sir.'

'What are you doing in my room?'

'Stitching a rent in your trousers,' he said, holding them up with long, spindly fingers. 'You tore them, so I am told, at the fete.'

'Did I? Thank you.'

'Don't mention it.'

I must have dropped off again because the light was fading when my eyes opened. As I stretched and sat up, I became aware of soft breathing.

'Hello, dear,' said Mrs Goodfellow, folding my chinos, hanging them in the wardrobe. 'Did you sleep well? Would you like something to eat?'

'Yes to both questions. What time is it?'

'Half-past nine. Would you like a cold beef sandwich?'

'I'd love one … Actually, I'd love some. I'm starving. With mustard would be nice.'

'Shall I bring them up here?'

'No, I'll come down.'

She left my room and a few minutes later, still in my pyjamas, I followed her into the kitchen.

She cut a freshly baked loaf into mouth-watering slices, spreading them with mustard, piling on the beef.

'Where's Hobbes?' I asked, detecting no signs of his presence; I could usually tell if he was in, even if he was being quiet.

'He's out with Dregs. He took Milord home and went to investigate another dead sheep.'

'Right,' I said. 'Umm … Milord?'

'The tailor. He came round to fix the old fellow's clothes and I got him to stitch the tear in your trousers that you made when you fell on the railings.'

'I fell on some railings?'

'After you'd put your head through the cider counter. Here you are.'

Handing me a plate of sandwiches, she poured me out a mug of tea. I sat at the table, chewing in confusion, with no memory of railings, then or ever. After I'd defeated the worst of the hunger, a thought occurred.

'Is he a lord, then – the tailor?'

'No, dear, whatever gave you that idea?'

'You called him Milord, didn't you?'

'It's his name: Milord Schmidt.'

'That's a strange name.'

'A strange name for a strange fellow, but his given name was Villy; he changed it when he settled here after the war, thinking it would impress people.'

'Did it?'

'Not really, dear. Still, he is a most excellent tailor and is always happy to look after the old fellow's clothes. They come in for a lot of wear and tear. He's especially good with trousers and zips – the old fellow calls him the Milord of the Flies. Not to his face, though: he's very highly strung.'

I nodded. Despite my rest and the wonderful sandwiches, my brain did not feel up to a long conversation with Mrs G. Still, another thought occurred.

'Did you say there was another dead sheep?'

246

'Yes, dear, out on a farm off the Pigton Road.'

'Do you know any details?'

'Sorry, you'll have to wait till he gets back.'

As I finished my sandwiches and tea, to my astonishment, I felt sleepy again and having yawned and stumbled upstairs, I slept until late the next morning. By then, I felt more or less better, though the previous couple of days remained hazy. It was almost like trying to remember dreams, when all that remained were flimsy, unconnected threads.

I washed and dressed, taking my time. On going downstairs, I found I was alone, which was fine; I needed peace and quiet. Having made myself tea and toast with marmalade, I sat at the kitchen table, munching and slurping with great pleasure, until, finishing, I picked up the *Bugle* from the table. The headline, 'Another Dead Sheep', was printed above a censored photo of the dear departed animal, whose throat, according to the article, had been torn out and who had been disembowelled. Local resident, Mr Robert Nibblet (42), had apparently stumbled across the gory remains when returning from an evening out. It took a second or two to register Skeleton Bob's real name and to realise he'd let the cat out of the bag, so to speak, having blabbed about his sightings. I couldn't blame him for wanting his moment.

'There have been,' the article continued, 'hundreds of big cat sightings across the country over the last few years. While some may dismiss them as fantasies, the evidence of this, a second mutilated sheep, suggests a truly terrifying wild beast may be at large in the vicinity of Loop Woods.'

I sniggered, reckoning he'd hit the nail on the head; Hobbes fitted the description perfectly, though I doubted he'd really dismember a sheep, unless he was extremely hungry and then he'd make sure to pay for it. However, if the victim had been Henry Bishop, I'd have had few doubts as to the perpetrator.

I flicked through a few more pages, finding only a short piece, about the music festival, of interest. It said that, although Tiny Tim Jones had, reluctantly, been forced to drop out because a court appearance had not gone according to plan, the organisers had managed to fill the gap with the Famous Fenderton Fiddle Fellows, or 4F to their fans. I was amazed they had any fans, having seen them once, when they'd played a New Year's dance in the Corn Hall, playing so atrociously that they'd cleared the place well before midnight. As most of the punters didn't have press cards like I did but had paid thirty pounds a head to get in, the consensus was that they'd suffered robbery with violins and the band had to be smuggled out the back to prevent a riot.

I cleared up my breakfast things, wondering what to do with myself until lunchtime, for, though I was feeling so much better, I was too lethargic to go anywhere.

The doorbell ringing, I walked to the front door and opened it.

The beautiful lady was standing at the top of the steps.

'Hello, Andy,' she said, smiling.

The unexpected apparition made my jaw drop, my legs lose rigidity, my heart pound, as I struggled for breath.

'Are you alright?' she asked.

Dancing black spots got in the way of the lovely vision as, head spinning, I made an idiot noise, feeling as if I'd fallen back into dreams, feeling the touch of her cool, soft hand on my wrist, smelling her warm, heady perfume, as she guided me to the sofa and sat me down. I remained there, confused, amazed, almost fainting, until she pressed a glass of water into my hand. When I bent forward to take a sip, sweat, dripping from my nose, rippled the surface.

How could she be in Hobbes's sitting room?

'I thought,' she said, 'that I'd come round to see how you're getting on. You had me worried at the fete but I bumped into Mrs Goodfellow in town and she said you were much better. I can see you're still poorly, though.'

'I … umm,' I mumbled.

'Would you like more water?'

'Eh?'

'More water?'

I shook my head. 'How did you … I mean … what do you want?' I felt I was not at my articulate best.

'Oh, sorry,' she said in her soft purr, a slight blush, making her even more striking, 'you probably won't remember me. We met briefly at the Wildlife Park? And at the fete?'

'Umm … fete … yes.' Of course I remembered her. It would take more than a mere brain trauma to drive her from my mind. Unfortunately, memory also threw up an image of what I'd done on her shoes.

'I'm sorry,' we said together and paused.

'Go ahead,' she said after a long few seconds.

'Umm … I'm sorry I was … umm … sick on your shoes. I hope you managed to clean them alright?' At the back of my mind a seed of worry was growing: had she come for compensation? Why else would she want to see me?

'Don't worry about those old things. You couldn't help it. I hope you are feeling better now. I've never seen anyone knocked out before and you looked so pale and ill.'

I nodded and, the conversation halting, she smiled again. Her teeth were white and regular. Mrs Goodfellow, I thought, would covet them.

'Would you like a cup of tea or coffee or something?' I asked, trying to stop the silence growing uncomfortable. 'Or ginger beer? It's home-made.'

'A cup of tea would be lovely.'

Dazed, I walked into the kitchen and put the kettle on. She *had* come to see me! My sense of confusion lifting, I grinned like a loon, performing an idiot arm-waving dance around the stove.

'No sugar, please, Andy,' she said, standing in the kitchen doorway, her eyebrows arched in amusement.

Feeling a blush flooding my cheeks, I made as if I'd been swatting a fly.

'Missed,' I said. 'Damn these bluebottles!'

I doubted my acting was very convincing, yet she smiled while I tried to stop staring at her like a fixated owl.

'You called me Andy,' I said. 'How do you know my name?'

'Mrs Goodfellow told me. We had a little chat while we were waiting for the ambulance. Oh, I'm sorry but I haven't introduced myself. I'm Violet. Violet King.'

'Oh, right. You must be related to Felix King. He helped me out when I had a spot of bother in town. Of course, I didn't know who he was until I saw him in the *Bugle*.'

'Felix,' she said, with a hint of grimace, 'is my big brother.'

248

'He seems very nice.'

'He is. Most of the time. At least, when he's not working.'

The kettle whistling, I made tea and carried it through to the sitting room. She sat down on the sofa and, so that I wouldn't appear too pushy, I pulled up one of Hobbes's old oak chairs.

'Would you like a biscuit?' I asked before sitting.

'No, thank you.'

'It's very nice of you to call round and see me. I'm feeling very much better now.'

'That's good ... Andy?'

'Yes?'

Her handbag suddenly chiming, she pulled out a mobile, answering it, with an apologetic smile. 'Hi Felix ... When was that? Oh ... That's unfortunate. Can't it wait?' She sighed. 'Right, I'll go straight round and sort them out ... OK ... bye.'

She rose to her feet. 'I'm ever so sorry, but I must go. It's business; I work with Felix.'

'What about your cup of tea?'

'Sorry.' Standing up, she walked towards the front door, stopped and turned round. 'Look, I'm sort of new to the area and I hardly know anyone. I wondered if you'd mind having dinner with me some time? Or lunch?'

'Umm,' I said, 'I don't know.'

'Oh. If you don't want to, I understand.'

'No. It's not that ... I wouldn't mind ... I'd love to ... only, well, I'm a bit short of money at the moment.'

'That's OK. I can pay – if you don't mind.'

'Of course not. I'd love to have dinner with you ... or lunch ... or breakfast, if it comes to that.'

As she raised her eyebrows, another blush burned my cheeks.

'Sorry, I didn't mean to imply I want to spend the night with you, I just meant I'd love to go out with you at any time that's convenient.' I had a feeling my response hadn't come out right. 'Umm ... it's not that I don't want to go to bed ... umm ... I mean I ....'

I wished I could rewind and start again.

To my amazement, she laughed. 'When you're in a hole, it's best to stop digging. I'll tell you what, how about if I pick you up tomorrow evening at eight?'

'That would be great.'

'You can decide where we go; I don't really know any places round here. Bye, Andy.'

'Bye.'

She walked away, closing the door behind her. Shortly afterwards, hearing a car's engine, I peeked out the window, watching as she drove away in a red, open-topped Lotus.

Sitting down, I poured myself a cup of tea and held it, watching it grow cold, my brain, having gone into overload, unable to cope with frivolities. I could hardly believe Violet King wanted to take Andy Caplet out to dinner. No one had ever done anything like that before. Might it be possible, I thought, that my concussion was causing hallucinations? Had the last few minutes all been a wonderful dream? Yet, I could still feel where she'd placed her hand on my wrist, still smell her perfume in the air.

'Wow,' I said at last, putting my mug down on the coffee table, standing up.

Mrs Goodfellow, arriving home a few minutes later, didn't seem surprised to see me dancing and emitting whoops of amazement and joy.

'Hello, dear, how's your head?'

'It's wonderful.'

Waltzing towards her, I hugged her, taking care to be gentle, for she looked all skin and bone, fragile as a dried twig, yet she'd once knocked me out with a single kick, having mistaken me for a ninja.

'I like it when you smile, dear,' she said, staring up at my mouth, 'you've got lovely teeth.'

'Not as lovely as hers,' I replied.

'Hers?'

'Violet King's. She came to see me and is going to pick me up and take me out for dinner tomorrow. She's lovely.'

'Ah, the charming young lady from the fete, the one with beautiful teeth? Well, if she's coming round again, I'll have to tidy up a bit after I've put the shopping away. I'd better get cracking.'

In the circumstances, I felt I should show willing. 'How can I help?'

'By keeping out of my way. You still need your rest, dear.'

Considering this a most satisfactory answer, I took myself upstairs for a lie down, ensuring I couldn't overdo things. I had not yet come to terms with the idea that Violet, what a lovely name, wanted to take me out for dinner and a cynical part of my brain kept suggesting that she was just playing a cruel joke. Awful thoughts stampeded through my mind. What if she never turned up, leaving me waiting on the doorstep? What if she took me to a swanky foreign restaurant and, unable to understand the menu, I ordered a dish of raw liver … or something worse? What if I chose somewhere that wasn't good enough and she walked out on me? My fears, overwhelming the euphoria, I sat on the bed, chewing my fingernails, fretting until Hobbes returned and Mrs G called me for lunch. Pulling myself together, I went downstairs.

The sitting room, smelling of bleach and polish, everything that could gleam gleaming, I doubted even the tiniest speck of dust had survived the onslaught, though the room had been spotless even before. I made my way through to the kitchen, where Hobbes was waiting at the table. When he'd said grace, Mrs Goodfellow served a wonderful mixed salad with the remains of yesterday's roast beef before vanishing. In all the months I'd been living there, I'd yet to see her eat anything, other than a taste to ensure whatever she was cooking was up to scratch.

I ate my lunch with great relish, something she made from onions, tomatoes and spices, something that, had she ever decided to sell it, would have made her a fortune, though I doubted she'd know what to do with the money. So far as I could see, she was happy looking after Hobbes, teaching Kung Fu and collecting teeth.

Hobbes, finishing, dabbed his lips with a napkin. 'I hear you've got a date tomorrow evening.'

'Yes.'

'Good for you, but I advise taking it easy on the alcohol. I must warn you, though; you'll miss a vindaloo.'

Normally that would have upset me for Mrs G made the most wonderful, aromatic, perfectly-spiced curries, but the prospect of being with Violet overcame everything else. Still, I couldn't pretend I didn't have a lingering regret.

'Anyway,' said Hobbes, 'there's been another big cat sighting, this morning. This one made the curate come off his motorbike.'

'Is he alright?' Kevin Godley, Kev the Rev, having helped me out on a number of occasions, I almost regarded him as a friend.

'He's fine, though his bike's a write-off. He says a big cat with a pheasant in its mouth ran from Loop Woods, straight across the road. He swerved, trying to miss it, but thinks there may have been an impact before he came off. By the time he'd stopped skidding and had climbed from a ditch, it had vanished.'

'So does that solve the mystery of the vanishing pheasants?'

'Possibly, though the cat would have to enjoy a fantastically healthy appetite to have eaten dozens of the birds in a matter of a few weeks.'

'Maybe,' I said, 'but, when I was a boy, our cat, Whisky, was forever bringing birds home. They were mostly sparrows and finches, but once he came back with a duck. The thing is, though he loved to hunt, he hardly ever ate them; he was too well fed.'

'That's an interesting thought,' said Hobbes. 'Are you suggesting the big cat is someone's pet? It's certainly a possibility. Perhaps someone lets it out at night, like a normal house cat. That could explain why it's not been found and why the pheasants keep vanishing. You might be onto something, well done.'

'Thanks,' I said, pleased, since he didn't often dish out compliments and their rarity gave them added value. 'Whisky used to torment the birds before killing them. Once, when I'd managed to get one away from him, Father made me give it back. He said it was natural for cats to play with their prey.'

'He's right,' said Hobbes, 'but pet cats aren't natural.'

'That's what I thought, so I tried to release them whenever I could, which wasn't easy, since Whisky soon realised what I was up to and, if he saw me sneaking up when he'd got a bird, he'd scarper. I spent many hours chasing him round the neighbours' gardens.'

Hobbes laughed. 'I suspect it might prove even more difficult to take a pheasant from a panther.'

'I guess so. But what about the dead sheep?'

'There's really no more information than appeared in the *Bugle*. By the time I got to the last killing, the rest of the flock had trampled the area, leaving no scent or trail. It's bad enough that sheep have been killed, and that some of the farmers are getting angry, but what if it attacked a member of the public? It's worrying.'

We went through to the sitting room, where Mrs Goodfellow brought us tea. I'd just taken my first sip when I noticed Hobbes stare at something and frown. I couldn't see why, the room looking the same as always, if possibly a little shinier. Then I noticed she'd placed her new skull on the mantelpiece as a rather gruesome centrepiece.

'What is that?' asked Hobbes, bounding over the coffee table to take a look.

'It's a skull.'

'I can see that. Where did it come from?'

'Mrs Goodfellow.'

Picking it up, he examined it, his frown appearing to be one of concern, rather than anger. 'Would you mind stepping in here, lass?' he shouted.

She came in from the kitchen, wiping her hands on her pinafore. 'Yes?'

'This skull,' he said, 'do you know what it is?'

'According to the dentists, it's from a man with an unfortunate dental condition. His teeth aren't pretty but they are most unusual.' She smiled, patting the dome.

'Most unusual,' he agreed. 'It's not from a man, though.'

'A woman's?' I asked.

'I don't believe it's human at all: not exactly.'

'Umm … What do you mean by not exactly?' I asked.

'I'm not quite sure,' said Hobbes, 'but it reminds me of something from years ago.'

'What?'

'A werewolf.'

Whereas Mrs Goodfellow merely nodded, I, my mouth dropping open, stared at Hobbes, dumbstruck for a few moments, thinking that he'd played cruel jokes on me before. I wasn't inclined to fall for this one, at least not without a fight.

'A werewolf?' I said at last. 'Come off it!'

'It's unusual, I admit,' said Hobbes, 'and I'm not absolutely certain, because it's so many years since I've seen one wolfifesting and, of course, he had his skin on at the time.'

'What the hell do you mean wolfifesting?' I asked.

'Language, Andy. Wolfifesting is the process whereby a werewolf transforms into wolf form; it's the opposite of manifesting.'

'No it isn't, you'll not get me this time,' I said, well aware that he'd proved himself adept at making me fall for ludicrous tall stories. The trouble was, some of the tallest had proved to be true.

'I'm not trying to.' Turning the skull round, he sniffed it. 'This one doesn't look quite right. I wonder if maybe he was killed mid-transformation.'

'Are you telling me that there really are werewolves?'

'Oh yes, dear,' said Mrs Goodfellow, 'of course there are, but I haven't seen any since old Wolfie Tredgrove passed away, and that must be over thirty years ago.'

'More like forty years,' said Hobbes. 'Poor old Wolfie. He grew very deaf in his final months, becoming more of a "what? wolf". Still, he was getting on, being well over ninety – I'm not sure what that would be in dog years – and it was the mange that got him in the end, an uncomfortable place to get it. Unfortunately, werewolves have grown scarce and increasingly shy since the invention of the gun. Many people are so intolerant of anything different and, in fact, this poor fellow was shot. See this?' He pointed to a small round hole towards the base of the skull.

I almost believed him. 'Umm … would you use silver bullets on a werewolf?'

He frowned. 'Of course not. Bullets can be very dangerous, even silver ones. You might hurt somebody.'

'I mean, would you use them if you wanted to kill one?'

'Why would I want to kill one?'

'Well, it if attacked you.'

'It'd hardly be likely to do that; wolves are shy creatures, werewolves doubly so. If one ever did get a little frisky, then a short, sharp rap on the nose with a rolled-up newspaper would do the trick.'

'But aren't they really dangerous?' I asked. 'I mean to say, I don't know much about them, only what I've seen in films, where they're usually portrayed as bloodthirsty monsters …' I paused, realising suddenly how completely I'd swallowed his story. Nearly completely, anyway.

'I'm afraid most people only see what they want to,' said Hobbes, shaking his head. 'They have a regrettable tendency to justify themselves when they've acted shamefully, such as trying to portray the wanton killing of a harmless creature as somehow heroic. I've never understood how using a high-powered rifle to kill an unsuspecting animal from a safe distance makes some feel courageous and manly. People can be very strange, but, getting back to your point, you are partly right, in that werewolves can be fierce when cornered.'

'So what would you advise then?'

'I'd advise not cornering them.'

I made a decision: should an opportunity arise, I would not, under any circumstances, attempt to corner one.

'You should see the pups,' said Mrs Goodfellow with a smile. 'They are adorable.'

Hobbes nodded. 'Though they can give you a playful nip if you get careless.'

'Would you turn into a werewolf then?' I asked, fascinated, despite the occasional twinge of scepticism.

'No.' He chuckled. 'You're confusing them with the silly old tales. With werewolves and I believe with vampires, it's genetic. However, should you chance to get bitten, I would recommend a course of antibiotics; they've never been keen on baths and you don't know what they might have been eating, or where they might have been. I wouldn't worry; there haven't been any round here since Wolfie.'

'That's a pity,' I said, though really I was glad. Whatever Hobbes said, I hoped never to meet one.

'Right,' he said, replacing the skull, 'I ought to get back to work. I intervened in an attempted mugging on the way home and the bad lad's probably had enough of hanging from a lamppost.'

I looked at him, shocked. 'You shouldn't have hung him from a lamppost,' I said.

He grinned. 'I didn't put him up it. He bolted up while attempting to evade arrest and refused to come down. Since I didn't want to be late for my dinner, I left him there.'

'I expect he's run off by now.'

'I doubt it. I left Dregs on guard. He knows his stuff.'

'Can I come with you?' It was always fascinating to watch Hobbes dealing with law breakers.

'No, you're still under doctor's orders and need rest.'

'Yeah, right. But I am going out tomorrow. I'm much better now.'

I went upstairs for a nap and fell asleep immediately; werewolves and panthers, red in tooth and claw, pursued me through dreams. Awaking, hot and sweaty, soft breathing tickling the back of my neck, I leaped up with a bellow of alarm.

Sleeping dogs, I discovered, can perform vertical take-offs. Dregs, rocketing from the bed, crashed to the floor, giving me such a reproachful look I was embarrassed, though my heart was going like the clappers.

'Sorry,' I said, patting his head.

The house shook as Hobbes, pounding upstairs, burst through the door. 'What's going on in here?'

'Umm …'

'Have you been teasing the dog?'

'No. It's just that, when I woke up, there was something breathing on my neck. I … umm … didn't know it was him. I thought it was a werewolf.'

Hobbes snorted with laughter. 'I suppose we need to make allowances for that bang on the head. Never mind, it'll soon be supper time.'

'I've slept right through the afternoon?'

'Yes.'

'Was the mugger still up the lamp post?'

'Of course and he'd drawn quite a crowd. He wouldn't come down and became quite obnoxious. In the end, I was forced to borrow a tin of pink salmon from an onlooker and knock him from his perch.'

'Was he hurt?'

'Apart from a small bump on his noggin, he was fine, but he didn't enjoy going to the station for a little chat.'

Having been present at a number of his little chats, chats that, even though they'd been directed at the suspect, had reduced me to gibbering terror, I understood. In fact, suspect was the wrong word. When Hobbes decided to arrest someone, he was never a mere suspect; he was a definite.

'When I was sure he'd seen the error of his ways,' Hobbes continued, 'I took him home and made him a cup of tea. I had to go out and buy him tea and milk because everything in his fridge was green.'

'Was he a vegetarian?'

'No. It was mainly sausages.'

'That's horrible,' I said, screwing up my face, trying to ignore the fact that the fridge in my flat had sometimes contained similar pestilential relics. I'd since grown accustomed to a more gracious standard of living.

Supper, a simple macaroni cheese, confirmed my opinion that Mrs Goodfellow possessed astounding alchemical skills, being able to transmute the basest ingredients into pure gold; I wished I knew the secret.

Afterwards, I washed up, since the old girl had gone to her Kung Fu class. I'd once considered joining, getting as far as listening outside the church hall, the sounds of screaming and thumping turning me into a quivering jelly, making me chicken out. Next day, I discovered I'd got the wrong part of the hall and that I'd been listening to the philately group's AGM: passions could evidently run high in stamp collecting. Since then, I'd never summoned sufficient courage to go back and, besides, I didn't need to know self-defence if Hobbes was around.

He was sitting at the kitchen table, finishing the crossword, as I scrubbed the last pan. 'Featherlight's in the cells again,' he said, putting down his pencil with a satisfied smile.

'What's he done this time?' I asked, turning the pan upside down to drain, reaching for a tea towel.

'He assaulted an assistant at the garden centre.'

'What was he doing in the garden centre?'

'He works there.'

'No, I mean, what was Featherlight doing there?'

'He said he'd decided to carry out some improvements to the pub.'

'Really? Well, I suppose it's about time,' I said, suspecting little had been changed, or cleaned, in the last fifty years.

'He's thinking of turning the back yard into a beer garden. At the moment it's full of cracked slabs, weeds and rubbish. He went to the garden centre looking for ideas.'

'But why assault the assistant?'

'I was coming to that,' said Hobbes, his mouth twitching. 'He says he was wandering innocently round the store when, in his words, a "spotty herbert" approached asking if he could be of assistance. Featherlight explained why he was there and the youth apparently said, "you need decking, mate". Featherlight decked him first, claiming self-defence, although he's twice the assistant's size.'

'If,' I said, 'anyone else had come up with such a lame reason, I wouldn't have believed it. In his case it could be possible.'

Hobbes nodded. 'I believe him, though it doesn't excuse him.'

'Is the spotty herbert alright?'

'Apart from a black eye, a thick lip and a mild concussion. I had to arrest Featherlight, though.'

'Did he come quietly?'

He shook his head. 'He never does anything quietly. He cursed and swore all the way to the station.'

I could believe it for Featherlight, as far as I could tell, was unique in lacking fear when confronting Hobbes. I had an idea this did not attest so much to his courage as to his stupidity.

'What'll happen to him?'

He shrugged. 'He'll go to court tomorrow and probably get off with a fine, as usual. I fear that one day he'll really get himself into trouble – and he'll deserve it, though he'll not have set out to cause any harm. He never does. I'll have to have a long chat with him sometime, when he's sober.' He sighed and stretched, 'Ah, well, sitting here and wagging chins won't get the dog walked.'

He took Dregs out and I, having Violet to consider, forgot about Featherlight's misfortunes. My main problem was where to suggest she might take me. While it couldn't be anywhere too expensive, in case she thought me a freeloader, it couldn't be anywhere too tatty, in case she thought me a low-life. The trouble was I didn't know many eating places not on the tatty side of the register; besides pubs, and the Greasy Pole, I hadn't a clue about dining out. There was the Black Dog Café, of course, but I feared I was still persona non grata there.

Resorting to careful study of the *Yellow Pages*, finding loads of restaurants but no inspiration about their suitability for dining with a sophisticated lady, a millionaire's sister, I was, after an hour, no nearer to a decision. Taking out my frustration on an innocent cushion, I punched it with great zeal, until it exploded, a soft cloud of feathers encircling my head, getting into my mouth and nose. I was spluttering and choking when Hobbes and Dregs returned.

Hobbes stared at the carnage and frowned. 'What's wrong?'

Fearing I was in trouble again, I tried to explain but only spat feathers.

'A little down in the mouth, eh?' he said with a chuckle.

Dregs bounded through the mess in great excitement, a white plume plastered to the black tip of his nose, sneezing.

'I had an accident,' I said and coughed.

'I'd never have guessed. What were you doing?'

'Looking for a suitable restaurant for Violet.'

'And why does that require a room full of feathers?'

'Umm … Sorry. I got fed up and punched a cushion and it burst.'

'I see,' said Hobbes. 'So did that give you any hints? Presumably, you're not going to take her to the Feathers?'

I shook my head. 'I don't know anywhere that's good. Do you have any ideas?'

'That depends on what you fancy. If it's a bit of curried Irish stew, why not try Bombay Mick's? Some people like it. Or Pavarotti's is excellent if you prefer spaghetti.'

'I want something a little more sophisticated – not overly expensive but still up-market.'

'In that case, Le Sacré Bleu might be your best bet. It's French and it's highly recommended by the Fat Man.'

'The Fat Man? Who's he?'

'The *Bugle's* food writer. Don't you know him?'

'Oh, yeah, but I've never read any of his stuff,' I said, remembering his occasional appearances at the *Bugle's* office. He was a tall, bearded man, a little doughy around the middle perhaps but not fat as such. With his battered leather coat and hunter look, he ought to have been a crime writer.

'You should, he's very good. He has a most inventive and ludicrous turn of phrase but, once you cut through that, he's a reliable and honest critic. He's brave too. About five years ago, having lunched at the Feathers, he wrote a scathing, though truthful, review of Featherlight's cooking, refusing to recant even when Featherlight dangled him from the church tower.'

It says something about Featherlight that I was more surprised to hear he'd squeezed his great bulk up the narrow, twisting staircase of the tower than that he'd dangled a man off it.

'What happened?'

'Featherlight dropped him onto the slabs below, where he made a splendid splash of colour on what would otherwise have been a rather grey winter's morning.'

'Did he?'

'Of course not. I managed to convince the lump that passes for Featherlight's brain that dropping the Fat Man would result in even worse publicity, so he put him down and went back to the kitchen. Of course, when the *Bugle* printed the story, people queued up for hours to enjoy the Feathers' experience.' He shook his head.

'So,' I said, trying to get back on track, 'you'd recommend Le Sacré Bleu? Have you ever eaten there?'

'Twice, when I've had work to do around there.'

'Where is it, exactly?'

'Out on Monkshood Lane at the bottom of Helmet Hill.'

'Oh right. That's near Loop Woods isn't it?'

'Yes.'

'D'you think it'll be safe? I mean with this panther about?'

He sucked his teeth. 'I shouldn't think so. Panthers are notorious for attacking customers in smart restaurants.'

'You're joking ... aren't you?'

He sighed. 'Look, panthers are shy beasts and, though it's possible one might lurk in the woods, it's hardly likely to lurk in a restaurant. Now, I think you ought to clean up your mess before the lass gets home.'

I nodded, reassured and pleased now I had somewhere suitable to take Violet. Strangely, I quite enjoyed picking up the feathers and stuffing them into a bin liner, since it seemed an age since I'd felt able to do anything. I still went to bed early and slept until late.

I awoke, refreshed, to a bright, warm morning. As consciousness returned, I grinned the smug grin of a man who, in a few hours, was to be taken out by a beautiful woman and wined and dined and ... I didn't dare consider any further possibilities. I knew so little about her, other than that her voice had a lovely, silky purr, that she was beautiful and sophisticated and that her brother was a millionaire. It wasn't long before my stomach contracted, for a nasty little voice in my head kept niggling, saying I didn't deserve her, I was nowhere near good-looking enough, I was pathetically lacking in dynamism and success. Nothing about me could possibly attract a woman like her: it was obvious she had other motives. Another voice, not so nasty, but equally insidious, suggested she only wanted me for my body and that, having used me, she'd discard me, broken-hearted. Although, for a moment, I wished I could call the whole thing off, hanging around with Hobbes had awakened my sense of adventure and I was determined to see it through, to accept whatever fate had prepared for me. Besides, I didn't know her phone number.

After breakfast, I just wished the day would get a move on. I spent my time pottering round the garden or loitering in the house, trying to avoid Mrs Goodfellow, who insisted on twinkling and digging me in the ribs. In mitigation, she did, at least, feed me with a world-beating pea and ham soup at lunchtime.

Afterwards, she helped me sort out some clothes for the evening: smart-casual was what she had in mind. Ferreting through cupboards, chests of drawers and wardrobes, she dug out a crisp white shirt, a silk tie bearing a crest that meant nothing to me, a navy-blue blazer with gleaming buttons, and a pair of white deck shoes. It all looked pretty good, though I did rebel, not wishing to appear foppish, when she produced a straw boater.

Apart from a brief encounter at breakfast, I didn't see Hobbes until he returned for his supper. Mrs Goodfellow's curry had been steaming and bubbling and enticing me with mouth-watering aromas for hours, and his evident delight as he devoured it proved too much to bear. I had to go and sit in the garden with Dregs until it was all over.

Then it was time for a bath, to get dressed, to ensure I was presentable. When, finally, reasonably satisfied with the results, I went down to the sitting room to fidget. Hobbes, who having finished the Demon Sudoku, was preparing to go out, told me that Henry Bishop, having dug out another shotgun, had taken a pot shot at one of Les Bashem's kids before running away. Though, fortunately, the child had not been hurt, he had decided to arrest Henry. Despite being more focussed on how long the clock was taking to reach eight o'clock, I felt a twinge of pity for the hunted man, who wouldn't, I suspected, get very far before retribution took him. Still, I thought as Hobbes left, the bastard deserved everything that was going to happen to him.

A car pulling up outside, I leaped up, looking out the window. It was a middle-aged couple in a Volvo. Sitting back down, I tried to keep still, watching the clock's hands, working in slow motion, at last reach eight o'clock and creep on to five past. I knew she wasn't going to turn up, knew my fears had come true; it had all been a cruel joke and she'd diddled me out of an exceptional curry. Sighing, I got to my feet, intending to hide my dis-appointment in my room.

The doorbell ringing, Dregs burst into the sitting room, barking madly.

'Shut up!' I yelled.

Since he hadn't quite forgiven me for shocking him the previous day, he retreated to the kitchen with a martyred look as I opened the door.

'Hi,' said Violet.

'Hi,' I said.

She looked stunning in a simple red dress, her smooth, tanned shoulders glowing in the evening light. Her hair was up and the soft curve of her neck took my breath away.

'Hello.' She smiled over my shoulder at Mrs Goodfellow. 'Shall we go, Andy?'

'Umm … yeah.'

'Make sure to have him home by midnight,' said Mrs Goodfellow. 'The lad needs his sleep.'

'Of course.' She waved goodbye, and led me to her gleaming red Lotus, parked a few yards down the street.

She started the engine. 'Where are we going?'

'To Le Sacré Bleu.'

I suddenly realised it was my responsibility to tell her how to find it and, though I had been out that way with Hobbes on many occasions, I'd mostly had my eyes shut: fortunately, the car had a satnav. Violet liked to drive fast but only when the road conditions permitted and I felt quite safe. The wind, the growl of the engine and the blare of the classical music she was playing meant conversation was impossible, which was just as well, because I couldn't think of anything to say.

After about fifteen minutes and one nearly wrong turning, when the satnav suggested a short cut via the River Soren, we crossed a bridge into the car park of Le Sacré Bleu.

Stopping the engine, she unbuckled her seat belt. 'Nice place,' she said.

It was. Before us was an ancient manor, its mellow, honey-coloured stone, clad in an ivy gown, snuggled in a hollow at the foot of Helmet Hill. The little River Soren, fringed with dancing reeds, dotted with jerky moorhens, wound past on the edge of a daisy-strewn lawn. A lazy heron flew above and sheep murmured in the surrounding fields. It looked idyllic, except that the car park was worryingly full.

'Shall we go in?' she asked. 'I'm starving.'

'OK.'

I gnawed my lip as we followed our long shadows down the stone-paved path to the entrance, cursing myself silently as an idiot for not having thought to book a table. A familiar, cold feeling had gripped my stomach and the memory of all those parked cars was twisting my insides. Still, I had no choice; I had to go through with it.

Violet ushered me inside into a pleasantly cool room, with dark beams, white tablecloths, sparkling glasses and gleaming silver, a room where rich aromas tempted all taste buds. Noticing every table in sight was occupied, I swallowed, trying to look suave.

'This is obviously the place to be,' said Violet. 'It's a great choice.'

I attempted a nonchalant smile as a tall man in a white shirt and bow tie approached.

'Bonsoir, monsieur, mademoiselle. Welcome to Le Sacré Bleu. How may I help you?'

'Umm ... a table for two, please?'

'Have you booked, sir?'

'Umm ... well ....'

The man sucked his teeth and glanced around him. 'I'm afraid we are rather busy tonight.'

'There's no problem is there, Andy?' asked Violet.

'Umm ....'

'Andy?' The man smiled. 'Ah, so you must be Monsieur Andy Caplet?'

'Must I? Umm ... yes, I suppose I must be.'

'Excellent. Then we have a booking for a table for two persons at eight-thirty. Follow me, please.' Picking up a couple of menus, he led us to a table by an open window, letting in a refreshing breeze and the scent of flowers.

'I see you have influence,' said Violet.

I nodded, trying to keep it together, dazed by what had just happened, ridiculously afraid another Andy Caplet would turn up, demanding his booking.

The man seated us and handed out the menus. 'Would you care for aperitifs?'

'No, we've brought our own.' I said, not thinking straight. 'Oh, you mean drinks?'

Violet laughed. 'Very funny. I'd like a pastis, please.'

'Very good, mademoiselle. And for monsieur?'

'A pint of lager ... umm ... on second thoughts, I'll have the same.'

As he departed, I smiled across at Violet, who smiled back. I smiled again and sent my gaze to wander round the room, searching for something to say.

'This is really nice,' she said before anything occurred. 'Isn't the view delightful? The river's lovely.'

'It is. I've never been here before but Hobbes reckons it's good.'

'He scares me,' she said. 'I don't know why.'

'He scares me a bit, too, sometimes – but he's been very kind.'

The introduction of Hobbes, coinciding with the arrival of our drinks, breached the dam and conversation began to flow. Suddenly, I was chatting to her like to an old friend, explaining about Hobbes, what he'd done for me, about his crime-busting, but I couldn't bring myself to expose his dark side or to mention the really odd bits. I didn't want to present him in a bad light. After all, he could do that well enough for himself.

When, a few minutes later, a waitress arrived to take our orders, we had to send her away as neither of us had got as far as opening the menu. When I did, my heart sank for most of the words, except for ratatouille and meringue, were in French.

'This is inspired,' said Violet. 'I think I'll start with the Pieds de Cochon Farci au Foie Gras et aux Langoustines. How about you?'

'Umm ... I might have the same.'

'Really? It's not everyone who likes pigs' trotters.'

'Oh … I didn't think … Sorry, but my French isn't very good.'

'Mine is.' She smiled. 'When I was a little girl we used to holiday in a chateau by the Rhone. I'll help you.'

It felt weird to admit my ignorance and not feel stupid about it, for something about her made me secure and I felt no awkwardness as she translated and explained. I even felt secure enough to tell her about my holiday on the Algarve, when I'd ordered chocos, expecting something chocolaty, instead being presented with a plate of cuttlefish. I'd put a brave face on it, forcing them down, bones and all. She laughed, seeming to find me very amusing. In the end, with her help, I settled for 'potage du jour' followed by 'Fillet of Venison and Confit of Shoulder with Dry Fruits Sauce'. She went for 'Shank of Pork Confit with Lentils Sauce and Bacon' and ordered a bottle of Château something.

The food was superb, nearly matching Mrs G's, though it felt disloyal to think so. Nevertheless, I didn't appreciate it as much as it deserved because Violet was taking so much of my attention. For some reason, and it wasn't the wine, because I was being sensible, I felt utterly relaxed in her company, absolutely comfortable. She laughed or offered sympathy in all the right places, smiling whenever our eyes met. In my opinion, and realising I'd only just met her, we were right for each other. If I'd have had time to think, I would have been amazed.

At length, excusing herself, she headed towards the Ladies. I watched her walk away, appreciating the sway of her hips, the way her dark hair gleamed in the candlelight, noticing with some indignation and, I admit, a touch of smugness, that she'd not gone unnoticed by other men. While I tried to look cool, as if accustomed to dining with a beautiful woman, I still found it unbelievable that she'd picked me and had to keep on trying to quiet the niggling part of my brain warning that good things didn't happen to me and that, if they did, the price I'd pay would be terrible.

Once she was out of sight, I permitted myself a sip of wine, savouring the smooth, mellow fruitiness for the first time. She obviously knew her wines, for even I could tell it was a cracking good one, nearly as good as Hobbes's.

Outside, a cow bellowed, a little owl yipped, and a couple of muffled pops suggested a farmer was waging a vendetta against the wood pigeon population. Inside, I was revelling in how much I was enjoying the evening, smiling complacently at other diners, occasionally peering out into the garden, which was already filling with dusk. Across the road, I could make out part of Loop Woods, which, beyond the shadow cast by Helmet Hill, glowed bright and brittle in the red light. In that moment I felt a chill, as if something was watching me. Perhaps, deep under the cover of the trees, a panther really was lurking. Taking a gulp of wine, I tried to ward off my foolish fears. Violet seemed to be taking her time doing whatever women do.

As I looked back into the restaurant, I glimpsed a movement from the garden, as if something had slipped from light into shadow. I jerked back, staring, unable at first to see anything out of the ordinary, nearly convinced my mind had been playing tricks. Then, without a doubt, there was a movement. Something darker than twilight was heading my way. It was nowhere near tall enough to be human and, though, it might have been as big as a panther, its lurching, uncoordinated movements were anything but feline. As it moved from my field of vision, I wished, for the first time that evening, that Hobbes was with me. I tried to persuade myself that I was being ridiculous. What danger could there be inside a crowded restaurant? But where was Violet? Feeling a sudden cold horror that she'd decided to step outside for a moment, I heard a cry from the garden.

I stood up and ran towards the door, side-stepping an astonished waiter, his arms full of plates, and jerked the door open. A hunched figure grabbed my blazer, whispered 'Help me' and fell face forward onto my feet. A woman screamed and the restaurant was in turmoil. Blood had splattered the stone floor, spotting my trousers; the figure, a man, making a low, bubbling groan, lay still.

'What's happening?'

Violet's voice, coming from behind me, I breathed a sigh of relief. The situation seemed to have paralysed everyone, except for her. Pushing through the gawping diners, brushing me aside, she knelt by the body and rolled it onto its back.

It was Henry Bishop, his shirt front dripping with the blood that gushed from a jagged wound in his throat.

Henry Bishop lay in a spreading pool of his own blood, as Violet, pressing her slim white fingers to his neck, fought to stem the dreadful flow. It was to no avail. He twitched, gurgled and her hands were drenched by one dreadful, final haemorrhage. His life had ended and, though he'd been a violent, wife-beating bully, no one deserved to die like that.

Everyone in the restaurant was standing in a wide, staring semi-circle around us: not quite everyone, for someone was vomiting.

'Is he alright?' asked the headwaiter, his face as white as his shirt.

'No, he's not all right,' said Violet in a quiet voice.

'Oh, Lord!' The headwaiter waved his hands in the air like a man distracted.

'Do you think he's dead?' asked a fat man in a too-tight dickey-bow. 'Have you checked his pulse?'

I doubted Henry had enough throat left to check.

'What are we going to do?' asked the headwaiter, teetering on the verge of hysterics.

Violet looked up, the hem of her dress dark with blood. 'Could someone get help?'

Nobody moved, all of them paralysed, shocked.

'I'll do it,' I said, 'if someone can lend me their phone?'

A young woman, looking horrified, scared, rummaged in her handbag and handed me her mobile. Calling 999, I requested an ambulance and the police before trying Hobbes's mobile. He didn't answer so, giving the phone back, I knelt to help Violet.

The headwaiter was clutching his head, moaning. 'We'll be ruined. What will become of us? What could have done such a thing?'

'Perhaps it was that panther,' said a bald, red-faced man.

Panic ensued, diners running, grabbing handbags and jackets. A plump, middle-aged couple headed towards the door, as though intending to paddle through the blood.

I stood up, feeling I had to do something. 'Everyone stay where you are,' I shouted. To my surprise, the stampede ceased, as all eyes looked to me for leadership and, though I could feel my cheeks reddening, I knew the procedure.

'No one else must touch the body, or leave the building until the police say so. We don't know what killed him yet and they may require statements.'

Some nodded, a few frowned but no one moved for the door. The woman whose phone I'd borrowed began to cry.

'If it's the bloody panther that killed him,' said the red-faced man, pushing towards me, 'it's not murder and there's no reason to stay. I want to leave.'

'We don't know a panther did it,' I said. 'Besides, if it did, who's to say it's not still outside?'

My argument striking home, the red-faced man returned to his table, where, to my astonishment, he sat down and carried on eating his steak. 'Shame to waste it,' he said.

Although some, agreeing with him, returned to their meals, most sat, grey-faced, waiting for the police.

'Andy,' said Violet.

She was still kneeling and, despite everything, I couldn't help admiring the sparkle of her eyes, her brave attempt at a smile, the hint of cleavage as I looked down.

'I need to wash,' she said.

I helped her to her feet, trying not to recoil at the sticky, congealing blood on her trembling hands, supporting her towards the door of the Ladies. 'Will you be alright?'

She nodded and I turned away, wiping my hands on a napkin before covering Henry's corpse with a white tablecloth. As it turned red, I had to fight the urge to throw up. People were looking at me as if expecting that I'd take charge but, having done my bit, I knew what had to be done next.

Beckoning the headwaiter, I asked him to fetch me a brandy.

For all the comprehension I saw in his eyes, I might have been speaking Swahili. 'Get me a brandy,' I said in slow, measured tones, 'a large one. Now!'

At last, he nodded, staggering to the bar. As he reached for a glass, his hand was shaking so much he shattered it. Though his second attempt was better, he still slopped more onto the counter than into the glass before finally filling it, handing it to me, and pouring one for himself. I took it back to our table, sipping, comforted by the fiery liquid searing its way to my stomach. Hearing an approaching siren, I glanced out into the garden.

Something large was moving in the deepening darkness, something stealthy, something approaching the restaurant. I gasped as Violet returned to her seat.

'What's up?' she asked in a small voice, 'is something out there?'

'I think so, but I'm not sure what.'

She was pale and trembling as I reached out to hold her hands.

'It'll be alright,' I said, 'the police will be here soon and, anyway, I'm sure we're safe inside.'

'Thank you,' she said, squeezing my fingers until I yelped.

Another movement caught my attention, much closer than before, caught in the beam of a car's headlights. A hefty figure, more ape-like than cat-like, was loping towards the window. I groaned.

Violet gazed into my eyes. 'What's the matter?'

I shook my head, unable to speak. Hobbes was out there, with blood on his face, a feral look in his dark eyes.

A few moments later, two policemen entered and took charge. I was soon too busy relating what I'd seen to think about Hobbes, except to avoid mentioning him. In my defence, I'd assumed he'd walk in to help with the investigation and could give an innocent and reasonable explanation.

Some paramedics, a pair of detectives and men in white suits turned up but Hobbes never showed.

After we'd all given our names and addresses, and an ambulance had taken away its gory cargo, we were allowed home. It had just gone midnight.

I was dazed as I left. I held Violet's hand while she led me to the car and strapped me in.

'You certainly know how to show a girl an interesting time,' she said with a grimace as she drove me home.

When at last we reached Blackdog Street, I asked her in for coffee, feeling a mixture of relief and sadness at her refusal, for my eyelids felt heavy, as if coated with lead, and I couldn't stop yawning. I'd known all along that the evening would end in disaster but could hardly believe it had gone so spectacularly wrong.

'Good night,' I said, though the words didn't sound appropriate. 'Thank you for dinner and I'm ever so sorry for everything.' I got out of the car.

'It wasn't your fault, Andy,' she said, her voice calm and flat. 'I'll call you.'

She drove away as I scaled the steps to the front door and went inside. Having dreaded telling Mrs Goodfellow what had happened, I was glad she'd already turned in. I went into the kitchen for a glass of water, finding Dregs dozing in his basket; he acknowledged my return by blinking and giving a single wag of his tail, which suited me, for I wasn't in the mood for enthusiasm. I hurried upstairs, washed and got ready for bed, terrified Hobbes would turn up so I'd have to talk to him, relieved when he hadn't appeared as I curled up in bed.

How could he have done it? I knew that, for a policeman, he took a somewhat personalised view of the law, but surely killing someone, even Henry Bishop, was murder. Certainly, the man had deserved punishment but not death. Though I tried to convince myself I'd imagined what I'd seen, that there'd be a reasonable explanation, the image of Hobbes with blood on his face and that wild look in his eyes would not go away. I lay in the dark, jumping at every noise, fearing his return, wondering if I dared challenge him, wondering if I should just tell the police, afraid they wouldn't believe me, scared what he might do if he learned what I'd witnessed.

Even more worrying was what he might do to Violet, if he thought she knew anything. I felt so sorry for her for, though I'd had little experience with women, I couldn't help feeling the killing must have quite ruined her evening, not to mention her beautiful dress. Still, I admired her courage. She'd been the only one trying to help the dying man and it wasn't her fault he'd already been beyond hope. Would I ever see her again? I doubted it, unable to escape from the fact that I'd only met her four times, three of which had been total disasters.

The last thing I expected happened. I fell asleep, sleeping well into next morning, waking in a sweat, all the blankets piled on top, as if I were an animal in its den. Since I'd not got round to drawing the curtains, I watched the dust-dancers twinkling and scintillating, living their moment in the sun's spotlight. From the kitchen came the rich scent of baking bread: from the roof, a blackbird's honey-throated singing. Life felt great until a deluge of memories swept all before it.

By the time I'd forced myself downstairs, I'd made a decision to say nothing to Hobbes – until the time was right.

Mrs Goodfellow was chopping vegetables at the table. 'Good morning, dear. How was your evening?'

'Not very good,' I said, wondering how much she knew. 'It started pretty well but then … well, umm … a man got killed, which rather spoiled things.'

She raised her eyebrows. 'I'm not surprised. What happened to him?'

'He had his throat torn out. Violet tried to help him but it was no good.'

'That's not nice. Did an animal do it?'

'I don't know. I suppose so.' I couldn't tell her what I was thinking.

'Was he anyone I know?'

'Henry Bishop.'

'Henry Bishop? No, I don't know him. I never will, now. Hold on, though, isn't he the one who hits his wife?'

'He used to. Didn't Hobbes tell you about it?'

'No, dear. He must have got up early and was out before I came down. He's taken the dog, too. He had Sugar Puffs for breakfast, so I suspect he's busy but, of course, he's bound to be busy if someone's been killed.'

'Of course,' I said, sitting down.

'Oh, well. Would you like any breakfast?'

'Just toast and marmalade. I'm not that hungry.'

'If you're sure.' She sliced some bread and put the kettle on.

The way she looked after me, though I did enjoy it, often made me feel uneasy, for she was Hobbes's housekeeper, not mine; I could, in theory, have looked after myself. With a shrug, I awaited service.

'We don't get many killings round here,' she said, buttering a thick slice of toast. 'The old fellow won't stand for them and he'll be in a right grumpy mood until he catches the killer, whatever it is.'

'He might be in a bad mood for some time,' I said.

'Why's that?'

'Oh, well, this time, he mightn't want to. He might think Henry deserved it; when he saw what he did to poor Mrs Bishop, he was more furious than I've ever seen him.'

'He'll still want to clear things up. He always has done, and he's good at it.'

I nodded, wondering how much had now changed. As I munched my toast, I again tried to work out how to proceed, for the police might just laugh at my suspicions; alternatively, if they took me seriously and came to arrest him, I doubted he'd go quietly. I wasn't even sure I could betray him after everything he'd done for me. Furthermore, I couldn't imagine how the old girl would take it. She idolised Hobbes, treating him with a peculiar mix of motherly pride and schoolgirl crush. Another important consideration was that, if I did turn him in, I'd have to move out and fend for myself, a prospect far from pleasant, yet, wasn't it still my duty, as a responsible citizen, to report what I'd seen? I couldn't do it, though whether through loyalty, fear, or selfishness, I couldn't decide.

Wondering whether the *Bugle* had reported the incident, I asked where the paper might be.

'I expect the old fellow took it. But, never mind that, did you get on well with your young lady?'

'Alright, in the circumstances I suppose. She's ever so nice but she's hardly going to forget an evening like that. It's all over before it's even started.'

'Did she say that?'

'No. She said she'd call me.'

'There you go. It couldn't have been so bad if she's going to call you.'

Putting on a brave smile, I nodded, finishing my breakfast. I'm sure the old girl would have loved me to talk more but I wasn't in the mood, responding to her questioning with grunts and one-word answers. My stock of optimism had run out and all that remained in store was a glut of gloom and misery.

'I need some air,' I said, wiping toast crumbs from my hands and heading for the street.

We were in the grip of a scorcher and, though the church clock showed it was not yet eleven, the town was oppressive as if it had been superheated. Rolling up my shirt-sleeves didn't make me any cooler, just allowing the sun to scorch my forearms.

I went into the library, which offered welcome shade, picked up the *Bugle* from a rack by the door and took it to an armchair in the corner. Though Henry Bishop's grisly death having made the front page wasn't a surprise, I was amazed the lead story was about Felix King's plans for the town. I ignored it, reading Phil Waring's article about Henry, which, to my astonishment, made no suggestion that Henry might have been murdered. The police, it reported, were keeping an open mind but there was a suggestion that a panther might have done it.

It seemed Hobbes had committed the perfect crime.

Except, it wasn't quite perfect; I was a witness, even though I hadn't actually seen him do the dirty deed.

Thoughts swirled through my head like snowflakes in a globe: images of Hobbes covered in blood, Henry's frightened face, Violet kneeling in his blood, the faces in Le Sacré Bleu. Unable to clear the dying man's last gurgle from my head, my brain felt full, as if it would explode. I fought to remain calm, to think rationally as I concentrated on the reported facts, sketchy as they were. According to the article, Henry's shotgun had been found by a tree. For a moment I tried to work out how a tree was capable of finding anything. Realising I wasn't making sense, that I needed air and space, I ran from the library.

I don't know what would have happened had I not stumbled across Billy Shawcroft, lying on the lawn outside.

Crying out in alarm and pain, he knelt up, rubbing his back.

'Sorry, I didn't see you there,' I said. 'Are you alright?'

'I was better before you trod on me. Can't a guy sunbathe in peace?'

'Sorry, I was distracted. I saw someone with his throat torn out last night.'

'What? That bloke in the paper that got done in by the panther? You were there?'

'I was.'

'They say he was a right bloody mess.'

'Yes.'

'But,' asked Billy, looking puzzled, 'didn't it happen up Monkshood Lane at some posh restaurant?'

I nodded.

'So, what were you doing there?'

'I was having dinner with … umm … a … lady.'

Billy's eyebrows going into orbit, a big grin split his face. 'You lucky bugger!'

'Not so lucky. The murder rather spoiled everything.'

'I suppose so, but it wasn't murder, was it? It was a panther.'

'Was it?' I asked, shaking.

Billy stared. 'You'd better come with me. I start work in ten minutes and you look like you could do with a drink but, take it easy won't you? I heard what you did at the fete.' Getting to his feet, slipping his shirt back on, he took me to the Feathers.

I walked with him, dizzy, swaying as if I'd already had a few, gasping in the midday heat. He led me inside, sitting me by the door, where a breeze ruffled my hair.

'What can I get you?'

'Umm ... I've no money.'

'My treat. Whisky?'

I nodded. 'And a lager, if you don't mind, I'm very thirsty.'

The drinks appearing before me, I swallowed half the lager and knocked back the whisky, which, as always, had an odd flavour. According to rumour, Featherlight's spirits were distilled in a disused warehouse in Pigton. It burned like liquid fire, melting my throat, numbing my brain, making me feel better, despite a burning sensation and a sour affliction of the stomach. Lost in my own thoughts, I lingered over the remnants of my lager until, the hands on the clock showing a quarter to one, it was time to go home for dinner.

'Cheers, Billy,' I said to the top of his head, all I could see of him as he poured a glass of cider for a man in a pinstripe suit.

Walking back to Blackdog Street with my stomach gurgling, I was unsure whether to blame the whisky, or the prospect of having to talk to Hobbes, something I'd have to do sometime, if I had sufficient nerve to confront him. If I hadn't, I wasn't certain I could stay with him, knowing what I knew.

From a purely intellectual viewpoint, I knew it would be better to do it sooner rather than later but cowardice was strong that afternoon and suggested silence would be easier.

Relieved on opening the front door to sense he hadn't yet returned, I found the fresh tang of salad and baked bread soothing. The church clock chiming the hour, the front door opened as I took my place at the table. A moment later Dregs was jumping all over me and Hobbes walked into the kitchen with a slight limp. Despite that, he looked remarkably cheerful, if a little weary. He grinned at me.

'I understand,' he said, 'that you took charge at the restaurant last night. Well done.'

I mumbled something non-controversial.

'I'm famished,' he said, washing his hands in the sink, 'and parched, too.' He sat at the table and poured a flagon of ginger beer down his throat. 'That's better. How was the Feathers?'

'How do you know I've been there?'

'Elementary, Andy. You reek of lager and the stuff he calls whisky and your forearms are stained with that unusual blend of old beer, cigarettes and general filth that only exists on tables at the Feathers.'

I glanced at the orange-brown stains. 'I see. Billy bought me a drink because ... umm ... I trod on him. Featherlight wasn't in.' It was hardly an adequate explanation, but Hobbes was distracted by the vast plate of salad and meats the old girl was carrying.

'Thanks lass,' he said as she laid it before him.

I received a similar, if smaller offering and, after the usual delay for grace, we tucked in, treating the meal with the reverence and deep appreciation it warranted. The only words he spoke until we'd finished were when he asked me to pass the pepper. After we'd finished every last morsel, I expected he would enjoy a mug of tea in the sitting room, as usual, giving me an opportunity to ask how he was getting on with the investigation. I gulped, because, at the appropriate time, I intended voicing my suspicions.

To my relief, things didn't go as expected. Instead of going through to the sitting room, he picked up his mug, threw in a fistful of sugar and said, 'I'm going to take forty winks.' Having stirred the scalding liquid, he licked his finger dry and turned to Mrs Goodfellow. 'I'll be out early tonight, so I'd be obliged if you'd prepare my supper for five o'clock.' He yawned.

'Of course,' said Mrs Goodfellow. 'I was planning beef rissoles.'

'Thanks, lass. That will be splendid. Make plenty of 'em; it may be a long night.' With that, he retired to his bedroom from where, a few minutes later, a series of bone-shaking snores emerged.

Taking my tea into the garden, I sat beneath the old apple tree as the afternoon grew still and humid. Surrounded by the hum of bees and the soporific, heavy scent of flowers, I, too, nodded off, awaking to the sound of thunder. The sky was leaden, the first fat raindrops were shaking the leaves, as I grabbed my mug, still half-full of cold tea, and fled inside. The kitchen clock showed five-thirty.

I was mostly pleased to see the old girl washing up Hobbes's dishes, to know he'd already gone out, despite realising that delay would only make accusations more difficult.

Dregs was dozing in the doorway to the sitting room. Stepping over him, switching on the television, I sat on the sofa, waiting for the news. Henry Bishop hadn't made the national headlines, only coming in third on the local news, behind reports of a political scandal in the council, and a devastating fire in a warehouse near Pigton.

'Good evening,' said Rebecca Hussy, a pretty, fresh-faced reporter in a crisp white blouse, addressing the camera outside Le Sacré Bleu. 'Last night, around ten o'clock, Henry Bishop, a respected local farmer and businessman, was discovered bleeding in the doorway of the exclusive restaurant behind me. Despite staff and customers battling desperately to save him and paramedics rushing to the scene, Mr Bishop died. According to unconfirmed reports, he had suffered severe injuries to his throat, injuries consistent with a vicious attack from a large predator. Terrified local residents say a big cat, probably a panther, has been sighted on numerous occasions recently. Red-faced officials admit they have not taken the reports seriously.'

So, the big cat story was holding up; Hobbes was not even a suspect. Rebecca went on to interview Mrs Bishop, who appeared distraught at the death of her husband, describing him as 'one in a million, the sort of man who would never have hurt a fly.' There was hardly anything new, except for one fact that made me gasp; both barrels of Henry's shotgun had been fired. Might that, I wondered, have explained Hobbes's limp? Flinching as a rumble of thunder rattled the windows, I dived deep into a dark pool of worry.

'Rissoles!'

Mrs Goodfellow's voice ringing in my ears, I jumped up, barking my shin on the coffee table. Her constant sneaking up on me could not be good for my heart.

'Your rissoles are ready,' she announced. 'You'd best eat them while they're hot.'

'Thank you,' I said, following her into the kitchen where she dished up a plate of rissoles and good brown gravy with a selection of nicely steamed vegetables. After the first bite, I decided, once again, to forgive her pretty much anything, so long as she continued to feed me, for although I hadn't been much looking forward to supper, having unpleasant memories of Mother's dry, tasteless cannonballs, the old girl's take on the humble rissole would have delighted the fussiest gourmet.

Later, relaxing in the sitting room with a nice, fresh mugful of tea while the old girl dusted the spotless room, my thoughts returned to Hobbes. 'Did he say what he was doing tonight?' I asked.

'No, dear, I expect it's something to do with the panther. He said he'd got a scent of it last night, so he'll probably try to catch it.'

'On his own?'

'I expect so. He wouldn't want anyone getting hurt.'

'But what if Henry Bishop wasn't killed by a panther? What if someone had murdered him and the panther was getting the blame?'

'Then, I'm sure the old fellow would have mentioned it,' she said, rubbing the television screen with her duster before returning to the kitchen to wash up.

I was neither convinced nor comforted. First, it had been Arthur Crud. Now, it was Henry Bishop. Who would be next? Furthermore, how many others might he have murdered in the name of justice? Though somewhere, in a dark corner of my mind, a vigilante was applauding what he'd done, the rest of me couldn't help but feel that the two men should, at least, have had a fair trial with a proper, human jury. I couldn't blame him for detesting rapists and wife-beaters but he held strong views on thieves and dangerous drivers (except himself) and I wondered where it might end. He had no right to act as judge, jury and executioner.

I wished I had someone to talk to. Violet would have been best but I could see no hope after what I'd put her through. Though I knew it hadn't been my fault, if I'd let her take me somewhere else, somewhere less swanky, she wouldn't have spent the evening kneeling in a dead man's blood. Yet, maybe, I reasoned, it had been for the best; I'd have screwed things up anyway, sooner or later. Some things were inevitable. The rain beat against the window, thunder crashed overhead, I jumped and unplugged the telly, sitting in the gloom, until the storm passed. When the rain stopped just before nine o'clock, I slipped out for a walk.

The evening air cooling my heated brow, I revelled in the fresh smell of the town's air, washed clean of car fumes and stagnant drains. As I stepped over a puddle, I thought, what the heck and jumped and splashed my way down The Shambles, going wherever my fancy took me, sometimes striding out, sometimes dawdling, or looking in shop windows. I half wished I'd taken Dregs, but having been asleep under the kitchen table, he didn't look like a dog that wanted to be disturbed.

After a while, the evening fading towards dusk, I realised, having walked in a near circle, that I was approaching Ride Park. The last time I'd been there, Hobbes had fallen from the tree, a time seemingly long ago, when I'd mostly trusted him. Grimacing, pushing through the gates, ignoring the path, I kicked through the sopping grass, enjoying the rich scent of damp earth, the fluttering and piping of birds getting ready for sleep, feeling pretty good. Perhaps, I thought, life wasn't so bad. It had its ups and downs and, admittedly, there were too many downs, but the compensations were great.

After half an hour or thereabouts, as I turned for home, I remembered noticing a sign saying that the park gates were locked at dusk. Yet, there was no need to panic, for, if all else failed, I could knock on the door of the park-keeper's cottage. He would let me out, I was certain, but only after I'd suffered a torrent of his pent-up frustrations about life and the idiocy of members of the public who ignored clear notices about closing times. I didn't fancy any aggravation of that sort and had an idea there was a side gate that might still be open about half a mile along a path through the woods.

The last glimmers of sunlight having all but faded, myriad stars twinkled in the velvet blackness, a faint glimmer of silvery light heralding the rising of the moon. A slight breeze blew up a mist, concealing my legs below the knee as I hurried on, with a shiver and a yawn, keen to put the park behind me, to get home, to get into my comfy bed.

I stepped beneath the canopy of the trees into what seemed utter blackness. Beneath my feet, a twig cracked like a shot in the stillness. Small woodland creatures going about their nocturnal business rustled and squeaked and, in the distance, a pair of owls hooted.

A deep growl nearly stopped my heart. Although I tried to convince myself it was a fox, or the park-keeper's dog, something about it chilled my blood. As I hurried on, not quite daring to run, far too scared to stop, the growl came again, closer and, surely, in front of me. Hesitating, half-turning to run, I tripped over my own feet and thudded into the soggy leaf mould. I lay still, my eyes wide open yet, with the dark and the clinging mist, I might just as well have been blind.

A faint hiss – the wind? Or soft breathing over sharp teeth? Whatever was out there was getting closer and all I could do was to stay still, to hold my breath, my heart beating in double time. A creature was out there, looking for me. Soon it would surely find me … and then what? I rolled onto my side in an ecstasy of terror, the breathing growing ever nearer. When hot, moist breath caressed my cheek, I thought my heart would stop. Something soft, something powerful, patted my head gently.

Since a human mind can only stand so much before primeval instinct assumes control, I leapt to my feet with a wild cry, running blindly into the night, expecting any moment to feel sharp claws in my soft skin, cruel jaws tearing at my throat. Yet, the pursuit never happened. Within seconds, I was close to the side gate, the glow of sodium streetlights offering safety. Risking a glance over my shoulder, for a heart-stopping moment I glimpsed two flashes of green, surely eyes: cat's eyes. As I blinked in the sudden headlight glare of a passing lorry, something slipped into the woods.

A rough voice yelled. 'What do you think you're doing?'

The park keeper was standing at the gate, a padlock in his hand. 'Don't you know we close at dusk?'

I couldn't even speak.

'What's the matter? Cat got your tongue?'

I nodded, pushing past him into the safety of Hedbury Road, my mind in turmoil again. On the walk home, every shadow, every unexpected noise, spooked me.

I reached Blackdog Street, where Mrs Goodfellow had already turned in and Hobbes had not yet returned. Dregs was curled up in his basket in the kitchen. Much to his indignation, needing reassurance, I lay beside him. It must have taken a couple of hours before I stopped trembling.

Something woke me. I was still lost in a sleep fuzz, surrounded by darkness, confused, my bed uncomfortable and smelling of dog. Recollection slowly returning, I knew where I was, why I had memories of fear. I was on my own, Dregs having deserted me, probably to sleep in my bed, if I was any judge of character. Though I was already shivering, a chilling realisation emerged from the depths of unconsciousness; a door had banged, the sound, I was nearly sure, having come from below. I longed to be under blankets, oblivious and if that meant sharing with the dog so much the better, for something was moving in the cellar.

When the wooden steps creaked, I crawled, without thinking, in a state of panic, across the kitchen floor, huddling into a corner, holding my breath, listening to the slow footsteps coming up, coming towards the kitchen. I'd spent long hours wondering about the mysterious door down in the cellar, the door hidden behind a heap of coal. Hobbes had once tried to deny its existence, making me doubt the evidence of my own eyes, but I knew what I'd seen. Later, when he'd refused to say what lay behind it, putting the fear of Hobbes into me when I'd pressed, I'd surmised, since he had no compunction in exposing me to the most nightmarish of situations, that something beyond averagely horrible was there.

The footsteps drawing nearer, terror rising, I suppressed a whimper and scrambled into the cupboard beneath the sink, lying there on my front, a scrubbing brush pressed into my soft bits. As I pulled the cupboard door to, I knocked over a bottle of disinfectant, the fumes soon stinging my eyes, making my nose run. Though the animal part of my brain was urging the need to make less noise than a sleeping mouse, I was sure my heart sounded like a kettledrum pounded by an enthusiastic gorilla, sure anyone could hear it two streets away. The door from the cellar to the kitchen opened and shut; footsteps entered the kitchen; there was an unearthly grunt as if from a wild beast. Then a dull thud suggested something solid had been dropped onto the kitchen table. I concentrated on not moving, keeping utterly quiet.

A sudden shaft of electric light stabbed through the crack where I'd left the cupboard door slightly ajar and I could see the kitchen floor and the vegetable rack in the corner. Despite part of me being desperate for a glimpse of what was out there, another part recoiled, fearing what would be revealed. Even worse, if I could see out, then it could see in.

'Who's there?' asked Hobbes.

Hearing it, though some of my terrors subsided on the principle of 'better the devil you know', I didn't move, hoping he couldn't have heard me, that the disinfectant would mask my scent.

'I require an answer, and quickly.'

Holding my breath, not moving a muscle, as his footsteps approached my hidey-hole, I wanted to scream.

The cupboard door jerking open, I looked up to see him staring down, scowling.

'Good evening,' I said, forcing a friendly smile.

'What are you doing in there?'

'Umm … I don't know … I …'

'If you're worried about personal hygiene,' he said, wrinkling his nose, 'I'd suggest taking a bath rather than disinfecting yourself. Out you come.'

Squatting down, seizing an arm and a leg, he dragged me out, lifting me, letting me dangle while he examined me, like a butterfly collector with a dubious specimen. Apparently satisfied, he set me down, his scowl holding me as firmly as tweezers grip a butterfly. 'Would you care to tell me what you were doing in there?'

I had no choice but to tell him, my story erupting like pus from a pierced boil. 'I went for a walk in Ride Park but there was a panther, I think, and it patted me on the head and I came home and stayed down here with Dregs, because I was still frightened. I must have fallen asleep and I think he's gone to my bed now. And … and then I heard something in the cellar and got scared again, scared something was coming for me.'

I felt a little better.

He nodded. 'What did you expect was coming from the cellar?'

'Umm … I don't know but I thought something had come through … that door.'

'I used the door. Now, tell me about the panther.'

I told him what I could, feeling powerless, something in his eyes compelling me to talk, though I had no intention of holding anything back.

His scowl relaxed into a frown, though it still held me tight. 'That's very interesting. You see, this evening, I was trailing a panther through Loop Woods and round Bishop's Farm. Since it couldn't have been in two places at once, there must be two panthers out there.'

'Did you catch the one you were after?'

'No, it gave me the slip. I haven't yet worked out how.'

'Did you actually see it?'

'I could smell it and I must only have been seconds behind. It's puzzling.'

His frown releasing me, I became aware that he was trying to stop me seeing whatever he'd lugged into the kitchen.

'But why did you come through the cellar?' I asked, trying, without making it too obvious, to catch a glimpse behind him, finding he was too close, blocking my field of view.

'That's police business,' he said, looking thoughtful. 'I need to examine something urgently and I want to examine it in my own way before anyone can tamper with it.'

'What is it?'

'Evidence.'

'Evidence of what?'

'I won't know until I've examined it. Now run along, you should be in bed.'

I tried to peep under his arm but his bulk blocked me.

His frown beginning to deepen once more, he stared into my eyes. 'You should be in bed. You must be feeling sleepy. Really sleepy.'

I nodded and yawned. Escorting me upstairs, he evicted a resentful Dregs from my bed. 'Sleep well,' he said, closing the door behind him, going back downstairs.

I undressed, put on my pyjamas and got into bed, certain sleep was out of the question, yet unable to keep my eyes open.

It felt as if I'd hardly lain down before I awoke. Getting up, I drew back the curtains, finding it was dull and grey outside, drizzle spattering the window. As usual, clean clothes had been laid out for me. I assumed Mrs G was responsible, though I'd never caught her at it. One day, I thought, I should thank her.

The stink of disinfectant was all over me, bringing the events of the previous night back into my head. I was still haunted by the panther's green eyes, again feeling the helpless terror as it had stalked me through the darkness. Worse memories returned, vague memories, almost as if I'd dreamt them: Hobbes emerging from the cellar, finding me cowering under the sink, questioning me. A horrific image squeezed back from when he'd pushed me from the kitchen and I'd glimpsed a reflection in the shiny bottom of a copper pan hanging on the wall. A man's body was lying on the kitchen table. Hobbes, I feared, had killed again. I wondered who his latest victim was, what he'd done.

Though unable to understand why he'd felt the need to bring the corpse home, it made me think of Whisky, the cat, who'd always done the same, usually keeping a little something for later; I'd once found a half-eaten rat under my pillow. Perhaps, I thought, Hobbes, too, liked to eat at leisure. The idea made me feel quite ill, yet I realised that, if he stored his leftovers behind the mysterious door, it was no wonder he didn't want me to see.

Yet, life had to go on and I was starving. So, steeling myself, rising above the ghastliness, I headed downstairs into the kitchen, where Dregs, bounding towards me with his usual morning enthusiasm, struck me as being a little wary, perhaps fearing I'd hug him again. Mrs Goodfellow, smiling, said 'Good morning', as I took my seat at the table.

Hobbes wasn't there. Neither was the corpse. Everything seemed so normal, I might have believed I'd dreamt the incident, had it not been for the lingering scent of disinfectant, nearly masked by the enticing aroma of the mushroom omelette Mrs Goodfellow was making. When she fed me, I found it as light as a cloud and utterly delicious, my appetite only slightly restrained by a nagging worry that Hobbes might not have scrubbed the table. It occurred to me, as I finished off the last bit of omelette and reached for the marmalade, that exposure to Hobbes had desensitised me. I doubted I'd have been so cool before my life in Blackdog Street.

After finishing breakfast, I helped Mrs G dry up, a rare event, but successful in that I didn't break anything and managed to locate the cutlery draw without prompting. We were chatting about the weather and pork chops when she told me she was going out to visit a dear old friend, who'd broken a leg falling off a trampoline.

'How old is she?' I asked.

'Eighty-eight.'

'Should she have been doing that at her age?'

'Well, dear, she's been doing it since she was sixty. Why stop when she enjoys it? I think her big mistake was jumping out the bedroom window to get a bigger bounce.'

'That sounds dangerous.'

'I suppose it does now you mention it, though it wasn't the big bounce that hurt her, but hitting the shed and landing on a pile of bricks. She's a silly old fool sometimes,

I don't know how many times I've told her to get a proper landing mat, but she always knows best.'

As often occurred in conversation with the old girl, I was soon out of my depth. I tried a change of subject. 'Where's Hobbes this morning?'

'At work. He was out very early and had Sugar Puffs for breakfast again. I'm worried he's not eating enough.'

'I'm sure he won't starve,' I said, suppressing a grimace.

'You're probably right.' She sighed. 'Still, I'll get him a good, big, juicy rib-eye steak for his supper. You like a steak, too, don't you?'

I nodded.

'That's alright, then. Thank you for your help and I'd better be off to the hospital.'

Having wiped her hands on her pinafore, she put a lead on Dregs and left me on my own.

Though I tried to think pleasant thoughts, I kept returning to Hobbes and the hidden door. Sitting back at the kitchen table, I realised I had the perfect opportunity to investigate, yet, had no idea what dangers lay behind it, assuming there really were any. One way or another, I needed to confirm my suspicions, or prove them false. I began trembling, torn between curiosity and self-preservation. Standing up, I marched round the kitchen trying to dispel my nervous energy. To my surprise, finding myself holding the handle of the door down to the cellar, the conflict in my head still raging, I decided there could be no harm in merely taking a quick look. I pushed open the door, turned on the light and started down the creaking wooden steps, breathing in air as moist and cool as a cavern, amazed as always by the extent of the cellar. On reaching the bottom, I stood a moment, taking a deep breath, before walking onto the old brick floor, past the enormous wine racks, noticing no dust or cobwebs on any of the hundreds of bottles down there. Mrs G's devotion to cleanliness and order was soothing.

The door, as I'd expected, was hidden behind a pile of coal that gleamed as if it had been polished. I laughed at the very idea, before forcing myself to calm down and to be serious. I could see that, if I really wanted to have a look at the door, heavy spadework would be required, so, picking up the broad, heavy coal shovel propped against the wall, I put my back into the task. Though it wasn't long before I was sweating, taking a moment for a breather, I saw I'd uncovered the top of the doorframe, having shifted about a third of the coal. Taking off my shirt, hanging it on the pedal of a penny-farthing, quietly rusting in the corner, I set to work again. Blisters tingled on my palms and, after another ten minutes, I had to stop to wipe the sweat from my eyes. I gritted my teeth and kept digging.

I was gasping for breath, a little light-headed, by the time I completely uncovered the door. After a moment's triumph, came a horrible moment when, cursing my stupidity, I realised I'd have to shift the whole lot back again. My plan, if I'd had one, was to get the coal out of the way, open the door, take a swift shufti and get the hell out of there, leaving no trace. Things had already gone awry, since I'd lost track of time, having no idea how long the old girl had been away, or when Hobbes would return. However, since I'd gone so far, I reckoned I might as well carry on and open it.

I reached out, taking the cold brass door knob in a shaking hand and turning it. Nothing happened and though I tried pushing and tugging, it was clear the door was locked.

'Bugger it!' I muttered, performing a stamping, fist-shaking dance of frustration, culminating in a wild kick at the door. It didn't help and, as I hobbled away, swearing like a bastard, I was glad Hobbes couldn't hear me.

'Right, Andy,' I said out loud, 'you've screwed this up right and proper. What are you going to do now?'

'Shut up and think,' was the answer.

Sitting on the coal, I thought: if the door was locked, then there had to be a key, a key that, perhaps, Hobbes kept hidden down there. Since taking a few minutes to search for it would make little difference to the mess I was in, since my only other option was to admit defeat, to shovel the coal back and walk away still ignorant, I started looking. The old Andy would no doubt have followed the second option but I'd developed into sterner stuff under Hobbes's tutelage.

I searched everywhere, trying to use my intelligence to work out where anyone might conceal a key. I looked under piles of flowerpots, through a cupboard full of ancient paint tins, even pulled a couple of loose bricks from the wall, without any luck. At last, in despair, making a decision to give up, to abandon my stupid plan, a feeling of utter relief surged through me. Dry of mouth, needing a glass of water, I walked slowly towards the steps, heading for the kitchen, hoping I'd have sufficient time and strength to shift all the coal back, to clean myself up, so no one would be any the wiser.

I didn't quite make it to the kitchen, for, hanging in plain view from a nail beneath the light switch, was a large black key. My stomach lurching, my heart thumping, I reached for it and picked it up. It was as long as my hand, weighty and old-fashioned. Taking it to the door, fitting it in the keyhole, I turned it. Its motion was smooth, silent, well lubricated, unnerving since I was anticipating a gothic creak.

The door being heavy, I had to lean against it, shoving hard until, just as I was about to give up, it swung open. I would have plummeted straight down the narrow flight of worn stone steps had I not grabbed a rusting rail, which supported me until it snapped. Stumbling forward, losing my footing, I landed hard on my bottom and slipped into the darkness, bumping and grazing my elbows on the way. Though I managed to regain my footing before the end of the stair, my momentum carrying me forward, I ran into a wall, knocking the wind out of me, making me fall backwards into a couple of inches of icy water. Gasping as it soaked my overheated body, I stood up, cracking the top of my head on something hard, falling back into the puddle, cursing and nursing what felt like a fine collection of bruises and scrapes.

As the shock and pain receded, I started to make sense of wherever I was. I groped back to where I could stand up safely, the reek of ancient stone and damp all pervasive, the only light, the feeble and distant remnants that made it down the narrow steps from above. I was in a tight, bare passageway, leading, so far as I could tell, towards the town. Since I'd got so far, self-esteem insisted on investigating a little more. I took a few steps forward, my hands held out like a mummy from a horror film.

I was sopping wet, my trousers clinging to my skin, shivering, more with nerves than with cold. Although the floor was smooth and regular, occasional projections from the wall proved dangerous and painful to my elbows. After no more than a dozen steps, finding myself in utter blackness, having gone far enough to satisfy honour, if not curiosity, I glanced back over my shoulder to reassure myself that I could still see the faint light from the cellar.

Unable to see anything, anything at all, my nervousness multiplied. Though reason suggested the passage was not quite straight, or, maybe, that the door had swung shut, I was gripped by a sudden horror that I might wander off into a maze of passages. Turning round, taking a step forward, I smacked straight into a solid wall. Sliding down onto my side, I lay stunned on the rocky floor and, by the time my head cleared, I'd lost any sense of direction.

Since the total silence amid the blackness was oppressive, I spoke out loud to myself. 'C'mon, Andy, stay cool and think. There are only two ways to go: backwards or forwards. If you take about twelve careful paces you'll be back at the steps, or if not, you'll be twelve paces further into the tunnel. If that's the case, all you have to do is turn again and take twenty-four paces and you'll be out. It's quite simple.'

I did my best to ignore the small voice in my head saying, 'What if there's more than one tunnel down here? Then you've had it. It'll serve you right, too; he told you not to come down here.'

The small voice made me forget to count. 'No problem,' I said to myself. 'Just count to twelve and, if there's still nothing, turn around and count up to, let's say twenty and then we'll be out. No problem.'

Having counted out twelve steps, all I could see, or rather, couldn't see, was darkness. The tunnel feeling like it might have widened, I made sure to keep my left hand against the wall. In the distance, a long way off, I thought I could hear running water.

'Oh well, that was the wrong way,' I said in a brave voice. 'About turn and you'll soon be out.'

I turned, groping along the opposite wall, counting out each step with a cheerful boy-scout optimism I didn't feel. I'd counted to fifteen when, reaching a dead end, my heart went into a frenzy of pounding, my breathing growing harsh and rapid. Trying to force myself to stay calm, I tried to think, aware that blind panic was lurking, ready to overrun any remaining good sense.

'There must be another tunnel,' I said. 'If I work my way back, I'll be able to find where I went wrong.' The trouble was, I didn't believe me.

Sometime later, I realised I'd been right not to believe me. Having no idea where I was, or to where I was heading, I just kept walking, on the dubious grounds that, sooner or later, I'd find a way out. The small voice in my head said, 'You've really done it, you've got yourself well and truly lost and I hope you're satisfied. Well done. You're in the labyrinth and you didn't even bring any string.'

Snippets of Greek mythology, learned at school, in particular, something about a Minotaur that lived in a similar place, devouring human flesh, kept flashing into my mind, the sort of memories I could have done without, for my imagination was already in full swing. The thing was, Hobbes, though warning of dangers behind the door, hadn't specified what they might be and I was conjuring up monsters, the sort previously only seen in nightmares, to scare me half to death. Since running was out of the question, I sat down on the hard stone floor, taking a breather, regretting my failure to get that glass of water for, by then, I would have been glad to drink from the puddle at the bottom of the staircase. Even in the midst of my terror and despair, I recognised that was a stupid idea, because, if I found the puddle, I'd be able to go to the kitchen. I listened for the running water I thought I'd heard, however long ago that had been, yet all I could hear was my own breathing.

Sitting there, calming myself, I wondered what on earth, or rather, below earth the tunnels were. I wasn't aware of any mine workings in the area and wondered if they could have been smugglers' tunnels, or part of an elaborate wartime bomb shelter, or maybe I was in one of those places where dead bodies were stored. What were they called? Catamarans? Something like that. Catacombs – that was the word. What a perfect place to hide a body.

I shouldn't have gone down there.

Vile images entered my mind, as bright as if I could really see them, of grinning skulls and heaps of rotten bones, and Hobbes sitting in the middle, chewing on some bit of somebody. Yet, I couldn't smell decay, which was some comfort. All my nose could detect was damp, soil and my own sweat. I was shivering, goose pimples erupting on my skin, teeth chattering, so I got to my feet, needing to keep walking or die of hypothermia. Anyway, I was bound to come across something eventually.

I couldn't stand much more of the darkness and the silence.

In fact, it wasn't quite silent. Something was moving, something I hoped wasn't rats, because there was nothing worse than rats, except for something bigger and fiercer. Whatever it was, it didn't sound as small as a rat: not by a long way.

Surely there wasn't another panther? Was it possible I'd stumbled into their daytime hideaway? But then, Hobbes would have known about it already, unless they were what he was hiding. Nothing made sense in that blackness, in my state of rising terror.

The noise getting louder, sounding horribly like paws, I held my breath, on the edge of blind panic, hearing something sniffing, something not far away. My nerves, or what was left of them, unable to take any more, I turned to flee, knowing it was hopeless.

'Stop! Stop right there!' said a voice that could not be disobeyed. 'Do not take another step. Stay exactly where you are.'

I stopped, terror giving way to fearful, almost tearful, relief.

'I'm lost,' I said, looking back over my shoulder, a futile thing to do in the blackness.

'Of course you are,' said Hobbes. 'Now do as I say, exactly as I say.'

'Alright.' My voice was surprising in its pitch, its feeble lack of timbre.

'Do not turn around. Take a step backwards … now another … and another … one more ought to do it. Now you can turn around, and put your right hand against the wall … your right hand! That's it. Now walk towards me, and slowly.'

I turned towards his voice, reassured by its calm authority, though the fear of whatever was behind goaded me into a scurry.

'Stop there,' he said, 'do not put your foot down.'

'Why not?' I gulped, keeping it raised.

'Because you'll tread on the dog.'

A cold nose pressing into my left hand, I stroked Dregs's head, safe for the first time since I'd lost my way. Hobbes's hand touched my shoulder.

'You shouldn't have come down here,' he said, 'there are more dangers than you can possibly imagine.'

'Like what?'

'Now is not the time for questions,' he said looping a length of cord around my neck. 'Follow me.'

The cord tightening, I followed, like a small child on a harness and, just like a child, I felt secure, wondering why, though I feared I was in for a severe telling off, I had no concerns about my well-being. There'd been no anger in his voice, only concern, and my suspicion that he'd murdered Henry Bishop and others no longer mattered; he was still my friend, someone I could rely on. It wasn't a ruthless application of logic that led me to this conclusion, it was just a feeling; sometimes feelings are worth more than logic.

Though Dregs's paws pattered quietly as we twisted and turned through the blackness, my feet scuffed and clattered, as I tripped and stumbled in the rear. Of Hobbes, other than a light pressure on my neck and the usual faint, feral odour, I could discern nothing, except on the occasions when he paused to sniff. I didn't care, so long as I got out of that horrible place, where the weight of aeons of darkness was crushing me, the unseen walls squeezing too tightly.

At last, so faint at first I doubted my own eyes, I began to see Hobbes's silhouette. As the outline sharpened, I could make out Dregs, padding to heel, two steps in front. Eventually, I could see my own hands, and then, a moment of bliss, the doorway. Though I longed to rush up the steps, to put the dark behind me, I had to climb up at Hobbes's steady, deliberate pace, until, at last, I was blinking in the dim light of the cellar. The dog yawned and shook himself, apparently sharing my feelings of relief as Hobbes shut and locked the door, pocketing the key.

'Thank you for getting me out of there,' I said, as a thought struck. 'Umm ... how would you have opened the door if I hadn't already moved the coal?'

'Quite easily. Now, you'd best get upstairs, get washed and make yourself respectable. We need to have a little chat, but it can wait till we've had some grub.'

Looking at myself, I was staggered how black, streaked and filthy I was.

As he picked up the shovel, shifting the coal back, I climbed the stairs to the kitchen, a flutter of butterflies taking wing in my stomach at the prospect of the little chat. Dregs bounded after me, pushing past at the top.

'Have you been having fun, dear?' asked Mrs Goodfellow, who was slicing bread at the table, apparently unsurprised by my appearance.

'It wasn't fun. I got lost.'

'Well, at least you didn't tumble into the bottomless pit of doom, or worse. Never mind, dear, you'll find clean clothes in your room.'

'Thank you,' I said, turning towards the stairs.

'But you'd better take those filthy things off first. I'm not having you messing up anywhere else. Anyone would think you've been rolling around in the coal.'

'But ...'

'But nothing. Hurry up.' She gave me what passed for her stern look.

Hobbes emerged from the cellar without a speck of dirt on him, having taken all of two minutes to put the coal back.

'C'mon, Andy,' he said, 'clean yourself up, and quickly. I'm famished.'

Giving up, I stripped to my underpants, which apparently passed muster for she nodded. 'Now hurry up. Dinner will be ready when you are.'

'Just one thing,' she said as I turned away, 'that young lady of yours called round when you were out.'

'Really?'

'Yes, really. Now move yourself.'

Although I hesitated, wanting to find out more, Hobbes's expression moved me on. My insides had been twisting themselves into knots at the prospect of the impending little chat, yet the mere thought of Violet blew away my immediate fears, as I tried to work out why she'd come round. It was hardly likely she wanted to see more of me, unless I'd misjudged everything. As hope sprouted, so did a sudden horror, for the old girl had said she'd called round, but hadn't actually said she'd left and the idea of her seeing me streaked with dirt and sweat, wearing only a pair of Y-fronts, made me cringe. Adopting stealth mode, creeping like a cat, I peeped nervously into the sitting room, as Dregs pushed past, making a circle of the room, sniffing and acting in an unusually manic way, before rushing back into the kitchen. I wasn't entirely sure if I was relieved or disappointed to find her gone.

I went upstairs and ran a bath. I was amazed how much black muck sloughed off me as I scrubbed away, using Mrs Goodfellow's long-handled back scrubber and a bar of soap. I had to change the water twice before it stayed reasonably clear. Afterwards, having dried myself and made some sort of effort to clean the bath, without completely removing the dark ring, I dressed and went downstairs.

For once, I didn't pay much attention to my lunch, though the crusty ham sandwiches didn't deserve such negligence. The problem was that, as the time for my little chat with Hobbes grew closer, my mouth was becoming as dry as talcum powder, despite the sluicing of a couple of pints of ginger beer down my throat. I wanted it to be all over, even if I really didn't want it to start, and he seemed to be lingering over his meal, as if he had all day. Though part of me wanted to urge him to hurry up, I suspected the waiting wouldn't be the worst part. At last, dabbing his lips with a napkin, he rose to his feet.

'Let's go through to the sitting room,' he said. 'I think some explanation is in order.'

I followed him, quaking. He appeared calm, but that meant little.

'Take a seat,' he said, indicating the near end of the sofa, planting his big backside on the far end. 'Make yourself comfortable.'

Nodding, I attempted a smile as, sighing, he rested his feet on the coffee table, just as Mrs Goodfellow came in with the tea. As she tutted, he shifted his feet onto the carpet with a sheepish grin.

'Thanks, lass,' he said as she returned to the kitchen.

'Now, then, Andy,' he said turning towards me, piling sugar into his mug, 'a few months ago, I told you not to use that door and I believe I suggested you would do better to forget all about it. Is that correct?'

I gulped, nodding.

Having stirred his tea with his finger, he took a long slurp and continued. 'Since it is often dangerous to seek out secrets, my intention was to instil such fear into you that you wouldn't dream of going in there. I thought, as the months went by, that it had worked.'

'It had,' I said, my voice a croak. 'Nearly.'

'I had good reasons, for there are untold dangers down there, dangers it would have been better for you to remain ignorant of. Unfortunately, I failed to take into account human curiosity. It was remiss of me and I apologise.'

I grunted, the little chat failing to live up to expectations.

'It must have been difficult to restrain yourself for so long. Was there something in particular that made you look?'

It was a tricky question and I squirmed before answering. 'Well, it was like this ... umm ... it was last night.'

'I see. Anything in particular?'

I was too bewildered to lie. 'The body you brought in.'

'I'd hoped I'd concealed it.'

'I saw the reflection.'

'I expect,' he said, 'that you want to know why I brought it back here?'

'Yes.' I nodded. 'Who was it and why?'

'You didn't recognise him?'

I shook my head. 'I only caught a glimpse.'

'It was the late-lamented Henry Bishop.'

'Oh ... but why?'

'Because I needed a really close look at the body before the pathologist mucked it up and it was easier to fetch him back here than to conceal myself in the morgue.'

'But how did you get him out of the morgue?'

'The tunnels run right across town and beyond. One of them goes by the morgue and there's a very useful manhole cover in the basement that allows access. Since hardly anyone even knows about the tunnels, I sometimes use them to move about without being observed, something I think is essential at the present.' Finishing his tea in one draught, he wiped his lips with the back of his hand.

'What's so special about the present?' I asked.

'I've sensed someone watching me. I don't know who yet, or why.'

'I see but ... umm ... why did you want to examine Henry Bishop's body?'

'I wanted to know what killed him.'

'Why didn't you have a look when you were at the restaurant?'

I experienced the rare pleasure of making Hobbes start. 'You saw me?'

'Yes and there was blood all over you and ... and when you disappeared, I thought you'd ... well, I didn't know what to think.' I still didn't and my nervousness returned.

'Ah!' he said. 'That explains it; I thought something was bothering you. Alright, I'll tell you what happened. If you recall, I was looking for Henry, following the incident with the Bashem's lad. It turned out he was a surprisingly good woodsman but I got onto his trail in the end and was only a few minutes behind when something crossed his path.'

'What?'

'A big cat that got to Henry before I could. Though he fired both barrels of his shotgun, it was to no avail and it attacked him. Managing to break away, bleeding badly, he made a run for the restaurant. I got some of his blood on me as I followed through the bushes.'

His explanation relaxed me enough that I was able to take a sip of tea. 'Umm ... why didn't you help him?'

'Because I hoped he'd be safe in the restaurant and believed it would be better to apprehend the cat before it caused any more trouble.'

'Shouldn't you have waited for backup? It might have been dangerous. And what happened?'

He frowned. 'Unfortunately, it gave me the slip, almost as if it had vanished. It was most peculiar and, since then, I've been aware of being watched from time to time. Since I'd venture to suggest such behaviour is unusual for a cat, it must be a person.'

'Why would anyone watch you? And why can't you catch the cat? It can't really vanish.'

'I don't know. It's a mystery.'

I scratched my head for Hobbes rarely admitted ignorance, and asked another question that had been bugging me. 'What are the tunnels for? Who made them?'

'I'll tell you what I can,' said Hobbes, 'but I'm no expert on tunnelling. I discovered them by chance many years ago while searching for a lost farthing. They are, I believe, ancient and, I suspect, may pre-date human settlement in this area. However, there are extensive crypts under the church that may have been part of the tunnels once upon a time.'

'Any idea who did make them?'

'Not for sure, but something still lives down there. I've picked up their scent now and again but I can't categorise it. I just think of them as troglodytes and if I use their tunnels I make sure to leave a gift of meat in payment. It always goes, and goes quickly.'

'Troglodytes? Do you think they're dangerous?'

'Probably, though they've never bothered me and, since they do not, to my knowledge, commit any crimes and, since they evidently don't wish to meet me, I leave them be. They are not the only dangers, though. You were right on the edge of a shaft when I found you. Two more steps and you'd have dropped right in.'

I shivered and, the phone warbling suddenly, spilled tea down my shirt. Fortunately it had cooled.

Hobbes shook his head. 'You'll need another clean shirt and it's still only two o'clock.' Chuckling, he reached for the phone.

'Inspector Hobbes,' he said, 'how can I help you? ... Yes, he is here. Would you like to talk to him? Right you are.' He winked at me. 'It's for you.'

Since no one ever rang me, I took the phone from Hobbes feeling confused.

'Hello?'

'Hi, Andy, it's me.'

'Violet?' My heart dancing ecstatically, I broke into a sweat. 'I wasn't expecting you.'

'Who were you expecting?'

She sounded a little hurt.

'No one. I just thought after ... well ... after last time you'd probably want to forget all about me.'

'It was hardly your fault, was it?'

'No ... but I just thought ...'

'I called round this morning, but Mrs Goodfellow said you were out. Didn't she say?'

'Well ... yes, she did. Umm ... I'm glad you've called.'

'Thank you. Did you go anywhere nice?'

'No, I got lost.'

'Where?'

Hobbes shook his head.

'I don't know ... I just found myself lost, if that makes any sense. I'm found now.'

'Good,' she said with a gentle laugh, 'because I was wondering if we might ... er ... meet again. If that's alright with you?'

'Umm ... OK,' I said. 'If you'd like.'

'Oh, you don't have to if you don't want.'

It dawned on me that my response might have suggested a lack of enthusiasm. The only excuse I could make was that I'd still been reeling from Hobbes's revelations when the surprise of hearing her voice had knocked me off balance; it was a good thing I still had the wits to realise in time. 'Sorry, that didn't come out quite the way it should have. What I mean is, I'd really like to see you again.'

'That's good, because I'd love to see you, too.'

My heart leapt. 'That's great ... fantastic. Umm ... when?'

'How about tomorrow afternoon? I finish at four on Fridays so I could come round straight after.'

I paused, as if checking through my varied appointments. 'Umm ... yeah, that sounds fine. What would you like to do?'

'I don't know,' she said, hesitantly. 'What would you like to do?'

'I don't know either ... umm,' I replied, my mind completely out of ideas.

'How about,' said Hobbes in what he evidently meant as a whisper, 'going to the pictures or for a picnic?'

'Good ideas,' said Violet. 'Are you alright? Your voice sounded hoarse.'

'I'm great. It wasn't my voice, but it was a good idea.'

'Which one?'

'Both, I suppose.'

'I'll just check the forecast,' said Violet, clicking computer keys. 'It says the rain's going to pass, so a picnic could be good fun.'

'Yes,' I agreed, 'so long as we steer clear of Loop Woods, with things being what they are.'

'I'll second that. Where would you suggest?'

She had me there. I caught myself 'umming', a bad habit I was occasionally guilty of. I just couldn't think of anywhere suitable.

'How about the arboretum?' said Hobbes.

'Umm … how about the arboretum?' I said.

'Why not? Where is it?'

'Umm …' I glanced at Hobbes for inspiration.

'The other side of Hedbury. About a ten-minute drive.'

I relayed the message, including an appropriate adjustment for normal driving. 'It's the other side of Hedbury. That's probably twenty minutes by car.'

'It sounds ideal. I'll come round just after four.'

'Sounds great … umm … but what about food?'

'Oh yes,' she said, laughing again, 'I'd forgotten that. I suppose we could just pop into a supermarket and pick up a few things. Anyway, I've really got to go now; I've got emails to send. I'll see you tomorrow. Bye.'

'Great,' I said, 'I'm looking forward to it. Bye.'

Putting the phone down, amazed, I turned towards Hobbes. 'She's going to pick me up tomorrow at four.'

'Who is, dear?' asked Mrs G, coming in from the kitchen, sagging beneath the weight of the sledgehammer on her shoulder.

'Violet is,' I said. 'We're going for a picnic at the arboretum.'

'Good for you, dear. I can make up a hamper if you'd like.'

'There's no need. We can get something from the shops.'

'You could,' she said, shaking her head, 'but I could make up something special.'

'I don't want to inconvenience you,' I said, thinking I ought to put on a little show of reluctance before accepting, for there was no doubt a spread she would rustle up would put any shop-bought stuff to shame.

'It won't be a problem, dear.'

'OK, then,' I said, as if doing her a favour, 'I'd be delighted.'

'I know,' she said, smiling, stumping upstairs, dragging the sledgehammer.

I have no idea what she did with it for I heard nothing after her door shut. I sat back next to Hobbes, expecting to continue our little talk when the phone warbled again.

'Inspector Hobbes,' he answered, 'how can I help you? What? … I see … How many? Right, just the one? Are you sure? Yes, I suppose one is enough … I'll be right over.' Slapping down the receiver, he turned to me and grinned.

'What's up?' I asked.

'It's not so much up as out.'

'Out? What's out, then?' I asked, puzzled by his gleeful expression.

'An elephant.' He rubbed his hands together, sounding like someone trying to grate a coconut shell, and pulled out his car keys.

'What?'

'You heard.'

'I know but I meant "why?" or "where?" I mean why is there an elephant out? Where is it? What's it doing?'

'I'll tell you in the car,' said Hobbes, 'if you'd like to come along … Dregs!'

Rain pattering against the window, I grabbed my mac as the dog bounded past.

'Come along, and quickly,' Hobbes urged, opening the front door, leaping down the steps, looking like an excited child, if you could ignore his bulk and his hairiness and his large, lumpy head, which I couldn't.

Dregs and I followed, running through the puddles, flinging ourselves into the car as he drove away. Somewhere, a horn blared but he gave it no mind, unlike Dregs who barked at the challenge. As I strapped myself in, hanging onto the seat, I wondered again about the folly that kept me following Hobbes. Time and time again I'd argued with myself that I didn't have to but, whenever the call came, I responded before my brain had a chance to stop me. Still, going anywhere with him usually lead to excitement and, much to my surprise, part of me that had never before manifested itself found it irresistible.

'Right,' he said, twisting the wheel as we screeched into Pound Street, 'about the elephant.'

'Go on,' I said.

'Apparently, it was being transported from one zoo to another. When the driver stopped for a cup of tea at the Greasy Pole it escaped and is now running amuck in the car park.'

'How could it escape?'

'You have as much idea as I do.' The car swerved and speeded up.

'What are you going to do?'

'I don't know, yet.'

'Will there be backup?'

'Oh yes, Derek Poll is on the scene and, of course, I'll have you.'

'Oh, great.'

In a matter of minutes we were screeching to a halt by the Greasy Pole café where thirty or more gawping people had gathered. PC Poll's long arms were holding them back. An athletic-looking young man in a dark suit, towards the front of the crowd, appeared vaguely familiar, though I couldn't place him. Besides, I was more interested in the rogue elephant, which, though I couldn't see it, I could deduce, using the detective skills I'd picked up from Hobbes, had recently been in the vicinity. It had clearly been on the café's patio – all over it in fact – and by the time I was out of the car, Dregs was sniffing at the steaming dung as if at a rare perfume. I suspected, however, that the pile of pooh had not yet registered with Eric Wyszynski, the café's owner, who, dressed in his habitual stained white jacket, his scrawny, tattooed hands clasped to his greasy hair, was staring at what remained of his café, a pile of rubble having appeared where there'd once been a wall. He wasn't taking his misfortune well to judge from the river of obscenities spewing from beneath his nicotine-stained moustache.

The elephant had presumably escaped from the box-trailer in the car park, a trailer that was, in my opinion, far too small to hold one in comfort for any time and, to judge from the state of it, it had been inside for a considerable time. Though I took the scene in within a few seconds, the star of the show was missing.

'Where is it then?' I asked.

In response, Hobbes, wrapping an arm around me, leaped backwards, completely over the car, landing on the grass verge behind. The shock, knocking the wind out of me, I was still struggling for breath as he set me back on my feet. Then, with a trumpeting and the pounding of heavy feet, the elephant lumbered over the spot where I'd been standing, heading directly towards the onlookers who scattered like dry leaves in the wind. Only one elderly man, standing beneath a black umbrella, didn't move a muscle. It was Augustus Godley, the oldest human in Sorenchester, who was still hale and well, despite the slowness of age.

As the elephant pounded towards him, I thought he'd had it, for I couldn't see how even Hobbes could rescue him in time. Yet, he didn't need to, for the beast, swerving, ran across the road, causing a big blue car to brake sharply and a small white one to run into the back of it. Neither driver got out as the elephant trundled into a meadow by the side of the river Soren.

'Are you alright?' I asked, running towards the old man, who was wearing a strange smile.

'Aye, lad,' he said, 'I'm grand. This takes me back to the time I was in India, when I had to shoot an elephant in my pyjamas.'

'Really?'

'How it got into my pyjamas, I'll never know.' A thin laugh wheezed between his lips.

'C'mon, Andy,' Hobbes shouted. 'And quickly, this is no time for listening to Mr Godley's jokes. There's an elephant to catch.'

'How? Won't you need a tranquilliser gun?'

'Let's hope not.'

'Oh, great.'

He loped across the road and into the meadow. The elephant, standing in the river, drinking, watched, flapping his great ears.

'Now then, my lad,' said Hobbes, approaching the beast, 'let's be having you. By rights you should be in your trailer.'

The elephant, shaking his massive tusks, lobbed a trunk-full of mud.

Hobbes sidestepped it and continued. 'That's enough of your nonsense.'

'Be careful, sir,' said PC Poll.

Hobbes looked back with a grin. 'Of course, but I'm sure Jumbo will come quietly.' As he reached for the elephant it shook its broad, grey head, seized him around the waist, lifted him high in the air and shook him like a terrier shakes a rat.

'An awkward customer, eh?' said Hobbes, dangling upside down over the river. With a grunt, he took the trunk in his hands, squeezing until, the elephant releasing him, he fell backwards into the river with a great splash and a yell. Jumping up in one fluid movement, grabbing a flapping ear, he half vaulted, half hauled himself onto the elephant's back. Dregs ran towards them, barking.

The great beast, taking fright, bolted along the river bed away from me, sending up curtains of foaming cappuccino-coloured water. Hobbes, somehow clinging to its back, despite the violent bouncing and scything attacks from its trunk, looked surprisingly small and vulnerable.

'Why doesn't he get down?' I muttered.

'He can't get down from an elephant,' said Augustus who, having shuffled to my side, was watching proceedings with a smile.

'Why not?' I asked, puzzled.

'Because, down comes from ducks.' He chuckled.

I groaned, staring at him. Hobbes might be killed any moment and all Augustus, an old friend of his, could do was make stupid, schoolboy jokes.

'I'd move, if I were you, sir,' cried PC Poll.

Dregs, tail between his legs, was rushing towards us, the elephant close behind, with Hobbes still clinging on, the grin on his face making him look like a child enjoying a free ride on the rollercoaster. PC Poll's advice seemed reasonable, so turning away, I fled. I'd only gone ten steps or so when, remembering Augustus, I hesitated, slowed, stopped and turned back. The elephant was again heading straight towards him, and I had no chance of reaching him in time. Since I could no longer see Hobbes, I assumed he'd fallen off. The elephant bellowed and wondering if, perhaps, he wasn't running quite so fast, reckoning I might just have a chance, I sprinted towards Augustus, who was watching calmly, unconcerned by the mountain of muscle bearing down on him. I reached him a moment before the elephant, still bellowing, came to a standstill, almost within touching distance.

Hobbes's voice rang out. 'Are you two alright?'

I still couldn't see him. 'We're fine,' I shouted. 'How about you?'

'A little wet.'

'Where are you?' I asked, peering along the river's sodden banks.

'Here.' His hand waved from behind the elephant, which was standing still, as if in deep thought.

In a slow and stately manner, it turned, stomping up the bank into the meadow, while Dregs bristled and growled from a safe distance. Hobbes, gripping its tail in one hand, seeming to have its undivided attention, guided it towards the trailer. I expected him to force it back inside. Instead, he shouted, 'Who's in charge of this poor animal?'

A stout, little man wearing greasy overalls and a faded denim cap, looking around, as if expecting to see someone, finally raised his hand. 'It looks like I am, guvnor. But I'm only the driver.'

'Alright,' said Hobbes, 'before he goes back, he needs feeding and I want the trailer cleaned out properly and a good supply of clean water and fodder put in. How long was he in there?'

'I don't know, guvnor, but I only picked him up a couple of hours ago.'

'Who was in charge before that?'

'I don't know. A bloke in a suit paid me five hundred quid to take the rig to Brighton Zoo. I only met him this morning.'

'Where did you pick it up?'

'At a service station, the other side of Birmingham. It took us the best part of two hours to get here. The bloke reckoned that, as it would take us another couple of hours to reach Brighton, it'd be a good idea to stop here and get a bite to eat. He said it was pretty good.'

288

I shuddered. In the past, having eaten at the Greasy Pole, I knew it wasn't good. Furthermore, Hobbes had hinted that he knew something about the place, something too horrible for my delicate ears. The only element in its favour was that it wasn't expensive.

'Where is the gentleman now?' asked Hobbes.

The little man shook his head. 'I wish I knew, guvnor. He hasn't paid me yet. All I know is that I was just sitting down with my burger and my mug of coffee when he says he has to step out, 'cause he's gotta make sure the elephant's alright. A couple of minutes later, all hell breaks loose, the wall comes down, the ceiling caves in, and we has to run for it.'

'I see,' said Hobbes. 'Do you know the gentleman's name?'

'I'm sorry.'

Hobbes sighed. 'Fair enough. Just get the trailer cleaned up and feed Jumbo.'

'Me? It's not my trailer. I'm just moving it.'

Hobbes growling, the little man ran up the ramp into the trailer, grabbed a bucket and shovel and set to work.

'I've got my hands full, Derek,' said Hobbes, turning to face Constable Poll, 'so would you ensure no one's been injured and then take statements from anyone who's got anything useful to say?' He beckoned me. 'Andy, find some food for this beast and plenty of it.'

'Umm … right. What do they eat?'

'Cabbage, bread, apples, bananas, carrots – that sort of thing. Try the kitchen. It looks like some of it's still standing.'

Eric appeared, wiping his eyes as if he'd been crying. 'He can't just go taking what he wants from my café.'

'Yes, he can,' said Hobbes. 'It would only go to waste otherwise. It's not like you're going to be in business for a while.'

Eric nodded unhappily and, oblivious to the rain, sitting on the kerb, sobbed like a broken man. Since I can't bear to see a grown man crying, I turned away and rummaged, finding several bags of white sliced bread, a bunch of browning bananas, a pile of cabbages and a crate filled with carrots, quite surprised to discover Eric could, apparently, have served vegetables with his stodge. Having piled a selection into a box, I hurried towards Hobbes, who was still holding the elephant's tail.

'Well done,' he said, 'but I believe that lot will do more good at the front end. He's quite calm now, but be careful.'

Plonking the box down in front of the elephant, I backed away, although I didn't feel in any danger. Picking up a carrot, it stuffed it into his mouth and, though I wasn't an expert, the way it tucked in suggested it hadn't been fed for far too long. As soon as it was absorbed in feeding, Hobbes released his grip, strolled round and patted its head. I noticed his thick, hairy toes were jutting from the ruins of his boots.

He followed my glance and shrugged. 'I appear to have worn out my boots. It takes a lot of leather to stop an elephant.'

The rain was still falling, Hobbes was soaked and splattered with mud – at least, I hoped it was mud – and I was nearly as wet, having, in all the confusion, never got round to donning my mac. We stood around, waiting until the elephant had eaten its fill, and the back of the trailer was nice and clean. Then Hobbes led it inside.

The stout little man, who answered to the name of 'arry, seemed a decent sort of bloke, who'd just been trying to earn a living and wasn't responsible for what had happened. Unfortunately, he couldn't give a detailed description of the man who'd employed him. All he could say was that his employer was young and fit, that he'd worn a dark suit and a blue tie emblazoned with a golden emblem. No one fitting the description could be seen, which didn't surprise me, for I wouldn't have wanted to take the blame had my elephant demolished a café.

It was one of those extremely rare occasions when I almost wished I was still working for the *Bugle*, for I couldn't yet see any reporters in the burgeoning crowd and wondered, for a moment, whether I might knock off a few hundred words to see how much Editorsaurus Rex Witcherley would pay for it. Yet, the prospect of having to face him again giving me the willies, I abandoned the idea.

Although Hobbes had the situation well under control, several police cars, two fire engines and an ambulance had rushed up, lights flashing. I couldn't blame them for wanting to be there, for it's not every day an elephant creates havoc in Sorenchester. With so many police officers attending, and the elephant happy and under control, there was no longer any reason for Hobbes to be there. So, leaving things in their hands, we left. I was glad to go, for I was shivering, dripping, sodden, and the rain was showing no signs of abating. As we walked towards the car, Dregs shook himself all over me and I was too wet to care. Even so, I was in a better state than Hobbes, for being dragged through a river by a rampaging elephant is one of the most effective ways of ruffling an individual's attire; his clothes had suffered almost as much as his boots.

For once, I didn't much mind his maniac driving, since it got us home quicker. When safely in the warmth, throwing off my soaked clothes, I wrapped myself in a dressing gown and drank hot tea, while he took first go in the bathroom, his roars suggesting he was enjoying his shower. When he'd finished, I took a long, hot and, as far as I was concerned, well-deserved bath. Afterwards, as if by magic, clean, fresh, dry clothes, nicely pressed and neatly folded, had appeared on my dressing table, while my soggy, dripping relics had vanished. Mrs G, I thought, was a marvel.

Going downstairs, I found Hobbes at the kitchen table, looking as clean and fresh as I felt. Dregs, on the other hand, having picked up on the idea of bath time, had wedged himself in the cupboard beneath the sink, and was resisting any attempts to remove him, until undone by Mrs G's low cunning. She dropped a scrap of meat into his bowl and, unable to control his hunger, he emerged, sealing his fate. Seizing him round the middle with her skinny arms, she carried him off to the bathtub of doom. To be honest, I didn't feel sorry for him, despite his hangdog appearance, having become convinced that he only exhibited token resistance for pride's sake and that, secretly, he rather enjoyed it.

I poured a fresh mug of tea and sat opposite Hobbes, who was staring out of the window in a manner suggestive of deep thought, or total paralysis. The rain having finally stopped, a glint of sunlight hinting the clouds were breaking up, a bird singing, I felt warm, relaxed and at peace with the world.

'Do you find it strange,' asked Hobbes, 'that someone would go to the bother and expense of transporting an elephant as far as Eric's café only to abandon it?'

I nodded. 'He must be bonkers – especially if he'd stopped there because he thought it was good. No one thinks the Greasy Pole is good.'

'Yet, according to Harry, the man had not acted at all strangely, other than being in possession of an elephant just outside Birmingham. And there's another thing, why would anyone come this way to get to Brighton? It's miles out of the way.'

'It just proves he's bonkers,' I said and shrugged. It didn't seem important.

'Maybe he is, as you say, bonkers. Yet the combination of events is striking. A mysterious young man offers to pay five hundred pounds, a generous sum for a few hours of work, to transport an elephant from Birmingham to Brighton. He then chooses a route taking them miles out of the way, stops at the Greasy Pole and steps outside for a minute, during which, the elephant, which is ravenous and bad-tempered, somehow escapes from a locked trailer and demolishes the café. By then our man is no longer to be seen. The whole scenario seems most unlikely.'

'Are you suggesting it wasn't an accident?'

'I think so. I asked one of the lads at the station to check who was supposed to be transporting an elephant to Brighton Zoo. He phoned back to say there isn't a zoo in Brighton. What's more, he'd checked round all the zoos within fifty miles of there and none of them was expecting an elephant.'

'That's very strange indeed, unless Harry got muddled up about where he was going.'

'Harry didn't strike me as a man who'd get muddled but, you're right, it is very strange, unless the man had a reason for letting an elephant loose at that particular spot. Perhaps, I'd better have a word with Eric and see if he's got any enemies.'

'He must have – anyone who's ever eaten there.'

Hobbes chuckled. 'I take your point but, really, I think a bad meal is unlikely to make anyone resort to such a bizarre scheme to get revenge, unless, of course, it killed someone. Mind you, that's unlikely. People are surprisingly resilient.'

'Isn't it weird,' I said, 'that this was another incident with a dangerous animal? It's like we've become infested with them.'

He nodded. 'It is unusual, even for Sorenchester, and I wonder if there might be a connection. I can't see any obvious link, but it's worth a little investigation.

'Right,' he said, standing up, 'I'd better go and see Eric. He's in hospital with shock so I'll go on my own; I don't want to alarm him. One more thing, Mr Catt at the Wildlife Park has agreed to look after Jumbo until things are sorted out. He's rather pleased.'

He walked away with a slight hobble. Even Hobbes wasn't entirely immune to elephants.

I sat at the kitchen table, staring into space, until Dregs, frenzied and exuberant, burst in on me. It was a hard job keeping him at a safe distance as he shook himself, trying his damnedest to rub his damp fur against my legs. Ending up in a sort of obstacle race round the kitchen, I found I was enjoying the chase almost as much as he was, and a cackling laugh from Mrs G, who'd appeared with a couple of grubby towels, suggested she appreciated the spectacle.

'Well, dear,' she said when we'd quietened down, 'have you any preferences for your picnic tomorrow?'

That was a poser. My memory stretched back to the rare occasions when mother had packed a picnic for a day on the beach or in the park. It had usually rained, or hailed, forcing us to spend long, gloomy hours in the steamy car, its plastic seats sticking to the backs of my bare legs, a faint aroma of vomit in the air. I'd been sick on the way to Great Aunt Molly's funeral and, although I'd only been sick on that one occasion, if repeatedly and profusely and, over the years, we'd had several cars, some with leather seats, the brain insisted on plastic seats and vomit. It also insisted on white bread and fish-paste sandwiches in greaseproof paper, packets of salt and vinegar crisps, which I didn't much like, and packets of cupcakes, which I loved, the whole lot being washed down with stewed, lukewarm tea from a tartan flask, a flask matching the rug on which we'd planned to sit.

In fairness to the past, I did recall an occasion when the sun had shone for us in a flower-strewn meadow beside a lazy river. I remembered the satisfying, rich, earthy aroma of the water, watching fish splash and jump, the way it all started to go wrong when father, smiling for once, biting down on a chocolate cup cake, was stung by a wasp. His tongue swelling up as big and purple as an aubergine, we had to pack everything away as quickly as possible and get him, groaning, back to the car, which had, in the meantime, been thickly plastered in pungent slurry by a careless farmer. I would never forget father's incoherent grunts of rage and pain as we rushed him to casualty. Since, so far as I could remember, that had been the Caplet family's most successful picnic ever, I began to panic about subjecting Violet to a similar fiasco and fretted, wondering if I should call the whole thing off, before any harm was done.

'Are you alright, dear?'

The old girl, interrupting my pondering, made me jump. 'Umm … yes. I'm alright, but I'm not sure what's best for a picnic.'

'Well, dear,' she said, her face crinkling with thought, 'how about a nice bit of cold beef? And there's some chicken in the fridge. I'll make a nice salad to go with it, and I could bake a veal and ham pie.'

'That sounds pretty good,' I said, my mouth beginning to water.

'That'll do for a start. Then I'll put in a crusty loaf and some biscuits, and I was thinking of baking a fruit cake.'

'Fantastic.'

'And some ginger beer and wine. How about hard-boiled eggs?'

'It sounds rather a lot,' I said, intending to impose some mild restraint, starting to worry about carrying it all. 'And that's without any fish-paste sandwiches.'

'I can do you some fish-paste sandwiches, if you really want.'

'No, please don't, but everything else sounds great!'

'Good,' she said, smiling. 'I haven't made a picnic since my old man went away and there's a nice hamper just gathering dust in the attic. I'll get it down after supper and make sure the mice haven't eaten it.'

'I can do that.'

'That's very kind of you, dear.'

'Not at all.' Since Hobbes had, at last, got round to fixing the loose planks in the attic, I was glad of any opportunity to look around up there, being half convinced that great treasures nestled among the piles of junk. 'I'll do it now, while I think about it.'

'Very good, dear. I think you'll find the hamper behind the trunk, the elephant's trunk that is, not the wooden one. That reminds me, Mr Goodfellow's old summer blazer is in the wooden one and you'll look really smart in it.'

'OK, then,' I said, turning away, heading towards the stairs.

The phone rang as I passed it. Hoping it might be Violet, I lifted the receiver, my heart pounding.

'Congratulations,' said a disembodied voice, 'you have won a guaranteed major prize in the Lithuanian State Lottery.'

I slammed the phone down, muttering a curse under my breath as I walked upstairs. They'd got me once. Never again.

I stood at the top of the loft-ladder besides the enormous stuffed bear, which was either a former resident or something salvaged from a skip, depending on whether you believed Hobbes or Mrs Goodfellow. The stiletto beam of sunlight stabbing through a crack in the grimy window added little to the feeble glow of a naked light bulb; I waited as my eyes adjusted. Since Mrs Goodfellow, regarding the attic as Hobbes's space, rarely visited, there was a sprinkling of dust and dirt everywhere. Most of the floor was covered in tatty piles of clothes, bits of old bikes, nameless junk and a rusty steel rack, concealing dozens of Hobbes's paintings. In my uneducated opinion, he had genuine talent, yet it seemed to embarrass him and he didn't like to talk about it. I found his work oddly beautiful and deeply disturbing in equal measure. Besides the paintings, something else about the attic made me a little uneasy, yet, since he'd never said I shouldn't go up, at least since he'd made the flooring safe, I reckoned I was reasonably safe.

Spotting the old wooden trunk I wanted beneath a large cardboard box, I went towards it. As I moved the box aside, the bottom dropped out and hundreds of photographs fell to the floor. Kneeling down, annoyed, intending to pick them up, to put them back, I made the mistake of looking.

They were in rough chronological order, the early ones showing sepia or faded black and white images of Sorenchester, and it was strange to see horses and carts on streets that had otherwise changed little over the years. Hobbes appeared in some, usually in his police constable's uniform, a splendid moustache obliterating most of his mouth. After I'd shuffled through a few dozen, Mrs Goodfellow made her first appearance, though she wasn't Mrs Goodfellow then, but a small, solemn-faced girl. She'd once told me how Hobbes pulled her from the smouldering wreck of a house after a bomb had killed the rest of her family during the war. I wondered about her family, what her name had been then, where she'd lived, realising how little I knew about her, feeling guilty that I'd never bothered to ask.

Still, time was passing so I pressed on, carrying out a botched repair on the box, placing it on a crate, apparently one containing a magic lantern, and began piling everything back, dropping a large, brittle brown envelope, spilling a pile of colour prints. They were holiday snaps, a little out of focus, faded in the way excessive washing fades summer clothes. Hobbes had barely changed, except that he was sporting a magnificent pair of sideburns and looked very casual in jeans and a t-shirt. Mrs Goodfellow, looking disturbingly young and attractive, wearing a variety of scandalously short skirts and huge straw hats, was with a man in flared scarlet trousers and a paisley-patterned waistcoat, whose shoulder-length dark hair was tied to his forehead with a beaded band. I guessed, although it was hard to make out any distinguishing features behind the mass of facial foliage, that he was Mr Goodfellow. A youngish woman I couldn't identify, with protuberant eyes and a long pigtail, wearing a loose brown kaftan, appeared in many of the prints.

On the back of one, Mrs Goodfellow had written *The old fellow, Robin, Froggy and me – Monterey, California, 1967*. Remembering something about the famous festival there, I giggled at the idea of Hobbes and Mrs G hanging out with hippies. It seemed so wrong.

As I flicked through them, I noticed how Froggy – I assumed that was the young woman's nickname – was usually by Hobbes's side, often with a hand on his shoulder, making him look rather nervous, and couldn't help wondering what sort of relationship they'd had. He'd never mentioned her, being reluctant to talk about his past; I had an idea this was more because he lived his life in the present than because of any reticence. Still, I could ask Mrs G, who was always happy to talk about him; the problem was shutting her up once she'd started.

As I began putting the photos back, I noticed one of Hobbes, messing around in the woods, shirt off, exposing a chest as hairy as a gorilla's. The image, being vaguely familiar, I wished I could remember where I'd seen it before.

I must have been up there for over an hour before I actually got a move on, putting all the photos back, starting the search for the picnic hamper, which, though it wasn't difficult to spot, was a pain to reach because of all the boxes and piles of old-fashioned police uniforms and other obsolete clothing in the way. Hobbes might have made a decent living as a theatrical supplier, if any actors matched his girth and shape. I dug through, shifting wooden boxes overflowing with cups and shields, suggesting he'd been some sort of sportsman in his day and, though he didn't have the physique of a typical athlete, I'd never come across anyone as healthy or so strong.

I struggled with a musty, old canvas tent in my way, hauling it aside, revealing a rusty crate, bound with heavy chains and padlocks. A wave of horror pulsed through me, the hairs on the back of my neck stiffening, my heart racing, because, for some reason, an idea that I'd stumbled across the last resting place of Arthur Crud burst into my head, making me realise I still didn't entirely trust Hobbes. The thought wouldn't go away, even though I was probably being ridiculous, the crate looking as if it hadn't been disturbed for decades. Grabbing the hamper, I turned around, wanting to be downstairs as quickly as possible, nearly forgetting the blazer.

I hurried back towards the trunk and opened it, finding the blazer neatly rolled on top. It turned out to be one of those red, white and blue striped affairs, not my style at all, yet possessing a certain je ne sais quoi, though I wasn't sure quite what it was. Grabbing it, I shut the lid and hastened towards the ladder.

'Hurry up, Andy,' Hobbes yelled from below, 'supper's ready.'

Catching my foot on something, overbalancing, I fell headfirst through the hatch, dropping my cargo. He caught me by the ankles.

'Thank you,' I said, grateful and uncomfortable if not especially shocked.

'I take it,' he said, flipping me the right way up, 'that you're hungry?' He set me down on the carpet and picked up the hamper and blazer.

'I am rather,' I said. 'I didn't realise I'd been up there so long.'

'Well you have, it's nearly half-past six and the lass is about to dish up rib-eye beef steaks. So wash your hands and come along, and quickly, because I'm starving.'

Doing as I was told, I tried to clear my mind, tried to convince myself I'd been imagining things. After all, why would he keep a body in a crate in his attic when he had all those tunnels? Disgusted with myself because, though he'd just saved me once again, I didn't entirely trust him, I resolved to try to be fair.

The aroma of frying steak and onions percolating upstairs proving far stronger than mere self-disgust, I headed for the kitchen, pondering how, since I'd been staying at 13 Blackdog Street, I'd always eaten so well and so much and yet my waistline had shrunk. I put it down to all the exercise, though nervous terror might also have played a role.

After the truly delicious, succulent rib-eye steaks with onions and wonderful crispy, fluffy chips, with a mug of tea in my hand and a satisfying fullness in my belly, I sat on the sofa, where Hobbes was deep in thought.

'How's Eric?' I asked.

'Eric? He's still undergoing treatment for shock. They tell me he'll be alright but he's not happy.'

'Well, you wouldn't be happy if an elephant had demolished your café.'

'I don't have a café anymore, but I take your point. Apart from swearing, he was almost speechless, yet I got the impression something was worrying him. Yes, I know an elephant demolishing his means of livelihood would worry him, but I had the notion there was more.'

'What d'you mean?'

'He seemed uneasy, as if he might be scared of something.'

'Or somebody,' I suggested, wondering if the reason for Eric's discomfiture might be sitting beside me.

'Or someone,' he agreed. 'What made you suggest that?'

'Umm … I don't know really,' I said, the familiar heat of a blush rising around my ears. It reminded me of the time Editorsaurus Rex overheard me calling him a fat, dozy prat. The consequences still made me cringe.

Hobbes took my remark at face value. 'Oh, well, I wondered if something had occurred to you, too. You see, I have a hunch the elephant incident was deliberate.'

'But why?' I asked, filled with scepticism. 'I can understand anyone getting upset with Eric, but using an elephant to get back at him is ridiculous. It must just have been a bizarre accident.'

'That's what everyone at the station says,' said Hobbes. 'They reckon it would be too complicated, too expensive and too ludicrous for anyone to go to the trouble of transporting an elephant merely to annoy Eric. Maybe they're right, or maybe that's what someone wants us to think. In any case, Eric is refusing to talk and I haven't been able to persuade him: the nurses were keeping too close an eye on me. I need to think.'

I would have liked to ask more but, turning on the television, he sat back, relaxing, apparently enthralled by the black and white cowboy film. I watched for a while until, a cougar attacking the hero, I got the heebie-jeebies and retreated to the kitchen.

Mrs Goodfellow, sitting at the table, having washed and polished bits of cutlery and wine glasses until they glittered, was replacing them in the picnic basket. 'I'm making sure everything's ready for tomorrow, dear,' she said, her false teeth grinning from the yellow duster by her side. They gleamed as bright as the cutlery.

'Thank you. That's very kind.'

'Not at all, it's nice to find a use for the old basket. It brings back such memories;

my husband bought it for me when we were in America.'

'Oh, yeah,' I said, 'I found some photos of you in America in the attic.'

'Happy days!' she said. 'At least they were happy for Mr Goodfellow and me, but the old fellow found it tough going.'

'It couldn't have been too bad; it looked as if he'd got himself a girlfriend.'

Mrs G frowned. 'She got him more like, and took advantage of him.'

'Really?' I asked, sniggering at the revelation. 'Shouldn't she have made an honest man out of him?'

'He always was honest. I mean she took advantage of his generous nature.'

'How?'

'She lied to him, making up stories of her hard, tragic life until he felt obliged to take care of her, sorting out her debts, giving her money he couldn't afford to lose. She was a nasty piece of work.'

'Was she called Froggy because of her eyes?'

'No.'

'She wasn't French was she?'

'No, dear, it was because she caught flies with her tongue, a very nasty habit, if quite useful in a field full of hippies.'

'You're having me on. Aren't you?'

She grinned. 'Actually, we called her Froggy because of her voice.'

'Wasn't that a bit mean?'

'I suppose so, but it was what her friends called her. Others called her "the Leech", which was as fitting a name as you could hope for.'

'What was her real name?'

'She said it was Enola-Gaye Johnson, but I think she was lying.'

'What happened to her?'

'I don't know. When the old fellow's money ran out she ran out too and we never saw her again, for which I, for one, was grateful. She'd left him so low on money he had to get a job.'

'What did he do? Detective work?'

'No, he got into the movies.'

'A film star?'

'He was hardly a star, dear. He was an extra.'

'Was he in anything?'

'Just one film, dear. He played a gorilla in *Planet of the Apes*.'

'Quite a stretch for him, then,' I said. I don't think she got the joke.

'Not so much as you might think, because he had acted before, playing the bear in the Sorenchester Players' production of *A Winter's Tale* in '62 and he was in their production of Frankenstein, though I can't remember what he played.'

'He must be a talented actor.' I smiled. 'And it's amazing he never became a star.'

'Maybe he would have been,' she said, 'if it hadn't been for the incident in the woods.'

'What was that?' I asked.

'It was so hot, we'd been skinny-dipping in a beaver lake,' she said, blushing, 'thinking no one else was around. After a while, the old fellow noticed a racoon rummaging around in our things and ran over to make sure it didn't do any damage, not realising he'd been spotted by a cameraman. Next thing we knew, he was headline news. They thought they'd filmed Bigfoot.'

'They thought Hobbes was Bigfoot?' I said, faking amazement, remembering the snippet of film I'd seen on the telly, understanding why the photo of him in the woods had looked so familiar.

'Yes, dear, which was quite ridiculous, because he looks nothing like Bigfoots. Or are they Bigfeet?'

'So you know what Bigfoot looks like?' I asked, chuckling.

'Of course, dear, we stayed with some for a few days. They're very nice, if a bit smelly.'

Once again my view of the world had widened. Of course, it was possible she was having me on but I didn't think so, being quite astute about such things. I'm not sure which concept my brain found it hardest to accept: Hobbes in a Hollywood movie, or the old girl staying with Bigfoot. Thinking about it gave me a headache and I turned in early.

I was enjoying the picnic with Violet, lying next to her in a sun-drenched clearing, when she stood up, saying she was hot and needed to cool off in the lake, the lake that had mysteriously replaced the trees. As I watched her walking, naked, into the water, wondering where my own clothes had gone, I ran forward, my feet becoming entangled in delphiniums, and fell, splashing and thrashing. When I was able to stand upright, I hugged her, amazed how strong and hairy she'd become, appalled to see it wasn't her anymore. Somehow, I'd got hold of Bigfoot and, pushing the beast away, I fled towards the shore, only running into deep water, where green-skinned girls licked up flies and croaked. Hobbes appeared in the trees riding an elephant, while Dregs snarled as he gnawed on a rotting corpse he'd dragged from a hole in the ground.

I woke up, refreshed if confused by the vivid dream, got up and drew back the curtains. Since brittle sunlight filled the room, it looked as though the weather forecasters had got it right; not that I relied on them, for Hobbes's predictions were far more accurate. Looking out on the day, my stomach lurched as hope, excitement and terror collided, remembering that, in only a few hours, Violet was going to take me on a picnic.

Still, a few nerves, the odd butterfly in my stomach, were not enough to put me off breakfast. Going down, I discovered Hobbes had eaten hours ago, and Mrs G was preparing scrambled eggs for me, scrambled eggs as yellow as primroses, as light and fluffy as … in truth, I doubted I'd ever eaten anything so light and delicious, except possibly her cheese soufflé, which, in my opinion, she didn't make often enough. Mind you, I thought that about all of her meals.

The problem was that, as soon as I'd finished, I began to feel twitchy, unable to work out how I'd fill the time until the picnic. Mrs G was already preparing food but refused my offer of help. Normally, I'd have felt relieved to have asked and got away with it, but I needed something to occupy my mind. I was saved by Hobbes appearing in his smart suit.

'Are you going anywhere nice?'

'Henry Bishop's funeral.'

'Can I come?' I asked, thinking it would at least get me out for a couple of hours.

'If you want to,' said Hobbes, sounding surprised, 'but get a move on, I'm going in five minutes. Make yourself respectable and don't wear the blazer you brought down last night.'

'I wasn't intending to,' I said, running upstairs and scrambling into Mr Goodfellow's dark-grey suit, a suit I'd never worn before but which, as I'd expected, fitted uncannily well. I checked its pockets for money, finding, to my regret, that they were empty, apart from a neatly pressed silk handkerchief, which I requisitioned, even though orange is not really my colour.

'You took your time,' said Hobbes, glancing at his watch, 'so we'll have to hurry, I'm glad to say. Excellent.' Clapping his hands, he grinned like a maniac.

'I wasn't that long,' I said, already regretting what I'd let myself in for.

'Long enough. Now let's move … not you, Dregs, you're staying.'

The dog's ears and tail drooped.

'There's no use you looking like that. You can't go until you learn how to behave with decorum.' Turning away, opening the front door, he led me to the car and drove to Henry Bishop's funeral in the manner of a man hurtling to his own. So much for decorum, I thought.

We arrived in time, parked outside and walked respectfully into the chapel. The funeral turned out to be a cremation.

'Mrs Bishop's taking no chances,' Hobbes whispered, as we took our seats at the back.

Despite, or because of my shock at his lack of respect, I sniggered.

'Now then, Andy,' he said with a frown.

It made things worse. I chuckled. Hobbes, shaking his head, trying to look stern, despite his lips twitching into a grin, failed to prevent a guffaw bursting from me and resorted to clamping his great hairy paw over my mouth. Though it dammed the stream of laughter, the build-up continued, with little snorts escaping from my nose, until that too was blocked. Tears welled up, overflowing down my cheeks, while my body shook with helpless laughter, though, with both nose and mouth blocked, I feared I would die laughing. Fortunately, Hobbes, knowing his stuff, managed to regulate the air supply, keeping me alive and (relatively) quiet.

A man in a black suit, one stinking of mothballs, leaned over the pew. 'Is he alright?'

'He's very upset,' said Hobbes.

'Did he know Mr Bishop well?'

'Not especially, he's just very sensitive.'

The organ music starting, I regained some control and he released me, though occasional titters and smirks still found their way out, some turning into strangled chuckles or broad grins. Several disapproving stares were directed my way, even though I was doing my utmost to avoid eye contact, aware the slightest stimulus might set me off again. As sanity returned, I was astonished how many had turned up to see the end of Henry. Some I recognised as local farmers and traders, yet there was also a number of smart, tough-looking young men in sharp business suits, suggesting Henry had enjoyed a wider circle of friends than I would have believed.

Mrs Bishop, her face concealed behind a black veil, the only representative of her sex, appeared grief-stricken, though I'd have thought she'd have been glad to get rid of the old bastard. Despite the manner of his death, I felt scant sympathy for him. The service began, dragging on, while my grins abated and gave way to yawns. The chapel was small and white, with a purple carpet and wooden pews, a coffin, presumably filled with Henry Bishop, at the front, beside a gold-coloured lectern, from where a bored-looking vicar spouted his stuff.

At length, it was Mrs Bishop's turn. Rising slowly, she approached the lectern and addressed us. 'Thank you,' she said, 'to all of you for coming to mourn my poor darling Henry. Of the people you meet, only one or two enter your life, touching you so deeply that forever after they remain a part of you. Some are but brief candles that flicker and blow out in the storms of life but Henry was like a bonfire, a beacon of warmth and light in my life. I hoped he would burn forever. He was my husband for nigh on thirty years and I don't regret a single day of it.'

My mouth dropped open in disbelief; Hobbes clumped it shut with the back of his hand as Mrs Bishop carried on eulogising her late husband in the same vein for several minutes, almost making me believe we'd gone to the wrong service. She told of meeting Henry in Portsmouth, when he was an able seaman, she a barmaid, saying it had been love at first sight. By the time she finished, I was blinking back tears. Human relationships were obviously far deeper and more complex than I'd have believed. Even so, I was glad when the coffin slid behind the curtains and we'd seen the last of Henry, and even more glad when the service ended.

Hobbes and I made our escape as the congregation began to disperse.

'Alas, poor Henry,' said Hobbes, grinning.

'I'm sorry about sniggering,' I said. 'I think it was nerves.'

'It did suggest a lack of respect for the dear departed, but I wouldn't worry about it; I think we covered it up.'

'What did you make of Mrs Bishop's spiel?' I asked.

'It was interesting and puzzling, yet I'm sure she'll get over him and see him in his true colours. I'd like to hope she'll soon be a merry widow.'

I nodded, wondering whether there'd been a hint of disappointment in his voice. My suspicion that he'd murdered Henry hadn't quite gone away. A puff of smoke billowed from the crematorium's chimney, and a faint whiff like cooking bacon made my mouth water, until a sudden suspicion the two were connected, nearly made me sick. My suit felt suddenly too heavy and restrictive, sweat trickled down my back.

'I wonder,' I said, trying to break my chain of thought, 'what's happened to the panthers. Have there been any more sightings?'

'Not that I'm aware of,' said Hobbes, strolling towards the car. 'Yet, perhaps it's not surprising. They're very good at hiding and it's been raining heavily.'

'Don't they like the rain?'

'I've no idea but people are less inclined to go out in it and so there are fewer eyes to see them.' He paused, staring at something. 'Of course, it's possible they have gone away.'

'I see,' I said.

He shook his head. 'No, you don't, you're not looking in the right place.'

'What do you mean?' I asked turning to where he was looking.

'Mice,' he said, pointing to a rubbish bin where three or four brown mice were scurrying and squeaking over a discarded packet of sandwiches.

'Fascinating,' I said. 'I've never been keen on rodents since a hamster savaged my ear.'

He raised his eyebrows. 'But don't you see what it means?'

'No.'

'While the cat's away, the mice will play.'

'That's just a saying.'

'There's often truth in old sayings.'

'Yeah, I know. But … really?'

He fixed me with an expression of such total innocence I knew he'd been playing with me. Probably.

The congregation was leaving the chapel, heading for the cars. Hobbes, raising his hand to shut me up, watched with hunter's eyes. I watched too, with no real interest, although one of the mourners, one of the tough-looking young men I'd noticed earlier, seemed familiar.

'The man in the dark suit,' I said, 'I've seen him before.'

'Nearly everyone's wearing dark suits, except Mrs Bishop,' said Hobbes, 'and you saw them all in the chapel.'

'That guy getting into the grey BMW – I saw him yesterday at the Greasy Pole and I was sure I'd seen him before.'

'There were many people at the Greasy Pole yesterday, and Sorenchester is such a small town it's not surprising you see the same ones now and again.'

'I know, but I'm sure he'd gone before you sorted it all out.'

'So did others. Some people are busy, you know?'

I didn't think the remark was directed at me, since he'd never hinted that he might consider me a freeloader, but it hit hard. I was probably feeling a little vulnerable, for it had crossed my mind that Violet might think me a loser. After all, she was holding down a responsible job, at least so I assumed, not actually knowing what she did, she was wealthy, she was gorgeous, she was sophisticated, she was intelligent. Surely I thought, she would tire of me, sooner or later and, though I hoped it would be later, I had an idea getting dumped would hurt more as time passed. Perhaps I'd have to enter a monastery to get over her: or an asylum, if such things still existed.

'Where do you go?' asked Hobbes, dragging me back to the present.

'What?'

'Where do you go when that vacant expression appears on your face?'

'Nowhere, really … I was just thinking.'

'About your young lady, I'll be bound.'

I nodded. Sometimes he could be quite astute.

'Right then, now you're back, I'm going to offer Mrs Bishop a lift.'

Henry Bishop's friends, who obviously held the poor woman in as much regard as Henry, had commandeered all the transport, leaving her stranded. I wondered how she'd react to Hobbes's offer but she smiled, getting into the car as he opened the door for her. 'You're very kind, Inspector,' she said. 'Of course, I didn't expect to be offered a lift by those bastards he called mates, but I'd got my bus fare ready.' She sighed. 'Thank God that's all over. Did you enjoy my performance?' She pushed the black veil from her face.

'It was very moving,' I said, getting into the back seat.

She turned to look at me as Hobbes introduced us. Her eye, though still bruised, was concealed beneath make-up and I was surprised to see no trace of tears.

'Moving?' she said and laughed. 'God knows, I should have been an actress. I might have been, too, if Henry hadn't banged me up. You should have seen him in his uniform, back in the day.'

'Was he good looking, then?' It seemed unlikely.

'Hard to believe, eh, seeing what he turned into, but that's what the drink did to him and he wasn't always so bad. He did do the right thing after getting me in the club. At least, we thought it was right at the time but it's a pity you can't see how things will turn out. We had our fair share of problems, not least poor little Mikey getting run over, and then the foot-and-mouth disease doing for his dad's farm that he was going to inherit. Still, he didn't have to deal with them by boozing and taking it out on me, did he?'

I shook my head, making sympathetic noises. Hobbes, I noticed, was driving with care and consideration, though his teeth glinted in a broad grin.

'How are you coping, since he passed away?' he asked.

'I'm coping just fine without the old devil,' said Mrs Bishop, with a broad smile, 'and I'm glad he's dead and burned. I hope he continues to burn! God knows he deserves to.'

'Will you be alright … for money and stuff?' asked Hobbes.

'I'll be fine. I've got my little nest egg, something I've built up over the years for when I left him. That should see me alright.'

'And you'll inherit his assets, won't you?' I said.

She shrugged. 'I suppose so. I'm seeing the solicitor next week to sort things out, though I doubt the old bugger made a will. He was too selfish to consider what might happen to me if he died. Still, I will probably be alright. He can't have drunk it all away and he's been getting paid pretty well, since he started working for King Enterprises.'

'King Enterprises?' I asked, anything to do with Violet interesting me.

'That's right, lad.'

'Do you know Felix King, then?'

'He's the boss right?'

I nodded.

'Of course not. Henry wasn't likely to be mixing in those circles. He worked for one of King's underlings, a rather unpleasant young man.'

'What did Henry do for them?' asked Hobbes.

'I'm not entirely sure. I think he may have collected rents and debts. Whatever it was, he seemed to enjoy it and got paid well enough – not that I ever saw a penny of it. He reckoned he'd soon be getting very much richer and that we'd be able to move into town.'

Hobbes, having steered into Mrs Bishop's yard, stopped the car and leapt out. He opened the door and offered his hand to help her out.

'You are very kind, Inspector,' she said. 'It's a fine day and it's a wonderful feeling to be coming home and know he won't be around.' She chuckled. 'Still, whatever you said to the old devil worked. He didn't lay a finger on me, though it didn't stop his foul mouth. For that I've got to thank a panther, apparently. Thank you for the lift.'

Hobbes walked her to the front door. 'Are you sure you'll be alright, Mrs Bishop?'

'I'll be better than alright. My sister's coming round this afternoon. I haven't hardly seen her since Henry turned bad. Thank you once again. Goodbye.'

She entered the house, smiling as she closed the door. Hobbes was right about her becoming a merry widow, though the transformation seemed a little rushed to me, possibly a little lacking in decorum. I couldn't blame her.

'Right,' said Hobbes, 'let's get back for dinner. Hanging round crematoriums always gives me an appetite.'

The mere prospect of spending more time alone with Violet unbalanced my mind so much that the next few hours were a little hazy; I couldn't even remember what the old girl prepared for lunch, though I'm sure I ate it alone, Hobbes having taken Dregs with him to work. Unable to settle, I kept looking at the clock, standing up, sitting down, walking round the house and garden, watching Mrs G at work and, generally, fidgeting. In the end, having had enough, she bundled me out the front door, saying she wouldn't let me back in until half-past three.

'Umm … but that'll only give me half an hour to have a bath and get ready.'

'That's more than enough,' she said, shutting me out and, although I had my key in my trouser pocket, I didn't try going back inside. She'd looked as if she meant what she said and it would have been quite wrong to try forcing my way back in; besides, I wouldn't have stood a chance.

Instead, having wandered aimlessly around the middle of town in a myopic daze, I came to rest on a bench in the shade of the church, surrounded by a coachload of tourists listening to some history stuff. A problem with my bench was that, even after the tourists moved inside the church, the parapet blocked my view of the clock tower, meaning I had to keep getting up to cross the road, from where I could see the clock's hands' lethargic progress. After repeating the procedure several times, becoming convinced the clock had slowed down, I hurried down The Shambles to a jeweller's shop, where ranks of clocks and watches in the window confirmed the church's infallibility.

Seeing all the shiny stuff laid out before me made me wish I could afford a new watch to replace the one I'd blown up in a microwave accident, though I was usually quite happy to be free of time's tyranny.

So much rushing around in the sun had got the sweat flowing, so, dabbing my face with the orange silk handkerchief, I retreated to the bench and fidgeted for several minutes, trying to keep cool. I was joined by the lanky figure of PC Poll, who, having marched up The Shambles, sat down beside me. Making a pretence that I hadn't seen him, for, despite Hobbes's influence, a uniformed police officer, even one I knew quite well, still made me feel guilty, I sat unusually still.

'So it was you, Mr Caplet,' he said. 'I might have known.'

'Hi … umm … Derek. What's up?' I said, turning to face him.

He smiled. 'You are. We had a report of a suspicious-looking character casing the jewellers. What have you been doing?'

'Nothing … I only looked in to check the time.'

'Wouldn't it have been easier to look up at the one on the church?'

'Well … umm … yes. Actually, I thought it might have stopped.'

'But,' said Poll, giving me a sceptical glance, 'the proprietor reported that you've been staring in his shop every couple of minutes, worrying his staff. He said you looked nervous and shifty, and he's correct. Are you sure everything's alright?'

'There's a perfectly simple explanation,' I said, feeling the blush coming.

'Go on.'

'It's sort of because I've … umm … got a date. I'm meeting a lady at four o'clock but Mrs Goodfellow won't let me back in the house till half-past three and I can't risk being late.'

'You've got a date?' said Poll.

Never before had I heard such doubt in his voice and, having always regarded him as far too nice and trusting to be a policeman, I wondered whether I should revise my opinion.

'Yes,' I said.

'Who's the unfortunate lady?'

There was, I suspected, a hint of a smirk on his face and I didn't like it. 'That's none of your business. And she's not unfortunate.'

'Oh, go on. I was only joking.' He smiled.

'Yeah, sorry,' I said, certain my cheeks must be glowing like a sunset. 'She's just someone I bumped into at the Wildlife Park. Her name's Violet and she's very nice.'

'OK, Andy,' he said, standing up, 'I believe you, thousands wouldn't. Please, just calm down and don't go frightening any more shopkeepers. See you.'

He wandered off along Vermin Street, stopping to chat with half a dozen locals on his way. Despite his long legs, he rarely got anywhere fast.

As he left, I decided a brisk walk around town might work off some of my nervous energy. It worked quite well and I was admiring the way some builders were transforming a near-derelict house into smart flats, when their radio informed me the three-thirty news was starting. I raced home, in a panic, sweating like a racehorse by the time I got in. Opening the front door, charging in, I galloped upstairs, threw off my damp clothes and oozed into the bathroom.

Though not a fan of cold showers, a lack of time and my red-hot body tempted me to make an exception. I hadn't forgotten Hobbes's plumbing but hoped, being prepared, to stand up to it. It was a mistake. Standing beneath the plate-sized rosette, I turned the tap on, producing a pathetic, tepid dribble. Turning it full on, disappointingly, seemed to make little difference, so, deciding I'd better make the most of it, I reached for the soap and lathered up.

The shower burped and an icy torrent struck me in the back with the power of a mountain waterfall, knocking me to my knees, then flattening me against the bottom of the bath. I gasped and squealed, trying to escape, when it stopped as suddenly as it had started. I raised my head, catching my breath and, with no warning, it started again, pressing me against the hard, white enamel. Helpless, I groped for the side, as the gentle trickle returned. I was already dazed, battered and disoriented before the following deluge demolished me again, staying full on this time, sometimes scalding hot, sometimes icy cold. In trying to drag myself clear, I pulled down the shower curtain, the pole striking my head a stunning blow, while the plastic sheet, clinging around me, turned my struggles to futility. Like a drowning man going down for the third time, panic set in, for I couldn't help believing it was curtains for me. When I opened my mouth to cry for help, nothing came out, because of the flood going in.

To my amazement, the inundation ended, the battering ceased, and I was saved. Raising myself on my arms, I rolled from the bath onto the lino, sucking dry air into my lungs, choking a while.

'Don't you go dripping all over the place,' said Mrs Goodfellow, holding out a fluffy white towel.

I pulled myself to my feet, wrapping the towel around my waist, and hugged her, any embarrassment having been swept away in a surge of relief and gratitude.

In all honesty, I was sure her arrival had saved me from a terribly silly end, the sort of bizarre death that makes newspaper readers snort with derisive laughter. At least, that's how they affected my father and one particular story came to mind, one he'd read to us at breakfast. It was about a burglar, who, having used a screwdriver to force open a skylight, had clamped the tool between his teeth while trying to climb down into the shop. When he slipped, he'd fallen on his face, forcing the screwdriver down his throat, choking him. I remembered the incident well for, not only had it been one of the rare occasions when my father had laughed out loud, but also because he'd pebble-dashed me with the cornflakes he'd been masticating.

'Are you alright, dear?' asked Mrs Goodfellow.

'I am now,' I said, hugging her again, grabbing at the slipping towel.

'Good,' she said, as she turned to leave the bathroom. 'I came to let you know it's ten-to-four, so you'd better get a move on. Your picnic's all packed and waiting by the door.'

I did get a move on, drying myself, dressing and grooming in record time, the shower having refreshed me no end, leaving me feeling tingling, alert and lucky to be alive. Examining myself in the mirror, trying my straw boater at various rakish angles, I indulged myself in a complacent smile. With the blue of my eyes matching the stripes on the blazer, my brown, wispy hair looking neat, I didn't think I looked half bad. Confidence rising, I went downstairs.

'Very smart, dear,' said Mrs Goodfellow. 'What lady could resist?'

When the doorbell rang, the lurch in my stomach came not from panic but from exhilaration and anticipation and I nearly skipped to the front door. I opened it. There stood Violet, smiling and divine.

'Hi,' she said and, just for an instant, her eyes widened, as if shocked at what she could see. Her smile stayed in place, but that one look convinced me my Technicolor blazer and straw hat were ridiculous. I wasn't surprised, for, after all, I was the same old, hopeless Andy, not the debonair gentleman I'd hoped to be.

'Hello,' I said.

Though she was wearing a simple red t-shirt and a faded denim skirt that must have seen a few years, even in such simple garments she retained, to my eyes, an air of elegance and sophistication. Yet something about her was different. Her expression showing a hint of stress, or possibly distress, I feared my appearance lay at the root of it.

The conversation exhausted, we looked at each other and squirmed. At least I squirmed, trying to work out if I had time to change into something more appropriate.

'Hello, dear,' said Mrs Goodfellow peering out at Violet from under my arm. 'How are you?'

'Very well, thanks.'

'Good. I've packed a picnic for you. Now, off you go and have a lovely time. Andy, why don't you pick up the hamper?'

'Umm ... right.' I squatted down to pick it up, alarmed, if not surprised, by its weight, as the old girl nudged me outside.

'Goodbye,' she said, 'have fun.'

I nodded, my confidence already shattered, and followed Violet down the steps.

'Where's your car?' I asked, looking around, hoping I wouldn't have to carry the hamper too far.

'It's just round the bend, behind that white van.'

Something in her voice suggested a problem. Stopping abruptly, she turned to face me.

'Look,' she said, 'there's no easy way to say this but my brother wants to come along and I hope it's alright with you. You see, Felix has a terribly stressful job and needs to unwind sometimes. He only said he wanted to come a few minutes ago and I couldn't really say no and there was no time to ask you. Anyway, it'll be a good chance for you to meet him. I hope you don't mind?'

'Oh, I'm sure it will be just fine,' I said, forcing a smile, my spirits sinking into my tennis pumps.

She smiled back, a little crookedly. 'Thanks. Do you think we'll need to get more food?'

I could answer that question with confidence. 'No, the old girl's used to catering for Hobbes so there'll be plenty and, as for cutlery and stuff, there's four of everything. We'll have loads, and there'll still be lots left over for feeding the ducks.'

'Will there be ducks? I like them but I thought there'd just be trees.'

'Umm ... I don't know, actually. I've never been there before, but there always seemed to be ducks when I went on picnics as a boy.' I remembered a flock of the flat-footed, quacking villains creating mayhem, decimating our sandwiches; that had been another unsuccessful Caplet family picnic.

We drew up to her car.

'Andy,' she said, 'this is my brother, Felix.'

I noticed with a mixture of anger and jealousy that he'd taken possession of the front passenger seat, that his clothes, khaki shorts and faded black polo shirt, were as casual as his sister's, yet he, too, looked smart and well-groomed, even if he had rather overdone the aftershave. He nodded at me, grinning, making me feel overdressed and awkward.

'Felix,' she said, 'this is Andy.'

'Hi,' I said, attempting to smile back, feeling like a phoney, a dissembler. 'But this isn't the first time we've met. Your brother helped me out when there was a misunderstanding in the bookshop.'

'Did I?' asked Felix, shrugging. 'I don't remember – but I'm glad I was of service, though I'm sure you were capable of sorting things out for yourself.'

'I expect so,' I lied. Things had a habit of blowing up in my face.

'Right,' he said, indicating the back seat, 'shove that hamper in the back and hop in.' Despite the car being a two-door model, he never offered to move.

My attempted casual vault into the back turning into a trip, I sprawled across the hamper, while trying to act cool. It wasn't easy.

'Let's go,' said Felix.

As Violet started the car, moving off, I struggled into a seat, retrieving my boater from the footwell, trying to look like a man enjoying myself. Violet, concentrating on her driving, didn't speak, Felix poked buttons on his mobile, while I fidgeted in the back, uncomfortable, the hamper pressing into my side. The journey was uneventful, except for my boater blowing off as we rounded a bend. Though I grabbed it, pleased with my reflexes, part of me wished I'd lost the ridiculous thing.

The silence being disconcerting, I was relieved when we reached the arboretum. Yet, I wasn't happy, for though I had reason to be grateful to Felix, I didn't want him there, even when he paid our admission money.

The car coming to a stop, he sprang out.

'Grab that basket, Andy.'

He didn't ask: it was an order.

'We'll find somewhere good to eat. I reckon over there's promising.' He gestured across the valley towards the trees on the far side.

It looked a pretty stiff walk for a man with a hamper.

'Or over there might be better,' I said, pointing in the opposite direction, towards a small meadow between stands of ornamental trees, no more than fifty metres away, 'It's got tables and benches. It looks ideal.'

'Oh, no,' said Felix. 'We don't want to be next to the car park and a brisk walk will do us all a power of good. Besides, while we're getting there I can update Violet on the project.'

He turned, putting his arm around his sister's shoulders. She gave a small, apologetic smile as he led her away down the hill. I struggled after them as best I could, sagging beneath the weight of the hamper, sweat prickling my skin, my shirt sticking to my back. I couldn't make out much of what Felix was saying, though it seemed to be mostly business talk about markets, investments and returns: pretty dull stuff, and not what I would have chosen to talk about on such an evening.

Nature, at least, was on my side. Butterflies dipped and swooped between banks of wild flowers, bumblebees busied themselves in patches of red clover and the air smelled fresh and earthy combined with the scent of warm grass and blossoms. I'm sure I would have appreciated it, had it not been for Felix hogging Violet, leaving me to struggle behind like a pack mule, the hamper seemingly gaining weight with every step. As we reached the bottom of the valley, starting upwards, the path became rough and uneven, the grass slippery, between spiky gorse bushes with yellow blooms. By the time we reached the woods, where roots were conspiring to trip me, my head was pounding with the heat, my breath coming in short gasps. A malevolent twig struck my head, knocking my hat to a ludicrous angle over my eyes, leaving me unable to see the snare of brambles about to hook my leg. I fell to my knees, letting loose an involuntary oath, yet holding fast to the basket.

'Here, let me give you a hand,' said Felix, taking the hamper from my outstretched arms. Violet, smiling, hesitated, as if about to help me up, but followed her brother as he strode away.

'He really is a stubborn fool,' said Felix, 'but he's willing to make a deal now he's seen what can happen, and if we can persuade that buffoon Binks about the need for progress, then we'll be getting somewhere. I'll get Mike to have a few words with him and see if he can't change his mind.'

Standing up, I brushed myself down, appalled how grievously the knees of my trousers had suffered, the crisp white cotton having been stained green from the lush grass, brown from the damp earth, the sharp creases having turned to saggy bags, tiny, bloody dots pointing to where thorns had penetrated. Muttering rude, biting words under my breath, arms and shoulders aching, I followed Violet.

'This will do perfectly,' said Felix, having carried the burden all of twenty steps into a glade.

To be fair, which I wasn't inclined to be, it was a great spot, the deep green carpet of turf beneath our feet as soft as fleece, a multitude of daisies everywhere, bright as stars in the night sky, the fragrance of wild flowers intoxicating.

'What did you do with the rugs?' asked Felix, setting the hamper down in a patch of buttercups.

'Rugs?'

'The ones you were sitting on when we drove here. You haven't left them in the car have you?'

'Me?'

'Yes, you.' He shook his head. 'You didn't expect me to carry them as well as the picnic did you? You'd better go and get them – it'll give me a chance to finish my conversation with Violet. We'll see you back here in a few minutes. OK?'

'But the grass is really soft,' I said. 'We won't need rugs. What do you think?' I turned to Violet who opened her mouth as if she might agree. She didn't get the chance.

Felix nodded. 'It's soft enough, I'll grant you, but it's still damp after all the rain. You wouldn't want my sister to catch her death would you?'

'No … but.'

'Of course not. Now, run along and get those rugs. The sooner you start, the sooner you'll return, right? If you wouldn't mind getting a move on, I'm quite hungry. By the way, when you're down there, you'll find a camping chair in the boot. You might as well bring that too, there's a good chap.'

Though dazed, confused and furious, for some reason I turned back towards the car.

'Oh, Andy!' He called me back after a few seconds. 'You'll need these.'

Violet handed him the car keys, which he threw towards me, or, rather, at me. Though it was some consolation to catch them cleanly, my mood was black as I stamped back towards the car.

The twig I'd run into earlier, still being up to no good, speared my boater, pulling it from my head. Putting it back on, though it now incorporated a dent and a finger-sized hole, I continued my long trek, muttering savage imprecations against picnics in general and picnics with Felix in particular, wishing I'd stayed at home, thinking about trying to hitch a lift back. Only the fear that no one would stop for a sweaty prat dressed like a dishevelled music-hall comedian and the realisation that I'd be leaving Mrs G's picnic basket behind stopped my escape. So far, Violet had barely spoken to me, while Felix was treating me like a lackey. Despite having known all along that it would go wrong with Violet, the end seemed to be approaching even faster than I'd anticipated, and prior knowledge didn't make the prospect any easier.

Nevertheless, I picked up the rugs and Felix's chair and lugged them all the weary way back. I guessed each trip must have taken me about twenty minutes, so I'd been in the arboretum for an hour and all I'd got was hot, dirty, sweaty, thirsty, angry, miserable and tired. Felix and Violet watched me all the way back. Reaching them at last, I dumped the gear on the grass.

'Good man,' said Felix, 'and now you must have a drink after all your exertions.'

I nodded, speechless, dripping.

'Come on, Violet,' he said, 'get the man a drink. He deserves one.'

She opened a bottle of ginger beer, filled a glass and handed it to me.

'Thank you,' I said, taking a swig, delighted it had stayed cool in its stone bottle, enjoying its spicy, sweet flavour.

She smiled. I smiled and took another pull at my glass. A drop going the wrong way, I started choking and gasping for air.

'Are you alright?' she asked, her hand on my shoulder.

'Does he sound alright?' said Felix. 'Take his glass. I'll sort him out.'

As soon as she took it, a blow between my shoulder blades felled me as if I'd been pole-axed. Sprawling in the grass, I groaned, forcing myself to stop choking for I couldn't have endured a repeat performance.

'Is that better?' asked Felix.

I nodded and he reached down, pulling me to my feet. He was much stronger than he looked.

'Good. Now spread those rugs and let's eat.'

Violet did as commanded and, as I helped her lay the food out, he erected his chair, sitting back into it with a sigh. Her hand brushing mine gently, deliberately, I hoped I'd been premature in pronouncing the death of the affair, if that's what it was.

'Excellent job, you two. Thanks,' said Felix, smiling as the last of the meal was set before him.

Somehow, those few simple words nearly made everything alright. I grinned up at him, repenting my evil thoughts, for though his earlier bulldozing had reminded me of Rex Witcherley, Felix could display a charm the Editorsaurus never would.

Nevertheless, I still felt like a dog at his master's feet, hoping for scraps. Not that there was any danger of being left with scraps, for the old girl, as usual, had excelled herself and I was delighted to see that, as well as ginger beer, she'd packed a couple of bottles of wine.

Violet picked them up. 'Red or white?'

'Red,' said Felix and I in unison.

'Just as well,' she said, 'they're both red.' She uncorked a bottle, pouring a glass for each of us, and handed them round.

Felix sniffed and took a sip, his eyebrows rising in appreciation. 'This is good,' he said, 'where did you get it from?'

'Umm …' I said, scratching my head, 'I think they're probably from Hobbes's cellar. He keeps a few down there and enjoys a drop now and again, when he's not working, of course.'

'Well,' said Felix, staring into the glass, 'this is truly excellent. Is it all as good as this?'

'Well … umm … it all tastes good to me. I don't know much about it, though I think this is the normal stuff. He's got a lot more that he keeps for special occasions.'

'The Inspector knows his wine, then. I'm surprised after what I've heard about him. Does he keep a large cellar?'

'Umm … pretty large, probably. Several hundred bottles I'd say.'

'Then he's a lucky man,' said Felix taking another sip. 'I don't suppose you know his supplier?'

'I don't. I've never actually seen him buy any; it's always just been there.'

'Well, it must have come from somewhere.' Felix leant forward, picking up the bottle. 'I don't recognise the label. What d'you make of it?' He glanced at Violet.

She sniffed the glass, rolling a drop round on her tongue, inhaling. 'It's like drinking bottled sunshine. This is beautifully balanced, elegant, sensuous, spicy wine. I've rarely tasted anything to equal it.'

'Me neither,' said Felix. 'And you say he's got hundreds of bottles of this? And keeps better ones? That's amazing.'

'Is it?' I asked, surprised. 'I mean I … umm … like the stuff, but I didn't think it was anything special.'

'It is very special,' said Felix, holding his glass up to the sky. 'I'd like to get hold of a few crates of it myself. Would you mind asking him from where he gets it?'

'No, of course not.'

'Good, man,' said Felix pausing. 'Still, I can't help wondering how an inspector can afford such quality. Police pay must be better than I thought.'

'Do you reckon it's worth a bit?'

'It should be. The only wine I recall coming close to this in the last few years was a vintage Burgundy from Domaine Chambourge. I think that one retailed at around five hundred pounds a bottle, if you could get it.'

I was stunned to learn anyone would spend so much on a bottle of wine. The most I'd ever paid had been ten pounds for a bottle of some white plonk I'd bought from a bloke in the Feathers, intending to impress a girl at a party. It hadn't worked and I could still remember the way she'd pursed her lips on realising I hadn't chilled it, the way she'd rolled her eyes when I drove a corkscrew through the screw-top, the way she'd clicked her tongue when I spilled a drop down her front, the way she'd walked out without a word after the first sip. I'd thought her overly judgemental until, taking a gulp to console myself, I felt as if the wine was stripping the enamel from my teeth, forcing me to drink about a gallon of water to douse the burning in my mouth and throat. Since then, I'd been happy to knock back any wine that left my teeth intact. Even so, I had enough palate remaining to have realised that Hobbes's stock was rather nice, without enough to realise it was exceptional. For a moment I wondered if they were having me on, yet their expressions as they sipped the stuff reminded me of one of the windows in the church, one depicting Saint somebody-or-other ascending to heaven, convinced me they meant it.

To me, the food, though no better than I'd expected, was even more impressive than the wine. As for Felix and Violet, after their first bite of one of Mrs G's cheese sandwiches, they ate in awed silence. Yet the sandwiches were the least of the delights, for she'd packed bite-sized meat pies that self-destructed in the mouth, leaving just a wonderful savoury taste, a crispy salad with a dressing that made me want to cry for joy, succulent cold meats and so many wonderful things that six of us could have dined with no hardship. As it was, I think we all rather stuffed ourselves, leaving little.

Felix sighed as he finished the last slice of fruit cake, refilled his glass and raised it. 'To Andy, who knows how to picnic. I haven't eaten so well in years.'

'It was no bother,' I said, truthfully, 'except that it was heavy to carry.'

'No problem,' he said, 'I'll carry it back. In the meantime, would you care for a top up?'

After he'd filled my glass, I stretched out on the rug.

'That was lovely,' said Violet, placing her hand on mine, giving it a squeeze, 'thank you.'

Feeling very full, very satisfied and very relaxed, as the shadows lengthened, I sprawled at Violet's side as we chatted about art and literature and business. In truth, Felix and Violet did the chatting, while I, trying to look intelligent, grunted occasionally to express agreement. Yet, when Violet leaned back with her head against my thigh, I felt as happy as I'd ever been.

'Isn't it a glorious evening,' I said.

'It is,' said Felix, 'and, of course, it's the solstice.'

'Oh yes,' said Violet, raising her head, 'I nearly forgot.'

'What is it?' I asked.

'The summer solstice,' said Felix, with a snort of derision, 'the longest day, the shortest night.'

'Oh, yes … of course … when the nutters prance round the stones on Hedbury Common.'

'So the local rag says,' said Violet, smiling, 'though I wouldn't go so far as calling them nutters; they're probably just having fun. After all, Midsummer's traditionally a time of celebration.'

'That's not how my father saw it,' I said, reflectively. 'He used to reckon it was all downhill towards winter from now on.'

'Sounds like a cheery soul.'

'Not really,' I said, about to relate an amusing anecdote from my childhood.

Felix's mobile phone chirruped, just as the evening sun disappeared behind a cloud.

'Excuse me,' he said, getting up, pulling the phone from his pocket. 'Felix King … Oh, it's you Mike … I said I wasn't to be disturbed … I see … Right, I'd best see to it at once … I'm at the arboretum, just past Hedbury, with Violet and her … friend, so pick me up in the lay-by in front of the kiosk as you come in …' He glanced at his wristwatch. 'I'll see you in about twenty minutes.' He pushed the mobile back into his pocket.

'Must you go?' asked Violet.

'I'm afraid so, something's come up,' he said and grinned. 'It's about time we had some good news on the project.'

Though I tried to look suitably sad at his imminent departure, my heart felt as if it were turning cartwheels of delight. Admittedly, things had improved considerably since we'd started the meal, but the food and drink, superb though they were, were not the real reasons for the picnic. What I wanted was to have her to myself, and it was beginning to look as if I might get my way. The affair was back on and, with the sun escaping the cloud's embrace, warmth flooded my soul.

'Actually, Andy,' said Felix, stretching, slicking back his hair, 'I was hoping to have a word with you this evening and, since I really must get a move on, I'd appreciate you walking back with me. It will give Violet a chance to pack up.'

Annoyed that he expected me to jump at his command, angered at his assumption that Violet would pack up on his say so, I should have just refused. Perhaps I would have, had I not been so polite, had Felix not been the sort of man who expected obedience and always seemed to get it. Without knowing quite why, I found myself walking with him.

'That was a splendid picnic and an excellent wine,' he said, 'and I'd really appreciate it if you could source it for me.'

'Sauce it?'

'Find out from where the Inspector obtains his supplies. Or you could ask him if he'd mind selling me a few crates. Money won't be a problem once this project comes to completion, and it's starting to move, so I won't quibble about the cost. Would you do that for me, Andy?'

'Umm … yes. I expect so,' I said, thinking his request not sufficiently important to drag me away from Violet, although the distant rumble of thunder suggested the picnic would have been curtailed soon anyway.

'Good man,' said Felix, pleasantly. 'And now there's something else I'd like to say, so you'd do well to listen.'

His voice had changed. All hint of friendliness had vanished, along with the commanding, yet reasonable, tones of a leader of men. In an instant it had grown cold, the tone reminding me a little of Hobbes when having a chat with a miscreant.

'I make a point,' he said, 'of taking a long, hard look at Violet's male friends. As her older brother, I've always looked out for her, always wanted what's best for her.'

'Good,' I said, wondering where he was going, fearing I could guess, 'I'm … umm … pleased to hear that.'

'She's very attractive, don't you agree?'

I nodded.

'But there are some, hangers-on, toadies, rogues and parasites, who find her wealth more attractive. Do you know what I mean?'

'Umm … yes. I suppose so.'

'So, which category do you fit into, Mr Caplet?'

'Me? None of them … I just like her and …'

'You say that, yet know nothing about her, except that she is rich. I, on the other hand, know rather a lot about you: you have no job, no home and no prospects. Am I right?'

'Well …'

'You live on Hobbes's charity and I have learned that Violet has already bought you an expensive meal. Is my information correct so far?'

'Sort of … umm … but …'

'It appears to me that you are a chancer and a parasite. She is smart, successful and cultured; you are a worthless waste of breath. Would you agree that a worthless waste of breath is not a suitable man for Violet?'

'Yes … but I'm not …'

'You seem to have taken her in for the moment but, in all honesty, I can't see what she sees in you. However, I do not intend her to be hurt again.'

'But … I … I'd never do that,' I said, feeling a chill run through me, shivering, despite the evening still being so warm.

'Men such as you have hurt her in the past and it has resulted in breakdowns. I will not go into the details. Suffice to say, I will not allow you to be the cause of such unpleasantness. When my car arrives, you will return to her, help her pack and carry the picnic and rugs back to her car. Afterwards, you will ask her to drive you straight home and you will not see her again. Understood?'

'Yes, I understand what you're saying, but surely it's her choice.'

'No, Mr Caplet. I expect you to do as I say, or you will regret it. Now, do you understand?'

'Yes … But …'

'Enough. I hope you know what's good for you.'

As he said this, we reached the car park and a glossy black Jaguar turned into the arboretum and stopped. As Felix marched towards it, a fit young man, who looked as if he might play rugby or some other manly sport, emerged, opening the back door for him.

'I'm glad we understand each other,' said Felix with a pleasant smile, his menace dissipated, 'because I really wouldn't want anything nasty happening to you. You can't help the way you are.

'Thank you so much for a delightful picnic and don't forget to ask the Inspector about his wine. Here's my card.' He pressed it into my hand, nodded and slid into the back of the car.

'Thanks,' I said, stupidly, standing there bemused as the young man, closing the door, climbed into the driver's seat and drove away.

I had much to think about while trudging back to Violet.

With the sun sinking and reddening, heavy clouds creeping up on the horizon, the heat and humidity seemed to be on the rise, the air feeling as thick as golden syrup. The gentle breeze that had maintained a little freshness in the air was growing fretful and capricious as the evening lengthened. Everyone else was heading for the exit and the birds had stopped singing. Not that I cared.

My legs were heavy, as if encased in concrete, and, although it was my fifth trek of the evening, it wasn't physical tiredness causing my weakness, for Felix's threats had knocked the stuffing out of me. I'd thought we'd been getting on tolerably well or, at least, that any animosity was on my side; he'd been saying nice things about the picnic and the wine, so his attack, shocking in its unexpectedness, had hit me like a punch to the jaw. Yet the threats weren't the worse of it, his brutal dissection of my character having really struck home, since I couldn't really refute his accusations: I really was out of work, reliant on Hobbes for shelter and food; I really was penniless (though not literally so, as I'd picked one up from the gutter); I really was useless. Such a realisation, hurtful though it was, was not nearly as painful as the prospect of ending it with Violet, for despite knowing our relationship was doomed, bound to smash into an uncharted reef sooner or later, it was still agony now the reef was just ahead and I had no means to steer away.

Yet, deep within, I felt a resistance movement stirring, my anger building, for her money meant nothing to me and I'd never have dreamt of hurting her. Who was Felix to tell me what to do or, for that matter, to speak for his sister? It had to be her decision to say when she was fed up with me.

I was in a dilemma, unsure whether to meekly give in or to damn the consequences and stand up to him, wondering if, perhaps, he'd just been testing me, giving me the chance to be a man, to prove myself worthy. Yet, I couldn't make myself believe he hadn't been deadly serious, or rid myself of the fear that he might not stop at cutting words the next time we met, unless I'd done what he'd asked. Even so, I could hardly bring myself to think that he, a respectable businessman, would really do anything to me, at least nothing violent. Yet if I was wrong and he did attack me, I was sure, his brief display of strength coming to mind, that I'd stand little chance of beating him. Even if I did get lucky, perhaps punching him out, I doubted Violet would be happy with me and running away from him would probably impress her even less than fighting.

There was another consideration: Felix might not have to do his own dirty work for Mike, his driver, had looked more than a bit handy.

He'd also looked familiar.

When I reached the clearing, Violet's smile drove away depressing thoughts.

'You took your time, slowcoach,' she teased, stretching out on the rug, back arched, slim arms behind her head. Her t-shirt, having pulled up to reveal an inch of soft, smooth belly, was tight across her breasts. 'I've packed everything away, apart from the drinks. I thought you might want something.'

'Yes … it's a long walk.' My throat was dry.

'You do look hot. Wine or ginger beer?'

'Both, please.'

As she sat up, reaching for the bottles, I sat down beside her, knowing with absolute certainty that I really did not give a damn about her wealth or what her brother thought of me. What I wanted was her, and I didn't mean physically: at least not just physically. Before anything, though, I needed a drink. As she handed me a glass of ginger beer, I gulped it down in one, glugging a glass of wine straight after it.

As I sat there, my thirst quenched, I came to a firm decision that, whatever Felix might do later, I was going to kiss her. I would, definitely, without hesitation, should an opportunity arise, in the fullness of time, kiss her. Finishing off the last bottle of ginger beer, throwing back the last dregs, I gazed into her gorgeous eyes.

Her face was just a few inches from mine and, taking myself by surprise, seizing the opportunity, I leaned forward and held her gently by the shoulders. Reassured by her easy sway towards me, I puckered my lips, looked deep into her dark eyes … and burped.

'Oh, God,' I said, recoiling, ashamed, 'I'm so sorry! I didn't mean it, it was all the fizz.'

Without trying, I'd blown it, done what Felix wanted, leaving me embarrassed, feeling like a total klutz.

However, she seemed to be taking it rather well. Rolling back onto the rug, she lay there rocking, little gasps of amusement soon becoming helpless laughter, continuing for what seemed like ages. When, at last, it looked as if she might be regaining control, she glanced up at me, catching my eye, starting again and setting me off. I collapsed on the rug beside her and, next thing I knew, she was lying half across me, her face buried in my blazer. Eventually, our laughter subsiding, she pinned me to the rug and kissed me full on the lips, making my head swirl as if I was on a fairground ride, the kiss lingering until, far too soon, she pulled away, sitting up abruptly. My lips still tingling, I reached for her hand.

'What was that?' she said, pushing me away.

'Just a kiss,' I said, deflated, disappointed. It had been good for me, the first real one I'd enjoyed in years, since Jenny Riley had pounced on me in the playground during a game of kiss chase; I'd been running away very slowly.

'Not that. Something's out there, didn't you hear it?' Wild-eyed, she stared into the woods.

'What do you mean?'

'An animal I think.'

I sprang to my feet, genuine dread gathering in my stomach. 'What sort of animal?' I asked, a big, dangerous cat springing to mind. 'Where?'

'I don't know.'

Taking my hand, she pulled herself to her feet, her body trembling as she snuggled against me. Suddenly alarmed, I put my arm around her shoulders, which certainly comforted me.

'We should probably go,' I said. 'What do you think?'

She nodded and, releasing her with regret, I threw the last odds and sods into the hamper, piled the rugs on top, and picked it up. Grabbing Felix's folding chair, she held it like a weapon, urging me back to the car, while I concentrated on keeping as close together as possible, feeling sure she was making a real effort not to run. At last, reaching the car park, hurrying towards her car, she rummaged frantically through her little hessian bag, her eyes as big as headlights.

'I can't find the keys,' she said, her voice shrill, on the edge of panic.

'It's alright,' I said, panting and sweating, resting the hamper on the bonnet, catching my breath.

'It isn't!' she said, shaking her head. 'I must have dropped them. I'm not going back to look. I'll call Felix and get help.'

'Don't worry,' I said, trying to be reassuring, 'I've still got them.'

'Thank God.' Her face was as white as a fridge door and her hand was trembling. 'Give them here.'

'They're in my pocket. I'll just put this down and ...'

Thrusting her hand into my trousers, she grabbed the keys, the touch of her warm hand in such an intimate spot like an electric shock through all my nerves, though not at all unpleasant. Even so, it paralysed me for a second or two, by which time she'd opened the car doors, sat down and was scrabbling to get the key in the ignition. Chucking the hamper into the back seat, I threw myself in beside her as, the engine bursting into life, we drove away in a plume of dust.

'Let's get out of here,' she said, through clenched teeth.

'Yeah, let's. But ... umm ... what was it? A panther?'

'No.' Shaking her head, turning the steering wheel, tyres screeching, she drove into the main road.

'What then?' I asked, the acceleration pinning me back.

'I don't know.'

'Do you think,' I said, noticing the speedo creeping up to ninety, 'we might be going a little fast?'

'We've got to get away.'

'But we're safe now,' I said, trying to calm her, worried that she was driving like Hobbes in a hurry, but without his reflexes.

Shaking her head, she leaned forward, hugging the wheel, as if urging the car ever faster.

I held my breath and the edge of my seat as we screeched round a bend. 'We must be miles away by now. It can't possibly catch us.'

Her manner, even more than her driving, scared me while Felix's remark about breakdowns made me doubt anything had been out there, for her change of mood had been so swift, she could easily have been mentally unstable, no doubt explaining why she'd taken a fancy to me. Perhaps my kiss had driven her over the edge.

'Please, slow down,' I said. 'You're starting to frighten me. This road's not very ...'

'Sorry, Andy. We've got to get away.'

'But I don't understand. What did you see? A fox, maybe?'

'It was no fox,' she shouted, her face flushed and angry.

Hitting a pothole, the car swerved, for a moment looking like it would veer into a tree, before she regained control.

'You must have seen something … umm … what was it?'

'Something in the woods.'

'Can you describe it?' I asked. 'Careful!'

We rounded a bend too close to the verge, the back tyres bumping.

'I didn't *see* anything,' said Violet, 'but something was there.'

'But what?'

'You wouldn't believe me.'

'I might but, please, slow down, for God's sake, we're coming to a village.'

Taking a deep breath, she nodded, slowing quite a lot as we approached the first house, a stone cottage with scruffy garden and leggy hollyhocks round the front. Bright yellow light was pouring from its open front door and a white pig with stuck up ears hurtled out, demolishing the garden gate, stopping in the middle of the road, sniffing something that had been squashed.

As Violet stamped on the brake, only my seat belt stopped me from kissing the windscreen. The tyres squealed. The pig looked like a goner. As we swerved, missing it by a grunt, we hit the kerb and lurched off the road. For a moment there was darkness, and then greenery, a thump and evening light. The car stopping at last, I turned towards Violet, who was slumped forward, still gripping the wheel.

'Are you alright?'

She didn't move.

Unbuckling my seat belt, I leapt from the car and ran round, pushing through a jungle of bamboo canes and clinging plants until I could pull the door open. 'Are you alright?' I asked again, reaching for her hand.

She turned towards me, blood oozing from her mouth and nose. 'I think so but my lip hurts. You?'

'I'm fine,' I said, leaning over, turning off the ignition, pulling out the key.

'Good,' she said. 'And the pig?'

'We missed it.'

She nodded. 'I'm so sorry, Andy.'

'Don't worry about me,' I said, 'there's no real harm done, that's the main thing.'

'No real harm done?' a man shouted. 'You've ruined my hedge and destroyed my runner beans.'

A hefty, bald-headed, middle-aged man in a checked shirt and olive corduroy trousers was striding towards us from an old stone cottage, his face, red and contorted with rage, complementing his voice. We'd crashed into a country garden, one that might have been idyllic before our arrival, with roses blooming around the cottage windows, a vine clinging to its walls and raised vegetable beds that were lush and green.

'I'm ever so sorry,' I said, holding up my hands in apology, the keys jangling, but a pig ran across the road and …'

'Sod the bloody pig!' the man bellowed, 'you were probably speeding. I know you lot with your flashy clothes and expensive motors, tearing up the countryside, wrecking people's gardens. Just look at my hedge! My great grandfather planted it a hundred years ago and you've just ruined it. I'll have the law on you, just see if I don't. You're going to pay for it and for what you've done to my runner beans. Now get off my bloody spuds!'

'Sorry,' I said, making sure to place my feet where they would cause least harm, making a big play of causing no further damage. Unfortunately, my attempted leap onto the path falling short, I stumbled backwards.

'Get off my bloody carrots!' the man screamed.

His face turning almost purple, his meaty hand seized my collar, dragging me off his precious vegetables onto the garden path. I was convinced he intended pulverizing me until Violet groaned. Turning my head, I watched her slide from the car, collapsing, lying still on the ground. The man, dropping me like a bit of litter, ran towards her. I couldn't help noticing that he went right through his carrots and potatoes.

'Are you hurt, my dear?' he asked, rolling her onto her back with surprising gentleness.

She didn't reply.

'What's wrong with you?' he bellowed. 'Why the hell didn't you tell me there was an injured woman in the car?'

'I was going to …'

'Shut up,' he roared at the top of his voice. 'Maureen!'

A stout, little woman with permed white hair and sallow skin hobbled from the cottage, looking confused. 'Yes, Tom?'

'Call an ambulance. Tell them there's been a road accident and that a woman's unconscious.'

'Yes, Tom,' she said, retreating.

Running towards Violet, I knelt at her side, feeling useless and terrified she was dying, holding her hand, shocked by how clammy and cold it felt.

Then I remembered my ABC.

A was for airways. Wiping blood and soil from her mouth and nose with the edge of my shirt, I made sure everything was clear.

B was for breathing. It was alright, her chest rising and falling, though faster than I'd have liked.

C was for circulation. Placing two fingers against her neck, finding the pulse, I was relieved beyond joy to feel how strong and regular it was.

The only blood was coming from a small split on her lower lip and from her left nostril.

'What's going on?' asked a tall, angular woman standing where the hedge had been.

'This idiot,' said the angry man, 'has crashed his car through my hedge and badly injured the young lady. Maureen's calling an ambulance but I fear it's too late.'

The woman stared at me through dead fish-eyes. 'I bet he's been drinking. They've always been drinking.'

'His breath stinks of it,' said Tom. 'They'll put him away this time, if there's still any justice in this country.'

'And good riddance,' added another spectator, an owl-faced man, peering at me.

Several people were soon at the gap, staring at me with contempt. Ignoring them as best I could, taking off my blazer, I laid it gently under Violet's head, trying to decide whether I needed to put her into the recovery position, longing for the ambulance to turn up. When at last her eyes opened, she stared up at me as if I were a complete stranger and tried to sit.

'No,' I said, placing a hand on her shoulder, 'it's best if you lie still until the ambulance gets here.'

'Where am I?' she asked, clawing my hand away roughly, sitting up anyway.

Though my hand stung, four little bleeding scratches showing where she'd made contact, I forced myself to ignore it. 'You're in this gentleman's garden,' I said.

'Felix?'

'No, it's me, Andy.'

'Are we having a picnic?'

'It's no bloody picnic,' Tom muttered.

'Did we catch many this time?' she asked, staring as if she thought she should know me, but couldn't quite place me.

'How many what?' asked Tom.

Her eyes suddenly coming into focus, she threw her arms around my neck. 'What happened?'

'You … umm … fainted after the accident.'

'Accident? Oh, yes … stupid pig!'

'Don't you go calling me names,' said Tom, standing over us, grumbling. By the smell of him, I wasn't the only one who'd been drinking.

Violet, letting go of me, glanced up. 'Do we know him?'

'No,' I said, 'but unfortunately we crashed into his garden and did a bit of damage.'

'A lot of damage,' said Tom, 'which someone's going to pay for.' He kicked a pebble savagely.

'Are they?' asked Violet, smiling, 'well, that's good news, isn't it? … I think I'm going to lie down again, I'm feeling a little woozy. Why is all that stuff on my car?'

'That's my hedge and beans,' said Tom.

'Just so long as we know.' Lying back, she closed her eyes.

A minute or two later, to the delight of the onlookers, several of whom seemed disappointed Violet wasn't dead, a police car arrived and a police officer strode towards us. To my dis-appointment, it was one from Hedbury, not someone I knew.

'What's going on here, then?' he asked.

'This idiot,' said Tom, jabbing his finger into my chest, 'crashed through my hedge and ruined my garden, not to mention injuring the young lady, who is lucky to be alive. I think I should point out that he's drunk.'

'I'm not dru …,' I began and stopped, realising Violet had taken a drink. So far as I knew, she'd only had one small glass of wine and a little ginger beer, which was only slightly alcoholic. Though she should have been fine, I hadn't been with her all the time and, if she'd had more than I thought, I'd be dropping her right in it.

'I was driving,' she said, making my hesitation redundant.

'Is that correct, sir?' asked the officer looking at me as if at a rat.

I nodded.

'Are you injured, miss?' he asked, squatting beside her.

'I don't think so. I hit my lip and bumped my head but I'm not really hurt … I just feel a bit funny.'

'I think she fainted after the accident,' I said, trying to be helpful. 'She's had a stressful evening.'

'Been out with you had she, sir?' asked the officer, standing up. 'Now, miss, just stay where you are while I ascertain a few facts.' Reaching into his shirt pocket for a notebook, he turned to me. 'Would you mind telling me what happened, sir?'

I did my best, with Tom interrupting and bemoaning his wrecked garden, judging it sensible to avoid mentioning Violet getting spooked in the arboretum, putting all the blame on the pig and whoever had let it out.

When I mentioned the house from which the pig had erupted, Tom nodded. 'That'll be Charlie Brick's place,' he said. 'He keeps pigs round the back.' He pointed. 'That's him by what's left of my poor hedge. Just look at it! Someone's going to pay for it.'

'I'm sure they will, sir,' said the police officer soothingly, beckoning over a little man wearing dirty white overalls.

Charlie Brick, dark, curly whiskers surrounding a pink face that made me think of a very intelligent monkey, loafed towards us.

The officer got straight to the point. 'Did a pig run from your house a few minutes ago?'

'It might have done, sir,' said Charlie in a slow drawl. 'The bugger, if you'll pardon my French, slipped through my fingers in the kitchen.'

'This gentleman alleges that it caused the young lady to swerve and crash.'

'Well, I'm sorry to hear that, but I expects she was driving too fast. Them's always driving too fast through our village.'

'Was she speeding, sir?' asked the officer, looking at me searchingly.

'I don't think so,' I lied. 'I'm not a driver myself, but I could tell she was slowing down before the accident, and I'm sure she wasn't driving any faster than anyone normally drives me.'

'I see.' The officer, making a note, turned towards Charlie. 'What happened to the pig?'

'I don't rightly know, sir,' said Charlie, scratching his head in a simian fashion, 'but I expects he'll be back when I feeds the others.'

'Where are the others?'

'In the sty, sir.'

'So what was that one doing in your kitchen?' asked the officer, looking confused.

'That's where I does my slaughtering – in the kitchen, if you understand me.'

'You were about to slaughter him?'

'Yes, sir, only he took fright when I started sharpening the knife and, well, sir, there ain't too many places to hold onto a pig. But he'll be back, the daft bugger … excuse me, and then I'll have him. There's nowt like home-cured bacon, sir.'

'Thank you,' said the officer. 'I must warn you that you may have committed an offence by allowing the animal to stray onto the public highway. You may not have heard the last of this.'

'Well, sir, I didn't exactly allow him to stray. I begged him to come back, but he wouldn't listen. That's pigs for you all over. Wilful they are, sir, wilful.' Charlie wandered away, shaking his head, scratching his ribs with a long, hairy hand.

The following flurry of activity left me quite bemused. The police officer kept asking questions and speaking into his radio. Violet groaned and was sick. The ambulance arrived at last and the paramedics, after a quick assessment, carried her away. Although I tried to go with her, they shut the doors in my face, leaving me at the roadside, watching her go, until a blaring horn made me jump out of the way. It was a tow truck. Tom's face turned an even deeper shade of purple as the car, attached to cables, was dragged from his garden, trailing a thicket of bamboo canes and bean plants through the hole in the hedge. As soon as the truck drove away, so did the police officer and, the show being over, the spectators went about their business, leaving Tom and I on our own. He wasn't very good company.

'Umm … could I use your phone?' I asked, realising I'd been left without transport, hoping Hobbes wouldn't mind picking me up.

'What?' asked Tom, his face attaining a darker tinge than I'd have believed possible. 'Use my phone? You think I'm going to let you into my house after what you've done to my garden? Not a bloody chance. There's a pay phone by the green. Now, get lost before I lose my bloody temper.'

As he stepped towards me, cracking his knuckles, I grabbed my blazer and fled, running until clear he wasn't following, stopping to take stock of my situation. It wasn't great, for I had an idea Blackdog Street was a weary walk away; a nearby signpost saying 'Sorenchester 14 miles', without any apology, concurred. Completely broke, apart from the penny I'd picked up, the pay phone was useless, even if it happened to be working, and it never occurred to me that I might be able to reverse the charges. Though there would, presumably, have been plenty of telephones in peoples' houses, I doubted anyone seeing my filthy white trousers, my ludicrous blazer, my soiled and bloody shirt and my battered and holed straw hat would let me in. In despair, I tried to calculate how long it would take me to walk home but, having little idea of my walking speed, my best answer was a long time.

My hand was sore, four long scratches beading blood where Violet had slapped it. Sucking it away, I sighed, starting the trek, realising within a few minutes that it had not just been Tom's face that had darkened; everything had darkened and not only from the advancing evening. A rumble of not-too-distant thunder hinting at what was to come, my mood dipped even further.

Even worse than the prospect of getting soaked and exhausted, was not knowing how Violet was, though I could take some comfort from the fact that she was in good hands. Although I was nearly sure she'd only fainted, that her injuries were trivial, my mind kept throwing up all sorts of what ifs that deepened my gloom and despondency. Furthermore, Felix's threats still haunted me, leaving me unsure whether I even dared check up on her. Thinking that, perhaps it was the right time to break things off, I still had to know she was alright.

I hurried on, trying to get as far as possible before the storm hit, though it was clear the mile or two I might put behind me would make little difference; I was in for a soaking.

The storm continuing to rumble with malice, I reached Hedbury, finding it battened down for the night, except for the pubs, which were doing good trade. As I passed the Jolly Highwayman, I looked in through the big bay window, seeing it full of jovial, happy people, wishing I could join them, even entertaining the possibility of begging for a drink, or the use of the phone. Yet pride or, more likely, an unwillingness to be seen in the state I was in, exerted itself and I pressed on.

I was just passing a sign saying 'Sorenchester 11' when the first heavy raindrops struck. Coming individually at first, as if the storm was still making up its mind whether to unload its cargo, they made little difference to me since I was already damp with sweat. Within minutes, however, I was immersed in a downpour. Turning up my collar, huddling into my blazer in a futile attempt at shelter, I trudged on, rain ricocheting off the tarmac up to my thighs, passing cars dousing me in a heavy mist. That was when I was lucky. When I wasn't lucky, sheets of water skimmed across the road from lorry wheels, drenching me. With none of the drivers showing any inclination to stop and pick up a suffering human being, I had to leap onto the verge many times when they didn't appear to even notice me. In fairness, I doubted they expected to see anyone out on such a night.

The roadside was thick with grass, thistle-infested and slick with mud. When I slipped, I slid into the ditch. Though it wasn't deep, it was swampy and even worse was a selvedge of stinging nettles that spitefully attacked my poor hands as I pulled myself out. The rain, though not a constant torrent, came and went with great persistence as the storm rumbled near and far. To start with I made an effort to avoid the puddles, but it wasn't long before, being as wet as a frog, I couldn't have cared less. My clothes clung around my body, making every movement a struggle and, in spite of the effort, my teeth started chattering. As black night engulfed everything, all I could do was to keep walking.

It seemed like hours had passed when, at last, I made out the faint glimmer of electric light from what had to be the town, as an oncoming white van forced me into a puddle, which turned out to be a pothole, turning my ankle. Sitting on the verge, I hugged my leg, trying to comfort it and, despite the pain, the cold and the wet, I laughed; the picnic had lived up to – and exceeded – the disasters expected of Caplet outings. Then I cried.

After several minutes, during which not a single vehicle passed, I wiped my nose on my blazer sleeve, stood up and limped on, nearly crying again when I realised the lights I'd seen were shining across the fields from Randle, a village not even on the same road, and that there were another four miles to go before I reached the outskirts of Sorenchester, and then the best part of another mile after that. The idea of curling up in the ditch and letting life slip away began to have its appeal, yet, before I died, I had to know Violet was safe. I kept going. My tennis pumps, limp and sodden, rubbed my feet, particularly the one attached to my good ankle and, discovering how extraordinarily difficult it was to limp on both sides, my progress was painfully slow. A stick poking from the hedge jabbed into my calf, tearing my trouser leg. Though I swore at it, it made a passable walking stick until, when it snapped, I fell hard, lying for a while in the road, winded, exhausted, sore, aching and shivering. Only a vast expenditure of willpower got me back to my feet. A lightning flash and simultaneous roll of thunder making me jump, I drew a deep breath.

The next flash, seeing, exposed in stark black and white, a figure staring at me from the other side of the road, my blood would have run cold had I not already been so chilled; the muscles in my legs would have turned to water had they not already been so weak and wobbly. I tried hard, really hard, to convince myself my imagination was playing tricks, that, on such a dark and stormy night, a mind could easily wander from reality, especially one weakened by fatigue, shock and pain.

It didn't work for I knew I really had seen a creature from nightmares, a creature with dark hair, glinting white teeth and reflective eyes, though nothing like a panther.

The thing was, it had been standing upright. I wished Hobbes was with me.

I wished I hadn't just seen a werewolf.

When the next flash split the night, it had vanished. I couldn't decide if that was reassuring or not. If it had gone, then all well and good, but how did I know it wasn't stalking me? What if it was already behind me, preparing to spring and tear me apart? Was that a twig cracking? Was that heavy breathing?

Out there in the dripping darkness all my being turned to fear and I learned what a sudden dose of adrenaline can do to a tired body. I ran like an Olympic champion, oblivious to the pain in my ankle, the rawness of my feet, my weary legs, only slowing when the streetlights of Sorenchester surrounded me, cocooning me in the safety of civilisation. When I looked back I was sure something dark slipped into the shadows. Yet, knowing it hadn't got me, the elation of survival spurred me on.

I hobbled through the deserted streets, the storm receding into distant rumblings, the rain turning to a light drizzle. It stopped completely when I reached Blackdog Street.

The house was quiet when I let myself in. I dragged myself upstairs, filled the bath with hot water, stripped off my filthy, sodden clothes and lowered myself in with a groan. Though my chilled skin protested, my feet stinging and throbbing, it was glorious to feel the warmth ooze back into my body. I would have fallen asleep had I not dropped the soap with a splash. I got out, dried myself, wrapped a towel around my middle and stumbled towards my room. Too tired to worry about anything, even Violet, I must have fallen asleep as soon as I'd got into bed.

14

On waking, I wished I hadn't. My head was throbbing with the power of a ten-pint hangover, my armpits had apparently been fitted with painful lumps, as big as golf balls, and my ankle kept going into agonising spasms on every heartbeat. Everywhere hurt and, weak as a newly-hatched chick, I was shivering, presumably because all my bedclothes had fallen off. Blindly groping on the floor failing to find them, I opened my eyes and whimpered, for even my eyeballs ached. The door clicked open.

'Good morning,' said Mrs Goodfellow. 'How are you today?'

Shaking my head in response proving a big mistake, my groan sounded as pathetic as I felt.

'Are you feeling poorly?'

'Yes,' I said through chattering teeth.

'You must be cold, dear, without any bedclothes or pyjamas,' she said, pulling the blankets over me and touching my forehead. 'You feel like you're burning, but I'll fetch you a hot water bottle.'

She left, returning a few minutes later with a grey rubber object that appeared to have been moulded in the shape of a deformed hippopotamus. I hugged it, enjoying the warmth, and snuggled down.

'Were you caught in the storm, dear? I thought you must have been because of the state of your clothes. I'm having 'em laundered and Milord should be able to fix the trousers and the blazer, but your pumps have had it and there's such a big hole in the straw hat I doubt there's any chance of fixing it. Now, can I get you something to eat?'

'No.'

'A nice hot drink, then?'

'Please … and some aspirins.'

'Aspirins? I don't think we've got any, though I do have a tincture that should make you feel as right as reindeer.'

As her footsteps receded, having an urgent need to relieve my bladder, I pulled myself into a sitting position, fearing any delay might prove disastrous and, though I hardly dared get to my feet, I had no choice. Wrapping a soft blanket around me, I hobbled to the bathroom, making it with seconds to spare, finding it a long way back.

The storm having passed, the sun shone painfully brightly through the closed curtains, as I curled up in bed, blankets piled high, the warm rubber hippo on my stomach, still shivering when the old girl returned with a mug of steaming something. Fluffing a couple of pillows, slipping them under my shoulders, she helped me sip the concoction. I'm not certain what was in it, though there might have been lavender. Finishing it, I lay back, feeling disconnected from the aches and pains in my body.

A scuffling woke me, or I think so, because everything was vague and fuzzy, almost as if

I was dreaming or hallucinating. The curtains having been drawn back and the window opened, I could hear the Saturday bustle of the town as I lay a while, blinking, fascinated by the scintillating patterns swirling in the sunlight. Trying to work out what was causing the peculiar misshapen shadow moving across the carpet, I looked up, seeing Hobbes's face upside down outside the window, winking at me from beneath a broad grin.

Puzzled, I closed my eyes. When I looked again, he'd been replaced by Milord Schmidt, hunched on a small stool, stitching a tear in my blazer.

'Good afternoon,' he said, peering over the top of his half-moon spectacles, stretching out his long, thin legs.

An unfamiliar middle-aged woman, smelling of disinfectant, was leaning over me, poking various tender places, shaking her head and frowning. When I opened my mouth to ask what she was doing, she popped in a thermometer, continuing the prodding occasionally saying 'um' or 'aah'. The 'ooh' came from me; her hands could have been warmer.

Retrieving the thermometer, she peered at it. 'You did well to call me in,' she said, ignoring me. 'He's certainly got a high fever, so it's no wonder he's feeling poorly. He would appear to have picked up a rather nasty infection, almost certainly a bacterial one, though I'll take a blood sample to make sure. In the meantime, I'll prescribe him a course of antibiotics. He should start it as soon as possible. I must say it's peculiar how the illness happened just like that, but I'd be surprised if it wasn't connected with the scratches on his hand.

'I almost think he should be in hospital, but I've an idea he'll be better off here. Make sure he has plenty to drink and he can eat a little when he feels up to it. Call me if he gets any worse, or if there's no improvement in the next two days.'

'Now,' she said, swabbing my arm with alcohol, 'you'll feel a little scratch.'

When she thrust the needle into my arm just below the elbow, I whimpered, nearly fainting as the little glass tube filled up with my blood. As she straightened up, turning away, I felt a momentary resentment that I hadn't been involved before drifting off.

Now and again Mrs Goodfellow shook me awake to pop some foul-tasting pills down my throat, washing them down with cool drinks. Sometimes I sweated, kicking off the bedclothes; other times I shivered, clutching them around me. The long night let loose dreams, leading me down nightmare alleys, where big cats with glowing eyes prowled, oblivious to something darker, something worse than panthers, lurking in the shadows. It was something looking like a man, except it was all wrong, though not in the way Hobbes was wrong. It was stalking Violet and I tried to warn her, only for Charlie Brick to release a herd of grinning pigs that ran squealing through a hole in the hedge, getting in my way. Unable to get close, I screamed for her to run.

'It's only a nightmare, dear,' said Mrs G.

I opened my eyes, blinking in the morning light, my chin rasping against the white sheets. I found it was surprisingly bristly.

'How are you feeling?' asked Mrs Goodfellow.

'Not so bad,' I said.

'That's good. You've been rather ill and Doctor Procter was quite worried – we all were – but the antibiotics seem to be working. Would you like any breakfast?'

'Umm … yes. Yes, I would. I really fancy scrambled eggs. I'm starving.'

Smiling, she walked away. After a few minutes, I sat up abruptly, feeling something terribly wrong around my waist. I put my hand beneath the sheets. Appalled at what I touched, I threw back the blankets and stared in absolute, horrified disbelief. Someone, and I didn't need to guess who, had encased my nether regions in a nappy.

A tray appeared at the bedroom door, followed by Mrs Goodfellow.

'Why,' I asked, pointing, 'am I wearing this?'

'To keep you dry.'

'But …'

'You needed it, dear, to stop you wetting the bed.'

'I did what?'

'Sorry, dear. It was for the best. You weren't able to get to the bathroom.'

'Oh, God,' I muttered, cringing, covering myself up, disgusted and ashamed, 'I'm really sorry.'

'You couldn't help it and, anyway, I saw a lot worse when I was nursing. Don't worry. Enjoy your breakfast.' Handing me the tray, she left me to it.

I shrugged. What had happened had happened, and didn't alter the fact that I was ravenous. She'd made scrambled eggs on toast and I wolfed them down at first, desperate to fill the emptiness. Only towards the end, the edge having been smoothed off my hunger, did I begin to appreciate their wonderful fragrance and fluffiness, though my taste buds didn't seem quite up to scratch. Even the tea tasted odd, though I still gulped it down.

I'd just finished eating when she returned with the *Bugle*. 'I brought you this. Would you like anything else, dear?'

'Yes, please. Could I have some toast and marmalade?'

'Of course. Would two slices do?'

'Better make it four … and some more tea would be great. Thanks.'

The headline was intriguing.

'Publican struck by lightning on battery charge.'

Underneath was a photograph of Featherlight Binks, wrestling with six police officers in front of the Feathers. I wasn't surprised, knowing how often he'd been arrested before.

What confused me was seeing it was in Monday's paper, which made no sense. The picnic had been on Friday evening, after which I'd walked home and gone to bed. It must, therefore, have been Saturday morning when I'd woken up feeling poorly, and now, somehow, it was Monday. Sunday had apparently come and gone without trace, which was weird, almost as if I'd been time travelling, skipping over a day of my life. Still, there was no point fretting. All I could do was to resume life where I'd rejoined it.

I forced myself to read the story. 'Leonard Holdfast Binks,' it said, 'landlord of the Feathers public house, was arrested on Sunday lunchtime, following allegations of a serious assault. According to Mr William Shawcroft, an eyewitness, when officers informed Binks, widely known as Featherlight, that he was under arrest, he adopted an aggressive stance, letting slip a tirade of foul and abusive language before attempting to absent himself from the premises via the back door. He was arrested after a struggle during which six officers received minor yet spectacular injuries. According to Mr

Shawcroft, Binks would probably have made good his escape had he not been under the weather, having been struck by lightning during Friday night's storm. Binks, he reports, is frequently struck, possibly on account of a metal plate in his head. Mr Shawcroft stated that Binks, who has several previous convictions for violence and cooking, is normally at his most placid following a lightning strike and that his behaviour was out of character. As Binks was dragged into the back of a police van, he denied assaulting anyone over the weekend and threatened anyone who disagreed with him with "a good shoeing".

'The victim, an as yet unnamed businessman, remains in hospital, where a spokesman reports that he is critical but stable.'

I'd just finished the article when Mrs Goodfellow returned with the toast and marmalade and more tea.

'I see Featherlight's in trouble again,' I remarked.

'It seems so,' she said, adjusting my pillows. 'Yet the old fellow has his doubts.'

'But, he injured six policemen,' I said, pointing at the photo. 'You can see what he did. There can't be any doubt.'

'He did that, but denies the original assault.'

'Well, he would, wouldn't he?'

'I doubt it. The old fellow reckons Mr Binks is honest. That is, though he may be involved in a multitude of nefarious schemes, he doesn't actually tell lies. Of course, what he perceives as the truth might differ from how you or I might see it.'

I laughed. 'You might be right, I'm sure he really believes he is a purveyor of fine ales and good food.'

'That's true, dear. Anyway, the old fellow believes him.'

'I still don't get it. If he didn't attack the businessman, then who did?'

'I have no idea, dear. Now, enjoy the rest of your breakfast and then you can tell me all about your picnic.'

After breakfast, while Mrs Goodfellow tidied up, I told my tale, though leaving out Felix's threats and the werewolf. I was still trying to come to terms with it all. When I'd finished, fearing the worst, I asked whether Violet had been in touch.

'No, I'm afraid not. I did wonder when she didn't call, if you two had fallen out.'

'I hope she's alright,' I said, a flock of worries fluttering round my stomach like frightened pigeons.

'I expect she is, dear. Otherwise we'd have heard something. Her brother would have let you know, wouldn't he?'

'Maybe,' I said, without feeling reassured. Still, I had an inkling that if anything really bad had happened, then Hobbes would have known and told the old girl. I still wasn't happy but the feelings of panic took wing.

After a bath, I brushed my teeth, removing a triple dose of morning breath, and went back to bed for a couple of hours. Waking just before lunch, I was strong enough to hobble downstairs, where Mrs Goodfellow had prepared chicken soup especially for me, Hobbes and Dregs having gone out for the day. Though I'd guess it was up to standard, my taste buds were still numb, for which I blamed the antibiotics, hoping the effect was temporary.

'The old fellow's supposed to be having the afternoon off,' said Mrs G, 'but he said he'd better take a close look at Loop's Farm.'

'Loop's Farm?'

'That's right, dear. The festival's on next weekend and those cats still haven't gone away – he says he nearly caught one on Saturday night. What's more, he believes something else is on the prowl, though it seemed to intrigue him rather than worry him.'

I nodded, coming to a decision. 'That's interesting,' I said, 'because I think I saw something when I was walking home, something odd.'

'Did you, dear?'

'Yes, it was when the lightning flashed. I saw it and it scared me so much I ran away as fast as my legs could carry me, and further than I'd have thought possible.'

'What did you see?'

Screwing up my eyes, I tried to pick out the image from a mess of memories. 'It was about man-sized and shaped, not as big as Hobbes or Featherlight, but big enough and it was sort of standing upright, yet kind of hunched, and it looked like it had hair and eyes. And teeth.'

'All the better to eat you with, dear.'

I laughed. 'But the crazy thing is I'm sure it was wearing trousers.'

'So you're telling me you saw what looked like a man wearing trousers? Extraordinary!'

'Yes,' I said, feeling slightly foolish, 'but it wasn't a man, I'm certain.'

'You haven't been very well. Perhaps the fever made you imagine things.'

'Maybe … but I don't think so. I don't think I was ill then.'

On reflection, I didn't believe I'd been hallucinating, remaining convinced something frightening had really been out there, something that was almost certainly a werewolf, though I didn't want to admit it, not even to myself. Once upon a time, before Hobbes, I'd have found it impossible to believe the evidence of my eyes, but I'd learned that strange folk lived among us, strange folk that went unremarked for the most part.

Still lethargic and tired, it was all I could do to slump in front of the telly, watching a heart-warming made-for-TV movie about a woman's brave fight for life and love after a horrific car crash left her with a collection of rather photogenic scars. Climaxing in a spurt of sickly sentimentality, it nearly turned my stomach, leaving me deep in melancholy.

Desperate for news of Violet, I could have kicked myself for not having thought to get her phone number, an obvious move, yet one that had never occurred to me, since she'd been the one to get in touch. I wondered if I'd been a little passive, whether some assertiveness would have been to my benefit, perhaps even impressing Felix. Realising that, if I'd shown any sign of being a man, I wouldn't have been me, I spent some time wallowing in a mire of self-indulgent misery. Yet, eventually, I roused enough to call the hospital. The woman I spoke to refused to answer any questions about Violet on the grounds that the law forbade it, refusing to budge even after I'd told her what I thought of the law.

I moped, having run out of options. Though, in truth, I knew I hadn't, I indulged my feelings of helplessness, unwilling to admit the most obvious course of action; I had

Felix's card and could phone him, if I dared. I fretted and dithered and, though it was a close call, my need to know won out in the end. Finding his card, dried out and creased, on the dressing table in my room, I took it to the phone and dialled the number.

'Mr King's office,' said an efficient female voice. 'Carol speaking. How may I help you?'

'I umm … I'd like to talk to Felix.'

'Mr King is out of the office. Can I take a message?'

'Umm …' I said, having failed to anticipate this contingency, 'yes … or perhaps you can help me? I want to know how Violet King is.'

'I'm afraid Miss King is off work. She was involved in a car accident.'

'I know. I was with her. How is she?'

'May I take your name, sir?'

'Yes, it's Caplet. Andy Caplet.'

'I thought it might be; Mr King informed me of the possibility you would call. He said anyone with a modicum of decency would have followed her to the hospital.'

'But I couldn't …'

'Mr King,' Carol continued, 'asked me to let you know that you are a self-centred, money-grubbing bastard.'

'I'm not …'

'And you are to leave his sister alone. Should you persist in importuning her, steps will be taken. That is all.'

'But is she alright?'

'That is all, Mr Caplet.'

'But please, I must know how she is.'

'You could have asked her yourself if you'd been bothered enough to visit her in hospital.'

'But I was seriously ill.'

'Were you?' she asked, the faintest hint of feminine sympathy in her voice.

'Yes … I've had a terrible fever and have only just risen from my sickbed,' I said, laying it on a bit thick, making my voice sound weak and feeble.

It worked.

'Alright, then,' she said, lowering her voice to a whisper, 'and don't tell anyone I told you, but Miss King is fine now. She had a mild shock with a few minor cuts and bruises and is taking a break until she feels better.'

'Thank you,' I murmured, though I don't know why I, too, felt the need to lower my voice. Things were going so well that I thought I'd push my luck. 'Umm … I wonder if you could let me have her address? Or her phone number?'

'Don't push it,' said Carol, 'I've already said more than I should have.'

'Please!'

'Sorry.' Her voice returned to normal. 'Thank you for calling, sir. Goodbye.' She put the phone down.

My first feeling was of relief that Violet was alright for, although, I'd had no reason to believe she wouldn't be, it was a great weight off my mind to be certain. My second feeling was of outrage. How dare Felix try to order me around? How dare he tell his secretary to insult me? The third feeling was of slow, cold fear. What if Carol told Felix

I'd called? The fourth feeling was more familiar: total bewilderment. I didn't know what to do next.

As afternoon rolled into early evening, I caught myself laughing at children's cartoons, feeling better the sillier they were, for they stopped me having to think. The early evening news put my problems into perspective, though other people's tragedies didn't make me feel any better about my own.

The front door bursting open, I was pounced on by Dregs who seemed delighted to see me downstairs and, though my battle to keep his tongue at a safe distance ended in an abject rout, his enthusiasm cheered me.

'Good to see you up,' said Hobbes, striding into the room, baring his great yellow teeth in a smile. 'How are you feeling?'

'Not too bad. I'm ready for my supper, though.'

'Me too,' he said as he bounded upstairs to wash his hands.

At supper, I was, once again, a little disappointed at the lack of response from my taste buds, despite Mrs G having cooked a magnificent shepherd's pie with Sunday's leftover lamb. Still, it filled me up perfectly and I would have been a relatively contented Andy, had Hobbes not poured himself a goblet of wine and drunk it with such evident enjoyment. Mrs G wouldn't allow me any alcohol while I was on antibiotics.

The wine reminding me of what Felix had said, I wondered if he'd regard me more favourably if I sorted something out for him.

'Violet's brother, Felix, asked me to ask you where you got your wine from.'

'And you've asked me,' said Hobbes with a chuckle. 'Well done.' He took another sip and sighed.

'The thing is, Felix reckons it's quality stuff and wants to buy some.'

'He's right about the quality, but he'll not find it on sale anywhere.'

'Why not?'

'Because it's a gift.'

'Who from?' I asked, resentful that no one ever gave me valuable presents.

'A friend.'

'Oh, well, in that case, Felix wanted to know whether he might buy any off you. He said you could name your price.'

'What price can you put on a gift from a friend?' asked Hobbes.

That stumped me, though I knew what price you could put on a gift from a mother. It was £5.99 in the sale – she'd left the price tag on the jumper she'd given me for my birthday. 'I don't know but I reckon he'd pay … umm … a hundred pounds a bottle.'

'As much as that?' asked Hobbes, raising his eyebrows. 'Doesn't he know he can pick up a drinkable wine from the supermarket for less than a tenner?'

'I doubt he'd consider drinking anything in that price range.'

'Why not?'

'Umm … I think he regards himself as a connoisseur, liking only the really good stuff. That's why he's so interested in yours.'

I felt I was really in there, fighting for Felix, doing exactly what he wanted me to do, though I wouldn't have been had I not wanted a chance with Violet. I still couldn't accept it was any of Felix's business what I did with his sister, as long as she wanted me. Of course, she hadn't called me and I seemed to be losing any chance of getting the wine for him.

'I'm sorry,' said Hobbes firmly, 'I can't sell the wine, though, since he's a friend of yours, he can have a crate as a gift.'

'What? Really?' I said, staggered by his generosity.

'Of course.' He drained his goblet. 'If he's a friend of yours, then he's a friend of mine. Right, I'm off to bed. I'm getting too old for all these nights out on the tiles. Thanks, lass for a delicious supper.' Yawning, he rose from the table and strode upstairs.

I sat back, feeling like a hypocrite, for, though I hadn't actually said Felix was my friend, I'd let him think it. Worse, I didn't care to think on my reason for helping Felix: getting him the wine in order to buy his favour, hoping he would then allow me to get off with his little sister. I didn't feel at all good about myself, despite my intentions being, more or less, strictly honourable. The whole episode had acquired a sleazy taint.

Mrs Goodfellow, materialising at my elbow, nudged me, resulting in a vertical take-off. 'A penny for your thoughts,' she said.

I landed back on my chair, shaking.

'You were looking very thoughtful, dear.'

'Yes … umm … I was just wondering where he gets his wine from.'

'From an old friend,' she said.

'Yeah, but which old friend?'

'It's from the Count.'

'His friend's a Count?'

'Yes, they met during the war, when the old fellow was able to do him a small service. They became friends and the Count sends him wine in gratitude.'

'Which war?'

'The Great one, dear. The First World War, you know?'

'I know,' I said, having seen the Victoria Cross in a tin in a drawer in his desk at the police station. Besides, Mrs Goodfellow had occasionally told me small details of his heroics, something he never spoke of. Though, somehow, I'd grown comfortable with the idea of his participation in a war a century ago, I was puzzled by his friend. 'I suppose the Count must be pretty ancient then?'

'I suppose he is, but he never forgets to send the wine.'

'Felix said he'd drunk a similar wine that cost five hundred pounds a bottle and the Count must send crates of it every year.'

'That's right, except during the Second War, when transport was a problem. He always sends half a dozen crates of the ordinary and one of the good stuff.'

'He must be very rich if he can afford to send all that, and generous.'

'He is very wealthy. He has a chateau perched on a hill with magnificent views all along the river – you should see it – and he is generous to a fault. Mind you he wouldn't have been either if it hadn't been for the old fellow.'

'Why? What did he do?'

'I'll tell you what I know,' she said. 'Years ago, when the old fellow had a week's leave and we visited the Count, he told me something of what had occurred. The Count is a charming fellow, by the way, with lovely white teeth; you'd like him. During the war he was a French Army lieutenant and was marching back from the front with his section when a shell struck the duckboards, throwing them all into liquid mud. Men would often drown if they fell in and that would probably have been their fate.'

'It must have been horrible,' I said, shuddering.

'It must have been, and all of them would probably have died had the old fellow not been passing and pulled them out. Afterwards, an officer reprimanded him for losing his boots.'

'That's typical!' I said, clicking my tongue.

'It wasn't really; he only lost them once. He seemed to hit it off with the Count, who ever since has expressed his gratitude with wine. That's about as much as I know, dear.'

'Thank you. I sometimes wish he'd talk more about the war.'

'He won't. He hardly ever says much about it these days. He reckons there's too much going on now to waste time on ancient history. Even so, he did once try to trace his ancestors but gave up.'

'He was adopted, wasn't he? Did he find anything?'

'Not that I know. Well, I can't stand round here all evening; I've got my Kung Fu to get to. We'll be looking after security during the festival. See you later, dear.'

She walked away, leaving me with Dregs who, having taken a leaf out of Hobbes's book, was lying on his back in his basket, an idiot grin on his face, emitting gentle snores. Leaving him to it, I hobbled through into the sitting room, wishing my feet weren't so sore, wondering if I could really let Hobbes give Felix the wine. If he did, I might yet have a chance with Violet, though, I couldn't help thinking that Felix would still detest me. In that case, he'd be the only winner.

I sat watching telly until the old girl got back, her face pink and shiny. Then, after a cup of cocoa and yet another antibiotic tablet, I went up to bed, sleeping as if I hadn't already slept for most of the weekend.

Next morning at breakfast, I sensed, once I'd filled my stomach enough to take notice of anything other than bacon and eggs, that Hobbes, the *Bugle* open but unread before him, stirring his tea and sucking his finger, was lost in thought. He stared at the ceiling apparently finding great interest in its network of cracks as I launched an attack on the toast and marmalade.

'There'll be no moon tonight,' he said.

'Won't there?' I asked, brushing crumbs off my chin.

'No, and furthermore, there'll be heavy cloud cover.'

'That's no good,' I said. 'It'll probably rain.'

'Yes, and it will be very dark in the woods.'

'I suppose so.' I wondered where he was heading.

'Which means those cats won't be able to see so well, which might give me a chance to nab them.'

'Are you sure? I thought cats could see pretty well in the dark.'

'They can, but it will be very dark tonight, which might be to my advantage.'

'Might it? Won't it be dark for you, too?'

'Of course, but that will not be a problem.'

'They'll still be able to hear and smell you, won't they?'

'Yes, and I'll be able to hear and smell them.'

'So, what are you going to do?'

'Think about it. By the way, I think something else is out there, something that might interest you.'

Something in the way he said it made my skin crawl. I could still see the creature in the lightning flash. 'What?'

'Something rare and rather exciting, I think.'

'Yes, but what?' My nerves tightened.

'Though I'm not entirely sure.'

'Please tell me.'

'I think we have a werewolf.'

'No!' I said, unwilling to believe him despite what I'd seen.

'Yes. Right, I'm off to work.' He rose from the table, leaving me open-mouthed and shaking.

'But what are you going to do about it?'

'Nothing, unless anyone makes trouble. Goodbye.' Calling Dregs, he left me to my thoughts.

I sat at the table, shaking, convinced he should be doing considerably more than nothing. Perhaps I was prejudiced, and he had insisted werewolves weren't dangerous, but I couldn't help feeling he should be raising a mob with flaming brands and pitchforks to destroy the monster. The merest glimpse had filled me with dread and I'd discovered how easily fear could turn to hatred. I wanted the thing dead so I would feel safe. Whether there was a genuine threat didn't matter.

15

Mrs Goodfellow took a break from washing the dishes to stand beside me and look sympathetic. 'Are you feeling poorly again, dear?'

'No,' I said, trembling, 'he thinks there's a werewolf.'

She smiled. 'Yes, isn't it exciting?'

'Exciting? It's terrifying.'

'Oh no, it's wonderful news. It would be lovely if they could make a comeback round here. I miss them; we used to have such fun.'

Either the old girl and Hobbes were quite mad, or I was.

'Yes,' she said, 'we used to have great times with old Wolfie. I wonder who the new one is? Wouldn't it be funny if it was someone we know?'

'Hilarious,' I said, grimacing, the very idea giving me the creeps.

'They've probably just moved into the area.' She chuckled. 'How long have you been in town, dear?'

'Long enough. I'm no freak.'

'Of course you aren't, dear,' she said.

'Umm … good. So long as that's clear.'

'We ought to go out one night, see if we can find it and make friends.'

'Well, not tonight, then. He said there'll be no moon.'

'That might make it a bit tricky for the likes of us, but it won't be a problem for him.'

'What I mean is there won't be any about. Don't werewolves only come out when there's a moon?'

'Of course not, dear. People believe such silly things and I think this myth came about since werewolves were most often spotted when the moon was out, so people assumed they only came out then.'

'Well, what's wrong with that?'

'The thing is, dear, if you're going to see anything at night it's likely to be under the moon, ideally the full moon – because of the light.'

'So they do come out at other times?'

'Of course.'

'So, one might be out tonight?'

'Yes.'

I decided I wouldn't be out that night.

It came as some surprise to find myself trailing through Loop Woods, a few hours later, wondering why I'd changed my mind so easily. I'd made my first mistake after finishing supper when I'd mentioned to Hobbes that Dr Procter had been round and pronounced me fit and well, so long as I was careful.

'In that case,' he said, 'do you fancy coming out tonight and having a go at nabbing those big cats?'

Though the sane bit of my brain, stunned for a moment, did not fancy it at all, my crazy mouth had already made my second mistake by saying, 'I'd love to'. The third mistake had been when the sane bit of brain, trying to get me to change my mind, wanting me to say no, had discovered that my crazy mouth was still refusing to cooperate. I could blame no one but myself.

It was already getting gloomy, an occasional fine drizzle a hint of what was to come. Anticipating heavy rain, I was wrapped up in an old mac and a flat cap, both Mr Goodfellow's cast-offs. Dregs led the way, his thick, dark hair a match for any weather. Hobbes sauntered at my side, wearing his tatty old raincoat, carrying a canvas bag and a chair from the kitchen. I was still more than mildly miffed he hadn't let me take one as well.

'Why couldn't I have a chair?' I asked. 'It might be a long night and I don't want to be sitting on damp ground.'

'Don't worry about that, I know a tree that'll give good shelter and be an excellent vantage point.'

'So what's the chair for? To give you a step up into the tree?'

'No. What I'll do is give you and Dregs a hand onto a safe branch and scramble up afterwards.'

'So what is it for?'

'For the cats. I've seen how lion tamers do it.'

'But you've never tried?'

'There has to be a first time for everything.'

'And what's in the bag?'

'A bullwhip. Lion tamers apparently use them, though I'm not sure why.'

I was getting a bad feeling about this venture and perching in a tree in darkness was no longer top of my worry list. 'But after you've successfully tamed it …'

'Them,' corrected Hobbes.

'Or them … What are you going to do then?'

'I've put a couple of dog collars and leads in the bag, so I expect I'll be able to work something out.'

'Have you actually thought this through?'

'No, improvisation is half the fun.'

Shaking my head, thinking it was more like madness, I kept with him, though it seemed that even Dregs, who was keeping within touching distance, was nervous. Hobbes loped through the quickly deepening gloom, his chair and bag slung across his back, his knuckles brushing the leaf mould, stopping now and again to sniff the air. A bird fluttered to its roost, giving a low warble, and that, besides the scuff and stumbling of my feet and the rustling of Dregs's paws was all I could hear. As usual, I was amazed how Hobbes, even with his great clumping feet, could move as silently as an owl when he wished. The breeze strengthening, the sun nearly down, I wished I'd put on a jumper. Pausing to get my bearings, I tried to come to terms with being there, thinking that, although on a warm, sunny afternoon I wasn't averse to a gentle stroll in the woods, with the night falling, hard, heavy clouds threatening torrents, dangerous animals about, I'd rather have stayed at home.

'Keep up,' said Hobbes, 'or you might get lost.'

I put on a spurt, having no intention of letting that happen.

Hobbes, stopping abruptly, held up his hand. 'Come here,' he whispered, 'and quietly.'

As Dregs stiffened and bristled, Hobbes reached out and grabbed his collar. My mouth felt dry, as if I'd been force-fed cream crackers; I couldn't even gulp, a sick feeling of cold fear filling my stomach.

'Shhh!' Hobbes murmured, 'over there, by the fallen tree.'

A giant tree trunk, moss covered and cracked, lay in gentle repose, gradually returning to the soil. Hearing what sounded like a cough and something purring, my mind said run, but my legs just shook. A grunt, as if from a man, was followed by a series of chattering squeaks and I suppressed a gasp as a sleek, grey animal with a black and white striped snout and small white-tipped ears gambolled into sight. Another launched itself over the tree trunk and the pair of badger cubs conducted a play fight, rolling and scrabbling in the leaf mould, driving away all of my fear. I'd never before seen wild badgers, apart from dead ones by the side of the Pigton Road, and hadn't realised how much I wanted to. A few moments later, a larger animal, the mother I supposed, ambled into view, rooting under the dead tree with powerful paws, grunting and coughing.

Though I would have been happy to stand and watch for hours, Dregs whined in a tone that meant he wanted to play, Mother Badger barked a warning, and all three trundled into the undergrowth.

'Oh well,' said Hobbes, smiling, 'we'd best get on'.

He loped away, leading us into denser woodland as the evening turned to night-time, any starlight being smothered by the trees and a sodden blanket of cloud. When an owl hooted, I felt Dregs jump. Raindrops pattered into the silent woods; I heard them long before I felt them.

'Here we are,' said Hobbes, patting the trunk of a tree that was barely visible in the darkness. His bag rustling, he squatted on his haunches, spreading something on the ground.

'What are you doing?' I whispered.

'Putting down some bait; Mrs Goodfellow bought me some marrowbones.'

'Will they work?'

'We'll see. Right, you two need to be out of the way.'

Before I could even think of objecting, he grabbed me round the waist, launching me upwards. Though I flailed in panic, I landed gently on something broad and solid. Groping around, I felt how a couple of sturdy, horizontal boughs, having interlocked, had formed a sort of small platform. I didn't know how high I was, what was above or what was below. All I knew was that I was up a tree and that I might just as well have been blind.

'Hold on,' said Hobbes, 'here comes the dog.'

'You can't throw him into a tree,' I said, reaching for some sort of handhold.

I was wrong. Dregs, landing beside me with a surprised yelp, sniffed around and proved he was made of sterner stuff than I by curling up as if to sleep.

'Where are you?' I called down to Hobbes.

'Up here,' he said.

'Eh? What?' Jerking back, staring blindly into the canopy, I nearly lost my balance.

His hand grabbed my shoulder, steadying me. 'I told you to hold on. Do as I say, and keep quiet. We may be here for some time.'

Finding a twisted cable, some sort of creeping plant that felt solid, I looped it round my left hand and sat still, as the rain started for real with a sound like a thousand tiny drummers and, though the leaves sheltered me and my cap kept off the worst of it, heavy dollops would, from time to time, explode into my face. My trousers, growing soggy, clung coldly around my legs. Though Dregs sighed every now and then, Hobbes might have sloped off minutes or hours earlier and I wouldn't have known; the concept of time seemed meaningless. Huddling against the rain as best I could, I wished again I'd stayed at home, deciding that almost anywhere was more comfortable than halfway up a tree in the rain. My bottom growing numb and wet, I wriggled in an effort to find a more comfortable position, letting out a soft groan.

'Shhh!' Hobbes hissed by my ear, clamping his hand across my mouth to stifle the gasp rising to my lips. 'Something's coming,' he whispered and was gone.

I held onto my precious creeper, waves of fear crashing through my body, scared that he hadn't said what was coming, giving me no clue as to whether it might be panthers, or a werewolf or just the badgers returning. Those next few moments rated well up my top ten most terrifying experiences. I couldn't see, all I could hear was rain, I was perched God knew how high up a tree, and all I could smell was the earthy scent of leaf mould and the stink of wet dog. When Dregs, all of a sudden, pressed his cold nose into my neck, I jumped, losing my grip, plummeting. In such a crisis, my brain must have worked faster than normal, because it had time to remember Hobbes's warning, to suppress a shriek, and still wonder how much I'd hurt myself when I hit the ground.

Instead of actually hitting the ground, I landed astride something soft, if not as soft as a man in my position might have wished. The thing snarled, twisting away from me and, despite the shock, all I could do was whimper, clutching my delicate parts, dropping to my knees. Two green eyes flashed and, by some trick of the light or of my imagination, I could see it clearly: it being a big, black cat. Judging by the way it was thrashing its tail, I'd annoyed it; judging by the way it was limping, I'd hurt it.

Strangely, I wasn't quite as scared as I had been in the tree. Perhaps the pain had something to do with it, but my fear of the dark unknown proved even worse than what was before me. It wasn't rational, of course, for anything has more potential for harm than nothing, and a big cat has more potential than most things. Neither was it rational to kneel there thinking such thoughts when I should have been fleeing for my life.

At last, I legged it, though not for long as I ran headlong into a spiky bush. Disentangling myself, I turned to face the panther. It was poised to spring.

'Whoa! Here, kitty, kitty,' Hobbes shouted from a distance: too great a distance.

As the panther leapt, I dropped and curled into a ball, my hands covering my face, an instinctive reaction that I doubted would help, yet the panther never touched me. Its great paws landed by my head and it ran. A moment later, something dark, hairy and heavy hurtled past, followed by Dregs, barking, with Hobbes bringing up the rear, bounding after them, almost silently.

I climbed back to my feet, trembling, sore, feeling horribly out of place. Not far away, something angry was growling and spitting and I wondered how many panthers infested the woods. The sounds of the chase were receding into the distance when an animal yelped in pain, a piteous sound, but it wasn't Dregs or Hobbes.

Though my first instinct was to run towards it and help, I didn't dare turn my back on the growling, spitting thing, hoping Hobbes had trapped it, fearing he hadn't, that the panther was winding up its fury before tearing me into little pieces. The tree I'd been in felt like sanctuary, though I doubted any panther would have trouble climbing it.

If I'd only had a light, I wouldn't have felt quite so vulnerable, yet the darkness had returned. I could see nothing. As a genius idea popped into my head, I plunged deep into the spiky bush, convinced nothing would be able to get at me, besides the wicked, scimitar thorns that raked my hands and face and stabbed through my trousers. It was fortunate my heavy mac, as impenetrable as chain mail, protected my vital organs. Despite superficial scratches, I was safe, but stuck.

The woods suddenly becoming uncannily quiet, except for the steady drip of rain-rinsed leaves, I tried to control my breathing, listening as hard as I could. Something was panting to my right and not far away I made out the faint rustling of furtive footsteps, heading to my left, towards where I'd heard the growling. I stayed put, the thorns giving me little other choice, all my senses on alert, as minutes rolled by like aeons and my nerves stretched.

'Are you alright there?' asked Hobbes from above.

My taut nerves snapping under the shock, I shrieked like a girl in a horror film until his hand clamped on my mouth to shut me up.

'It's only me,' he said, 'calm down and relax, alright?'

I nodded and he released me.

'What are you doing in that there briar patch?'

'Trying to get out,' I said, breathing hard, yet acting cool, until, an incautious movement resulting in a scratch on my neck, I yelped.

'I'll give you a hand.'

Grabbing my wrists, he lifted me straight upwards, so that I could just see his face, which being upside down, led me to believe he was holding onto a tree branch with his legs.

'Just hang in there a moment,' he said, 'until I find somewhere to put you down.'

I felt a swift, smooth motion as if he was sliding along a branch.

'This'll do,' he said, swinging me to one side and letting go.

Anticipating a long drop, I braced myself, rolling like I'd seen gymnasts do when I hit the ground, realising I'd only dropped a few inches and was lying on a soft litter of leaf mould and moss. Hobbes gave me a hand up.

'What just happened?' I asked, 'I mean … I don't get it, it was confusing.'

'OK,' he said, 'I was just arresting the first panther when you threw yourself onto the second one. Though it was brave, and I didn't think you had it in you, it was also a bit foolish.'

I tried a devil-may-care shrug.

He continued. 'I'd just got mine tied up, which it didn't seem to appreciate, when I realised the other one had the better of you. I came back to help, but there was no need; the werewolf got there first.'

'So that other thing was a werewolf?' I asked, shivering.

'Yes, which was lucky for you, because I might not have made it in time.'

I gulped, imagining hot, rank breath on my face, teeth tearing into my soft flesh. It didn't take much imagination, after what had happened to Henry Bishop. 'But what cried out? Was it the … umm …?'

'The werewolf,' said Hobbes, 'caught his foot in a wire snare. I'm going to have to have another word with Skeleton Bob about his poaching.'

'Is it … he … alright? The werewolf?'

'I expect he's got a sore leg but he managed to release himself and limped away. Dregs went with him.'

'Will Dregs be safe?'

'I expect so. The two of them seemed to be getting on very well.'

'Good … umm … Can I see the panther you caught?'

'I'm afraid not. It escaped.'

'How? Weren't your knots any good?'

'My knots,' said Hobbes, 'were fine. Unfortunately, someone cut them.'

'How?' I asked, intelligently.

'With a knife, a very sharp knife.'

'Who would do such a thing?'

'Someone with a sharp knife who wanted to release it. Now come along, we ought to investigate.'

'What about Dregs?'

'He'll find us, but if you're worried you can look for him. He went that way.'

Though I suppose he pointed, it was still too dark to see, yet, possibly, not so dark as it had been. I weighed up my options: I could search for Dregs, who was quite capable of looking after himself, on my own, in a wood full of werewolves and panthers, or I could stay where I was, on my own, in a wood full of panthers and werewolves, or I could follow Hobbes. Though none of them really appealed, the latter meant I'd at least have Hobbes with me.

'I'll come along,' I said. 'Just don't go too fast.'

'I'll try not to. Follow me.'

The rain returning, showing ambitions of becoming a deluge, I pulled up my collar and set out after him, a hopeless task, since after a few moments I couldn't see or hear him anymore. At first, I jogged in the direction in which I guessed he'd gone but after banging my knee on a fallen log, I resorted to slow walking. After a tree stump had barked my shin, I decided I might as well use it as a seat.

A twig cracked, leaves rustled and something was breathing heavily. I sprang into an alert crouch, facing – I hoped – whatever was approaching. After a few minutes, my knees starting to hurt, I had to stand up straight as something solid smacked into the backs of my legs, knocking me headlong into the ground with a soggy thud. Shocked and winded, raising my hands for protection, I felt a soft, wet tongue lick them and hugged Dregs's soggy fur, nearly crying with relief.

'Good dog,' I said, clambering to my feet with difficulty on account of the exuberant licking. When he shook himself, showering me, I didn't care and grabbed his collar as he bounced about me, feeling safe, which was foolish.

'Stay!' I said in my best commanding voice. 'The two of us might as well just hang around here until Hobbes gets back.'

Unfortunately, on hearing Hobbes's name, he set off to find him, his lunge taking me unawares, the collar tightening around my fingers, dragging me behind. Though I managed to keep up for a few steps, I soon realised it was extremely difficult to run in a crouch. How Dregs managed to keep going without choking, I had no idea. At last he stopped running and, groaning, muttering what I'd like to do to him, I managed to wrestle my hand from his collar.

'I thought you were supposed to be following me,' said Hobbes.

Though I ought to have been used to such shocks, I wasn't. 'I tried,' I said. 'I thought you were going to be slow.'

'I was, but you were slower. You'd have been faster if you hadn't stopped to play with the dog.'

'I wasn't playing … umm … did you find the panthers?'

'No, I lost them by the road. I don't know how they got away, but something very strange is going on.'

'You're telling me?'

'Yes. It's puzzling, because it's not difficult to track large animals through woods.'

'I know,' I said.

'And it should be even easier on a road, but they just vanished. I think there must have been a human with them but the scents were confusing.'

'Perhaps the human put them into a van and drove away.'

'That's plausible,' said Hobbes, 'because a vehicle had been parked by the roadside not so long ago.'

'Why,' I asked, 'would someone take panthers into the woods? It could be really dangerous.' Puzzled, I scratched my head, dislodging a number of leaves, as well as something soft and wriggly that made me shiver. Something smelled really bad.

'For exercise, maybe,' said Hobbes, 'but something smells wrong – and I don't just mean you. For future reference, rolling in fox dung is not effective with cats, who hunt mostly by sight and hearing. Smell is secondary.'

'I'll try to remember that,' I said, assuming nonchalance, trying to rise above the stink, which seemed to be all over me, stomach-turning and disgusting.

'Well,' said Hobbes, 'the lass won't allow that sort of fragrance into the house, but I know somewhere you can wash. Follow me …. Is this slow enough?'

'Umm … a little slower might be better.'

He took us through the woods as the rain clouds drifted away and the stars twinkled. With the prospect of a wash and going home to bed, I began to feel more cheerful, until I caught another whiff of myself. Dregs, on the other hand, finding me a source of delight, danced around, sniffing and whining with excitable good humour.

'What about the werewolf?' I asked, trying to divert my attention from the stink. 'Was it badly hurt?'

'No,' said Hobbes, 'I don't think so. They're as tough as old cow tails.'

'I wonder who it is?'

'I have a pretty good idea.'

'Who?' The night sky, glimpsed through a gap in the canopy, was definitely less dark.

'That would be telling. I'll let you know when I'm sure.'

'When will that be?'

'Soon … now mind this stile. It's slippy.'

He vaulted over while Dregs squeezed between the old planks of a tumbledown wooden fence. I scrambled after them, jumping down into the soft grass of a meadow, the woodland scents soon replaced by the great smell of sheep, at least when the fox dung wasn't overpowering everything.

'Where are we?'

'This is the edge of Loop Farm,' said Hobbes, striding forward. 'Henry Bishop's, or, rather, Mrs Bishop's place is just over there to the right.'

'Where can I wash then? Isn't it too late, or too early, to disturb people?'

'You won't disturb anyone, unless you yell too loudly.'

'Why would I yell?' I asked, more than a little wary.

'Because the water will be cold.'

'What water?' I asked, wariness turning to worry. I hung back, but not far enough.

'This water,' he said, seizing my shoulders, lifting me above his head and throwing me.

The water was cold: bloody cold. Going in backwards, I rose, gasping, to the surface, where he allowed me a couple of indignant breaths before dunking me again. I came up spluttering, seeing that he'd chucked me into a big, metal trough.

'Now let's have your coat,' he said, 'and I'll give it a good scrub.'

'But …'

I never had a chance to argue, for he unbelted and unbuttoned my coat, whipping it off, dunking me again before I could react. Grabbing the side of the trough, I tried to haul myself out, still gasping.

'One more time should do it.'

The last thing I heard before going down for the third time was his chuckle.

'Well done,' he said as I emerged, puffing. 'Give yourself a good rub down.'

'Do I have to?'

'I'm afraid so. I'll try to get some of the pong out of this.'

He began scrubbing and beating my coat against the metal sides of the trough. The water, once I was over the initial shock, didn't feel so bad, so I stayed put, rubbing at any dubious areas on my clothing, as Dregs joined in the jolly romp; cold water possessed none of the terrors of a warm bath.

'That'll do for now,' said Hobbes, lifting me onto the grass.

Dregs leapt out and delighted me by shaking himself all over Hobbes, who, shrugging it off, wrung the water from my coat. While Dregs rushed about, rubbing against the grass, I stood and dripped, seeing the distant blue-grey outline of hills standing out on the clearing horizon, hearing the birds chorusing from the woods and hedges.

'It's all very well,' I said, 'but how am I going to get dry?'

'Like this,' said Hobbes, his grin bright and clear, as he grabbed my wrist and ankle. 'Your very own spin dryer.' The world turned into a blur and I became aware I was yelling, with a mixture of indignation and exhilaration.

When, at last, he set me down, I tottered sideways for several steps like a drunkard, fell over and lay laughing in the grass. Hobbes sat next to me, Dregs flopping on my feet, as a pink glow over the hills heralded the dawn. Within minutes we were bathed in brittle, golden light, a fluffy mist lending an air of softness to the farmland. Across the glistening fields, I could see the festival stages had been set up. If the weather held, it looked like we'd be enjoying a great festival, despite the music.

'That,' said Hobbes, in a thoughtful voice, 'was a great night out.'

Looking at my sodden, grimy clothes, the scratches on my hands, I thought of how I'd been bruised and terrified.

'I wouldn't have missed it for anything,' I said, intending sarcasm. It didn't come out that way and I realised, I really wouldn't have missed it. Nevertheless, as the sun's warmth touched me, a great tiredness settled in my heart. I yawned, my head nodding, Hobbes's voice seeming very distant.

'C'mon, Andy, grab your coat, it's time to go home.'

Forcing myself to stay awake, I got to my feet and followed him, smiling as Dregs scouted ahead, his tail wagging happily, knowing just how he felt.

With a yawn and a stretch, I came awake, my hands sore, the rich aroma of oxtail soup pervading my room. Since I was in bed, with no memory of getting home, I guessed Hobbes must have put me there. Sitting up, I examined a selection of scratches that mapped the events of the previous night.

'Good afternoon,' said a heavily accented, guttural voice.

'Bloody hell,' I squeaked.

Milord, back-lit by sunlight, half-moon spectacles glinting, sat hunched on a three-legged stool by the window, a pile of my clothes at his side. He nodded.

'Is it afternoon already?' I asked, hoping a show of normality would mask my bemusement and shock.

'Yes, it is past noon.'

'Gosh, I must have slept like a baby.'

'No, this time you were not wearing a nappy.'

Bemusement turning to embarrassment, I tried to camouflage it behind a weak laugh and a question. 'How come you're always repairing my clothes in here?'

'Because you are always damaging them. You have become a great source of employment, for which, I thank you.'

'You're welcome. I mean to say … umm … why do you do it in my room? Haven't you got a workshop?'

'Of course, but Frau Goodfellow does not provide for me when I work there.'

'That is a good reason.'

Leaving him to it, for the soup was demanding my attention, I got up, dressed in the bathroom and trotted downstairs.

The old girl was cutting bread. 'Hungry, dear?'

'Ravenous,' I said, sneaking a slice of bread when she turned for a plate.

'Good, but we'd better wait for the old fellow.'

'Is he at the station?'

'No, he's at the hospital.'

'Is he alright?'

'He's fine, apart from some nasty scratches on his hands.'

'I've got a few of those and they don't half sting,' I said, holding up my hands, showing them off.

'They look like gardening scratches,' she said, peering. 'The old fellow's came from a panther's claws.'

I was ashamed of trying to play up my pathetic collection of injuries.

'I gather you boys had some fun last night?'

'Yes, I suppose it was pretty exciting, or was when it wasn't terrifying. But, if his scratches aren't serious, what's he doing at the hospital?'

'You remember Mr Binks was arrested for assault?'

'Yes, of course.'

'Well, the man he is alleged to have attacked died in hospital, so now it's a murder and the old fellow's on the case.'

'Oh no! Does that mean he'll be late for lunch?'

'Not likely,' said Hobbes strolling into the kitchen.

Dregs padded after him, flopped into his basket with a sigh, and was asleep within seconds. Late nights could obviously be too much for dogs, as well.

'Glad to see you up,' said Hobbes. 'D'you know you sleep like a baby?'

'Only when I was ill. I don't always wear nappies, you know.'

He laughed. 'I mean you suck your thumb.'

'Umm … it was probably scratched. But do you know what's happening with Featherlight?'

Hobbes, taking his place at the table, sighed. 'He's in a real pickle. I'll tell you after I've had my dinner.'

We feasted on the magnificent soup and fresh crusty bread before adjourning to the sitting room. Hobbes, having taken a slurp of tea, rested his mug on the coffee table.

'Featherlight,' he said, 'has been charged with the murder of the unidentified man who passed away in hospital this morning.'

'Does he still deny it?'

'Yes, though the evidence appears to be against him.'

'What evidence?'

'To start with, no fewer than twenty-three people witnessed an altercation between Featherlight and the deceased gentleman at the Feathers on Saturday evening. All agree that Featherlight punched him, put him in an armlock and dragged him outside. Approximately five minutes later, he was discovered unconscious in the alley by the side of the pub.'

'That would appear to be pretty conclusive.' I said. 'So why does he keep denying it?'

'He denies assaulting the man, who he says called himself Mike, or Mickey, but admits punching him.'

'What's the difference?'

'He claims the punch was in self-defence. He also admits putting him into an armlock and escorting him from the premises.'

I snorted. 'Escorting him from the premises? Is that what he said?'

Hobbes chuckled. 'Remember, he had been talking to a lawyer. What he means is that he thumped the man and threw him out.'

'In front of twenty-three witnesses.'

'Most of them entirely credible. They include Kevin Godley and Billy Shawcroft. They'll all stand up in court, if it goes there.'

'How will anyone be able to see Billy in the witness box?'

'Steps will be taken,' said Hobbes.

'But it sounds like Featherlight's not really got a case.'

'On the face of it, no.' He stroked his chin. 'However, there are some points that may be in his favour. Firstly, all the witnesses agree that he only punched the victim once when inside the pub, yet the man had received a thorough beating when he was found.'

'But he could have dragged the poor guy down the alley and done it.'

'True, though he'd have had to be quick and Billy is sure he was only outside for a matter of seconds. Of course, Featherlight can be surprisingly fast, in short bursts.'

'I know, I've seen him in action once or twice and he can be quite frightening.' I paused, as if to think and, to my surprise, a thought occurred. 'Who found the victim? If they found him only five minutes later, they might have seen or heard something.'

'Excellent,' said Hobbes, 'you're thinking well. A group of lads out on a pub-crawl found him and appear to have acted quite responsibly, despite being inebriated. One of them called for help on his mobile while the others did what they could to assist until the ambulance turned up.

'The strange thing is that we received another call about the incident a few seconds after the first.'

'Why was that strange?'

'Well, the caller, who wouldn't give his name, claimed to have witnessed Featherlight beating a man.'

'So, why didn't he stop him?'

'He said he tried to, but Featherlight attacked him and he had to run.'

'That sounds likely,' I said. 'I know I wouldn't like to mess with him. I reckon he did do it and is lying to save his skin.'

'That is possible,' said Hobbes, 'though he denies hitting anyone else.'

'Well, he would, wouldn't he?'

'Maybe, yet I've always known him to tell the truth, or at least the truth as he understands it. Still, I can't rule out the possibility that he is lying, especially with the charge being so serious. However, one of the lads who found him claims to have seen someone running away down the alley. Unfortunately, he couldn't give a description, other than that he thought it was a man. None of the others saw anything.'

'The guy was pissed, so how reliable is he?'

'I don't know,' said Hobbes, with a shrug, 'though I don't think he was as intoxicated as all that. Nevertheless, I might have agreed with your assessment, had it not been for that second phone call.'

'Which said Featherlight did it,' I said. 'I don't see how he's going to get out of this one. He's been close to going to jail for a long time and I can't see him keeping out of it again.'

Hobbes poured himself another mug of tea. 'He probably does deserve to go to prison, if only for his cooking, but I'm not convinced he's lying and wouldn't be surprised if the second phone call gets him off the hook. I think it would be very helpful if I could find whoever made it. There was one other thing, you know, that was extremely odd.'

'What?'

'Dregs. When we got there he refused to go down the alley. He stood at the entrance, trembling and bristling. The only time he's been like that before was at the Wildlife Park. What's more, I understood what was bothering him, because I sensed something wrong.'

'You were scared?' I couldn't believe it.

'No, not scared … stimulated more like …. I don't know … I'm still thinking about it.'

'But why?'

'I can't say for certain. There was something in the air, a scent, but it was strange, not exactly animal, and not exactly human.'

'Like a werewolf?'

'Not really. Besides, Dregs likes werewolves.'

He sat in thought for a few moments, the house silent, apart from Dregs snoring in the kitchen, until a car drove past, its occupants kindly sharing their music with the world.

'Of course,' said Hobbes, 'this case would be simpler if we knew the victim's identity. Unfortunately, he had no wallet, or keys, or anything that might identify him. That fact could be in Featherlight's favour, as he had nothing like that on him when he was arrested.'

'He could easily have hidden stuff.'

'He could, but I searched the area and found nothing. We are assuming, of course, that the victim had some personal effects to take and it's possible he didn't, though his expensive suit and shoes suggested he was well-off; in my experience, prosperous people usually have some identification about their persons. In addition, there was a white mark on his wrist, indicative of a watchstrap, but no watch. Again, Featherlight hadn't got it. Furthermore, he's never before robbed anyone he's thumped.'

'But there's got to be a first time for everything,' I said, 'and isn't it most likely that he did bash the poor guy and left him for dead in the alley? What if somebody else found him first, a tramp maybe, robbed him and then called the police because he had a bit of conscience.'

'It's one of the scenarios the CID lads are considering. It probably wasn't a tramp, though, since the second call was also made from a mobile.'

'You know,' I said, a thought occurring, 'I wouldn't be so sure that Featherlight has never robbed anyone. I saw him once thump a bloke called Lofty Peeke and take money from his pocket.'

'Ah yes,' said Hobbes, 'I remember the Lofty Peeke incident and, you're right, Featherlight did take money from him. In mitigation, he only took what he believed he was owed after Lofty had complained about his meal and refused to pay.'

'That's not much of an excuse.'

'No,' said Hobbes. 'But, there is another factor that must be taken into consideration: Billy says the Feathers has had considerably more awkward customers during the last month or so than is usual, all of them large, burly men, all of them looking for trouble. He reckons someone's trying to intimidate Featherlight.'

'I can't imagine him being intimidated by anyone – he's not even frightened of you.'

Hobbes held me in a disconcerting frown for a few seconds before laughing. 'You're right, he's not even frightened of me and, evidently, he wasn't intimidated by the victim, who was a large, burly man. Featherlight claims he'd attempted to be friendly, but that the man had, I quote, been a complete tosser.'

I shrugged. 'I can't imagine him being friendly with anyone, unless his idea of it is to knock someone's teeth down his throat.'

'True,' said Hobbes. 'He is not the most genial of hosts. By the way, I made a sketch of what the dead man might have looked like without two black eyes, a broken nose and a cracked skull.' Digging into his trouser pocket, he pulled out a crumpled sheet of paper.

Staggered, as always, at the dexterity of his massive fingers, I saw the image of a thickset young man with hard eyes and square jaw, an image that reminded me of someone.

'I think I know him,' I said.

'Really? Who is he?'

'Umm … I don't know.'

'So, in what sense do you mean you know him?'

'I've seen him around. His name's Mike.'

'So Featherlight said,' said Hobbes.

'Yes, but the thing is I think I saw this guy on Friday evening. He looks like the driver who picked up Felix after the picnic.'

'Are you sure?'

'Yes, if your drawing is accurate.'

'It's only a quick sketch, but, I flatter myself, it's a reasonable impression.'

I nodded, hot with excitement. 'What's more, I'd seen him before; I'm nearly sure he's the guy Featherlight knocked out when they were playing tennis and, come to think of it, his kit bag had a King Enterprises logo. It didn't mean anything at the time.'

Hobbes sat up from his habitual slouch. 'That's very interesting. How sure are you that it's the same man?'

'Quite sure … umm … I think. I wouldn't swear to it but I'd bet a tenner that it was, if I was a betting man and had a tenner.'

'That's good,' he said, 'though I'll need positive identification. How would you like to see the body?'

'Not at all,' I said, shuddering at the horrible thought, as an even worse one came to mind. 'You're not going to bring it back here are you?'

'Of course not. We'll go and take a look tonight, after supper, and make sure no one sees us.'

Something aroused my suspicions. 'We will go by way of the front door, won't we? That is, it will be an … umm … official visit, won't it?' Goosebumps were springing up all over.

'I wasn't thinking so much of going through official channels as going through the tunnels.'

'Why? Wouldn't it be best if I made an official ID?' I asked, not fancying going back underground, even with Hobbes.

'All in good time,' he said. 'For the moment, I think it would be better to keep what you said between ourselves.'

'But why?'

'Because, I don't want Felix King to know we've discovered the dead man's identity. I'm sorry he's a friend of yours but I suspect him of … not being entirely straight and don't wish to get his guard up.'

'He's not exactly a friend,' I said, 'not really. Not at all, in fact. He sort of …

umm … threatened me if I continued to see Violet.'

'Go on,' he said, slouching back onto the cushions.

I told him the entire story, including why I'd felt the need to ask about the wine. When I'd finished, he patted me on the shoulder quite gently. In fact, he barely left a mark.

'Never mind,' he said. 'I thought there might be a problem between you and that young lady. I now understand why you haven't seen her since the picnic.'

'It's not because I'm scared of Felix,' I said, 'although I am a bit, it's because I didn't get her telephone number or address. I can't believe how stupid I was.'

Smiling, he raised his eyebrows.

'Anyway, I got Felix's number off the card he gave me and called to check how she was getting on, but when his secretary realised who I was, she passed on his message that … umm … steps would be taken if I kept on importuning Violet. She did though, let on that Violet was alright but taking a few days off work.

'I wasn't importuning her. At least I don't think so; I'm not sure what it means. I just hoped the two of us had got, I don't know, something.'

'I would suggest,' said Hobbes, 'that you speak to her as soon as possible. I have observed that time can drive a wedge between friends who stop talking.'

'I'd love to, but don't know how to get hold of her. I was thinking of hanging around her office to see if I can talk to her when she gets back.'

'You could do that, or I could find her address for you. Besides, I think I'd enjoy a little chat with Mr King – concerning wine, you know? I might also try to find out about his driver, Mike.'

'When?'

'Right away. Would you like to come?'

'Me? Is that alright?'

'Of course, you can introduce us. Get dressed like a man of means, and quickly.'

Dashing upstairs, I put on a light-grey suit, a white silk shirt and, a rarity in Mr G's collection, a sober tie. It was only when I was adjusting the tie that I remembered Milord. He'd vanished, leaving behind a neat pile of perfectly repaired clothes.

'Very respectable,' said Hobbes, with an approving nod as I came downstairs, 'though I'm not quite sure about the slippers.'

Turning back, I put on a pair of glossy black brogues.

He was waiting by the door with two bottles of wine in his hand. 'Let's get going,' he said.

'Where to?'

'Mr King's offices, of course.'

'Where are they?'

'Didn't you look at his card?'

'Only at the phone number.'

'Go and get it.'

I ran upstairs, a bead of sweat trickling down my face. On reaching the top step, I remembered leaving the card next to the phone and, turning too fast, slipping, I bounced downwards with a series of undignified yelps.

'No need to rush, I've found it,' said Hobbes, handing me the bottles. 'Take these and let's go.'

Picking myself up, I hobbled after him and, since Dregs was still sleeping like a dog, I enjoyed the rare privilege of the front passenger seat and the feelings of terror and despair that came with it. I tried not to panic as he hurtled down The Shambles. The placard outside the *Bugle's* offices read, *Murdered Man Dies in Hospital. Police Suspect Homicide.*

'Where are we going?' I asked.

'Mr King's offices are in that new building off the Amor Lane Estate,' he said above the wailing of the brakes. 'Why is that Muppet slowing down?'

'Because he's approaching a busy roundabout,' I explained.

'Ah, a responsible driver.'

As we sped past the car, its driver, green-faced, goggle-eyed, stared, making me wonder why he was dressed as Kermit the Frog. I didn't wonder for long since Hobbes, taking the short, anti-clockwise route around the roundabout, despite the coach bearing down on us, drove everything else from my mind. Of course, we made it unscathed, leaving no casualties.

Within a few minutes, a sign for King Enterprises directed us towards a glistening, new steel and glass edifice, in a row with four similar buildings, adrift in a sea of car parks, grass and ornamental shrubs.

'I can't see any free spaces,' I said, looking around.

'This will do,' he said, driving onto a patch of lawn and stopping, 'but try not to trample the daisies. Follow me.'

He sprang from the car, slamming the door, marching towards the front of the building. As I scrambled after him, I dropped one of the bottles. Fortunately, my reactions were fast enough to catch it on my big toe. Picking up the bottle, I limped after him.

The door, one of those electronic ones that should open only after the correct code has been entered, gave way after one tug from Hobbes. Holding it open, he ushered me inside and up two flights of stairs; he didn't approve of lifts and I was just glad there were so few high-rise buildings in the area. At the top, we found ourselves in a shiny reception, smelling of newness, with potted plants, hard seats and a young woman with poodle hair and big glasses. She looked up, huge-eyed.

'Good afternoon, miss,' Hobbes boomed, 'we're here to see Mr King.'

'How did you get in?' she asked, her voice high and squeaky.

It wasn't Carol; I hoped her little kindness to me had not cost her.

'Through the door and up the stairs,' said Hobbes, advancing with what I assumed he meant as a friendly smile.

'Do you have an appointment?'

He waved his hand dismissively. 'I never bother with nonsense like that. Could you tell him Hobbes is here? It's about the wine.'

I held up the bottles.

'I'll see if he's available. Are you a wine merchant?'

'Just a friend,' said Hobbes, with a chuckle that turned her face white, despite the crust of make-up.

'And the other gentleman?' she asked, sticking to her guns.

'Is another friend.'

'Please, take a seat,' she said, leaving us at a brisk walk that became a rather undignified scurry as she exited the room.

Ignoring the seats, Hobbes followed her, so of course I followed him. The girl, hastening down a corridor, noticing we were on her tail, squeaked like a frightened mouse and plunged into a side room. When we got there, two burly security guards in black trousers and short-sleeved white shirts were waiting at the door. The girl was behind a table strewn with dirty mugs and even dirtier magazines.

'Excuse me, sir,' said the first guard, a tall man with a shaven head and a deep scar beneath one eye, 'I don't believe you have authorisation to be on these premises.' Stepping forward he placed his hand on Hobbes's shoulder. 'I'm going to have to ask you to leave.'

The other guard, shorter but broader, the possessor of an eternal stare, reached for Hobbes's other shoulder. I felt a weird mixture of relief that they weren't going to manhandle me, combined with indignation that they hadn't even appeared to notice my presence.

'Ask me then,' said Hobbes, smiling.

'Would you mind leaving the premises, sir?' asked the tall one, trying to push him back.

'Of course I wouldn't,' said Hobbes, 'after we've had our chat with Mr King.'

The guards, exchanging glances, pushed in unison. They had as much chance of moving him as the church tower. Adopting a different approach, they seized his arms, trying to drag him out, finding an old tree could not have rooted more firmly than he had.

'Please, leave the premises, sir,' said the tall one, red in the face and puffing, 'we wouldn't want to resort to force.'

'I wouldn't want you to either,' said Hobbes, pleasantly, 'because it wouldn't be worth it. As I believe I mentioned, we're not leaving until we've seen Mr King.'

In response, the shorter guard punched him in the stomach before spinning away, cradling his fist and groaning.

'Can we see him now?' asked Hobbes.

The taller one, adopting a karate stance, launched into a jumping kick, which might have looked quite impressive had the strip light hanging from the ceiling only been a couple of inches higher. As it wasn't, his leap being cut short by his forehead striking the fitting, his legs continuing forward with the momentum, he pivoted in mid-air, plunging down amidst a kaleidoscopic shower of splintered glass and would have landed flat on his back had Hobbes not caught him. Brushing the glass from the table, Hobbes laid the man, who was swearing, yet semi-conscious, on it.

Hobbes turned to the girl. 'Really, miss, wouldn't it be much easier if you just showed us into Mr King's office?'

She gulped, nodded and scuttled out like a nervous rabbit, while Hobbes busied himself with picking up the shattered glass and placing it in a bin.

'Did you have to do that?' I asked, feeling a certain sympathy for the security men, who'd only been trying to carry out their duties.

'Do what?'

'Umm ... whatever you just did.'

'I didn't do anything, did I?'

'No ... I know but ... umm ... couldn't you have not done it differently?'

'If I hadn't wanted to not do it in my own way.'

The conversation becoming tangled, I shook my head, giving up, sitting on the edge of the table, listening to the tall guard's incoherent cursing as a trickle of blood meandered down the side of his face into the shaven hair of his temple. The other guard paced up and down, rubbing and shaking his hand, avoiding eye contact.

Felix appeared at the door in a cloud of aftershave, the poodle-haired girl bobbing nervously behind him. I felt a little sorry for her, though not a lot, being unable to waste too much sympathy on anyone who would choose such a hairstyle.

'Andy, what a pleasant surprise,' said Felix, stepping forward, shaking my hand like a friend. Though his mouth smiled, there was no smile in his eyes, especially when they lighted on his two stricken guards. 'And this must be Inspector Hobbes.'

Hobbes nodded.

Felix, stepping forward, shook his hand without flinching. 'I'm delighted Andy has brought you to see me and I'm dreadfully sorry about the mix up. Had I known you were here I would, of course, have invited you straight in. It's not often I receive such a distinguished guest, but it's my secretary Linda's first day and she wasn't to know. She knows now of course and I trust she will prove more reliable than Carol, who let me down rather badly.' He glanced at me.

Though I felt incredibly guilty about Carol, I hoped she'd soon find a better employer.

'But enough of my business,' said Felix, 'let's go to my office.' He glanced towards his men. 'Get this place sorted out. I'll speak to you later.'

He took us from the side room, along a glass-walled corridor, past a rubber plant, a water dispenser and a number of cringe-worthy inspirational pictures, to his office. Full of daylight and gleaming metal, it dwarfed the reception and might have been considered a pleasant, airy room had his aftershave, or cologne, or whatever it was, not been so overpowering. Inviting us to sit on a soft, white leather sofa, he pulled up a matching chair for himself as we made ourselves comfortable.

Touching his fingertips together, Felix leaned back. 'It's very good of you to come. I appreciate you taking time out of your busy schedules to visit.'

I assumed he was having a dig at me.

'It's no trouble at all,' said Hobbes. 'I'm always glad to make the acquaintance of a fellow wine buff, and Andy reckons you are something of an expert.'

'Well, hardly an expert,' said Felix with a modest smile, 'merely an enthusiastic amateur.'

'If you say so,' said Hobbes. 'I thought you'd appreciate these. The '63 is reckoned to be an especially fine vintage. Andy, have you got the bottles?'

I placed them on the table in front of Felix.

Picking them up, he studied the labels. 'I expect he told you how much I'd like to get hold of a few crates of this. The thing is, I'm planning a celebration for when my current project is completed. In addition, I thought I'd like to market it. There would be, I'm sure, a great demand for a wine of such quality. We would, of course, split the profits equitably and, if it's all as fine as the bottle we enjoyed at the picnic, I think we would be in for a tidy sum. We'd have to make the label snazzier, of course, but, with a little advertising in select magazines we'd be onto a winner.'

Hobbes, shaking his head, looked sorrowful. 'Sorry but the wine is a gift from a friend and is not for sale.'

'But think of the money.'

'My friend has more than sufficient for his needs. He produces just enough wine to meet his own requirements and has no desire to expand his hobby.'

Felix sighed. 'A shame, but no matter, I respect his restraint. There are far too many people in my line of work who are only interested in accumulating money, even when they already possess far more than they could run through in a lifetime.'

'So, what is your motivation?' asked Hobbes.

'I can't deny that property development is a lucrative business, and I've made many killings over the years. Though I am a wealthy man, money is merely a means to an end.'

'And what is the end?'

'A better world, Inspector. I intend to play a role in the eradication of certain evils, evils that have plagued mankind since the dawn of time. That's my motivation.'

'What sort of evils?'

Felix's eyes gleamed. 'I intend to use my money to eliminate genetic mishaps.'

'That's a massive task.'

Felix nodded. 'I know. It's too much for one individual. I can't possibly rid the world of all its evils, but I might be able to make an impression on one or two of them. And, of course, it's not just me. A corporation such as this can achieve so much more, though it won't happen overnight. I'll have to see what I can do over the weekend.' He laughed, the gleam fading from his eyes.

'Philanthropy is a marvellous way to use your money,' said Hobbes, with great approval. 'I wonder ...' he paused, '... if it's not a bit cheeky, whether you might be able to do me a favour this weekend?'

'A favour?'

'Yes. You may be aware that there's to be a music festival? Well, a charity I'm involved with looks after underprivileged nippers, and I was wondering whether you might spare a car and driver to deliver them in the mornings and take them home afterwards. Andy mentioned that you have a driver ... Mike was it?'

It was the first I'd heard of any charity.

Felix shook his head. 'Alas, I can't help. Any other weekend, maybe, but I'm going to be busy.'

'You don't need to be involved at all,' Hobbes pointed out, 'other than by lending us a car and Mike – assuming he's willing, that is.'

'I'm afraid Mike Rook is no longer in my employment. I gather he inherited a plantation in Borneo, or some such place. He'd worked his notice, and was planning to fly out there last Saturday. I imagine he's there by now. It means, alas, that I am currently without a driver, which is inconvenient.'

'Not to worry,' said Hobbes. 'I can make other arrangements.' He glanced at a clock on the wall by Felix's desk. 'I say, is that the time? I'm afraid I have police business to attend to. I do hope you enjoy the wine and, if you do, I can let you have a crate for your party: as a gift of course.' He rose to his feet. 'Nice to meet you Mr King, but time and criminals wait for no man. Come along, Andy.'

Felix stood up and, to my regret, shook my hand again. 'Delighted you could visit. I hope we will meet again.'

'So long as it's not in my professional capacity,' said Hobbes with a pleasant laugh. 'Goodbye.'

'Goodbye, Inspector … Andy.'

As Hobbes and I walked back to the car, a small grey cat shot past, ears flat against its skull. It was lucky to escape the wheels of a reversing van.

'Stupid animal,' I muttered.

'No doubt she had a reason for her behaviour,' said Hobbes, opening the door.

'So,' I asked, 'what do you make of Felix?'

Resting his arm on the car's roof, he thought for a moment. 'Mr King struck me as a good man. He's obviously an intelligent businessman with a laudable vision of what he wishes to achieve and it's clear he has nothing to do with any of the recent funny business. Of course, I never thought it likely that he had. Sorenchester could do with more like him.'

As we got into the car, I was annoyed how Felix had fooled him so easily. Yet, when we were driving away he chuckled.

'What's so funny?'

'Mr King is. I hope I didn't overdo it, but flattery is like cream on a trifle; you can never lay it on too thickly.'

'What d'you mean?' I asked, confused.

'Mr King is not quite what he appears to be. I don't suppose you noticed him hiding in the shrubbery as we left? He got there extremely quickly and gave the cat a fright – it's lucky she wasn't squashed. I thought, since he was listening, I'd say something flattering.'

'He was listening? How? We weren't talking very loud.'

'He's got sharp ears.'

'Do you mean they're a bit pointed?'

'You noticed that did you? But I mean he has acute hearing.'

'Has he? ... Umm .... How did you know he was behind the bush?'

Hobbes's nose twitched. 'His aftershave is distinctive.'

'So, do you ... umm ... think Felix is actually involved in ... umm ... funny business? Did he attack Mike the driver?'

He shrugged. 'I don't know, yet, but I do know that he lied when he claimed Mr Rook was planning to leave; his name was still on the duty roster for next month.'

'What duty roster?'

'The one on the wall by his desk.'

'I didn't notice.'

'No, but I observe my surroundings. By the way, Miss King is now staying in London but will be returning on Friday.'

'How can you possibly know that?'

'There was a sticky note on his desk. But enough of that. Mr King worries me.'

'Me too.'

'There's something odd about him. Did you notice his scent?'

'I could hardly miss it.'

'No,' he said, shaking his head and slotting us into a minuscule gap between two cars, 'I don't mean his aftershave, I mean his own scent.'

'Are you saying he's smelly? I didn't notice but I think I know what you mean. One of my mother's larger friends didn't shower too often but slapped stuff on to cover it. The combination of perfume and stale sweat was overwhelming.'

'I don't mean that at all. The opposite rather … I couldn't pick up any scent from him. That stuff he wears seems to block everything.'

'Perhaps it's deodorant?' I suggested, having learned not to question his sense of smell, his nose seeming to match Dregs's.

'If so, it's a very effective one and he must use it all over, even on his hair. I wonder what he's hiding?'

'Perhaps he's embarrassed by body odours. Some people are.'

'Perhaps, but that's enough speculation. Hold tight.' He steered onto the dual carriageway, overtaking a convoy of lorries by driving along the verge.

I held my seat as tightly as I could, teeth rattling, until, having passed them all, we veered onto the road. 'Where are we going?'

'To have a word with Skeleton Bob, to tell him to be much more careful where he sets his snares. He might have hurt someone last night.'

'Some werewolf, you mean?'

'Werewolves are someone, too. Here we go.'

As he spun the wheel to the right, the car skipped through a gap in the crash barrier, straight across the opposite carriageway, dodging a petrol tanker bearing down on us. We made it, pursued by the discordant blaring of horns. Hobbes had once told me that if someone had time to sound the horn, he'd already decided there was no danger and was merely giving vent to his temper. I almost believed him.

We bumped off the carriageway onto the verge, up a steep slope, the engine straining and whining, across a patch of scrub and into the lane leading to Bob's place. The spherical Mrs Nibblet, glowing in a bright orange shell suit, reminding me of the space-hopper I'd had as a boy, was apparently picking nettles. She straightened up and frowned as we stopped.

'Oh, it's you again is it? What d'you want this time? Can't you go and arrest some real criminals instead of hassling us poor folk as is only trying to make a living?'

Hobbes, climbing from the car, bowed. 'Good afternoon, Mrs Nibblet. I'm not here to cause any unpleasantness; I just need a word with your husband.'

'Well, you can't. He's out. Goodbye.'

'Out you say? Then, that must be his identical twin peeking from the shed.'

'Oh, you bloody fool,' said Mrs Nibblet, rolling her eyes and shaking her head. 'You might as well come out now, why don't you?'

Skeleton Bob, emerging from the lopsided wooden shed by the house, scratched his head, smiling, displaying a set of coloured and disfigured teeth that even Mrs Goodfellow couldn't love. I wondered whether he'd ever visited a dentist.

'Hello, Bob,' said Hobbes.

Bob nodded, his eyes as wary as those of a hunted animal. 'What d'you want?'

'Just a pleasant little chat.'

356

Hobbes's smile didn't seem to reassure him.

Mrs Nibblet scowled. 'He's hardly left the house this last week. Don't you go nicking him for no good reason.'

Hobbes's eyebrows expressed shock. 'I wouldn't dream of it, madam. I'm not going to nick him, I'm here to offer a little friendly advice.'

Bob, his trousers heaving and writhing, as if containing a ferret, looked both suspicious and hopeful. Yelping, twitching, doubling up as if in pain, he reached into his pocket. 'Excuse me,' he said, pulling out a wriggling ferret by the scruff of the neck, walking towards the cage and dropping it inside. He turned back to face Hobbes. 'What do you mean?'

'All I want to do is to warn you …'

Mrs Nibblet sniffed. 'Threaten, more like.'

Hobbes beamed. 'I want to warn … no … encourage Bob, to take more care where he sets his snares.'

'They're nothing to do with me,' said Bob, trying to look innocent.

'Well you know best,' said Hobbes, raising his hands in mollification. 'I'll just say that one of those snares of yours might have caused a serious injury to a rare animal last night.'

'How do you know it was one of mine?'

'Oh, you fool!' Mrs Nibblet groaned. 'Just admit everything, why don't you?'

Hobbes tapped the side of his nose. 'I know many things. What do you set them for? Pheasants?'

Bob, with a glance at his wife, shook his head. 'No, I only set them for rabbits. When I want pheasants, I dazzle 'em with my lamp and catch 'em in my net.'

Mrs Nibblet slapped her forehead. 'Bob!'

'Oh, lawks,' said Bob. 'Now you've gone and snared me with all your clever words.'

Mrs Nibblet looked on the verge of tearing her hair out or punching her husband.

Hobbes, noticing my incredulous look, rolled his eyes. Skeleton Bob would never make it into Mensa. His name was on a long and varied criminal record, though he'd never been jailed, partly on account of the pettiness of his misdeeds, but mostly because the fines he paid far exceeded any harm he did. Though Hobbes tolerated his activities with just the occasional chat if he ever pushed his luck, more ambitious police officers, interested in meeting targets, took a less liberal view, with the result that Bob appeared in court every couple of months. It wasn't difficult to catch him or to get a confession.

'It doesn't matter, madam,' said Hobbes smiling. 'I know he's a poacher. You know he's a poacher. Even Andy knows he's a poacher. We also know he's not good at holding onto gainful employment and that money and food would be in short supply without his evening job. I also happen to know that he sells game to the milkman, who cheats him, and to the curate, who doesn't. Bob's not greedy, though, and doesn't take more than he needs.'

'That's true enough,' said Mrs Nibblet. 'He's soft in the head and I must be, too, for marrying him.' She smiled at her skinny spouse, who was hitching up his trousers again.

'No matter,' Hobbes continued. 'We were having a stroll through Loop Woods last night.'

'Did you see them?' asked Bob, looking as excited as his ferret, which was running bounding circuits of its cage.

'See what?'

'The big black cats. They were out.'

'Yes, we saw them.'

'I reckon,' said Bob, 'they may be dangerous, but they weren't the only things out. There was something else.'

'Bob!' cautioned Mrs Nibblet, shaking her head.

'I know there was,' said Hobbes, 'because it was that something else that got caught in your snare. I'm glad to say, it wasn't much hurt.'

'You see, Fenella?' Bob grinned. 'It's not just me. Mr Hobbes saw them as well and he's a policeman. Would you like a cup of tea?'

'That would be nice,' said Hobbes.

'We've only got nettle tea,' said Mrs Nibblet, 'we can't afford the shop stuff at the moment.'

'You can't beat a cup of nettle tea,' said Hobbes, smacking his lips.

I wasn't so sanguine. Nettles in my experience were horrible, nasty, vicious weeds that inflicted pain on the unwary. My worst memories came from a boiling hot day in the school holidays when, having sneaked from the garden I was meant to be weeding, I visited a little stream at the back of the playing fields. Since no one was around and since I was hidden by the weeping willows fringing the stream, I stripped to my pants for a paddle, making strenuous attempts at catching the wildlife that wiggled and darted through the muddy waters. I'd come close to landing some tadpoles and a stickleback when the sun's going in forced the goosebumps out. While trotting up and down the bank to dry off and warm up, a brilliant idea occurred: I could become Tarzandy, King of the Jungle. Though I had to contend with a scarcity of lions and a lack of creepers, it seemed to me that if I grasped a handful of the weepier branches, I could swing over the water and return safely to dry land.

It all worked beautifully, apart from the return safely to dry land part. Though I swung out in fine style, I'd failed to appreciate that my weight would bend the branches down. Despite my best efforts, my feet splashed up the water while my momentum was hurling me, at increasing pace, into the bank but not onto the bank. Raising my legs in desperation, I slid onto solid ground, cutting a path into the centre of a patch of stinging nettles. The more I struggled to get clear, the more they stung my bare skin, and by the time I got out, running home, howling and crying, I looked like a smallpox victim. I went off Tarzan after that.

When I came back to the present, Hobbes, seeming to know a great deal about the subject, was advising Bob how to set humane snares in rabbit runs where they would only be a danger to rabbits, thus sparing less-edible wildlife. They'd perched on a pair of discarded beer kegs that served as stools in the rickety, bramble-infested lean-to that pretended to be a porch. I joined them.

'I'll strive to be more careful in future,' said Bob.

Fenella waddled from the cottage bearing four non-too-clean mugs of nettle tea on a rusty tray. 'Here you go, lads,' she said, handing them round, lifting her ample backside onto a keg, which, being solidly made, groaned, but did not buckle.

My tea was in a cracked mug celebrating the coronation of Edward VIII, which seemed wrong somehow, though I couldn't work out why. Half thinking it might be a joke the others were in on and of which I was the butt, I sniffed the steaming liquid, a strange aroma reminding me of cut grass. Yet, as the others appeared to be drinking it, I risked a sip, finding it scalding hot, though not at all stingy, with an earthy, robust flavour that was quite pleasant.

Hobbes, taking a gulp, turned to Bob. 'So tell me about the other thing you saw in the woods?'

'Promise you won't laugh?'

'I promise.'

'Well, I'm not sure, but I think I saw … something I haven't seen before.'

'Go on.'

'Look, I've kind of felt something out there before, but last night was the first time I saw it proper. I was out setting my traps, trying to get 'em done before the rain came down, 'cause I could see we was in for a stinker.'

'And you were right, but what did you see?'

'I was coming to that,' said Bob, taking a slow sip and sighing. 'This is a lovely cuppa, love.'

Mrs Nibblet smiled.

He continued. 'I'd just got going when I felt the wood was … watchful, a bit like it is when the big cats come out, but not quite the same. It was sort of like the feeling when a fox is out, except this seemed more like curiosity than fear. I knew something was up, so I hid in a culvert and waited. I could feel it coming and then I saw it by a tree, cocking its leg like a dog.'

'What was it?' I had to ask.

'A werewolf.'

'Stuff and nonsense,' said Mrs Nibblet.

'No, really.' Bob glanced at Hobbes. 'You saw it too, didn't you?

'I did, and so did Andy. The creature saved him from the panther, only it got its paw snagged in one of your snares.'

'You see, Fenella?' Bob turned to her in triumph. 'They saw it too. Now what do you say?'

'That you're all soft in the head.'

Hobbes nodded. 'Unfortunately, that's the reaction you'll get if you tell anyone. They'll never believe you.'

'I know,' said Bob, his head nodding as if on a spring, 'I had enough grief when I told the boys down the pub about the big cats, and I was right about them an' all.'

'So it's best to keep things like this under your hat, then,' said Hobbes.

'That's the first sensible thing you've said,' said Mrs Nibblet. 'Perhaps you're not as daft as you look.'

'No one could be as daft as he looks,' I quipped, regretting my loose tongue as Hobbes's frown bored through me. 'Sorry.' I laughed nervously.

Then he chuckled, the Nibblets smiled, and I'd got away with it.

'We'd best be on our way,' said Hobbes, getting to his feet, 'or we'll be late for our suppers and it's cauliflower cheese tonight. Thank you for the nettle tea and your hospitality, Mrs Nibblet, and, Bob, remember what I said about snares. C'mon Andy, drink up. And quickly.'

I took a sip or two from my mug, though it was still scalding hot, and handed it back three-quarters full. Mumbling my thanks, I got back in the car. As we drove away, I was puzzled, if pleased, that Hobbes was driving with care and consideration, keeping within the speed limit. As we parked on Blackdog Street, the front wheel dropped off.

'I'll get Billy to fix it,' said Hobbes, getting out, bounding up the steps to the front door.

'Does he know about cars?' I asked, as I followed. 'I thought he was only a barman.'

'Only a barman? No, if you want anything mechanical fixed, Billy's your man.'

As soon as the door opened, Dregs, having obviously slept off last night's exertions, his delight in seeing us evident, overwhelmed me. Though I appreciated the welcome, I wished he hadn't knocked me down the steps and, though I assumed he hadn't meant to do it, he made a noise very much like a snigger as I sprawled in the gutter, before dancing around me with a toothy grin. Every time it had happened, I'd made mental notes to be more careful, but events nearly always erased them.

Picking myself up, slapping the dust from my jacket, I entered the house, showing as much dignity as I could muster with a party of excited camera-wielding Japanese tourists for an audience.

Still, all my woes fell away as we sat down for supper, for, having finished my course of antibiotics, my taste buds had returned to life. Their resurrection, combined with Mrs G's cauliflower cheese, outstanding even by her standards, was almost like a religious experience and brought tears to my eyes.

'Too hot for you?' Hobbes grinned. 'If I were you, I'd let it cool. Now, is there any more, lass?'

'It's fine,' I said, as the old girl refilled his plate. 'In fact it's perfect. A perfect end to the day.'

'Not quite the end of the day. You've got to identify a body first.'

I felt like a man who, clinched in a slow smooch with the most beautiful girl at a dance, has just realised the large, muscle-bound, tattooed hooligan approaching him is her boyfriend. I had once been that man and Leticia, for that had been her name, had used me to make her man, Crusher, jealous. Though things had worked out very well for Leticia and Crusher, my evening had ended in a skip.

'Do I have to? I'm tired and I don't want to go down those tunnels again.'

'Oh yes,' said Hobbes, 'the tunnels – I was joking but, since the car's out of action, the tunnels might be the easiest way of getting there.'

'What about a taxi?'

'I don't think that's a good idea; I can never bring myself to trust taxi drivers. No, you've convinced me, the tunnels are the best way.'

I had long ago realised that he didn't like being driven, perceiving most drivers, other than Billy, as dangerous. He had a point, I supposed: other drivers had accidents but, when he crashed, it was deliberate, or so he said.

We sat on the sofa watching a lousy film and, despite all my efforts, yawns kept breaking loose. I hoped Hobbes would regard them as a symptom of extreme fatigue and have pity. During a particularly wide and extended yawn, he turned to me.

'I see this film doesn't interest you. I'm not surprised. Anyway, the morgue will be as quiet as the grave now, so it's a good time to visit.'

I shivered. 'I hope it's quiet all the time. Do we really have to go?'

'Yes.'

'Can I take a torch?' I asked, fighting to stay calm.

'If you want. The lass keeps one in the drawer in the kitchen and it might have batteries. Grab it if you want; she won't mind; she uses it when she's cleaning the cupboards. Let's go.'

He got up, heading towards the cellar with Dregs at his heels.

Although the torch did contain working batteries, I'd have felt considerably happier had it been bigger and brighter than a cigarette lighter. I took it anyway, even if it provided more reassurance than light. When I reached the cellar, the coal pile was not in place and Hobbes was standing with his ear to the tunnel door, listening. So was Dregs. The hairs on my neck bristled.

'What's up?'

'Shhh!' He stepped back, a hairy finger pressed to his thick lips.

Dregs whined, standing alert in front of us as the doorknob slowly turned. Something was trying to get into the cellar and I felt a desperate urge to get out, though my legs, in a display of reckless loyalty, refused to leave Hobbes.

As the door swung back, I could hear shuffling footsteps, while cold, damp air seemed to be crawling around my feet. Shivering, I gulped, wanting to scream, to run, baffled as to why Hobbes was smiling and Dregs was wagging his tail. When something small and brown appeared in the doorway, I gasped; the last thing I'd been expecting was a shopping basket.

A small, skinny figure stepped into view.

'Hello,' she said. 'Can someone give me a hand with my baskets?'

Hobbes, took the basket from the floor, reached into the darkness for another and carried them upstairs. One contained a pair of steam irons and the other a large, bony-looking fish. I assumed she'd bought them somewhere, though I couldn't quite let go of the idea that she'd merely taken them for a walk.

As I watched Hobbes, Dregs and Mrs Goodfellow leave the cellar, I realised with a chill of horror that I was alone, standing with my back to the open door of the tunnels. Turning, I peered into the blackness below, fearing something was coming. The feeling was too much to bear, so, running forwards, wary of the steep steps, I grabbed the knob and pulled the door shut. A metallic chink came from behind it, repeating several times, diminishing like a fading echo. I was puzzled until I tried to lock the door.

'Sod it!' I muttered, clenching my fists, the fear of troglodytes, and God only knew what else, having access to the house, forcing me to act, to go below, to retrieve the key. After all, it would only be at the bottom of the steps; there would be no need to go any further, and I had a torch. What's more, Hobbes knew where I was and would, no doubt, follow in a matter of seconds. Though I could have waited, I had to prove something to myself.

Taking a couple of deep breaths, setting my jaw in a rugged, determined grin to underline my resolve, I turned the knob, pushed open the door and faced the void. My torch gleaming faintly, I stepped down, finding that, as the darkness deepened, its beam strengthened, revealing strange, intricate patterns carved into the dripping stone. I didn't dare spare any time examining them. Walking down took much longer than falling down and I had to force myself to continue. When I reached the bottom, the torch fading quickly, flickered and died. Though I shook and banged it, it was a goner. I became aware of a faint, distinct stink, like a combination of sour milk and day-old cabbage water.

In the dimness, I could just make out the key, lying in the puddle. I wondered whether the puddle was permanent, or just a result of heavy rain, and imagined it growing into a lake during the depths of winter. Bending down, groping for the key, I found the water so cold it hurt. The bad smell was growing stronger; I tried not to breathe it in.

As my hand closed round the key, there was a noise like the suckers on a rubber bath mat being pulled up, something plopped into the puddle, and the water swirled. I fled, taking the steps two or even three at a time. On reaching the cellar, I yanked the door closed behind me and locked it, though I didn't feel safe until I'd run upstairs into the kitchen.

The old girl was scaling the fish in the sink. 'Are you alright, dear?'

I nodded, panting too hard to speak, and slumped onto a chair. Hobbes was on the phone in the sitting room.

'So,' he said, 'we have a positive identity? Well, that saves me a job … Thank you … Goodbye.'

The receiver clicked down and Hobbes returned to the kitchen.

'That,' he said, 'was the station. The lab has confirmed the body is that of Michael Peter Rook. He'd served time for GBH, among other things, and they were able to match his fingerprints. Furthermore, he didn't die of his original injuries. He'd been smothered in his hospital bed. That's good news, eh?'

'Good news?' My voice was shaky. 'Why?'

'Well, firstly, it means Featherlight couldn't have been responsible for his death and, secondly, you don't have to identify the body. Thirdly, it's going to be fun finding out who did kill him … and why.'

'I see.' I could have punched the air at my reprieve. To be honest, I'm not sure I could have forced myself back down the tunnels, though I bet Hobbes could have.

'I'll just lock up,' he said.

'I've already done that.'

'Well done.'

'Thanks. Umm … I dropped the key and went to get it and I think something was clinging to the wall. It dropped into the puddle … I don't know what it was.'

'Nor do I,' said Hobbes, 'but those suckers stink.'

'They certainly do. Are they dangerous?'

'I expect so, but they've never done me any harm.'

Though he didn't reassure me, the relief of not having to go to the morgue made me euphoric, almost as if I'd downed a couple of bottles of wine. When Hobbes returned to the cellar to replace the coal, the existence of the extra barricade made me feel even better. I slipped across the kitchen floor and landed a kiss on the old girl's cheek, as warm and as soft as velvet.

'Thank you, dear,' she said and surprised me by blushing. Then she inserted a thin knife blade into the fish and its guts fell out, stinking and slimy.

'Fish tomorrow?' I asked.

'No, dear.'

I pointed at the mess in the sink. 'So, why are you gutting it?'

'It's something to do while I think.'

'What are you thinking about?'

'The festival. I'm just making sure I haven't forgotten anything. Ensuring the punters are safe and have a good time is very important.'

'I'm sure it is,' I said, smiling, thinking she wasn't a typical security guard.

'Ah, yes,' said Hobbes stepping back into the kitchen. 'I'm planning to go there first thing in the morning to make sure everything's safe before the crowds turn up. I thought I might turn in early tonight, as I doubt I'll be getting much sleep over the weekend. And Andy, make sure you pack a bag.'

When he went to bed, it was only nine o'clock. Though it seemed very early, after pushing a few clothes and other essentials into the old canvas kit bag that had been left by my bed, I too turned in.

When I awoke, it hardly seemed a minute had passed.

Despite the scent of frying bacon making my mouth water, the comfort of warm blankets, for a few minutes, was even more alluring. Even in my drowsy state I knew this to be unusual, the old girl's cooking having proved far more effective at getting me up than the alarm clock I'd relied on back in the days when I'd had a job. I couldn't understand why I was so heavy with sleep that I didn't want to move. Still, in the end, the bacon won. Sitting up, opening my eyes, I found it was so dark I feared we must be in for a storm, like the ones that had afflicted so many festivals I'd seen on the telly.

I dragged myself from bed, yawning across the room, and pulled open the curtains, surprised the street lighting was still on, as if in the middle of the night. Dazed, I washed, dressed and fumbled down the dark stairs to the kitchen, where I stood blinking in the doorway, fluorescent light battering my bleary eyes.

The old girl was at the cooker, sizzling bacon in a pair of blackened cast-iron pans that I struggled to lift. When she raised one in each hand to shake them, I feared her skinny wrists would snap, but she seemed as unperturbed as Dregs, who was still sprawled in his basket, emitting gentle snores. Hobbes, dressed alarmingly in his blue striped pyjamas and kitten slippers, leant across the table, slicing slabs of bread from a vast white loaf.

'Good morning,' he said.

'Is it?' I asked, too dozy to argue, sitting down at the table and yawning.

'You're up early,' said Mrs G by way of greeting.

'So are you. Why?'

Flipping a rasher, she examined it for defects and, finding none, flipped some more. 'Well, dear, it's going to be a busy day, so we thought we'd best make an early start. We weren't planning on waking you yet.'

'Thanks … but what are we going to do?'

'Keep people safe,' said Hobbes, waving the bread knife a little too close to my nose. 'The lass and her team will be ensuring there's no trouble with the festival-goers, while I'll be undercover, mingling, being inconspicuous.'

I tried not to laugh.

'And I'll keep an eye out in case other things cause trouble,' he continued.

'You mean the big cats?'

'I do in part, but I'll be policing as well, seeing that nothing goes on that shouldn't.'

'What can I do?' I asked, feeling like a spare part.

'You can enjoy the music … but keep alert and let me know of anything you think I should know. In the meantime, would you care to saw this bread while I get changed? When you've finished this loaf, there are three more in the pantry; that should be sufficient.' He handed me the bread knife.

'Sufficient for what?' Since he'd already carved a small hill of slices, I reckoned it might not all be for us.

'For you two and for my security lads,' said Mrs Goodfellow. 'They'll be getting to the farm for seven and I think it's only right and proper that they start the day with a decent bit of breakfast in their bellies.'

'And when do we get ours?' The aroma having wakened my stomach, it was grumbling and groaning quietly like a disappointed audience.

'When we get there.'

'So … umm … what time is it now?'

'Nearly four o'clock.'

I sighed, glancing out the window where a brittle, monochrome light was becoming apparent and a chaffinch began to sing. Twice in three days, I'd witnessed the sunrise and, much as I appreciated it, I hoped it wasn't habit forming.

I set to work, building a tottering tower of sliced bread, which the old girl, butter knife in hand, jar of home-made chutney chinking, converted into bacon sandwiches, hiding them away in a succession of brown paper bags. To my regret, not a single sandwich finding its way to me, I had to make do with a handful of the crumbs from the breadboard. Fortunately, there was a pot of tea and a couple of steaming mugs provided temporary respite. Still, I couldn't say I wasn't jealous when Dregs woke up and she treated him to a selection of bacon scraps.

I sat, watching as she scrubbed the dishes. She was wearing her normal checked skirt, a brown cardigan and, as a concession to the event, a pair of green wellington boots, very much down-at-heel.

'Shouldn't you have a uniform or something?'

'I have, dear,' she said, turning round, pointing to a badge pinned to the middle of her cardie. 'All the lads have them. Miss Pipkin typed them for us on her computer and Billy Shawcroft had them laminated. Nice aren't they?'

The badge read 'Festical Sexurity'.

'Shouldn't that be 'Festival Security'?'

'Yes, dear, but old Miss Pipkin's eyesight is not so good these days and I didn't want to upset her. Anyway, it might have been worse.'

'Much worse,' I said, smirking, 'though they won't do much for your authority, will they? Won't everyone laugh at you?'

'They might, if anyone notices. But that's not such a bad thing.'

'Isn't it?'

'No, dear. Laughter can dispel tension.'

'I suppose it can,' I said, thinking that not all laughter was well meant.

Hobbes's reappearance drove out such thoughts, replacing them with horror and a large dollop of amusement. Dregs, growling, retreated under the table, barking at Hobbes's hairy feet, which were enclosed in an ancient pair of leather sandals. I averted my eyes.

'It's time to load the car,' said Hobbes. 'Would you give me a hand?'

'Umm … yes.' I said, controlling myself, following him to the sitting room, wondering where the hell he'd found his clothes. Though I'd have been the first to admit my ignorance of things sartorial, even I knew the summer of love had run its course in 1967. I'd heard rumours of maroon velvet, flared trousers, but had never truly believed such things existed. He was also wearing what might have been an orange kaftan; if so, it was one for a much shorter person, barely covering his belly, the sleeves cut off at the elbow. His rectangular, blue-tinted sunglasses might have looked cool were they not beneath a stained, broad-brimmed, brown-suede hat, and I was sure his psychedelic glass beads would have been a bad idea at any point in history.

Even so, his clothes weren't the worst of it; even more alarming were the long, black, snaggly wig and the immense, droopy moustache. He was going to be as inconspicuous as a bull in a boudoir, though, in fairness, I doubted anyone seeing him would immediately think police officer.

I wondered why there was a pile of poles and tattered khaki rags on the floor.

'Right,' said Hobbes, 'let's pack the tents first.'

By the looks of them, he'd got them from Army Surplus at some point between the wars.

'I'll carry this lot if you open the boot. Take these.' Tossing me the keys, stooping, he scooped the whole lot into his massive arms.

Within a few minutes, we'd packed the car, all four of us squeezing into whatever space remained. I ended up with Dregs sitting on my lap, since he'd also been relegated to the back seat to make way for Mrs Goodfellow. Only when we were hurtling towards the festival site did I remember the front wheel, guessing Billy had fixed it overnight. I hoped he'd not been too drunk and, since we made it without any problems, I guessed he hadn't been.

As we arrived at Loop's Farm, Bashem and Bullimore, leaning on the gate in the same pose as when I'd last seen them, directed us towards a large, flat, grassy field where we parked in the farthest corner, beside a crumbling stone wall. The next field along, glinting green in the morning sun, sloped gently down towards a pair of stages between towering cliffs of speakers, awaiting the crowds. I had to admit it, everything looked surprisingly professional.

I got out of the car, clutching myself and groaning, for Dregs was never careful where he put his great paws when excited, and he was very excited. Racing across the field, he bounced around the farmers, as if they were old friends.

As Mrs G went to liaise with them, Hobbes and I carried the tents to a suitable spot. Truthfully, I only carried a tent peg that he dropped but I think my moral support was invaluable. His method for pitching tents involved a great deal of grunting and reminded me of Jonah being swallowed by the whale. I helped where I could, running round, lifting and pushing wherever it looked useful. Hobbes appeared to have gone down for the third time, when, emerging briefly, he handed me two lengths of twine.

'Hold tight and don't let go,' he said.

Only when both structures were up and he was battering the last pegs in with his fist did I realise I was holding both ends of a length of baler twine, with no connection with camping whatsoever.

'Well done, Andy, thanks,' he said, grinning through his new-fangled moustache, and pointing. 'This one's ours and that's for the lass and Dregs. Now, let's get the bedding inside.'

Whereas I'd hoped for camp beds and sleeping bags, we had a pile of rugs and blankets. The ground looked hard and lumpy.

We'd just finished when I was delighted to see the security crew turn up, which meant Mrs Goodfellow could dole out the bacon butties. She had, of course, prepared plenty for everyone, and there was enough left over to feed the pack of young Bashems who'd emerged from the farmhouse in great excitement.

After a couple of sandwiches, Hobbes, taking Dregs, vanished in the direction of Loop Woods, leaving the security crew to stand around trying to look important, giving the impression of being nervous. They weren't the big, rough lads I'd been expecting, apart from one hulking yet wobbly youth called Arnold, who was there with his dad, a slight, balding man with a paunch exaggerated by a knitted blue cardigan. The rest of them weren't much to look at either, being, for the most part, friendly, middle-aged blokes. One was actually wearing a red bow tie. Yet, the old girl, as she issued orders, exuded an air of quiet confidence that almost reassured me. Trucks and vans started arriving from nine o'clock, carrying caterers and stallholders onto the site.

I was free to mooch around, the only drone among the workers, a most pleasant sensation. The sun was warm, the scent of cut grass soothing, my belly full, as I stretched out in a patch of tiny, aromatic yellow flowers, watching the swifts and swallows swooping and soaring in the forget-me-not blue sky. Yawning, I shut my eyes, awaking to the strumming of an imperfectly tuned guitar.

I sat up, bleary, heavy-limbed, blinking in the bright summer sunshine, to see a line of cars and vans blocking the lane onto the farm, along with a mass of pedestrians. Mrs Goodfellow and Arnold's dad were at the gate, collecting tickets, letting the punters in and, since hundreds of tents had already sprouted like toadstools across the field, it took me a few moments to work out where ours were.

People were everywhere, talking, eating, strumming guitars and dancing. A spotty-faced troubadour, leaning against the wall, his hair like a failed experiment by a drunken basket-weaver, was twanging his instrument and chanting in a nasal monotone. Though a great believer in self-expression, I couldn't help thinking there should be limits.

I went towards the gates, looking for Mrs Goodfellow, hoping for food, finding only Arnold's dad addressing a group of hard-faced, shaven-headed, tattooed, young men.

'Sorry, gentlemen,' he said, 'I'm afraid you can't come in without a ticket, but I believe Mr Bullimore still has a few left, if you wish to purchase them.'

'We're not,' said a nightmare figure with a spider's web tattooed across his face, 'going to buy any tickets. Now, it's bloody obvious there's no way a fat, old git like you is gonna stop us getting in, so step aside and no one gets hurt. Right?'

'Sorry, my friends. No tickets, no entry.'

The men muttered and swore, bunching together, leaning over Arnold's dad.

'I'm not getting through to you, am I?' said the man with the facial tattoo, shoving Arnold's dad in the chest before dropping to his knees, moaning. 'Ooh, that hurt … that really hurt. What did you do that for?'

'I'm sorry to inconvenience you, sir, but I was merely ensuring my message got through to you and your friends. We have a rule: no tickets, no entry. I didn't make it, but I will enforce it.'

The group helped their sobbing friend back to his feet and led him away. He was walking slowly, with extreme concentration, and none of the rest seemed inclined to argue. Arnold's dad, smiling, continued to collect tickets, chatting to people as if nothing had happened.

As I wandered around, I caught up with Hobbes, sitting cross-legged on the grass, pounding a bodhran amidst an impromptu bunch of drummers before a crowd of admirers. That the crowd was mostly young and female both surprised and irritated me, though I had to admit he had a mean sense of rhythm.

'The big guy can't 'alf play,' said a skinny girl with too much eye make-up.

'Ah, but you should hear him sing,' I replied, which was nasty.

'Give us a song,' she cried, and the chorus joined in.

'Right on,' said Hobbes, screwing up his face, closing his eyes and bursting into a rendition of 'Puff, the Magic Dragon'.

Those nearby clamped hands to ears and fled, even his fellow drummers. Those further afield stopped whatever they were doing and looked stricken. It wasn't that he sang out of tune, which he didn't, or that he mangled the lyrics, which he did, it was the sheer, gut-tearing volume. Finishing, he opened his eyes, looking up as if anticipating applause and I think I detected a hint of surprise, or maybe disappointment, that I was the only one left.

He grinned. 'Hi, man, where've you been?'

'Sleeping in the sun, but I guess it must be lunchtime now. Do you fancy getting a bite?'

'Why not? There's a stall selling hot roast pork or beef rolls, how about one of them?'

'That sounds perfect.'

'Come on then.'

We strolled to the food zone, from where the most delicious smells arose, and bought a couple of enormous pork rolls with apple sauce.

'Thanks,' I said, taking mine. 'Umm ... I didn't know you could drum?'

'Yeah, man, though I haven't played much since I left the Army.'

We leaned against a mossy, old stone wall, munching, keeping it all together with difficulty, for the rolls were full to overflowing.

'Have you seen any signs of the panthers?'

'No. At least, no new ones. I did find some spoors, but they were at least two days old, which might suggest the cats have moved on. Then again, it might not. Still, I think everyone's likely to be safe. The sheer number of people here, not to mention the noise, should keep the creatures away.'

'What about ... umm ... the werewolf?'

'If he's around, he'll be no trouble, unless something upsets him.'

'What's going to upset him?'

Hobbes shrugged, pushing the remains of his roll into his mouth, chewing slowly, observing the crowd. Finishing my last piece of pork, I wiped my mouth with the serviette, which seemed to spread more grease than it absorbed.

'Right,' he said, walking away, 'I'm off to patrol. I'll see you later.'

I mooched about, listening, watching and absorbing the atmosphere. A couple of hours later, Hobbes reappeared.

'All seems well,' he said, with a smile. 'Hullo, something's about to happen.'

'Ladies and gentlemen,' said Bernie Bullimore, sporting a sparkling red waistcoat and a battered top hat, his voice booming over the sound system, 'welcome to the First Annual Grand Sorenchester Music Festival. I'm delighted so many of you are here and hope we've got a programme with something for everybody. Though we don't officially kick-off until five o'clock, we've had a young band turn up and they're desperate to play. I thought we'd given 'em a chance.'

Like many others, Hobbes and I headed towards the stage, passing an oddball bunch of hippie types, among whom even Hobbes would not have stood out too far. They were sitting cross-legged, facing the stage.

'Oh, no,' said one as Hobbes stepped round him, 'it's the Pigs.'

Bernie's voice roared out across the fields. 'Ladies and gentlemen, please give a massive Sorenchester welcome to the Pigs.'

To give the crowd its due, there was a spatter of cheering and even one or two whoops but, mostly, it clapped politely, as five lads shambled onto stage and picked up their instruments.

A tall, skinny youth grasped the microphone. 'Good afternoon, we're the Pigs. One, two, three … er …'

'Four!' prompted a loud mouth in the crowd, to much laughter.

The singer counted the band in again, punching the air when he reached 'four' and the song would probably have been more impressive had the sound system worked. We could hear the tinny, un-amplified drums and the guitarist's aggrieved moaning before the crowd's guffaws drowned it out. The Pigs slouched off stage, returning ten minutes later, when the problems had been rectified. An hour later, I think most agreed their first set had been the better one. Still, the lads had tried and, as they trooped off, fists clenched, they generated a smattering of applause, which, taking as a sign of approval, encouraged them to come back for an encore.

'Thank you, Sorenchester,' the singer bellowed and, something striking him on the forehead, collapsed face first onto the stage.

Having seen nothing, I was reluctant to point the finger at Hobbes, who, chuckling, wiped his hands on his velvet trousers as the band trudged off, bearing their stricken leader.

'Rock and roll,' said Hobbes. 'Who's on next, man?'

'Umm … It's the Famous Fenderton Fiddle Fellows at five. What time is it now?'

Hobbes, with a glance at the horizon, answered, 'Half-past four.'

I wondered how he knew, until I realised he'd been looking in the direction of the church clock, at least four or five miles away. I was impressed, though, for all I knew, he could have been lying. People were still arriving and I'd guess there were several thousand on the site, their tents as many and as close together as zits on a teenager's chin. Hobbes wandered off to make sure Mrs G was alright, although, with Dregs at her side, I didn't expect she'd have had much trouble, even if anyone had felt inclined to try anything. Besides, with the exception of the bunch Arnold's dad had turned away, everyone seemed in a friendly mood, gathering in small groups, chatting, laughing and occasionally singing. Queues snaked across the field towards the catering vans, beer tents and toilets.

I went over to watch a young man in motley garb juggling a handful of assorted cook's knives before a fascinated audience. We gasped with astonishment when, spinning a cleaver in a high loop, he bounced it off his forehead, carrying on as if it had been part of the act. Only when blood dripped into his eyes did he lose control, receiving several spectacular stab wounds and fainting as the knives responded to gravity. A team of St. John's Ambulance carried him away, along with the capful of small change he'd earned for his pains.

I wandered through the crowd seeing other, more successful, if less spectacular, jugglers, along with magicians, buskers and face-painters, narrowly avoiding getting my face painted by a hefty, determined lady in dungarees, escape only becoming possible when she discovered I was broke. I've tried to suppress memories of how she found this out, but it involved some pain and a loss of dignity. A number of brawny young blokes, their arms adorned with tangles of fantastic tattoos, laughed at my plight before heading towards the beer tent, which was doing a roaring trade.

To my surprise, when the Famous Fenderton Fiddle Fellows took to the stage, they'd transmuted from the drunken shambles I remembered into a good-time band, quite matching the spirit of the occasion. The crowd danced and sang and even I found my feet tapping. Hobbes was on the far side, apparently attempting to fit waltz steps to a rock beat, alternately smiling at the people around him and apologising when he stepped on them.

Towards the end of the set, a girl with long blonde hair and big hazel eyes, catching hold of my wrist, dragged me, protesting slightly, into a space where we and several others bobbed and gyrated to the music. The way she was smiling at everyone made me suspect the lager I could smell on her breath was not the only substance she'd taken. At the end, hot and sweaty, heart thumping, I dropped to the grass, my new friend, sprawling across me, kissed me hard on the lips.

I responded with a squeeze that made her giggle, until, pushing herself up on her arms she stared into my face with a look of disgust. 'You're not Wayne,' she said, getting to her feet, leaving me.

'Hello, Andy,' said a familiar voice, 'I'm glad to see you're enjoying yourself.'

Felix King, dressed in an immaculate linen suit, was looking down on me.

I sat up. 'Umm ... Hello ... I didn't know you'd be here.'

'It's always good to meet the locals. I'll see you around.'

He strolled away towards the camping field, a pair of large, intimidating young men in dark suits following and, to my horror, Violet walking in front. She was stunning in a diaphanous pale-green sundress, showing off her slim, tanned shoulders and I realised with dismay that she must have walked past when I'd been rolling in the grass with the strange girl. I wanted to run and explain myself, to tell her that what she'd seen wasn't what it looked like, but Felix, having caught up with her, putting his arm around her, glanced back at me, shaking his head.

My spirits plummeted. I feared I'd blown it and lost her forever. I pounded the turf with my clenched fists.

'What's that poor grass ever done to you, mate?' asked a bloke in a baseball cap, watching me with an infuriating grin. He walked away when I ignored him.

Getting back to my feet, I came to a decision that, whatever the risk, I was going to talk to her and explain. If she then told me to shove off, I was done for, yet there was a chance she'd listen and understand. As for Felix and his heavies, I didn't care; they could do their worst. Not that they were likely to do much in a packed field.

The crowd was swelling in anticipation of the next act, which I assumed, because of the cries of 'Come on Tim', was Tiny Tim Jones, who'd been released on parole. When at last I pushed my way through and out the other side, there was no sign of Violet, or Felix and his merry men. I walked around for a while, disconsolate.

Mrs G and Dregs were still by the gate. She was counting the ticket stubs out onto a table and frowning.

'Hello, dear,' she said, as I approached, 'are you enjoying yourself?'

'Yeah, I am,' I said, stroking Dregs's head. 'Umm … you look worried. Is something the matter?'

'Well, dear, the thing is, Mr Bullimore said he'd sold three-thousand tickets, but I've got more stubs than that.'

'Forgeries, maybe? At thirty quid a ticket, someone might have thought it worthwhile.'

'I fear you may be right, dear, but they all look genuine. I'll ask the old fellow when he turns up; he's good at spotting things. Have you seen him?'

'Yes, he was dancing.'

'I'm glad. He's good at it.'

'Umm … I'm not sure good is the right word, he was treading on people.'

'I expect it's because of this modern music and the grass. He can do a wonderful foxtrot on a sprung floor.'

'He looked more like a fox with the trots.' I smirked.

The old girl gave me her 'stern' look. 'Did you do any better?'

'Sort of. I danced with a young lady.'

'Good for you, but why are you looking so glum?'

'Because Violet saw me.'

'Well, a dance can't hurt.'

'Umm …' I said, squirming and blushing, 'we weren't actually dancing when she saw us … we were sort of rolling around in the grass.'

Mrs G's eyebrows rose and her eyes twinkled behind her glasses. 'I see.'

'No, you don't … I didn't mean it to happen … in fact, I'm not sure how it did happen and I wish it hadn't … At least not when she could see me. I want to explain it was all a mistake, but I can't find her and I don't know what she'll say if I do … and I'm not sure what Felix will do to me if … when I speak to her.'

'He won't do anything while I'm around.'

'Thank you. I'm going to talk to her whatever happens.'

'Well, take care, dear and don't do anything too foolish. I suspect millionaires won't be spending the night in a tent; if I were you, I'd check those camper vans on the edge of the site.'

'Thanks, I will, though I thought they were heading this way. Perhaps they're staying in the farmhouse?'

'I doubt it, dear. There can't be much room inside with six children, not to mention Mr and Mrs Bashem and Mr Bullimore.'

'Six? I thought there were an awful lot of them. Oh well, I expect they're all out enjoying the music.'

'I expect so, dear. Anyway, here's young Arnold come to take over the gate.'

Arnold wobbled towards us, a large paper cup of cola in one hand, an even larger burger in the other. He nodded with a greasy grin. Though, since living at Hobbes's, burgers had lost much of their appeal, the sight of it, combined with the scent of fried onions, made me realise I was quite hungry. I wondered what I could do about it.

'Well, unless anything happens, I'm off duty until midnight,' said Mrs G. 'I'll go and make supper. I expect you'll be hungry; I know the old fellow will be.'

'I was starting to feel a bit peckish,' I admitted. 'What are you going to do?'

'Chicken in the bucket.'

'Can I help?'

'No, dear, it's all prepared. I just need to mix it up and get it on the heat. It'll probably be ready after the next act.'

'Umm ... did you really say chicken in the bucket?'

'Yes, dear, though it's not really in a bucket; it's in a Dutch oven. You go and enjoy the music. I'm sure you'll find your young lady later.'

Taking Dregs with her, she walked away, and I headed back towards the stage in time for the end of Tim's short set, a complete racket. However, afterwards, we were privileged to witness a bizarre set from a lunatic calling herself Mad Donna. Though, when she started, some complained that she was not quite what they'd been expecting, her crazed antics and weird gibberings exerted a trance-like fascination, soon overriding any objections. She had a five-piece band, yet the music was strangely irrelevant. We finally cheered her off after three encores. I thought she'd be a hard act to follow, until I was strolling back to the tent and the scent of Mrs G's chicken in the bucket struck me.

The old girl, sitting cross-legged on the ground, was stirring an iron pot with a large wooden spoon or possibly a small paddle, with Hobbes squatting beside her, whittling a whistle from a small stick. Despite, or possibly because of, his weird costume and behaviour, I had to admit he'd done an amazing job at fitting in. No one would suspect him of being a policeman: he was quite obviously a nutter.

I sprawled on the grass next to Dregs while the old girl dished up, pulling in quite an audience. Sad people with hungry eyes swallowed, gazing at the steam swirling from the gurgling pot, the pot that was sending out such enticing aromas. When, at last, they turned away, trudging towards the burger vans, I had never before felt so privileged and lucky. When she handed me a bowl, with a hunk of fresh, crusty bread and a spoon, I could barely wait for Hobbes to say grace. Hunger, fresh air and exquisite cooking had given me an appetite and I regret I rather stuffed myself, fearful any might go to waste, or be offered to the passing throng. Though undoubtedly selfish, I'd challenge anyone to resist another bite of the old girl's cooking. A bottle of the good wine added extra zest to the meal.

When we'd finished, I asked if I could help with the washing up.

'Oh no, dear,' she said, smiling. 'Why don't you boys run along and enjoy yourselves.'

Sometimes, I thought, she had all the right answers. We sat watching Simon and Garth Ingle perform a set of whimsical folky songs, Dregs howling and, in my view, improving the performance. However, some people seemed to want to listen, so eventually we led him away, paying a quick visit to the beer tent.

'A pint of lager and two quarts of "Old Gutbuster" please, man,' said Hobbes to the barmaid.

Taking our drinks, we sat in the evening sun. Though Hobbes gulped down two pints in a matter of seconds, I sipped at mine, feeling far too full to take on copious amounts. My thoughts kept returning to Violet and, halfway through my drink, I came to a decision.

'I'm going to find Violet,' I said.

Hobbes nodded. 'Good idea. Would you like me to come with you? In case Mr King starts anything?'

'Thanks,' I said, 'but I'd rather do this on my own. I'll be alright. See you later.'

I got up, searching the crowd, examining every face, as bands came and went, some of them rather good, making me wish I could share them with her. I didn't see her, or Felix, or any of his men. In the end, when darkness had fallen except for the stage lighting, I gave up and watched No One You've Ever Heard Of. Their music was noisy with a pounding beat and the band, giving the performance of a lifetime, almost revived my spirits, making me cheer along with all the others. Hobbes joined me for a short time and then wandered off to ensure there was no trouble. I didn't think there would be; everybody seemed intent on enjoying themselves.

The band finishing, I returned to the tent, removing my shoes and crawling under the blankets. To start with, Dregs lay across my feet, welcome warmth, on a clear night with a steady breeze. I lay, yawning, trying to sleep, the ground even harder and lumpier than it had looked, people far too noisy. It became apparent that, despite exhaustion, I would never drop off. My fidgeting disturbed Dregs, who, sighing, wandered out into the night. After about half an hour, remembering I hadn't brushed my teeth, I dragged myself from beneath the covers, found my toothbrush and a towel and headed for the washrooms, shivering in the night air.

Just about everyone had moved away from the silent stage, now lit only by starlight and the crescent moon. Small groups of people, sprawling in the grass, sitting on stools, laughed and talked, as if no one else planned on sleeping that night. An assortment of teenagers were attempting rudimentary cooking on an open fire, impaling sausages on sticks, but the bottles and cans surrounding them suggested why they were not enjoying much success. As another sausage flared up in a blaze of glory, they roared with laughter. I doubted they'd get much to eat; they didn't appear to mind.

Finding the washrooms, I blinked under the strip light until, a basin becoming free, I brushed my teeth, made a brave attempt at washing in cold water, and headed back across the field. I paused to watch a bare-chested tumbler's wobbly one-man display. When he collapsed amidst great cheers, I turned away, bumping into a woman. Her perfume was powerful and heady.

'Oops … umm … sorry,' I said.

'Andy?'

'Oh … umm … Violet … Hi.'

'Well,' said Violet, 'I suppose I should be grateful you've remembered my name.'

'Of course I have,' I said. 'I'm so glad I bumped into you – I've been … umm … looking for you all night.'

She glanced at my towel and toothbrush. 'Have you?'

'Yes, really.'

Even in semi-darkness, she looked stunning, her eyes reflecting the crescent moon, her dark, lustrous hair gleaming over her shoulders. Another whiff of her perfume reached my nostrils. 'I've been trying to see you ever since the accident … I really have.'

'Oh, yes? I was in hospital; I assume you know where that is?'

She wouldn't look me in the face, despite my best efforts.

'Yes … but …'

'You couldn't even bother to get in touch when they released me. A token interest would have been polite.'

'I wanted to talk to you. I did try.'

'Did you? How hard is it to pick up a telephone?'

'But I hadn't got your number,' I said, realising how utterly useless I must be presenting myself.

'Ever heard of directory enquiries? Anyway, you could have asked Felix.'

'I did, but he wouldn't …'

'Wouldn't what?'

Her voice was harsh and cold and it hurt to hear it like that. I hesitated, wondering if I should just tell her what he'd said, fearing she wouldn't believe me.

'Umm … he … umm … suggested it might be better if I … we didn't see each other again.'

'And you didn't think it worthwhile to ask me?'

'Yes, I did … but …'

'Is this man bothering you?' asked one of Felix's men, tall, burly, with a head as smooth as a pickled-onion, approaching from the darkness.

Before she could answer, before I could think, but not before I could squeak, he frogmarched me across the field.

'It would,' he said, politely enough, had he not been crushing my shoulder, 'be an excellent idea for you to stop hassling Miss King. If you are tempted, resist it. If you don't, you are likely to find yourself in deep shit. You know what I'm saying?'

When I nodded, he released me.

'Good night,' he said, turning back the way he'd come.

Unable to see Violet anymore, I realised she might have been almost anywhere in the darkness, so all I could do was return to the tent and reflect on our chance meeting. It had not been a success and, although, the interruption hadn't helped, I couldn't fool myself that it had been going well before that. Knowing she believed I hadn't wanted to see her, hadn't even wanted to make sure she was alright, hurt as much as her cold voice. More painful though, was my shoulder, which, I suspected, would be displaying a hand-sized bruise by the morning.

My response to the henchman must have impressed her. If she'd been thinking 'what are you, Andy, man or mouse?' then my pathetic squeak would have confirmed her suspicions. I wished I'd had the guts to take Mrs Goodfellow's martial arts classes. If I had, I might not have been such a wimp.

It was too late of course, so, crawling back into the tent like the mouse I was, curling up under the blankets, I lay awake for what seemed like hours, futile regrets churning through my brain. I didn't expect to drop off.

Hobbes shook me from deep sleep. 'Wake up!'

'What's happening?' I asked, snuggling deeper into the blankets.

'Trouble.'

'Oh, right. I don't suppose you'll need me.'

Though my nose, my only exposed part, was cold, my bedding was warm and, to my astonishment, comfortable.

'Get your boots on,' said Hobbes, 'and quickly.' He tugged the blankets off me, except for the one I was clutching to my face.

I sat up, bleary and cross. He bundled me from the tent, sitting me down in front with my shoes. People were running backwards and forwards, making panicky noises as I struggled with my laces, the brisk breeze making me shiver and wrap my blanket around my shoulders. In the distance, a girl screamed, a faint orange glow became an intense red flame and I became aware of the stink of burning plastic. Something bad was happening.

'They're setting fire to tents,' said Hobbes. 'Follow me.'

Unable to make sense of shoelaces, I stumbled after him, shoes flapping, trying not to trip. When another tent flared up, his easy lope became a sprint and, on reaching it, he dived head-long into the inferno, as if into a swimming pool. Smoke and flames, bursting high into the night sky, rolled and twisted in the wind, casting shifting, fractured, red light over the crowd. People were coughing as the smoke billowed around the field.

The tent erupting with sparks and flaming fragments, Hobbes burst forth like a rocket from the launch pad, a limp body beneath each arm. I was still running as he laid them on the grass and, without thinking, pulling the blanket from my shoulders, I threw it over the nearest figure, beating out the smouldering patches, realising it was a young woman cocooned within a sleeping bag. Despite the smoke and fumes, I could smell the alcohol on her breath as she started to come awake.

'What the hell d'you think you're doing?' she asked, 'Get off me.'

An arm emerged and dealt a stinging slap across my face. With no time to explain, ripping the blanket from her, I spread it over the other figure, patting out any smoking bits. On looking up, I saw Hobbes rolling on the ground, his head ablaze. I grabbed the blanket but before I could get to him, he tore off his head and tossed it to the ground.

I screeched, an incoherent outpouring of horror, feeling sick, staring stunned and uncomprehending, as he leapt to his feet, stamping out the blaze. Only then did I realise that he'd simply torn off his hippie hat and wig.

'Are you alright?' I asked.

'Never better,' he said, 'though I was, maybe, a little hot-headed diving in like that, if not as hot-headed as I was getting out. I appear to be a little singed. It'll pass.'

Despite everything, I chuckled, before spluttering, the swirling, acrid smoke catching the back of my throat.

Hobbes, still smoking slightly, patted me on the back. 'You did well. It was good thinking to bring that blanket.'

He turned away and attended to the two he'd rescued. I knelt beside them as the girl, who looked familiar, unzipped herself.

'You!' she said, looking up at me and frowning.

'I'm still not Wayne,' I said.

'I'm sorry,' she said. 'I mean, I'm sorry I hit you, not that you're not Wayne.'

'Don't worry about it. I'm alright. You didn't hit me hard. Are you hurt?'

'I'm OK.' She coughed. 'Your lip's bleeding, I'm sorry; I thought you were Wayne trying it on. And I'm really sorry I stitched you up this afternoon.'

'What d'you mean? That was on purpose? Why?'

She looked away. 'Some bloke gave me twenty quid to jump on you.'

'Who?'

'I don't know. A tall guy in a suit … quite old: older than you, anyway. He said you were a bastard who was trying it on with his sister and I was to show her what you were like. I'm sorry.'

'Don't worry about it,' I said, despite seething – not at her, not much, but at Felix. Turning towards the other casualty, who was lying very still, I asked Hobbes how he was.

'He appears to be dead …'

The girl screamed, clapping a hand across her mouth.

Hobbes held up his hands, shaking his head. 'I was trying to say that he appears to be dead drunk. Otherwise, he seems alright apart from his hair. He'll not be needing a cut for a while.'

'Fetch water!' he roared at the crowd, getting to his feet, tearing down burning tents, three of which were already ablaze, others being in imminent danger as the breeze whipped up sparks and flame.

A few individuals, getting past the gawping stage, set up a chain from a standpipe, hurling containers of water onto the conflagrations. I joined them and, under the command of Mrs Goodfellow's team, with Hobbes's demolitions providing a firebreak, it wasn't too long before we were in control. When the fire brigade turned up, at last, there wasn't much left to do, other than damping down the remaining hot spots.

When, shortly afterwards, an ambulance arrived to take him away, Wayne had sobered up enough to realise his hair was a blackened frizz, and was seemingly more concerned about that than the loss of his tent and near immolation.

As order and calm gradually reasserted themselves, Hobbes took me across the field.

'It was very brave,' I said, 'to throw yourself into a fire. You were lucky you weren't hurt.'

'I was just doing my job.'

'But,' I continued, 'how did you know there was going to be a fire?'

'I didn't, but I had smelt trouble.'

'What sort of trouble.'

'Two panthers.'

'Won't the fires have scared them off?'

'Possibly.'

'Where did you see them?'

'I didn't see them,' he said, tapping the side of his nose.

'So, where didn't you see them?'

'Near the stage, heading towards the farmhouse.'

'OK, so what are we going to do?' I asked, with as much bravado as I could, worried he'd want to involve me in the trouble. Why else would he have woken me?

'Find them, if possible.'

'Will you need me?'

'Need? Probably not, but I thought you might be interested.'

'Interested is not the word,' I said, thinking terrified might be more appropriate.

'Good. Now follow me, keep close and keep quiet.'

I jogged behind, hoping the panthers had fled. As we reached the gate into the lane, he stopped suddenly.

I didn't. Bouncing off him, I sat down heavily. 'Oof!'

'Shh!'

'Sorry.'

'Shh!'

I used the gatepost to pull myself up, trying to see why he'd stopped, unable to see much at all, and certainly nothing to worry me, apart from Hobbes, of course.

'That's odd,' he murmured, sniffing the air.

'What's odd?'

'That scent. I know it. But from where?'

I couldn't smell anything, except for burned tent and a faint whiff of manure. The dark outline of the farmhouse stood out on the other side of the lane.

'It's familiar and strange. I noticed it at home recently. Just faintly. It'll come to me. In the meantime, duck.'

'You what?' I asked, puzzled.

He dragged me to the ground behind the wall as a spear of light stabbed through the darkness with a deafening retort.

'What's happening?' I asked keeping my head and voice low. 'Is someone shooting us?'

'No, someone shot at us. There's an important difference.'

'OK. But why shoot at us at all?'

'We'd better find out and stop them doing it again.'

'Can I do anything?'

'Yes, you can scream, as if you've been hit.'

'What?'

'Go on.'

'Agh,' I cried.

'No, like this,' he said, grabbing my wrist and pressing.

'Aaagh!' I screamed, writhing, until he released me.

'Much better. Now do that every few seconds.'

'OK, but for how long?'

He'd already vanished, so I lay where I was and screamed. A few seconds later I screamed again and then again, making sure it was a really good one, proud of its length, volume and pitch. A light flashed in my face, dazzling me.

'What's up with you?' asked a man.

'Nothing ... but I have a good reason.' There was no sign of Hobbes and a number of people were staring at me, while keeping at a safe distance.

'What reason?'

'Umm ... I don't know, exactly.'

'You're a dickhead,' said the man, and the group trudged away.

Once again, I screamed.

'Nutter!'

On the far side of the lane, someone's yell was stifled. I peeped over the wall to see Hobbes standing by the farmhouse, holding some poor devil by the collar, dangling him with his feet just scraping the ground. A shotgun with a broken back lay in the dirt until Hobbes booted it into a ditch, if he could boot anything with sandals on. Keeping my head down, creeping from the field, I went to see what was happening.

As he turned the man round, I saw it was Mr Bullimore, shaking like a man on the gallows.

'Good evening, sir,' said Hobbes. 'Perhaps you'd explain why you fired at us?'

'If I'd known who it was, I wouldn't have.'

'You shouldn't,' said Hobbes, 'be firing at anyone; it's against the law.'

Bullimore's voice shook. 'I apologise ... I thought it was them again.'

'Them?'

'Yes, them.'

'Right,' said Hobbes, 'I think we should go inside and have a little chat. Don't you?'

'No,' said Bullimore, shaking his head, 'we've got to find them.'

'Whom,' asked Hobbes, 'do we need to find and why?'

'Them!' Bullimore screamed, his scream far more convincing than any I'd managed.

Hobbes shrugged. 'Calm down, sir, let's go inside and then you can explain. Let's be having you, sir.'

Setting Bullimore back down, keeping a firm grip on his collar, he marched him round the side of the house to the front door, a great, solid, iron-studded creation, yet battered and cracked, as if it had withstood a siege. When he tried the handle it didn't turn. He knocked; a few moments later, he thumped it.

'Is anyone in?'

'Yes ... I hope so,' said Bullimore. 'I do have the key, though. There's only this one door.'

He stepped forward and tried to open it.

'I'm afraid,' said Hobbes, 'that it appears to be bolted, which suggests someone is in.' He pounded the door so that it shook, with a rhythm and volume that must have made people suppose another band had come on stage. When it stayed shut, he raised his fists as if contemplating demolition, hesitated and let his fists drop to his side. 'You

378

two stay here,' he said. 'I'll let myself in.'

I leaned against the gritty, old farmhouse wall in a state of hyper-nervousness, waiting with Bullimore, who might have been paralysed. Hobbes disappeared round the back of the house, glass shattered and, soon afterwards, the bolts on the door squealing, he reappeared in a blaze of electric light. As Bullimore rushed past him, I followed, stepping over a scattering of various-sized wellington boots, finding myself in an old-fashioned house, with a large plank table, a number of worm-eaten wooden chairs and very few modern comforts.

Mr Bullimore shouted, 'Helen? Les? Kids?'

No one replied. I knelt to tie my shoelaces hearing him running from room to room. As I got back to my feet, I became aware of a faint background odour, not dissimilar to Hobbes's feral scent, and noticed him sniffing the air and frowning while looking around.

Bullimore, white-faced and panting, pounded down the shiny, dark-wood stairs back into the front room. 'They're not here!'

'Someone must have bolted the door,' I said. 'So where are they?'

'I don't know,' he said, slumping heavily onto a creaky wooden stool.

Hobbes was crawling, toad-like, around the front room, sniffing, staring intently at the threadbare rug on the timeworn flagstones. Stopping, poking at a spot, he licked his finger. 'This is blood and it's fresh.'

Bullimore, groaning, held his head.

'Though,' said Hobbes, 'it's not human.'

Bullimore gave another, longer, groan.

Hobbes, quivering like a terrier in a barn full of rats, reached the back window. 'There are fresh scuff marks here ... and dried mud. Someone has gone out through the window.'

'When?' I asked.

'Within the hour, I'd say.'

Bullimore looked up, his eyes hopeful.

'Hello, hello, hello,' said Hobbes, pointing to the peeling cream paint on the woodwork, 'this is interesting.' Holding a long, thick, brown hair between thumb and fingernails, he examined it.

'Never mind that,' said Bullimore, despondent again, 'the window is locked and can only be locked from the inside. What you say doesn't make sense.'

Hobbes, standing up, pushed at the sash window, which moved easily and silently, sliding back into place when he let it go. 'The lock,' he said, peering at it, 'is broken. It appears to have broken a very long time ago.'

Bullimore groaned again, his face tinged grey.

'Now, sir,' said Hobbes, sounding urgent, 'I think it's time you told me what's going on. I want the truth, mind, no matter how peculiar.'

'I don't know how to tell you; you'll never believe it.'

'I'm very good at believing things. Try me. And quickly.'

Bullimore sighed, rocking backwards and forwards. 'I'm not sure where to start ... it's rather complicated and I really shouldn't tell you this.' He hesitated. 'In fact, I can't unless you promise not to tell anyone. You won't believe it anyway.'

'I said quickly,' Hobbes growled, 'and I meant it; we may not have much time.

Perhaps it would help if I told you that I already know about Mr Bashem? I already had a strong suspicion, but the blood and the hair confirm it.'

'What d'you know about him?' asked Bullimore, staring, looking nervous.

'That he's your son-in-law, that he's thirty-eight, that he and Mrs Bashem have six children, and that he's a werewolf.'

Bullimore's mouth dropped open, mimicking mine. I was stunned Hobbes would think Mr Bashem was the werewolf; he seemed such a nice man. Maybe he was a little hairy and, perhaps he could have done with taking a bath but …

'How did you know?' asked Bullimore.

'It's my business to know,' said Hobbes. 'Now, please, tell me what's going on, before it's too late.'

'I'll try,' said Bullimore. 'Do you know anything about werewolves? Anything at all?'

'A little.' Hobbes smiled. 'I was friends with one many years ago. He lived in a werehouse in town, next to the railway station.'

'There isn't a railway station in town,' I said.

'This was before your time, Andy. So, Mr Bullimore, I am familiar with the type.'

Bullimore sighed, looking relieved. 'That's good, because I didn't know how to start. You're absolutely right, Les is a werewolf. He's a good lad, though, or I wouldn't have let him near my daughter, being very protective after her poor mother died. I admit to being unsure about him to start with, and took steps to keep the wolf from the door when some of his behaviour struck me as barking mad. He'd scratch himself in public and wolf down his meals and, though I tried to put him off, he was dogged and one night he collared me and won me round. Of course, he'd long ago won Helen's heart.

'Well, to cut a long story short, they got married, with my blessing, and moved into a council house in Wolverhampton where, unfortunately, there were allegations about inappropriate use of lampposts and a misunderstanding over a cat that resulted in bad relations with the neighbours. A very unpleasant situation arose and Les was hounded by vigilantes. When he complained to the council, he was howled down and in the end they had to do a moonlight flit.

'They tried other places but similar things happened. It seemed that someone was always telling malicious tales to their new neighbours. Though they were lies or gross distortions the result was always the same; people weren't prepared to tolerate him, or Helen, or the young 'uns when they came along. They were spat at in the street and it began to get increasingly violent. In the end, in despair, they turned to me for help. As it happened, I'd long had an ambition to settle down in the country.'

'So you all moved here,' said Hobbes. 'Why?'

'Because Loop's Farm is mine. It's been in the family for generations and I inherited it from my grandfather, though he never lived here. It was always rented out in my time until the old boy who was the tenant passed away and we moved in. We're not great farmers, though the young 'uns have learned how to herd sheep, and money has been tight. That's why we came up with the idea of the festival. We thought it would make a bit of cash while, hopefully, getting people on our side. Things seemed to be going well until a couple of months ago. It all started with our neighbour, Henry Bishop.'

'I saw him die,' I said.

Bullimore stared at me, puzzled.

'This is not the time for idle chitchat,' said Hobbes. 'Please continue, sir.'

I didn't feel he was being fair. It wasn't chitchat; I had seen the man die, it had been horrible, and I'd suspected Hobbes. Though part of me still did, I began to wonder if Mr Bashem might actually have been the culprit.

'Did Les kill him?' I blurted out.

Hobbes scowled. 'If you don't keep quiet, I'll send you outside.'

Bullimore, ignoring me, carried on. 'Though Bishop was grumpy and miserable, he wasn't too bad at first and seemed harmless. Then he offered to buy the upper field, the one next to Loop Woods. We refused to sell, though the money would have been handy, but you don't just sell your heritage to get over being broke. Besides, it was such a ridiculously low offer, we reckoned he must have found out we were in a mess and tried to take advantage. It wasn't nice, it was business.

'After we rejected his offer, he turned nasty, objecting and complaining about everything, even the festival, though he'd made no complaint when we first told him. Not that it was anything to do with him – it wasn't going to have any impact on him or his land.

'Things took a turn for the worse when he took a pot shot at Les, though he claimed it was an accident and he was only after rabbits. We almost believed him until he had a go at the young 'uns. We had to ban them from anywhere he could see them.'

'I see,' said Hobbes nodding. 'You should have told the police.'

'We didn't want any more trouble. They aren't all like you, Mr Hobbes.'

'You're absolutely right there,' I said.

'Thank you,' said Hobbes, baring his great yellow teeth in a grin that would have terrified anyone without my experience.

'Things have been getting really bad, lately,' Bullimore continued. 'We've had tough men in suits come round here, causing trouble.'

'That'll be the Mormons,' I said, trying to lighten the mood.

'I warned you,' said Hobbes, grabbing my collar and the seat of my trousers, shoving me out the front door into the farmyard and shutting me out. Only by pressing my ear to the keyhole, could I hear.

'They've been offering a pittance, trying to force us to sell up. They said if we didn't accept their terms and get out there'd be trouble.'

'Do you know who they were?'

'Hired muscle, working for a bloke called Felix King, a developer, apparently.'

'That,' said Hobbes, 'doesn't entirely surprise me.'

'You know him? He's got a sister who's nearly as bad as him, a pity because she's a fine-looking lass. They say her name's Violet. We think it's short for Violent.'

Feeling a rush of fury that the fat, old farmer dared talk about her like that, I stood on the doorstep puffing, clenching and unclenching my fists. Though I knew my reaction was stupid, and despite being sure it was all over between us, I couldn't just stand there and let her be insulted. Actually, that was all I could do. That and fume.

Bullimore carried on. 'We hoped things would be better after Bishop died, assuming at first he was behind it; he turned out to have been just a pawn and the threats got worse. The truth is, Mr Hobbes, that we became suspicious of you, or, rather, of your friend. Les was trying to find out what they were up to and, having seen him with her at your house, followed them to the arboretum, where he hid in the woods, watching and listening. Your friend seemed very pally with them at first but it soon became very clear he was not one of King's cronies. In the end, Les, feeling sorry for him, kept an eye on him when he was going home after the accident.'

'So it was Les,' said Hobbes. 'I suspected so.'

'How did you guess?'

'I'd been hunting the panthers when I picked up a trail I didn't recognise. I was a little concerned when I became aware it was closing in on Andy, until I remembered the scent of werewolf.'

'Did you find the panthers?'

'No. I keep coming across their scent but it's usually blocked by something and, more puzzling, it often just stops. I think someone must be transporting them.'

'That's possible. I heard King used an elephant to break the guy who owns the Greasy Pole. He wants his land as well.'

'I'd suspected that. Mr King's driver was in the crowd when it happened and fitted the description of the man who'd released the creature. Unfortunately, he was murdered before I could interview him.'

'I'll bet King did that ... or his sister. They're ruthless.'

'It's likely,' said Hobbes. 'Anyway, I think that's enough history. What's been going on tonight?'

'King and his henchmen came round this afternoon, when I was on stage. He made another offer, worse than previous ones and, when Les told him where he could stick it, he received a beating for his trouble. I hope that's why you found the blood on the rug. When King left, he said Les would regret not getting out when he had the chance.'

Someone screamed. Across the field I could see people running.

Bullimore was still talking. 'They said they'd be back after dark. Les was going to bolt the door – it's really strong – but I feared it was only a matter of time before they tried the windows. Although they're not easy to reach, they're still the weakest part. That's why I went out with my shotgun. I thought I'd scare them off. I didn't mean to shoot at you.

'But now my family has gone, I've got to find them.'

At that point, I sort of forgave Mr Bullimore for shooting at us.

Something was happening in the field. Another tent flaring up, people were panicking and shouting, though I couldn't see what the problem was at first, for the fire brigade was still on site and could easily cope with a burning tent. I made out Mrs Goodfellow and Arnold's dad on the edge of the crowd, brandishing big sticks, for some reason. Then, I understood. Silhouetted, in the glare of yet another burning tent, I caught a glimpse of the dark, heart-stopping shape of a panther.

I banged on the door, yelling for Hobbes.

The door opened and Hobbes stepped out. 'What's up?'

'There's trouble again,' I said. 'I saw a panther and I think it's setting fire to tents.'

'Panthers aren't known as arsonists, but someone is out to cause trouble.'

An idea came to mind. 'Do you think it could be Felix?'

'I wouldn't be surprised. Violet, too, I'm afraid.'

'No, she can't be; she's not like him.' I still believed in her, despite what I'd heard.

'I hope you're right,' he said, gazing into the field. 'I'd better find the Bashems before it's too late.'

'Why? What do you think will happen?'

'Nothing good.'

'But what about all that?' I pointed to where chaos reigned.

'The lass is in charge and will sort it out with her boys – that's what they're here for – and the fire brigade can deal with the fires. I expect someone has thought to call the police by now.'

'Umm … can I do anything?'

'Stay with Mr Bullimore, and don't let him out of your sight. You should be safe here.'

'OK,' I said, thinking it didn't seem a very heroic role but, then, I wasn't feeling very heroic. One glimpse of panther had turned my muscles to water.

Hobbes was already loping down the lane, shoulders hunched, knuckles nearly grazing the cobbles, the twisting light of the fires casting a monstrous shadow on the stone wall. Though I almost wished I'd gone with him, I wouldn't have kept up with his pace for long, and the thought of being alone in the darkness with panthers and werewolves prowling, chilled me to the core. Shivering, I stepped into the house.

Mr Bullimore, still slumped in his seat, looked up through reddened eyes and I felt sorry for the old guy.

'Where's Mr Hobbes?' he asked.

'He's gone to look for your family.'

He nodded. 'He's a good man. There's something about him though …'

'You're right there.'

'He reminds me, well, of us. In a way.'

'What d'you mean by us?' I asked, suddenly wary.

'I mean he's not the same as other policemen, or other people. He's not like you.'

'That's true. But why did you say us? What are you trying to say?' My nerves were jangling.

'Les,' said Mr Bullimore, with a strange smile, 'isn't the only werewolf in the family. I'm part werewolf myself, on my mother's side. Maybe that's why I'm such a son of a bitch.'

'Oh yes?' I said, trying to ignore the urge to back away.

'Yes, though I can't change like Les can. About all I can do is to grow hair where I don't want it and fetch sticks. Not much use really.'

'But what about your daughter?'

'Just the sticks, but the young 'uns take after their dad; they're as fine a pack of werepups as you'll ever see. I hope Mr Hobbes finds them.'

He sniffed, looking at me with such a hangdog expression that it made me say something silly. 'Umm … I suppose we could go and help him.'

'He told me to stay here, but you're right, I can't just sit around when they might be in danger. Let's go.'

'OK,' I said, 'if you're quite sure. Or perhaps it would be better to wait? In case they come back. What d'you think?'

'Let's go.' He stood up, looking resolute and strong, putting on a battered tweed jacket, and striding towards the front door. Opening it, he glanced back. 'Are you coming?'

'I suppose so,' I said, already regretting my careless talk, hoping it wouldn't cost lives, particularly my own life, 'though I think we'd better stick together.'

As he stepped into the night, he nodded, which was some comfort as we marched along the lane, following in Hobbes's footprints – if he'd left any.

'Any ideas where to look?' I asked when Mr Bullimore halted by the gate.

'It depends if they're free or if King has kidnapped them.'

'Isn't the word dognapped?' I said unthinkingly, cringing as soon as the words were out.

Mr Bullimore stared hard as I apologised, before drawing a deep breath. 'We'll try the woods. Werewolves feel secure in woods.'

He stepped into the fields, walking quickly, not like Hobbes when he was in the mood, but fast enough to get me panting as I struggled to keep up. Ahead of us, deep within the shadow, loomed Loop Woods, and who knew what lurked within? A twig cracked and, at the same moment, catching my foot on something and stumbling, I thought I saw a movement on the edge of the wood. By the time I regained my balance, I'd lost sight of it.

'What was that?'

'What was what?' asked Mr Bullimore, walking on regardless.

'I … umm … think I saw something. Perhaps we should go back to the house and get torches?'

Turning back, he pushed an object into my hand. 'Take this. I always carry a couple in my pocket, just in case.'

For all its diminutive size, the torch had a powerful, if narrow, beam. Though it provided some reassurance, I'd much rather have returned to the farmhouse, despite it not feeling nearly so safe once Hobbes had left. However, it had thick, stone walls, a stout door and, most importantly, electric lights.

'Hurry up,' called Mr Bullimore.

All of a sudden his voice was too far away. Running towards it, I found I was on the edge of Loop Woods, becoming aware of a strange sort of stillness, as if someone was hiding, holding their breath, waiting to leap out with a yell and scare me half to death.

I glanced back over my shoulder seeing that the fires appeared to have been extinguished and that hundreds of torches were flashing, looking as far away as the stars. The headlights of a fire engine were reflecting on a stone wall, illuminating the still-smoking remains of a tent, as a bulky, dark-suited man appeared in the beam, brandishing a baseball bat at the frail, skinny figure advancing on him. It was Mrs Goodfellow, wagging her finger, as if telling him off. I felt sick and entirely helpless as he raised his club, yet, before he could bring it down, she, darting forward, appeared to tap him on the chin. As he toppled over backwards and Arnold sat on him, I felt enormously proud of the old girl.

'Did you see that?' I asked Mr Bullimore.

There was no reply, just a flicker of his torch beam between the black trunks. Hastening towards it, I realised I was entering a quite different part of the woods to where Hobbes had taken me, for, where there'd been wide spaces between massive trees, soft leaf litter beneath my feet and the odd thorn bush to break up the pattern, this place was crammed with massive, old conifers with few paths. Though I struggled to catch up, I was always being forced out of my way, my torch beam seemingly feeble beneath the dark ceiling, as if the thick, resinous carpet was absorbing all light. My feet sinking into the litter, sharp needles found their way into my shoes, forcing me to stop, take them off and shake them out. When I'd finished, having no idea where Mr Bullimore had got to, I gave up following him, concentrating instead on not getting lost, reasoning that I couldn't go far wrong so long as I didn't lose sight of the glimmer of light seeping in from the edge of the wood behind me.

Something rustled.

'Mr Bullimore?'

There was no reply.

I was trying to convince myself it had only been a rabbit or something, when I received a tremendous blow between the shoulder blades. Falling forward, my torch flew from my hand like a rocket, clattering into a tree, the light going out.

I came to, sprawled on my front, wondering if I'd gone blind. My head was throbbing, my back sore, and I could taste blood. Noticing a familiar, unwelcome smell, I groaned.

'Welcome back,' said a cold voice.

'Felix?'

His laugh made me shiver.

'Where are you?'

'Over here.'

Though I couldn't see him, as I pushed myself into a sitting position, it sounded like he was in front of me. I didn't feel too scared, being oddly reassured that I wasn't alone, not really believing he'd do anything too serious. I hoped Mrs G had already taken care of his henchmen.

'I think something hit me,' I said.

'Like this?' he said, from behind, as something thumped into my back, knocking me face first into the pine needles. I sat up rubbing my neck.

'Pain in the neck?' said Felix, which sounded more like an accusation than a question.

'That hurt.'

'It was meant to.'

'Why did you hit me?'

'Why do you think *I* did it?' His voice now came from my left side.

'Because there's only you here with me.'

'Are you sure?' he asked, now on my right.

'Where are you?'

'Here.'

A blow to my chest sending me crashing onto my back, I gasped with the shock and moaned.

'Shut your mouth! You're pathetic, and the fun's hardly started.'

As I rolled over and got to my knees, a stunning blow to the back of my neck sent me sprawling, a galaxy of spinning stars filling my head. Hot blood pumped from my nose, pooling in my mouth, and my only consolation was that I couldn't see it, as I attempted to staunch the flow.

I couldn't even try to fight if I couldn't see him. Screaming for help was an option but, before I could give it a go, a clout to my ear knocked me against the rough bark of a tree, leaving me dazed. By then I was filled with cold, hard fear.

'I thought I told you to shut your mouth? Did I tell you to shut your mouth?'

'Yes,' I said, spitting blood.

'So shut it before you make me angry.'

Something growled behind me. My heart was thumping, my breathing was too rapid, I felt sick and everything seemed distant. A cuff across the back of my head made pretty lights dance to the throbbing pulse of pain and all I could do was curl up into a ball like a hedgehog, wishing I had a hedgehog's sharp spines.

As I lay there stunned, my mind fogged with fear, a memory resurfaced of a holiday long ago. I was barefoot, playing in a sunlit garden, blotched with the long, dark shadows of enormous trees, a big, old house in front of me, with a patio on which my father, sitting on a stripy deckchair, was reading a newspaper. I must have been about six or seven, because my sister was there in her pushchair. A shiny blue and red ball lay in the long grass at the edge of the lawn and, as I ran to kick it, my sister's unexpected scream distracting me, I missed and felt a sudden pain. I fell down crying, blood oozing from several little holes in my foot, my father hurrying to see what was wrong. He picked me up, laughing, and pointed out the small, spiny creature curled up next to my ball.

'You know something, Andy?' Felix hissed, 'I don't like you.'

I'd already guessed as much.

'You won't do as you're told. I say, leave Violet alone and what do you do? You get her into a car crash, wait until she's recovered and try it on again. I might have respected you a little if you'd had the balls to stand up to me, or even if you'd visited her in hospital, but you haven't.'

'I would have visited if I could.'

'Shut up. What's more, you hang around with that freak Hobbes, which is not right. You should not associate with his sort. Even worse, you keep company with the vermin from the farmhouse down there and it makes me sick to the stomach to think someone like you has been with my sister, has touched her and shaken my hand.'

'I haven't "been with" her, whatever that means. I just want to be friends,' I said, sitting up, trying to get to my feet against the tree. Despite my fear, my anger was rising, until a thump to my solar plexus folded me up like a penknife.

'Did I give you permission to speak? No, I don't believe I did.

'What sort of person are you? Do you actually enjoy mixing with vermin? It's disgusting and shows you're no better than they are. If anything, you're worse, because that mongrel scum has no choice; they were born like it and they'll die like it, and the sooner the better.'

Spitting out another mouthful of blood, I tried to catch my breath, hoping my head would clear, groping for a stick, or anything to try defending myself, though, unless I could see, I doubted it would be of any use. His ranting, seeming entirely unhinged to me, was even more terrifying than the actual violence.

Although I thought I couldn't see a thing, I noticed there were two small, greenish glints, apparently hovering close together in mid-air just about where I guessed Felix might be. I stared at them, fascinated, while he continued his insane, though precise and articulate, diatribe against Bashem, Bullimore and Hobbes, until, when they blinked, I realised they were eyes, though human eyes wouldn't glint in the dark like that. Knowing Felix had a panther with him reduced me to a quivering jelly of a man, for even a beating had to be better than being mauled. I concentrated on being as still as I could, on keeping quiet and on controlling my breathing.

Felix stopped talking as distant shouts were followed by cheers. I guessed he was listening.

I tried to see things from his point of view: his not liking me was, perhaps, understandable, his protectiveness towards Violet was admirable, in a way, and I could see why anyone might regard Hobbes as a freak, since he often appeared pretty freakish to me. However, I could see no reason for hating the Bashems so much for, although they were undoubtedly werewolves, the mere fact making me nervous, despite all Hobbes's assurances, they'd done nothing, so far as I knew, to deserve the loathing Felix had heaped on them. Yet, since he was no longer spouting his nonsense, I hoped he might have calmed down, and risked opening my mouth.

'Why do you hate the Bashem family so much?' I asked, my voice sounding thin and shrill.

'Because,' he said, apparently in the mood to talk, 'those half-breed werewolves are nothing more than vermin that pollute the good earth.'

'But they don't … umm … cause any harm, do they?'

'They exist. What more harm can they do? Werewolves are an abomination and their mongrel spawn are even worse. It was one of them that frightened Violet and caused the crash. She might have been killed. Doesn't that mean anything to you?'

'Yes … but she didn't have to drive like that.'

'She had to get away from the filth. She was disgusted and knew you'd be no defence. You're not on their side, are you?'

'No … of course not. I didn't even know they were werewolves until Mr Bullimore told me tonight.'

'Yet you still stayed with him? Did it not disgust you?'

'I wasn't … umm … disgusted – not really. I don't know much about them but Hobbes says werewolves are shy and pretty harmless.'

'And you always believe what that hulking freak says?'

'Well, not necessarily,' I answered truthfully, still finding the whole werewolf concept deeply and fundamentally alarming. Yet it was the way Felix talked about Hobbes that disturbed me most. I wasn't sure why at first, since I'd thought much the same often enough, though not in the same words. Anyone might regard him as a freak – any police inspector who wasn't human was certainly abnormal. At length, I realised: most people just accepted him at face value, as a police inspector. He might make them uncomfortable or scare them, but hardly anyone recognised he wasn't human, at least not until they knew him well, and few knew him as well as I did.

I risked another question. 'Umm … why do you think Hobbes is a freak?'

'Because he is.' Felix laughed, though without any humour. 'He's degenerate, he stinks like a bear, he sniffs like a dog and he looks more than half like an ape. I don't know what he is but he's not human, though he seems to have you fooled.'

'Oh, no.' I shook my head. 'I worked that out long ago.'

'Well, then, since you're so clever, perhaps you'd explain what he is?'

'Umm … I don't really know. I just know he's … umm … unhuman.'

'And yet, you continue to share a house with him and that crazy old woman. How do you stand it? It makes me ill to think of it.' The noise he made, indicative of disgust, almost sounded like a growl.

'I've got used to it. He's not so bad when you get to know him … umm … most of the time he isn't. Anyway, he's nowhere near as strange as some of the other people round here.'

'There's truth in that,' said Felix. 'When I came to this backwater it was purely for business reasons; there was money to be made in developing this place. Parts of the town look like they haven't changed for centuries. It needs modernising and I'm the one going to do it.'

'By fair means or foul?'

That produced a genuine laugh. 'You're right there, Andy. I might occasionally break the rules, or someone's legs, but you've got to be ruthless to get on in my profession. I can't afford to let niceties get in the way of progress.'

'You got an elephant to demolish the Greasy Pole.'

Another laugh. 'Sometimes a flamboyant gesture pays dividends. Eric and I have since come to an arrangement that is mutually beneficial. I get his filthy café, for which I should get a medal, and he gets to keep his looks, such as they are.'

'And what about Featherlight?'

'That fat, filthy bar keeper,' said Felix, allowing a tone of grudging respect into his voice, 'is proving more difficult. He's a stubborn man and as tough as his steaks, though he's got no brains; that runt who works for him does the thinking.'

'Billy?'

'Yes, but that drunken dwarf won't be a problem much longer.'

'Why? What are you going to do to him?'

'Me? I'm not going to do anything but the poor little chap really should check his brakes more often.'

'That's despicable.'

'Thank you.'

A thought occurred. 'Umm … was it you killed Henry Bishop? And why?'

'I'm afraid the dear departed Henry got greedy and thought it might be a good idea to blackmail me, since I'd employed his skills on a couple of little schemes. He had to go.'

'So you set a panther on him?'

'If you like. I regret the incident spoiled Violet's evening. It was sheer bad luck you picked that place.'

'It was Hobbes's idea. He told me it was a good restaurant.'

'Hobbes, eh? He's behind all the problems round here.'

I shook my head. 'No, that's not true. Whatever you think of him, he's the one doing most to keep the peace. If it wasn't for him there'd be a lot more trouble. In fact I know some people choose to live here precisely because they've heard he's fair and won't let anything happen to them because of what they are.'

'That's just my point. Don't you see? If not for him, the weirdoes wouldn't keep coming here and, if any did, the decent folk could kick them out and good riddance. But Hobbes's days are numbered, like all the other freaks. After I've rid the area of the filthy werewolves, I'm going to drive all the weirdoes and deviants out, and make it a place fit for decent people.'

His voice, determined and utterly terrifying, boomed through the woods as if he were addressing a rally of his supporters. Furthermore, the pale eyes kept staring at me, adding an even darker dimension to my fear, though I knew one thing at least was good: so long as he was talking, he wasn't hitting or setting his panther on me. It appeared that he appreciated a captive audience, and I suddenly realised his words might be evidence, especially should a few intelligent questions prompt him to reveal more than he should.

'What d'you mean drive them out?' I asked.

'I intend to clean out the filth by whatever means necessary and if that means by force and fire, so be it.'

'And if they still won't go?'

'They'll go. I have my removal men.'

'Like Mike Rook?'

'Mike?' He laughed. 'Mike was merely my driver, though he had other uses until he started going soft, reckoning my plan to burn out Binks was a step too far.'

'Is that why you killed him?'

'I had him killed when he threatened to inform Hobbes.'

'He sounds like one of the decent folk you were making Sorenchester fit for,' I said, gulping, in case I was provoking him.

'Decent? He was only going to tell Hobbes if I didn't buy him off. He was nothing but a lousy blackmailer, like Henry Bishop.' He chuckled. 'Still, Mike did have an inventive mind, and his elephant scheme was a classic. Unfortunately, when he was no longer an asset, he had to go.'

'How did you get at him in the hospital?'

'Through a window. It wasn't difficult. Right, I've answered some of your questions and now it's your turn to answer some of mine. What do you know about the tunnels?'

'How do you know about them?'

'That drunken runt, Billy, told me after I bought him a lot of drinks, and Hobbes's sudden disappearances and unexpected re-appearances proved he hadn't been lying, though he knew little more than that they existed and ran as far as Blackdog Street. I expect one connects to Hobbes's wine cellar. Am I right?'

'Why do you want to know?'

'I'm just curious, like you are, Andy. I expect you'd like to know why I've been telling you all about my business affairs?'

'No, not really.'

'You really are stupid aren't you?'

'Umm …'

'Just accept it, man. Has it not occurred to you that everything I've told you could get me into serious trouble? If you told anyone that is.'

Though he still sounded calm, his voice had grown cold again. I shivered.

'But I won't tell anyone.'

'Promise?'

'Umm … I promise.'

'Do you know, I think I believe you. In fact, I know you won't tell anyone.'

His voice had grown louder, or was he closer? The eyes had disappeared.

'Can you guess why?'

The shock of his voice just next to my ear, his hot breath on my neck was too much. Giving in to terror, lurching to my feet, I ran.

'Come back,' said Felix. 'It'll be easier on you.'

Putting my head down, I fled, longing for light, unseen branches whipping my face, roots and logs trying to trip me, stumbling forward, breathing through my mouth. After a while, the fear he'd set the panther on me forced me to slow down and listen. My head was throbbing and I could feel blood congealing over my face and hands.

'You didn't answer my question.' His voice was in front of me. 'Go on, guess why I believe you.'

Green eyes and white teeth glinted where a hint of moonlight seeped through the heavy canopy. Putting my hands in my pocket, so he wouldn't see how much they were shaking, trying to be cool, unprovocative, I found my penny, hoping it was a lucky one.

'Alright, I'll tell you anyway. I trust you not to tell anyone because I'm going to kill you.'

The eyes approaching, I hurled the coin but I guess my aim was off, because it was Felix who cried out. Turning away, I ran, blindly, desperately.

It might have been a great escape had I not tripped and rolled into a hollow.

'You shouldn't have done that,' said Felix. 'You've made me angry. I was intending to make it quick and painless – well, quick anyway, but now you're going to die like Henry did.'

'Please, no!'

A shadow, even darker than night-time, was approaching and I feared I was going to die. Curling into a ball, I lay still, knowing I was trapped, that I was going to experience pain. The panther growled and I felt a thud as it landed at my side. Rank breath blew in my face, sharp claws raked my side. I cried for help, though my nose being stuffed with clotting blood, my scream sounded more like a duck call.

There was a sudden slight breeze, as if something had leapt over me, an angry hiss, as though from an infuriated cat, and I passed out.

Soft hands were stroking my forehead as I came to. 'I'm so sorry,' said a gentle voice.

'Violet?'

'Yes, you're going to be alright.'

'What happened?'

'You're safe, but I've got to go.'

'Don't leave me, please.'

'I must. They're coming to help you. Goodbye.'

As she moved away, I heard voices. Torch beams flashed between the trees.

'I'm over here,' I croaked.

'Are you alright, dear?' Light was around me and Mrs Goodfellow was peering into my face.

I blinked. 'Not really.'

'You are a mess, dear. We'd best get you back to the farm and clean you up. Can you walk?'

'I don't think so.'

Very soon I was being carried on a stretcher. The woods were left behind. In front was the comforting light of the farmhouse.

I didn't half feel ill when my eyes opened.

'He's in shock,' said a woman with a penetrating, brisk, no-nonsense voice that hurt my head.

Although I thought I recognised it, I struggled to work out why the ceiling looked familiar and why something was pressing on my mouth and nose.

'I thought so,' said Mrs Goodfellow.

'Indeed. He's displaying many of the classic symptoms: a rapid, weak pulse, shallow breathing, low blood pressure, clammy skin, blue lips …'

Raising myself on one arm to see what was happening, realising I was wearing a face mask with a plastic tube, I tore it off. 'Oh. Hello, doctor,' I said, seeing Dr Procter smiling down at me. Then, having vomited into a bucket that appeared in the right place, I slumped back onto my bed.

'Nausea is, of course, another classic symptom,' said the doctor, 'but the oxygen has taken care of the cyanosis and his lips are back to normal – the colour I mean. The swelling will go down, in time. He's evidently had a traumatic experience, but I gather he's quite used to them and, fortunately, he appears to have suffered no major physical injuries. His symptoms are already showing distinct signs of improvement and he should recover quickly. Nevertheless, he has taken quite a beating and it seems a cat's had a go at him again. I wonder what he does to annoy them. I'll write him a prescription for antibiotics; we wouldn't want him to catch whatever he had last time.'

'Is there anything else?'

'Not really. Keep him warm and quiet and give him plenty of fluids. You may notice some strange moods and behaviour as the psychological effects work themselves out.'

Mrs Goodfellow laughed. 'Strange moods and behaviour? How will I know?'

If I'd had the energy, I would have snorted with disdain, but, the blankets being warm, my bed feeling soft, I let myself drift back to sleep. Mrs Goodfellow woke me a couple of times to pour liquids into me or to thrust antibiotics down my throat. Though I'm sure they did me good, what roused me in the end was the pungent aroma of curry.

I got up, limping to the bathroom for a wash, shocked at the unfamiliar face looking back at me from the mirror, for, where there would normally have been pale, smooth, pinkish skin, there were lumps and purple marks, red eyes and a bottom lip, swollen as if someone had inserted half a saucer into it. Yet, my body showed no evidence of wounds or bruises at all, having been covered in bandages, like a mummy. A tentative poke suggested tentative pokes should be avoided.

After dressing, a slow, painful process, I hobbled downstairs towards the kitchen. When Dregs bounded towards me, I cringed, expecting the worst, but, seeming to understand my delicate state, he contented himself with licking my hand.

Mrs G, stirring a vast black cauldron, from where the delicious, enticing, smells were emerging, looked up from the stove. 'Hello, dear, I wondered if this might tempt you. I take it you're feeling better?'

'It did and I am, though I'm starving. Umm … when's supper ready?'

'At half-past six, as usual.'

'When's that?'

'In about twenty minutes, dear.'

'So long?'

'I'm afraid so. The old fellow will be back then.'

'Why isn't he at the festival? And … umm … shouldn't you be there, too?'

'It's been called off.'

'I'm not surprised,' I said. 'It was getting rather out of hand, though your boys did quite well … in the circumstances.'

'Thank you, dear. That's kind.'

I thought I ought to give her some support for, after all, it hadn't been her fault there'd been so much trouble and, in the circumstances, she really hadn't done badly. 'I saw you wallop the guy with the club. That was great.'

'No, it was regrettable, but I had to take him down when he wouldn't listen to reason and threatened to hurt people. The old fellow reckons he was acting under orders.'

'That's no excuse.'

'No, dear, though it is a reason. By the end of the night, we'd detained thirty young men, who were all acting under orders. Though most of them tried to put up a fight, a few ran and are being picked up by the police.' She looked glum for a moment, until a gummy smile broke through. 'On the bright side, I obtained six new teeth for my collection. Unfortunately, one was gold and another had a diamond in it, quite ruining it.'

'That is sad.' I grinned, my face hurting and giving rise to a worrying thought. 'Umm … I'm not sure I'll be able to eat properly. Just talking hurts enough and I'll never be able to chew.'

'Don't worry, dear, this is mulligatawny soup, so I'm sure you'll be able to manage.'

She wouldn't say any more about the events of the previous night, except that I should ask Hobbes. I tried to be cool and managed to sit quietly, with the exception of my stomach, which grumbled egregiously until he returned and took his place at the table. He looked tired and morose and, besides saying grace, didn't speak until we'd finished. I didn't mind, despite my curiosity, for I was fully engaged in the process of eating the thick, rich soup and, though my swollen mouth barely opened wide enough to let the spoon in, everything was chopped so finely I had no other problems eating.

Afterwards, while the old girl made tea and washed up, Hobbes and I sat on the sofa. He began twitching and growling, the overture to another bone-crunching episode I feared, until, after a short while, he turned to face me.

'I'm happy to see you up and recovering,' he said, 'and you'll be glad to hear I found the Bashem family safe and sound. They'd hidden in the crowd, which was sensible, and had taken Dregs, which was also sensible. They showed far more intelligence than you; you really shouldn't have gone out. I'd hoped you and Mr Bullimore had the brains to stay put.'

'Sorry, it was my fault; I thought we might be able to help find them. Is Mr Bullimore alright?' I was ashamed I'd never given him, or his family, a thought until then.

'Though he was mauled quite badly, he's a tough old dog and is getting better. He thought the panther was going to kill him, but, for some reason, it simply stopped the attack and ran off.'

'That's odd,' I said, 'because Felix set a panther on me and I think another one turned up and drove it away, which saved me.'

'That sounds like unusual behaviour for a panther,' said Hobbes, looking at me as if expecting more.

'Umm ... I expect it was unusual. But ...'

'But what?'

'But I think ... umm ... Violet brought the second one. I'm not sure quite what happened but, just after the first one ran off, she talked to me and stroked my head.'

'So, she was there, too? That is very interesting.'

'Yes and she said she was sorry, though I'm not quite sure why.'

Hobbes grinned. 'I suspect she has rather a lot to be sorry about, but that can wait till later. I think you may just have provided me with a vital clue.'

'Have I? That's great ... umm ... talking of clues, Felix told me quite a lot during the attack. I thought it might be evidence.'

'Tell me,' said Hobbes.

I told him everything Felix had said, or, at least, everything I could remember.

When I'd finished, Hobbes shook his head. 'I'll get Billy to check his brakes, but why do villains need to gloat and boast about their cleverness and ruthlessness when he could just have killed you and slipped away? That's what I'd do if I ever became villainous.'

I flinched at his casual attitude.

'Your evidence would be useful, should the case ever go to court, but, unfortunately, I doubt it will: not the real one. The lass and her boys have detained most of Mr King's henchmen, who are currently stewing in the nick, awaiting questioning. They will no doubt be prosecuted, yet, they weren't behind the events. Mr King was and he's vanished.'

I nodded, coming up with a phrase I'd once used in an article for the *Bugle*. 'You could say his men were just the cat's paws.'

I cringed, as memory pointed out that my article had not been a great success. It started with a lunchtime lager in the Feathers where, despite furious bellows from Featherlight, who was in dispute with some unfortunate customer, I'd overheard talk from a gang of shoplifters who'd just arrived in town. Having managed to identify the brains of the outfit, and where they were going to strike next, I rushed back to the office and typed up a couple of hundred words. I'd been extremely proud of the article and even Editorsaurus Rex had seemed pleased, until it turned out that my shoplifters had really been shop-fitters. Following a painful and unnecessarily prolonged interview with the Editorsaurus, I was rarely assigned to report anything other than pet shows and fetes.

Still, Hobbes chuckled. 'Cat's paws! That's a good one.'

'I still don't understand what's going on,' I said, feeling even thicker than usual.

'But I'm beginning to.' He smiled. 'Yet, I fear I've been slow; I had all the evidence and still couldn't fit it together, though, in fairness, it is an unusual case.'

I waited, puzzled, as he sat, eyes closed, as if in a deep trance.

'I couldn't understand,' he continued, 'why, though I could track the cats, their spore would suddenly vanish. I have an idea now.

'Are you absolutely certain both Mr King and Miss King spoke to you last night?'

'Yes.'

'Excellent. You see, I was stumped because having examined the place we found you, I found no trace of Mr King.'

'But he was there, honest.'

'I believe you. I did, however, find signs of two big cats and some tufts of fur that might suggest a fight, which agrees with your information. What I found really baffling was coming across clear signs a human had been there, though only around where you were lying. From the size of the footprints, I was almost sure it had been a lady, and I'm now confident it was Miss King. Strangely, she had bare feet and left no apparent trail either approaching or leaving.'

Having great faith in Hobbes's tracking skills, I was puzzled by such a failure. 'She must have done. She couldn't just appear out of thin air, unless she swung through the trees like Tarzan.'

'I did, in fact, check the trees and found nothing to suggest she'd been climbing. However, I think you may have provided the key to explain it all.'

'Go on,' I urged, unable to think of anything I'd said that was important.

'Right. Consider this. Both Mr King and his sister spoke to you, yet he, apparently, left no marks at all, while she only left them near where you'd fallen.'

'I still don't understand.'

Hobbes grinned. 'Yet, there were two distinct sets of big cat prints. Both had approached you and gone away.'

'Weird.'

'Precisely what I thought, so I had a word with Mr Catt at the Wildlife Park this morning. I showed him the fur I'd picked up and some casts I'd made of the paw prints and he was adamant they weren't from a panther, or any cat he's aware of.'

'So, what are you getting at?' I asked, starting to get an inkling, though my brain was having difficulties.

'There is an explanation that fits the evidence.'

At the moment an unearthly cackle announced that Mrs Goodfellow had brought in the tea and, had I not been so sore and stiff, I'd have jumped into orbit, as usual. Setting down the tray, she filled two mugs. Hobbes chucked in a handful of sugar, stirred his mug, sucked his finger and took a great swig. He sighed, the sigh of a contented police officer.

'Thanks, lass,' he said.

She nudged me and grinned. 'Well done – you've cheered him up again.'

'I'm not sure how,' I said, 'but I think I'm going to find out.'

As she headed back towards the kitchen, I took a sip of tea, squealing as it parboiled my split lip. Hobbes poured himself a second mug, giving me a few seconds to think. It didn't help.

'So,' he said, 'have you got it yet?'

'Umm … I'm not sure. You say Felix wasn't there but a panther, no … umm … some mysterious big cat was? So was it a talking cat?'

'You might say that.'

'Really?' I let the idea settle in my brain. 'And you reckon Violet also got there without leaving a trace, though she was there, and there were signs of two cats.'

'That's right. Do you get it yet?'

'No … not unless Violet and Felix could turn into cats!' I laughed.

Hobbes wasn't laughing.

'Come off it,' I said. 'It's bad enough the Bashems turning out to be werewolves, but now you're saying my girlfriend is a cat?' I shook my head. 'It's ridiculous.'

'Is it?'

'Of course. Look, if she was a cat, I'd know and would have taken cat food on the picnic and, what's more,' I felt myself blush, 'I have … umm … kissed her, and, I can tell you, she's a real woman.'

'What I mean,' said Hobbes, 'is that she and her brother are werecats.'

'You really mean she can change into a cat?' I asked, trying to maintain a front of scepticism, even though what he was suggesting made sense, in a thoroughly nonsensical way. 'You're saying she can somehow – what's the word? – wolfifest into a cat?'

'The word we use with werecats is transmogrify,' he said, 'though, apart from that, you've got it. Of course, they can revert to human form whenever it suits them.'

By then, I was too full of conflicting thoughts and swirling emotions to cope. Shaking my head, staggering upstairs, I collapsed onto my bed and curled up into the foetal position, my mind squirming with confusion, horror and doubt. After about ten minutes, feeling no better but still with an urge to know, I returned to the sitting room, where Hobbes had taken advantage of my absence to squeeze a third mug of tea from the pot. Dregs was dozing at his feet.

'You'd better tell me everything,' I said. 'Just take it that I believe you.' Though I wasn't sure I did, nothing else made sense.

'I will,' said Hobbes, finishing his tea and taking a deep breath. 'To start with, the big cat sightings only started after Mr King moved into the area, which, I admit, is purely circumstantial evidence. Then, as you know, they vanished whenever I tracked them and, since I often came across tyre tracks close to where I'd lost the trail, I assumed someone was transporting them. I now think it likely they drove themselves. Another thing which may be significant is that Mr King wears an overpowering aftershave or cologne, which I suspect he uses to mask any animal odours. Otherwise, I'm certain I'd have noticed something.'

'It put you off the scent?'

'Or, the scent put me off. And Miss King uses perfume, does she not?'

'Yes, though that's not unusual, is it?'

'No, not in itself, but she does use rather a lot. Furthermore, we only became aware of two big cats after she joined him here. There is one point, though: has she ever met the dog?'

Dregs, opening an eye, wagged his tail.

I thought for a moment. 'No, never. Except … umm … nearly that time at the Wildlife Park when something frightened him when he went inside …' I ground to a halt, seeing what Hobbes was getting at.

'Dogs have excellent noses and aren't easily confused by artificial perfumes. I suspect her animal scent scared him. Of course, my nose wasn't all it should be that day, with all that camel hair. You know something? I've a feeling Mr King might have got away with his intimidation of Eric and Featherlight and, I suspect, others who've sold property to him recently, had he not become aware of the Bashems. His schemes were overturned by his hatred of werewolves.'

'But why does he hate them? Aren't werecats and werewolves equally cursed?'

'It only becomes a curse if they let it become one. The Bashems are perfectly happy with their heritage. As for Mr King's hatred, I can only speculate that it started out as the usual cat and dog thing, but it seems to have grown out of all proportion. I fear he may be somewhat unbalanced.'

'He's stark raving mad,' I said, remembering his tirade in the woods and shivering, 'but what about Violet? She was nice to me.'

'I'm sorry, but I fear she used you to get information about me. I was obviously a threat, being what I am.'

'What are you?' I asked, hoping for insight.

'A police officer.'

'Of course. But, Felix sounded like he hated you personally.'

'He wouldn't be the first.'

Though it was hard to accept, I was starting to believe him. Once upon a time I wouldn't have, but, since being with Hobbes, I'd come to realise the world had more in it than I ever could have imagined.

When we'd finished talking, Hobbes took Dregs out, leaving me to struggle with my confused feelings for Violet. I'd believed she was special, though, in all honesty, I hadn't had much to compare with her. Without doubt, she'd brought glamour and yearning into my life and there'd been days when I'd barely been able to think of anything except her and, furthermore, there'd been whole hours when I'd dared to hope she was mine. Now it all boiled down to one fact, and there was no escaping it: she was a cat. I'd actually fancied a cat.

The realisation, especially since it was more than mere fancy, for even when she'd greeted me so coldly at the festival, I'd still warmed to her, left me utterly bewildered and bereft. I think I had really loved her and part of me still did, while another part couldn't help recoiling at the thought of what she was. Even so, such disasters just seemed to happen to me, my relations with women seemingly cursed. Then, at the back of everything, I was struggling to come to terms with one really odd fact, a fact that didn't make sense: when Felix had seemed certain to kill me, she'd come to my rescue, as if she'd really cared for me, and her last words in the woods still haunted me. I sat for a long time, brooding.

As the evening darkened, Mrs Goodfellow brought a cup of cocoa. Thanking her, I took it to bed and, after forcing my bruised body into a pair of clean, stripy pyjamas, I sat by the window, sipping my drink, still lost in a sea of baffling thoughts. As the lingering fronds of the day slipped away, I stared down into Blackdog Street, glinting silver beneath the glare of electric lights, seeing groups of people wandering past, no doubt on their way between hostelries. One guy, swaying down the centre of the street, collapsed with his head on the kerb, his legs stretched into the road, fortunate that no cars came by. Eventually, his mates lugged him up and dragged him away amidst ribald comments. The town settled into its usual background noise. Thuds nearby suggested someone was working hard at their DIY. In the distance, a dog barked and a plane flew high overhead, flashing red and green lights in the clear sky.

I was just about to turn in when, fancying I'd glimpsed a greenish flash from the roof opposite, I stared into the night, seeing nothing. Dismissing it, I got into bed. After only a few seconds, jumping back out, I shut the window and drew the curtains. Though it was silly, the flash had reminded me of the glowing eyes of the previous night and, stupidly, I blushed; if it had been Violet's flashing eyes out there, she might have seen me undressing. Not that I really believed anything, least of all her, was out there; it had certainly been a trick of the light, or of my imagination. Though I lay down and tried not to think, it didn't work as I needed time for my twisted thoughts to untangle.

The church clock struck eleven as someone sang an enthusiastic, if inaccurate, version of *The Green, Green Grass of Home*. Sometime later, the silence in the street outside suggesting the revellers and DIYers had called it a day, although I could have sworn I'd not slept, I jerked into full wakefulness and sat up.

My skin was crawling with goose pimples. I couldn't see anything, other than faint shadows cast by whatever light made it through the curtain, and couldn't hear anything beyond the hiss of my breathing and the tattoo drummed out by my heart. I tried holding my breath, listening, hoping not to hear whatever had alarmed me. My hope was fulfilled, which frightened me almost as much as if I had heard something.

The thing was, something felt wrong and, though I tried reasoning with myself, arguing against the likelihood of anything being in my room that shouldn't, I was scared, really scared. Grabbing the sheets, I pulled them tight around me, though why I thought that would help was beyond me. Then, at last, on the edge of hearing, yet distinct, I heard a faint sound, a little like Velcro being pulled apart. It came again ... and again. It was close, very close.

'Hello?' I said with quavering voice that tended to falsetto. 'Is somebody there?'

'Yes,' purred a soft voice by my head.

'Violet?' I gasped, knowing instantly what had been wrong: I could smell her perfume. It was too dark to see her. 'What are you doing here?'

'I came to make sure you're alright.'

'I'm OK. That is, I'm not too bad ... nothing's actually broken ... I'm a bit sore though. And you?'

'I'm fine. I'm glad you're alright.'

'I'll turn the light on,' I said, moving as if to get out of bed.

She pushed me back.

'That would not be a very good idea. It will be best if you stay where you are.'

'Why?'

'Trust me.'

'Alright,' I said and almost did, though a strange confusion of terror and elation was swirling through me. 'It's ... umm ... nice to see you again. I mean to say, I'm glad you're here. I've missed you.'

'I've missed you, too. I hoped you'd call after the picnic. Why didn't you?'

'I did try when I was better.'

'You were ill? What was the matter?'

'I got a bad fever, after I'd walked home in the rain.'

'Sorry about that … I had to get away from the arboretum … Something nasty was in the woods.'

'Ah, yes,' I said, 'the werewolf.'

There was a sharp intake of breath. 'You know about them?'

'Only what I've picked up recently. They still scare me.'

'Poor Andy, I really wish you hadn't got involved in all of this.'

'In all of what?'

'Our war against those vile, filthy abominations.'

'Well … they're a bit dirty, maybe, but Hobbes reckons they're alright.'

'He would do, but he's quite wrong. Felix thought you were one of them.'

'Me? A werewolf? That's crazy.'

'Not a werewolf, but a collaborator, which is almost as bad.'

'You're talking like him.' I said, not liking it at all, for she didn't sound like my Violet. Though I'd loved hearing her voice, always sounding soft and sweet, even when she'd been frightened or angry, the new, fanatical harshness scared and repelled me even more than what she was saying. I hoped, she hadn't meant it.

She continued. 'Felix talks a lot of sense. No one wants those freaks polluting our world.'

'They don't do any harm.'

'That's not the point. They exist. Therefore, they must be annihilated.'

'Why? Hobbes reckons we can all live together.'

'You are starting to sound like a collaborator and I thought you were one of the good guys … I liked you, despite what Felix said, but perhaps he was right, like he was with Arthur.'

'Who's Arthur?' I asked, suddenly, unaccountably jealous.

'Arthur Crud. He was my fiancé. Felix warned me about him.'

'Arthur Crud? The rapist?'

'That's him. He was like you, nice and harmless on the surface but a monster beneath.'

'He didn't …' I felt sick.

'Not me. Some other poor girl who worked for us. He'd be banged up in prison right now if your friend Hobbes hadn't got him off.'

'Hobbes did that?' The idea was appalling.

'Yes. And yet you admire him. I don't understand you.'

I felt like I'd fallen into an ocean of confusion. That Hobbes had his bad points, I'd have been the first to admit, though I found it hard to believe he'd help a rapist escape justice. It wasn't what he did and, whereas I knew he had his own take on the law, in my experience, he'd always aimed for justice, even if it might have been a rough sort of justice.

'But I thought Hobbes had killed Arthur Crud,' I said.

'Killed him? Felix would have had him killed if Hobbes hadn't interfered.'

'What?'

'Hobbes got Arthur away when Felix sent round some of the boys to deal with him.'

'Oh. But I'm not like Arthur Crud.'

'No? I saw you throw yourself onto that poor girl.'

'I didn't. She threw herself onto me!'

Though she laughed, it was a cold laugh. 'Don't flatter yourself, you're not that good looking. Actually, you're not bad. What lets you down is being friends with Hobbes, who's responsible for all the nastiness in this godforsaken town. You really should get away from here, and get away quickly.'

'I'm not really his friend,' I said, regretting it immediately, feeling a real traitor. Yet, he wasn't exactly a friend, for friendship implies a sort of equality and I didn't believe I was his equal in anything. Even so, there was something between us and I did care for him and his good opinion. In fact, it occurred to me that I often felt almost like a son, who needed his father's approval. The idea shocked me, though the time was not right for thinking about it. 'I'm only here because I've got nowhere else.'

'I'm glad to hear that,' she said, her voice softening again. 'My advice is to get out of here, to get out of here tomorrow. Then you'll have a future to look forward to, a future untainted by association. But time's getting on and I must say goodbye now. It's been interesting knowing you.'

'Has it? Good. Umm ... are you going somewhere?'

'We're leaving. We can't stay after what's happened, can we?'

'I suppose not, but why come to see me? Why not send a note? Surely, this is dangerous.'

'Yes, but I really wanted to see you again. I'd hoped, just for a few days, that you might be the special one because there is something in you ... I don't know what. The thing is, in the beginning, Felix asked me to befriend you as a way to get at Hobbes but I actually found that I liked you. You seemed different to other men and I hoped I might get you away from him and that I'd have you forever.'

Her voice was so gentle and sad I sat, entranced, quite forgiving her unforgivable behaviour.

'I'd hoped, too,' I said.

'Did you? It's such a shame. If those stinking werewolves hadn't turned up, it might have worked out. Given time, I would have convinced you to think and act right and saved you. I wish I still could. Maybe, Felix would have accepted you. Still, it can't be helped. Felix has done what had to be done and we've got to move on. Maybe, we'll be able to come back when the fuss dies down and people can see that we acted for the best.'

'You don't always have to do what he says.'

'My interests are his interests.'

'Are you sure?'

'He's my brother.'

'Did he tell you to attack Mr Bullimore?'

'He doesn't tell me what to do. That half-breed stinks of werewolf and had to be destroyed. I'm only sorry I failed.'

'Because you came to help me.'

'Yes.'

'Against Felix.'

'Yes.'

'You don't have to go with him. If you stay, I'm sure we can work something out. You're not like him.'

'I am very much like him. Sometimes we have to be ruthless, even if it hurts. We must always see the bigger picture. But you could come with me.'

'But what about Felix?' I asked, almost ready to risk his wrath, just to be with her. I was too late.

'Hobbes is coming,' she hissed. 'I must go. Goodbye, darling. I am truly sorry.'

Something soft and velvety brushed my cheek. There was a faint sensation of movement and a dark shadow before the curtains flapped and she was gone. Everything was quiet.

I sat, as if her leaving had turned me to stone, knowing I still loved her.

The front door opening, heavy feet pounded upstairs.

Hobbes burst into my room, turning on the light. 'Are you alright?'

'Yes,' I said and astonished myself by bursting into tears.

I would, no doubt, have found the next few minutes excruciatingly embarrassing, had I been capable of anything other than gut-wrenching grief. Though grown men weren't supposed to cry, I couldn't have cared less.

'Whatever is the matter?' asked Hobbes, raising his hand as if to console me, hesitating, and scratching his head.

I couldn't force out much intelligible in the gaps between the sobs. He stared and looked uncomfortable. Dregs hurtled upstairs, stopping just outside my room, and, picking up the mood, threw back his big black head and howled.

Mrs Goodfellow, shrouded in a voluminous white nightie, her thin grey hair coiled in rollers, arrived. 'What have you been doing to him?'

'Nothing,' said Hobbes. 'I sensed one of those big cats up here when I was coming up the street, so I thought I'd better make sure it hadn't eaten him.' He sniffed. 'It seems Miss King has been to see you.'

'She has,' I said, squeezing out words in the intervals between upheavals of my chest. 'She said she's got to go away from here.'

I don't think I'd ever felt such a cutting, debilitating sense of loss, at least not as an adult. Unable to help it, I cried, while Dregs bristled and howled.

After several seconds of mayhem, Hobbes roared, 'Be quiet!'

It shut us both up. Dregs, tail between his legs, mournful eyed, fled, while I sat up, blowing my nose on the tissue Mrs G had pulled from her pocket.

'Thank you,' said Hobbes, frowning. 'Now, maybe you'll explain what she was doing here?'

Though I did my best, it wasn't my most coherent narrative and yet he listened, appearing to understand my ramblings.

'Did she give any hint where they might be going?'

I shook my head. 'No. Not today … She did once mention a house in France, but I don't know.'

'Oh well,' said Hobbes, looking eager, 'I'd better look for her. I'll see you in the morning.'

Loping towards the open window, he vaulted out.

'I'll make you a cup of cocoa,' said Mrs G.

Dregs crept into the room as she left, laying his head on my hand. I stroked his rough hair, which comforted us both so much that, when the old girl returned a few minutes later, carrying a steaming mug, I'd more or less recovered from the crying fit, while Dregs was back to his normal self, though avoiding places where I guessed Violet had been.

'Your eyes are red, dear,' said Mrs Goodfellow, handing me the mug. 'It's hard when a loved one goes away.'

'I'm not sure I … umm … loved her.'

'I think you did, dear.'

She was right, though my feelings were too tender to admit to. Only much later did it occur to me that she knew what she was talking about, her husband having left her to find himself in Tahiti. I supposed she'd probably found his desertion hurtful.

'Drink it all up,' she said. 'It'll help you sleep.'

While I sipped, she went to her room for a hammer and nails and made the window secure. Though I was convinced Violet and Felix had gone forever, that it was unnecessary, it did make me feel safer to know he couldn't get in, even though I'd still have welcomed her. If only, I thought, I could have got her away from his malign influence, I could have loved her. I smiled, feeling a little better, wondering if I might be able to tame the wildcat. Though it was a silly thought, it made me giggle. The cocoa had an aromatic aftertaste.

'You put something in this, didn't you?'

'A little something to make you feel better. You'll sleep well.'

'I am feeling a little woozy.'

Waking to sunlight pouring into my room, I enjoyed a few moments of comfortable, hazy dozing until memories of the night's events dropped back into my mind like junk mail, filling it with confusion and a sense of utter loss. I made a decision to lie where I was forever, to refuse all sustenance and comfort, to allow my life to quietly slip away. It seemed the best course or, at least, the one with the least pain. Of course, my death might result in a small amount of grief for a few: Hobbes and the old girl, Billy, maybe, my parents, possibly. As I imagined their tears at my funeral, I hoped that maybe, just maybe, a mysterious, elegant woman, dressed all in black, would linger and drop a single flower on my grave.

I indulged this fantasy until a whiff of frying bacon put things in perspective, persuading me not to pine away.

A quick inventory suggested my injuries were getting better: my lip, though still sore, had shrunk to almost normal proportions, my bruises weren't quite so tender, and the scratches I could see looked clean and well on their way to healing. Getting up, I washed, dressed and made my way down to breakfast, finding Mrs Goodfellow alone with a frying pan. Dregs had been shut out. Occasionally, his head would bounce up at the window.

'Good morning, dear.'

After the usual enquiries, she fed me bacon and eggs, delicious, despite the lingering numbing effect of antibiotics. I felt surprisingly well, and even better after topping up with toast and marmalade.

'Where's Hobbes?' I asked, pushing my plate aside.

'He's still out hunting. It's not like him to miss his breakfast.'

'That's true. Do you think he's caught them?'

'I'm sure he'd be back if he had.'

I half hoped he had caught them; that is, I hoped he'd caught Felix and slung him in a cell, or a cage. At that moment, Hobbes, looking dishevelled and filthy, walked in, without saying a word, slouched across to the sink, picked up the washing up bowl and poured in a full box of Sugar Puffs and two pints of milk, before putting it on the table.

Not bothering with a spoon, he simply shovelled the mess into his mouth with his hands, hands criss-crossed by deep cuts. Finishing the last Sugar Puff, lifting the bowl to his mouth, he poured the remaining milk down his throat.

'That's better,' he said. 'Is there any tea, lass?'

The old girl handed him a steaming mugful, which he drank in one gulp. She refilled it and he repeated the procedure.

'Thank you. It's been a long night.'

'Did you catch them?' I asked, desperate to know about Violet.

'No.'

'So, why are you all scratched?'

'Oh, that,' he said with a glance at his hands. 'There was a fire at the Feathers, which I suspect was arson carried out by Mr King or his sister, possibly in revenge, or to keep me occupied and out the way. Whatever the reason, I had to abandon the hunt, break in to the Feathers and extinguish the blaze, finding, unfortunately, that Featherlight had just installed razor wire around every possible entrance. I had to tear it up to get in and it was lucky for Billy that I did; he was fast asleep behind the bar and drunk.'

'He must have been relieved when you turned up,' I said, memories of my terror and despair, when I'd burned down my flat and been pulled out by Hobbes, returning.

'He will be, when he sobers up.'

'Did you put the fire out?'

'Yes, though I had to shake up a couple of beer kegs and punch holes in them, since all the fire-extinguishers were empty.'

'Featherlight should be prosecuted for that,' I said, virtuously.

'No one was hurt.'

'Umm ... apart from you, no one was hurt, and Billy could have been killed.'

'Yet, I'm fine and so is Billy, so why add to Featherlight's problems?'

'Fair enough. Umm ... is he still banged up?'

'No, the murder charge was dropped, due, in no small part, to your evidence, and he's been released, which is just as well as we needed all the cells for Mr King's boys. Most of them, I'm glad to say, are inclined to talk, and their boss will be in a heap of trouble if we catch him. So, I'm afraid, will Miss King.'

'She only did it because he made her.'

Hobbes shook his head. 'Sorry, Andy, that might have been true once, but she had no cause to attack Mr Bullimore.'

'But she stopped attacking him to save me. That's got to be worth something.'

'I'm glad she did and, though there's obviously a better side to her, she murdered Henry Bishop.'

'No,' I said angered at the accusation, 'that's ridiculous. I was with her. She didn't do it.'

'I believe she killed Henry when he went into the restaurant.'

'But surely it was Felix who attacked him. She was having a meal with me.'

'True, but dead men don't open doors. Henry was still alive, badly wounded admittedly, but alive when he got through the door. Who was the first to react?'

'Violet: and she tried to save him.'

'That's what it must have looked like. You said the first thing she did was check his pulse?'

'Yeah.'

'That, I fear, was her cover for tearing his carotid artery, thus killing him instantly.'

Putting my head in my hands, I tried to think back. Henry had certainly been alive when he'd fallen at my feet, and Violet knelt beside him. I remembered her hand, such a pretty little hand, reaching out to his neck, my feeling of nausea as he haemorrhaged over that same hand. Could it have been as Hobbes was suggesting? I had to admit it; it could.

'If she did do it, she was trying to protect Felix,' I said, as if that excused her.

'I'm sure she was, though I have little doubt she administered the coup de grace after Mr King did the initial damage. Henry's sudden demise struck me as odd at the time, but I was led astray, taking her at face value.'

Mrs G, chuckling, poked him in the ribs with a bony finger. 'You always do where young ladies are concerned.'

Hobbes smiled and returned to his serious look. 'I'm also convinced Miss King murdered Mike Rook. I picked up a trace of her perfume in the room, though, unfortunately, since it was very faint and masked by all the hospital smells, I didn't recognise it until much later. Mr King was undoubtedly responsible for the initial attack, trying to ensure Mr Rook wouldn't speak to me. Since Mr Rook was a tough lad and showing signs of recovery, he arranged for his sister to finish the job.'

'But,' I said, unwilling to give her up without a struggle, 'she can't be a killer, she's too timid and gentle. What about when the werewolf frightened her at the arboretum? If she was like you say, wouldn't she have attacked it?'

'I suspect,' said Hobbes, 'it wasn't Les Bashem who frightened her. Even in werewolf form he offered no threat. He was merely keeping an eye on you two.'

'What then?'

'She was more concerned about her own reaction. Her instinct would be to transmogrify and attack. Yet, since you were there, she couldn't, because you wouldn't have been favourably impressed had she changed into a cat before your eyes. She didn't want to lose you.'

'But why not? I'm nothing special.'

'True … but you must have been something to her. I can't, for the life of me, understand why. Can you?' He turned to Mrs G.

'No. Not at all, though he does have excellent teeth.'

I was somewhat deflated by their opinions. Yet, when I looked up they were both grinning.

'Cheer up,' said Hobbes. 'You're not so bad, really.'

He raised a hand and, though I cringed, he patted me quite gently and I didn't cry out.

'Thanks,' I said.

'Don't mention it. I'm off for a nap before lunch.' Standing up, he belched. 'Pardon me; it's all the puff in the Sugar Puffs.'

'Before you go,' I said, as a thought occurred, 'what happened to Arthur Crud?'

'Mr Crud? The poor chap was maliciously accused. He's a gentle, bumbling, young fellow, not unlike you. Though the evidence I uncovered totally exonerated him and he was found not guilty, I had to hide him when someone, Mr King I now believe, whipped up bad feeling because he'd taken his sister to lunch on a couple of occasions.

Mr Crud is living safely in Cornwall for the time being.'

'Did you know the girl who accused him worked for Felix?'

'I did, though she was only a temporary assistant at his London office. At the time it didn't seem important.'

'Did Felix force her to accuse Arthur?'

'Possibly, but it's more likely he paid her. Apparently, she went missing a couple of weeks afterwards. The London boys couldn't find her and I fear Mr King disposed of a potentially dangerous witness. Right, I'm off.' Yawning, he stamped upstairs.

There were a couple of hours before lunch, which the old girl was just starting. It was going to involve chicken pieces. She could do wonderful things with chicken pieces, though why she was attacking them with a mallet was beyond me.

'I think I'll take the dog out,' I shouted over the thumping.

'Righto, dear. It's a lovely day. Enjoy yourself, if you're well enough.'

'I'm OK, I'll not go far.'

When I left the house, it felt great to be in the sun again, despite a fierce wind whipping up stinging dust from the dry streets. I was glad to reach the soft greenery of Ride Park. As I let Dregs off his lead, he ran free with a joyous bark and I wished I could enjoy such simple pleasures. Though I'd never expected my relationship with Violet to last, I had hoped.

Dregs, ran back with a long stick, dropped it at my feet and bounced and barked until I threw it, while I struggled to understand my feelings, for even after everything I'd learned about her, I was going to miss her. Though she might have been a murderer, she'd been good to me, and I still couldn't really believe that a woman so sweet and lovely had liked me, maybe even loved me. It was just my luck her turning out to be a cat.

Still, on reflection, I had always been a little afraid of her and, though it had never been the debilitating terror Felix had caused, it had been more even than my normal nervousness in the presence of an attractive woman. I couldn't help myself: I wanted her back, even if she was going to maul me.

As Dregs rushed back towards me, a harsh voice yelled.

'Oi, Caplet!'

Seemingly distracted, Dregs forgot to stop and his stick rapped my shins, making me hop and mutter. Someone laughed.

I turned to see Featherlight, standing on the edge of the woods, a can of beer in his hand.

'You make me laugh, you do.'

'Do I?'

'Yes. Now, when you see your mate Hobbes, tell him I said thanks for rescuing Billy and for putting the fire out and getting me out of the nick. And tell him he owes me for the two kegs of lager he used for putting out the fire.'

'What?' I said, outraged, 'that's not fair.'

'You tell him,' he said, displaying his horrible, big, yellow teeth in a grin, 'he'll understand.' He lumbered away, chuckling, a ring of pale flab flowing from beneath his vest, like a part-inflated rubber ring.

I guessed he'd been joking, though his usual attempts at humour involved pain and humiliation for whichever poor customer he'd picked on. I had, on several occasions, been that customer.

When Dregs was limp and panting, we returned home to find Hobbes was up, washed, groomed and back to normal. I passed on Featherlight's remarks.

He snorted. 'He was in a good mood, I suppose.'

'Well, you did get him off a murder charge, rescued his barman, stopped the Feathers burning down, and got rid of the crook who was trying to force him from his home.'

'I was only doing my job. Now, let's enjoy lunch.'

After he said grace, Mrs Goodfellow served a fantastic gazpacho, a real gazpacho, so very different from my disaster. I could hardly believe only three weeks had passed since then; life with Hobbes moved at a hectic pace.

'Would you like a bottle of wine?' asked Mrs G, as we were savouring the soup.

'Good idea,' said Hobbes. 'I intend to take it easy this afternoon.'

'Excellent,' said I.

'Sorry, dear,' she said, heading towards the cellar, 'you can't have any until Doctor Procter says so.'

She returned, holding two bottles, tutting. 'I really must clean down there. There's coal dust all over these.'

Having wiped them with a damp cloth, she opened one and poured it into a glass big enough for an adequate goldfish bowl. Placing it in front of Hobbes, she served the main course.

'What is it?' I asked, salivating. 'It smells fantastic. Is it Chinese?'

'That's right, dear, bang bang chicken.'

'I didn't know you could make Chinese food.'

'I do sometimes. I nursed there once.'

'When?'

'When I was a nurse.'

'Right … anyway … umm … it looks great.'

'Thank you, dear.'

It was, as I expected, excellent, aromatic, savoury, piquant and served with a refreshing simple salad, just perfect for a hot afternoon. Though, as usual, we ate in silent homage to the old girl's genius, unusually, not all of my attention was focussed onto the meal, part of it still being with Violet. I kept going back to her words about Felix having done what had to be done and, though I'd assumed she'd been referring to his business dealings, I wondered if there was more to them.

The old girl's remark about the coal dust on the bottle puzzled me for she normally kept the cellar as spotless as a surgery. Hobbes, raising his glass, sniffed the contents, making me realise how much I would have enjoyed a glass or two. I tried to concentrate on the bang bang chicken, thinking it was a funny name for a dish, though appropriate, considering the bashing she'd given it. It made me think about the banging I'd heard before Violet turned up.

Hobbes, opening his lips, tilted the glass, my own taste buds anticipating his pleasure.

My next move surprised both of us. Leaping up, my chair falling, clattering, to the ground, I shoved the glass from his hands, the wine splashing over us, the glass shattering onto the kitchen floor. He stared at me, then at his stained shirt front and then at the stem of the glass, still in his great fist.

'Have you recently joined the Temperance Movement?' he asked.

'No … I think … umm … that is … the wine might be poisoned.'

'No!' He roared.

I cringed, expecting storm-force anger, but the shout was directed at the dog, who was licking at the spillage. Dregs backed away, assuming his martyred look.

'Why do you think that?'

'I don't know. It might be.'

'It never has been before.'

'No, but I think … umm … Felix broke into the cellar last night. Someone was banging and I think it was him knocking the door in, because Mrs Goodfellow says there's dust down there and there shouldn't be any. I reckon he's poisoned the wine. Violet said he'd done what had to be done and I think she meant getting you out the way.'

'It smelt alright,' he said, dipping his finger in the mess and touching his tongue, 'and it doesn't taste as if anything's wrong with it.'

'Perhaps he used an odourless, colourless, tasteless poison.'

'Ah yes, one unknown to medical science. There are a lot of them about.'

'Are there?'

'No. Anyway, Dregs seems fine.'

Dregs, wagging his tail on hearing his name, was not the sort to hold a grudge.

'But Felix,' I said, 'might have poisoned some other bottles.'

'Let's take a look.'

Hobbes and I went down the steps. When Dregs stopped at the top, refusing to come any further, I gave Hobbes a significant look that he ignored. On first glance, nothing seemed wrong. However, as we passed the wine racks, we could see the tunnel door's lock had been smashed, a sledgehammer had been discarded in the corner, and the coal pile had been shoved aside. I had no doubt who was responsible. Hobbes, growling, looked around. The wine appeared untouched, except for several bottles of the best stuff having disappeared.

He was totting up how many, when we discovered the bomb.

Sniffing at it, pointing to the electronic counter wired to a number of off-brown sticks, he looked thoughtful. 'I suppose that shows how long we've got before it goes off.'

'Umm …' I replied, hypnotised by the flashing digits, 'I guess so. Is it counting in minutes or seconds?'

'Seconds by the looks of it.'

'So we've got thirty seconds. What are you going to do?'

'Twenty-five seconds now. Let me think.'

'OK.' Oddly, I felt quite calm.

It read twenty seconds when, grabbing the bomb, tucking it under his arm like a rugby ball, he charged across the cellar, and plunged down the steps into the tunnels.

Time seemed almost to slow down, though I was horribly aware it was running out far too fast. I hesitated, torn between wanting to help Hobbes, realising I couldn't, wondering whether I should make an attempt to get Mrs G and Dregs out of the house, though there was no time, and an urge to save myself.

Before I'd made up my mind, Hobbes bounded back into the cellar. On landing, he turned, jamming the door into place.

He'd got rid of the bomb. 'What did …?'

A tongue of hot red flame hurled him and the door across the cellar and, though it all happened so fast, I'm sure he whooped just before he slammed into the back wall. There was a deafening roar, a flash of heat and a rumble.

I picked myself up, coughing in the dust haze.

'Well,' said Hobbes, standing up, rubbing his elbow, 'that would have been more fun if the wall hadn't got in the way.'

Dregs rushed downstairs, barking and sneezing, Mrs Goodfellow close behind. Looking around, she shook her head. 'Look at the mess you've made.'

'It was a bomb,' I said. 'A great, big, bloody bomb!'

'Language, Andy,' said Hobbes, his face blackened like a coal miner's. 'I'll clean myself up and finish my dinner. Maybe you'll let me enjoy my glass of wine in peace this time.'

I stood there dumbfounded until Mrs G, setting to with dustpan and broom, chivvied me out the way. She didn't appear at all concerned that we might all have been killed.

That was pretty much the end of it, as far as we were concerned. We never heard any further news of Felix or Violet, but every time I read a story about a mysterious big cat sighting I wondered and, though Hobbes reckoned they'd probably gone abroad to continue their horrible schemes, I had a sneaking hope I'd reformed her.

The Bashems and Mr Bullimore, having picked up a small fortune in insurance money for the disastrous festival, continued to live on Loop's Farm. Though we became friends, I never felt quite comfortable if left on my own with them, especially after dark. Some fears were fundamental.

One lasting outcome was that the tunnel leading from the cellar collapsed. I was glad nothing could use it anymore, but I think it upset Hobbes. Another effect was that a section of Blackdog Street subsided, leaving a hole three metres deep. Although the council and gas board looked into it, they never got to the bottom of the mystery. They did, eventually, fill it in.

The day after the explosion, I began writing this memoir, thinking it might help me come to terms with losing her. It didn't.

Inspector Hobbes

and the Gold Diggers

Unhuman III

1

'This evening,' said the newsreader, just as my head was starting to nod, 'the quiet Cotswold town of Sorenchester was rocked by an explosion and small arms fire when a gang attempted to snatch gold with an estimated value in excess of one million pounds. Jeremy Pratt reports from the scene.'

I sat up agog as the familiar buildings of The Shambles appeared on television, with Jeremy Pratt, tall, thin and solemn, standing with a microphone in his hand. He was outside Grossman's Bank, which was enwrapped in police tape. In the background a van was smoking, while a fireman coiled up a hose as thick as an anaconda.

'Good evening,' said Jeremy, smiling with maximum condescension and minimum humour. 'At nine-thirty this evening, a gang, who were armed and wearing balaclavas, made a daring raid on the armoured security van behind me, which, a spokesman has confirmed, was being used to transfer a large consignment of gold sovereigns to the vault of Grossman's Bank. I have with me Mr Percival Longfellow, the driver.'

Jeremy turned to a tubby, balding man at his side, a man who looked utterly bewildered. 'Tell me, Mr Longfellow: is it true the robbers used explosives to break into the van?'

'Eh?' said Mr Longfellow, cupping his already prominent ears in his hands.

'Did the robbers use explosives to break into the van?'

'I can't hear very well since they blew the bloody doors off.'

'I see. Was anybody injured?'

'What?'

'Did the explosion hurt anybody?' asked Jeremy, articulating every syllable.

'You need to learn not to mumble so much, mate. I'm a little deaf since the explosion. They blew the doors off, you know.'

Jeremy raised his voice. 'And then what happened?'

'You what?'

'What happened after they blew the doors off?' Jeremy shouted, red faced and exasperated.

'No. What happened was they blew the bloody doors off and stole the money.'

'Amazing,' said Jeremy, looking baffled. 'Thank you very much, Mr Longfellow.' He shoved him out of shot.

'What?'

'Anyway,' Jeremy continued, 'it would seem that, after the gang had blown the van's doors off, they threatened a guard with firearms and there are unconfirmed reports of several shots having been fired. Then, having overpowered the guard, they seized the contents of the van, which, I have been led to believe, included a substantial quantity of gold sovereigns. They loaded them into the back of a get-away vehicle and made off with their ill-gotten gains. However, it appears they were thwarted by the local police, who have arrested three members of the gang and retrieved all of the gold.

'A police spokesman has, however, confirmed that two of the gang managed to escape and that the police are now looking for a white van with a large hole in its roof.'

The picture returned to the studio. 'Thank you, Jeremy,' said the newsreader. 'We'll come back to that story as soon as further details emerge. Now, over to Penny for the latest weather forecast.'

Once I was over the initial surprise, I was disappointed that I was missing all the excitement, for, much to my amazement, I'd become something of an adrenalin junkie since coming to know Inspector Hobbes of the Sorenchester Police. Anyone spending time with him needed to adjust, and quickly, to living with high intensity excitement: and fear. It had struck me just how often I'd been terrified since our first meeting and, although sometimes I wished I'd never set eyes on his huge, ugly frame, I'd survived and come to realise I wouldn't have wished to miss any of it. Life with Hobbes in it was interesting.

As I lounged in my chair, a number of thoughts kept resurfacing in my head. The first was why would anyone be taking gold to a bank at night? The second was how did the robbers know it was going to be there? The third was that if the robbers had been inside the getaway van, then how had the police retrieved the gold and arrested three of them? It all sounded weird to me, and since that was the case, I suspected Hobbes had been on the scene.

I was frustrated I wasn't there. A case of extreme bad timing had meant that I happened to be overnighting at my parents. Trying to get a good night's sleep on their ancient camp bed – uncomfortable, unstable and creaking with every breath – had proved a colossal failure and, giving up, I'd crept back into their lounge, switched on the television and slumped into an armchair, hoping the twenty-four hour news would be showing the usual boring stuff, and that I'd soon be lulled to sleep. Instead, I ended up sitting in front of the news for another two or three hours before, getting cold and there being no further developments, I returned to bed, where I supposed I must have dozed in between long intervals of tortured wakefulness.

I'd finally dropped into a deep slumber when there was a knock on the door and Mother walked in with a mug of tea.

'Good morning,' she said in a loud, cheerful voice. 'Rise and shine!'

She meant well, so, suppressing a groan, forcing a smile, I sat up and reached for the mug, muttering my thanks.

I should have taken more care, should have remembered how unstable the camp bed was. I didn't and it collapsed in a sequence of awkward stages, propelling my head backwards, flinging my feet upwards and resulting in a wave of hot tea breaking over my face as the mug caught me a mighty wallop on the bridge of the nose. As I thrashed about in the wreckage trying to break free, my big toe struck a bookcase at my side, but I had no time to fully appreciate that particularly exquisite agony, because I'd dislodged an old-fashioned alarm clock that dropped, with a merry jingle, into my right eye socket. Groaning, one hand reaching for my toe, the other clutching my face, I curled up, believing the worst was over. A foolish mistake. A deluge of books, all of them hardbacks, rained down, heavy wooden shelves battered me, and finally everything went dark. The bookcase had crashed down, like a coffin lid.

As I lay there, stunned and in pain, I heard the muffled voice of my father: 'What on earth is the idiot doing this time?'

'He's had an accident,' said Mother.

'He is an accident.'

'It wasn't his fault, really. It was the camp bed.'

'Pah! The boy's a fool. He takes after your brother.'

'You leave Harold out of this. He can't help it.'

I was unable to move, and interesting though my parents' discussion was, I wanted air. 'Help me,' I cried.

'Help me, what?' said Father.

'Help me, please.'

'That's better.' With a grunt, he lifted the bookcase, allowing me to roll free.

'Well, what do you say?' asked Father, as I got to my feet, shedding books like a moulting dog sheds hair.

'Ouch?'

'Bah!' Turning, he walked away, shaking his head and muttering.

Mother handed me a wad of tissues to staunch my bloodied nose and fetched a cold flannel for my eye, which was already swelling. Then Father insisted that I cleared up the mess I'd made, which took a surprising time, since all the books had to be replaced in alphabetical order.

Some good came of the accident, for my nose was so stuffed with blood clots I could barely taste the breakfast kippers. I'm not keen on them at the best of times, but the blackened, chewy relics Mother favoured were appalling. As a guest at Hobbes's, where I was fed daily by Mrs Goodfellow, his housekeeper, I now recognised and appreciated excellent food and knew just how terrible a cook Mother was. I could barely believe that, once upon a time, I'd thought she wasn't too bad.

Yet it was, indirectly, her cooking that had brought me to stay with them. The previous afternoon, she'd phoned in a panic, telling me Father was ill; dying, she'd suggested. Although we'd never got on, mostly because he'd always treated me as an imbecile, I'd felt compelled to do my filial duty. Arriving after a forty minute bus ride from Sorenchester and a long walk, and fearing the worst, I'd pressed the doorbell of *Dunfillin,* their new bungalow.

I'd been astonished when Father opened the door. He was not dying, but had merely been suffering extreme indigestion after overindulging on Mother's lasagne. Since it was late, I'd had little choice other than to pass the evening with them and to spend the night. Mother was, as ever, too clingy, while Father's sarcastic streak had broadened since he'd retired from dentistry and had no one to torture. Besides, now he ate all his meals at home, his chronic dyspepsia had not improved his temper.

Despite a slight nausea, fatigue, and being well battered, I volunteered to wash up after breakfast. I should have known better. It turned out that a kipper had exploded in the microwave and it took me over an hour before I was able to chip off the last few chunks. At least it gave me time to think about the robbery, though having no more information than I'd had last night, I had no idea what had really happened.

Eventually, having finished my chores and eager for further news, I went through to the lounge, where Mother was ironing socks, while Father read the newspaper, providing a running commentary on whatsoever caught his attention. Having learned in my youth not to disturb them when they were thus engrossed, I sat down, kept quiet and fretted. I thought of ringing Mrs Goodfellow and finding out what was happening but, having bought a bus ticket, I was short of cash and feared Father's acerbic comments should I not drop a substantial donation into the tin they kept by the hall phone. I wished I had a mobile. I'd had one once, when I, Andy Caplet, had been the worst-paid reporter on the *Sorenchester and District Bugle*, the *Sad B*, as it was affectionately known, but it had perished with the rest of my belongings when my flat had burnt down. Since then, having lost my job, I'd never had the money to buy a new one, or, to be honest, much need of one.

For the next half hour or more, I struggled to keep still, forcing myself not to wriggle, scratch or sigh. Instead, I stared at the deep, brown carpets, the heavy plush furniture, and the porcelain figurines that had to be dusted twice a day. It seemed like an aeon had passed when Father went to the bathroom, leaving the paper behind. I grabbed it, flicked rapidly through and was disappointed there was nothing about the robbery. I guessed the story had broken too late. Wishing the bungalow had thicker internal walls, I tried to ignore Father's rumblings.

'Did you know there was a gold robbery in Sorenchester last night,' I asked when he returned, still doing up his trousers.

'When are you going back there?' he asked. 'The sooner the better, I say, before you demolish the bungalow.'

'Oh, no,' said Mother. 'He's no trouble, really. He's going to stay with us for a few days, aren't you, Andy? I counted four changes of clothes in his bag and I can always wash them if he needs more. It'll be no bother. He's lost weight and looks like he could do with some good home cooking.'

'That would be really nice,' I said, 'but, since Father's better, I think I really must go back today. Hobbes might require my assistance.'

'God help him if he does,' said Father.

'Sorry,' I said, trying to ignore Mother's look of disappointment, 'but I'd better get there as soon as possible.'

My departure was hastened by the sight of the lump Mother disinterred from the freezer, intending to warm up for our lunch. Too polite to ask what it was, convinced nothing edible should be such a mottled grey, and certain it should not have such a peculiar, rainbow sheen, I made my excuses. Grabbing my bag, saying my farewells and promising to keep in touch, I set off for Sorenchester. It was approaching midday, and I was hoping to be back in time for dinner, as Hobbes habitually called lunch. Not that I was overly concerned about being late, because I was confident Mrs Goodfellow would rustle up something delicious, should I look hungry enough, and I had a talent for looking hungry. Just as importantly, I was desperate to find out about the attempted gold robbery, straight from the Hobbes's mouth.

My first problem arose on reaching the bus stop, when an increasingly frantic search through my pockets revealed a horrible truth: I'd lost my return ticket. In desperation, I counted out all the money on me, a scanty collection of silver and copper coins, my heart sinking as I realised it totalled less than one pound. Although I could have returned to *Dunfillin* and begged, I did have a modicum of pride, and besides, the bus was approaching. As it stopped, I made up my mind. I was nothing if not decisive.

The doors opened and I stepped aboard, where the driver, a spotty young man with short, greasy hair, smirked at me as if he'd never seen anything so funny.

'How far can I get for ninety-eight pee?' I asked, clutching my change in a sweaty grasp.

With a shrug and a long-suffering sigh, he consulted a dog-eared scrap of paper. 'Ninety pence will get you to the Deerstone stop.'

'Will I be over the hill, then?'

'Looks like you're already over the hill, mate,' said the driver, displaying an irregular set of teeth with a greenish tinge.

'I mean,' I said, 'will that take me past the top of Nobby Hill?'

'That it will, mate.'

'I'll do it!' Counting out ninety pence, I dropped it into the slot and picked up my ticket.

The bus was three quarters empty, with an ingrained residue of sweat mingled with diesel fumes. I took a seat by the window, reasonably pleased, because, after Nobby Hill, which was renowned both for height and steepness, the road to Sorenchester was relatively flat and I thought it would be a moderately easy walk from there. Certainly, it was going to be a long one, fifteen miles I'd guess, but it was a nice day and I hoped to thumb a lift. Even if I couldn't, I reckoned I'd make it to Sorenchester in four hours or thereabouts.

As we chugged though town, although glad to be going home, my mind was ticking over and barely aware of anything happening in the dusty streets, until we pulled up at a stop.

'All aboard,' said the driver, as the doors opened. 'Hurry up!'

'I am hurrying,' said a woman. 'I just need a moment to put my clothes on.'

Instinctively my head turned towards a pretty young student, dressed in tight jeans and t-shirt. She was shoving a large laundry bag aboard. I settled back down, amused, but disappointed.

It wasn't long before we reached Nobby Hill, where the bus, slowing to little more than jogging pace, strained to reach the summit. Massive trees flanked the sides of the road, glowing green under a sun that was still fierce for the time of year, although here and there a dash of tawny and the reddening of rowans hinted at the changing season. A pair of puce-faced hikers toiling up the hill made me even gladder I was riding the bus. Yet, all too soon, having reached the summit, we dipped towards the Deerstone stop.

'It's the end of the road for you, mate,' said the driver, as if I was thinking of staying put.

We stopped and I disembarked, pleased I'd remembered my bag. I watched the bus drive away, took a deep breath, slung my bag over my shoulder and began walking with my thumb stuck out in the time-honoured signal. Half a dozen cars and a lorry passed by almost immediately, all of them ignoring me, and then there was nothing: absolutely nothing. After about twenty minutes, I began to wonder if hitching a lift had been a fanciful idea, although it had seemed reasonable enough on a road that was normally busy. There was nothing I could do but shrug, keep walking, and wonder what had happened to the traffic.

The sun was making the road ahead shimmer. I guessed I'd been walking for an hour with nothing passing in either direction, and home felt a weary distance away, when, at last, I heard a car's engine. A muddy green Land Rover drove towards me along a rutted side road. Hoping it was heading for Sorenchester, I stopped, waggling my hitcher's thumb and trying to look like a perfect passenger. To my delight, the Land Rover slowed down and stopped.

The driver's window opened and I stepped forward, leaning in, seeing my benefactor, a young man in a checked shirt, corduroy trousers and a baseball cap, was looking at me expectantly.

'Can I help you?' he asked.

'Where are you going?'

'Home.' He pointed along the road to Sorenchester.

'Me too,' I said, nodding. 'Can I have a lift?'

'Yes, but, I'm going home …'

'That's fine. Just take me as far as you're going.'

'OK.' He shrugged. 'Suit yourself. Hop in.'

I hopped, shut the door and belted myself in. 'Thank you. It's very kind of you.'

'It's nothing.'

He was right. Setting off towards Sorenchester, he turned almost immediately into a dusty lane and came to a stop by the side of an old red-brick farm house.

'Home,' he said, grinning. 'I tried to tell you.'

'Thanks very much,' I said, gritting my teeth, getting out and trudging back the way we'd just come. At least it was downhill.

That was the only vehicle I laid eyes on, apart from a distant glimpse of a tractor in a field. The cylinder of hay it was carrying reminded me of a giant Swiss roll, an unfortunate analogy, as I was already starting to feel ravenous and guessed it was lunchtime. No doubt that was why the farmer had been heading home. The sun was at its zenith, sweat was sticking my shirt to my back and I had to keep moving my bag from shoulder to shoulder, aware they were starting to chafe, and, as if to distract me from that particular woe, a blister was coming up on my heel. Licking dry lips with a dry tongue, I wished I'd had the foresight to bring a drink and my thirst wasn't helped by seeing a sign to the Red Dragon Inn. I wondered how much ice-cold lager they'd let me have for eight pence. None whatsoever, I suspected. I trudged on.

The road really was remarkably empty. Nothing, besides the occasional bird, was moving, and I could almost believe I was the only human left in the world. I guessed there'd been a major accident or something that had meant the road was closed, and it now seemed a very long road, a very hot road, and one that was increasingly hard on my feet. Eventually, a most welcome downhill section took me to the tiny village of Northsorn, about half way to Sorenchester, where I beheld the Squire's Arms, a fine, old-fashioned, thatch-roofed pub, just off the road.

On reaching it, I loitered near the front door, which was wedged open, and stared longingly at the rows of beer pumps, considering my chances of begging for a drink. Unfortunately, there was a huge, shaven-headed, scowling man behind the bar. He reminded me, with his dim-witted, ugly, malevolent face, massive, thick arms and general look of belligerence, of 'Featherlight' Binks, the landlord of the Feathers in Sorenchester. He did not look the sympathetic type. Giving up on beer, I considered getting a drink from the tap in the gents' toilet but, since it was on the far side of the bar room and I'd have to walk there under the scrutiny of that scowl, I hesitated. When he glared at me, flexing his biceps, displaying an impressive red rose tattoo and giving an impression of great strength, I gave up. I'd just have to keep walking.

However, my situation wasn't quite as bad as it seemed, for the River Soren appeared out of the fields next to the Squires Arms and ran beside the road for a short distance. Coming across a flat, grassy spot beneath the shade of a fine old cedar tree, I laid down my bag, removed my shoes and socks, rolled up my chinos to my knees and plunged my feet into the stream. Although the initial shock made me gasp, it was soon blissful. I sighed, wiggling my toes as a large rainbow trout rose to inspect them before taking fright and concealing itself within a mass of streaming weeds. When my feet were sufficiently cool, I knelt on the bank, splashed my face and felt much better, despite still being desperate for a drink. Yet, the river, glinting, gleaming, gurgling and burbling, held enough drink for thousands. It was tempting, though I dithered a while, trying not to think of all the bugs it might contain and what the trout did in it. The temptation was too strong. Lying flat on my stomach, leaning over the stream, I opened my mouth and drank greedily. Though a little earthy, the river water was cool, fresh and delightful.

Gulping it down, drinking my fill, I was happy until rough hands grabbed my ankles and lifted them, plunging my head under the surface, causing water to pour up my nose, and explode into my sinuses. Panicking, in pain, desperate for air, flailing, writhing, squirming and kicking, unable to escape, I was certain I was going to drown until I was released to slide into the river. I grazed my hands on the pebbly bottom before, pushing up and kicking, I made it to the surface. Gasping for air, I floundered as the current took me.

'Help!' I screamed.

'We don't like poachers,' said the man from the pub, bending to pick up my bag and hurl it.

It hit the water in front of me and I grabbed it, clinging like the proverbial drowning man clings to a proverbial straw, and with about as much effect.

'I can't swim well!' I cried, raising my hands and sinking.

'Well, stand up, you daft bugger,' said the man. 'Then take your sodden bag and clear off.'

My feet touched bottom and I struggled to stand, finding the river was only waist-deep, though the flow was strong and the pebbles underfoot offered little grip. It was a relief to reach the bank, to drag myself ashore and to lie there panting, while my brutal assailant laughed his ugly head off. I wished Hobbes were there to sort him out.

Then, getting to my feet and drawing myself up to my full height, I turned to face him. 'Can I have my shoes back, please?'

He threw them. I nearly caught the first one. The second caught me on the ear.

'Now get lost,' he yelled, taking one giant step towards me.

Clutching my shoes and bag, I fled down the road until it felt safe to stop and catch my breath. After rubbing my ear, I sat on the verge to pull on my socks, which luckily I'd stuffed into my shoes. Then, to my surprise, I heard a car approaching. Unfortunately, it was heading in the wrong direction and was a police car that turned up the lane beside the Squire's Arms and sped into the hills.

Having put on my shoes, I stood back up and resumed my walk, leaving a trail of drips on the hot asphalt.

I could hardly believe what had just happened. Even Featherlight Binks had to be subjected to some degree of provocation before resorting to violence, and I'd noticed how he usually managed to restrain himself until he'd taken as much of a customer's money as he was likely to get before punching him or throwing him out. Besides, Featherlight had never, to my knowledge, tried to drown anyone in the river, although this might have been because the Soren was a five minute walk from the Feathers and his rage rarely lasted that long. However, according to Hobbes, he had once made an attempt at drowning a complaining customer in a pan of spicy cat stew.

I couldn't understand what I'd done to provoke the man, although I'd have been the first to admit I was not to everyone's taste. There'd been no reason for accusing me of poaching, although I had seen a trout when bathing my feet. I'd never heard of anyone poaching trout with their toes. Hobbes had once told me that he'd been fishing with bears, who'd used their paws to hook in salmon, but I had nothing in common with bears, other than that my bedroom had once been the den of a retired circus bear, called Cuddles, whose mortal remains, now stuffed, occupied the attic of 13 Blackdog Street. That was according to Hobbes; Mrs Goodfellow insisted he'd discovered it in a skip and brought it home as a curio.

Still, the dunking had cooled me, which was no bad thing as I still had a long way to trudge. All the water I'd taken in reached my bladder just as I was entering a lay by. Concealing myself behind a tree, I unbuttoned my flies, aware such bashfulness was silly with the road so empty.

I'd reached full spate when I was shocked by the sudden roar of car engines and a clang. Twisting my neck, I saw a white van had demolished the gate at the bottom of the recently ploughed field below and was being pursued by four police cars, which were tanking after it, spraying great clods of earth as they bounced and twisted over the furrows. The way the van was being driven, it was clear the driver had little regard for safety and was absolutely desperate. A man's torso popped up through a hole in the van's roof. He was holding a shotgun and fired both barrels at the pursuers. One of them, attempting to swerve out of harm's way, bounced high over a furrow, came down on its side, rolled onto its roof and skidded to a standstill. The others continued the chase, wisely hanging back out of range.

The white van seemed to be heading straight towards me and, as I retreated behind the tree, buttoning my flies with panicked haste, another car hurtled into the field, a familiar blue, rusting Ford Fiesta. I could make out Hobbes's vast figure wrestling the wheel, as the tortured engine screamed and the car bucked and bounced, leading a swarm of muddy clods. The van roared closer before veering towards a gap, where the thick hedge had been replaced by a section of wire fence. It smashed straight through, landing with a bone-jarring crash and hurtling off down the road, trailing wire and fence posts. Hobbes, who had already overtaken the police cars, waved as he shot past and, feeling somewhat foolish, I waved back, as his car, leaping suddenly like a startled lamb, plunged through the gap, careered down the road and disappeared around a bend. The other pursuers followed at a less breakneck pace.

Down in the field, two dazed-looking police officers crawled from the overturned car. Neither, so I gathered from their remarks, interspersed with bouts of swearing, was injured, so, since there didn't seem to be anything I could do to help, I continued homewards, mile after aching mile.

Tired of foot, with sore legs and dripping with sweat, I was nearing Fenderton, on the outskirts of Sorenchester, when the traffic started again. I wondered if that meant Hobbes had caught the van, and I hoped he hadn't been hurt, for, despite his strength and toughness, he wasn't immune to guns.

At last I reached town, where people kept staring and grinning. I guessed it was because of my clothes, which, although fully dried by then, were limp and filthy, my sharply creased chinos reduced to saggy bags and my shirt more like a cleaning rag. Then I caught a glimpse of myself in a shop window. My hair had dried into a sort of wild afro frizz and mud was smeared diagonally across my face, making me look like a new romantic who'd fallen on very hard times.

At least the mud concealed my identity, as well as my blushes, for as I turned into Blackdog Street, I was astonished by the crowd milling round the door of number 13. As I approached, a man walked up to the front door and rang the bell. No one answered.

Tapping someone on the shoulder, I asked: 'What's going on?'

He turned to face me, his eyes widening, a chuckle escaping. The camera round his neck and his jacket stuffed with notebooks and pens made it clear to me, a man who'd once worked for the *Bugle*, that he was a reporter, as was everyone else there, unless they were cameramen.

'It's the gold robbery,' he said. 'We want a word with the inspector.'

'He's out chasing the ones that got away.'

'Oh, really?' said the reporter, looking suddenly interested, 'and how would you know that?'

'Because I saw him.'

Taking a small recording device from his jacket pocket, he held it beneath my nose. 'Would you mind telling me who you are, and precisely what you saw?'

'I'm not sure I should say,' I replied, aware of having become an object of interest.

Reporters were jostling, thrusting microphones and cameras, shouting questions, and I wasn't enjoying my moment in the spotlight.

'I won't say anything unless someone tells me why you're all here.'

'After last night,' said the man I'd accosted, 'we want the low-down on this Inspector Hobbes.'

'Why?'

'Isn't it obvious?'

'Not really. What's he done?'

'You should check out the news. He was awesome.'

'I will,' I said, 'if you let me get to the door.'

'Do you live here?' asked a little, fat guy.

'What's your name?' asked a fierce looking young woman.

'What's your relationship with Hobbes?' asked someone I couldn't see.

The crowd was pressing from all sides. 'Look, I know nothing and my name is—'

'What?'

'—not important.'

Getting out my keys, ignoring questions, deflecting cameras, I shoved and dodged through the throng until I was in touching distance of the front door.

'Why are you so muddy?' asked a particularly pushy man, who looked vaguely familiar, and was trying not to let me pass. 'How old is Hobbes?'

It was Jeremy Pratt off the news. I shook my head. 'Sorry, I know nothing. No speakee English. Leave me alone.'

Managing at last to angle past him, to get up the steps and to stick my key in the lock, I opened the door, hoping I'd be able to stop them following me inside.

I needn't have worried. Out of the house, big, black and bristling, burst Hobbes's dog, Dregs. Brushing me aside, making the reporters scatter, he seized Jeremy Pratt firmly by the groin. Jeremy froze, his mouth open in a silent scream.

'Dregs,' I said in my authoritative voice, the one he usually ignored, 'drop!'

To my surprise he dropped, and Jeremy, clutching himself, teetered on the top step and stumbled back down to the street, moaning. I doubted Dregs had done any serious damage, for, beneath his ferocious exterior, he was quite benevolent. As I shut the door he leapt on me, delighted to see me again, and not happy until he'd given me a thorough licking.

'Get off!' I said, my authoritative voice having no effect until he'd finished.

'What on earth is going on out there?' I asked.

Dregs didn't know. At any rate, he wasn't telling. More to the point, there was no sign of Mrs Goodfellow, and worse, no smell of cooking. Heading to the kitchen, I helped myself to a flagon of cool ginger beer, gulping it all down in record time and burping freely. I washed my hands and face, put the kettle on and had a search around for food.

The result wasn't at all bad. I found a fresh, crusty loaf in the bread bin, a little butter, and some Sorenchester cheese in the pantry, and a selection of Mrs Goodfellow's home-made pickles in a cupboard. Although my attempts at slicing the bread wavered between slab thick and wafer thin, the sandwiches I put together tasted just fine. Sitting at the kitchen table, Dregs by my side, I tried not to stuff myself and to appreciate the delicate home-baked aroma of the bread and the wonderful, crumbly cheese with its sweet, tangy, almost nutty flavour. And then there were the pickles, which she made on wet autumn days and were, quite simply, the best I'd ever tasted. Hobbes had once remarked that she'd won the Parish Pungent Pickle Prize twenty-seven years in succession before stepping aside to let lesser cooks have a chance. Dregs watched every mouthful and drooled, though he knew I considered Sorenchester cheese was far too good for dogs and he didn't much like pickles anyway. When I'd finished, I made a pot of tea, rested my weary feet on a chair, and drank the lot.

Relaxed and fed, my leg muscles aching, my feet sore, I wondered where the old girl was, and why Hobbes had apparently not returned for lunch; even when busy, he usually made it.

A glance through the letterbox showed the reporters were still out there, so, turning on the television, finding a news channel, I sat back in the threadbare old sofa.

I didn't have long to wait. After a rather dull piece about a financial probe, the topic turned to the attempted gold raid. To start with, there was little more than an extended version of what I'd heard last night, plus something about the police closing the main road as they chased the remaining robbers, who had, unfortunately, escaped. I was a little surprised, for Hobbes, on the hunt, rarely came back empty-handed.

The matter-of-fact tone of the newsreader's voice changed: 'Last night, the gang had just finished loading the gold into their getaway vehicle when a plain clothes police officer arrived on the scene. A guest in a nearby hotel took this remarkable footage.'

There followed a rather wobbly video clip of the events. Black smoke was pouring from the back of the security van as four men appeared, their faces concealed in balaclavas. As they strutted, showing off a selection of guns, a white van, the one I'd seen earlier, roared into the picture and stopped to let three of the gang transfer a number of heavy-looking bags, while a fourth, a large man, holding a shotgun, covered the guard and two guys in business suits, who were lying face down on the pavement.

As soon as the last bag was loaded, the gang leapt into the back of the van, slamming the door behind them as they began to pull away up The Shambles towards the Parish Church. Hobbes came into view, sprinting, hunched up, his knuckles nearly scraping the road. He leapt at the van, holding on with one great hand and tearing at the loading doors with the other. Despite the van swerving from side to side, he somehow managed to open the doors and to swing inside. Unfortunately, as the van sped up the road, it went out of shot temporarily as the photographer changed his position.

The video continued, showing bags of gold rolling out and bursting in the road before, one after another, in rapid succession, three of the gang flew out the back and skidded along the tarmac. The final clip, just as the van disappeared from view around the corner, showed Hobbes swinging onto the roof.

The newsreader continued. 'The police officer, identified by witnesses as Inspector Hobbes, incredibly managed to knock a hole through the top of the van, despite coming under small arms fire. His amazing attempt at apprehending the entire gang only ended when the van crashed into a hedge and he was brushed off. Fortunately, he was reportedly unhurt and is already back on duty.

'Now, we're going over to Jeremy Pratt in Sorenchester for an update.'

The hapless reporter, dishevelled, and paler than usual, appeared on screen, with our house behind him. It was strange how different it looked on the television.

'Good afternoon, Jeremy' said the newsreader, 'is there any further news of Inspector Hobbes?'

'Good afternoon. Not much. However, a witness claims to have seen the remarkable inspector in hot pursuit of the fleeing villains.' He grimaced.

'Are you alright, Jeremy?'

'No, I am not. I have recently been indecently assaulted by a vicious dog, which bit me on the …'

'Thank you, Jeremy! We'll be back for more, later.'

It seemed Hobbes was hot news, which was hardly a surprise, for his heroics must have looked truly stunning to anyone who hadn't previously seen him in action. For me, who'd watched him playing leapfrog with rhinoceroses and arresting a rogue elephant, his behaviour had been, more or less, par for the course. I knew, though, how much he would detest all the publicity. It wasn't that he was shy – quite the contrary – it was just that he was naturally reticent about his own achievements, which, as soon as they were completed, belonged to the past. He preferred living in the present and looking forward to whatever came next.

There was, of course, another, huge reason why he never courted publicity; Hobbes wasn't exactly human. Although I'd never actually worked out quite what he was, I'd accepted his 'unhumanity' long ago and it rarely bothered me. When it did, on those, thankfully rare, occasions when he reverted to a wild and savage state, I was still not bothered. I was terrified, and, although he'd never attacked me during one of his little turns, part of me couldn't help feeling like a lamb in a lion's den, fearing that one day he'd have me. Most people failed to see past his veneer, the thin layer of policeman. He was a damn good one, even if he did not necessarily adhere too closely to the letter of the law. Furthermore, he was by no means the only non-human in town, for Sorenchester was a weird place and I'd never quite worked out whether he was the source of the weirdness or just a symptom of it.

I changed channels, switching to a local news programme, which, to my horror, was showing my arrival at 13 Blackdog Street. With my filthy, crumpled clothes, wild hair, muddied face, and the wounds from my battle with the alarm clock and bookcase, I, too, gave off an aura of weirdness, which was quite depressing. However, the look on Jeremy's face when Dregs nipped him in the bud quickly cheered me up. The clip was repeated in slow motion, before the grinning newsreader joked that the dog had been rushed to the vet with food poisoning. Turning off the television, I headed upstairs for a bath.

Sometime later, thoroughly soaked and deep cleansed, I went into my room and started putting on clean clothing. The street outside was still packed with reporters and cameramen, as well as a host of sightseers. At least the Black Dog Café down the road was doing extremely well, to judge by the number of cups and cakes I could see.

Feeling a little warm, I opened the window to let in some fresh air, and was thinking about combing my hair when a huge, horrible figure, wearing well-polished black boots, baggy brown trousers and a scruffy jacket, swung in through the window, and landed on the rug with barely a sound.

'Afternoon,' said Hobbes. 'Put the kettle on. I'm parched.'

Hobbes's unexpected arrival set my heart pounding, caused instant jelly legs and made me slump onto the bed, where I lay quivering, trying to control my breathing. It took a few moments before I felt able to get up and find my comb. I stared into the mirror, thinking that, despite my usually wispy short brown hair looking relatively neat, my face was not at its best, for although it had lost much of its pastiness and puffiness, my nose was swollen, a tender red split across the bridge merging into the bruise around my eye.

Before knowing him, I would, no doubt, have been feeling sorry for myself, and would most likely have stayed in bed to mope, but I'd grown accustomed to injury, because, in the same way as Hobbes attracted weirdness, I was a magnet for accidents and minor disasters. Although it would have been a lie to have claimed I took them in my stride, I could usually manage to stumble through.

At last, I went downstairs to the kitchen, put the kettle on and made tea. When it was nicely brewed, I handed a mugful to Hobbes, who was sitting at the table, with his hand on Dregs's head.

'I wasn't expecting you back today,' he remarked, stirring his steaming tea with a great, hairy finger. 'How is your father?'

'He's fine.'

'The lass told me he was at death's door.'

'That's what I thought, but it turned out there was nothing wrong with him, or at least, nothing a sensible diet wouldn't cure.'

'I'm happy to hear he's well.'

'Thank you. I was going to stay there for a couple of days, but I had a little accident …'

Hobbes chuckled.

'… and after seeing the news, I wanted to get back here.'

'Why? What's happened?' He looked puzzled.

'The gold robbery, of course.'

'Oh, that. It was nothing.'

'That's not what the press think, and they've been showing a film of you in action.'

He frowned. 'I was filmed?'

'By someone staying at the Golden Fleece,' I said, 'and it's been all over the news and it seems to have made everyone excited.'

'So, that's why all those people were loitering outside. I did wonder.'

'If you knew nothing about it, why did you come in through the window?'

'It was open,' said Hobbes, 'so I thought I'd take a shortcut.'

'Umm … wouldn't it have been quicker to park outside and come through the door?'

426

'It would, had I anything to park.'

'Why? What's happened to the car?'

'I broke it.' He grinned. 'It turns out it wasn't up to jumping walls, or, rather, it couldn't cope with landing afterwards. All the wheels came off – even the steering wheel. They don't make them like they used to. I'll have to buy another.'

'Won't the police buy you one?'

'No, we have an arrangement. I get what I want and they don't tell me how to drive it. It saves Superintendent Cooper a lot of stress.'

'That doesn't seem fair when you were on police business.'

He shrugged. 'Well, I was, it's true, but I was enjoying myself, too. I could have left the pursuit to the other lads, but why should they have all the fun?'

'Fun? Yeah, OK. But the robbers still got away.'

'For the time being.'

'You might have been hurt. I saw that police car crash.'

'I wasn't and nor was anyone else. As for the lads who crashed, it'll teach them to drive better next time.'

'Fair enough, but someone was hurt last night. There was the poor driver of the security van who got deafened.'

Hobbes scratched his head, sounding like someone brushing their feet on a coconut doormat. 'The driver wasn't deafened. I spoke to him.'

'Yes, he was, I saw it on the news. Some guy called Percival.'

'Are you referring to Percival Longfellow? He is most certainly hard of hearing, but he's been like it ever since getting too close to an explosion years ago in London.'

'But,' I said, 'didn't that happen last night? And wasn't he driving the van?'

'I think you are getting confused. The gang did indeed blow the doors off the security van last night, but Percival wasn't the driver. He hasn't worked in security for twenty years or more; not since a gang of jewel robbers blew open a bank vault he was guarding. He received a substantial amount of compensation for his deafness, which he invested in a nice flat in town. Nowadays, he manages a boy band.'

'I don't get it,' I said. 'A reporter spoke to him about the robbery.'

'Reporters have been known to get things wrong. You should know.'

I nodded, wondering if he'd made a dig at me. For far too many years, I'd been a cub reporter for the *Sorenchester and District Bugle*, and my failure to move up the pecking order in that time might have been down to the sackful of mistakes I'd made.

'What concerns me now,' said Hobbes, 'is how long those reporters are going to stay outside.'

'Probably until you give them a story.'

'In which case, they'll be there a long time.'

'Actually,' I said, thinking rapidly, 'it might be better to give them what they want now, because if you don't, they'll just stick around and make something up. That's what I used to do.' I didn't mention that most of my fictions had been discovered, sooner or later, resulting in embarrassing exposures to the Editorsaurus's sarcasm.

'No,' said Hobbes. 'It sounds like I've already got more than enough publicity and I don't intend to give them any more.'

'What if they make up something bad? And there's another thing to be considered: if they can't get to you, they'll try pumping anyone who might know you.'

Hobbes shook his head. 'I've got nothing to say. I was just doing my job.'

'They'll hang around and hassle people, at least until the next big story pops up. Think what it'll be like for Mrs Goodfellow when she goes shopping. By the way, where is she?'

'She's gone to Skegness for a long weekend.'

'She didn't say anything to me.'

'Because you weren't here. The lass thought she'd take the opportunity to visit her cousin Ethel, who runs a guesthouse. They normally only see each other once a year.'

'Oh no!' I said, stricken with a horrible realisation. 'What are we going to do for supper?'

'We'll manage.'

I groaned, remembering past culinary disasters when the old girl had been away, most of which had been my fault, or to be more truthful, all of which had been my fault.

'Tonight, for instance,' said Hobbes, 'I have been invited to dine by my friend Sid. Have you met him? Sid Sharples? He came to see me after I'd been shot the last time.'

'Umm … I might have done … I think. Well, I guess you'll be alright, but … umm …what about me?'

'That will not be a problem. Sid won't mind an extra body at the table and he's always glad of new blood in his circle. However, he's an old-fashioned sort of gentleman and likes his guests dressed for dinner.'

'If you're sure he won't mind, that'll be great. I think there's a dinner jacket and bow tie at the back of my wardrobe.'

One of the advantages of living at Hobbes's was that I'd acquired a whole new wardrobe and, more to the point, the clothes to fill it. They had once belonged to Mrs Goodfellow's husband, Robin, who, so far as anyone knew, was in Tahiti, attempting to found a naturist colony. Although most of his stuff might have been considered a trifle old-fashioned, I liked to believe it was classic tailoring, and was sure it gave me an air of distinction. I hoped so, anyway. Nonetheless, I still found it spooky that everything fitted as if made to measure.

'Excellent,' said Hobbes. 'He expects us at eight.'

'Does he?'

He nodded and poured himself more tea. 'There is,' he said casually – a little too casually – 'something I ought to tell you about him.'

'Go on.'

'Sid is a vampire.'

'Oh, is that all?' I said, trying not to look like a victim, my muscles turning to mush.

'But, don't worry, he won't hurt you, or harm you in any way, and he's a good cook and a generous host.'

Despite my best efforts, and Hobbes's reassurance, my hands shook. I was going to dinner with a real vampire; it had been bad enough meeting a wannabe vampire, in the form of my former editor's deranged wife, who had bitten me, leaving her false teeth sticking in my neck. If I looked under bright lights, I fancied I could still make out the scar.

When I felt able, I got up, walked calmly to the sink, picked up a cloth, returned to the table and wiped up the pool of tea I'd spilt when he told me. He watched, smiling wickedly, as I rinsed out the cloth, hung it over a tap, and returned to my seat.

'Sid,' he said, 'is quite harmless.'

'So, he won't want to drink my blood?'

'No. As is well documented, vampires only drink the blood of virgins.'

'That's alright then.' I forced a smile as if reassured.

Hobbes laughed. 'You have a very expressive face. I should tease you more often.'

'Is he really a vampire?' I asked, recalling numerous occasions when he'd made me fall for tall stories, although in fairness, some of the tallest had turned out to be true.

'He really is, though there's nothing to worry about, because although of the vampire race, he can't stomach the taste of blood.'

'So, what does he eat?'

'He particularly likes soup.'

'Soup?'

'Correct. He's getting on a bit, and finds it easy to digest and much more palatable than blood. No doubt he'll cook one for us tonight.'

'Umm …' I said, 'what sort of soup?'

'He usually goes for the meatier varieties, such as oxtail.'

'Good,' I said, slightly reassured, having had a horrific vision of him serving up a large bowl of something warm, red and frothy and passing it off as cream of tomato soup.

Although I did have a vague memory of Sid's visit, I couldn't picture him, yet my mind insisted that he was tall and slim, with slicked back hair, sharp teeth and a strange accent. Still, I told myself, he was only a vampire, so why worry? After all, I knew a family pack of werewolves quite well and, although they occasionally made me nervous, especially at night, particularly around full moon, they'd never hurt me, or, so far as I was aware, anybody else. They hadn't even bitten the postman. The worst I could say about them was that they had once given me fleas, and I'd still not completely recovered from the ignominy of being tricked by Mrs Goodfellow into sharing a flea bath with Dregs, who'd also been infested. Besides them, I'd eaten crumpets with the Olde Troll and was slowly learning not to give in to prejudice and to take people, of no matter what persuasion, on their individual merits.

Hobbes, finishing his tea, downed his mug, loped from the kitchen and returned a few moments later. 'Those reporters are still out there and showing no signs of moving on, so we'll need to get past them.'

'How?'

'I'll think about it, but not now. I'm going to take forty winks. It's been a long night and day.'

As he left, Dregs approached, sat by my side and tried to persuade me to take him for a walk. My attempts to ignore his hypnotic gaze soon crumbled.

'Oh, alright then,' I said.

Jumping up, thrashing his tail, he fetched his lead from the hook, waited for me to clip it to his collar and dragged me to the front door. In my naivety, I hadn't expected to spark much excitement, since I obviously wasn't Hobbes and looked relatively normal. I was wrong. As soon as I opened the door, we were confronted by cameras, flashing lights and thrusting microphones. However, Dregs's earlier actions had earned him a right of passage, and he only had to growl for the crowd to part, leaving a clear route. A nervous-looking Jeremy Pratt, dried slobber on his trousers the only evidence of his canine encounter, lurked towards the back of the mob as, ignoring the questions and the cameras, I let Dregs lead me to Ride Park.

Thankfully, no one followed us far and Dregs and I were able to pass an enjoyable hour or so. He chased squirrels, without ever getting near one. For him, all the fun was in running free and barking up the wrong tree. I mooched along, feet sore from the long trek, my leg muscles still aching, and appreciated the late afternoon sunshine, the buzz of insects and the changing tints of the trees, trying not to think about later, but wishing I'd asked Hobbes more about the robbery. I also wondered if I'd be on television again. I hoped not.

Despite my best intentions, one question kept buzzing round my head, as annoying as a wasp at a picnic: could a vampire really be as safe as Hobbes had suggested? I tried to believe him, to convince myself he wouldn't really put me into a dangerous situation, at least not on purpose. I knew, of course, that if I ever got into danger, he was the best person to get me out of it, but I was far from comfortable with the idea of visiting a vampire, even one with a preference for soup. Despite recognising my fear was based entirely on prejudice, my knowledge gleaned only from horror films, it was, nonetheless, genuine.

At length, all the squirrels having been treed, the evening approaching, and the temperature dropping, I called Dregs, clipped him to his lead and returned home, running the gauntlet of reporters. Again he proved invaluable and we got back inside without too much hassle.

Hobbes was already up and dressed. Having never seen him in his dinner jacket before, I was impressed. He looked almost smart and quite respectable, despite wearing a bow tie, a relic of the sixties I assumed, that looked as if a large velvet bat had seized him by the throat. Dregs apparently thought the same and growled and bristled until Hobbes let him sniff it. Then, relaxing, he waited for his dinner. While Hobbes was feeding him, I took a bulb of garlic from Mrs G's pot and secreted it in my pocket; I had an idea it might be useful.

'You'd better get ready,' said Hobbes.

'OK. Umm … have you worked out how to get past that lot outside?'

'Yes, though I suspect you might not like it.'

'Why not?'

'You'll see.'

He refused to elaborate and I went upstairs in a state of extreme trepidation. I'd already been shaky and his manner had really set me on edge. On reaching my room, I turned on the light and ferreted around in the wardrobe, finding a pair of black, sharply creased trousers, a crisply pressed dress shirt, and a dinner jacket. I laid them on the bed, and started to dress, popping the garlic bulb into my jacket pocket, finding its pungent aroma strangely reassuring.

I was doing just fine until the bow tie, a conundrum way beyond my abilities. Having made a right pig's ear of the whole rigmarole, frustration got the better of me and I punched the wall, a method that worked surprisingly well, since my yelp of pain and subsequent swearing brought Hobbes up to see what was the matter. He found me collapsed on the bed, clutching my hand and groaning.

Summing up the situation at a glance, he said: 'Bow ties can be tricky blighters.

Stand up, shut up, and I'll tie it for you.'

Taking me by the throat, he set to work, his massive hairy fingers tying the black rag into a beautifully neat bow. It was a little tight: a little too tight. Clutching at it, I struggled to breathe, until, recognising my antics as signs of distress, he loosened it with a deft twist.

'Thank you,' I croaked.

'Don't mention it. Now put on your jacket, and quickly. It's time to go.'

'So, how are you going to get past those reporters?' I asked, combing my hair and admiring myself in the mirror.

'By distracting them and going over the roof tops.'

'That's all very well for you,' I said, not liking the way this was developing, 'but what about me? Shall I take Dregs?'

'No, you're coming with me.'

'I can't. I'll fall off. No, it's impossible.'

'It is possible. I have a plan and you'll probably be fine. You'll see. First, however, I need something from the attic. While I'm getting it, open your window and turn off the light.'

'OK,' I said, my insides churning, but as usual, I realised I was going to let him do his stuff, and I was going to hope for the best. Turning off the light, I opened the window and looked down. Even from there, the street seemed a bowel-loosening long way below.

Hobbes returned, carrying an ancient canvas rucksack that looked just about big enough for a human body. Surely not, I thought, as he put it down.

'Get inside,' he said, grinning benignly.

'Do I have to?'

'Yes, and quickly.'

I stepped into it and made myself small, discovering my initial assessment of its size had been a little wrong, as my head and shoulders poked out the top. However, before I could object, Hobbes grabbed the straps, lifted me and swung me onto his back.

'Keep your head down,' he said.

'I can't keep it any more down and how are you going to distract that lot outside? They are bound to look up.'

'I'm not going to do anything.'

'Do I have to do anything?' I asked, peering over his shoulder, feeling precarious enough already.

'No. Just relax and keep quiet. It's time.'

A tremendous cacophony broke out in the street, as if a tone deaf brass band on steroids was performing.

'Here we go,' said Hobbes, springing lightly out the window.

Had my mouth not been dry, as if coated in peanut butter, I might have screamed. Twisting my neck, I stared down at the street, which was glittering under silvery streetlights and already looking much further away. The rucksack swung as Hobbes, twisting in mid-air, reaching out with one great, muscular arm, grabbed the top of the window frame, and hauled us up and onto the roof. As he scrambled on all fours to the summit, the tuneless braying ceased.

'Alright, Andy?'

'Umm … I suppose.'

'Good. Hold on tight.'

'Hold on to what?'

There was no reply.

Blackdog Street consisted of two parallel rows of tall, terraced houses and shops. Hobbes, as agile as a monkey, despite me swinging and bumping on his back, ran along the ridge towards the end of the street next to the Parish Church. Even in my terrified state, I was struck by how magnificent and strange the church looked from such an unusual vantage point. I tried to think about its architecture and not about what would happen should Hobbes slip, or should the frayed old straps on the rucksack snap.

He stopped and stood upright.

'Where does Sid live exactly?' I asked.

'Number one, Doubtful Street.'

'That's to the left, isn't it?' Below was the gentle curve of Pound Street. Doubtful Street, one of the oldest in town, led onto it.

'Yes.'

'How do we get down?'

'Getting down from a roof is easy, although getting down safely may be less so. Do you see that wall over there, the one around the big garden?'

I grunted an acknowledgment, fearing the worst.

'Well, once we're on that, it's an easy drop into Pound Street.'

'But, it's miles away! How can we possibly reach it? It's impossible.' I wished I'd decided to stay home and make do with toast.

'It's not impossible. I don't think so, anyway.'

'You're not going to … oh, God!'

Hobbes, having taken a few paces back, sprinted along the ridge until, when there was no roof left, he leapt. I didn't scream, the acceleration having squeezed all the air from my lungs, but I did manage a pathetic whimper that was instantly carried away in the wind rushing past my face. There was a sensation of weightlessness, a long moment when my heart seemed to have stopped and a thud that nearly bounced me from the rucksack. Within a few steps, we came to a halt.

We were on the wall.

Hobbes clapped his hands. 'I thought we'd make it.'

'You didn't know for sure?'

'Not for sure. I've never carried anyone before. It was fun.'

'We could have been killed.'

'But we weren't. Now, let's get down before somebody sees us and calls the police.'

The jump down seemed trivial, and I was suddenly safe, or as safe as anyone could be who was on their way to meet a vampire.

'You might as well walk from here,' said Hobbes, setting the rucksack down on the pavement.

Getting out wasn't as easy as getting in; my legs wobbled like those of a punched out boxer.

'Come along,' he said, swinging the rucksack onto one shoulder. 'We don't want to keep Sid waiting.'

432

'OK,' I said, struggling to keep up, trying not to think of how we'd get home, 'but can you explain something?'

'I can explain many things.'

'I know, but what made that awful racket?'

He laughed. 'That was Billy testing his new car horn. I phoned and asked him to put in an appearance. It worked rather well, don't you think?'

I nodded. Billy Shawcroft, a good friend of Hobbes, was a dwarf of no small ability, who had shown himself a very useful man in a crisis, and the reconditioned hearse he drove had proved its worth on several occasions.

Turning into Doubtful Street, we stopped outside number 1, a high, narrow, old house of dusty, lichen-encrusted stone, with a shiny black front door. Leaning forward, Hobbes gave the old-fashioned bell-pull a sharp downward tug and from within came the deep tones of bell. So far, so Gothic, I thought, closing my hand around my garlic bulb.

A moment later, there came a sound of shuffling feet and the door opened with a satisfyingly spooky creak. Inside, all was dark, except for the flickering light of a single candle held in a pale hand.

'Enter,' said a soft voice.

Nervously, I followed Hobbes inside, going down a corridor in which the candlelight cast grotesque flickering shadows onto dark, heavy-looking furniture. The front door closed behind us.

'Welcome to my humble abode,' said the soft voice. 'I'm dreadfully sorry it's so dark, but the bulb's just blown. Please, go into the kitchen.'

Hobbes, opening a door, led us into a large, comfortable, well-lit, modern kitchen, where he introduced me to Sid, who was not as I'd imagined. He was shorter than I and rather paunchy, with a balding head and plump, florid cheeks. Yet what surprised me most was his welcoming, white-toothed smile and friendly dark brown eyes.

'Delighted to make your acquaintance, young fellow,' he said, taking my hand in his soft pudgy one and shaking it vigorously.

'Pleased to meet you,' I said, wondering again whether Hobbes was playing a trick on me.

Sid nodded and then looked distressed. 'I'm afraid I'm having a bad day. First the bulb goes and then I discover I've completely run out of garlic.'

Reaching into my pocket, I held out my hand.

'Thank you,' said Sid. 'I don't suppose you brought any dill?'

The kitchen was mostly white, with every surface gleaming, and, above a sharp hint of bleach and a faint scent of apples, there was a beautiful, rich, delicious smell rising from a large copper pot bubbling on a vast wood-fired range. Sid, smiling at us over a bow tie that was nearly as large as Hobbes's, gestured towards the table and Hobbes and I sat down on cushioned pinewood chairs.

'It was lucky you had garlic with you,' said Sid, 'because the soup is not the same without it.'

'Umm … yes, it was. I don't usually carry it.'

'Was it anything to do with me being what I am?'

'Umm … well, yes, I suppose it was,' I said, more embarrassed than afraid.

'I expect,' said Sid, with a glance at Hobbes, 'that Wilber told you part of the story, just enough to get you worried.'

'Would I do anything like that?' said Hobbes, trying to look innocent.

'Yes,' I said, nodding, 'you would. Umm … Wilber?'

'It's short for Wilberforce,' said Sid.

'Wilberforce?' I said, staring. 'Is that his name?' I'd never dared ask, though I had noticed the signature on his paintings was W.M. Hobbes.

Sid nodded.

'In that case,' I asked, 'what does the M stand for?'

'His second name,' said Sid. 'is—'

'A secret,' said Hobbes, shaking his head and looking embarrassed.

'—is Makepeace.' Sid, breaking the garlic into cloves, sniffed them and nodded his approval.

Hobbes, putting his head in his hands, groaned. 'My awful secret is out. It was bound to happen one day.'

'Wilberforce Makepeace Hobbes?' I chuckled.

'Apparently both Wilberforce and Makepeace were popular names when I was a lad,' said Hobbes. 'I'm quite proud of them … really.'

'Anyway,' said Sid, 'before I was interrupted, I was trying to say that I love a bit of garlic and, furthermore, I have no adverse reaction to crosses, or holy water, or any of that nonsense.'

'I guess everything I think I know about vampires is wrong,' I said, feeling more at ease. 'Umm … what about stakes, though? Would a stake through the heart kill you?'

'Andy,' said Hobbes, 'that's not nice.'

Sid held up his hand. 'No, it's a fair question, if a little daft. So far as I'm aware, a stake through the heart would kill anyone and, before you ask, so would decapitation.' With a chuckle, he turned towards a chopping board, and selected a broad bladed knife.

'I'm sorry,' said Hobbes. 'He's not normally so forward. He's probably tired.'

'Don't worry, old boy,' said Sid. 'Most humans take a while to adjust. You can't blame them, really. There's so much piffle out there. Just try googling the word *vampire* and you'll find there are millions of hits and hardly any of them come even close to the truth.'

'I did tell him,' said Hobbes, 'that you would not dream of drinking his blood.'

'He did.' I agreed.

'That's alright then,' said Sid, examining the edge of the knife. 'Did he also mention that I prefer to dine on human brains?'

I shook my head, my mouth dropping open.

'I'm surprised,' said Sid. 'He usually does.'

Having crushed and chopped the garlic, he threw it into a small pot on the range, along with a knob of butter. The fragrance cut through everything else and made me even hungrier.

Hobbes was grinning and, I thought, looking somewhat sheepish.

'When the garlic is nicely browned,' said Sid, 'I'll add it to the soup and then we can have a good chat while it finishes. Help yourselves to wine while you're waiting.'

'Thanks,' said Hobbes, reaching for a bottle in the middle of the table. Pulling off the foil capsule, he gave three sharp smacks to the bottom of the bottle, making the cork rise up. Pulling it out with a gentle pop, sniffing it with a nod of approval, he flicked it across the kitchen, straight into a flip top bin.

'Would you care for a little, Andy?' he asked.

'Yes, please.'

Having filled three glasses with the dark red, almost purple liquid, he pushed one towards me and took one for himself. 'Cheers.'

'Cheers,' I said, sniffing, satisfying myself that it really was wine, and taking a sip. It was rich and fruity, with a warm velvety feel and was more than acceptable. Since living at Hobbes's I'd developed a rudimentary palate and considered I now knew enough to avoid anything likely to dissolve my teeth or blind me.

We sat in silence for a few moments, sipping, enjoying the flavour, relaxing as the sizzling garlic, combined with the other cooking aromas, set my mouth watering.

'Is he really a vampire?' I whispered.

'I really am,' said Sid, who was suddenly standing right behind me.

Jerking with shock, I knocked over my glass. Sid caught it and handed it back without a drop spilling.

'We have sharp ears as well as sharp teeth,' he said.

'Not to mention sharp reflexes,' said Hobbes.

'Hardly, old boy, I've slowed down with age.'

'Age?' said Hobbes, looking severe. 'More like your drunken life style.'

'Drunken? I haven't touched a drop since 1950.'

'Since it's only ten-past eight, now,' said Hobbes, 'you've lasted all of twenty minutes.' He handed a glass to the old vampire.

'Much obliged,' said Sid, raising it to his lips. 'Good health!'

If he was a vampire, and I had few doubts anymore, he was a cheerful one.

'The soup will be ready in just a few minutes,' he said, taking a seat at the head of the table.

'What is it?' I asked, raising my voice over the rumbling of my stomach.

'It's borscht, my own recipe and I hope you like it.'

'It smells great,' I said, unsure what borscht was, but unwilling to expose my ignorance.

'It does indeed,' said Hobbes and refilled his glass. 'It's very good of you to have us.'

'Not at all.'

'Your invitation was most opportune. You see, my house is currently under siege, and getting out is a trifle tricky.' Hobbes took a gulp of wine and stretched out his legs.

'Ah, yes,' said Sid, 'the barbarians at the gates. I've been keeping an eye on the news. I'm always a little nervous with crowds, because they are, in my experience, only one step removed from turning into mobs and taking up flaming brands and pitchforks.'

'You've had no more trouble of that sort since moving here, have you?' said Hobbes.

'No, and for that I give you thanks, old boy.'

'I'm just doing my job.'

'Like you were last night,' said Sid. 'It's regrettable someone caught your antics on camera, but otherwise you did well. I don't like losing our money.'

'Your money?' I said, surprised, for the news had suggested the gang was trying to steal over a million pounds in gold sovereigns and, although Sid's house suggested he was comfortably off, he didn't strike me as a millionaire.

'In a manner of speaking. The gold actually belongs to Colonel Squire, but since he was depositing it in my bank, I have a stake in it.'

Colonel Squire, the owner of Sorenchester Manor and several estates, was reputed to be very rich indeed.

'That's right,' said Hobbes. 'The colonel said he was diversifying his investments.'

'But why was he doing it at night?' I asked. 'Why not during normal banking hours?'

'There are two good reasons,' said Sid. 'Firstly, the colonel is rich enough to make the bank jump to his command. Secondly, he wanted me to accept the deposit personally and, if I have to go out, I prefer to do it at night. Now, if you'll excuse me, I'll serve the soup.'

Rising, he strolled across to the stove, very light on his feet for one so portly, and, returning with a vast tureen, ladled out generous portions into three large, white bowls. The soup was red and frothy.

I looked at it, then at Hobbes. He smiled.

'What is this?' I asked, trying to sound calm, trying to dispel a rising horror.

'Borscht,' said Sid, fetching a basket of thickly sliced, crusty bread and a butter dish. As if that explained everything.

'Yes, but what's actually in it, besides garlic.'

'I'll bet,' said Sid with a chuckle, 'that the colour is worrying you.'

I nodded, feeling sick.

'It's made with beetroot, and don't worry, there's no blood in it.'

'Oh, good,' I said, relieved. 'I didn't really think there would be.'

'Of course not,' said Sid, looking solemn.

I felt no fear. Whatever he was, he was no threat.

'Please, help yourself to bread,' said Sid, 'and eat. I hope you enjoy it.'

After Hobbes had said his customary grace, I did eat. The borscht had a robust, almost earthy flavour with a hint of sweetness, not to mention a satisfying nuttiness and a strong meaty flavour, with just a hint of sourness that piqued my taste buds. In fact, it was so good I even entertained the possibility that it might equal one of Mrs G's soups, though it felt disloyal to think so. Maybe it was because of my extreme hunger, or the contrast to Mother's well-meaning horrors.

I tucked in, listening with half an ear to Hobbes and Sid talking about Rocky, the Olde Troll, who'd apparently fallen asleep while out standing in his field, and had woken up covered in graffiti. Although the brisk application of a wire brush had restored him to pristine condition, Rocky had complained bitterly about the loss of his lichen patina. Then, when I might have expected more talk of old times and old acquaintances, the conversation turned to gold and banking. I was surprised to learn that Hobbes kept a deposit box in Grossman's Bank, a box he hadn't touched since 1922.

'Help yourselves to more borscht,' said Sid as I finished the bowl. 'There's plenty.'

'I don't mind if I do,' I said. 'It's delicious.'

'Delicious? I should jolly well think so. I've had plenty of practice since my wife died.'

'I'm sorry to hear that.'

'Don't be, young fellow. She had a good life. Until she married me, of course.'

Hobbes, with a laugh, helped himself to more and said: 'Your Queenie was a good woman; she was like a mother to the lass.'

Once again, I experienced the strange sense of dislocation that struck whenever I was confronted with the age of Hobbes and some of his associates. Although I'd never plucked up the courage to ask how old he was, I had ascertained that, despite appearances, he was old enough to have been a policeman for some years before joining up as a soldier in the Great War. Mrs Goodfellow, 'the lass' as Hobbes called her, had been orphaned during the Blitz in the next war, and yet still ran Kung Fu classes in the church hall. It was no great step to accept Sid as older, far older, than his smooth, plump skin suggested.

When we'd finished the borscht, Sid gathered up our bowls, stacked them in the dishwasher and returned to the table with three sundae dishes filled with another dark red, frothy substance. 'Raspberry mousse,' he said, before I could embarrass myself. 'I hope you like it.'

It was sweet and tart and fruity and smooth and utterly delicious. Hobbes didn't say another word until he'd scraped the dish clean. Then he said four words: 'Is there any more?'

Sid, looking well pleased, fetched him another dish, which went the same way. Although I would have loved to indulge my taste buds, I couldn't, for my belly was so tight I didn't dare and it was all I could do to find room for my wine.

Afterwards, Sid took us through to the lounge, painted a cosy, bright orange, dominated by an enormous book case, and containing a pair of magnificent green leather chesterfield sofas. A capacious armchair was positioned where its occupant might watch the vast television on the wall in total comfort, while benefiting from the fire that was dispelling any hint of autumnal chill and imbuing the air with the soft, soothing scent of warm, ripe apples. Hobbes and I, sprawling, replete, took a sofa each, while our host, having returned to the kitchen, brought in a steaming jug, whence arose the wonderful aroma of fresh coffee, adding to my feeling of comfort and ease. Having filled three translucent white porcelain cups and passed them to us, Sid approached a large, beautifully polished drinks cabinet.

'Could I interest either of you in a snifter of brandy?' he asked. 'I fancy one myself.'

Hobbes nodded.

'I'll stick to coffee,' I said. 'Brandy is a bit strong for me these days.'

'No problem,' said Sid, pulling out a pair of brandy glasses, filling them and handing one to Hobbes. 'Perhaps you'd like something else?'

'Umm … I don't know … I …'

'How about a cocktail? I suggest one the youngsters used to drink in the Old Country.'

'Maybe. Which old country? You don't really come from Transylvania, do you?'

He laughed. 'No, I come from a small village in Norfolk. The Old Country was a wine bar I used to own.'

'You wouldn't know it,' said Hobbes. 'It was way before your time. After he sold it, it became the Black Dog Café.'

'I'll tell you what,' said Sid, 'I'll make you one and see if you like it.'

With a sinister chuckle, he set to work with three bottles and a crystal glass.

'This,' he said, handing me the results of his alchemy, 'is a Brain Haemorrhage.'

It was an apt name. Floating in a colourless fluid was what appeared to be a small clump of brain with great bloody streaks running through.

Although I tried to act cool, I failed to suppress a shudder and a grimace. 'What is it?'

'Two parts peach schnapps, topped with a measure of Irish cream and drizzled with grenadine. It's normally drunk in a single quaff. I'm sure you'll like it. Enjoy.'

Though my brain said 'no' and my stomach said 'no room', I felt, for the sake of my honour, that I should give it a try. Taking a deep breath, I gulped it down, finding it wasn't nearly as bad as I'd feared. In fact, it was rather pleasant, with a sweet, fruity taste. Overcome with a sudden fatigue, I slumped in the chesterfield, resting my eyes, while Hobbes and Sid enjoyed a heated discussion on the subject of sticklebacks.

Having exhausted the topic, Sid asked about the investigation.

'It's too early to tell yet,' said Hobbes, 'but we have several lines of inquiry. Firstly, how did the gang know the gold would be delivered to the bank at that time?'

'Someone must have told them,' said Sid.

'That would seem likely, so we are working on the theory that it was an insider job. I'd be obliged if you'd let me have a list of anyone who knew, but it may not have been malicious; it may have been carelessness.

'Secondly, we're holding three of the gang in the nick, and I may persuade them to talk. Unfortunately, my first impression is that we caught the foot soldiers, who know very little and that the boss got away.

'Thirdly, there's the van. When we find it, it's likely to provide some clues – and it shouldn't be hard to find, as it's quite distinctive, having a hole in its roof and a huge dent where it hit a tree. I'd have caught them this afternoon, had my car not broken.'

'But, surely, old boy, they'll burn the van to get rid of any clues? That's if they haven't done so already.'

'I fear you may be right.' Hobbes sighed. 'Still, I do have one further line of inquiry, because I got a good view of the driver and I'd recognise him anywhere. In fact, I thought for a moment that I did recognise him. Unfortunately, I didn't get much of an impression of the other man, except that he was tall and wearing a tweed suit. I suspect that one was the boss.'

'What are you going to do next?' asked Sid. 'Won't all the reporters get in your way?'

'Maybe, but I don't really know what they want from me. Andy reckons they'll hang around until they've got a story, or they'll make one up.'

'He's probably right. They can be extraordinarily persistent until the next big news breaks. Do you remember what they were like that Walpurgis Night when Skeleton Bob Nibblet got stuck up the chimney? That could have become a very sticky situation. Another brandy?'

'Yes, please,' said Hobbes.

Sid got to his feet. 'Another Brain Haemorrhage, Andy?'

Although I could easily have dropped off in the warmth of the crackling fire, and my head, already fuzzy, felt as if it were spinning, I opened my eyes and sat up. 'Don't mind if I do,' I said, ignoring a sober portion of my brain whispering that I'd already had too much.

Sid fetched the drinks. 'Here's to solving crime … Cheers.'

'Cheers.'

Having taken a gulp of neat brandy, Sid, looking thoughtful, said: 'What I'd suggest is that you get away for a few days, until things quieten down. After all, you've already done enough. You saved the money and the bank's reputation and arrested three of the gang.'

'But at least two others are still free,' said Hobbes, 'and one of them is the brains and he might be planning something else.'

'Possibly, old boy, but he's more likely to be in hiding, afraid he's going to be arrested. Your police colleagues should be able to find him.'

'I don't like to leave a job half done.'

'Surely you don't want to take all the glory?' said Sid. 'Give someone else a chance. It was only an attempted robbery after all.'

Hobbes stared deep into his brandy as I gulped down my Brain Haemorrhage. They were moreish, so I didn't object when Sid fixed me another.

'Maybe you're right,' said Hobbes, after a long pause.

'I'm sure I am,' said Sid. 'Take a few days leave. I'll bet you've got a few accrued.'

Hobbes grinned. 'Superintendent Cooper reckoned I'd built up over four years and that was ages ago, so I dare say there's a few more now.'

'When did you last take a holiday?'

'Last week.'

'For how long?'

'All of Sunday morning.'

'What about a proper holiday?'

'I took a few days off last year, soon after I met Andy.'

Admittedly, my head was stupid with drink, but I couldn't think what he meant. 'The only time I remember you not going into work was after you got shot.'

'That's when I was thinking of,' said Hobbes. 'I spent a couple of days in bed.'

'That doesn't count as holiday,' I said. 'You're supposed to enjoy them.'

'He's right, old boy. You deserve a break.'

'But,' said Hobbes, a little peevishly, 'policing is so much fun. Why would I want a break?'

'It won't be so much fun with those vultures outside your door,' said Sid. 'You'll get a lot of attention. Remember back in '53 when they ran the story of you breaking the four-minute mile? They were after you for days, and it would probably have been much worse had it not been for the coronation.'

'I thought,' I said, 'the four-minute mile was broken in 1954.'

'Officially,' said Sid, 'but Wilber got there first.'

'I wasn't first,' said Hobbes, 'and it wasn't in a race and, I'm glad to say, never made the record books.'

'What happened?'

'I was in pursuit of a suspect,' said Hobbes.

'Who was on horseback,' said Sid. 'It was at Hedbury Races and Wilber was timed between mileposts before he made the arrest. According to the course clock, he'd covered the distance in well under four minutes'

'It wasn't a very good clock,' said Hobbes.

'But,' said Sid, 'the point is, it caught the press's attention and they swarmed around you like mosquitos, until the events in London distracted them.'

'True,' said Hobbes. 'It made my job a little difficult.'

'It'll be worse now. There are more of them, they've got telephoto lenses, they'll buy stories off people, and they'll use all sorts of unscrupulous methods.'

'Perhaps you're right,' said Hobbes, nodding. 'I suppose a few days off wouldn't hurt.'

'Quite right,' said Sid. 'You'll need to do something about the lass and Andy, or they'll be subjected to unwelcome scrutiny. More drinks?'

When they arrived, Hobbes was looking thoughtful and, maybe, a little wistful.

'Thanks,' he said, accepting another large brandy. 'I've decided to head up to Straddlingate. I don't know why, because I haven't been there for years, but it just popped into my head. I'll let the lass know what's happening and I'll mention it to the superintendent as well.'

'Good idea,' said Sid. 'Now that's settled, did you hear about Daft Abel?'

'Abel Clutterbuck? Not since he saw the headline in the *Bugle* saying man wanted for burglary and he went in and applied for the job,' said Hobbes.

'Well,' said Sid, 'Tom Pollack told me he'd had a postcard from him. He was on Easter Island and it seems there was this shark ...'

And I think that must have been when the final drink hit me.

I awoke, sorely afflicted by a raging thirst, a thumping headache and a bursting bladder, the latter of which was demanding urgent attention, despite my trying to wish it away and fall back into sleep. From the scent of apples and the absence of the underlying taint of Hobbes or Dregs, I knew I wasn't in my own bed and, since I was comfortable, with soft blankets pulled up to my chin, I wasn't at my parents'. Even after I'd prised open bleary eyes, I was still confused and lost, as the cold, grey light of early morning showed I was in a strange room, albeit one I felt I should recognise. I was lying on a chesterfield sofa. I sat up and realised I was still dressed, except for my jacket, bowtie and shoes. My head throbbed as I forced myself to stand, and I was panicking because I had no idea where the bathroom was and my need to reach it was rapidly approaching critical. As I staggered to the door, weak and shaky, my head was spinning and I came close to being sick.

I went into a gloomy hallway, where the scent of stale borscht made me understand that I was still at Sid's. The house was as quiet as the grave and, unable to see any stairs, my panic grew. A pair of large, matching china vases stood by the front door and I was seriously contemplating using one of them as an emergency pisspot, when I spotted a gap in the dark wooden panelling in front of me. Closer examination revealed a sliding door and, behind it, the stairs.

I would have run up them, had I dared. Instead I climbed steadily, concentrating on bladder control. At the top, faced with five closed doors, I came close to disaster, until my eyes adjusted to the gloom and I noticed the small china plaques on each door. Starting on the left, I read them: Bram's Room, Stephanie's Room, Sid's Room, Airing Cupboard, and finally, Batroom.

I opened the door and, seeing it was, indeed a bathroom, rushed inside, burst forth and stayed there for some time until the relief of Andy had reached its natural conclusion. As I tottered out, my headache more massive, my nausea barely under control, and my body shivering and weak, a small, ball-of-fluff cat hissed at me, put its ears back and fled downstairs. Taken aback, I stumbled, putting out a hand against a door to steady myself. The door flew open and I lurched inside.

Sid was staring at me, but he wasn't in bed. He was hanging by his ankles from a steel frame beside the wardrobe.

'I'm sorry,' I said, regaining my balance, 'the cat got in my way'.

'That's quite alright, young fellow. She's often in my way, too. My word, you do look rough, though it's hard to tell from this angle. Excuse me one moment.'

Grasping the side of the frame, he pulled himself upright, released his feet, stepped out of the contraption and slicked back his hair. For a moment, I almost forgot my hangover, paralysed by ancient preconceptions of vampires.

'Did I scare you?' he asked.

'Umm … no … yes.'

'I suppose you think I always sleep upside down, like a bat?'

'Don't you?' I asked unhappily.

'No,' he said, 'but, a few minutes inversion therapy does wonders for my stiff old back.'

'When my old editor had a bad back,' I said, grasping for normality, 'he swore by acupuncture. You could try it.'

'It's a little too close to being staked for my liking.'

'I see,' I said, and nodded, causing another wave of headache to break inside my skull.

'Hangover?'

I nodded again: a bad mistake.

'I'll fix you something that should help.'

'I don't want to be any bother.' I was desperate to lie down, to cover up, and to not move for hours.

'It'll be no bother.'

'What are you going to fix me?'

'A Bloody Mary.'

I might have guessed.

'It's my own recipe. It'll do you good, and I think you'll like it.'

Leading me back to the lounge, he propped me up on the sofa with cushions and headed for the drinks cabinet. With a laugh, like a mad scientist creating a monster, he selected a number of bottles and prepared his concoction.

'Get this down you,' he said, handing me a glass, 'and you'll soon be feeling more chipper.'

Grunting my thanks, I took it, mesmerised by the red, frothing contents and trying to think nice thoughts. Bracing myself, I took a sip. It was spicy and peppery and salty and thick. I wasn't sure I liked it but, before I'd come to a final conclusion, I'd finished it. Though I thought I felt a little better, less likely to throw up, my head was spinning again. Pulling the blankets to my chin, turning onto my side, I slept.

It must have been a couple of hours later, when I awoke again to full daylight, this time feeling like I might live, with the scent of roasting coffee making me want to. As I sat up, the door opened, the small, ball-of-fluff cat swaggered in, hissed, and scarpered, and then Sid was there with a steaming mug of coffee.

'Drink this,' he said, 'and your cure should be nearly complete.'

'Thank you.' I said. 'Is Hobbes here?'

'No, he's arranging a few days' leave.'

'That's probably a good idea. Did he stay last night?'

'No, he went home. He had some things to pick up and a dog to walk.'

'Why didn't he take me?'

'You were dead to the world, young fellow,' said Sid with a toothy smile, 'and it would have been cruel to wake you. Wilber was all for it, but I convinced him you needed plenty of beauty sleep. Drink your coffee. Then, take a shower if you wish; I've laid out towels and stuff in the batroom. When you're ready, come through to the kitchen and I'll fix you some breakfast.'

'That's very kind.'

'Nonsense,' said Sid with a pleasant smile that made me decide I liked the old vampire. I was rather pleased with how cosmopolitan my outlook had become.

He left me to my drink. When it started to hit my stomach, and was infusing my body with a rosy glow of well-being, I was able to get up and look around the room and to examine the contents of Sid's enormous bookcase. Mostly it was filled with handsome, leather-bound volumes with titles, so far as I could make out, in Latin. The exception was the middle shelf, full of lurid paperback detective novels. They were so tightly packed I didn't dare remove any, fearing I'd never be able to get them back.

Then, heading upstairs, I enjoyed a long, hot shower, a rare luxury, as the one at Hobbes's, which he'd installed for himself, put lesser users in mortal peril. The last time I'd used it, I might have drowned had Mrs Goodfellow not come to my rescue.

Glowing and clean, I dressed and headed for the kitchen, where Sid prepared a full English breakfast for me to devour. That, washed down with more coffee, left me buoyant and ready to face anything. I'd just finished when the doorbell rang and he went to answer.

A moment later he walked in with Hobbes, who was sporting a bushy beard, a matching moustache and sunglasses.

'Good morning, how are you?' said Hobbes.

'Quite well. Sid's been looking after me.'

'Good,' said Hobbes. 'Do you fancy going camping?'

'I don't know. When?'

'Now.'

'Umm ... where to?'

'Straddlingate.'

'Where's that?'

'It's in the Blacker Mountains,' said Hobbes. 'I haven't been back there for ages and it should be splendid this time of year.'

I could think of no reason why I shouldn't go. Perhaps I should have tried harder. 'OK then,' I said.

'Excellent,' said Hobbes. 'I've packed a tent and rations and clothes for both of us.'

'Umm ... how do we get there? You broke the car.'

'Billy's agreed to take us until the road runs out. After that, we're on our own.'

'Alright.'

'I've brought you some fresh clothes,' said Hobbes, handing me a small bag.

I took it, hurried upstairs and got changed. A tweed suit was not quite what I'd envisaged, but it was, at least, an improvement on evening wear. I went back down.

'Let's go,' said Hobbes, turning to shake Sid's hand. 'Thank you for supper last night, and for looking after Andy and for your advice'

'Always a pleasure,' said Sid. 'Take care.'

'Goodbye. I'll be in touch soon,' said Hobbes, bundling me from the house into the street.

Billy Shawcroft was leaning against his old hearse, which was glinting in the sunlight.

'Wotcha,' he said, looking up.

'Hi,' I said and was knocked onto my back.

Dregs, who'd been preparing for the journey against a lamppost, had leapt at me, greeting my return to his world as if I'd been away for a month. As his great, pink tongue snaked towards my face, I rolled to the side and pushed him off, alarmed by the white flecks around his jaws.

'Stop messing about,' said Hobbes, 'and let's get away before any reporters show up.'

Although there was plenty of room in the front of the hearse, I had to go in the back because Dregs insisted on riding there in case he wanted to stick his big, black head out the window. I wasn't much bothered for, despite having to share my space with a bagged tent and two bulging rucksacks, I could stretch out and relax. Billy, having strapped the wooden blocks to his feet that allowed him to reach the pedals, adjusted a pile of cushions and, when able to see over the steering wheel, drove away.

'I take it the reporters are still there,' I said.

'Yes,' said Hobbes. 'Even more than yesterday.'

'How did you get out of there with Dregs?' I asked, unable to imagine even Hobbes persuading him into a rucksack.

'I squirted shaving foam around his chops, opened the front door and shoved him out. As soon as the reporters saw him, they scattered like leaves in the wind, and I ran round the corner to meet Billy. I don't think anyone saw me.'

I laughed, impressed and amused by the brilliant simplicity of the plan. 'So how long will it take to get to wherever we're going?'

'About two hours,' said Billy. 'I've filled up, so we won't have to stop.'

He drove at a good speed, nowhere near as fast as Hobbes went, yet considerably faster than was normal, or decorous, for hearses. Fenderton passed in a blur and in no time we were heading upwards through lush green hills towards the dual carriageway. As soon as we were out of town, Hobbes peeled off his facial hair. He had a touching faith in his disguises, though his sheer size and enormous presence made him stick out like a panda in a poodle parlour.

When we reached the motorway, we headed north, maintaining a steady seventy miles per hour. Billy hummed along to the radio, switching stations whenever a tune failed to reach his standard. Hobbes was relaxed, his patience surprising for one more used to breakneck speed. Billy was just about the only other driver he trusted.

When the news came on, the attempted gold robbery had been relegated to third place, but Hobbes sat up when Jeremy Pratt reported a fresh development.

'Within the last few minutes,' said Jeremy, sounding both excited and pompous, 'a police spokesman informed me that a white van suspected of having been used in the attempted robbery was discovered burnt out on waste ground close to where it was last spotted. Although a forensic team is on the scene, it seems unlikely that any evidence will have survived the blaze.

'Of Inspector Hobbes, who, you will remember, heroically battled the gang, there has been no sign. There is speculation that he is actively pursuing the remaining gang members.'

Hobbes shrugged. 'Sid was right about the van, more's the pity. I'm glad to be taking a break. He was right about that, too.'

The journey continued peacefully, until Billy, running out of acceptable radio stations began singing. His high-pitched voice was strangely musical and soon I joined in, as did Dregs, who assisted on the high notes with howls, while supplying percussive barking and tail thumping where appropriate. Hobbes, despite claiming not to like this modern rubbish, sang along when the fancy took him and, fortunately, kept the volume down.

At last we left the motorway, heading west through fertile, undulating countryside, intersected with small rivers and streams. It was new territory to me, and the black and white cottages with their neatly thatched roofs, the fields and the orchards appealed, yet we quickly passed by, the road rising and narrowing as we headed towards the blue-grey of distant hills. A motorbike overtook at reckless speed.

'I'd have had him,' said Hobbes, 'if I was on duty. It's his lucky day.'

But it wasn't. A few miles further on, as we entered a village called Much Wetfoot, we stopped at a T-junction, something the biker had apparently failed to do, having ploughed straight ahead, demolishing a road sign, hitting a wall, flying over it and coming to rest amid the shattered glass of a greenhouse. A small crowd of local yokels had gathered to watch.

We stopped to help, but the biker was unhurt, seemingly more upset by the damage to the front forks of his bike than by his near death and the mess he'd caused, until Hobbes took him aside for a quiet word. As Dregs relieved himself on the bike's back wheel, a tall man in a battered jacket, his dark eyes strangely unfocussed, stared at Billy and me. His breath reeked of cider.

'Good day, sir' said Billy. 'What's the quickest way to get from here to Blackcastle?'

'Drive there,' said the man.

'But which way?' said Billy, with a glance at the demolished sign.

The man laughed and sat on the wall. 'Only joking, lads. Take the left fork.'

'How can we ever thank you?' I said.

'A drink wouldn't be a bad idea,' said the man, oblivious to my sarcasm.

'I'll sort it,' said Billy, taking something that rustled from his trousers, reaching up and stuffing it into the man's top pocket. 'Have one on us.'

'Cheers, lads,' said the man, with a grin and a cidery burp.

When we piled back into the hearse, I noticed our helpful friend was looking glum. 'What did you give him?' I asked.

'A sachet of drinking chocolate,' said Billy, chuckling. 'We were given free samples at the Feathers, only Featherlight won't do drinks like that. He says they're for wimps.'

A few miles on, the ground ever steeper, Billy asked where to turn.

'Soon,' said Hobbes. 'You see up there?' He pointed. 'That's the start of the Black Mountains.' He moved his finger a little to the left. 'That steeper ridge over there is the Blacker Mountains.'

'I hadn't even heard of them,' I admitted.

'I'm not surprised,' said Hobbes. 'No one lives there since the tenants were evicted and they can be dangerous. Even hill walkers give them a miss.'

'Dangerous?' I said. 'What d'you mean?'

'There are many perils up there for the unwary, but don't worry, I'm not unwary.'

I could feel the usual flocks of butterflies testing their wings in my stomach.

'What sort of perils?'

'Let me think. There are cliffs, caves, canyons, crevasses, screes, streams, gullies, rockslides, pitfalls, overhangs, marshes, icy waters, trackless wastes, mine workings and uncovered wells …'

'Oh, great.' The butterflies, having taken wing, were flapping madly.

'… but probably the biggest danger is the weather, which can change within minutes and there's precious little shelter, unless you know where to look.'

'So, why are we going there?'

'Because it seems like a good idea.'

'Why?'

'I'm not sure really. It's wild, beautiful in its way, and exciting. I used to wander there when I was a child.'

'Wasn't it dangerous?'

'Not for me.' He glanced towards Billy. 'See that milepost? Turn immediately after it.'

We turned into an overgrown lane, finding it blocked by two enormous boulders.

'Well,' said, Billy, braking, 'I guess that's about as far as I can take you.'

'Nonsense,' said Hobbes, getting out. 'I'll shift them.'

Dregs went with him to lend moral support.

Putting his shoulder to the smaller of the two rocks, Hobbes heaved. For a moment, nothing happened, except that his face grew redder and the veins in his neck bulged like hose pipes. Then a dandelion toppled, and the boulder rolled aside, leaving a deep hollow. As he turned to the other one, he removed his raincoat, and hung it on a bush.

'Do you want a hand?' asked Billy, freeing his feet from his wooden blocks.

Hobbes, smiling, nodded. Billy joined him and, though he only came up to Hobbes's waist, his expression was determined.

'On three,' said Hobbes. 'Three!'

They pushed and grunted. For a few seconds, I thought Hobbes had met his match and even considered offering my help. The boulder moved a fraction.

'Heave!' cried Hobbes and the boulder, ploughing a furrow through the stinging nettles, rolled to one side.

'That's far enough,' said Billy, his round face puce like a plum. 'I can squeeze through now.'

'That,' said Hobbes, wiping his brow on his handkerchief, 'was fun. We need to go about five miles down the lane. That will take us to an abandoned manor.'

Although I'd witnessed some incredible feats from him, this one took some beating, for the boulder was as tall as him and even broader, but, as he retrieved his coat, he frowned and dropped to his knees. I had a sudden fear he'd suffered a heart attack and jumped out to help, but he was crawling forward like a monstrous toad, sniffing the grass, and examining the track. He stood up, brushing dust from his knees, and looking puzzled.

'It appears,' he said, 'that a heavy vehicle passed this way, sometime after last week's rain. I can't tell which way it was heading, but, whichever way, someone would have had to roll the boulders aside and then put them back. Why would anyone want to drive up here?'

'I don't know,' I said, 'but we're going to.'

'Very true,' he said, as we got back into the car.

The next couple of hundred metres took us over rutted, bumpy land but, just as I feared my brains would be shaken out, the going became much easier, the lane smooth and covered with short grass. I suspected the abundance of rabbits kept the vegetation down. They certainly kept Dregs interested. He made several frantic attempts to squeeze out of the window as white bobtails bounded away.

The track ended at the manor, a long, single-storey building of grey rock, still showing traces of whitewash, though the roof had long since fallen in.

'This is the end of the road,' said Hobbes, as we stopped. 'Thanks for the lift. Do you fancy a coffee or anything before you go? I can have the kettle on in no time.'

'No,' said Billy. 'I'd better get back. I'm working this evening and Featherlight doesn't like me being late.'

We unpacked our gear and piled it by a wall. Billy turned the hearse about.

'Have a great time, guys,' he said, 'and, when you need picking up, you've got my number. See you.'

He drove away, leaving me with feelings of abandonment and panic. I wasn't used to the wild and the mountains and moors seemed to be gathering around, threatening me with their vastness.

'This old house belonged to the dowager Lady Payne,' said Hobbes, chewing on a blade of grass. 'I knew her well.'

'What was she like?'

'I don't know,' he said. 'I never met her.'

'Then how did you know her well?'

'I used to draw water from it. I could do with a nice hot cup of tea and this dog will need a drink before we set off, so I'd better find it. It was over there, I think. The kettle and the mugs are in the black rucksack and the stove is in the grey one, if you wouldn't mind getting them out.'

Taking a jerry can and a length of rope from the pile, he strolled towards the old barn, shoved a heap of rusting, crumbling, corrugated iron out of the way and uncovered a round, flat stone, about the size of a dustbin lid. As I dug through the rucksacks, he slid the stone aside, peered into the hole, gave me a thumbs up and returned with the can full of water. Within a few minutes, we had tea to drink. Afterwards, while I rinsed the tin mugs and Dregs's bowl, Hobbes sorted out the gear.

'Right,' he said, picking up the larger rucksack, 'let's get into the mountains.'

Within minutes, with the straps of the smaller rucksack digging into my shoulders that were still tender from the previous day's hike, I was struggling to keep up as Hobbes led me into a pathless waste of rank grass, bracken and heather. The odd sparse, stunted gorse bush appeared to cower in the occasional dips and hollows, though what they were hiding from I couldn't imagine. The sun was bright and I might even have been too warm, were it not for a gentle breeze whispering through the grass. Hobbes, striding along, was almost hidden beneath his massive grey rucksack and our supplies. He either didn't believe in modern, lightweight tents, or hadn't heard of them, for, bundled on top of his rucksack was a great, folded sheet of faded green canvas, a couple of heavy wooden poles, and a ball of tangled, thumb-thick ropes. At least he didn't need to carry a mallet, for I'd seen how he could drive tent pegs into the stoniest ground with a few blows from his great, hairy fist. Although Dregs, much to his annoyance, had been saddled with panniers full of tins, he soon got used to them and bounded ahead, making barking forays in the general direction of rabbits. A tapestry of muddy brown, green and khaki, interspersed with startling yellow swathes of gorse, stretched before us and, away to our right, a tiny waterfall, splashing over a low black cliff, filled the air with rainbows.

It wasn't long before our path grew steeper and rougher. Now and again there were patches of bare, black rock, corrugated with deep cracks that Hobbes and Dregs took in their respective strides, while I had to scramble on hands and knees. Despite the breeze, I was soon sweating like a wrestler, and, despite having filled up with tea, my mouth was as dry as custard powder. My stomach began grumbling that it was way past lunchtime and I hoped Hobbes had brought something good to eat that wouldn't take too long to prepare and that he'd stop soon – very soon. I had a horrible suspicion that Dregs's panniers contained only dog food, which he would eat if sufficiently hungry, but which had little appeal to me.

'Did you see that?' asked Hobbes, pausing by a deformed and stunted thorn bush.

'What?'

'The fox.'

'No.'

I trudged after him, beginning to feel light headed with hunger as we reached the top of a ridge, with a narrow valley stretching below us, hemmed in by moorland and sheer cliffs, broken up by massive boulders. As we began the descent, I made up my mind to not get lost, for, although Hobbes might be able to find his way around this horrible wilderness, I was certain I couldn't. A low-grade panic was building, forcing me forward, ensuring he never got too far ahead and, when he finally stopped and I caught up, I was panting and dripping. Apart from his load, he looked as if he'd just stepped from the office after a morning's paperwork.

'Did you see that?' he asked.

'What?'

'The red kite.'

'No,' I said, frustrated, but determined to keep my eyes skinned and to point something interesting out to him.

'Never mind. We'll stop here for lunch.' He swung his kit to the ground.

I wriggled free from my rucksack, enjoying the breeze, feeling my shirt sticking to my back. The day was somewhat cooler than it had been and the valley, to my eyes, was uninviting; bare, broken rock with now and again a whiff of stagnant water from a nasty, green bog at the bottom.

'Is there a reason for stopping here?' I asked, rummaging in my rucksack for my cagoule, already having had enough of the wind.

'There's fresh water.'

'I can't see any,' I said, peevish with hunger, wrinkling my nose, 'unless you mean that stinking stuff down there.'

'No.' He laughed, and said, 'There's a spring.'

'Where?'

'In the cave.'

'What cave?' I asked.

'This one,' he said, dropping to his knees and crawling into what I'd taken to be a hummock, where there was a fissure just big enough for him to squeeze through.

'Pass me the jerry can,' he said, disappearing, leaving only his hand remaining in the light.

I passed it, and can and Hobbes were gone. Although Dregs found the procedure most entertaining, he showed no inclination to follow and nor did I, for I'd had too many bad frights in dark places. Instead, I dug out the kettle, the stove, and a box of matches and waited, hoping Hobbes did not get himself lost or stuck. If my worst fears were realised, I would have to attempt a rescue, as I had no mobile phone and would undoubtedly get lost should I go looking for help. After a few minutes of silence, my stomach tightening with nerves, I dropped to my knees and stuck my head into the dark, narrow cave.

'Are you alright?' I yelled.

There was no response, so, I crawled inside.

'Hello!' I cried, my voice muffled.

'Are you shouting to me?'

I jumped, headbutted the low ceiling and groaned. Puzzled, but relieved, I reversed into the daylight.

'Umm ... how did you get here?'

'It's like a labyrinth in there,' said Hobbes. 'I came out another way.'

As I stood up, I considered punching him, and might have, had I believed it would hurt him more than it hurt me. Instead, I put the kettle on and, with a flourish like a stage magician pulling a rabbit from a hat, he produced a large, brown paper parcel from the rucksack. Inside was bread, cheese, pickles and salad, and two of Mrs Goodfellow's best china plates. I couldn't help thinking that he'd really catch it if we broke one.

I could barely restrain myself until it was time to eat and, as Hobbes passed me a plate, I fell to eating, like a wolf on the fold. Hobbes was more restrained, and Dregs was disappointed to get only water. The bread was fresh, crusty and fragrant, the Sorenchester cheese sweet and tangy, and the pickle pungent and perfect.

Hobbes, having filled two mugs with tea and given me one, took a slurp from the other. 'You'd better make the most of it. There's a meat pie for supper and after that we'll have to rely on what we can find or catch.'

'What,' I asked, staring at the desolate, empty landscape, 'is there to eat around here?'

'There are rabbits, hares, hedgehogs, stoats, fish, ducks and all sorts of roots and things. And there may still be wild strawberries, if we're really lucky.'

'But, how will we, umm … you catch them?'

'Strawberries don't usually require much catching,' he said, smiling. 'As for the others I will use stealth, cunning, and possibly a rock. If we're unlucky, there are emergency rations in Dregs's pannier.'

'What are the chances we'll need them?'

'We'll see.'

Although his answer failed to reassure me, I experienced the sudden realisation that I didn't *not* want to be there and that I would have hated giving up on the life adventurous. Sometimes, I doubted my own sanity, because when things became dark, dangerous and uncomfortable, as was frequent when Hobbes was around, I still wanted to be there. I had sometimes cursed myself for not sticking to safe, familiar ways, but not often.

Having rested and eaten my fill, I was in a fairly cheerful mood as we set off again, finding the going far easier on my feet than yesterday's road had been. It was hard to believe that had only been a day ago.

'Where, exactly, are we heading?' I asked breathlessly, having caught up.

'Straddlingate.'

'I know, but what is it? A camp site? Or a village?'

'It's a valley with an old quarry and some mine workings. It's said there was gold in these here hills, long ago.'

'Why are we going there in particular?'

'Something, I'm not sure what, is drawing me back. Possibly, it's because I always felt comfortable there, even though it can be a fearful place.'

'Fearful? What d'you mean?'

'I don't know exactly. Careful where you tread; that's a bog asphodel and it's quite rare.'

Looking down, I avoided crushing a plant with small orangey capsules and smooth stems, but only by stepping into a patch of thick, stinking, bubbling mud.

'Well done,' said Hobbes, as I extricated myself. 'Let's get a move on.'

As we strode deeper into the bleakness, he occasionally stooped to throw a stick for Dregs. Where Dregs had found a stick in such a desolate landscape was a mystery, but he was really in his element, his long legs making light work of the rough terrain.

It was a lot later when I realised that Hobbes had distracted me from questioning him about Straddlingate. Still, I reasoned that the company I was in would keep me fairly safe.

Hobbes stopped and pointed. 'Did you see them?'

'What?'

'The stoats.'

'No.'

He shrugged and carried on. I was annoyed with myself and feared he'd perceive me as a hopelessly unobservant clod.

The land remained bleak and lonely until we crested another ridge and started heading into a valley, where the air was fresh and clean, scented with gorse and some sweet herb. At the far end was a small pool, fringed by broken reeds, its dark waters backed up by a rugged cliff. I was feeling strangely euphoric, as if I'd cast off all the cares of the world, even though I'd never felt so far from the comforts and security of civilization, and even the tiredness of my leg muscles seemed pleasurable. I speculated that perhaps I was, at heart, a mountain man. Still, I was grateful when Hobbes said we'd arrived, for even Dregs had run out of bounds by then.

'Did you see that?' he asked as I stopped.

'Yes,' I lied.

'Then why did you step in it?'

My right foot was in the rotting, maggoty carcass of a crow or something. Its stench was such that even Dregs fled before it. I used a rock to prise it loose and finished the clean up on a tuft of heather.

'We'll camp down there,' said Hobbes, pointing towards a spring, bubbling from the side of the valley and forming a small stream that trickled and twisted down to the pool, where a grey heron, hunched on the far side, ignored us.

'This,' he said, still appearing as fresh as he'd been at the start, 'is Stradlingate. Let's get the tent up.'

Dropping my rucksack, I sprawled on a flat, sun-warmed rock and let him get on with it, for he knew what he was doing, and I would only have been in his way and got tangled up in all the lines. I did, however, pick up the bag of pegs, ready to hand to him, while Dregs, who believed Hobbes was being attacked by a vast canvas monster, growled encouragement and attacked any flapping edges. Yet, even with Dregs's contribution, it was not long before the tent was secure in the shelter of a gorse bush and Hobbes was punching in the final peg.

Although I couldn't stand up straight in it, there was plenty of room for all three of us. I just hoped the musty, dusty smell would go away. Dregs, accepting the transformation from monster to shelter with equanimity, lay down and went to sleep as soon as his blanket had been unrolled. I wasn't surprised that, instead of modern lightweight, micro-fibre sleeping bags, Hobbes had brought woollen rugs, which we piled on a pair of rubber-backed canvass groundsheets.

'That's yours,' he said, pointing to the left, 'and this is mine.'

'Will it be warm enough?' I asked. 'It must get pretty nippy at night.'

'We'll be fine … probably,' said Hobbes. 'I doubt the weather will turn bad for a day or two.

'I fancy a bit of a run up the Beacon. D'you want to come?'

'I think I've had quite enough exercise today,' I said, yawning. 'Where is the Beacon?'

Taking me outside, he pointed to a distant peak that rose high above the ridges. It was conical, covered with browning bracken on the steep sides, with bare rock as it reached the domed top, reminding me of Friar Tuck's tonsure. The sun, still bright and hot, was over the summit.

'It looks a long way off,' I said, glad I'd chickened out.

'Not really,' said Hobbes. 'I'll be back by dusk.'

'When's that?'

'When it starts to get dark.'

He left, his great loping strides taking him along the valley and then, via a cleft, towards the peak. I watched until he was out of sight and joined Dregs, who was snoring gently and twitching on his blanket. With a yawn, I lay down on top of my rugs, it being too warm inside to cover up, and rested my eyes for a few moments.

I awoke to Dregs's low growling, though that wasn't what had woken me. He was outside, bristling and ill at ease, and I understood, for something felt wrong, though I couldn't put my finger on quite what. I got up, surprised how gloomy the day had grown, and shivered, wishing Hobbes was back. Then I felt it, a weird sensation, an odd vibration, passing through my feet, up my body into my head. Though I couldn't have explained why, I decided it was coming from some distance, but as I left the tent, it stopped. In the distance, I could see Hobbes jogging towards us. Dregs rushed to greet him.

'Did you feel that?' I asked when they were back.

Hobbes nodded.

'What was it?'

'I don't know, but I remember something like it when I was a boy.'

I had never envisaged Hobbes as a boy. He gave the impression of having arrived fully formed, although he had made occasional remarks about his childhood, particularly about Auntie Elsie and Uncle Jack, who'd adopted him and guided him through his troubled youth. From what I'd gathered, he'd caused much of the trouble.

'It felt,' he said, 'like machinery in the mines.'

'Does that mean someone's mining?'

'Possibly,' he said, 'but I'd expect to see some signs.'

'Back when we left the road, you reckoned a heavy vehicle had been along before us.'

'That is true,' he said, 'but it seems unlikely they'd restart mining. They were all closed in the nineteenth century.'

'Then it's a mystery,' I said, with masterful insight.

'It is,' said Hobbes with a laugh, 'but it's nothing to do with us. All the land round here is private and what the owner does on it is his business.'

'What do you mean private land? We're not trespassing are we?'

'Only in the legal sense,' said Hobbes.

'What other sense is there?'

'Moral, or ethical. This whole area used to be common land, land that many families depended on. Then Sir Rodney Payne enclosed it and took it for himself, but his right to do so is debatable. What is not debatable is that Sir Rodney used considerable force and the enclosure was, in effect, robbery with violence.'

'How do you know all this?'

'Uncle Jack told me. His father used to have a small farm, grazing sheep on Blacker

Knob, until Sir Rodney threw him and his family out.'

'So, if he hadn't, would the farm have come to you eventually?'

'No. Uncle Jack was a younger son and, back then, inherited property went to the eldest.'

'When was that?'

'Late in the eighteenth century. Sir Rodney was widely regarded as the most odious man in the county and the same family still owns it. Most of them are no better than Sir Rodney, if the stories are to be believed. The point is, I have no compunction in being here. The Payne family may have the law on its side, but it does not have justice and, besides, we won't be doing any harm; there's nothing we could damage. Furthermore, we have the legal right to roam these days.'

'Good,' I said. 'Umm … when is supper?'

He laughed. 'You have a talent for getting back to what is really important. Supper's ready as soon as you've made tea and I've got the pie out.'

I filled the kettle and set it to heat on the stove, worried that there only appeared to be one gas cylinder, but hoping he had a plan for when it was used up; although he might not have had a problem with raw stoat, I certainly did and even Dregs preferred cooked meals. Still, that was a worry for later and the sight of the huge meat pie set my mouth watering. I made tea, Hobbes said grace and sliced the pie into generous chunks. We sat at a long, smooth rock that made a useful table, stuffing ourselves. Afterwards, he produced a bag of apples and, munching one, I began to feel comfortable and confident. The sun had long ago dipped beneath the Beacon, the temperature was dropping and night was falling fast. Hobbes lit a candle lantern, our only light.

'What are we going to do tonight?' I asked, hoping there'd be a cosy pub within easy walking distance, but fearing the appearance of being in the middle of nowhere was no illusion.

'We're going to wash up,' said Hobbes, 'and then I'm going to turn in. You can do what you like.'

'I hoped we might grab a beer or something.'

'The nearest pub is in Blackcastle. It's about eight miles due east of here. You can't miss it.'

'OK … Which way is east?'

'Over there.' He pointed. 'Roughly opposite to where the sun went down. Of course, to get there you'll have to cross Dead Man's Bluff.'

'I might give it a miss tonight.'

'Suit yourself.'

As soon as we'd washed up in cold water and stacked the plates to drip dry, he retired into the tent.

Wrapping my jacket around me, I lay on the flat rock, gazing at the stars. I'd never seen such abundance. Hobbes had once tried to teach me about them, displaying a vast theoretical and practical knowledge, but astronomy was way over my head. I could, at least, recognise the moon, half of which was rising, making the mountains shine with a pale, silvery light. Once or twice I noticed the flickering silhouettes of bats and, faraway, an owl screeched, emphasising the quietness and the isolation and filling me with a sense of melancholy and loneliness that was almost exhilarating. Sprawled, relaxed, contemplating the cosmos, I thought deep thoughts and pondered much on the meaning of life, until Dregs started licking himself. The mood shattered, I relieved myself in a gorse bush and decided to turn in. Anyway, I was starting to feel cold.

Hobbes, fast asleep, didn't stir as I snuggled into my pile of rugs. I was sure the ground was too hard and rocky and the rugs nowhere near thick enough to allow me to sleep, especially as Dregs had decided to lie on my feet.

When I awoke it was morning, and Hobbes and Dregs were already up. It took me a while to join them, because my back was rigid and my neck stiff and besides, it was warm where I was. Yet I had to move sometime, so, with a sigh, I crawled out into bright daylight and got to my feet, grunting good morning, stretching and yawning. Hobbes, having made a fire from old bits of gorse, was filleting several large trout.

'Where did you get those from?' I asked.

'Over there.' He pointed down the valley to the pool.

'Great. How did you catch them?'

'With difficulty, because they didn't want to be caught. I think they were nervous of the heron.'

When he started frying them, along with a handful of green leaves he'd found, the air was filled with delicious scents; they tasted even better. Fresh fish cooked and eaten in fresh air really piqued the appetite.

'I could get used to this,' I said, stuffing the last bit into my mouth.

'Yes. This is good living. There's plenty to eat around here and I doubt I'll have much trouble at this time of year. It's not so good in the depths of winter, though.'

'We won't be here that long, will we?'

'No. At least, I hope not, but it is October and the weather up here can change within minutes. Still, it should stay warm and sunny for the next few days. After that, I'm not so sure.' He sniffed the air and glanced at the sky. 'We'll see.'

'Do you think bad weather's on the way?'

'Maybe, but let's enjoy the good stuff while we can.'

Having never gone camping in really bad weather before, I wasn't much looking forward to the prospect, but Hobbes didn't concern himself with future problems that might not even arise. It struck me as a good way of living, one that I wished I could follow. Unfortunately, I had a tendency to worry, despite having learned that the worrying about a dreaded event was often far worse than the event itself. This wasn't always the case, for I had another tendency to drop myself into messes far deeper than I'd anticipated.

After we'd eaten and I'd scrubbed the dishes, I asked a foolish question.

'What do we do about washing ourselves?'

The pool was cool and clear and, once the shock of being thrown into it had passed, refreshing.

The next two days were glorious. We'd turn in as the light faded and wake early. I made it to the top of Beacon Peak, where I sat stunned by the vastness of the landscape as the morning mist dispersed. The hills looked pristine, as if human kind had never intruded, and it felt like we'd awoken into the first dawn of a clean, new world. When we got back down, Hobbes, naked and as hairy as a bear, his beard grown shaggy already, would plunge headfirst into the lake, often emerging with an eel or a trout between his jaws. Later, he would gut them, clean them and fry them for breakfast. The rest of the day, we would walk over the ridges and, despite Dregs's attentions, Hobbes would hunt for rabbits and hares, or scratch around for herbs and roots. He discovered a hunched, arthritic old apple tree, a remnant, so he said, of an ancient farmhouse, and roasted some of the ripe fruit on a sheet of corrugated iron that he unearthed in a cave. We ate like lords and never had to eat a stoat or open our emergency rations, though we had to drink our tea without milk.

By my reckoning, it was on the third day when our morning walk took us to Blacker Knob, a tall peak, where near the top, a pile of rocks might long ago have been a cottage. That was where our camping trip took a dark turn.

Hobbes was chasing a hare and, since he appeared to be enjoying his workout, I found myself somewhere sheltered to sit and watch. Dregs, for once not bounding after him, started barking, and something in the tone suggested urgency. I stood up, the wind blustering and raising goose pimples, and went to see what was bothering him. Bristling, excited and ill at ease, he was sniffing round a pile of small rocks and pawing at something.

'What is it?' I asked.

A smooth, round, white object, a bit like a child's ball, rolled towards me. Bending, I picked it up and was nearly sick. I had a human skull in my hand and, although my first instinct was to drop it, I couldn't let go. I stared into the empty eye sockets.

'Alas, poor Yorick!' I said, a long-forgotten incident popping unbidden into my head. 'I knew him, Dregs.'

It was a conditioned response and I was as unable to restrain myself as Pavlov's dogs could have stopped drooling at the sound of a bell. It all went back to when my class was studying the graveyard scene in Hamlet and I still remembered the malicious expression of Psycho Simms, our English teacher, who, book in hand, called me and 'Bill' Bailey to the front.

'Caplet,' said Psycho, 'although you are, perhaps, the most unlikely prince, you will recite Hamlet's part. Bailey, you play Horatio. Take it from where Hamlet picks up the skull.'

'Yes sir,' I said, my mind instantly going as blank as the freshly-wiped whiteboard. 'Alas ... umm ... alas ... alas ... alas ... umm.'

'Poor,' said Psycho.

'I'm sorry, sir. Oh, I see: that's what comes next.' I turned towards Bailey 'Alas, poor ... umm ...' I stared at his round, pimply face, struggling to recall the stupid name, growing ever more desperate, my mind empty of everything but embarrassment. As Psycho and the class waited and waited, someone sniggered and the blood burned my cheeks as my dramatic pause seemed to stretch towards infinity.

Bailey, taking pity, was mouthing the name.

I nodded, confidence flooding back, and, raising my hand dramatically, staring at an imaginary skull, I came out with the immortal words: 'Alas, poor Yogi!'

I never finished the speech. My role ended with a stunning rap on the head from the complete works of Shakespeare, mocking laughter from my classmates and having to write out the scene one hundred times.

Hobbes appeared with a brace of hares dangling limply from his belt.

'Hello, 'ello, 'ello,' he said. 'I take my eye off you for one minute and find you engaged in all sorts of skulduggery.'

I grimaced.

'I always knew you'd get ahead one day.'

'How can you joke about it?' I asked, trembling and hoping I'd only picked up a prehistoric relic, not a recently dead skull.

'Sorry,' he said, 'but humour soothes the sting of horror. Give it to me, please.'

I handed it over, nearly losing my breakfast when he sniffed it. He frowned, turning it over and round, running his hand over it, holding it up and examining it from all angles.

'It's only a few years old at the most and, judging by the size and the brow ridge, I'd say it belonged to an adult male human. It has received a severe blow to the top which caused a penetrating fracture. Of course, that might have occurred post mortem. I'm not an expert.'

Carefully, he put it down and began sifting through the rock pile, pushing aside a number of slabs to reveal a skeleton, still partially covered in ragged, faded scraps of clothing and with a pair of boots on the feet. I grabbed for Dregs's collar, but he made no attempt to go for the bones.

'Again,' said Hobbes, frowning and thoughtful, 'the hips suggest an adult male and, to judge from the long bones, quite a tall one.' He pointed to an arm. 'The upper bone plate and radius have fused, suggesting he was out of his teens, while the collarbone development indicates he was probably older than his late twenties.'

Squatting, he peered at the torso, where it was exposed beneath what might have once been a red-checked shirt. 'There is a little degeneration of the spine and that, together with the wear and tear on his teeth, leads me to speculate that our man was in his mid-forties.'

His calm assessments felt like soothing balm on my raw nerves and my brain started functioning again.

'How long has he been here?' I asked. 'And how did he get here?'

'It's not easy to be accurate,' he said, 'and as I said, I'm no expert, but I'll take a stab at it. The rocks and slates have protected the body from larger scavengers, so the skeleton is mostly intact and, although small animals have disturbed them to some extent, the bones are in reasonably good condition. The clothing and the boots are modern and appear to be of a type suitable for hill walking. I'd guess the cloth has made many a mouse nest cosier.

'I'd say he's probably been dead for two, maybe three years, and that someone killed him and carried him here to conceal the body.'

'It was murder then?' I said, my sick feelings returning.

'It seems likely. Clearly he didn't bury himself and the skull fracture suggests a violent attack. Assuming that's what killed him, the wound would have bled considerably, but there's no sign it bled round here, although that might be down to time and rain. I would also have expected a hill walker to have some sort of backpack and, at least, basic survival gear.'

'So,' I said, 'the poor guy was probably killed elsewhere and the murderer hid the body here. He didn't do a very good job.'

'No,' said Hobbes, 'but he wouldn't expect anyone to be up here.'

I shivered and it wasn't because of the cold wind.

'I suppose,' he said, scratching his chin, 'we should tell the authorities.'

'I suppose so.'

'The trouble is that I came here to escape publicity and, although I expect things have quietened down by now, I would rather not draw attention to myself again. You'll have to go into Blackcastle and tell the police. You could say you were out walking your dog and came across the skeleton on Blacker Knob, which is essentially the truth.'

'OK,' I said, reluctantly, 'but how do I … umm … get to Blackcastle?'

'I'll guide you to the outskirts. It's not far.'

'You said it was eight miles away!'

'Exactly.'

'Fine. How will I find my way back? I don't know where here is.'

'That's a good point,' he said. 'I'll lay a trail.'

We set off straight away, despite my hints that it was nearly lunchtime. He led Dregs and me to the outskirts of the little grey town, and handed me some money for a bite to eat and to buy a newspaper, asking me to check if interest in him had yet waned. Then he left us.

Dregs and I followed a potholed track into Blackcastle, walking past a row of seedy terraced houses that might have been transformed into something reasonably attractive had anyone been bothered. A slab pivoted, its front end going down, its back end rising and catching my foot, making me stumble and put my hand on a sturdy-looking garden gate. Giving a sad sigh, it crumbled into dust, falling onto a garden path that was ankle deep in dandelions and grass. As I hurried on, pretending it had been nothing to do with me, a terrier in the next garden along woofed once before relapsing into apathy and going back to chewing what appeared to be a flat cap. Dregs, knowing he was on a mission, ignored him and we turned onto a narrow street, hemmed in by squat, concrete buildings that I imagined estate agents might have referred to as bijou maisonettes. Their grey walls were stained and cracked, the paintwork bubbled and peeled and the doors and window frames were rotten.

Although some areas of Pigton, the nearest big town to Sorenchester, were rather rundown, I'd never before been anywhere as spirit draining as that godforsaken place. Even Dregs's normal bounding enthusiasm was dampened and he walked obediently to heel. As we reached the last house of the terrace, an old woman in a shabby brown cardigan appeared to be scavenging from a dustbin and, despite my friendly smile, she flinched and scurried inside, slamming the front door behind her. I blamed Dregs for alarming her, though I found his presence comforting.

We turned onto what appeared to be the main street, which took us towards an unexpectedly broad market square with a war memorial and a drinking fountain in the middle. The Badger's Rest, an old-fashioned and tatty pub, filled the nearest corner, while the police station, relatively modern, yet possibly even tattier, occupied the opposite one. A glance into the pub showed it was full of morose, down-at-heel drinkers. I led Dregs towards the police station, passing one small, dejected shop, allegedly a mini-supermarket, with its pathetic display of wrinkled, yellowing vegetables in a rack outside. The other buildings in the square appeared to be houses, one or two of them apparently derelict and covered in ragged posters for the approaching autumn fair. Near the police station, one place really stood out, looking clean, freshly painted in bright pink, with baskets bright with flowers hanging from brackets. A sign printed in large, frilly letters declared it was Pinky's Tearoom.

I took the most direct line towards the police station, striding there with due urgency, only to find it was locked. A faded sign pinned to the door said: 'back in 5 minuets'. I couldn't stop myself looking around for a dance hall.

'Are you after the cops, love?' asked a soft female voice.

I turned to see a plump, pretty, blonde woman, dressed in a trouser suit in the same shocking pink as the tea room.

'Yes,' I said, trying not to stare.

'They'll be down the Badger's. I'd look in there if I were you.'

'Thank you.'

'Don't mention it, love.'

'Umm … are you Pinky?'

Her big blue eyes widened in surprise. 'I am. How did you know?'

'Just a hunch.'

'Are you a detective?'

'No … not really … it's sort of a complicated story.'

'Well, come in for a cup of tea and tell me.'

Although I did fancy a drink and had money in my pocket, duty called. 'Maybe later, but I must tell the police something: something important.'

'Alright then. See you, love,' She turned and headed towards her tearoom in a cloud of perfume.

Leaving Dregs by the drinking fountain, I walked into the pub, its door opening with a horrible creak and the murmur of conversation immediately dying. The silence was broken only by the door creaking back and somebody coughing. As my eyes accustomed themselves to the gloom, I felt something zip past the tip of my nose and heard a clunk.

'Three!' said a male voice.

'That wanker put me off,' said a deeper, angry male voice.

I jerked backwards as the next dart flew past my face, wondering what sort of idiot would throw when someone was almost in the firing line, and what sort of idiot would position a dartboard between the door and the bar. It wasn't exactly welcoming, but then, as I looked around, nor was the rest of the pub. Dingy was the first word that came to mind, followed by dirty, dismal, disgusting, and smelly. As the third dart hit the board, I took my chance and scuttled towards the bar and, I hoped, safety. I couldn't see any policemen, just a bunch of drunken, scruffy men hunched on plastic covered stools, glasses in their hands, watching me. One man, flat on his back on the worn, sticky lino, began emitting blood-curdling snores.

The barman, a tall, skinny old man, whose cardigan was so riddled with holes it might have made a passable fishing net, nodded. 'You're not from around here, are you? I know that 'cos we don't get many strangers in here.'

'I can't understand why not,' I said, smiling, trying to establish friendly relations.

'Are you trying to be funny?'

'No… umm … it's quite quaint, really.'

'It's a total shit hole,' said the man. 'Are you blind?'

'I nearly was,' I said. 'Isn't it dangerous having the dartboard there?'

The barman shrugged. 'I didn't put it there. What's your poison?'

Although I hadn't intended buying a drink, I thought doing so might endear me. 'A half of lager, please.'

Someone sniggered.

'We don't serve poncey drinks in here, mate,' said the barman. 'We've got bitter or scrumpy.'

'OK … umm … I'll have a half of scrumpy.'

'We don't sell halves, except if it's for a lady.'

'I'll have a pint then.'

Turning, he sauntered towards a plastic barrel and poured my drink into a glass that was so chipped and greasy I feared it might be harbouring bubonic plague at the very least. He returned and placed it in front of me. I took a sip, surprised to find it wasn't bad.

'I went to the police station,' I said, adopting my most ingratiating expression and leaning on the bar, 'but it was closed. A lady said I might find a policeman in here.'

'You might,' said the barman, 'but that's none of my business.'

'Isn't it?' For a moment, I was stumped. Then I had an idea and addressed the drinkers: 'Is there a policeman in here?'

There was silence, apart from a thud from the dartboard, a very rude word and the deeper, angry male voice complaining that I'd put him off again.

'A policeman?' said a youngish man with a thin moustache and a plastic cigarette balanced on his lip. 'In that case, I reckon you'll be wanting Sam,'

'Who's Sam?'

'Sam,' said the man, grinning, 'is a police officer.'

'I gathered that, but where is he.'

'In here.'

'I see … umm … are you Sam?'

'No, but I, too, am a police officer.'

'Well, perhaps you could help me?'

'Perhaps I could, but you'll be wanting Sam.'

I addressed the pub again: 'Which one of you is Sam?'

Though there was no reply, everyone, except for the two playing darts, was watching me, as if I was a strange curio. Rare inspiration struck.

'It's him, isn't it?' I said, pointing at the man lying on the floor, who had stopped snoring, but had started drooling.

'Yep,' said the other police officer and, as if suddenly realising what he was supposed to do, rose to his feet, a trifle unsteadily, holding out his hand. 'I'm Constable Jones. Sergeant Beer is, regrettably, indisposed at the present time. How may I help?'

I shook his hand. 'My name is Andy Caplet and I have something to report.'

'Go on, then.'

'Umm … it might be better at the police station.'

'He's come to make a confession,' said the barman with a grin that was as lacking in teeth as the bar was in comfort. 'I reckon he's run over a sheep.'

'I haven't run over a sheep. I don't have a car.'

'Has it been stolen?' asked Constable Jones, pulling a notebook from the pocket of his trousers.

'No, I've never had one.'

'Then, how did you get here?'

'I walked.'

'I believe you, sir. What brings you to these parts?'

'I'm on holiday.'

This provoked a general guffaw from the onlookers. It seemed I was the best entertainment they'd had for weeks. With the exception of Sergeant Beer, I was the focus of everybody's attention and even the darts had stopped flying.

Constable Jones was shaking his head and grinning. 'No, really, what are you doing here?'

'I'm really on holiday.'

'Escaped from some sort of institution, have you, sir? We don't get tourists round these parts, and walkers don't usually wear tweed.'

'I haven't escaped from anywhere, I am on holiday and what I choose to wear is my own business. I really have got something terribly important to report.'

'Important, eh? Why didn't you say so?'

'I haven't had the chance.' I said, starting to get flustered. 'I've found a skeleton. Well, my dog did.'

The levels of public amusement increased.

Constable Jones made a pantomime of looking about him. 'Your dog, sir?'

'He's outside. He found a man's skeleton on Blacker Knob. It's been there for about three years.'

That stopped the laughter and Constable Jones's expression switched to serious. 'You'd better come with me, sir.'

Taking my arm, he led me outside, where Dregs introduced himself by thrusting his nose into the constable's groin before jumping up and licking his face. Jones, pushing him down, led us to the police station and unlocked the door.

'Come in, sir,' he said, 'and bring your dog. I'll open Interview Room number one and then I'd be obliged if you'd tell me your story.'

Blackcastle police station, its shoebox entrance hall painted a blotched khaki, the front desk chipped and covered in scrawls, wasn't much to write home about. The place stank of damp and feet, with an underlying aroma of urine. Jones, unlocking a battered door to the side of the desk, ushered me through a grim, open plan office, with three empty desks, towards Interview Room number 1, which was, so far as I could see, the only interview room.

'Take a seat, sir. Not the wooden one: that's mine. Would you like a cup of tea? Or would you prefer to finish your scrumpy?'

I sat down on the cheap, white, plastic chair, behind a manky, old wooden table and, realising I was still carrying my drink, gulped it down and asked for tea. Jones left us for a few minutes, giving me time to adjust. Besides the background stink, the room retained a residual pong of stale coffee and vomit. If I'd stretched out my arms, I could have touched two walls at the same time, had they not been blackened by mould. There was a tiny square of frayed, brown carpet beneath the table and Dregs, having sniffed it with evident interest, rubbed his bottom on it. I tried to ignore him.

'Right sir,' said Jones, returning with a chipped mug, containing industrial-strength tea, and setting it on the table in front of me, 'I'll need to take down a few details.'

Sitting down, taking out a notebook and a pencil, he prepared himself. I gave my name and address and, despite my concern that he'd react at the mention of Sorenchester, he did not appear to recognise it. Then I explained why I was in the area, avoiding any mention of Hobbes, and how Dregs and I had come across the skeleton.

'That, sir,' said Jones, pleasantly, 'is an interesting account, but I wonder if you could enlighten me on one point before we move on? When we were in the Badger's, you said the skeleton had been there for about three years. What makes you think that?'

'Umm … it was just a guess really. I've never seen a skeleton before, but there was no flesh on him and his clothes, or what was left of them, looked modern.'

'Him, sir? What leads you to suppose it was a male skeleton?'

'Well, I don't know really. It was quite big and the skull had brow ridges, but I'm just guessing.'

'You had no idea there'd be a body there?'

'None at all. I'd never been there before.'

'Could you point out the location on your map?'

'Umm … I'm not sure … I don't have a map.'

'I find it interesting that someone who has never been around here before manages to walk straight from Blacker Knob to Blackcastle without a map. How did you manage it?'

'I reckoned that, if I headed … umm … east, I'd find the town. I left a trail so I can take you back.'

'How did you know you were on Blacker Knob?'

'I didn't know,' I said, surprised at the acuity of Jones's questioning and getting agitated, '… I think someone must have told me.'

'Who? When?'

'I can't remember.' As I floundered, I wished I'd paid more attention to Hobbes when he was giving me a cover story.

'I'm forming the opinion,' said Jones, 'that you are withholding information. I wouldn't advise you to do that, sir.'

A small flare of anger erupted. 'Look,' I said, 'the important thing is that I've found a skeleton. The man may have been murdered and …'

'Murdered, sir? That's a new one. What makes you think he might have been murdered?'

'I don't know … it looked like he'd had a bump on the head.'

'Did you bump him off, sir?' Constable Jones's gaze held me in a tight grasp.

'No … no. It wasn't me,' I said, squirming, but unable to break his stare.

An electric bell rang, making me jump.

'Wait here,' said Jones.

When he left, I tried to reassure myself that I hadn't done anything wrong and, consequently, had nothing to fear. Unfortunately, I was still worried about what was going to happen, even though I had, essentially, told the truth and had held nothing important back. All I had omitted was Hobbes; admittedly that was a rather large omission and I wished he'd turn up and explain. I finished my mug of tea, which wasn't as bad as it looked, and burped as the scrumpy bubbled back, with a sharp overtone of onion, or was it garlic? Dregs seemed to be taking my discomfiture in his stride, or rather his sleep.

Jones was talking. I assumed he was on the phone, until I heard a woman speaking.

The voices faded and I sat in silence for a few minutes until Constable Jones returned, wearing hill walking gear.

'Sorry about the wait, but I had to brief Mrs Duckworth about your information.' He said the name as if he expected me to recognise it.

'Who,' I asked, 'is Mrs Duckworth?'

'Councillor Hugh Duckworth's wife.'

I shrugged and looked blank.

'Councillor Duckworth,' said Jones, 'vanished in mysterious circumstances, just over three years ago.'

'I see. Umm … do you think it's him?'

'Quite probably and so does Mrs Duckworth. She insists on accompanying us. It's against regulations, but I have no intention of stopping her.'

'But what about your sergeant? Shouldn't he come too?'

'He may not be capable.'

'Of course I'm capable,' said the booming voice of Sergeant Sam Beer. He walked in, tall, fat, red in the face, stinking of beer and sweat and wearing dirty khaki shorts, a faded Black Sabbath T-shirt and a pair of flip-flops. 'Since it's the first interesting thing to happen in this godforsaken town in the last three years, I'm not going to miss it. Let's get a move on.'

'Shouldn't you change your clothes, sir?' asked Constable Jones.

'Nonsense. I'll be fine.'

The two police officers escorted me from the station and into the market square, where Sergeant Beer thrust his head under the drinking fountain for so long I feared he'd drown himself. Then, standing up, shaking himself like a dog, he smoothed back his greying hair and stood upright, relatively alert and ready to go. After a few moments, Mrs Duckworth, a small woman about my age or possibly a little younger, joined us and, with her dark eyes, soft brown hair and neat figure, was, in my opinion, highly attractive. Having such thoughts in the circumstances filled me with guilt, for I was going to take her to see what were probably the mortal remains of her husband.

'What are we waiting for?' asked Sergeant Beer.

'For Mr Caplet to stop staring at Mrs Duckworth and show us the way,' said Constable Jones.

'Oh,' I said, 'I'm awfully sorry. It's this way.'

As I turned away, I thought I glimpsed a moving shadow on the rooftop opposite and wondered whether Hobbes was keeping an eye on me.

I led my posse through the deserted streets, rarely seeing anything move, besides an occasional pigeon or sparrow. As we were leaving town, an old tom cat, big, ginger and fierce looking, swaggered by, giving us a disdainful glance. Dregs made a point of not noticing him.

On leaving Blackcastle, I came to the conclusion that it was the most depressing place I'd ever visited, which was saying something for one who'd endured so many Caplet family holidays. Father, never having been one for spending more than he had to, was drawn to any apparent bargain, no matter how unsuitable. We'd once spent a week in the middle of an industrial estate, staying in a dingy flat above a derelict abattoir. It had rained nearly every day and petrol was, according to Father, too expensive to take us anywhere, without good reason. Merely enjoying ourselves was not good enough. Effectively marooned, I'd had to make my own entertainment, playing with the rats that lived downstairs and even thinking I'd made friends with one, until it bit me on the lip. The trip to hospital for a tetanus jab and a stitch was the highlight of the holiday.

My spirits lifted as we headed back into the wilderness, following Hobbes's trail, which he'd made by breaking off gorse branches, chewing off the spines and the bark, gnawing one end into a spike and driving them into the ground at regular intervals. I had no idea why he'd used his teeth, since he had a perfectly serviceable pocket knife. The pale stakes, standing out against the green and brown, were easy to follow and we made good progress. Anyway, Dregs seemed to know where he was going.

We walked silently in Indian file until Mrs Duckworth caught up with me.

'Mr Caplet,' she said, 'I understand you are here on holiday?'

'Yes.'

'It's a funny place to choose.'

'Umm ... yes, I suppose so, but he ... umm ... I mean ... I wanted somewhere quiet and off the beaten track.' I hoped she'd not noticed my little slip.

'He?' she said.

'What?' I replied.

'You mentioned a *he*.'

'Did I? I meant Dregs.'

'Are you saying you came here because your dog wanted to?'

There was a hint of suspicion in her voice, which otherwise, was soft and rather pleasant. I tried to allay her worries. 'I'm sorry, I didn't mean to say he. It's just that I've been a bit distracted since I found the bones. He reckons ... I reckon it might have been murder.'

'There's that *he* again. Are you here with someone?'

'Just my dog,' I said, putting on a spurt, trying to avoid catching her eye, and attempting to project an aura of honesty and reliability. I suspected I'd only made myself look shifty.

Mrs Duckworth caught up again, frowning. 'Don't take me for a fool, Mr Caplet. Your story doesn't ring true.'

I was aware the two policemen were listening in and couldn't stop myself blushing and biting my lip, making it look as if I really did have something to hide, something to be ashamed of. I tried to be firm.

'Look, the truth is that I've never been anyway near here before and just happened to come across the bones while out on a walk with Dregs. As soon as I found them, I immediately went to Blackcastle to inform the police.'

'For which we thank you,' said Constable Jones. 'It was very clever of you to find your way to us, without a compass or map and it's puzzling that, having managed so well, you had to mark the path.'

'Umm … I didn't … or rather, I sort of did. I … umm … thought the sun might dazzle me on the way back.'

It wasn't a very convincing response, but I was getting in a flap. The constable was obviously no fool and I feared I was going to drop myself into some serious trouble, unless I mentioned Hobbes. Instead, feigning deafness, I strode on, as fast as I could go.

We made good progress, climbing steadily, and had reached what might once have been a lane, when I found myself on the horns of a dilemma for, although I was merely a little out of breath and sweaty, Sergeant Beer's face was as red as a raspberry and he was panting like an old steam train. I was worried I'd have another body on my hands if I didn't call a halt, but if I did, they'd start questioning me again. I had not yet come to a decision when I heard something.

'What's that?' I asked, though it was obviously a car's engine revving hard.

Sergeant Beer, slumping against a rock, sighed. 'Trouble. How did he hear about it?'

The engine noise grew louder and a gleaming, white Land Rover with mirrored windows rounded the bend, heading straight at us, not bothering to brake until the last possible moment. If the driver was trying to intimidate us, and I thought he was, then he only partially succeeded, as I was the only one who dived for cover. At least I amused Dregs and, by the time I'd pushed him off and got to my feet, a tall, dapper man, sporting a clipped moustache, was stepping from the Land Rover.

'Ah,' he said in a posh drawl, 'it's Sergeant Beer and his mob. Would you explain what you're doing on my land?'

Sergeant Beer, standing straight, mopping his brow with a grim, grubby handkerchief, said: 'Some say it is common land, Sir Gerald.'

Sir Gerald laughed. 'Not according to the law, which you are, are you not, paid to uphold?'

'Yes, of course, sir, but that's neither here nor there.'

'I'm astonished to hear a police officer speak so lightly of the law of the land. Now, would you mind escorting these … people … off my land?'

'Let me explain, Sir Gerald.'

'I wish you would.'

Sergeant Beer took a deep breath. 'We are here to investigate a report that a body has been discovered.'

'Nonsense. No one comes here, so how could anyone discover a body?'

'This gentleman,' Sergeant Beer pointed at me, 'claims to have discovered a human skeleton on Blacker Knob.'

'Preposterous! What was he doing on Blacker Knob?'

'He says he's on holiday.'

'He must be an idiot.' Sir Gerald spared me a glance. 'He certainly looks like one, doesn't he?'

'That's not for me to say, sir,' answered Sergeant Beer, 'but we must investigate.'

Sir Gerald shrugged. 'It sounds like a wild goose chase to me. I'd arrest the blighter for trespass and wasting police time, if I were you.'

'I can't do that yet, sir.'

'We have to check,' said Mrs Duckworth.

Sir Gerald peered at her, as if noticing her for the first time. 'Oh, it's you,' he said. 'I might have known you'd be at the bottom of this. I suppose you think the bones belong to that waster of a husband of yours. What was his name? Pugh?'

'Hugh.'

'Well, don't go raising your hopes. It's most likely your old man left town with some floozy. You're wasting your time. This fellow's probably just stumbled across a dead sheep.'

I didn't much like being referred to as *this fellow*. 'It wasn't a sheep.'

Sir Gerald, giving me a most condescending smile, turned back to the sergeant. 'Well,' he said, 'your time is evidently not as valuable as mine and, since I'm obviously not going to stop you, I'd be obliged if you'd let me know what happens. Then I can say I told you so.'

Nodding dismissively, he got back into the Land Rover, allowing me a glimpse of the driver, a bald, thickset man, whose bare arms were plastered in tattoos. The Land Rover drove away.

'Who was that?' I asked.

'That,' said Mrs Duckworth, 'was Sir Gerald Payne.'

'He's a big landowner round these parts,' added Sergeant Beer.

'Does he really own this land?'

'So he claims, sir, and he's got a court order to prove it.'

'But Hob … but I was told it's really common land.'

'So some say,' said Constable Jones. 'Mr Duckworth was one of them.'

'That's right,' said Mrs Duckworth. 'He spent a lot of time trying to prove this was all common land. But we need to get a move on.'

As the way steepened, we carried on without further talking, other than Sergeant Beer muttering that his flip-flops were giving him gyp. I had time to think about Mrs Duckworth. Her softly accented voice was melodious and pleasant, her pretty face suggested a friendly nature, but I was glad our conversation had been interrupted; I'd had enough interrogation for one day.

When, at last, we reached Blacker Knob, I pointed out the position of the skeleton and sat down out of the way with Dregs. The wispy morning clouds had congealed into a heavy grey mass, and the afternoon was as dark as early evening. I pulled my jacket tight to keep off a wind that kept thrusting chilly fingers everywhere it could reach and realised I hadn't yet had any lunch. My stomach was grumbling so much that Dregs was staring, as if he expected an alien to burst forth.

The voices of Mrs Duckworth and Sergeant Beer were carried on the wind.

'Those boots certainly look like Hugh's,' she said, 'and he used to wear a shirt like that.'

'Are you sure it's him?' asked Sergeant Beer, still breathless.

'Of course not, but I think it's likely.'

She spoke clearly and firmly, without any sign of the tears I'd been expecting. I admired her courage. Constable Jones, talking on his mobile, drowned out the rest of their conversation as he called for a forensics team. I heard him mention a helicopter. When he'd finished, putting his mobile back into his pocket, he sat beside me and shivered.

'It's a lonely place to die,' he said.

I nodded.

'It's not somewhere I'd choose to go for a walk,' he said, 'and I wouldn't want to come round here for my holidays.'

'I don't think I'll come back,' I said, 'but it seemed a good idea at the time.'

'I prefer Spain, or Greece, somewhere warm with a bit of nightlife.' The constable stretched out his legs. 'Where are you staying?'

'We're ... umm ... camping.'

'We?'

'Me and Dregs,' I said, covering my slip brilliantly.

'Where's your tent?'

'Umm ... it's over there somewhere,' I said, waving a hand in what I hoped was the right general direction.

'If you don't mind me saying, you don't much look like a hill walker.'

'I'm not normally much of one.'

He sighed. 'Mr Caplet, I'm sorry if I'm bugging you with these questions, but I get the feeling you're hiding something.'

'I've told you the truth,' I said.

'But not the whole truth, eh?'

'I've told you everything that's important.'

He laughed and patted Dregs. 'I'm inclined to believe you about finding the skeleton, but, come on, you're not this dog's master, are you?'

'What do you mean?'

'I can see he knows you well enough, but I've had experience with dogs and it's obvious you're not his master. Plus, it's clear that someone else marked the path and that you haven't got a clue where we are and what's up here.'

'Umm ...'

'Don't worry. I won't press. I think you are honest and, no doubt, you have your reasons.'

I nodded. The constable was much sharper than his sergeant, who was standing on a tussock, adjusting his shorts and complaining about his poor feet, while staring blankly at the bones.

Mrs Duckworth joined us and although her face showed strain, she was still in control. I just wished she wouldn't look at me with such deep suspicion. Still, I was used to similar reactions in women who didn't know me and even in some who did.

Only once had I really believed I'd got lucky. Her name was Violet, and I'd nearly been sure she loved me, as I thought I loved her. Unfortunately, love's course had failed to run true since the girl of my dreams wasn't quite as she appeared and had bloody murder on her conscience, if, indeed, she had a conscience. I might have let myself feel sorry for myself again, had it not been for Mrs Duckworth's example.

'I'm sorry,' said Constable Jones.

'I suppose I already knew he was dead,' she said. 'He wasn't the type who'd run away when he had a cause to fight and he was convinced all of this,' she waved her hand to encompass the Blacker Mountains, 'is common land, whatever Sir Gerald Payne might claim.'

'Still,' said the constable, 'it must be a shock to find him. Assuming it is him.'

'I'm almost sure it is. It's those boots. He got them in Peru. As for a shock, I guess it is, though I've already done my grieving. In any case, we'd grown apart, because he was too interested in his good causes to waste much time on anything else.'

Constable Jones pulled a sympathetic face. 'That was a shame.'

'Maybe,' said Mrs Duckworth. 'Although, if he hadn't left me to my own devices so often, I'd never have had time to study.'

'What are you studying,' I asked, feeling left out.

'That's none of your business.'

'No, of course it isn't. Sorry.'

'I'm sorry, too. I wasn't fair. I studied archaeology, something that's always fascinated me, and I have a degree now. Recently, I've been conserving some amazing Viking pieces.'

'I suppose,' said Sergeant Beer, approaching, 'archaeology is a bit like police work. We also dig things up and make deductions from the evidence. In this case, though, I don't think there's much to be investigated. It looks like he got caught in a storm and tried to build himself some sort of shelter. I'd guess he died of exposure. That's what does for a lot of hill walkers.'

'But,' I said, 'what about his fractured skull?'

'Your dog probably did that when he dug it out.'

'He barely touched it,' I said with a glance at Dregs, who was innocently sitting by Mrs Duckworth, wagging his tail.

Sergeant Beer shrugged. 'Bones become fragile with exposure to the elements and there are a lot of elements up here. Aren't I right, constable?'

'Well, yes, Sarge. Blacker Knob is reputed to have some of the worst weather in the country. That's one of the reasons no one comes up here. It's dangerous.'

'It doesn't seem so bad,' I said.

'Well, sir,' said Sergeant Beer, 'I don't suppose you've been here when the winds come up sudden, like, from the south-west. It can be terrible and there are many tales of people dying in the old days. Old Walt, who runs the Badger's, told me that when he was a child, he was up the Beacon. The wind was really strong and he saw this little fluffy cloud blowing towards him. It knocked him down. It turned out to be a waterlogged sheep. Not sure I believe him. Old Walt's not quite right in the head since then.'

He glanced towards the bones. 'The thing is, it's still dangerous up here, so I'd take care if I were you, Mr Caplet, because my feet reckon the weather's turning. I hope the

468

chopper gets here soon, because I want to be getting back before it starts. I'd strongly advise you to get out of here.'

'I'll be fine,' I said, trying to look resolute and intrepid while my insides quaked.

Still, I'd have Hobbes with me and was confident he'd know what to do, though I had some concern that his concept of bad weather might differ from mine. I wondered where he was, for although I'd kept an eye out, I'd seen no further sign of him. That was probably unsurprising, but I was puzzled that Dregs, who had curled up at Mrs Duckworth's feet, had shown no indication that he was anywhere near.

I got to my feet, looking around casually as if admiring the view and, to be fair to Blacker Knob, it was picturesque in a rugged and bleak sort of way and it was difficult to see why it had such a bad reputation. It appeared to my, admittedly inexperienced, eyes to be excellent walking country, for any who liked such exercise. I wasn't yet convinced I was one of them, for although I did appreciate fresh air and scenic views, I wasn't so keen on the actual walking bit. My legs were already tired and I had a horrible suspicion I'd have to go back to Blackcastle to make a statement or something, and I'd bet there would be no room for me in the helicopter. Turning up my collar, I sat back down. The wind was strengthening and I was sure I felt a spot of rain on my cheek.

I shivered. 'How long will we have to wait?'

Sergeant Beer shrugged. 'As long as we must.'

'They said it'd be here within the hour,' said Constable Jones.

'As long as it's here before the rain,' said Mrs Duckworth.

I prepared for a long wait that never happened. The helicopter arrived within minutes, its downdraught showering us with debris and dust. I held my hands to my ears and half closed my eyes until it landed and the rotors had slowed to a standstill. A door opened and a man and a woman in white coveralls emerged. Sergeant Beer stepped forward to greet them.

'You two had better stay here,' said Constable Jones, joining the newcomers.

I nodded, having grown accustomed to keeping out of the way when Hobbes was investigating. Mrs Duckworth, on the other hand, was not so experienced and, fearing she'd get up and interfere, I thought I should try to take her mind off what was about to happen.

'Umm …' I said by way of a start, 'what do you do?'

She turned towards me, frowning. 'I beg your pardon?'

'What do you do for a living?'

'I work. How about you?'

That was a poser. 'I used to be a reporter for a newspaper, but I'm sort of freelance now.'

'I had some experience of reporters when Hugh went missing. They didn't strike me as very nice and I couldn't get rid of them.'

'I know what you mean,' I said, nodding.

'I very much doubt it.'

'I really do. We had loads of reporters outside when … I mean … umm … What I mean is, I've seen them in action.' Again, I'd nearly let slip too much and it was just lucky I'd still got my wits about me and could cover it up. I continued. 'I never got the hang of pestering people. That's probably why they sacked me. Umm … one of the reasons anyway. I wasn't very good.'

She laughed. 'I can believe that.'

Her response, better than I'd expected, came across as only slightly hostile and I ventured another question: 'Have you lived round here all your life?'

'No, I only came to Blackcastle because of Hugh.'

'Because of me?'

'Not you, Hugh!' She laughed again, this time genuinely amused. 'Yes, his family were originally from these parts and we moved here when he found a job. Things were fine until he discovered some documents linking his family to sheep farming and quarrying and got obsessed by researching them. I must say that I'll be glad to leave. I've never liked the place.'

'You're moving then?'

'I've got myself a job in a museum miles away from here.'

'Where?'

'That really isn't your business.'

'No, I suppose not. Sorry.'

'I intend to put all of this behind me,' she said. 'I see it as moving on mentally as well as physically and I do not intend to allow what's happened to spoil my future. That's why I'm only telling family and friends where I'm going. You are not the only one who can withhold information, Mr Caplet.'

After this exchange, we sat in near silence, watching what little of the action we could see, which wasn't much.

After no more than an hour, the two white-clad people loaded a black plastic bag into the helicopter and, following a brief discussion with Sergeant Beer and Constable Jones, climbed inside. As soon as the policemen retreated, the helicopter took off, turned slowly, and departed into the darkening sky.

Sergeant Beer walked back, looking glum. 'They're off,' he said, 'and they wouldn't take me. We'd better start moving before this storm hits.'

As if to reinforce his words, a spatter of rain propelled by a squally wind struck.

'Do you need me to go with you?' I asked, hoping the answer would be 'no'.

I was pleasantly surprised when that turned out to be the response.

'There's no need, sir,' said Sergeant Beer. 'We have your details and can contact you should we require anything further. I doubt we will though. This looks to me like an unfortunate accident and Forensics agreed. But, thanks for your help, sir. It's much appreciated. We don't get too many cases out here, but it's still satisfying to tick one off the list. Enjoy the rest of your holiday, but seriously, I would advise you to get off the tops soon. These hills really can be dangerous and besides, you are technically trespassing. Good day, sir.'

With that they left me. I watched them go, disappointed Mrs Duckworth hadn't acknowledged me, other than by a single, cold nod. I didn't blame her, for it's not every day a woman has to identify her husband's skeleton and I imagined she'd found it somewhat distracting. Maybe as distracting as I'd found her.

'Well,' I told Dregs, 'we're on our own now. I suppose we should find Hobbes.'

Dregs put his head to one side.

Then, remembering that I'd promised to buy a newspaper, I groaned and decided to return to Blackcastle anyway. Dregs, refusing to come, trotted away, heading back to the tent, I supposed.

Drizzle stung the back of my neck and made me shiver, but at least there was shelter in the lee of Blacker Knob as I descended. Despite my leg weariness, I was making good time, though the sky had darkened to the colour of the slates on the roofs in Blackcastle.

It wasn't long before punching rain took over from the drizzle and my tweed jacket and trousers, so good at keeping out the wind, proved to have the absorbency claimed by the manufacturers of certain brands of kitchen towel. Before long I was drenched, weighed down, as if in a suit of armour, and with icy trickles running down my legs and back. It was like being under a waterfall, except the rain seemed to be falling parallel to the ground. I could barely see and my feet slipped several times. Twice I was nearly blown over. I needed shelter, and quickly, and could have kicked myself for not heeding the warnings. The Blacker Mountains were, indeed, dangerous.

Giving up on any idea of fetching the newspaper, I turned around, heading back to Blacker Knob, hoping I'd be able to find the tent from there. I hadn't gone far when a white stick slalomed past on the torrent. I tried to convince myself that even I couldn't get lost between stakes.

It turned out that I could, and after perhaps five minutes I turned to retrace my steps, hoping to find where I'd been, but very soon, unable to see much of anything, I had to accept that I was utterly lost and in dead trouble. Failing to think of a brilliant plan, I turned again, heading upwards, hoping to stumble upon Blacker Knob, because from there I would, no doubt, be able to find the tent. I hoped so. I really hoped so.

Walking against the flow of water, I kept losing my footing on the sparse grass, which might just as well have been oiled for all the grip it offered. Reaching a rocky area which was a little less slippery, I followed it, moving with renewed confidence until it became suddenly steeper, forcing me to crawl on hands and knees. If anything the storm was intensifying, and it felt like marbles were being hurled into my eyes, making them feel bruised and sore. Blinking, I groped forward, because I didn't know what else to do, having lost all chance of finding Blacker Knob, but hoping still to chance upon some sort of shelter.

From somewhere, I found the strength to keep going, clinging onto hope, trying to believe Hobbes would find me and trying to choke off the insidious growth of despair. Then, I was no longer climbing, but sliding, horribly aware there was nothing in front of me.

A roaring wind, blowing full in my face, swallowed my cries and, although I scrabbled, grabbing at anything that might be solid, I plunged into nothingness. Yet even as I dropped, my left hand, by no conscious action, seized a sturdy root or something and I was left swinging by one arm. This was the moment, so experience told me, when Hobbes would put in an appearance. He didn't.

Sometimes I'd been able to make quick decisions and I made one then; I was not going to let go. Still, the weight of my sodden suit, plus the slipperiness of my hands, conspired against my decision and I began to slide, until somehow I managed to get a grip with my other hand. For a moment I was euphoric, a bizarre sense of relief flooding my nervous system, before my predicament struck home. I was dangling over what I assumed was a precipice, and my situation was not helped by a gush of water that seemed determined to sluice out my mouth. I had to act and, fuelled by adrenalin, using sheer muscle power, something I'd never believed I possessed, I hauled myself up, hand over hand, my shoulders agonising, until, just before my strength failed, with one final, valiant effort, I dragged myself over a lip of rock and lay face down, gasping like a landed fish and just as wet.

After a while, the heat my efforts had generated leaking away, my teeth began chattering, reminding me of the wind-up ones sold in joke shops, and making me laugh like a madman. As the hysteria subsided and I pulled myself together, congratulating myself on a lucky escape, I got wearily to my feet and tried to get my bearings.

A sudden, huge blast of wind caught me off guard, blowing me over the edge.

Too surprised to react, even to scream, I plummeted, fearing and expecting a bone-shattering encounter with sharp rocks, but, instead, I squelched into soft mud up to the waist. Although for a few moments, despite the bad-egg stink I'd let loose, I considered myself fortunate, it wasn't long before I had to reconsider. I was stuck and struggling to get free only seemed to drive me deeper into the mire. The storm showed no signs of abating and I was getting colder. The only good thing was that I didn't sink any further if I stayed still. It wasn't much of a good thing.

'Help!' I yelled as loudly as I'd ever shouted, realising my chances of being heard in that wilderness, in that wind, were infinitesimal.

Nevertheless, I wasn't going anywhere, so, every few minutes, I unleashed a lung-busting bellow in the hope that Hobbes, or anybody, might hear me, pull me out and take me somewhere warm and dry, somewhere I could have a hot drink and something to eat. I still hadn't had my lunch. At the back of my mind a terrifying thought was growing; no one was going to hear me. I was going to die of hypothermia, unless I struggled and drowned first.

As time passed, my cries became weaker and less frequent, while the invading cold overcame all resistance. My throat was sore, even though, by tilting my head, I could swallow rain, and I was exhausted and hopeless. Although I desperately wanted to lie down and rest, I was stuck in a standing position, but even so, my head lolled, my chin rested on my chest, and I fell into an odd sort of semi-conscious doze.

'Hello, dear.'

I raised my head. A small, yellow wigwam was addressing me, in Mrs Goodfellow's voice. Could hypothermia cause hallucinations, I wondered?

'Are you having a nice paddle?'

'No,' I said, wondering why I was in conversation with a wigwam, 'I'm stuck.'

'Then I suppose we ought to pull you out.'

At least the hallucination was talking sense, but I could see a problem: 'I'm stuck fast,' I said, 'and you're too small a wigwam to do much good.'

'Nonsense, dear. Billy will help me.'

'He's a good man, that Billy, but he's in Sorenchester.'

'No, mate. I'm here.' The wigwam had swapped to Billy's voice.

'Clever wigwam,' I murmured, which was difficult as my teeth were chattering again and my eyelids were too heavy to keep open.

Both of the wigwam's voices spoke, there was a racking pain in my shoulders, a pop, and a sudden sense of release.

'It is very strange,' I said to myself, 'that I feel warm and the rain has stopped.'

I still couldn't move and thought the bog still had me until, realising I was lying down, I opened my eyes. For reasons I was unable to fathom, I was on my back, swaddled in blankets, as immobile as an Egyptian mummy. The rock ceiling above me was flickering red. Something smelt good, making my mouth water.

'Where am I?' I asked of no one in particular.

'In one of the old mine workings,' said Mrs Goodfellow. 'How are you feeling?'

'Stiff … and hungry,' I said, turning my head to see her. 'What happened?'

'Billy and I pulled you out. You were stuck fast and getting dozy.'

'Thank you. I … umm … seem to remember a yellow wigwam talking to me in your voice.'

She laughed. 'I was wearing Mr Goodfellow's old cycle cape. It came in very handy on such a wild night. It kept the rain off both of us.'

'Both of you? Oh, yes, I remember, Billy was there. That's why the wigwam had two voices.'

'That's right, dear. He drove me here.'

'But why? I mean … what are you doing here?'

'We came to let the old fellow know the press has moved on and that he can come home when he wishes.'

'How did you know where to find us?'

'You'd better have something to eat and drink before we talk any more. Sit up.'

'I can't. The blankets are too tight.'

Leaning across, she tugged a corner, freeing me. I sat up, dislodging a hot water bottle in the shape of a deformed hippopotamus, and looked around. A brisk fire was burning in the entrance and there was a pile of twisted, dark logs by the far wall. Outside it was pitch black, the wind still blustering and howling, the rain still pounding the rocks. There was no sign of Hobbes, or Billy, or Dregs, but I was far more interested in the pot bubbling on the fire, which was sending out tendrils of steam and, more to the point, enticing, savoury, warm smells.

Mrs Goodfellow ladled out a bowl of what turned out to be stew, stuck a spoon in it and handed it to me. I stuffed myself until there was nowhere left to be stuffed, almost crying with delight, and it was only when I was on to my second bowl that I could really appreciate the flavours: vegetables, stock and a variety of meats expertly blended into one delightful whole. My ordeal almost began to feel worth enduring for such a reward. It was another of the old girl's masterpieces.

When I finished, she took the bowl away and handed me a mug of tea and, by the time I'd drained it, my spirits were quite restored, though my arms and legs were heavy and aching.

'That was wonderful. Thank you … and thanks for getting me out of that horrible bog.'

'You're welcome, though I might have struggled without Billy's help. He crawled over the top and prised you out with an old pit prop, while I pulled on a rope. You came out with a slurp and a cloud of stinky marsh gas. At least that's what he said it was.'

'Well,' I said, 'I'll thank him when I see him. Where is he?'

'He's with the old fellow and Dregs. They've gone for a walk.'

'Out there?' I said, with a glance at the storm. 'But, it's horrible.'

'No, in here.'

'I don't understand'

'They've gone into the mine.'

'Isn't that dangerous?'

'That's how the old fellow likes it.'

'I suppose, but … umm … why does he want to go for a walk in a mine?'

'He's interested in mining.'

'Is he? He's never mentioned it.'

'He's interested in many things that he never mentions, unless he has a reason.'

'I thought he was only interested in crime and art … and music … and films … and … and aubergines.'

'Oh, no, dear. He likes zoology and astronomy and gastronomy and history and politics and economics and geology and rheology and theology and agriculture and oceanography and sport and …'

'Enough!' I said. 'I get the point.'

'That's why he's so interesting.'

'I'm not sure that's why. But, tell me, how did you find me?'

'We were looking for your campsite when we heard shouting.'

'I was lucky. These hills are huge and you might not have come anywhere near.'

'Well, dear,' she said, 'I expected he'd stay somewhere around Stradlingate, because that's what he usually did when he came up here. I think it comforts him.'

'I'm not comfortable,' I said, shivering as a blast of wind howled outside and made the fire spark.

'Shall I adjust your blanket, dear?'

'No, I don't mean that. I mean this place … this whole area … there's something wrong with it. It spooks me, if you know what I mean.'

'Not really, dear. It is wild and lonely, but it's beautiful in its own way.'

'Perhaps,' I said, doubtfully, 'but Blackcastle is the pits.'

'It was quite prosperous long ago, but it's fallen on hard times since the Paynes stole the land.'

'The Paynes? I saw a bloke called Payne today … Sir Gerald. I didn't like him.'

'There aren't many round here have a good word for the Paynes, especially the current crop.'

'I guess,' I said, 'it's the old story of the aristocracy trampling the peasants underfoot.'

'Not really. It's odder than that, according to Roger Jolly's Pirate Miscellany.'

'What's that? I've never heard of it.'

'It's a very old book and very rare, because the Paynes tried to destroy all the copies. A few have survived and the old fellow has one. I imagine it's valuable.'

'I've never seen it.'

'No, dear, he keeps it in a strongbox in the attic.'

'Tell me about the Paynes,' I said, stretching out my legs.

'Once upon a time,' said Mrs Goodfellow, 'late in the seventeenth century, a child was born to a small farmer who scratched a bare living on Blacker Beacon. Such a life was not for Greville, who ran away when he was twelve and joined the navy. Being a bright, active lad, he did well, until he was wounded during the Wars of the Spanish Succession.'

I nodded wisely, pretending I was familiar with the history.

'He lost an eye,' she continued, 'and while recuperating met Edward Teach.'

I must have looked blank, because she explained.

'Better known as Blackbeard the pirate?'

'I've heard of him,' I said.

'When Greville met him, he was still a privateer, but, when the war ended, he took up piracy. Greville became mate of his ship, the *Queen Anne's Revenge*, and prospered, until Blackbeard shot him during a dispute about dried peas. Greville, however, was made of tough stuff and survived.

'He came home with enough wealth to buy a small farm, but was not a success, until he discovered gold and began mining.'

'So, the Paynes' money came from piracy and gold mining.'

'In part, dear, but his fortune bought power and influence and after he performed some small service for King George the Second, he was made a baronet. He was generally well liked, or at least tolerated, by local folk.'

'When did people turn against the Paynes?'

'His son, Sir Rodney, was a greedy and devious man, who inherited the estate and made use of the Inclosure Act to acquire land over which he had no rights. Ever since, the Paynes have been a blight on local people, although Gerald's father did try to make some sort of amends. Unfortunately, Sir Gerald reversed most of his father's improvements.'

'A bad family.'

'On the whole, dear.'

'I wonder,' I said, 'how long the others will be.'

Mrs Goodfellow shrugged. 'I doubt they'll be long. I'll put the kettle on again.'

As the wind outside howled with increased volume, I snuggled into my blankets and looked forward to a fresh cup of tea. It had been a long and trying day and I'd been incredibly lucky to survive. I wondered whether Sergeant Beer might have been correct about Hugh Duckworth's death; a storm such as the one raging outside could kill a man so easily, and perhaps he had just been caught out by its suddenness. It could have been that he'd just run out of luck, and I couldn't help feeling he must have used up a fair amount in attracting such a fine woman as Mrs Duckworth. Though she'd, perhaps unsurprisingly, been cool and distant, she'd still displayed flashes of compassion and passion that made her very appealing. Besides, she wasn't at all bad looking and her soft brown eyes were lovely. I couldn't deny having been attracted to her, which was a bit off in the circumstances. Not that it mattered, for I wouldn't see her again.

Something, beside the wind, was howling, something becoming louder, something coming from inside. It was an echoing, confusing, almost musical sound, rising and falling, with voices in it.

'What's that?' I asked, trying not to sound too nervous.

Mrs Goodfellow poured steaming water into a teapot and stood upright. 'It's the lads coming back.'

As the eerie noise drew nearer, it became apparent that Dregs was making the howling as he backed up the rich, if raucous, baritone of Hobbes and Billy's reedy treble. The echoes distorted everything, producing a weird, twisted, pulsing beat and it was a long time before I could make out the words: 'Heigh-ho, heigh ho'.

Standing up to greet them, discovering I was naked, I clutched at the blankets and wrapped them around me like a toga. Yet I was deceived by the acoustics, for it must have been five minutes before they appeared round a bend.

Dregs, abandoning his backing vocals, charged, nearly knocking me down in his eagerness to say 'hello'. I could only think that he was trying to make amends for his earlier desertion, though I had to admit, he'd shown far more sense than I had.

'Hiya,' said Billy.

Hobbes nodded. 'How are you feeling?'

'I'm fine, now,' I said. 'Thank you.'

'I expect you boys will be wanting a cup of tea and a bite to eat,' said Mrs Goodfellow.

About half an hour later, Hobbes wiped his lips and rose from the rock on which he'd been sitting down to eat. 'That was delicious, thanks, lass,' he said, throwing another log on the fire and staring out into the dripping darkness. 'This weather is set for the night, so we'd better make the most of it and get some sleep. It'll be better in the morning.'

'It's a good job you brought everything in here.' said Billy. 'I wouldn't fancy going out in it.'

'There'd be nothing left,' said Hobbes. 'The tent would have been torn to shreds and the contents scattered over the hillside.'

'Where did you go?' I asked, bursting to know.

'We have been exploring the mine,' said Hobbes.

'I know, but why? And weren't you scared of getting lost? Or of a cave-in, or something?'

Hobbes grinned. 'Which question shall I answer first?'

'The first one.'

'I wanted to see if there was any evidence of renewed mining.'

'Was there?'

'Not as such, but people have been working on the third level. There was some powerful new drilling equipment but nothing for rock crushing or cutting.'

'Perhaps they're just getting ready for mining,' I said.

'Perhaps. As for your other questions, I wasn't afraid of getting lost because I remember these old workings from way back and many of these tunnels have been here for centuries without coming down, so the chances of one falling when we were passing were remote. I'm going to have a lie down.'

Yawning, he stretched himself out by the entrance, his feet towards the fire, his head resting on his hands. Dregs, who'd been allowed to finish the stew and was looking very satisfied, slumped beside him and, within a few minutes, both were snoring gently.

Mrs Goodfellow, perched on a rock, was deep in thought, planning breakfast I hoped. Billy, having washed and stacked our dishes, came and sat next to me, wrapping a blanket around his shoulders.

'Wotcha,' he said. 'It's been puzzling me. How did you end up right in the middle of the bog?'

I told the tale of my ordeal, grateful for his interest, for I'd been a little hurt no one had asked. Although I might have embellished things a little, attempting to present myself in a slightly more heroic, slightly less idiotic light, it didn't seem to work. Billy, having started chuckling near the beginning of my saga, was rolling round on the floor by the end. I hadn't realised how callous he was, and I would have expected more from Mrs G, who I noticed wiping away tears of mirth. I forgave her on account of the stew and Billy on account of getting me out the bog. It was big of me.

Sometime later, I fell asleep.

Cold, clinging, stinking mud was sucking me down, drowning me. I yelled, waking myself up and finding the fire had burned low, though it was still glowing and throwing out heat.

'Bad dream?' asked Hobbes, who was standing in the entrance, staring inwards. Dregs, at his feet, had his head on one side as if listening.

'Umm ... yes,' I said as my senses woke up.

I could make out a throbbing hum on the very edge of hearing.

'What's that?' I said.

'A machine. I'll take a look.'

'Shall I come, too?' I asked, feeling I should show willing, despite my fear of deep, dark tunnels.

He shook his head. 'No, you'd better keep guard here.'

'OK,' I said, as if reluctantly sacrificing adventure on the altar of duty, though, at the time, I would have given my breakfast to avoid going.

He strode off into the darkness, Dregs keeping pace a few steps behind, and they were soon out of sight. For a while, I could hear the faint clicks of the dog's toe nails, but nothing of Hobbes. It still amazed me that he could move more silently than a cat when he wished. Then all I could hear was the distant hum and the occasional crackle from the fire.

Getting up, gripping my blanket against the cool, damp air, I walked over to the fire and threw on a couple of logs. They caught almost immediately and I warmed my hands, looking out into the night, where the storm, as Hobbes had predicted, had blown itself out, leaving only a soft, cool breeze and the occasional spatter of fine drizzle. The nearly-full moon, getting low on the horizon, lit up ragged tails of shredded clouds and an owl yelped in the distance. I shivered and leant against the wall, pulling the blanket over my head and standing guard and, although I wasn't sure what I was guarding against, I intended doing a good job.

I must have fallen asleep where I was standing, sliding down the wall to sprawl on the hard, stony ground, still wrapped in my blanket, because I awoke with bright sunlight flooding in. Outside, I could hear Mrs Goodfellow and Billy making breakfast. Unwrapping myself, I got up, got dressed in my spare clothes and stepped into the morning.

The hills had forgotten their dark rage of the previous night and the sun's gentle warmth fell on my face. I smiled, blinking as my eyes adjusted. Billy was scowling with concentration as he poured boiling water into the teapot and Mrs Goodfellow was heating a frying pan.

'Good morning, dear,' she said as I yawned. 'You have lovely teeth.'

'Thank you,' I said, although they felt in urgent need of a vigorous brushing. 'Where's Hobbes?'

'I expect he's taken the dog for a walk. He was up before us.'

'Ah, yes,' I said, remembering. 'He got up in the night to investigate a funny noise down the mine. I do hope he's alright.'

'I'm sure he will be,' said Mrs Goodfellow.

I nodded, though I couldn't rid myself of a nagging worry. What if he had got lost? Or trapped? Who was going to search for him? Mrs Goodfellow, soothingly, began frying bacon and eggs, as I fretted.

Then Dregs appeared, bounding over Blacker Ridge, running down towards us, with Hobbes loping into view a moment later, a bulging hessian sack bouncing on his shoulder. Dregs greeted us in his usual exuberant fashion and we were still trying to push him off when Hobbes reached us and dropped his sack.

'That smells good, lass,' he said. 'I was worried I'd miss my breakfast.'

Sitting lazily in the sunshine after such a traumatic day, eating bacon and eggs prepared with all the old girl's skill, it was not surprising that I over indulged. As a result, I was bloated and lethargic and quite unwilling to offer any objections when Billy volunteered to wash up. Instead, I mooched about, groaning whenever I had to bend over to pick up Dregs's stick that he kept insisting I throw for him. His night-time excursion had not diminished his enthusiasm for running. As Billy dried the dishes and tidied them away into a hamper, the breeze began to strengthen and a curtain of iron-grey clouds appeared on the horizon.

Hobbes, who'd been sitting hunched up, scowling at a lump of rock in his hand, sprang to his feet. 'It's time to get back to Sorenchester. I've been away too long.'

'What?' I said. 'Now? On such a lovely day? Why can't we just enjoy the sun for a while?'

'No,' said Hobbes, shaking his head. 'We need to go … and quickly. The weather's on the turn.'

'I've packed everything,' said Mrs Goodfellow, emerging from the mine.

Within five minutes we were marching downhill and, although the ground was squelchy and slippery, we made good progress and I soon kicked off my lethargy, managing to keep up despite aching legs. I might even have felt proud of myself, had Mrs Goodfellow and Billy not been carrying more than I was, though admittedly, I was carrying a lot more in my stomach. Hobbes's load, of course, was far greater than any of ours for, in addition to the camping gear and his enormous rucksack, he was also lugging along the heavy sack he'd brought back with him. Dregs, alert like a wolf on a mission, led the way.

It was well we'd started when we did, for the breeze had developed teeth, turning into a cold, biting wind, a reminder of the approaching autumn, and by the time we reached flatter ground the sky was darkening, though it was not yet midday.

'I wouldn't be surprised,' said Hobbes, looking back, 'to see a foot of snow up there by supper time.'

'Snow in October?' I said. 'It's hardly likely is it?'

'It's not as rare as you might think in these hills. Let's get back to the car while the going's good. And quickly!'

Billy's hearse, parked next to the derelict manor, was already spattered in a slushy, grey sleet when we reached it. Having loaded as quickly as possible, we drove away and, when I glanced back, I noticed the higher peaks were already wearing thin, white caps. I should never have questioned Hobbes's ability to read the weather.

I was delighted to be leaving those wild, barren hills and to be in the comfort and warmth of Billy's car. In the end they had been too much for me, though Hobbes had seemed completely at home, more so even than in Sorenchester.

Although Billy put his foot down as soon as we reached the main road, we soon came across a flood and were forced to make a diversion through Blackcastle. The ancient hearse could reach no great speed but Billy drove sufficiently quickly that people in town stared. The market place was bustling, with a small travelling funfair, stalls, and several hundred people, despite the sleet and the wind. I kept my head down, not wanting anyone to recognise me and think me a liar for having claimed I only had Dregs for company. There was one person in particular I hoped wouldn't notice me and think bad of me, though I kept an eye out, hoping to see her. I didn't.

'What's going on?' I asked. 'It was practically deserted last time.'

'It's the Autumn Fair,' said Hobbes.

'Surely,' I said, suspecting the good folk of Blackcastle of being even dafter than I'd first thought, 'it would make more sense to hold a fair at the weekend?'

'It is the weekend, dear,' said Mrs Goodfellow.

'No, it can't be,' I said. 'We came here on Sunday, didn't we?'

'Yes,' said Billy.

I totted up on my fingers. 'So, we camped for three nights before I found Mr Duckworth's bones. That must have been Wednesday. Therefore, today must be Thursday. Right?'

'Wrong,' said Billy. 'It's Saturday.'

'It can't be.'

'It can,' said Hobbes. 'We'd been camping for five nights before you found the body.'

Although I was at first inclined to argue, a poster, proclaiming Blackcastle Autumn Fair was being held that weekend, took the wind from my sails. Going back over everything we'd done, I just could not make my memory tally with the facts, even when I tried working out what I'd had for breakfast each day. It was as if I'd fallen into a Rip Van Winkle-like sleep and my sense of confusion could hardly have been worse had I really slept for a hundred years.

'I don't understand,' I said. 'I've lost two days.'

'I wouldn't fret, dear,' said Mrs G, patting my arm. 'You probably relaxed so much you just lost track of time.'

Although I nodded, I sat in near silence for the rest of the journey, worrying about losing my mind. It wasn't for the first time since I'd known Hobbes, but at least getting back to Blackdog Street meant that unpacking and lugging our gear inside distracted me. Yet my concern about the lost days remained, becoming just one more item on my worry list whenever I woke in the night and was unable to get back to sleep. Fortunately, such nights were rare, for my list was long and growing, as anyone who has nearly been buried alive by ghouls, has been bitten by a wannabe vampire, has been trailed by a werewolf, and has kissed a werecat might understand.

It felt good to be back home, especially when Mrs Goodfellow fed us a late and extremely welcome lunch, a huge plate piled with cheese and chutney sandwiches, washed down with plenty of fresh tea. Billy ate with us and, afterwards, pulling a chair over to the sink to stand on, washed up. I, feeling extremely virtuous, dried and put the dishes away.

'Thank you for lunch,' said Billy, finishing the last knife and jumping down. 'Now I gotta get to work, because Featherlight doesn't like it if I take time off and I said I'd be back in this afternoon.'

'Thanks for everything,' said Hobbes, who was still at the table and frowning at a rock. 'Mind how you go.'

I went upstairs and lay down. I had a slight headache, with a lot of questions churning in my mind and no answers forthcoming. But, when I heard Hobbes take Dregs out for a walk, I took the opportunity to answer one question: what had he brought back in that sack? It was lying in the corner of the kitchen and, knowing him as I did, I opened it with some trepidation.

I was disappointed to find it contained nothing but rocks, just like the one he'd been frowning at earlier, and that, as rocks went, they weren't at all impressive, looking just like any other in the Blacker Mountains. They were strange souvenirs.

Baffled, I went through to the sitting room, turned on the television and found that watching a rather good black and white gangster film helped take my mind off things. The hero, a hard-bitten cop, reminded me a little of Hobbes until he drew his gun and fired; Hobbes preferred a more hands-on approach to crime fighting. As the hard-bitten hero filled the baddy with lead and ran inside the burning house to rescue the damsel in distress, there was a commotion in the street outside.

A car's engine roared, tyres squealed, and a horn blared. A moment later the front door opened and Dregs bounded in, pinning me to the sofa and licking me in great excitement.

Hobbes followed him in. 'Alright, Andy?'

'Ugh!' I said, curling up into a ball, and clutching myself. Dregs was never careful where he put his feet.

'Good,' said Hobbes, smiling and looking really pleased with himself.

As Dregs galloped after him into the kitchen, I unwound, wondering how he could be chatting with Mrs Goodfellow, because she hadn't been in the kitchen and I was certain only Hobbes and Dregs had gone past. Maybe she'd been in the cellar, dusting the coal, or selecting root vegetables for our suppers.

The phone rang. It was Billy, though it took a while before a lull in the background racket allowed me to hear him clearly.

'Andy,' he said, 'we've got trouble. Ask Hobbesie to come here, pronto.'

'Are you at the Feathers?'

'Of course.'

'Why can't Featherlight sort it out?'

'He's not in. Get Hobbes. Now!'

Glass shattered, someone screamed and the phone went dead.

I raced into the kitchen, where Hobbes was sitting, reading the *Bugle*.

'That was Billy.' I said. 'There's trouble at the Feathers.'

'I'd better sort it out, then,' he said.

'You had, because Featherlight's not there.'

'Let's go,' he said getting up, grabbing his old raincoat and running to open the front door.

Dregs and I followed.

'You better hurry,' I said, the scream having really spooked me. 'Don't worry about me. I'll only hold you up.'

'It's alright' said Hobbes, as he ran into the street, 'we'll take the car.'

I hesitated in the doorway, worry about possible danger competing with a thrill at the prospect of action, until Dregs barged into me and made me lunge down the steps. Before I could object, Hobbes had dragged me into the car and I was fitting my seatbelt. Dregs, for once, accepted the back seat.

The acceleration as he launched us up Blackdog Street seemed to crush me into the seat and I was just getting my head up when we screeched into Pound Street, ignoring the red light and the traffic coming at us. Although The Shambles was packed with Saturday shoppers and tourists, Hobbes was in no mood to slow down, even when a pair of old ladies crossed the road in front of us. It turned out that there was just enough pavement for a car to squeeze past without touching them.

It was only when we'd turned onto Lettuce Lane and the Feathers was already in sight that I realised he shouldn't have a car any more.

'Where did this come from?' I asked, wondering if he'd commandeered it.

'Billy made the arrangements and it arrived this afternoon. Hold on!'

Although I gripped the seat with both hands, the top of my head still whacked the ceiling as we bounced onto the pavement and screeched to a standstill outside the Feathers. A fat man crashed through the pub's window in a shower of glass shards in best western movie tradition, but unlike in westerns, he didn't pick himself up, shake himself down and dive back into the fray. Instead, as we got out of the car, he lay there, groaning and bleeding from a number of cuts. Hobbes stepped over him and strolled inside, with Dregs at his heel. I considered helping the casualty but, since his wounds didn't look severe and he was swearing like my father used to when hauling on an obstinate wisdom tooth, I walked past, intending to take a tentative look inside. Holding the door open, I peeked round it, ducking as a chair smashed into the wall where my head would have been. I was still congratulating myself on my reflexes, when something spinning like a Frisbee struck me full on the forehead with a resounding clang.

As if in slow motion, I sank to my knees and the door, swinging back, struck me on the ear. Although too dazed at first to register pain, I touched my hand to my forehead and wasn't in the least surprised to see blood and, with the realisation of injury, my head began to pulse with a deep, dull throb while the world became distant and muffled.

Crawling forward, I cowered behind an overturned table, pressing my handkerchief to my wound, which felt as if it was on fire, and tried to make sense of what was happening. At least twenty men were brawling, while half a dozen more sprawled unmoving on the filthy, matted floor covering that had, presumably, started life as a carpet.

'Stop this at once,' said Hobbes in a quiet, friendly voice. He was standing just in front of me, watching the action, smiling, with Dregs at his side.

To my surprise, everyone ceased pummelling each other and turned to face him. About half of the brawlers were local tough guys, who were harmless enough, so long as you didn't catch their eye, look at their girlfriends, or spill their beer. The opposition, all of them dressed in a similar smart casual fashion, with their hair cropped short, was unfamiliar.

One of the locals, a large, slow-witted lout, who often frequented the Feathers and liked to be referred to as Hammerfist (though his real name, as I recalled from my brief stint as deputy, temporary, stand-in crime reporter, was Tarquin Sweet), spoke.

'I'm sorry, Mr Hobbes. I didn't come here for no trouble, but these bastards were up for it.'

'That's alright, Tarquin,' said Hobbes. 'Put your stool down and wait for me outside. I'll speak to you later. That goes for the rest of you, too.'

Although the local lads, apologising and carrying three of their unconscious mates with them, hurried outside, the newcomers were not inclined to be cooperative.

A tall, thickset man, with a flat nose and a mouthful of gold teeth, grinned. 'So, you're Hobbes, are you? We've been looking for you.'

'I've been on my holidays,' said Hobbes. 'Why do you wish to see me?'

'We don't exactly want to *see* you.'

'They say you're hard,' said a tattooed oaf, who was nearly as broad as he was tall, 'but we don't think you are.'

'Everyone,' said Hobbes pleasantly, 'is entitled to their opinion. Would you care to discuss the issue, sir?'

'We're not going to discuss anything,' said the first man.

'Fair enough. There's no reason why you should, but since you have contributed to the mess in here, you could start making amends by tidying up.'

'Why don't you make us,' said the second thug.

'I was hoping,' said Hobbes, 'that you'd do it because it's the right thing to do.'

'We're gonna do you,' said the second thug, forming an impressively sized fist with his right hand.

'I really don't think you should,' said Hobbes.

The tattooed oaf, lunging forward, swung a brutal haymaker at Hobbes who, swaying away from harm, raised his hands in a gesture of peace and could not be blamed if the man's wild swing unbalanced him, so he stumbled and his jutting chin struck Hobbes's outstretched palm. Slumping to the floor, he lay peacefully.

'It would be so much pleasanter and easier if we could all be civil,' said Hobbes, opening his arms as two more of the gang charged. It was not his fault that, as he embraced them in a friendly hug, their heads cracked together. As he laid them gently on the bar, out of harm's way, three more of the gang, experiencing unfortunate collisions with Hobbes's knee, foot and elbow, lay down and slept. The others backed away and fled and, to judge from the sounds outside, our locals didn't waste any time in continuing the relationship. Only one man, the tall, thickset one, remained facing Hobbes.

'Very impressive,' he sneered. 'Now, let's see what you're really made of.'

All of a sudden, a long, slim knife appearing in his hand, he lunged only to find Hobbes had swayed to one side. He made a wild slash at Hobbes's face but, unfortunately for him, Hobbes, as fast as a striking snake, displaying the reactions of a well-trained police dog, seized his wrist in his mouth. Although he made an attempt to punch with his free hand, he went limp, crying like a child as Hobbes, growling, increased pressure and Dregs, bristling, butted him in the groin. As the knife dropped, Hobbes kicked it into the dart board that had come off the wall and was lying in a corner. By then, all the fight had drained from the man and, besides his whimpering and the occasional groan from the ranks of the fallen, all was peaceful.

That was when I saw red and my eyes began to sting. Blood was dripping into them. I wiped it away with my handkerchief, which was sopping, and blinked. Looking down, I saw I'd been struck by a battered, rusty beer tray, and got to my feet a little unsteadily. Hobbes released the sobbing thug and sat him on a bar stool.

I leaned against a wall, swaying slightly, and fearing what Hobbes had done to him. After all, someone who I'd seen crunching up raw marrowbones with his teeth was quite capable of biting off a man's hand. I was relieved when everything appeared to be where it ought to have been.

'What did you do to him?' I asked.

'I just gave him a quick nip on a pressure point. It's something the lass showed me and it's remarkably effective, though I have modified the technique slightly. He'll be over it in a few minutes with no harm done.'

'Well done.'

'It was nothing,' said Hobbes. 'A policeman has to be able to deal with high spirits every now and then.

'I see you are bleeding, Andy. Are you alright?'

'It's nothing,' I said bravely.

'Good,' said Hobbes and tossed me a bar towel. 'This will mop it up, until you get it treated.'

Despite many misgivings about what horrible bugs the towel might contain, I pressed it to my forehead.

'Now, sir,' said Hobbes, addressing the weeping man, 'what have you done with the barman?'

He shook his head, looking puzzled. 'Nothing,'

'Then where is he?'

'I don't know. He was here when it all kicked off.'

A Billy-sized groan arose from beneath one of the prone figures. Hobbes ran across and rolled an unconscious troublemaker, one I knew as Sam Jelly Belly, to one side to reveal Billy, who was looking extremely cross.

'The big bully fell on me,' said Billy, and I thought he was going to put the boot in until a glance from Hobbes dissuaded him.

'I don't think he had much say in the matter,' said Hobbes, pointing to an impressive lump on the man's head. 'Are you alright?'

'Apart from my dignity,' said Billy. 'What are you going to do with this lot? Our lads were having a quiet drink when this mob from Pigton burst in looking for trouble.' He glanced around him and grinned. 'It looks like they found it.'

'I am going to have a quiet, friendly chat with these boys,' said Hobbes, 'and then they can help tidy up the mess.'

Billy chuckled. 'Featherlight won't recognise the place.'

'In the meantime,' said Hobbes, 'you'd better call an ambulance. There's some here that need patching up.'

He went over to the dart board, pulled out the knife, which must have been a foot long at the least, and snapped the blade off at the hilt with his bear hands. Handing the hilt back to the thug, who was blowing his nose on his shirt, he slipped the blade into his coat pocket. 'That can go in the recycling,' he said.

Hobbes had such a convincing way with his little chats that within ten minutes seven Pigton penitents were clearing up. The others, plus a couple of local boys, were taken away by ambulance.

When they were all working to his satisfaction, he turned to me. 'You'd better get yourself seen to.'

'I'll be fine,' I said, though I was feeling light headed.

'That cut could do with a couple of stitches and, from the look of that tray, you'll need a tetanus shot.'

'Do I have to? I hate needles.'

'You have to. Billy will take you. On your way. And quickly.'

So, while the great clean-up of the Feathers continued and Hobbes, backed up by Dregs, was organising an impromptu whip-round to pay for the damage, Billy drove me to the hospital, where, I regret to say, too many people recognised me as an old customer. Nearly all my injuries had occurred since I'd known Hobbes.

Two hours later, stitched, heroically bandaged, and shot full of tetanus vaccine, I got back to Blackdog Street, where Mrs Goodfellow enjoyed having a patient to fuss over and I did nothing to spoil her enjoyment, playing the part of a wounded soldier most convincingly until she went to prepare supper.

Hobbes returned and was telling me what a great job his cleaning gang had done, when the doorbell rang and he went to answer it. A woman with orange hair and large, slightly protuberant eyes was standing at the top of the steps, a big red suitcase on wheels at her side.

'Hi,' she said in a soft American accent, 'I'm your daughter.'

11

Since I'd grown accustomed to seeing Hobbes cope with just about any situation, including a pair of rhinos charging at him, without even flinching, it was a shock to hear him gasp and to see him stagger. For a moment, I thought he might collapse, until, pulling himself together with a jerk, he grabbed Dregs, who was attempting to charge the door.

'Could you repeat that, madam?'

'I'm your daughter,' she said, breathing hard, though whether from emotion or the shock at seeing him I couldn't tell.

'But,' said Hobbes, 'I don't have a daughter.'

'Surprise!' Although she looked anxious, she smiled.

'There must be some mistake.'

'I don't think so. Mom recognised you straight away on YouTube.'

'I'm not on YouTube … am I?'

'You sure are.'

'I don't understand.'

'You were chasing bad guys. Mom recognised you at once. You're famous, Daddy.'

'You'd better come in,' said Hobbes, his face troubled. 'We need to talk. Mrs? Miss?'

'Miss Johnson. Kathleen Johnson,' said the woman, walking into the sitting room as if she owned it.

'Johnson?' said Hobbes. 'That name rings a bell.'

'It should do. It's my mom's name.'

'Shift up, Andy,' said Hobbes. 'Give Miss Johnson some space.'

'Yeah … Of course,' I said, sliding to the end of the sofa, because she looked as if she'd need most of the rest. 'Can I take your coat, Miss Johnson?'

Ignoring me, she parked her ample rear. Hobbes watched her, looking bewildered, but keeping a firm grip on Dregs. After a moment of staring and looking nonplussed, he dragged the over-excited dog into the kitchen, came back and pulled up one of the heavy, old oak chairs. As he sat down, facing her, apparently lost for words, I took the opportunity for a good look at the interloper.

My impressions weren't favourable. She was a stout, lumpy woman, a few years older than me, at a guess, with protuberant, dull-brown eyes, puffy, flabby, sallow skin and with short, orange hair (dyed by her own hand, I assumed) that appeared to have been hacked by a hedge trimmer, although for all I knew, it might have been a fashionable and expensive cut where she came from. She was wearing an unbuttoned green coat and a purple dress that was a little too tight and bulged. So far as I could see, her only attractive parts were her even, white teeth.

'This is a nice little house,' she said, looking around.

'Thank you, Miss Johnson,' said Hobbes.

'Please call me Kathy.'

As he nodded, she smiled at him. He was still looking bewildered and I'd rarely seen him at a loss, except the time when my ex-editor's wife shot him, and when he was stricken by acute camel allergy.

'I'm forgetting my manners,' said Hobbes. 'May I offer you a cup of tea?'

'Thank you, Daddy,' she said, 'but I'd prefer a coffee and I'm famished with all the excitement and the travelling, so I wouldn't say no to a few cookies.'

'I'll have the lass see to it,' said Hobbes, standing up and leaving at such a pace I almost suspected him of running away.

'And who might you be?' she asked.

'I'm Andy ... Andy Caplet.' I held out my hand.

After a slightly uncomfortable pause, she shook it.

'So, what's wrong with you?'

'Eh?'

'Your head.'

'It ... umm ... got in the way of a beer tray during a pub brawl.'

'Why were you brawling?' she asked, looking at me with distaste.

'I wasn't. I was with Hobbes, your father that is, when he was stopping it.'

'Oh, I see,' she said, 'so, you're a police officer, too.'

'No, I'm not ... not exactly.'

'So, what are you?'

'I dunno really,' I said, flummoxed and squirming. 'I just help him out now and then.'

'How?'

'In any way I can.'

She frowned, looking suspicious. 'What *do* you do if you're not *exactly* a police officer? What is your job?'

'I don't ... umm ... actually have a job.' I feared my face was turning red.

She shook her head. 'I don't understand. What is your connection with my daddy?'

'He's my friend ... sort of ... and I do try to help him out.'

'I see. Well, Mr Caplet, I need to have a long talk with him. We have a great deal to catch up on and it would be better if we were alone. Do you understand? I think you should go home now.'

'This is my home.'

'You live here? You're a paying guest?'

'Well, I don't exactly pay.'

'So, what exactly is your relationship with my daddy?' she asked, raising her pencilled eyebrows.

I didn't like the way she was thinking, or at least, I didn't like the way I thought she might be thinking. 'I'm his friend. We've just got back from a camping trip, but I normally stay in his spare room.'

'For which you don't pay rent?'

'No.'

'And you don't have a job.'

'No. Your father is a very kind man. So is Mrs Goodfellow ... no ... she's not a man, but she is kind.'

'And who is Mrs Goodfellow?'

'The housekeeper.'

'He has a housekeeper? I guess he must be loaded.'

'I don't really know. He doesn't live like a rich man, but he doesn't seem short of money.'

'I see,' she said, looking thoughtful and, to my mind, greedy and calculating. 'It seems to me he must be wealthy to have a house like this and a housekeeper, and to afford a freeloader – no offence – staying with him. What does he drive?'

'Umm … a car.'

'No shit. What sort of car?'

'The little red one outside. I don't know what sort it is. He only got it today.'

'That piece of junk? Jeez!'

'The old fellow asked me to bring you this,' said Mrs Goodfellow, appearing with a tray and making Kathy jump. She placed it on the coffee table. 'There's coffee and hobnobs. I haven't had time to bake.'

'You must be the housekeeper,' said Kathy with a nod. 'That will be all for now.'

Mrs Goodfellow stiffened, but returned to the kitchen without another word as Hobbes reappeared, his dark, bristly hair damp around his face.

'Help yourself to biscuits … or should I say cookies,' he said. 'Sorry, Andy, would you mind leaving us alone for a bit? Miss Johnson …'

'Kathy, please.'

'… Kathy and I need to talk. The lass is making a pot of tea.'

'Umm … yes … of course.' I got to my feet. 'Bye.' I walked away, unwanted.

Going into the kitchen, I closed the door behind me, pulled up a chair and sat at the table. Mrs Goodfellow was battering a lump of meat with a wooden mallet while Dregs, to judge from the snorting and scratching at the back door, had been confined to the garden.

'Fancy Hobbes having a daughter,' I said. 'Who'd have thought it?'

Mrs Goodfellow, sniffing, continued pounding the innocent meat to a pulp.

'She says,' I continued, 'that her name is Kathleen Johnson. I wonder who her mother is. Well, I expect it might be Mrs Johnson. Why isn't her surname Hobbes?'

'I knew her mother,' said Mrs Goodfellow, the mallet still in her hand. She turned to face me, looking fierce: fierce for Mrs Goodfellow, that is. 'And that woman in there has a definite look of her, a real taint.'

'How did you know her?' I asked, fascinated.

'It was when we were in America, back in 1967. I think you saw the photographs in the attic?'

I nodded, remembering the bizarre snaps of Hobbes hanging out with a bunch of hippies, including a much younger, and confusingly attractive, Mrs Goodfellow. One young woman had always seemed particularly close to Hobbes and it dawned on me that she had looked something like Kathy, particularly about the eyes.

'So,' I said, 'her mother is the one you used to call Froggy, isn't she?'

'Yes,' said Mrs Goodfellow, nodding, brandishing the mallet like a club. 'She used to hang around him like a bad smell and the old fellow couldn't get rid of her until she'd spent all his money. She was off like a shot, taking his car, when it ran out. I knew she was a nasty piece of work all along, but the old fellow wouldn't see it. You know he can't see any bad in a woman until it's too late.'

'That's true,' I said. He'd been completely taken in by Narcisa, my former-editor's wife, until she imprisoned him, starved him and shot him. Not that my record with women was anything to boast about; it had taken me ages to accept that my last girlfriend was a werecat, even after I'd caught cat scratch fever off her.

'What do you make of her in there?' asked Mrs Goodfellow, nodding towards the sitting room.

'Well,' I said, trying to be fair, 'I can't say my first impression is very good, but it's unfair to judge her when she's probably tired and nervous. I'm sure she doesn't think much of me, though. Do you really think she's his daughter?'

'I can't see it,' she said, shaking her head. 'I don't think Froggy and the old fellow were ever … intimate, but it was so long ago and times were very different.'

I shuddered at the mere idea of him being intimate with a woman. It wasn't that I was jealous, or not especially because of that, it was just that I couldn't, or didn't, want to believe it. For one thing, I doubted any human woman was tough enough to survive a night of passion with him. It just didn't bear thinking about. I tried not to.

'What's for supper?' I asked.

'Beef wellington,' said the old girl, who also seemed pleased to change the subject. 'I haven't baked one for years, but the fillet of beef looked so tender and succulent and I had a basket of mushrooms that needed using.'

'If the beef is so tender,' I asked, 'why are you bashing it?'

'That's just a bit of shin for Dregs, dear.' She laughed and then sighed. 'I wonder what's going to happen with that … woman?'

My diversion hadn't worked for long.

'I don't know. Perhaps he'll send her packing.'

'That would probably be best, but what if she tells him a sob story? He's got too soft a heart for his own good.'

I had to agree for, beneath his rough exterior, he was often startlingly kind and, moreover, he tended to treat women with a gentle, old-fashioned courtesy. At least until they started shooting at him, when his feral side could emerge, quite terrifying, even to an innocent bystander such as me. In the quiet that followed, I could hear the murmur of Hobbes and Kathy talking and, although I couldn't make out what they were saying, Hobbes's chuckle suggested they were getting along just fine.

My insides went suddenly cold as I was struck by a horrible fear that something momentous was happening, something that would not be to my advantage. Though my conscious mind couldn't work out why I was so worried, it conceded that my insides might be correct. Somehow, I felt as if a jury was debating my case, that my case was not a strong one and that my future was in someone else's hands. I tried to keep calm by drinking tea.

The old girl, having cut some butter into chunks the size of sugar cubes, was mixing them with flour and salt in a bowl, when the kitchen door opened and Hobbes entered.

'Kathy will be staying for supper,' he said, 'if that's alright?'

Mrs Goodfellow nodded. 'There should be enough beef wellington to go round.'

'Thank you,' said Hobbes, returning to the sitting room.

A few seconds later, he returned, looking a little embarrassed. 'I explained what beef wellington was and she said she didn't think she'd like it. She asked if there was anything else?'

Mrs Goodfellow was silent for a long minute, during which he tried to smile.

'I suppose,' she said, 'I could make hamburgers.'

'Thanks, lass. I'll see if that's alright.'

He turned, walked away and checked. 'That will be fine. She'd like French fries as well.'

'I'll see what I can do,' said Mrs Goodfellow.

Hobbes fled.

'At least it's good news for the dog,' said Mrs Goodfellow.

'Why?' I asked.

'Because he'll get some beef wellington for his supper. I think *he* will appreciate it.'

'I thought you were giving him that bit of old shin you were battering.'

She grinned gummily.

'Oh,' I said, 'I get it.'

I watched her feed the shin through a mincer and then bustle about with pots and pans and meat and vegetables and pastry. Although I tried to pretend that I was thinking deeply, I wasn't. Any intelligence I possessed had been swamped by a flood of vague worries.

At six-thirty, just as the old girl was dishing up, in walked Hobbes and Kathy. He pulled out a chair for her and she sat facing me and nodded. I nodded back and smiled, feeling I ought to appear friendly for the time being. After all, I might be seeing a lot more of her. When she smiled back, a brief smile to be sure, I hoped I'd made a breakthrough, though I feared I might just have come across as gormless.

When Hobbes said grace, as was his wont, Kathy looked a little startled, but went along with it. Then it was time to eat. The fillet, succulent and pink at the centre, burst from its golden crust, filling the world with subtle scents and flavours, helped along by a pungent, breathtaking horseradish sauce. Hobbes and I ate in a reverential rapture while Kathy wolfed her two large burgers and fries, ignoring the salad. She didn't, she said, 'do rabbit food'.

When she'd finished, she leant back in her chair and said: 'That wasn't bad. What's for dessert?'

'I'm sorry,' said Mrs Goodfellow, appearing as if from nowhere, 'but I haven't made one.'

'I see,' said Kathy, raising her eyebrows.

'We don't usually have dessert,' said Hobbes, 'except on Sundays.'

Kathy pouted. 'Do you call that a meal? I heard British meals were insufficient, but … I'm sorry. Thing is I'm still famished.'

My mouth dropped open. Mrs Goodfellow had always struck me as an extremely generous supplier. Certainly I'd never had cause to complain. Nor had Hobbes, even with his colossal appetite.

'I'm sure the lass can rustle up something,' he said.

'Well,' said Mrs Goodfellow, 'there are still some biscuits left, or there's bread and jam.'

'Come on, lady,' said Kathy, 'you must have something in the freezer.'

'We don't have a freezer.'

'Jeez!' She looked shocked. 'No freezer? How do you store things?'

'I make them fresh every day.'

'No kidding? I'll bet you don't have a microwave either?'

Mrs Goodfellow shook her head.

'Fancy that,' said Kathy. 'I had no idea. I guess that means you made the crusty beef thing and my hamburgers … and the fries.'

'Of course,' said Mrs Goodfellow.

'Then,' said Kathy, 'I apologise for putting you to so much trouble. I had no idea what I was asking.'

'It was no trouble,' said Mrs Goodfellow, smiling. 'You weren't to know that the old fellow insists on good home cooking.'

'I do indeed,' said Hobbes, 'and the lass does us proud.'

'She really does,' I said, gushing. 'She's brilliant.'

Mrs Goodfellow blushed, but looked pleased.

'I'm glad to hear my daddy's so well looked after,' said Kathy, reaching out and patting his arm.

'He is,' I said, 'though he can look after himself. We've just been camping up in the hills and he cooked really well. He even caught most of what we ate. Apart from the leaves and roots.'

Kathy nodded. 'Mom said he was kinda practical. And that he loved the outdoors.'

Hobbes grinned and scratched his head and I almost believed that he, too, blushed.

'I'll tell you what,' said Mrs Goodfellow, 'I can rustle up pancakes in a few minutes. How would that suit you?'

'That would suit me just fine, Mrs Goodfellow.'

The old girl beamed and, having cleared the table, set to with flour, milk and eggs in her massive mixing bowl. Without even being asked, I started on the washing up, trying to prove what a useful addition to the household I was, or at least trying to demonstrate that I wasn't a complete waste of space. When I'd finished, I found a tea towel and not only dried up, but also began to put bits and pieces away, until Mrs Goodfellow stopped me.

'I'll do the rest, dear. I'd like to be able to find them again.' She turned to Kathy: 'I'd normally rest the batter for a few minutes but, since it's urgent, I'll just go ahead.'

Opening a cupboard, she took out a pair of enormous black frying pans that anyone might imagine would snap her bony wrists.

'Would you boys care for a pancake?' she asked.

'No thank you, lass,' said Hobbes. 'I've had an elegant sufficiency already.'

Although not at all hungry, I had too many fond memories of the last time she'd made pancakes to resist. 'I … umm … wouldn't mind a small one.'

They turned out so delicious and so fluffy that I overrode the fullness in my stomach and overdid the gluttony. Even so, I utterly failed to keep up with Kathy's unhealthy appetite. When, six pancakes and most of a tin of golden syrup later, she'd finally finished, it was clear how she'd achieved her bulk.

Hobbes led her back to the sitting room, while I helped make coffee, finding, under direction, the correct cups. Kathy had turned her nose up when offered tea.

Mrs Goodfellow allowed Dregs back in and presented him with a plate of beef wellington, which, rather than wolfing down, he ate slowly, with his eyes half closed, savouring every mouthful, like the gourmet he imagined he was. I'd even seen him sniffing the cork from a bottle of Hobbes's good wine, looking every bit the connoisseur.

'What do you think of Kathy now?' I whispered. 'Perhaps she's not all that bad.'

'We'll see, dear' said Mrs Goodfellow. 'I'll make an effort to like her for the old fellow's sake, but she reminds me too much of her mother, and not at all of him.'

'She takes after him in the eating stakes,' I said.

'No, she doesn't. He appreciates good home cooking and he'll have a pudding now and again because he knows I like making them, but he hasn't really got a sweet tooth. Anyway, he's not as fat as … he's not fat.'

Later, while making my way up to my room, I overheard Kathy and Hobbes.

'Yes,' she said, 'I sure would love to stay for a few days.'

'Good,' said Hobbes.

My mind was in turmoil and the dull ache gripping my guts was nothing to do with how much I'd eaten. There were only three bedrooms, so where was she going to sleep? It seemed most likely she'd be offered my room and, although I was supposedly only staying there until I'd found a place of my own, the truth was that I hadn't looked for anywhere else, having found a comfortable berth that was more homelike than anywhere else I'd ever stayed. Even though there had been a time when I would have given anything to get away from Hobbes to find somewhere safe, those days were long gone. I'd developed a quite unexpected regard for him and, besides, there was the old girl's cooking, not to mention her eccentric kindness. Finally, there was Dregs, who'd scared me silly (or sillier, according to Hobbes) when he'd first arrived with his delinquent ways, but I'd grown used to the shaggy beast and liked having him around. He'd become part of the family and it was beginning to look as if I wouldn't be for much longer.

I stretched out on my bed. It wasn't mine, of course: nor was the room. I was merely the occupier, with no more right to stay there than the spider Mrs Goodfellow had evicted earlier in the day. I hadn't felt so insecure for a long time.

I'd grown complacent. I'd not had a job in ages, had no income, nowhere else to live, and was entirely dependent on Hobbes's generosity. That wasn't all, for, in a strange way, I'd become addicted to excitement and got a real buzz from the way things happened when he was around. Yet, like other addicts, part of me suspected it wasn't quite healthy.

It was dark when I crept downstairs, hoping for a cup of tea or cocoa. Hobbes heard me and called me into the sitting room.

I walked in, blinking in the brightness.

Kathy, looking perfectly at home, was sprawling comfortably on the sofa, at the end where I normally sat. Hobbes was on the oak chair.

'Take a seat,' he said, gesturing towards the sofa.

Kathy, shifting fractionally, allowed me to squeeze in.

'I thought you should know,' said Hobbes, 'that Kathy will be staying for a few days.'

'At least,' she said.

Hobbes smiled. 'But, obviously, there aren't enough bedrooms.'

I nodded, guessing what was coming.

'So,' he continued, 'a little reorganisation will be required.'

The cold, heavy feeling in my stomach spread to my legs.

'So, just for tonight, Kathy is going to sleep in my room and I'll sleep on the sofa.'

'No,' I said, grateful that I wasn't going to be kicked out immediately, 'that's not fair. I can sleep on the sofa. Anyway, you won't fit.'

Hobbes shook his head. 'I'll be fine. I've slept in far worse places.'

'But,' I said, reluctantly, knowing I was cutting my own lifeline, 'it's your house. If Kathy is going to stay, I'll have to move out.'

Kathy nodded. 'He's right, you know, but I don't want anyone to be put out on my account.'

I smiled back and felt rotten. *Put out*: she could hardly have chosen better words. A cat gets put out, evicted from warmth and comfort and forced out into the bleak, cold night, but at least I wasn't going to be put out that particular night. I put on a brave mask.

'That's very good of you to offer,' said Hobbes, 'but you have nowhere else to go, unless you want to go back to your parents.'

I shook my head. 'I'd rather not, but I should be able to find somewhere to stay round here.'

'It won't be easy,' said Hobbes, 'without any money. You'd have to get a job.'

'I know. I've … umm … been meaning to.'

'Everyone should have a job,' said Kathy. 'Otherwise, how they gonna live?'

'I don't want you to leave,' said Hobbes. 'I've thought about it and, as you say, it is my house and in matters such as this I will make the decisions. Therefore, as I said, I will sleep on the sofa tonight, and tomorrow I'll clear some space in the attic. The lass has been saying I should. I think she's worried the weight will bring the house down.'

Kathy snorted as she suppressed a laugh.

'There's plenty of room up there for me to make up a bed,' he continued, 'and I will be perfectly comfortable.'

'It doesn't seem fair,' I said, though the relief almost made me dizzy.

'I agree,' said Kathy. 'I don't see why my daddy has to give his bed up.'

Hobbes shrugged. 'Nevertheless, that is my final word.'

His tone of voice indicated that he meant it.

I found it difficult to relax that night, being acutely aware of the stranger in the room next door, as well as feeling guilty that Hobbes was downstairs. It wasn't that there was anything wrong with the sofa, besides a little old age fading and scuffing, but it was no place for such a big guy to spend the night and I don't know how he managed, for next morning, after mowing his overnight bristles, taking a shower and dressing in his smart suit, he showed no hint of tiredness or stiffness. Despite the Sunday morning clamour of the church bells and the scent of frying bacon, Kathy was a no-show for breakfast. Although conceding the possibility that she was jet-lagged, I was more inclined to put it down to laziness.

Hobbes had just finished his third huge mug of tea when the phone rang and he went to answer it.

'That was Sid,' he said, on his return. 'There was a break in at the bank overnight.'

'A break in?' I said, always quick on the uptake. 'Was anything stolen?'

'It's unlikely someone broke in to make a deposit. Now I have a slight problem. I was intending to escort the lass to church this morning, so would you mind going with her instead?'

'Of course,' I said, biting back on my objections, hiding my disappointment that I would not be taken to the crime scene and still determined to be on my best behaviour. 'It'll be my pleasure.'

'Thank you, dear,' said Mrs Goodfellow, who'd just reappeared in her Sunday best, a slightly-too-big green frock, patterned with orange flowers. She had inserted her previously-owned false teeth and had topped off the entire creation with a saggy, baggy black hat with artificial daisies. 'Go and put on a suit. A good thick one would be best as it's chilly outside.'

'OK ... I'll wear the dark one.'

'And quickly, or you'll be late,' said Hobbes, heading out. 'I'll be off. Dregs, stay.'

Dregs, a connoisseur of crime scenes, slumped under the table as Hobbes left.

Hurrying upstairs, I pulled out the heavy, dark woollen suit that, like my entire wardrobe, had once belonged to Mr Goodfellow and which, like everything else, fitted uncannily well. The last time I'd worn it had been to the funeral of a murdered man, when, although I hadn't realised until later, my then girlfriend had been the killer. In fairness to her, the victim hadn't been nice. Then I tentatively removed the bandage round my head and gazed in the mirror for a moment, impressed by the rainbow colours beneath.

'Very smart, dear,' said Mrs Goodfellow as I came downstairs ready for action. 'Let's go. You can carry this.'

She handed me a large paper bag. To my surprise, it was full of aubergines.

Leaving the house, turning left down Blackdog Street, we headed for the church.

The wind was tossing litter and leaves around, ruffling my hair, making me shiver as if it were thrusting icy fingers through my clothes. I wished I'd put on an overcoat, and maybe a trilby, though I doubted it would have stayed on long. A brief shaft of sunlight stabbing through the heavy grey cloud only seemed to make the day colder, and I was pleased when we reached the church door and could leave the wind to its mischief.

Someone was playing a sprightly tune on the organ and the ancient stonework was decorated with flowers, fruits, and sheaves of wheat and barley. Although not a churchgoer, except for the occasional wedding, funeral or christening, it seemed busy to me, with plenty of bums on seats. I recognised a few of them from the Feathers and elsewhere.

'There's always a good congregation for the harvest festival,' said Mrs Goodfellow, guiding me towards a pew.

After apologising for standing on an old gentleman's gouty foot, and nodding at my friend Les Bashem and his pack of young werewolves, I sat down beside her.

'Is the harvest festival today?'

She nodded.

'Is that why we've brought aubergines?'

She nodded.

'Is that the vicar coming in?'

She nodded a third time, adding a slight frown.

'Should I shut up now?'

She nodded and the service started. Although I made an effort to pay attention, I was itching to find out what had happened at the bank and kept drifting away. It seemed strange that Sid's bank had been targeted twice in such a short time. I wondered why, and what had been taken. After all the publicity last time, I couldn't believe anyone would be so rash, or stupid, to risk the wrath of Hobbes.

Mrs Goodfellow nudged me. I was the only one still seated, apart from a very old chap in a wheelchair. Embarrassed, I rose to my feet and joined in the singing of 'We Plough the Fields and Scatter', rather enjoying myself, until I realised everyone else was singing 'Come Ye Thankful People, Come'. That was probably the highlight for me, and by the time the vicar took to the pulpit for his sermon, my mind had moved on to lunch; in particular, the magnificent fruit pie I'd noticed the old girl had baked. As a result, I couldn't remember much of the vicar's spiel, except for a bit about someone toiling in the vineyard of the Lord, which struck me as odd, since there were no vineyards round Sorenchester. Even so, I made a real effort to fidget as little as possible, lowered my head to conceal my yawns, and tried to look intelligently interested, though my eyes seemed terribly heavy. The thump of my forehead striking the pew in front and the pain it caused made me yelp. I avoided looking towards Mrs Goodfellow, who I feared would be seriously annoyed. Fortunately, my cut didn't reopen.

At least I was awake when the curate, Kevin Godley, known as Kev the Rev because of his motor bike obsession, got up to do a reading from the Bible. Since he was a far better speaker than the vicar, it wasn't difficult to pay attention and a phrase struck me as apposite: 'And having food and raiment let us be therewith content.' I did, I reflected, have food and raiment and was quite content, or would have been had I a little money to call my own.

As if reading my mind, Kev continued: 'For the love of money is the root of all evil'.

I shrugged off the attack, for I neither loved, nor needed money, getting on pretty well without it. A warm glow of self-righteousness spread through me, a most welcome sensation in the draughty old church.

'They that will be rich,' said Kev, 'fall into temptation and a snare, and into many foolish and hurtful lusts, which drown men in destruction and perdition.'

Not being rich, or ever likely to be, it was unlikely I'd succumb to that particular temptation and I enjoyed a sudden feeling of righteous superiority over my less fortunate, if much richer, neighbours.

My happy complacency lasted until the vicar resumed control and announced it was time to present harvest gifts. Mrs Goodfellow sent me to the front with the bag of aubergines. As I stood up, I realised I was the only adult, a giant among the children. I was thinking I should sit down again when Mrs Goodfellow gave me the look. Realising the futility of trying to be inconspicuous, aiming for nonchalant good humour, I stepped into the aisle, swinging my bag casually, as a little girl with a wicker basket full of shiny apples rushed past, eager to reach the front. I was on the down swing and my bag smacked her full in the face. She fell, emitting a wail of distress, and my bag split, spilling its bounty in a wide arc. A tubby boy with freckles, the next in line, stepped on a very ripe aubergine, skidded and crashed into a pew, causing his magnificent marrow to explode. He burst into tears and the vicar, hands raised, looking aghast, rushed to help.

'I'm … umm … ever so sorry,' I said and bent down to help the child.

It was simply bad timing that the girl's mother was already rushing to the rescue. As her knees hit my back, she went right over the top, crashing down and felling the onrushing vicar, whose sprawling demise caused a domino effect among the children, and a shower of tomatoes and freshly laid eggs.

'I didn't mean it,' I said, standing up, rubbing my back, stunned by the carnage I'd caused.

'It's that man again!' cried a lady with blue-rinsed hair and a face that looked like it could chop through logs. 'He's always trouble.'

'Not always,' I said, 'and it was an accident.'

'What have you done to my wife and my little girl?' asked a burly, balding man, striding forward, his face as red as the squashed tomato beneath his foot. As he slid past, arms flailing like a novice ice skater, he demolished the poor vicar, who was just getting back to his feet, his once pristine surplice horribly egged and slimed.

A firm hand grabbed my shoulder. It was shaking with indignation and I was fully expecting painful retribution from an outraged parent, but it turned out to be Mrs Goodfellow's. People were sniggering, trying to look suitably outraged, except for the young werewolves who were howling with laughter.

'I think,' she said, 'it's time to go.'

My cheeks aflame, hanging my head in shame, muttering apologies to anyone who caught my eye, I allowed myself to be frogmarched through the church and evicted into The Shambles.

'I am so sorry,' I said, hoping to calm her anger with a show of penitence, although it really hadn't been my fault. 'I didn't mean any harm. It was just an unfortunate accident.'

'What are you, dear,' she said, looking me right in the eye, 'some kind of Doomsday machine?' She exploded into laughter, leaning against me, her eyes streaming. 'That was the best service I've been to in years, and I don't know about the rest of them, but I feel thoroughly invigorated. Thank you.'

Wiping her eyes, she patted me on the back, as I stood before her, nonplussed and still horrified by what I'd done. From inside came the singing of 'We Plough the Fields and Scatter'. My antics had not held things up for long.

'Anyway,' she said, her hysterics subsiding, 'let's go home and see to the dinner.'

'Great,' I said, feeling immediately better. 'What is it?'

'Nothing special. It's slow roasted belly pork with mashed potatoes, glazed carrots, peas and a nice apple sauce, using some of the windfalls.'

'That sounds delicious, but is that all?' I said, joking.

'No, dear,' she said, seriously. 'I've also made a blackberry and apple pie.'

'I saw it,' I said, wishing dinnertime would hurry up, 'and it looked absolutely marvellous. Let's hope Kathy will be alright with it.'

Mrs Goodfellow shrugged. 'I hope she'll like it.'

'And another thing,' I said, feeling a little sorry for her, 'what will she do when she wakes up and finds no one's home?'

'She'll be fine. I left a note, telling her to help herself to whatever she wanted for breakfast.'

I grimaced, recalling the first time I'd had to make my own breakfast at Hobbes's. Things had not quite gone according to plan and I'd come perilously close to torching the kitchen while trying to make a cup of tea.

'Let's hope she's better at it than you were,' said Hobbes.

I must have leapt a good foot skyward. 'Where did you come from?' I asked on landing.

'From across the road, I've done what I had to at the bank and was just leaving when I saw you two having a laugh.' He glanced at the clock on the church tower. 'You're out early.'

'Yes,' said Mrs Goodfellow, regaling him with my misadventures as we strolled home.

His guffaw resonated off the church walls like the sound of a great bell. 'How do you manage it?' he asked.

'I only wish I knew.'

'How many did you actually bring down?'

'Only two directly, I think, though a few more came down in the aftermath.'

'It reminds me,' said Hobbes, 'of when Bob Nibblet went to church.'

'Skeleton' Bob Nibblet, the skinniest man in the county, was its most unsuccessful petty criminal and a notorious drinker. The two were not unconnected. I wouldn't have reckoned him a churchgoer.

'Bob was experiencing a run of bad luck,' said Hobbes, 'having been caught red-handed five times in a week. On the sixth evening, he decided to forego poaching and to drown his sorrows. At throwing out time, having taken on board a gallon of Old Bootsplasher Ale, some joker bet him ten pounds that he couldn't vault the car park wall. Eager for easy money, Bob accepted the bet and successfully cleared the wall.'

'Good for him,' I said, as we crossed into Blackdog Street, 'but what's this got to do with church?'

'I was coming to that. Although he got over, he had quite failed to look before he leapt. He landed in a parked car.'

'Don't you mean on it?'

'No, it was parked parallel to the wall and he crashed straight through the driver's window.'

'Was he hurt?'

'He broke his leg. Worse for Bob was that the car belonged to Colonel Squire, the magistrate who'd just fined him one hundred pounds for poaching.'

'That was bad luck.'

'It was, and more so for the colonel, who had just enjoyed a pleasant meal with Mrs Squire. Fortunately, Bob is not the burliest fellow in the world, but it is still not pleasant to have a fully grown man wearing hobnail boots land on your face.'

'I expect not. But what has this got to do with church?'

'I was coming to that.' He paused at the bottom of the steps outside the house. 'Next morning, after a night of being plastered, and having learned that he'd been summonsed, charged with being drunk and disorderly, he realised Colonel Squire's fiery temper would not have been improved by a broken nose and several loose teeth. Therefore, he decided to seek comfort in the church.

'It turned out that a visiting evangelist was leading the service and the vicar, disapproving of the young man's style, had taken refuge in his office.'

'I remember,' said Mrs Goodfellow. 'The evangelist's name was Gordon Cursitt.'

'That's right,' said Hobbes. 'He preached about the healing power of the Lord and, Bob, carried away by the power of his words, struggled to the front of the church, threw aside his crutches and cried "Alleluia!"'

'That's amazing.'

'Gordon Cursitt rushed to tell the vicar of the miracle and the vicar, remorseful for his scepticism, hurried out to see what had happened, but there was no sign of Bob.'

'Where was he?'

'Behind the font, groaning and clutching his leg.'

He chuckled, bounded up the steps and opened the door. I hoped the story was true, though I had to admit I sometimes doubted Hobbes's veracity. The savour of roasting pork drove lesser considerations from my mind as I followed Mrs Goodfellow into the house.

Kathy was sitting at the kitchen table, an empty plate and a glass of water in front of her.

'Good morning,' said Hobbes, as Mrs Goodfellow let Dregs into the garden, 'did you sleep well?'

'Not really. That pesky dog was under my bed. He snores.'

'You should keep the door closed,' said Mrs Goodfellow.

'I did. He must have snuck in when I went to the bathroom.'

'I'm sorry,' said Hobbes. 'You should have pushed him out.'

'He growled.'

'I'm sorry to hear that,' said Hobbes. 'I'll tell him not to do it again.'

'Did you find everything for breakfast?' asked Mrs Goodfellow with a friendly smile, displaying her false teeth.

'Not really. The bread wasn't sliced and you don't appear to have a toaster, I couldn't find the coffee machine and there were no sodas in the ice box.'

'Sorry,' said Hobbes, 'but the lass bakes her own bread and slices it with a bread knife. There's a grill on the cooker and she makes coffee on the hob. Would you like one now?'

'Yes, please. I've only drunk water from the faucet and I can't face the day without my coffee.'

'I'll make you some,' said Mrs Goodfellow. 'Did you find anything to eat?'

'Only a pie,' said Kathy. 'I made do with that.'

'I see,' said Mrs Goodfellow.

'I hope that's alright,' said Kathy.

'I'm sure it is,' said Hobbes. 'If you're hungry, you must eat.'

I couldn't believe she'd guzzled the whole pie, for, unlike Hobbes, I looked forward to my puddings. A slice of that pie would have been the perfect finale to the roast pork and she had deprived me of a real treat. I would have liked to have said something fine, biting and sarcastic, at least, if I'd been able to think of anything, but instead, still trying to be on my best behaviour, I was reduced to a sort of mental spluttering. The whole pie? The old girl was a generous cook and there were always seconds and leftovers and, though Kathy was a large lady (I was still on my best behaviour), I couldn't get my head around it. The whole pie? Succulent with apples and ripe with blackberries? I could have wept and it wasn't because I was obsessed with food, for although I had a healthy appetite, I enjoyed a wide range of interests; anyone fortunate enough to have eaten one of the old girl's pies would have understood my point of view.

Except for Kathy.

'I didn't much like it,' she said. 'It was too fruity.'

'It was a fruit pie,' I said, gritting my teeth.

'Yeah, well,' she said, 'I guess it was at that.'

Hobbes smiled. 'We'd best get out of here and give the lass some space. Shall we all go through to the sitting room?'

'Yes, Daddy.'

I went upstairs, changed out of my suit and into more normal wear, olive chinos and a crisply ironed white shirt. Going back down, I had to squeeze myself in beside Kathy on the sofa. I thought Hobbes looked a little ill at ease on the oak chair, but I approved that he'd got her away from Mrs Goodfellow. I'd have hated the cooking to be disrupted.

'What are we doing this afternoon?' asked Kathy with a smile for Hobbes. 'After luncheon, that is.'

'I really must get back to work.' said Hobbes. 'There was a break in at the bank last night.'

'Wow, I didn't realise how crime-ridden this quaint little town is.'

'Perhaps Andy can look after you? Until I'm free.'

'Do I have to?' I said, wondering about kicking him; I might have had he not been so hard and had I not reminded myself that I was on my best behaviour. 'That is … umm … I don't want to interfere with Kathy's plans.'

'I have no plans … I was just hoping to spend a few hours with my daddy.'

'Unfortunately, I have a job to do, and will probably be busy all afternoon. Andy will show you the sights. Won't you?'

'I guess so,' I said, unable to see why she couldn't go with him. He had, after all, taken me to numerous crime scenes without any problem. Perhaps he thought she would eat the evidence. I smiled, putting on a brave face. 'Actually, I'll be glad to.'

'Thanks,' said Hobbes.

'In the meantime,' I said, 'tell us what happened at the bank.'

'Person or persons unknown drilled into the vault from the cellar of the shop next door.'

'I noticed one of the shops was being renovated,' I said.

'That's the one. The builders weren't at work yesterday, yet witnesses report hearing heavy machinery.'

'So, the builders didn't do it?'

'It would seem not. The perpetrators apparently used an unusually powerful drill that made short work of the old bricks in the cellar and the reinforced concrete walls of the vault. They must have known precisely where they were going.'

'Umm ... does that mean an insider job?'

'It's a possibility, but the buildings down The Shambles are old and it's possible that documents or plans fell into the wrong hands.'

'Did they leave the drill behind? That might give some clues.'

'No, there was nothing,' said Hobbes. 'They evidently had plenty of time to clear up.'

'But wasn't the vault alarmed?' asked Kathy.

He looked puzzled and then smiled. 'I take it that you're asking whether there was an alarm in the vault. Yes, there was. Only it wasn't working, because the wires had been cut by the drill. Unfortunately, it was not a modern alarm, which would have had back up power.'

'Cut to the chase,' said Kathy. 'What was stolen?'

'Bank officials are still checking records, so they don't yet know about everything. However it is clear that Colonel Squire's gold has gone, along with at least two other gold deposits.'

My mind made a connection. 'Was Colonel Squire's gold the same stuff that you retrieved from the gang?'

'It was.'

Another connection popped into my head. 'And don't you have something in there?'

'I did,' said Hobbes. 'That was also stolen.'

'Hey,' said Kathy, 'Inspector Hobbes is back and this time it's personal. I can see why you have to get out there. I'll bet you want to kick some butt.'

'I will do my job in my normal manner.'

'But, how can you just sit here when the bad guys have gotten your property?'

'Because,' said Hobbes, 'I want my dinner.'

'It's important to get your priorities sorted out,' I said, repeating a lesson I'd learned from him and that, one day, I hoped to apply to my life.

She shrugged. 'Well ... OK ... I suppose. But, what if the bad guys get away? It's yours, Daddy. Was it cash? How much was there?'

'I can't remember,' said Hobbes.

'I'm not surprised,' I said. 'Sid reckoned you hadn't looked at it since nineteen t…'

Hobbes's cough interrupted me. He shook his head ever so slightly.

'Dinner's ready!'

Mrs Goodfellow's shrill voice made me jump. I'd never worked out how she moved so silently, and wished she didn't, for my nervous system must have been damaged by all the shocks. Still, it was some consolation to see Kathy's reaction was even more extreme. I'd never before seen such a hefty woman do a vertical take-off.

'Excellent,' said Hobbes. 'Shall we go through?'

Dinner was, of course, superb, the pork succulent and tender, the apple sauce fresh and sharp, the mashed potatoes fluffy, the glazed carrots and peas bursting with sweetness and flavour, and to top it all, there was the crackling, which just exploded into the taste buds and I think even Kathy was impressed, for she ate far more slowly than the previous evening. I put this down to her appreciation of what was before her, although it may have been connected with being full of pie. Even so, she still managed to find room for the apple dumplings Mrs G had somehow managed to rustle up, which made me appreciate the fruit at a new level and almost not regret the pie.

Afterwards, Hobbes sat back with a smile. 'That was delicious, lass, thank you.' He grinned at Kathy. 'Now, perhaps you understand why I didn't want to miss my dinner?'

Kathy nodded. 'Yes, it was pretty good. Thanks a lot, Mrs Goodfellow.'

'And now,' said Hobbes, getting to his feet, 'I've got bank robbers to catch. I hope you two have an enjoyable afternoon.'

He and Dregs departed and Mrs Goodfellow began the washing up.

I smiled at Kathy. 'Is there anything you'd like to do?'

She shrugged, staring at me as if I were a cockroach. 'What is there to do in this one horse town?'

'I could … umm … show you the sights?'

'What do you mean? Building sites?'

'No … umm … there's the church … and … and the park … and the museum … and the town. The museum's got some sort of exhibition on, according to *Sorenchester Life*.'

'OK, Mr Caplet, why don't you wow me?'

'I'll do what I can, but you'd better make sure you wear something warm because it's nippy … cold … out there.'

'Let's do it.'

She went upstairs to get ready. I waited on the sofa. I wasn't much looking forward to the next few hours.

I waited and waited and then waited some more, before Kathy reappeared, wearing a red Puffa jacket that did nothing to hide her bulk, and a pair of tight blue jeans tucked inside cowboy boots. I sincerely hoped she'd never used them for actual riding, as I was quite fond of horses, so long as they kept their distance, for the feeling was not reciprocated. When I was small, a Shetland pony that was supposed to be taking me for a short ride along the beach had bolted and thrown me headlong into the sea. When I'd reached my teens, a larger and meaner specimen had chased me round and round a field, trying to kick me in the head whenever it wasn't trying to bite me. On a third occasion, as I reported on a pet show, a dray horse had used me as a convenient scratching post, crushing me painfully against a stone wall. Still, on balance, I felt I would rather spend the afternoon with a horse than with Kathy, although the two were not entirely dissimilar.

'Let's do it,' she said.

From her expression, she was looking forward to the afternoon with as much enthusiasm as I was, which, for some reason, felt like a snub. Nevertheless, I rose to the challenge, faking a cheerful smile, hoping to generate genuine cheerfulness.

I got up and, as I put on my overcoat, I told her that I liked her jacket. Although a blatant lie, I thought it might smooth the way.

'Thank you, Mr Caplet,' she said.

'My friends call me Andy.'

She paused, just long enough to worry me, before smiling. 'OK, Andy, show me the town.'

I escorted her along Blackdog Street towards the church and, although it would have been nice to have engaged in a scintillating conversation, I couldn't think of anything to say until we were waiting to cross into The Shambles.

'How did you get to Sorenchester?'

'I caught a bus from London Heathrow Airport.'

'So you flew to Britain?' Sometimes I could catch on quickly.

'Of course.'

'How was your flight?'

'Long and uncomfortable.'

'But worth it to see your father?'

'I guess so. I hope so. Are we going to cross this road, or do you plan to stand here freezing our butts off all afternoon?'

'Oh, right … come on.'

We walked towards the entrance to the church. I had more than a few qualms about going back inside.

'This,' I said, 'is the church. It's very old.'

'How old?'

'Umm … I'm not sure … I'd guess at least six hundred years, maybe more. It was around long before Shakespeare.'

'Did Shakespeare come here?' she asked, sounding almost interested.

'No, I was just trying to put it in perspective.'

'OK. It's not very big, is it?'

'This is just the porch. Let's get inside and away from the wind.'

As we entered beneath the Gothic archway, our footsteps echoing on ancient, patterned tiles, I continued, recalling the few facts I could remember: 'Actually, it is quite big for such a small town. You see, hundreds of years ago, Sorenchester became very prosperous on account of the wool trade and the merchants decided to build something that would demonstrate their wealth.'

'What a bunch of show-offs!'

'Well … maybe.'

When we reached the main body of the church, I was impressed that there was no sign of the mess I'd caused. She showed little sign of being interested in the architecture, which many regarded as a first-rate example of English building, appearing equally unimpressed by the towering stone columns, the magnificent wood-vaulted ceiling, the spectacular carved fifteenth century rood screens and the superb stained glass medieval windows.

'It's smelly in here,' she said.

'It is a little,' I acknowledged. 'I've always put it down to generations of unwashed peasants worshipping in here, though it might be because of the damp. I think the roof leaked last winter.'

We walked slowly around until we came to a glass covered recess in a pillar.

'That,' I said, pointing at the gold goblet, 'is the Roman Cup.'

'Oh yes?' she said, suppressing a yawn.

'It's made of pure gold, though it's not actually Roman.'

'Then it's a stupid name.' She perked up. 'Pure gold you say?'

'It's priceless and it's not actually a silly name, because it was donated to the church by Mr Roman, a Romanian refugee. Some believe it was once owned by Vlad Tepes, or, as he is more generally known, Dracula.'

Kathy raised her eyebrows. 'No kidding? If it's so valuable why isn't it kept somewhere safe?'

'Oh, it's quite safe here. That recess is lined with inch-thick toughened steel and the glass at the front is bullet proof. What's more there are all sorts of alarms and CCTV watching it. It was stolen some time ago, but your father and I got it back.'

'You mean Daddy did and you tagged along?'

'No … it really wasn't like that. It's a long story…'

'Then, save it for the long winter evenings.'

'Alright.' I said, deflated, for it was a good story and I had saved Hobbes and another man from being murdered, not to mention helping solve the crime. Admittedly, things would have turned out very badly for me had Mrs Goodfellow not turned up in the nick of time, but I had, I considered, been quite heroic.

'Let's get out of here,' said Kathy. 'Show me something else.'

Leaving the church, we strolled around town. I pointed out Grossman's Bank, which, like the shop next door, was festooned in police tape. It was guarded by Constable Poll, stamping his feet and blowing onto his long, bony fingers.

'Afternoon, Derek,' I said, assuming an easy familiarity with the lanky cop. 'How you doing?'

'Fine, except that it's a nippy afternoon to be standing guard.'

'That's true. Is Hobbes in there?'

'No, he looked in for a minute with his dog and left with Mr Sharples.'

'Mr Sharples? Oh you mean Sid, the va … I mean, the director of the bank?'

'That's right,' said Poll with a glance at Kathy.

'Oh … umm … This is Kathy. She's staying with us for a few days and I'm showing her around until Hobbes is free. She's his … umm … I mean she's new in town. From America.' I hoped he didn't think she was my girlfriend.

Constable Poll smiled. 'You should take a look in the museum. It's got a fantastic new exhibition of Viking gold that was found in a field over towards Hedbury.'

'That' said Kathy, 'sounds like a great idea, and it would get us out of this goddam wind. My ears are frozen.'

'Where are you from?' asked Constable Poll.

'California most recently,' said Kathy. 'I'm not used to this.'

'What a great place,' said Poll. 'I went there on my holidays – my vacation I should say – two years ago.'

'Yeah, it's a blast,' said Kathy grinning, 'though your little town is kinda cute. Andy's just been showing me the church. It's so quaint and I love all the history. You have a pretty neat accent.'

'So do you,' said Constable Poll, grinning back. Then, standing to attention, he whispered: 'I'll have to stop chatting now. Superintendent Cooper is coming.'

The superintendent, an attractive woman in her late forties, with friendly eyes that belied a steely streak, was approaching. Although we'd only met a couple of times, I'd formed the impression she didn't think much of me.

'Thank you, Constable,' I said, in a loud, unconvincing manner. 'That was most helpful.'

He nodded and we turned away.

'Nice guy for a cop,' said Kathy.

'Yes, Derek's alright. Would you like to see the museum now?'

She shrugged. 'Is it far?'

'No, it's just around the corner.'

'Let's go.'

When we reached Ride Street, although I pointed out the genuine Roman stone arch forming the entrance and the poster showing a golden crown to advertise the Viking hoard exhibition, Kathy ignored them, pushed straight past and joined a long queue.

'Do you come here often?' asked Kathy as we inched forward.

'No, not really. I haven't been in here since your father brought me here on a case. I don't know why, because they've got some really amazing stuff.'

'I'm looking forward to it.'

After about ten minutes, as we advanced another few inches and were next in line to pay, a sudden thought twisted me up inside.

'Kathy,' I whispered, the blood rising to my cheeks, 'do you have any British money on you?'

'What d'you mean, "on me"?'

'Do you have any British money with you? Now?'

'No. Why?'

'Well … umm … the thing is, I haven't either. I forgot. I'm sorry.'

'You really are something else. Jeez!'

'I just didn't think.'

'I can believe that, but, don't worry, I'll get us in.'

'How?'

'Watch and learn, buddy.'

But, just as the young couple in front had paid for their tickets and were heading inside, she groaned, swayed and tottered forward.

'Pardon me,' she said in a feeble voice, 'I'm feeling faint.'

The young man, fortunately a strong young man, caught her as she dropped into his arms and, although his knees sagged, he held firm.

'May I sit down for a moment?' she murmured, exuding fragility.

The young man, with minimal assistance from me, supported her to a bench and the young woman, her face all concern, sat beside her, holding her hand, asking if she was alright. It was clear to me that she wasn't and I was shocked how quickly it had come on.

'Perhaps,' said Kathy, 'I might have a glass of water?'

'I'll fetch you one,' said the woman at the till, hurrying away.

'Shall I fetch Mrs Goodfellow?' I asked, panicking and feeling useless. The old girl always seemed to know exactly what to do in a crisis.

'No,' said Kathy. 'Stay with me, please.'

When the till lady returned with a glass of water, Kathy took it and sipped, before swaying and groaning. For a moment, I thought she was going to pass out.

'Shall I call an ambulance?' asked the till lady, taking the glass back.

'No,' whispered Kathy. 'I'll be alright in a few minutes. I have these turns now and again. It's low blood sugar and comes on when I haven't eaten enough. I've hardly had a bite all day, but I'll be alright in a minute. I always am.'

My mouth gaped. How could she say such a thing?

'Andy, would you sit with me?'

'Yes, of course.'

She took my hand in her soft, pudgy one and gave it a gentle squeeze, leaving me puzzled and slightly alarmed.

'Can we do anything else?' asked the young woman.

'No, but thank you so much for helping me. I'm a little better already. I'm sure I'll be fine in a moment. Please, go and enjoy the museum.'

Kathy smiled bravely and leant forward, head in her hands, as the couple departed, and the till lady returned to her till.

'Right,' said Kathy, glancing around and standing up, 'let's take the tour.'

As we headed towards the first exhibition hall, the till lady called out: 'Excuse me, but you haven't paid yet.'

'We have,' said Kathy. 'Andy had just picked up the tickets when I had my turn.'

'That's not how I remember it,' said the lady.

'Well,' said Kathy, 'you are very busy. Andy, show the lady our tickets.'

'Eh?' I said, wondering whether her brain had been affected.

'They're in your pocket.'

Embarrassed, I went through a pantomime search and was astonished and confused to actually find a pair of museum tickets. I showed them to the till lady.

'He sometimes gets so worried when I have a turn,' said Kathy with a big smile, 'that he forgets what he's just done.'

The till lady smiled, looking at me as at a well-meaning, but hopeless, idiot. 'Sorry,' she said, 'my mistake. Enjoy your visit.'

'I'm sure we will,' said Kathy, beaming.

As we entered the first hall and I realised what had just happened guilt surged through me and I began shaking. I wanted to confess. I wanted to run away.

'Hold it together,' she said. 'Stay cool, or we'll never pull this off.'

'I'll try. I would never have had the nerve to do that. I thought you were really ill.'

'Is it your perceptiveness that Daddy finds so helpful?'

'Yes ... umm ... no,' I said, 'but you can't just go round breaking the law willy nilly. Don't forget your father is a police officer.'

'Who's Willy Nilly?'

'It doesn't matter. But, what about that nice couple who helped you? You stole their tickets.'

'They were already inside, so what's to complain about? No one was hurt.'

'We might have been caught!'

'We weren't, so chill out and enjoy yourself.'

Filled with a strange mixture of admiration for her cool ingenuity, fear we'd yet be found out, wild elation that we'd pulled it off, and guilt, I might have confessed had she not grabbed my arm and hauled me towards the exhibits. She surprised me by wanting to see everything.

We began at the beginning and it was fascinating, even to me, who was ignorant of archaeology and possessed but a sketchy knowledge of history. There were prehistoric stone tools, exquisite Bronze Age brooches, Roman pillars and statues and amazing relics of the Wars of the Roses and the English Civil War. I could have kicked myself for not having spent time there. In fact, the only thing I didn't much like was all the people milling about, looking at what I wanted to look at and getting in the way.

'How weird is this?' said Kathy, grabbing my arm. 'Look!'

She pointed to a black and white photograph of a group of locals that, according to the caption, had been taken following the discovery of a Roman mosaic during renovations to an inn in 1935.

'Sorenchester as it used to be,' I said. 'It hasn't changed all that much, except there weren't many cars back then. It looks better without them, doesn't it?'

'Yeah, I suppose.'

'I think the inn is the Bear with a Sore Head,' I said, 'though it was probably still called the Ram in those days. Hobbes ... your father ... keeps the original bear with the sore head in the attic. It's ... umm ... stuffed of course. It all began with a darts match and ...'

'Yeah, yeah' said Kathy, 'I'm sure it's a very interesting story, but have you seen this guy?'

'The one with the shovel?'

'Doesn't he look like Daddy?'

It was definitely Hobbes.

'Yes,' I admitted, hoping to put her off the scent, 'it does a bit, except for that ridiculous moustache.'

'Shave it off and it could almost be him. It must be a relation of some sort, I guess.'

'I guess,' I said cautiously, afraid she'd realise how old he was and freak out.

'And that guy in the vest, the one leaning against the wall, he looks a bit like Daddy as well. I guess he had family hereabouts.'

I stared in amazement for, although the other man did indeed look a little like Hobbes, he looked a lot more like Featherlight Binks, the landlord of the Feathers. Several ideas tried to get in my head, but I turned them away, not wanting to think about it.

'Actually,' I said, jerking from my daze, 'he once told me he was an orphan and was adopted and raised in the Blacker Mountains. I don't think his family was from around here at all.'

'Oh, well.' She shrugged. 'I guess it's just coincidence.'

'Let's go and see the Viking stuff,' I said.

We entered a twilight world where the only light came from glass cases and stands. The Viking hoard, silver coins, gold arm rings and bracelets, hack silver, precious stones, rusted remnants of weapons, made a marvellous display. What most impressed me was a massive silver goblet engraved with fantastic figures of long ships and warriors and, despite not being gold, it was even more beautiful than the one in the church. I wondered who'd buried it and why he or she had never retrieved it and was amazed it had been in the ground for so long, with generations walking over it, oblivious to the unimaginable wealth beneath their feet. It left me quite melancholic.

We sat on a bench and watched an educational video. One William Shawcroft, a local metal detectorist, had uncovered the hoard in a field by the River Soren. I only realised who it was when a historian, a tall, thin, grey-haired woman, interviewed him. Despite his piping voice and diminutive stature, he came across as authoritative and knowledgeable.

'That's Billy!' I said, 'I know him.'

'The little guy?' asked Kathy.

'Yes, he's a friend of Hobbes … your father, but I never knew he was into this, though, come to think of it, he did once show me a Roman coin he'd found in Ride Park.'

'Suddenly,' explained the on-screen Billy, 'I had a massive signal on my detector, so I dug down a couple of inches and found a coin. When I cleaned it, I could see it was gold and from the reign of King Athelstan, in the tenth century AD. I went a little deeper and came across the goblet and knew at once I'd discovered something truly amazing.'

The video showed that, before cleaning, the find had looked exactly like something dug up from a muddy field, more like a crushed turnip than something valuable. Then, moving on to the conservation of the articles, it showed the techniques. I was fascinated by how much effort had gone into scraping out the tiny bits of embedded dirt, using porcupine quills and electrical vibrations.

Just before the end, the focus pulled from a bracelet in the process of being cleaned to show the person cleaning it.

I gasped. 'That's Mrs Duckworth!'

'You seem to know a lot of folk in the treasure business,' said Kathy, sounding sceptical. 'Is she a friend of yours, too?'

'No, I've only met her once, but it was last week, just after I'd found her husband's skeleton.'

'Bullshit!' said Kathy. 'Are you some sort of crazed fantasist?'

'No, it's all true. It was when we were camping. I was with Dregs and he found the skull.'

'So you didn't find it. The dog did. If you're gonna impress folk with tall tales, you gotta be consistent.'

'I was with the dog. The police reckoned there'd been an accident, but I don't think so. The man had been buried under rocks and Hobbes thinks he might have been murdered. At least I think that's what he thinks.'

'I've heard enough of your ravings. Let's get out of here.'

'Alright, but I am telling the truth. You should ask your father.'

'I will, too.'

A wall clock showed the time was approaching five o'clock, or, as the museum staff called it, closing time, but she insisted on looking round the gift shop before we left. Although I was nervous, fearing she'd steal something using me as a decoy, all she did was browse a booklet about the hoard. It had been written by Daphne Duckworth, whose photograph was inside.

So that was her name! I liked it: Daphne. I was saddened that I'd never see her again. Not that I could expect anything if I ever did, because I was sure she hadn't thought much of me. Still, getting to know someone over the dry bones of her husband was not ideal and, perhaps, had circumstances been different …

'Sometimes,' said Kathy, 'I think you're not really with me.'

'I'm sorry,' I said, falling back into reality, 'I was thinking of something.'

'Congratulations. What are you gonna show me now?'

'Well … umm … it's getting late, so nothing much will be open now.' Nothing, I thought, except some of the pubs. I didn't half fancy a pint, or two, of lager, but being penniless, that was out of the question. 'We might as well go home. The old girl will make us a cup of tea, or coffee if you prefer.'

She nodded. 'That sounds like a plan.'

We walked out into the street where the lights were already glowing bright and the cold wind was nipping at ears and fingers. I put my hands in my pockets.

'Let's get a move on,' she said, shivering.

We hurried back along Ride Street towards Blackdog Street. A middle-aged woman, carrying a pair of heavy string bags, was a few steps in front when a hooded figure darted from the shadows and shoved her. She fell with a cry, spilling groceries over the pavement. The figure ran away.

'He's got my handbag!'

I picked up a tin as it rolled into the gutter and hurled it, watching as it arced through the evening sky, completely missing the target, but smashing the back windscreen of a parked car. The mugger, running round a bend, went out of sight.

I started after him, as a furious woman got out of the car. She was pretty. She was also familiar.

'What,' she said, holding up the tin, 'did you do that for?'

'Sorry,' I said, biting my bottom lip, 'it was an accident.'

She stared at me and her frown deepened. 'I know you, don't I?'

'Yes, Mrs Duckworth. It's Andy. I found your husband.'

'What are you doing here?'

'I live here. I've just been showing her round the museum.' I pointed at Kathy who was helping the victim retrieve her shopping. 'We saw you on the video. I thought it was very interesting.'

'Great. I'm flattered, but why were you throwing tins of beans?'

'I was trying to stop a mugger. He's got that poor lady's handbag.'

'Then shouldn't you go after him?'

'Umm ... yes ... I suppose. Sorry about your car. Bye.'

I ran, looking along Goat Street and up Hedbury Road, but it seemed he'd got away. On the point of giving up, I heard an empty drinks can being kicked. It came from the car park on Hedbury Road. A hooded head popped up before ducking back behind the wall.

Stupidly, I ran across the road and vaulted the low wall into the car park.

'Now I've got you,' I said in triumph, intending to prove that I really was packed full of the right stuff. I was going to show Kathy what I was made of and, hopefully and more importantly, I was going to impress Mrs Duckworth: Daphne.

The mugger, the handbag still tucked under his arm, stood up, eyes glinting from the depths of his hood. He was wearing baggy blue jeans and a pair of boots that looked as if they could kick a man in half, but what I most noticed was that he was taller than me.

'Give me the bag, at once,' I said holding out my hand. Despite my bravado, my voice quavered.

'Piss off!' he yelled, his voice harsh.

'Not until you let me have it,' I said, fighting against leg-wobbling fear.

The mugger, a man of few words, pulled out a knife. 'I'll really let you have it unless you back off.'

'Put that down,' I said, filled with a sudden bravery and a sense of elation. 'Just give me the bag, and no one gets hurt.'

'You having a laugh, mate? Get out of here now, or I'll stick you.'

I really did laugh. 'Honestly, it will be so much better for you if you just drop the knife and give me the bag.'

Although I couldn't see his face, his body posture suggested hesitation, or confusion. Taking a hesitant step forward, he waved the knife.

'Sorry,' I said, shaking my head, 'but I did warn you.'

Hobbes, silent as a hunting tiger, leapt from the shadows and rammed a wheelie bin over the mugger's head, jamming it down, pinning his arms to his sides. The knife dropped with a clatter, the handbag dropped with a thud, and the mugger fell to his knees amid an outpouring of swearing and maggots. Dregs, sniffing him, bristled and growled.

'Evening, all,' said Hobbes, leaning on the bin. 'Did you and Kathy have a good afternoon?'

'Umm … yes … it wasn't bad,' I said, patting Dregs. 'We went to the museum.'

'I'm pleased to hear it. Now, what did you do to annoy this fellow?'

'Nothing … he mugged a lady and stole her handbag, so I went after him.'

'That's very public spirited of you, but it might have been dangerous.'

I nodded, still a little weak at the knees. 'I wasn't half glad to see you coming. I thought you'd be hunting the bank robbers.'

'All in good time,' said Hobbes. 'I had to take some rocks for analysis. By the way, where is Kathy?'

'She's just round the corner helping the poor lady that got mugged. Umm … what rocks?'

'Now is not the time. We'd better check on the ladies. Shift yourself – and quickly.'

'Yeah, but what about him?' I pointed at the bin.

'I'd better bring him along as evidence. Would you mind picking up the handbag? And the knife. It's dangerous to leave them in car parks.'

Grabbing the bin in both arms, turning it over, he carried it towards Ride Lane, with the mugger's legs kicking wildly out the top, the volume of his cursing increasing, and Dregs growling. We found Kathy with her arm around the victim, who, although crying, was unhurt. The lady cheered up immediately as I handed back the bag,

'Thank you,' she said, looking at Hobbes. 'I thought I'd lost it and it would have been awful, because it's got my keys and my credit card and all sorts of stuff.'

'Just doing my job, Mrs Brown,' said Hobbes.

Since I thought I'd done rather well in the circumstances, I was a little miffed to get no credit. Admittedly, I would have been in trouble had Hobbes not showed up in the nick of time, but I had found the mugger and stopped him getting away. Even so, I realised my heroics had been somewhat dimmed by what I'd done to Daphne's car. I looked around to apologise again, but she'd gone. I sighed, though I'd probably not done my chances with her any harm at all. I must merely have hardened her dislike for me.

The lady, thanking Hobbes again, insisting she was fine, picked up her bags and left.

'Good job, Daddy,' said Kathy, smiling proudly. 'Now what are you going to do with this hoodlum?'

'I suppose,' said Hobbes, 'that I should get him cleaned up. It's not very pleasant inside that bin, as his rather incontinent language would suggest.' He glanced at the church clock. 'We'd better get a move on. I wouldn't want us to be late for tea.'

When we reached the steps outside the house, Hobbes upended the bin and the mugger, still swearing, slithered onto the pavement, along with a disgusting, putrid stench. Pushing back his hood, dislodging a selection of wriggling maggots and bits of rotten vegetables, he revealed himself as a slim young man with short, blond hair and a narrow face, bursting with acne. He cowered away from Dregs, who was still bristling and growling, before looking up and seeing Hobbes for the first time.

'Please, don't hurt me,' he said, suddenly more like a frightened schoolboy than a hardened criminal: a very dirty, smelly schoolboy, to be sure.

'I have no intention of hurting you,' said Hobbes, 'but accidents can happen. I try to avoid them.'

I was sure, at least I thought I was sure, that he meant it as a mere statement of fact, but I could understand how the mugger might take it the wrong way, especially with Dregs's aggressive posture suggesting a likely cause of an accident.

'Take the dog inside, please, Andy,' said Hobbes.

Dragging him up to the front door, I fumbled for my key. I was still proud Hobbes had trusted me with it, for my parents had never done the same and, until I'd left to find my own way in the world, I'd had to be back home by ten-thirty, which was their bedtime. It had done little for my social life, or my reputation. Opening the door, I shoved Dregs inside, much to his annoyance.

When I turned round the mugger, back on his feet, had adopted a sort of fighting stance. Though Hobbes was smiling, he'd positioned himself where he could protect Kathy from any sudden lunge.

'I warn you,' said the mugger, 'I'm a fifth Dan in Karate and my feet are lethal.'

'Thank you for the warning,' said Hobbes. 'Have you tried washing them with soap and water and applying talc?'

'Are you taking the piss? I don't like it when people take the piss.'

'Nor do I,' said Hobbes, 'and I ask you to mind your language when a lady is present. Now, stop fooling around, or you'll hurt yourself.'

'I'll hurt you.'

'That is not going to happen. Your stance is all wrong and you don't know how to form a fist.'

'I'll show you,' said the mugger, shuffling forward, throwing a few air punches.

'No,' said Hobbes, shaking his head, 'you're doing it all wrong. If you close your hand like this,' he formed a fist that would have cowed a mad bull, 'then you're far less likely to injure yourself.'

The mugger charged in a blur of swinging arms and foul language.

'Stop it,' said Hobbes, ducking and swaying, avoiding or deflecting all the punches.

The mugger's momentum carried him forward until, falling over Hobbes's outstretched leg, he landed full on his face and lay groaning, bleeding from the mouth and the nose.

'I told you to be careful,' said Hobbes, 'and now you really have gone and hurt yourself. That's enough nonsense. I'm going to get you cleaned up and then we're going to have a little chat.'

'Ain't you gonna cuff the creep, take him down the station and book him?' asked Kathy, who'd been watching the encounter with shining eyes.

'I don't think that will be necessary,' said Hobbes. 'He's going to behave now. Aren't you?'

The mugger grunted, and Hobbes, taking this as assent, hauled him back to his feet and handed him a handkerchief.

'Hold this to your nose,' he said and turned to me. 'Would you mind taking the bin back? I borrowed it from the side of the Firefly.'

For a moment, I was inclined to sulk, thinking that he was exploiting my good nature on such a night. I then reflected that Kathy might consider I'd been exploiting his good nature ever since I'd taken up residence, and, since I was still determined to prove I was an asset, I agreed.

As I pushed the bin back towards the Firefly restaurant, I hoped Mr Yau, the owner, wouldn't spot me. The trouble was that the old man, watching me using chopsticks for the first time, had started to laugh, becoming so helpless that he'd fallen from his stool. Even the pain of a broken wrist had not been sufficient to curb his amusement and, although the incident had occurred five years ago, the mere sight of me still reduced him to giggles; although the Firefly had a great reputation, I went out of my way to avoid it if I could. Just a glimpse of Mr Yau's bald head and wispy beard would set me galloping to safety. I was mighty pleased to complete my mission without being spotted.

I hurried back towards Blackdog Street, my head awash with thoughts and, although Sunday tea drifted there, as did speculation about the mugger's fate, the image of Daphne Duckworth floated highest. It had been a bizarre twist of fate to bring her to Sorenchester and to park just where I would throw a tin of beans through her back windscreen. I really had a way of impressing a woman and I'd sometimes wondered whether I'd been cursed always to be unlucky in love. Had I only been able to throw accurately, I might have been basking in her admiration. It was a fine line between being a hero and someone fit only to return a wheelie bin, and I was always on the wrong side.

When I got home, Kathy was on the sofa, sipping from a mug of steaming coffee. She nodded.

'Where's the mugger?' I asked, hanging up my coat, pleased to see a pot of tea awaiting my pleasure.

'In the bathroom.'

'Fair enough. He needed a good wash.' I poured myself a drink and sat on the hard chair.

'Does Daddy often bring home freaks off the streets?'

'No, not often.'

'Is that where he found you?'

'No, I came here to interview him when I was a reporter. Umm … do you think I'm a freak?'

'I dunno. Maybe. He sure seems to attract them. There's you and the old woman and that dratted dog.'

'I don't think that's fair,' I said, for although I had noticed how oddballs and weirdoes were drawn to Hobbes, I'd never considered myself as one of them. 'Anyway, you're here, too.'

She nodded and thought for a moment. 'Yeah, I guess you're right.'

As she spoke she looked lost and vulnerable, almost like a little girl, despite her size, and I felt sorry for her; a lonely woman in a strange land, among strange people, trying to build a relationship with a father she'd never met, a father who was as strange as could be.

A shriek from upstairs nearly stopped my heart.

'What was that?' asked Kathy, leaping from the sofa with a grace and fluidity quite at odds with her figure.

'A shriek.'

'But whose? Why?'

Her coffee had spilled down her white blouse and she was pale and big-eyed with fear.

'I'll … umm … go and find out. By the way, where is Hobbes?'

'He went out for some sodas.'

'So, Mrs Goodfellow's alone with that thug?'

'Yes,' said Kathy, clapping a hand to her mouth.

'Oh, the poor guy,' I said, running upstairs.

He was in the bath. Mrs Goodfellow, holding the scruff of his neck, was scrubbing vigorously with a sponge and, although he was trying to protect his dignity, it was hopeless. He cast a despairing look in my direction as the sponge went to work below the waterline. Although I shrugged and shook my head, grimacing, trying to show that I, too, had suffered, his humiliation was temporary and fully deserved, and cleanliness was better than stinking like the Firefly's bin.

I returned to the sitting room to reassure Kathy. 'It's OK, he's fine, but Mrs Goodfellow is sponging him down.'

'Eeuw!'

A few minutes later, the front door swung open and Hobbes returned, a couple of giant plastic cola bottles in his left hand. He took them to the kitchen and returned with Dregs, who was looking a little nervous. Bath time, anybody's bath time, always took him like that, for he was another of the old girl's victims, and had soon learned that resistance was useless. I could understand his concerns, for big black dogs should not smell of lavender and rose water.

However, lavender and rose water was a definite improvement for the mugger, who lurched into the sitting room, wrapped in the flamboyant silk dressing gown that had once belonged to Mr Goodfellow.

'This is Rupert,' said Mrs Goodfellow, following him. 'He would like to say something. Come on Rupert.' Taking his arm, she pulled him into the centre of the room.

There was a stunned, lost expression in his eyes, as if he believed he'd fallen into a surreal nightmare from which he could not wake. He shuffled his feet and stared at the carpet. 'I'm sorry I was bad,' he said, his voice, low and hesitant, sounding well-educated.

'Well done,' said Mrs Goodfellow. 'Now, take a seat next to Kathy and I'll get tea ready. Are you hungry?'

'Yes. Very.'

'Good lad.'

She left us, followed by Dregs, who was not impressed by Rupert's scent and who was hoping for scraps before supper, although the old girl was always very strict with his mealtimes. Still, he remained an optimistic dog.

When Rupert apologetically shuffled next to Kathy, her expression could not have been more disgusted had Dregs left a deposit there. Rupert sat hunched up, with downcast eyes and trembling hands, with Hobbes looming over him like a potential avalanche.

'Well, Rupert,' he said, quite gently for him, 'I want you to tell me why you assaulted the poor lady and stole her handbag and why you threatened Andy with a knife?'

'I'm ever so sorry,' said Rupert, 'I hope I didn't hurt her, and I would never have used the knife.'

'You were lucky,' said Hobbes, 'that she was shaken up and upset, but uninjured. If she had been, you might have made me angry and you wouldn't like me when I'm angry.'

'He's right,' I said. 'You wouldn't.'

'Thank you, Andy,' said Hobbes, keeping his gaze on the squirming Rupert. 'Why did you do it?'

'I was desperate. My wallet got stolen and I haven't eaten all day. I just wanted to go home.'

'I'm sorry to hear that,' said Hobbes. 'Did you report the stolen wallet to the police?'

'No.'

'I see. Where do you live?'

'A long way from here, in the Blacker Mountains. The nearest town is Blackcastle, but you've probably never heard of it.'

'We ...' I said and stopped, aware of Hobbes's frown.

'We have heard of the place,' he said. 'What brings you to Sorenchester?'

'I had a job to do ... for my father.'

'I see. Aren't you a bit young to be working?'

Rupert blushed. 'I'm eighteen.'

'Old enough, then, but why didn't you ask him for help if you'd lost your money?'

'I couldn't ... because ... I had no money at all.'

'But,' said Hobbes, 'the lass gave me this.' He held out a very swish-looking smartphone. 'It was in your pocket and it works and it's charged.'

Rupert's voice dropped to a mumble. 'I forgot.'

Hobbes laughed. 'You forgot? I'm afraid I don't believe you.' His voice rose just a little in volume, but several notches in threatening, as he examined the device. 'It appears that you made several calls today. Didn't you?'

'Yeah,' he admitted, looking absolutely miserable.

'So, you didn't forget, did you?'

'No,' said Rupert, staring at the carpet as if he hoped a big hole would open up and swallow him. He sighed.

'Good,' said Hobbes, his bright smile displaying a worrying jawful of teeth, 'now, tell me the truth.'

'I'd rather not.'

'Why doncha kick the punk's bony ass?' said Kathy. 'Then he'll spill the beans.'

'I'm sure there'll be no need for that,' said Hobbes smiling. 'Rupert will cooperate, sooner or later.'

'It's a goddam funny way of policing. Back home, the cops would have busted his ass and thrown him in the slammer.'

'Language, Kathy,' said Hobbes.

'You're a cop?' asked Rupert, looking up, seeing Hobbes's nod and cringing.

'Yes, didn't I say?'

'Am I under arrest?'

'Not yet and maybe not at all, if you answer my questions truthfully and fully.'

'But I can't.'

'Of course you can. What have you got to hide?'

'I'm saying nothing.'

Hobbes shrugged. 'Can you at least tell me how you lost your wallet?'

Rupert nodded. 'I went into a pub for a pint and a bite to eat. After I'd paid, I put my wallet back in my pocket. It wasn't there when I left, so someone must have nicked it.'

'Which pub were you in?'

'One called the Feathers. The landlord's a real big ba … I mean a real big bloke, like you, but I spoke to the little guy behind the bar.'

'Go on,' said Hobbes.

'I went straight back when I noticed it had gone,' said Rupert, 'and had a look around, but couldn't see it. The little guy kept grinning at me, so I figured he'd got it, but he denied it.'

'I see,' said Hobbes, 'and what did you do?'

'I asked him to turn out his pockets. I did get a bit angry.'

'Then what happened?'

'The big ba … man charged across the room, picked me up by my neck and trousers and threw me into the street.'

'You got off lightly, my lad,' said Hobbes.

I nodded. Featherlight's temperament might be compared to that of a wild bull and the slightest incident could set him off, which would frequently lead to blood being spilled, though it was a comforting part of his character that he didn't stay angry for long. It was usually, however, long enough for his victim to need a visit to casualty. How he wasn't in prison was a mystery, though he did receive some protection by being a tourist attraction. Some people just seemed to find him fascinating, and a few thought it might be amusing to provoke him, usually not realising their folly until they came round. Still, it's an ill wind that blows no good and Mrs Goodfellow's tooth collection had acquired many of its finest specimens from the Feathers, as well as a few that made me despair for British dentistry.

'Now, tell me,' said Hobbes, 'what did you do last night?'

'I went into the church, hoping for shelter, but a fierce woman with blue hair made me leave when she started locking up. After that, I tried sleeping under a bush in the park, but it was far too cold. That wind!' He shuddered. 'In the end, I just wandered the streets until morning.'

'That can't have been much fun,' said Hobbes.

'It was horrible.'

Rupert looked so miserable that I would have felt sorry for him, had he not pulled a knife on me an hour ago. Thinking about what might have happened, I began shaking and, despite a noble struggle to keep myself together I could easily have gone to pieces, had Mrs Goodfellow not announced that tea was ready.

Hobbes, putting his great paw on Rupert's shoulder, pulled him up and propelled him to the kitchen. Kathy followed, looking utterly perplexed and shaking her head. Making an effort, I shrugged and smiled, trying to indicate that I was completely cool with the situation and that, if she intended staying, she would have to get used to a lot. From experience, this wasn't always easy and there had been occasions early on when I'd come close to running into Blackdog Street, screaming. Since then, I'd learned to cope: mostly. It was worth hanging in there because I'd seen so many things I wouldn't have otherwise. It was true some of them gave me nightmares, but it was great to have a life and to be building up a store of memories.

Another thing that made life worth living was Mrs Goodfellow's Sunday tea. It was only sandwiches and cake, but such sandwiches and such cake! At first Kathy looked a little disappointed, but after Hobbes had embarrassed Rupert by saying grace, she took a bite from a sandwich. A smile spread across her face, for, although it was a simple cheese and chutney sandwich, the cheese was the tangy, nutty, sweet Sorenchester cheese and the bread, like the spicy, mouth-watering, chutney, was home-made and utterly delicious. Rupert kept quiet and stuffed himself. He'd probably told the truth about not having eaten all day.

Mrs Goodfellow opened a bottle of red wine and offered it round. Hobbes, smiling and friendly, kept Rupert's glass topped up. I wondered what he was up to because, while it wasn't unusual for him to treat criminals in an unorthodox manner, he was usually rough, if not brutal, with anyone who'd attacked a woman. Yet, since tipping him out of the bin, he'd shown kindness and understanding towards Rupert. If it was an attempt to impress Kathy it was failing for, whenever her mouth wasn't full, she would glower at Rupert, as if planning a lynching. All I could do was wait and see how things turned out.

After the meal, Hobbes took us back to the sitting room, while Mrs Goodfellow washed up and Dregs hung around, waiting for his supper.

'Did you enjoy your tea?' Hobbes asked, guiding Rupert to the sofa and making sure he didn't spill his wine.

'Yes,' he said, sprawling, making himself comfortable, grinning and emitting a hiccup, 'I was starving, but that was great. I feel fine now.'

'Good,' said Hobbes, topping up his glass. 'It's not at all pleasant to be penniless, without food and shelter, especially now the nights are getting so cool. That's why I'm so surprised you didn't ask for help.'

'I couldn't. My father …'

'Who is your father?'

Rupert sat up straight. 'Sir Gerald Payne. He's a very important man.'

'That must be *the* Sir Gerald Payne,' said Hobbes. 'I've heard he owns a little land around Blackcastle.'

'A lot of land, actually. Well over a thousand acres and we … he owns all sorts of property around there.'

'That does sound a lot,' said Hobbes, 'but I don't suppose it gives him a huge income. I mean, the Blacker Mountains are barren and can hardly bring in much cash at the best of times, and they say times are hard there. I don't suppose the rents are very high.'

Rupert grinned. 'That's all true. It is hardly worth our while to rent out the properties.'

'I don't know how he makes ends meet,' said Hobbes, shaking his head sympathetically. 'Unless, of course, he has other income streams? I'll bet he's a shrewd investor.'

'Of course,' said Rupert, his voice dropping to a confidential whisper. 'And the best thing is that we've just reopened the family gold mine.'

'Gosh,' said Hobbes, his eyes wide. 'A gold mine? It's lucky to have one of those to fall back on, just as the price of gold is rising.'

'Luck doesn't come into it,' said Rupert, his smile broad and smug, his words slurred. 'My ancestor Sir Greville Payne discovered the gold and scrimped and saved for years until he could buy the land and open the mine. That's where the family fortune came from.'

'Good for Sir Greville.'

Kathy and I exchanged glances. Hobbes seemed excessively friendly with this young crook.

'But,' he continued, 'if your family has a fortune and a gold mine, and your mobile was working, I don't understand why you couldn't phone for help.'

'He said he'd kill me if I fu … messed up again.'

'He can hardly blame you for being robbed, can he? More wine?' He refilled Rupert's glass.

'Thanks. You don't know him. My father can be a right bastard.'

'But he wouldn't really kill you, would he?'

'He bloody would … Well, not literally kill me, but he gets really angry. I say, this is awfully strong wine.'

Hobbes nodded. 'I expect that, when you've done the job, he'll be pleased with you?'

'The thing is,' said Rupert, 'that I haven't done it. I'm going to be in deep sh … trouble.'

'Maybe not,' said Hobbes. 'Perhaps I can help. After all police officers are here to help the public.'

'What?' said Kathy, looking furious.

Hobbes raised his hand.

'Could you?' asked Rupert, his words increasingly slurred. 'That's very decent of you.'

Hobbes smiled. 'I'm just doing my job. What do you have to do?'

Rupert hiccupped, scratched his head and shifted awkwardly. 'I've got to find where someone lives.'

'Can't you look in the phone book?'

'No, she's just moved here and is ex-directory. My father says she's trouble.'

'Who, exactly, are you looking for?'

'I don't think I should tell anyone.'

'Quite right, you shouldn't tell anyone, but you can tell me.'

'Can I?'

Hobbes nodded.

'OK. I gotta find Daffy Duck.'

'Are you sure?' asked Hobbes, raising an eyebrow.

'No, that's not right. It was something like it.'

'Donald Duck?' I suggested.

'Quiet, Andy' said Hobbes. 'Rupert will get there in a moment.'

'I know. I've got to find Daphne Duckworth.'

'Daphne?' I said, suddenly hot and angry. 'What do you want with her?'

'Shh,' said Hobbes quietly.

I shushed, despite feeling a strange desire to protect her, although I wasn't quite sure from what.

'What,' asked Hobbes, 'are you going to do to the lady?'

'Nothing. I've only got to find out where she lives and what she's doing.'

'Why?'

'I dunno. My father says she's trouble like her old man was, but I don't know what he wants with her. Maybe he just wants to keep an eye on her, but he can be a right bastard sometimes.'

'So,' asked Hobbes, his smile still friendly, though his voice was sharp, 'do you think she might be in danger?'

Rupert shrugged. 'Dunno. He doesn't employ Denny to be nice to people. He's not nice to me.'

'So, you suspect your father might get this Denny to do something unpleasant to Mrs Duckworth.'

'Maybe. I say, my head's spinnin' and I'm feelin' all sleepy.'

His eyes closed and his breathing became deep and regular, interspersed by the occasional snort.

'Well, that was an effort,' said Hobbes.

'What just happened?' asked Kathy, looking at the sleeping Rupert with deep loathing and then at Hobbes with confused admiration.

'I got him to talk. The gentle touch often works with someone who's not too bright and is scared even sillier than he is naturally.'

'It cost you a meal and a bottle of wine,' said Kathy. 'Why didn't you just beat the crap out of him?'

'I am not in the habit of beating people,' said Hobbes. 'Besides, his fear of his father would have stopped him talking until he'd been hurt badly. His brain works too slowly to make sensible decisions in a short time.'

'Mom told me that you once totally demolished a biker gang. She said there were twelve of them and you beat them all unconscious. Is that true?'

'No,' said Hobbes, shaking his head. 'There were fifteen of them.'

'Even better,' said Kathy, with a sudden, proud grin. 'What happened?'

'It was a long time ago. It doesn't matter.'

'I'd still like to know.'

Hobbes sighed. 'The boys were out of their minds on something and completely out of control. Some of them were armed and all of them were dangerous. When I chanced on the scene, they'd already injured several people. All I did was stop their misbehaviour with the minimum amount of force necessary. It so happened on that particular occasion that the minimum amount was considerable.'

'How did you do it?'

'As quickly and efficiently as I could.'

'Mom said you hit them with a chair.'

'Two chairs, a table and a frozen chicken, if I remember rightly, but it was long ago and best forgotten. What is important now is ensuring the safety of Mrs Daphne Duckworth. I am somewhat concerned.'

I was still feeling protective and worried. 'What d'you think they'll do to her?'

'Nothing,' said Hobbes, 'if I have anything to do with it.'

'And what you gonna do with this creep?' asked Kathy pointing a plump, manicured finger at Rupert.

'That's a good point,' I said. 'He can't sleep here.'

'He appears to be doing just that,' said Hobbes.

'But, where will you sleep? You haven't had time to tidy the attic yet.'

'Anyway,' said Kathy, sounding frightened, 'when he wakes up, won't he steal stuff or murder us all in our beds?'

'There's no fear of that,' said Hobbes. 'I'll get Dregs to keep an eye on him.'

'You're gonna trust a hoodlum to that dumb dog?'

Hobbes nodded. 'He knows his stuff. Right, anyone fancy helping me clean out the attic?' He sprang to his feet.

'Umm ... OK, then.' I said.

'I'll give you a hand,' said Kathy.

Hobbes grinned. 'Thank you. Come along then. And quickly.'

From my first visit, the attic, lit only by a single, low-powered light bulb, had impressed me with a weird sensation of being in a treasure house, a museum, a junk room and Aladdin's cave all thrown into one. There was a frisson whenever I went up there, for I always imagined I'd discover something exciting. Kathy was still puffing upstairs, as I followed Hobbes up the ladder and past Cuddles the bear, the stuffed guardian of the relics of Hobbes's past. Although he had occasionally talked about Cuddles, claiming my room had once been his, I'd never got him to explain why there was a stuffed elephant's trunk up there, nor why he kept the heaps of old clothes and the various bits of penny-farthings that lined the walls. To my eyes, though most of it was probably junk, there were treasures as well, not least the paintings he'd done, which I found strangely beautiful, if deeply disturbing. In addition, this was where I'd found the fading photographs of Hobbes and Froggy, Kathy's mother. I'd never yet penetrated the darker reaches, where mysterious shapes lay concealed beneath old blankets and rags.

'The lass was right,' he said, 'it is a mess. Where shall we start?'

'Umm … I don't really know. It depends on what you want to throw out and what you want to keep.'

He scratched his head, sounding like someone sawing wood. 'I suppose if we piled things higher, there'd be enough space for a bed.'

'I suppose so.'

'What the hell is that?' said Kathy, at the top of the ladder, staring wide-eyed into the bear's maw, wrinkling her nose.

'That,' said Hobbes, 'is Cuddles. He won't hurt you, he's stuffed.'

'You gotta get rid of it! All that fluff is coming out of it and it stinks of old socks and who knows what.'

He nodded, a little shamefaced.

She stepped up, looking around with amazement. 'You're not really gonna sleep up here?'

'I'll be fine.'

'But it's cold and it doesn't look like it's been cleaned in a century.'

'I replaced the floor boards not long ago,' he said.

'Jeez! What a mess. Doesn't your housekeeper ever tidy up?'

'This is my space. She leaves it alone, unless I ask.'

'This whole house is your space.'

'Yes, but I like up here as it is. All I need to do is make sufficient floor space for a bed.'

'How you going to get a bed up here?'

'There's one under this.' Kicking aside a spiked German helmet, he pulled back a blanket with a magician's flourish.

The air was suddenly full of mice, spinning and squeaking, and Kathy, with a squeal, covering her head with her hands, turned and ran in a blind panic, straight towards the hatch. Before the last mouse had even landed, Hobbes, diving full length, caught her around the waist with one long arm, but her momentum dragged them both through. There was a scream, a crash, and a groan as, horrified, I rushed to see what had happened, fearing he must have crushed her like an elephant falling on a kitten, albeit a rather overgrown kitten, but he was lying on his back with Kathy cradled to his chest, amid the junk his trailing foot had hooked out.

'Are you alright?' I asked, scrambling down.

Kathy looked up and nodded, her face a mix of relief, shock and amazement.

'Oof!' said Hobbes, opening his eyes.

As I helped her back to her feet, not an easy task, Hobbes sat up with a groan, rubbing his side. Dregs bounded up the stairs followed by Mrs Goodfellow, who, keeping pace, was panting like the dog.

'What happened?' she asked. 'Is anyone hurt?'

'I fell, but Daddy caught me,' said Kathy in a weak voice. She looked down. 'I'm OK, I think. Are you hurt?'

Hobbes pushed himself to his feet, still rubbing his side. 'I reckon I've bust a rib.' Holding onto the balustrade, he grinned. 'Still, mustn't grumble, it could have been worse.'

'We'd better get you to the emergency room,' said Kathy.

'Oh no,' he said, 'I'll be fine after a good night's sleep.'

'But …' said Kathy and stopped, staring at a photograph that had come down with the mess. Bending, she picked it up and gasped. 'It's … Mom and you, but … you look just the same!'

'Hardly,' said Hobbes, taking a glance. 'Look at those trousers! And I wouldn't wear my hair that long these days.'

'I don't mean the clothes, I mean you. You don't really look any different now and this must have been taken in the sixties. I don't get it. How come you haven't grown older?'

'I have grown older, just like everyone.'

'You don't look any older,' she said, staring.

'Put it down to healthy living,' I said.

'And good food,' added Mrs Goodfellow.

'And good genes,' I continued.

'No,' said Kathy, screwing up her face. 'Mom looks like an old lady and you don't.'

'That's because he's not a lady,' I said, helpfully.

She glared.

'I suppose I've just been lucky,' said Hobbes. 'Who's going to help me get a bed ready?'

She shook her head. 'No, I need to know, because there's an even older photograph in the museum and one of the guys in it looks just like you. Andy sort of convinced me it was just a coincidence, but it really was you, wasn't it?'

He shrugged, looking nervous.

'And,' said Kathy, her voice rising in pitch and volume, 'you fall through the goddam hatch and catch me and then get straight back up? You should be dead. What are you?'

'I,' said Hobbes, 'am a police officer.'

'Mom warned me you were a weird kinda guy, but she put that down to you being English. That's not the reason is it? You're not normal. You're not right. And what does that make *me*?'

Detecting the onset of hysteria, I considered slapping her. The trouble was, I wasn't sure it would work. Furthermore, I feared she'd slap me back with interest, and, if she'd inherited only half of Hobbes's power, she'd knock me into the middle of next week. Before I'd made up my mind she stopped talking, turned pale, and swayed. Hobbes, leaping towards her, held her as she collapsed, and grimaced as he took her dead weight.

'Is she alright?' I asked.

'I think she's fainted,' said Hobbes.

He carried Kathy's limp body into his room and laid her gently on the bed.

'Should we get a doctor?' I asked, worried, for it had been a spectacular collapse, and far more convincing than the one at the museum.

'I don't think that will be necessary,' said Mrs Goodfellow, who claimed to have once been a nurse, checking her pulse and looking into her eyes. 'He's right. It is just a faint. It'll be from emotional stress. I'll keep an eye on her, but she'll be alright in a few minutes.' Taking the pillows, she placed them under Kathy's legs.

Hobbes sent me for a moist flannel and applied it to her face.

After a minute, she opened her eyes and gulped. 'What happened?'

'You fainted,' said Hobbes. 'How are you feeling?'

'Bad.'

Mrs Goodfellow checked her pulse again. 'Do you faint often?'

She shook her head and groaned. 'I want to sleep now. Please leave me alone.'

We walked away. Then Mrs Goodfellow turned around, went back in and prised Dregs from under the bed. Hobbes winced as he bent to pick up some of the junk that had fallen through the hatch.

Mrs Goodfellow noticed and gave him her sternest frown. 'Don't even think of trying to clear out that attic now. You'd better rest.'

'But where?' I asked.

'You'd best take Andy's room. Lie down and I'll bring up some of my cordial.'

'Thanks, lass, but where's he going to sleep?'

She thought for a moment. 'I'll call Sydney.'

So it was that an hour or so later, clutching a small overnight bag, I found myself back at the old vampire's house, this time having arrived conventionally.

'Come in,' said Sid, beaming a sharp-toothed smile. 'How the Dickens are you?'

'I'm fine, but Hobbes thinks he's bust a rib.'

As the front door closed behind me, it struck me that I was about to spend the night under a vampire's roof. I felt very brave.

'A bust rib?' said Sid. 'I expect that'll slow him down for a day or two. Come on into the kitchen. Have you eaten? I've got some soup in the fridge if you're hungry.'

'No, thank you.'

'A drink? I usually have a mug of hot milk before I turn in.'

'Can I just have water?'

'I gather,' he said, pouring me a glass, 'that Wilber's long-lost daughter has turned up.'

'Yes,' I said and explained the situation with Kathy while he heated up his milk.

'Who'd have thought it?' he said, with a strange smile. 'I hope, though, that with the excitement of a new daughter, plus an injured rib, he won't forget about solving the robbery. I've had Colonel Squire threatening to sue me unless I retrieve his gold.'

'He can't do that can he?'

'I don't know, young man. We've never before had a successful robbery at the bank. With Wilber on the case, I'm hoping the situation will be resolved soon, before too much harm is done.'

'I hope so,' I said, 'but he may also be distracted by Rupert.' I filled in the details, glossing over the tin of beans incident.

Sid didn't seem surprised.

'Hobbes,' I said, 'is going to help him to do a job for his father, but I don't really understand what he's up to.'

The old vampire looked rather down in the mouth and I wasn't sure how to cheer him up, for I couldn't help wondering whether Kathy's arrival had unhinged Hobbes. She certainly had me worried and I was sure Mrs Goodfellow wasn't happy. Only Dregs, after a suspicious start, seemed pleased to have her in the house. Perhaps the beef wellington had something to do with it.

'The odd thing is,' I continued, 'that I encountered Rupert's father, Sir Gerald, when we were camping. Although it was only for a couple of minutes, I could understand why the lad might be scared of him. He was really arrogant and rude.'

Sid's eyebrows rose. 'I was introduced to Sir Gerald a few months ago at Colonel Squire's Summer Ball. He was a real Payne in the … well, you get my drift.'

'That's the one,' I said. 'It's a small world.'

Sid nodded. 'Although we only spoke for a few minutes, he tried to persuade me to invest in his gold mine. I wasn't interested. It seemed an unlikely proposition and one the bank should have no part of.'

'Rupert mentioned that his father had just reopened it. It must be nice to have something like that and I suppose it explains why the Payne family evicted all their tenants from the land and why Sir Gerald didn't want us around.'

'He'd certainly want to protect his assets. The price of gold has risen quite substantially this year and looks like going higher, which I suppose is why he feels it worthwhile. I guess he found someone to invest.'

I finished my glass of water and yawned. 'I'm sorry, but all of a sudden, I'm feeling terribly sleepy.'

'You can use Bram's room, young fellow,' said Sid. 'It's all made up.'

Taking my bag, he escorted me upstairs and led me into a bedroom. 'Here you go. You know where the batroom is. Just watch out for the cat. I'll leave you to it. Sleep well.' With a toothy smile, he left.

The bedroom was small, with old football posters on the wall; the bed was by the window. I had just enough energy for a trip to the batroom and to get into my pyjamas before losing control of my mouth, which went into a spasm of deep yawning. I crawled into bed, unfazed by the black satin sheets. They smelt clean and fresh and, having turned out the lamp on the bedside table, I fell asleep as soon as the blankets settled.

So far as I know, I slept through the night and awoke with a start to find the sun streaming into the room. I grasped for memories of dreams, finding them as fragile as the mist that had filled them, but all I could recall were vague, fractured images: Sid clinging to the wall outside, snatching at moths; Sid crawling across the ceiling in pursuit of spiders; Sid's blood red eyes. Although I knew they were merely dreams, they were strangely disturbing. As I tried to bring back more images, the church clock struck nine times.

It seemed I had slept both well and long, and my stomach thought it high time to remind me of breakfast. I wasn't certain Sid would provide one and was wondering whether I'd have to return to Blackdog Street. Yet, before anything, the batroom beckoned. I washed and shaved, checking, despite my better judgement, that there were no puncture marks in my neck. Satisfied, I dressed and went downstairs, finding Sid in the kitchen, reading the newspaper at the table. A mug of coffee steamed on the table in front of him.

'Good morning,' he said. 'Did you sleep well?'

'Yes.' I nodded. 'Thank you.'

'Excellent, young fellow. Now, would you care to break your fast here?'

'That's very kind.'

'Nonsense. We're old friends now. Blood brothers you might say.'

I wondered what he meant, but a more urgent matter was the question of what to eat. I decided on coffee, and toast and marmalade, finding, to my surprise, that the marmalade was every bit as good as Mrs Goodfellow's. It was less of a surprise to learn she'd actually made it. Sid read his paper as I ate my fill and I was brushing the crumbs from my lips when he spoke again.

'The gold price has gone up.'

'I guess Sir Gerald will be pleased,' I said.

Sid nodded. 'But Colonel Squire won't. The bank will make good what he lost in the robbery, if necessary, but only at the price of gold at the time. The colonel will no doubt be preparing another salvo of sarcasm about his theoretical losses even as we speak. Let's hope Wilber does his stuff quickly.'

'Let's hope so. Of course, he lost something in the robbery as well. I guess it was valuable if he kept it in the vaults.'

'You would think so,' said Sid. 'More coffee?'

'No thanks. It's perked me up considerably.'

'Good,' said Sid, 'because you were looking a little pale.'

'Was I? Well, I'm fine now.' I laughed, thinking it fitting that I should be pale after a night in a vampire's house. Though I felt absolutely safe, I couldn't deny a slight, nagging unease. 'Anyway, I should be getting out now and see what's happening.'

'Ask Wilber to keep me up to date with any developments.'

I nodded, thinking he would, assuming there were any to report. I hoped he wouldn't be wasting too much time with Rupert. In my opinion, he ought to have been protecting Daphne, rather than helping the unpleasant youth spy on her.

Taking my leave, I stepped out into the morning sun, pulling my jacket close against a chill wind, trying to ensure there were as few chinks in my armour as was possible. Denied entry, it expended its fury by whipping up dust and fallen leaves, though there were no trees nearby. I decided not to walk straight back to Blackdog Street, but to make a loop past the museum and, although I pretended I was acting on a whim, deep down, I was hoping to bump into Daphne. I had a vague idea that I could give her a fulsome apology for the can of beans and had a feeble hope that she'd laugh, forgive me and agree to meet me sometime.

I was utterly amazed when that was precisely what did happen. She was walking towards me and agreed to stop and talk. We didn't have long, since she didn't want to be late, explaining that she's just started working at the museum, but, importantly, she agreed to meet me at half-past twelve. Leaving her outside the museum, I walked the rest of the way home in a daze, wondering how to fill the next three hours until our rendezvous at the Black Dog Café.

'Oh, it's you,' said Kathy as I walked in, shutting the door behind me. 'What are you grinning at?'

'I'm just feeling cheerful,' I said. 'It's a beautiful day.'

'Huh! It's goddam freezing. This dump doesn't have central heating.'

'Put a jumper on.'

'A what?' She snapped shut the book she was holding.

'A sweater.'

'I'm wearing two sweaters.'

'Well, how about a brisk walk? That'll warm you up.'

'How about I kick your butt? That'll warm us both up.'

'Is something wrong?'

'Wha'd'ya mean?'

'Well,' I said, 'you're not in a very good mood.'

She hurled the book. It struck me on the ear and smashed a glass vase on the rebound. Although I believed this proved my hypothesis, I didn't hang around to make the point, for she was already reaching for a mug. Rubbing my ear, I fled towards the kitchen, where Mrs Goodfellow was kneeling on the table, scrubbing with a chunk of sandstone.

'What's up with her?' I asked.

'It's lack of sleep, dear. Young Rupert woke in the night and needed the bathroom. He tripped twice on his way upstairs, banged his head on the bathroom door and then fell into the bath. He lay there moaning until I went in and pulled him out. Then he tumbled downstairs. After that, he thought it would be a good time to start a sing-song and wouldn't be quiet.'

'So what happened?'

'Since I reckoned the old fellow needed his rest, I gave Rupert a tap on the chin to shut him up.'

'Did it work?'

She nodded. 'He slept as quiet as a corpse, but woke with a bit of a headache. I think that was from all the wine he'd put away.'

'Where is he now?'

'Out for a walk with the old fellow and Dregs. The old fellow's rib is still a bit sore.'

'I'm not surprised, after catching Kathy like that. There's a lot of her.'

'Shut up!' said Kathy who was at the kitchen door, glowering.

Mrs Goodfellow caught the mug an inch from my nose. 'Calm down,' she said, mildly.

'Make me,' said Kathy, walking into the kitchen, looking mean and dangerous.

'If you want, dear.'

Moving with the speed of a striking falcon, she patted Kathy's neck with an open hand. Kathy's eyes opened in surprise and closed in unconsciousness and Mrs Goodfellow, catching her as she dropped, laid her on the table.

'What have you done?' I asked.

'I've just relaxed her. She'll sit up soon.'

'But how?'

'I could tell you, dear, but then I'd have to kill you.'

I laughed, assuming she was joking. 'Umm … I'll not be in for lunch today. I'm … umm … meeting someone.'

'Oh yes? Anyone special?'

'I'm not sure. I hope so, I think.'

'Good for you, dear. You'll be wanting some pocket money, I expect.'

'Umm …' I said, cursing myself for having once again forgotten my penniless state. 'I hadn't thought of that.'

She rummaged in the pocket of her pinafore, pulled out her purse and handed me a wad of notes. 'Take this, dear.'

'I couldn't possibly,' I said.

I didn't feel good about myself, but I did take it.

Having gone upstairs and changed, I strolled into town, intending to mooch about and see what was going down on the street. I was, in fact, planning to waste time until lunch, but, after an hour or so, somewhat bored, and with money in my pocket, I thought I'd treat myself to a cappuccino and a doughnut at the Café Olé, a hot and happening new coffee shop on Vermin Street, or so the posters led me to believe. On entering, I stood in the doorway, disappointed by the cheap plastic tables and chairs, until the waiter, finishing his obviously-important phone call, showed me, the only customer, to a seat with its very own icy draught. After a brief glance at the menu he'd slapped onto the table in front of me, and a sharp intake of breath at the prices, I got up to leave.

Although I considered myself a man of the world, one well used to verbal abuse, I was shocked by the vileness and vitriol of the waiter's language as I walked out. Trying to ignore him, I marched nonchalantly away, even when he burst out after me, launching barrel-loads of filthy words in my general direction. I couldn't help but think the café's future would be a short one, although, in fairness, Featherlight had successfully used a similar strategy at the Feathers.

He kept on coming and, losing my nerve, I fled ignominiously up Vermin Street towards The Shambles, seeking sanctuary in the church, which was almost empty. I ducked down into a pew just as he burst in, still swearing, and lay flat until I heard him leave. I stretched out, catching my breath, letting my heart rate drop. Someone else walked in and sat down a few rows away. Since I was comfortable and it would have been embarrassing to pop up suddenly like a piece of toast, I stayed put, contemplating the ornate carvings on the ceiling, wondering why some craftsman long ago had carved a cat pursuing a mouse.

'Hello, boss,' a deep, rough, male voice whispered. 'No, I haven't found him. He was in a pub in town yesterday, but no one I've spoken to has seen him since. The little guy in the pub told me he'd found the kid's wallet down the back of a bench and had handed it in at the cop shop.'

My mild curiosity at eavesdropping a stranger's conversation changed to serious interest.

'Yes, boss, I have found where she lives and she's got a job at the museum … No, as I said, no one seems to have seen him and I've already been everywhere I can think of. Sure, boss, I'll keep looking. Should I do anything about her? … Yes, boss.'

I heard the pew creak as he stood up, the heaviness of his feet as he walked away, and sat up to see who it was. Unfortunately, a group of tourists had just come in and blocked most of my view and all I got was a glimpse of a large man with a bald head. He reminded me of someone, but I couldn't work out why. It was frustrating.

I sat for a few minutes, trying to puzzle out what I'd just heard, convinced the man was the one Rupert had mentioned, the one that had made him nervous. After rummaging through the mess in my head, the name Denny came to mind and, I thought, it was just as well he hadn't spotted me eavesdropping, for the vast acreage of his back had suggested massive strength.

What worried me most was the *her* he'd mentioned. Unless I was making a right hash of things, something I was admittedly perfectly capable of, *her* meant Daphne and I had a horrible feeling she was in danger. I'd learned from Hobbes that feelings, or instincts, came from the subconscious and should not be ignored since they were often more reliable than the intellect, especially when the intellect was mine. Sometimes I worried about my brain and wondered if it had a mind of its own.

I stood up, hurried out and looked around, but Denny had long gone. Making my way to the museum, I loitered outside, like a sentry guarding Buckingham Palace, hoping my mere presence might be some protection for her.

After a while, despite stamping my feet and rubbing my hands together, I was getting cold, as well as attracting puzzled glances from passers-by. Realising I was not the usual impecunious Andy, but Andy with a wad of cash in his pocket, I paid the entrance fee and went inside.

Having smoothed down my hair, I made a quick reconnaissance. There was no sign of Daphne and, since there were few visitors, none of whom looked a likely threat, I relaxed and took another look at the photo of Hobbes.

Without Kathy to entertain, I took the opportunity for an in-depth examination. I had no doubt it was him, the notion of seeing him in really old pictures no longer striking me as remarkable, but it was his companion who was the real puzzle. If I hadn't known better, I would have sworn it was Featherlight. Several minutes of staring later, I wondered if I knew anything at all, for he did look uncannily like Featherlight, admittedly, minus a couple of chins and belly rolls and sporting a Clark Gable moustache, yet it had to be him. No one else could have looked like that, and, furthermore, he might almost have passed for Hobbes's brother.

The implication took my breath away, as well as the strength from my legs and, had a bench not been within staggering range, I might have collapsed. As it was, I landed heavily and sat gasping and limp. An old lady with fluffy white hair and red glasses asked if I was alright and, although, I nodded, she brought me a glass of water anyway.

'Honestly,' I said, as she tried to make me drink, 'I'm alright. I just need a few moments to recover. I've had a bit of a shock, that's all.'

Huge eyed through thick lenses, she smiled. 'You look awful, but you'll feel better once you've had a sip of water.' She forced the glass towards my lips.

As I opened my mouth to protest, she tilted the glass and cold water gushed in, making me choke and jerk and knock the glass from her hand. The shock of cold water pouring down my neck made me gasp and then choke even more. My eyes streamed and I gurgled, struggling to breathe as I got to my feet. Even in my death throes, the idea that I would go down in history as the man who drowned in Sorenchester Museum struck me as amusing: a silly end for a silly man.

A vivid memory of a long-forgotten incident resurfaced. My little paddleboat had capsized because of the reckless stupidity of older children and I felt the chill of the water, the panic, the fear, as I struggled upwards, only to find myself trapped in blackness beneath the upturned hull. Knowing I couldn't hold my breath any longer, unable to escape, I was going to drown, until a hand grabbed me, dragging me from blackness, and back into the sunlight. I'd choked and spluttered, until my saviour, a large woman with a small, bedraggled dog, thumped my back and set me on the bank.

A thump on my back sent water gushing from my throat like a fountain and knocked me back into the present. I coughed and, as air wheezed into my lungs, I thought I might just live. Wiping my eyes, I turned to face my rescuer. It was Daphne.

'Are you alright?' she asked, her expression a confusion of concern and amusement.

I nodded, still unable to speak.

'I knew a sip of water would make him feel better,' said the old lady, smiling and walking towards the shop.

'She nearly drowned me,' I whispered.

When Daphne laughed, I couldn't help but laugh as well.

'It's nice,' she said, 'to meet a man who lives for excitement. Seriously, though, are you OK, now?'

'Yes … I think so,' I said, pulling myself together.

'You do look rather wet.'

Since my shirt and trousers were dripping, I took the comment at face value. 'I am a bit,' I admitted. 'I'd better try and dry myself off.'

She smiled. 'You do that. Then come and see me in my office. My door's the one at the end of the corridor.' She pointed past the Roman antiquities.

'The one with "private" on it?'

'That's the one. Would you like a cup of tea … or are you a coffee man?'

'Thank you … umm … I prefer tea.'

'I'll put the kettle on.'

Turning, she walked across the hall and down the corridor.

I watched her go, noticing her navy blue trouser suit was, perhaps, a little too large and didn't really suit her as well as it should. Still, she looked pretty good to me and she'd smelled nice.

'Cor, look at 'im,' said a wizened old man walking past, looking like a goblin, speaking at a volume suggesting his antiquated wife was very deaf, or that he was just very rude and didn't care who heard him, ''e's gone and wet himself.'

I headed for the gents, where I discovered the hand dryer was so positioned that it was nearly, but not quite, impossible to use on trousers. After persevering, getting a contemptuous glance and a completely uncalled-for remark from a fat man who wished merely to dry his hands, I succeeded in making a difference. Looking reasonably presentable, I took a deep breath, made another attempt at controlling my hair and went in search of Daphne's room.

It looked more like a store cupboard than an office, although it had a desk, two chairs, a telephone, a wastepaper bin, a computer and a filing cabinet squeezed into it. She was on the phone, but indicated that I should sit. The window behind her was open, allowing a cool breeze to ripple the papers on the desk.

At last, she put the phone down and smiled. 'I hope you don't mind the window being open, but it was rather stuffy.'

I shook my head.

'How do you take your tea?'

'White, no sugar, please.'

'Me too.' Lurking behind the filing cabinet was a tiny table, supporting a kettle. She filled a couple of mugs and handed one to me.

'Thank you,' I said, taking a sip. It wasn't great, but it was hot and wet and I avoided choking on it. 'Umm …' I said, 'are you the new curator?'

'I'm afraid not. I'm only the new temporary deputy curator. Why do you ask?'

I told her about Mr Biggs, the previous curator, who, having got himself involved in various nefarious activities, culminating in Hobbes nearly losing his life, had fled to France.

'I had no idea,' she said, 'that this town was such a hot bed of crime. Are the police here as bad as the gruesome twosome we were saddled with in Blackcastle?'

I shook my head. 'No, they're pretty good on the whole – especially Hobbes.'

'Hobbes was the big, ugly copper on top of the getaway van, right?' she said. 'I saw the video.'

I nodded.

'That was impressive, but I don't think I'd like to meet him in a dark alley.'

'You'd have nothing to fear,' I said, 'unless you were seriously up to no good. He's one of the good guys at heart. Mind you, he can be utterly terrifying when it suits him.'

'Do you know him?'

'Very well,' I said, surfing a swell of self-importance. 'He's my friend.'

'Really?'

'Yes. He stopped me getting stabbed yesterday when I went after that mugger. Rupert had just pulled a knife when he scooped him up in a wheelie bin.'

'Rupert? Are you on first name terms with all the local criminals?'

'I only know his name because Hobbes decided to take him home and feed him instead of taking him down the police station.'

'Why?' she asked, looking at me with interest, which I hoped wasn't all on account of my story.

'I'm not sure. He's like that sometimes. It's maddening, but he usually has a reason, although I'm not always convinced he knows what it is. Still, it usually seems to work out, and it did help him learn that Rupert's father is Sir Gerald Payne and—'

Daphne gasped, her face suddenly pale. 'Sir Gerald? I'd hoped I'd got away from him. What's he up to?'

I wondered if I'd said too much. Then again, maybe I hadn't said enough. I didn't want to alarm her, but perhaps she deserved to know what I knew and, I thought, I owed her some sort of explanation.

'I don't want to alarm you, but … umm … Rupert said he came looking for you.'

'No! Is your friend, Hobbes, going to do something about it?'

'I suppose he is, sort of, but, at the moment … umm … he appears to be giving him a hand.'

'You mean he's actually helping him?'

She looked scared and angry – and pretty.

'I'm sure he has a good reason.' I said, forcing a confident smile. 'Probably, anyway.'

'But,' she said, 'I came here to get away from the Paynes. They've made my life a misery, even before Hugh died.'

'Hobbes won't let Rupert harm you in any way,' I said. 'You're one of the public and I'm sure he'll want to protect you.'

'I'm not worried about that young idiot, Rupert! He'd be harmless enough without his father. He's the one who scares me, because he's ruthless and vindictive and he's not stupid. What's more he has Denzil to do his dirty work.' She shivered, seeming to shrink into herself.

'Rupert mentioned someone called Denny. Is that him?'

'Yes, Denny hurts people. He once smashed Hugh over the head with a trombone when Hugh remonstrated with him for attacking a brass band.'

'Why didn't the police do something?'

'They tried. Sergeant Beer did, anyway, and Denny nearly killed him. He's not been the same since and he's terrified of Sir Gerald and Denny. Constable Jones is too inexperienced to make a difference.'

'But,' I said, 'how do they get away with it? Can't somebody do something?'

She shook her head and sighed. 'It seems not. Most are too scared to press charges and Sir Gerald knows the ones who aren't and … well, he has means to persuade them.'

'That's terrible,' I said.

'Yes.' She paused to sip her tea. 'I thought I was getting away from all of that. It seems not.'

'But, why you? What has he got against you?'

She stared at me for a long moment, a frown creasing her forehead. I was struck, and deeply impressed, by how calm she'd become again.

'Sorry, Andy,' she said, eventually. 'I can't tell you. Not yet. Maybe later, when I know you better.'

'If you don't trust me, I understand. I can wait.'

'It's not that. Well, maybe it is that. I *don't* know you yet and after what you said about Hobbes and Rupert, I'm not sure quite what to think.'

As I reached for my cup of tea, I came to a startlingly quick decision and acted on it. Leaping forward, ignoring her gasp and look of alarm, I seized her shoulders and dragged her to the floor. Something missed her by a hair's breadth and hit me on the forehead. White lights and black spots boxed in front of my eyes until the blackness won a knockout.

A woman was speaking to me. I liked the lilt in her voice almost as much as the note of concern. I was on the carpet, lying on my side, my head sore. When I touched it, there was pain and a warm wetness. I groaned.

'Andy?'

There was that woman again. There was something familiar …

'Do I come here often?' I asked.

'Are you alright?'

'What happened?'

'A brick hit you,' said Daphne. 'Well, half a brick.'

I opened my eyes and pushed myself onto my knees.

'Why?' Everything was hazy and distant, apart from her face. It was pretty, but looked worried.

'Someone chucked it at me, but you headed it into the waste paper bin. Thank you.'

Again I touched my head and glanced at my hand. Although there was some pain and wetness, there was no blood.

'It's tea,' she said. 'You knocked my mug.'

'Ah … umm.' Although things were starting to make sense, I wasn't sure I was and, when I tried to stand, I needed guidance to reach my chair. 'My head is a bit sore, but I think I'm alright.'

'You were really lucky,' she said as I sat down, 'that it was only a glancing blow. It could have killed you.'

'If I was really lucky, it wouldn't have hit me at all.'

She laughed. 'That's true. Any idea who threw it?'

'Yes,' I said, 'a big bloke … bald, with a rose tattoo on his arm. I think it was …'

'Denny,' said Daphne.

'He might have hurt you. Should I call the police?'

She thought for a moment and shook her head. 'No, but I suppose I'd better tell you what's going on, now you're involved. I'll shut the window first.'

As she neared the window, she cried out as a huge, hairy hand, seizing her by the wrist, started to drag her forward, her feet scuffing the floor and kicking wildly. Leaping from my chair, overriding the pain in my head, I grabbed her around the waist, pulling back with all my strength, making her groan. Despite my efforts and her managing to get a grip on the window frame with her free hand, it was no good. A sudden jerk broke my hold and I nearly fell backwards. I dived forward, trying but failing to hold her ankles. She screamed as she was dragged outside and all that was left of her was her left shoe.

Although, following a number of unpleasant incidents, my normal maxim was to look before I leapt, my impulsive vault through the window worked in our favour. Time seemed to move into slow motion. I had a brief vision of Daphne, lying face down in a narrow alley, with a huge, shaven, tattooed man crouching over her. Then my feet, with all my weight behind them, crashed into the side of his head, knocking him down. I landed with a splat onto paving stones, winded and dazed. As I got back to my feet, my heart was pounding and my stomach churning with the thought of what he would do next, certain my intervention would not have improved his behaviour. He began to get up, but she bashed him on the head with the heel of her remaining shoe, leaving him flat on his face and groaning.

'Come on!' she said, grabbing my hand and pulling me after her.

We ran. Denny's lunge barely missed as we hurdled him and, without breaking stride, fled down the alley along the side of the museum and out onto the pavement, where we paused, gasping.

'What now?' I asked.

'Back into the museum.'

We ran inside.

Daphne shouted to the ticket lady: 'Call the police!'

The lady stared, shocked. 'Why?'

'I've been attacked.'

Putting down her magazine, the lady pointed at me. 'Was it him? I saw him lurking outside earlier and thought he looked like he was up to no good.'

'No,' said Daphne. 'Do you think I'd be holding his hand if it was?'

We were still holding hands, which, despite the circumstances, made me feel on top of the world, until there was a shadow at the door. Denny lurched in and, although his face was smeared with blood, it could not mask the rage in his eyes. Without thinking, I pushed Daphne behind me and faced him, wondering what to do next, for chivalry is all fine and well, but would serve no purpose if I couldn't back it up. As he advanced, cracking his knuckles like rifle shots, I raised my fists in a pathetic gesture of defiance, but I couldn't just stand there, and there was nowhere to run to.

As he took a step towards us, beckoning with both hands, I had an idea. I'd have been the first to admit it wasn't one of my finest, but I had to try something.

'Stop where you are!' I said, using my authoritative voice, the voice that mostly failed on Dregs. 'What do you mean by attacking Mrs Duckworth? If you take one more step towards us, you will force me to make a citizen's arrest.'

Behind me, Daphne gasped. Before me, Denny stopped, shaking his head as if he hadn't heard correctly. Then, a slow, chilling sneer spread across his face and he laughed. The sheer contempt in that laugh aroused something unexpected in me: something dangerous. Adrenalin surged, my heart quickened and my breathing grew more rapid. I had, of course, experienced the fight or flight response many times and had, traditionally, favoured the latter option. This time was different. Rage swept through me, the world changed colour and I saw Denny, red as a devil in hell. Primeval instincts kicking in, I hurled myself at him, with the sole intention of destroying that sneer. Never before had I experienced a feeling of such strength; never before had I felt so coordinated, so whole, so alive, so un-Andy-like. The next few seconds remain vivid in my memory.

Ducking beneath his punch, I swung with all my might, feeling his nose crunch as my left fist struck and, as my right fist thudded onto the point of his jaw, he went over backwards. I fell with him, landing on top, punching, kicking and biting, shrugging off his attempts to grapple until he seized my wrists and tossed me aside. Landing on my back, I slid across the marble floor, but was back on my feet in an instant and landed several swinging punches without reply.

It couldn't go on forever. His massive fist thumped into my solar plexus. I doubled up like a broken deckchair and collapsed, gasping for breath that wouldn't come.

That was the end of my heroics. I was helpless and knew it and expected worse, far worse, to follow. Yet nothing worse did happen and things began to improve considerably. Daphne's arms closed around me and I could feel her warmth and her heart beating, even through my own trembling.

'Are you alright?' she asked, over and over, although I was unable to reply.

I nodded and, at last, air filled my lungs. I sucked it down as the gut pain receded into a dull ache. My knuckles were raw and bleeding. The kiss she gave me as I sat up took my breath away in an entirely different way.

'I'm OK,' I said, looking around fearfully while she helped me stand up. 'What happened? Where did he go?'

'It was strange,' she said, her eyes teary. 'Just as you went down, your big black dog burst in and launched himself at Denny, who ran away.'

'That sounds like Dregs,' I said, knowing it wasn't the first time the brave beast had saved me. 'He's actually Hobbes's dog. That is, he stays at Hobbes's and helps him with his cases.'

As I spoke, I was shocked to realise just how similar my situation was, and wondered whether Hobbes regarded Dregs as just another house guest, or whether he regarded me as just another pet.

'That is one fierce animal,' said Daphne.

'He's a softy, really,' I said, 'though, to be honest, he scared me when he first came along. He was wild and dangerous back then. He isn't now. Not normally.'

Leaning forward, she kissed me again. 'I'm glad he was fierce then, because Denny looked in the mood for murder.'

'I'm glad, too.'

She smiled. 'And thank you. Most men wouldn't have the guts to fight him and you knocked him down, twice.'

'Well … the first time was a bit of luck.'

'But the second time wasn't. You really went for him.'

'I did, didn't I? I … umm … didn't know what else to do. I'm not normally a fighter.'

She helped me get back to my feet. I was shaking, my knuckles were stiff and sore and my mind seemed to be turbocharged with conflicting emotions. There was pride that I'd fought Denny, though deep down I knew I'd just been desperate, like a cornered rat, and I didn't like the fact that I'd lost control. It took me back to an incident at school, when I'd been nine or ten. Timothy Walsh had grabbed my pencil and run away with it, laughing. Although Timmy was a friend, the pencil had belonged to my sister before the accident and my behaviour regulator had malfunctioned. Instead of treating it as a joke, I'd pursued him, thrown him to the ground, knelt on his arms and raised my fists to pound him. The memory of his face, shocked, scared, and confused remained. Although I'd stopped myself in the nick of time, I'd scared myself as much as him and had always feared unleashing that emotion, the beast within, as Hobbes described it.

A sudden movement in the doorway made my stomach lurch.

'Alright, Andy?' asked Hobbes, peering in.

'More or less,' I said.

'Has someone thrown a rock at you?'

'No, it was a brick and it wasn't thrown at me.'

'Then,' said Hobbes, turning towards Daphne, 'may I deduce that it was aimed at you, Mrs Duckworth?'

Her eyes widened. 'Yes, but how do you know my name?'

'I'm a detective,' he said. 'I take it that the large bleeding man currently being pursued by Dregs is Mr Denzil Barker?'

Daphne nodded. 'Yes. He threw the brick at me, but Andy got me out the way. Then Denny dragged me out the window, but Andy knocked him down. Then he came in here and Andy fought him.'

Hobbes grinned. 'That was extremely well done.'

I blushed. 'It was nothing. Dregs saw him off.' Inside, part of me basked in the praise, while another part wouldn't stop reminding me that I'd just got lucky, that I'd resorted to violence, and that I was a pet, like Dregs, but less useful.

'No,' said Hobbes, 'it's something to be proud of, so don't put yourself down. According to Rupert, Mr Barker is given to bouts of extreme violence and has seriously injured many, including, I regretted to learn, some police officers. To come away from the encounter with a bruise on the head, a wallop in the guts and bloody knuckles is to have acquitted yourself well. I begin to have great hopes for you.'

'Thanks,' I said, embarrassed. 'But what have you done with Rupert? And, if it comes to that, where's Dregs?'

Hobbes shrugged. 'I'm afraid Rupert ran away when I was dealing with a stampede at the Farmers' Market. I expect he'll turn up sometime, probably after getting in trouble.' He put his head to one side as if listening. 'As for Dregs, if I'm not very much mistaken, he's on his way back.'

Daphne was watching him, her expression a strange mix of horror, amazement, and puzzlement. 'You're Inspector Hobbes, aren't you?'

To my surprise, he gave a theatrical bow.

'I am,' he said, grimacing and rubbing his ribs. 'I should have introduced myself.'

'Andy said you were helping Rupert Payne spy on me. Why?'

'It's true that I was trying to help the lad and that he was sent to spy on you, but I wasn't helping him in that. In fact, I strongly discouraged him. I was hoping he'd lead me to Mr Barker, because I want a word with him.'

'I see,' said Daphne, as if she didn't.

With a clicking of toenails and a wagging of tail, Dregs reappeared, a dirty blue rag in his jaws. Having luxuriated in our praise and patting for a few moments, he allowed Hobbes to take it. It was a piece of torn denim.

Hobbes held it up to the light and sniffed. 'That's funny,' he said.

I stopped stroking Dregs's rough, black head. 'What is?'

'This cloth, formerly part of Mr Barker's trousers, has a strange scent, yet it is familiar, if very faint. I can't put my finger on quite why. It'll come.'

'Excuse me,' said the ticket lady, looking rather bored, 'but do you still want me to call the police?'

'No,' said Hobbes. 'I am the police.'

Nodding, she went back to reading her magazine, as if gladiatorial contests between man and monster took place in the museum's foyer every day.

'Inspector,' said Daphne, 'what do you want to talk to Denny Barker about?'

'It's to do with a crime,' said Hobbes, looking thoughtful. 'I would like to rule him into my investigation, but I'm afraid that's all I can say for now.'

She nodded. 'I understand. But can you tell me what brought you here?'

'Of course, Mrs Duckworth. I happened to be approaching the foyer when I saw Mr Barker, who appeared to be in an agitated state, enter the building. Unfortunately, I have a busted rib and can't get around like I usually do, so I sent in the cavalry, in the form of Dregs. He's handy in a brawl, so long as he knows whose side he's on.'

'But,' she continued, 'if you're injured, what were you going to do about Denny?'

'I would have talked to him and tried to dissuade him from doing anything he might have later regretted.'

'No, seriously? He only listens to Sir Gerald.'

'Well, if a little chat didn't work, I would have dissuaded him by other means.' Hobbes smiled.

She frowned. 'But you don't know him. He's really dangerous. Honestly, I've seen him beat up four men at the same time. He might have hurt you badly.'

'He might have, and I suppose he'll have his chance when I find him. Thank you for the warning, but I'll take him as he comes. Are you two alright? It is not pleasant to be attacked.'

'I'm a bit shaky,' said Daphne, 'but I'm alright, apart from scrapes and bruises from when that brute pulled me through the window ... and my trousers will never be quite the same.'

'I'm OK, too,' I said, 'except for a sore head ... and I'm a bit tender.' I patted my stomach and winced. 'I'll get over it, but my hands are very stiff.'

'I'm not surprised,' said Hobbes. 'I'd get some ice on them, if I were you, and the lass will have something to soothe them. Now, Mrs Duckworth, could you show me your office?'

She looked puzzled. 'Yes, I suppose so. This way.'

She led us to the room where he sniffed about for a few moments before picking up a frame of metal bars.

'Last time I was in here,' he said, 'the security grille was on the window.'

'It was until this morning,' said Daphne, retrieving her lost shoe. 'I took it down so that I could open the window and let in a bit of air. It was so stuffy, it smelt like a bear pit.'

'I very much doubt it,' said Hobbes. 'Bear pits have a most peculiar and pungent aroma, but I can quite believe it gets stuffy. However, I would advise keeping the grille in place, at least until I can ensure Mr Barker won't be up to any more mischief.'

'Makes sense,' she agreed.

Lifting the grille, he slotted it into place and held it while she locked it securely with a key from the desk drawer.

'Right,' said Hobbes, 'my work here is done for now. I'd better catch some villains, or Sid will give me an ear bashing. Good to meet you, Mrs Duckworth. I'll see you at supper time, Andy. The lass is making a pork vindaloo. Goodbye. Come on, Dregs.'

'Right,' said Daphne, as they left, 'are you ready to get some lunch?'

The puny, shrouded midday sun only seemed to underline the damp chill and blustery wind as we left the museum. I was still shaking, coming down from my adrenalin high, but Daphne appeared quite cheerful.

'I don't know about you,' she said, 'but I could really do with a stiff one. I don't normally drink at lunchtime, but it's been one hell of a morning. Is there anywhere round here?'

'Sounds like an excellent idea … umm … the Black Dog Café does a decent lunch, and it serves wine or bottled beers.'

'I could do with something a little stronger.'

'I know,' I said, inspired by an advert I'd seen in *Sorenchester Life*, 'there's a new place opened on Rampart Street called the Bar Nun and it's said to serve good food. I haven't been there yet, but it's only a two or three minute walk away.'

'Lead me to it.'

As we walked the short distance we talked, and I was comfortable, as if I'd known her for years; I was amazed she was smiling and laughing at my witticisms, some of which were, even to my ears, incredibly naff.

The Bar Nun had been done out to resemble a sort of Hollywood idea of a nunnery. The walls had the look of ancient, rough-hewn stone, the floor tiles appeared medieval, and there were rows of polished wooden refectory tables set along the walls, with dark wooden benches to sit on. Two months previously, it had been an expensive and spectacularly unsuccessful shoe shop, but now it smelt of cooking, beer and paint. Some of the tables were walled off by wooden partitions, like little cells, and offered privacy. I thought we'd choose one of them, but first we headed to the bar, where a pretty young woman wearing a skimpy black habit smiled at us.

'Hello, sir, madam,' she said. 'How can I help you?'

'What would you like?' I asked Daphne, patting the comforting wad in my breast pocket.

She paused for a moment. 'I rather fancy a cocktail.'

'That's a good idea,' I said, as if accustomed to ordering them, and turned to the barmaid. 'Do you do cocktails, miss? Or should I say, sister?'

The girl grimaced. 'Yes, we do the normal ones plus a few specialities of the house.' She pointed to a list on a blackboard above the bar and, while we examined it, served an elderly couple, the only other customers, who wanted milky coffees.

'I think,' said Daphne, when the barmaid turned back to us, 'I'll have a Godchild.'

'Excellent choice,' I said, craning to see what the barmaid put in it: a measure of brandy, something creamy from a rectangular bottle and a small mountain of ice.

The barmaid, placing it on a coaster, looked at me expectantly.

'Right,' I said, with the easy confidence of an ignoramus, 'I rather fancy one of your house specialities. Give me an Ecstasy of Saint Theresa, please. Shaken not stirred.'

'Are you sure, sir?' asked the barmaid.

I nodded and she busied herself with a worrying number of bottles and a shaker. 'Here you are,' she said at last, handing me a glass filled with a clear, innocuous-looking fluid with floating ice, a sliver of lime, and salt crystals round the rim.

'Thank you,' I said. 'Cheers!'

'Cheers,' said Daphne, sipping her drink and smiling.

I took a gulp of mine and instantly regretted it, for it was, quite simply, the nastiest liquid that had ever passed my lips, which was saying something. I shuddered, my tongue went numb and my throat burned, despite the chill of the ice.

'Water! Pleathe!' I said, shocked that I couldn't help but lisp, and found the barmaid had already placed a pint glass of iced water in front of me. Grabbing it, I swilled it down.

'Most customers need water after one of those,' she said with a merry laugh, quite inappropriate for a nun.

'Thank you,' I said, thinking she might have given me prior warning. 'Do people drink this for pleasure?'

'No, sir. Mostly we have to force them.'

Daphne was reading the menu. 'We'd better get something to eat or we'll end up squiffy. I'll have Chicken Madras. Andy?'

'I do like a curry, but since I'm having one for supper, I'll … umm … have a chilli.' I hoped it would be a really spicy one, something that would neutralise the taste of the cocktail. I wished I'd just stuck to lager, which was usually safe.

After ordering, we sat in one of the small cells, towards the back. As a drinker more used to the Feathers and its veneer of filth that nearly masked the squalor beneath, I was delighted to find the table was clean and not at all sticky.

'What a morning!' said Daphne with a shiver. 'I'm so glad you were there. I don't know what might have happened otherwise.'

I smiled and shrugged. 'I'm glad I was there, too.'

'I'm sorry I wasn't very nice when we first met,' she said. 'I had you down as a waster.'

I stared at my drink for a long moment. 'I'm … umm … afraid you're not far from the truth. I've tried to kid myself I'm not, but when it comes down to it, I live on Hobbes's charity and the only reason I've got any money for lunch is because Mrs Goodfellow, his housekeeper, is so kind.'

'I thought you were a reporter?'

'Not any more. I did work for the *Bugle*, but I was fired. Since then, I've sort of pretended I've gone freelance, but I haven't actually written anything, except stuff about Hobbes, which I can't do anything with, because … because he hates publicity. I'm a bit useless really.'

'No,' she said, shaking her head, 'you're not. The way you went for Denny showed what's inside.'

'I couldn't think of anything else to do.'

'Precisely! You followed your instincts and did the right thing. You should trust yourself more often.'

'I don't know when to. I've let myself and others down too often.'

She reached out and put her hand on mine. 'Give yourself a break.'

I nodded. Her hand was warm and soft and smooth and, despite my sore knuckles, I liked its touch. The barmaid placed our cutlery and meals in front of us.

To my eyes, it looked like a terrible curry, a thin, watery, yellow sauce poured over rubbery lumps of boiled out chicken with overcooked rice. Perhaps Mrs Goodfellow had spoiled me, but Daphne ate it without a murmur of complaint. My chilli con carne was edible, if a little bland, and distracted me sufficiently that I took another glug of my cocktail. If anything, it was even nastier second time around. I stared at it, like at a mad dog that I had to get past.

'You're really not enjoying that are you?' said Daphne, finishing her Godchild. 'Why not just give up on it and try something else?'

'Yeth,' I croaked, wondering why I hadn't thought of such a simple solution. 'Would you like another drink?'

'I'll just have a coffee: black, no sugar, please. I'll nip to the ladies while you're getting them.'

I went up to the bar, aware of a man striding briskly past. I was heading back, trying not to spill any coffee, taking sips off the top of my lager, when another man entered. As he walked past, I recognised him as Colonel Squire. I sat back at our table, pleased the lager was diluting the cocktail's lingering aftertaste.

'Ah, there you are, Gerry,' said Colonel Squire, presumably to the first man, who was out of sight, although I could just about hear him. 'Shall I get the drinks in?'

'Good to see you, Toby,' said the first man. 'Make mine a whisky and soda.'

There was something hard and arrogant in his voice and yet it was oddly familiar. I flicked through my memory and, slightly to my surprise, found a match. It was Sir Gerald Payne, I was almost certain.

Colonel Squire, a tall, neat man in a grey business suit, was carrying two glasses back to his table when Daphne returned. As she sat, I put my finger to my lips and leant over to where I could hear. She looked puzzled, but did as I wanted.

'Bottoms up, Gerry,' said Colonel Squire.

'Cheers, Toby,' said Sir Gerald. 'How goes the hunt for your gold?'

'Not at all well. I keep getting on to old Sharples, but he's hopeless, and the police don't seem to be making any progress whatsoever.'

'What about that big ugly devil who stopped the first attempt?'

'Hobbes? He seems to be a great one for being the action hero, but he doesn't seem to be much good as a detective.'

How little he knew, I thought.

Sir Gerald laughed. 'Well, he can't be any worse than the police around us. We've been lumbered with a matching pair of complete idiots. Anyway, if the worst comes to the worst, you'll get your money back.'

'To an extent, but the price of gold has risen and Sharples says I'll only get the market rate at the time of the robbery. I stand to lose thousands.'

'Just as well you can afford it,' said Sir Gerald with a laugh.

'That's not the point. I intend to make sure I don't lose out at all and I hold Sharples personally responsible. One way or another, I'm going to make him pay. I entrusted him with my gold, he was in charge of security, and he failed. Therefore, he owes me. And it's not just the value of the gold, because some of the coins were quite rare and worth a great deal more than their weight.

'Well, that's enough of my woes. How are things with you, Gerry?'

'They are going very well. It's an ill wind that blows no one any good and the rise in the gold price has meant it is economical to reopen the mine. It's back in production, we've dug up some top-class ore, and have smelted our first ingots. It's the first Payne gold for over one hundred years.'

'Lucky for you,' said Colonel Squire. 'Not many chaps get to inherit their own goldmine.'

'True, but there are not many chaps get to inherit thousands of acres of prime Cotswold farmland as you did.'

'One must count one's blessings I suppose. If my gold isn't recovered, and I'm not hopeful, then at least I'll get plenty of cash, even if it's not nearly as much as it ought to be.'

'I'll tell you what,' said Sir Gerald, 'if you still mean to keep your own gold reserve, I could sell you some ingots from the mine. I know it's not much recompense for those rare coins, but I could mark them with your family crest, and I'm sure I could arrange a most generous discount, since we won't have to go through any brokers.'

'That's very decent of you.'

'Not at all. After all, I partly blame myself for your loss. It was I who persuaded you to put it in Grossman's Bank. I just thought it would be safer there than in your cellar. It *had* a good reputation.'

'Not your fault at all,' said Colonel Squire. 'It was sensible advice and you can't be blamed if the country's going to the dogs. All these robberies in town! We should hang a few more ruffians. That would make them think twice about robbing. And maybe we should start hanging a few bankers as well. Old Sharples should be the first.'

Rage burst up in me and I might have said something had Daphne not been there.

'I tell you what I'll do, Toby,' said Sir Gerald, lowering his voice to a whisper, 'I'll get my man to have a word with Sharples and ensure he gives you what you deserve. He can be most persuasive.'

'Thank you, an excellent suggestion. That'll give the old bloodsucker something to think about. Show him what looking after your customer is all about, eh?'

'That's right.'

'But,' said Colonel Squire, 'first reassure me that he won't go too far and that there will be no way I might be held responsible. People round here respect me as a magistrate and I wouldn't want things to become embarrassing.'

'Don't worry. He knows what he's doing. Besides, even should he happen to go too far, he has no links to you. You'd still be in the clear.'

'What if he's caught?'

'I doubt,' said Sir Gerald, 'that any officer round here could arrest him.'

'What about Hobbes?'

'I'd bet my man against him any day and, even if by some freak chance I'm wrong, then he's loyal and knows to say the right thing. He's been in the family for more years than I care to remember and would do nothing that might cause me trouble. He is an extremely useful chap to have around and I'll make sure he gives Sharples a damn good … talking to.' Sir Gerald laughed.

I didn't mean to, but I gasped. It just slipped out, because, from what I'd seen, talking wasn't Denny's speciality and I feared for the old vampire's well-being.

'I think someone might be listening,' said Sir Gerald quietly.

I heard him stand up, heard his footsteps approaching and, knowing he'd recognise Daphne, fearing he'd do something, I was paralysed for an instant. Then, before he could see us, inspiration struck. I threw my arms around her, drew her towards me and gave her a passionate kiss on the lips, amazed how easily she participated. I maintained my grip, aware Sir Gerald was looking at us, aware he could not see our faces, so long as we stayed in the clinch.

With a disapproving snort he walked away, but, although my ploy had worked brilliantly and the danger had passed, I didn't pull away from her, or she from me. The kiss lingered for what might have been several minutes and only ended when, in manoeuvring for breath, I knocked over the remains of my lager.

She was looking at me with a strange expression. I was euphoric, for being kissed by a lovely woman was a rare experience. There had been Violet, of course, but she'd turned out to be a werecat and Daphne was the real thing. Despite barely knowing her, I felt I could be anything: her friend, her lover, her protector. I could even get a job and make something of myself.

'Well,' she said, smiling, 'that was unexpected.' She sipped her coffee.

I nodded, realising I was in an awkward situation. The kiss had been wonderful, but I was wondering whether I needed to tell her my reasons. Although I took a breath and opened my mouth to speak, I asked myself why I should spoil the moment. Deciding to say nothing was, in all honesty, the right decision. The only trouble was that I couldn't think of anything to say instead, so for a moment I must have looked like an idiot, or worse.

'I'll get you another drink,' said Daphne.

'No,' I said, keeping my voice low, 'I'm fine.'

Admittedly my fears of Sir Gerald attacking her in there were probably exaggerated, for the bar had filled up considerably and I was almost certain Colonel Squire would not sanction violence, especially in front of witnesses. He had far too much to lose. Still, I thought it prudent to get out as soon as possible.

She shrugged. 'Well, I ought to be getting back to work soon. It's my first proper week and already I don't know what they must be thinking of me, so … I can't afford to go back late and reeking of alcohol.' She finished her coffee.

'OK,' I said. 'Let's get out of here.'

As we left, I held her hand and whispered in her ear. 'I'm sorry if I was acting a little strangely, but Sir Gerald Payne was sitting behind us and talking about the gold robbery with Colonel Squire. Did you hear any of it?'

She shook her head and I told her what I'd heard.

'It might,' she said, looking serious, 'have become unpleasant, if he'd recognised me.'

'I'll walk with you back to the museum,' I said, as we left the bar, 'but then I really must warn Sid. He's a nice old va … chap and I wouldn't want him to get hurt.'

'You must,' she said, 'but, please, be careful when you're out. Denny Barker is a really dangerous man and he won't be happy that you've bested him twice. Next time he sees you, there's no knowing what he might do.' She squeezed my hand very gently, for which I was grateful.

I tried to look nonchalant and hoped Hobbes would be around next time I met Denny, although I hadn't much liked Sir Gerald's confidence in his man. Besides, there was always the possibility that I'd be on my own, probably down some dark alley, when next I bumped into him. I almost wished I'd finished my cocktail, for after one of those, anything would be bearable.

The weather hadn't turned any warmer and few people were out and about. There being no sign of Denny or Sir Gerald, I started to relax. We were just passing the end of Blackdog Street when I heard a familiar voice.

'Hi, Andy,' said Kathy, enormous in her red Puffa jacket, smiling as she approached, 'Where are you going to take me this afternoon?'

'Oh,' I said. 'Umm …'

'Who's this?' asked Kathy.

'Oh … Right, I should introduce you. Kathy, this is Daphne. Daphne … this is … umm … Kathy.'

Daphne nodded. Kathy did not. I squirmed.

'I'm glad you two have met,' I said, with a feeble smile. 'Kathy is staying with us at the moment and I've been showing her around.'

'I see,' said Daphne.

'Daphne works at the museum,' I said.

'So, shouldn't she be *at work*?' asked Kathy.

'Yes, I probably should,' said Daphne. 'I'll see you around, Andy. Nice to have met you … Kathy.'

'Ditto.'

'Take care,' I said.

As Daphne turned away, Kathy, heavy with scent, enveloped me in a massive, suffocating bear hug, which was about as welcome as it would have been from a real bear and I was just as powerless. I couldn't understand why she was doing it. She really wasn't my type, if she was anybody's, and her sudden show of affection was as puzzling as it was alarming. Still, part of me felt sorry for her, even though I wished she hadn't just turned up, or, in fact, come into our lives at all.

'Have you seen Daddy?' she asked on releasing me.

'I did before lunch. He'd lost Rupert.'

'I knew he should have slammed that punk in jail. He kept me awake all night.'

'I'm sorry to hear that.'

'And I'm sorry I was a little sharp this morning. I was tired and cold and the coffee hadn't kicked in. I'm not at my best without a strong black one in me.'

'That's alright. I'm not at my best when I'm tired either. Still … umm … I don't throw mugs.'

'Well, I didn't hit you, did I?'

'Not with the mug … but you might have done.'

'Might have wins no prizes. I wouldn't have a cow about it.'

'I won't.'

Smiling, she hugged me again. I tried not to breathe in the scent fumes, which wasn't too difficult as she was squeezing so tightly. All I could do was hope I wouldn't be crushed like an empty beer can and that Daphne couldn't see this unseemly behaviour. When at last she let me go I stepped out of reach.

'Right,' she said, 'since my daddy is nowhere to be found, I'm relying on you to show me a good time. How about it, Big Boy?'

'What?' I said, caught off guard. 'I … umm … don't know what to suggest.'

'Well, what d'ya normally do for kicks in this neck of the woods?'

'There's not much to do on a cold afternoon. You've seen the church and the museum.'

'Too true.'

'Well, I sometimes used to go for a drink.'

'Why the heck not? What's the wildest place in town, buddy?'

'Oh … probably the Feathers. There's usually something happening down the Feathers.'

'Great, let's go.'

'I must warn you it's a bit grotty and the landlord is … well … umm … different, and it can sometimes be dangerous there.'

'It sounds fun.'

We set off, although I wasn't at all sure it was a good idea, but it had been my best shot at short notice and there was no place quite like the Feathers and she had allowed no time for any other suggestions. I just hoped Hobbes would forgive me. She kept squeezing my sore hand, talking and laughing, as if she were the happiest woman in the world. I really did not understand her.

Even the first sight of the Feathers, all peeling paint and grubby windows, didn't dampen her spirits. As we approached the front door it opened, a young man flew out and landed with a splat and a curse on the pavement. Picking himself up, he wiped a smear of blood from his nose and swaggered away as if well satisfied with his experience.

Plucking up courage, I ushered her inside, where Featherlight was resting one of his bellies on the bar, and wiping his hands on his stained and torn vest.

'Caplet,' he said, 'didn't I tell you not to show your ugly face in here again?'

'No, I don't think you did.'

'Well I bloody should've. Who's the lady?'

'This is Kathy.'

'A fine looking bit of skirt. You're a lucky bastard.'

Kathy giggled and patted me heartily on the back. As I stumbled towards the bar, Billy's head appeared.

'Wotcha, Andy. The usual?'

'Please … and what would you like, Kathy?'

'I'll have a Margarita.'

'Not in here you won't,' said Featherlight, mopping up a puddle of spilled beer with his vest.

'Well, what can a girl drink round here?'

Billy grinned. 'Beer or white wine. I wouldn't trust the spirits.'

'Gimme a beer then, buster.'

'Bitter? A pint?'

'Sure … whatever.'

Billy poured the drinks, raising his eyebrows when I handed him actual money, but saying nothing to embarrass me. A large gulp of lager, cool and crisp, washed away the cocktail's hideous residue.

Kathy took a hefty swig of her bitter, frowned and shrugged. 'What the heck is this?'

'Hedbury Best Bitter,' said Billy.

'Jeez! What's their worst bitter like? It's warm and it tastes like … I don't know what the heck it tastes like. Is there something wrong with it?'

I cringed, expecting Featherlight to explode at the slur. Billy reached under the counter for the steel helmet he'd taken to wearing in times of crisis as Featherlight turned to face her.

'She didn't mean it,' I said. 'She's just not used to British beer. She's from America.'

Featherlight's habitual frown had been replaced by a smile, showing off a mouthful of large, insanitary teeth. 'I can tell where she's from, Caplet. You think I'm so daft I can't place an American accent?'

'No … I was just pointing it out.'

'Well, don't. Sit down, shut up, and drink, while I talk to the young lady.'

Taking my glass to a sticky seat, I sat at an even stickier table as Billy removed his helmet. Featherlight, drawing up a barstool, wiped it with his vest in what was, for him, a gallant gesture.

'Have a seat, miss,' he said, giving a low bow.

She sat as requested and, to give her some credit, without a shudder.

'Can I offer you something different?' asked Featherlight, gesturing at her beer.

Billy's mouth dropped open at this unprecedented offer.

She shook her head. 'No thanks, buddy. I'll get used to it.'

'Well then, Miss Kathy,' said Featherlight, 'what brings an American beauty to my humble establishment?'

'It was Andy's suggestion.'

'Well, I never thought I'd say this, but I'm grateful to him. It's not often we get a genuine American lady in here, but he shouldn't have brought you. This can be a rough place.'

Kathy smiled. 'It looks fine to me and I reckon you're big and tough enough to protect a gal should there be any rough stuff.'

He inclined his head. 'I guess you're right at that. But,' he said, glaring at his customers, 'don't any of you lot think of trying anything.'

There was an outbreak of mumbled denials and much head shaking among the half-dozen or so desperate drinkers.

Featherlight, nodding, turned back to Kathy, still maintaining his disconcerting smile. 'Are you here on holiday?'

'Not exactly. I'm visiting family.'

'Caplet?'

'No, he's just been kind enough to show me around town.'

'Mrs Goodfellow, then?'

'No.'

'Who?'

'Inspector Hobbes is my daddy.'

'Hobbes?' Featherlight raised his hairy eyebrows. 'I didn't think he had it in him.'

'Do you know him?'

'Yes, Miss Kathy. We go way back.'

'I bet you do. You remind me of him a little, except of course, you're much better looking.'

Featherlight's face took on an even ruddier tint than normal and his smile broadened.

I sat, elbows on the table, open-mouthed, for, although I could think of many words to describe him, good-looking was not one that sprang immediately to mind, even in comparison to Hobbes. Like me, Billy was watching, wide-eyed and engrossed by the show. Unlike me, he was not recovering from a toxic cocktail, and the fact that I was enjoying gulping down lager at the Feathers proved just how awful it had been. Still, as my mouth and throat recovered, I was able to concentrate on my kiss with Daphne and felt well-disposed to Featherlight for taking Kathy off my hands, allowing me time to indulge my memory. The trouble was, something kept nagging, a vague, guilty feeling, as if I ought to be doing something urgent. The day's events churned through my head in a random stream until a stray thought snagged my conscience. Knocking back what was left of my drink, I peeled myself off the seat.

'I've just thought of something,' I said. 'I've got to go.'

I ran from the pub to warn Sid.

I was legging it towards Grossman's Bank, skilfully weaving between shoppers and charity collectors, hoping I wasn't already too late, when a thought stopped me outside a tea shop. What if Sid was not at the bank? Might he not be at home? Or enjoying lunch somewhere? Or was he somewhere else entirely? After deliberating, panting from the run for a minute or two, I reasoned that I should try his house first, because if he was there, he was likely to be on his own, whereas there would be other people at the bank, not to mention some sort of security. I set off again, just as a little, white-haired old lady stepped out of the tea shop. Tripping over the wheeled basket she was towing, knocking it over, I landed in the gutter. I picked myself up, apologising, retrieved her spilled groceries and listened to a long and bitter lecture, criticising the young people of today. Although at other times I might have been flattered to be considered young, I had a job to do and, turning away with a final word of apology, I ran.

'Stop thief!' she cried.

I was still holding her handbag. Stopping, apologising again, I threw it back and fled.

Reaching Doubtful Street, I stood outside Sid's house, ringing the bell and pounding on the door, without a response. Taking a deep breath, I turned around and headed for the bank at a gentle jog, there being no gallop left in me.

When I was halfway down The Shambles, the bank already in sight, a big hand seized my shoulder and dragged me into an alley, nearly causing my heart to burst from my chest.

'Don't hurt me,' I said, cringing.

Hobbes's deep chuckle gave me instant comfort.

'Oh, it's you. What's up?' I asked.

'We've been told to look for someone fitting your description. The suspect allegedly mugged an old lady before hurling her own handbag at her, striking her a blow on the head.'

'I hit her on the head? Is she alright? I didn't mean it.'

'So it was you. I suspected as much and, no doubt, you'll be pleased to know the lady is fine, apart from being extremely annoyed with the youth of today, by which she means you. Tell me what happened.'

I explained, adding what I'd overheard at lunch and why I'd been in such a hurry.

'It could only happen to you, Andy.' He laughed and paused for a moment, his face screwed up with thought. 'However, your information is revealing. Things are finally starting to make sense.'

'What things?'

'The robbery, the rocks, Hugh Duckworth's death.'

'Not to me they're not. Tell me what rocks?'

'Rocking chairs?'

'No, I mean, what rocks are you talking about?'

'The ones I took from Sir Gerald's mine.'

'I thought you said they were just ordinary ones.'

'They are, which is precisely why they are so important.'

I scratched my head. Conversations with Hobbes didn't always make sense.

'What about Sid?' I asked.

'Don't worry, he can look after himself, but I suppose I should have a word with him.'

'Do you really think he'll be alright?'

'He always has been and I doubt this time will be any different.'

'But what about Denny?'

'I'm sure he'll be alright too, just as long as he keeps out of Sid's way.'

'What? Denny's really strong and he's really mean.'

'You'd be surprised what Sid can do. You're forgetting what he is.'

'He's a nice old man.'

'No, he's not. He's an old vampire, who chooses to be nice. I'm far more worried about Denzil Barker's well-being, and I'd like to give him a word of warning before he does anything else he'll regret.'

'Good,' I said uncertainly, but slightly reassured. 'There's another thing – Sir Gerald was confident Denny could beat you, and don't forget, you are injured.'

He shrugged. 'I hope it won't come down to violence, but if it does, well, who knows?'

Some of my reassurance evaporated, but the jut of his chin suggested he was not to be argued with. 'OK,' I said, 'but could you explain about the rocks?'

'I showed them to a geologist who had them analysed.'

'And what did he discover?'

'*She* confirmed they are perfectly ordinary rocks, just the same as any other in that region of the Blacker Mountains.'

'Well, in that case,' I said, 'it hardly seems worth the effort.'

'On the contrary, it was most illuminating.'

'I don't see why. And what's it all got to do with Hugh Duckworth's death?'

'Mr Duckworth was, I understand, an amateur geologist as well as being a historian. He was planning to publish a booklet on the Blacker Mountains.'

'But what has that got to do with his death?'

'I think,' said Hobbes, 'that it is likely that his research had the potential to reveal a certain inconvenient truth.'

'What truth?'

'That the rocks around Blacker Hollow are quite ordinary.'

'You keep saying that, but it doesn't make any more sense. I don't get it.'

He shook his head. 'I'll leave you to think about it for a while longer. It'll do you good. In the meantime, let's go and tell Sid your news. Come along. And quickly.'

As he strode from the alley, I followed, even more confused than usual. The rocks completely baffled me, because I could see no significance to them at all. Had they been valuable I might, perhaps, have seen a motive for keeping them secret, even for killing someone, but they weren't.

However I looked at what had happened, it seemed to me that Hugh Duckworth had been murdered and that someone, possibly Hobbes, even though it had taken place outside his jurisdiction, should be investigating. I suspected Denny and it was chilling to know that I'd given him a reason to hold a grudge. Perhaps Daphne also suspected him. She was certainly afraid of him and with good reason. Even so, I didn't know why he'd attacked her after she'd left Blackcastle. I wondered if she had something Sir Gerald wanted. Could it be information? Possibly the inconvenient truth Hobbes had mentioned? Yet, despite my fear of him, I recognised that Denny was the hired help and that he was only doing what he was told to do. It was clear Sir Gerald was behind her problems, although it would be difficult to prove. I really hoped Hobbes would help her and make her well-being his priority, despite the importance of recovering the stolen gold and catching the rest of the gang.

As we crossed The Shambles, heading for the bank, which although still festooned in police tape, was open for business, Hobbes asked about Kathy, reminding me of what was apparently his true priority. 'She was a little dispirited at lunchtime,' he said, 'and I hoped you might bump into her and keep her amused for a while. It's a shame I'm so busy at the moment because I'd like to spend more time getting to know her. By the way, where is she?'

'At the Feathers,' I said, embarrassed. 'She was talking to Featherlight. They appeared to be getting on very well.'

He frowned. 'You left her at the Feathers?'

I nodded. 'I had to find Sid. She'll be alright.'

'I hope so, but it's no place for a lady, especially one on her own.'

'But Featherlight was looking after her. He wouldn't try anything on, would he?'

'No. In his own peculiar way, Featherlight is an honourable man. I'm just not so sure about some of his customers.'

'He can take care of them.'

Hobbes brightened. 'Of course he can.'

We entered Grossman's Bank, a solid, dark, heavy-barred building that looked as if it had not changed since Queen Victoria was sitting on the throne. My footsteps rang on black and white tiles as we approached a varnished door with a gleaming brass handle. Hobbes knocked and a diminutive, skinny man with pointy elbows, wearing a tight black suit and steel-framed, half-moon glasses, opened the door.

'Good afternoon, Siegfried,' said Hobbes. 'Is Mr Sharples in?'

'Good afternoon, sir,' said Siegfried, with a slight Germanic intonation, giving us a quaint bow. 'He's in his office. Please, go straight through. He's expecting you.'

'Thank you,' said Hobbes, leading me down a gloomy corridor to the enormous, polished, panelled door at the end, a door intended to impress. It bore a brass plaque with the legend: 'Dr Sidney Sharples, manager.' As he knocked, it swung open without a sound.

Sid, immaculate in a navy blue, pinstripe business suit, was behind a vast desk in an old-fashioned and rather grand office, with half a dozen armchairs arranged in a semicircle around a log fire. Rising from his green leather chair, he removed his spectacles and smiled.

'Wilber, Andy, welcome.'

Walking around the desk, he approached with his hand held out. As I shook it, I was again struck by the delicacy and softness of his plump fingers and couldn't see him faring well should Denny ever catch up with him.

'How can I help you? Would you like a cup of tea? Or can I arrange an overdraft?'

'I never say no to a cup of tea,' said Hobbes, sitting in a leather-covered armchair.

'Yes please,' I said, 'tea would be nice.' I wriggled onto the chair next to Hobbes, finding it was surprisingly deep and astonishingly comfortable, and stretched out my hands, warming them at the blaze.

Sid pulled a cord on the wall and Siegfried entered, once again treating us to his bow.

'A pot of tea for three, if you'd be so good,' said Sid.

Siegfried bowed and departed.

Sid sat down with us and I wondered if his smile was a little forced, though I believed his welcome was sincere.

'It's good of you to drop by. It makes a pleasant change from Colonel Squire. I suppose he has a good reason for shouting and threatening, but it doesn't help. Still, I suspect the colonel is all bluster and is mostly harmless, which is more than can be said of his friend, Sir Gerald.

'But, enough of my woes! How are you getting on with the investigation, old boy? Any progress?'

'Some,' said Hobbes, 'and Andy has recently provided me with some interesting points that, combined with the physical evidence, are quite revealing.'

'Well done, young fellow,' said Sid.

I smiled, looking suitably modest, which wasn't difficult as I had no idea what I'd done that was so significant.

'Furthermore,' Hobbes continued, 'Andy informs me that Sir Gerald plans to send his manservant, Mr Denzil Barker, commonly known as Denny, round to talk to you.'

'One more won't make much difference,' said Sid with a shrug.

'Mr Barker,' said Hobbes, 'is not noted so much for his talking as for his extreme acts of violence.'

Sid nodded. 'I see. Any idea when I might expect him?'

'No, except that it's unlikely to be in full public view. Mr Barker, I have been led to believe, favours encounters down dark alleys and on lonely footpaths. He is, according to a young lad I was talking to, particularly handy with a sock filled with sand.'

'Thank you for the warning. How will I recognise him?'

'Tell him, Andy.'

'Oh … umm … right. He's a big, brawny man, like Hobbes and just as ug … umm … unusually strong, and he has a bald head and a tattoo of a red rose on his right arm.'

'Thank you,' said Sid.

'Besides that,' said Hobbes, grinning, 'Andy is too modest to mention that Mr Barker has a variety of superficial injuries to his face, including a bloodied nose and a split lip that he obtained when Andy knocked him down.'

'Well done that man,' said Sid with approval and some amusement.

'And there's one other thing. Mr Barker may be somewhat lacking in trouser material on his rump following an encounter with Dregs.'

'I get the picture,' said Sid. 'What do you want me to do about it?'

'When you meet him, go as gently as you can,' said Hobbes. 'He's suffered enough for one day.'

'No, he hasn't,' I said, shocked. 'Not nearly enough. He attacked my girlfriend today and he's threatened her in the past and I reckon he killed her husband, but more to the point, he is a big, dangerous bastard.'

'Language, Andy,' said Hobbes, frowning.

'Sorry, but he is,' I continued. 'You need to stay out of his way. I got lucky, but I doubt he'll be careless again. I wouldn't want you to get hurt.'

Sid beamed. 'Thank you for your concern. I really appreciate it, but there's nothing to worry about.'

'Yes, there is. I've met him – I know what he's like.'

'You don't,' said Hobbes, shaking his head. 'You've only seen him when he's working and, for all you know, he might be a friendly fellow in his spare time.'

'No,' I said, feeling, as I sometimes did with Hobbes, that I was in a madhouse. 'He really is dangerous and he's going to hurt Sid. He needs to be stopped.'

'Don't vex yourself about my safety, young fellow,' said Sid. 'I may have slowed down now I'm so advanced in years, but I am still a vampire.'

'What's that got to do with it?'

'Vampires,' said Hobbes, 'are extremely strong, extraordinarily fast and uncannily agile.'

'It's true,' said Sid, complacently.

I shook my head, not understanding how they could be so cool.

'I see you don't believe me,' said Sid. 'I'll show you something. Do you see that glass paperweight on the table in front of you?'

'Yes, of course.'

'Good. Pick it up, if you would.'

'Alright,' I said, more confused than ever, but doing as I was told. It was a pretty thing, made of glittering crystal with a dandelion head entombed. 'Now what?'

'Throw it at me. As hard as you can.'

'I can't do that. It's really heavy. I'd hurt you.'

'Honestly, you won't. Give it a go. I'll be fine.'

'Well, alright, if you're quite sure?'

With a shrug, I pulled my arm back ready to throw and found my hand was empty.

'What do you think of that, then?' asked Sid, strolling back to his chair, bouncing the paperweight in his hand.

'OK,' I admitted, not having even seen him stand up, 'that was fast.' I'd always been impressed by Hobbes's speed, but Sid was something else. I was trembling: not with fear, but awe.

'You should have seen me in my heyday,' he said, his eyes seeming to focus on the distant past.

'I couldn't even see you then,' I said.

The old vampire chuckled. 'Aye, well, maybe I'm still not so slow.'

There was a knock on the door and Siegfried entered, carrying the tea on a silver tray, setting it down and pouring us each a cupful, before departing with a bow. Although I'd never been great at recognising faces, a major handicap for a reporter, I couldn't help thinking I knew him from somewhere. Then I realised how similar he

550

was to Hobbes's tailor. 'He looks like Milord Schmidt.'

Hobbes nodded. 'He's Milord's younger brother.'

'Indeed he is,' said Sid. 'He's been with the bank since before the war and I couldn't do without him.'

Although I'd have guessed Siegfried was in his early forties, I'd come to accept that normal human lifespans didn't apply to everyone in town and it was getting to the stage when I sometimes wondered whether actual humans might be in the minority. Not that it mattered because, somewhat to my surprise, I rather enjoyed living in a town with so many oddballs. As I sipped tea, I mused on my life, luxuriating in the comfort of the chair and recovering from the shock of Sid. At some point, I stopped paying attention to the conversation. I could scarcely believe I'd just described Daphne as my girlfriend and that it had felt perfectly natural, perfectly reasonable, to do so, though I barely knew her. Moreover, there was an even stranger fact. For some reason, I didn't believe I was going to screw things up with her. Something made me feel as if she might put up with me, despite my shortcomings, which were legion.

I hated that she was under threat and kept going back to whatever it was that made her a target. It was obviously something important for Sir Gerald to go to such extraordinary lengths, but why should a wealthy landowner with a working goldmine feel threatened by a widow? There had to be something and I suspected it had to be something connected with the Blacker Mountains and, if Hobbes was to be believed, some ordinary rocks. My brain, not up to sorting out such complex problems, directed me to enjoy my tea.

'Thank you for the chat,' said Hobbes, standing. 'Keep your chin up, because I believe I'm onto something and it's exciting. The only trouble is that it means I'm neglecting poor Kathy. She's come all the way from America to see me and I keep having to tell her I'm busy. I regret it, but it is necessary for the time being. On your feet, Andy.'

I would have been happy to stay there all day, but Sid rose to see us out.

'With any luck' said Hobbes, as I got to my feet, 'I will soon have good news.'

'Excellent, old boy,' said Sid, opening the door. 'I'll make sure to keep Colonel Squire in the dark, though. Goodbye.'

When we left the bank, The Shambles was already showing early symptoms of dusk; the lights were coming on and passing people were even more huddled than earlier.

'There'll be a frost later,' said Hobbes, sniffing and walking away.

'I can believe that,' I said, pulling up my collar and thrusting my hands into my jacket pocket. 'Umm … can you explain why Sid wants to keep Colonel Squire in the dark? You can't suspect him of stealing his own gold, surely?'

'Stranger things have happened,' said Hobbes, 'but, no, I don't. I took a look at his accounts and, with or without the stolen gold, he's a very wealthy man.'

'Did he show you them? I thought he was a very private individual.'

'He didn't actually *show* me.'

'What do you mean?' I asked, for his expression suggested he'd been up to something. 'You didn't break into his house, did you?'

'I didn't break anything. I did, however, enter it.'

'Doesn't he have security? Alarms and things?'

'He has, and dogs and CCTV. It was fun getting past that lot.'

'Weren't you scared of being caught?'

'No.' He strode on, turning right past the Bear with a Sore Head.

'Why not?'

He shrugged and I could see he wasn't in the mood to say any more.

'Where are we going?' I asked, struggling to keep up.

'To make sure Kathy is alright.'

As we approached the Feathers, a group of men had gathered around a figure lying supine on the pavement outside. Hobbes ran. I followed, a horrible, sick feeling filling my stomach. Although I didn't care for Kathy, I didn't wish her any harm and, besides, I should have been looking after her, even though she seemed quite capable of looking after herself.

It wasn't Kathy. She was inside, yelling. It was Constable Poll.

'See that he's alright,' said Hobbes, pointing at the fallen constable and bursting through the door.

'Umm … right.' I said to the crowd, 'let me through, I'm an … umm … interested party.'

'Wotcha, Andy,' said Billy, who was kneeling at Constable Poll's pointy end. 'You missed all the fun.'

'How is he?' I asked, squeezing between two fat men, who stank of stale beer, sweat, and cigarettes.

'He'll be alright,' said Billy. 'His breathing's fine and he's not bleeding much. I expect he'll come round soon.'

'Did Featherlight hit him?'

'Sort of, but it wasn't his fault and this guy started it.'

'Really?' Derek Poll was the most amiable, peace-loving policeman I'd ever met. 'Why?'

Billy grimaced. 'It started when Featherlight decided to impress the lady with his rat in the trousers trick.'

'He didn't!' I shuddered. 'That's disgusting. Was she impressed?'

'It certainly made an impression on her, if that's what you mean. To start with, she actually seemed to find it amusing, but it all went pear-shaped when the head came off. Unfortunately, when she screamed, the copper was passing. He rushed in, just as Featherlight was trying to wipe the blood off her face.'

'Not with his vest?'

Billy nodded.

'Ugh! That's horrible.'

'The copper saw her trying to fend him off, jumped to the wrong conclusion, charged at Featherlight, called him a dirty, rotten scoundrel and tried to punch him on the nose.'

'I don't suppose he liked that very much.'

'No, and he looked as if he was going to flatten the copper, but the lady shook her head and he sidestepped instead.'

Constable Poll groaned and twitched.

'In that case,' I asked, 'how did he end up like this?'

'Well,' said Billy, 'he turned to have another go, but stepped in some spilt beer, skidded and fell, head-butting Featherlight's knee on the way down. The copper got to his feet, staggered into the street and passed out. It was a complete accident.'

'Why is Kathy screaming and yelling?'

'Featherlight stepped on her foot.'

I pulled a face; there was an awful lot of him.

'I don't think he did much damage,' said Billy, 'but she can't half make a fuss.'

Constable Poll, groaning again, sat up and rubbed the side of his head. 'What am I doing here? What happened?'

'You had a strop and headbutted the boss's knee,' said Billy. A couple of eyewitnesses confirmed his story.

'Oh, yes,' said Poll, 'it's all coming back.' His pale face took on an angry tinge and he moved as if to stand up. 'What on earth was he doing to poor Kathy? I'll kill him!'

'No, you won't,' said Billy pushing him back. 'Just calm down for a moment.'

'Why should I?'

'There's loads of reasons, mate. Firstly, he was only showing her his conjuring trick.'

Poll blanched again. 'Not the one with the rat in his trousers? He wouldn't!'

'He would,' said Billy, 'although I tried to warn him. The point is, he didn't mean to cause offence and was actually trying to be friendly.'

Poll shook his head. 'Is there something wrong with him?'

'I have often thought so,' said Billy. 'I think, though, he has just taken a bit of a shine to Kathy.'

'I suppose I can't blame him for that,' said Poll, still looking extremely angry, 'but you said there were lots of reasons. Tell me another, or I really will go inside and punch him.'

'Another reason is that he'd flatten you.'

Poll nodded. 'You're probably right.'

'Besides, it doesn't look good if a police officer starts a brawl in a pub over a girl.'

'Yeah. Enough. I'm calm now,' said Constable Poll, getting to his feet, swaying as if still groggy. 'Hi, Andy,' he said, noticing me for the first time, as I helped steady him.

'I'm glad you're OK, Derek,' I said, 'but that's some bump on the head you've got.'

'I'm alright,' he said, 'but you're a fine one to talk about bumps on the head. What *have* you been doing?'

I raised my hand for a tentative touch to the tender spot. 'Someone threw a brick at me.'

'And the other side?'

'Oh yeah, I'd nearly forgotten that one. Someone threw a beer tray at me.'

Poll laughed, heartlessly. 'And your knuckles?'

'I was defending a lady against a brutal attacker and had to resort to my fists.'

'Yeah,' said Poll, 'pull the other one.'

It went quiet inside the Feathers and Hobbes emerged, holding Kathy by the hand. She was crying and his face was flushed and scowling.

'Is she alright?' I asked. 'What's up?'

'I'm taking her home,' said Hobbes. 'We need some time alone.'

They walked away, turning up Vermin Street, out of sight. Featherlight appeared, rubbing his knee and looking grim.

'What's up boss?' asked Billy.

Featherlight scowled. 'Someone is going to be in big trouble.'

That was all he would say.

The crowd dispersed and I was left outside with only Derek Poll, who was staring at the point where Kathy had left his vision. Inside, Featherlight roared and one of the fat men burst out and ran down the road. I knew him as a regular customer, a man who knew to keep out the way until Featherlight's rage had run its course. It would not be too long.

'Kathy will be alright, won't she?' asked Poll, his brow furrowed.

'Yes,' I said, 'she'll be safe with Hobbes. He'll take care of her but there's something strange going on.'

'She's beautiful, isn't she?' said Poll, his face reddening.

I'd heard that beauty was in the eye of the beholder, but couldn't help thinking an ophthalmologist would have his work cut out curing any eye that beheld Kathy as beautiful. He seemed to be expecting a positive answer. 'Umm … I suppose so.' I said.

'Yeah,' said Derek, 'she's some looker and she seems really nice, too.'

Unsure how to react, I nodded, though it was true that sometimes she could be quite pleasant, particularly when she wasn't throwing things at me. Still, she could not compare to Daphne, who I just couldn't imagine throwing anything in anger and, since Hobbes was so busy with Kathy, it seemed Daphne's well-being was going to be down to me again. This thought didn't make me feel heroic at all, but scared, and not scared for myself.

'What time is it?' I asked.

Poll looked at his watch. 'Quarter past five. It's getting dark early.'

'I have to go now,' I said. 'Are you sure you're alright?'

'I'm great,' he said, grinning the soppy grin of a police officer newly in love.

I might have returned a similar grin had I not thought of Denny lurking out there in the gathering dusk. Leaving Poll to his thoughts, I hurried to the museum, strange, conflicting thoughts and emotions struggling for superiority. As I jogged up Vermin Street, I caught myself scanning every shopper, every passer-by, just in case they might be Denny in disguise, but, with no sight of him, the dull ache in my stomach began to recede.

As I reached the end of Vermin Street, a young man, very much like Rupert, alighted from the Pigton bus at the stop outside the church. He was wearing a smart coat and carrying an expensive-looking briefcase and, although I was almost sure it was him, I had doubts because he now looked so prosperous. A big blue van blocked my view and, by the time it had passed, he'd vanished. I dismissed him from my thoughts. Daphne's well-being was my primary concern and, although he was probably still some sort of threat, he was not Sir Gerald or Denny.

Turning left down Rampart Street, passing the Bar Nun, I reached Goat Street and approached the museum, just as the church clock struck five-thirty: closing time.

Taking up a strategic position by the door, I waited for her.

It was growing darker and I wondered whether it might be cold enough for snow. So, pulling up my collar, I tucked my hands into my pockets and stamped my feet, watching the last visitors make their way out. Shortly afterwards, some of the museum staff left. She was not among them. Still I waited until, just as the clock struck six, a young man in a duffel coat came out and started to lock the doors.

'Excuse me,' I asked, 'has Daphne Duckworth left?'

'Yeah, she went early.'

'Why?' I asked, my worry level rising.

'I think there was some sort of problem. It might have been to do with her flat.'

'Do you know where she lives?' I asked, with a rising fear.

He turned to face me, suspicion in his eyes. 'Who wants to know?'

'I do. I'm a friend.'

'If you are her friend, why don't you know where she lives?'

'Because she hasn't told me. Not yet, that is.'

'Good friends are you?'

'Yes.'

'Sure you are. I heard she had some trouble today.'

'She did, but I was the one who looked after her. I'm the good guy here and I'm worried.'

'I think I'd better call the police,' said the young man, reaching into his coat pocket and pulling out a mobile.

'Don't bother,' I said, turning away. 'You'll just be wasting their time.'

As I left him, I booted a Coca-Cola can furiously into the gutter, yet I could see his point of view. With all the bumps and bruises on my face, I probably looked a real desperado and he, no doubt, assumed he was doing her a favour.

His assumptions were irrelevant. The point was that I didn't know where to start looking for her and, since she hadn't mentioned any problems with her flat, my fear was growing into stomach-gripping panic. I had a desperate urge to do something, but, since nothing occurred, I ended up walking into Blackdog Street and pacing up and down outside the house, biting my nails and fretting. I considered getting in touch with Hobbes, but, since I had nothing definite to say, it seemed pointless worrying him about what was probably nothing, especially when he had Kathy to deal with and a gold robbery to solve.

Since I could think of nothing sensible to do, other than to wander around town in the hope of spotting her car or stumbling over some other clue, I cursed myself for not asking where she lived. The trouble was that I couldn't shut up a nasty, nagging, negative part of my brain that kept pointing out that, as she hadn't offered to tell me, she might not want me to know. Perhaps I was already expecting far too much of our relationship, if it was a relationship yet. I had past form in that respect. Despite this, and whatever her feelings were for me, if she was in trouble, I was going to help … if I could.

Glass smashed not far away and a man shouted angrily. Fearing the worst, I sprinted along Blackdog Street and into Pound Street.

It was a false alarm. A van driver, attempting a three-point turn and failing to take account of the ladder jutting from the back of the van, had smashed an antique shop's window, and, judging by the few words from the shop's owner that weren't blasphemous, had also destroyed a rare Georgian mirror. Ordinarily, as a fan of street theatre, I might have stayed to watch. Not this time. I turned away, desperate to find Daphne, and bumped into a dark-cloaked figure.

The impact, like walking into a tree, knocked me backwards.

'Careful, young fellow,' said Sid, grinning to show off his sharp, white teeth and grabbing my arm to keep me upright.

'Thank you,' I said.

'Don't mention it. Now, why are you looking so wild?'

'I need to find a lady ...'

'I see,' said Sid, raising an inquisitive eyebrow.

'... who's in danger. At least, she might be ... I think. Her name is Daphne.'

'I take it,' said Sid, 'that the lady in question is your young lady, and that she's being threatened by Sir Gerald Payne and his wicked henchman.'

'Yes. I think she's probably at home, but I don't know where it is and I don't know who to ask.'

'Would she be Mrs Daphne Duckworth?'

'Yes,' I gasped. 'How did ...?'

'A lucky guess. Daphne is not such a common name these days, but we had Mrs Duckworth open an account with us a few days ago.'

'That makes sense.' I said, hope rising. 'She's just moved here. I don't suppose you remember her address?'

'I'm afraid not; we have hundreds of customers.'

'Damn it! Wait, though, could you perhaps look it up?'

'I could, but that would take some time. There are all sorts of locks and timers and alarms to turn off before I can get into my office.'

'Oh, no.' My worry levels were rising again and, forgetting my sore and swollen knuckles, I slammed my clenched fist into my palm in frustration and yelped.

Sid wrapped his cloak around him, frowning, thinking, while my feet performed a stilted dance of frustration.

'There may be a quicker way,' he said. 'I could ask Siegfried. He remembers everything and he'll be at home now.'

'Great! Let's go.'

He hesitated, biting his lip hard enough to produce a pinprick of blood. 'I'll take you, but only if you agree to do exactly what I say.'

'Of course,' I said.

'Alright then, follow me. It's not far.'

He took me down Pound Street and turned left into Sick Hen Lane, allegedly the most ancient part of town, where small, dark houses huddled together, leaning over the cobbled street. After a few steps Sid stopped.

'Shut your eyes, please,' he said.

'What?'

'Please, do as I say. And keep them shut until I tell you to open them. Got it?'

I nodded, closing my eyes, puzzled, but trusting as Sid, grabbing my shoulders, spun me several times until I was disoriented. He nudged me forward and I might have stumbled had he not steadied me.

After a few quick strides, our footsteps echoing as if in a narrow passage, he stopped me and knocked three times on a door. After a short wait, there was a click and a creak and he guided me forward into warm air with a scent of burning logs and spice. A door closed behind us.

'You can open them now,' he said.

I was standing on time-worn flagstones in a narrow, low-ceilinged room, lit only by two small candles on a low table and a log fire blazing in a small, black grate, with three solid-looking oak chairs gathered around it. There was a pair of three-legged wooden stools beneath the heavily curtained window and an old-fashioned clock ticking on the mantelpiece. I would have been fascinated had I not been in such a hurry.

'Good evening, sir, good evening Mr Caplet,' said Siegfried, bowing. 'I am honoured you would choose to visit our humble abode.'

'Ah, Siegfried,' said Sid, returning the bow, 'it is always a pleasure. Are your brothers well?'

'Quite well, sir,' said Siegfried with a glance at the clock. 'It is just past six of the clock, so they return imminently. May I offer you some refreshment?'

'I regret,' said Sid, 'that we cannot stay long. My young friend here requires a little of your expert knowledge. He believes a young lady, one who has recently opened an account with us, may be in great danger. Unfortunately, he does not know her address.'

Siegfried studied me, his blue eyes enormous behind his glasses. 'What is the lady's name, sir?'

'Daphne Duckworth.'

'Ah, yes, I remember the lady. She is a widow, I believe, and hers is a most tragic story.'

'That's her.' I said. 'Do you know where she lives?'

'Please excuse me for one moment,' said Siegfried, closing his eyes. 'Yes, sir, I recall her address.'

'Can you tell me?'

'I should not, sir, since there is her privacy to consider.' He paused for a second. 'However, as it is an emergency, I am prepared to break my rule. She resides in Flat two, number two Spire Street, Sorenchester. Do you know where that is, sir?'

'Umm … yes, I do,' I said, overwhelmed by a tsunami of amazement. Once upon a time, in the bad old days, I'd lived in that same flat, had accidently set fire to it and come horribly close to incinerating myself and the entire block. Since then, the building (so I'd read in the *Bugle*, having never dared go back and talk to my old neighbours) had been repaired, refurbished and gentrified.

'Excellent,' said Sid. 'Thank you, Siegfried, and I bid you a very good evening.'

'Good evening, sirs,' said Siegfried, bowing low.

'Thank you,' I said.

Sid's hand grasped my shoulder. 'Alright, you know the drill. Close your eyes.'

'Of course.'

He spun me round, the door clicked open, and he nudged me forward. The door closed behind us, our footsteps echoed for a few moments and then the cold wind made me shiver. After another spin, I was allowed to open my eyes.

'Sorry I had to do that,' said Sid, 'but Siegfried and his brothers value their privacy. Now you'd better find your young lady.'

558

'Yes,' I said, 'I will. Thank you so much.'

With a nod of farewell he strode away, his cloak flapping, but despite the urgency, I couldn't help lingering for a few moments, my mind befuddled by the strange and quaint household I'd just visited and, although I looked hard, there was no sign of a house down a passageway. I never did discover where Siegfried and his brothers lived, and was left with an eerie feeling that, briefly, I'd stepped into the fairy realm. Yet, time was not on my side and so, steeling myself for action, I started to run, praying she was safe, hoping my fears were unfounded.

Leaving Sick Hen Lane, turning past the church, I stampeded down The Shambles, past the offices of the *Sorenchester and District Bugle*, where the lights were still burning as the latest hot news was forged by skilled reporters and editors. I'd never really fitted in there. Sprinting along Up Way and Down Way and crossing Mosse Lane, I turned into Spire Street and slowed down. Although I was sweating and panting, I was alert by the time I reached number 2, a two-storey purpose-built block, dating from the nineteen-seventies, a modern building by Sorenchester standards. The place looked much smarter, more upmarket, than when I'd lived there.

Unable to see Daphne's car in the car park, I swore under my breath, trying to control my fear, my frustration, and to reason clearly. If she wasn't home, she might be almost anywhere and so might Denny. Yet, remembering what I'd done, I considered it quite possible that her car was being repaired. I didn't give up, thinking she might still be home. Never despair, I thought, approaching the block's front entrance.

I was immediately thwarted by an electronic system that restricted entrance to residents and invited guests, an innovation since my day. Undaunted, I pressed the bell marked Flat 2. There was no reply. I pressed again, hoping to hear the intercom crackle into life, but nothing happened. Standing back a few paces, I looked up to see there was a light on in her flat. I tried to convince myself that she was probably fine, that she'd popped out for a minute, or was taking a shower, or listening to loud music on headphones. There were all sorts of reasons why she didn't answer and yet ... and yet I couldn't rid myself of an image of her lying up there injured, or about to be injured: or worse.

A revving engine made me glance over my shoulder to see a gleaming, white Land Rover with tinted windows pulling up in the car park. My adrenalin levels reached critical as I darted behind a holly bush, out of sight, and watched Sir Gerald emerge, carrying a canvas shopping bag that, to judge by the way he was holding it, contained something heavy.

He was joined by Denny, looking particularly mean and dangerous, and something in his expression triggered a memory of a hot day not so long ago when a big bully with tattoos had dunked me in the river. The man I'd believed was the landlord of the Squire's Arms had undoubtedly been Denny and I couldn't believe I'd failed to make the connection long ago. Yet, even as I was beating myself up, I was struck by a thought. Why had he been there? Had it just been a bizarre coincidence? He couldn't have been hunting for Daphne, because she'd still been in Blackcastle. Maybe it had merely been bad luck that I'd bumped into him, for, had the road not been closed in the aftermath of the attempted gold snatch, I would almost certainly have been able to hitch a lift.

As Sir Gerald and Denny headed towards the entrance, I was pleased to see Denny limping, and felt proud to have made the bruises on his ugly face. Yet, I was puzzled by his subservient attitude, for it was quite clear who was the master. Denny pressed Daphne's doorbell, but she was still not answering. Then, looking around in as furtive a fashion as anyone his size could achieve, he reached into his coat, pulled out a crowbar and set to work on the door. After a couple of tortured creaks, it burst open and he stepped back, an unpleasant grin on his face, to allow Sir Gerald inside.

When both had entered, I was left in a quandary: would I be of more use if I rushed in after them? Or would it be better to find a phone box and call Hobbes? Or should I run to the police station and fetch help? It was a sticky situation and there was no time to weigh up the possibilities and be rational. Despite a bowel growling terror gripping me, I came to a decision. I was going to rush to the rescue, although it was more than likely that Denny would simply punch my lights out as soon as I was in range. Yet, I reasoned, I'd been lucky twice before, and I might make a difference, might buy her some time and, if I made enough noise, one of the neighbours would probably call the police. Taking a deep breath, trying to control the fear, I emerged from behind the bush and stepped towards the broken door. I would have liked to have walked with a determined stride, but, the truth was, it took all of my will power to move at all.

I had reached the entrance, vaguely aware of a car pulling into one of the parking bays and a car door slamming, when an unexpected voice called out: 'Hi, Andy.'

It was Daphne. She waved and smiled and turned as if to lock the car.

'Get back in,' I cried, running towards her, 'and drive! We have to get away from here. And quickly.'

'What's up?

'Denny is. We need to go. Now!'

I would have liked to believe it was my authoritative tone that got through to her, but honesty made me suspect it was my look of terror. With a nod, she slid into the driver's seat, started the engine, and reversed out of the parking space as I threw myself into the passenger seat. A glance over my shoulder showed Denny pounding towards us, brandishing the crowbar above his head like a battleaxe.

'Quickly!' I squeaked.

She threaded the car between two others, taking what I considered unnecessary care with Denny catching up so rapidly. As he swung for us, she put her foot down and he missed the back of the car by a cat's whisker. Still he lunged, though the danger seemed over, for we were going faster than him and our exit was just ahead. Just as escape and safety seemed inevitable, a small red car swung across the road, blocking the way out and forcing Daphne to stamp on the brake. I headbutted the windscreen, the impact sufficient to stun and bring pain to my already tender bruises. Since then I have never really questioned the value of seat belts.

Denny's cry of triumph rang in my ears and, as if in slow motion, I turned to see him raise his crowbar and smash it down on the back windscreen. Daphne ducked as a shower of glass twisted over her. Then, as the window at her side shattered, she threw herself towards me. Denny's massive, tattooed hands reached in, one unbuckling her seatbelt, the other seizing her by the throat. He began to drag her out. Even in my dazed state, there was no way I was going to allow that sort of thing and so, grabbing his right hand, I tried to prise it off her. It had no effect whatsoever. Desperate, I lunged forward and sank my teeth into his little finger. Bellowing in pain and rage, he released her and the next thing I saw was his enormous fist powering towards my face. Shutting my eyes, raising my hands in a pathetic attempt at a block, I awaited pain that never happened.

'Urk!' he said, unexpectedly.

I thought it an odd remark.

Something smashed into the side of the car and, as Daphne flopped back into my arms, trembling as much as I was, I opened my eyes. Hobbes was leaning in at the window.

'It's alright,' I said, 'it's Hobbes.'

'Hobbes?' Her voice was weak and tremulous.

'Are you injured, madam?' he asked.

'No, not really. My throat is sore ... and there's glass in my hair, but I'm OK.'

'Andy?'

'I banged my head on the windscreen, but I'll be alright in a moment.'

'Yes,' said Hobbes, 'I saw that. What have I told you about seatbelts?'

'Umm ... seatbelts are for wimps?'

'No ... well, I may have said it once, but I also said that you should wear one.'

'There was no time ... umm ... What happened to Denny?'

'Mr Barker is taking a little nap.'

'I see and Sir Gerald? He was here too.'

'I regret he didn't stay to make my acquaintance and made off in the Land Rover.'

'He and Denny broke into the flats,' I said. 'They were looking for Daphne.'

As Hobbes stood up straight, holding his side and smiling, I could feel her relax and only then did I realise I had encircled her in my arms. Since she was snuggling against me, I guessed she didn't mind.

'I suppose,' she said, 'that I should see what damage he's done.'

'Quite right, madam,' said Hobbes, wrenching open the buckled car door for her to get out.

I was very sorry when she broke away but, with a sigh, I got out as well, despite still feeling a little fuzzy round the edges. Denny was lying on his back, eyes closed, a happy smile on his ugly face and with the crowbar bent into a horseshoe around his neck. In addition to the car's shattered rear windscreen and driver's window, there was a dent in the door, about the size of Denny's head, and the inside was sprinkled with glinting diamonds of glass.

'I'd only just picked it up from the garage,' said Daphne, staring and shaking her head. 'I've had it for four years without a single problem and then I decided to come to Sorenchester ...'

'I'm sorry, Mrs Duckworth,' said Hobbes. 'I came as quickly as I could.'

'I'm really glad you did,' I said, 'but why?'

'Sid phoned to say you might need a little help.'

'That was good of him. I should have asked you, but I thought you were busy.'

'I was,' said Hobbes, 'but public safety is important. I'd better check on the flat, now I'm here, but first, I'll move Mr Barker out of the way and then we can put the cars somewhere sensible.'

He dragged Denny onto a patch of grass and left him there, before parking both cars in marked spaces. Then, with a frown at the shattered door, he led us into the building and upstairs. Daphne's front door had been jemmied open and her sitting room was reminiscent of my old sitting room in that it was a complete mess. Everything that could have been turned over had been turned over. I had to hand it to Denny and Sir Gerald; they were fast. I doubted they'd been inside for more than a minute.

She shrugged. 'I'm just glad I wasn't here. It's only stuff. Everything can be put back or replaced.'

'Stay outside,' said Hobbes, going in, sniffing and examining things, seemingly at random. 'It would appear they were searching for something. Have you any idea what?'

'Not exactly,' said Daphne, 'but I think it may have something to do with Hugh's notes. I'm not sure.'

'Get out!' said Hobbes, turning and running at us. 'And quickly!'

'Eh? What?' I said, as quick on the uptake as ever.

Gathering us up in his great arms, he bundled us down the stairs. We'd just reached the bottom when there was a white flash, a surge of heat, a bang that made my ears ring and a hail storm of debris and dust.

He set us down outside and dusted himself off. Daphne's eyes were wide and frightened.

'What just happened?' she asked.

'A gas explosion. I haven't seen one of those for years.'

'Did they cause it?'

'That,' he said, 'would appear very likely.'

'But why? They might have killed me.'

Hobbes shrugged, and took off his coat, the back of which was smouldering. 'Without evidence or questioning them, I can't know for certain. However, it would be reasonable to speculate they were attempting to get rid of whatever they were looking for. That suggests they didn't find it and that they wanted to destroy it at any cost. I wonder if Mr Duckworth had learned the secret of the rocks?'

Dropping his coat, he stamped on it until it stopped smoking.

Faces were appearing at windows and footsteps were running towards us.

'What about the rocks?' I asked.

'Later,' he said. 'I'd better go back in and make sure everyone is safe. Stay out here, unless I call.'

He ran back up the stairs.

Daphne looked at me and smiled bravely. I put my arms around her, feeling her body shake and kissed her on the cheek. It was wet and her tears somehow made me feel like a hero. We were still hugging when the sirens announced the arrival of the fire brigade and a police car. In moments, firemen were running around, unreeling hoses.

Constable Wilkes approached. 'Are you two hurt?'

I shook my head.

'Good,' said Wilkes. 'Do you know if anyone's inside?'

'Hobbes is.'

'Oh, no, he isn't,' said Hobbes, leading a white-haired couple to safety. They looked oddly familiar, but it took a moment to recognise them as the young newlyweds who'd moved in next door to me about a month before I'd moved out. I hadn't known them, except to nod to, but they'd both had dark hair back then. Only when the woman sneezed and shed some of the whiteness did I realise they were liberally coated in a fine powder, like flour.

Hobbes went back in and returned a few moments later with a furious, dusty, frazzled ginger cat. As soon as he released it, it hissed and ran up a tree. A bunch of firemen rushed into the block, dragging hoses.

Daphne, her face streaked and puffy with tears, pulled away and turned towards Hobbes. 'Is everyone alright?'

'Besides shock and dust, they will be,' he said. 'However, I fear my coat is beyond hope.' Picking it up, he peered through a black-ringed hole about the size of his head in the back. 'I doubt even Milord will be able to do much with this.'

'Oh, well, the lass has been on at me to get a new one since the Big Freeze of sixty-three, but I doubt I'll be able to get one like it now.' He shrugged. 'We'll have to find Mrs Duckworth somewhere safe for the night.'

'I'll be alright,' she said. 'I can stay in a hotel. I'll be perfectly safe now you've caught Denny.'

'I'm afraid,' said Hobbes, looking around, 'that Mr Barker may still be a threat.'

Denny had gone, and so had Hobbes's car.

'You should have cuffed him,' said Daphne.

'Since he'd struck his head and was unconscious,' said Hobbes shaking his head, 'I could see no reason to cuff him, as I don't condone gratuitous brutality ... or do you mean, why didn't I put him in handcuffs?'

Daphne nodded, looking confused.

'With hindsight, perhaps I should have, but I'm not sure where mine are. I think I had some once.'

'It doesn't matter,' I said, trying to get the situation back under control. 'What does matter is what happens next?'

'That's easy,' he said. 'We will go home and enjoy some supper. The situation will seem clearer on a full stomach and the lass is cooking a vindaloo tonight. Would you care to join us, Mrs Duckworth?'

Her face suggested nervousness and uncertainty.

As she hesitated, I jumped in. 'That's a really good idea. The old girl does the best curries I've ever had, much nicer than anything you'd get in a restaurant. The spices she uses are to die for.'

'I can't just turn up out of the blue. It wouldn't be fair.'

'She'll be delighted to see you,' said Hobbes.

'It's true.' I said.

Although I could tell she was far from convinced, Daphne's resistance crumbled. 'OK. That will be nice. Thank you, Inspector.'

Hobbes, with a nod, went to have a few words with Constable Wilkes and one of the firemen. He returned smiling.

'The fire's out and the gas supply has been made safe until the engineers get here and ensure everything stays that way. It appears that no major structural damage was done, although there'll need to be a proper inspection before anyone can stay in there. I'm afraid, Mrs Duckworth, that your kitchen is wrecked. The fireman says it appears that someone turned the gas on and left an incendiary device. They will investigate further.'

'What's going to happen to the other residents?' asked Daphne. 'They have nothing to do with this. It's not fair.'

'Constable Wilkes has contacted the council, who are sorting out temporary accommodation for those that need it. By the way, the next-door neighbours recognised you, Andy, and suspected you might be the culprit again. I put them right.' He chuckled.

'Why would anyone suspect Andy?'

'It's a long story,' I said, blushing.

'And an embarrassing one,' said Hobbes. 'We can talk about it later, but essentially their suspicions were based on him having previous form. We'd better get a move on. I wouldn't want our suppers to spoil.'

Although we struggled to keep up as Hobbes route marched us back to Blackdog Street, I had sufficient breath to explain how I'd set fire to my flat, and she had enough breath to laugh. For some reason, I was happy with that; it didn't make me feel like a fool, or, rather, no more of a fool than usual.

The church clock was striking half-past six as we entered 13 Blackdog Street to be greeted by a delicious, mouth-wateringly pungent aroma. Mrs Goodfellow had already set the table for the three she was expecting and Kathy was sitting there, picking at a chapatti impatiently. Hobbes introduced Daphne and, following a very quick wash and brush-up, we rearranged the seating. Mrs Goodfellow, having noticed and tutted over the state of my knuckles, applied a strange-smelling yellow ointment that provided instant, tingling relief.

When satisfied I could hold my knife and fork comfortably, she served us, Hobbes said grace and we tucked in to a totally brilliant curry, a perfect combination of flavour and fire, with the most delicious, tender, melting pork and her special rice and chapattis. Daphne, after her first taste, looked delighted and turned to thank the old girl, who had, as usual, vanished.

'You weren't joking.' said Daphne when her plate was clean. 'That really was the best curry I've ever tasted, and I've had a few.'

'Thank you,' I said, accepting the credit with due modesty. 'Mrs Goodfellow is the finest cook in Sorenchester … and probably in the entire Cotswolds.'

Kathy, who had not said a word since we'd reached home, sniffed loudly. Although at first I assumed she was just being her usual sniffy self and was preparing to defend the old girl's cooking, she stood up before I could say anything, clutched a handful of tissues to her face, and rushed from the kitchen.

'What's up with her?' I asked.

'She's trying to come to terms with herself,' said Hobbes, looking, I thought, a little awkward and quite sad.

'What do you mean?'

'She is acquiring self-knowledge and insight, which can be a painful process. I'll talk to her when she's had chance to compose herself. In the meantime, let's go through to the sitting room and have a cup of tea.'

As we took our seats, I was grateful that he took one of the hard oak chairs, leaving Daphne and me to sit together on the sofa, where her warmth against my leg made the world a better place. Mrs Goodfellow, reappearing with a well-laden tray, beamed gummily and winked at me before taking her leave, for it was Monday evening and time for her Kung Fu class. As often happened, Dregs accompanied her, though he had little to learn about self-defence. Hobbes, having poured the tea, sat back with a sigh and took a great slurp.

'An interesting day,' he said, 'but at least nobody was seriously hurt. Still, losing my car is a nuisance, especially as Billy had only just got it for me. Oh well, I can always get another if I must and, Mrs Duckworth, if it suits you, I'll ask him to fix yours. He's very good.'

'Thank you,' said Daphne, 'I would appreciate that, but it's my flat that worries me most. It's an awful thing to happen just as I was getting it comfortable. What sort of person would do such a thing?'

'Umm … a bad one?' I suggested.

'That's undoubtedly true,' said Hobbes, 'but it also suggests something more.'

'I don't understand,' I said. 'Wasn't it just nastiness?'

'I wouldn't have thought so,' he said. 'It strikes me that causing a gas explosion and fire is an act of desperation. The risk of being caught was high. It was fortunate you weren't home, Mrs Duckworth. Have you really no idea what they want from you?'

'No … well yes, I sort of know, but I don't know why. Just after Hugh disappeared, Denny Barker forced his way into my house and demanded his notes. When I told him I didn't have them, he ransacked the place, but didn't find anything. He came back several times, just threatening me at first, but becoming increasingly violent when I denied all knowledge of them. The last time he turned up, I had to go to hospital.'

'Why didn't you tell the police?' I asked, maintaining a superficial calm while I was seething internally, although part of me was ecstatic that I'd managed to hurt Denny, if only a little. It felt like revenge.

'Because,' said Hobbes, 'I suspect that Mrs Duckworth had found out that Sir Gerald and Mr Barker had already rendered the local police impotent by means of bribery and terror.'

'That's right,' she said.

'But,' said Hobbes, 'you do know the whereabouts of Mr Duckworth's notes, do you not?'

She hesitated before nodding.

'Where are they?'

'Under a layer of megalodon teeth in a box in the museum's storeroom.'

'Where did you keep them before?' I asked, impressed and proud that she'd managed to thwart Sir Gerald, while at the same time my loathing for him and Denny was rising.

'In the back garden. I wrapped them in plastic bags to keep them dry and hid them in a big conifer.' She smiled. 'After wrecking the house, Denny took the shed apart and dug up the garden, but I don't think he ever thought of looking upwards and, even if he had, he wouldn't have seen much. The branches were really dense and I don't think he ever suspected.'

'Well done, indeed,' said Hobbes, his chuckle rumbling through the room. 'May I be permitted to examine the notes when we've finished our tea?'

'I'm afraid not,' said Daphne, shaking her head. 'At least, not easily. I don't have a key to the museum yet and even if I had, I haven't been briefed on how to disable the alarms. Security is quite tight. Apparently there was a break in a few months back.'

'There was,' said Hobbes, 'and Andy was of considerable assistance to me in apprehending the perpetrators.'

Although I gave him a glance conveying gratitude, he didn't acknowledge it, so perhaps he was only speaking the truth. Not that it mattered, for she favoured me with a huge smile.

'But,' he continued, 'you wouldn't mind me looking through your husband's notes when we can get to them?'

566

'No, not at all. I'd love to know what all the trouble has been about. Do you have any ideas?'

'I wouldn't be surprised to find it's all connected to the rocks in the Blacker Mountains.'

'What about them?' I asked.

'I'll tell you when I have confirmed my suspicions,' he said, putting his empty mug back on the tray and standing up. 'Now, I have work to do. I'm not sure when I'll be back, so, if I were you, Mrs Duckworth, I would stay here tonight. You can sleep in Andy's room and Andy can take the sofa. Look after Kathy if she comes down, please.'

'But where will you sleep?' I asked.

'Don't worry about me, I'll be fine. Goodnight.'

He left us alone.

'I don't want to turf you out of your bed,' said Daphne.

'It's alright,' I said, 'you won't have to.'

'Andy!' she said, opening her eyes wide, 'What are you suggesting?'

'Umm … nothing … What I … umm … meant was that I was turfed out of my room yesterday. I didn't mean to imply that I intend sharing it with you.'

For a moment I was worried I'd offended her. Then, she laughed and I laughed, too. Although I realised she'd been teasing, the mere idea of sharing my bed with her turned me hot and cold in turn.

'Who, exactly, *is* Kathy?' she asked, after a long pause.

'She's Hobbes's daughter,' I said. 'She turned up out of the blue a few days ago and I think she shocked him. He hadn't realised he had a daughter. Why do you ask?'

'I'm just curious. You see, I caught a glimpse of someone, who I now believe was Rupert Payne, hand something to her this morning. I'd quite forgotten with all the excitement, but I remember thinking that something … shady was going on.'

'That's interesting,' I said, 'because I'm almost sure I saw Rupert getting off the bus this evening. He was looking very smart and prosperous, which was odd as he was sleeping rough yesterday.'

Daphne shrugged. 'Don't forget, his father is in town. The boy probably just got his pocket money.'

'Oh, yes,' I said, 'I hadn't thought of that, though last night he sounded scared of his father and I formed the impression he wouldn't dare approach him for money, because that would mean admitting he'd lost his wallet. I wonder what he was doing with Kathy. Perhaps he got money off her.'

'Who knows? You could ask her.'

'I could,' I said, 'but she can be … unpredictable. Sometimes she's not too bad and I can tolerate her, but at other times she's awful. She's thrown things at me and been rude to Mrs Goodfellow and she's selfish and …'

'Don't talk about me behind my back,' said Kathy, entering the sitting room and staring at me through red-rimmed eyes. 'It's not fair.' Running to the front door, she opened it and fled into the night, slamming the door behind her.

'Oh, no …' I said, ashamed and sorry. 'I didn't mean …' I turned to Daphne. 'I didn't think she was listening, or I wouldn't have … I didn't mean to upset her.'

'I know.'

'I'd better go and find her. I feel somehow responsible for her.'

'I'll come too.'

'No, I'd better go alone. Hobbes said you should stay here.'

'I think he meant *we* should stay here, but, if you're going out, I'm going with you. I don't want to be left here on my own.'

Although I had a ton of misgivings, I couldn't dissuade her, and anyway, she had a point. Getting up, we put on our coats and set out.

The heavy clouds had blown away and the moon, ripening towards fullness, lit up a clear sky that still held a faint hint of pink towards the west. A man down the street was scraping ice from his car's windscreen and somewhere in the distance I could hear a gritting lorry. I wasn't at all surprised that Hobbes had been correct about the frost.

'Chilly, isn't it?' I said.

Daphne nodded, pulling up her collar. 'Any idea where she'll be?'

'No, not really. She doesn't know her way around too well. She seemed to like the Feathers, though, so we could try there first.'

We walked through town, hardly seeing anyone, except for some shivering tobacco addicts huddled outside the Barley Mow in a cloud of smoke. On the way, I tried to prepare Daphne for the full horror of the Feathers, but it was peaceful and almost homely when we arrived. A coal fire was blazing in the fireplace and two old boys were playing darts, while Featherlight slouched against the bar, a mug of beer in one hand, shovelling pork scratchings into his mouth with the other.

'Evening, Caplet,' he said, spraying crumbs. 'And with yet another beauteous lady, I see. Welcome, my lady.'

For a moment I was nonplussed and disconcerted by his affability, but then he'd always managed a certain old-fashioned charm with women in his pub – not that there were many.

'What can I get for you, this cold evening?' he asked.

'Umm … nothing actually … the thing is, I …umm … we want to ask you a question. Is that OK?'

'If that was the question,' said Featherlight with a chuckle, 'then, yes, it was OK.'

'What?'

He sighed. 'Oh forget it. Fire away, Caplet.'

'Right … umm … have you seen Kathy?'

'Of course I have, you dolt,' he said frowning. 'What sort of stupid question is that? You brought her in here yourself.'

'No, have you seen her since then? In the last few minutes?'

'I regret I have not set eyes on the fair Kathy since Hobbes took her away.'

'Thanks.' I looked at Daphne and shrugged.

'Hiya, Andy, what's up?' said Billy, emerging from the cellar, looking dusty and pink in the face.

'We're looking for Kathy.'

'What?' Featherlight roared, the furrows in his forehead deepening. 'Why? What have you done to her? I'll smash your face in.' He took a step towards me, his face taking on a purple tinge.

'Stop,' said Daphne. 'Andy didn't do anything. She overheard something, got the wrong end of the stick and stormed out. We just want to make sure she's alright.'

Featherlight stopped. 'Sorry, my lady. I didn't mean any harm. I'm just worried about her. She's sweet, but she may have problems.'

'What sort of problems?' asked Daphne.

'Well, besides having Hobbes as a father, and hanging around with Caplet, there's the other thing.'

'What other thing?'

Looking around, lowering his voice to a whisper, he leaned towards us, smothering us in beer fumes: 'Drugs.'

'Really?' I said.

'No, not really,' said Featherlight, the purple tinge returning, 'it's the sort of thing I'm always joking about. Sometimes, Caplet, you can be a real clod!'

'Sorry,' I said. 'I didn't know. What sort of drugs?'

'How the hell would I know? Hobbes found out, though.'

'Is that why he was so angry when he came out of the pub?'

'No, it was because of the parlous state of the economy.' He shook his head. 'Of course that's why he was angry, you idiot.'

'Oh, right.' Strangely I didn't feel fear, for he was in a comparatively mellow frame of mind, thanks to Daphne's presence.

'Have you any ideas where she might be now?' she asked.

'Sorry,' said Featherlight, shaking his big head. 'My conversation with her was, alas, too brief. Why don't you ask Hobbes to find her?'

I hesitated. 'I don't think—'

'That is obvious,' said Featherlight.

'No, I don't think I should disturb him. He's really busy and there's no reason to believe she's in danger. I'd just like to find her and make sure. The only thing is, I don't know where to start looking.'

'I've an idea,' said Billy. 'If Hobbes took her drugs away, she might want to score some more.'

'She might,' I agreed, 'but I can't see how that helps.'

'It could,' said Billy.

'How?'

'Well, we had a young guy come in yesterday who I reckon was a small-time dealer. He dropped his wallet and I found it when I was cleaning up. It was stuffed with cash.'

'That was Rupert Payne,' I said, 'but just because he had money doesn't mean he's a drug dealer.'

'Of course not,' said Billy, 'but I know something about dealers. I've met a few in my time and, well, he gave off that vibe. So what I'm trying to say is that if you can find the guy, you might find her as well.'

'It's a possibility,' I said, 'but we have no idea where he might be. I thought I saw him near the church a couple of hours ago, but he could be anywhere by now.'

'We haven't anything else to go on,' said Daphne, 'so we might as well start there. He might still be around, or someone might have seen him.'

'It's worth a try,' I said. 'Let's go.'

Featherlight nodded. 'You do that. We'll keep an eye out for her back here.'

'The way I see it,' I said, as we walked out into the freezing night, 'Rupert can be dangerous, so it might be better if I take you home before looking for him.'

She shook her head. 'You don't get rid of me that easily.'

'I don't want to get rid of you—'

'I'm glad to hear it.'

'—but I'd rather you were somewhere safe.'

'And I'd rather you were somewhere safe, but we ought to find her and we'll be alright together. No more arguments.'

'Oh … umm … alright,' I said, unsure that I felt good about this. Then again, it meant she would be with me.

As we walked back along Vermin Street, I was too nervous to talk and Daphne seemed to feel the same way. The streets were almost deserted and the church was in darkness. The church hall's windows, by contrast, glowed bright with electric light, while yells, screams and thuds penetrated the walls.

'That,' I said, 'sounds like Mrs Goodfellow's martial arts class.'

'Isn't she a bit old for that sort of thing?'

'You'd think so, but she's the teacher and enjoys it. Mind you, it's possible it's her marital arts class.'

'You're joking … aren't you?'

'No, she really does teach marital arts. It started with a printer's error and she didn't want to disappoint people.'

Laughter steamed from her mouth. 'Liar!'

I couldn't blame her, though the story was entirely true.

'We could try there.' I pointed to an alley, which led to Church Fields.

She nodded and hand in hand we walked into it, only a faint glimmer from somewhere ahead to show our way through the darkness. Neither of us spoke, both of us on tiptoe, trying to make as little noise as possible, though I wasn't sure why. When something moved deep within the shadows ahead, Daphne gasped and I pushed her behind me, but it turned out to be nothing more than a fat ginger tom cat, who swaggered past, his insolent eyes radiating indifference to our pounding hearts. Breathing heavily, we continued through the crushing gloom until we were in Church Fields, where the pale light of a single, old-fashioned lamppost revealed a nightmare landscape of ancient gravestones and crumbling tombs.

I could honestly say that I wasn't nervous. I was, in fact, suddenly terrified, reminded of the time, albeit in a different churchyard, when a pair of grave-robbing ghouls had tried to bury me. Back then, Hobbes had dissuaded them with a well swung shovel, but he wasn't with us and neither, fortunately, were the ghouls. I doubted they went there because the medieval bones beneath Church Fields had surely crumbled to dust long ago.

Squeezing Daphne's hand to reassure us, I whispered: 'No one's here. Let's move on.'

'Let's,' she murmured.

We walked away, heading by the back of the church and plunging into total darkness beneath a massive yew tree, a tree Hobbes had once told me pre-dated the church by centuries. A layer of dry needles muffled every sound and all I could hear was our breathing. I began to think we were on a wild goose chase.

Far away, someone screamed.

'Did you hear that?' I asked, hoping she'd say no, hoping I'd imagined it.

'Yes,' she said, getting even closer.

'Do you think it might have been a fox?' I asked, grateful for her presence. I could feel at least one of us was trembling.

'No.'

'Nor do I. I suppose we'd better go and see what's happening. Maybe it's just kids mucking about.'

'On a night like this?' she said. 'Someone's in trouble and it might be Kathy. Come on, I think it came from over there.'

We ran from the tree's cover, and there was just enough light from the moon to make out the broad lawns that were leading us down towards Church Lake. My stomach, already tight with worry, contracted when another scream rang out.

'That didn't sound like a woman,' said Daphne.

There was a yell, a splash and a white flash of disturbed water. As we neared the edge, I saw an arm emerge some way out, followed by a head and another arm. The arms flailed wildly and slid beneath the surface.

'I think someone's fallen in,' I remarked, as perceptive as ever.

'No, he couldn't have. He's too far out.'

She was right again, for when the head reappeared, I realised it was probably ten metres from the bank.

'Perhaps he jumped?' I said doubtfully.

'A long jump, but it doesn't matter. We have to help.'

'Umm … yeah … how?' I asked as we reached lake side, both of us breathing hard, the ground getting soggy.

'Could we throw something?' asked Daphne. 'If we can't, someone will have to wade out to him, unless there are any boats?'

'Not at this time of year. What could we throw?'

'Isn't there a lifebelt around here somewhere?'

'Yes, there is,' I cried, thinking back to a lazy summer afternoon. 'There's one over by the bench. At least, there was in August. Let's get it.'

We turned and ran along the bank where, missing my footing I stumbled in, gasping as extremely cold water filled my shoes, but fortunate it was only ankle deep. I scrambled out, my feet squelching, and we continued towards the bench, finding the lifebelt hanging on a post. As I grabbed it, the man yelled again, a frightened, panicky cry and we hurried back to the water.

'Throw it!' said Daphne as I tried to gauge the distance.

Once, twice, three times I swung, building up a good momentum before hurling it with a cry of encouragement.

It was a good throw again: far too good. There was a thud, a splash, a groan, and silence.

'I think,' said Daphne, 'that you hit him. And shouldn't you have held onto one end of the rope?'

'Damn it,' I stepped into the dark water, 'I'll have to wade.'

It didn't feel quite so shockingly cold as it had done the first time, or, rather, it didn't until it reached my knees. I hoped it wouldn't get much deeper.

'Careful!' said Daphne.

I looked back over my shoulder, nodded and took another step. At least, I intended to. Instead, my feet sank into the ooze and were gripped in its soft, clinging embrace, preventing any movement, other than a wild windmilling of my arms that only ended when I fell, face first. I came up, spluttering and gasping and all I wanted was to be back on solid ground. Had Daphne not been there, I would probably have given up. Instead, I decided to play the hero and swim to the rescue. I soon discovered that my heavy overcoat and tweed jacket had other ideas, restricting all movement in my arms so that it was like trying to swim in a straitjacket. I was barely making any progress and, where a more sensible man might have turned back and stripped off, I continued, floundering and gasping.

'I'm coming,' I yelled between breaths, even though I could no longer see the casualty. 'Where are you?'

'Go away.'

The voice was familiar.

'Rupert?'

'Sod off. You hit me in the face.'

Still, I kept going, although the cold was getting to me, stabbing into muscles that were already crying out for oxygen and finding my gasping lungs weren't up to the task. At last I spotted him. Grasping the life belt, he was kicking for the far shore for all he was worth.

A couple of minutes later, I was in trouble.

'Have you found him yet?' shouted Daphne.

My chest felt as if it was being crushed and all I could manage was a feeble whisper: 'I think I might need help.'

Rupert meanwhile, ignoring, or, to be charitable, ignorant of, my plight, was dragging himself from the lake. Icy water splashed my face and shot up my nose and it struck me how much easier it would be to swim if I took off my coat. Although my hands were too cold to be cooperative, I trod water and, following a brief struggle, undid the buttons. Buoyed by my success, I tried to wriggle from its smothering embrace, only to have it pinion my arms behind my back. The more I struggled, the more it seemed to push me under and the earthy, stagnant flavour of lake water filled my mouth. I raised my face to breathe, the coat over my head and it wasn't long before I realised I was losing the fight. As the dark waters closed over me again, I kicked frantically back to the surface, managing half a breath of air. It wasn't nearly enough and it took all my failing will power not to breathe water as I went down again. Though not prone to panic, I came close in the next few seconds. I really thought this was it, the end of Andy.

Just before despair gripped me, a hand did, seizing my collar, supporting me and keeping my head above water. I flapped like an idiot and tried to grab whoever was there until a sharp slap on my cheek knocked some sense back into me.

'I've got you,' said an authoritative female voice. 'Lie back, relax and let me do the work.'

Still supporting me, she whipped off the overcoat, turned me onto my back and towed me towards the shore.

'Is he alright?' asked Daphne.

'I guess,' said Kathy, 'though why he wanted to undress himself in the middle of a lake beats me. Sometimes he's an idiot.'

'I was trying to rescue Rupert,' I said through chattering teeth.

'That was Rupert?' said Daphne.

'Yes. I thought I'd knocked him out with the life belt.'

'I hope you knocked the punk's teeth out,' said Kathy. 'Can you stand now?'

'Umm … yeah.'

'So, why don't you?'

I put my feet down and we waded to shore, where Daphne helped us out.

'What happened out there?' she asked. 'I couldn't see you properly and then you started splashing.'

'Tell her on the way home,' said Kathy, 'otherwise we'll freeze our butts off.'

My tale of woe was apparently much funnier in the telling than it had felt at the time, and my chattering teeth only added to the amusement. I wasn't half glad to get back to Blackdog Street. Unfortunately, my front door key was still in my coat pocket and my coat was still in the lake. I stood and shivered while Kathy rang the bell. It seemed a long time before Mrs Goodfellow, still pink from her exertions at Kung Fu, answered the door.

'Have you two been swimming?' she asked. 'You'd better come in at once and warm up. I'll get you some towels and put the kettle on.'

Kathy and Daphne helped me into the light and the warmth and the night was shut out. I enjoyed a wonderful hot bath and a cup of cocoa before being tucked up in my bed. Daphne kissed me on the cheek and the light went out. It had been an eventful day and that last act made all the pain and the fear seem worth it.

A knock on the front door catapulted me from bed, instantly awake, alert, fearing that Denny had found us. I stumbled into a pair of trousers and was still fumbling with the buttons as I rushed downstairs.

'Hello,' said Mrs Goodfellow, opening the door, 'can I help you?'

'Good morning,' said a soft voice that seemed strangely familiar and had an accent similar to Daphne's.

Since it was a woman, my fears were partially assuaged and I continued down at a safer pace, ensuring my trousers were properly secured.

'I'm sorry to disturb you, but I wondered if you might know something about my friend.'

'I wonder if I might,' said Mrs G.

'The thing is, that I passed her flat this morning, but there was police tape everywhere. A nice policeman said there'd been a gas explosion, but that no one had been injured and that Inspector Hobbes might help me find her. Do I have the right address?'

'You do,' said Mrs G, 'but, unfortunately, he's out.'

She was talking to a slightly plump, blonde woman with enormous blue eyes, who was wearing a long, pink coat with a pink fur collar, pink trousers and pink shoes. I instantly recognised her as Pinky of Pinky's Tearoom and, although she'd seemed very pleasant back then, I was suspicious.

'What's your friend's name?' asked Mrs Goodfellow.

'It's Duckworth ... Daphne Duckworth. Do you know where she might be?'

'Don't tell her,' I said, as I reached the front door.

'Why not, dear?'

'Because, for all we know, she might be working for Sir Gerald.'

Pinky's look of puzzled recognition, twisted into one of anger. 'I would never work for that loathsome man. What's he been doing?'

Although she sounded sincere and I was inclined to believe her, I wasn't yet prepared to take the risk.

'I'm sorry,' I said, 'but we must be careful.'

'You seem familiar. Haven't I seen you somewhere before? Weren't you in Blackcastle?'

I nodded.

'Do you know her?'

'Yes, we're friends.'

'Aren't you the so-called tourist who found Hugh's remains?' Now she was sounding suspicious.

'How do you know about that?'

'She told me. She didn't tell me you were friends though. In fact, I had the impression she didn't much like you.'

'Things have changed since then.'

'Well,' said Mrs Goodfellow, 'you'd better come in, rather than letting all the heat out. Then maybe we can help you.'

Although Pinky still looked suspicious, Mrs G's gummy smile seemed to reassure her. 'Alright.' She stepped inside.

'You'd better get dressed, dear.'

Suddenly embarrassed by my naked torso, I fled upstairs.

When I came back down, washed, shaved and dressed in the neatly pressed clothes that had been laid out for me, Pinky was on the sofa sipping a mug of tea. She looked up and smiled.

'Mrs Goodfellow explained about you and Daphne.'

'Good. I'm Andy Caplet. Andy.'

'And I'm Lillian Pinkerton. Most people call me Pinky. Nice to meet you again.'

'After what I've just been told, I can understand why you were wary, but, if you give her a call at work, you'll be able to trust me. We've been friends since she and Hugh moved into Blackcastle.'

'I don't have her number.'

'But you do have one of these.' Putting down her mug and getting to her feet, she went to the telephone table, pulled out the directory and opened it. After running her finger down the page, she picked up the phone and dialled.

'Good morning,' she said. 'Could you put me through to Mrs Duckworth, please?'

After a moment, she handed me the phone.

'Hello?' said Daphne, her voice electronically flattened, 'is anybody there?'

'Yes, it's me …'

'Andy! How are you today?'

'I'm fine, but … umm … do you know Lillian Pinkerton?'

'Pinky? Of course. She's a good friend. Why do you ask? Has something happened?'

'No, nothing's happened. It's just that she's with me now.'

'At the inspector's house? Why?'

'She came to make sure you were alright.'

'That's nice. Can you put her on?'

I handed back the phone and, leaving them to talk, headed to the kitchen in a quest for tea and breakfast, for I was still muzzy headed and would have preferred to go back to bed for an hour or so. The events of the previous night were trying to resurface from the depths of my mind, but I forced them back under. They would have to wait until I was ready.

There was fresh tea in the pot, but I was reduced to making my own breakfast, since Mrs Goodfellow was rushing out, claiming to have a dental appointment. I didn't wish to doubt her but, since all her own teeth, plus countless others, were kept in jam jars, it sounded unlikely. Still, it was none of my business, so, cutting a couple of slices of bread, grilling them until they were nicely brown, plastering them with fresh butter and marmalade, I sat down to eat. Although I regretted the lack of bacon and eggs, I could not really feel hard done by, for the old girl's marmalade was the best. It was a mystery how she did it, for I'd watched her make it and she hadn't appeared to use anything other than oranges and sugar, yet the flavours she produced just tingled the tongue and set the palette on fire.

'Daffy says Inspector Hobbes is with her,' said Pinky, standing in the kitchen doorway.

'Oh … right. He wanted to take a look at something.'

'Yes, Hugh's notes, so she said. Do you have any idea why?'

She walked over and took a seat, facing me across the table.

'It's apparently something to do with rocks,' I said, after swallowing the last crumbs.

'Rocks?'

'Yes, I think there must be something terribly important about the rocks in the Blacker Mountains.'

'I doubt it,' said Pinky, shaking her head. 'They're just rocks.'

'Umm … yeah. That seems to be what's significant about them, though I haven't a clue why. I think Hobbes was hinting that there's some sort of connection between them and why Sir Gerald wants Hugh Duckworth's notes destroyed, but it didn't make any sense to me.'

Hearing the front door open and shut, I assumed Mrs Goodfellow had forgotten something, or that Hobbes had returned.

'It might, you know,' said Pinky, looking thoughtful.

'How?'

'Well, I heard Sir Gerald has reopened the old gold mine.'

'He has,' I said. 'So what?'

'So, perhaps the rocks contain gold ore. Does gold come as an ore?'

'I don't know. I thought it came in nuggets. But Hobbes said there was nothing unusual about the samples he took from the mine. He said they were just ordinary rocks, like all the others in the Blacker Mountains, and ordinary rocks don't have gold in them.'

'In which case,' said Pinky, 'how can the Paynes have a gold mine?'

'That's a good point,' I said.

'Inspector Hobbes is the one that was on the telly? The one that chased down the gold thieves, isn't he?'

'That's right.' A thought struck me. 'You don't suppose there's a connection between the rocks and the robbery?'

Pinky shrugged. 'I don't know, but it might explain why Sir Gerald was getting so desperate. I mean, what if his gold mine was a sham?'

'You mean,' I said, 'that it could be a cover? A way of making stolen gold seem legitimate?'

'Maybe. I don't know.'

'It sounds a little far-fetched, doesn't it?'

'Does it? It could explain what's been going on. Hugh was always keen on his geology so what if he'd discovered the mine was a fake? Might that be why Sir Gerald killed him?'

'But *I* didn't kill him,' said a deep drawl from the kitchen door.

Shocked, I leapt to my feet, banging my knees on the table. I rubbed them and stared, open-mouthed, at Sir Gerald.

'Good morning, Pinky,' he said. 'I see you've put on weight. Such a shame. There was a time when you were quite … acceptable.

'And it is regrettable to find you in such low company. Do you know this fool takes his holidays in the Blacker Mountains, and pretends he's up there on his own? As if he could last five minutes!'

'How did you get in?' I asked, ignoring the insults, something I was used to.

He held up a key.

'That's mine! How did you get it?'

'That should be obvious, even to an idiot like you. Quite clearly, it was in the pocket of your coat, which Denzil fished from the lake. By the way, your antics last night were most entertaining and you were lucky Hobbes's daughter rescued you.'

I hung my head, ashamed that until then, I hadn't spared Kathy a single thought or shown any gratitude for what she'd done.

Pinky got to her feet. 'What are you doing here, Gerry?'

'I could ask you the same question, Pinky.'

'She's a guest,' I said, 'and you are not. Give me my key, please, and leave the house.'

'That's not very welcoming. Wouldn't you like to know why I'm here?'

'Why are you here?'

'I'm so glad you want to know. Please, both of you, sit down.'

Pinky sat back down, fear and loathing in her big, blue eyes. Still rubbing my bruised knees, I hobbled towards my chair.

'Take your time,' said Sir Gerald.

'Are you both sitting comfortably?' he asked, when I'd finally planted myself on the seat. 'Then I'll begin. I'm here because I wish to obtain Hugh Duckworth's notes.'

'We don't have them,' I pointed out, confused and afraid that Denny would not be far away.

'I'm aware of that. Mrs Duckworth has them and that uncouth fellow Hobbes is with her.'

'So, what do want from us?'

'I would like you to pass a message to him.'

'If I were you,' I said, 'I would leave here before you anger him. He can be dangerous and you underestimate him at your peril.'

Sir Gerald smiled. 'I don't underestimate him, or overestimate him. I know his sort. Denzil has, after all, been in my family for years and I expect Hobbes is much like him – strong in the arm, but weak in the head.'

'What do you mean his sort?'

'The Evil Ones. The Mountain Folk,' said Sir Gerald. 'Call them what you will, they're the last of a dying breed that few will miss when they finally die out for good. But, I have to say, Denzil has proved most useful.'

'Evil Ones? Mountain Folk? What are you talking about?'

'The vagrants that used to infest our mountains. Now, kindly stop your blathering. I want you to pass this message to Hobbes.'

'What?'

'Tell him his daughter will come to no harm if he does precisely what I say.'

'What have you done to her?' I said, bouncing back to my feet and taking a step towards him. At least I had the satisfaction of seeing his eyes widen in alarm. He was obviously aware of my violent tendency.

'Calm yourself,' he said, recovering his composure in an instant. 'She's fine. Nothing has happened to her, and I hope nothing will. Tell Hobbes to bring Duckworth's notes to the Squire's Arms at Northsorn at three o'clock this afternoon. Tell him to come alone and that any funny business might have a serious effect on the lady's well-being. Finally, he's not to tell anyone. I have eyes and ears all around the town and, should he try anything stupid, I'll know, and, let's say, there will be consequences.'

'But,' I said, 'what's the point? Hobbes will have read the notes. He'll have worked out what's going on. What's more,' I pointed to Pinky, 'we know.'

'What Hobbes might think he knows is of no consequence without the evidence, and you know nothing, except for wild speculation. Besides, I happen to be friends with the right sort of people, who can ensure nobody will ever believe your malicious attacks on an honourable family. Not that anyone would be likely to believe you anyway. Let's see, we have Pinky, a woman seething with resentment, and you, a failed reporter for a pathetic local rag, a complete incompetent. Oh, no, you'll not be any problem.'

'You may be right,' I said, 'but can you tell me something?'

'Try me.'

'If you didn't kill Hugh Duckworth, who did?'

'Let's just say it was his curiosity. Those mountains are dangerous and anyone who fails to take sufficient care can quickly come to grief.'

'But how did he die?'

'Painfully, but quite quickly. Now, that's enough banter. You're boring me. Tell Hobbes what I said.

'Goodbye, Pinky, darling. It's such a shame to see what time and spite have done to you. I'll let myself out. Nice to have made your acquaintance again, Mr Caplet.'

Tossing me the key, he turned and walked away. The front door opened and shut.

'Are you alright?' I asked.

Pinky was trembling and deathly white. She nodded. 'It's just that I hate him so much.'

'Any particular reason?'

'There are many reasons. Too many. You'd better get that message to the inspector quickly and I hope his daughter's alright. I don't trust Gerry and, if he's here, Denny Barker won't be far away and he really is dangerous.'

'He was hanging around yesterday,' I said, and couldn't stop myself adding: 'We had a couple of encounters and I knocked him down.'

'You did? How?' asked Pinky, sounding a little sceptical.

'Umm … I jumped out of a window onto his head when he was trying to kidnap Daphne and then I knocked him down again.' I showed her my knuckles, which were still raw, though the swelling and soreness had subsided.

Although she nodded and looked impressed, it seemed she didn't quite believe me. I suspected her doubts were nothing compared to mine about my well-being should I ever encounter Denny again and yet, at that moment, my fears for my safety were nothing like my worries for Kathy.

'When you see Hobbes,' said Pinky, 'you'd better warn him that Sir Gerald is a devious man and it sounds to me as if he's setting a trap.'

'Does it? You might be right, but he'll know what to do. I hope. I'll get my coat …
oh, no, it's still in the lake … I'll go and find him. He's probably still at the museum.'

'Or you could use the phone,' she said.

'Oh yes. I never think of that.'

We hurried through to the sitting room. I called the museum and, within five
minutes, Hobbes, accompanied by a very excited Dregs, burst through the front door. I
introduced them both to Pinky, whose evident nervousness at the sight of them was not
helped by the ravages of Dregs's tongue, despite my best efforts to keep her dry, or by
the heavy, blood-stained, brown paper bag in Hobbes's hand. His feral scent was far
stronger than usual and he was twitching, with a wild expression in his dark eyes.

'Welcome to Sorenchester, Miss Pinkerton,' he said and turned to me. 'Spread some
papers in the corner and get her out of here … and quickly. I have a bone to pick.'

Knowing what was coming, I threw a few copies of the *Bugle* onto the carpet, went
to grab my coat, remembered where it was, and bundled a bewildered Pinky into the
street.

'What's happening?' she asked.

'You don't want to know.'

'I do.'

'Umm … it's quite warm today, isn't it? I mean compared to yesterday.'

'Don't try to change the subject. What's wrong with him?'

I was unsure how to respond, for I knew that Hobbes, having bought himself a
large, raw marrowbone, had undoubtedly already pounced on it, like a leopard onto a
tender young antelope, and was crunching it up in his great jaws. Having witnessed the
whole process, I found it disgusting and terrifying and made sure to keep out of the
way whenever the fit came over him.

'Sorry,' I said at last. 'The thing is, he has his own way of working off stress and it's
best to avoid him until it's all over. We should give him half an hour.'

She frowned. 'He's going to crunch up a bone, isn't he?'

'Eh?' I said, confused. 'How would you know?'

'He's one of the Mountain Folk, like Denny Barker, isn't he? I've been there when
Gerry threw Denny a bone to entertain his guests.'

'I think I know where you're coming from,' I said, 'because that's what he'll be
doing, but Hobbes is one of the good guys. I thought he was unique, until recently.'

'But he looks like Denny and no one else I know eats raw bones. There's something
about them, something weird, something dangerous.'

I nodded. 'Hobbes is certainly weird and he might be dangerous sometimes, but
he's the best I know. Do you really think he's like Denny?'

'Absolutely.'

'Wow.' I paused, letting the thought sink in. 'Look, do you want to get a coffee or
something while we wait?'

'No, I've just had a cup of tea,' said Pinky. 'We could go and see Daphne.'

'She's at work,' I said. 'It's a new job and she hasn't really had a very good start. I
think we should give her some peace.'

Instead, we strolled around town for the next half hour or so and I told her
everything that had happened to Daphne recently. To my regret, Pinky was far more
interested in my accident with the baked bean tin and my near disaster in the lake than

with my heroic battles with Denny. She told me a little about herself, claiming she was thirty, though I'd have guessed she was a good few years older than that, that she'd lived in Blackcastle all her life and that she was divorced.

We glimpsed Featherlight riding a bicycle that was far too small for him at the far end of Vermin Street.

'There's another of them!' she said, pointing. 'Until I came here, I really thought Denny was the last of them and now I find two others within a matter of minutes!'

'But, what are they?' I asked.

'The Mountain Folk?'

'Yes.'

We carried on walking and had turned down the Shambles when, stopping to look at a hat shop's window display, she took a deep breath. 'I don't know really. For a long time, I thought they were just a legend … a story to frighten the kids and I really don't know much.'

'You know more than I do.'

'OK, this is what I remember, though I'm not sure how much is true anymore, because most of what I know came from my granddad, who used to work for Sir Digby, Gerry's grandfather. Sometimes, when he'd knocked back a few beers, he'd tell me tales of the Mountain Folk.

'They used to turn up from time to time, though there were never that many of them and they mostly kept themselves to themselves, except at the end of summer when they'd find work with the farmers, taking in the harvest, or in the spring, when they'd help with the shearing. They were hard workers, good with animals and skilled with their hands. Granddad reckoned they built all the drystone walls in the area.'

'They must have been very useful,' I said.

'I suppose they were, but people were suspicious of them. They used to camp under Blacker Knob, which had an evil reputation.'

'People are often suspicious of anything different.' I said. 'I was suspicious of Hobbes once and, even now I'd call him a friend, he can sometimes terrify me, although he's got me out of sticky situations so many times.'

Pinky nodded, a lock of blonde hair falling over her eye. Brushing it aside, she fixed her gaze on a livid pink pixie hat. 'People began to say that they stole things, that they spoiled food, soured milk and swapped their offspring for human babies. What was more, they never attended church and it was rumoured that they were fiends, in league with the Devil. That's why some called them the Evil Ones.'

'Hobbes sometimes goes to church,' I said, feeling weirdly that I should be protecting him and his kind. 'He always goes on Remembrance Sunday. He was in the Great War and won a Victoria Cross.'

I feared I'd said too much, but she didn't appear surprised.

'That just convinces me he's one of them, because Granddad said they lived much longer than other men. When he was young, he sometimes used to work with Denny Barker and he reckoned Denny was the last of them.'

'What happened to the others?'

She shook her head. 'I really don't know. Granddad would always change the subject when I asked. All he'd say was that they'd gone away. It was my impression that something bad had happened and I tried to get some answers from the other old boys.

They would never say much, but one suggested I might find something in the Parish records.'

'Did you?'

'I tried, but it turned out that they'd been burned when the old town hall caught fire.'

'When was that?'

'During the Second World War.'

'Was it bombed?'

She laughed. 'No, I don't think Blackcastle was ever of any strategic importance … or of any sort of importance at all. According to the *Blacker Times* archive from 1941, the cause of the fire was a mystery. It was put down to faulty wiring, though there was some suspicion of arson. That's really all I know about the Mountain Folk. It's not much.'

'Maybe not, but it's interesting. I've often tried to work out what Hobbes is exactly. I can't tell you how much of a shock it was when I first realised he wasn't strictly human. I wonder if he knows anything about them?'

'Ask him.'

'That wouldn't work,' I said, shaking my head. 'He doesn't normally like to talk about the past … his past anyway … and I wouldn't even have found out that he'd won the Victoria Cross if I hadn't been a bit nosy. On the other hand, Mrs Goodfellow likes to talk about him. He adopted her you know?'

Pinky turned from the window to face me. 'Although that seems so wrong, because she looks so much older than him, I can believe it.

'Do you think he's finished his bone yet?'

A glance up Vermin Street to the church clock tower showed the time was approaching midday. 'Probably. Let's go.'

When we got back, Mrs Goodfellow was tidying up the newspapers while Hobbes was upstairs, roaring and singing in the shower. Dregs was barking in the back garden.

'Hello, dear,' said Mrs Goodfellow as we walked in. 'Would your friend like to stay for dinner?'

'Umm … I don't know. I hadn't thought. Umm …Would you?'

'Thank you,' said Pinky, 'but I can't. I have an appointment with my bank at one.'

'Isn't that a bit inconvenient?' I said. 'Why here?'

'I'm thinking of moving here and opening a new café. The thing is, there's not much trade in Blackcastle and Gerry has put the rent up again. I have no intention of filling that bastard's coffers any more.'

'But why here?'

'Because I have a friend here.' She glanced at her watch. 'I'd best be on my way. I'm not quite sure where to go.'

'Which bank?'

'Grossman's. I figured that, since they'd had two robberies, they'd probably tightened up security.'

'We passed it earlier. It's halfway down The Shambles, not far from the hat shop.'

'Thank you,' she said and took her leave.

A few minutes later Hobbes reappeared, looking clean, relatively civilized, and tidy. He was chuckling and grinning.

'What's up?' I asked.

'I have my car back. It was abandoned on Green Way.'

'Good. What are you going to do about Kathy? Shouldn't you be doing something now?'

'All in good time. Firstly though, I'm going to do the crossword and the Sudoku and then it'll be lunchtime. The Butcher of Barnley delivered some of his best pork and leek sausages last night and the lass is making toad in the hole.'

'Last night? Doesn't he always deliver punctually in the afternoons?'

'Normally, but he was delayed.'

'Really? Why?'

'He slipped and sat on the mincer. It meant he got a little behind in his sausage making.'

'Sounds painful.'

'Probably.' He chuckled again.

'Are you joking?'

He winked. 'The point is, I like a good toad in the hole, his sausages are excellent and the lass makes a great batter.' He patted his stomach. 'I'll need a good dinner to set me up for this afternoon.'

'You've still got room after that bone?'

'Of course. Picking a bone just piques my appetite. I'm surprised more people don't try it.'

I couldn't stop myself shuddering, being a little squeamish when it came to raw meat. This, I suspected, dated back to the time when I was a small boy, and Mother had attempted to quick roast a joint of beef she'd only just removed from the freezer. The result had been a crumbling outer layer of charcoal, with cold, bloody meat inside and a core that was still solid. It hadn't stopped her serving it and the sight of bright red mashed potato and the taste of iced blood had made me vomit on the table. I reassured myself, because, with Mrs Goodfellow in charge, there would be no similar problems. My only slight worry was that Hobbes, in his weirdly euphoric mood, might slip a real toad onto my plate.

Sitting down on the sofa, he reached for the *Bugle* and a pen and started scratching at the crossword. I couldn't believe how relaxed he was. My nerves were jangling and I just wanted to rush out and rescue Kathy, though I didn't understand how Sir Gerald had got his hands on her.

'What are you going to do?' I asked, sitting down beside him. 'And can I help?'

'I intend,' he said, 'to visit the Squire's Arms at the appropriate time and pick her up. I don't want you there, because Sir Gerald requested me to go alone. Hmm … it's tricky.'

'It could be a trap.'

'I think it's probably apatosaurus.'

'What?' I said.

'Five across: a large plant-eating dinosaur of the Jurassic period … apatosaurus.' He filled in the squares and frowned.

'Oh, I see. But you ought to take precautions this afternoon.'

He glanced up. 'Ought I? Why?'

'Well, it might be dangerous.'

'I do hope so. Stilton. So, that means two down must be titular.'

Getting up, I left him to his puzzle and paced about the house until Mrs Goodfellow called us through. The toad in the hole was so magnificent, the batter so light and fluffy, the sausages so robust and satisfying, the gravy so aromatic and delicious that it took my mind off poor Kathy and what Sir Gerald and Denny might have in store for Hobbes. But afterwards, a mug of tea in my hand, my nerves returned, for it was my opinion that he was being far too complacent. I decided that, whatever he thought, I would be close at hand. My idea was to stow away in the car boot.

When he went upstairs to put on his boots, I took my opportunity. I rummaged in his coat pocket for the keys, sneaked outside, opened the car boot, rushed back inside and returned the keys.

'I'm just going out for a walk,' I said casually, as he came downstairs. 'I hope Kathy's alright.'

'Thank you,' he said. 'I'll see you later.'

Hurrying into the street, I climbed into the boot and pulled down the lid, making sure it didn't quite click. It was smelly in there, as if the previous owner had used it for transporting manure and, as it was also uncomfortably cramped, it didn't take much time before I felt I'd already been there too long. I was just beginning to wonder whether I was making a huge mistake when I heard a car pull up nearby.

'Wotcha,' said Billy.

'Afternoon,' said Hobbes. 'Thanks for coming.'

Dregs was sniffing and scrabbling at the boot. It suddenly clicked shut.

'Let's go,' said Hobbes, his voice muffled. 'And quickly.'

Billy's car drove away down Blackdog Street, leaving me a prisoner.

Although I'd have been the first to admit to having made some rotten plans in my time, this one was turning out to be a real stinker. Hobbes was gone and I feared he was walking blindly into a trap, and I was going to be as helpful to him as whatever it was that was sticking into my back. There was some comfort in knowing that Billy was taking him and that Dregs would also be there, although, after what he'd done to Denny, his presence might only make matters worse. I hoped Billy would keep out the way. He was far too small to be of any use.

Unable to see anything, other than a fringe of faint light around the top of the boot, I groped around as much as I could, which wasn't much, since I was pinned down. Even so, my hands explored wherever they could reach, hoping to chance on some sort of release mechanism and, despite starting with hope, I was soon entering the realms of despair, especially when my shoulders began to cramp.

Forcing myself to relax, taking long, deep breaths, I tried to think. My first thought was that I was well stuck. The second was that I was stuck in an embarrassing situation. The third was that this was not the time to think useless thoughts. Somehow, I had to find a way to get out and, furthermore, I had to do this sooner rather than later, for it was already getting stuffy in there and I was starting to worry about how well sealed it was and how much oxygen might be left. I tried to imagine what Hobbes would do and came to the simple conclusion that he would not have put himself into such a stupid situation in the first place.

Although everything, other than my own breathing, was muffled, I could still make out sounds from the street, which I assumed meant that passers-by would hear me, should I make sufficient noise. Even so, I had to overcome the massive embarrassment of having to beg for help and of having to explain how I'd got there and I couldn't bring myself to do it for several minutes. Besides, I was in something of a quandary, for screaming would use up my oxygen faster, whereas keeping quiet might just mean I'd die more slowly. In the end I realised I had no choice. I lay as still as a corpse, trying not to breathe more than necessary, until I heard footsteps approaching.

'Help,' I bellowed, banging on the boot lid, 'I'm stuck!'

The only response was heartless laughter and a most unfeeling remark. As the footsteps receded, I ground my teeth and tried to relax.

More footsteps approached and this time, my pleas received no response whatsoever. More footsteps: again nothing. As panic closed in, throwing caution to the winds, I yelled and banged, sweated and gasped.

A crunch and screeching of tortured metal hurt my ears. Then I was blinking in bright sunlight with something dark looming overhead. A vision in pink came into view as my eyes adjusted. Pinky was staring down, looking puzzled.

'What on earth are you doing in there?' she asked.

'Good question,' said a familiar voice.

'Sid?'

'At your service,' said the old vampire who, dressed in a long black cloak and a Homburg hat, was twiddling a crowbar in his fingers.

'Would you mind helping me out? My legs won't move.'

Passing his crowbar to Pinky, he reached in, his surprisingly strong hands grabbed me around the waist, lifted me and sat me on the steps.

'Thank you,' I said. 'I was stuck.'

'Obviously,' said Pinky, 'but why?'

'I was trying to help Hobbes.'

'In a car boot?' Her tone suggested she considered me beyond all hope.

As the feeling returned to my legs as pain, I groaned and stretched. 'I didn't mean to get locked in. He was going alone and I thought he might need some help. I tried to hide in there, but the lid closed and, then he went off in Billy's car.'

'Billy Shawcroft?' asked Sid.

'Yes. Do you know him?'

'Everyone knows Billy. He's a good man in a crisis.'

'But what can he do? He's so small.'

'There's more to him than you'd think,' said Sid. 'He's a man of no small talent and ability.'

'I suppose he is. Umm … I thought your sort didn't go out in daylight.'

'Bankers don't normally,' said Sid, 'because they're at work.'

'Oh. I thought you couldn't stand sunlight?'

'It's alright. Too much gives me wrinkles.'

'What's the matter?' asked Pinky, again looking puzzled. 'You're talking as if Mr Sharples were a vampire.'

'Only joking,' I said, 'but what brings you two here?'

'Miss Pinkerton mentioned that Wilber's daughter was in trouble, so I thought I'd offer my services. Alas, it would seem I am too late.'

'I wish we could go after him,' I said, 'because I'm sure he's walking into a trap. It's all Kathy's fault for getting herself kidnapped.'

'Don't blame her,' said Sid. 'She's in danger and he's going because he has no choice. He must help her. That's what he does.'

'I'm sorry. I wasn't really meaning to blame her, but I'm worried. About both of them.'

'Of course you are,' he said, glancing at his watch. 'Look, it's still only quarter to three and we'll probably just about get there in time if we use the Batmobile.'

'The what?' asked Pinky, looking thoroughly bewildered.

'My car,' said Sid. 'That's what Billy calls it on account of it being black and looking like it should have wings.'

'Great!' I said. 'Umm … where is it?'

'In the Batcave. Before you ask, that's my garage. Follow me.'

He led us along Blackdog Street and into Pound Street at a steady jog. I wondered where we were heading, for there'd been no room for a garage near his house. The mystery was solved when, having crossed the road, he opened an iron gate in the old stone wall and led us into a courtyard surrounded by eleven garages, their doors painted in all colours. The one he approached was the black one, bafflingly numbered 39. He opened it, tugged at a tarpaulin and uncovered a huge, black, gleaming, very old-fashioned, very American car.

'That's lovely,' gasped Pinky, applying a lace handkerchief to her face, which now matched her clothes. 'What is it?'

'That, young lady, is a 1958 Cadillac, Series 62, Extended Deck Sedan. A true classic.'

'Is it? Good, but does it go?'

'Does it go?' asked Sid, chuckling and then looking worried. 'I hope so. I haven't actually used it for some time.'

He squeezed into the driver's seat and a moment later the engine roared. He opened the window as he drove out: 'That's a 365 cubic inch V8 engine, packing 310 horsepower. A marvellous machine. Hop in, there's plenty of room for all of us in the front.'

Exchanging amused, if slightly puzzled glances, Pinky and I got in, sliding along the bench type seat, with me in the middle. It soon became apparent that, despite its mighty-sounding engine, it was a sedate car, comfortable, but totally lacking in zip. It felt slow: frustratingly slow.

'What time is it now?' I asked as we reached the outskirts of Sorenchester.

'Ten to three,' said Pinky. Her watch, I wasn't surprised to see, was pink. 'How long will it take us to get there?'

'About ten minutes,' said Sid.

'Can't we go any faster?'

He shook his head. 'She was designed for long, straight American highways, not these twisting Cotswold roads.'

Clutching my hands into fists, forcing myself to sit still, I fought against a repeated urge to ask whether we were nearly there yet, a question that had once so exasperated my father that he'd turned the car around and headed straight back home, instead of to the caravan in Wales he'd rented for a week. The disappointment of that day, of that lost week, still resonated, despite the fact that we had stayed there before. The caravan had been cramped, freezing at night, roasting during the day, mildewed and at the very bottom of a marshy field. It had no facilities, other than a tap at the farmhouse, a good ten-minute trudge away, and an old spade for digging holes when nature called, yet I'd loved it because of the mountains rising imperiously behind, the restless sea over the dunes, the little trout stream, and the space and the freedom. Thinking about it helped slacken off my taut nerves.

Even so, it seemed an age before, rounding a sharp bend, we came in sight of the Squire's Arms and the River Soren. There was no sign of Billy's hearse, or of any movement, except for the languid munching of a herd of black and white cows in a meadow on the other side of the road, below an ancient and ridiculously massive church. Sid, slowing to thirty in accordance with the speed signs, was immediately overtaken by a dark-blue van. Ignoring it, he signalled and turned right over the bridge into a lane leading towards Northsorn, with the Squire's Arms on our right. Its car park was empty, and there was a large, handwritten sign saying: 'Sorry, closed due to bereavement'. I presumed, and hoped, it was just to deter visitors.

'Is it three o'clock yet?' I asked.

'Two minutes to,' said Pinky.

'I don't like it.' I said. 'It's too quiet.'

Sid parked by a hedge and we got out into a cool breeze, though the sun was bright.

'Well,' said Pinky, looking around, 'what are we going to do now?'

'Umm … I don't really know.'

'I think,' said Sid, 'we should stay out of sight.'

'I agree,' I said, 'but then what?'

'How about,' said Pinky, 'finding a place where we're hidden, but from where we can see what's going on? Then we might be able to do something, if there's any trouble.'

Sid pointed downhill. 'There's a footpath running behind the pub. We'll try that, but keep your voices down … and stay alert. This might be dangerous.'

Having no better suggestion, I went with them, feeling horribly conspicuous until, as we reached the path, there were hedges and bushes to hide behind. The path was sticky with mud, with a collage of human and canine footprints indicating what it was mostly used for. As we tiptoed past a hawthorn tree, glowing bright with red berries, we could see a gate leading towards the back of the Squire's Arms, where the footprints suggested many dog walkers sneaked in for a crafty pint. From there, we could also see one side of the pub, part of the front and most of the car park. As we looked around, wondering if it was the best place, a sudden, stealthy movement ahead made us duck back under the hawthorn's shade.

A diminutive figure in black from boots to hood, slipping through the gate into the pub's backyard, concealed himself behind a stack of gleaming kegs, his arms outstretched.

'That's Billy,' Sid whispered. 'What's he up to?'

'Hiding,' I murmured.

'Shh!' Pinky cautioned. 'Someone's coming.'

It was Hobbes, walking a little stiffly, I thought, through the front entrance of the car park, sporting a new gabardine raincoat and, unusually, with a trilby pulled low over his eyes. He approached the front of the Squire's Arms, stopped, folded his arms across his chest, and said: 'I am here.'

His voice was so hoarse and tense I wouldn't have recognised it had he not been standing there.

'Very punctual,' said Sir Gerald, sauntering through the open doorway. 'I knew you would be. Your kind has never exhibited any originality.'

'Where's Kathy?' asked Hobbes, barely loud enough for us to hear.

'She's currently enjoying a glass of lager with my son. She apparently prefers it to English ale, which is her loss. Did you know this pub gets an honourable mention in the Good Beer Guide?'

'I'd like to see her,' said Hobbes.

'Of course you would, but first I want Duckworth's notes.'

'How do I know she's alright? I want to see her.'

'This,' said Sir Gerald, 'is my game and we will play it by my rules. You'll see her as soon as I have the notes.'

'How do I know I can trust you?'

'You have my word.'

'That's good enough for me,' said Hobbes.

'It will have to be,' said Sir Gerald.

Reaching into his coat pocket, Hobbes brought out a notebook and held it up.

'And the rest of them,' said Sir Gerald.

He produced three more battered notebooks.

'Good,' said Sir Gerald. 'You can't imagine the trouble I've had getting hold of them.'

'But why do you want them? They're only books, full of scribbles. They looked worthless to me.'

'Because you're a fool! If any geologist saw them, my little game would be up for good.'

'This is not a game,' said Hobbes.

'It's the game of life. There are winners and losers. I am one of the winners. You and your kind are the losers.'

'Games have rules.'

'Oh, rules!' said Sir Gerald with a sneer. 'A man of vision knows when to use them and when to break them.'

'I want to see Kathy.'

'Give me the books.'

'Not till I see her.'

'Very well. If you swear there'll be a fair handover, I'll let you see her.'

'I swear.'

'Good. Put the notebooks down and step away from them.'

Hobbes did as he was told.

'Very well,' said Sir Gerald, looking over his shoulder. 'Denzil, would you care to escort the young lady out here?'

Denny appeared, gripping Kathy by the shoulders. She tried to break away, but his hold was firm.

'Get your paws off me,' she said, squirming.

Suddenly, with a grimace and a cry of pain, she stopped struggling.

'Calm down, please' said Sir Gerald. 'I'd appreciate your cooperation for just a little longer and then you can go home with your father and we'll all be happy.'

Pinky couldn't help snorting. Sid put a finger to her lips.

'Do you expect to get away with this?' asked Hobbes.

'Yes, I do,' said Sir Gerald, smiling.

'Your scheme might have worked for your ancestors, but times have changed.'

'No, they haven't. Not really. You'll still find that a little money, judiciously applied, will sway things the right way, especially when there's a modicum of threat to back it up.

'And now, Inspector, to prevent any unfortunate misunderstandings, I must ask you to move back and to lie face down on the ground with your arms stretched out in front where I can see them.'

Hobbes did as he was told.

'Don't move a muscle,' said Sir Gerald. 'I have you covered.'

As he swaggered towards the notebooks, which were fluttering on the tarmac like autumn leaves, Rupert stepped from behind a bush, aiming a double-barrelled shotgun at Hobbes, who appeared to be entirely unaware of the danger.

'Look out!' I yelled, 'he's got a gun!'

Ignoring Sid's horrified expression, I ran towards the car park gate. I had no plan, just a desperate urge to do something.

Sir Gerald, glancing over his shoulder, saw me and turned back. 'I said, "Come alone". If you had, no one would have been hurt.' He shook his head and glanced at Rupert and then at Denny. 'Kill them!'

As Rupert stepped towards Hobbes, the shotgun aimed at his back, a powerful engine roared and a dark-blue van, the one that had overtaken us earlier, hurtled along the footpath directly at Sid and Pinky, giving them no chance of escape. I stood aghast, horrified by what I'd done, hearing her scream, seeing her flying backwards, her arms and legs flailing wildly. I stood there, helpless, appalled, paralysed and unable to flee as two burly men, armed with axes, leapt from the van. One of them charged towards me. Over by the pub, Kathy cried out.

Although my brain was frozen, some deep-seated survival instinct threw me to the ground, just avoiding an axe blow that would have split my skull. Kicking out wildly, I caught the man behind the knee, knocking him down, and jumped back to my feet.

Denny was holding Kathy above his head as if he meant to smash her into the ground. For a moment, he hesitated and frowned.

'Do it,' cried Sir Gerald. 'Now!'

Denny nodded. Shifting his grip, he hurled her at the ground, but, as he did, a vast figure, appearing as if from nowhere, moving with feline grace at cheetah speed, dived full length and caught her.

The axeman came at me again and, as the gleaming blade scythed towards my side, I lurched forward, avoiding the sharp edge and receiving a mighty smack in the ribs from the shaft that knocked me headlong into a bush. I sprawled, winded, bruised and groaning, but, despite the pain, I was back on my feet before the axeman regained his balance.

A shot made us both jump and look towards the car park. Rupert had fired into the body of Hobbes, who was lying motionless on the tarmac. I was still frozen in horror when my assailant, with a cruel grin, raised his weapon and this time I seemed to have no chance of surviving, until a high-pitched howl rang out. It distracted him just long enough to allow me to duck out of harm's way, but, tripping over my own feet, I fell and was utterly at his mercy, something I doubted he possessed in any quantity. As I cringed and expected pain, a small, solid, black figure leapt up with a fierce cry and nutted the axeman right between the eyes. He went over backwards like a felled tree and the small, solid, black figure pulled back his hood.

'Wotcha, Andy,' said Billy, rubbing a graze on his forehead and grimacing. 'I reckon that got him a good one. I just wish he didn't have such a thick skull.'

'Thank you,' I said, getting to my feet.

'Are you alright?'

I nodded, though I wasn't really, feeling bruised and shocked and appalled at what had happened to Hobbes, who was sprawled on the tarmac, with Rupert, white-faced, standing over him, staring at the shotgun. I ran towards the gate into the car park and stopped, open-mouthed, doubting my sanity. Another Hobbes, this one hatless, was in the process of kicking the legs from under Denny, who collapsed like a dynamited factory chimney. Kathy, sitting on a bench, was staring, her eyes as wide as my mouth.

I heard the second axeman scream and looked back to see him throw his weapon aside and run, his face cauliflower white, his eyes bulging like a rabbit's.

As I turned back, Sir Gerald pulled a pistol from his pocket.

'He's got a gun, too!' I shouted.

'Oh do shut up!' he said, pointing it at me and pulling the trigger.

A shot cracked, as I was flinging myself to the ground behind the beer kegs. Billy dived in beside me. Another shot showered us with brick dust and I looked up to see a crater in the wall above.

'This is a bit of a mess,' I said between shocked gasps.

'We had a plan,' said Billy, 'and it was all going smoothly until you mucked it up. You weren't supposed to be here.'

'Sorry,' I said, getting to my knees and peering out.

The other Hobbes was talking to Kathy, who was staring at him and nodding, while Denny lay groaning on the floor. Rupert, apparently in shock, had dropped the shotgun and looked like he was crying.

'There are two Hobbeses. I don't understand,' I said.

'I'll tell you later,' said Billy. 'Just keep your head down before you get it shot off.'

Although it was undoubtedly good advice, I felt a compulsion to keep watching.

'Leave the girl alone,' said Sir Gerald.

Hobbes turned to face him.

'I told you to come alone,' said Sir Gerald. 'If you had, and you'd done what I asked, I'd have spared her.'

'I very much doubt it, sir. You couldn't afford to have her as a witness.'

'Maybe I could,' said Sir Gerald with a shrug. 'I'm not a monster. Unfortunately, you've forced my hand and, alas, you will all have to die.'

'What would be the point?' said Hobbes, his voice calm and soothing. 'It's all over now. Too many people have seen what's happened. Why don't you just put the gun down, sir?'

'Do you really imagine,' said Sir Gerald with a harsh laugh, 'that I'm going to give up just like that? I might be in a tight corner, but I'm still in the game.'

'Please, give me the gun,' said Hobbes, taking a step forward, holding out his hand. 'You can't possibly get away with it.'

Sir Gerald raised the gun.

Still Hobbes advanced, his voice quiet and calm: 'Don't be a fool, sir. Put the gun down. Put it down!'

'I'll put you down,' said Sir Gerald.

'I wouldn't do that, Gerry,' said Pinky marching forward, muddied but unbowed, aiming Rupert's shotgun at Sir Gerald.

He turned towards her, his face shocked.

'Today,' said Pinky, her soft, pretty face frozen as hard as ice, 'I get my revenge.'

She pulled the trigger. The retort echoing off the walls made me clutch my ears and duck. Ears ringing, I looked up, puzzled to see Sir Gerald still standing, and apparently unharmed. Frowning, she squeezed the trigger again but she was out of ammo.

'Did you miss me, Pinky?' said Sir Gerald, trying to look composed, though his voice quivered. 'I suppose, when it came down to it, you couldn't bring yourself to do it. You always were weak.'

He raised his pistol.

'Stop!' cried Hobbes.

But before he could intervene, Denny, back on his feet, fury in his eyes, massive fists bunched, clobbered him in the side of the head, making him cartwheel to the ground.

Sir Gerald, with a nasty grin, took aim at the defenceless Pinky, his finger tightening on the trigger. Before he could shoot, there was a blur of movement and Pinky was suddenly lying flat on the tarmac, beneath Sid. His face distorted by rage, Sir Gerald started to adjust his aim, only to find Sid was already back on his feet, diving forward, his arms stretching out his cloak into the semblance of wings. Sid engulfed him and the pistol dropped harmlessly to the ground.

Hobbes, already back up, blood smeared across his face, deflected a bone-breaking clout from Denny with his forearm, ducked beneath the follow up, a wild scything haymaker, and punched him once in the solar plexus. Denny, deflating like a punctured football, crumpled into a foetal position at Hobbes's feet. It was, I thought, the only time I'd ever actually seen Hobbes hit anyone.

'That's enough, Sid,' said Hobbes, glancing over his shoulder. 'You can put him down.'

Sid, though shorter than Sir Gerald by a head, was holding Sir Gerald off the ground by the lapels of his jacket. Yet there was still fight in the man and, as soon as Sid released him, he made a dive for the pistol. Sid, shaking his head, stepped forward and stamped on his hand as it closed around the butt. Sir Gerald screamed and curled into a ball, cradling his mangled fingers as Hobbes ran across, grabbed the pistol and ejected the magazine.

'Have you quite finished yet?' asked the prostrate figure of the first Hobbes, ''cause I want to take this corset off. It's chafing my nipples something rotten.'

'Yes, you can get up now,' said Hobbes, 'and many thanks for your assistance.'

The first Hobbes, the one I'd thought had been shot, got to his knees, removing his hat and revealing himself as Featherlight.

'Give me a hand up,' he said to a bewildered, red-eyed Rupert, 'or I'll tear your bloody head off for shooting me.'

'I'm sorry, sir,' said Rupert extending a shaking hand. 'I didn't mean to. It just went off.'

'Well, no harm done,' said Featherlight, getting to his feet and taking off his coat, beneath which, in place of his habitual grubby vest, he was sporting an extremely tight and uncomfortable-looking whalebone corset. 'Now, you can unlace me. This bloody thing is squeezing my bits into something awful.'

'But I don't understand,' said Rupert. 'I was pointing right in the middle of your back. You should be dead.'

'You'd better thank Billy that I'm not and that you're not on a murder charge,' said Featherlight. 'Now, let me loose, or I really will tear your head off.'

Pinky and Kathy, neither of them apparently hurt, but both looking shocked and confused, stood up. Hobbes gave Kathy a quick hug, before attending to Denny who was groaning where he lay, clutching his stomach and vomiting.

'You're a big man,' said Hobbes, 'but you're in bad shape. For me it's a full time job. Now behave yourself.'

Denny nodded feebly and threw up again.

Hobbes grinned at me. 'I've always wanted to say that. Now is everyone alright?'

'No,' said Pinky, 'I'm all covered in mud!' She pointed an accusing finger at Sid. 'He threw me into a ditch!' She grinned. 'Thank you. You saved my life.'

It turned out that the only ones with any serious hurts were Sir Gerald, whose fingers were sticking out in emetic directions, and Denny, whose capacious stomach was still emptying itself. Hobbes's face, a bloody split beneath his eye, was already starting to bruise. It looked like it would be a good one.

'Well, that's a good result,' he said. 'I suppose I'd better let the superintendent know what's happened and I should call an ambulance for Sir Gerald.' He reached into his pocket for his mobile.

I sidled up to Sid. 'What did you do to that bloke with the axe? He looked absolutely terrified.'

'Nothing much. All I did was look at him.'

'That doesn't sound too bad.'

'It can be, if I do this!'

I wish he hadn't. I had nightmares for weeks.

Hobbes rested his feet on the still recumbent Denny and talked to Kathy, holding her hand, while Sid, Pinky and Featherlight disappeared into the pub, leaving Billy and me to keep our eyes on Sir Gerald and Rupert.

'How is it,' I asked, 'that Featherlight and Sir Gerald weren't killed when they were shot? No one can miss at that range: not with a shotgun.'

'There is,' said Billy, 'a perfectly simple explanation.'

'What is it?'

'I'd tampered with the cartridges.'

'Why?'

'Hobbesie had it all planned. One of my jobs was to take care of any firearms. I sneaked into the pub, found the shotgun and removed all the shot and most of the powder from the cartridges.' He showed me a handful of small, grey balls from his pocket.

'That was well done,' I said.

'It would have been,' he continued, 'if I'd realised Sir Gerald had a Walther PPK.'

'A what?'

'His pistol was a Walther PPK, the sort James Bond uses.'

'Really? It was lucky he missed,' I said, pointing towards the bullet crater in the wall.

'Yes,' said Billy, 'that was close, but not as close as the other one.'

He pointed up at my armpit. Just below it, passing right through my jacket and shirt, was a small, neat hole and, although it hadn't touched me, my legs turned to jelly.

'You got lucky,' said Billy, guiding me to a seat, 'but you really shouldn't have been involved. We had the situation under control. Featherlight was the distraction, Hobbes was to take down the villains, and I was to do the guns and the video.'

'I thought I was helping,' I said, ashamed.

'By barging in and putting civilians in the firing line? It's a good job one of them was Mr Sharples or that pink lady would have been killed. Do you have any idea why she tried to shoot Sir Gerald?'

'I don't know,' I said, 'but I don't think she likes him.'

'That explanation had, of course, never occurred to me. Are you feeling any better?'

I nodded and turned to see Hobbes approaching, a handkerchief in his hand, wiping a trickle of blood from his face.

'Andy,' he said, 'your intervention was not at all helpful. You should have stayed in the car boot, safely out of harm's way.'

'I'm sorry. I just saw the gun and panicked ... You knew I was in the boot?'

He nodded. 'Oh well, no major harm was done.' He glanced at Billy. 'Did you get it all?'

'Nearly all. I did miss a few moments when I was looking after Andy, and when Sir

Gerald started shooting at us. Still, we should have recorded something on Trilbycam.'

'What,' I asked, 'is Trilbycam?'

'The camera in Featherlight's hat to record the events automatically.'

'That's clever,' I said, 'but … umm … tell me, why your arms were outstretched?'

'To ensure a good stereo recording. I've got a mike up each sleeve,'

'So, you're carrying a tape recorder?'

'What century are you living in?' said Billy, shaking his head. 'Everything's digital these days.'

'So, you really did have it all planned,' I said, crestfallen.

It didn't take long for a police car and an ambulance to arrive. Hobbes, the side of his face swelling impressively, went across and explained the situation, pointing out Sir Gerald, who was sitting cross-legged on the tarmac, clutching his fingers and whimpering like a baby, Rupert, who was pale, sweating and incoherent, and, lying stretched out on the bench, the axeman Billy had nutted. The axeman was still out for the count and was, I suspected, going to wake up with a mighty headache. While the casualties were being loaded and driven away, Hobbes perched a dazed-looking Denny on a keg and gave him a stern talking to, a talking to incorporating far more than the standard quantity of finger wagging. By the end, had there been a world record for head hanging and looking contrite, then Denny would have won it by a mile.

'Excellent,' said Hobbes, looking pleased. 'Now it's time to break up our little gathering. I suppose I really should do some paperwork and afterwards I'll go and retrieve the gold.'

'You know where it is?' I said.

'Indeed I do. It's hidden, but I know exactly where.'

'How?'

'Mr Barker is proving very cooperative.'

'Can I come with you? I've always wanted to find treasure.'

'We'll see. Maybe, if you behave yourself and do as you're told. It will require something of a journey. Now Billy, let's get back to Sorenchester … and quickly.'

He walked away, depositing Denny in the police car and collecting Featherlight and Kathy.

'Where's your car?' I asked Billy as he was leaving. 'I didn't see it.'

'Over there,' he pointed across the road, 'behind the village church.'

Realising I'd completely forgotten about the dog, feeling suddenly ashamed, I asked: 'Is Dregs in it?'

'No, Hobbesie took him to guard that nice lady at the museum before we came here.'

'Daphne?' Shocked that I'd hardly given her a thought in all the excitement, my shame rose into the red.

'Come along, Andy,' said Sid as I stood, watching Billy cross the road, 'we really must get Miss Pinkerton home, or she'll catch her death of cold.'

She was shivering, despite being wrapped in Sid's black cloak.

'Good idea,' I said, snapping out of it. 'Where are you staying?'

'I don't know,' she said indistinctly through the staccato clatter of teeth. 'I was hoping to stay with Daphne, but that's obviously out of the question. I suppose I should get a hotel for the night, but I don't know what's available.'

'We can work something out,' said Sid. 'Let's get a move on.'

As we hurried back to the car, leaving two constables to do whatever police constables do at crime scenes after the event, I put my arm round Pinky's shoulder to keep her warm and, though it didn't appear to do her much good, I rather enjoyed the softness of her body, despite her new scent of stagnant ditch mud.

'I've been thinking,' said Sid as we drove away. 'You could stay at my place tonight, Ms Pinkerton. It will save you having to search for a hotel. There's plenty of room.'

'Oh, I couldn't possibly,' said Pinky, in a tone that meant yes, please.

'Excellent. That's settled then. I can make you quite comfortable and I'll be glad of your company. Do you like soup?'

'I love it,' said Pinky, who was obviously a pushover.

The two of them chatted happily all the way back, leaving me confused and completely puzzled by my feelings. Fortunately, I kept my mouth shut, because otherwise I might have said something stupid. I knew I was being silly, but, for some reason, I was getting worked up about her moral welfare and, apparently, my concerns were much greater than hers. The thing was, I really didn't think a young, well, youngish, woman should stay overnight with Sid, a known vampire, and, although I had almost no fear he'd bite her neck and drain her dry, I'd seen far too many films in which vampires exerted an unhealthy fascination on vulnerable women to be entirely at ease. I was worried that, to judge from her smile and conversation, she was relishing the idea.

It wasn't that I was jealous, or perhaps it was, but I shouldn't have been, because I had Daphne, or at least so I hoped. As my thoughts turned to her I began to feel better, for she had a certain something that made me a better man. Pinky had something about her, too, but given the choice, I'd have definitely picked Daphne. At least I thought I would have.

Once back in Sorenchester, Sid parked his monumental vehicle half up on the pavement outside his house.

'I shouldn't really stop here,' he said, 'but Ms Pinkerton ...'

'Pinky, please!' she said.

'... Pinky needs a hot bath as quickly as possible. So, I'll see you soon, Andy. It has been a most interesting afternoon.'

'Alright then,' I said as we got out and my confusing feelings flooded back. 'Bye.'

Turning away, I tried not to mind her delighted giggle as Sid, with a deep bow and a toothy smile, opened the front door and showed her inside.

I headed towards the museum to check on Daphne, to ensure she was coping with Dregs, who could be a handful. It turned out that I had no cause to worry, for I met her outside with Dregs, who was walking to heel like the hero in a Disney film about a very good, heroic dog.

'Hi, Andy,' said Daphne, smiling and stroking his shaggy black head, 'we're just going for a comfort break in the park.'

'Hi,' I said, suffering an unreasonable stab of jealousy. 'How are you?'

'I'm fine. How's the inspector's daughter?'

'She's safe. He had a plan to rescue her and I nearly screwed it up, but it all ended well. Sir Gerald's under arrest, but he was taken to hospital because Sid trod on him. Rupert was taken away, too.'

'I'd love to hear all about it,' she said, 'but later. I'm still at work, but the dog wanted some air. I finish at five-thirty, so I'll see you here in,' she glanced at her watch, 'about forty minutes.'

'Great.' I said. 'I'll take him for his walk.'

Handing me the lead, kissing me on the cheek, she headed back. His tail drooped as she went inside and it was only when we reached Ride Park and he'd chased a rabbit that his spirits revived. As the minutes passed until I could go and meet her, my mind kept churning over the facts and one in particular kept bubbling to the surface. I had come within millimetres of being shot and, although I'd learned that new sensations and new experiences helped prevent one getting stuck in a rut, there was something about bullets that made ruts seem attractive. I might have been wounded, or killed. It would, I reflected, have been just my luck to get killed in action when things were beginning to look promising with Daphne.

Yet the bullets hadn't touched me and the truth was that it had been just my luck to have survived unscathed when things were beginning to look promising with Daphne. I clung to this far more comforting point of view, hoping it was a sign my luck was changing, because, in my opinion, good luck was long overdue. A wave of euphoria broke over me, engulfed me, and deposited me gently back in Ride Park. The case had been solved, the bad men had been thwarted, if my luck held I was going to find gold, and, to top it all, I was meeting Daphne very soon.

I asked an old chap throwing a ball for a yappy miniature poodle, whether he had the time.

'Five twenty-five.'

'Thank you,' I said, fearing I'd be late.

I called Dregs, who was making a point of ignoring the poodle, and attached his lead.

'Come on,' I said, 'let's go and find Daphne.'

On hearing her name, he took off like a greyhound and I only just managed to keep up by taking unfeasibly long strides. Still, the burst of speed worked, for we arrived at the museum just as she emerged. Seeing her, Dregs put on an extra spurt and self-preservation forced me to drop his lead.

Looking up, she smiled. Dregs accelerated, running faster than I'd ever seen him, running straight towards her, despite my calling him back. I was convinced she was going to get flattened.

Instead, avoiding her by a whisker, he leapt at the hooded figure who had just stepped from the shadows behind her. The man screamed as Dregs's sharp white teeth closed on his wrist and the momentum sent him spinning to the ground. A knife skidded into the gutter as the man's hood fell back. It was Rupert Payne.

'Get it off,' he cried, blood spurting from his wrist as Dregs, growling savagely, kept him pinned down. I could have called him off, he might for once have obeyed, but I didn't.

'Drop,' said Daphne in a quiet voice.

Dregs dropped and gazed at her, wagging his tail.

'Good dog.'

'I'm hurt,' said Rupert, in the moments when he wasn't rolling around on the pavement, clutching his arm. 'He bit me. I'm bleeding.'

'Good,' I said with feeling as I ran to Daphne's side. She looked far less shocked than I felt.

'I didn't mean any harm,' Rupert whined. 'I wasn't going to hurt anyone.'

'You had a knife,' I said, 'and you threatened me with one on Sunday.'

'But, I didn't use it, did I? I only pulled it out because I was scared.'

'Were you scared of me?' asked Daphne.

'No, Mrs Duckworth. I only wanted to talk, but, when I saw the horrible dog coming for me, I panicked and pulled the knife to protect myself. I didn't use it, though, because I didn't want to hurt the inspector's dog after he'd been so kind.'

He groaned. 'My wrist is ever so painful and I'm bleeding. Please, help me.'

He sounded sincere and I nearly believed him, nearly distrusted the evidence of my own eyes. Yet I knew what I'd seen. The knife had been in his hand long before he could possibly have seen Dregs. Daphne stooped, reaching for his arm.

'We'll take care of you,' she said. 'Let's have a look at it.'

As fast as a weasel, he seized her scarf, pulling her down with him, and lunged for the knife. She gasped, trying to break free, but his grip was firm.

Sid had shown me what to do next and I was already in position as Rupert's hand closed around the hilt. I stamped down hard and his wrist snapped with a stomach turning crack. With a scream, he slumped face forward into the road.

'Are you alright?' I asked.

'I'm fine,' said Daphne, pushing herself up. 'Are you?'

I shook my head. The pavement seemed to be rolling, my vision was blurred and her voice reverberated through my skull. I had a vague awareness of people and a voice shouting: 'look at that guy's wrist!' The feel and sound of it overwhelmed me.

'Come on Andy, wake up,' said Constable Poll.

A soft, warm hand stroked my brow.

A hot, wet, stinky tongue licked my face as I opened my eyes. A crowd had gathered to stare.

'What happened?' I asked, sitting up, feeling sick.

'You fainted …' said Constable Poll.

I would have hung my head in shame had it not already been lolling. Fainting was not manly.

'… and I'm not surprised, because the sight of the lad's wrist made me a bit queasy. It's not pretty, but you did well to disarm him.'

'It was Dregs that stopped him,' I said.

'At first, but I'm sure he was going to stab me,' said Daphne. She turned to Poll. 'Andy was brilliant – again.'

I couldn't hold back a self-satisfied grin as she hugged me, because, although I wished I hadn't hurt Rupert quite so badly, I had been brilliant. Still, I thought I should show some concern. 'How is he?'

'Apart from a very nasty compound fracture of his right wrist,' said Poll, 'dog bites, and serious psychological issues, he's doing fine. Mrs Goodfellow is looking after him until the ambulance arrives.'

'I don't understand,' I said. 'I saw him put into an ambulance about an hour ago. Why isn't he already in hospital?'

'He ran off as soon as they took his father into surgery,' said Poll. 'Superintendent Cooper ordered us to keep a look out for him, because he was believed to be armed and dangerous.'

I was on top of the world by the time the ambulance arrived and the moaning figure of Rupert was carried on board. Constable Poll got in beside the paramedic, although I doubted Rupert was likely to be troublesome for some time. With the ambulance's departure, the crowd dispersed and Mrs Goodfellow approached.

'How about a nice cup of tea?' she said.

'Yes please,' I said. 'Can Daphne come?'

'Of course, dear, and she can stay for supper if she likes.'

Daphne agreed and we walked back to Blackdog Street.

'Look what Mr White, the dentist, gave me.' said Mrs Goodfellow, pulling a brown paper bag from somewhere in her cardigan and opening it with a worrying rattle.

'Lovely,' I said, wondering how Daphne would react to a bag full of human teeth. All she did was nod gravely and smile politely.

Ten minutes later, we were drinking tea in the kitchen, with Dregs curled up at Daphne's feet. Although an array of warm, enticing, delicious smells arising from the oven made me hungry, I concentrated on not drooling and related the afternoon's events. When I showed the bullet hole beneath my armpit, Daphne paled and squeezed my hand so hard I feared I'd be following Sir Gerald and son to hospital, where the hand and wrist surgeons must have been very busy. Fortunately, she slackened the pressure when I yelped and so the hospital was spared another casualty. Best of all, the way she was looking at me made me feel important and heroic.

We helped Mrs Goodfellow set the table for supper and waited for Hobbes and Kathy to return. A little before six-thirty the front door opened. Dregs's tail wagged once and then he stood up, bristling, growling, standing protectively in front of us and staring at the kitchen door as it opened. In walked Denny.

My heart began to pound and a sick feeling gripped my stomach. Daphne gasped and sat down, as if her legs had given way. Mrs Goodfellow, a steaming wooden spoon in one hand, grabbed Dregs's collar with the other and stepped forward.

'Good evening,' she said. 'Who are you, and what are you doing here?'

Denny, tidier and cleaner than I'd yet seen him, touching his forelock and bowing with an old-fashioned gesture, smiled. 'Good evening, ma'am,' he said and turned towards Daphne and me, repeating the bow. 'Good evening, Mrs Duckworth. Good evening, sir. I'm Denzil Barker. I'm here to apolo … apolo … to say sorry for what I done. Mr Hobbes had a long talk with me and taught me that what I been doing was wrong. I am sorry, ma'am, Mrs Duckworth, sir. I didn't want to hurt nobody, but I thought I had to do what the master said. Mr Hobbes says I don't have to do that no more.'

'I am very pleased to hear it,' said Mrs Goodfellow. 'Where is Mr Hobbes? I expect he let you in.'

'Yes, ma'am. He's taking Miss Kathy upstairs, 'cause she's feeling a bit poorly and wants to lie down.'

'Oh, the poor girl,' said Mrs Goodfellow, whose innate kindness overwhelmed her suspicions, 'I'd better go and make sure she's alright.'

'There's no need,' said Hobbes, entering the kitchen and patting Denny on the shoulder. 'She just needs a little time on her own. What's for supper?'

'Sorenchester hotpot,' said Mrs Goodfellow. 'Is Mr Barker going to eat with us?'

Denny nodded. 'I would like that very much, ma'am. I am very starving hungry and I like the smell of what you got cooking. Thank you, muchly.'

'You are welcome, dear' said Mrs Goodfellow. 'There's plenty to go round.'

Still shaking, still very much surprised, still utterly bewildered, I took my seat next to Daphne, whose face showed a weird mixture of fear, suspicion and relief. Denny sat on my other side and Hobbes, at the head as always, said grace. It was a bizarre occasion and, to start with, my nerves were stretched so tightly I was sure they'd snap, until the old girl served us and it was clear she'd excelled herself as usual, when I allowed myself to relax by small degrees. Sometimes I suspected her of witchcraft, for it was clearly impossible for every meal to be better than the previous one, but if I was under a spell, I was in no rush to break it.

Denny, polite and calm, ate in awed silence and when seconds were offered accepted them with alacrity. The same went for thirds and fourths. By the end of supper, I had accepted his presence. He no longer felt like a threat, reminding me instead of an overgrown, over-aged, none too intelligent child. Hobbes had achieved many remarkable feats, but the taming of Denny struck me as one of his most amazing.

Denny volunteered to wash the pots. Hobbes, letting him get on with it, answered Daphne's questions about Nutcase Nugent, a notorious former resident of Blackcastle, who'd featured in Hugh Duckworth's notes. I went upstairs to relieve myself, and had just finished washing my hands when I overheard Kathy talking on her mobile. She was angry and sounded even more American than usual.

'No,' she said, 'I won't do it. Not now, not ever. This game of yours stops here … How could you tell me such a pack of lies? … Baloney, Mom! When have you ever done anything for *my* good? … Yes, I am going to tell him … Tonight. He deserves to know … He's been really kind … no, he's nothing like you described him … Well, sure, he is one big, ugly dude, but he's a good man … I wish he really was my daddy.'

As I headed back downstairs, I wondered how Hobbes would react to suddenly not having a daughter again.

Daphne was helping Denny put things away, while Hobbes, a mug of tea in his hand, was telling them the legend of the Blacker Mountain crocodile that had finally put an end to Nutcase Nugent.

Kathy entered the kitchen, her eyes rimmed with red, breathing heavily, but in control.

'Excuse me for butting in,' she said, 'but I have something important to say. I just wish I didn't have to. I wish everything was different.' Facing Hobbes, she gulped and took a deep breath. 'I'm not your daughter.'

'I know,' said Hobbes with a sad smile. 'I always did. We saved you some supper.'

Kathy stood and faced us, tears rolling down her cheeks, her eyes puffy with crying. I could see no nastiness or arrogance in her, just unhappiness and, strangely, dignity. She wiped her face. 'I'd like to explain myself before anything else.'

'Very well,' said Hobbes.

'We'd better leave you to it,' I said, getting up, embarrassed.

'No, Andy, please stay,' she said. 'Mrs Goodfellow, too. All of you stay, if you don't mind. I'm fed up with secrets. I'm sorry Dad … Inspector, but I've only just found out that some of what I told you, some of what I believed, was completely wrong.'

I sat back down.

Denny shrugged his massive shoulders and stood in the corner by the sink, as immobile as a sculpture. Mrs Goodfellow pulled up a chair and joined us at the table.

Kathy stood quite still, except for the rise and fall of her chest as she fought to stay in control, her fists clenched, her face as white as skimmed milk.

'I want to apologise,' she said.

'That's the word I wanted to say,' Denny murmured and resumed his silence.

'I didn't intend to deceive you,' said Kathy. 'I didn't intend to deceive anyone. I really thought I was your daughter. I hope you believe me?'

'We'll see,' said Mrs G, trying to look stern.

'I'll start at the very beginning,' said Kathy.

'A very good place to start,' I responded, before a frown from Hobbes quelled my attempt at lightening the mood.

'I've lived with my mom most of my life and for most of the time it was just the two of us. She told me my daddy hailed from England and that she'd met him when he was on vacation, but he'd gone home before I was born. She said he was a cop and his name was Hobbes.'

Mrs G snorted and shook her head. Hobbes held up his hand to quiet her. 'Go on,' he said.

'I never thought I'd ever meet him, because Mom had no idea where he lived. Anyway, we got by somehow or other, even though we moved about all over the States when I was little. Mostly this was because she kept getting into trouble and running away. For a long time she used drugs and sometimes she was put in jail. At those times, nice folk looked after me and I had a bit of schooling. After I graduated high school, we kind of settled down. I found a job waitressing and Mom got herself clean of drugs.'

'That is good,' said Hobbes. 'I warned her of the risks back in'67, but she was young and foolish then.'

'She's still foolish,' said Kathy, a snap of anger in her voice.

'So,' I asked, 'why did you take drugs yesterday?'

'I didn't knowingly. That punk, Rupert, put something in my soda.'

'Is that why you threw him in the lake?'

'Pardon me, sir,' said Denny. 'Miss Kathy di'n't throw him in. It was me. Master Gerald wanted the young master to feel what failure was like.'

That I'd almost forgotten him testifies to the change Hobbes had already wrought, and made me wonder whether he might always have been quiet and respectful had it not been for the rottenness of the Paynes.

'OK,' I said, trying to compute the new data and staring at Kathy. 'How come you were there?'

'I was getting my head together and I heard a scream.'

'Andy,' said Hobbes, 'interesting as your misunderstandings are, can you please let her continue?'

'A few years ago,' said Kathy, 'Mom persuaded me to use the few dollars I'd saved and go into business.'

'What sort of business?' I asked, unable to envisage her as a businesswoman. She didn't seem the type.

'We opened a shop selling bison products.' She grimaced.

'Bison?'

'Yeah, we called it *Buy Some Bison*. Neat, huh?'

'What did you sell?' I asked, suddenly intrigued.

'Bison leather goods mainly: belts, shoes, coats, trousers, wallets, bags and hats. We also sold fresh and canned bison meat, which is low in fat and cholesterol. The trouble was, when I say sold, I really mean stocked. We never sold too much of anything, but somehow, we kept going for a few years. In the end it became clear, even to Mom, that it was just a matter of time before we went big time bust. It was then she chanced on the video of you on YouTube.'

'So, she still recognised the old fellow,' said Mrs Goodfellow.

Kathy nodded. 'At once and, I tell you, it was one helluva shock for her. I wondered what was wrong and thought she was going to faint, but she showed me and said I was your daughter. Then she took up a bottle of Tequila and drank herself unconscious. She took two days to sober up, which gave me time to think.' She wiped her eyes again. 'I wanted to see my daddy.'

'And get some money off him?' asked Mrs Goodfellow with a disapproving sniff.

With a wry smile, Kathy nodded. 'I'll not pretend that it didn't cross my mind, but I really wanted to meet you … him. Ever since I was a kid, I suppose I'd always had this crazy idea that one day you … he would come along and rescue me, but really, I just wanted to see you and talk and find out something about you. I hoped you'd help me understand something about myself. So, I booked a cheap plane ticket to England and found my way here, hoping you'd welcome me and … and you did. You really did, even though I must have been a shock.'

Hobbes, frowning, nodded.

'At first, I was totally scared of you. Mom had said you were a big guy, but I hadn't realised how big. I put on a front and I hope I didn't offend anyone too much. I guess I might have come across as rude.'

'Perhaps a little,' said Mrs Goodfellow, her face betraying a smile.

'I'm sorry,' said Kathy. 'I soon came to like you, and then when you caught me that time I fell, it was like I'd really come home. I'd dreamt of living in a place like this and leaving all my problems behind but … but …'

'You worked out that I wasn't your father,' said Hobbes.

'You couldn't be. You're just too … different. You're different to everyone, except to Featherlight and Denny. They're just like you.'

'Indeed, they are not!' said Mrs Goodfellow, a look of almost comic indignation on her face.

Hobbes, holding up a hand to quiet her, couldn't hold back a smile.

Kathy wiped her eyes and blew her nose on the tissue Mrs Goodfellow offered her. 'I don't mean you're like them in everything, but seeing the three of you together this afternoon made me certain. I don't know what you are and it doesn't matter, because you're a good man anyway, but you are different. D'you know what I mean?'

'I believe I do,' said Hobbes.

I was impressed. It had taken me far longer to conclude that Hobbes wasn't like the rest of us and I was still amazed at my insight, though it puzzled me why more people hadn't made the jump. Even so, and despite few being as close to him as I was, I often felt I didn't really know him at all. It was difficult enough to understand another human's thoughts, and it was almost impossible to know precisely what was going on in an animal's head. It wasn't that I considered him an animal, except so far as we were all animals. He was a man, but a non-human one, if that made any sense.

'Mr Hobbes is a Mountain Man, jus' like me,' said Denny suddenly, 'and so is Mr Featherlight. I didn't think there was any others like me till I came here. They said our kind was evil. I think I was.'

'But,' said Hobbes, 'you aren't anymore.'

'Whatever you are,' Kathy continued, 'I knew you couldn't be my daddy and, when I called Mom tonight, I finally made her admit it. My real daddy's some guy she met in Pittsburgh long after you'd left her.'

'The old fellow didn't leave her,' said Mrs Goodfellow. 'She left him when his money ran out. She even took his car.'

'I gave it to her,' said Hobbes. 'Her father was ill and she needed it to visit him in Detroit.'

'Her father was killed in Korea in 1952,' said Kathy, 'and granny never remarried. Neither of them ever lived in Detroit. Mom lied.'

'She always did,' said Mrs Goodfellow, smiling at Hobbes, 'only you were too much of a gentleman to acknowledge it. She would have taken your trousers if she'd thought there was money to be made from them.'

A tint of red appeared on Hobbes's cheeks. 'She did take them, which made things awkward. I had to improvise.'

'Was that when you started wearing that awful tarpaulin caftan?' asked Mrs Goodfellow. 'I did wonder.'

Hobbes nodded.

'So,' said Kathy, 'I'm not your daughter, but I didn't mean to trick you. Mom lied, although tonight she said you were the best man she'd ever known. I think that might have been true.'

'I doubt it,' said Hobbes with a sudden grin that was swiftly eclipsed when he saw Kathy's expression of sadness.

'I'm sorry,' she said, 'for everything. I really didn't know. I've packed my bags and

I'll find myself a hotel and get out of your lives.'

'There's no need to be hasty,' said Hobbes. 'You're welcome to stay for as long as you want.'

'But there's no room,' she said.

'We can always make room, can't we, lass?'

Mrs Goodfellow nodded. So, to my surprise, did I.

'Thank you.' The relief in Kathy's voice was echoed in her face.

'That's settled then,' said Hobbes, smiling.

'But, there is one thing,' said Kathy. 'How did you know I wasn't your daughter?'

'I calculated dates and times. I did the math, as you Americans say, and it was impossible.'

'Oh,' I said, surprised, 'I thought it was because you hadn't … umm.'

'Hadn't what?' asked Hobbes.

'Hadn't … umm … hadn't noticed enough similarity.'

'There was that as well,' said Hobbes. 'Although I knew, it appeared to me that you genuinely believed it …'

Mrs Goodfellow shook her head and chuckled.

'… and,' Hobbes continued, 'I didn't want to let you down. Now you've discovered the truth, I hope we can still be friends?'

Getting up, he embraced her in an immense bear hug.

My eyes moistening, I had to blink until they cleared. Daphne gave my hand a little squeeze.

Hobbes released Kathy, who was displaying a genuine, all-American smile that lit up her face. I could almost see her from PC Poll's point of view.

'Well,' he said, rubbing his hands together, sounding like a carpenter sanding rough wood, 'I'm glad that's all sorted because Denny is going to show me where the stolen gold is. Andy, there'll be room for you, too, but I must warn you, it will be a long night.'

Although a small part of me would have preferred to stay behind with Daphne, I could not turn down the opportunity to go on a treasure hunt, and within a few minutes I was sandwiched in between Featherlight and Denny in the back of Billy's hearse. All I could do was to look out through the windscreen between Hobbes and Billy as the headlights lit up the streets of Sorenchester. Soon we were on the dual carriageway, sided by fields, stark and empty, under a moon that was a little past fullness. The halo around it suggested there'd be a frost later.

'Where are we heading to?' I asked.

'You'll see,' said Hobbes, looking over his shoulder with an infuriating grin. 'Eventually.'

I had to be content with that, and since neither he, nor any of the others seemed in the mood for talking, I tried to relax. It was warm and the drone of the engine and the pulse of the tyres on the road lulled me to sleep.

When I awoke, the car was stationary, the windows misty with condensation, and I was on my own. Bleary-eyed, feeling a little sick and headachy, I climbed out, shivering as I pulled up my collar and tried to get my bearings. The place looked familiar, yet strange under the moonlight, and it took a moment to realise I was back in the Blacker Mountains and that we were parked beside the derelict manor house, where Billy had dropped us off just over a week earlier. It seemed incredible that so much had happened in such a short period, but that was so often the way with Hobbes.

I was annoyed and a little worried that the others had deserted me, until voices from the ruins suggested they were not far away. It was almost as bright as daytime and, as I walked towards the voices, my moon shadow flickered before me over the rocky ground.

'Hello?' I said, with no response.

As I reached the house, I touched its cold, grey, stone wall and called out again, a little louder than before.

'Andy?'

Hobbes's disembodied voice, deep and sepulchral, made me start: 'Did you have a good sleep?'

'Yes … thanks.'

'Good. Are you going to join us?'

'I would if I knew where you were.'

His hand grabbed my ankle and would have made me jump into orbit had its grip not been so strong.

'We,' said Hobbes, 'are in the cellars.'

All I could see of him was his hand and his big, yellow teeth, glinting in the moonlight, grinning from the bottom of a steeply sloping shaft. He released me.

'How do I get down?' I asked, my poor heart pounding.

'Just slide down this here coal chute and I'll catch you at the bottom.'

Sitting down, slotting my bottom half into the tight, damp, steep chute, I braced myself for action, but just before I let go I had a thought. The chute was not wide enough for him, or for Denny and definitely not for Featherlight.

'How,' I asked, 'did you get down there?'

'We used the steps.'

As I tried to extricate myself, he gave a tug and, with a little shriek, I slid into the darkness, where, to give him his due, he did catch me and set me down on an uneven floor. There was a stink of mildew and age and, when my eyes had adjusted, I saw I was in a long, low room with a crumbling, dripping, brick ceiling festooned with a crop of what appeared to be small stalactites. Around the chute, everything was mossy, with pale ferns and spiders' webs. In the further reaches I could make out a mess of rusting junk, crumbled rock, and rotting leaves.

'Take care,' said Hobbes, 'it's slippery in places.'

'Where are the others?

'In the wine cellar.'

'So, what's this?'

'The coal cellar.'

'Ah … that would explain the coal chute.'

'I'll make a detective of you yet,' said Hobbes, leading me to the far end, where half a dozen cracked steps led down into another brick chamber. I could barely see him so, reaching out, I gripped the edge of his jacket.

'There are more steps,' he warned after a few paces across the lumpy floor, 'and they are worn and broken in places. Take care.'

At least twenty steps took us down to an echoing chamber where it was noticeably colder and damper, but where a faint light meant I could make out that we were in a wide space that, to judge by its ceiling, had been hacked from the bedrock. I followed Hobbes, walking briskly as he turned into yet another large chamber, one lined with rotting wine racks. It was a little disappointing as a generous gulp of wine would have fortified me nicely.

At the far end, Featherlight and Billy were holding torches as Denny shoved one of the racks aside.

'This is the door,' he said, putting his shoulder against a section of what I'd taken to be solid brickwork. With a creak it swung open to reveal a small vault.

As Featherlight aimed his torch, my eyes were caught by the pale gleam of metal. Rushing forward impulsively, intending to be first in, I was shocked when Denny shoved me roughly aside. As I fell and sprawled on the cold, wet ground, a rock, bigger than Hobbes's head, crashed down just where I would have been standing.

'Thank you,' I said, getting back to my feet.

'You must always wait. Master Gerald said Mr Duckworth di'n't wait and the rock cracked his bonce, so I had to hide him on Blacker Knob. Master Gerald said it served him right for poking his nose in where it weren't wanted. It's alright to go in now.'

Instead of being first, I was left outside, peering in, looking round Featherlight's back, while Billy opened two solid-looking steel boxes. The first one contained hundreds, maybe thousands of gold coins: the second, gold bars and papers.

Hobbes smiled. 'Well done, Denny. Thank you.'

'Pleased to help, Mr Hobbes.'

'I take it,' I said, peering in, 'that those are Colonel Squire's gold sovereigns?'

'Correct,' said Hobbes.

'And the other box?'

'That's mine.'

'That's a lot of gold,' I said, wide-eyed.

'It was a gift from a lady. I've never been sure what to do with it.'

'For a gift,' said Billy, 'that's not bad. The last one I got was a tie which was too long.'

'Sorry about that,' said Featherlight, 'but it was too tight on me.'

At the very end of the vault, in the corner, lay a small, worm-eaten, wooden chest. Billy opened it. It contained a few pieces of jewellery.

'Denzil,' asked Hobbes, 'do you know anything about this?'

'It was here when I first come down here with Master Gerald. He said it was very old.'

'How did he know?' I asked.

'It was written about in a mouldy old book Master Gerald found in the attic. He said Sir Greville had wrote it, but I don't know Sir Greville.'

'I know about him,' said Hobbes, 'because he was in Roger Jolly's Pirate Miscellany, which claimed that he sailed with Blackbeard, though the Payne family denied it and used their influence and money to suppress the book. Few copies still exist, but I have one. If I were a betting man, I'd wager that box is the last of Sir Greville's ill-gotten treasure.'

'You could well be right,' said Billy, who'd been rummaging through the contents. 'This stuff would appear to date from the late seventeenth century and contains some exquisite examples of Spanish workmanship. We'll have to tell someone.'

'Of course,' said Hobbes.

'But what are we going to do now?' I asked, suddenly aware of the lateness of the hour.

'Load it into the car and return to Sorenchester,' said Hobbes. 'Sid will be delighted to get his gold back. The robbery upset him far more than he lets on and Colonel Squire will no longer have anything to rant about.'

'I'll give you a hand,' I said, squeezing past Featherlight and attempting to pick up one of the metal boxes. I couldn't move it, couldn't even shake the coins.

Featherlight guffawed. 'Put your back into it, Caplet.'

'He'll put his back out if he strains anymore,' said Billy.

It was left to Featherlight and Denny to lift the boxes and to carry them to the hearse. Afterwards, Hobbes removed a few souvenirs from Featherlight's pockets.

'How did they get in there?' asked Featherlight, attempting a look of wide-eyed innocence that suited him as well as lipstick suits a fish.

'I have no idea,' said Hobbes, taking his mobile from his pocket. 'I'd better inform the local boys and then it'll be time to head back.'

As soon as he'd finished speaking to Sergeant Beer we started for home and, although it must have been a long, tiring drive for Billy, I slept most of the way.

I was woken by Featherlight nudging me in the ribs.

'Wake up, Caplet, you lazy git,' he said.

I rubbed my neck and blinked. 'What's happening?'

'We're back.'

We were outside Grossman's Bank, where a tired-looking, but beaming Sid, wrapped in his cloak, his breath steaming in the grey, dawn air, was waiting. I couldn't stop myself from wondering how much of his smile was down to getting his gold back and how much to having spent the night with Pinky. As I yawned and shivered, Hobbes and Denny carried the gold inside, where Siegfried was waiting.

Then we said our goodbyes and went home. I was barely awake enough to drink a cup of tea while Hobbes explained to the others what we'd been up to. Then, to my delight, Daphne kissed me, led me to my own bed and tucked me in. The sheets still retained some warmth from her body as well as a comforting hint of her scent. I slept until lunch time.

Hobbes must have been the only reason that Denny Barker was never arrested or even charged with any crime, and, despite everything he'd done, it felt like justice had been served. Without Sir Gerald's malign influence, he was a friendly, if rather dim, sort of soul, who was eager to please and help out. He stayed with us while Hobbes was tying up the last strings of the case and number 13 Blackdog Street, with Daphne and Kathy still in residence, was consequently very crowded. Despite having to sleep on the sofa, I found it a happy time. The only real problem was that Hobbes and Denny had contrived to sling hammocks in the attic and, most nights, Denny fell out with a frightful crash.

After a week, Kathy, who turned out to be quite likeable, returned to America. We all went to wave her off at the airport with promises to keep in touch, and I knew I was going to miss her. A week after that, Daphne moved back into her flat, which had been restored and was even better than before. I used to go round to see her every evening and we'd meet at lunch times too, when she could make it.

Life in Blackdog Street returned to what passed as normal, except that when I took Dregs for a walk, I had to take Denny as well. He proved no better than Dregs at catching squirrels. Then, one raw morning, just after breakfast, when Denny and Mrs Goodfellow were washing up, Hobbes put down his mug and cleared his throat.

'I'm going away for a while,' he said. 'I'm taking Denny home.'

'OK,' I said. 'How long will you be gone?'

'A while.'

Later that morning, Billy drove them away.

With their departure, the house felt empty and quiet. I was often at a loose end and Dregs kept wandering around morosely, as if he'd lost something. Daphne's visits always consoled him, almost as much as they did me and, after a few days, we settled into a sort of routine. Mrs Goodfellow, to my surprise, wasn't as upset by Hobbes's absence as I'd thought she would be.

'It's alright, dear,' she said. 'A week or two in the Blacker Mountains will do him a power of good.'

He didn't return in a week or two.

If possible, her cooking reached new heights, as if she was trying to lure the old fellow back, and the result was that Dregs and I, and frequently Daphne and occasionally Sid and Pinky, were exceedingly well fed. Pinky, who'd hit it off amazingly well with Sid, had taken up permanent residence and her tea room, on the site of the unloved Café Olé, was already doing a brisk trade. We enjoyed some fine times and my feelings for Daphne grew, so that, for some time, she occupied my thoughts most of the day and quite a lot of the night.

Halloween came and went, as did Bonfire night and still there was no sign of Hobbes.

I read in the *Bugle* about Sir Gerald's trial in mid-November when, having pleaded guilty to theft, conspiracy to rob, assault, arson and attempted murder, he received a substantial prison sentence. Young Rupert Payne, having been diagnosed with serious mental health problems, was detained indefinitely in an institution.

As the end of November approached, Daphne and I were spending more and more time together. One evening, after we'd been to the cinema in Pigton, and were enjoying a cuddle on the sofa in her flat, she pulled away and sat up, looking serious.

'Andy,' she said, 'I would like you to stay the night. What d'you think?'

I was so taken by surprise, I was reduced to making fish faces for several seconds, before I heard myself say: 'I think I would like that.'

The following day, I moved in with her. I expected Mrs Goodfellow would be upset when I told her. Instead, her eyes twinkled and she spent a good half hour embarrassing me and poking me in the ribs. It was all very trying, but I forgave her on account of all her past kindness, especially when she invited us to a celebratory supper. It was of course the best meal I'd ever tasted, which was saying a lot, and was washed down with a bottle of Hobbes's best red wine. It made me realise how much I was going to miss her cooking and it said something about my feelings for Daphne that this seemed a fair price to pay.

The next surprising event came the following day when, by chance, I found a job, even if it was only a part-time one. We were at Pinky's Tearoom and I was telling Sid about our last supper, getting so carried away with enthusiasm for the old girl's beef and oyster pie that phrases like 'love in a crust' and 'fresh as an ocean breeze' sprang to my lips.

A young man approached.

'Hi, Andy,' he said. 'Sorry to interrupt you.'

'Oh … Hi, Phil,' I said, recognising Phil Waring, who'd been my colleague at the *Bugle*, and whose life I'd saved when he was about to become an unwilling blood donor to a wannabe vampire. Since then, our careers had diverged. I was unemployed; he was the editor.

'I couldn't help overhearing you,' he said.

'Sorry.'

'What I mean is this. Can you write about food as well as you talk about it?'

'Umm …' I began, before catching Daphne's look, 'yes, I expect so. Why?'

'Well,' said Phil, 'the Fatman is retiring and the *Bugle* needs a new food writer. How about it?'

'Great,' I said. 'When do I start?'

'How about next Monday?'

'Why not? I'll see you then.'

December arrived with still no word from Hobbes. On Christmas Eve, I went to see Mrs Goodfellow, taking her a little something bought with my first pay. After fighting off Dregs's friendly exuberance, I was enjoying a cup of tea, while discussing Christmas dinner, to which Daphne and I, Sid and Pinky, Featherlight and Billy had been invited. The old girl was chatting about teeth, while working out how to fit an ostrich-sized turkey into the oven, when Dregs leapt to his feet with a deafening volley of excited barking.

In walked Hobbes, as if he'd never been away.

'Afternoon,' he said, pulling up a chair. 'Is there any tea in the pot?'

Inspector Hobbes

and the Bones

Unhuman IV

1

The man walking past the coach stop had his raincoat hood pulled low against the morning drizzle, but I barely noticed him until he punched me on the nose. Fearing another blow, I cowered and covered my face, and by the time I felt safe enough to look up, he was sauntering away as if nothing had happened. I blinked away tears and spluttered meaningless sounds of shock and outrage while warm blood dripped between my fingers. Eventually, I managed to construct a coherent question.

'Why?'

If he heard, he ignored me.

I mopped up some of the gore with a ragged tissue from my coat pocket, and, as the pain kicked in and rage grew, considered the possibility of pummelling him into the ground. I'd even got as far as taking a tentative step after him, when a big black Mercedes with tinted windows drove by, splashing me with filthy, slushy water. It pulled up next to the man, who got in without looking back and was driven away, leaving me infuriated, if more than a little relieved, since I've never really been a fighter, and he'd looked a solid, muscular sort of bloke. Instead, I shook my fist and exorcised my frustration and temper by shouting insults, though not too loudly in case he heard. In all the excitement, I forgot to note the car's number plate, a practice my friend Inspector Hobbes of the Sorenchester Police had tried to instil in me when I used to help with his more difficult cases.

Much had changed since those days. I was married and had become, I hoped, a better and more confident person. Other than what had just happened, no one had hit me since my marriage to Daphne, but two years had passed and she was leaving me, which hurt far more than a mere bloody nose. I turned around, hoping for one last glimpse, but the National Express coach with her aboard had already pulled out of sight onto the Pigton Road. On impulse, I reached for the smartphone she'd given me for Christmas, but what was the point? She was heading for the airport, and there was no way she could come back to comfort me, even if she'd wanted to. I'd just have to cope, and get used to being alone again.

I realised I hadn't spoken with Hobbes for at least a couple of months, though, now and again, I'd spotted his vast ugly frame loping along The Shambles in the town centre, and had been reassured to see him out there, fighting crime and setting the world to rights in his own bizarre 'unhuman' fashion. Feeling suddenly lonely, I decided to pay him a visit. Lunchtime, I thought, would be good, because he'd almost certainly be home then, and I'd stand an excellent chance of a free meal. My mouth started watering at the mere thought, as anyone who'd been treated to the cooking of Mrs Goodfellow, his brilliant, if eccentric housekeeper, would understand. The only trouble was that I'd only recently breakfasted, and would have to wait until one o'clock.

Pulling myself together, the soggy tissue still pressed to my dripping nose, I turned towards the office, where I had to look in from time to time in case they were missing me. I crossed the road, heading towards The Shambles, and five minutes later entered the *Sorenchester and District Bugle's* front door, inhaling the familiar scent of printers' ink and stale coffee as I trotted upstairs to the main office. Phil Waring, the editor, as elegant and well-groomed as ever, was speaking to Basil Dean, a grizzled old hack, whose strange left eye was already aimed at me while the other concentrated on his computer screen.

'Hi, Andy,' said Phil. 'All right?'

I nodded.

'What happened?'

'Someone punched me,' I said, 'but it's nothing.'

'I'm glad to hear it.'

'Umm … when I say nothing, it's actually incredibly painful, but I'll be okay.'

'Excellent.' He turned back to Basil. 'Okay. We'll run the one about the university rugby team's unprecedented success as it is, but are you sure about the weather one?'

'It's based on the Met Office's long-range forecast,' said Basil, whose accent still marked him as a Liverpudlian, though he'd lived in the Cotswolds for over forty years. 'I'm always a bit sceptical about this sort of thing, but it does look as if we're in for a right good deluge, like, and with all that snow still in the hills …'

Disgruntled by their lack of sympathy, I headed to the gents and examined my battered hooter in the mirror. It wasn't as bad as I'd feared. It had already stopped bleeding, appeared as straight as ever, and wasn't nearly as sore as it might have been. I was still baffled by why the guy had attacked me, for I couldn't think of anything I'd done to provoke him, and I hadn't even recognised him. Perhaps I'd just had the misfortune to meet a random nutter, as had happened now and then, though it had usually been the more systematic ones that worried me. However, there was nothing I could do about it, so I decided to put it from my mind and get on with writing my review of Bombay Mick's Indian restaurant. I splashed water onto my face, wiped away the blood stains, dried myself and returned to the office.

Phil had recruited me as the food critic, giving me a second chance at the *Bugle,* and my career had been going comparatively well. I believed I'd become accepted and reasonably respected by my colleagues, which had never been the case during my previous stint. This time, despite only being a part-timer, my name, Andy Caplet, appeared regularly on bylines, and I was enjoying the work. It took me out and about and gave me an opportunity to sample a wide variety of foods and locations. Mostly, it was the eating that was the best part, even if no restaurant I'd visited had yet reached Mrs Goodfellow's culinary standards.

The previous week I'd reviewed Big Mama's Canteen. Big Mama was a large and formidable woman, though welcoming enough, and the place had been neat and friendly. I'd given it a favourable write-up, saying that it was an appealing little place, where I'd enjoyed some fine dishes and where the house Barolo had left my palate singing. I'd even submitted the piece, plus a courtesy copy to Big Mama's, via my smartphone, which, given my technophobic tendencies and awkward fingers, had been a miracle.

While my computer booted up, I made myself a mug of instant coffee, before sitting down and bashing out my piece. It was rather easy since Bombay Mick's food had been nicely spiced and tasty, unlike its rival, Jaipur Johnny's, where everything had been over-spiced and burnt, forcing me to write a real stinker, but only after a period of confinement in the bathroom with a nasty case of the Jaipur trots. After an hour or so, I finished my five hundred words and emailed it. I checked a few things, got up to leave, and was putting on my coat when Phil called me over.

'Thanks for the review,' he said. 'It reads well. And I've got a bit of news for you. It seems your articles have come to the attention of some influential people.'

'I'm sorry,' I said. 'What's wrong with them?'

He laughed. 'Nothing. In fact they like them and you're going to be syndicated in both *Sorenchester Life* and *Cotswold Hodgepodge*.'

'That's great,' I said, relieved not to be getting a bollocking, aware that old habits and thought patterns still lurked in dark corners of my mind, though Phil was nowhere near as terrifying as Editorsaurus Rex Witcherley, the previous editor. Plus, since I'd once saved Phil's life, I figured he would never be too nasty.

'It'll mean you get paid a bit more.'

'Brilliant! Thank you,' I said. 'Right, I'd better be off. See you.'

I bounced downstairs in a state of mild euphoria, wishing there was someone to share my good news with, for I'd never before had a pay rise. Looking back, I'd never deserved one since my early career had been one long chain of largely self-made disasters. What had changed me was meeting Hobbes.

I stepped out into The Shambles, deciding it was still too early to direct my feet towards number 13 Blackdog Street, where he lived, and recalling the first time I'd visited there in my capacity as deputy stand-in crime reporter, when I'd been nervous of his reputation. Since then, despite episodes of terror, pain and horror, my life had improved beyond measure.

A woman shouted. 'Look out!'

A black Mercedes mounted the pavement and sped towards me, forcing me to dive headlong into the entrance of Grossman's Bank. The car drove away, jumping the red light, and turned into Pound Street.

'Are you okay?' the woman asked, running towards me as I sprawled.

She was young and pretty. In fact, she was beautiful, and her soft green eyes were expressing concern. She was dressed in something fluffy that emphasised her attractions without being at all slutty.

'Umm … yes, I think so,' I said, getting to my feet, almost oblivious to the stares of the bank's customers, and enchanted by a whiff of her perfume. 'Thank you for warning me.'

'It looked deliberate,' she said, frowning and pushing back her long blonde hair.

'You mean someone was trying to run me over? Why would anyone do that?'

She shrugged. 'Who knows? Are you sure you're all right? My name's Sally.'

'Andy. I'm fine, and I'm sure it was just an accident. No one would have any reason to hurt me.'

'I suppose not.' She hesitated, biting her lip in the most fascinating and charming manner. 'Look, Andy, I don't normally do this sort of thing, but can I treat you to a coffee?'

I knew I shouldn't, but I hesitated and was lost. 'Umm … okay.'

'Shall we go to Pinky's?' she asked. 'I hear that's good.'

'Umm … why not try that one?' I pointed down the road.

'Café Nerd? What's it like?'

'I've never been in, but it might be brilliant,' I said. 'Anyway, it's closer.'

The truth was that Pinky was Daphne's best friend, and although having a coffee with a ravishing young woman who'd just saved my life was entirely innocent, for some inexplicable reason the idea of her seeing us together was making me feel guilty.

'Fine,' she said, taking my arm.

I was sure every passer-by was staring at us and thinking bad thoughts about me, so I was glad to get inside Café Nerd. It was nothing to write home about, being a bland, white plastic sort of place, with walls plastered in posters from comic books, but it looked comfortable enough.

'What would you like?' I asked, reaching into my pocket.

'Put your wallet away,' she said, squeezing my hand. 'This one's on me.'

'Very kind,' I said. 'In that case, I'll … umm … have a cappuccino.'

She ordered from a smiling young guy with a red bowtie and I managed to lead her to a booth in the corner, out of sight of the front window. I took off my coat and sat down by the wall, expecting her to take the seat facing me. It was disconcerting when she slid along the bench by my side, and despite my budging up as much as possible, she came a little too close. Not that it wasn't pleasant, but I think I'd have preferred more space, and I was baffled why she was gazing into my face with those alluring green eyes.

'It's not a very nice day,' I said, wishing I'd given myself an escape route, and trying to fill an uncomfortable silence.

At least, I found it uncomfortable, but, Sally appeared quite relaxed. I tried to match her, and might have succeeded had she not touched my knee.

'Did you know,' she murmured, 'that you are a most attractive man?'

'Me? Come off it. I'm nothing special.'

'Oh, but you are, Andy.'

I think I blushed and was only saved further embarrassment when the guy came with our drinks.

I grabbed my cappuccino, and took a gulp. It was scalding hot, but I forced it down, guessing she wouldn't be much impressed if I spat it all over the table, and it did at least give me a few moments to think, though I couldn't think of anything.

'Gosh, I was thirsty,' I said, fighting off the pain and putting down the cup.

'So I see. You strike me as the sort of man who knows what he wants and how to get it. It makes you extremely desirable.'

'Does it? I'm flattered, but I've got to tell you I'm married.'

'So? We're only having a coffee. What's wrong with that?'

'Nothing, I suppose, but …'

I gulped as her hand strolled on fingertips a little higher up my thigh.

'What harm can it do? Besides, you're not your wife's property are you?'

'Well, no. Not as such.'

'You're not her chattel. You're a free man.'

'Yes, of course, but …'

'And I'm a free woman.' She paused and nibbled her lip again.

It was a most charming little habit.

'I'm normally very shy,' she said, 'but you're so sweet and so very handsome …'

With no further warning she threw her arms around my neck, pulled herself even closer and kissed my lips. Taken aback, I didn't stop her. I doubt I could have, though I knew it was wrong, and, indeed something about the whole experience felt weird. Even so, I let it happen. The small part of me that enjoyed what was happening, that was flattered, over-rode any guilt and suspicions and somehow, I was kissing her and she was in my arms, her body warm and soft, her scent enchanting but discreet. The whole café lit up for an instant.

'Thanks, mate, that'll do nicely,' said a gruff male voice.

It was all over in a flash. Sally broke from my embrace, slid from the bench and walked straight from the café without a backward glance. The man who'd spoken was stout and balding with a long grubby mac, his nicotine stained fingers holding a camera. He took a few more snaps of my shocked face, glanced at the screen, grinned and turned away.

'What are you doing?' I asked, looking around and feeling confused.

'Taking photographs,' he said over his shoulder. 'Thank you for your cooperation.'

'But why? What's going on?'

'Doubtless all will be made clear shortly. Nice to have met you, Mr Caplet.'

'How do you know my name? Who are you?'

He waved and walked out.

Determined to extract more information, I grabbed my coat and started for the door.

'Excuse me, sir,' said the waiter, blocking my path. 'You haven't paid for your coffees.'

'She said she'd do it.'

'She didn't.' He glanced at a paper bill in his hand. 'That will be five pounds and fifty pence, sir.'

'For two coffees? You've got to be joking.'

He pointed to the sign above the counter. 'All our prices are clearly displayed.'

I glanced up and coughed up, pleased to have the cash, which was still somewhat of a novelty. When I eventually got outside, I looked up and down The Shambles, but Sally and the photographer had gone. To my mind, the whole incident had all the ingredients of a set-up, particularly since he'd known my name. It must have been, and they were intending to blackmail me, but why? I wasn't rich or anything. However, I feared I'd find out all too soon, and there was nothing I could do but wait.

I decided to head for Blackdog Street, although it was only eleven-thirty and still far too early for lunch. I expected Hobbes would be out policing, but Mrs Goodfellow would probably be home and I had no doubt she'd offer me a cup of tea in exchange for a chat. By then I really was thirsty, having been too occupied to take more than just the one gulp of super-heated cappuccino. Deep in thought, wondering about the odd stagnant taste in my mouth, but back to my normal self, I strolled up The Shambles, avoiding the market stalls in the middle where I was well known as a sucker. I passed the stately old Cotswold-stone church and waited for the lights to change so I could cross the road into Blackdog Street, feeling as if I were going home, because I'd lived there for several months when Hobbes took me in after I'd accidently burned down my flat and lost my job. It was only then, aged thirty-seven, that I felt my adult life had begun, and that everything before had been a sort of pupation, a period when I'd achieved almost nothing other than survival. Those days were gone and I'd emerged like a butterfly from a pupa to enjoy the fruits of adulthood. Well, maybe not a butterfly, but I had definitely emerged from darkness into light and things had been going so well.

As I waited, a black Mercedes with tinted windows approached in the midst of a stream of traffic. A rifle barrel pointed from the back window, and I turned to run. There was a sudden sharp pain in my left buttock and I fell forwards with a cry.

'Are you all right, mate?' asked an innocent bystander.

'I've been shot,' I said, numb with horror, except in the buttock area.

'Where?'

'Just here.'

'No, where are you hurt?'

I pointed at my bottom.

'Ooh! I bet that smarts. Who did it?'

'I don't know and it's not important. Call an ambulance!'

'Why?'

'What do you mean why? I've been shot!'

'You'll get over it. It'll sting and you might get a little bruise, but it's nothing to get so worked up about.'

And then the unfeeling, heartless swine just walked away.

I touched the spot, expecting blood, but there was none. However, my probing fingertips located a small hard lump stuck in the fabric of my trousers. It turned out to be an air gun pellet that had passed right through my coat and jacket but not through me. A little ashamed, if still sore, I got to my feet and, seeing the lights had changed and the traffic had stopped, hobbled across into Blackdog Street, heading for the terrace of old stone houses at the end. When I reached number 13, I limped up the three stone steps to the glossy black front door with its shining brass knocker, and reached into my pocket for my key, which wasn't there. Of course it wasn't, because I'd given it back after moving in with Daphne. I reached for the doorbell.

'Hello, dear,' said a familiar high quavering voice that made me jump.

Although I looked down the grille into the cellar, up at the windows, and down the street, I couldn't see her. 'Hello, Mrs Goodfellow. Umm … where are you?'

'On the roof, dear.'

Dressed in a red cardigan and skirt, and a matching headscarf, she was leaning over and waving with no visible means of support. My stomach lurched to see such a frail old woman in such a precarious place.

'Why?'

'The old fellow reckons we're in for torrential rain and gales, so I'm making sure the tiles are all safe and secure and that the gutters are clean.'

'But it must be really slippery up there with all this drizzle. I don't think you should be doing it at your age, and especially in this weather.'

'Far better to do it now than in a gale, dear. That really would be dangerous, and what's my age got to do with anything?'

She had a point, I suppose, but I wasn't happy.

'Nearly finished,' she said, 'so if you give me a moment, I'll come down and let you in. It's nice to see you.'

Arms outstretched for balance, she slid along, squatted, scooped up some gunk with a trowel and threw it into an old sack. Then, looking like a diminutive Santa who'd been on a strict diet, she slung the sack over her shoulder and trudged up the tiles to the summit.

'I'll be with you in a minute,' she said and disappeared.

A minute later, the front door opened.

'Come in, dear. How are you?'

'Fine,' I said, stepping into the neat, if faded, sitting room. With its homely flowery wallpaper and slightly tatty furniture, it looked comfortingly familiar and unchanged, and I started drooling at the aroma of something rich and savoury that was cooking, and which almost, but not completely, overpowered the feral odour I associated with Hobbes.

'You don't look fine,' she said, peering up into my face. 'Have you been fighting? And you've got a bit of a limp.'

'Well, actually, someone punched me on the nose, and then someone shot me in the bottom with an air rifle.' I showed her the tiny pellet and sat down carefully on the sofa.

She laughed. 'Do you want me to take a look at it?'

'No, not really,' I said, ignoring her callous attitude, though I knew how kind she'd be if I'd genuinely been hurt. 'How are you?'

'Very well.'

'And Hobbes?'

'The old fellow's much the same as always. He'll be back for his dinner at one o'clock. Would you care to join him? It's nothing special, just mutton chops.'

'If you're sure there'll be enough, then yes, please.'

'That'll cheer him up. He's been a little bit down since … since he had to deal with something nasty.'

'But, he often deals with nasty things – he's a policeman.'

'Of course, but this was out of the ordinary.'

'I can't remember seeing anything too bad in the *Bugle* … or do you mean that killing in Barnley?'

'No, dear. That was just a drunken fracas that got out of hand when a silly argument became a punch-up. A young man fell, hit his head and died. It was sad and unpleasant, but easily solved. No, I gather it was far, far worse.'

'What then?'

'He hasn't talked about it. All I know is that something happened on Hedbury Common, and that it was not a normal police case. I'm glad I don't know any more. Would you like a cup of tea?'

'I would,' I said, unsure whether to be upset at missing out on the action, or relieved I'd been spared.

'I'll go and make one. Do you like celeriac dauphinoise?'

'I expect so.'

'Good, then make yourself at home.'

'Thank you. Umm … is Dregs out with Hobbes?' I asked, missing the big, black delinquent dog who, though he'd once terrorised me, had become a firm friend.

'He's out courting some bitch, and I'm not sure when he'll be back.'

She went into the kitchen, leaving me with just the latest issue of *Sorenchester Life*. I took it from the coffee table and flicked through, more interested than normal now my reviews would be in it. It was a sure sign I was rising up the social standing, since the glossy magazine was clearly designed for posh people, and largely featured posh people. I'd sometimes wondered why Mrs Goodfellow ordered it, for she was anything but posh and Hobbes was … Hobbes.

Most of the magazine struck me as rather pointless, particularly a long, boring piece about the university rugby team's unexpected recent run of success, but one article about a prize pig called Crackling Rosie grabbed my attention. It wasn't that I was especially interested in pigs, although she looked to be a fine specimen of the Sorenchester Old Spot breed, but because her owner was a local man called Mr Robert Nibblet, better known to me as 'Skeleton' Bob. Bob was the skinniest man in Sorenchester, and widely known as a spectacularly unsuccessful petty criminal and poacher. The police largely tolerated his unlawful activities, since the fines and compensation he had to pay dwarfed the proceeds of his crimes. He'd won Crackling Rosie when bowling for a pig at St Stephen's Church Fete, and was now claiming to be on the straight and narrow. I laughed out loud, for, although it was possible I'd grown old and cynical, I had little doubt he'd be back in the crime pages of the *Bugle* soon. A voice in my ear made me jump.

'Here's your tea, dear,' said Mrs Goodfellow, and placed a mug on the table.

I nodded, shocked as always by her abrupt appearances. How she could move as quietly as a cat was beyond me, but then, compared to Hobbes who, when he wanted, could be quieter than a mouse in felt slippers, she clumped around like a rhinoceros.

'Thank you,' I said when I'd got my breath back. She'd already gone.

The tea was delicious and fragrant, and when I'd drunk it, I considered offering my help in the kitchen, though my culinary skills, unlike my appreciation of them, were not great. However, I had learned an awful lot from Mrs Goodfellow and most of my recent efforts had turned out reasonably edible, unlike many of Daphne's. Although I'd never told her, and never would, she was almost as bad a cook as my mother, who'd even been known to devastate tinned soup. My palate had of course been spoiled by the delights Mrs Goodfellow had bestowed upon my unworthy plate and, although Daphne had undoubtedly been the best thing that had ever happened to me, I'd still experienced occasional nostalgia pangs for life at Hobbes's, especially when meal times were approaching. It occurred to me that I had so much to thank the old girl for; without her, my appreciation of good food would never have developed, and I would never have been able to do my job.

The front door swung open.

A vast figure in well-polished black boots, baggy brown trousers and a flapping gabardine raincoat stood framed in the doorway. As he pulled the door behind him, his eyes scrutinised me from beneath a tangle of dark, bristly eyebrows, and his ugly face broke into a display of grinning yellow teeth.

'Andy! What a wonderful surprise,' said Hobbes. 'Are you staying to lunch?'

I got to my feet and shook the hand he was proffering. It was as hard and as hairy as a coconut and made mine feel as small and weak as a baby's.

'Yes,' I said. 'Mrs Goodfellow invited me. I hope that's not a problem?'

'Of course not. How are you?'

'Apart from being punched on the nose, nearly run over, and getting shot at from a car this morning, I'm fine.'

He chuckled. 'I'm glad to see you've still got your taste for adventure. Take a seat and tell me about it.'

I sat back down and recounted the events of the morning, leaving out the kissing part, and let him examine the pellet that I'd kept in my pocket. When I'd finished, he looked thoughtful.

'It seems someone is out to intimidate you.'

'Or kill me.'

'Shooting you in the backside with an air rifle pellet does not count as an assassination attempt.'

'What about trying to run me over?'

'Then why did the girl warn you? I'm interested in her role in this, but doubtless everything will become clear in good time. Have you annoyed anyone recently?'

'Not that I can think of.'

'Have you written any particularly scathing reviews?'

'No … well yes, a couple of days ago at the start of my curry house special, but it's not been published yet.'

'I remember one from a few months back,' said Hobbes. 'It was about The Italian Job in Hedbury. That was a stinker, though from what I've been told, accurate.'

'I suppose so,' I said, gratified he'd actually read it. 'Do you think they might be behind the attacks?'

He scratched his jaw with his thumb, producing a sound rather like someone sawing a log. 'It would seem an overreaction, but some of these restaurateurs and chefs can be rather precious and thin-skinned. Do you remember what happened to your predecessor?'

'The Fat Man? Do you mean when Featherlight dangled him from the church tower to make him apologise, after a bad review.'

Len 'Featherlight' Binks, the landlord of the Feathers, the most disreputable pub in town, claimed to have once been an army chef and prided himself on his cooking, despite what it did to his customers. Oddly, the pub maintained a loyal clientele and was so shockingly awful that it attracted tourists looking for an experience. For a fair number, their experience ended, for one reason or another, in the hospital.

'Dinner's ready,' said Mrs Goodfellow.

'Thank you, lass,' said Hobbes and smiled as the shock of her voice launched me from the sofa.

It was always the same, but I knew I'd forgive her as soon as I'd started to eat. Hobbes ushered me into the kitchen, which was just as I remembered, and we took our places at the well-scrubbed wooden table in the middle of the red brick floor, as the old girl dished up. The aroma was so delicious I'd already picked up my knife and fork before remembering that Hobbes always said grace, a habit imposed during his far-distant childhood. Trying not to fidget, I waited until he'd finished.

Although I'd had a slight fear that memory had built up her powers too high, that she'd only seemed so brilliant in comparison to my mother's dreadful concoctions, along with the abominations from the Feathers and the Greasy Pole, and that my recent fine dining might have spoiled me, the first morsel made me realise just how foolish my concerns had been. She was, quite simply, the best cook I'd ever known, and by such a distance I wondered if I'd been far too generous in most of my reviews. Indeed, many of the restaurants I'd assessed as excellent now seemed merely adequate, for her mutton chops, slow cooked in a rich tangy sauce were a taste of heaven, the celeriac dauphinoise was fragrant and substantial and the sautéed leeks worthy of their own paragraph of effusive praise at the very least. As usual, Hobbes and I ate in reverential silence until our plates were clean.

'That was delicious,' said Hobbes as she came to clear up, and I nodded, fearing an emotional breakdown if I tried to say anything.

'How is Daphne?' asked Hobbes, when the old girl had served us tea in the sitting room.

'Fine, I think.'

'That's a strange answer,' he said, tipping sugar into his mug and stirring it with his finger.

'She's gone away.'

'Where to?'

'Egypt. She left this morning.' I glanced at my watch. 'I expect she'll be on the plane by now.'

'Is she on holiday?'

'No, she's got a secondment on an archaeological dig. Apparently, they think they might have discovered a lost city beneath the sands, but she didn't know where, because it's all secret to protect it from grave robbers.'

'That sounds interesting,' he said. 'If it weren't for all the camels, I'd like to go back there some time.' He took a huge slurp from his mug.

'I didn't know you'd ever been,' I said and took a tiny sip of tea. It was still scalding.

'It was after the Great War.'

'Why?'

'I was sent to sort out a rogue anubis.' To my surprise, he shuddered.

'What's one of those?'

'A so-called mythical creature, and that's all I'm prepared to say. It was not a happy experience … for either of us. Besides, it was where I developed my camel allergy.'

Since I'd long ago learned that he could not be persuaded to say more than he wanted, I dropped the subject, just adding it to the pile of mysteries. I'd once believed my slow realisation that he was not strictly human, that he was, in fact, 'unhuman', had been his greatest mystery, but, since then I'd learned such snippets of his history that mere 'unhumanity' seemed almost unremarkable.

'What are you doing these days?' I asked, changing the subject.

'Surprisingly little since a nasty case up on Hedbury Common before Christmas. Yesterday, I investigated some petty vandalism in Stillingham, but it didn't take me long to nail the culprit, a fifteen-year old lad who'd got bored and smashed some windows. I've had a word with him and I doubt he'll be any trouble now.'

'That's good,' I said.

'It is for the public, but it's not very exciting for me. Still, I'm sure something will turn up soon. It usually does.'

Hobbes finished his tea and got to his feet, saying he was heading back to the police station. Having decided to tag along, I was soon in the once familiar position of scurrying behind, breathing heavily, and trying to keep up with his long, lazy lope. When we turned into Vermin Street I was suddenly and unexpectedly enveloped in a big black dog.

'Get off!' I said, wrestling with Dregs who, having not seen me for a while, was determined to make up for lost time. I was delighted to meet him again, despite his long wet tongue. In addition, I was rather proud he'd failed to knock me to the ground, as he'd done so many times before.

'Have you finished courting for today?' asked Hobbes.

'What?' I said, taken by a sudden fear that he'd heard something.

But he was talking to Dregs, who wagged his tail and contrived to look smug.

'Should he be out on his own?' I asked.

'I doubt it, but he insisted.' He paused and looked down the road. 'Hallo, 'allo, 'allo, what's going on here then?'

A spaghetti-thin man in a threadbare jacket and stained trousers, tears rolling down his bony face, was running towards us shouting. 'Mr Hobbes! Mr Hobbes!'

'Calm down, Bob,' said Hobbes. 'Whatever is the matter?'

'It's Rosie,' said Skeleton Bob as he drew near. 'Some swine has murdered her.'

'Rosie who?' asked Hobbes, frowning and reaching for his notebook.

'Bob's prize pig,' I said. 'It was in *Sorenchester Life*. I forgot to tell you I'm going to be published in *Sorenchester Life!*'

'When did this happen?' asked Hobbes.

'This morning,' I said. 'Phil Waring told me.'

'Thank you, Andy, but I was asking Bob.'

'It must have happened overnight, Mr Hobbes. I went to feed her this morning and there she was, dead. Murdered! She was such a sweet pig.'

'Tell me what happened,' asked Hobbes, who to his credit was still looking concerned.

'Someone must have broken down the wire around her yard and attacked her in her house. There was blood all over and she was dead. Stabbed I reckon. She was a lovely animal.'

'Most unpleasant,' said Hobbes. 'Have you informed the police yet?'

'We don't have a phone because we couldn't pay the bill. I had to walk and I've only just got here and I'm really tired.'

'But your cottage is only five miles out of town. It shouldn't have taken you more than an hour and a half,' I said.

'I had some things to deliver,' said Bob. 'I have to do them all on foot since they took my van away. They reckoned it wasn't roadworthy.'

'I heard you drove it into a pond,' said Hobbes.

'Yes, but I could've got it out.'

'I also heard it had no brakes and that all four tyres were as bald as eggs and that there was a big hole in the floor.'

'But it still went like a bomb.'

Hobbes smiled. 'I'll give you a lift home and take a look at the crime scene. My car's at the station. Do you fancy a trip out, Andy?'

I nodded and he led the way down Vermin Street and through a dank and mossy alley, before we reached the back of the police station where his latest ridiculously small car, a rusty Nissan Micra, was parked. Bob and I had to cram into the back since Dregs preferred riding up front. The engine started.

'Hang on,' I muttered.

The car hurtled through town, Hobbes ignoring red lights and road signs, until we hit the main road to Bob's place where he could really crush the accelerator. Although Bob whimpered occasionally, I, acting on the principle that ignorance was bliss, screwed my eyes closed and thought happy thoughts until we'd stopped. Hobbes's driving hadn't got any better, though in fairness he never had accidents unless he meant to, when presumably they should have been called deliberates.

'Where's the crime scene?' he asked, getting out and looking around at the red brick hovel and the chaotic yard that was littered with rusting metal and nameless junk. Dregs, to his chagrin, was not allowed out and moped in the car. At least he was spared the drizzle.

'Behind the cottage,' said Bob. 'It's not a pretty sight.'

'No, it isn't, but I expect new windows and a lick of paint would help,' I said.

Bob frowned. 'I meant the crime scene. It's in the orchard.'

He showed us round the back, which involved an undignified scramble over what might, in a previous existence, have been a tractor. Although the so-called orchard contained a number of bare trees, they didn't look likely to bear fruit, and I'd have guessed they were sycamores. However, the pig run in the corner looked well kept, apart from the broken wire fence and the bloodied carcass. She'd been a big pig. Hobbes glanced at me.

'I remember the routine,' I said. 'I have to stay back ... or should I say sty back?'

'No, you shouldn't.' He was already in the pig run, looking, poking and sniffing.

If anyone had asked me, I'd have said the only smell was pig.

Kneeling down, he examined Crackling Rosie and the muddy ground. He nodded as he got back to his feet and leant into the brick pig house, a solid structure about the size of a medium-sized garden shed.

'Yes,' he said. 'Rosie is certainly dead, and your surmise that she was killed is entirely justified. However, I don't believe the culprit was human.'

'D'you mean aliens did it?' I asked, and was ignored.

'You see,' Hobbes continued, 'there are two sets of trotter prints.'

'Two?' said Bob. 'But I've only got ... I only had the one.'

'And Rosie's wounds appear to have been caused by tusks, so I believe she was attacked by a wild boar.'

'I thought they were extinct in this country,' I said.

'They were,' said Hobbes, 'but some were brought back in collections, and, of course, a few escaped and bred. I wasn't aware of any around here, but there would appear to be at least one.'

'Are they dangerous?'

'Apparently,' said Hobbes, with a glance at Rosie. 'However, the occasional ones I've met have been quite charming.'

'What are you going to do about it?' asked Bob, still tearful. 'She was a lovely pig and didn't deserve to be murdered by a fence-crashing boar.'

I sniggered and Bob stared at me, nonplussed, looking forlorn in the increasing drizzle.

'I will report the incident,' said Hobbes. 'Perhaps I'll track down the culprit and assess the risk to the public.'

'Do you think it might attack someone?' I asked.

'Possibly,' said Hobbes, 'and it might cause a road accident.'

'I guess it's likely to be a road hog,' I said.

Hobbes acknowledged my little jest with a nod, but it soared way over poor Bob's head.

I wished I'd thought to bring an umbrella since my tweed jacket, as absorbent as kitchen towel, was growing heavier, and stinking like Dregs did before it was necessary to give him a bath – a wild and messy procedure.

'I'm ruined,' said Bob. 'I was banking on breeding from her and now I'll have no money coming in at all. How will I pay the bills? How will I eat?'

'At least you'll have bacon,' I said, trying to help him see the bright side.

He burst into tears.

'That was a little tactless,' said Hobbes. 'Cheer up, Bob. I'll ask your wife to make you a cup of tea.'

'Fenella isn't home. She said I was spending too much time with Rosie and that I had to choose between the two of them. I couldn't, so she walked out and went to stay with her mum.'

'I know how you must feel,' I said. 'My wife's just gone to Egypt.'

'You don't understand,' said Bob, his head in his hands. 'She'll come back now Rosie's gone.'

Hobbes led him into the house, sat him down on a stool, made him a pot of tea, and left him to sob as we returned to the car.

'Where are we going?' I asked once I'd broken free of Dregs, who'd scrambled over the seat to take a good long sniff at my jacket.

'To the Wildlife Park,' said Hobbes. 'It's possible they've lost a boar, though I don't remember seeing any there.'

'There were some guinea pigs in the petting zoo,' I joked. 'Perhaps it was one of them?'

'Despite the name they are not actually pigs, and they're far too small to be a threat to a porker like Crackling Rosie. I do recall Red River Hogs there, but I think it unlikely that the park would let anything escape. However, they might have some information about them.'

I sat back, closing my eyes, as he stamped down on the accelerator. Now and again car horns blared, but I remained blissfully ignorant as to the cause.

After a few minutes, we slowed and turned and I risked a look. We were approaching the Wildlife Park by way of a long driveway between fields. Last time I'd gone there, it had been on a glorious summer's day with hundreds of visitors, but the car park was empty now, and even the fields appeared deserted, though I did eventually spot a morose bunch of Bactrian camels sheltering under a tree.

A notice board next to the narrow green ticket booth bore the message: Have we got Gnus for you! Moving into pastures gnu, our gnu herd of wildebeests!

Another board read: Visit our South American bird collection and meet the rhea of the year! See how our Peruvian Pelican's bill holds more fish than his belly can!

The attempts at humour made me suspect they were the work of Mr Catt, the director.

A well-wrapped man emerged from the booth, holding up a gloved hand, and approached the car. Hobbes opened the window.

'Two adults, is it?' asked the man.

'Police business,' said Hobbes, showing his ID.

The man rolled his eyes and tutted. 'I've been freezing my arse off all day and the first visitors turn out to be cops. It was a complete waste of my time coming in!'

'Cheer up, sir,' said Hobbes. 'At least you'll be paid.'

'I bloody won't. I'm a volunteer.'

'You must love animals,' I said.

'Used to, until the blasted giraffe started pissing on me from a great height.'

'Sorry to hear that, sir. Where can we find Mr Catt?'

'In the aquarium.'

'I hope he brought his towel,' I quipped.

'Thank you for your help, sir,' said Hobbes, ignoring me.

He parked the car and we headed into the aquarium, where it was pleasantly warm, and lit only by the soft glow of fish tanks. Mr Catt, a chubby, red-faced little man in a dishevelled safari suit, was staring into one of the smaller tanks that was home to a variety of brightly-coloured little fish, some with torn fins. A young woman in blue overalls and thick glasses was standing on a step ladder, trying to scoop up a small orange and white fish that kept darting into a big greenish globby thing.

Mr Catt turned as we approached. 'Mr Hobbes,' he said, 'good afternoon.'

'Good afternoon, sir,' said Hobbes, saluting.

'You find us trying to trap a clown fish, *Amphiprion percula*.' He nodded at the woman. 'This is Annette. Annette's essential for catching fish.' He chuckled.

'What's wrong with him?' I asked, as Dregs, an avid observer of wildlife, sat and stared.

'Percy is looking green around the gills, and has been attacking all the other fish, apart from Derek the domino fish, *Dascyllus trimaculatas,* who he won't allow to move away from him or the anemones.'

'Is that unusual?'

'No,' said Mr Catt, giggling like a silly kid. 'Clown fish like to keep their friends close and anemones closer.'

'Most fascinating, sir,' said Hobbes, 'but we're here on business.'

'Of course, Inspector. How may I be of assistance?'

'Do you keep any wild boar?'

'*Sus scrofa?*' said Mr Catt, shaking his head. 'Why do you ask?'

Hobbes explained.

'Very sad,' said Mr Catt, 'but, no, we don't have any in our collection. However, it was only a matter of time before they reached this part of the world, and from what you said it sounds like there may only be the one so far. It'll be interesting if they start breeding nearby. That could cause a lot of problems.'

'What sort of problems?' asked Hobbes. 'Are they likely to attack the public?'

'They're normally afraid of people, so attacks are quite rare, but possible in certain circumstances. They are, however, quite likely to go for pet dogs if they feel threatened, and they've been known to spook horses, causing riders to fall. In addition, they can cause traffic accidents, and since they're so big, hitting one at speed is likely to be extremely serious. They can also create mayhem on farmland and in gardens.'

'Yes!' cried Annette, having finally trapped Percy. She transferred him into a polythene bag of water and climbed down.

'Oh, well done!' said Mr Catt. 'Plop him in the holding tank and I'll take a look when I'm finished here.'

As she turned to go, Mr Catt glanced at his watch and called after her. 'And then would you go to the office? Our *Latrodectus hesperus* is due for delivery in five minutes.'

'What's that?' I asked.

'A black widow spider for our arachnid collection. It proved difficult to source her until we looked on the web.' He sniggered as Annette walked briskly away, shaking her head.

Not being a fan of creepy crawlies, I shuddered. 'Aren't they poisonous?'

'I doubt anyone's tried to find out, because they don't look very appetising. They are, however, venomous, if that's what you mean, though they rarely bite humans, and their bites are hardly ever fatal.'

'Fascinating,' said Hobbes, 'but where is a boar likely to live?'

'They prefer mixed woodland but can exist in a variety of habitats, provided there is sufficient shelter and adequate food and water. Are you going to do anything about it?'

'I might have to. Mr Nibblet was most upset. Is there any reason why the boar attacked Crackling Rosie?'

'Hard to say. It could have been territorial; sometimes a pig won't accept other porcines in its boardom.'

'What?' I said, puzzled.

'A king has a kingdom. Therefore, a boar has a boardom.' Mr Catt explained, smirking. 'I thought everyone knew that.'

'Umm … are you sure?'

He shrugged and continued. 'It might have been a fight over food, or it's just possible that it's an unusually aggressive specimen.'

'A psycho killer?' I suggested.

'Could be,' Mr Catt agreed.

There was a small glass box with a perforated lid in the corner that I only noticed when something thin and brown, partly hidden by twigs, moved inside. 'What's that?' I pointed, a little nervously, fearing it might be a snake.

Mr Catt walked over, picked up the box and showed me. Inside was an insect with an evil wedge-shaped head, bulbous eyes, and with spiky front legs held out in humble supplication. 'This little beauty is a Chinese praying mantis, *Tenodera sinensis*. She's waiting to be introduced to her soon-to-be-late husband. The females tend to devour the males during the very act of copulation, so her husband is not long for this world. But what a way to go, eh!' He sniggered.

I was grateful for having been born human.

'Is that all?' asked Mr Catt.

'I believe so,' said Hobbes. 'Thank you.'

'A pleasure, as always, Inspector. I'd better get on. I must see what is ailing Percy, and I have to check on one of our carp who keeps hiding away.'

'It's probably just a little koi,' I said, grinning.

'No, he's a silver carp, *Hypophthalmichthys molitrix*,' said Mr Catt seriously, 'and rather a fine specimen. Good afternoon, gentlemen. When I've finished in here I need to check on our bipolar bear. My work is never done.'

The rain was heavy as we ran back to the car.

'What next?' I asked as we got inside. 'Are you going to hunt it down?'

'No. We'll head back to town,' said Hobbes. 'It would be difficult, not to mention unpleasant, to go on a wild boar hunt in this rain, and, besides, you're not really dressed for outdoor activities.'

'That's true,' I said, pleased he'd noticed, though slightly disappointed, since hunting with Hobbes was an exciting, if occasionally terrifying, experience.

Still, the weather was really horrible, and I'd grown accustomed to comfort, warmth and stability since marrying. I didn't regret the marriage, not at all, even though I'd admit to days when I'd missed the visceral thrill of being out and about with Hobbes. If everything was running to plan, Daphne would be flying south-eastwards across Europe and would soon be crossing the Mediterranean to Egypt. I hoped she'd do well, for I'd not forgotten her excitement at being offered the chance to use her archaeological skills on a new site. And yet, I wasn't happy she'd chosen to be so far away, particularly as I didn't know how long she'd be there.

Hobbes dropped me off outside our flat, the one Daphne had bought when she first moved into town, and coincidently the one I'd previously lived in until I'd accidently burned it down. Since I'd caused so much damage, the whole building had required refurbishment, with the result that it was far smarter than it had been in my solo days. Really, I'd done everyone a favour.

'If you have any more trouble with attackers,' he said before driving away, 'then call me. This sort of thing is prone to escalation, and I would advise taking care for the immediate future. I'll see if I can find out what's going on, because I can't have members of the public attacked and you are my public. Mind how you go.'

I poked in the number to unlock the building's door, and went inside, a little shaken by what he'd said, for in my naiveté I'd decided the worst had already happened. The idea that there might be more attacks had simply not occurred, and, as I trotted upstairs and opened our front door, I began to worry again. Why had the guy taken photographs of Sally and me? Had she really liked me, or had she just been toying with my affections? I feared the latter, though not as much as the prospect of being blackmailed.

I made myself a drink, sat down in the kitchen, and thought that Hobbes might have had a point in suggesting some disgruntled restaurateur held a grudge against me. That could explain the punch on the nose, and the Mercedes intimidation, but a blackmail plot, if that's what it turned out to be, seemed far-fetched. After all, what could anyone expect to get from me? I wasn't rich, had no possessions of great value, and wasn't in a position of any real influence. The whole thing seemed so unlikely. Perhaps I'd misinterpreted the whole incident. Maybe Sally had been the target and I'd merely been collateral damage. However, this shaky hypothesis collapsed since I had to admit that young women were not normally so smitten by my manly charms that they flung themselves into my arms. I would have to wait and see, though it was an unhappy thought that any day I might receive an envelope with photographs, and a letter made up of words clipped from newspapers, if that's how it was still done. The only good I could see in the situation was that Daphne was away, and I hoped I could sort things out before she returned, for there was no denying the photos would be what the press always called 'compromising'.

The rest of the afternoon I frittered away on her old laptop, scaring myself when reading of possible terrorist activity in Egypt and, although it was probably nowhere near where she'd be, I couldn't stop worrying. She'd insisted that any threat was negligible, and it probably was, but I still fretted and intended to continue fretting until she was safely home.

In the early evening, I ate baked beans on toast, watched some telly and went to bed. Although I took a book, I became sleepy almost at once and, having turned off the bed-side light, fell asleep.

4

When I surfaced from a plunge into deep sleep, rain was battering the windows and the wind was howling. It was nearly four o'clock, and clamping pillows to my ears didn't drown out the din, which, even in my dozy state, struck me as unusual as our flat was triple-glazed and we could usually hear nothing of what was going on outside. I gave up on getting back to sleep, mooched into the lounge, and pulled back the curtains.

I could see little out in the blackness other than frills of rain rippling down the window, until a lightning flash lit up a world of wind and water. Almost simultaneously, thunder roared like an artillery bombardment, or at least like I imagined an artillery bombardment might sound. The weather forecasters had got it about right for once, though if anything they'd underestimated the storm. Yet, warm, dry and safe inside, I found it all quite exhilarating, until the window shattered.

All the lights blinked out and something bashed into me, sending me flying across the room. Although I don't think I quite lost consciousness, I was stunned, winded and discombobulated and it must have taken several minutes before my brain engaged a gear and worked out that I was on my back, pinned down by a crushing weight. The storm had become deafening, rain was in my face and I was shivering and goose pimply, pyjamas not being adequate for the occasion. It took another couple of minutes before I worked out that one of the massive old trees in the communal garden had come down and smashed through our flat. Wriggling free wasn't easy because of the smooth, wet, laminated flooring, and it took several minutes of grunting and groaning before I got a grip on Daphne's heavy oak sideboard and pulled myself free. The manoeuvre tore my pyjama bottoms in two lengthways, and as I stood, they fell around my ankles, exposing me to the elements.

After a rummage, I unearthed a small torch in the sideboard and turned it on. The tree had not only smashed through the window, but had also knocked in a large chunk of the wall, and, to judge by the broken tiles, part of the roof. I was covered in scratches, grazes and bruises, but these, and losing my pyjama bottoms, seemed a small price to pay for having escaped. It could have been so much worse, but I wondered what Daphne would think when she reached camp and phoned me. If she could, when our phone was somewhere under the tree.

I heard shouting and, thinking I might be able to help or fetch help, ran to the front door, opened it, stepped boldly into the hallway, before retreating in a bashful panic, realising in a flash of lightning that I wasn't presentable. Besides, it seemed sensible to ensure I was adequately dressed for the storm. Turning back, I clambered over the tree's dripping branches towards our bedroom, and shoved open the door. I came within a whisker of plunging into a gaping void where the floor had been, but, somehow, my grip on the door handle stayed firm and allowed me to haul myself back to safety, my heart pounding, my insides squirming.

The outside had come inside, and vice versa, and our bed and all our things were downstairs on our new neighbours' flattened flat. They'd only moved in a couple of weeks earlier, and I hadn't even met them. I shouted down, but got no response, and feared I never would. The situation was clearly far worse than I'd imagined, but the gust of wet wind around my nether regions reminded me that I was in no state to parade around. Yet, since all my clothes, not to mention the wardrobe that had contained them, were now downstairs, I was nonplussed until I remembered Daphne's dressing gown. She kept it on a hook behind the bedroom door, and, unless it had blown away, it might still be there. Groping around the back, terrified of the drop in front, I found it at last and jiggled it loose. Although it was sopping wet, small and pink, it was far better than nothing.

I put it on, tied the cord, and scrambled back over the branches to the hallway, where Mrs Rodgers, a large and normally cheerful divorcee of indeterminate age, and Mr Hussain, a slight, bald man in his late fifties, were talking in her doorway. Both were holding candles. Both gaped when they saw me.

'D'you know what's happened?' asked Mr Hussain.

'A tree came down,' I said. 'It's smashed up our flat and our bedroom floor has fallen on top of the new people below.'

'Aubrey and Hilda Elwes?' said Mrs Rodgers, her eyes widening. 'That's awful.'

'Have you called the emergency services?' I asked. 'My phone's gone.'

Mr Hussain shook his head. 'No, we had no idea what was going on.'

'I'll do it now,' said Mrs Rodgers and disappeared into her flat with Mr Hussain tagging behind.

'I'll see if anyone needs help,' I said, though I doubted they could hear me.

I ran downstairs, where a tall, slim young man was banging on the Elweses' front door, shouting at the top of his voice. He turned his torch on me when he heard my approach. I thought he looked vaguely familiar, and suspected he might be a neighbour.

'A tree's smashed into the building,' he said, looking panicked. 'I can't get a reply from Aubrey and Hilda.'

'Our bedroom's fallen on them. Mrs Rodgers is calling the emergency services.'

'Do you think we should break in?' he asked.

'Umm … good question. If they're hurt, they may need our help quickly. I'll do it.'

Filled with unusual bravado, I charged their front door, only to bounce off like a tennis ball. Groaning, I sank to my knees, and rubbed my shoulder.

'Or we could wait for help,' he said.

'I wish I'd thought of that.' I got back to my feet.

Although he carried on banging and shouting, no one else appeared, and I began to fear other flats had been destroyed. I ran to the next front door along and pounded on it.

'Are you all right in there?' I cried, but there was no response.

'You're wasting your time,' said the young man. 'That's my place, and I'm here.'

'Oh, right. I think I'll take a look outside.'

'Okay, but hadn't you better adjust that … thing you're wearing?'

I retied the cord, using a double knot, ran to the block's back door and opened it. As I stepped out, a shrieking wind nearly blew me back inside, and might have done had the spring-loaded door not slammed. The night air was so full of rain it was a struggle to even breathe, and my puny torch barely made a glimmer in the blackness. Hunched against the storm, clutching the dressing gown, I stumbled and groped my way through the communal garden until there was a lull in the wind. It gave me the opportunity to run, but, unfortunately, I ran into something that knocked the wind from my lungs, as it knocked me onto my back, where I lay stunned for a few moments with rain pouring up my nose. When my lungs re-inflated and my head cleared, I tried to stand up, but struck my head and fell back, moaning. By the feeble glow of my torch, I saw I'd again been flattened by the tree. My teeth were chattering and, although sense told me to concede defeat and to retreat into the dry, a tiny seed of resolve was growing. Getting back to my feet, I forced myself onward, battling the elements, imagining myself a hero such as Scott of the Antarctic, though memories of his tragic end were not encouraging. Onward I went, through branches and twigs, getting scratched and battered, until I reached a massive hole in the wall containing a huge chunk of tree. I scrambled into what had been the inside.

'Hello?' I yelled. 'Is anyone there?'

There was no reply.

'Mr and Mrs Elwes, are you all right?'

'If you mean us, then yes,' said a soft male voice from behind. I assumed it was Mr Elwes.

Two figures appeared in my torchlight.

'What have you done to our flat?' asked a hooded woman who was almost as tall as the man at her side.

'Me? Nothing.'

'Where's it gone then?' Her voice was sweet and sounded amused.

'The tree came down on it.'

'I wondered what it was doing there,' said Mr Elwes. 'We were out.'

'In this?' I gestured at the weather.

'Why not?'

'It's horrible.'

'Or exhilarating,' said Mrs Elwes.

I shook my head, and shivered, thinking there were some odd folk about. 'I'm getting really cold and I'm going back inside. Mrs Rodgers is calling for help.'

'Okey dokey,' said Mr Elwes, who did not sound much concerned.

Above me I could hear something moving, as if it was sliding. For a moment I wondered what it might be, and then it hit me.

I could smell hospital, and a familiar voice was asking how I was feeling. Despite a dull, throbbing headache, I opened my eyes to see a thin lad in a white coat, with a stethoscope around his neck.

'Dr Finlay,' I said, and shook his hand.

He nodded. 'Indeed. You haven't been in for ages. Nice to see you again.'

'Thank you … umm … what happened? What am I doing here?'

'You received a nasty blow to the side of the head from half a roof tile. It was lucky your neighbours were there to rescue you, because I gather the rest of the roof collapsed moments after they got you out.'

'No, that can't be right. I went to rescue them … I think. Umm … things are a little blurry.'

'That's perfectly normal with a concussion.'

'Another one? Why me?'

Dr Finlay shrugged. 'Wrong place at the wrong time. Now, I have a few questions…'

'Fire away, doc.'

'Do you know your name?'

'Of course.'

'Well, what is it?'

'What's what? Who are you? … Only joking. I'm Andy … Andy Caplet.'

'Excellent, and how are you feeling?'

'Fine, apart from a bit of a headache, and I'm a little sore here … and here.' I felt around and wasn't surprised to find a bandage on my head.

'Excellent. How many fingers do you see?'

'Eleven. Including the finger of fudge in your top pocket.'

'Very amusing. It's a snack for later … if I'm not too busy.'

'That's a point. I'm feeling rather hungry. What time is it?'

'Twenty past ten,' said Dr Finlay after glancing at a wall clock.

'Really? How long was I out?'

'No more than two minutes after the tile hit you, according to your neighbours, but longer after the second incident.'

'Second incident?'

'You were lying on a trolley in triage awaiting initial assessment when you decided you needed to visit the bathroom.'

'Oh, yes,' I said, as memory juddered back into focus. 'I really needed to go. What happened?'

'According to Nurse Dutton, you leapt to your feet, ran around frantically, tripped over that rather fetching dressing gown you were wearing, and head-butted the reception desk. You were in and out of consciousness for over an hour then, but you appear fine now.'

'I rather think I am. I've been told I've got a thick skull. By the way, was anybody else hurt? In the flats I mean.'

'Just you.'

'Good. Umm … do we get fed soon?'

'Not until lunchtime, but you'll be out before then. We'd normally keep you in longer for observation, but the density of your cranium is well known to us, and, anyway, we're full and need every available bed.'

'But there's a tree in my flat! Where will I go?' As full recollection came back, I was gripped by a sudden panic. 'And I've got no clothes!'

'Don't worry,' said Dr Finlay. 'We contacted Mrs Goodfellow who'll be bringing something for you to wear.'

A massive surge of hope washed through me; if the old girl was involved everything would turn out all right.

'She'll be here before twelve o'clock, and suggested you could stay with them while you sort things out. I have other patients to see now, but someone will be with you in a few minutes to run through a bit of paperwork and then, assuming you're still feeling well, you're free to go. Nice to meet you again. Keep safe. Bye.'

'Bye, doc. I'll give it a try.'

Despite his youthful appearance, Dr Finlay had treated me several times in the past, but when Daphne had been around I'd gone unscathed. Left to my own devices, I'd managed to stay out of hospital for less than a day. I hoped she'd have a good laugh when I told her, but how was I going to tell her when my mobile was in the Elweses' flat and the landline and my laptop must have been smashed by the tree? The plan had been that she'd text or email me when she'd reached camp, but that was clearly out of the question. I supposed I could do the contacting, because I knew it was possible to get my email on another computer, but I had an awful feeling I'd need a password and I hadn't a clue what mine might be, since Daphne had set up my account. All in all, it seemed I wasn't doing a great job of coping.

As soon as I was free to go, Mrs Goodfellow, clad in a daffodil-yellow rain cape and green wellingtons, stomped into the cubicle, lugging a battered leather suitcase.

'Hello, dear,' she said. 'I've brought you some clothes.'

'Thanks,' I said, taking the case, and leaning down to receive a kiss on the cheek. 'It's been a difficult couple of days.'

I explained how I'd got there while I turned my back and dressed, glad to rid myself of the totally inadequate – and draughty – hospital gown.

'That's a nasty-looking bruise on your bottom,' Mrs Goodfellow remarked. 'Was that where you got shot, dear?'

I nodded and pulled up my pants. Although she'd seen me naked often enough and there should have been no need to feel bashful, I still was. Embarrassment was a concept she seemed unable to grasp. However, as I'd expected, all the clothes, including a fabulous tweed jacket, fitted as if bespoke, though they'd formerly belonged to her errant husband, who'd last been heard of setting up a windsurfing school in Bali, called Washed Up. His previous enterprise had been a naturist colony on Tahiti, until the authorities clamped down and he could bare it no longer. When I'd finished dressing, I noticed she'd brought a gabardine raincoat and an old pair of black wellies.

'Is it still raining?' I asked.

'Worse than ever, dear. It's wild out there. Trees have come down all over, roofs have blown off, there are already some floods, and now the river looks like it's going to burst its banks. The old fellow's helping with the evacuation and is worried the rain is turning into a drownpour.'

'D'you mean a downpour?'

'No, dear. It's getting so bad there's a risk to members of the public.'

'I just can't imagine the Soren bursting its banks. It's such a placid little river.'

'But not today, and it has flooded in the past. About thirty years ago it filled our cellar with six inches of filthy water.'

'That must have been unpleasant.'

'It was, though we weren't the worst affected by far. The houses across from Church Fields were flooded three feet deep and had to be pumped out!'

'Well, let's hope it stops soon. I'm ready now. Shall we go?'

'Yes, we'd better. I've still got his dinner to prepare. Would you like to join us?'

Had there not been a number of sick and injured people about, I might have whooped for joy. Instead, I smiled and said, 'I'd love to. Thank you.'

She led me through the A&E department towards the exit. 'You can use your old room if you'd like, until you've sorted out somewhere else. The old fellow reckons your block of flats is structurally unsound and will have to be demolished.'

Although I'd assumed the tree must have caused a great deal of damage, I'd barely thought about the consequences. I was, or rather we were, homeless, and although for me the flat had just been a pleasant place to live, for Daphne it had represented a whole new life, a break from the past after the loss of her first husband, whose bones Dregs and I had once stumbled across.

'Oh, dear,' I said, inadequately. 'I suppose I'd better go round and see if I can salvage anything … after we've eaten of course. '

'You can't, dear,' said Mrs Goodfellow. 'No one is allowed in. It's too dangerous.'

'It's a disaster then. I guess it'll be tricky to find anywhere good to live when all our neighbours are looking for places as well.'

As we reached the exit, the old girl unfurled a large umbrella that just seemed to appear in her hand, and stepped out into the storm, which was at least as bad as it had been in the night, if not quite as dark, and I was dressed more appropriately. It was not surprising that hardly anyone was walking, and that even traffic was scarce. Those few cars and vans that were out were crawling along, their wipers going full tilt. Water sluiced off every surface, drains overflowed, the roads were already ankle deep and it was a struggle to even walk with gale force gusts threatening to blow me over, though Mrs Goodfellow, snug beneath her oversized umbrella, seemed to have no problem. I put it down to her diminutive size, since the wind obviously couldn't be bothered to knock her about when it had me to batter, though how she managed to stop the umbrella from blowing away or turning inside out was a mystery. Blackdog Street was a little uphill from the hospital and I was gasping like a heavy smoker in a marathon when we reached number 13, and she let us in.

'Wow!' I said, as she closed out the weather.

She nodded. 'It's worse than ever. I hope the old fellow's all right. He doesn't swim too well.'

'I thought he did everything well, and I've seen him diving for eels.'

'Not everything, dear. He doesn't like to be out of his depth.'

'I'm sure he'll be fine,' I said, delighted to discover something at which I might best him. It wasn't that I was such a great swimmer, but Daphne had given me lessons and I'd become confident in water, as long as it wasn't too cold or too deep.

'I'd better get on with dinner, dear. I'll do something substantial, because he'll need it, and I expect you're hungry, too?'

'I certainly am. I didn't have any breakfast today … and I only had beans on toast last night. What are you cooking?'

'Smoked haddock soufflé with herb champ.'

'Marvellous,' I said, although not entirely sure what herb champ was.

However, it had always been one of the delights of the old girl's cooking that, although she had a set of particularly wonderful dishes based on the seasons and whatever turned up in the shops, her repertoire was seemingly endless. She had no need of cookbooks or scales, and I'd sometimes watched her at work, noting every ingredient and how she treated it. Since moving in with Daphne, I'd attempted my own versions, and on the whole, the results had not even come close to the originals, though they'd mostly been tasty enough for Daphne to declare me a good cook. Compared to her, I probably was.

I relaxed by watching the end of a black and white cowboy film on the telly. It turned out to be rather a good one. Westerns had once been a bit of a no-go area until Hobbes persuaded me to watch a few, and I discovered there was something brave and spirited in the best of them, while the landscapes were often breathtaking. He'd visited the American West back in the sixties and I think he enjoyed the familiarity.

The front door opened, bringing in rain and the chime of the church clock striking one. Hobbes nodded at me, shook out his coat, hung it on the bullhorn coat rack in the corner, and closed the door behind Dregs, who, soggy but exuberant, insisted on drying himself on me. Hobbes ran upstairs to wash his hands, returning just as Mrs Goodfellow announced in a loud voice from behind my ear that dinner, as he typically called lunch, was ready.

Had I not been pinned down by the dog, I would have leapt from my skin. As it was, my alarmed twitch threw him off and onto the rug, where he blinked and looked confused, clearly wondering how he'd got there, but giving me the chance to escape. The aroma of smoked haddock as I entered the kitchen was mouth-watering.

'How's things?' I asked when Hobbes took his seat.

'Not good. If this rain keeps up, and I think it will, the Soren will burst its banks this afternoon. The environment people don't think it will cause much of a problem, but I'm not convinced. The trouble is there'll be so much run-off from the hills, and the ground is already saturated.'

'Here you are,' said Mrs Goodfellow, placing plates in front of us.

Hobbes, dismissing his worried frown, smiled, thanked her, and said grace before giving his full concentration to the soufflé and the champ, which turned out to be mashed potato with green herbs and a pool of melted butter in the centre. It was a treat, and, since I realised it would re-calibrate my appreciation of good food, I suspected the next restaurant I visited professionally would suffer in comparison. We ate, as ever, in silence and, as usual, Mrs Goodfellow disappeared. I assumed she took food, but I couldn't remember ever seeing her do so, other than tiny tastes to ensure a dish met the mark.

Yet, as soon as we'd finished, she was back to receive our praise, to clear away the plates and to start washing up. Hobbes was extremely well looked after, as I'd been when I'd lived there, and I had to admit that moving in with Daphne and having to share the household chores had come as a real shock. Neither of us had found the transition easy. I didn't think I was completely to blame, since I'd been spoiled, firstly by my mother, and then by the old girl. In between, I'd lived a bachelor's life with a bachelor's disregard for housework of any kind other than what was absolutely essential.

'I'm afraid I'll have to forego my cup of tea,' said Hobbes, getting to his feet. 'I must get back to work. I fear there'll be serious flooding.'

'Can I come along?' I asked, looking forward to an afternoon of excitement.

'No,' said Mrs Goodfellow. 'You've had a head injury and must take it easy for the rest of the day.'

'But ...'

'Doctor's orders,' she said.

'I don't remember that.'

'Which just goes to show why you need to take it easy,' she said, giving me her stern look.

'I'll see you later,' said Hobbes, chuckling as he left the kitchen.

'But what am I going to do all afternoon?' I asked.

'I think you should take a nice nap,' said Mrs Goodfellow.

'I don't want one.'

'You'll do as you're told, young man!'

And so I did. I went upstairs, undressed, put on a pair of blue striped pyjamas, and got into the bed I'd once called my own. The sheets were crisp and white and held a delicate fragrance of lavender, but I wasn't tired. After about five minutes, the old girl brought me up a mug of tea. I inhaled the aroma and sipped. No one could make tea like she could, but as soon as I'd emptied the mug, the dull headache that had been bothering me receded and I became incredibly sleepy. I lay down, pulled up the blankets and closed my eyes. The last thing I heard was rain battering against the window.

Still fuzzy with sleep and convinced I was home in bed with Daphne, I rolled over for a cuddle, only to experience a moment of apparent weightlessness and confusion before I smacked onto floorboards. It was too dark to see and, as I got up, struggling to remember where I was, I turned the wrong way, stubbed my toe against something hard, and flopped back onto the bed with an oath. I groaned and cuddled my foot, finding it a poor substitute for a wife, and a painful reminder that she'd gone away and that I was back at Hobbes's. My watch showed it was six o'clock, meaning that supper, as he called his evening meal, would be ready in half an hour. The fact helped soothe the pain.

I found the light switch, dressed and opened the bedroom door, wondering why there was no sound, other than wind and rain on the windows, and, more importantly, why there were no cooking aromas. A horrible idea that I'd missed supper and had slept right through until morning had to be put to rest, so I rushed downstairs. The house felt deserted, and I re-checked my watch, and even turned on the television news, but both pointed to the conclusion that it really was just after six o'clock in the evening. The only times Mrs Goodfellow had not cooked Hobbes's supper were when she'd gone on holiday or to a dental conference, and I'd been hoping for some really comforting food. I felt I needed comforting. Ideally, I'd have liked to talk to Daphne, but hadn't yet worked out how and, anyway, I wasn't much looking forward to telling her my news.

It was not a great story. Left alone, I'd been punched, been nearly run down, made myself liable to blackmail, been shot in the buttock, lost the flat, and I suspected, most of our possessions, had been in hospital, and was now back as a guest at Blackdog Street. Although I didn't think any of it had been my fault, and it could all have happened to anyone, I feared it wouldn't sound too good. In addition, I didn't quite believe the part about none of it being my fault, for I had to concede that the blackmail incident, if that's what it proved to be, might have been partly down to my folly. I should have thanked Sally for her warning and just walked away, but I'd always found it hard to say no to a pretty face – not that I'd had many opportunities to say it.

However, I'd always prided myself on an ability to prioritise and, even with the guilt circling in my head, it struck me that food and drink was my most urgent need, and, although I hoped Mrs Goodfellow would return soon, I thought I'd better have a contingency, just in case. I decided to visit Heaven, a new bar and restaurant that had recently opened on Rampart Street. This would mean I'd get a meal, I could persuade them to forward the bill to the *Bugle*, and I'd get paid for writing about it. In the circumstances, it didn't seem a bad idea.

My stomach rumbled, time passed, and I fretted as six-thirty marched towards seven when I gave up and hit the road to the restaurant, which was only about a ten-minute stroll away. Suitably clad for such a short walk, I opened the front door and looked out, still hoping to spot the old girl coming back. I didn't, and I couldn't see anyone out, though there were sirens and shouts in the distance. Rain was still teeming down and the road was a river, with the last of the snow piles sinking like doomed islands. It was only after I'd shut the door behind me that I remembered I didn't have the key anymore. I tried to convince myself that it would not be a problem, because Hobbes and Mrs Goodfellow would certainly be back by the time I returned. Almost certainly.

I jumped down the steps and turned right, heading for Goat Street before veering left onto Rampart Street. As I walked, I noticed how deep the water in the road had become, and realised it would be tricky to cross without filling my shoes. The wellies Mrs Goodfellow had given me were behind the door at Hobbes's, though they might as well have been in Siberia for all the good they could do. I kept going, hoping there'd be somewhere to cross dry-shod, but I was out of luck. With filthy brown water starting to spill across the pavement, it became clear that if I was going to get anywhere, I'd do so with soggy feet. I took the plunge at the junction, gasping as icy water gripped my toes and despite emptying my shoes on the other side, I squelched with every step.

As I was climbing the three steps to Heaven, its front door opened and a skinny young man in a white shirt and black bowtie looked me up and down.

'You're not the sandbag guy, are you?' He sounded disappointed.

'No, I'm here to eat, though I don't have a reservation. I hope that'll be all right?' I glanced inside, reassured by the absence of diners.

'I'm sorry, sir, but we've had to close.'

'Why? I'm really hungry.'

'It's the flood, sir,' he explained as if to an idiot.

'Flood? It's only a bit of rain spilling over.'

'With respect, sir, it isn't. The Soren has burst its banks, Colonel Squire's lake is overflowing, water is pouring into town – can't you see it? It's still rising.'

'So, that's why you want sandbags.'

'Yes, but so do loads of other people, and there may not be any left. It might be too late for us anyway, because there's already water running into the kitchen.'

'Well, I'm sorry to hear that, but … umm … do you know if anywhere else is still serving food?'

'I don't, sir, but we're not the only place having to shut the doors tonight. Good luck, and come back when we're dry.'

I sloshed away, my stomach growling like a famished bear. The Bar Nun was also closed, as was Big Mama's, Jaipur Johnny's, Thai Po, and even my last resort, The Leaning Tower of Pizzas. Many businesses and houses were already sand-bagged and, as I turned away, hoping for better luck elsewhere, I wondered where the fire brigade had got to.

I found them around Pound Street and Ditch Lane, where they were pumping out basements and cellars, trying to flush the waste down drains that were already overflowing, while all sorts of people struggled to build dams. The water was around my ankles, but I'd reached the stage where it seemed I had no option but to press on.

'Hello, dear! Are you feeling better?'

Mrs Goodfellow, clad in her yellow cycle cape and wellington boots, was among the workers. As she spoke, she tossed a sandbag to the next guy in the team, who I recognised as Kev the Rev, the church curate.

'Much better,' I said. 'I wondered where you were. Is Hobbes here?'

'He was, but he went to help with the evacuation on Spittoon Way and Dribbling Lane and around there. Church Lake is overflowing, the river's pouring out across the land, and some folk are in real difficulty. What are you doing out?'

'Actually, I was looking for somewhere to eat,' I said, ashamed. 'I hadn't realised things were so bad. Umm … can I help?'

'I wouldn't worry, dear. We've nearly done as much as we can for now. I'm sorry I haven't had time to make supper, but, as you can see, it's all hands to the pumps.'

'In that case, I'll see if I can help Hobbes.'

'I'm sure he'll be delighted to see you up and about. Dregs is with him.'

I splashed towards Dribbling Lane, which, from what I could see, might, more accurately, have been renamed Torrent Lane. By then the flood had reached my calves and, despite my heavy tweed trousers, I was shivering and my feet had lost all sensation. I was up to my knees when I reached a mass of miserable people huddled beneath the strange, open-sided pillared building that Hobbes reckoned had once been part of a medieval hospital. Hobbes himself waded into view, with a tubby middle-aged woman on his shoulders and a child beneath each arm. Dregs followed, looking embarrassed, probably because of the basket of kittens in his mouth and the bedraggled tabby cat riding his back. Despite his fierce appearance, he could be quite a softy. He took his passengers into the shelter and sat back and watched them.

'Good evening,' said Hobbes, grinning, water dripping off him. 'Are you here to help, or are you just sightseeing?'

'I was looking for food, but I'll do what I can.'

'Good man. I'll put Mrs Harrison and her children into the dry, and then you can help rescue the Vernons.'

He carried the woman and the children to safety, spoke with them for a few moments, his voice soft and reassuring, and came back to join me.

'How are you with boats?' he asked.

'Umm … I've never had much to do with them since I was a kid. One overturned and I got stuck under it. Why?'

'We're going to need one to reach the Vernons at the end of Hairywart Close.'

'The big house in the hollow?' I asked, following as he loped towards Church Fields.

He nodded. 'But, the hollow is now a pond, and water is already lapping the bedroom windows.'

'Umm … where are we going to get a boat?'

'Church Lake,' said Hobbes, maintaining a pace that meant I had to jog.

'Aren't they only there in summer?' I asked, breathing hard.

'That's when they're for hire. The rest of the time they're stored on the island.'

'But, won't the island be under water?'

'Of course,' he said, turning towards the lake, 'but I expect the boats are floating.'

'How will we reach them?'

'I have an idea,' he said, 'though you might not like it.'

'What?' I shivered – not because of the icy water lapping my thighs, though that didn't help, but because I'd had previous experience of ideas that he thought I might not like.

'You can float out and retrieve them.'

'Me? On what?'

'On an emergency lifebuoy.' He turned to grin at me.

'But, the water's freezing, and I'm already half-frozen.'

'Then the exercise will warm you up.'

'Why can't you do it?'

'I'd give it a go if you weren't here, but I suspect the lifebuoy might not support me, and I don't float well.'

Though unconvinced, I kept following him down the slope, the icy water taking my breath away as it lapped my groin. His plan was clearly crazy, and anyone in his right mind would have just walked away, but for some reason I knew I was going to do it. When we reached the lifebuoy, a ring about an arm's length across, he pulled it from its mounting and held it out.

'There are two ways you could do this. You could either put it over your head and shoulders and swim, or you could sit in it and paddle. Take your pick.'

I had a flashback to when the Caplet family was enjoying, if that was the word, a week's holiday in Devon, and when Granny Caplet had given me a little spending money. I'd not known what to do with it, until I fell in love with a little inflatable canoe in the beach shop. Though Father said it was a silly toy for a seven-year old, it was a ship to me, and I planned to explore distant islands where I'd find exotic beasts, friendly natives, and, of course, pirate treasure. I remembered the pungent aroma of vinyl, the effort to inflate her, and the run to the sea to launch her. Granny's money had not quite stretched to a paddle as well, but I reckoned my hands would make a reasonable substitute. Not being a fool, I decided to make myself familiar with how she handled before attempting any oceanic crossing, and so I paddled parallel to the shore, a few feet out. Everything went really well for a minute or two, and my confidence grew until a big wave picked me up, carried me up the beach and tipped me out face first into the sand. The worst part had not been the pain, or hearing the big kids laughing, but seeing my vessel bubbling and hissing from a gash in one of the tubes. That was the end of my nautical adventures for, despite sticking a plaster over the rip, I could never afterwards get it to stay up.

'Are you still there?' asked Hobbes.

'I was just thinking,' I said, almost as excited as I'd been back then. 'I'll sit in it and paddle with my hands, like I used to. Umm … I can't see the island.'

'I strongly suspect it's beneath where those trees are poking through,' he said. 'The boats are stored on the other side.'

'It looks quite a long way.' I peered into the night, shivering, and on the verge of changing my mind. 'I'll freeze my butt off.'

'Then you'd better move yourself, and quickly,' said Hobbes. 'Don't worry, butts may freeze, but they don't usually come off.'

Not having really expected sympathy, I decided to get it over with as soon as possible. 'Okay, but could you help me aboard?'

He scooped me up and plumped me down right in the middle of the ring. For a horrible moment I thought I was going to drop right through or capsize, but a helping hand from him and some severe muscular exertion on my part allowed me to balance.

'Off you go,' he said, shoving me in the right direction. 'Be careful, and don't take any unnecessary risks.'

I nodded, gritted my teeth and set off like a hero, wobbling through the darkness, awkward and ungainly, but paddling with all my might, though my craft, particularly its keel, was not exactly streamlined. Progress was slow, my shoulders were soon aching, and my hands were numb, but the warmth from the effort meant hypothermia seemed a little less certain.

'You're doing well,' he said. 'You'll soon be there.'

I didn't waste breath on a reply but kept paddling until the trees were in reach. As he'd said, the boats floated just behind, but he'd not mentioned that they'd be upside down and tied together in a line. I tried to release the first one, but, unable to see much, finding the knots tight, the rope soggy and frayed, and my fingertips numb, soft and squidgy, I made no progress. I nearly gave up, but the heroic flame that had sparked up had not yet burned out, and I thought I might as well have a go at the next boat along. By a miracle, and with the assistance of some severe muttered swearing, a knot parted and I had my prize, or rather prizes, because I had no way of getting rid of the first boat. Yet, it was far too cold to dither, so I looped the rope around the lifebuoy and headed back, taking the long way round the trees, trying to avoid entanglement. Upside down boats are neither manoeuvrable nor streamlined, so progress was painfully slow, and my shoulders and stomach muscles were soon burning. I'm not sure I would have made it, but, as soon as I'd cleared the trees, I began gliding forwards, riding on a bow wave and leaving a wake. Hobbes was hauling me in with the lifeline.

'Well done,' he remarked as I came alongside.

'No problem,' I said and levered myself out, thinking the worst was over.

But it was yet to come.

As my feet touched bottom, there was a sudden eruption. Filthy, foaming water was everywhere and, I was dragged under, spinning around as if in a whirlpool. Blind panic and good luck brought me back up, gasping with the cold.

'What was that?' I cried, grabbing the lifebuoy, though I was already standing.

Hobbes didn't reply. In fact, there was no sign of him. Fearing he'd also been sucked under, I groped around in the black water for what seemed like an age, and was despairing until Dregs arrived at a gallop. He dived underwater, like a bear hunting salmon, but bobbed up again almost immediately. Then, he swam out a little, plunged and disappeared. I was just starting to believe I'd lost him as well when he broke surface like a hairy submarine with Hobbes's coat collar in his teeth. A moment later Hobbes himself appeared. He scrambled to his feet, coughed up half a pint of water, and patted Dregs on the head.

'That wasn't much fun,' he said, shaking himself like the dog. 'Are you all right, Andy? You look as if you've just seen a ghost.'

'Yeah ... umm ... it's just that I found something down there. It ... umm ... felt like ... I don't know.'

'Where?'

I pointed.

He came towards me and started groping around in the murky water. 'I can't feel anything.'

However, Dregs, who was enjoying the time of his life, dived again and surfaced almost immediately with what looked horribly like a human skull in his mouth.

'Not again,' I said.

'Give,' said Hobbes, and took the skull from the dog's mouth. He ran his hands over the dome, and sniffed. 'It's human, but there's no meat left on it.'

'Now what?' I asked, staring at him with horrified fascination.

'I'll put it back for now, since it's not a fresh one. The dead will have to wait until the living are safe. Would you still like to help me rescue the Vernons?'

To my surprise, I nodded, though what I really wanted was warmth and dryness and a total absence of skulls. Most of all, with my body running on empty, I wanted ample supplies of hot, delicious food. I feared I'd soon succumb to cold or famine, and that I'd fall in when I fainted through lack of sustenance. In my mind's eye I pictured fishes gnawing at me as I sank into the slime, leaving my bones to roll in the deep alongside the skull we'd found.

I said none of this to Hobbes who, having untied and righted the boats, had launched himself into the first one, with Dregs scrambling in after him.

'You'd better take the other one,' said Hobbes.

I hauled myself aboard and watched him lean forward, fiddle under his seat for a pair of oars and slide them into the rowlocks.

'Follow me,' he said. 'And quickly.'

He set off, with Dregs sitting in the bow like a figurehead. I groped for my oars, but couldn't find any. Instead, there was a single long pole, and it struck me that my boat was not the same as Hobbes's, in that it had a flat bottom, didn't have a pointy bit, and had a platform at one end. I stared, dumbfounded, for a moment before realising I'd got myself a punt, a vessel with which I'd had no experience. However, Father had once dragged me along to a dentists' conference in the days when he was still trying to interest me in the dark arts, and I'd watched students mucking around in them on the river. That would be sufficient knowledge, or so I hoped.

I tottered towards the platform, and wobbled there a while, gripping the pole like a tightrope walker, certain disaster was approaching fast. Yet, I didn't fall in, and when I'd set one end of the pole firmly down in the mud, everything became much more stable and I felt almost secure. Of course, merely balancing successfully was no good to anyone. I had to follow Hobbes, shoving my boat along with the pole without losing it, or falling in, and although spectacular failure and ignominious splashdown seemed imminent, it wasn't quite as difficult as I'd imagined. When I pushed, the punt slid forward, and I soon discovered how to use the pole as a sort of rudder. I went after him, and, despite the occasional lurch, I didn't fall. The rain was still teeming down.

My progress, though slow, was steady, and I made it to the Vernons' house, where Hobbes was already helping the family to escape through a bedroom window. Between us, we took all eight of them aboard, and headed back. Soaked to the skin, I shivered all the way, but, despite feeling light-headed with hunger, nothing went wrong.

I was glad to reach land, where Mrs Goodfellow and other kind people helped us into the shelter of the old hospital building. Kev the Rev had magically organised hot drinks and blankets, and the mug of hot, sweet coffee was just what the doctor would have ordered. I held it in both hands, making the most of its warmth as I sipped, and after a while my teeth stopped chattering, and I was able to devour some biscuits. Still, I'd had enough of being heroic and just wanted to be warm, and to have proper food set before me. Fortunately, I didn't have long to wait before Hobbes decided we'd done all we could and led us home.

'I'm sorry, lads,' said Mrs Goodfellow on the way, 'but I haven't had time to cook.'

'You've been very busy,' said Hobbes. 'Perhaps we can get a takeaway?'

'I'm not sure anywhere will be open,' I said, my voice slurred as if I'd had a few too many lagers.

'There's no need for takeaways,' said the old girl with a sniff. 'I can throw a stir-fry together using Sunday's leftover pork, and it shouldn't take more than a few minutes. How would that suit you?'

'Just fine,' said Hobbes, and I grinned like a condemned man whose reprieve had just come through.

The pavement along Blackdog Street was mostly submerged and a number of houses had sandbag dams that were holding back the waters. Others, ours included, had water pouring through the grates into their cellars.

'There's nothing we can do for now,' said Hobbes with a shrug. 'Let's get inside. And quickly.'

It was wonderful to be out of the weather, and even better to immerse myself in a hot bath, though, with supper already cooking, I wallowed for no more than ten minutes before emerging, glowing with the warmth. I dried off, wrapped myself in a heavy old dressing gown and hurried downstairs, led by the enticing aroma of stir-fried pork with onions and ginger.

Unfortunately, supper wasn't quite ready, so, after Mrs Goodfellow had re-bandaged my head, I perched on the sofa and drank more hot sweet coffee, trying to be a model of polite restraint and patience until Hobbes, having showered and changed, joined me.

It looked like being a grand end to a trying day, until the phone rang.

Hobbes picked up the receiver.

'Inspector Hobbes,' he said. 'How may I help you?'

He listened for several minutes, saying nothing except for 'Yes, Ma'am,' just before he replaced the receiver.

'That was Superintendent Cooper,' he said, looking grave. 'The dam at Fenderton Mill is about to collapse and it's serious. I'm going over there now.'

'You won't be able to drive in these floods,' I pointed out.

'No, so we'll have to pick up the boats again.'

'We?'

'If you're up for it.'

Like an idiot, I nodded. 'Let me finish my coffee and get dressed.'

'Quickly,' said Hobbes. 'When the public's in peril, there's no time to lose.'

Any sensible person would have backed down, mentioning that he was exhausted, recovering from concussion and hypothermia, and that he'd already been quite heroic enough for one day, but my crazy mouth, having gulped down the coffee, overrode any sense left in me and said something stupid I'd once heard in a film. 'Let's get ready to rock and roll!'

He seemed to get my meaning and I ran to my room where there was scuffling under the bed and a strong smell of wet dog. However, Dregs, evidently suspecting a dastardly plot to get him in the bath, stayed where he was while I dug out warm clothing and waterproofs, preparing myself for action. I could still have backed out, my excuses being reasonable enough, but I'd been missing excitement since my marriage, and a part of me wanted to be involved. Besides, if people were at risk, I should help, and do something to make Daphne proud of me. Of course, I really should have been trying to establish communications with her, but I had to admit that a small part of my brain thought that a little worry might do her good, and might teach her not to be so dismissive of my concerns. I tried to pretend I wasn't being childish, but didn't quite convince myself.

I jogged downstairs. 'I'm ready to go as soon as I've put my wellies on.'

Hobbes was already in his coat, his only concession to bad weather. I sometimes wondered if he only wore it so Mrs Goodfellow wouldn't nag him about catching a chill, though he did find the pockets useful for holding his notebook and pencil. I pushed my feet into my boots and was ready to go.

As soon as Hobbes opened the front door, Dregs bounded downstairs to join us. Then he saw the weather, put the brakes on and scarpered back upstairs. I didn't blame him. I just hoped he'd stay under my bed and not get in it, or bury a bone under the pillow as he'd once done.

We stepped out into the street and away on our mission of mercy, with Hobbes striding at a pace I struggled to match, especially as we were splashing through calf-deep water. A vicious cold wind fired heavy volleys of rain that stung my face, and by the time we reached Dribbling Lane I was already breathing hard. I'd half hoped the boats had gone and that I'd have another excuse to chicken out, but they were still sheltered beneath the roof of the old building. The people, though, had gone. I hoped they were somewhere safe, warm and dry and that they'd had something to eat.

'Do you want the punt again?' asked Hobbes, 'or would you prefer to change?'

'Umm … do you think we'll need both of them?'

'We might.'

'I … umm … suppose I'll take the punt.'

We launched our vessels, climbed aboard and set off towards Fenderton, Hobbes rowing at a frantic pace and, though I really put my back into it, the heavy old punt was, at best, a sedate craft and I soon fell behind. Still, I couldn't help notice that his technique was open to improvement, since much of his effort went into lifting the boat, almost pulling it clear of the water before it crashed down with a massive splash. If he'd only managed to get all that power into forward motion I'd have lost sight of him in seconds.

It was strange to be floating between houses, and the feeling grew as I reached the inland sea where there'd been Fenderton Road and fields on the previous day. The street lights were still working, casting orange reflections and shadows on the dark waters, making me imagine I was on the coast, though fortunately there were no real waves. I just kept punting, maintaining my balance, letting my mind wander, and keeping warm with all the exercise.

'Wotcha, Andy!' said a high-pitched voice, seeming to come from about water level. 'Mind the current ahead.'

I came within a flea's whisker of overbalancing. It was Billy Shawcroft, the dwarf, a good friend of Hobbes's and mine, who was in a kayak.

'Hi,' I said, as he drew alongside. 'What current?'

'The river's still there, you know, though you can't really see where it starts. It's running fast, but if you give yourself a mighty shove now, you'll make it across. Careful, though, because it'll hit you hard, and you'll need to keep your balance.'

I did as he said, feeling the sudden punch of the river thrusting me sideways. Had he not turned up, I reckon I'd have gone in, but he had and I didn't. Not quite.

'Where are you off to?' he asked when I'd reached still water.

'To Fenderton. The dam is collapsing and I'm going to help.'

'I'll come, too. I've just been helping out at the butchers down The Shambles. Most of their meat has washed away in the flood – it was a bit choppy down there. Is that Hobbesie splashing ahead?'

'Yes. He left me with the punt. I didn't know you were a kayaker.'

Billy smiled. 'I love to get out on water, and I built this myself, because the ones in the shops are all for big people like you.'

Although I'd never considered myself big, being only of average height, I could see his point of view. Little in modern life was designed for small people, yet he was a cheerful guy and adept at overcoming the many difficulties that were thrown at him. He gave the impression that he could do anything, and was certainly a man of no small ability. I'd soon come to understand why Hobbes always treated him with the utmost respect.

'I'll go on ahead and catch up with him,' he said, 'in case anyone is in immediate danger. See you.'

He set off, powering through the flood like a shark, leaving me floundering in his wake. It only took him a few minutes to pull alongside Hobbes, and he must have passed on some words of advice, because Hobbes was soon rowing like an Olympian. Within a minute or two they'd both passed out of sight into the gloom. I kept going, despite a blister growing on my right hand, and it must have taken me half an hour to reach the outskirts of Fenderton which was almost unrecognisable. A few minutes more and I caught up with Hobbes, who was hauling a bedraggled man aboard his boat to join four other people hunched miserably in the middle.

With a powerful thrust on my pole, I went alongside. Had Hobbes not put his arm out and stopped me, I would have smacked into a wall.

'What can I do?' I asked.

'The dam's gone, so use your eyes and ears, and if someone's in trouble, pull them out. Keep your centre of gravity low so you don't overturn.'

'Then what?'

He pointed up the slope. 'They'll be safe there. It's where I'm taking these good people.'

After he'd rowed away, I heard a cry for help and spotted a man waist deep in a torrent roaring down the hill. On his shoulders was a small child in a red raincoat.

'I'm coming!' I yelled, turning the punt towards him.

As he nodded, he lost his footing and went under. I pushed along, taking care to avoid the worst of the flow, while moving as fast as I dared. The man bobbed up, spluttering and gasping, and looking around helplessly for the child. A sick, helpless feeling welled up in my stomach and only a massive exertion of will stopped me panicking, for I knew that if I thought about it too long, I'd confuse myself and dither. The kid needed rescuing quickly if it was to have any chance, and that meant keeping in control of myself and the punt, and acting immediately. So, without any kind of plan, I pushed off, crouching on my platform and peering into the turbulent, shadowy waters, hoping for a glimpse of red. The flow swept me towards what were normally water meadows, and the glimmer from the Fenderton street lights began to fade with every second.

Within too short a time I was in near darkness and beginning to despair. Then there was a splash to my left and, maybe, a hint of red. I flung myself to the side, nearly overturning, and plunged a hand into the water. To my amazement I felt something, grabbed it and held on. It was the kid's coat, and the kid was still in it. When I hauled him aboard, for he turned out to be a boy of about three or four years old, he took one look at me and began to scream. Taking my coat off, I covered him, and strained my eyes searching for the man, his father I supposed, though I could barely see anything other than streetlights receding into the distance.

I shouted without response, except for an increased volume from the kid up front, whose screaming was already getting on my nerves and not helping in any way. No doubt he'd had a shocking and unpleasant experience, and I was trying to be sympathetic, but it was no way to carry on in an emergency.

'Stiff upper lip, old chap!' I said, with no effect whatsoever.

The punt had begun bucking, rolling, shaking and picking up speed towards the bright lights of town and I guessed we'd drifted into the Fenderton Brook, its normal sluggish flow now a churning nightmare. With a lurch of horror and panic, I realised I had to get us out before it joined the river, but when I reached for the pole, it had gone. Dimly, I remembered a splash when I was rescuing the noisy, ungrateful brat up front, who didn't seem to care that we were helplessly adrift. I quickly discovered that swearing didn't help, but the worst thing, something that nearly sent me into a panic, was that I had a horrible feeling that the brook joined the river just before the road bridge near the end of Dribbling Lane. With the height and ferocity of the waters, I really couldn't imagine us getting through there in one piece. In desperation, I knelt and paddled, my hands pulling frantically, but I might just as well have tried to propel a battleship with a button.

I could now make out the course of the river, streaked with white foam where it was smashing into the bridge, and I guessed the arch below was completely submerged. We were cannoning towards it far too quickly, and there was nothing I could do to prevent a smash. I was going to be broken, or drowned, or both, and so was the boy.

'Help!' I yelled, my voice loud, though cracking with fear.

There was nothing else I could do, though I didn't really expect anything. However, a woman appeared on the bridge.

'Are you all right?' she asked.

Even in the midst of terror, I thought it a stupid question. Did I look as if I was all right? However, it was not the time for sarcasm.

'No,' I shouted above the river's roar, 'and I have a child with me.'

'Then you should be ashamed of yourself.'

I bit down on a waspish response, lurched to the front end and picked up the kid, which at least stopped him screaming, though it started him kicking me in the stomach.

The bridge was horribly close.

'I'll throw him up.'

'You can't. I'll drop him.'

'No, you won't.'

'What's his name?'

'Don't know.'

'Then what are you doing with him?' Her voice was sharp with suspicion.

There was no time left.

'Ready?' I screamed.

The woman, looking shocked, nodded, the punt bounced and rolled, and I lifted the kid above my head. Despite receiving a kick in the teeth for my efforts, I launched him and felt the woman take his weight just as the punt smashed into the bridge and disintegrated. For an instant, I glimpsed her white face and blue hair as she dragged the boy to safety, and then the river had me. The shock of the cold water was dreadful, as was the immense violence of the current. Everything went dark and I knew I was under the bridge, desperate to breathe, though all around was water, cold and blackness. Hard things struck from all sides and I was tossed around like a leaf in a gale, sure I was going to die. Just to add to the fun, the bandage around my head started to unravel and wrap itself around my throat, threatening to strangle me. It was, at least, an alternative to drowning.

Incredibly, my face came up into air, and I was gasping and sobbing, knowing I'd made it through in one piece. I was shooting feet-first towards where the bank would normally have been and when a tree root came into view, I grabbed it, held it, and rejoiced in its strength and solidity, using it to haul my battered body into relatively placid, thigh-deep water and safety. The woman was standing on the bridge clutching the wriggling boy to her chest, and shouting at me, though I couldn't catch any words. I was just pulling myself clear, and thinking of heading back to Blackdog Street for a well-deserved meal in the warmth, when I glimpsed something shooting from under the bridge.

It was a man, face down and limp. The river thrust him across to the far bank, where there were no roots, just a rough stone wall against which the waters crashed and foamed. I called out, but he didn't even twitch. I looked for help, but there was none, and, I knew I was his only hope, assuming he was still alive. Having no option, though unsure whether I'd survive another immersion, I plunged back in.

The current struck. It ducked and pummelled me, and I couldn't reach him, until I had a brainwave. I lassoed him with a loop of my bandage, pulled us together and turned him face up. After that, I was effectively stuck, with one hand keeping his head above water and the other grasping the wall. There was no chance of dragging us back across the churning Soren to relative safety, and I knew if I tried that we'd both be swept away, like the shattered debris of my punt. From what I could see downstream, where there were other bridges, our chances of surviving would be negligible, but if I stayed put, I doubted I'd be able to cling on for long. I was shivering so much the whole world seemed to be shaking as the cold leached the last strength from my body. Within minutes it was all I could do to keep both our faces above water. Then the man coughed and groaned, and the knowledge that he was alive kept me hanging on for a little longer. Still, the end seemed very close.

'Chin up, Andy.'

It was Hobbes, and I clung on with renewed hope, the last of my energy and determination kicking in. He was rowing towards us and, though he now looked like he knew what he was doing, I still wished he'd do it faster.

As he drew near, he jumped in, the water reaching his waist. He waded towards us.

'Careful,' I cried, my voice taking on a weird vibration as my teeth chattered, 'it gets deep.'

As he reached the river, his boat was swept away and he went down, the dark waters closing over his head. I feared he was lost, and was on the verge of despair when his hands grabbed my waist, lifting both me and the casualty from the water, and carrying us back across the current. With a powerful surge, he reached the shallows, and his head burst into the night. I felt the blast of air as he exhaled. He stood still for a moment, sucking down a great lungful of air, his face eerily pale in the sodium light, still holding us in his great arms.

'Thank you,' I said indistinctly over the chattering of my teeth.

He pitched face forward into the water, spilling us. Keeping tight hold of the man, I groped hopelessly for Hobbes, who'd sunk without trace and would surely have been a goner if Billy hadn't turned up, handling his kayak as if it were part of him. Powering towards the spot where Hobbes had sunk, leaning so far over it was incredible he didn't capsize, he plunged his stubby arms deep into the water. Then, somehow, he was dragging Hobbes's head and shoulders across the deck, and, although his kayak listed like a torpedoed ship and he was only able to paddle on one side, he dragged him up to the bridge. Though exhausted and chilled to my soul, I followed, hauling the semi-conscious man with me, until I could put him down. Remembering enough of my first aid course to check he was breathing, I rolled him into the recovery position, reassured by his moans.

I helped Billy pull Hobbes clear of the water, but when we laid him down on his back he wasn't breathing. Fearing the worst, I dropped to my knees, but Billy dived head first into his abdomen. Hobbes coughed, a plume of water shot from his mouth like a fountain, and he spat and sat upright, looking dazed. Billy rolled off, and got to his feet a little unsteadily, rubbing his head, and I was nearly in tears.

'That,' said Hobbes, following a long cough, 'was not as much fun as it might have been. I really began to think I wasn't going to make it. That current is strong. How is the casualty?'

'Moaning and throwing up,' said Billy.

'Good,' said Hobbes, still breathing heavily, but pushing himself onto his feet. 'I'll take a look.'

He knelt at the man's side, checking him over. 'It's Nathan Pegler. He should be fine, but I suppose I should get him to hospital.' He glanced at me. 'I saw what you did. It was brave. You saved his life, as well as the boy's. Well done.'

Since praise from Hobbes was almost as rare as dogs on unicycles, I was taken aback. Then, realising what I'd actually done, I basked in a warm glow of satisfaction; it was the only warm thing around.

'Inspector, I demand that you arrest that man!'

The woman who'd caught the boy walked towards us holding him by the hand. Her voice, shrill and grating, was aimed at Hobbes.

'Which man, madam?' asked Hobbes.

'That one,' she said, pointing at me.

I recognised her severe face and the blue hair poking from under her headscarf, as well as the glare she was aiming through horn-rimmed glasses. Unfortunately, we'd met several times before and her opinion of me was, to say the least, unfavourable.

'He's a bad lot,' she insisted, 'and I should know. I've caught him thieving.'

I cringed, because I couldn't deny it. She had once caught me in the act of pilfering a pamphlet from the church, and although I'd had a particularly good excuse, needing the information in it to save Hobbes from a terrible fate, she'd never forgiven me. Her distrust and dislike had multiplied after I accidently hit her in the face with a dead rat. Ever since, whenever we met, she'd keep her gorgon glare on me until I'd slunk away, and, since she frequented the church in the centre of town, I'd done a great deal of slinking and slipping away down backstreets and alleys to avoid crossing her path. At least she wasn't carrying her umbrella, which she'd once used to beat me, and I realised she didn't need it. The rain had stopped at last.

'Mrs Nutter,' said Hobbes, his voice hoarse but patient, 'that was all in the past and has been explained. What's he done this time?'

'He's been gallivanting on the river in a stolen punt – and I know it's stolen because it belongs to Mr Nelson, my neighbour, who runs them – and he's been putting this little lad at risk. If you want my opinion, I don't even believe the child is his, so you should arrest him for kidnapping as well.' She glared at me. 'Is he your son?'

'Umm … no … but …'

'He admits it, Inspector. When are you going to arrest him?'

'Mrs Nutter,' said Hobbes, 'I have no intention of arresting him.'

'Then, I shall inform your superiors.'

'Madam, I have no superiors, just some people who get paid more.'

I was a little surprised at his bold statement, but, knowing Hobbes, it was probably just a statement of fact. It did, however, shut her up for the moment.

'Andy was rescuing Pegler junior from the flood,' he continued. 'I saw what he did, and I must also commend you, Mrs Nutter, on a most fine catch in difficult circumstances.'

'Oh. Thank you, Inspector,' she said, mollified. 'I couldn't let the poor boy down.'

'Of course not. Now, I need to attend to Pegler senior. Would you be so good as to look after the boy for a minute?'

'Of course,' she said, all smiles.

Hobbes glanced at Billy, who was ensuring Mr Pegler was comfortable, or at least as comfortable as he was likely to be after being immersed in icy water and lying on a bridge. 'Would you mind heading back to Fenderton and inform Mrs Pegler that her husband and son are safe, and that there is nothing to worry about, but that I'm taking them to the hospital as a precaution?'

Billy nodded, returned to his kayak and paddled away. Though he was one of the most capable people I'd ever met, his diminutive stature often led people to treat him like a child. It had taken me a while to realise, and he still sometimes surprised me. He was a good man in a crisis, as Hobbes often remarked, though, of course, not without faults; sometimes he drank too much, and he had a reputation as a card sharp, although no one, not even Hobbes, had ever caught him out.

'How are we going to get them to the hospital?' I asked.

'I'll carry them, but I'd suggest that you head straight home and take a hot bath. This water may be contaminated and there have been warnings of rising pee levels and worse. You'd better take my key in case the lass is out again.'

He handed it to me and I splashed homewards, shivering and close to exhaustion, but, for once, pleased with myself. He passed me at a gallop on Spittoon Way, with Mr Pegler in his arms and the boy perched on his shoulders, urging him on as if he were a pony.

At last I reached Blackdog Street, where I was surprised to see a number of people messing about on air beds and inner tubes, making the most of the flood, even though others were still pumping out basements or building barriers. There was no sign of Mrs Goodfellow outside, which I hoped suggested she was home and that food would be available. My hunger pangs had not gone away, and the thought of eating intensified the emptiness.

I walked inside to be a greeted by a massive smelly dog hug, while a whiff of cooking made the world feel right, though I was a little surprised to already be thinking of there as home again. It reminded me that I should get in touch with Daphne, and that I ought to find out what was happening with the flat. However, I put such thoughts to the back of my mind and, fighting off Dregs, hurried into the kitchen.

'Hello, dear,' said Mrs Goodfellow with a cheerful smile. 'You look wet and cold. Have a quick bath, and by the time you get down your supper will be ready.'

'Thanks,' I said. 'It smells fantastic.'

'How's your head? Do you want it bandaging again?'

'No, it'll be fine.' I hurried to the bathroom.

By the time I was clean, dressed in my pyjamas, and ready to eat, Hobbes was already at the kitchen table, wrapped in his dressing gown, kitten slippers on his feet, a massive mug of steaming tea in his fist.

'You took your time,' he said. 'Let's eat.'

He rattled off the most rapid grace ever, and we unleashed ourselves on stir-fried pork in a most delicious tangy sauce and served with a mountain of fragrant rice. The hot, spicy food almost made up for all the privations and suffering of the day.

'That was fantastic,' I said when my belly was as tight as was decent. 'What was it called?'

'Stir-fried pork and stuff,' said Mrs Goodfellow. 'I just threw in what was available, and I'm glad you liked it.'

'Praise from a food critic,' said Hobbes with a smile, 'is praise indeed.'

The old girl blushed and grinned her toothless grin. 'I'll clear up and make you boys another pot of tea.'

However, I was too full to even contemplate adding more to my stomach. Warm, and relaxed, I began to feel very sleepy.

'How are the Peglers?' I asked, forcing my eyes to stay open.

'Very well. There was nothing much wrong with the boy, and he was happy to be reunited with his mother. Mr Pegler had a touch of hypothermia and a minor head injury, but was fully conscious and feeling much better when I left.'

'Good.' I said and, giving up the struggle, took myself straight up to bed. Although I had an idea I should be doing something, it didn't keep me awake for long.

Although my sleep was long, it was not especially peaceful. I kept dreaming of Daphne, certain I had something important to tell her, but she was too far away and, although I tried to reach her, something always blocked my way, and by the time I'd dealt with it she was even more distant, becoming at last a tiny dot on the horizon. My final desperate attempt to catch her was thwarted by Sally, who was pounding a drum and forcing me to dance to her beat.

When I began to surface, rising from dreams into the grey light of a new day, the drumming continued, but it was only when I heard Mrs Goodfellow open the front door that I worked out someone had been knocking. I sat up in bed, yawning, stretching and listening.

'Hello, dear,' said the old girl. 'What brings you here so urgently?'

'Have you heard anything from Andy?' asked a woman.

It was Daphne's friend, Pinky.

'Yes, dear. He's upstairs in bed.'

'So, he's here. I've just had a frantic phone call from Daphne, wondering why she couldn't get in touch, and when I went round to their flat it had been destroyed. I thought he might have been killed. Is he all right?'

'He's fine.'

'Well, that's good, I suppose, but why didn't he call her?'

'He was rather busy.'

'Too busy to send an email, or Skype her, or use a telephone? I don't believe it.'

By then, I was out of bed, in a clean shirt and underpants, and pulling on a pair of trousers, buttoning them up as I galloped downstairs. A little more caution would have been advisable, since my bare feet skidded on the steps and I bounced to the bottom on my bottom.

'Hi,' I said, getting up with a light laugh, as if my pratfall had been just a jolly little jape, though it had actually hurt quite a lot, and I could feel I'd have a bruise or two to add to my collection.

'Andy, what were you thinking of? Daphne's distraught, and I've been worried, too.' Though Pinky frowned, her big blue eyes expressed concern.

'Sorry.'

'Is that all you can say?'

'Come in, dear,' said Mrs Goodfellow.

Pinky came in and sat with me on the sofa.

'Would you like a cup of tea? Or a coffee?' asked Mrs Goodfellow.

'No, thank you,' said Pinky. 'I can't stay long. I've got to open the café.'

'I'd like a cup of tea, please,' I said.

Mrs Goodfellow hurried away and I smiled at Pinky, who was dressed in her trademark pink trouser suit, with a low cut pink blouse. She'd lost a little weight I thought, and looked beautiful, and I had to force myself not to stare, though she'd always been too pretty to ignore.

'How are you?' I asked.

'Never better, but Daffy's worried sick. She reached camp yesterday and has been trying to contact you ever since. She saw about the floods online. You should have let her know you were well.'

'But, I lost the computer and the phone and my mobile when the flat was hit.'

'There are other computers and telephones,' said Pinky, frowning. 'You could have come to us. Sid wouldn't mind you using his laptop, or you could've tried that new internet place you wrote about.'

'Gollum's Logons? I suppose I could've, but I was in hospital with a head injury.' I pointed to the lump, although it was no longer evident, 'and then I was rescuing people from the flood.'

'You must still have had a few minutes!'

Overwhelmed by a sudden shame, I hung my head, knowing I could have made time had I really tried, and that a peevish, childish part of me was sulking, wishing to hurt her because she'd gone away. Also, I had an idea that I was already struggling without her, which did nothing to raise my self-esteem.

'I'm sorry,' I muttered again.

'It's no use apologising to me. Call her now.'

'Umm … but I don't know her number. You see it was in my mobile, and I hadn't written it down, and I can't remember her email.'

I knew I must be coming across as pathetic and incompetent, and that was without admitting that I'd also forgotten my own logon. After all, once Daphne had set me up, I hadn't needed to remember.

'I'll write the camp's number and her email down for you,' said Pinky in a voice she might have used to an imbecile.

She took a notebook and pen from her pink handbag, scribbled on it, tore off the leaf and handed it to me. The paper, too, was a delicate shade of pink, and the only thing that surprised me was the black ink. I thanked her.

'I've got to open the café,' she said, getting up.

'How is it?'

'Fine. Sid put down sandbags, and nothing got past.'

'How are the floods?'

'Not quite as bad today, though everywhere near the river is still awash. I must go.'

Mrs Goodfellow, who'd just reappeared and placed a mug of tea before me, opened the front door.

'Call her,' said Pinky as she left.

'What should I do?' I asked Mrs Goodfellow after she'd shut the door.

'Call her. Use our phone.'

'But won't it be the middle of the night there?'

'No, dear, it'll be approaching midday. Egyptian time is only two hours ahead.'

'Can I have some breakfast first?'

'No.'

I grabbed the phone, dialled and waited, hoping she'd be in.

'Hi,' I said when I heard it picked up. 'I'm really sorry I haven't called, but the flat's been knocked down by a tree, and I was in hospital with a head injury, and then I was rescuing people from the flood, but I'm all right now. How are you? I love you.'

'Thank you, sir, I am well, but who is speaking?' asked a man with a strong Egyptian accent.

'Oh … sorry. My name is … umm … Andy.'

'Ummandi? I do not know you, sir. Why you say you love me?'

'It was a mistake. I don't really.'

'Why not? What have I done?'

'Nothing. I thought you were my wife.'

'I not your wife! I married already.'

'I know …'

'How you know I married?'

'I didn't …'

'Then you lie!' He was sounding really pissed off.

'No … umm … me make big mistake … me think you my wife,' I said getting flustered, and knowing I needed to remain calm, and to explain myself clearly. However, panic getting the better of me, I slammed the phone down.

'She wasn't in,' I said.

Mrs Goodfellow gave me her stern look. 'Try again, dear,' she said, crossing her spindly arms across her sparrow chest and tapping her foot.

I did as I was told. Had I not, she might have refused to feed me.

This time when someone picked up, I waited for a response.

'Hello?' said Daphne.

'It's me.'

'Oh, thank god! Where've you been? I've been trying to call you since last night, and you haven't answered my emails.'

'I've had a few … umm … problems.' I told her of my misfortunes, leaving out any mention of Sally. Other than my heroic rescue of Mr Pegler and son, it was a sorry tale.

'I see,' said Daphne. 'So you're back at Inspector Hobbes's. Well, at least that should keep you out of mischief for a while. But what's going to happen with the flat? Have you called the insurance company?'

'Not yet,' I admitted. 'As I said, I've been rather busy.'

'Well you'd better, as soon as possible.'

'Umm … okay … who are we insured with?'

'All the details are on the computer … That's not much help is it?'

'Not much. Even if I can find it, I suspect it's smashed or flooded.'

'Never mind. The insurer is The Pigton Insurance Company. Mr Sharples helped me arrange it, so he may be able to help.'

'Oh, good. I'll go round and see him some time.'

I rather liked Sid Sharples, the manager of Grossman's Bank, and an old friend of Hobbes. We'd got to know him quite well since Pinky had moved in with him shortly after she'd turned up in Sorenchester. The fact that he was a known vampire did not appear to bother either of them, and I tried not to let it bother me, though I could never quite relax in his company without the assistance of alcohol.

'Yes,' said Daphne, 'and you'll have to find some place for us to live. You can't keep imposing on the inspector and Mrs Goodfellow.'

'I know, but it's not a good time at the moment. Half the town is under water and loads of people will be looking for some place to stay while their homes dry out.'

'Fair enough, but don't leave it too long.'

'I won't. How are you?'

'I'm great. This dig looks like it's going to be fascinating. Mahmoud's been showing me around and I'll start work properly tomorrow.'

'Who is Mahmoud?'

'Professor Mahmoud El-Gammal. I told you about him. He's the leader of the excavation and was the one who found the tomb of Rameses the Idiot ten years ago. Don't you remember?'

'Yes, of course,' I said, as if I had the first clue who Rameses the Idiot was, though I vaguely remembered hearing the name. I suspected he was an ancient Egyptian. 'Is it hot out there?'

'Like you wouldn't believe, and it's still winter. Mind you, I could believe it last night – it was literally freezing. You should have seen the stars though. They were brilliant, and so many of them.'

'Great. How's the food?'

'Not too bad. It's mostly been beans and flat bread so far, which is tasty enough and quite filling. I expect you've had better, though. Could you send Mrs Goodfellow out here?'

I laughed.

'Anyway,' she said, 'I've got to go. Mahmoud's in a bad mood. He received a crank phone call a few minutes ago.'

'Oh … umm … so they get that sort of thing in Egypt, too. Who'd have thought it? Right in the middle of the desert. How strange!'

'So, it was you, Ummandi,' she said with a chuckle. 'I won't tell him. Goodbye. I'm glad you're all right. Love you.'

That was it. The phone went dead and I was left with so much I wanted to say, specifically that I loved her and missed her, and though it was a cliché, it was true. I really was much better with her than without her, despite the good food at Hobbes's, and, of course, the excitement.

'Is everything all right?' asked Mrs Goodfellow.

I nodded, too emotional to risk speaking.

'I'll get you some breakfast. Would a full English suit you?'

I nodded again and replaced the receiver as she returned to the kitchen. A couple of minutes later, the mouth-watering aroma of bacon infiltrated the sitting room and I felt ready to start the day. Indeed, I was almost back to my normal self when she called. I went through and, having demolished the contents of the enormous plate she set before me, still found room for a couple of slices of toast and marmalade.

'Thank you,' I said as I finished the last crumb. 'Where are Hobbes and Dregs?'

'They left early. The old fellow said they had something to attend to from yesterday.'

So much had happened since then that, incredibly, I'd forgotten the horror of what I'd found. I told her about it.

'I wonder if it might have anything to do with the old abbey,' she suggested. 'You know, the medieval one that got knocked down.'

'I don't know much about that. Was it one of those that Henry the Eighth got rid of?'

'Yes, dear.'

'So, that might mean the skull came from a medieval monk,' I said, relieved, since ancient remains held little of the horror of recent ones.

'I don't know, dear. I expect we'll find out soon enough.'

'I expect so, but I think I'll take a stroll down there and see what's happening.'

It was a bright cold morning and the church clock was striking ten. The pavements were no longer awash, though the road still looked like a canal, and the streets sounded eerily quiet, despite plenty of townsfolk going about their business. It was a while before I realised this was down to the lack of traffic noise. I turned towards The Shambles, which was comparatively dry, and headed down the narrow alley at the back of the church, passed through the old graveyard, and into Church Fields. The lake looked at least three times bigger than normal.

The long lanky form of Constable Poll and a petite figure in white were talking together outside a tent on a grassy knoll above the water level, while Hobbes, fully dressed, was up to his waist in the lake. Dregs was doggy paddling by his side. They exchanged glances and ducked beneath the surface. When they popped up, Dregs began barking excitedly.

'There are more,' said Hobbes, and dived again.

He came up holding a pair of long bones and handed them to the woman in white before plunging back into the flood.

Constable Poll, who'd always struck me as far too friendly and easy-going to really be a police officer, nodded as I approached.

'What's up, Derek?' I asked.

'The inspector's found some sort of collapsed vault and has been fishing bones out all morning. We've already got remains from at least sixteen individuals, according to Doctor Ramage. By the way, have you met Doctor Cynthia Ramage, our new forensic pathologist?'

'Pleased to meet you. I'm … umm … Andy.'

She turned to face me and smiled. She had short dark hair and big brown eyes, and would have been rather attractive, had she not been mummified in those baggy white overalls.

'Are the bones from the monks at the old abbey?' I asked, hoping to appear intelligent.

'Probably not,' she said, 'since some appear to be from women and children.'

'So, what are they doing here?'

'I don't know yet, but I have a suspicion that there might have been an ossuary, or bone house, on the site. Or it's just possible we've stumbled upon a medieval plague pit.'

'So the bones are old?'

'They appear so.'

'I … umm … suppose it's hardly likely they are the results of a modern massacre.'

'I think we might have been aware of one of those,' said Constable Poll.

'Derek is right,' she said. 'The ones so far have the appearance and fragility of old bones, though I'll have to test them back in the lab to be quite certain.'

'So why is Hobbes bothering with them?'

'Because we can't just leave them out in the open,' said Poll. 'It's best to collect them before the floods go down and the public and dogs and wild animals can get at them, especially if it was a plague pit. Can you imagine what might happen if there was still infection?'

'I thought the plague came from rat fleas,' I said.

'The spread of the Black Death can be blamed on rodent fleas,' said Cynthia, 'but there was more than one type of plague, and people of those times were prone to all sorts of nasty illnesses. I'll learn more when I've got them back to the lab, but I'm ninety-nine percent convinced they'll prove of more interest to the archaeologists than to the police. Still, it makes a change.'

'There's a whole one in the drain,' said Hobbes.

'What do you mean?' I asked.

'A complete human body. I'll bring it out.'

He plunged again, emerged and began walking backwards towards us, his arms around the torso of what had once been a man. The corpse was dressed in a grey suit and white shirt with a red and white striped tie.

'He can't have been dead for all that long,' said Cynthia as Hobbes laid him gently on his back at the waterside.

Though pale and bloated, the body was intact and the features were quite recognisably those of a middle-aged man, a little chubby, of less than average height, with short greying ginger hair and a wide bald spot on the crown.

'He was a monk,' I said, fighting a wave of nausea. 'I thought there weren't any round here anymore.'

Hobbes, dripping wet, examining the body, looked up, puzzled. 'What makes you say that?'

'His hair's cut like a monk.'

'It looks more like male-pattern baldness,' said Cynthia, squatting at his side. 'Besides, he's wearing a modern suit.'

'Sorry,' I said. 'I was getting carried away by history. What do you think killed him? Did he drown?'

'It would appear that he died before the flood,' said Cynthia.

'This may have had something to do with his demise,' said Hobbes, turning the head to reveal a horrible swollen gash around the temple. 'It's not a pretty sight.'

Constable Poll's loud vomiting started me off. Otherwise, I might have been all right, although my legs felt as if the bones had been replaced by wet spaghetti, and my head was swimming like a tadpole.

'Yes, indeed,' said Cynthia. 'Exposing the brain like that would cause instant unconsciousness, and, without urgent treatment, death would follow very quickly.'

'What caused the wound?' asked Hobbes. 'An axe?'

'It was certainly caused by a blade, but it would appear a little too narrow for an axe. A machete, maybe?'

'I see what you mean. Let's see if he has any identification.' Hobbes folded back the man's jacket, reached inside and pulled out a soggy leather wallet.

660

'What's in it?' I asked as curiosity overrode the nausea.

'A wad of bank notes and credit cards,' he said, unloading the contents. 'The credit cards are all current and in the name of Mr Septimus Donald Slugg. Aha! There's also a driving licence. It appears Mr Slugg lived at 10 Umbrage Crescent, Tode-in-the-Wold.'

'That'll be useful,' I said.

'It might well be,' said Hobbes. 'For the present, I'll work on the assumption that the information is correct and that this photograph is of the deceased. The features, as far as I can tell, match. Doesn't he have tiny ears?'

Cynthia nodded, and then looked thoughtful. 'I might know something about him.'

'Go on,' said Hobbes, looking up.

'Wasn't he that politician with the long hair and the green eyes? The one who said he wanted lots of new development in Sorenchester? The guy who formed the Sorenchester Needs Improvement Party? The SNIP? He seemed charismatic and persuasive when he was on television, but his ideas didn't make much sense when they were spelled out.'

'I remember,' I said. 'No one voted for the SNIP.'

'Actually,' said Hobbes, 'I believe that was Mr Solomon Slugg, who lives in Fenderton.'

'Yes, you're quite right,' said Cynthia. 'And do you remember when he got drunk and someone took photos of him lying face down in a bed of lettuce? What was the headline in the *Bugle?*'

'A Slugg in the Salad,' I said, nodding as the pictures came to mind.

'Yeah, that's it, and the article claimed he was more Slugg than Solomon. His campaign rather fizzled out after that.'

'Completely,' I said. 'Mind you, his manifesto was so ridiculous I doubt many would have voted for him anyway.'

'If anyone had bothered to read it,' said Cynthia. 'It's an odd name, though.'

'The surname is certainly unusual,' Hobbes agreed, 'so I think it possible that our Septimus was related to him.'

'I'd have thought almost certainly,' I said.

'But not necessarily, since there's little to suggest a family resemblance. Mr Solomon Slugg, as I recall, was tall, whereas Septimus is rather short.'

He pulled a dripping mobile phone from his pocket, poked a few buttons and frowned. 'I've flooded it again.' He turned to Constable Poll. 'Derek, I'd be obliged if you'd call Superintendent Cooper and let her know what we've found. And, Andy, since this now appears to be a crime scene, I'm going to ask you to step away.'

'Oh, yeah … right,' I said, disappointed, but familiar with the procedure. 'What about Dregs?'

'He knows how to behave.'

A thought stopped me as I was turning away. 'Umm … would you mind if I wrote a short piece about this for the *Bugle?*'

Hobbes thought for a moment. 'I can't stop you doing what you want, but from a police point of view it would be helpful if you would hold off for a short time, so the news does not alert the culprit.'

'Can I report about the old bones, then?' I asked, willing to do what he said for the sake of friendship, though a crime scoop would have been a massive boost to my career.

'Again, Andy, I'd prefer that you didn't for the time being.'

'OK,' I said, frustrated, though proud of myself for having even thought about writing an article. I suspected I'd missed a whole lot of news during my first stint as a reporter, when I'd been too focussed on myself to use my eyes and brain for the newspaper. On one occasion, I'd failed to notice that a bus had lost control and demolished a shop front, even though I must have stepped through the rubble when I was hurrying to a dog show. 'Editorsaurus' Rex Witcherley, my editor at the time, had not been impressed, especially when I told him the dog show had been cancelled. He'd been even less impressed when the reason for the cancellation emerged: there'd been a rabies scare, a fact I'd not considered newsworthy. Looking back on those times, I'd been less a newshound and more a short-sighted lazy lapdog, and had been incredibly lucky the Editorsaurus had kept me on for so long. But that was all in the past. With Phil Waring at the helm of the *Bugle,* I believed I might succeed, despite only being a part-time food critic.

Having carried the mortal remains of Septimus Slugg into the tent, Hobbes waded back into the flood, where Dregs was in hot pursuit of a passing coot.

10

I walked to our flat, or what was left of it, intending to see if anything was worth salvaging, but found it surrounded by a chain-link fence and signs warning of imminent collapse. Looking at the wreckage, it seemed incredible that everyone had got out without serious injury, for even the parts that hadn't been flattened looked ruinous.

As I walked around the perimeter, a quick movement caught my eye. Someone was scrambling about in the debris of our flat. My first thought was looters, and I reached into my pocket, intending to call the police, before remembering that my mobile was somewhere amidst all that rubble, if it had survived. The intruder was a tall, slim woman with long dark hair and a strikingly beautiful face. She looked up and waved.

'Andy, how are you?'

Hers was a soft, mellifluous voice with a musical lilt, and although I didn't recognise her, there was something familiar.

'Umm … I'm fine … and you?' I asked, playing for time, hoping for inspiration.

'Very well, thank you,' she said, stepping gracefully from the debris into the garden. 'How is your head?'

'Umm … much better. What are you doing in there?'

'It's our flat.'

Inspiration struck. 'Mrs Elwes?'

'Hilda, please.'

'OK, Hilda. The sign says it's dangerous.'

She shrugged, a most graceful movement, and smiled. 'What's life without a little danger?'

'Safe?'

Her laugh was tuneful, almost angelic. 'I suppose it is, but a safe life is not an exciting one, is it?'

She gazed at me, rarely blinking, her green eyes so bright and alluring they made me nervous, though I could have stared into them forever.

'Probably not,' I admitted. 'How did you get in?'

'Over the fence. It's quite easy. Are you going to join us?'

'I don't know. I'd like to have my mobile and my laptop, but they're almost certainly smashed, so it may not even be worth looking.'

'Was your laptop the shiny red one?'

'Yes, have you found it? I also had a white smartphone.'

'I'm afraid your laptop is beyond help, but Aubrey found your mobile and it appears undamaged. Would you like him to fetch it for you?'

'If it's not too dangerous.'

'It's not dangerous at all. I'll ask him to bring it over. We found your wallet as well.'

She stepped back inside and a moment later, a tall elegant, well-dressed man with long hair that looked good on him emerged and walked towards me.

'Hi, Andy,' he said, smiling as he approached. 'More conventionally clad than last time.'

'Last time?' I said. 'Have we met?'

'Of course. We had a nice long chat while we were waiting for the ambulance. Don't you remember? I'm Aubrey Elwes.'

'No. Well, not much.'

'At least your head came off better than the tile. That smashed into a million fragments. You seemed all right at the time, apart from a small cut.'

I shook my head. 'It's almost a complete blank. We talked after the accident?'

'Yes, and you were most informative on the subject of aubergines. We had no idea they were so fascinating. Do you grow them?'

'Aubergines? No, but … umm … I have a friend who does.' It was one of Hobbes's hobbies, and although he had talked about them on occasion I hadn't realised I'd taken much in. 'I'm sorry if I rambled on.'

'Not at all. Hilda and I are always grateful for new knowledge, whatever the source. We also learned quite a bit about Egyptology. How's Daphne?' He handed me my wallet and mobile, squeezing them through the links.

'Thank you. She's fine. She's reached the camp and has been familiarising herself. She starts work tomorrow.' It was odd and disconcerting to be chatting to this man, who was, to all intents and purposes, a stranger.

'Have you found a place to stay?' asked Aubrey.

'Yes, I'm staying with a friend.'

'Inspector Hobbes?'

I nodded.

'I expect all this flooding is keeping him busy.'

'It is, and things are going to stay busy because …' I ground to a halt, aware I'd nearly said too much to this friendly man, who already knew more than I was comfortable with.

'Because of what?'

'Because he found something interesting. That's all I can say. It's police business, of course.'

'Of course. Well, nice to catch up with you, Andy. I'd better go back and help Hilda tidy up.'

He strolled back to the wreck of the building, leaving me dazed, confused and slightly unnerved – not an unfamiliar sensation, except for an added dimension of weirdness. He'd treated me as more than a mere acquaintance, almost like a friend. The fact was that I'd never been good at making friends, although I'd acquired a few after meeting Hobbes, and a few more after marrying Daphne. The trouble with the latter ones was my certainty that the thing they most liked about me was her. Still, why should I worry about being befriended? I was doing all right today, and it was nice to have my phone back, not to mention my wallet, which I checked, was still full of money and credit cards.

Lunchtime was not far away, and, having cash in my pocket, I decided to treat myself to an aperitif before returning to Blackdog Street. I turned along Spire Street and headed towards Mosse Lane and the Feathers, where Billy worked behind the bar.

For reasons I'd never fathomed, he seemed to enjoy it there, and had proved astonishingly loyal to Featherlight, the landlord, whose short temper and violent outbursts had become a tourist attraction for reckless visitors.

As I drew near, I was surprised the old pub had a new door and double glazed windows. Featherlight was not known for his improvements, though he had once put down decking in the backyard in the hope of creating a beer garden. Although it had been a complete failure because he'd hadn't bothered to put tables or chairs out there and had neglected to water the potted plants, it did provide a useful area for guests to recover consciousness.

Featherlight himself, bloated, multi-bellied, and wearing a stained vest and shorts, was standing in the doorway behind a barricade of sandbags, glowering at the floodwater as if he longed to punch it.

'Good morning,' I said cheerily.

'What's so good about it, Caplet?'

'Well, it's not raining.'

'Didn't I ban you?'

'Umm ... no, I don't think so.'

'I'm losing my touch then.' He spat into the water. 'Do you reckon I can advertise my beer garden as a riverside terrace now?'

'Umm ... probably not. I think the floods will be gone soon.'

'Oh well, it was just a thought. Will your good lady be joining you?'

'No, she's in Egypt.'

'A reasonably safe distance. What on earth does she see in you? It beats me.'

'To be honest, it beats me too.'

'Well, you're punching above your weight with that one, you lucky bastard.'

'True,' I said, pleased to find him in one of his affable moods.

'Enough of your blather. Are you coming in to spend money?'

'I thought I'd have a pint.'

'Well stop wasting my time, get inside, and don't splash unless you want to feel the business end of my boot.'

I stepped into the familiar fug, a heady mix of sweat, stale beer, old tobacco, bad cooking and years of engrained filth, the latter persisting despite Billy's best efforts. During quieter periods he could often be spotted hard at work with various patent cleaning products, and although he'd made little impression on the overall seediness, the last environmental health inspection had rated kitchen hygiene there as adequate, a colossal improvement. There'd been a time when I would sometimes eat there, and, somewhat to my amazement, I'd survived without any major internal horrors, although I suspected I'd been served spicy cat stew at least once.

My feet felt sticky on the greasy greyish floor covering that, according to the old-timers, had once been a carpet, and I felt strangely at home with the nicotine-stained walls and ceiling. I'd read how some modern establishments used a similar colour of paint in an attempt to make them look old and lived in, but the Feathers was the genuine article, and it had taken generations of heavy smokers and shoddy cleaning to produce the authentic effect of squalor, misery and degradation. Furthermore, the colour scheme was still developing, since Featherlight consistently ignored the smoking ban. No one, to my knowledge, had challenged him about it since a tourist, a huge, shaven-headed guy, had demanded that he stop smoking when serving food. To start with, Featherlight had merely ignored him, and it might have stopped there had he not coughed his cigarette butt into the man's curry. Courteously for Featherlight, he had immediately dug it out and put it back in his mouth, but the tourist, leaping to his feet, showing himself to be even taller than Featherlight, had insisted on a replacement meal. Featherlight, who has never appreciated that sort of thing, having asked him to sit down and shut up, though not quite as politely, had pushed him back into his chair. The tourist had sprung up again like a jack-in-a-box and punched Featherlight on the jaw. To everyone's surprise, Featherlight had not hit back immediately. Instead he'd invited him to step out the back.

The subsequent brawl had lasted as long as it took for the posturing tourist to get his guard up and to land on the decking. He turned out to have been an aspiring cage fighter who'd been looking for an opportunity to test his skills and gain publicity. Rumour had it that he gave up martial arts on regaining consciousness, and had to live on soup for six months. Since then, Featherlight had led a comparatively peaceful life, which was good for the over stretched resources of the local A&E, if not so good for Mrs Goodfellow's tooth collection.

'Wotcha, Andy, what can I get you,' said Billy's voice from behind the bar.

I leant over to see him polishing a glass.

'Hi,' I said. 'A pint of lager, please.'

He walked to a pump, climbed on to an upturned bucket and began to pour my drink.

'How's business?' I asked.

'Good. Despite the storm, most of our regulars checked in last night, and we had a number of displaced people as well. The sandbagging has prevented any real flooding, though the cellar is somewhat damper than usual. We got off lightly. Some folk really had it rough.'

I nodded and fiddled in my wallet for the money, apologising for its dampness as I handed it over and took my glass.

'Cheers!' I said.

'Cheers to you too,' said Billy. 'By the way, I've got something to tell you.'

'What?'

'Skeleton Bob came in a few minutes ago. He was scared and bedraggled and reckoned he'd had to flee his cottage on an airbed because a huge, fierce grey creature was approaching through the flood. He reckoned it was a hippopotamus or something, and that it must have escaped from a zoo.'

'Was he drunk?'

'I don't think so. I think something had really scared him, so I tried to call Hobbesie, but couldn't get through.'

'He's drowned his mobile again.'

'I'm worried Bob'll do something daft.'

'Dafter than usual, you mean.'

'Yes. He was wittering on about borrowing a harpoon.'

'Where from?'

Billy shrugged. 'I've no idea, mate, but he seemed convinced he could get one. You'd better warn Hobbesie.'

'There are other policemen, you know. You could always have called the police station.'

'I could've, but most of the cops aren't as sympathetic to Bob and his ways, and he'll do almost anything to avoid them.'

'Anything except not breaking the law. Never mind, I should be seeing Hobbes at lunch, though he's very busy. The fact is I found something in the flood yesterday, and, well, it seems to have become a crime scene.'

'What sort of thing?' asked Billy.

'I can't say. It's … umm … police business, and there's a press blackout.' If I exaggerated, it was only because I was showing off.

'Was it in Church Fields? I saw something going on there when I came by.'

'I can't say,' I said. 'It's an official secret.'

'It sounds interesting then.'

I nodded and took a big slurp from my glass. 'Hey, what's up with the lager?'

'Nothing. It's the same rubbish as usual.'

'But it's good. There's none of that vinegary aftertaste.'

'Maybe it's because I cleaned out the pipes,' said Billy. 'The boss was in court last week and I took the opportunity to run the cleaner through them three times. I'm not sure anyone had bothered this century, and I'm not saying there was all sorts of horrible gunk came out, but it now takes me half as long to fill a glass, and people have started enjoying their beer. Even the boss didn't complain when he had his breakfast pint.'

I took another long, slow pull on my glass. 'Surely it's his job to clean the pipes.'

'Are you trying to tell me how to run my pub, Caplet?' Featherlight's great hand landed on my shoulder like a side of beef, and spun me round.

His face had just a hint of the stormy tint that was an early warning of violence.

'No,' I said, cringing, although he'd never hit me since I'd become friends with Hobbes. It wasn't that he was frightened of Hobbes, or anything as mundane as that. In fact, he was just about the only person in town who wasn't scared to face his wrath. I'd been puzzled for years until I'd discovered the reason; Featherlight was as 'unhuman' as Hobbes.

'You'd better not. Now, drink up and get out before I boot you out.'

Gulping down the remains of my lager, I removed myself from harm's way.

As I walked back to Blackdog Street, I felt as if I was going home, even though I'd only lived there for a relatively short time as a temporary non-paying guest, and had been away for a couple of years. It did, however, lack the one ingredient that would have made it perfect, which was Daphne.

Thinking of her, I checked my mobile, and was ashamed to see she'd made nineteen attempts to call me. Although there'd been genuine difficulties and obstacles, I could and should have tried harder to let her know I was safe, and check that she was well and happy. She really should have been my priority. Still, as Featherlight liked to say, there was no use crying over split lips. I was back in contact, and all was well, apart from the loss of our flat and most of our possessions, and that thing with me and Sally.

The Sally problem kept running through all my thoughts, bringing a constant nagging horror that I'd soon receive a mysterious and sinister letter, unless blackmailers had moved to more modern methods like texts or emails. I both hoped and feared I'd find out really soon and that I'd sort everything out before Daphne returned. I felt how I imagined a criminal might feel after being found guilty but before sentence had been passed; full of fear yet dreaming that the judge might yet be lenient. Of course, my case was entirely different as I hadn't really done anything wrong, though, unfortunately that wasn't how it would look. I dreaded Daphne's response should she ever see the photographs. What if she refused to believe my perfectly reasonable explanations and pleas of innocence? What if she convicted me on the evidence? Deep down I believed her to be amazingly tolerant of my faults and foibles, and I was deeply in love with her, as I hoped she was with me and I wasn't sure I'd be able to manage if she walked out of my life. Yet, despite knowing her as well as anyone might expect, I couldn't guess how she'd respond. At such times I really needed to talk to someone, such as Hobbes or Mrs Goodfellow, but I was far too ashamed.

When I got in, Hobbes and Dregs were already home, cleaned and dried. The good thing was that Dregs, having just been bathed, was in a subdued mood when he greeted me, and not inclined to rough me up or give me a good licking. Hobbes was on the sofa, doing the *Bugle's* Cunningly Cryptic Crossword, a task he seemed to enjoy, though it rarely took him longer than ten minutes. I was lucky if I worked out one clue in a week, though I could usually manage a decent stab at the concise version.

He finished, put the paper down and looked up. 'How was the Feathers?'

'Quiet and dry. Umm … how did you know I'd been there?'

'The place has a unique aroma, and the grubby patch on your left elbow shows you leant on the bar.'

I glanced at the brown smudge on my sleeve. 'Umm … did you find any more bodies?'

'If you mean fresh ones, then no, though there are still plenty of bones to be retrieved. There appears to be quite a spacious chamber down there, and I've advised Superintendent Cooper to call in a diving team to take a proper look. Doctor Ramage has taken Septimus Slugg's remains back to her lab, and the other recovered bones, which she still believes are hundreds of years old, are resting in peace in my office for the time being.'

'Couldn't you have just left them for now? I mean, what harm could come to them?'

'You'd be surprised what people will do sometimes, and don't forget there are ghouls about.'

He meant real ghouls, not just ghoulish humans. I'd had an alarming experience with a couple of them shortly after I'd first met him and was still disgusted that such creatures were allowed to live in town. Yet, so long as they didn't break the law too obviously, and didn't leave opened graves, he tolerated them, pointing out that the only real harm they did was to old bones, which they'd grind into ghoul hash. I was amazed they hadn't found these bones before, for they had an extraordinary talent for locating them.

It was then I remembered to tell him what Billy had said about Skeleton Bob.

'I'd better go and see him,' said Hobbes. 'I was thinking I ought to check up on him anyway. He was rather distraught after the loss of his pig.'

'How will you get there?'

'By boat, but since we broke the ones we used yesterday, I'll have to get another … I know, I'll ask Sid if he still has his canoes. He won't mind lending me one.'

Though I knew Sid Sharples was a vampire, I hadn't known he was a canoeist as well. Mind you, I also hadn't known he flew a black micro-light until he buzzed me one afternoon in Ride Park, nearly causing heart failure.

'Dinner's ready,' announced Mrs Goodfellow, nearly causing heart failure, and making me reflect that life can sometimes be a series of repeating patterns.

I headed into the kitchen and sat down, soothing my strained nerves as Hobbes said grace. The food was excellent, even though it was just an egg and cheese salad. I'd not been a great fan of salads until I'd tried one of the old girl's, since never before had I realised that cucumber could be so fragrant, that lettuce could be so crisp, and that tomatoes could be so sweet. Besides, she had a way with boiling eggs and I was always a sucker for the nutty, crumbly Sorenchester Cheese, especially when taken with a dollop of her prize-winning pungent pickle. I was a very contented Andy by the time we'd finished and were back on the sofa, drinking tea. Hobbes made a phone call to Sid.

'D'you fancy a canoe trip?' he asked when he put the receiver down.

'Yes, why not?' I gulped down as much of the scalding liquid as I could before grabbing my coat and rushing out with him and Dregs.

We paid a quick visit to Sid's lock-up where Sid, unusually short, paunchy, balding and affable for a vampire, helped us take down a big red fibreglass canoe that had been slung from the beams. I helped Hobbes carry it down to the junction of Dribbling Lane and Spittoon Way by not getting in his way. He set the canoe down on the water, and we prepared for the voyage. Taking a paddle, I scrambled to the front, with Dregs, tail wagging like an old seadog, sitting himself in the middle. Then Hobbes plumped himself down in the back. The canoe pivoted, his end plunged, and mine rose, nearly catapulting me out, and leaving me high and dry. I grabbed the side and looked over my shoulder as Dregs slid backwards and raised me even higher.

'This will need a little re-organisation,' said Hobbes whose backside was within a whisker of the water line.

I splashed down as he sprang out.

'Right, I'd better take the middle, Dregs had better sit at the back, and you might as well stay where you are.'

Although Dregs was reluctant to take up the inferior position assigned to him, Hobbes insisted, and within a couple of minutes we were on our way to Bob's place, and I believe I made a contribution to our progress, though most of it was down to Hobbes, who seemed far more at ease in a canoe than he had been in a rowing boat. I said as much.

'I once spent some time in British Columbia,' he said, 'and found that canoes were often the best way of travelling any distance, though they weren't fibreglass in those days.'

'What were you doing out there?'

'Hunting a fugitive wendigo.'

'Were you on secondment?'

'No, it was a special assignment.'

'Did you catch him?'

'I caught *her* and I still have the scars to remind me.'

He would say no more, which was infuriating since I still wanted raw material so I could write about him. My original plan had just been to draft an article. Later, I thought I'd get a book out of him, and by then I was wondering whether a series might be possible. Unfortunately, though I'd picked up some amazing details, I was certain many of the really fascinating parts of his story remained locked up in that great ugly head of his. As far as he was concerned, the present was far more interesting than the past and only now and again, usually when he'd dredged up an old memory relevant to a current case, would he let slip an intriguing hint of old times.

Instead of giving in to frustration, I decided to make the most of the trip and to treat it like a jaunt. We took the direct route to Bob's, crossing flooded fields, gliding through submerged copses and over hedgerows and walls. It was quite pleasant, despite my worries about the beast Bob had spotted, but, other than a fierce-looking swan and some water-logged sheep gathered on a mound, I saw nothing to alarm me. After about twenty minutes we approached Bob's cottage, which, despite being in a relatively raised position, had water lapping the perimeter fence. A small brown dog, splashing around the edge, woofed, sparking a barking match with Dregs.

'Ahoy!' cried Hobbes's foghorn voice when we were a hundred metres or so away.

Bob's head poked round the side of the house. 'Hello, Mr Hobbes.'

'Good Afternoon,' said Hobbes. 'Permission to land?'

'Granted,' said Bob, his grin displaying despicable dentition.

Seeing the small dog walk up to us, its tail wagging like a propeller, and thinking I'd make myself useful, I grabbed the painter Hobbes had laid along the bottom of the canoe, and stood up, expecting to step into calf deep water.

'Not yet,' said Hobbes, a fraction too late to stop me.

I went in with a splash and a deal of astonishment, going under as if I'd stepped into the deep end of a swimming pool. Coming up, spluttering with the shock of sudden immersion, I swam, puzzled that the little dog was still walking at my side. Its movements were perhaps a little stiff.

'Hold on,' said Hobbes as I grabbed the painter.

I was expecting him to pick me up, not to tow me behind like hippo bait, but after a moment or two my feet touched the bottom and, like an idiot Robinson Crusoe, I dragged myself onto dry land. Bob tied the canoe to a fence post.

'Why did you throw yourself in?' he asked as Hobbes and Dregs stepped onto dry land.

'I didn't think it was very deep. I mean, that little dog was walking around without any problems. I don't understand it.'

Bob guffawed. 'That dog is a Stillingham Stilthound.'

'A what?'

'You heard,' he said, grinning from ear to eternity.

'I've never heard of such a thing.'

'That's because the working dogs have become quite rare,' said Hobbes, who was also chuckling. 'They were originally used for duck hunting in the days when they'd flood the water meadows around Stillingham every winter.'

To illustrate his point, the dog strolled ashore and greeted Dregs. It was a sturdy little animal with wooden stilts attached to powerful legs. Dregs looked up at him, seemingly as amazed as I was.

'Stumpy is staying here a while. He belongs to my old mate, Jake, who's having to dry out his house,' said Bob.

'Would that be Jake Custard, the council's flood expert?' asked Hobbes.

'That's him.'

'Is he all right?'

Bob nodded. 'He's bearing up, but will be better when he can move back home and have his dog back.'

'Good,' said Hobbes. 'Now, tell me about your mysterious sighting.'

'Oh, that,' said Bob, his face turning as red and shiny as a cricket ball. 'I was mistaken.'

'Were you drunk again?' I asked, shivering, dripping, and grateful for a sliver of sunlight that had broken cover to emit a tiny hint of winter heat.

'No, it was a mistake anyone could have made.'

'Robert Nibblet, what have you done this time?' asked a breathless woman's voice from inside the cottage.

'Nothing really,' said Bob, suddenly looking as pale as a white mouse, a nicotine-stained finger to his lips, his eyes pleading.

'Your wife's back,' I said. 'When did she return?'

'This morning, when I was in town,' said Bob.

'But, how did she get here?' I asked, with a gesture at the floods.

Hobbes, chuckling for a reason that escaped me, clamped his hairy hand across my mouth.

'Good afternoon, madam,' he said, as Fenella Nibblet filled the doorway. 'Just a routine visit.'

'Thank you,' Bob mouthed.

'Oh, is that all? I feared he'd been up to his old tricks again. It would be just like him to mess things up when I'm away,' said the spherical Mrs Nibblet, squeezing through the doorway and rolling from the house, wearing a close-fitting orange onesie that made her look like an enormous animated pumpkin.

'Delighted to see you again,' said Hobbes, releasing my mouth and snapping off a smart salute.

She nodded. 'So why are you here?'

Bob shook his head almost imperceptibly.

'There were just a couple of details I wanted to clear up regarding the attack on Crackling Rosie,' said Hobbes, with what must have been his attempt at a pleasant smile.

'Well don't waste too much time. That Rosie was a menace, but at least she'll make some good sausages.'

'Don't,' said Bob, with a sob. 'She was a lovely animal.'

'She was a lump of vicious lard,' said Mrs Nibblet.

'Well, so are you,' he retorted.

For a moment he stood there, angry and defiant, until realisation of what he'd said dawned. Mrs Nibblet directed a storm-force glare at him, and he attempted a smile. It came out as a grimace.

'What did you say?'

'It was just a joke, my dear, just a silly joke.'

Then, his nerve broke, and he fled, with his wife in hot pursuit, the pair of them bringing to mind a bowling ball chasing a skittle. Dregs and the stilthound, both barking excitedly, joined in the fun.

'What will she do to him?' I asked as they vanished around the side of the cottage. 'Do you need to protect him? I mean to say, she must be three times his weight.'

'More than that,' said Hobbes, 'and if there was a chance she'd hurt him I would, of course, intervene. However, as they've been married for over twenty years and Bob has survived entirely unscathed, I think he's safe. At heart, and despite appearances, Mrs Nibblet is a kind and loving wife, though many might consider him a most provoking husband.'

'There again, his survival might say more about how fast he is on his feet,' I suggested as Bob emerged from the other side of the cottage, having opened up a five second gap on Fenella, whose beetroot face was clashing horribly with the onesie. Dregs and Stumpy the stilthound were keeping up, their tails wagging as if this was the game of the century.

'Possibly,' said Hobbes, 'but Bob reckons her bark is worse than her bite.'

'Has she ever bitten him?' I asked as Bob headed for the dark side of the cottage.

'Not to my knowledge. And now she's using her brain.'

Mrs Nibblet had stopped running and was lying in wait at the corner of the house, breathing so heavily I could hear her from twenty paces. When Bob, bug-eyed like a rabbit, reappeared, she made a grab for him, but he ducked and slipped through her arms. Then, mystifyingly, and much to Hobbes's amusement, he carried on running round the house. She seized him on her second attempt.

'Robert Armstrong Nibblet,' she said, holding him by the scruff of the neck as if he were a naughty puppy, 'you apologise. You apologise now!'

'I'm sorry, dearest. Truly I am,' said Bob, squirming. 'Please forgive me.'

She glared for a long moment, before hauling him towards her and giving him a hug. I was just starting to fear she was crushing him, like a python crushes a deer, when she let go. He stepped back to breathe and when he grinned at her, she smiled back. The dogs, seeing the excitement was over, returned to splashing about in the water.

'I wish all domestic disputes were resolved so happily and quickly,' said Hobbes.

'And so entertainingly,' I said.

'Indeed. Let's leave the happy couple to their own devices. Get in the boat. Are you cold?'

'Yes. Especially now the sun's gone back in.'

'You'd better cover yourself with this,' he said, taking off his gabardine mac. 'Come here, Dregs.'

With a lingering look of regret for the breaking of a new friendship, Dregs hopped aboard, taking up his position in the stern. Hobbes shoved off with his paddle.

When we'd gone some distance, he began laughing.

'What's so funny?'

'Bob's hippopotamus.'

'Yeah, that was strange. I thought you'd question him about it. Umm ... what do you think he saw?'

'Mrs Nibblet coming home.'

'That's a bit unfair,' I said. 'I know she's rather a large lady, but no one would mistake her for a hippo ... and, anyway, didn't he say the beast was grey?'

'He did.'

'Well it can't have been her then. She was in orange.'

'I take it you didn't observe what was hanging on the washing line next to the airbed?'

'No, but what's that got to do with anything?'

'Everything.'

'What was it then?'

'A jumbo-sized grey wetsuit ...'

A glance over my shoulder proved he wasn't joking.

'... which I strongly suspect is hers. It certainly isn't Bob's – he'd be able to fit all of him into one of the legs.'

'Why would she have a wetsuit?'

'For scuba diving. Bob once mentioned she'd joined the local club.'

'There's a diving club in Sorenchester?'

'The *Sorenchester and District Orcas*. I had a try-dive with them once.'

'Really? What happened?'

'Firstly, they couldn't find any kit to fit me, and secondly, I sank, even when I shouldn't have. But never mind that, let's get you home and then I'll get back to work.'

Digging the paddle in, he sent us skimming across the water. Dregs sat at the back, his nose raised into the wind, his tail thumping. I expect I would have enjoyed the ride, too, had I not been so cold.

We were just approaching the outskirts of Sorenchester, cruising between parallel lines of Cotswold stone, where the tops of the inappropriately named drystone walls bordered a lane, when Dregs began barking. Hobbes stopped paddling and we drifted to a standstill next to a man who was chest deep in water, and breathing heavily.

'Are you all right, sir.'

'I'm just taking a breather. I'll be glad to get back home though. This water is not exactly tropical, is it?'

'No, sir,' Hobbes acknowledged, 'it isn't. Would you like a lift?'

'Thank you, but I'm on my bike. I'm training for the Tour of the Cotswolds and my schedule is all out because of the awful weather.' He glanced at his watch. 'I really should be going now.'

'Enjoy your ride,' said Hobbes, speeding us away.

Looking back, I could see the man peddling, or paddling, hard but not exactly moving at high speed. 'That's dedication,' I said.

Hobbes nodded.

'Though some might call it lunacy,' I continued.

'Possibly, Andy. It's all down to results. If he does well, it will be called dedication. If he doesn't it will be lunacy.'

When we'd reached dryish land, Hobbes and Dregs returned the canoe, allowing me to head straight home for yet another hot bath and change of clothing. The clean clothes remained something of a mystery, for they would always be ready, neatly folded and laid out, whenever I needed them. Even better, my filthy wet clothes would vanish and then reappear a day or two later, magically cleansed of all dirt and hurt, pressed and ready to go. I suspected Mrs Goodfellow was responsible, but had never caught her in the act, though one day I intended thanking her and judging her reaction to test whether my Sherlockian intellect, having eliminated the impossible, had come up trumps.

Hobbes and Dregs returned for a cup of tea before heading back out to check on developments at the bone site. Feeling warm, clean and drowsy, I took the opportunity for a quick nap. When I awoke it smelt like it was almost supper time, which was no bad thing, though I felt groggy and headachy as the sleep cleared.

I was at the table, willing and ready, when Mrs Goodfellow served up creamy fish chowder that, besides being utterly delicious, seemed entirely appropriate with all the water about. Just for a moment I'd had a slight worry that she'd managed to hoik the fish out of the street, but, since some of it was smoked haddock, I relaxed. Although it was obviously impossible for her to surpass herself with every meal, she seemed to manage it. I wished Daphne could cook half as well as her, though I'd have been just as happy if I could. I'd really missed the old girl's food, despite all my visits to restaurants. Even the best ones lagged way behind and I couldn't always choose the best, as Phil insisted that I visit all sorts of places. A few, with all due respect, stank: some literally so. On the bright side, the truly appalling ones were rare and made me appreciate the others.

Another admirable aspect of the old girl was that, unlike certain so-called celebrity chefs, she never got flustered or swore, though I'd once heard her mutter something that might have been unladylike when a starling fell down the chimney, blundered into the kitchen and belly flopped into the magnificent trifle she'd spent several hours working on for an old folks' supper. If it had been me, that bird would have breathed its last where it floundered. Since it wasn't, she dug it out, leaving behind a perfect sooty impression of every feather, washed it under the tap, dried it with a hairdryer and released it. Only then had she turned her attention to a replacement, somehow producing a superb Eton Mess just in time for Hobbes to deliver it to the church hall. Where she'd found strawberries in December was beyond me, though I'd occasionally speculated that she had magical powers. The truth was more mundane; she was simply outstanding at what she did and knew every shopkeeper, farmer and gardener who had whatever she required.

When we'd finished eating, and Hobbes and I were drinking tea, I asked how his investigations were going.

He thought for a while. 'The situation is not at all straightforward. I've had to inform the duty sergeant and call in other detective resources because of the murder of Mr Septimus Slugg. However, preliminary tests have confirmed that most of the other bones date from medieval times.'

'Most?'

'It turns out that not all of them are so old.'

'What do you mean?'

'The divers discovered an intact male skeleton this afternoon. It was still showing fragments of clothing, as well as something you wouldn't expect on a medieval corpse.'

'What?'

'A digital watch.'

'Wow,' I said, stunned. 'So that does make it recent.'

'Indeed,' said Hobbes. 'The watch in question is a mass produced Casio, and the model dates from the late nineteen eighties.'

'So that's when he died?'

'That is the earliest possible date, though, of course, he might have worn the watch for many years before his death.'

'Are there any indications what killed him? Was it another murder?'

'It would appear so. Dr Ramage pointed out some skull injuries that suggest he'd been bludgeoned. Besides, it's clear he didn't stick himself down there.'

'But I don't understand where all the bones are coming from.'

Hobbes sighed. 'That remains to be determined. However, I have spoken to Mr Spiridion Konstantinopoulos …'

'The local historian,' I remarked. 'I saw one of his books once.'

'He informed me that there are no records of any plague pits around the town and he agrees with Dr Ramage that the old bones were probably in an ossuary, or charnel house. That fits in with the discovery of the large chamber. It is, of course, underwater now, but it would normally have been underground.'

'Does that mean the killer knew where it was and hid his victims there?' I asked.

'It's a possibility, though I doubt it. It's more likely that the killer, or killers, dumped the bodies in the old culvert that runs alongside. Apparently, that was what collapsed under us and knocked down the ossuary wall.'

'It was a most unpleasant experience.'

'It was, but it may have been fortunate in that something was revealed that someone hoped would not be revealed.'

'Do you think the bodies might have blocked the culvert? Could that be why the flooding was so bad this time?'

'It wouldn't surprise me.'

'I wonder who did it and why?'

'So do I, and I intend to find out,' he said with a sudden grin.

'Good … can I come with you?'

'I expect so. At least for some of the time.'

'Excellent,' I said, and though I was genuinely delighted, a timid, or sensible, part of my brain was, as usual, screaming 'no!' Sometimes, my newly acquired courage astounded me, but mostly it scared me. Yet, investigating crimes with Hobbes always made me feel more alive, even when it left me half dead. The paradox had long puzzled me.

'Of course,' he continued after a slurp of tea, 'investigation will be tricky until the roads are clear. I really need to see Mr Solomon Slugg.'

'Couldn't you just phone him?'

'I could, but then I'd be unable to see him.'

'Or smell him?' I suggested.

He nodded and changed the subject. He always seemed a little reticent about his unusual abilities, but it had been the way he sniffed out clues at crime scenes that had given me my first inkling that he wasn't quite human.

That evening we stayed in. I watched the telly, while he read the paper. It was barely nine o'clock when he yawned and went up to bed. His yawn set me off, too, and I crashed out only a few minutes later. This time, so far as I could remember, I enjoyed a dreamless sleep.

Next morning, I sat alone at the table as the old girl ladled porridge into my bowl. The house was really quiet.

'Where are they?' I asked.

'Out. Somebody telephoned in the middle of the night.'

'I didn't hear anything.'

'I'm not surprised. You looked exhausted and you slept like the dead, except that you were snoring.'

'I didn't know I snored. Do I do it often?'

'Only when you're asleep, dear.'

I concentrated on eating my porridge, still amazed how she could transmute it into haute cuisine, and remembered the distasteful grey, lumpy mess Mother used to slop out, a sludge that was barely palatable even when laced with golden syrup. Nowadays, I looked forward to getting my oats, even though it meant I'd missed out on some other delight. I'd learned to accept whatever was on offer, and to await further delectation.

I'd just scraped my bowl clean and was wondering whether there was space for anything else when Dregs burst into the kitchen, heralding the return of Hobbes, who was looking rather bedraggled. He poured a mug of tea and took a big slurp.

'That's better,' he said, and spoke no more until he'd drained three further mugs and had spooned down a titanic volume of porridge.

Dregs, who'd lapped up a bowl of water, sprawled beneath the table and was soon fast asleep, twitching, and kicking my feet at odd intervals.

'Did you have an interesting call-out?' I asked, having restrained my curiosity for as long as seemed possible without bursting.

'Yes,' said Hobbes, buttering a slice of toast, 'but it was puzzling.'

'Who called you out?'

'Superintendent Cooper.'

'She must have been working late.'

'No, she was in bed when Sergeant Dixon phoned, and she decided she needed to call me.'

'What was it about?'

'A report had come in concerning intruders at a house in Fenderton.'

'One of the flooded ones?'

'No, one on the hill. However, I needed to borrow Sid's canoe again to get there, though the waters have receded quite a lot.'

'But why did she call you? It sounds more like a job for the ordinary police ... the ones in uniform that is.'

Hobbes applied marmalade to his toast and ate it slowly, while I waited.

'That would normally be the case. However, the house is on Elphinstone Road ...'

'So?'

'… where a number of very distinguished and wealthy people live.'

'So, they get special treatment? That's not fair.'

'Of course they don't get special treatment, but the house in question belongs to Mr Solomon Slugg.'

'I see,' I said. 'So you got to talk to him?'

'No, I didn't, because he wasn't there. No one was.' He scratched his chin, his fingers rasping on his morning stubble.

'Who made the phone call then?'

'According to Sergeant Dixon, the caller did not give his name and hung up abruptly before he could be questioned.'

'So how did he know where the call came from?'

Hobbes laughed. 'Andy, you really are a luddite! The number was recorded and Dixon looked up the address. When he saw whose house it was, he called the superintendent. He's a bright one is young Reg.'

I nodded and turned to Mrs Goodfellow. 'Is there any more tea?'

'I've just made another pot, dear.' She carried it over and refilled our mugs.

Beneath the table, Dregs was snoring gently.

'Did you find anything?' I asked and took a sip of fresh tea.

'Only the mysterious disappearance of Mr Solomon Slugg.'

'Do you think he's been kidnapped?'

'It's a possibility. The back door had been left open, and someone had been in the house recently.'

'How did you know?'

'There was fresh mud on the floor.'

'Umm … couldn't that have been Solomon? He might have opened the door and fled.'

'That wouldn't explain it.'

'Unless he ran out and back in and back out again. Perhaps he forgot his coat or something?'

Hobbes nodded and drained his mug. 'Good try, but there were two sets of muddy prints going in and out, and I'd suggest one of them was made by a woman.'

'Well, maybe he had a female friend round, and they both forgot something.' I was starting to think my reasoning was getting a little far-fetched.

'I'll keep an open mind, but, since someone telephoned about intruders, I would suggest that intruders are more likely, don't you agree?'

'Yeah, you're probably right. Was there any sign of a struggle?'

'There were signs of a hasty departure, but there was no blood, or any other damage.'

'Had the back door been forced?'

'No,' said Hobbes, 'but there were a few tiny scratches around the keyhole that might suggest lock picks. I don't often see them used these days, but this was an old-fashioned lock, and if I'm correct someone made a very neat job of it.'

'So the big question is, who did it?' I said, pleased with my insight.

'Or, more importantly, where is Mr Solomon Slugg?'

'Oh, yeah. There's that.'

'I'll go back later, have another nose around, and see what turns up. Now, I'm going to get myself neat and tidy.'

He finished his tea, marched upstairs and shortly afterwards I heard his heavy duty electric razor at work, followed by his yells as he stood under the dangerously powerful shower. A few minutes later, he returned, fully dressed and ready to go.

'Right,' he said, 'I'm off to work.'

'Can I come?' I asked, hoping.

'I'm going into the station to do paperwork, and to see if there's any new information on the bodies. I don't suppose that will interest you very much, but I intend to head up to Mr Slugg's place afterwards. I'll look back in here before I go, so if you'd like a trip out, then you'd be most welcome.'

'That'll be great,' I said, as he left.

Shortly afterwards, having pulled my feet from under Dregs, who'd somehow contrived to lie across them in his sleep, I took a look outside the front door. The floods were definitely going down, and other than hoses pumping filthy water into drains that now seemed prepared to take it away, things looked reasonably normal. The sun wore only a thin film of gauzy cloud, and there was, maybe, a hint of warmth in the air, a reminder that spring was not so very far away. There was still little sign of moving traffic, and I wondered how many vehicles had survived the deluge. The worst thing was the foetid stench of sewage.

I went back inside and telephoned Daphne, who, to my delight, was in the office, and in a sparkling mood, fizzing with enthusiasm about what she'd seen and done, and what was happening. The dig, she said, had uncovered a number of interesting artefacts, one of which was possibly unique and might point to the existence of a previously unknown Pharaoh. I formed the impression that the team was hoping for something to rival the tomb of Tutankhamen. She laughed off my concerns about a possible curse, and despite knowing my fears were silly, anything seemed possible since I'd fallen into Hobbes's world. I reserved the right to worry.

Afterwards I was unsettled and lonely, feeling every one of the thousands of miles between us, and despite her being the one in a strange land, I was the one who seemed to be struggling, and although we'd parted with statements of love, I feared she was enjoying herself far too much. What if she found so much fulfilment and excitement out there that she never came back? After all, what could I, a part-time journalist in an insignificant Cotswold town, offer a dynamic, fascinating and lovely woman like her? She was bound to meet someone quite different to me, someone like Professor Mahmoud El-Gammal, who was, I convinced myself, tall, slim and handsome, with dark seductive eyes and exquisite manners. I sat on the sofa, growing morose and self-pitying until Dregs woke up and bullied me into taking him for a walk.

We used the park's Hedbury Road entrance, which was above flood level. Looking back down the slope towards town, the fields were still mostly under water, and the church tower appeared to rise above them like a lighthouse. I let the dog off the lead to run and bark and sniff. The ground squelched with every step, making me glad of my Wellington boots, but Dregs's tail was wagging in ecstasy, for cold, preferably muddy, water held none of the horrors of a bath. It was sad really, because he was dirtying his undercarriage so much that Mrs Goodfellow would insist on dunking him straight into the tub when we got back. Still, since he'd never worked out the link between getting filthy and ending up in the dreaded bath, he was perfectly content for the time being. I followed his meanderings, daydreaming about the allure of the other women I'd met recently, and wondering why I couldn't quite bring the charm and beauty of Sally and Hilda to mind when it was so easy with Pinky and Dr Cynthia, and Daphne, of course.

'Oi, Caplet!' Featherlight's harsh voice smashed through my reverie like a sledgehammer through a fruitcake.

'Good morning,' I said.

'Good morning be damned. Shift your arse and take a look at this.'

'What?' I asked.

'Shut up and I'll show you.'

He turned away, his bellies following a moment later, and headed for the trees, walking with a slight forwards lean, his arms at his sides as if pushing a heavy wheelbarrow. I couldn't help remembering Mother's advice about not following strange men into the woods, particularly as few were as strange as Featherlight. Still, he was obviously in a benign mood by his standards and I was likely to be quite safe. Besides, I had Dregs to look after me, which he could do if he felt like it.

After a brisk and muddy walk, we reached an overgrown stone quarry that had become a convenient place to tip old junk, and scrambled down a slimy slope. After skirting the murky puddle or pond in the middle we reached the far end where Featherlight called a halt. Dregs, who was running a little ahead, sneezed and retreated, his hackles rising.

'What's up?' I asked.

'See that?' said Featherlight, pointing at a perfect circle of flattened crushed grass about the size of the old vinyl long-playing records Hobbes occasionally played. In the middle was a star within a hoop made of split twigs.

As I stepped forward to examine it, Featherlight's heavy hand clamped onto my shoulder and dragged me back.

'I wouldn't do that if I was you, Caplet,' he said.

'Why not?' I asked, wondering why a bit of rustic tat worried him so much.

'It's dangerous.'

I laughed. 'Come off it! It's just a corn dolly, or something.'

'Even a mutton-brained numbskull can tell it's not a damned corn-dolly,' he growled.

He really did growl, like a huge angry dog, except there were words in it. The only other person I knew who could do such a thing was Hobbes, though he usually required something serious to tip him into angry mode. Featherlight's temper, however, was like a mantrap with a hair trigger: the slightest incident could set it off. I'd known him long enough that I should have known better, and I did know better, but some reckless impulse overrode sense and I tried to wriggle free. The next thing I knew, I was dangling by my collar from a branch, my feet kicking helplessly, while a purple-faced Featherlight roared improbable anatomical abuse into my face. When my wellies slipped off, Dregs bounced up to lick my feet, pleased to join in this jolly game.

All things considered, I'd got off lightly, and Featherlight, whose rages tended to be short, if often painful to anyone within range, was back to relative affability.

'That thing is dangerous, you wazzock,' he said.

'Fine,' I said. 'I believe you, but what is it?'

'It's a sign of trouble. Tell Hobbes.'

'I will, but what sort of trouble?'

'Bad trouble. Big trouble. Trouble with a capital T.'

'But why?'

'Ask Hobbes. I'm busy.'

'OK … umm … but before you go would you mind letting me down?'

It testified to his good mood that he deigned to unhook me.

'See you,' I said, as he stomped away.

'Not if I see you first.'

I put my boots back on, despite Dregs's best efforts, and considered picking up the star thing as soon as Featherlight was well out of sight. For once, caution, or maybe an inkling of unease, got the better of me and I turned for home.

When we got back to Blackdog Street, Hobbes was fiddling with the car.

'I'm just going to see Mr Slugg,' he said. 'Do you still fancy coming?'

Without thinking, I nodded and a moment later I was getting into my accustomed place in the back seat, with Dregs making himself comfortable in the front.

'D'you think the roads are clear enough yet?' I asked.

Hobbes shrugged. 'We'll soon find out. The car should be fine. Billy came round and dried out the works, so it runs all right, but I apologise that it's still somewhat damp inside.'

Somewhat damp was the understatement of the year, for he could have grown rice in there. Fortunately, he'd covered the seats with sheets of polythene, which, despite keeping my backside reasonably dry, were as slippery as wet fish. I belted up, expecting that we'd soon be hurtling along Blackdog Street. However, I was surprised that he drove with such care that I felt it reasonable to keep my eyes open and see how he was avoiding puddles and ensuring he never splashed anyone or created a wash that might flood houses. We continued at the same sedate pace as we turned left by the church onto Pound Street, headed onto Spittoon Way and carried on towards Dribbling Lane, which was still awash, though nowhere near as deep as it had been. Unfortunately, the main road to Fenderton, slightly raised above the flooded meadows, was dry. He put his foot down.

I closed my eyes, clinging to the door handle, and despite my seatbelt, I slid from side to side and back. At last we turned and I opened my eyes for a moment, seeing that we were on Uphill Way, ascending at such a speed my ears popped. A few moments later we slowed down and I could breathe again and look around.

'Here we are,' said Hobbes, bringing the car to a stop on a broad gravelled driveway in front of an old-fashioned wooden garage set in a small, slightly unkempt garden. 'Let's see if Mr Slugg's in. I hope he is, because I'd really like a word with him.'

We got out of the car and I tried not to show how shaken I was, for my tolerance of his driving, though probably still better than most, had lessened since I'd been away. Dregs, left behind, moped.

We were outside a medium-sized house that looked in good nick, though the paintwork was a little tired. Hobbes strode up to the solid, heavy-looking front door and pressed the doorbell. An electronic Big Ben chime sounded within the bowels of the house, and then, besides Dregs bounding around in the car, there was silence. After a minute or so, Hobbes tried again. Then he knocked so hard a lesser door might have burst open.

There was still no reply.

'He's not in,' I said when Hobbes showed no sign of movement. 'Perhaps the intruders kidnapped him.'

'I suspect not,' he murmured, with a glance at a tiny security camera on the wall above.

'Umm … now what?'

He took out his warrant card, held it to the camera and rang the bell again.

There was still no reply.

'Are you going to knock the door in?' I asked.

'Of course not.' He shook his head. 'Although I would like to talk to Mr Slugg, there's no immediate urgency. He is not suspected of anything and Superintendent Cooper takes a dim view of shattering doors without due cause. I should know.'

'So what happens next?'

He shrugged. 'We could go home and have a cup of tea.'

'Is that all?' I'd been hoping for a bit of excitement and felt let down.

We returned to the car, reversed from the driveway and headed downhill. After a few seconds, he stopped and parked by the kerb.

'Why have we stopped?'

'Because I heard movement inside the Slugg residence.'

'From here?'

He chuckled. 'No, when we were outside.'

'It might not be him,' I said. 'It could be his dog or something.'

'If it was a dog it would have barked, and besides I heard the television being turned off, which is not something dogs generally do. Therefore, I conclude someone is home.'

'Perhaps they aren't dressed yet,' I suggested.

'Perhaps,' he said, 'or perhaps somebody doesn't wish to talk to me. I think I'll try a surprise visit, and this time Dregs can come.'

We got out, closing the doors quietly, and, having sneaked back up the road, ducked behind the shoulder-high privet hedge surrounding Mr Slugg's garden.

'There, you are,' said Hobbes, peering through the foliage. 'I told you someone was home.'

A tired old chap wearing tinted glasses, and with long grey hair down to his tweedy shoulders, was looking from the large downstairs window. He turned away.

'Stay out of sight, and wait,' said Hobbes, 'I'm going in.'

He took a few steps back, sprinted forwards, hurdled the hedge and landed on all fours on the front lawn, looking like an ape in a raincoat. His knuckles grazing the grass, he jogged towards the window, knelt below it, and gave a low whistle. Dregs, who'd been sitting patiently by my side, leapt up and, barking his big head off, galloped round the hedge towards him.

Mr Slugg returned to the window, frowning and presumably wondering why a large, clearly mad dog was bounding into his garden.

'Dig!' Hobbes whispered.

Still barking, Dregs began digging on the lawn, his tail a blur of excitement. After a moment, the front door opened and Mr Slugg thundered forth, clutching a heavy wooden walking stick.

'Clear off!' he yelled, brandishing his stick like a sword and charging at Dregs, who stopped digging long enough to dodge a vicious blow that left a deep dent in the lawn.

'I'd be obliged if you would leave the dog alone, sir,' said Hobbes, stepping in front of the doorway.

'I'll have you as well,' said Mr Slugg, turning and rushing Hobbes, who ducked under a scything swipe.

'That's enough of that, sir.'

'Get out of my garden,' bellowed Mr Slugg, his face red, the veins in his neck sticking out like firehoses.

'I would appreciate a few minutes of your time, sir.'

'Clear off!'

He aimed another wild whack at Hobbes, who deflected the blow with his forearm, which threw Mr Slugg so far off balance that he fell nose-first into the wall.

'Are you injured, sir?' asked, Hobbes, his voice full of concern.

Mr Slugg groaned and rolled onto his back, his nose pumping blood. Hobbes confiscated the stick and handed him a clean white handkerchief.

'That must be painful, sir. Let me help you inside. Come on, Andy.'

Lifting the moaning casualty over one shoulder, he carried him into the house, dropping him gently onto a large black leather sofa. Mr Slugg, the handkerchief at his snout turning bright scarlet, groaned. We were in a comfortable living room, with two matching armchairs, a vast television on the wall, an impressive iron stove that was throwing out a tremendous heat, and a small bookcase filled with old paperback thrillers. The walls were covered in the sort of wallpaper that looked as if someone had hurled small splats of porridge at it before painting it a dull beige, and the carpet was thick and brown, reminding me of the tasteless soup I'd enjoyed, if that was the word, at Gollum's Logons. There was a faint stagnant odour in the house.

Hobbes stood back and saluted. 'I'm Inspector Hobbes of the Sorenchester Police, as you well know, having seen my ID. These are my associates, Andy and Dregs.'

'Andy's a ridiculous name for a dog,' said Mr Slugg with a sneer.

'I'm Andy,' I said.

'Don't I know you?' asked Mr Slugg, fixing his gaze on me.

'I … umm … don't think so.' For some reason, I wished he did.

He shrugged.

'I'd like to ask you some questions,' said Hobbes, 'and I'd like you to answer them, if that's all right, sir?'

'It doesn't seem as if I've got any choice, does it?' said Mr Slugg.

'Of course you do, sir. You don't have to answer, but if you don't, or don't to my satisfaction, I will have to get you to talk by other means, which you may find rather less easy.'

'A threat eh? Let's get it over then.'

'Not a threat, sir, just a fact. Firstly, may I have your full name?'

'No, firstly, what's all this about, Inspector? I haven't done anything.'

'Then you have nothing to worry about. Your name?'

'Solomon Slugg.'

'Thank you. And this is your residence?'

'Yes.'

Mr Slugg's voice had changed, becoming relaxed and mellifluous, while his pleasant smile made him appear at least twenty years younger. In fact he was nowhere near as old as I'd first thought, and was actually tall, slim and rather aristocratic in bearing. Now he'd stopped being aggressive, he seemed like a nice chap, the sort of hearty fellow you could enjoy a pint of lager with.

'Do you know Mr Septimus Slugg?' asked Hobbes.

'Mr who?'

'Septimus Slugg.'

He sighed. 'Unfortunately, Inspector, I do. He's my brother, though I haven't seen him in ages.'

'Why's that, sir?'

'It's not my fault. The truth is that he borrowed money off me – rather a lot of money – and has never seen fit to repay it. Not that I'd care if he'd made any sort of effort, but he was always a dead beat.'

'I'm sorry to hear that, sir,' said Hobbes, looking sad.

'Though, of course, I regret the estrangement, I'm better off without him in my life. But, why are you asking? What's he done this time?'

'I regret to inform you, sir, that we believe he is dead.'

'I'm not surprised. I suppose it was the drink?'

'It appears he might have been murdered.'

Mr Slugg shrugged. 'Well, I can't say I'm too surprised. I feared he'd come to a bad end one day. He always used to prefer low company and I'd guess he probably owed money to one of his so called mates who killed him for it. How did it happen?'

'I'm afraid that a person, as yet unidentified, struck him with a weapon.'

Mr Slugg shook his head. 'Poor Septimus. Oh, well.'

'Are there any other relatives we should inform?' asked Hobbes.

'No. Not any more, as far as I know.'

'You had other siblings?'

'No, it was just the two of us, and our parents are long dead.'

'Fair enough,' said Hobbes, looking thoughtful.

'I hope you catch the culprit. Do you have any leads?'

'Not yet, sir, but your information might narrow the field down a bit. You wouldn't happen to know the names of any of the low company he used to keep?'

'I'm afraid not. I purposefully kept myself free of that kind of association. A man in my position can't afford to have dirty little secrets, so I've always done my best to keep myself squeaky clean, and completely free of scandals.'

'Except for that time you got photographed when you were drunk and face down in the lettuce bed,' I said, butting in and receiving a frown from Hobbes.

'I was not drunk,' Mr Slugg said, anger in his voice, his face reddening and scowling for a moment. He pulled himself back together. 'On that occasion I was taken suddenly ill at my smallholding and collapsed. It was a shabby trick to photograph me and make political mischief of my misfortune. I'm certain those photographs ruined my campaign. I could have done so much good for this area.'

'There are all sorts of low tricks in politics, so I'm led to believe,' said Hobbes, a portrait of sympathy.

'I'm sadly afraid that is true, Inspector. However, I have always tried to play straight, though it would appear that honesty and integrity are not much valued these days.'

'You may be right, sir. Before I go, would you happen to have any photographs of your brother?'

'No. I disposed of them. I do not like being reminded of my younger days, which were difficult through no fault of my own.'

'All right, sir. Would you happen to know where he lived?'

'As I said, I have had nothing to do with him in ages.'

'That's not a problem, sir.'

'Let me tell you frankly, Inspector, that I'm not sorry he's dead. I never wished him any harm, but if the fool managed to get himself hit on the head by a billhook, then I'm really not surprised. You may think I'm being callous, but you didn't know him. He was a wrong'un from birth. We were always so different that I could hardly believe we were related.

'Now, if that's all, Inspector, I have a busy day.'

'That is all,' said Hobbes. 'We'll be off now and thank you for your co-operation. Andy, Dregs, come along. Goodbye, sir.'

Turning away, he led us from Mr Slugg's house, shutting the front door behind him, and took us back to the car.

'So, did you get any useful information?' I asked.

'I believe I did,' said Hobbes and started the engine.

'What? Because I didn't get much from it. He seemed a nice chap.'

'Didn't he just?' said Hobbes, driving away. 'However, several interesting points came up that I will pursue. The first is to discover what's frightening him.'

'He didn't seem frightened to me. Just rather angry until you explained what was happening.'

'Then why didn't he answer the door? And why did he have that heavy stick to hand?'

'He might need it to walk. He is getting on a bit you know … or perhaps he isn't … he was much younger than I first thought.'

Hobbes glanced over his shoulder at me. 'He didn't need a stick when he ran from the house. Besides it was weighted with lead at the business end.'

'Like a weapon?'

He nodded.

'Why didn't you arrest him for attacking you?'

'No harm came from it, except to his nose. Hold on!'

As we reached the bottom of the hill and he turned the wheel, launching us into the main road, I slid across the seat and smacked my head against the side window. It was at such times that I especially wished I was safe with Daphne. I closed my eyes and wondered what she was doing, what treasures she was unearthing, and whether she'd find as many bodies as we had. At least that would be something to brag about next time I was being browbeaten by her intellectual colleagues. I reckoned I'd easily out-skeleton most of them.

As we were heading back towards town, Dregs suddenly leapt up and started barking and Hobbes stamped on the brake. I was mighty pleased the seat belt was so sturdy.

'There, I suspect, is Bob's murderer,' said Hobbes.

'What? Who? Where?' I asked, opening my eyes and slightly below my coherent best.

'There.' He pointed ahead.

Crossing the road was a huge brown, bristly beast with a brush of long dark hair standing upright along its back, as if it were sporting a Mohican. It turned to stare at us through a pair of pale, piggy eyes, giving us a good view of three-inch long tusks and alert, erect ears. Had I been foolish enough to get out and stand beside it, I reckon its shoulders would have reached up to my chest.

'The murderer?'

'Of Crackling Rosie,' said Hobbes. 'He's a big one.'

'Huge!' I said, awestruck and more than a little scared.

'He looks like he could do a lot of damage if he chose to, though Mr Catt reckoned they are shy creatures, and that it's unusual to see one out in the open during daylight hours.'

'It's probably hungry,' I said.

'Probably. This road will become busy soon, so I ought to make sure piggy doesn't get in anyone's way.'

'What are you going to do?'

'Arrest him. Stay here.'

Although I'd feared he'd say that, I didn't think it would be a good idea. I opened my mouth to comment, but he'd already gone, leaving me with a highly excited dog.

'Now my lad,' said Hobbes, taking a step towards the boar, 'you are going to cause an accident if you keep wandering into the road like that.'

The boar grunted and took a step back. Hobbes took another step forward. The boar took a further step back. The sequence continued for thirty seconds or so, the distance between them remaining the same, though the interval between steps grew shorter. Then the boar turned tail and fled into the meadow by the Soren, splashing through the dark waters, with Hobbes pounding along behind. Despite his bulk, he was all muscle and had a most impressive turn of speed. Much the same could have been said of the boar.

Dregs, who'd ceased barking, was watching intently, alert and whining, clearly wanting to be part of the chase. Hobbes put on a spurt and dived, grabbing for the boar, just as it jinked sideways. He made an enormous splash as he stretched his length in the water and sank from sight. The boar kept running, heading for the river, where it jumped in and was swept away in the rapid current.

Getting back to his feet, and shaking himself like a dog, Hobbes made a move as if to follow, shook his head, and turned back to the car.

'He got away,' I said, amazed, having developed a massive respect for his hunting abilities.

'I noticed.' He got back in and took his seat with a squelch.

'I didn't think he would,' I said.

'Nor did I, but he zagged when I expected him to zig, and when I saw he'd taken to the river I realised I couldn't catch him. Not this time anyway. All I got was this.' He held up a few hairs. 'I nearly had him by the tail, which would be nowhere near as much fun as catching a tiger by the tail.'

'Have you ever done that?'

'Just the once. I wouldn't care to repeat the experience.'

He started the engine, the car leapt forward, and we were soon heading back into Sorenchester, which still looked like the Cotswolds' answer to Venice. Gondolas wouldn't have looked out of place, though the waters had receded even since we'd been out.

'Where are we going?' I asked. 'Home?'

'To see if Dr Ramage has discovered anything new.'

Dr Ramage, looking incredibly young and pretty even in ugly white overalls that could have made her look like a snowman, was in her office, typing into an old-fashioned computer. She smiled as we entered, not appearing to notice that Hobbes was leaving puddles wherever he went. Dregs greeted her enthusiastically.

'I'm glad you're here,' she said.

My heart leapt, until I realised she was addressing Hobbes. I berated my heart for inappropriate leaping, since I was a happily married man, and it had no business leaping for other women, no matter how gorgeous.

'Is there anything new?' asked Hobbes.

'A couple of things. Firstly, I can confirm the majority of the bones are medieval.'

Hobbes nodded.

'Secondly, the recent skeleton was a man, probably in his late thirties. He was shorter than the average height, and had received a severe blow to the back of his head, fracturing the skull.'

'Was that the cause of death?' asked Hobbes.

'Such an injury would undoubtedly cause immediate unconsciousness and would probably be fatal unless the victim received immediate medical attention, and even then …'

'Clearly he did not receive immediate medical attention,' said Hobbes. 'I think I can work on the premise that he was unlawfully killed and disposed of.'

'Another point of interest,' said Cynthia, 'is that the state of the medieval bones indicates they'd been stored in a dry environment until very recently, whereas the modern skeleton came from a wet one.'

'That's ridiculous,' I said, 'since they all came from the same place.'

'Not at all,' said Hobbes. 'It confirms that the old bones were kept in the ossuary, assuming that's what it is, and the new ones had been stuffed into the culvert that runs alongside. The flood waters probably pushed them along to where we found them.'

'That's how I see it,' said Cynthia.

'Was there anything else of significance with the old bones?' Hobbes asked.

'Not really. I'll put all the details down in my report. And now to the cadaver.'

'Septimus Slugg?' I said.

She nodded and led us to the lab, the stench of which, a hint of putrefaction along with some pungent chemical, nearly turned my stomach. It would have done once.

The bones of the full skeleton were laid out on one metal table, and the body of Septimus was covered up on another. As she pulled back the sheet, I turned away, though not quickly enough to avoid a glimpse of bloated greyish skin.

'The body had been immersed in water,' she said, 'though I'm not precisely sure for how long. I would estimate for at least a month, but it might have been up to two months, because if he'd been hidden there in December or January, the cold weather would have helped preserve the soft tissues.'

Hobbes grunted acknowledgement and she continued. 'He was definitely killed by this blow to the head, and I can confirm the wound was made by a machete, or something very similar. In addition, there are these injuries to the arms. As you can see, there are three cuts to the left ulna from the same blade that caused the head wound, as well as a deep slash across the right palm.'

'Suggesting he tried to defend himself,' said Hobbes, sounding grave.

A horrible flutter passed through me as I imagined the pain and fear of the poor man's final moments. I wondered who would do such a thing, and why. Murder was uncommon around Sorenchester – Hobbes didn't approve of it – but it was clear a killer was on the loose. I was glad Daphne was well out of it.

'Mr Slugg,' Cynthia continued, 'despite being a small and slightly built man, was healthy at the time of the attack and might have put up quite a struggle.'

I heard her pull the sheet back up and turned around, trembling and breathing hard.

'Thank you, Dr Ramage,' said Hobbes, touching his forehead in an old fashioned salute. 'That was most illuminating. Is there anything else I should be aware of?'

'Not yet, Inspector. I have a couple more tests to perform, but I've given you the gist. I'll probably be able to finalise my report today.'

We said goodbye and re-joined Dregs, who we'd left in the corridor on account of the bones, although it was unlikely he'd have done anything to really embarrass us, because, like me, he'd become a gourmet since his introduction to the delights of Mrs Goodfellow's cooking.

'Now what?' I asked, fighting against Dregs's severe licking, and fearing I'd soon be as wet as Hobbes.

'Home. I need dry clothes and I could do with some grub. Visits to the mortuary always give me an appetite.'

He grinned, so it was likely he was making a joke. I chose to believe so.

Following an exceptionally fine chicken pie with fragrant buttered greens and leeks, I was sitting on the sofa, drinking tea. I remembered what Featherlight had said in the park and told Hobbes, treating it as something of a joke, until I noticed his serious expression and gave him the full details.

'Are you absolutely sure it was a seven-pointed star?' he asked.

'Umm … yes … pretty sure …'

'It couldn't have been eight-pointed?'

'Does it really matter?'

'Yes. If it really was seven, then we might have a problem.'

'What sort of problem?'

'A nasty one. Sup up your tea, because you'd better show me where it is.'

Two minutes later, my tongue slightly scalded, we were marching towards Ride Park. Dregs was leading the way until we reached Keeper's Cottage, a small house backing onto the park, where he gave us a quick, apologetic look, leapt the wall and disappeared into the back garden.

'Where's he off to?' I asked.

'I expect he's courting again,' said Hobbes. 'He'll join us when he's done.'

No one else was in the park and the sun was drawing a faint mist from the sodden ground. No birds were singing and I was nervous, though I couldn't work out why. I tried to ignore the feeling and concentrated on the task in hand, making only one tiny navigational error by taking us into the woods a little too early. The detour did have one good outcome in that Hobbes spotted a set of boar prints, though they were several days old. Moving on, I soon found the quarry and the trampled circle of grass.

The star thing had gone.

'It was here,' I said, 'and Featherlight saw it, too.'

'I believe you,' said Hobbes, dropping to his knees, examining the area, and sniffing a great deal.

'The ground's too wet,' he said a few moments later.

'So you can't discover anything?'

'Beyond the obvious, no.'

'What's the obvious?'

'Clearly two people made the ring a few nights ago, probably the same night as the storm. The only visitors after that were you, Featherlight and Dregs and one other person, until a number of children came here later. I imagine they found the star and took it.'

'I suppose all that was evident,' I lied, 'but Featherlight reckoned the star thing was dangerous, though he wouldn't say why. Do we need to find those kids and warn them?'

He shook his head. 'Children by their nature would not be at risk.'

'What risk could there be from a star made from twigs?'

'None as such,' said Hobbes, 'unless they were spiky or poisonous ones, but since it was made of hazel …'

'You never even saw it, so how can you possibly know that?'

He pointed to a bush on the edge of the grass ring. 'This is hazel, and these twigs were cut with a razor-sharp blade.'

'What does that mean?'

'That someone has a sharp knife, and knows the proper way to prune. Can you see how the cuts slope slightly downwards from the buds?'

I nodded. 'But I don't understand why Featherlight was worried.'

'I do,' he said. 'I think I need a word with him.'

He got to his feet, apparently oblivious to the sogginess of his knees, and set off towards the Feathers, and since I could barely keep up with him, I had no breath to waste on questions.

The Feathers looked much the same as last time, except for the ambulance outside and the bloodied man who was limping towards it, supported by a paramedic.

'Hallo, 'allo, 'allo,' said Hobbes, 'what's going on here, then?'

'This unfortunate gentleman received an injury to his head when the dartboard fell on him,' the paramedic explained.

'Is that correct, sir?' asked Hobbes.

The man, a burly lout, nodded and groaned as he stepped aboard the ambulance. The doors closed.

'Do you believe him?' I asked, 'because I certainly don't. He had far too many injuries.'

'I believe a dartboard may have been involved at some point.'

We entered the Feathers, where Billy was helping an elderly table back to its legs, while Featherlight, grinning broadly, was hanging up the dartboard, the metal rim of which showed a head-sized dent. A handful of customers, seeing Hobbes, tried to appear as if their drinks were of immense interest, while totally failing to look cool, relaxed and as if nothing out of the ordinary had happened.

'Good afternoon,' said Hobbes.

The customers turned around, feigning surprise, and he was greeted by over-enthusiastic messages of welcome. Billy looked up, which was his default position, and Featherlight grunted.

'Make sure that dartboard is secure,' said Hobbes. 'They can inflict a lot of injury when they fall on somebody … apparently.'

'It did fall on him,' said Featherlight.

'After you'd punched him three times?'

Featherlight glowered. 'That's a lie … it was four times.'

'Four? I only made out three sets of knuckle prints on his face. Are you losing your touch?'

Featherlight grinned, displaying his horrible, discoloured teeth. I'd thought Hobbes's were bad enough, though they were always clean, except after he'd crunched

690

up a raw bone.

'It was definitely four,' Billy piped up. 'A quick one to the belly, followed by three to the head.'

'What's this all about,' asked Featherlight. 'I did nothing wrong. The bloke came here looking for trouble, and I gave him some. It's what we in the business know as giving the customer what he wants. He'll live and he didn't complain, did he?'

'He did not,' said Hobbes, 'but I'd appreciate a bit more restraint in future. Casualties from your establishment put a strain on an already over-burdened health service. Superintendent Cooper asked me to point that out.'

'I was bloody restrained,' said Featherlight. 'He kept all his teeth and was able to walk out. I merely connected with my customer in a meaningful way, like it says in my management book. That's all. What more do you want from me?'

'Just be careful,' said Hobbes. 'Now, I have a question for you.'

'If I get the answer right, do I win a prize?'

Hobbes shook his head. 'How many points were on the star you showed Andy?'

'Why don't you take a look instead of bothering me? Even a rank bonehead like Caplet should be capable of finding it.'

'He was, and we examined the scene, but it had already gone. Some youngsters may have taken it.'

'Shouldn't they have been at school?'

'Most schools are still closed because of the floods.'

'In that case,' said Featherlight, 'I'll tell you. It had seven points.'

'Are you absolutely sure?'

'Even after all these years, I think I can recognise one of their heptagrams when I see one,' said Featherlight.

Hobbes looked worried, which was worrying, because hardly anything worried him.

'So, they're back,' said Featherlight.

Hobbes shrugged. 'It would appear so. I'd already seen something on Hedbury Common that had made me wonder.'

'But what's so bad about a star made of twigs?' I asked.

'It's not just any star, Caplet, it's a heptagram, sometimes called a septacle,' said Featherlight in such a soft voice that I had to look again to confirm it was actually his.

'Umm … what does that mean?'

'I don't know, but I fear it was made by the sly ones,' said Featherlight, 'and the last time I saw one of those there were deaths.'

'Whose deaths?'

'Public deaths, probably,' said Hobbes, 'though we never identified who they were because there was nothing left to recognise, and we failed to make any arrests.'

'Even though we knew who'd done it,' said Featherlight.

Hobbes nodded. 'However, it doesn't necessarily follow that history will repeat itself. It might mean nothing.'

'But, what about the murders?' I said without thinking.

'Enough, Andy,' said Hobbes sharply. 'We've got to go.'

He thanked Featherlight, turned and shoved me out into the street. I was apologetic, fearing I'd angered him, but he appeared merely thoughtful.

'I still don't understand about this star thing,' I said as we were walking along

Mosse Lane.

'I'm not surprised,' said Hobbes.

'Umm … could you tell me about it?'

'I could,' he said, breaking his stride to swing a boot at a plastic wheelie bin, 'if I knew enough.'

The bin resounded and he kicked it again and again before turning away as it split and fell, spewing out storm damaged rugs and cushions. I'd never before seen him display such violence against an inanimate object, and it scared me.

'Featherlight looked anxious.' I said when we'd moved on a bit.

Hobbes sighed. 'He may well have cause. The last time we saw a heptagram like that was in the fifties, and before that there'd been one at the start of the Second World War. Shortly afterwards, on both occasions, we noticed those he calls the sly ones around town and there were some nasty goings on.'

We turned up Vermin Street, which was busy, a number of shops having re-opened, though a few were still pumping out. Someone shouted, 'Thief!'

A tall, slim, hooded figure, all in black, burst through the doorway of Hound's Jewellers, pursued by the tiny rotund figure of Harry Hound. The hooded one, his head down, made the mistake of running in our general direction, though Hobbes was still so deep in thought I wondered if he'd noticed, and even considered taking action myself.

He had, of course, noticed and, stepping sideways, he held up his right hand. 'Stop!'

The thief, running full tilt, did stop, but only on impact. His legs swung up, his body levelled out, and he crashed to the pavement where he lay whimpering. Hobbes bent down and retrieved a gold necklace.

'Yours I believe, Mr Hound,' he said, handing it back. 'What happened?'

'Thank you, Mr Hobbes,' said the jowly jeweller. 'This young rascal came in, saying he wanted a gift for his girlfriend, and asked to see a number of items. He grabbed this and ran when I turned my back.'

'I see.' Hobbes hoisted the thief to his feet, where he stood, swaying slightly, head bowed. 'Push your hood back, and quickly.'

The bad man revealed himself as a youth of about seventeen, who might have been quite good looking were it not for his expression of wide-eyed terror, and the acne. His face reminded me a little of a pizza with added sweetcorn.

'Daniel Duffy,' said Hobbes. 'I'm surprised at you. Why d'you do it, Danny?'

'Wanted something for Angie for Valentine's Day. The necklace looked nice, only I couldn't afford it. I didn't want to disappoint her.'

'Pah!' said Mr Hound. 'As if the poor girl could be any more disappointed than having you for a boyfriend.'

'I'm sure the young man is not all bad,' said Hobbes.

'What are you going to do to me?'

'Good point,' said Hobbes. 'That largely depends on what Mr Hound decides.' He turned towards the jeweller. 'Any ideas?'

'The ruffian must be charged with theft, and I'd like to see him in prison,' said Mr Hound, who'd grown exceedingly red in the face. 'Hanging's too good for him. I don't know what young people are coming to. It was never like this in my day.'

'Was it not?' asked Hobbes. 'Perhaps you don't remember the laundry incident?'

692

'Oh … er …yes, maybe I was forgetting.' He grinned. 'Come to think about it, I won't press charges … just so long as you have a word with the rascal. We were all young once.'

'I'll make sure I do,' said Hobbes, 'when I'm less busy.'

'That sounds fair enough,' said Mr Hound, chuckling and grinning for some reason that escaped me.

'Very good, sir,' said Hobbes.

'Am I going to prison?'

'No, Danny, not on this occasion, but I will be round to see you very soon, and then we will have a friendly little chat.'

'And then what?'

'Then you might wish you were in prison,' said Hobbes, with a sudden grin that showed his huge yellow teeth to their best advantage.

Danny cringed, looking more like a frightened little boy than a hardened criminal. His eyes bulged and his knees knocked so hard I could actually hear them over the street sounds.

'But for now,' said Hobbes, 'I have things to do, so let's have no more nonsense. How much is the necklace worth?'

'One hundred and fifty pounds,' said Mr Hound.

'Here you are then,' said Hobbes, drawing a fistful of notes from his wallet, handing them to the bewildered shopkeeper and turning back to Danny with the necklace. 'Take this, give it to Angie, and behave yourself from now on, if you know what's good for you. I will see you soon.'

He strode away, leaving Danny and Mr Hound open-mouthed and staring.

'That was an extraordinary thing to do,' I said, when I'd caught up, 'but why? He's a thief.'

'He certainly attempted to be one. However, I happen to know young Angie, who's a sweet girl and has been having a hard time. I wouldn't wish to make it any harder. As for Danny, his head is like an old empty barn – there's nothing in it, though his heart is in the right place. If I'd arrested him, he might have gone to prison, which would not benefit anyone. After we've had our little chat, I doubt he'll steal again. My way means he gets what he wants, Angie gets a nice surprise tomorrow, and Mr Hound gets his money. No one loses out.'

'Except you. You're a hundred and fifty pounds down on the deal. That doesn't seem right.'

He shrugged. I guessed he could afford it for he seemed wealthy enough, although few would have known, since he preferred a simple life, and rarely spent money on himself. Yet, he could be extraordinarily generous when the mood took him, as he had often been to me. However, the main thing I took from the conversation was a useful reminder that Valentine's Day was coming up, since with all the recent excitement it had almost slipped my mind. Even so, I was proud that I had remembered before Daphne left, and had secreted a nice card with a lovey-dovey message, along with a small box of her favourite chocolates from Chocolate Ears, a posh new shop on Rampart Street. I smiled to myself, thinking about what she'd say when she found them, and made a plan to head for Gollum's Logons in the morning and use one of its computers to send her a nice, soppy email. In fact, as I mulled it over, I decided there was nothing to stop me sending one right then while the idea was fresh in my head.

'I … umm … think I'll head to Gollum's Logons and send Daphne an email.'

'Good idea,' he said. 'I read your review of the place, but haven't looked in there yet. I'll come along and I might just try the coffee.'

We turned down Rampart Street, passing Chocolate Ears which, despite having been flooded, was doing a roaring trade, and headed for Goat Street, which had escaped the worst of the recent events. I'd been a little confused by my previous visit to Gollum's Logons, an unusual attempt at an internet café with a Lord of the Rings theme, and with pretensions to high class restaurant cuisine. Although the coffee had been pretty good, the wine acceptable and the service passable, my meal had been greasy, cold and tasteless and the broadband hadn't quite been adequate. It had taken me most of a week to get the right balance in my review of that one.

Somewhere, a woman screamed.

'No coffee for me I'm afraid,' said Hobbes and loped away at sprint speed.

How he could move so fast with his knuckles nearly scraping the ground was beyond me. When I'd experimented, I'd run headlong into a lamppost and given myself a fine head lump. The worst part, other than pain, had been trying to explain exactly what I'd been attempting to a passing American tourist who'd stopped to help me as I lay in the road. He'd listened patiently, thought for a moment, and called me a dumb-ass, an epithet I'd probably richly deserved. Hobbes, of course, never ran into anything he didn't mean to. As he turned out of sight, I considered following to see what all the fuss was about, but decided to attend to Daphne first.

There weren't many customers in Gollum's Logons, other than a couple of burly young guys I suspected were students on account of their Sorenchester University rugby shirts, and a strikingly good looking young woman with a rucksack by her side. I nodded at the little waitress, who was looking rather self-conscious, probably because she was dressed as a hobbit. She directed me to a computer and took my order for a cappuccino. It took me a while and a couple of attempts to remember how to logon to my email account, but I got there and felt quite proud of myself.

I scrolled through the list. The first two mails were suggesting remedies for my being tragically under-endowed, so I deleted them as probable spam. After that came eight from Daphne, which I started opening in chronological order. The first seven, her attempts to contact me, were filled with love and concern and were quite heart-warming, although part of me resented the implication that I might be incapable of looking after myself.

Then I opened the latest one. It was entitled 'Chocolate' and I grinned to myself, wondering what nice things she'd say. My complacent mood lasted until I clicked on it.

> *Andy, what the hell were you thinking? Were you actually thinking at all, or are you just an idiot? Whatever possessed you to do such a thing? (I'm assuming it was you – after all who else could it have been?) When I came back to my tent this lunchtime, I found it had been overrun by millions of little yellow ants. Millions! They were all through my luggage, in my clothes and even in my bed. Everywhere! And can you guess why? They'd been attracted by the sticky brown goo that was oozing from my holdall! When I opened it up, there was a box of chocolates that had melted and run through everything. It has completely ruined my smart dress which I needed for tonight, when I'm supposed to be meeting an important guest.*

> *I'm really angry with you right now and I going to let my temper cool before I write again, which might take a while as it's nearly fifty degrees out here. I've got a headache and I'm tired and I can't lie down until I've got rid of all these ants. They bite, too, and I'm covered in unsightly itchy blotches.*

> *Thank you so much and I hope you're satisfied.*

That was all. There was no message of love, no indication that she was missing me, and no hope. She hadn't even signed off with her name. First I felt sick and confused, and then I became furious with myself.

'You really are a complete idiot,' I muttered, grinding my teeth. 'You're a total ass...'

'Excuse me, what did you say?' asked one of the students, who was close by.

'Umm …' I said, 'did I say that out loud? I didn't mean to.'

'You shouldn't even have thought it. I've never done anything to you, have I?'

'No, but …'

'Apologise.'

'But …'

'If you don't, I'll make you,' said the student, springing to his feet.

I couldn't help notice how tall and powerfully built he was. His face had taken on a similar tinge to the one exhibited by Featherlight in a rage.

'All right, but …'

As he walked towards me, bunching his fists, which, while not in the same league as Hobbes's or Featherlight's, were on the massive side, I kicked backwards, making my chair scoot across the floor. I bumped into something that screamed like a girl. Crockery shattered, and the hobbit, a tray still clutched in her hands, was sprawling among a debris of white plates, glittering cutlery and devastated confectionery.

'Sorry,' I said, getting to my feet and ducking under a straight punch from my assailant, who, to judge from his expression, was as unimpressed by my manoeuvre as I was by his fearsome breath.

'First you insult me …' he said swinging again.

I blocked the punch with my left forearm, something I'd once seen Hobbes do, only he'd not squealed like I did. It really hurt, and my hand went numb and tingly hot at the same time.

'And then,' he continued, as I retreated, 'you attack that poor girl.'

His next punch, a real swinging clubbed effort, would probably have taken my head off, but I was on a roll – a cheese and onion one by the smell of it – and slipped. Missing threw him off balance and he lurched towards me as I fell backwards over the unfortunate hobbit girl who'd just got into a kneeling position. As my head went down, my feet flew up and booted him on the point of the chin. He collapsed as if poleaxed, going face-down into a sponge cake, which at least gave him a soft landing.

Apologising profusely to everyone who could hear, I got up. The other student was on his feet, looking furious, but dithering, clearly wanting to give me a damned good thrashing, but thinking he should first check on his chum, from whose face the hobbit girl was scraping jam and cream with a spoon.

The other woman, the attractive one, smiled. 'Cool moves, dude,' she said in a strong American accent.

Making a show of nonchalance, I gave her my best devil-may-care grin, and sauntered towards the door. As soon as I was in the street and out of sight, I fled, congratulating myself on having got away unscathed. I'd just glanced back to ensure I was not being pursued when rough hands seized me. A coarse sack, stinking of garlic, was pulled over my head and my arms were pinioned to my sides, rendering me helpless, though I struggled and kicked as well as I could. The hands shoved me along, making me stumble up some steps. A door clicked shut and the muted sounds made me think I was indoors.

'I've got you now,' said a voice that, even accounting for the sack over my head, sounded muffled and strange. 'I'm going to teach you what happens when you don't show respect.'

Something hit me across my legs. I fell and, as I lay there writhing, I was pummelled all over. The only good thing was that whoever was doing it spared my face. The beating continued until I passed out.

When I came awake, I almost wished for oblivion again for my body was a mass of aches and I was shivering. It took a while, but I freed my arms and pulled the sack from my head to find myself surrounded by thick bushes and in semi-darkness. I had no idea where I was but, as I tried to rub life back into my hands, the church clock struck the quarter hour. To judge by the loudness, it was nearby. I rolled onto my hands and knees, groaning at the pain in my ribs, and crawled through the branches and twigs until I emerged onto a squelching lawn. I was in the old graveyard by Church Fields, right beside the tomb of the unknown worrier. Down the slope, the lake was still flooded, and a faint pink glow on the horizon made me suppose it was shortly before sunrise. I needed the support of a tree to stand up, and then staggered towards the gate, which, with its rusting steel bars, reminded me of a medieval portcullis, especially as it was shut with a heavy chain and a massive padlock. Outside, the streetlamps were still lit, and the streets seemed deserted. My watch had been smashed in the beating, and I couldn't see the church clock from where I was, but it was clearly next morning. Without expecting anything, I rattled the chain and tugged at the padlock. The result was just as expected.

I called for help, and even resorted to screaming, but no one was around yet, and kicking the gate did little to relieve my frustration, though the exquisite torment of my toes took my mind off the other aches and pains for a few moments.

Climbing over was an idea, though the barbed wire on top made it a poor one. However, doing nothing was not a great option either, because my clothes were damp, the sky was clear and there was a hint of frost. I feared I'd freeze to death before the good townsfolk were up and about.

Seeing no other possibilities, I made a bold attempt at scaling the gate, only to find the bars were covered in condensation and as slithery as wet fish. It was only luck that I didn't hurt myself as I slipped and fell. Since it seemed I would just have to endure and hope for release, I pulled my jacket closer, stuck my frozen hands into its pockets, and could have kicked myself in frustration. I might have, had I not already been too sore for such nonsense. Instead, I had to be content with calling myself an idiot, for only an idiot would have forgotten his mobile phone. I pulled it out and tried to figure out where Hobbes's number was listed. Finding it at last, I pressed to call.

It was answered almost immediately.

'Inspector Hobbes. How may I help you?'

'It's me, Andy,' I said. 'I'm sorry to wake you …'

'I wasn't asleep. Are you calling to say you won't be back for supper?'

'No, I'm stuck … umm … what do you mean supper?'

'I mean the meal we are accustomed to eat in the evening. You know that. Are you all right?'

'Not really. I'm locked in the old graveyard and can't get out. I've been here all night … umm … I think I have. Actually, what time is it?'

'Quarter past six, and you haven't been out all night. It's still Thursday. I'll come and get you. Are you at the gate?'

'Yes.'

'Well, don't go away.'

'I can't.'

Only a minute or two later, Hobbes came loping along Blackdog Street towards me. As he crossed the road, his grin changed into a look of concern. 'What happened to you?'

'I got put in a sack and I've been beaten up and I'm cold.'

'I'll have you out of there in a jiffy.'

On reaching the gate, he took the chain in his bear hands, stared at it for a moment, gritted his teeth and twisted until one of the links came apart with a groan like a man suffering a bad hangover. As he unwound the chain and released me, I stumbled out, and, like a maiden swooning in an old film, collapsed into his arms.

'Thank you,' I said, my teeth chattering.

'You're welcome.'

As I headed homewards, leaning on his arm, ashamed of my weakness, I explained what had happened as well as I could. He helped me up the steps into the house where Dregs, with a noticeably hangdog expression, looked up from his place on the mat, wagged his tail once and slumped.

'What's up with him?' I asked.

'I fear his courting went awry,' said Hobbes.

The air, besides the usual feral taint and a slight doggy odour, was filled with delicious savoury aromas that, despite my pains and shivers, set my mouth to watering. I would have been glad to go straight into the kitchen and eat, but Mrs Goodfellow saw me first and half-dragged, half-cajoled me upstairs and into yet another hot bath.

In all honesty, it was a wise decision, for, although my stomach and salivary glands might have disagreed, the warm water soon began to revive me, despite the embarrassment of having the old girl clucking over my collection of bruises and scrapes. After adding a curious minty-smelling green gunk to the tub, she called Hobbes, who appeared in the doorway and, much to my discomfiture, examined my collection of injuries.

'Somebody has certainly worked you over. Do you have any idea who did it?'

'No, not really. There was a sack over my head. I ... umm ... did have a bit of trouble beforehand, but I don't think it could possibly have been connected.'

Hobbes took another look at my back. 'It appears the attacker used a stick for a few blows, but most of your injuries are from boot or fist. Whoever did it must have unusually large hands and feet. Do you know anyone who fits that description?'

I shook my head and squawked as a pain stabbed between my shoulder blades. 'Only you and Featherlight,' I said.

'I can assure you it wasn't either of us. Enjoy your bath, but don't take too long, because I'm in need of my victuals.' He left us to it.

'Are you fit enough to bathe yourself, dear?' asked Mrs Goodfellow.

'I think so.'

As she left, I relaxed. I'd never felt comfortable with having no clothes on in front of her, despite her claims to have been a nurse and to have seen far worse than I'd ever showed. Still, feeling self-conscious didn't actually harm me, and her cooking and kindness had always led me to forgive her, even after she'd dunked Dregs and me together in the same flea bath when we'd become infested after hanging out with werewolves.

I wallowed for a while, contemplating my bruises while the warmth soothed away much of the pain. Unfortunately, it gave me time to think about the terrible thing I'd done to Daphne, as well as to remember that I'd never got round to sending her my Valentine's Day email. I was filled with a horrible fear that my thoughtless gift, though well-meaning, might mean I'd lost her, and the mere idea nearly made me feel sick.

The knocking on the bathroom door brought me back. 'Supper's ready as soon as you are,' said Hobbes, 'so you'd better get a move on. And quickly!'

A few minutes later, wearing neatly pressed, clean clothes, I headed downstairs, where the cooking smells encouraged me to believe that life was not so bad. Mrs Goodfellow started dishing up as soon as I appeared. Though the meal was only slow-cooked beans and bacon, a simple dish, it had been transformed by the old girl's golden touch into a delight fit for a king. I said as much when my plate was empty and my stomach was as full as was practical.

'It truly was a dish fit for a king,' said Hobbes. 'King George III instigated an annual bean feast after tasting it during a visit to Woolwich Arsenal.'

'King George III? Did you ever meet him?' My question was a cheeky attempt to get an idea of his age. I knew he was unfeasibly old, but how old?

'Of course not,' he said. 'I've rarely had sufficient time to meet royalty. Shall we go through to the sitting room?'

Thwarted, I nodded and followed him. I'd once asked Mrs Goodfellow his age, but she hadn't known, other than that he'd been a police officer before the war, by which she meant the First World War. When I'd enquired if she thought he was immortal, she'd shrugged and said that he had been so far. Dying, she'd said, would be the last thing he'd ever do.

As we sat down on the sofa, a thought crossed my mind. 'When you ran off earlier, what was that all about?'

'A lady who works as a cleaner at The Italian Job was throwing some rubbish bags into the bins at the back when she was surprised by the wild boar.'

'In town? But I thought they were shy.'

'He is shy. As soon as he saw her he fled.'

'So, it's not dangerous.'

'I wouldn't go as far as that,' said Hobbes. 'Had she been in his path, and there was no other way out, he might have attacked. Fortunately, she wasn't, and, fortunately, she's not the sort that is easily cowed …'

'Or do you mean boared?' I said with a chuckle.

'… cowed. She was keen to get back to work after a stiff brandy.'

'Good for her.'

'However, if the boar has taken to coming into town, the danger to the public has increased considerably. I'll have to do something about him, if there's time, because I do have a murderer to catch, and that business on Hedbury Common has not yet reached a satisfactory conclusion.'

'What did happen there?'

He sighed. 'Horrible things. I wish to interview somebody who might be able to assist me with my enquiries, but she has not yet turned up.'

'She?'

Hobbes nodded. 'The name she uses is Matilda Kielder.'

'Umm … do you think she might be in danger?'

'No, I fear she is the danger … but here's the tea! Thank you, lass.'

Mrs Goodfellow set the tray on the table before us. Hobbes leant forward, filled two mugs, handed one to me, piled a pyramid of sugar into his and stirred it with his index finger, a trick that still alarmed me. How his finger wasn't cooked was beyond me, since the tea was volcano-hot. He raised his mug, quaffed it in one and poured himself another, as I sipped mine, protecting my lips and tongue. I'd barely wet my mouth when he got to his feet, drained his mug and yawned.

'I'm going to bed,' he said, though it was only seven-thirty. He loped upstairs.

Since there was nothing interesting or amusing on the television, I thought of going out for a lager, but didn't really fancy one, or want to risk any more trouble. Instead I just sat and thought. It had been another difficult day. Being on my own and staying with Hobbes and Mrs Goodfellow had been a pleasant change of routine, but I wanted Daphne back, and was desperately worried how she'd react to my thoughtless gift. Reason told me she wasn't likely to stay mad forever, but old insecurities kept sneaking in whenever I dropped my guard.

'Are you all right, dear?'

Mrs Goodfellow's question from just next to my right ear made me jump to my feet and crack my shin on the coffee table. My yelp of pain brought Dregs in from the kitchen to stare.

'I was,' I said, rubbing the bruised bit. 'Why?'

'You looked troubled.'

'I was just thinking …'

'Ah, that would explain it.' She smiled.

'… If you must know, I was thinking about Daphne, and how much I miss her. You have no idea …'

'I think I do,' she said.

'Umm … yes … I suppose you must do. I was forgetting.' I was ashamed of myself. Mrs Goodfellow's husband was still believed to be in Bali. 'How do you cope?'

'I keep busy. The old fellow takes a bit of looking after, and then there's my Kung Fu and marital arts classes. Still there are times …'

I nodded and thought sad thoughts, until I recalled something Hobbes had mentioned. 'Do you know a woman called Kielder?'

'Matilda Kielder? I know of her but I only actually saw her once, and then only briefly.'

'Do you know anything about her?'

'Not a great deal, dear. She brought a lot of bother to the old fellow a few years ago. I gather she was something of a man-eater.'

'Do you mean she fancied him?' I'd always struggled to believe any woman, or at least any human woman, could have the hots for Hobbes. There was just something too feral about him. Besides, not even his mother would have considered him good looking, though, in fairness, there was a rough gallantry about him.

'No. She ate men. Really. Well, bits of them. Perhaps she was more of a man taster.'

'I suppose she couldn't eat a whole one, especially a whole Hobbes.'

'Not in one sitting, dear, and so far as I know, she never took a bite out of him.'

'How come I've never heard of her before? And how come she's not locked up?'

'I can't explain your ignorance,' she said with a gummy grin, 'but she's not locked up because she was never caught.'

'I thought Hobbes always got his man.'

'So he does, but Miss Kielder is a woman, and you know how he can be with them.'

I nodded, remembering how close he'd come to death after trusting Narcisa Witcherley, my former editor's criminally insane wife, who'd shot him. I, too, had taken a bullet during those desperate hours, but had still acted heroically, at least by my standards. It served as a good reminder of the danger of getting involved, though, for reasons I couldn't quite understand, I rather enjoyed the excitement, or I did when I wasn't too terrified or in too much pain. Yet no one could have denied how much my life and my character had improved since I'd first met him, and the old girl, of course. The thought cheered me up a little, and when I eventually went to bed, carrying a cup of cocoa, I was in a far better frame of mind than earlier, despite lingering concerns. In all honesty, I had a whole litany of things to worry about beyond the normal background level, including the attacks on my person, possible consequences for having knocked out the student, blackmail, man-eaters and murderers. However, Daphne was foremost in my mind.

I suspected I'd enjoy little sleep that night, with all my anxieties, the bodily injuries, and a sore throat that was developing. However, just as I was starting to think I'd never drop off, I dropped off. On waking next morning to a dull grey day, I suspected the old girl had put a little something into my cocoa, and, not for the first time, I was grateful. My bumps and bruises didn't feel too bad when I tested them, so I got up and prepared for a new day.

Although I went downstairs looking forward to breakfast, I couldn't stop thinking about Daphne. I couldn't decide whether to call her as soon as possible or to give her more cooling-off time. Despite longing to be decisive, I sat and dithered and the result of my deep thought was that I had no recollection of actually eating, though I must have done. Hobbes, however, devoured a vast bowl of Sugar Puffs, a sure sign something was bothering him.

When he'd finished, I asked how his investigations were going.

He shook his head and looked glum, which was not a normal expression for him. 'Not well, I'm afraid. I've made little progress with the Septimus Slugg murder, and none with the earlier one, although Dr Ramage has given me a rough sketch showing an impression of how the skeleton's face might have looked in life. In addition, it'll be a chore to catch that boar, and I'll have to become a magic wielder to arrest Miss Kielder, if she really is back.'

'On the bright side,' I quipped, 'your poetry is improving.'

'I beg your pardon?'

'Chore, boar. Wielder, Kielder … you're a poet and you didn't know it.'

'I see. I'm not convinced accidental rhyming counts as poetry, though it might pass as doggerel, I suppose. I would rather regard poetry as the interpretation of nature and the understanding of humankind written in a style that blends delicacy of words with grace of harmony and rhythm.'

'Really?'

'There are, of course, other opinions. I respect them, even if I can't agree with them.'

'I thought it was all about rhyming.'

'No, dear,' said Mrs Goodfellow. 'Poetry is when emotions find the right thoughts, the thoughts find the right words, and the words find the right form.'

'Is it?' I asked.

'It can be,' said Hobbes, 'but I must away, because, although I'd be happy to discuss poetry until the lowing herd winds slowly o'er the lea, I have interviews to conduct.'

'Eh? What lowing herd?'

'He means he could discuss poetry until the cows come home,' said Mrs Goodfellow. 'He's misquoting Gray.'

'Of course,' I said. 'Umm … what's grey?'

'Thomas Gray the poet, dear, from his *Elegy Written in a Country Churchyard*.'

'Yes, I thought it was,' I bluffed.

'You can come along if you'd like,' said Hobbes. 'It might keep you out of trouble.'

'I'd love to, but … umm … I really should call Daphne. It is Valentine's Day, after all. Is that all right?'

'I'm in no rush. You can still come if you hurry up about it.'

'Thanks.'

'And hurry up now,' said Hobbes a few moments later. 'What's stopping you?'

'They've had a row,' said Mrs Goodfellow. 'Haven't you, dear?'

I nodded. 'How do you know?'

'It's written in your face, and your behaviour.'

'My behaviour?'

'It has been rather distracted, dear. You poured tea into the sugar dish instead of your mug and drank it, and you buttered two slices of toast, put them in a bowl and added milk and marmalade. Then you ate the mess without apparently noticing. You are showing classic symptoms of having fallen out with your beloved.'

'True,' said Hobbes, 'but your classic symptoms are more extreme than most. Go and make that call … and quickly!'

I did as I was told. The only trouble was that nobody answered. After the third attempt, I slammed down the phone.

'Not in?' said Hobbes.

I shook my head.

'You could always text her.'

'I suppose I could, but I'd rather speak to her.' The truth was that, while I did know how to text, I had clumsy fingers and, anyway, I was suspicious that my phone had been possessed by imps since it had a tendency to put my words through the blender, changing them into utterly incoherent gibberish, or occasionally into downright insulting rudeness. My last attempt had been a couple of weeks earlier, when Daphne had texted to say she'd be back early, but would have to be heading out for a lecture on Egypt within an hour. When I'd replied, attempting to let her know that I'd prepare an early dinner, the imps had struck and I'd instead informed her that I'd preserve a warty donger. Subsequent attempts at correction had resulted in such a bizarre stream of balderdash that she'd come straight home, worrying I'd had a stroke.

'You know best,' said Hobbes. 'Are you ready now?'

'Yes.' I grabbed my coat and followed him out the door. 'Where are we going?'

'We are going to see Mr Godley.'

'Old Augustus or Kev the Rev?'

'Augustus. I want to show him Dr Ramage's picture.'

'Why? I know she's very pretty, but at his age?' Augustus Godley, having survived for over one hundred years, was the oldest human in town.

'I meant the sketch Dr Ramage gave me,' said Hobbes, striding along Blackdog Street, 'not a portrait of her.'

I kept up, though the effort cost me. The streets had somewhat dried, though huge puddles still remained in places, and pumps were still pumping out. We crossed onto Moorend Road, where Mr Godley occupied the first of an impossibly cute row of alms-houses. Piles of sandbags against the wall suggested they'd been well protected against the deluge. Hobbes opened the garden gate, and we walked to the diminutive stone porch with its distinctive crust of lichens and moss. He rang the doorbell.

It was a long wait, for Mr Godley, though mentally acute, had physically slowed to sloth pace. After a few minutes, the door opened and he stood before us, his face as wrinkled as desiccated walnuts, his hair and bushy whiskers as white as vampire's teeth, his narrow shoulders stooped with age. His blue eyes, however, were sharp and alert.

'Sergeant Hobbes … I mean Inspector Hobbes. How nice to see you. I suppose you want my help?'

'If you can spare the time, Mr Godley.'

'I was just getting ready for my parachute club, but I've got a few minutes. Come in and bring young Sandy with you. Where's your dog? Is he all right?'

'He's moping,' said Hobbes, following Mr Godley along the musty dusty and gloomy stone-paved corridor that led to his small, cluttered sitting room, where a coal fire burned brightly and dispelled any chills. 'He's been unlucky in love and wants to spend some time with his thoughts.'

'How very sad. He's a fine animal. Would you like a cup of tea?'

'No, thank you very much. We've just breakfasted.'

'Where's your budgie?' I asked, missing the little blue chatterer and fearing the worst.

'Taking a shower in the kitchen,' said Augustus, lowering himself into one of the faded velvet-covered armchairs and indicating that we should occupy the others. 'Now what are you here for?'

Hobbes pulled a sheet of paper from his pocket, unfolded it and handed it to the old man, who smoothed it flat, and peered at it.

'Not bad,' he said after a minute or two, 'but, if you don't mind, I'd say it's not up to your usual standard.'

Hobbes chuckled. 'It's not one of mine.'

'Then why show it to me? The technique is adequate, but the face has no animation. Who did it?'

'A forensic pathologist,' said Hobbes, 'and you'll probably forgive the lack of animation when I tell you this is a rough impression of how a recently discovered skeleton might have appeared in life. I was hoping you might recognise him.'

'I don't.' Mr Godley stared at the sketch again and shook his head. 'Is that all? Because my taxi will be here any time now.'

'That is all,' said Hobbes, taking back the paper. 'It was a long shot, but worth taking. Thank you.'

As Hobbes and I were getting to our feet, Mr Godley raised his hand and frowned. 'Actually, there may be something …'

'What?' said Hobbes.

'I remember there was this boy at my school, and it's not that your sketch looks much like him, or even as I imagine he might have been as an adult, but there's something.'

'Well done,' said Hobbes. 'What was his name?'

'Alas, that I can't remember. He was a couple of years younger than me, so a lower form of life to a ten year old …'

Hobbes shrugged.

'… but there may be a record of him in the old school annals.'

'Which school?' said Hobbes, brightening.

'The Green Coat School. Do you remember it?'

'Yes, of course, but it must have closed over sixty years ago.'

'However, there may still be school records and photographs in existence. I believe they went into the *Bugle's* archive.'

'I doubt it,' I said. 'I work there and there's no room for much of an archive. There's a small store room, but that's mostly full of ink and chemicals they used in the olden days.'

'I expect much of the archive is on those new-fangled computers,' said Mr Godley, 'but there may still be physical records. I'd ask the editor, or the owner.'

'That is very helpful. Thank you again,' said Hobbes, and we took our leave.

As we left the house, I had to ask a question that had been bugging me. 'He doesn't really go parachuting, does he?'

'Not anymore, but he's still a member of the club. He sometimes pilots their plane.'

'You're joking … aren't you?'

'No. His body might have slowed, but his hands and brain are still quick, and he hasn't crashed since he was last shot down. He flew Spitfires in the war, you know.'

'I never knew that. He doesn't look very heroic.'

'Heroes don't on the whole. I think we should pay a visit to the *Bugle* and see if they do have the archive.'

'Yes, I suppose we should. Why was it called the Green Coat School? It's a funny name.'

'Because the pupils originally wore green coats as part of the school uniform. There's a statue of one in the church. Haven't you seen it?'

'Yes, I believe I have. I didn't know what it was, but it looked very quaint. Mr Godley didn't dress like that, did he?'

Hobbes shook his head. 'The statue represents how the pupils dressed in Victoria's day. He's not quite that old.'

As we turned onto Moss Lane I attempted to match his stride length while chatting, but caught my foot on a flagstone the flood had raised. I would have stretched my length in the gutter had he not grabbed my shoulder. For the rest of the walk, I kept quiet, concentrating on keeping upright and not entangling my feet, annoyed by my clumsiness, which I used to consider as the root of many of my problems, until Hobbes had pointed out that I was probably no more clumsy than average, but had a tendency to inflate any mistakes to the size of a hippopotamus. Since then, although not entirely convinced by his argument, I had frequently chastised myself for this failing, adding it to my ever-lengthening list of imperfections.

Swaggering towards us were five large young men, who appeared to belong to the rugby-playing tendency, an impression confirmed by their Sorenchester University Rugby Club hoodies. I recognised two of them, noting that the one I'd kicked had a sticking plaster on his chin. Butterflies took wing in my stomach when he pointed.

'That's the runt who kicked me in the face!'

'Let's scrag him and teach him to respect his betters,' said one, who was even bulkier than the first.

'I'm sorry about yesterday,' I said, 'but it really was just an unfortunate accident.'

They didn't seem to be in the mood for listening to reason and quickly surrounded us.

'There will be no scragging,' said Hobbes, smiling. 'What's all this about?'

'Stay out of it, old man,' said a third, probably the most thickset and burly of the lot. 'It's not your business. Back off, unless you want some, too.'

'Some what?'

'Some pain, granddad. Clear off. Your little chum attacked James, and we don't stand for that sort of thing.'

'Nor do I,' said Hobbes, pleasantly. 'What exactly did you do, Andy?'

'Nothing.' I squirmed, suspecting my face was turning red. 'Well, I did sort of knock that guy out, but I didn't mean it.'

'He insulted me for no reason,' said James, 'and when I remonstrated, he kicked me in the face. We're going to teach him some manners.'

'Everybody calm down,' said Hobbes, with a reassuring smile.

'Please don't hurt me,' I said, getting worried, as the pack drew in. 'I'm truly sorry for what happened. Let me explain …'

I never felt the first blow, or the next. In fact I didn't feel any at all. Hobbes blocked the lot.

'Stop it,' he said after a few moments. 'This is unseemly behaviour.'

The students, having retreated a step or two to rub bruised arms and shins, charged, front, side and rear. He never even raised a finger. Instead, picking me up by the shoulders, he ducked, dodged and weaved. Within a few seconds, which I saw mainly as a series of blurry images, four of the students contrived to collide, and lay in a moaning heap on the pavement. The last one standing, seeing the carnage, turned and ran. Unfortunately for him, he ran straight into a wall. Putting me down, Hobbes grabbed him as he fell and laid him to rest with the others.

'Thank you for that,' I said, still a little dizzy, and explained what had happened. 'So, you see, it really was an unfortunate set of calamities.'

'I see,' he said, checking no serious damage had been sustained by the students. 'I might doubt the story if others told it, but with you, Andy, it has the ring of truth. These hearty young fellows are clearly prone to aggressive behaviour, and I fear someone will get hurt, one of these days.'

To judge by their groans, they'd been hurt already, but I didn't point that out, just grateful Hobbes had been with me. He seemed thoughtful.

'What's up?' I asked.

'Well,' he said, 'although it's by no means unusual for some of the students to display arrogance and to be a little boisterous, they are not usually so much trouble, and physical violence is rare. However, these young fellows seemed overly belligerent, don't you think?'

I nodded, although I had provoked similar hostility in others before. Still, he was right. This lot had seemed a little unhinged.

'Another thing that interests me,' he continued, 'is why they were using an internet café, or rather an internet restaurant, when they almost certainly have their own devices.'

He dropped to his hands and knees, sniffing the bodies, which was puzzling to me as they smelled of changing rooms even from where I was. It reminded me of the school gym, where I and my classmates had spent many a miserable hour being tormented by the psychopathic games teacher. After a few moments Hobbes reached into one of their trouser pockets and pulled out a small plastic bottle. 'Aha!' he said.

'What's that?'

'It's a small plastic bottle.'

706

'Yes, but what's in it?'

He unscrewed it, poured a number of seven-sided pink pills into the palm of his hand and wrinkled his nose as if at an unpleasant smell.

'What are they?'

'Anabolic steroids.'

'The things that give you big muscles?'

'They can do, and sportsmen have been known to use them to improve performance and stamina. In high doses they can also increase irritability and aggression.'

'Well that certainly seems likely. Are they legal?'

'That rather depends on where they come from, what they are used for, and what the precise ingredients are. Though some are legitimately prescribed by doctors, they are often sold on the black market, and if they're used without supervision and knowledge they can be dangerous, and not only to the users. Their use is certainly not permitted in sports.'

'What are you going to do?' I asked. 'Arrest them?'

'I'd rather not. The cells are already full.'

'I didn't know there'd been a crime wave.'

'There hasn't. They are temporarily occupied by members of the public whose homes have been flooded, since there's a scarcity of alternative accommodation. The church halls and other suitable locations are also full to bursting. Happily, more long-term arrangements are being worked out.'

'So, what are you going to do with this lot?'

'I'll confiscate their pills, and have a quiet chat with them when they are in a more receptive mood.'

'Like when they're fully conscious?'

'That would help.'

'But you can't just leave them lying here.'

'I can you know.'

'But shouldn't they be taken to the hospital?'

'The hospital is busy with flood casualties.' He squatted down, sorted the heap into individuals, examined them and rolled them into a neat line next to a wall. 'None of them has any serious injuries and I've made them comfortable enough. They'll wake up soon and may well have headaches and some bruising, but, being rugby players, they'll be used to that sort of thing.'

'Perhaps it'll teach them a lesson,' I said.

'I doubt it,' said Hobbes, 'but my little chat will. Let's go.'

As we walked away, they were all starting to sit up and were looking utterly bewildered. We carried on past the Feathers, where no violence was taking place, and crossed into The Shambles towards the offices of the *Bugle*.

Basil Dean was alone, keeping an eye on us while the other appeared to be checking the football scores. He nodded and stood up.

'Hiya. How may I help, Inspector?'

'Good morning, Mr Dean. Do you have the Green Coat School papers in your archive?'

Basil shook his head.

'Can't you check?' I asked.

'There'd be no point. The archive was here – we kept it in the basement for many years – but space is tight and we had a clear out. We removed a century of clutter. Some material was scanned and stored on computer, but I clearly remember Editorsaurus Rex taking the Green Coat School boxes away. He thought that, though they might have historical significance, they were unlikely to contain anything newsworthy.'

'What did Mr Witcherley do with them?' asked Hobbes.

'I imagine he chucked them into a skip, or took them down the dump, but I don't know for certain. You could ask him. Here's his phone number.'

Basil reached into his desk drawer and handed Hobbes a card.

'Thank you, Mr Dean,' said Hobbes. 'May I use your phone? Mine had a dunking and I haven't had time to replace it.'

'Be my guest. You can use that desk.'

Hobbes poked in the numbers.

'Good morning, Mr Witcherley,' he said after a short pause. 'Inspector Hobbes here … Yes, I am fully recovered … There are some scars, but nothing to worry about … How is Mrs Witcherley? … I'm sorry to hear that … and she's still being treated? … It must be a worry … Yes, there is a reason. Can you recall what you did with the archives from the Green Coat School? … In your attic? Excellent … May I see them? … When? … I'll be with you within the hour. I'm mostly interested in records from the nineteen-twenties … I'll be bringing Andy, if that's all right with you … No, not Capstan, Caplet … Yes, it is an odd name … French I believe … Goodbye, sir.'

I gulped for I'd always found the Editorsaurus intimidating. Yet, since he'd retired to look after his murderously insane wife, Narcisa, I'd had time to reflect on how he'd treated me back then, and had been forced to concede that he'd been far kinder and more forgiving than I'd deserved. I'd begun to recognise that I'd been lazy and almost useless when I'd first worked there. Besides, I'd had a bad attitude, stemming from resentment at being the longest-standing cub reporter the *Bugle* had ever employed, at never having had a pay rise, and because I'd rarely been assigned to any good, juicy news stories. My reporting back then had mostly been confined to dog shows, church fetes and whist drives, and, when I'd finally been given a proper assignment, the one that had introduced me to Hobbes, it had only been because no one else was available. Of course, it was largely down to Hobbes that I'd changed, that I'd met Daphne and that I'd got a job again. I actually had a lot to thank the Editorsaurus for.

'Stop dreaming,' said Hobbes, giving me a nudge that nearly flattened me. 'We need to get back to Blackdog Street, pick up the car and visit Mr Witcherley. Goodbye, Mr Dean.'

'Ta-ra for now,' said Basil, one eye looking up.

Hobbes bustled me from the office, down the stairs and onto The Shambles. Within ten minutes, we were in the car, hurtling towards Fenderton. I'd absent-mindedly taken the front seat, and, despite being fully aware of his driving record, still came close to screaming when I opened my eyes as he threaded the car through a line of speeding traffic into Alexander Court.

Halfway up the hill, hiding behind a thick yew hedge, was the Witcherley residence, an impressively large house even in a street packed with impressively large houses. Gravel scrunched beneath the tyres as we turned into the driveway. Hobbes parked by the garages, we got out and approached the front door. Despite the Editorsaurus no longer having power over me, I could feel flocks of butterflies beating against my insides as Hobbes raised his finger to ring the doorbell. Last time I'd been there, I'd been awed by the polished wood, the gleaming brass on the front door, and the glittering glass, but now the woodwork looked tired, the brass was dull, and the windows were smeary. I glanced into the porch, which must have been as big as the sitting room at Blackdog Street, and saw mud streaking the tiled floors, a pile of dirty boots in one corner, and a dead plant in the middle.

A few seconds later Editorsaurus Rex appeared, wearing a grubby white shirt and stained jeans. He'd lost weight and with it some of his imposing appearance. His skin looked greyish, and his bare ankles were thin and shocking as he crossed the porch and opened the door.

'Good day, and thank you for your help, sir,' said Hobbes, snapping off a sharp salute.

'I'm always pleased to help you, Inspector. Come in. You, too, Capstan.'

'Caplet,' I said.

'What?'

'Nothing,' There was little point in asserting my right to be called by my given name. He'd failed to get it correct during all my years working for him, and I just couldn't be bothered any more.

'Please excuse the mess. My cleaning lady's on holiday,' said Rex, leading us to the lounge where he pushed aside a pile of old papers and magazines to reveal a sofa, and gestured for us to sit, while he went into the next room.

I was surprised to see layers of dust on the surfaces, and red wine stains disfiguring the deep-pile of the rich cream carpet. During my previous visit, I'd had the feeling that the house was too smart and neat to really be lived in.

Rex returned with a dusty old cardboard box and a musty tang.

'This one has the years you were interested in,' he said, handing it to Hobbes. 'You're lucky I've still got it, because Narcisa got fed up with the smell and stuck it in the attic. I had intended to take it to the dump sometime, but I sort of forgot about it, because of … well, you know.'

I knew he was alluding to the events surrounding his wife's incarceration in a secure unit, after she'd turned from an efficient business woman into a wannabe vampire.

'Thank you, sir,' said Hobbes as he took the box.

It was full of yellowing papers and tatty books with faded covers. He leafed through them, piling them on my lap, until he emptied a manila envelope onto the carpet. The contents were a number of faded black and white photographs of the school's staff and pupils, with the teachers seated at the front and a mass of urchins standing behind in rows. He examined them closely.

'That's Mr Barry,' he said, pointing at a large, whiskered man in the middle, 'the legendary headmaster.'

'Why legendary?'

'Because he'd fly into rages and threaten to chop naughty children with his axe. They called him Barry the Hatchet.'

'But he never did, did he?' I asked, shocked.

'No. Even in those days dicing the pupils was frowned upon, but the mere threat stopped most bad behaviour. Those it didn't deter were caned, which was a popular pastime for teachers back in the day. Spare the rod and spoil the child was the thinking, but in Barry the Hatchet's case it was more like wield the rod and spoil the trousers. He was a vicious man.'

'I remember my grandfather talking of him,' said Rex. 'I thought he was exaggerating, like the old ones do.'

'All too true, I'm afraid,' said Hobbes, continuing to stare at the pictures. 'This one's got young Augustus in.'

I wouldn't have guessed the fresh-faced kid in the woollen jumper was the same person as the old man I knew, though there was something about him that made me accept the identification.

'Aha!' said Hobbes, holding up another photograph.

'What is it?' Rex and I asked in unison.

'This young fellow here,' he jabbed at it with his finger.

'What about him?' said Rex.

'He is of interest in regards to an inquiry.'

'But he probably died decades ago,' said Rex.

'Very probably,' said Hobbes, 'but he may still have living descendants.'

'But you can't blame them for whatever he did,' said Rex.

'Of course not, but I'm not investigating this young fellow.'

'Can I see?' I asked, feeling left out.

Hobbes was pointing to a small grinning lad in a tatty coat, who looked much like the other boys around him.

'What's so special about this one?'

'Something about him is remarkable, and it might be significant. Can you see it? Or I should say can you see them?'

I stared, but failed to make out what he was seeing.

'It's the ears, isn't it?' said Rex.

'That's right, sir,' said Hobbes. 'Now do you see, Andy?'

'Umm … not really. The kid seems to have the requisite number, and they might stick out a bit.'

'But, they're unusually small,' said Rex, 'with tiny lobes.'

'I … umm … suppose they are, especially if you compare them to those on the other boys. Yeah … I see what you mean, but so what?'

'I'll tell you later,' said Hobbes. 'In the meantime, let's see if we can identify him.'

Unfortunately, no one had bothered to record the pupils' names on any of the photographs, not even on the back. I thought we'd have to give up, but Hobbes began sifting through all the documents, muttering to himself on occasion. Rex and I sat back and waited and I'd just reached the yawning and fidgeting stage when Hobbes grunted.

'What?' I asked, sitting up.

'I've just found something interesting in the punishment book. There's a line here that, on January the fifteenth, Samuel Slugg received six strokes of the cane for fighting in the playground.'

'Samuel Slugg?' I did a swift calculation. 'Could that be Solomon and Septimus's father?'

'The age would fit.'

'Who are Solomon and Septimus?' asked Rex.

'They are … umm …' I began.

'… people who may be of interest in an enquiry,' Hobbes broke in before I could say too much. 'Let's take another look at that photograph.'

He examined it again, and checked the next three or four in chronological order. 'It would appear that young Samuel Slugg, assuming I've identified him correctly, was always shorter than the other boys in his class.'

'It wasn't his fault,' I said, 'and why does it matter how tall or short he was?'

'It might not, but, then again, it might,' said Hobbes, infuriatingly. 'Well, Mr Witcherley, I believe I've taken up enough of your valuable time. The information I have discovered may well prove useful. Thank you very much.'

'Always pleased to help,' said Rex. 'Drop in any time. You too, Capstan.'

'Caplet,' I muttered.

Hobbes stood up. 'Come along, Andy. We'll see ourselves out.'

I got up, and shook Rex's proffered hand. It was large and soft, and a little moist. As we left I couldn't help feeling sorry for him; he seemed rather lonely and lost in his big house, with his wife locked up.

We were just about to drive away when a red sports car drove onto the drive and parked next to us. A smart and striking woman in her mid-thirties got out, smiled and, having taken a key from her bag, unlocked the front door and entered the house.

'I wonder who that was, and what she's doing here,' I said.

'It's probably his cleaning lady returned from her holiday,' said Hobbes.

I left it at that, and wondered whether my sympathy for Rex had been misplaced.

One of the things that still puzzled me about Hobbes was what he knew about sex, because sometimes he seemed a little naïve, though there'd been occasions when his knowledge and wisdom had struck me as incredible. Thinking about it, my main problem was that I doubted he could have a sex life, because I'd never seen an 'unhuman' woman of the right type, and I was convinced he was far too rough and ugly for any human woman. And yet, I wasn't entirely sure because Daphne's friend,

Pinky, had once remarked, after a few glasses of chardonnay, that she found him rather sexy. Still, she was undoubtedly weird, being in a relationship with a gentleman of the vampire persuasion, albeit a charming one who had no inclination to suck people dry.

As we were driving away, I asked a question that had been bugging me. 'Was that really a useful visit, or were you just being polite?'

'It was very useful. I learned something I didn't know and have been reminded of a number of interesting facts that, taken on their own, might not mean a lot, but together are suggestive.'

'Like what?'

'That Septimus Slugg and the skeleton are almost certain to have been related to Samuel Slugg. I suspect they were two of his children.'

'Two of them? That suggests you think there were more. How do you work that out?'

'Septimus is from the Latin for seventh, which suggests at least six older siblings.'

'I didn't know you knew Latin.'

'It was compulsory at my school, like at many back then.'

'But there was more?'

'I was reminded of something. Many years ago there was a greengrocer's shop in Stillingham called Sam S Lugg's.'

'So?'

'Andy, if you don't mind me saying, you can sometimes be a little dense. If you think about it, being a Slugg in charge of lettuces might not be good for business, so, if someone had that name it might make sense to change it to Lugg, and …'

'Might?' I said, peevishly, 'but there might really have been a Sam S Lugg, who had nothing to do with the Slugg family, and, besides, I can't see what an old greengrocer's shop in Stillingham has to do with anything anyway.'

'If you'd let me finish,' he said. 'Mr Sam S Lugg was clearly the small boy in the photograph who'd grown up. And before you start, I know that because I recognised him. In those days I used to go over to Stillingham quite often to quell the cheese riots, and I distinctly remember asking a local hard case, named Brian Madde, to desist from hurling a brick through Sam S Lugg's shop window.'

'And did he?'

'He did. Unfortunately, he threw it at me instead and it rebounded off my helmet and smashed the post office's window.'

'Were you hurt?'

'No, but the point is that I remember Mr Lugg, as I thought he was called, having several children.'

'I believe you, but I still can't see what you're getting at.'

'If I recall correctly, and I usually do, all the family, except for his wife of course, had a certain look. I mean they all had small ears and were below average height.'

'Which means?'

'Think about it. The skeleton we found was of a short man, who had noticeably small ears.'

'Small ears? How on earth can you say that? Skulls don't have ears.' My doubts about this line of reasoning were growing fast.

'You should have been listening to what Dr Ramage was saying instead of staring at her bosom.'

'I wasn't … was I?'

He nodded and continued. 'There were, of course, no ears on the skull. However, there was clay adhering to one side of it and the clay held a good impression of the ear.'

'Clay? Where did that come from?'

'The ground. And then we get to the body of Septimus Slugg who, again, was a man of short stature with small ears, which we can see, and which I remarked on.'

'Yes … but …' I floundered trying to think of an objection.

'What's wrong with Dregs?' said Hobbes, swinging the wheel and sending the car twisting across the road onto the pavement beside the flooded meadows.

'What?'

'Over there, by the river.'

The dog was staggering through water up to his chest, his left back leg dragging.

'He's hurt himself,' I said, observantly. 'I wonder how?'

'That doesn't matter,' said Hobbes, leaping out as Dregs collapsed.

Before I could make another comment, he was sloshing towards the dog, who was paddling feebly, barely keeping his nose above water. Hobbes scooped him up and waded back, his face grim, and a crimson trail following. As he laid Dregs on the back seat, the dog whimpered and wagged his tail.

'What's the matter?' I asked. 'Did the boar get him?'

'Look at that,' said Hobbes, pointing to a bloody puncture mark.

'Is that all? It's tiny!'

'But it's deep. We'd better get him to the vet.'

'For that? Can't you just take him home? I'm sure Mrs Goodfellow could clean it up and put on a plaster. What caused it anyway? A bite?'

Hobbes shook his head. 'I once saw a similar injury to a cat in Pigton, so I'm fairly sure someone has shot him with an air rifle. It must have been a powerful one, or very close, or both, to break the skin and penetrate so deep.'

'An air rifle? I know just how that feels. Poor dog.'

Dregs looked mournful as Hobbes covered him with a rug and ran back to the driver's seat, where he crushed the accelerator, making the tatty old car leap forward like a stung bullock. Any supposed tolerance I'd built up to his driving was nowhere near sufficient when he was in a hurry, for whereas, normally it was merely terrifying, it became paralysing. I couldn't shut my eyes, or even gibber. All I could do was to sit still, my hands clutching the seat, and let fate have its way. Of course, we reached the vets without injury to ourselves or anybody else, although the sparks that flew when we screeched round bends or landed after taking off over speed-bumps suggested the car might need some attention.

Hobbes was out and sweeping Dregs into his arms almost before we'd stopped.

'Lend a hand, Andy,' he said, as he sprinted towards the surgery door.

I gazed at him through unblinking eyes.

'And quickly!'

The last command, a roar, jerked me from my stupor and, having unlocked my hands and my seatbelt, I stumbled out and ran to open the surgery door for them.

'It's an emergency,' I shouted, bursting in, making the large man in the white coat by the counter jump, and causing a small ginger cat to break from its cage and circle the room at head level, apparently getting a grip on the wallpaper. 'Our dog's hurt.'

The man in the white coat, stared blankly, and I was on the verge of saying something rude, when the surgery door opened and a small girl in a dark green smock emerged.

'Bring him straight in, Inspector,' she said, 'and put him on the table.'

Hobbes did as asked, and I stood leaning against the door.

'Close it,' said the girl.

'Yeah, okay, but I'm holding it for the vet!'

'Hello, Mrs Collyer,' said Hobbes, interrupting. 'I believe he's been shot.'

'She's the vet?' I said as realisation and embarrassment struck together, making me blush, though no one was paying me any attention.

'So I see,' said Mrs Collyer, examining Dregs' leg and poking about.

Dregs gave a muted yelp, raised his head, wagged his tail and flopped.

'I'll need the nurse,' said the vet, pushing me aside and opening the door. 'Nick. Can you come here at once, please?'

The man in the white coat looked around, but seemed far more concerned by the cat's antics. I was infuriated by his lack of urgency and dumb idiocy.

'Shift yourself,' I yelled, glaring. 'Can't you see it's an emergency?'

He pointed to his chest, looking gormless, shook his stupid head, and shrugged.

I was thinking of something really biting to say when another girl in a green smock appeared. 'I'm coming as fast as I can,' she said, grabbing the cat by the scruff of the neck and stuffing it back into its cage.

'Oh … umm … sorry … I … umm …'

As the spring from which words normally gushed dried up, I was left red-faced and silent, trying to work out a form of words to explain my gaffe, or, to be honest, my gaffes, and to make the point that it had been the man's white coat that had confused me, and was not because I was sexist or anything.

However, no one was paying me any attention, so I just stood and cringed internally.

'I need to take this dog's blood pressure,' said the vet.

Nurse Nick, Nichola I assumed, nodded and fetched a trolley with electronic stuff on it and, after a glance at Dregs, reached into a drawer and pulled out a cuff. 'This one?'

Nodding, Mrs Collyer took it and wrapped it round Dregs's foreleg. 'His BP is low,' she said after several beeps.

'Is that because he's bled so much?' I asked, breaking my silence.

'Possibly, but shock is more likely … I'm going to give him saline.'

Nurse Nick took a bag of clear fluid, a length of plastic tubing and a small plastic packet from a cabinet. When she removed a hypodermic needle from the packet, I began to feel weird and hot.

My brain was trying to work out why I was lying on my side on the floor. My eyes opened and focussed on a large rat that was watching me with interest. When I recoiled, I bashed the back of my head on what turned out to be a chair leg.

Rolling over, rubbing the bumped bit, I sat up. I was in the waiting room, but couldn't work out how I'd got there.

'Don't mind, Stanley,' said the man in white. 'He won't hurt you.'

'Good … umm … pleased to hear it.' My head cleared. 'Who's Stanley?'

'My rat. He's here with his piles.'

'So, you don't work here?'

'No, of course not. I'm a chef.'

'Where?' I asked, professional curiosity asserting itself.

'Gollum's Logons,' he said. 'Haven't you been one of our customers?'

'Yes.'

'I thought I recognised you.' He held out a big hand. 'I'm able.'

'Good … umm … able to do what?'

He laughed a long slow laugh as he engulfed my hand and shook it. 'My name is Abel. Abel Seaman.'

'With a name like that you should be a sailor.'

He grimaced. 'Used to be. I was cook on the QE3 until the company went under.'

'QE3? I don't know that one, but I do remember the old QE2. My parents sailed on it once, before they had me. It was their honeymoon, I think.'

He looked puzzled. 'That's odd. I didn't think the Quality Export ships ever took passengers. I didn't catch your name, by the way.'

'It's Andy … Andy Caplet.'

Abel nodded. 'I thought it might be. You're the critic who gave us a rotten review.'

'It wasn't all that bad. I said I liked the coffee, but I'm sorry if I caused any offence. I didn't mean to. The thing is I see my job as pointing out areas where things could be improved. It's all for your benefit in the long run.'

'Isn't it to sell newspapers?'

'Well, yes … but if a restaurant improves as a result of something I've written, it's got to be better for the restaurant, and for the public, hasn't it?'

Had I not been so groggy, I might never have been so honest. Now I had, I began to worry what he might do, for he was a hefty man with meaty hands that looked capable of bunching into formidable cudgels, and I remembered Hobbes's comment that the man who'd beaten me had big fists.

He shrugged. 'Perhaps you're right. In fact, I did think the soup you described was rather inadequate, but it's all down to the ingredients, and, frankly, the boss is a cheapskate. Actually, the thing that most annoyed him was that you spelt our name wrong.'

'Did I?'

'Yes. There's only one "L" and no apostrophe in Golums. That was careless.'

'Sorry.'

I was about to ask the name of his boss when the surgery door opened and Hobbes appeared, with a huge smile and a thumbs up. 'Mrs Collyer has extracted the pellet, cleaned him up and stitched him. He'll be sore for a few days, but he'll soon be back to his normal self.'

'Great,' I said, my smile matching his. 'Can I see him?'

'Of course,' said Hobbes, 'but he's still sleeping. How are you?'

'Better, I think, but I don't know what happened.'

'You keeled over when the needle went into him.'

'I've never been fond of them since Father used to practice on me.'

'Mr Seaman?' said the nurse. 'Mrs Collyer can see Stanley now.'

'Let's get out of here,' said Hobbes, stepping aside to allow Abel and his ailing rat into the surgery.

'It's time for dinner,' said Hobbes with a glance at his watch.

'Already? Umm … how long was I out?'

'About an hour and a half. I've let the lass know what's been happening and I've asked her to get some bones in.'

Although the road conditions were reasonably good around town, our return to Blackdog Street was at a leisurely pace, which was alarming, since he normally only drove responsibly when there was a real danger to people, or when something was troubling him. I kept quiet, and vowed to stay clear of the sitting room after we'd eaten, because I had no need to guess what would happen then, and knew he'd put the fear of Hobbes into me if I was too close. It was an unfortunate and deeply disturbing quirk of his to release excess stress by crunching up a pile of raw bones. At such times, which were happily rare, there was something so feral and dangerous in his manner that it gave me the shakes, as if I were a helpless little lamb in a tiger's den, and, although he'd never actually done anything to hurt me, he'd given the impression of being out of control, of having cast off the veneer of civilisation. I'd seen the savage horror of his 'unhuman' self, and had been truly terrified.

On the plus side, there was lunch to look forward to.

The scent on entering 13 Blackdog Street, a heady mix of freshly baked bread and something rich and savoury, immediately set me drooling, though I had to endure a cruel wait while Hobbes updated the old girl about the dog's condition, and lingered forever over saying grace. Still, the wait was worth it when she presented us with a magnificent golden pea soup, so thick my spoon almost stood up on its own, with croutons that were so light and crunchy that I nearly wept for pleasure. It was served with warm, buttered freshly-made garlic bread that was so toothsome it drove the forthcoming dread from my mind.

For a short while.

As soon as we'd finished, a change came over Hobbes. Mrs Goodfellow, with a nod at me, a warning to stay clear, picked up a handful of old newspapers and took them through to the sitting room. Hobbes followed, growling and twitching, his dark eyes as cold as a shark's. She returned, took a blood-stained brown paper parcel from the larder, carried it to the sitting room door, and threw it in. I heard Hobbes snarl, and felt the thud as he pounced on the parcel.

Then, I blocked my ears so I didn't have to hear the slathering and the shocking cracks as his great teeth crunched through the bones as easily as mine did through digestive biscuits. I could only feel relief that the fit had not come upon him at the mortuary.

After a short while, Mrs Goodfellow handed me a mug of sweet tea and it was all over. I thanked her and sipped as Hobbes's footsteps clunked upstairs. Moments later he was roaring, only this time, there was pure exhilaration in his voice as the dangerous shower washed away the meat and bone scraps, and any residues of stress. I'd just started on my second mug when he returned, clean, in fresh clothes, and with a grin on his face.

'By heck, I needed that,' he said and accepted a mug of tea. 'Thank you, lass, for getting the bones in at such short notice.'

'You're welcome.' She smiled, looking at him as if she were an indulgent grandma who'd dished out a bag of toffees to a naughty but loveable child.

Hobbes heaped sugar into his mug, stirred it and drank. When he'd finished and poured himself another, he reached into his pocket and held out his hand. 'This is what Mrs Collyer dug out of Dregs.'

It was a small pellet, just like the one that had stung my bottom. I said as much.

'It is exactly like the one that hit you, in that it is the same calibre and from the same manufacturer.'

'Does that mean it was fired from the same gun?'

'Not necessarily. It's a fairly common type of ammo, widely used by shooters. However, as there have been very few incidents of crimes involving air rifles round here, and none to my knowledge, other than your misfortune, within the last five years, it would not surprise me. I'll get Dr Ramage to take a look and see if there is anything to confirm this.'

'But, if they were both fired from the same gun, does it mean someone shot Dregs to get at me?'

'It's a possibility,' said Hobbes, 'but I suspect a fairly remote one. Dregs can be annoying, too.'

'I suppose so … hey! What do you mean?'

He chuckled, reached out a long arm and patted me gently on the back, knocking the wind from my lungs.

As breathing and the power of speech returned, a thought popped into my head. 'Umm … when we were at the vets, I met the chef from Golums Logons. He thought I'd given the place a bad review, and he had big hands. Do you think he could have been the one that's been attacking me?'

Hobbes shrugged. 'Maybe. Did you catch his name?'

'Yes, I did … what was it … something nautical.'

'A strange name,' said Mrs Goodfellow.

Having forgotten she was still there, her unearthly cackle made me jump, bang my knee and groan. Dregs always loved this particular comedy routine, and the silence that followed showed how much he was missed.

'Actually, his name was Abel Seaman,' I said.

'I know Abel,' said Mrs Goodfellow. 'He's a kindly soul, always rescuing small animals and helping old ladies.'

'Yes,' said Hobbes, 'I'd heard he was back, but I would say that, unless going to sea has completely changed him, he's unlikely to have done you, or anyone else, any harm.'

'But what about his boss? Abel said he'd been annoyed, although that was mostly because I'd spelled the place's name wrong.'

'In what way?' asked Hobbes.

'I put an extra "L" in it. Apparently, there's only one in Golums … I expect that's for copyright reasons or something. And there's no apostrophe.'

His expression instantly changed to one of quiet thought. 'Only one "L" you say?

Now that is interesting.'

'Umm … Good … Why?'

'Would you get me a pencil and paper, please?' he asked.

Mrs Goodfellow obliged.

'Thank you,' he said, taking them and spreading the paper out.

'What are you doing?' I asked, getting up and trying to peer over one shoulder while Mrs Goodfellow tried the other. He leant back to let us see.

He'd written two lines, one directly above the other.

G O L U M S L O G O N S
S O L O M O N S L U G G

'I see,' said Mrs Goodfellow. 'That is interesting.'

'I don't see,' I said, feeling my usual confusion.

'Both lines have the same number of letters,' said Hobbes.

'I see that, but, so what?'

'Exactly the same number of letters.'

I must have looked blank for he took his pencil and drew lines, connecting the same letters on top to those below. At last, I got it.

'It's exactly the same number of exactly the same letters!' I said.

'Or to put it another way, Golums Logons is an anagram of Solomon Slugg.'

'I get it.' A wave of excitement washed over me, but still left me high and dry. 'Yeah, but what does it mean?'

'That remains to be seen,' he said, 'but I'd hazard a guess that Mr Slugg is the owner.'

'That's brilliant,' I said.

'Elementary, but it may not mean much. However, any little scrap of information may prove valuable to a detective.'

'How big were Solomon Slugg's hands,' I asked.

'About average for a man of his size.'

'Then it wasn't him that beat me … unless he got someone to do it for him.'

Hobbes nodded. 'That is possible, although I didn't think your piece on Golums Logons was particularly scathing. I thought its tone was more encouraging and helpful, and it did make me think that I should look in some time for a coffee, or even a meal next time the lass is away.'

'That's what I was aiming for,' I said, delighted that, once again, he knew my work.

'Then you scored a bullseye.'

'Yes,' said Mrs Goodfellow. 'I always look out for your articles in the *Bugle*. They are most entertaining, and, Mrs Fitch at the newsagents says they are becoming quite influential in raising standards.'

Unused to praise, I found it hard to deal with and embarrassing, although I couldn't deny how gratifying it was to hear it. All I could do was to stammer out thanks and look bashful.

I was saved by the bell.

Hobbes went to answer the phone, and returned a few minutes later. 'That was Dr Ramage, with some interesting news.'

'Go on,' I said.

'She sent samples from the two more recent bodies for DNA testing, and has received the preliminary results.'

'That was quick.'

'I gather her fiancé works there and did her a favour.'

'She has a fiancé?' The news was disappointing, though I couldn't, or wouldn't, understand why.

'Yes. He's called Roger, and I gather he's nice and very intelligent.'

'Good for him,' I said, struggling to keep quite unreasonable jealousy from my voice, and to get back on track. 'But what were the results?'

'They indicate the two deceased individuals were closely related. In fact, they were probably brothers.'

'As you suggested.'

He nodded.

'But, what does it mean?' I asked, having taken up my familiar position of bafflement.

He smiled. 'It means I should do a little more investigation into the Slugg family.'

'Family? Umm … but didn't Solomon Slugg say he only had the one brother?'

'He did and I've been wondering about that since.'

'Because Septimus should have been the seventh child. Are you going to arrest him?'

'Hold on there, Andy. I can't arrest someone for not telling the whole truth about his family when he wasn't even under caution. He claimed he'd been ashamed of Septimus, so perhaps he has the same opinion of the others.'

'True. Septimus sounded like a real liability.'

'He did,' said Hobbes, nodding, 'though we only have his brother's word for it.'

'D'you think he lied?'

'I have no means of knowing until I've established more facts. I'll start by investigating Septimus Slugg. I have his address, and the roads are dry enough now for a visit to Tode-in-the-Wold.'

'Can I come?'

'No,' said Mrs Goodfellow, from just behind my left ear.

'Why not?' I asked, when my speech returned.

'Because you have to talk to you wife, dear. Have you forgotten what day it is?'

'It's Friday.'

'It's St Valentine's day,' said Mrs Goodfellow, looking shocked.

'I know,' I said, 'but … umm … I don't think she'll want to talk to me. I covered all her clothes in chocolate and ants. It was an accident.'

'I know, dear,' said Mrs Goodfellow.

'How?'

'Because she telephoned when you were out.'

'Did she? Why didn't you tell me?'

'I just did, dear. I couldn't tell you earlier, because I know what you're like at meal times, and it didn't seem appropriate when the old fellow was … busy.'

'I see. Thank you. Did she say anything?'

'It would have been a strange call if she hadn't, like the ones I used to get from that

Gordon Bennett.'

'Was he the guy you arrested for flashing?' I asked Hobbes, who was heading towards the kitchen door.

'I did arrest Mr Bennett, but it wasn't for that, since I'd already convinced him that a cover up was required. Sadly, a few weeks later, he started making nuisance phone calls and I had to confiscate his phone. After that, he turned to car crime and I had to book him when he used violence against a member of the public. I'm afraid Mr Bennett is in prison now. Unfortunately, he appears to be one of those that can't help themselves. I gave him a second chance, and a third, but I fear he'll never break the habit. He gets it from his father and grandfather who were much the same back in their day.

'I'm off now, but the lass is right. You should call your wife as soon as possible. Goodbye.'

Despite knowing in my heart that he and the old girl were correct, I just sat for a while and wondered what to do and when to do it.

'You can use our telephone,' said Mrs Goodfellow, who'd been observing my inertia with increasing annoyance, 'unless you want to Skype or send an email, in which case you'll have to go elsewhere.'

'Umm ... right ... thank you. What did Daphne tell you?'

'That it was very hot, and that Mahmoud had driven her to the nearest town, which is sixty miles away across the desert.'

'Mahmoud? Why?' Pangs of jealousy and suspicion stabbed through me.

'He has a car, and she needed new clothes, because of your little gift.'

The jealousy was replaced by guilt. 'Umm ... yes. I was a little foolish.'

'Only a little, dear?'

'Okay, a lot.' I admitted. 'I just hadn't thought it would be so hot in February, even in the desert. On reflection, chocolates were a pretty stupid idea.'

'But you meant well,' said Mrs Goodfellow, 'and she knows that. Now, call her.'

'Right,' I said, hoping I agreed with the old girl's assessment, 'I think I will.'

'Good lad ... well, what are you waiting for?'

'Nothing ... umm ... I was just wondering if she'd be around. What do you think? Wouldn't it be best to try later?'

'Since I'm not blessed with the second sight, I have no idea when she'll be around. What I do think, dear, is that you're prevaricating.'

'No, I'm not doing that. I was just starting to think I should wait a little. In the evening perhaps?'

Mrs Goodfellow gave me what I supposed was meant as a fierce glare. 'Call her now, or it'll be dry bread and water for your supper.'

Although I was almost certain she didn't mean it, the risk was too great, so I nodded. I would, at least, test the temperature by sending Daphne an apologetic email.

'I'm off to Golums Logons,' I said, grabbing my coat and fleeing into Blackdog Street, scurrying away, in case the old girl came after me.

My head was full of confusion, and I had to think, even though for some reason I seemed incapable of making a decision. Her absence was already disturbing my equilibrium. Part of me really wanted to talk to her, to tell her how much I loved her,

722

and how much I was missing her. Another part feared she'd still be angry, and that any attempts to mollify her would make matters worse, leading me to say or do something that would be like the proverbial last straw and break the camel's back. I stopped that line of thought, for comparing her to a camel would not endear me. A final small but nasty part wanted her to suffer for her anger, though I knew a stupid attempt at punishing her might have terrible repercussions. Then I realised that if I didn't speak to her soon, she might think I didn't care.

Deep gloom gripped me as I turned onto Rampart Street, my feet finding their own way, since my brain had no room for ideas of navigation, or, as it turned out, road sense. The shriek of brakes brought me back, and I realised I'd just walked out in front of a car. The driver shook his totally bald head at me and mouthed something that looked rude, before driving around and speeding away. The volume of traffic appeared to be more or less what it was normally, but it took the horn of a white van to make me understand that I'd drifted off again and was still standing in the middle of the road.

'Sorry!' I mouthed, and ran to the pavement, where I stood awhile in thought in a clothes shop's doorway, getting my wits back, such as they were. And then, like someone switching on the light, I understood that I'd been on the verge of sabotaging my happiness because the negative part of my personality, the bit that believed Daphne was far too good for the likes of me, had briefly gained the upper hand. The knowledge helped me overcome it, and I hurried towards Golums Logons. When I reached it, I looked up and ascertained that it really did have one 'L', and no apostrophe.

I pushed open the door.

'Well done, dear,' said Mrs Goodfellow, making me jump as if she'd pricked me with a pin.

'You followed me,' I said, turning and getting smacked in the butt as the door swung back.

'I thought you might need some encouragement. Are you going in?'

'Umm ... yes.'

'I say, it's that runt again,' drawled a posh male voice as I entered, 'and this time he hasn't got the big bastard with him.'

Two of the rugby types stood up from their computers and stepped towards me with intent.

'Go get him, Guy! You and Toby can give him a damn good thumping,' said a third, who'd handed a wad of money to a vaguely familiar hooded man. The money looked tiny in his hands.

'Yeah, go for it,' said the hooded man, who had something a little foreign in the way he spoke, 'and give him one for me.'

As they advanced, Mrs Goodfellow thrust me aside and stood in front, her spindly arms folded across her chest.

'Oh look,' said Guy, 'he's brought his nanny!'

They laughed.

'You'd better stand aside, old woman,' said Guy, 'because we don't want to hurt you.'

'But we do want to hurt him, don't we?' said Toby.

'We certainly do. Would you care to join in the fun, James?'

The third one, having completed his transaction, strode towards us, nodding and grinning as the hooded man slipped away through a back door.

'Calm down, lads,' said Mrs Goodfellow. 'No one needs to get hurt.'

James tried to push her aside, which was a mistake. The old girl just took his hand turned it gently, and dumped him face first onto the carpet. His mates charged, no longer going for me, but for her. They failed most miserably, and, to judge from their cries, most painfully too. At a guess, I'd say the fight lasted five seconds, and ended with all three of them on the carpet, whimpering like kicked puppies.

Mrs Goodfellow drew herself up to her full height, which was about four foot ten, and wagged her finger. 'I want no more of this nonsense. Start behaving yourselves at once, or someone is going to get hurt.'

'I'm already hurt,' moaned Toby.

'No, you're not, my lad. It will pass in a minute or two. However, if I get to hear that any of you is mean to my friend, you will know what being hurt really is … and that's not a threat, it's a promise. Get up, get your things, and get out.'

The three of them, looking sheepish and puzzled did exactly as she told them. I'd just been guided to a terminal by the hobbit girl, who appeared rather wary of me, when the door opened and James filled the doorway. I turned, expecting more trouble.

'We're very sorry, madam,' he said.

'That's all right, dear,' said Mrs Goodfellow, smiling gummily. 'Now, run along and be good.'

'We will. Again we are all truly sorry. Goodbye.' He turned and walked away.

'A nice, polite, well-brought up young lad,' said Mrs Goodfellow.

'Then why does he keep attacking me?'

'That is a very good question. Now sit down and talk to your wife.'

'Yes,' I said, and logged into my account.

Daphne had sent me an email. Since it was entitled *Sorry*, I hoped it was a sign that she'd forgiven my stupidity. Then again, what if it meant 'I hope you are sorry for what you did'? Or even 'I'm sorry the marriage didn't work out'. Or …

'Aren't you going to open it, dear? There's nothing to worry about.'

I nodded.

'When?'

'Now … but … but …'

'No more buts, dear. Open it. I promise I won't look.'

'Okay.' I took a deep breath and clicked.

Dear Andy,

I'm ever so sorry, and hope you can forgive me for my bad temper yesterday. I was just too hot and too tired, and an ant had bitten me on the eyelid, and seeing all the mess in my things was the last straw. I hadn't remembered it was Valentine's Day today, and I now understand why you put the chocolates there. It was a nice idea, and you weren't to know it would be unusually hot here for the time of year. And thank you for the lovely card, too. It's a bit chocolatey, but it's lovely. I hope you're not feeling too neglected and think I didn't get you one, because I did. I hid one in my bedside table, and planned to tell you today, but I suppose it must have been destroyed.

Have you made any progress with the insurance claim yet? Or found anywhere to live?

I really miss you, and would love to hear your voice. I rang earlier, but you were out.

Love, Daphne

I released the breath in a long happy sigh.

'There you are, dear. I told you there was nothing to worry about.'

'Yes … and you also promised not to look!'

'I didn't, dear. She'd already told me what she'd written.'

I was feeling so much better that, had I been somewhere less public, I would have let loose a mighty whoop, or even burst into song. As I wasn't, I restricted myself to a grin.

'You do have lovely teeth, dear,' Mrs Goodfellow remarked. 'I'm so glad you look after them well.'

She'd long ago put in a request that when I had no further use for them, they would go to her collection. Although I'd agreed at the time, being in a panic, I wondered whether Daphne might want a say in the distribution of my body parts, should anything untoward befall me. Of course, I'd naively assumed my teeth would be safe from falling into the old girl's clutches, because, being so old, she would almost certainly die long before me, but she seemed so fit, that I'd developed doubts. Not that it would bother me if I was dead, but I'd sometimes wondered if our verbal agreement was legally binding, and suspected Daphne might not like it.

'You'd better reply, dear, or you could call her now you know there's nothing to worry about.'

The truth was that there were many things to worry about, such as putting in an insurance claim, and finding a new flat, but I'd had little chance to do anything so far, and there seemed to be no immediate rush. In addition, and potentially more serious, the photographs of me and Sally were bound to turn up sooner or later, and I was on tenterhooks, not knowing if my unknown and known assailants might strike again. In fact, I had a host of worries jostling for attention at the back of my mind, but they would just have to wait their turn.

'I'll send her an email now,' I said, resolute for once, 'and I'll ring her later, if you're sure you don't mind me using your phone.'

'Of course not, dear, and you can always use your mobile. Daffy says you keep forgetting you've got one.'

'That's true. I'd got so used to being without one that I just can't get into the habit.' I took it from my pocket. 'It needs recharging.'

'Use ours then.'

'I will later, after I've emailed.'

'Good lad.' She left me to get on with it and I composed a reply.

Dear Daphne,

Happy Valentine's Day!

It was great to receive your email. Don't worry about losing your temper, because it really was all my fault. I hadn't thought it through properly. I hope your new clothes are wonderful, and I hope your bite is getting better. I wish I could have found your card, but I imagine it's still in what's left of the Elweses' flat. I haven't been able to do much about that, because everything has been really difficult here with the floods, but they aren't quite so bad now. I've also been helping Hobbes with a double murder, and with looking after Dregs who got shot by someone with an air gun, but he will be all right, according to the vet.

I will talk to you soon. I'll be going back to Blackdog Street and Mrs Goodfellow says I can use their phone while my mobile recharges.

I love you and miss you,

Andy

P.S. When I say I'm helping Hobbes with a double murder, I don't mean helping him commit them, I mean we are investigating them.

I sent it, paid for my session and, feeling as happy as I could be when she was thousands of miles away, walked into the street and turned homewards.

That was when I saw the first one.

A poster, about the size of a paper-backed book, had been stuck on a lamppost in Rampart Street, and my unfortunate little dalliance with Sally was now made public. Although I'd been expecting something, it took my breath, chilled my blood, set my heart racing and made my chest hurt. I felt sick, convinced every passer-by was staring at me, seeing my apparent infidelity and judging me a rotter. My legs trembled so much I dropped to my knees, staring up at the image as if through a long dark tube. It was me, and though little of Sally was recognisable, she was clearly not Daphne.

'You praying to that lamppost, mate?' a man asked. He laughed and walked on.

I had to endure what felt like an aeon of shaking, sweating and blackness before I could force my legs to stand on my own two feet. Though I tore the poster down, there was another further on, and as I lurched towards it, I spotted the next, and the next, and the next … all along the street. My image seemed to be everywhere, and it was unmistakeably me, despite the face I was pulling, a weird mix of elation, incomprehension and (I hoped) reluctance. I was convinced people were pointing and smirking.

Cringing, avoiding eye contact, I hurried homewards, tearing down any posters I saw. As I turned into Goat Street, Featherlight's harsh voice broke into my nightmare, almost as a welcome distraction.

'Oi, Caplet! Unless my eyes mistake me, and they don't, that lady is not your wife. What've you been up to, you dirty dog?'

He lumbered towards me, one of the posters in his hand, one of his bellies protruding beneath his greasy singlet.

'Oh, hi,' I said, and failed to pull off a nonchalant smile. 'It's not what it looks like.'

'What are you playing at, you idiot? You've got yourself a fine woman – far better than you deserve – and yet as soon as she's out of sight you fling yourself at a floozy. What's wrong with you, knucklehead? I've a good mind to teach you a lesson.'

'Please don't,' I whined. 'It was a set up and now it's a complete nightmare. Do you really think I … umm … wanted to kiss her?'

'I can't see you putting up much of a fight.'

'A camera doesn't always show what really happened. She took me by surprise.'

'Several times by the looks of it,' said Featherlight, scowling. 'If I had a woman like Daphne, I wouldn't go snogging any young doxy who crossed my path. Are you trying to mess up your marriage?'

'I wasn't. It was all just a horrible mistake, and I'm scared Daphne'll find out and not understand. I don't know who's been sticking these things up, or why. Who'd hate me so much they'd do something like this?'

'Anyone who's met you, I expect,' he said, shaking his head and making his chins wobble. 'Look, Caplet, if it was just you I'd let you flounder in your own mess, but since

I have a great admiration for your good lady wife, except for her poor taste in husbands, I'll tell you that I saw the bloke who's posting them turn down Vermin Street about five minutes ago.'

'Who was it?'

'A bloke.'

'Could you describe him?'

'He was a bloke wearing a black hoody … average height … quite muscular … bit of a belly …'

'Is that all?' It didn't seem much to go on.

'… and he had hands like a mole.'

'What? Muddy?'

'Big.'

'But you didn't recognise him?'

'No, but you might, if you hurry.'

'What?'

'Use what passes for your brain. He might still be around, mightn't he?'

'Umm … yes … I suppose so … Vermin Street? Thanks.'

I scurried away, hoping to spot the fiend, while hoping he wouldn't spot me, for I'd not forgotten the size of his hands, and had already linked them to the bruises from my beating. Fighting to overcome a sense of terror, my hunting instincts buzzing, I kept my eyes skinned, but other than posters on lampposts, there was no evidence of him. I even asked a number of passers-by, but no one admitted to having seen anything. I rushed around town like a mad thing, tearing down poster after poster, but never spotted him. The horror was immense and my panic was growing. I leant against a wall and clutched my head, despairing until a heady, spicy fragrance surrounded me, renewing hope that things might work out.

'Good afternoon, Andy,' said the soft, honey-coated voice of Hilda Elwes. 'I see you've been enjoying yourself. When the cats away, eh?'

'Umm … hello.' I turned to face her, and forced myself to be normal. 'It's not that. It's all a big mistake … honestly.'

'I'm not judging you,' she said. 'Everyone has their own little foibles and weaknesses.'

She was wearing a flimsy purple dress and high heels, looking so stylish and summery among the drab winter clothes that she might have been modelling for one of the fashion magazines I'd flicked through in doctors' waiting rooms. Her smile was comforting, and her jade eyes were soft and forgiving. For a moment I wondered if she might be trying it on, having seen evidence that I was such a soft touch, and I made up my mind not to succumb to her charm, although it was immense. However, I must have misread her, for she continued on an entirely different tack.

'I'm told the engineers have made the flats safe, so, if you want to see if anything can be salvaged, I'd report to the council. They'll give you a pass to get on-site.'

'Thank you,' I said. 'I will … when I have time … umm … how are you managing?'

'Managing, Andy?'

'I mean since that night. Have you found anywhere to stay?'

I realised how lucky I was to be back with Hobbes and Mrs Goodfellow, and how little thought I'd given to my neighbours who'd had no such friends.

'Oh yes.'

'Where?'

'Over that way.' She waved her hand vaguely in the direction of Ride Street.

'With friends?'

'No, just the two of us.'

'Good … umm … Good.' My conversational skills having dried up, I resorted to an inane grin, and thought desperately. 'Someone shot Hobbes's dog.'

'Was he mad?'

'He wasn't happy about it, but the vet took an air rifle pellet out and reckons he'll be all right. What kind of person would shoot a dog? I mean … he's a big daft brute, but he's good natured.'

Hilda's uncanny gaze was still fixed on me. 'I don't know, but Aubrey saw a man with an air rifle shooting at rabbits in Ride Park last night.'

'You think it might be the same person?'

She shrugged. 'Who knows?'

'Umm … how could he be shooting in Ride Park? It's closed at night. I know because I nearly got locked in once.' I shuddered, recalling a terrifying walk through dark woods, with a big cat on my tail.

'So I've heard. Colonel Squire doesn't like plebs in his park at night.'

'But he lets your husband in?'

'Not as such, but Aubrey likes a moonlit walk. So do I … and he's not my husband … he's my cousin.'

Her smile made me feel like a puppy dog, desperate to ingratiate himself. There was something enchanting about Hilda Elwes.

'I see.' For a moment my suspicion that she was coming onto me returned, though her eyes suggested she merely found me amusing, but she was so charming and lovely. With an effort, I got back to the subject in hand. 'Did he see who was shooting?'

'No, he kept well out of the way.'

'Oh … never mind … thank you … umm …'

'I mustn't keep you, Andy, I'm sure you are very busy. Farewell.'

She walked away, leaving a hazy cloud of fragrance and a feeling of total confusion. I thought her an alluring woman, although I wasn't entirely sure. She was certainly elegant, or probably was, but oddly I couldn't picture her. However, I was sure I didn't fancy her … and yet, she did something to me, and when she was around I wished I had a tail to wag. Now she'd gone, I felt suddenly tired and drained.

I found myself back at 13 Blackdog Street, where the steps up to the front door felt like climbing a mountain. As I opened the door I sneezed. Then I sneezed again and again as if my head was exploding.

Mrs Goodfellow appeared. 'Are you all right, dear?'

I shook my head and shivered.

'You look very pale.'

'I feel very pale.' I sneezed. 'And my throat hurts.'

'You'd better go upstairs and lie down. You've probably caught something. It's not surprising after all the soakings and the dirty water.'

I forced myself upstairs, stripped and fell into bed, where I lay shivering until Mrs Goodfellow appeared with a hot drink. She put her hand on my forehead.

'You're a little feverish. Never mind, drink this.'

It was hot and tasted of honey and lemon combined with something I couldn't quite place, though I didn't care, for it was warming and soothed my throat.

'You should sleep, dear,' she said, closing the curtains.

'But I've got to call Daphne,' I said, remembering and making a feeble attempt to get up.

Mrs Goodfellow pushed me back. 'Stay where you are. I'll call her, and say you're ill.'

'All right. Say I'll try later.'

I was soon in a deep sleep that was, as far as I could remember, dreamless. At some point, I think I came awake and staggered to the bathroom and back. At another point, Mrs Goodfellow fed me chicken soup, but after that I knew nothing until morning, when I sat up with a slight headache and a nose that was as well stuffed as a marrow. I had breakfast in bed, lunch in bed and even dinner in bed and only got up for calls of nature. The rest of the time I slept.

The following day, my headache was better, the stuffiness was gone, and the sore throat was almost a memory. I bounced from bed, washed, dressed and went downstairs where I was greeted by Dregs, who, if not quite his usual self, and who looked unbalanced with his left back leg shaved and in a white dressing, was delighted to see me. The feeling was mutual.

Hobbes was already at the table. 'Glad to see you back on your feet.'

'Me or Dregs?'

'Both of you.' He grinned.

'I thought he'd be wearing one of those plastic lampshade things, so he can't pull his dressing off,' I said, remembering the time Granny Caplet's wicked orange cat, having got himself into a brawl, had needed stitches. They'd left him even more bad tempered than usual, and when I'd laughed at his stupid plastic cone, he'd upped and scratched me on the nose, which Granny had said served me right.

'Mrs Collyer thought he should have one, but I had a quiet word with him and he knows to leave the dressing well alone,' Hobbes explained.

Mrs Goodfellow presented us with creamy scrambled eggs on thick buttered toast, the toast somehow staying crispy, and the eggs as fluffy as only she could make them. My appetite was as hearty as that of the proverbial condemned man, and I followed up with more toast, this time with a new batch of marmalade, a perfect melding of sweet and sour with just a hint of smokiness. The latter flavour was something of a mystery because I'd watched her at work and the only ingredients had been Seville oranges and sugar.

'It's good to see you back to normal,' said Mrs Goodfellow as I finished off the last crumbs. 'That was a nasty bug.'

'I think it might have been flu,' I said, 'but that stuff you gave me worked wonders. What was it?'

'Honey and lemon, dear.'

'And?'

'And a secret ingredient.'

'And some of my best Islay malt whisky,' said Hobbes, looking grumpy.

'Just a drop,' she admitted.

'Well, it was good stuff. Thanks.'

'You're welcome, dear. Now, I'd better get on with the washing up and get the dinner in the oven before I get ready for church.'

'It's Sunday is it?' I said, pleased to have spotted the clues.

'It is,' said Hobbes.

'I should telephone Daphne. I was going to do it yesterday … no … on Friday. She'll be worried.'

'No, she won't,' said Mrs Goodfellow, 'because I told her you were under the weather. But, yes, you should call today.'

'I'll do it now, if I can use your phone?'

Hobbes nodded, and I hurried through to the sitting room and, after a bit of thought, poked in her number. I got through.

'Hello,' I said. 'Daphne?'

'No, buddy,' said a deep voice with an American accent. 'Mike Parker. Mrs Caplet is busy with the professor, and he said they should not be disturbed until they've finished.'

'The professor?'

'Professor Mahmoud El-Gammal.'

'Him again,' I said, flushed with jealousy. 'What are they doing?'

'They're in the bedchamber, making out …'

'What?'

'… making out an inventory.'

'I see. Just the two of them?'

'Yep.'

'Why?'

'Why what? Excuse me, but who are you?' asked Mike.

'I'm Daphne's husband.'

'Thought you might be. How you doing, buddy?'

'I'm fine.'

'Great, because I heard you were sick.'

'I was. Umm … why are she and the professor working alone?'

'Because there's no room for anyone else in there.'

'There's usually space for more than two in a bedroom,' I said.

He laughed. 'It's not actually a bedroom. It's a chamber where we found a bed and some other artefacts.'

'I don't get it. What's the difference?'

He laughed again. 'Daffy said you're a dude who'll always choose the wrong end of a snake to poke. I'll explain. When we were investigating what might prove to be a tomb, we came across a small chamber that just happens to have a bed in it.'

'Like in Tutankhamun's tomb?' I asked, trying to show how switched on, intelligent and knowledgeable I was.

'Nothing like that. That was a magnificent piece, fit for a pharaoh, but the one we got is a piece of worm-eaten junk.'

'So, why are you interested in it?'

'We may not be.'

'Why not? It's old isn't it?'

'Oldish, and that's as much as I'm willing to say, because anything else would be speculation. I'll let Daffy know you called, and ask her to call back, or d'you wanna leave a message?'

The answer was yes. I wanted to tell her how much I loved her and missed her, and how much I wanted her back, but I couldn't bring myself to say these things to Mike, who seemed far too familiar with her. Besides, I really didn't like her being alone with Professor Mahmoud El-Gammal.

'Umm … no. Just say I'll try later.'

'OK, buddy, I'll do that. Ciao.'

'Chow?'

He hung up, and I was just about to sit down when the phone rang. Excited, I picked it up.

'Daphne, how are you?'

'Bonehead,' said Featherlight. 'If you had an identical twin, the pair of you wouldn't have the brains to make a whole idiot.'

'Sorry,' I said. 'I thought you were her, because …'

'If you've started to think I'm your lovely wife, then you've got even more problems than are obvious.'

'I didn't know it was you until you spoke. Sorry, Featherlight.'

'It's Mr Binks to you, Caplet, and I don't want you calling me Daphne again. Got it?'

'I won't. Now, how can I help you?'

'You can't even help yourself. Just tell Mrs Goodfellow that Billy was having a tidy up and came across a bag of mixed teeth which no one has claimed. She can have 'em.'

'I'm sure she'll be delighted,' I said with a grimace.

He hung up, and I went into the kitchen, only to find Mrs Goodfellow wasn't there. How she wasn't there was a puzzle, because she couldn't have got by me without my noticing. I looked out into the back garden, where Dregs, all alone, was enjoying a good sniff, his breath curling like dragon's smoke. As I watched, he turned his head as if intending to lick his wounded leg, but paused, and resumed sniffing. I returned to the sitting room as the old girl came downstairs dressed in her Sunday best, a long green winter coat and a longer turquoise skirt, the effect a little spoiled by the tatty black Wellington boots. She beamed when I passed on Featherlight's message.

'Thank you, dear. He's such a thoughtful man, isn't he? I'll pick them up after church.'

Although he was not at all a thoughtful man in my opinion, there was still something about him that was weirdly disarming. That was the reason, I supposed, why there were so many regular customers at the Feathers, even though there were far nicer pubs in town. Thinking about it, all the other pubs were nicer, but they didn't have Featherlight. According to Hobbes, he meant well, though it wasn't easy to tell, especially for those who got on his wrong side and felt his fists, which, like his bellies, were big, but which, unlike his bellies, were as hard as granite. Happily, his temper rarely lasted more than a minute, though it was a minute too long for most. Another peculiar facet of his personality was the old-fashioned courtesy he always extended to women, even though few ventured into the Feathers to experience it, being repelled, so I'd been told, not by the smell or the dirt, but by the customers. However, the few who did enter had nothing to fear since he'd swiftly sort out any man who stepped far out of line, and most of us – them, rather – did not dare explore how far that might be.

As Mrs Goodfellow left for church, Hobbes came downstairs, and I wondered why he wasn't escorting her, which he normally did unless snowed under with work. He was poking at a rather smart new mobile he must have acquired when I'd been afflicted and didn't appear too busy, despite the murders and the boar.

'I'm going to take Dregs for a walk,' he said.

'Is that wise? With his leg?'

'With all of his legs. The vet said he should take exercise, so long as he doesn't overdo it. Are you fit enough to go out?'

'I think so,' I said, having checked it wasn't raining.

'Well, if you want to come, get yourself ready while I fetch him.'

I grabbed my coat, and, realising I was wearing slippers, rushed upstairs for my boots. When I returned Hobbes was ready and the dog, unusually, was on his lead.

'Why did you put that on?' I asked.

'I don't want him rushing off at the moment. He knows he should take it easy, but there are too many distractions. Let's go.'

We headed up Hedbury Road towards the side entrance of Ride Park. Just as we approached Keeper's Cottage, Dregs tucked his tail between his legs and bristled.

'What's up?' I asked.

He said nothing, but growled and bared his teeth.

'Interesting,' said Hobbes.

'Yeah,' I agreed, putting on a spurt to keep up. 'Why?'

'Because he's not happy, and this is where he left us to go courting.'

'So it is. D'you think she rejected him?'

'A big, handsome fellow like Dregs? I doubt it.'

'Well, something's upset him,' I said as we passed the cottage.

'But he's over it now,' Hobbes observed.

Indeed, Dregs, his tail wagging again, was marching in front, straining against his lead, eager to reach the park despite his injured leg. Hobbes released him as soon as we got there, and though I expected him to run off like the mad thing he usually was, he walked with us, obviously heeding the vet's advice, even when a squirrel ran across the path. As I huddled into my coat against the bitterly cold wind, I'd have liked to question Hobbes about what he'd been up to, but, since he appeared to be in deep contemplation, I reined in my curiosity.

The park wasn't quite as deserted as I'd first thought, though only a handful of people were out and about, mainly walking with dogs. I guessed it was too raw for most. Still, after a day in bed, I was delighted to be in the open, and to feel so well, since my previous bad cold had left me bedbound for a week, and lethargic and drained for a further week. Admittedly, I might have made a little more of it than had been strictly necessary, since I'd rather enjoyed Daphne fussing over me.

I wondered what she was doing all alone with that professor, and why she hadn't mentioned Mike, who sounded like a big, confident kind of guy, the sort any woman would want to have around. For some reason the world became tinged with green, and for a moment I thought it might be a side effect of jealousy. It turned out we'd walked into a small copse festooned with ivy and almost enclosed by holly.

Hobbes stopped and stared at the ground.

'What's up?' I asked.

He held up his hand in warning and stepped into the dense undergrowth, Dregs on his heels, while I stayed put, scared in case he'd discovered something dangerous, like, for instance, a wild boar's nest. However, Dregs's body-language, ears up, tail up, wary but calm, suggested interest rather than alarm. I still held my breath as Hobbes dragged aside a curtain of bramble and ivy, but since nothing horrible appeared, I relaxed.

He stood to the side to let me see. 'Someone's been camping here.'

Hidden deep in the vegetation was a small hut made of sticks, woven twigs and grass, with stones around the base. He pushed aside a woven screen of sticks and ivy and revealed the interior, a snug space, lined with moss and dry leaves. A pair of hammocks, again cunningly woven by nimble fingers from whatever grew around, had been stretched between the walls.

'I wouldn't have wanted to sleep out in this with all the rain we've had,' I said.

'I suspect you'd have been fine,' said Hobbes, looking around, 'though it appears, in fact, to have been built since the storm. These twigs have been cut very recently.'

'Who would make such a thing? Kids?'

'It's far too well built for children. Whoever made this knew precisely what they were doing, because I reckon it would keep out even the heaviest weather. It looks nearly windproof, and it's well insulated and is just about as well put together as it could be without timber and nails.'

'I still wouldn't want to live here though,' I said.

'Maybe not if you had a choice, but this place, although it clearly lacks modern comforts, would be acceptable. It's not so long ago that most people round here had to live much like this, though in more permanent structures. I'd guess it's only a temporary dwelling.'

'You didn't answer my question. Who could have done it? I mean, who would have the right skills and knowledge?'

'I don't know, but I have some suspicions.'

'Go on.'

'Do you remember the heptagram?'

'The star thing? Of course.'

'Well, whoever made that probably made this. The handiwork is very similar to ones I've seen before.'

'Yeah, I suppose it's possible, but since you don't know who made the star, it doesn't really help, does it?'

'I don't know their names, and I may not need to. It's not a criminal offence to live in this manner, although Colonel Squire is hot-headed enough to do something against the law if he finds someone using his land without permission and without paying rent. I'm inclined to think the people who built this shelter may have come here after being flooded out.'

'Or maybe their flat was demolished by a tree,' I said as a couple of random thoughts came together and stuck.

'Do you know something?'

'I might do. You see, the Elweses, the couple whose flat ours fell on, weren't home at the time, which was lucky for them, though I thought it strange, because … well … I mean to say, it was a rotten night to be out in, wasn't it?'

Hobbes nodded.

'And when I bumped into her earlier, we had a chat, and she said something …'

'It would have been rather one-sided if she hadn't.'

'She said her cousin, Aubrey, had seen a man with an air rifle in the park last night, and I wondered about that because …'

'Because the park is locked at dusk,' said Hobbes, nodding. 'I don't suppose he recognised the shooter?'

'I asked the same question, because I thought it might have been the bloke who shot Dregs and me, but she said Aubrey hadn't seen him clearly.'

'Thanks,' said Hobbes. 'You may well be right about this being their accommodation.'

'Thanks, but … umm … thinking about it again, I'm not so sure. She, Hilda that is, was really smartly dressed, at least I think she was, and she didn't look like she'd been sleeping in a hut.'

Hobbes shrugged. 'If she's what I suspect she is, she could easily appear smart to one such as you.'

'What d'you mean "one such as me"?'

'A member of the public,' said Hobbes. 'Let's put their screen back and get out of here. By the way, have you noticed anything unusual about this place?'

'Not really. What do you mean?'

'Something is missing.'

As he picked up the screen, I took a last look around inside and stepped out into the open.

'Umm … a bathroom?'

He fitted the screen and turned away. 'They could do their business in the woods, like bears are reputed to do, and there are facilities in town. No, I mean something fundamental.'

'Umm … wardrobes?' I hazarded, following as he marched away.

'No. Let me put it this way. If you were building a shelter at this time of year, besides making it weatherproof, what would you want to include?'

I screwed up my face with the effort of thinking while Hobbes rearranged the undergrowth so that no one would know there was a hidden shelter.

'Yeah,' I said at last, 'I've got it … somewhere to cook!'

'Well, yes, it could be used for that, but I was thinking more generally of a fire.' He sniffed the air, dropped to his knees and crawled towards a small holly bush. When he pushed it, it fell to reveal a shallow pit with stones around the top and charred wood and ash at the bottom. 'I thought so. Most folk would want some sort of fireplace. It gets dark at night, and cold.'

'It's not so warm now,' I said, shivering as he replaced the holly.

'A brisk walk will warm you up, and give me time to think.'

A brisk walk for him and Dregs was close to a fast jog for me, and as I followed them around the park, gasping for air, I reflected that my fitness was not as good as when I'd been staying with them full-time, and yet I reckoned I was already fitter and a little slimmer than I'd been when Daphne had left. I hoped I could pleasantly surprise her when she came back, whenever that was. Soon I hoped, and nearly choked – not too soon would be better, since I needed to sort out my little problem with the compromising photographs first. I would have liked to ask Hobbes for advice but was too embarrassed and ashamed, and, anyway, he had two murders to solve, though he seemed not to be doing very much about them.

And yet, there'd been other occasions when I'd not noticed him doing anything, when in reality I just wasn't following the process. It would have been nice if he'd chosen to let me know more of what he was thinking, though, in fairness, he had discussed some cases with me. In fact, there'd been occasions when he'd thanked me for my help in resolving them, although, in all honesty, I'd entirely failed to grasp the significance of what I'd said or done until much later. After one instance, when I'd felt frustrated by his thought processes, I'd asked Mrs Goodfellow how he did it.

'Well, dear,' she'd said, after a good cackle at my vexed expression, 'to make a cake, you have to mix all the ingredients together, put the mixture in the right pan, and put it in the oven at the correct temperature for the correct time. If you're impatient and take it out too soon, you end up with half-baked goo that is no good to anyone. You've got to wait until it is ready.'

Although I'd not entirely grasped her point, my brain being confounded by thoughts of cake, the outcome had been pleasing, since the analogy had inspired her to bake the lightest, fluffiest, richest, most delicious English sponge I'd ever tasted.

I was so much into my own thoughts that I failed to notice Hobbes had stopped until I walked into his back, which was about as soft as a brick wall. Getting back to my feet, a little stunned, I realised we'd left the park and that Dregs was growling and bristling. Once again we were outside Keeper's Cottage.

'There's something about this place that upsets him,' said Hobbes, 'which, together with the information you gave me earlier, makes me think I should have a bit of a nose around.'

'What information?' I asked.

'The man with the air rifle.'

'I see … umm … possibly. Do you think he lives here?'

'I think it's a distinct possibility since it gives him easy access to the park.'

'So do a lot of places,' I pointed out.

'True, but Dregs only reacted to this one.'

'So what?'

Hobbes sighed. 'So, it's possible the man with the air rifle in the park, is the individual who shot him.'

'That's what I thought! Are you going in?'

'Not until Dregs is away from here. He's not happy, so you'd better take him home.'

Though I would have preferred to stay and watch the fun, the dog was evidently in so much distress that I nodded and led him away. As soon as we were past the cottage, he perked up and headed for home at a sedate pace, in keeping with his invalid status. Unfortunately, this didn't last. After a couple of minutes he seemed to forget he was an invalid and broke into a run, overcoming my attempt to restrain him, and dragging me towards Blackdog Street at a speed I would once have described as breakneck, but which, since my neck remained intact, could more properly have been described as traumatic.

It was busy in town, and despite having to exert an immense amount of concentration on merely staying on my feet, I couldn't understand people's reactions. I was not used to inspiring shock, fear, and horror. Many fled as we approached, some of them screaming, and by no means all of them women. Realisation dawned appallingly slowly that they weren't actually looking at me or Dregs, but at something following us. This left me with a dreadful dilemma since I couldn't look back without losing my balance, unless I released Dregs's lead first, in which case I would slow down and whatever was behind would catch up. I still hadn't solved the problem, when Dregs made it academic by swerving around a red pillar box, a manoeuvre inertia would not permit me. Releasing the lead, I made a desperate attempt at a leapfrog, getting one leg over, but catching the other. For a moment I straddled the top, and then, as gravity took over, flopped back, and landed astride something that was large, bristly and muscular. It had huge, erect hairy ears, fearsome tusks, and squealed like a pig. A man in my position has two choices: to try to hang on, or to fall off. I chose the latter, or rather the boar chose for me, when after a number of steps that caused immense grief to my groin department, it executed a series of pirouettes that sent me spinning into the gutter.

All the breath was knocked out of me, and it seemed ages before I was able to re-inflate my lungs. As breathing returned, I asked my brain what I could do should the boar attack, and, for once, it responded really quickly; I could do nothing at all, except squeal, which was exactly what I did when something touched my shoulder.

'Are you all right?' asked Hobbes.

'Umm … yes. At least I think so.'

'Good. Now, what made you decide to ride the boar?'

'I didn't actually decide. It was an accident.'

'Oh well, it was entertaining while it lasted.'

'Great, but … umm … where's it gone now?'

'Away. It turned left at the end of the road, so I expect it's heading towards the river, or Church Fields.'

'Where did it come from?' I asked as he helped me back to my feet.

'Keeper's Cottage. When I hopped into the back garden, there he was. My arrival must have spooked him, and he leapt the wall like a show jumper and fled into town. I must say I was impressed by your turn of speed when you realised he was behind you.'

I nodded modestly, but said nothing. We turned into Blackdog Street.

'However, your attempt at hurdling the pillar box was less impressive. Ah! Here he is.'

Dregs, looking around suspiciously as if expecting attack from every shadow, was trotting towards us, dragging his lead and, other than a slight limp, appeared unscathed. He gave us an enthusiastic greeting and seemed keen to get home, where he enjoyed a noisy drink before settling down in his basket for a well-deserved rest.

'Are you going back to Keeper's Cottage?' I asked Hobbes.

He shook his head. 'Not until later. It's nearly dinner time.'

I glanced at the clock, surprised it was already half-past twelve, though the aroma of roasting pork ought to have alerted me. 'But where is Mrs Goodfellow?'

'Good question,' he said. 'She should be back by now.'

'She did mention going to the Feathers after church to pick up a bag of teeth.'

'Oh dear,' he said.

'Why? They're lost teeth no one wants anymore and she'll give them a good home.'

'Yes, I'm sure she will, but I was thinking more of our dinners.'

'She hasn't gone far. She'll be back soon … won't she?'

'Possibly not. There's the sherry you see.'

'Sherry? What sherry?' I asked. 'Where's she going to get sherry from?'

'Featherlight will offer her a glass.'

'Sherry? At the Feathers? You're having me on.'

'I wish I was,' said Hobbes looking gloomy. 'He keeps some in for his lady customers.'

'He gets lady customers?'

'Not often,' he admitted, 'but he always keeps some in on the off chance, and the trouble is that the lass has a bit of a weakness for it. She'll occasionally take a sip of other drinks, but sherry …'

'You think she'll drink too much?'

He nodded. 'And she can't hold it.'

'At her age, she should know her limits,' I said.

'She knows them well enough, but ignores them.'

At that moment, the front door bell rang. Dregs looked up and barked, and decided he was still too much of an invalid to go charging around. Hobbes answered it.

It was Featherlight, wearing the old girl across his shoulders like a cape. He ducked his head and she rolled into Hobbes's arms.

'I know who you are,' she said opening her eyes, looking up and burping. 'Pardon me!'

'Sherry?' asked Hobbes.

Featherlight nodded and treated us to his broadest grin, which was not pleasant on an empty stomach. 'I'll leave her to you,' he said. He started to turn away and paused. 'I had a customer in last night ...'

'Amazing!' I said, and was rewarded with a glare.

'... who said something interesting.'

'About what?' said Hobbes, cutting me off before I could make a facetious reply.

'About a wild boar. He was reading about it in the *Bugle,* and said he'd delivered one to a smallholding near Fenderton a couple of months back. He was a bit vague because he'd had a few drinks, mind.'

'Do you think it's the same boar?' I asked.

Featherlight shrugged.

'Thank you very much,' said Hobbes. 'I don't suppose you caught the gentleman's name? Or asked the address where he'd delivered it?'

Featherlight shook his head. 'I'm not a copper any more. I leave that kind of stuff to you. He was just a van driver.' He paused. 'I think his name was 'arry, but he was heading for Birmingham today.'

Then he glared at me. 'There's more of those posters gone up. It looks like you've been a naughty boy, and if Hobbes wasn't here I'd give you such a clout that'd teach you to treat your marriage vows with respect.'

Featherlight turned away, raising a hand in farewell and leaving me to panic again.

'Posters?' said Hobbes.

'Oh ... umm ... they're nothing much, but they're ... umm ... a little embarrassing. I'll deal with them.'

'All right then,' he said and shut the front door.

I was by no means convinced I could do anything sensible, but it was my problem, and I was too guilt-ridden to talk about it. Besides, it could hardly be his priority, and hopefully it would sort itself out.

'I need to give some thought to that boar,' said Hobbes, 'but first I'd better put the lass to bed.'

'I'm not a bore and it's not bedtime,' said Mrs Goodfellow, yawning. 'I'm not tired.'

'Why would somebody want a boar?' I asked as he carried her upstairs. 'I reckon they'd be a bit fierce for a pet.'

'Who knows,' said Hobbes. 'Some folk like fierce things. I once knew a chap in Hedbury who kept a crocodile as a pet. He said it was friendly and only gave him love bites. One day it bit his head off.'

'My granny had a mad bad cat,' I said, 'but he was only fierce to me.'

Having carried the old girl to her room, he laid her on her side on the edge of the bed. 'You'd better get her a bucket,' he said.

I fetched a heavy galvanised bucket and set it on the floor beneath her face and we left her, snoring.

'What about lunch?' I asked as we went back downstairs.

'The pork will be fine, but we'll have to manage the vegetables between us.'

'What should I do?' I asked when we were in the kitchen.

'Fetch some spuds up from the cellar, and make sure they're the starchy ones. While you're doing that I'll start on the greens and take the meat out to rest.'

He grabbed the hugest knife in the rack, one that reminded me of a cutlass, and selected a pointy cabbage, leeks and broccoli from a box. I headed into the cellar, and since I had reason to be nervous of things that had lurked in the dark down there, I was relieved the light was working, as well as being pleased the rickety old steps had been replaced by sturdy new ones. Although occasional and usually carried out just before whatever he was working on entirely turned up its toes, Hobbes's handiwork was effective and reliable. He was the only person I knew who could drive nails into wood with his knuckles, or turn a screw with his fingernails, though I suspected Featherlight might be capable of similar feats, should he ever feel the need to repair anything, which, going by the state of the Feathers, he didn't often.

The flood was evidenced by dark, dank puddles, a stagnant stench, and a watermark a third of the way up the walls, but the old girl's roots, like Hobbes's wines, were safely stored on wooden racks above the high tide mark. There were baskets of parsnips, turnips, swedes, carrots and some long, weird vegetables I didn't recognise, but I had a bit of trouble finding potatoes. I eventually spotted some on a rack in the corner. They were, perhaps, a little on the small side, and had a few too many roots sprouting, but they felt firm, and I reckoned they looked starchy enough, whatever that meant. I selected a generous handful of the bigger specimens and carried them upstairs.

'Peel 'em, cut 'em into quarters and boil 'em for fifteen minutes with a pinch of salt. Then drain 'em, mash 'em with a masher, add a knob of butter, and serve 'em,' said Hobbes, who was hacking cabbage into tiny strips.

The task was fiddly and hard going, even though I'd selected a knife almost as massive as Hobbes's. However, I finally triumphed and placed the peeled, chopped spuds in a saucepan, with sufficient, but not too much, water and a pinch of salt. Hobbes, having poked the resting pork, lit the gas under the saucepans.

'Keep an eye on those,' he said, 'while I check on the lass.'

He left me to it, and I discovered the truth in the old adage about watched pots never boiling. Getting bored, I picked up the *Bugle* and read about the boar, only to be disappointed that the article contained less information than I already knew. At some point, I was vaguely aware of a sort of hiss but I didn't register what it was until I smelt gas. When I glanced up, all the pans had boiled over and dowsed the burners, leaving the top of the cooker awash. I got up, took a match from the drawer, and struck it as I approached the cooker.

The flash and the heat took me by surprise, but left me unhurt, though I wondered about the unpleasant sulphurous smell as I tried to calm Dregs, who was barking and excited. Hobbes burst in and, to give him credit, ascertained that neither of us had been hurt before laughing long and loud. It was by no means the first time I'd come close to disaster in there.

'What is it with you and kitchens?' he asked, when his guffaws had subsided into grins.

'I don't know. I do my best, but this one seems to have it in for me. I'm sorry.'

'Never mind,' he said. 'No real harm's been done. I'm sure it'll all grow back.'

'What will?'

'Your eyebrows and the hair at the front.'

'Oh, no ... how long?'

'As long as it was before, but it'll take a few weeks.'

I ran upstairs, peered in the mirror, and groaned. The frizzed hair on my forehead, coupled with the blank canvas where my eyebrows should have lived, left me looking like an alien. I just knew people would point me out in the street and laugh, that dogs would bark at me and that little children would flee in horror. And what would Daphne say when she saw me?

I returned to the kitchen where Hobbes, having brought the cooking back under control, was carving the meat, and to be fair, not making a bad job of it. The pan with the meat juices was simmering nicely, emitting pleasant aromas, and I began to hope we'd managed without the old girl.

'How can I help?' I asked.

'Mash the potatoes, please.'

I did as he asked, draining them and pummelling them with the masher, although the task, and the spuds, were much harder than I'd anticipated. As soon as I'd thrown in a little butter, Hobbes began plating up.

I took my place and waited while he said grace. It looked like we'd done a reasonable job, though the vegetables were perhaps a little watery. Hobbes shovelled a fork-load of mashed potato into his mouth, and looked puzzled.

'What did you do to this?' he asked.

'Nothing I shouldn't have.'

I sampled a little. The texture was all wrong and the taste, though not exactly unpleasant, was exactly unlike what I'd been expecting, being a curious mixture of carrot, celery and water-chestnut.

'I don't believe this is potato at all,' said Hobbes with a chuckle.

'Umm ... it must be. What else can it be?'

He laughed again.

'What's so funny?'

'Where did you find them?'

'In the cellar, like you said.'

'On the vegetable racks or the one in the corner?'

'The one in the corner. That's where they were, and it's not my fault they taste funny.'

'They taste of what they are.'

'What?'

'Congratulations, you have prepared a fine dish of mashed dahlia roots. The lass stores them down there ready for planting out in the spring, and she won't be happy we've eaten them. I'd make the most of this dinner if I were you, because you'll be on dry bread and water when she sobers up and realises what you've done.'

Although I knew he was joking, the thought of missing out on her cooking made my stomach lurch.

'They're not poisonous are they?' I asked, as he helped himself to a large fork load.

'No,' he said when he'd swallowed. 'The Aztecs cultivated them for food.'

'But didn't they die out?'

'Their culture did, and many of the people, but, don't worry, it wasn't dahlia tubers that killed them. I believe it was smallpox.'

'How do you know all this stuff?'

'I read – you should try it, but in this case, I was told when I was in Mexico.'

'I didn't know you'd been there … when?'

'Long ago.'

'Why?'

'They asked me to police an outbreak of chupacabras.'

'What?'

'Dangerous beasts.'

I would love to have probed more, but a deep frown dissuaded me and I left him to his dinner, which, all things considered, wasn't too bad, and was far better than many pub meals I'd enjoyed before I'd acquired a gourmet's palate.

Afterwards, I cleared the dishes and, feeling extremely virtuous, washed up while Hobbes made a pot of tea. We were reasonably successful at both tasks; I only chipped one plate, and the tea was drinkable. We repaired to the sitting room and sat down.

'So, apart from the boar, did you see anything else of interest at Keeper's Cottage?' I asked, as he stirred sugar into his mug.

'I believe I met Dregs's love interest, a sweet Samoyed bitch, who, to go by the tag on her collar, is called Mimi.'

'What's a Samoyed?'

'A breed of dog,' said Hobbes.

'I guessed that. I mean what are they like?'

'Medium-sized, white, fluffy and doggy. The breed was once used for pulling sleds in Siberia.'

'So, a bit like a husky?'

'A bit, but smaller and fluffier. Her behaviour worried me.'

'Why?'

'She was scared.'

'I'm not surprised with that boar around.'

'No, by me. She seemed quite relaxed with the boar.'

'That's unusual,' I said, for Hobbes had something about him, his feral odour I suspected, that dogs seemed to like. I'd once thought of analysing it, bottling it, and selling it to postmen and the like, but hadn't quite got round to it.

'It is, and it's also unusual to keep a timid dog on a heavy chain. I suspect she's being ill-treated, so I intend to make a further visit.'

'When?'

'When I've finished my tea.'

The phone rang. Hobbes put down his mug to answer. 'Inspector Hobbes, how may I help you? … Good afternoon, Derek … Mr Marco Jones? Are you sure? … I see … and did you find out the other thing? … Now that is interesting … What about Golums Logons? … Yes, I suspected so … Thank you very much indeed.'

Having replaced the receiver, he returned to the sofa, looking thoughtful.

'Who was that?' I asked.

'Constable Poll. He's been doing a bit of investigation for me.'

'That's nice. So … umm … who is Marco Jones?'

'The tenant of Keeper's Cottage.'

'You sounded really interested. Why?'

'Because Derek found out who actually owns the cottage.'

'And?'

'It's Mr Solomon Slugg.'

'Him again? It's probably just a coincidence?'

'Possibly. Coincidences happen all the time, but not so often that I wouldn't check them. According to Poll, Mr Slugg also owns Golums Logons, and has a majority holding in Big Mama's Canteen, where Mr Marco Jones works.'

'Well, he is a local businessman. Wouldn't you expect him to have an interest in a few local concerns?'

'Of course,' said Hobbes. 'However, Mr Slugg is really starting to interest me.' He drained his mug and poured himself another.

'Because of Septimus?' I asked, 'Or is there something else?'

'During my visit to Tode-in-the-Wold, I asked a number of people about Mr Septimus Slugg and it turned out that he was quite well known there. However, no one I spoke to suggested he might be a wastrel or a drunkard. He was, in fact, the town librarian, and though he used to enjoy the occasional pint in the Green Dragon and often took part in its pub quiz, he was never known to be drunk or to cause trouble. I confirmed that he had no police record.'

'That doesn't fit in with Solomon's account,' I observed.

'Certainly not,' he agreed. 'Furthermore, Septimus was indeed the seventh and youngest child of Mr Samuel Slugg, also known as Samuel S Lugg. Two of his brothers have died, but the other siblings, two sisters and a brother, are alive and well in Australia, to where they emigrated in the sixties. According to his phone records, Septimus kept in regular contact, and his passport showed he'd visited there about three years ago. So, it seems to have been a happy family, other than Solomon. I contacted his sister Emily, who is now Mrs Boon, and informed her of Septimus's death. She was understandably upset, though she'd suspected something was amiss since he hadn't been in contact, which was unlike him. In addition, she gave me some interesting information about Solomon.'

'What?' I asked, agog, my tea cooling.

'She said he was nearly a recluse. He lived alone, rarely left the house, and was financially dependent on a trust fund set up for him by his late father. The family sent him birthday and Christmas cards, and occasional letters, but he never responded and hardly ever allowed them to visit. None of them had actually set eyes on him since nineteen ninety five.'

'Except for Septimus,' I pointed out. 'She must have been lying for some reason, because we've met Solomon who's rather a charming gentleman, and not at all reclusive.'

'No,' he admitted. 'He didn't give that impression.'

'So you could discount her evidence.'

'I could, but I won't. I can think of no reason for her to lie about him.'

'In that case, he must have changed, though isn't it more usual for people of his age to become set in their ways rather than to suddenly decide to go into politics and business?'

'It depends on the individual,' he said, 'but I have a suspicion that whatever has changed, it was not Mr Slugg's personality. There's a numerical element to this case that is intriguing.'

'You've lost me now. We know what he's like, and, if you believe what his sister says, he must have changed considerably, which doesn't make sense.'

'I think it might,' he said, grinning in the infuriating way he had when he was trying to get me to think.

I was spared by a thump and a clang from above.

'What was that?'

'The lass falling out of bed, I expect,' he said, standing up, and loping to the rescue.

I followed, nearly getting bowled over by Dregs who, fully restored by his nap, was keen to see what was happening.

Mrs Goodfellow's normally pale face held more colour than was usual; it was green. She was sitting on the floor, groaning.

'I think I may have imbibed a trifle too much sherry, dear,' she said as Hobbes helped her up. 'Take me to the bathroom. Now!'

He took her at a gallop, and shut the door behind her, which at least muffled the horrible retching and splashing. After a few minutes, she tottered out and he helped her back to bed.

'How are you feeling?' I asked.

'A little delicate.'

'Can I get you anything?'

She nodded, groaned, and held her head. 'Could you go to my drawer in the kitchen and fetch my tonic? And I'd like a glass of water too, if it's not too much bother.'

I hurried away, filled a glass and found the bottle she wanted beneath her set of nunchakus. Instead of pushing them aside and leaving them well alone, I thought it might be fun to give them a quick whirl, like Bruce Lee in the movies. I was mistaken. When I'd recovered enough to stand up straight, I vowed never to touch the things again. I took her tonic and water upstairs.

'You've been playing with her nunchakus,' said Hobbes as I reached the old girl's room. 'I can tell by the way you're walking.'

'Those things are dangerous.'

'Not when they're in the drawer, dear,' said Mrs Goodfellow, taking the glass and shaking in a few drops of her tonic, which was thick and red, like tomato ketchup, but which smelt of unwashed feet. She gulped down the contents in one, and lay back with a groan.

A moment later, she performed a vertical take-off, crashed down and went rigid, the manoeuvre making Dregs bound around the room, barking like a mad thing.

'Is she all right?' I asked.

Hobbes held up his hand.

She sat up, blew her nose on a tissue and smiled. 'Thank you, dear.' Then she fell back unconscious.

'She'll sleep for a couple of hours now,' said Hobbes, 'and will wake feeling better, after which she'll swear off drink, and adhere to her pledge. Until next time.'

'Does she do it often?'

'About once a year.' He covered her with a blanket and opened the plastic bag she'd been clutching. 'Let's see what she got.'

'That sounds like teeth,' I said, horribly familiar with the rattle.

He nodded and showed me. There must have been a hundred, in all shades from snow white to slush brown: molars, premolars, canines and incisors. Once the sight, and the knowledge of why they'd left their owners in the Feathers, would have made me sick, but I'd grown into sterner material and a slight shudder sufficed. Even so, when one fell to the floor and I bent to pick it up, I recoiled.

'You can't handle the tooth,' said Hobbes, who had no such qualms.

'That's a good haul,' I said as he dropped it back into the bag. 'Do you think Featherlight is putting dentists out of business, or is keeping them busy repairing the damage?'

'That is a question to which I suspect we'll never know the answer. Right, I'm heading back to Keeper's Cottage, where I hope to have a word with Mr Jones.'

We left her bedroom. Then Hobbes turned, went back, and retrieved Dregs, who'd been attempting to sneak onto the bed.

'Can I come with you?' I asked when we were heading downstairs.

'Yes, but Dregs had better stay.'

The dog's tail drooped as he heard the fateful word 'stay', and he looked up at Hobbes with a pleading expression.

'No,' said Hobbes. 'You might find it upsetting.'

Dregs whined, wagged his tail and twisted his mouth into a passably endearing grin.

'Oh, all right then. Just behave yourself.'

A minute or two later, suitably clad against drizzle so fine it was almost mist, we started towards Keeper's Cottage. A man in a hooded mac was walking ahead, and although I thought there was something familiar about him, it took a few moments to work out why, by which time he'd turned towards Keeper's Cottage and gone inside. Dregs started growling again until Hobbes reminded him to behave.

'I saw that man in Golums Logons when Mrs Goodfellow sorted out the students,' I told Hobbes. 'He was taking money. Quite a lot of it, I think.'

'Thank you,' said Hobbes, walking up to the door and ringing the doorbell. The door opened almost immediately and the man stood there. Although he was of less than average height and rather thick around the waist, he looked powerful, like a bodybuilder.

'Who are you?' he asked, frowning, his accent an odd mix of local with a smidgeon of Welsh and a pinch of something foreign.

'Mr Marco Jones?' asked Hobbes, showing his ID card.

'Maybe. What do you want?'

'I want a world of harmony and peace ...' said Hobbes.

'You what?' said Mr Jones, looking confused. When he saw me, he bit his lip as if my presence alarmed him, which was not an effect I normally had on people.

'... and I'd like to see your dog, sir.'

'I don't have a dog.'

'In that case, I'd like to see the dog in your garden.'

'Which one?'

'The one at the back of your house.'

'Why?' asked Mr Jones.

'Why not?' asked Hobbes with a smile.

From the bafflement on Marco's face, I suspected he might not be overly endowed with brains.

'Er ... Because she's dangerous,' he said after a long pause.

'All the more reason for me to see her,' said Hobbes. 'If she's dangerous, it might mean she's a threat to the public, and we can't allow that sort of thing, can we? It's bad enough having that wild boar running about.'

'Have you seen one?' asked Mr Jones, looking suddenly interested.

'Why? Have you lost one, sir?'

'Er ... no ... of course not ... er ... what would I be doing with a boar? They can be dangerous, and I wouldn't keep a dangerous animal.'

'Apart from your dog?'

'It's not mine.'

'I trust you haven't stolen her, sir,' said Hobbes with a stern expression.

'No … I'm … er … keeping her for … a friend … because his smallholding is flooded. Yes, that's it.'

Having had some experience of Hobbes's interviews, I was growing suspicious of Marco Jones.

However, Hobbes merely nodded and smiled. 'A friend in need is a friend indeed, sir. Just to satisfy my curiosity, could you tell me your friend's name and address?'

'His name is … er … er …'

'One of the Gloucestershire Er-Ers, I presume. Does he have a first name?'

'Eh?'

'So, Mr A Er-Er. Quite unusual, sir.'

'No,' said Marco, squirming. 'You've got it wrong and you're making fun of me. I don't like it.'

'Sorry, sir. Your friend's name?'

'It's on the tip of my tongue … it's … John … er … Johnson … and he lives in … that place that got flooded …'

'Atlantis?' I suggested.

'No, Fenderton.'

'By the Soren, I expect,' said Hobbes, nodding. 'I know the area well, but I'm not aware of any Mr John Johnson. I wonder why?'

'Er … that's because he's … er … only just moved there. … Yes, that's right.'

'Have you known him long, sir?'

'A few years.'

'Very good, sir.'

Marco blew out his cheeks, as if he thought he'd just sailed unscathed through the hazardous straits of thought. But Hobbes was not finished.

'Where did you first meet?'

'At the Bellman's Arms. Do you know it?'

'Indeed, I do, sir. It's on The Shambles, near to the *Bugle's* offices … but, hold on a minute, that sounds a little strange. Are you quite sure?'

'Yes.'

'Then perhaps you could enlighten me how you met Mr Johnson at the Bellman's a few years ago, when he's only just moved here, and you yourself have not been in town for very long?'

It was a good point that Marco failed to appreciate. 'Are you calling me a liar?'

'No, of course not, sir, but I am suggesting you may have got a little confused.'

It may have been a trick of the light, but Hobbes appeared to have grown both in height and breadth, and was looming over Marco like a thundercloud over a picnic. Marco was suddenly as pale as the snowdrops that had recently emerged from their long sleep, and was as twitchy as I'd been when infested with werewolf fleas.

'Yes, I am a little confused.'

'It can happen so easily,' said Hobbes. 'I suppose you must be flustered because you're not used to being asked questions by a police officer. I am right, aren't I, sir?'

'Yes.'

'And I suppose you would like me to leave you in peace?'

'Yes.'

'But you'd be happy to let me see the dog first?'

'Yes ... er ...'

'Thank you, sir. Is this the way?'

Not forgetting to wipe his feet on the doormat, he squeezed past Marco, who looked utterly bamboozled.

'Come along,' he said.

Dregs and I followed, with Marco clumping along at the rear, apparently lost for words, though he was making a strange whimpering noise. Dregs never took his eyes off Marco. The cottage itself, though weather-beaten Cotswold stone on the outside, had been modernised within so that, although it still retained much of its rustic charm and character, it was warm and comfortable, with varnished floorboards, fine furniture and cream plastered walls. It was discreetly lit by small strategically positioned lamps, was neat and tidy, and smelt fresh and citrusy. It was not as I would have expected, had I got around to expecting anything.

'Very nice, sir,' observed Hobbes, looking back over his shoulder. 'Is this the way to the back door?'

Although Marco nodded, his mouth moved as if it wanted to say something, if only his brain had managed to think of anything.

Hobbes led us through the kitchen, past a polished plank table and wooden chairs painted a pale blue, between a tall dresser covered with plates and other crockery on the left, and, on the right, a cream Aga range with a row of gleaming copper saucepans above. He opened the back door and we entered the back garden, where a beautiful, long-haired white dog was tethered to a stake by a heavy chain padlocked to a steel collar. She cringed and whimpered on seeing us, until Dregs burst past and ran towards her, whining and wagging his tail, like she was an old friend. She relaxed, and allowed us to stroke her, though she flinched if a hand went close to a small scab on her neck. Whenever Marco moved, she cringed.

'She's a fine looking dog,' said Hobbes, 'but I fail to understand why you have her chained up like this, especially without food, water or shelter. I would like an explanation, and one that doesn't have any reference to the fictional Mr John Johnson.'

'He's not fictional, he he ...' Marco began and stuttered to a halt, stunned, I imagined, by Hobbes's inter-continental scowl.

'No more untruths, sir. It'll be so much better for you if you start answering honestly while you have a choice, rather than later when I get angry. You wouldn't like it when I'm angry.'

'No, you really wouldn't,' I said as Marco looked to me for guidance.

I shuddered, recalling those rare occasions when I'd been caught in the fallout of Hobbes's rage, which although not directed at me, had been dreadful. He could be amazingly lenient with petty offenders, if having to endure one of his little talks could be described as lenient, but would come down harder, heavier and faster than a concrete slab on those he suspected of cruelty or of abusing positions of authority. Of course, when he allowed himself to get in a rage the recipients were no longer mere suspects, but definites.

Marco, wide-eyed and rubber legged, stared around, as if searching for sanctuary. None was available.

'Speak to me, Mr Jones,' said Hobbes, towering over him.

'He's fainted,' I observed, as the man went down like a punctured airbed.

'So I see,' said Hobbes with a wicked grin, 'and, since an unconscious man is clearly incapable of caring for a dog, I feel I ought to take charge of her.'

He carried the casualty to the white-leather sofa in the sitting room and, having ascertained that his vital signs were okay, returned to the garden and picked up the dog's chain. Expecting a demonstration of his phenomenal strength, I was disappointed when he simply unbuckled her collar. The released dog bounded around us, nuzzling and playing with Dregs, and Hobbes sent me into the kitchen to fetch her some water. I returned with a brimming copper pan which she lapped dry as soon as I put it down.

'I'd like to get her out of here as soon as possible,' said Hobbes. 'Would you take her home?'

'Yeah … why? What are you going to do?'

'I am going to ensure Mr Jones is comfortable, and I might take the opportunity for a bit of a nose around.' He tapped the side of his rather large hooter and chuckled.

'You planned this, didn't you?'

'How could I plan for Mr Jones to faint?'

'I don't know,' I admitted, though it had struck me as odd that so many of those he was interviewing passed out at the most convenient moment.

'You'd better put her on Dregs's lead, because she may not be very good in traffic, or meeting people.'

'But her collar is still padlocked to the chain.'

'So it is,' said Hobbes and took the padlock in his great fist, squeezing until there was a crack. He handed me the collar.

'Thanks,' I said, taking it. 'Come on, Mimi.'

She looked up on hearing her name and trotted towards me, allowing me to refit her collar, and to clip on the lead. I said goodbye to Hobbes, who was on his knees and sniffing in the kitchen, and headed home with Dregs who, though normally a connoisseur of police work, chose to join us, walking at Mimi's side, his thick black tail wagging as if he might take off like a helicopter.

When I reached home, Mrs Goodfellow, looking bleary and wan, was at the kitchen table, splitting hairs with the enormous cleaver she used for slicing tomatoes.

'Hello, dear,' she said, giving me a toothless smile. 'Who's the bitch?'

'Mimi,' I said. 'Hobbes thinks we should look after her, because the man who's supposed to have been doing it is unconscious.'

The old girl nodded, groaned and clutched her head. 'I'm never ever going to drink sherry again,' she announced, fulfilling Hobbes's prophecy.

'Can I get you anything?' I asked, sympathising, for I, too, had over consumed alcohol on occasions, and had been glad of any small kindness.

'No thank you, dear. My tonic is working and I'll be fine after a cup of tea.'

'I'll put the kettle on,' I said.

'Thank you, dear. I'd better feed Mimi. She looks like she needs something.'

'You're probably right. She was very thirsty earlier, and Hobbes thinks she's been mistreated. Umm … what can we give her?'

'There are a few dog food tins in the cupboard. We can open one of those for now, and after that there's some venison in the cellar that needs using up.'

'Is there? I didn't see any and I was down there at lunchtime.'

'Billy brought it round a few minutes ago. That's why I'm awake already.'

'Where did he get it from? The shops only seem to be selling basics at the moment.'

'Off Pigton Road.'

'Road kill?'

'Mercedes kill, if the mark on the poor beast's flank is anything to go by.'

'Is it all right to eat?'

'It's fresh and has been tenderised.'

'Umm … okay … shall I go and fetch it?'

'I thought you were putting the kettle on, dear.'

'I am,' I said, picking up the old copper kettle, filling it and putting it on to boil. 'I'll get the venison now.'

'No, dear. It's a little heavy, so you'd better leave it to me. You can open a tin for Mimi.' She got up, groaning, and headed for the cellar.

There had been a time when my manly ego would have insisted on lifting heavy things for her, but I'd learned to look past her frail appearance and advanced years and see the strength within. Leaving her to get on with it, I patted Mimi, who acknowledged the gesture with a thump of her tail and went back to nuzzling Dregs, who was a most smug-looking dog.

'You're a lucky fellow,' I told him.

Wagging his tail, he whined and woofed, and, from the way she snickered and glanced in my direction, I could only believe he'd told her something about me that wasn't entirely complimentary. It might merely have been my paranoia talking, but I think it was Dregs.

I opened a tin, popped the meat into a bowl and set it down. Both dogs came up, and though Dregs merely sniffed at it, Mimi wolfed the whole lot down within seconds. As soon as she'd finished, she lay down and licked her lips.

Now and again a bump sounded from below. After a particularly loud one, I thought I ought to check.

I headed for the cellar door. 'Are you all right?'

'I'm fine,' she gasped, and came into view, hunched under a massive carcass.

'Bloody Hell!' I exclaimed, 'What on earth is that? Are you sure it's a deer? It's as big as a cow!'

'It's a red deer, dear, and mind your language.'

'Sorry … but it can't be … where are its horny things? I mean its antlers? Shouldn't it have them if it really is a deer?'

'The males drop them this time of year …'

'Very careless,' I said.

'… but this is a doe, dear, and so never had any.'

'I see. Do you want any help?'

'No, thank you.' She continued upwards, moving the carcass far more easily than I would have. Always helpful, I got out of her way.

When she reached the middle of the room, she dropped her right shoulder and twisted her scrawny old hips, depositing the deer onto the table. Both dogs watched with interest, but only Mimi approached for a sniff. I wasn't surprised, since Dregs had developed an aversion to meat unless it had been prepared and cooked to his satisfaction. In this regard he was more civilised than Hobbes. Mrs Goodfellow stood upright and stretched.

'Now what?' I asked.

'Now we butcher the carcass. First we skin it, and then we cut it into joints.'

'We?' I said.

'Only if you want to, dear.'

Accepting this as my cue to exit, I fled to the sitting room, for although I didn't believe I had a weak constitution, I was concerned the smell would turn my stomach as easily as I could turn a door knob. It made me wonder how a charming young woman like Dr Cynthia could cope with the sights and stinks she must meet on a regular basis, and I could only marvel at her fortitude. Her job was not one that appealed, although I could understand she might get some sort of intellectual thrill from uncovering hidden secrets, much like Daphne must have been finding with her tombs and bedchambers.

I flopped onto the sofa, overcome by the weight of thoughts in my head: Daphne, the murders, the bones, the poster vendetta, the boar, the dog shooter, the psychopathic rugby players, what Hobbes suspected about Solomon Slugg, my getting syndicated in *Sorenchester Life,* and what I ought to be doing about the flat and contacting the insurers. Although it seemed reasonable to deal with the insurance first, it was the least interesting on the list, though Daphne would struggle to understand why I hadn't done it, and I would struggle to explain myself. It was clear I ought to contact the insurers soon, and afterwards that I should search for accommodation. Yet, I couldn't stop thinking that, if I failed to deal with the posters and the threat of blackmail, Daphne might not want me any longer. Before she'd left, and after hard reflection, I'd concluded that the best thing I'd brought to the marriage had been loyalty, and, although I still was loyal really, albeit I had briefly allowed myself to be flattered by a beautiful face, she might not see it like that.

Every now and then my thoughts were punctuated by thuds, and occasional cries of 'get down, Mimi' from the kitchen. The distractions meant that I hadn't quite come to a conclusion about my next move when Hobbes returned, looking rather pleased with himself.

'How did it go?' I asked.

He hung up his coat and sat beside me. 'Firstly, I believe I have confirmed why Dregs was upset in the vicinity of Keeper's Cottage.'

'Go on.'

'When I was nosing around I came across an air rifle and ammunition hidden at the back of a wardrobe. There's nothing wrong with that as such, though the pellets match the one taken from Dregs's leg.'

'So, you think it was Marco who shot him? I thought the pellets were common.'

'So they are, and they would mean little had Mr Jones not volunteered a confession when he came round and was shown the evidence.'

'Volunteered?'

Hobbes had the grace to chuckle. 'He volunteered the information when I pressed for an answer as to why he possessed such a weapon. It is possible that he formed the impression that possessing a powerful air rifle was illegal, and confessed to spare himself more distress, but I don't know where he got that idea from. It would not be unreasonable to suggest that he is not conspicuously intelligent.'

'Did you charge him?'

'No, I negotiated with him, and since he was worried how his mother would react to his being arrested, he was inclined to be helpful.'

'He has a mother?'

'Everyone has, or had, one. His runs the restaurant where he works. I suspect few others would employ him.'

'She's Big Mama?'

'Indeed. She is a formidable lady.'

A series of thuds came from the kitchen.

'What's the lass doing?' he asked.

'Butchering a dead deer for the dogs.'

'Well, she would hardly butcher a live one,' he said, a little uncertainly.

'I would hope not.'

'So would I. I think I've put a stop to that sort of thing, but she can be a little forgetful.'

'I suppose she is getting on a bit,' I said.

'So she is, but her memory is better than when she first came to stay.' He sighed, and shook his head. 'Anyway, to return to Mr Jones, he did confirm that Mr Solomon Slugg has a controlling stake in the restaurant and is often there.'

'Him again? But, isn't it confirmation that his sister's comments were just wrong?'

'Only if we accept Mr Slugg at face value,' said Hobbes.

'What do you mean?'

'I mean I have strong suspicions about him.'

'I don't see why. He's charismatic and charming, and yes, I understand he's a bit of an oddball, but there's nothing wrong with being eccentric, or owning a restaurant, or even in being a politician.'

'You are essentially correct,' he said, 'though some might quibble about the latter.'

'But, you can't really suspect him of killing his own brother?'

'I don't believe he killed either of his brothers.'

'Either? And aren't you sure the skeleton was Solomon's brother?'

'Quite sure.'

'And … umm … didn't you say his surviving brother is in Australia?'

He nodded.

'Then that can't be right … unless his sister lied.'

'She didn't,' he said, grinning.

'All right, I'll accept that for the moment,' I said, my brain hurting with the effort. 'The important thing is, if you don't think Solomon killed them, who do you think did?'

'If you stop to think about the numbers here, you might begin to suspect he did.'

'You just said he didn't!'

'No, what I said was that I didn't think he'd killed *his* brothers.'

'Now you're just confusing me.'

His smile was infuriating. 'I'm going to see whether the lass needs any help. I'll leave you to mull it over.'

He headed into the kitchen, and I sat back, scratching my head and hoping I hadn't picked up fleas again. It turned out to be just the one and I quickly caught and crushed the little perisher, suspecting Mimi as the source, since Dregs had learnt that Mrs

Goodfellow wouldn't allow that sort of thing in the house. Freed from the itch, I was able to devote myself to deep thought. The problem, as I saw it, was that Hobbes suspected Solomon of the murders, and at the same time didn't suspect him. Perhaps he'd meant it philosophically, in that he suspected everybody in general, but nobody in particular, and yet I reckoned he'd meant more than that. It was an impossible conundrum. How could he have murdered the two brothers and, yet, not have murdered his brothers? I'd almost convinced myself that Hobbes had been talking nonsense, when I became aware of a thought at the back of my mind, just out of reach. I forced myself to think outside the box, as Phil had often encouraged me.

The facts were that two brothers had been murdered, one of them being Septimus, the seventh and last of his family. Two others had died long ago, one lived in Australia, and there were two sisters. I counted them up. Seven. That was right. I wondered what Hobbes had been getting at with his talk of numbers. There'd been seven siblings in the family, and I'd accounted for them all.

I slapped my head in frustration, which caused the thought to come loose. As it drifted closer, I snatched at it and held on.

I'd got it! At least I thought I had.

I'd forgotten to include Solomon. That meant there were seven plus one: eight siblings. So, assuming the sister wasn't lying, there appeared to be an extra brother.

The problem was starting to resolve itself. What if the charming man who'd identified himself as Solomon Slugg wasn't really him? Wouldn't that explain why he'd been so different to his sister's description? Despite his beguiling personality, he could be an imposter. That thought opened the possibility that he had killed two brothers, but they were not actually *his* brothers because he was not Solomon. It was a simple solution to what had seemed a crazy conundrum, though why he'd done it was a question to answer later.

Elated by my triumph, I got up and ran to the kitchen to check my answer, quite failing to notice Dregs stretched out in the doorway. Tripping over him, making him yelp, I fell, splatting into the kitchen floor, skidding over the red bricks, and coming eyeball to anus with a sleeping Mimi, who, clearly a dog of delicate sensibilities, leapt to her feet with a yelp, and tried to clear the table at a single bound, just as Mrs Goodfellow's heavy, gleaming cleaver swung down. It would have split Mimi in two had Hobbes not flung himself into harm's way. The cleaver missed the dog, but struck the top of his head with a horrible crunch like cabbage being chopped, and, as I looked in horror at what I'd done, I was showered in hot blood. I got up, trying to help, but found my legs had turned to mush.

When I came to, I was staring at Dregs between my legs and the legs of the chair I was sitting on. Seeing my eyes were open, he wagged his tail. I pulled myself upright, still feeling groggy, and wondered why my face was so sore.

'Are you all right, dear?' asked Mrs Goodfellow who was still hacking, though the carcass had been mostly reduced to joints of meat.

'I think so.' I nodded, trying to shake my brain back to life, vaguely aware something had happened.

'Good, but you're still very pale.'

'Did I faint?'

She nodded. 'You went out like a light and fell face first into a chair. You've got a lovely pair of shiners, but I've put a little of my tincture on them, so, in a day or two, they'll be as right as reindeer.'

'Thanks.' I became more my normal self and remembered. 'Hobbes! Is he all right?'

'He's fine.'

'But he can't be … I saw you chop him … didn't I?'

'Yes, dear, but he's a tough nut.'

'But, I'm all covered in his blood!'

'Then you'd better wash it off, and change your shirt as soon as you feel up to it.'

'Right. Where's Mimi?'

'In the back garden with the old fellow. The poor bitch is very nervous after what you did to her and he's calming her down. Dregs tried, but what he had in mind didn't suit her, so he's confined in here for now. Would you like a glass of water?'

I nodded, and after washing her hands she handed me a drink. The coolness soon made me feel better, and I sluiced it down, washing away an unpleasant metallic taste, and trying not to think where it had come from. I'd just finished when the garden door opened and Hobbes entered, his head turbaned in white bandages.

'Feeling better?' he asked.

I nodded. 'You?'

'I'll be fine. It's not the first time someone's tried to scalp me. On the other hand, poor Mimi was distressed by the whole incident. She's a highly strung creature.'

'What are you going to do with her? Are you going to take her back to Marco?'

'No, but I would like to find her owner.'

'Surely that'll be easy? A pedigree like her is bound to have been microchipped. You just need to get her scanned.'

'It probably would have been easy had her chip not been cut out.'

'That nasty scab on her neck?' asked Mrs Goodfellow, taking a break from hacking. Hobbes nodded.

'Well,' I said, 'what about her tag?'

'It's new,' he said, 'and the address on the back is Jones at Keeper's Cottage.'

'That means Marco really did lie about her belonging to John Johnson. That was well spotted.'

'It was obvious, and it's possible she's not really called Mimi.'

'You think she was stolen, but why?'

'I suspect she was taken to be used as a breeding mother. According to Constable Poll, who knows about such things, pure-bred Samoyed puppies go for a lot of money – three thousand pounds each or more. They usually have four to six puppies at a time, and can have two litters a year.'

'So Marco could easily make thirty-six thousand pounds every year. That's not a bad sideline.'

'It wouldn't all be profit, because he'd have to feed her, though I'd imagine he could do much of that with scraps from the restaurant, and he'd need a male Samoyed, at least for a short time. Of course, if he was intending to breed pedigrees it would be a reason for shooting Dregs. He wouldn't want a dog whose ancestry is obscure hanging around her. However, I don't actually believe the scheme was concocted by Mr Jones.'

'No,' I agreed, 'he didn't strike me as a man of ideas, but we know he's working for someone. His mother?'

Hobbes shook his head. 'I have a better candidate.'

'Who?'

'Mr Solomon Slugg, or whatever his real name is.'

'So, I was right,' I exclaimed. 'I worked out that he wasn't who he said he was. But are you sure? He can't be behind everything.'

'No, not everything. However, I've often found that someone I arrest for committing one crime later admits to many others.'

'Maybe, but you don't really see the guy as a one man crime wave, do you?'

'I do.'

'But he doesn't seem the sort. He's a respectable businessman and a politician. What evidence do you have?'

'Firstly, he's not who he says he is, and secondly, he owns a controlling share in Big Mama's Canteen, and I suspect is responsible for leading Mr Marco Jones into bad ways.'

'That'll not convince a jury.'

'I'll admit the evidence is circumstantial at the moment, but it'll be fun finding proof, and there are other things to consider …'

'Like what?'

'Such as how the boar came here, the intruders at Mr Slugg's house, why he was so evasive, and who has been supplying the steroids to the rugby players. I would very much like to know the true identity of the man claiming to be Mr Solomon Slugg.'

'So, what are you going to do?' I asked.

'The cryptic crossword.'

'No, really.'

'Really. It's a fine way of clearing the mind of other problems, and creating space for thoughts to grow. You should try it. After I've finished that, I might pay another visit to the Slugg residence.'

He headed to the sitting room, picked up the *Bugle* and a pen, and sat down on the sofa.

'Do you mind if I try calling Daphne again?' I asked before he became engrossed.

'Hmm? Daphne? Of course I don't mind.'

As I reached for the phone, it rang. I grabbed the handset. 'Daphne?'

'You what, mate? Have I got the wrong number? Who are you?'

The voice, though distorted by the phone, was familiar.

'Is that you, Bob?'

'I think so, but I wanted Inspector Hobbes. Have I used the right number?'

'You have.'

'You don't sound like him. Are you sure?'

'I'm not.'

'You're not sure? Are you winding me up?'

'No, I'm not Inspector Hobbes.'

'Why did you say you were?'

'I didn't.'

'You bloody well did.'

'No, I said you had the right number for Inspector Hobbes.'

'I know I've got the right number for him – it's on the card he gave me, but I wanted to know if I'd dialled it right.'

'You did. Would you like to speak to him?'

'I wouldn't have gone round to Mr Custard's house and used his telephone to call Mr Hobbes if I didn't want to speak to him, would I?'

'No, I suppose you wouldn't … umm …' By this point I was confused, and relieved when Hobbes took over.

'Inspector Hobbes. How may I help you? … Yes it is me … The idiot? … Oh, that was Andy … yes, his telephone technique could be better … now what do you want, Mr Nibblet? … I see. When? … And it's still there, is it? … Well done … I'll be round as soon as I can. How are the floods? … Goodbye, Mr Nibblet.'

'What's happening?' I asked.

'Bob's caught the boar,' he said, putting the phone down.

'Really? How?'

'He turned up looking for food and Bob trapped him in Crackling Rosie's pen.'

'But that had a big hole in it. How can he keep it inside?'

'I gather he's persuaded Mrs Nibblet to guard it. Apparently, she's very handy with a piece of plywood and a stick.'

'But that huge beast is really dangerous.'

'That's no way to talk about Mrs Nibblet,' he said. 'I'll grab my coat and go straight there. Are you coming?'

'Yes, please … but … umm … what are you going to do with it?'

'I thought I'd wear it.'

'Not your coat, the boar.'

'I suppose I'll have to arrest him.'

'And then what?'

'Put him in secure accommodation, until I can determine where he's come from.'

'Where?'

'That's a good point. Sergeant Bert gets upset when I keep livestock in the cells, and, besides, they are still filled with displaced members of the public, though I hope not for much longer.'

'Where then?'

'He'll have to stay here.'

'I feared you might say that. Umm … you're not thinking of bringing the creature back in the car, are you?'

His expression told me that he was. 'Actually,' I said, 'though I'd love to go with you, I really must phone Daphne. Do you mind if I give this one a miss?'

'Of course not.'

He left me to feelings of relief that I wouldn't have to share the car with such a fierce and powerful animal, and disappointment that I'd miss seeing Fenella Nibblet's pig wrangling.

I phoned Daphne and after three rings someone answered.

'Daphne?'

'No, sir,' said a deep American voice. 'Mike Parker. Are you Randy?'

'That's none of your business … Oh, I see … my name's Andy.'

'My mistake, Andy. How may I help?'

He sounded tired.

'I'd like to speak to my wife, Daphne.'

'You can't, she's in bed with the professor and half the others …'

'What?' I snapped, my jealousy rising like a hungry trout to a mayfly.

'Let me finish. They are all in bed …'

'I don't believe you!'

'… because they've gone down with a bad case of gippy tummy – that's what you guys call it, isn't it?'

'Oh, I see … sorry.'

Mike chuckled, a deep resonance in my ear. 'Don't worry yourself, buddy. I might have phrased it better … my bad.'

'Is she all right?' I asked, jealousy standing aside to allow worry through.

'No, not really. A doctor's on his way from Cairo, but he won't be here for a few hours.'

'What's wrong with them?'

'It's likely something they picked up from unwashed dates. The cook bought some in the market and they were shared round before he could rinse them. I'm only okay because I don't like them, but those that do are quite ill. I hope it is just gippy tummy.'

'Why?' I asked, fear upwelling, and my stomach churning. 'What else might it be?'

'Someone suggested it might be amoebic dysentery. That's bad.'

'How bad?'

'Pretty bad, but it is treatable. At the moment those of us who are still fit are making sure they get enough to drink. Dehydration can be a big problem out here.'

'Is there anything I can do?'

'Not from England, buddy. Call back in a couple of hours and maybe I'll have better news.'

'Right … yes … umm … thanks, Mike.'

'No problem, Randy,' said Mike, hanging up before I could correct him.

I slumped onto the sofa and worried, and the worst part was that, for all my fretting, there really was nothing I could do.

A sharp rat-a-tat shocked me from my gloom. I went to the front door and opened it. Billy Shawcroft was looking up at me.

'Wotcha, Andy, I'm back again. I like what you've done to your face. Is Hobbesie in?'

'No, sorry. He went out a few minutes ago to arrest the boar. Can I take a message?'

'I suppose so, matie. It's from Featherlight.'

'What does he want?'

'He asked me to tell Hobbesie that he spotted a pair of them hanging around in Ride Park.'

'A pair of what?' I asked.

'He didn't elucidate. He said Hobbesie would understand.'

'Do you have any idea what he meant?'

'Not really, except that he looked worried, and when he gets that look, there's usually something to worry about.'

'In that case I'll make sure to tell Hobbes as soon as he gets back. Umm … would you like to come in for a cup of tea, or something?'

Billy glanced at his watch. 'I'd love one.'

'Great. Mrs G will be pleased to see you. She's been hacking up that deer so she can feed the dogs.'

'Dogs?' said Billy, stepping inside.

I shut the door and explained about Mimi as we headed towards the kitchen, where Mrs Goodfellow, having finished hacking, was simmering something in a jumbo-sized copper saucepan, and unleashing delicious aromas into the world. Mimi was far more interested in the cooking smells and only spared Billy a short glance, as he took a seat, but Dregs was delighted to see him and to act as a rest for his little legs.

We drank tea and engaged in trivial banter for a pleasant twenty minutes, until, feeling relaxed and convivial, I accidentally mentioned Solomon Slugg.

'Solomon Slugg?' said Billy, looking interested. 'Is Hobbesie interested in him?'

'Yes, because he seems to think Solomon might be involved in a couple of murders and other stuff ….'

Mrs Goodfellow frowned.

'Umm … I shouldn't have said all that. Don't tell anyone, please.'

'Don't worry. I know the ropes,' said Billy. 'It's just that the name stuck in my mind, because it's unusual, and because I remember seeing his picture in the *Bugle* and thinking he looked familiar. I reckon I used to know him years ago …'

'His sister says he was a recluse, but now he runs businesses and has tried his hand at politics.'

'The man I knew was never a recluse, worse luck. He was charismatic and plausible, but underneath he was a nasty piece of work, always causing trouble in a mean sort of way. Of course, he went by a different name back then.'

'So, how come Hobbes doesn't recognise him?'

'Probably because the guy I knew didn't live here. He was a drifter, but often hung around Tode-in-the-Wold when I lived there.'

'I didn't know you lived there.'

'Yes, well, I don't often talk about that part of life. You see, I was a bit of a bad lad then. I was a conman, and my trick was to pass myself off as a psychic, using it as cover for collecting information from my customers, which I'd then use to make money. To cut a long story short, it all went badly wrong one day, and I had to go on the run.'

'There was an article in the *Bugle*,' said Mrs Goodfellow, stirring the pot. 'It had that funny headline. What was it?'

'"Small Medium at Large."' Billy grimaced. 'It was a bad period in my life and who knows what would have happened if I hadn't run into Hobbesie when I did.'

'How did that happen?' I asked.

'I jumped on a bus and fled to Sorenchester, hoping no one would know me here, but a copper spotted me and I scarpered down the alley by the church and literally ran headfirst into Hobbes. Anyway, I came round in hospital, and he had a long talk with me, after which I gave up being a crook.' He shivered and looked thoughtful for a few moments. 'It wasn't easy, because it had never really been about the money, but more about the buzz, and when I went straight, I took to drinking too much. Hobbesie saw what was going on and now he kindly involves me in some of his work, so, along with all the bother at the Feathers, I still get some excitement, but don't have to spend all my time in courtrooms and with lawyers.'

'The old fellow's always said there's much more to policing than upholding the law,' said Mrs Goodfellow.

I nodded, realising again how little I knew of him, though I was sure I knew much more than nearly everybody else. I really wished he'd give me permission to write his life story, but I doubted he ever would because, for him, the past was dead, buried and best forgotten, except when he needed to exhume a memory pertinent to a case.

'I really must go,' said Billy, with another glance at his watch. 'Thank you for the tea.'

'You're always welcome, dear,' said Mrs Goodfellow.

As I let him out, I had a thought. 'I was just wondering how you … umm … manage to reach the door knocker?'

'I have an extendable tool.'

'That must be handy,' I said as he went down the steps. 'By the way, you don't recall the name used by the bloke claiming to be Solomon Slugg, do you?'

'No, mate … not really … maybe it was something like Elvis … but I can't quite put my finger on it … and the name I knew him by might not have been his real one anyway. See you.'

'See you, Billy. Take care.'

I watched the diminutive figure wander away along the drizzly street, before heading back inside and stumbling over Dregs again, to the evident delight of Mimi, who'd temporarily abandoned her kitchen watch to observe my antics. Hearing Dregs's snicker as I hit the deck made me suspect he'd done it on purpose. Perhaps it was his way of showing Mimi how harmless I was. Whatever, from that moment, she became very friendly, although she took to staring at my face with an embarrassing intensity, as if she saw something hilarious there.

As I got back up, an alarm bell started ringing in my brain, a warning that something wasn't right. It took a moment to work it out. Then I rushed back to the front door, opened it and looked up and down the street. Another poster had appeared on the nearest lamppost, and I knew what it was without even having to take a look. I ran outside and tore it down. It showed a different photograph, one in which I appeared to be gazing at Sally with big, soulful eyes while holding her hand, which just went to show how a picture could lie. Other lampposts were similarly decorated, and I tore down two more on Blackdog Street and a further half dozen on Ride Street before giving up and retreating to the warmth and dryness of number 13.

'What have you got there, dear?' asked Mrs Goodfellow as I shut the front door behind me.

'Nothing,' I said, hiding the crumpled sheets behind my back.

'Then why are you blushing?'

'I'd rather you didn't see them. They make me look bad.'

'I'll be the judge of that,' she said. 'Let me see.'

I tried to escape, but should have known better.

Darting forward with cobra speed, she grasped my upper arm between finger and thumb and squeezed gently. I found myself helpless as she took the posters from my paralysed hand and released me. I regained control of my body, but it was too late. She'd already seen enough.

'I see,' she said, giving me her stern look.

'It's not what you think.'

'I think it is what I think.'

'It isn't!'

'What do you think I think, dear?'

'That I've been messing about with other women when Daphne's away.'

'I don't think that, dear. I think there's only been the one.'

'There was, but I didn't mean for anything like that to happen. She was the one who saved me when I was nearly run down. I only went for an innocent coffee with her and before I knew what was going on she was all over me, and then a man with a camera turned up. I guess I was unlucky.'

'No, dear, I guess you were lucky ...'

'How?' I asked. 'I didn't want the attention at all.'

'But it could have been so much worse.'

'I don't see how!'

'Maybe not yet, dear, but, then you don't know who she is ...'

'She's called Sally.'

'But she's also known as Matilda Kielder.'

'The one Hobbes has been after?'

'Yes, dear. It's a much nicer picture of you than on those other posters.'

'You saw them?'

'Of course. They were all around town.'

'Why didn't you warn me earlier?'

'To be fair, dear, the others didn't show much of her that was recognisable, and she's changed her hair colour since I saw her. You were lucky the cameraman turned up when he did, or she would have lured you away to a terrible fate. Did I mention she was a man-eater?'

'You did. I sort of thought you were joking. I know I'm gullible at times – Daphne said so. I'm quite worried about her because she's poorly after eating some bad dates.'

I explained what had happened, enjoying the ensuing sympathy and gratified the old girl cared about my wife, though I might have wished Mimi wasn't sitting on my foot and staring into my face.

'She seems to like you,' Mrs Goodfellow observed, turning towards the kitchen, 'I wonder why? Right, I'm going to get back to supper.'

'Great. What are we having? Venison?'

'Not tonight, dear. I'm cooking beef, slow braised in Hedbury stout, with creamed potatoes and glazed carrots.'

'That sounds great,' I said, anticipating true greatness. Then, since I didn't wish to just sit and drool until suppertime, I decided to take a look around town.

Having put on my coat and escaped from Mimi, I left Blackdog Street and wandered aimlessly around, brooding on my luck and quaking every time I thought about myself having been on Matilda Kielder's menu. I happened to pass Travis's, an estate agent's at the top of Vermin Street, where I was struck by how useless I'd been at finding somewhere to live. The window was filled with photographs and details of properties of all sizes and locations, and it was depressing how few were in our price range. To be completely honest, I suspected that none of them was in our price range, unless we won the lottery or something. It was clear we'd have to rent unless we moved somewhere cheaper like Pigton.

Bowed beneath a weight of gloom, I walked away from Travis's and stumbled over a broken broomstick on the pavement. Being a good citizen, I picked it up and looked around for somewhere to dispose of it.

My mobile rang and I answered, surprised to see it was on.

'I've arrested the boar,' said Hobbes. 'I'll bring him home and he'll have to go in the back garden for now.'

'Good,' I said, wondering why he'd felt the need to call me.

'I expect you're wondering why I called,' he said, 'and the answer is that I need you to ensure both dogs are out the way. I suggest putting them in my bedroom while I get the boar through the house, because I'm not sure how they'll interact. Can you be back at Blackdog Street in ten minutes?'

'Yes, I expect so. How did you know I wasn't at home?'

'Because you sound as if you're outside. I can hear the drizzle …'

'That's well heard,' I said, impressed.

'… and I've just spoken to the lass, who said you'd gone out.'

'I'm starting back now. I'll see you soon.'

As I turned for home, a dented black Mercedes drove past and stopped just outside Big Mama's. A sturdy man, undoubtedly Marco Jones, got out and walked into the canteen. Again I forgot to note the car's number plate.

I was almost certain it was the same car that had taken away the man who'd punched me, and, other than its damaged front, it could easily have been the one from which I'd been shot. Besides, Marco was a strong man with big hands who owned an air rifle. Then I remembered his strange reaction at the door of Keeper's Cottage. Had that been guilt? I wondered who owned the Mercedes, because whoever it was must have known what was going on. Perhaps it was Marco's mum – Hobbes had said she was a formidable woman. There again, the evidence for someone else being involved was purely circumstantial, and it could easily just have been Marco who had it in for me, though I couldn't think of anything I'd done to upset him. My review of Big Mama's had been generally favourable, since the food there had been good and wholesome and I'd marked it as one of the best in the Cotswolds for informal friendly dining.

I was within sight of home when Hobbes's little car drew up by the kerb. He leapt out, grinning. I wondered why he'd phoned me for help, when Mrs Goodfellow could just as easily move the dogs. Perhaps she was too busy cooking.

'I'll unleash the beast!' he said, walking round to open the passenger door.

Fenella Nibblet, carrying a huge white sports bag, emerged like a balloon squeezing from a box and stood up, wheezing and groaning.

Aghast at his lack of manners, I'd already opened my mouth to tell him off when I found myself staring into a pair of piggy eyes in a long hairy face. The boar was sitting on the back seat.

As Hobbes let it out, I noticed it was not restrained by anything other than a red ribbon around what I imagined was its neck. It turned towards me, flicking its tail like Granny Caplet's mad cat used to before it bit me. I eyed up the distance to the front door, estimating my chance of getting inside before I was run down and tusked – somewhere between slim and fat, probably. Running down the street, screaming my head off, was pointless as I'd already experienced its pace. I dithered, and stood still. It trotted towards me, stopped, and sniffed. For some reason, I dropped my hand and stroked its bristly head. It responded like a big friendly dog.

'He likes you,' said Hobbes, walking up the steps to 13 Blackdog Street. 'It seems he's friendly and that he's quite used to being in people's company.'

'I'm almost sorry to lose him,' said Fenella. 'Robinson's rather a lovely pig, and not at all vicious like that horrible Rosie, despite what Bob would have you believe. Well, I'd better be on my way. Thank you for the lift, Mr Hobbes, and I hope your head is better soon.'

'You're welcome, Mrs Nibblet, and thank you for looking after Robinson so well, and, of course, for the nettle tea. I hope you enjoy your Zumba class.'

'Robinson?' I said as she rolled out of earshot.

'That's what she's been calling him. Are you going to help get him in?'

'Of course … umm … how?'

'Say "heel" in a commanding voice, and walk towards me.'

'OK. Will he follow?'

'Maybe. Let's see.'

'Heel!' I said, in my firm voice, the one that Dregs ignored unless it suited him. Taking one end of the ribbon firmly in my left hand, I started walking. To my astonishment, he came with me.

A couple of elderly passers-by gaped.

'That is the ugliest guide dog I've ever seen!' the old man announced in a loud voice. 'Almost as bad as his owner.'

'Shh!' said the woman equally loudly. 'He's blind, not deaf. Don't be rude.'

'Why did they think I was blind?' I asked Hobbes as they walked away.

'I'd suggest it was because of your stick,' said Hobbes, 'and because your black eyes could be mistaken for sunglasses at a distance and when seen with failing eyesight.'

Until then I hadn't realised I was still holding the broomstick. I must have had a vague idea it would come in handy.

'What I want you to do,' said Hobbes, 'is run inside and ensure Dregs and Mimi are out of the way, so I can allow Pig Robinson through to the garden. I expect things would be fine, but interactions between animals can sometimes get a little out of hand. In addition, please ask the lass to go to her room. Have you got that?'

'Yes, but … umm … why does she have to go to her room?'

'Because pigs are scared of her. I don't know why.'

'What does she do to them?'

'Nothing normally, but for some reason they take one look at her and flee, though they're usually fine once they get to know her. The initial meeting can be … messy.'

I nodded, despite not understanding how a powerful boar could be frightened of a skinny old lady. Perhaps it was pheromones or something. I handed the boar's ribbon to Hobbes and headed inside. Mrs Goodfellow was cleaning the kitchen, removing the evidence of butchery, while Dregs and Mimi rushed me as I entered, knocked me down and gave me a right good licking. Though part of me was gratified, the outside parts were wet and sticky. It must have taken a good two minutes before I shook them off and got to my feet, with a chuckling Mrs Goodfellow being of no assistance whatsoever.

'Are you ready yet?' asked Hobbes looking in at the front door.

'Not quite,' I said.

Mimi was entirely relaxed about the situation and seemed pleased to follow me upstairs to Hobbes's room. I expected trouble with Dregs, but he charged up with her and allowed himself to be locked in. It was Mrs Goodfellow, pouting and stubborn, who had to be coaxed.

'It's not my fault I frighten them,' she said.

'No, I'm sure it isn't, but he asked me to ask you to go to your room until he's got Robinson in the garden.'

'Robinson, dear?'

'No, Robinson Pig. Mrs Nibblet named it.'

'After the Beatrix Potter character, I presume,' said the old girl.

'She was a writer, yes?' I said, displaying my literary gem like a medal.

'Well done, dear. I suspect that was the last book Fenella read.'

'Can I bring him in now?' Hobbes yelled from the front door.

'Not quite. I still have to move something.'

'All right, dear,' said Mrs Goodfellow and sighed. 'I'll go.'

I went to the front door as soon as I heard her in her bedroom, and in burst the boar. Then came Hobbes and between us we managed to steer a course to the kitchen, without any mishap, other than when I trod in Dregs's water bowl. My squelching feet seemed to amuse the boar, and we got him through the back door into the garden.

'That was easier than I thought,' said Hobbes, strolling out after him.

'It certainly was,' I said, standing in the doorway, watching as Robinson started to explore his new home.

'That's a fine animal,' said Mrs Goodfellow, leaning from her window.

Robinson squealed, a sound like a knife on a shiny plate but much louder, did an about turn, and rushed towards me, trying to get inside. Unable to shut the door in time, I tried to block him. He brushed me aside and I had a horrible thought that the front door was still open and that we'd lose him again. Acting on impulse, I grabbed his tail, there being few other handholds on a pig, but his momentum was far too much, and he jerked me off my feet onto my front. I slid easily across the kitchen floor, feeling, I assumed, the warm glow of friction on my belly as Robinson, clearly under the illusion that he was still a dainty little piglet, ran straight for the kitchen table, apparently believing he could fit beneath.

He couldn't. His ridged back hit the table hard. For a moment it skittered in front of us until, snagging against a chair, it toppled onto its side. Squealing, Robinson kept going, the table in front like a bulldozer, scooping chairs and the kitchen bin towards the sitting room. How he knew where to go was a puzzle since the table must have blocked his vision, but, fortunately, the whole lot wedged in the kitchen doorway. Hobbes vaulted over us, miraculously not braining himself on the door jamb, and slammed the front door shut.

'Well held, Andy,' he said, 'though you clearly find pig handling is a drag. You can let him go now, and I'll take it from here.' He dropped to his knees and whispered into the pig's ear, while stroking its back with unusual gentleness, until it quietened down.

I was very glad to let go, for my shoulders felt as if they were about to pop from their sockets, and my hands were tired and stiff. Although I hadn't been bitten or trampled, I suspected I'd picked up any number of bruises to add to my tally. Still, I was pleased with myself, until I became aware of a pungent new aroma that was overwhelming the cooking smells and the normal odour of Hobbes.

'Could you clear up in here?' he asked, 'while I take him outside again.'

'All right,' I said, thinking it would be a small job, just putting the kitchen furniture back where it had been.

The smell was getting stronger, my shirtfront was feeling clammy, and I realised the warm glow I'd experienced had not been the result of friction, but Robinson's lamentable lack of bodily control. I was horribly plastered and a smudged brown trail crossed the kitchen, charting our progress.

Despite trying to convince myself that he'd only meant for me to clear up the furniture, I knew what I had to do, and could have kicked myself for having agreed so readily, though I felt it would be some re-payment for all his generosity. Drawing a deep breath, which was a mistake in the circumstances, I gritted my teeth and set to work with bucket, rags and cleaning materials, making occasional forays to the back door for fresh air. Most of the time I spent on my knees, scrubbing and rubbing, and it took me about twenty minutes before I was reasonably satisfied. When I'd finished, I stood up to admire my work, hoping it would be good enough for Mrs Goodfellow, and wondering where she'd got to.

'Well done, dear,' she said, from the stove, where she was stirring something in a pot.

'You were upstairs,' I pointed out when my voice came back under control. 'Now you're here. How?'

'I came to check on the dog meat,' she said, which was no answer at all.

'Robinson is settled,' Hobbes announced, walking in. 'I've given him some water, but he'll need feeding soon.'

'What would he like to eat?' asked Mrs Goodfellow.

'Acorns,' I said, vaguely remembering something I'd seen on telly.

'Where am I going to get acorns from at this time of year?'

'Wild boars do indeed eat acorns in the autumn,' said Hobbes with a smile, 'but they're omnivorous, so they'll eat nearly anything. At the moment, I would suggest a large bowl of porridge.'

'Do they prefer it with salt or sugar, or both?' asked Mrs Goodfellow, pulling a sack of oats from a cupboard.

'Neither, I think,' said Hobbes. 'We can also feed him bread and vegetables and meat scraps, which should keep him going until I can sort out where he's going to live.'

'So, he's not going to be here permanently?' I asked, relieved.

'No. He needs space, and it won't be long before I have to start preparing the soil for my spuds and aubergines and flowers. He'll have to be gone by then, or he'll dig the lot up when he's rooting around, and I wouldn't like that. Besides, I suspect he belongs to someone. He's nervous around people, though he's clearly used to them. I suspect ill treatment.'

'Like with Mimi?' I said.

He nodded. 'You'd better change your shirt, and you can let the dogs out now.'

I ran upstairs, opened the door and found the pair of them in a rather compromising position. Dregs glared, until, muttering profuse apologies, I retreated and shut them back in.

'They're not ready yet,' I announced, when I returned downstairs, washed and in a fresh shirt and trousers. 'I'd give them another few minutes.'

'I see from your delicate blush what they were up to,' said Mrs Goodfellow. 'Do you think Dregs will make a good father?'

'Umm … I don't know.'

'I don't suppose Mr Marco Jones and his boss will be best pleased,' said Hobbes. 'Whatever Dregs's merits might be, he is by no stretch of the imagination a pedigree Samoyed.'

'You mean the pups won't be worth anything?' I said.

'Well, they won't fetch anywhere near as much money, though I'm sure they'll be fine dogs.'

'Assuming there are any,' said Mrs Goodfellow. 'For all we know Dregs is firing blanks.'

'What makes you say that?' I asked. 'He seems fit and well in every other respect.'

'Yes, dear, but he hasn't fathered any other pups, though I suppose that may just be because he's incredibly ugly.'

'He's not that bad,' I said, defending him, and wishing the conversation would move towards other matters.

The dogs joined us, Dregs smug and Mimi looking extraordinarily coy. How they'd let themselves out of Hobbes's room was beyond me. It was possible I hadn't shut the door properly, but I reckoned Dregs had been showing off.

Mrs Goodfellow put down some stewed venison for them. Dregs, ever the connoisseur, ate slowly as if savouring every bite; Mimi gulped hers down within seconds and then started on his, growling and snarling when he attempted to regain possession of his bowl. He sat back on his haunches, pained by her ill manners, and then sighed as if realising that allowances had to be made for her previous privations, and lack of education. Fortunately, he wasn't hungry for too long since she soon retired to the blanket Hobbes had laid out for her, and seconds were served.

After a really beefy supper, feeling gloriously full and slightly drowsy, I was sipping tea while Hobbes browsed a book on pig management.

'Billy asked me to tell you something,' I said, having just remembered.

'Go on,' said Hobbes, looking up.

'He … umm … said to tell you that Featherlight told him to tell you that he'd seen a pair of them in Ride Park. He said Featherlight said you'd know what he meant.'

'When was this?'

'Earlier.'

'Clearly,' he said. 'Today?'

'Yes.'

'Morning or afternoon?'

'Afternoon.'

'Thank you, though you should have told me earlier. I'm going to see Featherlight. Are you coming?'

He dropped his book on the coffee table, slurped his tea, and stood up, reaching for his raincoat. As I got ready, he removed the bandage from his head, revealing a wound as long as the cleaver. Though the surrounding hair was bristly with congealed blood, it seemed to bother him less than a paper cut did me.

'Come along,' he said and opened the front door.

Dregs joined us, looking keen, which I suspected was only because Mimi had gone to sleep. Then, our breath steaming like old-fashioned locomotives, we stepped into the night.

'There's going to be a sharp frost tonight,' said Hobbes, sniffing the air and yomping towards the Feathers.

'That'll be fun with all the standing water,' I said.

He nodded. 'The problem is that some people will always try to skate on ice, no matter how thin, and there'll be accidents. I've already got enough bodies to deal with, though I've seen no recent sign of Matilda Kielder, which might be good news.'

'Oh, her.' I felt a blush develop and spread. 'Umm … you know I mentioned a girl saving me?'

'I remember.'

'The thing is … umm … there was a bit more I should have said. We went for a coffee and she started kissing me, though I didn't want her to, and since then someone's been putting up photographs of the two of us. I've been tearing them down, but Mrs Goodfellow saw the last lot, and she reckons the girl in the picture was Matilda Kielder.'

'Actually, I've seen some of them. You were very clear, but not much of her was showing.'

'Yes, but this last lot were different. You could see her face and my … umm … embarrassment.'

'Interesting,' said Hobbes, continuing to walk at an uncomfortable pace.

'The old girl recognised her right away. She said she'd seen her once.'

'She did, maybe thirty years ago, when … when there was some trouble. The lass actually stopped her murdering a man, by hitting her with a mouldy grapefruit before too much harm was done. I think, Andy, you had a lucky escape.'

'Thirty years ago? No, that can't be right. She must be thinking of someone else. The girl I kissed, umm … I mean the girl who kissed me … couldn't have been more than twenty.'

'The truth is, Andy, that there's something about them that confounds the senses.'

'Them?'

'People of her type.'

'Which people? Who are they?' I asked, putting on a spurt to catch up.

'I don't know.'

'Well they must be called something.'

'I suppose so,' he said, 'but putting a label on a group of people doesn't help much since they're all individuals with their own stories and behaviours. Featherlight, however, has all sorts of names for them, some of them mythical, many of them unrepeatable.'

'He called them the sly ones.'

'Sly may be apt, though it has connotations,' he said, looking troubled. 'Perhaps he's right since the word encompasses cunning and covert as well as sneaky. What I know about them is that individuals and small groups turn up every now and then, and there's often trouble when they do, though not every time, and it's not always them that start it. I've found that, while some of them have carried out the most dreadful acts, others are quite decent.'

'You mean they're good law-abiding citizens?'

'Absolutely not.' He shook his head. 'I don't think any of them have regard for our human laws. The one known as Matilda Kielder is, unfortunately, of the dreadful sort. I suspect she ate someone on Hedbury Common recently, but there wasn't enough left to identify him, not even for DNA testing. She'd sucked him dry.'

'I know what you mean. She was all over me, and I couldn't do anything about it,' I said, though thinking back to that morning in Café Nerd, I wasn't absolutely sure I couldn't have done a little more to get her off. However, such was my story, and I intended sticking to it.

'I'm sure you tried,' said Hobbes, 'but if you hadn't been interrupted when you were, she'd have taken you somewhere quiet and …'

'I don't want to know any more,' I said, shuddering, although I was sweating, despite the falling temperatures.

'It's probably best not to,' he said.

Since, according to Mrs Goodfellow, even Hobbes, with his hippopotamus-thick skin and years of police experience, had been appalled by whatever Matilda Kielder had done, I was starting to believe I really had been lucky. Yet I was puzzled, since he seemed to know more about her people than he was willing to divulge and I found his attitude worrying. He seemed nervous, if not scared, and that was almost unheard of.

Normally he relished danger and enjoyed pitting himself against any villainy, the bigger the better. That, and the thought that she was still out there, and might be anywhere, left me with churning guts and a dry mouth.

A light came on in a window across the street, and I glimpsed a woman's face before she pulled down the blinds. She didn't look anything like Sally, yet how could I be sure now? I caught myself staring at every passer-by, just in case I saw anything to alarm me, which had the effect that everything alarmed me. Even so, part of me could only think of her as sweet and pretty, and I struggled to dislike her, even as Matilda Kielder.

I was twitching and starting like a nervous rabbit by the time we reached the Feathers, where a chalked sign on the door announced it was quiz night, which was odd, as Featherlight didn't believe in entertainment that involved him handing out prizes. As we entered the warm fug, his voice was booming out from the bar on which he was sitting, a chipped pint mug wedged between a couple of his bellies. 'What do you mean there's no such country? I assure you there is. I've been there.'

'But it hasn't been called that for decades,' said a familiar posh voice, the middle-sized one of the rugby playing students. The one called Guy.

'Well, aren't you a clever dick,' said Featherlight, 'but the country is still there even if the name's changed, and the question is the same. What's the capital city of Upper Volta?'

'It's Burkina Faso now.'

'Wrong. It's Ouagadougou.'

'That's the capital of Burkina Faso and you've just told us the answer,' said Guy, shaking his head.

'You're an overweight idiot!' the one known as James sneered.

Featherlight twitched, his face darkening like the evening sky before a storm.

'You can't even run a proper quiz, never mind this so-called pub of yours,' James continued. 'You couldn't even organise the proverbial in a brewery. What a retard!'

'Absolutely right,' said the one called Toby, and deliberately poured his beer onto what had once been the carpet. 'This place is the pits, your customers are swine, and you,' he pointed at Featherlight, 'are an absolute ar …'

But we never heard the pearls of wisdom Toby intended to cast before us, for Featherlight lurched to his feet, the mug popping from his belly folds like a cork from a champagne bottle and arcing across the room with a beery comet tail. Billy, who was already sporting the helmet he'd taken to wearing when trouble was brewing, caught it as Featherlight, snorting like an enraged bull, lunged in a blur of swinging arms. He demolished all three students before they'd even managed to get to their feet. Then, one by one, he lifted them by the seat of their trousers and the necks of their shirts and hurled them into the street, where they lay, groaning and spurting blood from flattened noses. Although Hobbes frowned, he did not intervene.

'Quiz Night is cancelled,' Featherlight announced, his words evidently a relief to the regulars who could return to their normal pastimes of serious drinking, darts, and incoherent arguing about darts and drink.

'What can I get you gentlemen?' asked Billy, removing his helmet and walking beneath the flap to behind the bar.

'A pint of your best bitter for me,' said Hobbes, a pint of lager for Andy, and a shandy for Dregs, who's still an invalid. Have one for yourself if you'd like, and one for your boss.'

'Thank you,' said Billy, reaching for a bowl with his tool.

Featherlight came back grinning, his big brown teeth a dental horror show. 'Before you start, I'm still giving my customers what they want, and I left those students with a couple of questions to answer.'

'What questions?' I asked.

'Where am I? And what hit me?'

'Still they were correct in saying that Upper Volta is now known as Burkina Faso,' said Hobbes, accepting a glass from Billy, and putting the bowl of shandy down for Dregs, who lapped it up noisily and messily.

'I know,' said Featherlight, 'but those blockheads have been trying to provoke me since I started running the quiz, and I just needed an excuse to rid myself of them.'

'Do they come here often?' asked Hobbes.

'They've been visiting now and again since last year, and, as students go, they weren't too bad at first. However, since their blasted rugby team started doing well they've become increasingly arrogant and aggressive, and they've taken to throwing their weight about and causing trouble.'

'I thought you liked trouble,' I said, and took a slurp of lager.

'Only if it's fair trouble, and I won't have them pushing the old timers around.'

Once again he'd taken me by surprise. Beneath his horrible exterior, there were traces of something decent, though they could only rarely be glimpsed. His bad temper had vanished like a gust of wind, unlike the gust of wind he released on sitting down, which hung around like a smog cloud.

'It's interesting that their behaviour changed when they became successful,' said Hobbes.

Billy nodded, handed a glass to Featherlight and began pouring a beer for himself. 'I've seen that sort of behaviour in body-builders when they started taking anabolic steroids.'

'I reckon you're right,' said Hobbes. 'I confiscated a bottle off them, and when I've got time I intend to ask them politely who their supplier is.'

'No need,' said Billy. 'It's that thick bloke from Big Mama's. He came in here, trying to sell his stuff, but the boss kicked him out.'

'And it was a good kick,' said Featherlight, laughing. 'He must have flown ten feet through the air, and I had to buy a new pair of boots.'

'I suspected it might be him,' said Hobbes. 'Still, I'll have to get proof and some other witnesses … or perhaps he might be inclined to confess.'

'Actually,' I said, 'I might be a witness. I think I saw him taking a wad of money from one of those students in Golums Logons. I didn't know who he was at the time, and it didn't cross my mind that it might be for drugs.'

'A mind as sharp as a banana,' said Featherlight. 'It amazes me he can walk and breathe at the same time.'

'He has his lucid moments,' said Hobbes with a laugh. 'He did remember to tell me your message … eventually. He said you'd spotted a pair of them. Is that correct?'

'Yep. They were in Ride Park this morning. One male and one female. There'll be trouble, mark my words. There always is when the bloody sly ones turn up.'

'Who and what are they?' I asked.

'As to who, I don't know,' said Featherlight, scowling. 'As to what they are, all I know is they're dangerous troublemakers.'

'Umm … what sort of trouble?'

'Big trouble,' said Featherlight, banging down his glass on the bar with such force that it shattered and beer and blood spilled. 'Dammit! I've just mugged myself.' He held up his hand and glared at the gore dripping from his thumb as if he could cauterize it with a look. 'Give me a towel and make it fast.'

Billy wrapped one of the filthy rags that served as bar towels around Featherlight's hand.

'Thanks,' he grunted.

'At least your glass was half-empty,' I remarked.

'It was more like half-full. Pour me another. These sly ones make me nervous.'

'You're bleeding through,' Hobbes observed, as blood dripped onto the floor. 'You need to get that cut stitched. Have you got a needle and thread?'

'There's some by the till. Shall I do it?' said Billy. He pulled a black cotton reel from a canvas bag and threaded a needle.

'Make it sew,' said Featherlight.

'You'll feel a bit of a prick,' he said, taking Featherlight's massive paw in his own little hand.

'No more than I do now,' said Featherlight with a grin. 'It was a stupid thing to do.'

Although I had to look away as Billy went to work, the sound of sewing still reached my ears and travelled all the way down to my stomach. I had to put my drink down and concentrate very hard on not jettisoning my supper. Featherlight never made a sound throughout the procedure, and Hobbes merely commented on the neat job Billy was making. I took his word for it, studiously looking away, even when it was all over and Billy poured a tot from a bottle of what Featherlight laughably claimed was whisky over the wound.

Featherlight grunted his thanks, and continued talking. 'If I've seen a pair of them, I'll bet there are others.'

'You'd win your bet,' said Hobbes. 'Andy had a run in with the one that calls herself Matilda Kielder. She's his poster girl.'

'The one Caplet was snogging? He's lucky to have escaped intact.'

'Very lucky,' I said, quivering, and still a little queasy and faint.

'If you'd gone with her,' said Featherlight, 'she'd have got you alone somewhere and then she would've taken your …'

Shortly afterwards, cold water splashed across my face, and I sat up spluttering, wondering why I was on the floor with an audience of grinning faces. Featherlight was laughing, and when I remembered what he'd been saying I came close to passing out again.

He turned back to Hobbes. 'So, this Matilda Kielder has eaten someone again, and has escaped justice so far by using her feminine wiles. Is that correct?'

Hobbes, looking as grave as I'd ever seen him, nodded.

'There's something strange in this,' said Billy.

'Stranger than man-eaters?' I asked, trying to stand, but finding my legs were still infirm.

Billy shrugged. 'It's just that I'd assumed the photos were taken to blackmail Andy and that she was part of the plot, but she doesn't sound the sort of girl who'd do that.'

'You're right,' said Hobbes, 'but don't mistake her for a girl. I've known of this one since the Hedbury Horror of 1956.'

Featherlight creased up. 'Caplet's been snogging pensioners. I always knew he was weird.'

'I didn't know she was that old,' I said, 'and, what's more, I didn't snog her. She snogged me.'

'Poor innocent little lamb,' said Featherlight. 'She took advantage of him.'

'She did, and I can't see why that's so funny.' I scowled at the grinning faces, although it caused hysteria throughout the pub.

I stood up with all the dignity I could muster in the circumstances, though the effect was somewhat marred when my feet slipped in Featherlight's spilt beer and I came as close as I ever could, and far closer than I'd ever wanted, to doing the splits. The laughter would have been unbearable pre-Hobbes, but I'd developed a sort of immunity. I knew I had a tendency to being a clumsy oaf, but I wasn't always, and it didn't always matter, and when I realised I hadn't torn anything, I found I was laughing with the rest of them.

'Was there anything else?' asked Hobbes when order had been restored.

'Only that I reckon they might be living in Ride Park, and I reckon that heptagram was a declaration of war or something like that,' said Featherlight.

'There again, it might just have been a warning, like Keep off the Grass,' said Hobbes, 'or, for all we know, it was a message to one of them.'

There were times when I was confused, and this was one of them. Danger was close, and both Featherlight and Hobbes were worried, yet they wouldn't, or couldn't, say who these sly ones were or why they were such a danger. Since the pair of them could look after themselves, I felt it reasonable to be alarmed. I found one possible atom of comfort: it seemed unlikely that Sally, or Matilda Kielder, or whatever she was really called, had come after me specifically. Yet, the posters were still going up, and I had no idea who was behind them. Was the photographer responsible? Unlikely, since I hadn't recognised him. It seemed more probable that he'd been a hired gun, sent out to catch me doing something embarrassing, but by whom? And what about the man with the big hands, and, more to the point, fists? Was he the same one who'd punched me, or had that been yet another hired goon? As I thought, I came to suspect the Mercedes driver might be behind it all, but why?

One thing remained certain; I was in a mess and really did have to extricate myself before Daphne returned, though, if I couldn't, I retained a hope that Hobbes and Mrs Goodfellow might persuade her I'd been brave and lucky to have escaped Matilda Kielder's clutches.

Hobbes was saying goodbye. I supped up my lager and, having nodded my farewell, followed him out.

'What now?' I asked as we strode into the night.

'I'm going after them.'

'The ones Featherlight saw?'

He nodded.

'Why are they so dangerous?'

'They might not be, since not all of them are malicious, though I doubt I could persuade Featherlight of that, since one was responsible for the death of his wife and unborn child.'

'Featherlight was married?' I gasped, half assuming he was joking, even though his mood was grim.

'He was, and he only took to the drink after losing them. Before then he'd been a fine police constable. One of the best.'

'What happened?'

'Murder, and that's as much as I'm prepared to say.'

'Did you catch who did it?'

'No, but some of the killer's people did, and carried out their own form of justice.'

'But who are they?'

'Hidden people … an ancient people … cunning people … they're outside the law.'

'Outlaws?'

'An outlaw was formerly someone declared outside the protection of the law, but these folk don't recognise our laws and have always been outside them, though they apparently have some sort of code that most adhere to. I understand the term outlaw is now used for anyone who consistently violates the law, but these people are simply not a part of it.'

'I don't understand,' I said, catching up as Hobbes and Dregs waited on the kerb for a car to pass.

'Nor do I. All I know is that certain populations in this land have always been here and have always gone about their business with little or no regard for humans, whom they treat as upstarts. Normally, fortunately, there is little interaction, and when there is it usually turns out badly for us.'

I was surprised and a little touched that Hobbes, for all his 'unhumanity', regarded himself as one of us. It was reassuring that he was on our side.

'And yet on the whole they don't seek conflict,' he continued, as we crossed towards Goat Street. 'Problems begin when one or more turn renegade and live among us. You see even the best of them have traditionally regarded humans as little more than animals, while the renegades have tended to treat them like vermin.'

'But what about you?' I asked. 'I mean to say, you're … umm … not exactly human. How do they treat you?'

'Much the same. Now, what do you want to do? Come with us? Or would you prefer to go home?'

'Where are you going?'

'To Ride Park.'

'It'll be locked.'

'Probably, but that's no problem.'

'I'll … umm … think about it,' I said.

'Be quick then, for here is where you must decide. You can either turn right and go home, or turn left and follow us. It might be dangerous.'

'I want to … go with you … I think.' I said, certain my decision was not rational, but too intrigued to turn away, even though my brain kept reminding me of all the important things I should have been doing.

'Good,' said Hobbes. 'Now, follow, and keep quiet.'

We hastened along Hedbury Road, Dregs hard on Hobbes's heels, me puffing along behind, already regretting my foolish curiosity. Keeper's Cottage was all in darkness. I assumed Marco was working in Big Mama's. The park gate was locked, and the park was apparently secure behind its stone wall.

Hobbes and Dregs stopped. So did I, though only in my head. In practice, my feet slid from under me, and I went down with a thud and an oath.

'Careful,' said Hobbes, 'it's icy.'

'I noticed,' I whispered, trying to divert Dregs from licking me where I lay.

'Get up,' said Hobbes, 'and keep quiet.'

I got to my feet, trying to stay away from slippery bits, which wasn't easy. 'What are we going to do now?'

'Go in.'

'How?' I asked, though I should have known better.

'Like this,' he said, grabbing me round the waist and hurling me skywards.

Had I not been accustomed to this type of treatment, and had I not been warned to keep quiet, I would have shrieked. Instead, I kept my mouth clamped until I landed atop the wall, when a sound somewhere between oof and a whimper escaped.

'Shhh!' he hissed.

Looking over my shoulder into the park, I could make out little, though a silvery glow filtering through trees on the horizon suggested the moon was on the rise, and the coal black sky scintillated with myriad stars. Their beauty was reassuring and calming.

'Catch!' said Hobbes.

There was a muted yelp, and Dregs was in my arms, the impact coming close to knocking me backwards from my perch, but before I could think of complaining, Hobbes was squatting by my side, sniffing the air.

'What now?' I asked.

'We jump down, of course.'

'Umm … it's too dark to see. I'll hurt myself.'

'I'll lower you. Keep a tight grip on Dregs.'

I started to point out that, since Dregs was a born wriggler, I'd need both arms to hold him, and, in consequence, had nothing by which I could be lowered. However, my hypothesis was disproved by his picking me up by my coat collar, dangling me like a rag doll, and lowering me to the ground. He was at my side before I could even put Dregs down.

'Follow me,' said Hobbes, 'and quickly.'

'Of course, but, please, not too quickly, I don't want to get lost.'

'You can't possibly get lost in Ride Park. It's far too small.'

'It's nearly four thousand acres!'

'Exactly.'

As someone who'd gone astray in many places, I wasn't convinced. A particularly traumatic incident from schooldays came to mind when, engrossed in desperate last minute revision, I'd walked into a storeroom instead of the classroom two floors below where I was due to take a maths exam. Although it shouldn't have been a problem, the door handle had come off in my hand, and by the time anyone heard my cries for help, the exam was long over. The worst part had been trying to explain to Father why I'd failed maths, despite two terms of after-school tutoring.

'Hurry up,' Hobbes hissed.

I followed the darker darkness ahead. The park walls and trees blocked virtually all light and, although I had no fear of the night as such, I was nervous of things that might be out in it.

A scream, as if someone was being cruelly murdered, nearly stopped my heart, and I blundered blindly forwards, only to run headlong into something as solid as a tree.

'Careful, Andy,' said Hobbes softly, as I held my head, 'or you'll hurt yourself.'

'Did you hear that?' I whispered, pushing Dregs's shaggy head away from my groin, and thinking it a stupid question. Of course he'd heard. So, why was he not rushing to help the poor victim?

'D'you mean the fox?'

'Oh. Sorry. Umm … where exactly are we going?'

'Towards the shelter we found.'

'Are we nearly there yet?'

'Nearly. Keep up.' He walked away, quieter than a flying owl.

I did keep up, refusing to become distracted by the churning sea of thoughts that kept vying for attention, some of which were actually most important, but not just then. We weaved through trees for maybe twenty minutes before I heard something.

'What's that?' I whispered, feeling strangely disoriented, and putting it down to the lager. Perhaps Featherlight had stopped watering it down.

'Singing. Now, keep quiet.'

As we continued, I began to make out two voices. Their song was soft and sad and beautiful, though the words, if any, meant nothing to me.

There was a flicker of orange light ahead. I gasped.

'Shhh!' said Hobbes, holding out an arm to stop me. 'It's just a fire. Stay here with Dregs, and I'll see who it belongs to, though I suspect we know.'

Handing me Dregs's lead, at the far end of which Dregs was alert and bristling, he slipped away into the darkness, invisible and silent. We waited nervously. Well, I was nervous, with any unexpected sound setting my heart rate to overdrive, and there were many unexpected sounds. I regretted my rash decision, wishing I was warm and safe with a cup of tea back at Blackdog Street rather than shivering in Ride Park. Yet, maybe it wasn't quite as dark as it had been, for the edge of the moon, only a couple of days past its fullest, was peeping through the branches and the utter blackness was replaced by a faint silvery twinkle. It might have eased my stretched nerves, had it not enabled me to make out dark shapes, walking on two legs, like twisted little people with wedge-shaped heads, their sharp teeth glinting in narrow mouths, their eyes gleaming black voids. They were about the size of cats, and there were dozens of them, not actually close, but not so far away that I could watch with detachment. Dregs, however, did not react in the slightest, not even when one, approaching much closer, nearly brushed the tip of his nose.

'Come along, Andy,' said Hobbes, his voice seeming to come from a great distance.

Although I was feeling disconnected from my body, I followed, shaking my head, trying to clear it.

'What are they?' I asked at last, my voice slow and slurred.

'What are what?' asked Hobbes.

'The small walking things with the teeth!'

'I didn't see anything. Perhaps they were rabbits, or maybe you were dreaming.'

'I wasn't … I don't think,' I said, though I dimly recalled similar childhood nightmares after my sister died.

'Well, whatever you saw, they're not here now are they?'

I looked around, but it was still too dark to see much, and there was nothing I wouldn't have expected. 'No.'

'Good. Now, shift yourself and come and say hello. I'll introduce you.'

I followed him into the light with some trepidation.

'Andy,' said a honeyed female voice. 'How nice of you to drop in. The no eyebrow look really suits you.'

'It is indeed a great pleasure,' said a deep, cultured male voice.

'Mr and … umm … Miss Elwes!'

'Aubrey and Hilda, please,' said Aubrey. 'We're old friends now.'

'So, you do know each other,' said Hobbes, nodding.

'Of course. Aubrey and Hilda were our downstairs neighbours, until that horrible night.'

'Which is no doubt why you're living out here,' said Hobbes. 'Does Colonel Squire know?'

'I very much doubt it,' said Hilda with a musical laugh.

'But why in the park?' I asked. 'Couldn't you find somewhere warm and comfortable? It's cold out here, and scary.' As if to emphasise my point, I shivered.

'We're fine,' said Aubrey. 'Come on in, pull up a chair, and warm yourself at the fire.'

I did as he suggested, sitting down on a most comfortable and enticing armchair, which part of my brain registered as being a little out of place, and warmed my hands at the blaze. Dregs lay in front of me, and we basked in the warmth and the light and the night. The little horrors felt a long way away.

'Can I get you a drink?' asked Hilda, her voice as rich and sweet as melted fudge.

Her eyes were sparkling like starlight. I gazed into them and nodded. 'Yes, please.'

'What would you like?'

'Umm … if you've got it, I'd like a sweet hot chocolate … umm … please.'

'Such beautiful manners in this one,' she remarked, making me smile, as I remembered smiling when Miss Morgan, my favourite ever teacher, used to say nice things to me when I was seven. 'I'll fetch your drink.'

Hobbes and Aubrey were talking, and although I could have reached out and touched them, their voices came to me as if from some distant place, and for a moment I could have sworn I saw them on some ice-clad mountain, frozen under starlight. Yet, when I shook my head and looked again, they were sitting at my side by the fire. Hilda, her smile as bright as a full moon, handed me my drink, and I took it eagerly, mumbling thanks, feeling even more like a child.

'I hope it's not too hot or too sweet,' she said.

I sipped and it was perfect: warm without scalding, sweet without being sickly, and it was as fragrant as spring flowers and as delicious as … Before I could put my thoughts into words, I was drinking it, almost oblivious to anything else, except for Hilda's beauty, and Aubrey's majesty. Hobbes, his voice as harsh as a crow's, looked like a deformed ape, and I knew I was just a silly little boy, with scabby knees and runny nose, who was only tolerated because they were so kind. I tried to listen to the grown-ups' spellbinding conversation, as I had in church when the man in the black dress would talk about things my young mind couldn't comprehend. The names Solomon Slugg, and Matilda Kielder came up now and again, amongst others that meant little to me. Aubrey spoke of his family, and Hilda of laws and punishment, while I listened, spellbound by the beauty of their voices that rose and fell harmoniously like music. I was glad Hobbes only rarely spoiled it by interrupting. The fire was hot, the drink heady, and the night blurred into dreamscapes of strange lands and alien skies.

I became aware of Hobbes's voice and found we were walking under streetlights. Dregs was at my side.

'Are you all right now, Andy?' Hobbes asked.

I thought for a moment and nodded. 'Umm … where am I?'

'Walking along Hedbury Road. I'm glad you're back, and I'm sorry I exposed you to that. I hadn't realised they had so much power.'

'What happened?' I asked, some of the fuzzy heat in my head dispersing, leaving me shivering and disoriented. Everything felt wrong, as if I'd fallen asleep as a child in my bed and woken as an adult in a cold street.

'You fell for their charm,' said Hobbes.

'What do you mean?'

'You were enthralled. I've seen it affect people before, but never quite so strongly. Perhaps it was the moonlight and music.'

'I thought I was somewhere else. Did she put something in my chocolate? Some sort of drug?'

'You were gone before that, and she only gave you cold water.'

'No, it was definitely hot chocolate. Wasn't it comfortable in the woods? It was so much better than I could ever have imagined. That armchair was so soft.'

'Imagined is the right word,' said Hobbes. 'You were sitting on a log.'

I shook my head but, if I concentrated really hard, part of me knew he was right. As so often in my excursions with him, I was bewildered, so I just kept walking, while the sense of being detached, of being intoxicated, faded slowly.

'Were they trying to harm me?' I asked, as we turned into Blackdog Street.

'I don't believe so,' he said, 'but you just happen to be sensitive. According to what they told me, they have no desire to cause any mischief to the general public, and I have no reason to doubt them.'

'Okay … good, but … umm … does that mean they do wish to cause mischief to somebody?'

'They are hunting two individuals of their sort.'

A glimmer of their conversation returned. 'Solomon Slugg and Matilda Kielder?'

'Yes, though those aren't their real names. They never use their own.'

When we reached home at last, Dregs bounded up the steps and waited impatiently to be let in. Whether that was because he wished to escape the frost or because he wished to reacquaint himself with Mimi wasn't clear.

By the time Hobbes opened the door, I was yawning my head off, and went straight upstairs, flopping face-first onto the bed as soon as I reached my room. I was probably asleep before I landed.

When I awoke, I was tucked up in bed and wearing pyjamas. My mouth was dry and tasted as if I'd been eating compost. Memories of the previous evening, or at least the bit after we arrived in the park, were vague and elusive, and it took me several minutes to grasp any of them; huge chunks had slipped away for good, or ill. One thing was crystal clear – there really was something fascinating about Hilda Elwes, who I remembered as sparkling like spring flowers in sunshine after gentle rain, and yet I couldn't quite picture her, and was uncertain whether she was tall, or petite, blonde or brunette, fair skinned or dark. I couldn't envisage Aubrey either, though I didn't try so hard. Even so, the nobility and dignity he exuded had the power to make me feel small, and grateful he'd paid any attention to my unworthy presence.

Fortunately, the scent of frying sausages had sufficient power to bring me back to Blackdog Street. I hurried through my ablutions, dressed, and headed for the kitchen, where Mrs Goodfellow was turning delicately spiced Sorenchester Old Spot sausages in an enormous cast-iron frying pan. A pan of mushrooms simmered alongside and, awaiting transformation was a saucepan of beaten eggs. Though I was nearly always hungry in the mornings, that particular morning I was ravenous and could barely wait.

'Good morning, dear.'

'Good morning,' I replied. 'That smells delicious. Umm … where's Hobbes? And the dogs?'

'Out for a walk. They'll be back soon.' Turning the gas on beneath the eggs, she stirred the pan gently, as I sat, fidgeting and drooling, hoping they wouldn't be long.

They returned with just enough time for Hobbes to wash his hands and sit down before the old girl started dishing up. I had to fend off twice the normal quantity of dogs' tongues before they allowed me to tuck in. Not a word was spoken until we'd finished.

'Last night was interesting,' I said when Mrs Goodfellow was clearing away our plates, 'but I can only recall odd bits.'

'I'm surprised you remember anything at all,' said Hobbes. 'You were in a most peculiar place. They really dazzled you, didn't they?'

'I think so. I saw things that weren't there, even before I met the Elweses, and way before I drank the hot chocolate. It tasted delicious last night, but this morning my memory is only of cold muddy water.'

'They do that to humans, and I don't think it's something they can control, but at least the Elweses, as they call themselves, don't appear to have any malicious intent.'

'I'm confused, because … umm … you say Matilda Kielder is one of them, whatever they are, but she looked nothing like them. I don't think she did, anyway.'

'Of course not,' said Mrs Goodfellow. 'She'd appear to you just as she'd want to appear.'

Hobbes nodded. 'And, unless you normally cavort with strange women as soon as your wife is out of sight, her perceived glamour fascinated you.'

'I … umm … see what you mean. I've never done anything like it before, and I tried to resist, though I didn't do very well. Who, exactly, is she?'

'As far as I can understand, she is what we'd call the Elweses' cousin. They were keeping her under restraint after what she did thirty years ago and before, but she escaped last year. When Aubrey and Hilda tracked her down, they coincidently discovered the one we know as Solomon Slugg, who is another cousin.'

'He's one of them as well? But he looks nothing like the Elweses or Matilda.' Even as I said it, I realised how foolish it was.

'You see him how he wants to be seen. I wonder how he'd appear if you had a clear mind?'

'Do they influence you? Or other animals?' I stopped, realising what I'd just implied.

He shrugged. 'To an extent they do, but I've met them a few times and nowadays I can largely maintain control when they do their thing. At least I can, if I know what I'm going into. However, I was taken unawares, and may have been somewhat deceived by Alvin Elwes, though I had suspicions about him.'

'And who is Alvin Elwes?'

'He's the one we've been referring to as Solomon Slugg.'

'How do you know?'

'The one calling herself Miss Hilda Elwes told me last night, when you were sitting on that log with an idiot smile on your face and burbling about burbots.'

'What is burbots?' I asked, wondering if he was making a joke at my expense.

'They are a type of freshwater fish and are regarded as extinct in this country, though I know a few deep lakes where they still thrive.'

'But I've never heard of them, so how could I have been saying anything?'

'I don't know, but you sounded very familiar with preparing, cooking and eating them,' said Hobbes. 'You recited several recipes.'

I shook my head, but he appeared to mean what he was saying.

'What are you going to do about our visitors?' asked Mrs Goodfellow from just behind my right ear.

'Firstly, I'll question Mr Alvin Elwes, aka Solomon Slugg, since I believe he has committed at least two murders.'

'Has he really?' I asked. 'Who?'

'Septimus Slugg and the real Solomon Slugg.'

'What? No! I thought he was just a bit of a rogue, and an unfortunate politician. How can you tie him to the murders?' Even as I spoke, I had a strong feeling of déjà vu, and knew he was telling the truth, though I couldn't remember why.

'I'll tell you later. Do you want to come and see the fun?'

'I'd like to, but can I make a phone call first? I need to check how Daphne's getting on.'

'If you're quick,' he said. 'I intend taking both dogs, so there won't be much room in the car.'

'You're not planning on arresting Alvin, are you?' I asked as I stood up.

'I might be.'

'But where would you put him if the car's already full?'

'I'll think of something, should the need arise. Now, call your good lady wife, and quickly!'

I hurried to make my call.

The deep, resonant American voice of Mike Parker answered. 'Hi, how can I help you?'

'It's Andy,' I said, wondering why he'd sounded so down.

'Hiya, buddy. I'm afraid we've had some bad news today ...'

I was instantly transformed into panic-stricken Andy. 'What's happened? Is it amoebic dysentery? Is she all right?' I felt as if cold strong hands were twisting my guts into knots.

'Daphne's on the way to Cairo.'

'Cairo hospital?' The panic was rising.

'No, it turns out she only had a nasty tummy bug and she's over it now. She's gotta call in at the university.'

'But why?'

'Because Professor Mahmoud has cancelled the dig – that's our bad news. What we found wasn't what we'd hoped for. It seems to be some sort of nineteenth-century junk store.'

'Not a tomb, then?'

'The prof thinks it might have been built as a tomb, but there's no evidence it was ever used for that purpose. As it happens, there were one or two interesting items among the crap, but it's not even clear whether they're genuine.'

'So, what's happening with Daphne?'

'She'll be heading home soon, and I guess she'll call you when she knows more. There's some paperwork she needs to deal with first, but she should be with you in a day or two, when she can get a flight. I'm in the process of winding down the camp, and paying off the local staff.'

Panic had mutated into euphoria. She was coming home! However, I felt I should say something appropriate, and feeling every bit the hypocrite, injected a tone of sadness into my voice. 'I'm so sorry to hear that.'

'So are we,' said Mike. 'I need to get on now. It's been good to talk to you. So long.'

'So long, Mike. All the best.'

I put the phone down and was in the process of punching the air when panic struck again. I still hadn't sorted out the problem with the posters ... and then there was finding somewhere to live ... and getting the insurance sorted out ... and ...

'Ready?' asked Hobbes.

I nodded, and before I could say anything he'd bundled me and a tangle of dogs from the house, and towards the car, which was white with frost. He scraped the windows with his fingernails, ploughing deep furrows in the ice until they were clear. Since Dregs and Mimi were happy to be together in the back, I was allowed the privilege of riding up front, which, although it felt like a promotion, also meant there was far less in front to crumple and cushion me should we smash into a lamppost. He started the engine.

'Seat belt, Andy.'

I obeyed, and the car sprang forward like a greyhound from a trap, hurtling along

Blackdog Street while I closed my eyes and clung on, one hand gripping the door handle, the other the edge of my seat. It was something to do, though it didn't divert my mind from the imminence of oblivion as the journey, taken at his normal breakneck speed to the usual accompaniment of angry car horns, was unusually terrifying, because of the icy road, which, combined with his sharp braking, mad acceleration and cornering, caused us to skid several times. At some point, I'm sure we careered backwards around a bend.

'Here we are,' said Hobbes at last. 'You can wake up now.'

'I wasn't sleeping, I was resting my eyes,' I said, blinking and looking around.

We were outside the home of Solomon Slugg, or, as I'd now have to think of him, Alvin Elwes. Hobbes and the dogs seemed entirely unconcerned by the ride, and, although I was shaking, I forced myself to appear nonchalant, an act that was growing easier with practice. One day, if I survived long enough, I hoped it would no longer be an act.

Dregs was alert, leaning forward between the seats and blowing dog breath into my face. Mimi looked nervous.

Hobbes glanced back at her. 'It looks like she's been here before. I suspected she might have.'

'Does that mean you think Marco Jones stole her from here?' I asked.

He shook his head. 'I think it more likely that Mr Jones stole her on behalf of his boss, Mr Alvin Elwes.'

'Right. I get it … umm … actually I don't. Why?'

'I had Constable Poll check a few things, and it appears Big Mama's Canteen was in deep financial trouble after Little Papa ran off with the waitress and the cash. Mr Elwes, in the guise of Solomon Slugg, invested in it and, although it undoubtedly saved the business, it left the Joneses heavily in his debt. Marco, who was brought up to be obedient and was heavily under the man's charm, felt he had to do whatever he was told to do, even though he knew some of it was wrong. He kept it from his mother. I think, in his way, he was trying to protect her.'

'That's reassuring.'

'Perhaps, though he still shouldn't have done what he did. However, he is beginning to realise and is already somewhat repentant. He's not a villain at heart, but he will feel a lot more repentant when I have my next little chat with him. At least he now accepts that he's done wrong and I've convinced him that I'm his only chance of staying out of prison, so I expect further cooperation. In addition he admitted to the attacks on you, though he says they were not intended to cause any serious harm.'

'I see … umm … sort of. But why?'

'Later. There's work to be done.'

'So, what are we going to do now?'

'I'm going to have a quick look in there.'

He got out of the car, walked towards the garage, peeped in through the window, and beckoned me over. Standing on tiptoe, I looked. Inside was a Mercedes with tinted windows.

'Do you recognise that?' he asked.

'Umm … I think it might be the one that picked up Marco after he'd hit me, and it could be the one that shot me, if you see what I mean, but it's got a dent in now.'

Hobbes nodded. 'Which I suspect was caused by running into the deer. See how its badge is bent?

'And now, let's have a talk with Mr Alvin Elwes.'

'Do you think he'll even open the door when he sees who it is?'

'The door will open.'

'And then what? Are you going to arrest him?'

'An imminent arrest is certainly a possibility.'

'And then are you going after Sally … Matilda Kielder … umm … Elwes, or whatever her name is?' I asked, feeling that if anyone had a legitimate interest in keeping her off the streets and away from vulnerable young men, it was me.

'If I can find her. She's possibly even more dangerous than her cousin Alvin at the moment, and I might need help. Right, I'm going in. Come along if you want, and bring the dogs if they wish.'

He loped towards the house and rang the doorbell while I released the dogs, who sniffed around in the hedge, their breath smoking. Having no wish to get my head bashed in by Alvin's leaded stick, I stayed back with them and shivered, wondering if he'd used the same weapon to bludgeon the real Solomon Slugg. Yet, even then, I had doubts, for, despite everything I'd been told and seen, I couldn't see him as a killer; he was far too charismatic and pleasant. A distant part of my brain suggested that perhaps he was still exerting an influence, though I had no idea how, since I didn't believe I was the sort of weak-minded individual who could easily fall under someone's spell when I'd been forewarned.

There again, perhaps I was. Who could say what was true with these people? And why did I believe what Hobbes told me? Could it be that he was the one exerting the influence? If so, it certainly wasn't through his charm, though it might explain why I was following him around when I should have been sorting out my own problems.

Hobbes rang again and knocked, shaking the door on its hinges. Neither Alvin Elwes nor his big stick appeared.

'Now what?' I asked.

Hobbes scowled, his features hardening from ugly to gargoyle. He knocked a third time and, after waiting a minute, leant forward and struck the door with both fists. It cracked and burst open, a number of locks and chains hanging uselessly from the jamb.

'Stay here until I tell you it's safe,' he said, charging in, his face unusually grim, and although I feared for Alvin's wellbeing should he be home, I felt in no danger.

I stood in the front garden, keeping an eye on the dogs, until I heard a door crash shut from the back of the house. A moment later, Alvin was running towards me, and I smiled, pleased to see an old friend, though something didn't feel quite right. Perhaps it was because he was wielding a billhook, or was it because his noble features were distorted by murderous rage? It was interesting to speculate, but at the last moment I registered that a maniac was bearing down on me, and my animal body overrode my brain. I fled, despite knowing he was already too close and too fast, and that I'd left it too late. Any moment, I expected to feel the blade bite into my head or back, but I'd reckoned without Mimi.

Until that moment, I'd regarded her as little more than a fluffy bundle of fur. I had to revise that assessment when she transformed into a seething mass of muscle and snarling white fangs and sprang. She knocked me aside as if I were an empty bottle, and

Alvin shrieked like a trapped rabbit. Mimi, growling like a furious bear, struck him in the chest, flattening him. His left hand struggled to hold her off, her teeth inches from his face, but his right hand groped for the billhook he'd dropped. As his fingers closed around the handle, Hobbes strolled from the house and trod on them, a remarkably effective, if painful, technique for disarming a man. Alvin screamed again and, to add insult to his injury, Dregs, who'd been watching the performance with interest, swaggered forwards, cocked a leg and widdled on his face.

'That's enough,' said Hobbes. 'Drop.'

As Mimi released her grip, Hobbes picked Alvin up by the collar and let him dangle. His left forearm was punctured and bloody and his right hand hung uselessly. As he moaned and writhed in Hobbes's grasp, I was amazed I'd ever considered him good looking. In fact, he was sharp faced, looking a bit like an old rat, and though the pain was evident in his expression, it did not override the fury and cruelty in his eyes. His long hair had fallen in such a way that one of his ears was revealed. It was large and pointed, most unlike the tiny Slugg family ears. I wondered what Matilda's ears looked like beneath all that long, golden hair.

'Are you going to call him an ambulance?' I asked, shaken, and not trying to hide it.

'Later, perhaps,' said Hobbes.

He dragged Alvin, half-walking, half-stumbling, and moaning piteously, into the house and nodded, which I took as an invitation to follow. I felt no sympathy for Alvin, thinking that it served him right, and though the thought was callous, the look in his eyes made me think I was thinking right. The dogs and I entered the house, where Alvin, who was trying to cradle both arms at the same time, was sprawled on the sofa in the lounge.

'This is police brutality and entirely uncalled for,' he said, his voice soft and sad, as if he'd been cruelly wronged, but sought no vengeance.

'I merely prevented you from re-acquiring a potentially lethal weapon, sir,' said Hobbes, 'and I used the minimum amount of force I deemed necessary in the circumstances.'

'You set your dog on me!'

'I did no such thing and she's not my dog, sir. I suspect you know much more about her than I do.'

'That's slander,' said Alvin. 'I've never seen her before in my life.'

'Yet, she appears to know you, sir.'

Mimi, her hackles high, her teeth bared, was growling at Alvin, while Dregs was staring at her, looking puzzled.

'Get that brute away from me,' Alvin's voice was harsh again.

'She won't hurt you, as long as you stay where you are,' said Hobbes, with a glance at Mimi who sat down and relaxed, though without taking her eyes off Alvin.

'She's already hurt me. Call me an ambulance.'

'Very good, sir. You're an ambulance.' Hobbes smiled. 'Mr Godley told me that one.'

'Who the hell is Mr Godley?' asked Alvin, his mellow voice cracking, so the end of his question came out as a squawk.

'An old fellow who knows a lot, Mr Elwes.'

'That's not my name. I am Solomon Slugg. I don't know anyone called Elwes.'

'We'll see about that,' said Hobbes. 'Perhaps I'll fetch your relations here and have them identify you.'

'My brother is dead and my sisters live in Australia.'

'But, didn't you tell me your family was just you and Septimus, sir?'

'Er … yes… maybe … I'd forgotten about them … because of the distress caused by his death.'

'Solomon Slugg's brother is dead,' said Hobbes, 'because you killed him, with, I suspect that billhook, which is a fearsome weapon in the right hands. And, by the way, when we had our earlier chat, you let slip that Septimus Slugg was killed by one, which I hadn't known until then. I took that as an indication of your guilt.'

'He was going to use it on me,' I said, 'and would have, if Mimi hadn't bitten him.'

Mimi broke off trying to outstare Alvin to give me a big adoring glance. It was getting embarrassing.

'I had no intention of using it on you, young man,' said Alvin, smiling through his pain, his words dripping sincerity and good intentions. 'I was rushing out to protect you from that ferocious dog.'

I almost believed him … and yet, was that a sly look in his eyes?

'She's not ferocious,' I said, struggling against his beguiling manner. 'She only became that way when you showed up.'

'Let's give you the benefit of the doubt for now, sir,' said Hobbes. 'Perhaps you could inform me what it was about Mimi that made you believe she was a threat to Andy.'

'I know that breed of dog. They are highly aggressive, and had I been elected, I would have done my utmost to ensure they were muzzled at all times when out in public.'

'How do you know this sort of dog, sir? Did you have one once?'

'No, never. I did, however, know of someone who owned one. One day, it turned on him, and he had to get rid of it. It had become a grave danger to people.'

'Exactly where did it bite you, sir?' asked Hobbes sounding and looking sympathetic.

'On my … on his calf.'

'Yours or his, sir?'

'His of course. You confused me for a moment.'

'Yes, sir, I understand how a perfectly straightforward question might be confusing.'

'Damn you!' said Alvin, springing from the sofa, the rage taking over. 'I'm going to phone my solicitor.'

'I won't stop you, but first I need to check something, and I apologise for what I'm about to do to you, sir.'

His next move certainly took me by surprise.

Stepping forward and squatting, Hobbes grabbed the waistband of Alvin's trousers, tugged them down, tore them off and tossed them into the corner, where Mimi, growling ferociously, pounced on them.

'What do you mean by this outrageous behaviour?' Alvin shrieked. 'I'm going to have words with your superintendent, and I can tell you, Inspector, you're in a heap of trouble.'

Hobbes by Wilkie Martin

I must admit to thinking that he might be right, for Hobbes had surely gone too far this time. He was staring at Alvin's spaghetti-thin legs.

'Those are impressive scars, sir,' he said, shoving Alvin back onto the sofa. 'They look just as if they were the result of a recent dog bite.'

'So what?' asked Alvin, whose face was red, and whose voice was drained of all its honey, leaving only sharp ill-humour. 'I got bitten by a dog. That's all.'

'This dog, I suppose,' said Hobbes, with a glance at Mimi, who was shaking the trousers as if she'd got hold of a rat.

'Not at all. I was attacked when taking my morning constitutional three weeks ago. It's nothing to do with that bitch.'

'And yet, I'd make a bet that her teeth match your wounds. Shall we try them for size, sir?'

'Certainly not. I am injured and in pain and demand immediate medical attention.'

'Of course, sir. How remiss of me. Where are your first aid supplies? In the bathroom? I'll have a look.'

'You can't search my house without a warrant. You are only making things worse for yourself.'

'I'm not searching your house, sir. I am merely looking for your medical supplies. You do have some, don't you?'

'It's no business of yours. Call me an ambulance!'

'I've already done that, sir,' said Hobbes as he headed upstairs. There were a few bumps and bangs and other noises, suggestive of rummaging.

Alvin glared. 'What's he doing up there? He has no right.'

'Looking for your first aid kit, I expect,' I said, keeping a wary eye on him, though I felt surprisingly relaxed.

'Who the hell are you?' he asked, his glare reaching near-Hobbesian power.

'I'm … umm …Andy.'

'And what do you do when you're not helping that brute harass law-abiding citizens.'

'I'm a food critic …'

'What?' He spluttered, his bafflement almost concealing the rage on his face. 'Why are you here?'

'Umm … he asked me if I wanted to come.'

'Do you get a sick thrill from seeing a gentleman in difficulties and in pain?'

'No … umm … not as such. Seeing Hobbes at work can be very educational and …'

'Shut up a moment,' said Alvin. 'Andy, you said?'

I nodded, unable to look away.

'I know who you are now. You're that snotty food critic from the *Bugle*. I just wish he'd hit you harder.'

'How do you know about that?' I asked.

'None of your damn business. Yes, I know you. You were trying to ruin Big Mama's, which I have an interest in. How could you write that it was appalling? The food there is not, by any stretch of the imagination, fiendish, and the wine is definitely not minging – I chose it myself.'

'I never wrote anything like that.'

'Liar. Marco showed me your text. That's what it said.'

788

'It didn't. I gave it a very good review. I said it was appealing, and that there were fine dishes and that the wine left my palate singing.'

Alvin snorted. 'I know what I saw. Don't lie. You deserved what you got and you should have got more.'

I started to argue, and stopped, realising I'd again been a victim of predictive text. That and clumsy fingers.

'What a useless parasitical occupation you have,' Alvin continued. 'It's so easy to criticize and lambast hard-working people when you don't have to do it yourself, and couldn't if you tried. You remind me of one of those horrid boys who pull the wings off butterflies for sport. I've a good mind to finish what Marco started.'

He made a move as if he was going to get up, but a growl from Mimi changed his mind. Having torn the trousers to shreds, she was bristling again, while Dregs gazed as if amazed.

'Get that animal out of here,' Alvin demanded.

'Certainly, sir,' said Hobbes, reappearing. 'Please, leave the room, Andy.'

'What?' I said, jerking like a sleep walker awaking.

'I meant the blasted dog,' said Alvin.

'But, I'm sure she means no harm,' said Hobbes, 'though she would appear to bear a grudge against you. I wonder why that would be.'

'I have no idea.'

'And I suspect you're going to claim to have no idea why there is a dog cage in your back garden.'

'You've been tramping all over my garden as well, have you?' said Alvin. 'My solicitor is going to have so much fun putting you in your place.'

'Actually, sir, I glanced out the window when I was looking for your first aid kit.'

'Did you find it?' I asked.

'I did, and I've taken the liberty of removing some bandages, a dressing and a bottle of TCP. If you'd allow me, sir?'

He opened the bottle, took Alvin's wounded arm and poured a drop of the pungent liquid into the punctures.

'That stings,' Alvin moaned, writhing and trying to break away.

'That shows it's working,' said Hobbes with a pleasant smile, 'and suggests there's no nerve damage. Isn't that good news, sir?'

Having torn open a couple of packets, he dressed the bites and then examined the hand he'd stepped on.

'It's bruised, that's all. Stop whining and give me an explanation for these.' He reached into his pocket and pulled out a handful of small bottles.

'What are those?' I asked.

'A handful of small bottles. However, they are full of pills and I'd like Mr Elwes to explain why he was keeping them in the recess under his bath.'

'They're nothing to do with me,' said Alvin. 'You must have planted them. I've done nothing wrong, but you've attacked me, ransacked my home and planted illegal amphetamines on me. I want my solicitor.'

'Are they illegal amphetamines, sir?' asked Hobbes innocently.

'Well, I … er … think they must be, otherwise you wouldn't have planted them. I don't know what you suspect me of, Inspector, but I'm innocent …'

Hobbes by Wilkie Martin

'I don't suspect you, sir.'

'Then get out of here, and take your savage dogs and that idiot food critic with you.'

'Not when we're getting on so well,' said Hobbes in a light, conversational tone. 'The fact is, Mr Elwes, that I don't suspect you, because I know what you've done. You murdered Solomon Slugg and Septimus Slugg, and used Solomon's identity, you stole one Samoyed bitch for the purposes of breeding and selling the pups, you stole a wild boar ...'

'Well, you got that one wrong, smartass. I paid for that boar fair and square. I have the receipt. It's just that he escaped.'

'So, you admit the rest?' asked Hobbes.

'I admit nothing, and I'm saying nothing more.'

'That is, of course, your right, sir. In the meantime, I am arresting you for the murder of Solomon and Septimus Slugg. Other charges may be brought later.'

'You can't arrest me without reading me my rights.'

'I can, sir, but, if you like, I can caution you to start telling the truth or your situation will become even worse than it is already.'

'Worse? What do you mean?'

'I might become angry.'

'Which is not a pretty sight,' I said.

'Thank you, Andy. Now, Mr Elwes, are you going to come to the police station quietly?'

'Yes, but when I get there, I intend to kick up such a fuss that you'll regret ever being born.'

'That is your right, sir.'

'And I warn you that I know your superintendent, and the chief constable.'

'So do I, sir,' said Hobbes, and jerked him to his feet.

'I'm not leaving the house without trousers.'

'Of course not, sir. It's awfully chilly out there, and I wouldn't want you to catch a cold. Shall I fetch you a pair, or would you prefer to get them yourself?'

'I'll do it myself. Just keep that damned hellhound away.'

'Andy,' said Hobbes, 'would you mind holding Mimi's collar?'

I did as asked while Mr Elwes headed for the stairs. Hobbes's grin suggested he was up to something, though I had no idea what.

'Stay here,' he said, walking from the room.

A moment later, I looked through the window and saw him heading up the drive.

'What's his game?' I asked.

The dogs didn't say, though Dregs snickered, and I could have sworn there was a knowing expression in his dark eyes. Mimi, having exhausted the possibilities of trousers, made herself comfortable on the sofa, exuding an element of defiance, as well as of fear, as if she believed she was being a bad dog, but didn't care. I let her settle, wondering how long Alvin would take to get dressed, and hoping Hobbes would be back before then, since I didn't fancy facing a murderer on my own.

A window creaked open upstairs.

'He's trying to get away!' I yelled, but there was no sign of Hobbes.

I ran and looked out the front door. Alvin was climbing down the trellis.

'Stop!' I said.

There was a triumphant grin on his face as he prepared to jump the last bit, but as he let go, Hobbes's car, its engine revving madly, screeched backwards down the drive with its boot wide open. Alvin dropped right in. Hobbes, grinning, sprinted round before he could move and shut him in.

'You were wondering how we'd all fit in the car if I arrested Mr Elwes,' said Hobbes. 'I found a solution.'

'Umm … did you plan that?'

'No. I merely went to collect my handcuffs, because his sort is dangerous. Get the dogs and we'll head back to town.'

Alvin kept kicking and cursing, which, although annoying, was a distraction from the driving.

'I can't breathe!' he screamed after about five minutes.

'Shouldn't you let him have some air?' I asked.

'There's plenty,' said Hobbes, his voice booming. 'At least there will be if he doesn't waste it.'

Alvin quietened down for the rest of the journey. I hoped he hadn't snuffed it, for even Hobbes would struggle to get away with asphyxiating a suspect. Not that Alvin was technically a suspect by then; he was a definite in Hobbes's eyes.

After parking outside the police station, Hobbes opened the boot and Alvin sprang up, trying to make a run for it.

'Stop messing about,' said Hobbes, seizing him by the collar and making him squeal. 'I need to get you booked in. Andy, would you mind taking the dogs home? I'll be along as soon as he's safely in a cell. I'll not be long, because I want my dinner.'

A glance at the church clock showed it was nearly lunchtime and that the morning had passed really quickly. I intended to stroll home, but it wasn't long before the wind had bitten through my coat and forced me to adopt a brisk, hunched walk, with the dogs bounding about, seemingly pleased to have seen the back of Alvin. Without a lead, I'd had some worries about Mimi, but she appeared to have acquired Dregs's traffic sense, which he'd picked up from Hobbes. I reflected that it hadn't been so long ago when he'd been a wild and potentially dangerous animal. Dregs that was. Hobbes was still wild and potentially dangerous.

I led the pack back into 13 Blackdog Street and took off my coat, enjoying the feeling of warmth and wondering what we'd have to eat. Besides food, I had two further reasons for being cheerful: Daphne was coming home, and I hadn't spotted any more embarrassing posters. There were down sides to both points, since she would want somewhere to live, and the posters might reappear, but I still hoped to deal with both situations in time. I checked my mobile, but there were no new messages.

The old girl was in the kitchen, stirring magical aromas from a gleaming copper pot. 'Hello, dear. Dinner's nearly ready. Did you have a good morning?'

'Not bad. Hobbes arrested Solomon Slugg, who's also Alvin Elwes, and, who is apparently, my neighbours' cousin. It was him that murdered them.'

Mrs Goodfellow looked baffled. 'Alvin Elwes murdered your neighbours?'

'No.'

'So, who did murder them?'

'No one did. They are both well.'

'I don't quite follow. Was it your neighbours that murdered someone?'

'Umm … no … not as far as I know. I'll start again.' I took a deep breath, thinking myself lucky that my job involved writing rather than speaking. 'What I was trying to say is that Alvin Elwes killed Solomon Slugg and pretended to be him, and then murdered his brother … umm … that is to say he murdered Solomon's brother, Septimus.'

'Then I'm not surprised the old fellow arrested him, and that sounded like the front door. Go and wash your hands, and I'll start ladling out the soup.'

Hobbes had returned and three minutes later he and I were enjoying a rich and hearty soup, made with winter vegetables, basil and chunks of Italian sausage. Together with freshly-baked crusty bread and primrose-yellow butter, it was a feast made in heaven, and one to drive away all vestige of winter's chill.

We were nicely full and sipping tea in the sitting room when a mobile rang and I pulled mine from my pocket, hoping it was Daphne. I stared at it baffled for a moment, wondering when I'd turned it off.

'Good afternoon, Billy,' said Hobbes on his new phone. 'What's happening? I see … Thanks … I'll be with you as soon as possible. I'll bring the dogs, and would you ask Featherlight to keep close, but not too close, and to be ready on his mobile?'

'What's up?' I asked.

'The game is afoot.'

'Is it? What game?'

He was already up and putting on his mac. 'A dangerous one.'

'Can I come and watch?' I asked, and, on seeing his grim, worried face, wished I'd bitten my tongue off instead.

'No. It would be better if you stayed here out of harm's way. I'm going out and I may be some time.'

I sat for a while after he'd gone, my brain a battlefield between two conflicting thoughts. The first was the sensible reasoning of a sensible married man with responsibilities that he ought to be dealing with. However, just when it seemed sense would triumph, the idiotic part of me launched an attack, using notions of excitement and bravery, and swept aside all opposition before it could be reinforced. I grabbed my coat, and rushed out, jealous that Billy, Featherlight and the dogs were part of whatever was going on, and I wasn't invited.

Although Hobbes was out of sight, his car was still parked at the kerb. Surmising he was on foot, I ran to the end of Blackdog Street and into The Shambles where I glimpsed him on Vermin Street. He turned down the alley towards the police station.

I ran, my legs like pistons, my lungs burning, my breath steaming, and my heart thumping, as the good shopper folk of Sorenchester parted before me. Sweat trickled down my back, as I reached the chemist's shop and turned into the alley. A few steps later, I stopped and backed into the shadows. A twitching in my stomach suggested all was not well, though my brain could not identify any specific reason.

My position gave a good view of the back of the police station, where all appeared quiet and normal, apart from Hobbes who was squatting by a skip, apparently mumbling to himself. He nodded and scratched his chin as if in deep thought, and I wondered if something might have moved high up on the edge of vision. I craned my neck, hoping for a better sighting, but whatever it had been had gone. The sensible part of me rallied, wanting to get the hell out of there, but idiocy, or something, had control of my will. I stayed where I was, watching, and reassured to hear people walking up the alley behind me. Then their voices dropped, their footsteps faltered, and they hurried back the way they'd come, though they couldn't possibly have seen anything.

The back door of the station opened and the lanky figure of Constable Poll staggered out as if he'd been punched. He would have fallen had Hobbes not leapt up, caught him and lugged him over his shoulder. As he did so, a small dark shape moved from the shadows by the skip and I tried to call out a warning. Only a cracked croak escaped. For a moment, I feared it was one of the things I thought I'd seen in the park, but it was only Billy in his ninja outfit. After a quick word with Hobbes, he slipped back into the shadows.

A strange confusion began to cloud my brain, and a terrible feeling of dread was growing. Then I heard a voice.

'I thought I told you to stay at home,' said Hobbes, looming above me.

'Umm … you did … but … I …'

'Didn't do as you were told,' he said and sighed. 'Well, since you're here, you'd better look after Derek.'

He swung Constable Poll down and sat him with his back propped against the alley wall.

'What's wrong with him?'

'He appears to have been dazzled by her charms.'

'Her charms?'

'Matilda Kielder's. She is inside the station, doing what she does best.'

'Why? Is she going to eat somebody?' I shivered, reflecting on my own lucky escape.

'Possibly, but I suspect she's here to release Alvin.'

Hobbes turned back towards the police station.

'She's so beautiful,' Constable Poll murmured, staring with wide, unfocussed eyes as I leant over him. 'You're not, though. What have you done to her?'

'It's me, Andy,' I said. 'Andy Caplet. Snap out of it, man.'

'Take me back to her.'

'Her? Do you mean Matilda?'

'The angel lady. She's so beautiful, and her perfume is …'

'That's nice, but she's a man-eater? You'll get over her.'

'Won't.'

'I bet you will. I have, I think. She wanted to eat me.'

'You filthy lying swine,' said Poll, making a feeble effort to punch me but keeling over and sliding onto his side. He lay still, burbling to himself, a stupid grin on his face, his enormous pupils obscuring the blueness of his eyes.

'What about the others in there?' I asked, but he was in a happy world of his own, and I wondered if I'd been in a similar state that day in the café. It seemed so long ago, though it was only about a week.

Hobbes was walking towards the back door of the police station, something in his hunched movement reminiscent of a desperate gun fighter in one of the old westerns he loved. I wished I knew what he was planning, and what he was up against, because, although normally he could cope with anything life threw at him, there'd been occasions when he'd seemed incredibly vulnerable. The way the chills were running down my spine suggested this might be another of them. I wanted to help, to be the trusty sidekick who saves the day, but I was held back by fear, almost like a physical barrier. In addition, an unhappy thought came to me that, all too often, it was the trusty sidekick who got gunned down.

Trying to focus, I reminded myself that I wasn't in the Wild West and that a gunfight was unlikely. Although I'd never been keen on guns, I'd grown even less enamoured of them after the Editorsaurus's wife shot me in the leg. Admittedly I'd not been the target – she'd been trying to shoot her own trusty sidekick – and the bullet that hit me had ricocheted and was nearly spent, but it had stung and broken the skin, and I fancied I could still make out the scar under bright lights. Daphne had agreed when I pointed it out, though I suspected she might have been humouring me.

Constable Poll giggled as if drunk.

'Are you all right?' I asked.

'It's all too beautiful,' he said, making a feeble attempt to get to his feet, but slumping face down onto the moss-encrusted pavement.

'What are you doing?' I asked. 'It's cold, damp and filthy down there.'

'I'm resting my eyes in shades of green,' he said, and snored.

Since he seemed quite relaxed and there was no sign of immediate danger, I thought I could safely leave him for a short time. The main threat to him seemed to be the biting wind, so I covered him with my coat and wondered whether my next move would count as one of my finer moments, or would just increase my tally of stupid ones. Despite every better instinct, despite the fear, I was going in.

'Don't go away,' I told the sleeping policeman, and scurried towards the station.

It was only a few steps away, though it felt longer, as if I was running into a strong, cold wind. Gritting my teeth, I butted forward, swaying as if the earth was shaking, and I was making reasonable progress until a small dark figure darted out, grabbed my legs and squeezed them together. I crashed down right in front of the door.

'What do you think you're doing?' said Billy, rolling me over and sitting on my chest. 'Hobbesie didn't want anyone else involved, and you should be safe back at Blackdog Street. It's really dangerous in there.'

'I'm ... umm ... worried about him and came to help.'

'I'm worried too, mate, but you're not going to be any use if something happens to you.'

'What could happen? Derek Poll's all right, other than being completely out of it.'

'You think being completely out of it is all right?'

'No … I suppose not, but I'm feeling kind of strange myself. What about you?'

'Yeah, a little.'

'But why?'

'I wish I knew, mate. It's just something these people do.'

'But who are they?'

'Dunno. I'd never heard of them before, but Featherlight reckons they just turn up and cause trouble. He's banned them from the Feathers, though that doesn't mean much. He's banned most people, including me a few times, and I'm the only barman who'll work there.'

I got an impression of movement.

'I think someone's on the roof,' said Billy.

'Yes, I thought I saw something when I got here.'

He scanned the roofline. 'I can't see anyone now. Get out of here while you can.'

He rolled off me and dived back into the shadows while I retreated to the alley, where Constable Poll was snoring and occasionally giggling. My desire to get inside the police station had become a compulsion, and, although I was still worried about Hobbes, that was not the reason. It was as if something like a magnet was drawing me in, weakening my sense of fear.

I lost control and sprinted for the door. Billy, cursing, dived out and got a grip on my ankle, but I kept going, dragging him with me.

'Stop!' he cried. 'Don't be stupid!'

I shook my head, unable to understand why I was doing it, and trying to kick him off. He proved a persistent little sod, but eventually I caught him a good one, and left him clutching his ribs, though he still managed to block the back door. I felt myself drawn round to the front entrance, feeling a bit like a fish must feel when hooked and being reeled in. When I scuttled inside, Sergeant Dixon, a youngish man built like a docker, was lying on his back by the front desk, grinning and chuckling like Poll. His outstretched legs were propping open the door to the inner station.

'Are you all right?' I asked, stopping briefly.

All I got by way of reply was a soppy grin that reminded me of something, though it took a few moments to remember that it was the same goofy expression I'd worn in our wedding photographs, and, I suspected, when I'd been with Violet, the lovely woman who'd taken an unexpected shine to me, and who had then, even more unexpectedly, turned out to be a werecat.

There was no sign of Hobbes.

Despite fear building up, something was drawing me further in. I stepped over Dixon, who waved and giggled, and entered the main corridor. On my right was the main office, where everything appeared much like the last time I'd been there, though some desks had a neglected look as if they were no longer regularly used. One thing was decidedly different; the officers, civilian and uniformed alike, were sprawling on the floor, smiling and helpless. A skinny, grey-haired little woman in brown slacks held out her arms.

'Love me,' she demanded.

'Umm … what?' I said, maintaining my ability to communicate in awkward situations.

My voice seemed to take her aback. 'You're not him. You're an imposter!'

'Not who?'

'Not the beautiful one.'

'You don't mean Hobbes, do you?' I asked, astounded, though I'd noticed with huge mystification that some women seemed at least half-attracted by his feral Hobbesness.

'Don't be silly.' She shook her head and smiled as she lay back down, her eyes glazing over. I walked past her and looked inside the canteen, which, other than vending machines, Formica-covered tables and orange plastic seats, appeared empty, though an enchanting feminine fragrance made me linger.

'Why, it's Andy,' said a sweet voice that reminded me of Daphne and Violet and every other charming woman I'd had a crush on, though it was softer, gentler and more alluring.

A beautiful young woman with huge, emerald green eyes full of desire and delight gazed at me from the doorway that led into the kitchen.

'Sally!' I cried and took a clumsy, lumbering step towards her, my arms held out like a clock stuck at quarter-to-three.

Deep down I had an inkling that something was terribly wrong. I fought to regain control, trying to resist her charms, reminding myself that I loved Daphne, and that so much beauty was unnatural. For a moment I held back. Then she smiled and I was lost. I lurched forwards, shaking as if I were about to attempt a tight rope walk over a ravine, and my heart filled with desire and love for this wondrous apparition.

'Come to me, you delightful man,' she said, her voice sweeter and thicker than honey. 'I love your new frizzed hair, and not having eyebrows really suits you.'

'Thank you,' I murmured, and, like a fly about to ensnare itself hopelessly in a honeydew plant, I went to her, enraptured by her perfume, her voice, her loveliness.

'Andy, no!'

A harsh, high-pitched squawk grated on my nerves. I looked down at the diminutive black-clad figure who was standing between me and my heart's desire and shoved him aside.

'Well done, darling,' said Sally. 'Come to me. We were meant to be and should never have parted. Come to me now. I'm so hungry for love.'

'I'm coming,' I said.

'No,' said Billy, but I ignored him.

'Come to me, my own true love.'

I nodded, my eyes fixed on the spellbinding vision, my head pounding.

'It's a trap, Andy,' Billy cried, his voice muffled by the blood rush through my brain. 'She's not what you think she is, and you know it.'

'Be quiet, little man,' said Sally, her voice cold and sour. 'Get out or expect a bitter fate.'

I couldn't have said the spell was broken, yet for a second I was more myself, and able to take in my surroundings. Billy was on his hands and knees, blood dripping through his ninja mask, though what had happened to him was beyond me.

'You've been warned,' Sally snarled. 'Get out or I'll introduce you to my cousin, and he's not as nice as I am.'

Something must have gone wrong with my eyes because for a moment she looked nothing like my lovely Sally, and there was something about her that made me think of the praying mantis from the wildlife park.

Then she smiled again and beckoned, and despite my body shaking with terror, I was drawn to her, and in those moments, though they felt as long as hours, I would willingly have died for her. The mix of terror and ecstasy and being entirely out of my own control was most peculiar, and reminded me of when someone had slipped something into my beer at a party and I'd come awake in a park where an electric-blue gorilla was playing bagpipes.

'Andy!' Her call was that of the Siren.

'Sally,' I cried.

'That's not who she is,' said Billy's voice, as if from a great distance. 'She's Matilda Kielder, the man-eater.'

'She can eat me whenever she likes,' I murmured, though I so much wanted to run and save my life, and Billy's.

I was intensely aware of all my flaws: frizzed hair, bald eyebrows, a slightly misaligned front tooth, a chin that might have been better shaved, breath that stank, a nose that was too big and had a tiny pimple, and the clumsiness of my lumpen body. It was clear I was unworthy of the vision before me, and, though I really ought to crawl away and die, grateful for having glimpsed such perfection, her compassion was so vast that she could love even a wretch like me. I dragged my hopeless ungainly body towards her welcoming arms, and though an image of Daphne, the woman I loved, flashed before my eyes, it did not deter me.

What might have happened next had I not been such an uncoordinated oaf is something I never dared dwell upon. My huge, disgusting feet became entangled and, instead of flinging myself into her arms, I tripped, lunged forward, and head-butted her in the midriff.

Her screech, more the bellow of an enraged and ferocious animal than a woman's cry, scared me, making me desperate to get away, but I was still falling, going down on her as she clawed at me with astonishing strength. There was no softness in her body as we hit the floor. She gasped, a weirdly primeval noise that made me stare into her face, which had become dark and desiccated, like a mummy's. Her mouth was a nightmare of shark-like teeth, and a repulsive stagnant smell was all around.

Though winded and fuzzy headed, I leapt up and tried to flee, only to be brought back down by a grip like contracting steel around my ankle. She was dragging me towards her, despite my attempts to crawl away; no traction was to be had on the smooth linoleum flooring. I screamed for help, but Billy was curled up against the wall, not moving. When I turned to look at the woman, I saw no beauty, and she now reminded me of one of the prehistoric bodies that occasionally turned up in peat bogs, deflated, leathery, and half-rotten. How I'd ever seen her as the least bit attractive was beyond me. The spell fell apart, and even in my panic and despair, I felt relief.

'What do you want with me?' I asked, my voice quavering. I was hoping she'd explain herself and that my brilliant ploy would, at worst, buy me some time, and, at best, would end with her changing her mind and letting me go.

She was not in a talkative mood.

She leapt on me, her scent overly sweet and repulsive, like the stink of slow decay. Her sinewy limbs were unnaturally strong and there was nothing wrong with her teeth so far as sharpness went, though Mrs Goodfellow would have found fault with the bubbling grey film coating them.

'Help!' I cried, and she giggled, sounding for a moment just like my darling Sally.

'Kiss me!' she breathed, her mouth a hideous pucker.

'Shan't,' I said, closing my lips as tight as I could and turning my head aside.

Kissing, I feared, was not what she had in mind, and those sharp teeth served to remind me, if I could have forgotten, that she was a man-eater.

She leaned forward and I was drowning in her breath, my head spinning, losing all hope and wondering how I'd explain my death to Daphne.

A massive thud shook the room and made her look up, giving me an opportunity to escape, though I was in no condition to take it. All I could manage was a feeble wriggle, like a maggot on a hook. Another thud, booming even louder than the first, stirred up dust that twinkled and scintillated for a moment in a stray beam of sunlight.

'What's that?' said Matilda.

There was a third massive bang and the wall burst inwards in a whirlwind of debris with Hobbes at the centre. He landed on top of her. Only he stood up.

'Oof!' he said, and grinned. 'I always thought a door would come in handy there. All right, Andy?'

I nodded and coughed as plaster and flakes of paint showered us, giving him the appearance of a white-haired old man with appalling dandruff. He shook himself like a dog, and returned to his more normal appearance, such as it was.

He poked the unconscious monstrous thing sprawled at his feet with the toe of his boot, but she didn't respond. In her stillness, she, if that pronoun applied, looked even more like a bog body.

I sat up, shaking. 'I was wondering when you'd blow in. Where were you? She was going to eat me, I think.'

'I only knew you were here when I heard your cry for help. You were supposed to be looking after Derek.'

'Oh, yes, well … umm … I thought he'd be all right where he was … I did cover him up … He wasn't himself though.'

'No, he got a full blast of Matilda's charm, but, like you, he's tougher than he appears, and managed to get out on his own.'

'I'm tougher than I appear?' I wasn't sure whether to feel pleased or insulted.

'You resisted more than some, though you'd had prior experience.'

I nodded, the fuzzy headed feeling clearing a little. 'But where were you? I saw you come in … I think …'

'I was on the roof, negotiating with Aubrey and Hilda Elwes. It took some time, so I only got away a few moments ago.'

'Aubrey and Hilda? What are they doing up there?'

'They were planning to bust Alvin out.'

'Bust him out? But I thought they were the good guys … sort of.'

'Perhaps they are … sort of.' Hobbes half-smiled. 'They intended taking him into their own custody and I've not yet decided whether to grant their wish.'

'But you can't. He's a double murderer.'

'It's true that he's killed at least twice.'

'You think there may be others?'

He shrugged. 'Maybe. Anyway, the point is moot since Matilda got to him first, and freed him. His current whereabouts are unknown, though he can't have gone far.'

'That's worrying.'

He nodded and glanced towards Billy. 'What happened to him?'

'I … umm … don't know.' I had a vague memory of violence, but was nearly certain I wouldn't have hurt my friend.

Hobbes went towards him, but paused. 'Maybe I should restrain her before anything else. She may still present a danger.'

He pulled a set of old-fashioned handcuffs from his pocket, looked at her inert form for a few moments, and put them back. 'Maybe not. She doesn't look as if she'll cause any more trouble for a while.'

'Are you sure?' I asked, but he was already looking after Billy.

When he turned him over, I gasped.

'He's been beaten up,' said Hobbes, removing the little fellow's ninja hood. Blood was oozing from his nose and mouth.

'Is he all right?'

He checked Billy's vital signs. 'He's got a strong pulse and he's breathing well.'

'Umm … who could have done such a thing?'

'Come here.'

I hobbled over, drained and dizzy as if I'd been drinking long and hard.

'Kneel down and make a fist.'

I knelt, clenching my fingers and wrapping my thumb around them tightly, as Mrs Goodfellow had once shown me, and tried to work out why my knuckles were skinned and bruised. He took my fist and fitted it to one of the bruises on Billy's face.

'But I only pushed him away,' I said. 'He was being really annoying and trying to stop me going to Sally… ' I hesitated. 'I don't remember hitting him … and she was just an illusion, wasn't she? He was trying to save my life and if he hadn't slowed me down …'

Hobbes wiped blood from Billy's face.

'Sorry,' I said. 'I must have done it, but I don't remember. I didn't know what I was doing.'

'Do you ever?' said Billy and sat up with a groan.

'How are you feeling?' asked Hobbes.

'As well as anyone who's just been bashed by a maniac,' said Billy and wiped a fresh trickle of blood from his nose, which was bent far enough that he'd be able to sniff around corners.

'I'm sorry,' I repeated, feeling as thoroughly ashamed of myself as anyone who'd just beaten up an innocent dwarf should feel, though all I could recall was giving him a bit of a shove. I wanted to deny everything, but the evidence was compelling.

'Forget it, mate.'

'Thank you,' I said, and turned to Hobbes. 'Does he need an ambulance?'

'He don't need an ambulance,' said Billy. 'I'll be fine.'

'But, your nose!'

He touched it, grimaced, and pulled it straight with a sickening scrunch that nearly made me faint.

'Ouch,' he said, as if reading my mind. He grinned, and mopped his face with a black handkerchief.

'Good. All's well as ends well,' said Hobbes, and helped him to his feet.

'What are you going to do with her?' I asked, jabbing a thumb in the general direction of Matilda, who, other than twitching slightly, had not moved. 'Are you going to sling her in the cells?'

'I ought to find her cousin,' said Hobbes, 'but I suppose I should lock her up first.'

'Yes, and then we can hunt him down,' I said, elated to have survived another horror. 'And he'll be easier to deal with.'

'What makes you think that?' asked Billy, his voice rather nasal.

'Well, you know what they say, don't you? The female of the species is more deadly than the male.'

'So I've heard,' said Hobbes, 'but, I don't know who they are that say such things, and I'm not sure it's true. Both genders of these people can be equally dangerous, depending on circumstances.'

'Even Aubrey and Hilda?' I asked. 'They seem rather nice, and she's awfully pretty.'

'You still haven't quite worked them out, have you?' said Hobbes. 'If they so chose, Aubrey and Hilda could be at least as dangerous as their cousins, and you can't judge by their appearances.'

I nodded, feeling utterly confused, which was at least within my comfort zone. 'You mean she doesn't look like what she looks like?'

'I mean, she does look just like she looks like, but it's all a mirage, and the same goes for him. However, these debates, though clearly fascinating, can be left for later. In the meantime, I'd like to put Matilda somewhere safe,' said Hobbes in a loud clear voice.

The canteen door flew open and smacked against the wall.

'Oh no, you don't,' said a familiar voice.

It was Solomon Slugg. That is, it was Alvin Elwes.

'Shift yourself, Knuckledragger,' he said, giving a glance over his shoulder.

Marco Jones, looking dazed, followed him into the canteen, a double-barrelled shotgun in his big hands. He pointed it at Hobbes, and occasionally at Billy, but clearly did not consider me a threat. I suppose I should have been insulted, but I wasn't, because it meant I wasn't in immediate danger. Even so I thought it wise to step away from them as I tried to figure out how long it would take him to reload if he shot at Hobbes and Billy, and whether that would give me sufficient time to get out of there in one piece. Given the volume of adrenalin surging through me, I reckoned I'd be halfway up Vermin Street by the time he was ready. I hoped it wouldn't come to that.

Alvin looked at us, smiling sadly, and it struck me how much we'd wronged him, because there was no way such a noble man could possibly murder anyone, and it was obvious that all his business interests were entirely legitimate. I wondered if he might become my friend, since he was evidently a far superior kind of person to Hobbes, and way above Billy, though everybody was way above that little runt. I stared at them, finding it unbelievable that I'd never noticed just how ugly they both were. Of course I'd known Hobbes was no oil painting, but I'd never before been struck by how hideous and uncouth he was. There were gargoyles and grotesques on the church with better features, and more social graces. As for Billy, small, and stubby, I couldn't believe I'd ever considered him a friend. What had possessed me to believe I wanted to hang around with such freaks, such monsters? Hobbes nodded at Billy and I was sickened by how lumpish his every movement was. I was soothed by Alvin's voice. How beautiful were his words, like lyrical poetry. How gentle and charming was his voice.

Something about the word charming triggered a warning. I shook my head and blinked, trying to disperse a fog of confusion and found I'd drawn closer to Alvin, whose brilliant eyes were fixed on mine. He really was a fine looking man, honest and decent, and yet, if I concentrated and my eyes were shut, I knew it was all deception. Hobbes, was standing still, his shoulders hunched, looking defeated. Billy held a mobile phone in his hand. As I watched, he pressed a button.

'Throw that down, little man,' said Alvin, his voice sweet, yet not at all wholesome, and containing something of sickness and decay.

Billy dropped the phone, and gave a barely perceptible wink to Hobbes, whose lips twitched into a quick smile. Feeling more myself, I took a step towards my friends, towards Hobbes and Billy, though it took such an effort of will that I almost cried with the pain.

'Welcome back from the dark side,' Billy whispered.

'Fool,' said Alvin, addressing me. 'I thought you were the clever one. You could have joined me, to both of our benefits. I could have done so much for this town, and you could have helped me and risen high in the world. Never mind. It's clear you belong in the gutter with those freaks.

'Now, give me back my cousin, if you'd be so good. It's time for us to go.'

'I'll not stop you,' said Hobbes, standing aside to allow him access to Matilda, 'but are you sure you want to leave us? Aubrey and Hilda are waiting outside.'

'Liar!'

'I never lie,' said Hobbes. 'They've been looking for you. I've persuaded them to wait, but if they see you making a run for it they will have you, and I won't be able to help.'

For a moment, Alvin sagged, looking like a bog body in a business suit. Then his fine-chiselled chin jutted defiantly and he looked heroic, distinguished and thoroughly admirable. 'They won't get me. Was it them that broke into my house?'

'So they said,' said Hobbes, 'but you ran away.'

'As I'd already seen their heptagram asking for news of Matilda, I suspected they'd tracked me down too, so I made a strategic withdrawal.' He glanced at Marco. 'Pick up the telephone.'

Marco looked around stupidly at the tables. 'What telephone? There isn't one.'

'The one on the floor next to the dwarf.'

'The mobile phone?'

'Yes, Marco, the mobile phone. Pick it up and give it to me.'

Marco did as he was told, his body as slow as his mind.

Alvin took the mobile, poked a few buttons, shook his head and laughed. 'What sort of message is that?' he asked. 'Dogged by misfortune, release the hounds.''

Billy shrugged. 'It was a joke.'

'I don't get it.' said Alvin. 'It's not very funny.'

'No,' admitted Billy, stone-faced.

'Why don't you give yourself up, sir?' asked Hobbes. 'It will be better for you.'

'Because, Inspector, I have no intention of going to one of your prisons. They used to be a piece of cake to escape from, but I'm not so sure these days.'

'Modern times, sir. I don't suppose even you can charm an electronic lock,' said Hobbes sympathetically. 'But, tell me why you murdered Solomon Slugg.'

'I didn't murder him. It was self-defence, and it's something I regret, though it was necessary.'

'I wish I could believe you, sir. Perhaps you can convince me. Where did you defend yourself?'

'In the house. He wanted me to leave it and I wasn't ready. He manhandled me.'

'And you unfortunately killed him.'

'Yes. He wouldn't keep quiet.'

'Fair enough,' said Hobbes. 'I can see why that might have been annoying.'

I could see that too and Alvin's case seemed convincing, and one no reasonable person could argue against.

'I do have a question, though,' Hobbes continued. 'What were you doing in his house?'

'Taking possession of it.'

'And he objected, sir?'

'Indeed he did. Violently. In the subsequent fracas I accidently hit him on the head.'

'That seems clear,' said Hobbes. 'You broke into his house ...'

'I didn't break in. I entered through an open window.'

'That obviously makes a difference, sir, but would you confirm the sequence of events? You entered his house via an open window, he objected to your presence ...'

'Strongly objected ...'

'And in the ensuing struggle you accidently bashed him over the head repeatedly with your lead-weighted stick.'

'Correct, Inspector. Well done.'

'And how did Mr Septimus Slugg die?'

'Oh, him. He came to visit when I was gardening and refused to accept my explanation of why I was there. He said he was going to tell the police, so I dissuaded him with my billhook.'

'And you disposed of both bodies in the culvert by the church. Why there, sir?'

'It was deep and old, and no one knew about it.'

'Thank you, sir. That was useful. You'd have got away with it too had it not been for the flood and Andy's luck.'

'I will still get away with it, Inspector. You won't profit from what I've told you, since I have the upper hand.'

'In what way, sir? You're in a police station, and, despite your protestation of innocence I am not convinced, so I intend to re-arrest you for the murders of Solomon Slugg and Septimus Slugg, to which you have admitted in front of witnesses. I rather think I have the upper hand.'

'Not while I have Marco with me. I find a shotgun trumps all arguments.'

'But Marco won't use it.'

'He damned well will when I tell him to.'

'I doubt it, sir.'

'Why, Inspector? He's a useful idiot and does what he's told.'

'Not anymore. He'll put the gun down and walk away.'

'Why would you think that? His will is mine.'

'You may think so, sir, but if he doesn't put the gun down I'll tell his mum.'

'Enough!' said Alvin, his face ugly with rage as he glanced at Marco. 'Shoot him, and then shoot the homunculus.'

'But he said he'll tell ma,' said Marco, his eyes wide. 'And I don't know what a homunculus is.'

'Just do as you're told. Shoot the big one and then the little one!'

'Put the gun down, Marco,' said Hobbes gently, 'because if you don't, I really will tell her, and she'll be ever so cross. Can you imagine what she'll say if I have to tell her you've shot us?'

Despite a lingering and persistent fuzziness in my head, I wondered if Hobbes's logic might be flawed, but no such doubts seemed to afflict Marco.

'Please don't tell, Mr Hobbes. I don't mean any harm. I'll put it down.'

He bent and placed the shotgun carefully on the floor.

'Thank you, Marco,' said Hobbes. 'You may go now, if you wish.'

Looking dazed, Marco nodded, turned and ambled away, humming to himself.

For a moment Alvin seemed nonplussed. Then, as swift as a foraging ferret, he sprang forward and grabbed the shotgun. 'If a job's worth doing,' he said, 'do it yourself.'

'I really wouldn't if I were you, sir,' said Hobbes, shaking his head.

'Don't tell me what to do, you freak. I'm in charge here.'

'You're really not, sir. Please put the gun down. I don't want you to get hurt again.'

'It's not me who's going to get hurt,' said Alvin, raising the shotgun.

Hobbes shook his head. 'OK,' he said. 'Get him.'

'What?' said Alvin, turning towards the sudden scrabbling from the corridor.

It was dogs' claws accelerating on lino. Dregs barged in, closely followed by Mimi. Alvin screamed as they leapt, knocking him flat onto his back, while Hobbes, diving forwards, caught the shotgun. Dregs, knowing police business, stepped off Alvin, and stared at his face, alert and ready for action. Mimi, however, was a dog possessed and, her hackles up, her teeth bared, she went for any bit of Alvin she could get her teeth into, and there turned out to be lots of bits.

'Drop!' said Hobbes and passed the shotgun to Billy.

Mimi glanced up, and, clearly unused to being spoken to in that way, resumed her attack, getting a firm grip on Alvin's ankle, which she was trying to shake as if it were a scrawny rat, while he shrieked, his voice sharp and harsh, lacking any of the honeyed sweetness of a few seconds earlier. I could see why Hobbes had entrusted the shotgun to Billy rather than to me; I might have been convinced to use it against the wrong targets. In fact, I was still feeling ridiculously amiable towards Alvin, who had never done me any harm, so far as I knew, whereas Hobbes kept putting me into the firing line, and Billy had hurt my knuckles on his face …

Hobbes gently tried to prise Mimi off Alvin's groin, to which she'd become quite attached, having had her fill of ankles. I shook my head again, and had to keep reminding myself that Hobbes and Billy were my friends, and that Alvin was a sick and twisted individual, whose ugly interior was now mirrored by his ugly exterior. As he lay there, screeching and groaning, with skinny tea-brown limbs, a narrow, leathery face, stained teeth and pale, sunken eyes, he really did look like something dragged into the daylight after millennia festering. He smelt that way as well.

'Get the savage brute away from me!' Alvin yelled.

'I'm doing my best, sir,' said Hobbes, lifting Mimi to one side, and holding her still as she wriggled, bristling and snarling, clearly convinced her task had only just begun. To be fair, parts of Alvin remained unbitten.

Despite his desiccated appearance, Alvin appeared to be rather talented at leaking blood, and, despite my improved ability to cope with gore (so long as it wasn't my own) I was becoming increasingly light-headed and wobbly. Billy must have noticed, because, having laid the shotgun carefully in the corner, he came across and helped me to a chair. I plumped down heavily, my head lolling, and tried not to faint.

'I'll get you a glass of water,' he said and trotted into the kitchen.

Hobbes, with a little assistance from Dregs, wrestled Mimi out into the corridor, and shut the door behind them, leaving me alone with Alvin. I wasn't concerned, because he clearly was in no state to do anything, except moan and groan, at which he was proving himself an expert. I shut my eyes, fighting a sense of increasing confusion, until something hard and cold jabbed under my nose.

I flinched and gasped, looking up into the face of the woman I'd have died for a few minutes earlier. Somehow I'd forgotten about Matilda, or Sally, or whatever her real name was, or rather, I'd just assumed she was no longer a threat. Sadly she still was, especially now she had the shotgun.

'Did I wake you, Andy?' she said, and the allure was back in her voice, though I fought it.

I trembled, watching how the shotgun followed my every movement.

'Did you do that?' she asked, pointing at Alvin, who was groaning and writhing.

'Umm … no … It was a dog.'

'A dog, Andy? I see no dog. Do you mean that uncouth inspector?'

'No, and he's not uncouth. Well, he is a bit, but he doesn't go round biting people … not often, anyway.'

'Stand up!'

I got to my feet, confusion overridden by fear, for, although I could occasionally catch a glimpse of my lovely Sally, I could mostly see scrawny, leathery Matilda, who bore scant resemblance to a living woman, and who, to judge from the dark emptiness in her eyes, would have no compunction in blasting me into eternity.

'What are you going to do?' I asked.

'Get out of here with my cousin.'

'Good plan. You won't need me for that, will you?'

'I think I might. Firstly, you'll make a good hostage, in case anyone thinks about doing something stupid, and secondly, you will assist my cousin, who needs a supporting hand. Help him to his feet, Andy, like a good lad.'

Although repulsed and almost sickened by the dry parchment feel of his skin that seemed to crackle over his bones, I helped him to get up, trying to ignore his blood on my hands.

'Take him into the corridor, and don't think of running away or you'll get a blast of hot lead.'

Despite his emaciated appearance, Alvin hung like a lead-weight on my arm as I dragged him towards the exit.

'Here's your water,' said Billy, walking back through the kitchen door as I was struggling to lug Alvin into the corridor.

Dropping the glass, he ducked back into the kitchen and slammed the door behind him. Although I couldn't blame him, for he was only a little guy and the shotgun was big and in the hands of a merciless killer, I couldn't help but feel disappointed. I'd been hoping he'd do something amazing. Still, I wasn't despondent, certain that Hobbes would get me out of the predicament.

Neither he nor the dogs were in the corridor, or anywhere else to be seen.

'Take Alvin out the front,' Matilda commanded, 'and don't think of doing anything silly.'

'I wasn't thinking of anything … and … umm … what are you going to do when we're out? He won't get far like this.'

'We'll take a car. You can drive.'

'No, I really can't,' I said, gasping under Alvin's weight as I man-handled him to the front desk, where Sergeant Dixon was still propped against the wall, grinning and singing to himself.

'I don't believe you,' said Matilda.

'It's true. I've never learnt, and last time I tried I knocked over a tree … it was in the *Bugle*.'

'In that case, I'll drive,' she said.

'That would be wise and then … umm … then you wouldn't want me, would you?'

'You will still be my hostage, until you have no further use.'

'And then you'll let me go?'

'Of course,' she said, smiling.

I wanted to believe her.

'Now what?'

'Get me to a car,' said Alvin, his first articulate sound for some time. He returned to groaning, and continued dripping blood from any number of punctures.

'Shouldn't we give him first aid?' I asked.

'That will have to wait,' said Matilda, opening the front door and stepping out. 'We need to get away from here before that big bruiser comes back. Now move!'

That was the moment when I saw my chance to escape. All I had to do was throw Alvin at her, slam the doors behind them, and barricade myself in the kitchen with Billy. Unfortunately, just before I acted, Sergeant Dixon muttered something about truth and beauty, and I realised I'd be leaving him, and the others, in danger. I couldn't do it, and my chance had gone.

Matilda made a gesture with the shotgun that removed any lingering idea of escape, and I did as she demanded, helping Alvin through the door, bearing his weight while she peered up and down the street.

'It's all clear,' she said, with a smile that allowed me another glimpse of Sally. 'Come along. Let's find a car.'

I looked around for Hobbes, but there was no sign of him, and the whole area was quiet. In fact, it appeared to be deserted, and I began to feel very much abandoned, fearing he'd taken the dogs back home after they'd done their bit, and that he was sitting there, probably with his feet up and with a mug of tea in his hand. However, it would be wrong to suggest it was then when I began to feel sorry for myself, since I'd been feeling that way since I'd first bumped into Sally, and yet part of me was almost enjoying my new role as tragic hero, who, rather than leave a helpless police sergeant to a dreadful fate, was bravely marching to a martyr's death. It was a *far, far better thing* that I was doing, than I had ever done, though I wished Alvin wasn't so heavy.

Then everything went heavy, and the only possible direction of movement was downwards. I hit the ground, with Alvin at my side and Matilda just in front. Despite struggling, I was helpless, as were the others, though perhaps if Matilda had put as much effort into trying to move as she did into screaming obscenities, she might have got away, for she was only just beneath the wide-meshed net that had entrapped us. As for me, the more I fought it, the more entangled I became until all I could move was my head.

There was nothing else to do, so I tried to relax as much as was possible when flat on my back on an icy cold pavement with my legs bent beneath me. I stared at the sky, by then a pleasant pale blue without a hint of cloud, and waited for something to happen. Then I glanced down my body. The shotgun was pointing at my crotch, and Matilda's finger was still on the trigger. She was face down and furious, but when she saw what I'd seen she grinned. No charm remained.

'Inspector Hobbes,' she shouted, 'get me and my cousin out of this net, or I'll ruin Andy's day.'

I waited, hoping.

'I mean it.' Her finger twitched.

'Please, don't!' I cried, but there was no response from Hobbes.

But there was a response.

'You might as well give up now, dear cousin,' said the smooth voice of Aubrey Elwes.

Matilda's hiss made me even more nervous.

'He said they were here,' said Alvin. 'I didn't believe him.'

'Both of them?' asked Matilda.

'Yes, cousin dearest,' said Hilda her voice sweet, like a honeyed-up bee with a sting in its tail.

'Let us go, or I'll blow the hostage in two.'

'No, don't,' I said, though I doubted anyone was listening.

'You must know your threat means nothing to us,' said Hilda. 'Whether he lives or dies is irrelevant.'

'No, it isn't!' I said, for although I'd been in plenty of uncomfortable situations, this was possibly the most terrifying, and besides, I'd thought Hilda and Aubrey were my friends. However, in those desperate moments, disappointment was not my main concern.

'Liar,' said Matilda. 'You two were always soft on these upstarts. Let us out, or I'll blast him.'

'Do what you want,' said Aubrey, 'but it won't help you. All you'll get is his gizzards splashed on your nice frock.'

'I'll do it.'

'She really will,' said Alvin, leaving off moaning for a second.

'So what?' said Hilda. 'Do it if you must, but we'll still catch you. And then we will take you to Auntie, who is already angry that you two have turned out to be killers.'

'I'm not a killer,' said Alvin.

'Yes, you are,' I corrected him. 'You killed Solomon and Septimus Slugg.'

'I admit it, but, I'm not a killer. I'm someone who has killed. There's a difference.'

'Umm … I'm not sure there is.'

'Of course there is. I admit to having killed two people. I didn't want to, I didn't enjoy doing it, and I don't make a habit of it. I merely did what had to be done. Now, my adorable cousin …'

'Shut up,' said Matilda.

'… gets a kick from killing …'

'Shut up.'

'And she likes to chew the fat of her latest sweetheart.'

'Shut up,' said Matilda.

'No, go on,' said Aubrey. 'Your account is most illuminating.'

Matilda, hissing like a maddened snake, was fighting furiously and I really hoped she was being careful with her trigger finger, for I couldn't even move my legs together, which might have been a small comfort. All I could do was raise my head slightly and watch as she finally freed herself with a convulsive heave. I hoped Hobbes would turn up, but he didn't. I hoped Aubrey or Hilda would disarm her, but they didn't. Matilda got to her feet, holding the shotgun with a casual menace that wouldn't have looked out of place in the old gangster movies Hobbes loved to watch.

She pointed the double barrels at my head. I wasn't sure this was an improvement.

'Let my cousin go,' she yelled, 'or we'll find out whether lover-boy here has any brains in his thick skull. My bet is that he doesn't.'

'You'd lose,' I said. 'I had a scan and …'

'You talk too much. Just shut up.'

I shut up and she checked the streets and rooftops.

'You'd better show yourself, Inspector Hobbes, because my beloved siblings seem strangely unmoved by your friend's plight.'

Nothing happened, but at least Aubrey and Hilda refrained from encouraging her.

'Get me out of here,' said Alvin.

'Leave him there,' said Hilda.

'Get lost,' said Matilda. 'Remember, there's two barrels in this gun, so there'll be one left for you.'

'Why waste one on me?' I asked. 'I'm no threat to you, but they are. You might need both barrels.'

'I'll shoot whomever I want,' said Matilda. 'If your precious inspector doesn't show himself within ten seconds, and release my cousin from this net, then you're going to get it.'

'By it, I don't suppose you mean the net?' I said.

She laughed. 'I'm going to miss you, Andy.'

'I really hope you do.'

She laughed again, sounding almost like my Sally, but when she spoke her voice was harsh and shrill. 'Ten seconds, Inspector. The countdown starts now. Ten … nine … eight …'

'Help!' I cried.

'Seven … six … five …'

There was no sign of Hobbes, and Aubrey and Hilda were just lounging by the police station wall, smiling.

'Four …three …'

'Two and three quarters,' I hinted.

'Two … one …'

'Please don't,' I pleaded.

'Too late, Inspector,' she said. 'You had a chance to save your foolish friend, but you blew it, and now I'm going to blow his head off.' She stood over me, her leathery face cracked into a malicious leer.

Still there was no sign of Hobbes.

'I don't know what I ever saw in you,' I said, hatred momentarily getting the best of fear. 'You're hideous.'

'Shut up! You're no oil painting yourself with that stupid frizzed hair and no eyebrows … and the rest. What did you do?'

'It's a long story,' I said. 'It all began when I was a child …'

I was hoping to buy time. It didn't work.

'Enough. I've really had enough of you,' she said. 'I reckon I'm doing the world a favour.'

Her finger tightened on the trigger and I stared death in the face. It was no less horrible than her.

I was lying on something soft, and swaying slightly as if I was on a boat. My knuckles were sore. There were voices nearby, and, since they didn't sound at all angelic, I concluded I wasn't in the afterlife. As consciousness crept back, they began to sound very much like those of Hobbes and Billy. I opened my eyes. The sky was blue and cloudless.

'Ah, Andy, you're back,' said Hobbes.

'Wotcha, Andy,' said Billy, sounding as if he needed a handkerchief.

'What happened?' I asked, struggling to sit up. 'She was going to blow my head off.'

'She would never have shot you,' said Hobbes.

For an instant my mind took me back to smiling, lovely Sally. 'You mean she still liked me?'

'Of course not.'

'Then … umm … why?'

'Because I'd already taken the shells from the gun,' said Billy, pulling them from his pocket.

'I didn't know that!'

'I don't suppose you did,' said Hobbes.

'I thought I was going to die.'

'Sorry,' he said, and I was gratified that he did look a little shame-faced. 'However, you shouldn't have been there. It was a dangerous situation, which was why I told you to stay away.'

'I thought I could help.'

'Actually, in a way you did,' said Hobbes with a grin. 'It's possible that if you hadn't got yourself into such a predicament, I would have relented and taken the pair of them into custody.'

'Pleased I could help, but are you saying they're not in custody. You mean you let them go? They're killers. Well, Alvin reckons he isn't exactly, and Sally … umm … Matilda can be quite charming and lovely …' I stopped, still confused, but relieved to find it was mostly my normal confusion, and not the confusion they'd put in me.

'They are both killers,' said Hobbes. 'When I arrested Alvin I intended charging him and putting him before a jury.'

'But why didn't you?' I was outraged. 'They're really dangerous.'

'They were,' said Hobbes, his expression shifting from grin to grim.

'What have you done?' I asked, fearing something awful. It wasn't the first time I'd suspected him of murder, though last time he'd been entirely innocent, other than possibly having bent a few laws in the cause of real justice.

'Let me explain,' he said. 'I was going to ensure they had a fair trial, even though they would not have recognised the court.'

'So why didn't you?' I asked, feeling let down.

'Because when I saw how they charmed you and the others, I realised just how easily they manipulated people, even a roomful of people.'

Light began to dawn. 'So you reckoned they'd do their charm thing on a jury and get off?'

'No. I suspect they would have charmed their way out of the cells well before any trial. It has happened before.'

I thought about this for a moment, and it made sense. They'd really messed up my mind, and I'd been by no means the worst affected. 'So where are they now? What did you do?'

'He left them to their cousins,' said Billy.

'Hilda and Aubrey, but why?'

'Because, they can deal with their own without distractions. I doubt Matilda and Alvin will trouble us again.'

'What will they do to them? Sal … umm … Matilda seemed scared. They both did.'

'I don't know,' said Hobbes.

'It might be best not to,' Billy suggested, and wiped a smear of blood from his nose.

I nodded, and then stared at him. 'What happened to you?'

'You did, mate. Don't you remember? You laid into me with your fists when I got in your way.'

'I didn't—' I started, and fell silent, struck by an overpowering sensation of déjà vu. Had I been in a similar conversation not so long ago?

'You did, mate.'

'I don't remember … I've got fractured images in my head, but they're like those weird bits you remember from dreams in the morning … umm … sorry for what I did. I didn't mean it.'

'It's all right,' said Billy. 'You weren't yourself.'

'Who was I?'

'You'd fallen under their spell, particularly under Matilda's,' said Hobbes. 'At least, that's how I understand it. Alvin had almost completely beguiled you before, of course. Remember how you found it difficult to believe him a villain, even when the evidence was right before your eyes? And when you met her, you were enchanted because in your eyes she was a beautiful young woman. You've always been susceptible to a pretty face, haven't you?'

I nodded unhappily.

'But if it's any consolation, you stood up to her better than all the lads in the station. Derek put up some sort of resistance but even he crumbled quickly.'

'It is some consolation,' I said, 'but there's just one thing I don't understand …'

'Just one thing?' said Billy with a lop-sided smirk.

'… among the many things I don't understand is that there were women in there, and they, too, were completely out of it.'

'That was Alvin,' said Hobbes. 'Dr Ramage seemed particularly spellbound.'

'Spellbound?'

'The word seems appropriate.'

'Will everyone recover?' I asked. 'Will I?'

'Those affected seem much better already,' said Hobbes, 'and you are nearly back to what passes for normal.'

'Thanks … umm … what do you mean passes for normal?'

'The phrase seems appropriate.' He grinned, and it was clear his natural humour was back.

'Now what?' I asked.

'If you're feeling well, you can get up, and get on with your life.'

I made a move, realising too late that I'd been resting on the net that had been strung between two lampposts like a hammock. As my legs swung round, the whole thing swayed and tipped me face first into the gutter. Typically, the street was busy again, so I had a small but appreciative audience.

Holding out his huge hairy paw Hobbes yanked me back onto my feet.

'Right,' said Billy, 'I'm off. I need to clean up and change into my work clothes. I'll let the boss know you didn't attack me on purpose. See you.'

'Thanks for your help,' said Hobbes, 'and thank Featherlight for letting the dogs go on cue.'

'Sorry I beat you up, Billy,' I said as he walked away.

It was typical that one of the passers-by was the blue-rinsed Mrs Nutter, whose gorgon glare, focussed though horn-rimmed spectacles, would have turned me to stone had I not fled for sanctuary inside the police station. Sergeant Dixon and Constable Poll were standing by the front desk, comparing notes on what had just happened to them.

'The coast is clear,' said Hobbes, grinning round the door a moment or two later. 'All right, Reg? All right, Derek?'

The two police officers, looking sheepish, nodded.

'Good,' said Hobbes. 'I'm going to get the dogs and then I'm off home for a cup of tea. Coming, Andy?'

After we'd released the dogs from internment in his office, we walked home, for once at a relaxed pace. The cool fresh air cleared my head with every breath and I was able to appreciate a beautiful afternoon, and, though it was still cool, it felt like spring might not be far away. As if in confirmation, the first shoots of crocuses and daffodils were showing in their planters around Pansy Corner. All of this added to the elation of having survived yet another crisis, and I felt fantastic.

It didn't last, because, by the time we reached Blackdog Street my limbs were heavy and I couldn't stop yawning. I barely stayed awake long enough to drink a cup of tea, before tottering upstairs and crashing out.

33

I awoke with bright morning light filtering through the curtains. Beneath the mouth-watering scent of frying bacon I noticed an earthy animal odour as well as a pleasantly fresh feminine scent. However, a pressing matter had to be attended to before anything else, so I sprinted to the bathroom. Afterwards, as I was washing my hands, I realised I'd slept right through the night, and had missed my supper. It was a bitter disappointment, though much mitigated by the prospect of breakfast. I shaved, washed, and, having dressed with extreme haste, headed downstairs.

There were women's voices in the kitchen. I assumed Mrs Goodfellow was entertaining some of her friends, a mob of cheery and disreputable old ladies, whose eccentricities were legendary. They always liked to fuss over me, and I just hoped they wouldn't interfere with my eating.

It wasn't them. Two younger women were at the table. The one with her back to me was tanned, with short brown hair and a trim figure. The one facing me was blonde, blue-eyed and breathtakingly beautiful in pink.

'Hi, Pinky,' I said, wondering what she was doing there, and fearing I'd done something wrong again.

The other woman turned and my heart leapt at her lovely smile and soft dark eyes, though the surprise of seeing her knocked my brain out of gear.

'Good morning,' she said, laughing at my impromptu impression of a goldfish.

Unable to find words, I ran towards her, just as Mimi appeared from nowhere and tripped me, making me fling myself into Daphne's arms.

'He's still keen,' said Pinky.

I didn't respond, being locked in a kiss that I wanted to continue forever.

Eventually, though, we both had to come up for air.

'When did you get here?' I asked.

'About an hour ago. I got a late flight yesterday, but it was delayed, and we only landed at about six this morning. After that, I took a coach and came straight here. Mrs Goodfellow has been looking after me.'

'Fantastic,' I said, as I fought off Mimi, 'but why didn't you wake me?'

'We tried,' said Mrs Goodfellow, 'but you were determined to get your beauty sleep. Not even Pig Robinson could rouse you.'

'You put that creature in my bedroom?'

'Yes,' said Daphne. 'Isn't he sweet?'

'Is he? I suppose he is in his way, though we thought he might be dangerous to start with.'

'He seems quite safe to me,' said Mrs Goodfellow. 'He's certainly never come close to blowing up my kitchen, unlike some folk I could mention.'

'Which explains the frizz and the bald eyebrow look, I expect,' said Pinky.

'I … umm … was a bit careless with the gas.'

'It'll soon grow out,' said Daphne, holding my hands and gazing into my face. She looked thin and tired, though her face had tanned to the colour of toffee.

'I expect you'll be wanting your breakfast?' said Mrs Goodfellow.

'Yes … I expect I will,' I said, though Daphne's return had driven hunger away.

It came back with a rush when the old girl set a plate of bacon and eggs and fried bread and toast before me.

'Excuse me,' I said, 'but I'm famished. I didn't have my supper.'

'Go ahead,' said Daphne. 'Mrs Goodfellow's been telling me some of what you've been up to. You've been busy.'

'I'd better be off to work,' said Pinky, glancing at her pink watch. 'It's great to have you back, Daffy, and nice to see you Mrs G. Goodbye.'

I ate well, though without pigging out, while Daphne told me about the dig. It was only when I'd finished that I wondered where Hobbes was.

'He and Dregs went to have a word with those students you fell out with,' said Mrs Goodfellow as she cleared the dishes.

I had to explain to Daphne what had happened.

'These things could only happen to you,' she said, laughing.

I laughed too, and stopped abruptly as a horrible thought swooped into my mind; I still hadn't sorted out the posters, and she was going to be so upset when she saw them. A ridiculous notion of taking her away someplace where no one knew me came into my head, though I doubted it would work. Sooner or later she'd see one, or someone would talk. Unable to come up with a better idea, I decided to confess.

'That wasn't the only thing that happened,' I admitted, hot faced and ashamed. 'There was this woman, well, it turned out she wasn't actually a woman … but nothing happened anyway, and it wasn't my fault …'

'You'd better tell me all about it,' said Daphne, looking straight into my eyes while I squirmed.

'Well … umm … what happened was that a car tried to run me down and this woman warned me and saved me … and then we went for a cup of coffee …'

'I see. Was she pretty?'

'Umm … no … well … I thought she was at the time, but …'

'Carry on,' she said, frowning, and folding her arms – a bad sign if ever I saw one.

'Right … umm … when we were in the café she sort of threw herself onto me and, though I tried to get her off …'

'I bet you tried really hard,' she said, her frown deepening, her eyes teary.

'I did actually, but she'd cast some sort of spell on me …'

'Well, that's original. Go on.'

I stared at the table, and forced myself to speak. 'Then she made me kiss her …'

I cringed at her sudden intake of breath, expecting a tearful outburst, and, maybe the beginning of the end of our marriage.

'I'm truly sorry,' I said, forcing myself to look her in the face, fearing the worst.

She chuckled once, opened her mouth as if to say something, and fell into a long fit of helpless laughter. Every time it looked as if she was regaining control, she'd look at my puzzled face and her giggles restarted. At last, wiping her eyes, she overcame the paroxysm.

814

'What's going on?' I said.

'Assuming you mean the woman on the posters, Mrs Goodfellow has already told me about it. You are talking about that one, aren't you?'

'Yes,' I said, still feeling apprehensive and guilty. 'I don't know what came over me.'

'Nor do I. She looks like something dragged from a bog.'

'On the posters?' I asked, confused.

'Where else? And, since I once helped excavate a bog body, I know what I'm talking about.'

'Excuse me a minute, I need the bathroom,' I said.

I ran upstairs and stared at the poster I'd hidden beneath the handkerchiefs in the bedside table. Daphne was quite correct. Now Matilda's spell was broken, she looked like what she was, a hideous skeletal, leathery-skinned thing who barely even looked female. I tore the poster into tiny bits, flushed them down the toilet and went back to be with my wife.

We stayed with Hobbes and Mrs Goodfellow while we sorted ourselves out, filling in forms, and searching for a new flat. In truth, Daphne did most of the difficult stuff while I helped Hobbes clear up a few things, including locating Mimi's real owners, a retired couple from Stillingham. Handing her back was rather traumatic since I'd grown fond of her, and had half hoped I could keep her. However, her evident delight at the reunion gave me reason to believe she'd be happy.

We also found Pig Robinson a good home. Skeleton Bob, on the explicit instructions of Fenella, adopted him and, since he turned out to be a champion truffle hunter, he provided a massive boost to the Nibblets' income.

The university rugby team's fortunes took a nose dive after their supply of anabolic steroids dried up, though the lads who'd had it in for me, after experiencing one of Hobbes's little talks, became model citizens. Except for the one called Guy, who dropped out of his course and switched to dentistry.

I never saw any of the Elwes family again, which was probably for the best, though I wouldn't have minded seeing Hilda. She'd been so charming.

A few weeks later, when life had settled down again, I entered the Bear with a Sore Head, a town pub that had recently gone upmarket. I was combining business with pleasure, since I intended reviewing the menu for my new syndicated column while enjoying lunch with Daphne. She'd just started her new job, which was excavating and cataloguing the medieval charnel house I'd discovered, and had texted to say she'd be a few minutes late.

I passed the time with a pint of lager, and was trying to get a sense of the pub's ambience and clientele when I noticed a stout balding, sleazy-looking man in a long grubby mac sneaking up on a couple at a table in the corner.

'What are you doing?' I asked.

The man spun around. He was holding a camera, and his fingers were yellow with nicotine.

'You!' I said.

He looked puzzled for a moment, and then smiled as if at an old friend. 'Why, it's Mr Caplet! How nice to see you again. Did you like the photos? I thought you came out

815

really well.'

'No, I didn't, but why did you take them?'

'It was a job. Nothing personal.'

'Really? Well, then … umm … who do you work for?'

'Anyone who pays me.' He reached into his pocket and handed me a card. 'If you ever need my services …'

'Victor Ludorum, private detective? But why me? I'd done nothing wrong.'

'As I understand it, my client believed you were trying to ruin his restaurant and wanted some … leverage. Unfortunately, he seems to have disappeared and still owes me. Now, if you'll excuse me, I'm working …'

He turned back, but the couple he'd been sneaking up on had already escaped. Mr Ludorum, if that was his real name, shrugged. 'Never mind. I'll catch up with them later. Jealous husbands can be strung along with snippets for weeks, and it doesn't pay to peak too early.'

'Sorry I'm late,' said Daphne, walking towards me.

'Another beauteous woman,' murmured Mr Ludorum with a wink. 'How do you do it?'

'Pure charm,' I replied.

The private detective hurried away.

'Who was that?' Daphne asked.

'A chance acquaintance, of no importance. Let's get something to eat.'

Wilkie Martin

Wilkie Martin's Unhuman series is available in ebook, paperback, hardback and audio. This collection contains the first 4 books in the series. A further Unhuman book is planned so keep a look out for it. His next book, also based in and around the fictional town of Sorenchester, is currently called Razor and is due to be published in 2018. He also has a little book of silly verse — Relative Disasters.

He lives in the Cotswolds, UK, which is where these novels are based.

Find out more at his website, where you can also signup for his newsletter to receive updates on his next book: wilkiemartin.com

Or like his facebook page: tinyurl.com/wilkiemartinfacebook

Use these links to share samples of the books, audiobooks, and video trailers, and introduce your friends to Inspector Hobbes: tinyurl.com/unhumanI tinyurl.com/unhumanII tinyurl.com/unhumanIII tinyurl.com/unhumanIV

CPSIA information can be obtained
at www.ICGtesting.com
Printed in the USA
LVHW082150130321
681492LV00032B/879